PENGUIN MODERN CLASSICS

REMEMBRANCE OF THINGS PAST

Marcel Proust was born in Anteuil in 1871. His father, an eminent Professor of Medicine, was Roman Catholic and his mother was Jewish, factors that were to play an important role in his life and work. In his twenties he became a conspicuous society figure, frequenting the most fashionable Paris salons of the day. After 1899, however, his suffering from chronic asthma, the death of his parents and his growing disillusionment with humanity caused him to lead an increasingly retired life. From 1907 he rarely emerged from a cork-lined room in his apartment on the Boulevard Hausmann in Paris, in order to insulate himself against the distractions of city life as well as the effect of the trees and flowers which he loved but which brought on his attacks of asthma. He slept by day and worked by night, writing letters and devoting himself to the completion of *A la recherche du temps perdu*. He died in 1922 before the publication of the last three volumes of his great work. With *A la recherche du temps perdu* Proust attempted the perfect rendering of life in art, of the past recreated through memory. It is both a portrait of the artist and a discovery of the aesthetic by which the portrait is painted, and it was to have an immense influence on the literature of the twentieth century.

For this three-volume edition, based on the Pléiade text (1954), Terence Kilmartin has revised C. K. Scott Moncrieff's original English translation and incorporated new material. Volume One contains *Swann's Way* (*Du côté de chez Swann*, 1913) and *Within a Budding Grove* (*A l'ombre des jeunes filles en fleurs*, 1919). Volume Two contains *The Guermantes Way* (*Le côté de Guermantes*, I and II, 1920 and 1921) and *Cities of the Plain* (*Sodome et Gomorrhe*, I and II, 1921 and 1922). Volume Three contains *The Captive* (*La prisonnière*, 1923), *The Fugitive* (*Albertine disparue*, 1925) and *Time Regained* (*Le temps retrouvé*, 1927).

D0064408

MARCEL PROUST

REMEMBRANCE
OF THINGS PAST

"When to the sessions of sweet silent thought
I summon up remembrance of things past . . ."

VOLUME ONE
SWANN'S WAY
WITHIN A BUDDING GROVE

Translated by C. K. Scott Moncrieff and
Terence Kilmartin

PENGUIN BOOKS

Penguin Books Ltd, Harmondsworth, Middlesex, England
Penguin Books, 625 Madison Avenue, New York, New York 10022, U.S.A.
Penguin Books Australia Ltd, Ringwood, Victoria, Australia
Penguin Books Canada Ltd, 2801 John Street, Markham, Ontario, Canada L3R 1B4
Penguin Books (N.Z.) Ltd, 182–190 Wairau Road, Auckland 10, New Zealand

This translation first published in Great Britain by Chatto & Windus 1981
Published in Penguin Books 1983

Reproduced, printed and bound in Great Britain by
Hazell Watson & Viney Ltd, Aylesbury, Bucks
Set in Garamond

A Monsieur

GASTON CALMETTE

*Comme un témoignage de
profonde et affectueuse
reconnaissance*

MARCEL PROUST

CONTENTS

*

CONTENTS

NOTE ON THE TRANSLATION

C. K. Scott Moncrieff's version of *A la recherche du temps perdu* has in the past fifty years earned a reputation as one of the great English translations, almost as a masterpiece in its own right. Why then should it need revision? Why tamper with a work that has been enjoyed and admired, not to say revered, by several generations of readers throughout the English-speaking world?

The answer is that the original French edition from which Scott Moncrieff worked (the "abominable" edition of the *Nouvelle Revue Française*, as Samuel Beckett described it in a marvellous short study of Proust which he published in 1931) was notoriously imperfect. This was not so much the fault of the publishers and printers as of Proust's methods of composition. Only the first volume (*Du côté de chez Swann*) of the novel as originally conceived—and indeed written—was published before the 1914-1918 war. The second volume was set up in type, but publication was delayed, and moreover by that time Proust had already begun to reconsider the scale of the novel; the remaining eight years of his life (1914-1922) were spent in expanding it from its original 500,000 words to more than a million and a quarter. The margins of proofs and typescripts were covered with scribbled corrections and insertions, often overflowing on to additional sheets which were glued to the galleys or to one another to form interminable strips—what Françoise in the novel calls the narrator's "*paperoles*." The unravelling and deciphering of these copious additions cannot have been an enviable task for editors and printers.

Furthermore, the last three sections of the novel (*La prisonnière*, *La fugitive* and *Le temps retrouvé*) had not yet been published at the time of Proust's death in November 1922 (he was still correcting a typed copy of *La prisonnière* on his deathbed). Here the original editors had to take it upon themselves to prepare a coherent text from a manuscript littered with sometimes hasty corrections, revisions and afterthoughts and leaving a number of unresolved contradictions, obscurities and chronological inconsistencies. As a result of all this the original editions—even of the volumes published in Proust's lifetime—pullulate with errors, misreadings and omissions.

In 1954 a revised three-volume edition of *A la recherche* was published in Gallimard's Bibliothèque de la Pléiade. The editors, M. Pierre Clarac and M. André Ferré, had been charged by Proust's heirs with the task of "establishing a text of his novel as faithful as possible to his intentions." With infinite care and patience they examined all the relevant material—manuscripts, notebooks, typescripts, proofs, as well as the original edition—and produced what is generally agreed to be a virtually impeccable transcription of Proust's text. They scrupulously avoided the arbitrary emendations, the touchings-up, the wholesale reshufflings of paragraphs in which the original editors indulged, confining themselves to clarifying the text wherever necessary, correcting errors due to haste or inadvertence, eliminating careless repetitions and rationalising the punctuation (an area where Proust was notoriously casual). They justify and explain their editorial decisions in detailed critical notes, occupying some 200 pages over the three volumes, and print all the significant variants as well as a number of passages that Proust did not have time to work into his book.

The Pléiade text differs from that of the original edition, mostly in minor though none the less significant ways, throughout the novel. In the last three sections (the third Pléiade volume and the third volume of this present translation) the differences are sometimes considerable. In particular, MM. Clarac and Ferré have included a number of passages, sometimes of a paragraph or two, sometimes of several pages, which the original editors omitted for no good reason.

The present translation is a reworking, on the basis of the Pléiade edition, of Scott Moncrieff's version of the first six sections of *A la recherche*—or the first eleven volumes of the twelve-volume English edition. A post-Pléiade version of the final volume, *Le temps retrouvé* (originally translated by Stephen

Hudson after Scott Moncrieff's death in 1930), was produced
by the late Andreas Mayor and published in 1970; with some
minor emendations, it is incorporated in this edition. There
being no indication in Proust's manuscript as to where *La
fugitive* should end and *Le temps retrouvé* begin, I have followed
the Pléiade editors in introducing the break some pages earlier
than in the previous editions, both French and English—at the
beginning of the account of the Tansonville episode.

The need to revise the existing translation in the light of the
Pléiade edition has also provided an opportunity of correcting
mistakes and misinterpretations in Scott Moncrieff's version.
Translation, almost by definition, is imperfect; there is always
"room for improvement," and it is only too easy for the late-
comer to assume the *beau rôle*. I have refrained from officious
tinkering for its own sake, but a translator's loyalty is to the
original author, and in trying to be faithful to Proust's meaning
and tone of voice I have been obliged, here and there, to make
extensive alterations.

A general criticism that might be levelled against Scott
Moncrieff is that his prose tends to the purple and the precious
—or that this is how he interpreted the tone of the original:
whereas the truth is that, complicated, dense, overloaded
though it often is, Proust's style is essentially natural and
unaffected, quite free of preciosity, archaism or self-conscious
elegance. Another pervasive weakness of Scott Moncrieff's is
perhaps the defect of a virtue. Contrary to a widely-held view,
he stuck very closely to the original (he is seldom guilty of
short-cuts, omissions or loose paraphrases), and in his efforts
to reproduce the structure of those elaborate sentences with
their spiralling subordinate clauses, not only does he sometimes
lose the thread but he wrenches his syntax into oddly un-
English shapes: a whiff of Gallicism clings to some of the
longer periods, obscuring the sense and falsifying the tone. A
corollary to this is a tendency to translate French idioms and
turns of phrase literally, thus making them sound weirder,
more outlandish, than they would to a French reader. In
endeavouring to rectify these weaknesses, I hope I have
preserved the undoubted felicity of much of Scott Moncrieff
while doing the fullest possible justice to Proust.

Pace those Proust scholars who feel that "Remembrance of Things Past" distorts the meaning of Proust's title and who would prefer a more literal rendering, Scott Moncrieff's title has been retained for this edition. Of the titles of the seven separate sections, only one has been altered: "The Sweet Cheat Gone" (never Scott Moncrieff's happiest invention) becomes *The Fugitive*, in conformity with the Pléiade edition, which reverts from *Albertine disparue* to Proust's original title *La fugitive*, discarded in 1922 when a book of that title by Rabindranath Tagore was published in France.

There could of course be no question of reproducing the elaborate Pléiade "Notes and Variants" in an English edition, but I have included as addenda a selection of passages which, for one reason or another, did not find a place in Proust's final text. The most substantial of these—the tragi-comedy of the Princesse de Guermantes's unrequited passion for Charlus—will be found at the end of Volume Two and should on no account be overlooked.

I should like to thank Professor J. G. Weightman for his generous help and advice and Mr D. J. Enright for his patient and percipient editing.

Terence Kilmartin

Numerals in the text refer the reader to explanatory notes while asterisks indicate the position of textual addenda. The notes and the addenda follow the text in each volume.

SWANN'S WAY

OVERTURE

For a long time I used to go to bed early. Sometimes, when I had put out my candle, my eyes would close so quickly that I had not even time to say to myself: "I'm falling asleep." And half an hour later the thought that it was time to go to sleep would awaken me; I would make as if to put away the book which I imagined was still in my hands, and to blow out the light; I had gone on thinking, while I was asleep, about what I had just been reading, but these thoughts had taken a rather peculiar turn; it seemed to me that I myself was the immediate subject of my book: a church, a quartet, the rivalry between François I and Charles V. This impression would persist for some moments after I awoke; it did not offend my reason, but lay like scales upon my eyes and prevented them from registering the fact that the candle was no longer burning. Then it would begin to seem unintelligible, as the thoughts of a former existence must be to a reincarnate spirit; the subject of my book would separate itself from me, leaving me free to apply myself to it or not; and at the same time my sight would return and I would be astonished to find myself in a state of darkness, pleasant and restful enough for my eyes, but even more, perhaps, for my mind, to which it appeared incomprehensible, without a cause, something dark indeed.

I would ask myself what time it could be; I could hear the whistling of trains, which, now nearer and now farther off, punctuating the distance like the note of a bird in a forest, showed me in perspective the deserted countryside through which a traveller is hurrying towards the nearby station; and the path he is taking will be engraved in his memory by the excitement induced by strange surroundings, by unaccustomed activities, by the conversation he has had and the farewells exchanged beneath an unfamiliar lamp that still echo in his ears amid the silence of the night, and by the happy prospect of being home again.

I would lay my cheeks gently against the comfortable cheeks of my pillow, as plump and fresh as the cheeks of childhood. I would strike a match to look at my watch. Nearly midnight. The hour when an invalid, who has been obliged to set out on a journey and to sleep in a strange hotel, awakened by a sudden spasm, sees with glad relief a streak of daylight showing under his door. Thank God, it is morning! The servants will be about in a minute: he can ring, and someone will come to look after him. The thought of being assuaged gives him strength to endure his pain. He is certain he heard footsteps: they come nearer, and then die away. The ray of light beneath his door is extinguished. It is midnight; someone has just turned down the gas; the last servant has gone to bed, and he must lie all night in agony with no one to bring him relief.

I would fall asleep again, and thereafter would reawaken for short snatches only, just long enough to hear the regular creaking of the wainscot, or to open my eyes to stare at the shifting kaleidoscope of the darkness, to savour, in a momentary glimmer of consciousness, the sleep which lay heavy upon the furniture, the room, the whole of which I formed but an insignificant part and whose insensibility I should very soon return to share. Or else while sleeping I had drifted back to an earlier stage in my life, now for ever outgrown, and had come under the thrall of one of my childish terrors, such as that old terror of my great-uncle's pulling my curls which was effectually dispelled on the day—the dawn of a new era to me—when they were finally cropped from my head. I had forgotten that event during my sleep, but I remembered it again immediately I had succeeded in waking myself up to escape my great-uncle's fingers, and as a measure of precaution I would bury the whole of my head in the pillow before returning to the world of dreams.

Sometimes, too, as Eve was created from a rib of Adam, a woman would be born during my sleep from some strain in the position of my thighs. Conceived from the pleasure I was on the point of consummating, she it was, I imagined, who offered me that pleasure. My body, conscious that its own warmth was permeating hers, would strive to become one with her, and I would awake. The rest of humanity seemed very remote in comparison with this woman whose company I had left but a moment ago; my cheek was still warm from her kiss, my body ached beneath the weight of hers. If, as would sometimes happen, she had the features of some woman whom I had known in waking hours, I would abandon myself altogether to the sole quest of her, like people who set out on a journey to see with their eyes some city of their desire, and imagine that one can taste in reality what has charmed one's fancy. And then, gradually, the memory of her would dissolve and vanish, until I had forgotten the girl of my dream.

When a man is asleep, he has in a circle round him the chain of the hours, the sequence of the years, the order of the heavenly bodies. Instinctively he consults them when he awakes, and in an instant reads off his own position on the earth's surface and the time that has elapsed during his slumbers; but this ordered procession is apt to grow confused, and to break its ranks. Suppose that, towards morning, after a night of insomnia, sleep descends upon him while he is reading, in quite a different position from that in which he normally goes to sleep, he has only to lift his arm to arrest the sun and turn it back in its course, and, at the moment of waking, he will have no idea of the time, but will conclude that he has just gone to bed. Or suppose that he dozes off in some even more abnormal and divergent position, sitting in an armchair, for instance, after dinner: then the world will go hurtling out of orbit, the magic chair will carry him at full speed through time and space, and when he opens his eyes again he will imagine that he went to sleep months earlier in another place. But for me it was enough if, in my own bed, my sleep was so heavy as completely to relax my consciousness; for then I lost all sense of the place in which I had gone to sleep, and when I awoke in the middle of the night, not knowing where I was, I could not even be sure at first who I was; I had only the most rudimentary sense of existence, such as may lurk and flicker in the depths of an animal's consciousness; I was more destitute than the cave-dweller; but then the memory—not yet of the place in which I was, but of various other places where I had lived and might now very possibly be—would come like a rope let down from heaven to draw me up out of the abyss of not-being, from which I could never have escaped by myself: in a flash I would traverse centuries of civilisation, and out of a blurred glimpse of oil-lamps, then of shirts with turned-down collars, would gradually piece together the original components of my ego.

Perhaps the immobility of the things that surround us is forced upon them by our conviction that they are themselves and not anything else, by the immobility of our conception of them. For it always happened that when I awoke like this, and my mind struggled in an unsuccessful attempt to discover where I was, everything revolved around me through the darkness: things, places, years. My body, still too heavy with sleep to move, would endeavour to construe from the pattern of its tiredness the position of its various limbs, in order to deduce therefrom the direction of the wall, the location of the furniture, to piece together and give a name to the house in which it lay. Its memory, the composite memory of its ribs, its knees, its shoulder-blades, offered it a whole series of rooms in which it had at one time or another slept, while the unseen walls, shifting and adapting themselves to the shape of each successive room that it remembered, whirled round it in the dark. And even before my brain, lingering in cogitation over when things had happened and what they had looked like, had reassembled the circumstances sufficiently to identify the room, it, my body, would recall from each room in succession the style of the bed, the position of the doors, the angle at which the daylight came in at the windows, whether there was a passage outside, what I had had in my mind when I went to sleep and found there when I awoke. The stiffened side on which I lay would, for instance, in trying to fix its position, imagine itself to be lying face to the wall in a big bed with a canopy; and at once I would say to myself, "Why, I must have fallen asleep before Mamma came to say good night," for I was in the country at my grandfather's, who died years ago; and my body, the side upon which I was lying, faithful guardians of a past which my mind should never have forgotten, brought back before my eyes the glimmering flame of the night-light in its urn-shaped bowl of Bohemian glass that hung by chains from the ceiling, and the chimney-piece of Siena marble in my bedroom at Combray, in my grandparents' house, in those far distant days which at this moment I imagined to be in the present without being able to picture them exactly, and which would become plainer in a little while when I was properly awake.

Then the memory of a new position would spring up, and the wall would slide away in another direction; I was in my room in Mme de Saint-Loup's house in the country; good heavens, it must be ten o'clock, they will have finished dinner! I must have overslept myself in the little nap which I always take when I come in from my walk with Mme de Saint-Loup, before dressing for the evening. For many years have now elapsed since the Combray days when, coming in from the longest and latest walks, I would still be in time to see the reflection of the sunset glowing in the panes of my bedroom window. It is a very different kind of life that one leads at Tansonville, at Mme de Saint-Loup's, and a different kind of pleasure that I derive from taking walks only in the evenings, from visiting by moonlight the roads on which I used to play as a child in the sunshine; as for the bedroom in which I must have fallen asleep instead of dressing for dinner, I can see it from the distance as we return from our walk, with its lamp shining through the window, a solitary beacon in the night.

These shifting and confused gusts of memory never lasted for more than a few seconds; it often happened that, in my brief spell of uncertainty as to where I was, I did not distinguish the various suppositions of which it was composed any more than, when we watch a horse running, we isolate the successive positions of its body as they appear upon a bioscope. But I had seen first one and then another of the rooms in which I had slept during my life, and in the end I would revisit them all in the long course of my waking dream: rooms in winter, where on going to bed I would at once bury my head in a nest woven out of the most diverse materials—the corner of my pillow, the top of my blankets, a piece of a shawl, the edge of my bed, and a copy of a children's paper—which I had contrived to cement together, bird-fashion, by dint of continuous pressure; rooms where, in freezing weather, I

would enjoy the satisfaction of being shut in from the outer
world (like the sea-swallow which builds at the end of a dark
tunnel and is kept warm by the surrounding earth), and where,
the fire keeping in all night, I would sleep wrapped up, as it
were, in a great cloak of snug and smoky air, shot with the
glow of the logs intermittently breaking out again in flame,
a sort of alcove without walls, a cave of warmth dug out of
the heart of the room itself, a zone of heat whose boundaries
were constantly shifting and altering in temperature as gusts
of air traversed them to strike freshly upon my face, from the
corners of the room or from parts near the window or far from
the fireplace which had therefore remained cold;—or rooms
in summer, where I would delight to feel myself a part of the
warm night, where the moonlight striking upon the half-
opened shutters would throw down to the foot of my bed its
enchanted ladder, where I would fall asleep, as it might be in
the open air, like a titmouse which the breeze gently rocks
at the tip of a sunbeam;—or sometimes the Louis XVI room,
so cheerful that I never felt too miserable in it, even on my
first night, and in which the slender columns that lightly
supported its ceiling drew so gracefully apart to reveal and
frame the site of the bed;—sometimes, again, the little room
with the high ceiling, hollowed in the form of a pyramid out
of two separate storeys, and partly walled with mahogany, in
which from the first moment, mentally poisoned by the unfamiliar scent of vetiver, I was convinced of the hostility of
the violet curtains and of the insolent indifference of a clock
that chattered on at the top of its voice as though I were not
there; in which a strange and pitiless rectangular cheval-glass,
standing across one corner of the room, carved out for itself
a site I had not looked to find tenanted in the soft plenitude
of my normal field of vision; in which my mind, striving for
hours on end to break away from its moorings, to stretch
upwards so as to take on the exact shape of the room and to
reach to the topmost height of its gigantic funnel, had endured
many a painful night as I lay stretched out in bed, my eyes
staring upwards, my ears straining, my nostrils flaring, my
heart beating; until habit had changed the colour of the
curtains, silenced the clock, brought an expression of pity to

the cruel, slanting face of the glass, disguised or even completely dispelled the scent of vetiver, and appreciably reduced the apparent loftiness of the ceiling. Habit! that skilful but slow-moving arranger who begins by letting our minds suffer for weeks on end in temporary quarters, but whom our minds are none the less only too happy to discover at last, for without it, reduced to their own devices, they would be powerless to make any room seem habitable.

Certainly I was now well awake; my body had veered round for the last time and the good angel of certainty had made all the surrounding objects stand still, had set me down under my bedclothes, in my bedroom, and had fixed, approximately in their right places in the uncertain light, my chest of drawers, my writing-table, my fireplace, the window overlooking the street, and both the doors. But for all that I now knew that I was not in any of the houses of which the ignorance of the waking moment had, in a flash, if not presented me with a distinct picture, at least persuaded me of the possible presence, my memory had been set in motion; as a rule I did not attempt to go to sleep again at once, but used to spend the greater part of the night recalling our life in the old days at Combray with my great-aunt, at Balbec, Paris, Doncières, Venice, and the rest; remembering again all the places and people I had known, what I had actually seen of them, and what others had told me.

At Combray, as every afternoon ended, long before the time when I should have to go to bed and lie there, unsleeping, far from my mother and grandmother, my bedroom became the fixed point on which my melancholy and anxious thoughts were centred. Someone had indeed had the happy idea of giving me, to distract me on evenings when I seemed abnormally wretched, a magic lantern, which used to be set on top of my lamp while we waited for dinner-time to come; and, after the fashion of the master-builders and glass-painters of gothic days, it substituted for the opaqueness of my walls an impalpable iridescence, supernatural phenomena of many colours, in which legends were depicted as on a shifting and transitory window. But my sorrows were only increased thereby, because this mere change of lighting was enough to destroy the familiar impression I had of my room, thanks to which, save for the torture of going to bed, it had become quite endurable. Now I no longer recognised it, and felt uneasy in it, as in a room in some hotel or chalet, in a place where I had just arrived by train for the first time.

Riding at a jerky trot, Golo, filled with an infamous design, issued from the little triangular forest which dyed dark-green the slope of a convenient hill, and advanced fitfully towards the castle of poor Geneviève de Brabant. This castle was cut off short by a curved line which was in fact the circumference of one of the transparent ovals in the slides which were pushed into position through a slot in the lantern. It was only the wing of a castle, and in front of it stretched a moor on which Geneviève stood lost in contemplation, wearing a blue girdle. The castle and the moor were yellow, but I could tell their colour without waiting to see them, for before the slides made their appearance the old-gold sonorous name of Brabant had given me an unmistakable clue. Golo stopped for a moment and listened sadly to the accompanying patter read aloud by my great-aunt, which he seemed perfectly to understand, for he modified his attitude with a docility not devoid of a degree of majesty, so as to conform to the indications given in the text; then he rode away at the same jerky trot. And nothing could arrest his slow progress. If the lantern were moved I could still distinguish Golo's horse advancing across the window-curtains, swelling out with their curves and diving into their folds. The body of Golo himself, being of the same supernatural substance as his steed's, overcame every material obstacle—everything that seemed to bar his way—by taking it as an ossature and embodying it in himself: even the door-handle, for instance, over which, adapting itself at once, would float irresistibly his red cloak or his pale face, which never lost its nobility or its melancholy, never betrayed the least concern at this transvertebration.

And, indeed, I found plenty of charm in these bright projections, which seemed to emanate from a Merovingian past and shed around me the reflections of such ancient history. But I cannot express the discomfort I felt at this intrusion of mystery and beauty into a room which I had succeeded in filling with my own personality until I thought no more of it than of myself. The anaesthetic effect of habit being destroyed, I would begin to think—and to feel—such melancholy things. The door-handle of my room, which was different to me from all the other door-handles in the world, inasmuch as it seemed to open of its own accord and without my having to turn it, so unconscious had its manipulation become—lo and behold, it was now an astral body for Golo. And as soon as the dinner-bell rang I would hurry down to the dining-room, where the big hanging lamp, ignorant of Golo and Bluebeard but well acquainted with my family and the dish of stewed beef, shed the same light as on every other evening; and I would fall into the arms of my mother, whom the misfortunes of Geneviève de Brabant had made all the dearer to me, just as the crimes of Golo had driven me to a more than ordinarily scrupulous examination of my own conscience.

But after dinner, alas, I was soon obliged to leave Mamma, who stayed talking with the others, in the garden if it was fine, or in the little parlour where everyone took shelter when it was wet. Everyone except my grandmother, who held that "It's a pity to shut oneself indoors in the country," and used to have endless arguments with my father on the very wettest days, because he would send me up to my room with a book instead of letting me stay out of doors. "That is not the way to make him strong and active," she would say sadly, "especially this little man, who needs all the strength and will-power that he can get." My father would shrug his shoulders and study the barometer, for he took an interest in meteorology, while my mother, keeping very quiet so as not to disturb him, looked at him with tender respect, but not too hard, not wishing to penetrate the mysteries of his superior mind. But my grandmother, in all weathers, even when the rain was coming down in torrents and Françoise had rushed the precious wicker armchairs indoors so that they should not get soaked, was to be seen pacing the deserted rain-lashed garden, pushing back her disordered grey locks so that her forehead might be freer to absorb the health-giving draughts of wind and rain. She would say, "At last one can breathe!"

and would trot up and down the sodden paths—too straight
and symmetrical for her liking, owing to the want of any feeling
for nature in the new gardener, whom my father had been
asking all morning if the weather were going to improve—her
keen, jerky little step regulated by the various effects wrought
upon her soul by the intoxication of the storm, the power of
hygiene, the stupidity of my upbringing and the symmetry of
gardens, rather than by any anxiety (for that was quite unknown
to her) to save her plum-coloured skirt from the mudstains
beneath which it would gradually disappear to a height that
was the constant bane and despair of her maid.

When these walks of my grandmother's took place after
dinner there was one thing which never failed to bring her
back to the house: this was if (at one of those points when her
circular itinerary brought her back, moth-like, in sight of the
lamp in the little parlour where the liqueurs were set out on
the card-table) my great-aunt called out to her: "Bathilde!
Come in and stop your husband drinking brandy!" For,
simply to tease her (she had brought so different a type of
mind into my father's family that everyone made fun of her),
my great-aunt used to make my grandfather, who was forbidden
liqueurs, take just a few drops. My poor grandmother would
come in and beg and implore her husband not to taste the
brandy; and he would get angry and gulp it down all the same,
and she would go out again sad and discouraged, but still
smiling, for she was so humble of heart and so gentle that her
tenderness for others and her disregard for herself and her
own troubles blended in a smile which, unlike those seen on
the majority of human faces, bore no trace of irony save for
herself, while for all of us kisses seemed to spring from her
eyes, which could not look upon those she loved without
seeming to bestow upon them passionate caresses. This torture
inflicted on her by my great-aunt, the sight of my grandmother's
vain entreaties, of her feeble attempts, doomed in advance, to
remove the liqueur-glass from my grandfather's hands—all
these were things of the sort to which, in later years, one can
grow so accustomed as to smile at them and to take the
persecutor's side resolutely and cheerfully enough to persuade
oneself that it is not really persecution; but in those days they

filled me with such horror that I longed to strike my great-aunt. And yet, as soon as I heard her "Bathilde! Come in and stop your husband drinking brandy," in my cowardice I became at once a man, and did what all we grown men do when face to face with suffering and injustice: I preferred not to see them; I ran up to the top of the house to cry by myself in a little room beside the schoolroom and beneath the roof, which smelt of orris-root and was scented also by a wild currant-bush which had climbed up between the stones of the outer wall and thrust a flowering branch in through the half-opened window. Intended for a more special and a baser use, this room, from which, in the daytime, I could see as far as the keep of Roussainville-le-Pin, was for a long time my place of refuge, doubtless because it was the only room whose door I was allowed to lock, whenever my occupation was such as required an inviolable solitude: reading or day-dreaming, secret tears or sensual pleasure. Alas! I did not realise that my own lack of will-power, my delicate health, and the consequent uncertainty as to my future, weighed far more heavily on my grandmother's mind than any little dietary indiscretion by her husband in the course of those endless perambulations, afternoon and evening, during which we used to see her handsome face passing to and fro, half raised towards the sky, its brown and wrinkled cheeks, which with age had acquired almost the purple hue of tilled fields in autumn, covered, if she were "going out," by a half-lifted veil, while upon them either the cold or some sad reflection invariably left the drying traces of an involuntary tear.

My sole consolation when I went upstairs for the night was that Mamma would come in and kiss me after I was in bed. But this good night lasted for so short a time, she went down again so soon, that the moment in which I heard her climb the stairs, and then caught the sound of her garden dress of blue muslin, from which hung little tassels of plaited straw, rustling along the double-doored corridor, was for me a moment of the utmost pain; for it heralded the moment which was bound to follow it, when she would have left me and gone downstairs again. So much so that I reached the point of hoping that this good night which I loved so much

would come as late as possible, so as to prolong the time of
respite during which Mamma would not yet have appeared.
Sometimes when, after kissing me, she opened the door to go,
I longed to call her back, to say to her "Kiss me just once
more," but I knew that then she would at once look displeased,
for the concession which she made to my wretchedness and
agitation in coming up to give me this kiss of peace always
annoyed my father, who thought such rituals absurd, and she
would have liked to try to induce me to outgrow the need,
the habit, of having her there at all, let alone get into the habit
of asking her for an additional kiss when she was already
crossing the threshold. And to see her look displeased destroyed
all the calm and serenity she had brought me a moment before,
when she had bent her loving face down over my bed, and
held it out to me like a host for an act of peace-giving
communion in which my lips might imbibe her real presence
and with it the power to sleep. But those evenings on which
Mamma stayed so short a time in my room were sweet indeed
compared to those on which we had guests to dinner, and
therefore she did not come at all. Our "guests" were usually
limited to M. Swann, who, apart from a few passing strangers,
was almost the only person who ever came to the house at
Combray, sometimes to a neighbourly dinner (but less frequently since his unfortunate marriage, as my family did not
care to receive his wife) and sometimes after dinner, uninvited.
On those evenings when, as we sat in front of the house round
the iron table beneath the big chestnut-tree, we heard, from
the far end of the garden, not the shrill and assertive alarm
bell which assailed and deafened with its ferruginous, interminable, frozen sound any member of the household who
set it off on entering "without ringing," but the double tinkle,
timid, oval, golden, of the visitors' bell, everyone would at
once exclaim "A visitor! Who in the world can it be?" but they
knew quite well that it could only be M. Swann. My great-
aunt, speaking in a loud voice to set an example, in a tone
which she endeavoured to make sound natural, would tell the
others not to whisper so; that nothing could be more offensive
to a stranger coming in, who would be led to think that people
were saying things about him which he was not meant to hear;

and then my grandmother, always happy to find an excuse for an additional turn in the garden, would be sent out to reconnoitre, and would take the opportunity to remove surreptitiously, as she passed, the stakes of a rose-tree or two, so as to make the roses look a little more natural, as a mother might run her hand through her boy's hair after the barber has smoothed it down, to make it look naturally wavy.

We would all wait there in suspense for the report which my grandmother would bring back from the enemy lines, as though there might be a choice between a large number of possible assailants, and then, soon after, my grandfather would say: "I can hear Swann's voice." And indeed one could tell him only by his voice, for it was difficult to make out his face with its arched nose and green eyes, under a high forehead fringed with fair, almost red hair, done in the Bressant style,[1] because in the garden we used as little light as possible, so as not to attract mosquitoes; and I would slip away unobtrusively to order the liqueurs to be brought out, for my grandmother made a great point, thinking it "nicer," of their not being allowed to seem anything out of the ordinary, which we kept for visitors only. Although a far younger man, M. Swann was very much attached to my grandfather, who had been an intimate friend of Swann's father, an excellent but eccentric man the ardour of whose feelings and the current of whose thoughts would often be checked or diverted by the most trifling thing. Several times in the course of a year I would hear my grandfather tell at table the story, which never varied, of the behaviour of M. Swann the elder upon the death of his wife, by whose bedside he had watched day and night. My grandfather, who had not seen him for a long time, hastened to join him at the Swanns' family property on the outskirts of Combray, and managed to entice him for a moment, weeping profusely, out of the death-chamber, so that he should not be present when the body was laid in its coffin. They took a turn or two in the park, where there was a little sunshine. Suddenly M. Swann seized my grandfather by the arm and cried, "Ah, my dear old friend, how fortunate we are to be walking here together on such a charming day! Don't you see how pretty they are, all these trees, my hawthorns, and my new pond,

on which you have never congratulated me? You look as
solemn as the grave. Don't you feel this little breeze? Ah!
whatever you may say, it's good to be alive all the same, my
dear Amédée!" And then, abruptly, the memory of his dead
wife returned to him, and probably thinking it too complicated
to inquire into how, at such a time, he could have allowed
himself to be carried away by an impulse of happiness, he
confined himself to a gesture which he habitually employed
whenever any perplexing question came into his mind: that is,
he passed his hand across his forehead, rubbed his eyes, and
wiped his glasses. And yet he never got over the loss of his
wife, but used to say to my grandfather, during the two years
by which he survived her, "It's a funny thing, now; I very
often think of my poor wife, but I cannot think of her for
long at a time." "Often, but a little at a time, like poor old
Swann," became one of my grandfather's favourite sayings,
which he would apply to all manner of things. I should have
assumed that this father of Swann's had been a monster if my
grandfather, whom I regarded as a better judge than myself,
and whose word was my law and often led me in the long run
to pardon offences which I should have been inclined to
condemn, had not gone on to exclaim, "But, after all, he had a
heart of gold."

For many years, during the course of which—especially
before his marriage—M. Swann the younger came often to see
them at Combray, my great-aunt and my grandparents never
suspected that he had entirely ceased to live in the society
which his family had frequented, and that, under the sort of
incognito which the name of Swann gave him among us, they
were harbouring—with the complete innocence of a family of
respectable innkeepers who have in their midst some celebrated
highwayman without knowing it—one of the most distinguished members of the Jockey Club, a particular friend of
the Comte de Paris and of the Prince of Wales, and one of the
men most sought after in the aristocratic world of the Faubourg
Saint-Germain.

Our utter ignorance of the brilliant social life which Swann
led was, of course, due in part to his own reserve and discretion, but also to the fact that middle-class people in those days

took what was almost a Hindu view of society, which they held
to consist of sharply defined castes, so that everyone at his
birth found himself called to that station in life which his
parents already occupied, and from which nothing, save the
accident of an exceptional career or of a "good" marriage,
could extract you and translate you to a superior caste. M.
Swann the elder had been a stockbroker; and so "young
Swann" found himself immured for life in a caste whose
members' fortunes, as in a category of tax-payers, varied
between such and such limits of income. One knew the people
with whom his father had associated, and so one knew his own
associates, the people with whom he was "in a position to
mix." If he knew other people besides, those were youthful
acquaintances on whom the old friends of his family, like my
relatives, shut their eyes all the more good-naturedly because
Swann himself, after he was left an orphan, still came most
faithfully to see us; but we would have been ready to wager
that the people outside our acquaintance whom Swann knew
were of the sort to whom he would not have dared to raise
his hat if he had met them while he was walking with us.
Had it been absolutely essential to apply to Swann a social
coefficient peculiar to himself, as distinct from all the other
sons of other stockbrokers in his father's position, his coefficient would have been rather lower than theirs, because,
being very simple in his habits, and having always had a
craze for "antiques" and pictures, he now lived and amassed
his collections in an old house which my grandmother longed
to visit but which was situated on the Quai d'Orléans, a
neighbourhood in which my great-aunt thought it most
degrading to be quartered. "Are you really a connoisseur,
now?" she would say to him; "I ask for your own sake, as
you are likely to have fakes palmed off on you by the dealers,"
for she did not, in fact, endow him with any critical faculty,
and had no great opinion of the intelligence of a man who,
in conversation, would avoid serious topics and showed a
very dull preciseness, not only when he gave us kitchen recipes,
going into the most minute details, but even when my grandmother's sisters were talking to him about art. When challenged
by them to give an opinion, or to express his admiration for

some picture, he would remain almost offensively silent, and would then make amends by furnishing (if he could) some fact or other about the gallery in which the picture was hung, or the date at which it had been painted. But as a rule he would content himself with trying to amuse us by telling us about his latest adventure with someone whom we ourselves knew, such as the Combray chemist, or our cook, or our coachman. These stories certainly used to make my great-aunt laugh, but she could never decide whether this was on account of the absurd rôle which Swann invariably gave himself therein, or of the wit that he showed in telling them: "I must say you really are a regular character, M. Swann!"

As she was the only member of our family who could be described as a trifle "common," she would always take care to remark to strangers, when Swann was mentioned, that he could easily, had he so wished, have lived in the Boulevard Haussmann or the Avenue de l'Opéra, and that he was the son of old M. Swann who must have left four or five million francs, but that it was a fad of his. A fad which, moreover, she thought was bound to amuse other people so much that in Paris, when M. Swann called on New Year's Day bringing her a little packet of *marrons glacés*, she never failed, if there were strangers in the room, to say to him: "Well, M. Swann, and do you still live next door to the bonded vaults, so as to be sure of not missing your train when you go to Lyons?" and she would peep out of the corner of her eye, over her glasses, at the other visitors.

But if anyone had suggested to my great-aunt that this Swann, who, in his capacity as the son of old M. Swann, was "fully qualified" to be received by any of the "best people," by the most respected barristers and solicitors of Paris (though he was perhaps a trifle inclined to let this hereditary privilege go by default), had another almost secret existence of a wholly different kind; that when he left our house in Paris, saying that he must go home to bed, he would no sooner have turned the corner than he would stop, retrace his steps, and be off to some salon on whose like no stockbroker or associate of stock-brokers had ever set eyes—that would have seemed to my aunt as extraordinary as, to a woman of wider reading, the thought of being herself on terms of intimacy with Aristaeus and of learning that after having a chat with her he would plunge deep into the realms of Thetis, into an empire veiled from mortal eyes, in which Virgil depicts him as being received with open arms; or—to be content with an image more likely to have occurred to her, for she had seen it painted on the plates we used for biscuits at Combray—as the thought of having had to dinner Ali Baba, who, as soon as he finds himself alone and unobserved, will make his way into the cave, resplendent with its unsuspected treasures.

One day when he had come to see us after dinner in Paris, apologising for being in evening clothes, Françoise told us after he had left that she had got it from his coachman that he had been dining "with a princess." "A nice sort of princess," retorted my aunt, shrugging her shoulders without raising her eyes from her knitting, serenely sarcastic.

Altogether, my great-aunt treated him with scant ceremony. Since she was of the opinion that he ought to feel flattered by our invitations, she thought it only right and proper that he should never come to see us in summer without a basket of peaches or raspberries from his garden, and that from each of his visits to Italy he should bring back some photographs of old masters for me.

It seemed quite natural, therefore, to send for him whenever a recipe for some special sauce or for a pineapple salad was needed for one of our big dinner-parties, to which he himself would not be invited, being regarded as insufficiently important to be served up to new friends who might be in our house for the first time. If the conversation turned upon the princes of the House of France, "gentlemen you and I will never know, will we, and don't want to, do we?" my great-aunt would say tartly to Swann, who had, perhaps, a letter from Twickenham in his pocket; she would make him push the piano into place and turn over the music on evenings when my grandmother's sister sang, manipulating this person who was elsewhere so sought after with the rough simplicity of a child who will play with a collectors' piece with no more circumspection than if it were a cheap gewgaw. Doubtless the Swann who was a familiar figure in all the clubs of those days differed hugely from the Swann created by my great-aunt when, of an evening, in our little garden at Combray, after the two shy peals had sounded from the gate, she would inject and vitalise with everything she knew about the Swann family the obscure and shadowy figure who emerged, with my grandmother in his wake, from the dark background and who was identified by his voice. But then, even in the most insignificant details of our daily life, none of us can be said to constitute a material whole, which is identical for everyone, and need only be turned up like a page in an account-book or the record of a will; our social personality is a creation of the thoughts of other people. Even the simple act which we describe as "seeing someone we know" is to some extent an intellectual process. We pack the physical outline of the person we see with all the notions we have already formed about him, and in the total picture of him which we compose in our minds those notions have certainly the principal place. In the end they come to fill out so completely the curve of his cheeks, to follow so exactly the line of his nose, they blend so harmoniously in the sound of his voice as if it were no more than a transparent envelope, that each time we see the face or hear the voice it is these notions which we recognise and to which we listen. And so, no doubt, from the Swann they had constructed for themselves my family had left out, in their ignorance, a whole host of details of his life in the world of fashion, details which caused other people, when they met him, to see all the graces enthroned in his face and stopping at the line of his aquiline nose as at a natural frontier; but they had contrived also to put into this face divested of all glamour, vacant and roomy as an untenanted house, to plant in the depths of these undervalued eyes, a lingering residuum, vague but not unpleasing—half-memory and half-oblivion—of idle hours spent together after our weekly dinners, round the card-table or in the garden, during our companionable country life. Our friend's corporeal envelope had been so well lined with this residuum, as well as various earlier memories of his parents, that their own special Swann had become to my family a complete and living creature; so that even now I have the feeling of leaving someone I know for another quite

different person when, going back in memory, I pass from the
Swann whom I knew later and more intimately to this early
Swann—this early Swann in whom I can distinguish the
charming mistakes of my youth, and who in fact is less like his
successor than he is like the other people I knew at that time,
as though one's life were a picture gallery in which all the
portraits of any one period had a marked family likeness, a
similar tonality—this early Swann abounding in leisure,
fragrant with the scent of the great chestnut-tree, of baskets
of raspberries and of a sprig of tarragon.

And yet one day, when my grandmother had gone to ask
some favour of a lady whom she had known at the Sacré Cœur
(and with whom, because of our notions of caste, she had not
cared to keep up any degree of intimacy in spite of several
common interests), the Marquise de Villeparisis, of the famous
house of Bouillon, this lady had said to her:

"I believe you know M. Swann very well; he's a great friend
of my nephew and niece, the des Laumes."

My grandmother had returned from the call full of praise
for the house, which overlooked some gardens, and in which
Mme de Villeparisis had advised her to rent a flat, and also
for a repairing tailor and his daughter who kept a little shop
in the courtyard, into which she had gone to ask them to put
a stitch in her skirt, which she had torn on the staircase. My
grandmother had found these people perfectly charming: the
girl, she said, was a jewel, and the tailor the best and most
distinguished man she had ever seen. For in her eyes distinction was a thing wholly independent of social position. She
was in ecstasies over some answer the tailor had made to her,
saying to Mamma:

"Sévigné would not have put it better!" and, by way of
contrast, of a nephew of Mme de Villeparisis whom she had
met at the house:

"My dear, he is so common!"

Now, the effect of the remark about Swann had been, not
to raise him in my great-aunt's estimation, but to lower Mme
de Villeparisis. It appeared that the deference which, on my
grandmother's authority, we owed to Mme de Villeparisis
imposed on her the reciprocal obligation to do nothing that

would render her less worthy of our regard, and that she had
failed in this duty by becoming aware of Swann's existence and
in allowing members of her family to associate with him.
"What! She knows Swann? A person who, you always made
out, was related to Marshal MacMahon!" This view of Swann's
social position which prevailed in my family seemed to be
confirmed later on by his marriage with a woman of the worst
type, almost a prostitute, whom, to do him justice, he never
attempted to introduce to us—for he continued to come to
our house alone, though more and more seldom—but from
whom they felt they could establish, on the assumption that
he had found her there, the circle, unknown to them, in which
he ordinarily moved.

But on one occasion my grandfather read in a newspaper
that M. Swann was one of the most regular attendants at the
Sunday luncheons given by the Duc de X——, whose father
and uncle had been among our most prominent statesmen in
the reign of Louis-Philippe. Now my grandfather was curious
to learn all the smallest details which might help him to
take a mental share in the private lives of men like Molé,
the Duc Pasquier, or the Duc de Broglie. He was delighted to
find that Swann associated with people who had known them.
My great-aunt, on the other hand, interpreted this piece of
news in a sense discreditable to Swann; for anyone who chose
his associates outside the caste in which he had been born
and bred, outside his "proper station," automatically lowered
himself in her eyes. It seemed to her that such a one abdicated
all claim to enjoy the fruits of the splendid connections with
people of good position which prudent parents cultivate and
store up for their children's benefit, and she had actually
ceased to "see" the son of a lawyer of our acquaintance because
he had married a "Highness" and had thereby stepped down—
in her eyes—from the respectable position of a lawyer's son
to that of those adventurers, upstart footmen or stable-boys
mostly, to whom, we are told, queens have sometimes shown
their favours. She objected, therefore, to my grandfather's
plan of questioning Swann, when next he came to dine with
us, about these people whose friendship with him we had
discovered. At the same time my grandmother's two sisters,

elderly spinsters who shared her nobility of character but lacked her intelligence, declared that they could not conceive what pleasure their brother-in-law could find in talking about such trifles. They were ladies of lofty aspirations, who for that reason were incapable of taking the least interest in what might be termed gossip, even if it had some historical import, or, generally speaking, in anything that was not directly associated with some aesthetic or virtuous object. So complete was their negation of interest in anything which seemed directly or indirectly connected with worldly matters that their sense of hearing—having finally come to realise its temporary futility when the tone of the conversation at the dinner-table became frivolous or merely mundane without the two old ladies' being able to guide it back to topics dear to themselves— would put its receptive organs into abeyance to the point of actually becoming atrophied. So that if my grandfather wished to attract the attention of the two sisters, he had to resort to some such physical stimuli as alienists adopt in dealing with their distracted patients: to wit, repeated taps on a glass with the blade of a knife, accompanied by a sharp word and a compelling glance, violent methods which these psychiatrists are apt to bring with them into their everyday life among the sane, either from force of professional habit or because they think the whole world a trifle mad.

Their interest grew, however, when, the day before Swann was to dine with us, and when he had made them a special present of a case of Asti, my great-aunt, who had in her hand a copy of the *Figaro* in which to the name of a picture then on view in a Corot exhibition were added the words, "from the collection of M. Charles Swann," asked: "Did you see that Swann is 'mentioned' in the *Figaro*?"

"But I've always told you," said my grandmother, "that he had a great deal of taste."

"You would, of course," retorted my great-aunt, "say anything just to seem different from *us*." For, knowing that my grandmother never agreed with her, and not being quite confident that it was her own opinion which the rest of us invariably endorsed, she wished to extort from us a wholesale condemnation of my grandmother's views, against which she hoped to force us into solidarity with her own. But we sat silent. My grandmother's sisters having expressed a desire to mention to Swann this reference to him in the *Figaro*, my great-aunt dissuaded them. Whenever she saw in others an advantage, however trivial, which she herself lacked, she would persuade herself that it was no advantage at all, but a drawback, and would pity so as not to have to envy them.

"I don't think that would please him at all; I know very well that I should hate to see my name printed like that, as large as life, in the paper, and I shouldn't feel at all flattered if anyone spoke to me about it."

She did not, however, put any very great pressure upon my grandmother's sisters, for they, in their horror of vulgarity, had brought to such a fine art the concealment of a personal allusion in a wealth of ingenious circumlocution, that it would often pass unnoticed even by the person to whom it was addressed. As for my mother, her only thought was of trying to induce my father to speak to Swann, not about his wife but about his daughter, whom he worshipped, and for whose sake it was understood that he had ultimately made his unfortunate marriage.

"You need only say a word; just ask him how she is. It must be so very hard for him."

My father, however, was annoyed: "No, no; you have the most absurd ideas. It would be utterly ridiculous."

But the only one of us in whom the prospect of Swann's arrival gave rise to an unhappy foreboding was myself. This was because on the evenings when there were visitors, or just M. Swann, in the house, Mamma did not come up to my room. I dined before the others, and afterwards came and sat at table until eight o'clock, when it was understood that I must go upstairs; that frail and precious kiss which Mamma used normally to bestow on me when I was in bed and just going to sleep had to be transported from the dining-room to my bedroom where I must keep it inviolate all the time that it took me to undress, without letting its sweet charm be broken, without letting its volatile essence diffuse itself and evaporate; and it was precisely on those very evenings when I needed to receive it with special care that I was obliged to take it, to snatch it brusquely and in public, without even having the time or the equanimity to bring to what I was doing the single-minded attention of lunatics who compel themselves to exclude all other thoughts from their minds while they are shutting a door, so that when the sickness of uncertainty sweeps over them again they can triumphantly oppose it with the recollection of the precise moment when they shut the door.

We were all in the garden when the double tinkle of the visitors' bell sounded shyly. Everyone knew that it must be Swann, and yet they looked at one another inquiringly and sent my grandmother to reconnoitre.

"See that you thank him intelligibly for the wine," my grandfather warned his two sisters-in-law. "You know how good it is, and the case is huge."

"Now, don't start whispering!" said my great-aunt. "How would you like to come into a house and find everyone muttering to themselves?"

"Ah! There's M. Swann," cried my father. "Let's ask him if he thinks it will be fine to-morrow."

My mother fancied that a word from her would wipe out all the distress which my family had contrived to cause Swann since his marriage. She found an opportunity to draw him aside for a moment. But I followed her: I could not bring myself to let her out of my sight while I felt that in a few minutes I should have to leave her in the dining-room and go up to my bed without the consoling thought, as on ordinary evenings, that she would come up later to kiss me.

"Now, M. Swann," she said, "do tell me about your daughter. I'm sure she already has a taste for beautiful things, like her papa."

"Come along and sit down here with us all on the verandah," said my grandfather, coming up to him. My mother had to abandon her quest, but managed to extract from the restriction itself a further delicate thought, like good poets whom the tyranny of rhyme forces into the discovery of their finest lines.

"We can talk about her again when we are by ourselves," she said, or rather whispered to Swann. "Only a mother is capable of understanding these things. I'm sure that hers would agree with me."

And so we all sat down round the iron table. I should have liked not to think of the hours of anguish which I should have to spend that evening alone in my room, without being able to go to sleep: I tried to convince myself that they were of no importance since I should have forgotten them next morning, and to fix my mind on thoughts of the future which would carry me, as on a bridge, across the terrifying abyss that yawned at my feet. But my mind, strained by this foreboding, distended like the look which I shot at my mother, would not allow any extraneous impression to enter. Thoughts did indeed enter it, but only on the condition that they left behind them every element of beauty, or even of humour, by which I might have been distracted or beguiled. As a surgical patient, thanks to a local anaesthetic, can look on fully conscious while an operation is being performed upon him and yet feel nothing, I could repeat to myself some favourite lines, or watch my grandfather's efforts to talk to Swann about the Duc d'Audiffret-Pasquier, without being able to kindle any emotion from the one or amusement from the other. Hardly had my grandfather begun to question Swann about that orator when one of my grandmother's sisters, in whose ears the question echoed like a solemn but untimely silence which her natural politeness bade her interrupt, addressed the other with:

"Just fancy, Flora, I met a young Swedish governess today who told me some most interesting things about the co-operative movement in Scandinavia. We really must have her to dine here one evening."

"To be sure!" said her sister Flora, "but I haven't wasted my time either. I met such a clever old gentleman at M. Vinteuil's who knows Maubant quite well, and Maubant has told him every little thing about how he gets up his parts. It's the most interesting thing I ever heard. He's a neighbour of M. Vinteuil's, and I never knew; and he is so nice besides."

"M. Vinteuil is not the only one who has nice neighbours," cried my aunt Céline in a voice that was loud because of shyness and forced because of premeditation, darting, as she spoke, what she called a "significant glance" at Swann. And

my aunt Flora, who realised that this veiled utterance was
Céline's way of thanking Swann for the Asti, looked at him
also with a blend of congratulation and irony, either because
she simply wished to underline her sister's little witticism, or
because she envied Swann his having inspired it, or because
she imagined that he was embarrassed, and could not help
having a little fun at his expense.

"I think it would be worth while," Flora went on, "to have
this old gentleman to dinner. When you get him going on
Maubant or Mme Materna he will talk for hours on end."

"That must be delightful," sighed my grandfather, in whose
mind nature had unfortunately forgotten to include any
capacity whatsoever for becoming passionately interested in
the Swedish co-operative movement or in the methods employed by Maubant to get up his parts, just as it had forgotten
to endow my grandmother's two sisters with a grain of that
precious salt which one has oneself to "add to taste" in order
to extract any savour from a narrative of the private life of
Molé or of the Comte de Paris.

"By the way," said Swann to my grandfather, "what I was
going to tell you has more to do than you might think with
what you were asking me just now, for in some respects there
has been very little change. I came across a passage in Saint-
Simon this morning which would have amused you. It's in
the volume which covers his mission to Spain; not one of the
best, little more in fact than a journal, but at least a wonderfully well written journal, which fairly distinguishes it from
the tedious journals we feel bound to read morning and
evening."

"I don't agree with you: there are some days when I find
reading the papers very pleasant indeed," my aunt Flora broke
in, to show Swann that she had read the note about his Corot
in the *Figaro*.

"Yes," aunt Céline went one better, "when they write about
things or people in whom we are interested."

"I don't deny it," answered Swann in some bewilderment.
"The fault I find with our journalism is that it forces us to
take an interest in some fresh triviality or other every day,
whereas only three or four books in a lifetime give us anything

that is of real importance. Suppose that, every morning, when
we tore the wrapper off our paper with fevered hands, a
transmutation were to take place, and we were to find inside
it—oh! I don't know; shall we say Pascal's *Pensées?*" He
articulated the title with an ironic emphasis so as not to appear
pedantic. "And then, in the gilt and tooled volumes which we
open once in ten years," he went on, showing that contempt
for worldly matters which some men of the world like to
affect, "we should read that the Queen of the Hellenes had
arrived at Cannes, or that the Princesse de Léon had given a
fancy dress ball. In that way we should arrive at a happy
medium." But at once regretting that he had allowed himself
to speak of serious matters even in jest, he added ironically:
"What a fine conversation we're having! I can't think why we
climb to these lofty heights," and then, turning to my grandfather: "Well, Saint-Simon tells how Maulévrier had had the
audacity to try to shake hands with his sons. You remember
how he says of Maulévrier, 'Never did I find in that coarse
bottle anything but ill-humour, boorishness, and folly.' "

"Coarse or not, I know bottles in which there is something
very different," said Flora briskly, feeling bound to thank
Swann as well as her sister, since the present of Asti had been
addressed to them both. Céline laughed.

Swann was puzzled, but went on: " 'I cannot say whether
it was ignorance or cozenage,' writes Saint-Simon. 'He tried
to give his hand to my children. I noticed it in time to prevent
him.' "

My grandfather was already in ecstasies over "ignorance or
cozenage," but Mlle Céline—the name of Saint-Simon, a "man
of letters," having arrested the complete paralysis of her
auditory faculties—was indignant:

"What! You admire that? Well, that's a fine thing, I must
say! But what's it supposed to mean? Isn't one man as good
as the next? What difference can it make whether he's a duke
or a groom so long as he's intelligent and kind? He had a
fine way of bringing up his children, your Saint-Simon, if he
didn't teach them to shake hands with all decent folk. Really
and truly, it's abominable. And you dare to quote it!"

And my grandfather, utterly depressed, realising how futile

it would be, against this opposition, to attempt to get Swann to tell him the stories which would have amused him, murmured to my mother: "Just tell me again that line of yours which always comforts me so much on these occasions. Oh, yes: 'What virtues, Lord, Thou makest us abhor!'[2] How good that is!"

I never took my eyes off my mother. I knew that when they were at table I should not be permitted to stay there for the whole of dinner-time, and that Mamma, for fear of annoying my father, would not allow me to kiss her several times in public, as I would have done in my room. And so I promised myself that in the dining-room, as they began to eat and drink and as I felt the hour approach, I would put beforehand into this kiss, which was bound to be so brief and furtive, everything that my own efforts could muster, would carefully choose in advance the exact spot on her cheek where I would imprint it, and would so prepare my thoughts as to be able, thanks to these mental preliminaries, to consecrate the whole of the minute Mamma would grant me to the sensation of her cheek against my lips, as a painter who can have his subject for short sittings only prepares his palette, and from what he remembers and from rough notes does in advance everything which he possibly can do in the sitter's absence. But to-night, before the dinner-bell had sounded, my grandfather said with unconscious cruelty: "The little man looks tired; he'd better go up to bed. Besides, we're dining late to-night."

And my father, who was less scrupulous than my grandmother or my mother in observing the letter of a treaty, went on: "Yes; run along; off to bed."

I would have kissed Mamma then and there, but at that moment the dinner-bell rang.

"No, no, leave your mother alone. You've said good night to one another, that's enough. These exhibitions are absurd. Go on upstairs."

And so I must set forth without viaticum; must climb each step of the staircase "against my heart,"[3] as the saying is, climbing in opposition to my heart's desire, which was to return to my mother, since she had not, by kissing me, given my heart leave to accompany me. That hateful staircase,

up which I always went so sadly, gave out a smell of varnish
which had, as it were, absorbed and crystallised the special
quality of sorrow that I felt each evening, and made it perhaps
even crueller to my sensibility because, when it assumed this
olfactory guise, my intellect was powerless to resist it. When
we have gone to sleep with a raging toothache and are conscious
of it only as of a little girl whom we attempt, time after time,
to pull out of the water, or a line of Molière which we repeat
incessantly to ourselves, it is a great relief to wake up, so that
our intelligence can disentangle the idea of toothache from any
artificial semblance of heroism or rhythmic cadence. It was
the converse of this relief which I felt when my anguish at
having to go up to my room invaded my consciousness in a
manner infinitely more rapid, instantaneous almost, a manner
at once insidious and brutal, through the inhalation—far more
poisonous than moral penetration—of the smell of varnish
peculiar to that staircase.

Once in my room I had to stop every loophole, to close the
shutters, to dig my own grave as I turned down the bedclothes, to wrap myself in the shroud of my nightshirt. But
before burying myself in the iron bed which had been placed
there because, on summer nights, I was too hot among the rep
curtains of the four-poster, I was stirred to revolt, and attempted the desperate stratagem of a condemned prisoner.
I wrote to my mother begging her to come upstairs for an
important reason which I could not put in writing. My fear
was that Françoise, my aunt's cook who used to be put in
charge of me when I was at Combray, might refuse to take
my note. I had a suspicion that, in her eyes, to carry a message
to my mother when there was a guest would appear as flatly
inconceivable as for the door-keeper of a theatre to hand a
letter to an actor upon the stage. On the subject of things which
might or might not be done she possessed a code at once
imperious, abundant, subtle, and uncompromising on points
themselves imperceptible or irrelevant, which gave it a resemblance to those ancient laws which combine such cruel
ordinances as the massacre of infants at the breast with prohibitions of exaggerated refinement against "seething the kid
in his mother's milk," or "eating of the sinew which is upon

the hollow of the thigh." This code, judging by the sudden obstinacy which she would put into her refusal to carry out certain of our instructions, seemed to have provided for social complexities and refinements of etiquette which nothing in Françoise's background or in her career as a servant in a village household could have put into her head; and we were obliged to assume that there was latent in her some past existence in the ancient history of France, noble and little understood, as in those manufacturing towns where old mansions still testify to their former courtly days, and chemical workers toil among delicately sculptured scenes from *Le Miracle de Théophile* or *Les quatre fils Aymon*.[4]

In this particular instance, the article of her code which made it highly improbable that—barring an outbreak of fire —Françoise would go down and disturb Mamma in the presence of M. Swann for so unimportant a person as myself was one embodying the respect she showed not only for the family (as for the dead, for the clergy, or for royalty), but also for the stranger within our gates; a respect which I should perhaps have found touching in a book, but which never failed to irritate me on her lips, because of the solemn and senti-mental tones in which she would express it, and which irri-tated me more than usual this evening when the sacred character with which she invested the dinner-party might have the effect of making her decline to disturb its ceremonial. But to give myself a chance of success I had no hesitation in lying, telling her that it was not in the least myself who had wanted to write to Mamma, but Mamma who, on saying good night to me, had begged me not to forget to send her an answer about something she had asked me to look for, and that she would certainly be very angry if this note were not taken to her. I think that Françoise disbelieved me, for, like those primitive men whose senses were so much keener than our own, she could immediately detect, from signs imperceptible to the rest of us, the truth or falsehood of anything that we might wish to conceal from her. She studied the envelope for five minutes as though an examination of the paper itself and the look of my handwriting could enlighten her as to the nature of the contents, or tell her to which article of her code she ought to refer the matter. Then she went out with an air of resignation which seemed to imply: "It's hard lines on parents having a child like that."

A moment later she returned to say that they were still at the ice stage and that it was impossible for the butler to deliver the note at once, in front of everybody; but that when the finger-bowls were put round he would find a way of slipping it into Mamma's hand. At once my anxiety subsided; it was now no longer (as it had been a moment ago) until to-morrow that I had lost my mother, since my little note—though it would annoy her, no doubt, and doubly so because this stratagem would make me ridiculous in Swann's eyes—would at least admit me, invisible and enraptured, into the same room as herself, would whisper about me into her ear; since that forbidden and unfriendly dining-room, where but a moment ago the ice itself—with burned nuts in it—and the finger-bowls seemed to me to be concealing pleasures that were baleful and of a mortal sadness because Mamma was tasting of them while I was far away, had opened its doors to me and, like a ripe fruit which bursts through its skin, was going to pour out into my intoxicated heart the sweetness of Mamma's attention while she was reading what I had written. Now I was no longer separated from her; the barriers were down; an exquisite thread united us. Besides, that was not all: for surely Mamma would come.

As for the agony through which I had just passed, I imagined that Swann would have laughed heartily at it if he had read my letter and had guessed its purpose; whereas, on the contrary, as I was to learn in due course, a similar anguish had been the bane of his life for many years, and no one perhaps could have understood my feelings at that moment so well as he; to him, the anguish that comes from knowing that the creature one adores is in some place of enjoyment where oneself is not and cannot follow—to him that anguish came through love, to which it is in a sense predestined, by which it will be seized upon and exploited; but when, as had befallen me, it possesses one's soul before love has yet entered into one's life, then it must drift, awaiting love's coming, vague and free, without precise attachment, at the

disposal of one sentiment to-day, of another to-morrow, of
filial piety or affection for a friend. And the joy with which I
first bound myself apprentice, when Françoise returned to tell
me that my letter would be delivered, Swann, too, had known
well—that false joy which a friend or relative of the woman
we love can give us, when, on his arrival at the house or
theatre where she is to be found, for some ball or party or
"first-night" at which he is to meet her, he sees us wandering
outside, desperately awaiting some opportunity of communicating with her. He recognises us, greets us familiarly,
and asks what we are doing there. And when we invent a story
of having some urgent message to give to his relative or friend,
he assures us that nothing could be simpler, takes us in at
the door, and promises to send her down to us in five minutes.
How we love him—as at that moment I loved Françoise—the
good-natured intermediary who by a single word has made
supportable, human, almost propitious the inconceivable,
infernal scene of gaiety in the thick of which we had been
imagining swarms of enemies, perverse and seductive, be-
guiling away from us, even making laugh at us, the woman
we love! If we are to judge of them by him—this relative
who has accosted us and who is himself an initiate in those
cruel mysteries—then the other guests cannot be so very
demoniacal. Those inaccessible and excruciating hours during
which she was about to taste of unknown pleasures—suddenly, through an unexpected breach, we have broken into
them; suddenly we can picture to ourselves, we possess, we
intervene upon, we have almost created, one of the moments
the succession of which would have composed those hours,
a moment as real as all the rest, if not actually more important
to us because our mistress is more intensely a part of it:
namely, the moment in which he goes to tell her that we are
waiting below. And doubtless the other moments of the party
would not have been so very different from this one, would
be no more exquisite, no more calculated to make us suffer,
since this kind friend has assured us that "Of course, she will
be delighted to come down! It will be far more amusing for
her to talk to you than to be bored up there." Alas! Swann
had learned by experience that the good intentions of a third

party are powerless to influence a woman who is annoyed to find herself pursued even into a ballroom by a man she does not love. Too often, the kind friend comes down again alone.

My mother did not appear, but without the slightest consideration for my self-respect (which depended upon her keeping up the fiction that she had asked me to let her know the result of my search for something or other) told Françoise to tell me, in so many words: "There is no answer"—words I have so often, since then, heard the hall-porters in grand hotels and the flunkeys in gambling-clubs and the like repeat to some poor girl who replies in bewilderment: "What! he said nothing? It's not possible. You did give him my letter, didn't you? Very well, I shall wait a little longer." And, just as she invariably protests that she does not need the extra gas-jet which the porter offers to light for her, and sits on there, hearing nothing further except an occasional remark on the weather which the porter exchanges with a bell-hop whom he will send off suddenly, when he notices the time, to put some customer's wine on the ice, so, having declined Françoise's offer to make me some tea or to stay beside me, I let her go off again to the pantry, and lay down and shut my eyes, trying not to hear the voices of my family who were drinking their coffee in the garden.

But after a few seconds I realised that, by writing that note to Mamma, by approaching—at the risk of making her angry —so near to her that I felt I could reach out and grasp the moment in which I should see her again, I had cut myself off from the possibility of going to sleep until I actually had seen her, and my heart began to beat more and more painfully as I increased my agitation by ordering myself to keep calm and to acquiesce in my ill-fortune. Then, suddenly, my anxiety subsided, a feeling of intense happiness coursed through me, as when a strong medicine begins to take effect and one's pain vanishes: I had formed a resolution to abandon all attempts to go to sleep without seeing Mamma, had made up my mind to kiss her at all costs, even though this meant the certainty of being in disgrace with her for long afterwards—when she herself came up to bed. The calm which succeeded my anguish filled me with an extraordinary exhilaration, no less than my sense of expectation, my thirst for and my fear of danger. Noiselessly I opened the window and sat down on the foot of my bed. I hardly dared to move in case they should hear me from below. Outside, things too seemed frozen, rapt in a mute intentness not to disturb the moonlight which, duplicating each of them and throwing it back by the extension in front of it of a shadow denser and more concrete than its substance, had made the whole landscape at once thinner and larger, like a map which, after being folded up, is spread out upon the ground. What had to move—a leaf of the chestnut-tree, for instance—moved. But its minute quivering, total, self-contained, finished down to its minutest gradation and its last delicate tremor, did not impinge upon the rest of the scene, did not merge with it, remained circumscribed. Exposed upon this surface of silence which absorbed nothing of them, the most distant sounds, those which must have come from gardens at the far end of the town, could be distinguished with such exact "finish" that the impression they gave of coming from a distance seemed due only to their "pianissimo" execution, like those movements on muted strings so well performed by the orchestra of the Conservatoire that, even though one does not miss a single note, one thinks nonetheless that they are being played somewhere outside, a long way from the concert hall, so that all the old subscribers—my grandmother's sisters too, when Swann had given them his seats—used to strain their ears as if they had caught the distant approach of an army on the march, which had not yet rounded the corner of the Rue de Trévise.

I was well aware that I had placed myself in a position than which none could be counted upon to involve me in graver consequences at my parents' hands; consequences far graver, indeed, than a stranger would have imagined, and such as (he would have thought) could follow only some really shameful misdemeanour. But in the upbringing which they had given me faults were not classified in the same order as in that of other children, and I had been taught to place at the head of the list (doubtless because there was no other class of faults from which I needed to be more carefully protected) those in which I can now distinguish the common feature that one succumbs to them by yielding to a nervous impulse. But such a phrase had never been uttered in my hearing; no one had yet accounted for my temptations in a way which might have led me to believe that there was some excuse for my giving in to them, or that I was actually incapable of holding out against them. Yet I could easily recognise this class of transgressions by the anguish of mind which preceded as well as by the rigour of the punishment which followed them; and I knew that what I had just done was in the same category as certain other sins for which I had been severely punished, though infinitely more serious than they. When I went out to meet my mother on her way up to bed, and when she saw that I had stayed up in order to say good night to her again in the passage, I should not be allowed to stay in the house a day longer, I should be packed off to school next morning; so much was certain. Very well: had I been obliged, the next moment, to hurl myself out of the window, I should still have preferred such a fate. For what I wanted now was Mamma, to say good night to her. I had gone too far along the road which led to the fulfilment of this desire to be able to retrace my steps.

I could hear my parents' footsteps as they accompanied Swann to the gate, and when the clanging of the bell assured me that he had really gone, I crept to the window. Mamma was asking my father if he had thought the lobster good, and whether M. Swann had had a second helping of the coffee-and-pistachio ice. "I thought it rather so-so," she was saying. "Next time we shall have to try another flavour."

"I can't tell you," said my great-aunt, "what a change I find in Swann. He is quite antiquated!" She had grown so accustomed to seeing Swann always in the same stage of adolescence that it was a shock to her to find him suddenly less young than the age she still attributed to him. And the others too were beginning to remark in Swann that abnormal, excessive, shameful and deserved senescence of bachelors, of all those for whom it seems that the great day which knows no morrow must be longer than for other men, since for them it is void of promise, and from its dawn the moments steadily accumulate without any subsequent partition among offspring.

"I fancy he has a lot of trouble with that wretched wife of his, who lives with a certain Monsieur de Charlus, as all Combray knows. It's the talk of the town."

My mother observed that, in spite of this, he had looked much less unhappy of late. "And he doesn't nearly so often do that trick of his, so like his father, of wiping his eyes and drawing his hand across his forehead. I think myself that in his heart of hearts he no longer loves that woman."

"Why, of course he doesn't," answered my grandfather. "He wrote me a letter about it, ages ago, to which I took care to pay no attention, but it left no doubt as to his feelings, or at any rate his love, for his wife. Hullo! you two; you never thanked him for the Asti," he went on, turning to his sisters-in-law.

"What! we never thanked him? I think, between you and me, that I put it to him quite neatly," replied my aunt Flora.

"Yes, you managed it very well; I admired you for it," said my aunt Céline.

"But you did it very prettily, too."

"Yes; I was rather proud of my remark about 'nice neighbours.'"

"What! Do you call that thanking him?" shouted my grandfather. "I heard that all right, but devil take me if I guessed it was meant for Swann. You may be quite sure he never noticed it."

"Come, come; Swann isn't a fool. I'm sure he understood. You didn't expect me to tell him the number of bottles, or to guess what he paid for them."

My father and mother were left alone and sat down for a moment; then my father said: "Well, shall we go up to bed?"

"As you wish, dear, though I don't feel at all sleepy. I don't know why; it can't be the coffee-ice—it wasn't strong enough to keep me awake like this. But I see a light in the servants' hall: poor Françoise has been sitting up for me, so I'll get her to unhook me while you go and undress."

My mother opened the latticed door which led from the hall to the staircase. Presently I heard her coming upstairs to close her window. I went quietly into the passage; my heart was beating so violently that I could hardly move, but at least it was throbbing no longer with anxiety, but with terror and joy. I saw in the well of the stair a light coming upwards, from Mamma's candle. Then I saw Mamma herself and I threw myself upon her. For an instant she looked at me in astonishment, not realising what could have happened. Then her face assumed an expression of anger. She said not a single word to me; and indeed I used to go for days on end without being spoken to, for far more venial offences than this. A single word from Mamma would have been an admission that further intercourse with me was within the bounds of possibility, and that might perhaps have appeared to me more terrible still, as indicating that, with such a punishment as was in store for me, mere silence and black looks would have been puerile. A word from her then would have implied the false calm with which one addresses a servant to whom one has just decided to give notice; the kiss one bestows on a son who is being packed off to enlist, which would have been denied him if it had merely been a matter of being angry with him for a few days. But she heard my father coming from the dressing-room, where he had gone to take off his clothes, and, to avoid the "scene" which he would make if he saw me, she said to me in a voice half-stifled with anger: "Off you go at once. Do you want your father to see you waiting there like an idiot?"

But I implored her again: "Come and say good night to me," terrified as I saw the light from my father's candle already creeping up the wall, but also making use of his approach as a means of blackmail, in the hope that my mother, not wishing him to find me there, as find me he must if she continued to refuse me, would give in and say: "Go back to your room. I will come."

Too late: my father was upon us. Instinctively I murmured, though no one heard me, "I'm done for!"

I was not, however. My father used constantly to refuse to let me do things which were quite clearly allowed by the more liberal charters granted me by my mother and grandmother, because he paid no heed to "principles," and because for him there was no such thing as the "rule of law." For some quite irrelevant reason, or for no reason at all, he would at the last

moment prevent me from taking some particular walk, one so
regular, so hallowed, that to deprive me of it was a clear
breach of faith; or again, as he had done this evening, long
before the appointed hour he would snap out: "Run along
up to bed now; no excuses!" But at the same time, because he
was devoid of principles (in my grandmother's sense), he could
not, strictly speaking, be called intransigent. He looked at me
for a moment with an air of surprise and annoyance, and then
when Mamma had told him, not without some embarrassment,
what had happened, said to her: "Go along with him, then.
You said just now that you didn't feel very sleepy, so stay in
his room for a little. I don't need anything."

"But, my dear," my mother answered timidly, "whether or
not I feel sleepy is not the point; we mustn't let the child get
into the habit . . ."

"There's no question of getting into a habit," said my
father, with a shrug of the shoulders; "you can see quite well
that the child is unhappy. After all, we aren't gaolers. You'll
end by making him ill, and a lot of good that will do. There
are two beds in his room; tell Françoise to make up the big
one for you, and stay with him for the rest of the night.
Anyhow, I'm off to bed; I'm not so nervy as you. Good night."

It was impossible for me to thank my father; he would have
been exasperated by what he called mawkishness. I stood there,
not daring to move; he was still in front of us, a tall figure in
his white nightshirt, crowned with the pink and violet cash-
mere scarf which he used to wrap around his head since he
had begun to suffer from neuralgia, standing like Abraham in
the engraving after Benozzo Gozzoli which M. Swann had
given me, telling Sarah that she must tear herself away from
Isaac. Many years have passed since that night. The wall of
the staircase up which I had watched the light of his candle
gradually climb was long ago demolished. And in myself,
too, many things have perished which I imagined would last
for ever, and new ones have arisen, giving birth to new
sorrows and new joys which in those days I could not have
foreseen, just as now the old are hard to understand. It is a
long time, too, since my father has been able to say to Mamma:
"Go along with the child." Never again will such moments

be possible for me. But of late I have been increasingly able to catch, if I listen attentively, the sound of the sobs which I had the strength to control in my father's presence, and which broke out only when I found myself alone with Mamma. In reality their echo has never ceased; and it is only because life is now growing more and more quiet round about me that I hear them anew, like those convent bells which are so effectively drowned during the day by the noises of the street that one would suppose them to have stopped, until they ring out again through the silent evening air.

Mamma spent that night in my room: when I had just committed a sin so deadly that I expected to be banished from the household, my parents gave me a far greater concession than I could ever have won as the reward of a good deed. Even at the moment when it manifested itself in this crowning mercy, my father's behaviour towards me still retained that arbitrary and unwarranted quality which was so characteristic of him and which arose from the fact that his actions were generally dictated by chance expediencies rather than based on any formal plan. And perhaps even what I called his severity, when he sent me off to bed, deserved that title less than my mother's or my grandmother's attitude, for his nature, which in some respects differed more than theirs from my own, had probably prevented him from realising until then how wretched I was every evening, something which my mother and grandmother knew well; but they loved me enough to be unwilling to spare me that suffering, which they hoped to teach me to overcome, so as to reduce my nervous sensibility and to strengthen my will. Whereas my father, whose affection for me was of another kind, would not, I suspect, have had the same courage, for as soon as he had grasped the fact that I was unhappy he had said to my mother: "Go and comfort him."

Mamma stayed that night in my room, and it seemed that she did not wish to mar by recrimination those hours which were so different from anything that I had had a right to expect, for when Françoise (who guessed that something extraordinary must have happened when she saw Mamma sitting by my side, holding my hand and letting me cry unchided)

said to her: "But, Madame, what is young master crying for?"
she replied: "Why, Françoise, he doesn't know himself: it's
his nerves. Make up the big bed for me quickly and then go
off to your own." And thus for the first time my unhappiness
was regarded no longer as a punishable offence but as an
involuntary ailment which had been officially recognised, a
nervous condition for which I was in no way responsible:
I had the consolation of no longer having to mingle appre-
hensive scruples with the bitterness of my tears; I could weep
henceforth without sin. I felt no small degree of pride, either,
in Françoise's presence at this return to humane conditions
which, not an hour after Mamma had refused to come up to
my room and had sent the snubbing message that I was to go
to sleep, raised me to the dignity of a grown-up person,
brought me of a sudden to a sort of puberty of sorrow, a
manumission of tears. I ought to have been happy; I was not.
It struck me that my mother had just made a first concession
which must have been painful to her, that it was a first abdication on her part from the ideal she had formed for me, and that
for the first time she who was so brave had to confess herself
beaten. It struck me that if I had just won a victory it was over
her, that I had succeeded, as sickness or sorrow or age might
have succeeded, in relaxing her will, in undermining her
judgment; and that this evening opened a new era, would
remain a black date in the calendar. And if I had dared now,
I should have said to Mamma: "No, I don't want you to, you
mustn't sleep here." But I was conscious of the practical
wisdom, of what would nowadays be called the realism, with
which she tempered the ardent idealism of my grandmother's
nature, and I knew that now the mischief was done she would
prefer to let me enjoy the soothing pleasure of her company,
and not to disturb my father again. Certainly my mother's
beautiful face seemed to shine again with youth that evening,
as she sat gently holding my hands and trying to check my
tears; but this was just what I felt should not have been;
her anger would have saddened me less than this new gentleness, unknown to my childhood experience; I felt that I had
with an impious and secret finger traced a first wrinkle upon
her soul and brought out a first white hair on her head. This

thought redoubled my sobs, and then I saw that Mamma, who had never allowed herself to indulge in any undue emotion with me, was suddenly overcome by my tears and had to struggle to keep back her own. When she realised that I had noticed this, she said to me with a smile: "Why, my little buttercup, my little canary-boy, he's going to make Mamma as silly as himself if this goes on. Look, since you can't sleep, and Mamma can't either, we mustn't go on in this stupid way; we must do something; I'll get one of your books." But I had none there. "Would you like me to get out the books now that your grandmother is going to give you for your birthday? Just think it over first, and don't be disappointed if there's nothing new for you then."

I was only too delighted, and Mamma went to fetch a parcel of books of which I could not distinguish, through the paper in which they were wrapped, any more than their short, wide format but which, even at this first glimpse, brief and obscure as it was, bade fair to eclipse already the paintbox of New Year's Day and the silkworms of the year before. The books were *La Mare au Diable*, *François le Champi*, *La Petite Fadette* and *Les Maîtres Sonneurs*. My grandmother, as I learned afterwards, had at first chosen Musset's poems, a volume of Rousseau, and *Indiana*; for while she considered light reading as unwholesome as sweets and cakes, she did not reflect that the strong breath of genius might have upon the mind even of a child an influence at once more dangerous and less invigorating than that of fresh air and sea breezes upon his body. But when my father had almost called her an imbecile on learning the names of the books she proposed to give me, she had journeyed back by herself to Jouy-le-Vicomte to the bookseller's, so that there should be no danger of my not having my present in time (it was a boiling hot day, and she had come home so unwell that the doctor had warned my mother not to allow her to tire herself so), and had fallen back upon the four pastoral novels of George Sand.

"My dear," she had said to Mamma, "I could not bring myself to give the child anything that was not well written."

The truth was that she could never permit herself to buy anything from which no intellectual profit was to be derived,

above all the profit which fine things afford us by teaching us
to seek our pleasures elsewhere than in the barren satisfaction
of worldly wealth. Even when she had to make someone a
present of the kind called "useful," when she had to give an
armchair or some table-silver or a walking-stick, she would
choose "antiques," as though their long desuetude had effaced
from them any semblance of utility and fitted them rather to
instruct us in the lives of the men of other days than to serve
the common requirements of our own. She would have liked
me to have in my room photographs of ancient buildings or
of beautiful places. But at the moment of buying them, and
for all that the subject of the picture had an aesthetic value, she
would find that vulgarity and utility had too prominent a part
in them, through the mechanical nature of their reproduction
by photography. She attempted by a subterfuge, if not to
eliminate altogether this commercial banality, at least to
minimise it, to supplant it to a certain extent with what was
art still, to introduce, as it were, several "thicknesses" of art:
instead of photographs of Chartres Cathedral, of the Fountains
of Saint-Cloud, or of Vesuvius, she would inquire of Swann
whether some great painter had not depicted them, and preferred to give me photographs of "Chartres Cathedral" after
Corot, of the "Fountains of Saint-Cloud" after Hubert Robert,
and of "Vesuvius" after Turner, which were a stage higher in
the scale of art. But although the photographer had been
prevented from reproducing directly these masterpieces or
beauties of nature, and had there been replaced by a great
artist, he resumed his odious position when it came to reproducing the artist's interpretation. Accordingly, having to
reckon again with vulgarity, my grandmother would endeavour to postpone the moment of contact still further. She
would ask Swann if the picture had not been engraved,
preferring, when possible, old engravings with some interest
of association apart from themselves, such, for example, as
show us a masterpiece in a state in which we can no longer
see it to-day (like Morghen's print of Leonardo's "Last
Supper" before its defacement). It must be admitted that the
results of this method of interpreting the art of making presents
were not always happy. The idea which I formed of Venice,

from a drawing by Titian which is supposed to have the lagoon in the background, was certainly far less accurate than what I should have derived from ordinary photographs. We could no longer keep count in the family (when my great-aunt wanted to draw up an indictment of my grandmother) of all the armchairs she had presented to married couples, young and old, which on a first attempt to sit down upon them had at once collapsed beneath the weight of their recipients. But my grandmother would have thought it sordid to concern herself too closely with the solidity of any piece of furniture in which could still be discerned a flourish, a smile, a brave conceit of the past. And even what in such pieces answered a material need, since it did so in a manner to which we are no longer accustomed, charmed her like those old forms of speech in which we can still see traces of a metaphor whose fine point has been worn away by the rough usage of our modern tongue. As it happened, the pastoral novels of George Sand which she was giving me for my birthday were regular lumber-rooms full of expressions that have fallen out of use and become quaint and picturesque, and are now only to be found in country dialects. And my grandmother had bought them in preference to other books, as she would more readily have taken a house with a gothic dovecot or some other such piece of antiquity as will exert a benign influence on the mind by giving it a hankering for impossible journeys through the realms of time.

Mamma sat down by my bed; she had chosen *François le Champi*, whose reddish cover and incomprehensible title gave it, for me, a distinct personality and a mysterious attraction. I had not then read any real novels. I had heard it said that George Sand was a typical novelist. This predisposed me to imagine that *François le Champi* contained something inexpressibly delicious. The narrative devices designed to arouse curiosity or melt to pity, certain modes of expression which disturb or sadden the reader, and which, with a little experience, he may recognise as common to a great many novels, seemed to me—for whom a new book was not one of a number of similar objects but, as it were, a unique person, absolutely self-contained—simply an intoxicating distillation of the

peculiar essence of *François le Champi*. Beneath the everyday
incidents, the ordinary objects and common words, I sensed a
strange and individual tone of voice. The plot began to unfold: to me it seemed all the more obscure because in those
days, when I read, I used often to daydream about something
quite different for page after page. And the gaps which this
habit left in my knowledge of the story were widened by the
fact that when it was Mamma who was reading to me aloud
she left all the love-scenes out. And so all the odd changes
which take place in the relations between the miller's wife
and the boy, changes which only the gradual dawning of love
can explain, seemed to me steeped in a mystery the key to
which (I readily believed) lay in that strange and mellifluous
name of *Champi*, which invested the boy who bore it, I had
no idea why, with its own vivid, ruddy, charming colour.
If my mother was not a faithful reader, she was none the less
an admirable one, when reading a work in which she found the
note of true feeling, in the respectful simplicity of her interpretation and the beauty and sweetness of her voice. Even
in ordinary life, when it was not works of art but men and
women whom she was moved to pity or admire, it was touching to observe with what deference she would banish from her
voice, her gestures, from her whole conversation, now the note
of gaiety which might have distressed some mother who had
once lost a child, now the recollection of an event or anniversary which might have reminded some old gentleman of
the burden of his years, now the household topic which might
have bored some young man of letters. And so, when she read
aloud the prose of George Sand, prose which is everywhere
redolent of that generosity and moral distinction which
Mamma had learned from my grandmother to place above all
other qualities in life, and which I was not to teach her until
much later to refrain from placing above all other qualities in
literature too, taking pains to banish from her voice any
pettiness or affectation which might have choked that powerful
stream of language, she supplied all the natural tenderness,
all the lavish sweetness which they demanded to sentences
which seemed to have been composed for her voice and which
were all, so to speak, within the compass of her sensibility.

She found, to tackle them in the required tone, the warmth of feeling which pre-existed and dictated them, but which is not to be found in the words themselves, and by this means she smoothed away, as she read, any harshness or discordance in the tenses of verbs, endowing the imperfect and the preterite with all the sweetness to be found in generosity, all the melancholy to be found in love, guiding the sentence that was drawing to a close towards the one that was about to begin, now hastening, now slackening the pace of the syllables so as to bring them, despite their differences of quantity, into a uniform rhythm, and breathing into this quite ordinary prose a kind of emotional life and continuity.

My aching heart was soothed; I let myself be borne upon the current of this gentle night on which I had my mother by my side. I knew that such a night could not be repeated; that the strongest desire I had in the world, namely, to keep my mother in my room through the sad hours of darkness, ran too much counter to general requirements and to the wishes of others for such a concession as had been granted me this evening to be anything but a rare and artificial exception. To-morrow night my anguish would return and Mamma would not stay by my side. But when my anguish was assuaged, I could no longer understand it; besides, to-morrow was still a long way off; I told myself that I should still have time to take preventive action, although that time could bring me no access of power since these things were in no way dependent upon the exercise of my will, and seemed not quite inevitable only because they were still separated from me by this short interval.

And so it was that, for a long time afterwards, when I lay awake at night and revived old memories of Combray, I saw no more of it than this sort of luminous panel, sharply defined against a vague and shadowy background, like the panels which the glow of a Bengal light or a searchlight beam will cut out and illuminate in a building the other parts of which remain plunged in darkness: broad enough at its base, the little parlour, the dining-room, the opening of the dark path from which M. Swann, the unwitting author of my sufferings, would emerge, the hall through which I would journey to the first step of that staircase, so painful to climb, which constituted, all by itself, the slender cone of this irregular pyramid; and, at the summit, my bedroom, with the little passage through whose glazed door Mamma would enter; in a word, seen always at the same evening hour, isolated from all its possible surroundings, detached and solitary against the dark background, the bare minimum of scenery necessary (like the decor one sees prescribed on the title-page of an old play, for its performance in the provinces) to the drama of my undressing; as though all Combray had consisted of but two floors joined by a slender staircase, and as though there had been no time there but seven o'clock at night. I must own that I could have assured any questioner that Combray did include other scenes and did exist at other hours than these. But since the facts which I should then have recalled would have been prompted only by voluntary memory, the memory of the intellect, and since the pictures which that kind of memory shows us preserve nothing of the past itself, I should never have had any wish to ponder over this residue of Combray. To me it was in reality all dead.

Permanently dead? Very possibly.

There is a large element of chance in these matters, and a second chance occurrence, that of our own death, often prevents us from awaiting for any length of time the favours of the first.

I feel that there is much to be said for the Celtic belief that the souls of those whom we have lost are held captive in some inferior being, in an animal, in a plant, in some inanimate object, and thus effectively lost to us until the day (which to many never comes) when we happen to pass by the tree or to obtain possession of the object which forms their prison. Then they start and tremble, they call us by our name, and as soon as we have recognised their voice the spell is broken. Delivered by us, they have overcome death and return to share our life.

And so it is with our own past. It is a labour in vain to attempt to recapture it: all the efforts of our intellect must prove futile. The past is hidden somewhere outside the realm, beyond the reach of intellect, in some material object (in the sensation which that material object will give us) of which we have no inkling. And it depends on chance whether or not we come upon this object before we ourselves must die.

Many years had elapsed during which nothing of Combray, save what was comprised in the theatre and the drama of my going to bed there, had any existence for me, when one day in winter, on my return home, my mother, seeing that I was cold, offered me some tea, a thing I did not ordinarily take. I declined at first, and then, for no particular reason, changed my mind. She sent for one of those squat, plump little cakes called "petites madeleines," which look as though they had been moulded in the fluted valve of a scallop shell. And soon, mechanically, dispirited after a dreary day with the prospect of a depressing morrow, I raised to my lips a spoonful of the tea in which I had soaked a morsel of the cake. No sooner had the warm liquid mixed with the crumbs touched my palate than a shudder ran through me and I stopped, intent upon the extraordinary thing that was happening to me. An exquisite pleasure had invaded my senses, something isolated, detached, with no suggestion of its origin. And at once the vicissitudes of life had become indifferent to me, its disasters innocuous, its brevity illusory—this new sensation having had on me the effect which love has of filling me with a precious essence; or rather this essence was not in me, it *was* me. I had ceased now to feel mediocre, contingent, mortal. Whence could it have come to me, this all-powerful joy? I sensed that it was connected with the taste of the tea and the cake, but that it infinitely transcended those savours, could not, indeed, be of the same nature. Whence did it come? What did it mean? How could I seize and apprehend it?

I drink a second mouthful, in which I find nothing more than in the first, then a third, which gives me rather less than the second. It is time to stop; the potion is losing its magic. It is plain that the truth I am seeking lies not in the cup but in myself. The drink has called it into being, but does not know it, and can only repeat indefinitely, with a progressive diminution of strength, the same message which I cannot interpret, though I hope at least to be able to call it forth again and to find it there presently, intact and at my disposal, for my final enlightenment. I put down the cup and examine my own mind. It alone can discover the truth. But how? What an abyss of uncertainty, whenever the mind feels overtaken by itself; when it, the seeker, is at the same time the dark region through which it must go seeking and where all its equipment will avail it nothing. Seek? More than that: create. It is face to face with something which does not yet exist, to which it alone can give reality and substance, which it alone can bring into the light of day.

And I begin again to ask myself what it could have been, this unremembered state which brought with it no logical proof, but the indisputable evidence, of its felicity, its reality, and in whose presence other states of consciousness melted and vanished. I decide to attempt to make it reappear. I retrace my thoughts to the moment at which I drank the first spoonful of tea. I rediscover the same state, illuminated by no fresh light. I ask my mind to make one further effort, to bring back once more the fleeting sensation. And so that nothing may interrupt it in its course I shut out every obstacle, every extraneous idea, I stop my ears and inhibit all attention against the sounds from the next room. And then, feeling that my mind is tiring itself without having any success to report, I compel it for a change to enjoy the distraction which I have just denied it, to think of other things, to rest and refresh itself before making a final effort. And then for the second time I clear an empty space in front of it; I place in position before my mind's eye the still recent taste of that first mouthful, and I feel something start within me, something that leaves its resting-place and attempts to rise, something that has been embedded like an anchor at a great depth; I do not know yet what it is, but I can feel it mounting slowly; I can measure the resistance, I can hear the echo of great spaces traversed.

Undoubtedly what is thus palpitating in the depths of my being must be the image, the visual memory which, being linked to that taste, is trying to follow it into my conscious mind. But its struggles are too far off, too confused and chaotic; scarcely can I perceive the neutral glow into which the elusive whirling medley of stirred-up colours is fused, and I cannot distinguish its form, cannot invite it, as the one possible interpreter, to translate for me the evidence of its contemporary, its inseparable paramour, the taste, cannot ask it to inform me what special circumstance is in question, from what period in my past life.

Will it ultimately reach the clear surface of my consciousness, this memory, this old, dead moment which the magnetism of an identical moment has travelled so far to importune, to disturb, to raise up out of the very depths of my being? I cannot tell. Now I feel nothing; it has stopped, has perhaps sunk back into its darkness, from which who can say whether it will ever rise again? Ten times over I must essay the task, must lean down over the abyss. And each time the cowardice that deters us from every difficult task, every important enterprise, has urged me to leave the thing alone, to drink my tea and to think merely of the worries of to-day and my hopes for to-morrow, which can be brooded over painlessly.

And suddenly the memory revealed itself. The taste was that of the little piece of madeleine which on Sunday mornings at Combray (because on those mornings I did not go out before mass), when I went to say good morning to her in her bedroom, my aunt Léonie used to give me, dipping it first in her own cup of tea or tisane. The sight of the little madeleine had recalled nothing to my mind before I tasted it; perhaps because I had so often seen such things in the meantime, without tasting them, on the trays in pastry-cooks' windows, that their image had dissociated itself from those Combray days to take its place among others more recent; perhaps because of those memories, so long abandoned and put out of mind, nothing now survived, everything was scattered; the shapes of things, including that of the little scallop-shell of pastry, so richly sensual under its severe, religious folds, were either obliterated or had been so long dormant as to have lost the power of expansion which would have allowed them to resume their place in my consciousness. But when from a long-distant past nothing subsists, after the people are dead, after the things are broken and scattered, taste and smell alone, more fragile but more enduring, more unsubstantial, more persistent, more faithful, remain poised a long time, like souls, remembering, waiting, hoping, amid the ruins of all the rest; and bear unflinchingly, in the tiny and almost impalpable drop of their essence, the vast structure of recollection.

And as soon as I had recognised the taste of the piece of madeleine soaked in her decoction of lime-blossom which my aunt used to give me (although I did not yet know and must long postpone the discovery of why this memory made me so happy) immediately the old grey house upon the street, where her room was, rose up like a stage set to attach itself to the little pavilion opening on to the garden which had been built out behind it for my parents (the isolated segment which until that moment had been all that I could see); and with the house the town, from morning to night and in all weathers, the Square where I used to be sent before lunch, the streets along which I used to run errands, the country roads we took when it was fine. And as in the game wherein the Japanese amuse themselves by filling a porcelain bowl with water and steeping in it little pieces of paper which until then are without character or form, but, the moment they become wet, stretch and twist and take on colour and distinctive shape, become flowers or houses or people, solid and recognisable, so in that moment all the flowers in our garden and in M. Swann's park, and the water-lilies on the Vivonne and the good folk of the village and their little dwellings and the parish church and the whole of Combray and its surroundings, taking shape and solidity, sprang into being, town and gardens alike, from my cup of tea.

COMBRAY

COMBRAY at a distance, from a twenty-mile radius, as we used to see it from the railway when we arrived there in the week before Easter, was no more than a church epitomising the town, representing it, speaking of it and for it to the horizon, and as one drew near, gathering close about its long, dark cloak, sheltering from the wind, on the open plain, as a shepherdess gathers her sheep, the woolly grey backs of its huddled houses, which the remains of its mediaeval ramparts enclosed, here and there, in an outline as scrupulously circular as that of a little town in a primitive painting. To live in, Combray was a trifle depressing, like its streets, whose houses, built of the blackened stone of the country, fronted with outside steps, capped with gables which projected long shadows downwards, were so dark that as soon as the sun began to go down one had to draw back the curtains in the sitting-room windows; streets with the solemn names of saints, not a few of whom figured in the history of the early lords of Combray, such as the Rue Saint-Hilaire, the Rue Saint-Jacques, in which my aunt's house stood, the Rue Sainte-Hildegarde, which ran past her railings, and the Rue du Saint-Esprit, on to which the little garden gate opened; and these Combray streets exist in so remote a corner of my memory, painted in colours so different from those in which the world is decked for me to-day, that in fact one and all of them, and the church which towered above them in the Square, seem to me now more insubstantial than the projections of my magic-lantern; and at times I feel that to be able to cross the Rue Saint-Hilaire again, to engage a room in the Rue de l'Oiseau, in the old hostelry of the Oiseau Flesché, from whose basement windows used to rise a smell of cooking which rises still in my mind, now and then, in the same warm and intermittent gusts, would be to secure a contact with the Beyond more marvellously supernatural than it would be to

make Golo's acquaintance and to chat with Geneviève de
Brabant.

My grandfather's cousin—by courtesy my great-aunt—with
whom we used to stay, was the mother of that aunt Léonie
who, since her husband's (my uncle Octave's) death, had
gradually declined to leave, first Combray, then her house in
Combray, then her bedroom, and finally her bed, and now
never "came down," but lay perpetually in a vague state of
grief, physical debility, illness, obsession and piety. Her
private apartment looked out over the Rue Saint-Jacques, which
ran a long way further to end in the Grand-Pré (as distinct
from the Petit-Pré, a green space in the centre of the town
where three streets met) and which, monotonous and grey,
with the three high sandstone steps before almost every one
of its doors, seemed like a deep furrow carved by some
sculptor of Gothic images out of the block of stone from which
he might have fashioned a calvary or a crib. My aunt's life
was now practically confined to two adjoining rooms, in one
of which she would spend the afternoon while the other was
being aired. They were rooms of that country order which—
just as in certain climes whole tracts of air or ocean are illuminated or scented by myriads of protozoa which we cannot see—
enchants us with the countless odours emanating from the
virtues, wisdom, habits, a whole secret system of life, invisible,
superabundant and profoundly moral, which their atmosphere
holds in solution; smells natural enough indeed, and weather-
tinted like those of the neighbouring countryside, but already
humanised, domesticated, snug, an exquisite, limpid jelly
skilfully blended from all the fruits of the year which have
left the orchard for the store-room, smells changing with the
season, but plenishing and homely, offsetting the sharpness of
hoarfrost with the sweetness of warm bread, smells lazy and
punctual as a village clock, roving and settled, heedless and
provident, linen smells, morning smells, pious smells, rejoicing
in a peace which brings only additional anxiety, and in a
prosaicness which serves as a deep reservoir of poetry to the
stranger who passes through their midst without having lived
among them. The air of those rooms was saturated with the
fine bouquet of a silence so nourishing, so succulent, that I

never went into them without a sort of greedy anticipation,
particularly on those first mornings, chilly still, of the Easter
holidays, when I could taste it more fully because I had only
just arrived in Combray: before I went in to say good morning
to my aunt I would be kept waiting a moment in the outer
room where the sun, wintry still, had crept in to warm itself
before the fire, which was already alight between its two
bricks and plastering the whole room with a smell of soot,
turning it into one of those great rustic open hearths, or
one of those canopied mantelpieces in country houses, beneath
which one sits hoping that in the world outside it is raining
or snowing, hoping almost for a catastrophic deluge to add
the romance of being in winter quarters to the comfort of a
snug retreat; I would pace to and fro between the prie-dieu
and the stamped velvet armchairs, each one always draped in
its crocheted antimacassar, while the fire, baking like dough the
appetising smells with which the air of the room was thickly
clotted and which the moist and sunny freshness of the morning
had already "raised" and started to "set," puffed them and
glazed them and fluted them and swelled them into an invisible
though not impalpable country pie, an immense "turnover"
to which, barely waiting to savour the crisper, more delicate,
more reputable but also drier aromas of the cupboard, the
chest-of-drawers and the patterned wall-paper, I always returned with an unconfessed gluttony to wallow in the central,
glutinous, insipid, indigestible and fruity smell of the flowered
bedspread.

In the next room I could hear my aunt talking quietly to
herself. She never spoke save in low tones, because she believed
that there was something broken inside her head and floating
loose there, which she might displace by talking too loud;
but she never remained for long, even when alone, without
saying something, because she believed that it was good for
her throat, and that by keeping the blood there in circulation
it would make less frequent the chokings and the pains from
which she suffered; besides, in the life of complete inertia
which she led, she attached to the least of her sensations an
extraordinary importance, endowed them with a Protean
ubiquity which made it difficult for her to keep them to

herself, and, failing a confidant to whom she might communicate them, she used to promulgate them to herself in an unceasing monologue which was her sole form of activity. Unfortunately, having formed the habit of thinking aloud, she did not always take care to see that there was no one in the adjoining room, and I would often hear her saying to herself: "I must not forget that I never slept a wink"—for "never sleeping a wink" was her great claim to distinction, and one admitted and respected in our household vocabulary: in the morning Françoise would not "call" her, but would simply "go in" to her; during the day, when my aunt wished to take a nap, we used to say just that she wished to "be quiet" or to "rest"; and when in conversation she so far forgot herself as to say "what woke me up," or "I dreamed that," she would blush and at once correct herself.

After waiting a minute, I would go in and kiss her; Françoise would be making her tea; or, if my aunt were feeling "upset," she would ask instead for her tisane, and it would be my duty to shake out of the chemist's little package on to a plate the amount of lime-blossom required for infusion in boiling water. The drying of the stems had twisted them into a fantastic trellis, in the interlacings of which the pale flowers opened, as though a painter had arranged them there, grouping them in the most decorative poses. The leaves, having lost or altered their original appearance, resembled the most disparate things, the transparent wing of a fly, the blank side of a label, the petal of a rose, which had all been piled together, pounded or interwoven like the materials for a nest. A thousand trifling little details—a charming prodigality on the part of the chemist—details which would have been eliminated from an artificial preparation, gave me, like a book in which one reads with astonished delight the name of a person one knows, the pleasure of finding that these were sprigs of real lime-trees, like those I had seen, when coming from the train, in the Avenue de la Gare, altered indeed, precisely because they were not imitations but themselves, and because they had aged. And as each new character is merely a metamorphosis from something earlier, in these little grey balls I recognised green buds plucked before their time; but beyond all else the rosy,

lunar, tender gleam that lit up the blossoms among the frail
forest of stems from which they hung like little golden roses—
marking, as the glow upon an old wall still marks the place
of a vanished fresco, the difference between those parts of
the tree which had and those which had not been "in colour"
—showed me that these were indeed petals which, before
filling the chemist's bag with their spring fragrance, had
perfumed the evening air. That rosy candleglow was still
their colour, but half-extinguished and deadened in the
diminished life which was now theirs, and which may be called
the twilight of a flower. Presently my aunt would dip a little
madeleine in the boiling infusion, whose taste of dead leaves
or faded blossom she so relished, and hand me a piece when it
was sufficiently soft.

At one side of her bed stood a big yellow chest-of-drawers of
lemon-wood, and a table which served at once as dispensary
and high altar, on which, beneath a statue of the Virgin and
a bottle of Vichy-Célestins, might be found her prayer-books
and her medical prescriptions, everything that she needed for
the performance, in bed, of her duties to soul and body, to
keep the proper times for pepsin and for vespers. On the other
side her bed was bounded by the window: she had the street
in full view, and would while away the time by reading in it
from morning to night, like the Persian princes of old, the
daily but immemorial chronicles of Combray, which she would
discuss in detail later with Françoise.

Scarcely had I been five minutes with my aunt before she
would send me away for fear that I might tire her. She would
hold out for me to kiss her sad, pale, lacklustre forehead, on
which at this early hour she would not yet have arranged the
false hair and through which the bones shone like the points
of a crown of thorns or the beads of a rosary, and she would
say to me: "Now, my poor child, off you go and get ready for
mass; and if you see Françoise downstairs, tell her not to stay
too long amusing herself with you; she must come up soon
to see if I need anything."

Françoise, who had been for many years in my aunt's
service and did not at that time suspect that she would one day
be transferred entirely to ours, was a little inclined to neglect

my aunt during the months which we spent in her house. There had been in my early childhood, before we first went to Combray, and when my aunt Léonie used still to spend the winter in Paris with her mother, a time when I knew Françoise so little that on New Year's Day, before going into my great-aunt's house, my mother would put a five-franc piece into my hand and say: "Now, be careful. Don't make any mistake. Wait until you hear me say 'Good morning, Françoise,' and tap you on the arm, before you give it to her." No sooner had we arrived in my aunt's dark hall than we saw in the gloom, beneath the frills of a snowy bonnet as stiff and fragile as if it had been made of spun sugar, the concentric ripples of a smile of anticipatory gratitude. It was Françoise, motionless and erect, framed in the small doorway of the corridor like the statue of a saint in its niche. When we had grown more ac-customed to this religious darkness we could discern in her features the disinterested love of humanity, the tender respect for the gentry, which the hope of receiving New Year bounty intensified in the nobler regions of her heart. Mamma pinched my arm sharply and said in a loud voice: "Good morning, Françoise." At this signal my fingers parted and I let fall the coin, which found a receptacle in a shy but outstretched hand. But since we had begun to go to Combray there was no one I knew better than Françoise. We were her favourites, and in the first years at least she showed for us not only the same con-sideration as for my aunt, but a keener relish, because we had, in addition to the prestige of belonging to "the family" (for she had for those invisible bonds which the community of blood creates between the members of a family as much respect as any Greek tragedian), the charm of not being her customary employers. And so with what joy would she welcome us, with what sorrow complain that the weather was still so bad for us, on the day of our arrival, just before Easter, when there was often an icy wind; while Mamma inquired after her daughter and her nephews, and if her grandson was a nice boy, and what they were going to do with him, and whether he took after his granny.

And later, when no one else was in the room, Mamma, who knew that Françoise was still mourning for her parents, who

had been dead for years, would speak to her kindly about
them, asking her endless little questions concerning their lives.

She had guessed that Françoise was not over-fond of her
son-in-law, and that he spoiled the pleasure she found in
visiting her daughter, with whom she could not talk so freely
when he was there. And so, when Françoise was going to
their house, some miles from Combray, Mamma would say
to her with a smile: "Tell me, Françoise, if Julien has had to
go away, and you have Marguerite to yourself all day, you'll
be very sorry, but you will make the best of it, won't you?"

And Françoise answered, laughing: "Madame knows everything; Madame is worse than the X-rays" (she pronounced the
"x" with an affectation of difficulty and a smile of self-depreca-
tion at the notion of an unlettered woman daring to employ a
scientific term) "they brought here for Mme Octave, which
see what's in your heart"—and she went off, overwhelmed
that anyone should be caring about her, perhaps anxious that
we should not see her in tears: Mamma was the first person
who had given her the heart-warming feeling that her peasant
existence, with its simple joys and sorrows, might be an object
of interest, might be a source of grief or pleasure to someone
other than herself.

My aunt resigned herself to doing without Françoise to
some extent during our visits, knowing how much my mother
appreciated the services of so active and intelligent a maid,
one who looked as smart at five o'clock in the morning in her
kitchen, under a bonnet whose stiff and dazzling frills seemed
to be made of porcelain, as when dressed for high mass;
who did everything in the right way, toiling like a horse,
whether she was well or ill, but without fuss, without the
appearance of doing anything; the only one of my aunt's
maids who when Mamma asked for hot water or black coffee
would bring them actually boiling. She was one of those
servants who, in a household, seem least satisfactory at first
to a stranger, doubtless because they take no pains to make a
conquest of him and show him no special attention, knowing
very well that they have no real need of him, that he will cease
to be invited to the house sooner than they will be dismissed
from it, but who, on the other hand, are most prized by

masters and mistresses who have tested and proved their real capacity, and care nothing for that superficial affability, that servile chit-chat which may impress a stranger favourably, but often conceals an incurable incompetence.

When Françoise, having seen that my parents had everything they required, first went upstairs again to give my aunt her pepsin and to find out from her what she would take for lunch, it was rare indeed for her not to be called upon to give an opinion, or to furnish an explanation, in regard to some important event.

"Just fancy, Françoise, Mme Goupil went by more than a quarter of an hour late to fetch her sister: if she loses any more time on the way I shouldn't be at all surprised if she arrived after the Elevation."

"Well, there'd be nothing wonderful in that," would be the answer.

"Françoise, if you had come in five minutes ago, you would have seen Mme Imbert go past with some asparagus twice the size of mother Callot's: do try to find out from her cook where she got them. You know you've been serving asparagus with everything this spring; you might be able to get some like those for our visitors."

"I shouldn't be surprised if they came from the Curé's," Françoise would say.

"I'm sure you wouldn't, my poor Françoise," my aunt would reply, shrugging her shoulders. "From the Curé's, indeed! You know quite well that he never grows anything but wretched little twigs of asparagus. I tell you these ones were as thick as my arm. Not your arm, of course, but my poor arm, which has grown so much thinner again this year . . . Françoise, didn't you hear that bell just now that nearly split my skull?"

"No, Mme Octave."

"Ah, my poor girl, your skull must be very thick; you may thank God for that. It was Maguelone come to fetch Dr Piperaud. He came out with her at once and they went off along the Rue de l'Oiseau. There must be some child ill."

"Oh dear, dear; the poor little creature!" Françoise would sigh, for she could not hear of any calamity befalling a person unknown to her, even in some distant part of the world, without beginning to lament.

"Françoise, who were they tolling the knell for just now? Oh dear, of course, it would be for Mme Rousseau. And to think that I had forgotten that she passed away the other night. Ah! it's time the good Lord called me too; I don't know what has become of my head since I lost my poor Octave. But I'm wasting your time, my good girl."

"Not at all, Mme Octave, my time is not so precious; the good Lord who made it doesn't charge us for it. I'm just going to see if my fire's going out."

Thus Françoise and my aunt between them made a critical evaluation, in the course of these morning sessions, of the earliest events of the day. But sometimes these events assumed so mysterious or so alarming a character that my aunt felt she could not wait until it was time for Françoise to come upstairs, and then a formidable and quadruple peal would resound through the house.

"But, Mme Octave, it's not yet time for your pepsin," Françoise would begin. "Are you feeling faint?"

"No, no, Françoise," my aunt would reply, "that is to say, yes; you know quite well that there's very seldom a time when I don't feel faint; one day I shall pass away like Mme Rousseau, before I know where I am; but that's not why I rang. Would you believe that I've just seen, as plain as I can see you, Mme Goupil with a little girl I didn't know from Adam. Run and get a pennyworth of salt from Camus. It's not often that Théodore can't tell you who a person is."

"But that must be M. Pupin's daughter," Françoise would say, preferring to stick to an immediate explanation, since she had been perhaps twice already into Camus's shop that morning.

"M. Pupin's daughter! Oh, that's a likely story, my poor Françoise. Do you think I wouldn't have recognised M. Pupin's daughter!"

"But I don't mean the big one, Mme Octave; I mean the little lass, the one who goes to school at Jouy. I fancy I seen her once already this morning."

"Ah! that's probably it," my aunt would say. "She must

have come over for the holidays. Yes, that's it. No need to ask, she will have come over for the holidays. But then we shall soon see Mme Sazerat come along and ring her sister's door-bell for lunch. That will be it! I saw the boy from Galopin's go by with a tart. You'll see that the tart was for Mme Goupil."

"Once Mme Goupil has company, Mme Octave, you won't have long to wait before you see all her folk going home to their lunch, for it's not so early as it was," Françoise would say, for she was anxious to return downstairs to look after our own meal, and was not sorry to leave my aunt with the prospect of such a diversion.

"Oh! not before midday," my aunt would reply in a tone of resignation, darting an anxious glance at the clock, but furtively, so as not to let it be seen that she, who had renounced all earthly joys, yet found a keen satisfaction in learning that Mme Goupil was expecting company to lunch, though, alas, she must wait a little more than an hour still before enjoying the spectacle. "And it will come in the middle of my lunch!" she would murmur to herself. Her lunch was such a distraction in itself that she did not wish for any other at the same time. "I hope you won't forget to give me my creamed eggs on one of the flat plates?" she would add. These were the only plates which had pictures on them, and my aunt used to amuse herself at every meal by reading the caption on whichever one had been sent up to her that day. She would put on her spectacles and spell out: "Ali Baba and the Forty Thieves," "Aladdin and his Wonderful Lamp," and smile, and say: "Very good, very good."

"I would have gone across to Camus . . ." Françoise would hazard, seeing that my aunt had no longer any intention of sending her there.

"No, no; it's not worth while now; it's certainly the Pupin girl. My poor Françoise, I'm sorry to have brought you upstairs for nothing."

But it was not for nothing, as my aunt well knew, that she had rung for Françoise, since at Combray a person whom one "didn't know from Adam" was as incredible a being as any mythological deity, and indeed no one could remember, on

the various occasions when one of these startling apparitions
had occurred in the Rue du Saint-Esprit or in the Square,
exhaustive inquiries ever having failed to reduce the fabulous
monster to the proportions of a person whom one "did know,"
either personally or in the abstract, in his or her civil status as
being more or less closely related to some family in Combray.
It would turn out to be Mme Sauton's son back from military
service, or the Abbé Perdreau's niece home from her convent,
or the Curé's brother, a tax-collector at Châteaudun, who had
just retired on a pension or had come over to Combray for
the holidays. They had on first appearance aroused the exciting
thought that there might be in Combray people whom one
"didn't know from Adam," simply because they had not
been recognised or identified at once. And yet long beforehand Mme Sauton and the Curé had given warning that they
expected their "strangers." Whenever I went upstairs on
returning home of an evening, to tell my aunt about our walk,
if I was rash enough to say to her that we had passed, near the
Pont-Vieux, a man whom my grandfather didn't know:

"A man grandfather didn't know from Adam!" she would
exclaim. "That's a likely story." None the less, she would be
a little disturbed by the news, would wish to have it cleared
up, and so my grandfather would be summoned. "Who can
it have been that you passed near the Pont-Vieux, uncle? A
man you didn't know from Adam?"

"Why, of course I knew him," my grandfather would
answer. "It was Prosper, Mme Bouillebœuf's gardener's
brother."

"Ah, good," my aunt would say, reassured but still slightly
flushed. "And the boy told me that you passed a man you
didn't know from Adam!" After which I would be warned
to be more circumspect in future, and not to upset my aunt
so by thoughtless remarks. Everyone was so well known in
Combray, animals as well as people, that if my aunt had
happened to see a dog go by which she "didn't know from
Adam" she never stopped thinking about it, devoting all her
inductive talents and her leisure hours to this incomprehensible
phenomenon.

"That will be Mme Sazerat's dog," Françoise would suggest,

without any real conviction, but in the hope of appeasement, and so that my aunt should not "split her head."

"As if I didn't know Mme Sazerat's dog!" My aunt's critical mind would not be fobbed off so easily.

"Well then, it must be the new dog M. Galopin brought back from Lisieux."

"Oh, if that's what it is!"

"They say he's a very friendly animal," Françoise would go on, having got the story from Théodore, "as clever as a Christian, always in a good temper, always friendly, always well-behaved. You don't often see an animal so gentlemanly at that age. Mme Octave, I've got to leave you now; I haven't time to dilly-dally; it's nearly ten o'clock and my fire not lighted yet, and I've still got to scrape my asparagus."

"What, Françoise, more asparagus! It's a regular mania for asparagus you've got this year. You'll make our Parisians sick of it."

"No, no, Mme Octave, they like it well enough. They'll be coming back from church soon as hungry as hunters, and they won't turn their noses up at their asparagus, you'll see."

"Church! Why, they must be there now; you'd better not lose any time. Go and look after your lunch."

While my aunt was gossiping on in this way with Françoise I accompanied my parents to mass. How I loved our church, and how clearly I can see it still! The old porch by which we entered, black, and full of holes as a colander, was worn out of shape and deeply furrowed at the sides (as also was the font to which it led us) just as if the gentle friction of the cloaks of peasant-women coming into church, and of their fingers dipping into the holy water, had managed by age-long repetition to acquire a destructive force, to impress itself on the stone, to carve grooves in it like those made by cart-wheels upon stone gate-posts which they bump against every day. Its memorial stones, beneath which the noble dust of the Abbots of Combray who lay buried there furnished the choir with a sort of spiritual pavement, were themselves no longer hard and lifeless matter, for time had softened them and made them flow like honey beyond their proper margins, here

oozing out in a golden stream, washing from its place a florid
Gothic capital, drowning the white violets of the marble floor,
and elsewhere reabsorbed into their limits, contracting still
further a crabbed Latin inscription, bringing a fresh touch of
fantasy into the arrangement of its curtailed characters, closing
together two letters of some word of which the rest were dis-
proportionately distended. Its windows were never so sparkling as on days when the sun scarcely shone, so that if it was
dull outside you could be sure it would be fine inside the
church. One of them was filled from top to bottom by a
solitary figure, like the king on a playing-card, who lived up
there beneath his canopy of stone, between earth and heaven,
and in whose slanting blue gleam, on weekdays sometimes,
at noon, when there was no service (at one of those rare
moments when the airy, empty church, more human somehow
and more luxurious, with the sun showing off all its rich
furnishings, had an almost habitable air, like the entrance hall—
all sculptured stone and painted glass—of some hotel in the
mediaeval style), you might see Mme Sazerat kneel for an
instant, laying down on the seat next to hers a neatly corded
parcel of little cakes which she had just bought at the baker's
and was taking home for lunch. In another, a mountain of
pink snow, at whose foot a battle was being fought, seemed
to have frozen against the very glass itself, which it swelled
and distorted with its cloudy sleet, like a window to which
snowflakes have drifted and clung, illumined by the light of
dawn—the same, doubtless, that tinged the reredos of the
altar with hues so fresh that they seemed rather to be thrown
on it momentarily by a light shining from outside and shortly
to be extinguished than painted and permanently fastened on
the stone. And all of them were so old that you could see,
here and there, their silvery antiquity sparkling with the dust
of centuries and showing in its threadbare brilliance the
texture of their lovely tapestry of glass. There was one among
them which was a tall panel composed of a hundred little
rectangular panes, of blue principally, like an enormous pack
of cards of the kind planned to beguile King Charles VI;
but, either because a ray of sunlight had gleamed through it
or because my own shifting glance had sent shooting across

the window, whose colours died away and were rekindled by turns, a rare and flickering fire—the next instant it had taken on the shimmering brilliance of a peacock's tail, then quivered and rippled in a flaming and fantastic shower that streamed from the groin of the dark and stony vault down the moist walls, as though it were along the bed of some grotto glowing with sinuous stalactites that I was following my parents, who preceded me with their prayer-books clasped in their hands. A moment later the little lozenge panes had taken on the deep transparency, the unbreakable hardness of sapphires clustered on some enormous breastplate behind which, however, could be distinguished, dearer than all such treasures, a fleeting smile from the sun, which could be seen and felt as well here, in the soft, blue stream with which it bathed the jewelled windows, as on the pavement of the Square or the straw of the market-place; and even on our first Sundays, when we had come down before Easter, it would console me for the blackness and bareness of the earth outside by quickening into blossom, as in some springtime in old history among the heirs of Saint Louis, this dazzling, gilded carpet of forget-me-nots in glass.

There were two tapestries of high warp representing the coronation of Esther (tradition had it that the weaver had given to Ahasuerus the features of one of the kings of France and to Esther those of a lady of Guermantes whose lover he had been), to which the colours, in melting into one another, had added expression, relief and light: a touch of pink over the lips of Esther had strayed beyond their outline; the yellow of her dress was spread so unctuously, so thickly, as to have acquired a kind of solidity, and stood out boldly against the receding background; while the green of the trees, still bright in the lower parts of the panel of silk and wool, but quite "gone" at the top, brought out in a paler tone, above the dark trunks, the yellowing upper branches, gilded and half-obliterated by the sharp though sidelong rays of an invisible sun.

All this, and still more the treasures which had come to the church from personages who to me were almost legendary figures (such as the golden cross wrought, it was said, by Saint Eloi and presented by Dagobert, and the tomb of the sons of Louis the Germanic in porphyry and enamelled copper),

because of which I used to advance into the church, as we
made our way to our seats, as into a fairy-haunted valley,
where the rustic sees with amazement in a rock, a tree, a
pond, the tangible traces of the little people's supernatural
passage—all this made of the church for me something entirely
different from the rest of the town: an edifice occupying, so to
speak, a four-dimensional space—the name of the fourth being
Time—extending through the centuries its ancient nave,
which, bay after bay, chapel after chapel, seemed to stretch
across and conquer not merely a few yards of soil, but each
successive epoch from which it emerged triumphant, hiding
the rugged barbarities of the eleventh century in the thickness
of its walls, through which nothing could be seen of the heavy
arches, long stopped and blinded with coarse blocks of ashlar,
except where, near the porch, a deep cleft had been hollowed
out by the tower staircase, and veiling it even there by the
graceful Gothic arcades which crowded coquettishly around
it like a row of grown-up sisters who, to hide him from the
eyes of strangers, arrange themselves smilingly in front of a
rustic, surly and ill-dressed younger brother; raising up into
the sky above the Square a tower which had looked down
upon Saint Louis, and seemed to see him still; and thrusting
down with its crypt into a Merovingian darkness, through
which, guiding us with groping finger-tips beneath the
shadowy vault, powerfully ribbed like an immense bat's wing
of stone, Théodore and his sister would light up for us with
a candle the tomb of Sigebert's little daughter, in which a
deep cavity, like the bed of a fossil, had been dug, or so it was
said, "by a crystal lamp which, on the night when the Frankish
princess was murdered, had detached itself, of its own accord,
from the golden chains by which it was suspended on the site
of the present apse and, with neither the crystal being broken
nor the light extinguished, had buried itself in the stone,
which had softly given way beneath it."

And then the apse of Combray: what can one say of that?
It was so crude, so devoid of artistic beauty, even of religious
feeling. From the outside, since the street crossing which it
commanded was on a lower level, its great wall was thrust
upwards from a basement of unfaced ashlar, jagged with

flints, in which there was nothing particularly ecclesiastical, the windows seemed to have been pierced at an abnormal height, and its whole appearance was that of a prison wall rather than of a church. And certainly in later years, when I recalled all the glorious apses that I had seen, it would never have occurred to me to compare with any one of them the apse of Combray. Only, one day, turning out of a little street in some country town, I came upon three alley-ways that converged, and facing them an old wall, rough-hewn and unusually high, with windows pierced in it far overhead and the same asymmetrical appearance as the apse of Combray. And at that moment I did not say to myself, as I might have done at Chartres or at Rheims, with what power the religious feeling had been expressed therein, but instinctively I exclaimed: "The Church!"

The church! Homely and familiar, cheek by jowl in the Rue Saint-Hilaire, upon which its north door opened, with its two neighbours, Mme Loiseau's house and M. Rapin's pharmacy, against which its walls rested without interspace, a simple citizen of Combray, which might have had its number in the street had the streets of Combray borne numbers, and at whose door one felt that the postman ought to stop on his morning rounds, before going into Mme Loiseau's and after leaving M. Rapin's, there existed, nonetheless, between the church and everything in Combray that was not the church a clear line of demarcation which my mind has never succeeded in crossing. In vain might Mme Loiseau deck her window-sills with fuchsias, which developed the bad habit of letting their branches trail at all times and in all directions, head downwards, and whose flowers had no more important business, when they were big enough to taste the joys of life, than to go and cool their purple, congested cheeks against the dark front of the church, to me such conduct sanctified the fuchsias not at all; between the flowers and the blackened stone against which they leaned, if my eyes could discern no gap, my mind preserved the impression of an abyss.

The steeple of Saint-Hilaire could be distinguished from a long way off, inscribing its unforgettable form upon a horizon against which Combray had not yet appeared; when from the train which brought us down from Paris at Easter-time my father caught sight of it, as it slipped into every fold of the sky in turn, its little iron weathercock veering in all directions, he would say: "Come on, get your wraps together, we're there." And on one of the longest walks we used to take from Combray there was a spot where the narrow road emerged suddenly on to an immense plain, closed at the horizon by a jagged ridge of forest above which rose the solitary point of Saint-Hilaire's steeple, so slender and so pink that it seemed to be no more than scratched on the sky by the finger-nail of a painter anxious to give to such a landscape, to so pure a piece of "nature," this little sign of art, this single indication of human existence. As one drew near it and could see the remains of the square tower, half in ruins, which still stood by its side, though without rivalling it in height, one was struck most of all by the dark-red tone of its stones; and on a misty morning in autumn one might have thought it, rising above the violet thunder-cloud of the vineyards, a ruin of purple, almost the colour of Virginia creeper.

Often in the Square, as we came home, my grandmother would make me stop to look up at it. From the tower windows, placed two by two, one pair above another, with that right and original proportion in their spacing which gives beauty and dignity not only to human faces, it released, it let fall at regular intervals, flocks of jackdaws which would wheel noisily for a while, as though the ancient stones which allowed them to disport themselves without seeming to see them, becoming of a sudden untenantable and discharging some element of extreme perturbation, had struck them and driven them out. Then, having crisscrossed in all directions the violet velvet of the evening air, they would return, suddenly calmed, to absorb themselves in the tower, baleful no longer but benignant, some perching here and there (not seeming to move, but perhaps snapping up some passing insect) on the points of turrets, as a seagull perches with an angler's immobility on the crest of a wave. Without quite knowing why, my grandmother found in the steeple of Saint-Hilaire that absence of vulgarity, pretension, and meanness which made her love, and deem rich in beneficent influences, nature itself—

when the hand of man had not, as did my great-aunt's gardener, trimmed it—and the works of genius. And certainly every part of the church that one saw distinguished it from any other building by a kind of innate thoughtfulness, but it was in its steeple that it seemed most truly to find itself, to affirm its individual and responsible existence. It was the steeple that spoke for the church. I think, too, that in a confused way my grandmother found in the steeple of Combray what she prized above anything else in the world, namely, a natural air and an air of distinction. Ignorant of architecture, she would say:

"My dears, laugh at me if you like; it is not conventionally beautiful, but there is something in its quaint old face that pleases me. If it could play the piano, I'm sure it wouldn't sound tinny." And when she gazed up at it, when her eyes followed the gentle tension, the fervent inclination of its stony slopes which drew together as they rose, like hands joined in prayer, she would absorb herself so utterly in the effusion of the spire that her gaze seemed to leap upwards with it; her lips at the same time curving in a friendly smile for the worn old stones of which the setting sun now illumined no more than the topmost pinnacles and which, at the point where they entered that sunlit zone and were softened by it, seemed to have mounted suddenly far higher, to have become truly remote, like a song taken up again in a "head voice," an octave above.

It was the steeple of Saint-Hilaire that shaped and crowned and consecrated every occupation, every hour of the day, every view in the town. From my bedroom window I could discern no more than its base, which had been freshly covered with slates; but when, on a Sunday, I saw these blaze like a black sun in the hot light of a summer morning, I would say to myself: "Good heavens! nine o'clock! I must get ready for mass at once if I am to have time to go in and kiss aunt Léonie first," and I would know exactly what was the colour of the sunlight upon the Square, I could feel the heat and dust of the market, the shade thrown by the awning of the shop into which Mamma would perhaps go on her way to mass, penetrating its odour of unbleached calico, to purchase a handkerchief or something which the draper, bowing from the

waist, would order to be shown to her while, in readiness
for shutting up, he went into the back shop to put on his
Sunday coat and to wash his hands, which it was his habit,
every few minutes, even in the most melancholy circumstances, to rub together with an air of enterprise, cunning, and
success.

And again, after mass, when we looked in to tell Théodore
to bring a larger loaf than usual because our cousins had taken
advantage of the fine weather to come over from Thiberzy
for lunch, we had in front of us the steeple which, baked
golden-brown itself like a still larger, consecrated loaf, with
gummy flakes and droplets of sunlight, thrust its sharp point
into the blue sky. And in the evening, when I came in from
my walk and thought of the approaching moment when I
must say good night to my mother and see her no more,
the steeple was by contrast so soft and gentle, there at the close
of day, that it looked as if it had been thrust like a brown
velvet cushion against the pallid sky which had yielded
beneath its pressure, had hollowed slightly to make room
for it, and had correspondingly risen on either side; while the
cries of the birds that wheeled around it seemed to intensify
its silence, to elongate its spire still further, and to invest it
with some quality beyond the power of words.

Even when our errands lay in places behind the church,
from which it could not be seen, the view seemed always to
have been composed with reference to the steeple, which
would loom up here and there among the houses, and was
perhaps even more affecting when it appeared thus without
the church. And, indeed, there are many others which look
best when seen in this way, and I can call to mind vignettes
of housetops with surmounting steeples in quite another
category of art than those formed by the dreary streets of
Combray. I shall never forget, in a quaint Norman town not
far from Balbec, two charming eighteenth-century houses,
dear to me and venerable for many reasons, between which,
when one looks up at it from the fine garden which descends
in terraces to the river, the gothic spire of a church (itself
hidden by the houses) soars into the sky with the effect of
crowning and completing their façades, but in a style so

different, so precious, so annulated, so pink, so polished, that
one sees at once that it no more belongs to them than would
the purple, crinkled spire of some sea-shell spun out into a
turret and gay with glossy colour to a pair of handsome,
smooth pebbles between which it had been washed up on
the beach. Even in Paris, in one of the ugliest parts of the town,
I know a window from which one can see, across a first, a
second, and even a third layer of jumbled roofs, street beyond
street, a violet dome, sometimes ruddy, sometimes too, in the
finest "prints" which the atmosphere makes of it, of an ashy
solution of black, which is, in fact, none other than the dome
of Saint-Augustin, and which imparts to this view of Paris
the character of some of the Piranesi views of Rome. But
since into none of these little etchings, whatever the discernment my memory may have been able to bring to their execution, was it able to contribute an element I have long lost,
the feeling which makes us not merely regard a thing as a
spectacle, but believe in it as in a unique essence, so none of
them keeps in its thrall a whole section of my inmost life as
does the memory of those aspects of the steeple of Combray
from the streets behind the church. Whether one saw it at
five o'clock when going to call for letters at the post-office,
some doors away from one, on the left, raising abruptly with
its isolated peak the ridge of housetops; or whether, if one
were looking in to ask for news of Mme Sazerat, one's eyes
followed that ridge which had now become low again after
the descent of its other slope, and one knew that it would be
the second turning after the steeple; or again if, pressing
further afield, one went to the station and saw it obliquely,
showing in profile fresh angles and surfaces, like a solid body
surprised at some unknown point in its revolution; or if, seen
from the banks of the Vivonne, the apse, crouched muscularly
and heightened by the perspective, seemed to spring upwards
with the effort which the steeple was making to hurl its spire-
point into the heart of heaven—it was always to the steeple
that one must return, always the steeple that dominated everything else, summoning the houses from an unexpected pinnacle,
raised before me like the Finger of God, whose body might
have been concealed below among the crowd of humans

without fear of my confusing it with them. And so even
to-day, if, in a large provincial town, or in a quarter of Paris
which I do not know very well, a passer-by who is "putting
me on the right road" shows me in the distance, as a point to
aim at, some hospital belfry or convent steeple lifting the peak
of its ecclesiastical cap at the corner of the street which I am
to take, my memory need only find in it some dim resemblance
to that dear and vanished outline, and the passer-by, should he
turn round to make sure that I have not gone astray, may be
amazed to see me still standing there, oblivious of the walk
that I had planned to take or the place where I was obliged to
call, gazing at the steeple for hours on end, motionless,
trying to remember, feeling deep within myself a tract of soil
reclaimed from the waters of Lethe slowly drying until the
buildings rise on it again; and then no doubt, and then more
anxiously than when, just now, I asked him to direct me, I
seek my way again, I turn a corner . . . but . . . the goal is in
my heart. . . .

On our way home from mass we would often meet M.
Legrandin, who, detained in Paris by his professional duties
as an engineer, could only (except in the regular holiday
seasons) visit his house at Combray between Saturday evenings
and Monday mornings. He was one of that class of men who,
apart from a scientific career in which they may well have
proved brilliantly successful, have acquired an entirely different
kind of culture, literary or artistic, for which their professional
specialization has no use but by which their conversation
profits. More lettered than many men of letters (we were not
aware at this period that M. Legrandin had a distinct reputation
as a writer, and were greatly astonished to find that a well-
known composer had set some verses of his to music), endowed
with greater "facility" than many painters, they imagine that
the life they are obliged to lead is not that for which they
are really fitted, and they bring to their regular occupations
either an indifference tinged with fantasy, or a sustained and
haughty application, scornful, bitter, and conscientious. Tall
and handsome of bearing, with a fine, thoughtful face, drooping fair moustaches, blue eyes, an air of disenchantment, an
almost exaggerated refinement of courtesy, a talker such as we

had never heard, he was in the sight of my family, who never ceased to quote him as an example, the very pattern of a gentleman, who took life in the noblest and most delicate manner. My grandmother alone found fault with him for speaking a little too well, a little too much like a book, for not using a vocabulary as natural as his loosely knotted Lavallière neckties, his short, straight, almost schoolboyish coat. She was astonished, too, at the furious tirades which he was always launching at the aristocracy, at fashionable life, at snobbishness—"undoubtedly," he would say, "the sin of which St Paul is thinking when he speaks of the unforgivable sin against the Holy Ghost."

Worldly ambition was a thing which my grandmother was so little capable of feeling, or indeed of understanding, that it seemed to her futile to apply so much heat to its condemnation. Besides, she did not think it in very good taste for M. Legrandin, whose sister was married to a country gentleman of Lower Normandy, near Balbec, to deliver himself of such violent attacks upon the nobility, going so far as to blame the Revolution for not having guillotined them all.

"Well met, my friends!" he would say as he came towards us. "You are lucky to spend so much time here; to-morrow I have to go back to Paris, to squeeze back into my niche. Oh, I admit," he went on, with the gentle, ironical, disillusioned, rather absent-minded smile that was peculiar to him, "I have every useless thing in the world in my house there. The only thing wanting is the necessary thing, a great patch of open sky like this. Always try to keep a patch of sky above your life, little boy," he added, turning to me. "You have a soul in you of rare quality, an artist's nature; never let it starve for lack of what it needs."

When, on our return home, my aunt would send to ask us whether Mme Goupil had indeed arrived late for mass, not one of us could inform her. Instead, we increased her anxiety by telling her that there was a painter at work in the church copying the window of Gilbert the Bad. Françoise was at once dispatched to the grocer's, but returned empty-handed owing to the absence of Théodore, whose dual profession of choirman, with a share in the upkeep of the church, and of grocer's assistant gave him not only relations with all sections of society, but an encyclopaedic knowledge of their affairs.

"Ah!" my aunt would sigh, "I wish it were time for Eulalie to come. She is really the only person who will be able to tell me."

Eulalie was a limping, energetic, deaf spinster who had "retired" after the death of Mme de la Bretonnerie, with whom she had been in service since her childhood, and had then taken a room beside the church from which she would incessantly emerge either to attend some service or, when there was no service, to say a prayer by herself or to give Théodore a hand; the rest of her time she spent in visiting sick persons like my aunt Léonie, to whom she would relate everything that had occurred at mass or vespers. She was not above adding occasional pocket-money to the small annuity paid to her by the family of her former employers by going from time to time to look after the Curé's linen, or that of some other person of note in the clerical world of Combray. Above a mantle of black cloth she wore a little white coif that seemed almost to attach her to some Order, and an infirmity of the skin had stained part of her cheeks and her crooked nose the bright red colour of balsam. Her visits were the one great distraction in the life of my aunt Léonie, who now saw hardly anyone else, except the Curé. My aunt had by degrees erased every other visitor's name from her list, because they were all guilty of the fatal error, in her eyes, of falling into one or other of the two categories of people she most detested. One group, the worse of the two, and the one of which she rid herself first, consisted of those who advised her not to "coddle" herself, and preached (even if only negatively and with no outward signs beyond an occasional disapproving silence or doubting smile) the subversive doctrine that a sharp walk in the sun and a good red beefsteak would do her more good (when she had had only two wretched mouthfuls of Vichy water on her stomach for fourteen hours!) than her bed and her medicines. The other category was composed of people who appeared to believe that she was more seriously ill than she thought, in fact that she was as seriously ill as she said. And so, of those whom she had allowed upstairs to her room, after considerable hesitation and only at Françoise's urgent request, and who in the course of their visit had shown how unworthy they were of the honour which had been done them by venturing a timid: "Don't you think that if you were just to stir out a little on really fine days . . .?" or who, on the other hand, when she said to them: "I'm very low, very low; nearing the end, I'm afraid" had replied: "Ah, yes, when one has no strength left! Still, you may last a while yet," all alike might be certain that her doors would never be opened to them again. And if Françoise was amused by the look of consternation on my aunt's face whenever she saw from her bed any of these people in the Rue du Saint-Esprit looking as if they were coming to see her, or whenever she heard her door-bell ring, she would laugh far more heartily, as at a clever trick, at my aunt's devices (which never failed) for having them sent away, and at their look of discomfiture when they had to turn back without having seen her, and would be filled with secret admiration for her mistress, whom she felt to be superior to all these people since she did not wish to receive them. In short, my aunt demanded that whoever came to see her must at one and the same time approve of her way of life, commiserate with her in her sufferings, and assure her of ultimate recovery.

In all this Eulalie excelled. My aunt might say to her twenty times in a minute: "The end is come at last, my poor Eulalie!," twenty times Eulalie would retort: "Knowing your illness as you do, Mme Octave, you will live to be a hundred, as Mme Sazerin said to me only yesterday." For one of Eulalie's most rooted beliefs, and one that the formidable number of rebuttals which experience had brought her was powerless to eradicate, was that Mme Sazerat's name was really Mme Sazerin.

"I do not ask to live to a hundred," my aunt would say, for she preferred to have no definite limit fixed to the number of her days.

And since besides this Eulalie knew, as no one else knew, how to distract my aunt without tiring her, her visits, which took place regularly every Sunday, unless something unforeseen occurred to prevent them, were for my aunt a pleasure the prospect of which kept her on those days in a state of expectation, agreeable enough to begin with, but swiftly

changing to the agony of a hunger too long unsatisfied if
Eulalie happened to be a little late. For, if unduly prolonged, the rapture of waiting for Eulalie became a torture,
and my aunt would never stop looking at the time, and
yawning, and complaining of each of her symptoms in turn.
Eulalie's ring, if it sounded from the front door at the very
end of the day, when she was no longer expecting it, would
almost make her ill. For the fact was that on Sundays she
thought of nothing else but this visit, and the moment our
lunch was ended Françoise would be impatient for us to leave
the dining-room so that she might go upstairs to "occupy"
my aunt. But—especially after the fine weather had definitely
set in at Combray—the proud hour of noon, descending from
the steeple of Saint-Hilaire which it blazoned for a moment
with the twelve points of its sonorous crown, would long
have echoed about our table, beside the blessed bread which
too had come in, after church, in its familiar way, and we would
still be seated in front of our Arabian Nights plates, weighed
down by the heat of the day, and even more by our heavy meal.
For upon the permanent foundation of eggs, cutlets, potatoes,
preserves, and biscuits, which she no longer even bothered to
announce, Françoise would add—as the labour of fields and
orchards, the harvest of the tides, the luck of the markets, the
kindness of neighbours, and her own genius might provide,
so that our bill of fare, like the quatrefoils that were carved
on the porches of cathedrals in the thirteenth century, reflected to some extent the rhythm of the seasons and the incidents of daily life—a brill because the fish-woman had
guaranteed its freshness, a turkey because she had seen a
beauty in the market at Roussainville-le-Pin, cardoons with
marrow because she had never done them for us in that way
before, a roast leg of mutton because the fresh air made one
hungry and there would be plenty of time for it to "settle
down" in the seven hours before dinner, spinach by way of a
change, apricots because they were still hard to get, goose-
berries because in another fortnight there would be none left,
raspberries which M. Swann had brought specially, cherries,
the first to come from the cherry-tree which had yielded none
for the last two years, a cream cheese, of which in those days I

was extremely fond, an almond cake because she had ordered one the evening before, a brioche because it was our turn to make them for the church. And when all this was finished, a work composed expressly for ourselves, but dedicated more particularly to my father who had a fondness for such things, a chocolate cream, Françoise's personal inspiration and speciality would be laid before us, light and fleeting as an "occasional" piece of music into which she had poured the whole of her talent. Anyone who refused to partake of it, saying: "No, thank you, I've finished; I'm not hungry any more," would at once have been relegated to the level of those Philistines who, even when an artist makes them a present of one of his works, examine its weight and material, whereas what is of value is the creator's intention and his signature. To have left even the tiniest morsel in the dish would have shown as much discourtesy as to rise and leave a concert hall before the end of a piece under the composer's very eyes.

At length my mother would say to me: "Now, don't stay here all day; you can go up to your room if you are too hot outside, but get a little fresh air first; don't start reading immediately after your food."

And I would go and sit down beside the pump and its trough, ornamented here and there, like a Gothic font, with a salamander, which impressed on the rough stone the mobile relief of its tapering allegorical body, on the bench without a back, in the shade of a lilac-tree, in that little corner of the garden which opened, through a service door, on to the Rue du Saint-Esprit, and from whose neglected soil there rose, in two stages, jutting out from the house itself, and as it were a separate building, my aunt's back-kitchen. One could see its red-tiled floor gleaming like porphyry. It seemed not so much the cave of Françoise as a little temple of Venus. It would be overflowing with the offerings of the dairyman, the fruiterer, the greengrocer, come sometimes from distant villages to dedicate to the goddess the first-fruits of their fields. And its roof was always crowned with a cooing dove.

In earlier days I did not linger in the sacred grove which surrounded this temple, for, before going upstairs to read,

I used to steal into the little sitting-room that my uncle
Adolphe, a brother of my grandfather and an old soldier
who had retired from the service as a major, occupied on the
ground floor, a room which, even when its opened windows
let in the heat, if not actually the rays of the sun which seldom
penetrated so far, would never fail to emit that oddly cool
odour, suggestive at once of woodlands and the ancien régime,
which sets the nostrils quivering when one goes into an
abandoned shooting-lodge. But for some years now I had
not gone into my uncle Adolphe's sanctum, for he no longer
came to Combray on account of a quarrel which had arisen
between him and my family, through my fault, in the following
circumstances: Once or twice a month, in Paris, I used to be
sent to pay him a visit, as he was finishing his luncheon,
wearing a plain alpaca coat and waited upon by his man-
servant in a working-jacket of striped linen, purple and white.
He would complain that I had not been to see him for a long
time, that he was being neglected; he would offer me a biscuit
or a tangerine, and we would go through a drawing-room in
which no one ever sat, whose fire was never lighted, whose
walls were decorated with gilded mouldings, its ceiling painted
blue in imitation of the sky, and its furniture upholstered in
satin, as at my grandparents', only yellow; then we would
enter what he called his "study," a room whose walls were
hung with prints which showed, against a dark background,
a plump and rosy goddess driving a chariot, or standing upon
a globe, or wearing a star on her brow—pictures which were
popular under the Second Empire because there was thought
to be something about them that suggested Pompeii, which
were then generally despised, and which are now becoming
fashionable again for one single and consistent reason (not-
withstanding all the others that are advanced), namely, that
they suggest the Second Empire. And there I would stay with
my uncle until his man came with a message from the coachman, asking him at what time he would like the carriage. My
uncle would then become lost in meditation, while his servant
stood there agape, not daring to disturb him by the least
movement, curiously awaiting his answer, which never varied.
For in the end, after a supreme crisis of hesitation, my uncle

would utter, infallibly, the words: "A quarter past two," which the servant would echo with amazement, but without disputing them: "A quarter past two! Very good, sir . . . I'll go and tell him. . . ."

At this date I was a lover of the theatre: a Platonic lover, since my parents had not yet allowed me to enter one, and so inaccurate was the picture I had formed in my mind's eye of the pleasures to be enjoyed there that I almost believed that each of the spectators looked, as through a stereoscope, at a scene that existed for himself alone, though similar to the thousand other scenes presented to the rest of the audience individually.

Every morning I would hasten to the Morris column to see what new plays it announced. Nothing could be more disinterested or happier than the day-dreams with which these announcements filled my imagination, day-dreams which were conditioned by the associations of the words forming the titles of the plays, and also by the colour of the bills, still damp and wrinkled with paste, on which those words stood out. Nothing, unless it were such strange titles as the *Testament de César Girodot* or *Oedipus Rex*, inscribed not on the green bills of the Opéra-Comique but on the wine-coloured bills of the Comédie-Française, nothing seemed to me to differ more profoundly from the sparkling white plume of the *Diamants de la Couronne* than the sleek, mysterious satin of the *Domino Noir*; and since my parents had told me that, for my first visit to the theatre, I should have to choose between these two pieces, I would study exhaustively and in turn the title of one and the title of the other (for these were all that I knew of either), attempting to snatch from each a foretaste of the pleasure it promised, and to compare this with the pleasure latent in the other, until in the end I succeeded in conjuring up such vivid and compelling pictures of, on the one hand, a play of dazzling arrogance, and on the other a gentle, velvety play, that I was as little capable of deciding which of them I should prefer to see as if, at the dinner-table, I had been obliged to choose between rice *à l'Impératrice* and the famous cream of chocolate.

All my conversations with my friends bore upon actors,

whose art, although as yet I had no experience of it, was the first of all its numberless forms in which Art itself allowed me to anticipate its enjoyment. Between one actor's tricks of intonation and inflection and another's, the most trifling differences would strike me as being of an incalculable importance. And from what I had been told of them I would arrange them in order of talent in lists which I used to recite to myself all day and which ended up by hardening in my brain and hampering it by their immovability.

And later, in my schooldays, whenever I ventured in class, as soon as the master's head was turned, to communicate with some new friend, I would always begin by asking him whether he had already been to the theatre, and whether he agreed that our greatest actor was Got, our second Delaunay, and so on. And if, in his judgment, Febvre came below Thiron, or Delaunay below Coquelin, the sudden volatility which the name of Coquelin, forsaking its stony rigidity, would acquire in my mind, in order to move up to second place, the miraculous agility, the fecund animation with which the name of Delaunay would suddenly be endowed, to enable it to slip down to fourth, would stimulate and fertilise my brain with a sense of budding and blossoming life.

But if the thought of actors preoccupied me so, if the sight of Maubant coming out of the Théâtre-Français one afternoon had plunged me into the throes and sufferings of love, how much more did the name of a "star" blazing outside the doors of a theatre, how much more, seen through the window of a brougham passing by in the street, its horses' headbands decked with roses, did the face of a woman whom I took to be an actress, leave me in a state of troubled excitement, impotently and painfully trying to form a picture of her private life.

I classified the most distinguished in order of talent: Sarah Bernhardt, Berma, Bartet, Madeleine Brohan, Jeanne Samary; but I was interested in them all. Now my uncle knew many of them personally, and also ladies of another class, not clearly distinguished from actresses in my mind. He used to entertain them at his house. And if we went to see him on certain days only, that was because on the other days ladies might come

whom his family could not very well have met—so they at
least thought, for my uncle, on the contrary, was only too
willing to pay pretty widows (who had perhaps never been
married) and countesses (whose high-sounding titles were
probably no more than *noms de guerre*) the compliment of
presenting them to my grandmother, or even of presenting
to them some of the family jewels, a propensity which had
already embroiled him more than once with my grandfather.
Often, if the name of some actress were mentioned in conversation, I would hear my father say to my mother with a
smile: "One of your uncle's friends," and thinking of the
weary and fruitless novitiate eminent men would go through,
perhaps for years on end, on the doorstep of some such lady
who refused to answer their letters and had them sent packing
by the hall-porter, it struck me that my uncle could have spared
from such torments a youngster like me by introducing him
to the actress, unapproachable by all the world, who was for
him an intimate friend.

And so—on the pretext that some lesson, the hour of which
had been altered, now came at such an awkward time that it
had already more than once prevented me, and would continue
to prevent me, from seeing my uncle—one day, not one of the
days which he set apart for our visits, taking advantage of the
fact that my parents had had lunch earlier than usual, I slipped
out and, instead of going to read the playbills on their column,
for which purpose I was allowed to go out unaccompanied,
ran round to his house. I noticed in front of his door a carriage
and pair, with red carnations on the horses' blinkers and in
the coachman's buttonhole. As I climbed the staircase I could
hear laughter and a woman's voice, and, as soon as I had rung,
silence and the sound of shutting doors. The manservant
seemed embarrassed when he let me in, and said that my
uncle was extremely busy and probably could not see me; he
went in, however, to announce my arrival, and the same voice
I had heard before said: "Oh, yes! Do let him come in, just
for a moment; I should so enjoy it. Isn't that his photograph
there on your desk? And his mother (your niece, isn't she?)
beside it? The image of her, isn't he? I should so like to see
the little chap, just for a second."

I could hear my uncle grumbling angrily; finally the man-servant ushered me in.

On the table was the same plate of biscuits that was always there; my uncle wore the same alpaca coat as on other days, but opposite him, in a pink silk dress with a great necklace of pearls about her throat, sat a young woman who was just finishing a tangerine. My uncertainty whether I ought to address her as Madame or Mademoiselle made me blush, and not daring to look too much in her direction, in case I should be obliged to speak to her, I hurried across to embrace my uncle. She looked at me and smiled; my uncle said "My nephew!" without telling her my name or giving me hers, doubtless because, since his difficulties with my grandfather, he had endeavoured as far as possible to avoid any association of his family with this other class of acquaintance.

"How like his mother he is," said the lady.

"But you've never seen my niece except in photographs," my uncle answered brusquely.

"I beg your pardon, dear friend, I passed her on the staircase last year when you were so ill. It's true I only saw her for a moment, and your staircase is rather dark; but I could see well enough to admire her. This young gentleman has her beautiful eyes, and also *this*," she went on, tracing a line with one finger across the lower part of her forehead. "Tell me," she asked my uncle, "is your niece's name the same as yours?"

"He takes most after his father," muttered my uncle, who was no more anxious to effect an introduction by proxy by mentioning Mamma's name than to bring the two together in the flesh. "He's his father all over, and also like my poor mother."

"I haven't met his father," said the lady in pink, bowing her head slightly, "and I never knew your poor mother. You will remember it was just after your great sorrow that we got to know one another."

I felt somewhat disillusioned, for this young lady was in no way different from other pretty women whom I had seen from time to time at home, in particular the daughter of one of our cousins to whose house I went every New Year's Day. Apart from being better dressed, my uncle's friend had the same quick and kindly glance, the same frank and friendly manner. I could find no trace in her of the theatrical appearance which I admired in photographs of actresses, nothing of the diabolical expression which would have been in keeping with the life she must lead. I had difficulty in believing that she was a courtesan, and certainly I should never have believed her to be an ultra-fashionable one, had I not seen the carriage and pair, the pink dress, the pearl necklace, had I not been aware, too, that my uncle knew only those of the top flight. But I asked myself how the millionaire who gave her her carriage and her house and her jewels could find any pleasure in flinging his money away upon a woman of so simple and respectable an appearance. And yet, when I thought of what her life must be like, its immorality disturbed me more, perhaps, than if it had stood before me in some concrete and recognisable form, by being thus invisible, like the secret of some novel or some scandal which had driven out of the home of her genteel parents and dedicated to the service of all mankind, which had brought to a bright bloom of beauty and raised to fame or notoriety, this woman the play of whose features, the intonations of whose voice, reminiscent of so many others I already knew, made me regard her, in spite of myself, as a young lady of good family, when she was no longer of any family at all.

We had moved by this time into the "study," and my uncle, who seemed a trifle embarrassed by my presence, offered her a cigarette.

"No, thank you, my dear," she said. "You know I only smoke the ones the grand duke sends me. I told him that they made you jealous." And she drew from a case cigarettes covered with gilt lettering in a foreign language. "But of course," she began again suddenly, "I must have met this young man's father with you. Isn't he your nephew? How on earth could I have forgotten? He was so nice, so exquisitely charming to me," she added, with an air of warmth and modesty. But when I thought to myself, knowing my father's coldness and reserve, what must actually have been the brusque greeting which she claimed to have found so charming, I was embarrassed, as though at some indelicacy on his part, by the

contrast between the excessive recognition bestowed on it
and his want of geniality. It has since struck me as one of the
most touching aspects of the part played in life by these idle,
painstaking women that they devote their generosity, their
talent, a disposable dream of sentimental beauty (for, like
artists, they never seek to realise the value of their dreams,
or to enclose them in the four-square frame of everyday life),
and a wealth that counts for little, to the fashioning of a fine
and precious setting for the rough, ill-polished lives of men.
And just as this one filled the smoking-room, where my uncle
was entertaining her in his alpaca coat, with the aura of her
charming person, her dress of pink silk, her pearls, the elegance that derives from the friendship of a grand duke, so in
the same way she had taken some casual remark of my father's,
had delicately fashioned it, given it a "turn," a precious title,
and embellishing it with a gem-like glance from her sparkling
eyes, tinged with humility and gratitude, had given it back
transformed into a jewel, a work of art, into something
"exquisitely charming."

"Look here, my boy, it's time you were off," said my
uncle.

I rose. I had an irresistible desire to kiss the hand of the
lady in pink, but I felt that to do so would require as much
audacity as a forcible abduction. My heart beat loud while I
repeated to myself "Shall I do it, shall I not?" and then I
ceased to ask myself what I ought to do so as at least to do
something. With a blind, insensate gesture, divested of all the
reasons in its favour that I had thought of a moment before,
I seized and raised to my lips the hand she held out to me.

"Isn't he delicious! Quite a ladies' man already; he takes
after his uncle. He'll be a perfect 'gentleman,' " she added,
clenching her teeth so as to give the word a kind of English
accentuation. "Couldn't he come to me some day for 'a cup
of tea,' as our friends across the Channel say? He need only
send me a 'blue' in the morning?"

I had not the least idea what a "blue" might be.[5] I did not
understand half the words which the lady used, but my fear
lest there should be concealed in them some question which it
would be impolite of me not to answer made me keep on

listening to them with close attention, and I was beginning to feel extremely tired.

"No, no, it's impossible," said my uncle, shrugging his shoulders. "He's kept very busy, he works extremely hard. He brings back all the prizes from his school," he added in a lower voice, so that I should not hear this falsehood and interrupt with a contradiction. "Who knows? he may turn out a little Victor Hugo, a kind of Vaulabelle, don't you know."

"Oh, I love artistic people," replied the lady in pink. "There's no one like them for understanding women. Apart from a few superior people like yourself. But please forgive my ignorance. Who or what is Vaulabelle? Is it those gilt books in the little glass case in your drawing-room? You know you promised to lend them to me. I'll take great care of them."

My uncle, who hated lending people books, said nothing, and ushered me out into the hall. Madly in love with the lady in pink, I covered my old uncle's tobacco-stained cheeks with passionate kisses, and while with some embarrassment he gave me to understand without actually saying that he would rather I did not tell my parents about this visit, I assured him with tears in my eyes that his kindness had made so strong an impression upon me that some day I would most certainly find a way of expressing my gratitude. So strong an impression, indeed, had it made upon me that two hours later, after a string of mysterious utterances which did not strike me as giving my parents a sufficiently clear idea of the new importance with which I had been invested, I found it simpler to tell them in the minutest detail of the visit I had paid that afternoon. In doing this I had no thought of causing my uncle any unpleasantness. How could I have thought such a thing, since I did not wish it? And I could not suppose that my parents would see any harm in a visit in which I myself saw none. Every day of our lives does not some friend or other ask us to make his apologies, without fail, to some woman to whom he has been prevented from writing, and do not we forget to do so, feeling that this woman cannot attach much importance to a silence that has none for ourselves? I imagined, like everyone else, that the brains of other people were lifeless and

submissive receptacles with no power of specific reaction to
anything that might be introduced into them; and I had not
the least doubt that when I deposited in the minds of my
parents the news of the acquaintance I had made at my uncle's
I should at the same time transmit to them the kindly judgment
I myself had based on the introduction. Unfortunately my
parents had recourse to principles entirely different from those
which I intended them to adopt when they came to form their
estimate of my uncle's conduct. My father and grandfather
had "words" with him of a violent order; as I learned indirectly. A few days later, passing my uncle in the street as
he drove by in an open carriage, I felt at once all the grief,
the gratitude, the remorse which I should have liked to
convey to him. Beside the immensity of these emotions I
considered that merely to raise my hat to him would be
incongruous and petty, and might make him think that I
regarded myself as bound to show him no more than the
commonest form of courtesy. I decided to abstain from so
inadequate a gesture, and turned my head away. My uncle
thought that in doing so I was obeying my parents' orders;
he never forgave them; and though he did not die until many
years later, not one of us ever set eyes on him again.

And so I no longer went into the little sitting-room (now
kept shut) of my uncle Adolphe; instead, after hanging about
on the outskirts of the back-kitchen until Françoise appeared
on its threshold and announced: "I'm going to let my kitchen-
maid serve the coffee and take up the hot water; it's time I
went off to Mme Octave," I would then decide to go indoors,
and would go straight upstairs to my room to read. The
kitchen-maid was an abstract personality, a permanent institu-
tion to which an invariable set of functions assured a sort of
fixity and continuity and identity throughout the succession
of transitory human shapes in which it was embodied; for we
never had the same girl two years running. In the year in
which we ate such quantities of asparagus, the kitchen-maid
whose duty it was to prepare them was a poor sickly creature,
some way "gone" in pregnancy when we arrived at Combray
for Easter, and it was indeed surprising that Françoise allowed
her to run so many errands and to do so much work, for she

was beginning to find difficulty in bearing before her the mysterious basket, fuller and larger every day, whose splendid outline could be detected beneath the folds of her ample smock. This last recalled the cloaks in which Giotto shrouds some of his allegorical figures, of which M. Swann had given me photographs. He it was who pointed out the resemblance, and when he inquired after the kitchen-maid he would say: "Well, how goes it with Giotto's Charity?" And indeed the poor girl, whose pregnancy had swelled and stoutened every part of her, even including her face and her squarish, elongated cheeks, did distinctly suggest those virgins, so sturdy and mannish as to seem matrons rather, in whom the Virtues are personified in the Arena Chapel. And I can see now that those Virtues and Vices of Padua resembled her in another respect as well. For just as the figure of this girl had been enlarged by the additional symbol which she carried before her, without appearing to understand its meaning, with no awareness in her facial expression of its beauty and spiritual significance, as if it were an ordinary, rather heavy burden, so it is without any apparent suspicion of what she is about that the powerfully built housewife who is portrayed in the Arena Chapel beneath the label "Caritas," and a reproduction of whose portrait hung upon the wall of my schoolroom at Combray, embodies that virtue, for it seems impossible that any thought of charity can ever have found expression in her vulgar and energetic face. By a fine stroke of the painter's invention she is trampling all the treasures of the earth beneath her feet, but exactly as if she were treading grapes in a wine-press to extract their juice, or rather as if she had climbed on to a heap of sacks to raise herself higher; and she is holding out her flaming heart to God, or shall we say "handing" it to him, exactly as a cook might hand up a corkscrew through the skylight of her basement kitchen to someone who has called down for it from the ground-floor window. The "Invidia," again, should have had some look of envy on her face. But in this fresco, too, the symbol occupies so large a place and is represented with such realism, the serpent hissing between the lips of Envy is so huge, and so completely fills her wide-opened mouth, that the muscles of her face are strained and contorted,

like those of a child blowing up a balloon, and her attention—
and ours too for that matter—is so utterly concentrated on the
activity of her lips as to leave little time to spare for envious
thoughts.

Despite all the admiration M. Swann professed for these
figures of Giotto, it was a long time before I could find any
pleasure in contemplating on the walls of our schoolroom
(where the copies he had brought me were hung) that Charity
devoid of charity, that Envy who looked like nothing so
much as a plate in some medical book, illustrating the compression of the glottis or the uvula by a tumour of the tongue
or by the introduction of the operator's instrument, a Justice
whose greyish and meanly regular features were identical
with those which characterised the faces of certain pious,
desiccated ladies of Combray whom I used to see at mass and
many of whom had long been enrolled in the reserve forces of
Injustice. But in later years I came to understand that the
arresting strangeness, the special beauty of these frescoes
derived from the great part played in them by symbolism,
and the fact that this was represented not as a symbol (for the
thought symbolised was nowhere expressed) but as a reality,
actually felt or materially handled, added something more
precise and more literal to the meaning of the work, something
more concrete and more striking to the lesson it imparted.
Similarly, in the case of the poor kitchen-maid, was not one's
attention incessantly drawn to her belly by the weight which
dragged it down; and in the same way, again, are not the
thoughts of the dying often turned towards the practical,
painful, obscure, visceral aspect, towards that "seamy side"
of death which is, as it happens, the side that death actually
presents to them and forces them to feel, and which far more
closely resembles a crushing burden, a difficulty in breathing,
a destroying thirst, than the abstract idea to which we are
accustomed to give the name of Death?

There must have been a strong element of reality in those
Virtues and Vices of Padua, since they appeared to me to be
as alive as the pregnant servant-girl, while she herself seemed
scarcely less allegorical than they. And, quite possibly, this
lack (or seeming lack) of participation by a person's soul in

the virtue of which he or she is the agent has, apart from its aesthetic meaning, a reality which, if not strictly psychological, may at least be called physiognomical. Since then, whenever in the course of my life I have come across, in convents for instance, truly saintly embodiments of practical charity, they have generally had the cheerful, practical, brusque and un-emotioned air of a busy surgeon, the sort of face in which one can discern no commiseration, no tenderness at the sight of suffering humanity, no fear of hurting it, the impassive, unsympathetic, sublime face of true goodness.

While the kitchen-maid—who, all unawares, made the superior qualities of Françoise shine with added lustre, just as Error, by force of contrast, enhances the triumph of Truth—served coffee which (according to Mamma) was nothing more than hot water, and then carried up to our rooms hot water which was barely lukewarm, I would be lying stretched out on my bed with a book in my hand. My room quivered with the effort to defend its frail, transparent coolness against the afternoon sun behind its almost closed shutters through which, however, a gleam of daylight had contrived to insinuate its golden wings, remaining motionless in a corner between glass and woodwork, like a butterfly poised upon a flower. It was hardly light enough for me to read, and my sense of the day's brightness and splendour was derived solely from the blows struck down below, in the Rue de la Cure, by Camus (whom Françoise had assured that my aunt was not "resting" and that he might therefore make a noise) upon some dusty packing-cases which, reverberating in the sonorous atmosphere that accompanies hot weather, seemed to scatter broadcast a rain of blood-red stars; and also from the flies who performed for my benefit, in their tiny chorus, as it were the chamber music of summer, evoking it quite differently from a snatch of human music which, heard by chance in high summer, will remind you of it later, whereas the music of the flies is bound to the season by a more compelling tie—born of the sunny days, and not to be reborn but with them, containing something of their essential nature, it not merely calls up their image in our memory, but guarantees their return, their actual, circum-jacent, immediately accessible presence.

This dim coolness of my room was to the broad daylight of
the street what the shadow is to the sunbeam, that is to say
equally luminous, and presented to my imagination the entire
panorama of summer, which my senses, if I had been out walking, could have tasted and enjoyed only piecemeal; and so
it was quite in harmony with my state of repose which (thanks
to the enlivening adventures related in my books) sustained,
like a hand reposing motionless in a stream of running water,
the shock and animation of a torrent of activity.

But my grandmother, even if the weather, after growing too
hot, had broken, and a storm, or just a shower, had burst
over us, would come up and beg me to go outside. And as I
did not wish to interrupt my reading, I would go on with it
in the garden, under the chestnut-tree, in a hooded chair of
wicker and canvas in the depths of which I used to sit and feel
that I was hidden from the eyes of anyone who might be
coming to call upon the family.

And then my thoughts, too, formed a similar sort of recess,
in the depths of which I felt that I could bury myself and remain
invisible even while I looked at what went on outside. When
I saw an external object, my consciousness that I was seeing
it would remain between me and it, surrounding it with a thin
spiritual border that prevented me from ever touching its
substance directly; for it would somehow evaporate before
I could make contact with it, just as an incandescent body that
is brought into proximity with something wet never actually
touches its moisture, since it is always preceded by a zone of
evaporation. On the sort of screen dappled with different
states and impressions which my consciousness would simultaneously unfold while I was reading, and which ranged from
the most deeply hidden aspirations of my being to the wholly
external view of the horizon spread out before my eyes at the
bottom of the garden, what was my primary, my innermost
impulse, the lever whose incessant movements controlled
everything else, was my belief in the philosophic richness and
beauty of the book I was reading, and my desire to appropriate
them for myself, whatever the book might be. For even if I
had bought it at Combray, having seen it outside Borange's—
whose grocery lay too far from our house for Françoise to be

able to shop there, as she did at Camus's, but was better stocked as a stationer and bookseller—tied with string to keep it in its place in the mosaic of monthly serials and pamphlets which adorned either side of his doorway, a doorway more mysterious, more teeming with suggestion than that of a cathedral, it was because I had recognised it as a book which had been well spoken of by the schoolmaster or the schoolfriend who at that particular time seemed to me to be entrusted with the secret of Truth and Beauty, things half-felt by me, half-incomprehensible, the full understanding of which was the vague but permanent object of my thoughts.

Next to this central belief which, while I was reading, would be constantly reaching out from my inner self to the outer world, towards the discovery of Truth, came the emotions aroused in me by the action in which I was taking part, for these afternoons were crammed with more dramatic events than occur, often, in a whole lifetime. These were the events taking place in the book I was reading. It is true that the people concerned in them were not what Françoise would have called "real people." But none of the feelings which the joys or misfortunes of a "real" person arouse in us can be awakened except through a mental picture of those joys or misfortunes; and the ingenuity of the first novelist lay in his understanding that, as the image was the one essential element in the complicated structure of our emotions, so that simplification of it which consisted in the suppression, pure and simple, of "real" people would be a decided improvement. A "real" person, profoundly as we may sympathise with him, is in a great measure perceptible only through our senses, that is to say, remains opaque, presents a dead weight which our sensibilities have not the strength to lift. If some misfortune comes to him, it is only in one small section of the complete idea we have of him that we are capable of feeling any emotion; indeed it is only in one small section of the complete idea he has of himself that he is capable of feeling any emotion either. The novelist's happy discovery was to think of substituting for those opaque sections, impenetrable to the human soul, their equivalent in immaterial sections, things, that is, which one's soul can assimilate. After which it matters not that the actions, the feelings

of this new order of creatures appear to us in the guise of truth,
since we have made them our own, since it is in ourselves that
they are happening, that they are holding in thrall, as we
feverishly turn over the pages of the book, our quickened
breath and staring eyes. And once the novelist has brought us
to this state, in which, as in all purely mental states, every
emotion is multiplied ten-fold, into which his book comes to
disturb us as might a dream, but a dream more lucid and more
abiding than those which come to us in sleep, why then, for
the space of an hour he sets free within us all the joys and
sorrows in the world, a few of which only we should have to
spend years of our actual life in getting to know, and the
most intense of which would never be revealed to us because
the slow course of their development prevents us from perceiving them. It is the same in life; the heart changes, and it is
our worst sorrow; but we know it only through reading,
through our imagination: in reality its alteration, like that of
certain natural phenomena, is so gradual that, even if we are
able to distinguish, successively, each of its different states,
we are still spared the actual sensation of change.

Next to, but distinctly less intimate a part of myself than
this human element, would come the landscape, more or less
projected before my eyes, in which the plot of the story was
taking place, and which made a far stronger impression on my
mind than the other, the actual landscape which met my eyes
when I raised them from my book. Thus for two consecutive
summers I sat in the heat of our Combray garden, sick with a
longing inspired by the book I was then reading for a land of
mountains and rivers, where I could see innumerable saw-
mills, where beneath the limpid currents fragments of wood
lay mouldering in beds of watercress; and near by, rambling
and clustering along low walls, purple and red flowers. And
since there was always lurking in my mind the dream of a
woman who would enrich me with her love, that dream in
those two summers was quickened with the fresh coolness of
running water; and whoever she might be, the woman whose
image I called to mind, flowers, purple and red, would at once
spring up on either side of her like complementary colours.

This was not only because an image of which we dream

remains for ever stamped, is adorned and enriched, by the association of colours not its own which may happen to surround it in our mental picture; for the landscapes in the books I read were to me not merely landscapes more vividly portrayed in my imagination than any which Combray could spread before my eyes but otherwise of the same kind. Because of the choice that the author had made of them, because of the spirit of faith in which my mind would exceed and anticipate his printed word, as it might be interpreting a revelation, they seemed to me—an impression I hardly ever derived from the place where I happened to be, especially from our garden, that undistinguished product of the strictly conventional fantasy of the gardener whom my grandmother so despised— to be actually part of nature itself, and worthy to be studied and explored.

Had my parents allowed me, when I read a book, to pay a visit to the region it described, I should have felt that I was making an enormous advance towards the ultimate conquest of truth. For even if we have the sensation of being always enveloped in, surrounded by our own soul, still it does not seem a fixed and immovable prison; rather do we seem to be borne away with it, and perpetually struggling to transcend it, to break out into the world, with a perpetual discouragement as we hear endlessly all around us that unvarying sound which is not an echo from without, but the resonance of a vibration from within. We try to discover in things, which become precious to us on that account, the reflection of what our soul has projected on to them; we are disillusioned when we find that they are in reality devoid of the charm which they owed, in our minds, to the association of certain ideas; sometimes we mobilise all our spiritual forces in a glittering array in order to bring our influence to bear on other human beings who, we very well know, are situated outside ourselves where we can never reach them. And so, if I always imagined the woman I loved in the setting I most longed at the time to visit, if I wished that it were she who showed it to me, who opened to me the gates of an unknown world, it was not by the mere hazard of a simple association of thoughts; no, it was because my dreams of travel and of love were only moments—which I isolate artificially to-day as though I were cutting sections at different heights in a jet of water, iridescent but seemingly without flow or motion—in a single, undeviating, irresistible outpouring of all the forces of my life.

Finally, continuing to trace from the inside outwards these states simultaneously juxtaposed in my consciousness, and before reaching the horizon of reality which enveloped them, I discover pleasures of another kind, those of being comfortably seated, of sniffing the fragrance of the air, of not being disturbed by any visitor, and, when an hour chimed from the steeple of Saint-Hilaire, of seeing what was already spent of the afternoon fall drop by drop until I heard the last stroke which enabled me to add up the total, after which the long silence that followed seemed to herald the beginning, in the blue sky above me, of all that part of the day that still remained to me for reading, until the good dinner which Françoise was even now preparing and which would strengthen and refresh me after the strenuous pursuit of the hero through the pages of my book. And as each hour struck, it would seem to me that a few moments only had passed since the hour before; the latest would inscribe itself close to its predecessor on the sky's surface, and I was unable to believe that sixty minutes could have been squeezed into the tiny arc of blue which was comprised between their two golden figures. Sometimes it would even happen that this precocious hour would sound two strokes more than the last; there must then have been an hour which I had not heard strike; something that had taken place had not taken place for me; the fascination of my book, a magic as potent as the deepest slumber, had deceived my enchanted ears and had obliterated the sound of that golden bell from the azure surface of the enveloping silence. Sweet Sunday afternoons beneath the chestnut-tree in the garden at Combray, carefully purged by me of every commonplace incident of my personal existence, which I had replaced with a life of strange adventures and aspirations in a land watered with living streams, you still recall that life to me when I think of you, and you embody it in effect by virtue of having gradually encircled and enclosed it—while I went on with my reading and the heat of the day declined—in the

crystalline succession, slowly changing and dappled with foliage, of your silent, sonorous, fragrant, limpid hours.

Sometimes I would be torn from my book in the middle of the afternoon by the gardener's daughter, who came running wildly, overturning an orange-tree in its tub, cutting a finger, breaking a tooth, and screaming "They're coming, they're coming!" so that Françoise and I should run too and not miss anything of the show. That was on the days when the cavalry from the local garrison passed through Combray on their way to manoeuvres, going as a rule by the Rue Sainte-Hildegarde. While our servants, sitting in a row on their chairs outside the garden railings, stared at the people of Combray taking their Sunday walk and were stared at in return, the gardener's daughter, through the gap between two distant houses in the Avenue de la Gare, had spied the glitter of helmets. The servants had then hurried in with their chairs, for when the troopers paraded down the Rue Sainte-Hildegarde they filled it from side to side, and their jostling horses scraped against the walls of the houses, covering and submerging the pavements like banks which present too narrow a channel to a river in flood.

"Poor boys," Françoise would exclaim, in tears almost before she had reached the railings, "poor boys, to be mown down like grass in a meadow. It's just shocking to think of," she would add, laying a hand over her heart, where presumably she had felt the shock.

"A fine sight, isn't it, Mme Françoise, all these young fellows not caring two straws for their lives?" the gardener would ask, just to "draw" her. And he would not have spoken in vain.

"Not caring for their lives, is it? Why, what in the world should we care for if it's not our lives, the only gift the Lord never offers us a second time? Oh dear, oh dear! you're right all the same, they don't care! I can remember them in '70; in those wretched wars they've no fear of death left in them; they're nothing more nor less than madmen; and then they aren't worth the price of a rope to hang them with; they're not men any more, they're lions." For by her way of thinking, to compare a man with a lion, which she used to pronounce "lie-on," was not at all complimentary.

The Rue Sainte-Hildegarde turned too sharply for us to be able to see them approaching at any distance, and it was only through the gap between the two houses in the Avenue de la Gare that we could glimpse more helmets flashing past in the sunlight. The gardener wanted to know whether there were still many to come, and he was thirsty besides, with the sun beating down upon his head. So then, suddenly, his daughter would leap out as though from a beleaguered city, would make a sortie, turn the street corner, and after having risked her life a hundred times over, would reappear bringing us, together with a jug of liquorice-water, the news that there were still at least a thousand of them, pouring along without a break from the direction of Thiberzy and Méséglise. Françoise and the gardener, reconciled, would discuss the line to be followed in the event of war.

"Don't you see, Françoise," he would say, "revolution would be better, because then no one would need to join in unless he wanted to."

"Oh, yes, I can see that, certainly; it's more straightforward."

The gardener believed that, as soon as war was declared, all the railways would be shut down.

"Yes, to be sure; to stop people running away," Françoise would say.

And the gardener would assent, with "Ay, they're the cunning ones," for he would not allow that war was anything but a kind of trick which the State attempted to play on the people, or that there was a man in the world who would not run away from it if he had the chance to do so.

But Françoise would hasten back to my aunt, and I would return to my book, and the servants would take their places again outside the gate to watch the dust settle on the pavement and the excitement caused by the passage of the soldiers subside. Long after calm had been restored, an abnormal tide of humanity would continue to darken the streets of Combray. And in front of every house, even those where it was not as a rule "done," the servants, and sometimes even the masters, would sit and watch, festooning the doorsteps with a dark, irregular fringe, like the border of shells and sea-weed which a stronger tide than usual leaves on the beach, as though trimming it with embroidered crape, when the sea itself has retreated.

Except on such days as these, however, I would as a rule be left to read in peace. But the interruption and the commentary which a visit from Swann once occasioned in the course of my reading, which had brought me to the work of an author quite new to me, Bergotte, resulted in the consequence that for a long time afterwards it was not against a wall gay with spikes of purple blossom, but against a wholly different background, the porch of a gothic cathedral, that I saw the figure of one of the women of whom I dreamed.

I had heard Bergotte spoken of for the first time by a friend older than myself whom I greatly admired, Bloch. Hearing me confess my admiration for the *Nuit d'Octobre*, he had burst out in a loud bray of laughter like a bugle-call, and said to me: "You really must conquer your vile taste for A. de Musset, Esquire. He is a bad egg, one of the very worst, a pretty detestable specimen. I am bound to admit, natheless, that he, and even the man Racine, did, each of them, once in his life, compose a line which is not only fairly rhythmical but has also what is in my eyes the supreme merit of meaning absolutely nothing. One is '*La blanche Oloossone et la blanche Camyre*,' and the other '*La fille de Minos et de Pasiphaë.*' They were submitted to my judgment, as evidence for the defence of these two runagates, in an article by my revered master, old Leconte, beloved of the immortal gods. By which token, here is a book which I haven't the time to read just now, recommended, it appears, by that colossal fellow. He regards, or so they tell me, its author, one Bergotte, as a most subtle scribe; and, albeit he exhibits on occasion a critical mansuetude that is not easily explicable, still his word has weight with me as it were the Delphic Oracle. Read you then this lyrical prose, and, if the titanic rhymester who composed *Bhagavat* and the *Lévrier de Magnus* speaks not falsely, then, by Apollo, you may taste, *cher maître*, the ambrosial joys of Olympus." It was in an ostensible vein of sarcasm that he had asked me to call him, and that he himself called me, "*cher maître*." But, as a matter of fact, we each derived a certain satisfaction from the mannerism, being still at the age in which

one believes that one gives a thing real existence by giving it a
name.

Unfortunately I was unable to set at rest by further talks
with Bloch, in which I might have insisted upon an explanation, the doubts he had engendered in me when he told me
that fine lines of poetry (from which I expected nothing less
than the revelation of truth itself) were all the finer if they
meant absolutely nothing. For, as it happened, Bloch was not
invited to the house again. At first he had been well received
there. It is true that my grandfather made out that, whenever I
formed a strong attachment to any one of my friends and
brought him home with me, that friend was invariably a Jew;
to which he would not have objected on principle—indeed
his own friend Swann was of Jewish extraction—had he not
found that the Jews whom I chose as friends were not usually
of the best type. And so whenever I brought a new friend
home my grandfather seldom failed to start humming the
"O, God of our fathers" from *La Juive*, or else "Israel, break
thy chains," singing the tune alone, of course, to an "um-ti-
tum-ti-tum, tra-la"; but I used to be afraid that my friend
would recognise it and be able to reconstruct the words.

Before seeing them, merely on hearing their names, about
which, as often as not, there was nothing particularly Hebraic,
he would divine not only the Jewish origin of such of my
friends as might indeed be Jewish, but even at times some
skeleton in their family cupboard.

"And what's the name of this friend of yours who is coming
this evening?"

"Dumont, grandpapa."

"Dumont! Oh, I don't like the sound of that."

And he would sing:

> Archers, be on your guard!
> Watch without rest, without sound.

And then, after a few adroit questions on points of detail,
he would call out "On guard! on guard," or, if it were the
victim himself who had already arrived, and had been unwittingly obliged, by subtle interrogation, to admit his origins,
then my grandfather, to show us that he had no longer any

doubts, would merely look at us, humming under his breath the air of

> What! do you hither guide the feet
> Of this timid Israelite?

or of

> Sweet vale of Hebron, dear paternal fields,

or, perhaps, of

> Yes, I am of the chosen race.

These little eccentricities on my grandfather's part implied no ill-will whatsoever towards my friends. But Bloch had displeased my family for other reasons. He had begun by irritating my father, who, seeing him come in with wet clothes, had asked him with keen interest:

"Why, M. Bloch, is there a change in the weather? Has it been raining? I can't understand it; the barometer has been 'set fair.'"

Which drew from Bloch nothing more instructive than: "Sir, I am absolutely incapable of telling you whether it has rained. I live so resolutely apart from physical contingencies that my senses no longer trouble to inform me of them."

"My poor boy," said my father after Bloch had gone, "your friend is out of his mind. Why, he couldn't even tell me what the weather was like. As if there could be anything more interesting! He's an imbecile."

Next Bloch had displeased my grandmother because once, after lunch, when she complained of not feeling very well, he had stifled a sob and wiped tears from his eyes.

"How can he possibly be sincere," she observed to me. "Why, he doesn't know me. Unless he's mad, of course."

And finally he had upset the whole household when he arrived an hour and a half late for dinner and covered with mud from head to foot, and made not the least apology, saying merely: "I never allow myself to be influenced in the smallest degree either by atmospheric disturbances or by the arbitrary divisions of what is known as time. I would willingly re-introduce to society the opium pipe of China or the Malayan kris, but I am wholly and entirely without instruction in those infinitely more pernicious and moreover quite bleakly bourgeois implements, the umbrella and the watch."

In spite of all this he would still have been received at Combray. He was, of course, hardly the friend my parents would have chosen for me; they had, in the end, decided that the tears which he had shed on hearing of my grandmother's indisposition were genuine enough; but they knew, either instinctively or from experience, that our impulsive emotions have but little influence over the course of our actions and the conduct of our lives; and that regard for moral obligations, loyalty to friends, patience in finishing our work, obedience to a rule of life, have a surer foundation in habits solidly formed and blindly followed than in these momentary transports, ardent but sterile. They would have preferred for me, instead of Bloch, companions who would have given me no more than it is proper to give according to the laws of middle-class morality, who would not unexpectedly send me a basket of fruit because they happened, that morning, to have thought of me with affection, but who, being incapable of inclining in my favour, by a simple impulse of their imagination and sensibility, the exact balance of the duties and claims of friendship, would be equally incapable of loading the scales to my detriment. Even our faults will not easily divert from the path of their duty towards us those conventional natures of which the model was my great-aunt who, estranged for years from a niece to whom she never spoke, yet made no change in the will in which she had left that niece the whole of her fortune, because she was her next-of-kin and it was the "proper thing" to do.

But I was fond of Bloch; my parents wished me to be happy; and the insoluble problems which I set myself on such texts as the "absolutely meaningless" beauty of *La fille de Minos et de Pasiphaë* made me more exhausted and unwell than further talks on the subject would have done, unwholesome as those talks might seem to my mother's mind. And he would still have been received at Combray but for one thing. That same night, after dinner, having informed me (a piece of news which had a great influence on my later life, making it happier at one time and then more unhappy) that no woman ever thought of anything but love, and that there was not one of them whose resistance could not be overcome, he had gone on to assure me that he had heard it said on unimpeachable authority that my great-aunt herself had led a tempestuous life in her younger days and had been notoriously "kept." I could not refrain from passing on so important a piece of information to my parents; the next time Bloch called he was not admitted, and afterwards, when I met him in the street, he greeted me with extreme coldness.

But in the matter of Bergotte he had spoken truly.

For the first few days, like a tune with which one will soon be infatuated but which one has not yet "got hold of," the things I was to love so passionately in Bergotte's style did not immediately strike me. I could not, it is true, lay down the novel of his which I was reading, but I fancied that I was interested in the subject alone, as in the first dawn of love when we go every day to meet a woman at some party or entertainment which we think is in itself the attraction. Then I observed the rare, almost archaic expressions he liked to employ at certain moments, in which a hidden stream of harmony, an inner prelude, would heighten his style; and it was at such points as these, too, that he would begin to speak of the "vain dream of life," of the "inexhaustible torrent of fair forms," of the "sterile and exquisite torture of understanding and loving," of the "moving effigies which ennoble for all time the charming and venerable fronts of our cathedrals," that he would express a whole system of philosophy, new to me, by the use of marvellous images that one felt must be the inspiration for the harp-song which then arose and to which they provided a sublime accompaniment. One of these passages of Bergotte, the third or fourth which I had detached from the rest, filled me with a joy to which the meagre joy I had tasted in the first passage bore no comparison, a joy that I felt I was experiencing in a deeper, vaster, more integral part of myself, from which all obstacles and partitions seemed to have been swept away. For what had happened was that, while I recognised in this passage the same taste for uncommon phrases, the same musical outpouring, the same idealist philosophy which had been present in the earlier

passages without my having recognised them as being the
source of my pleasure, I now had the impression of being
confronted not by a particular passage in one of Bergotte's
works, tracing a purely bi-dimensional figure upon the surface
of my mind, but rather by the "ideal passage" of Bergotte,
common to every one of his books, to which all the earlier,
similar passages, now becoming merged in it, had added a
kind of density and volume by which my own understanding
seemed to be enlarged.

I was not quite Bergotte's sole admirer; he was the favourite
writer also of a friend of my mother's, a very well-read lady;
while Dr du Boulbon had kept all his patients waiting until he
finished Bergotte's latest volume; and it was from his consulting room, and from a house in a park near Combray,
that some of the first seeds were scattered of that taste for
Bergotte, a rare growth in those days but now universally
acclimatised, that one finds flowering everywhere throughout
Europe and America, even in the smallest villages, rare still in
its refinement, but in that alone. What my mother's friend
and, it would seem, Dr du Boulbon liked above all in the
writings of Bergotte was just what I liked, the same melodic
flow, the old-fashioned phrases, and certain others, quite
simple and familiar, but so placed by him, so highlighted,
as to hint at a particular quality of taste on his part; and also,
in the sad parts of his books, a sort of roughness, a tone that
was almost harsh. And he himself, no doubt, realised that
these were his principal attractions. For in his later books, if
he had hit upon some great truth, or upon the name of an
historic cathedral, he would break off his narrative, and in an
invocation, an apostrophe, a long prayer, would give free
rein to those exhalations which, in the earlier volumes, had
been immanent in his prose, discernible only in a rippling of
its surface, and perhaps even more delightful, more harmonious
when they were thus veiled, when the reader could give no
precise indication of where their murmuring began or where
it died away. These passages in which he delighted were our
favourites also. For my own part I knew all of them by heart.
I was disappointed when he resumed the thread of his narrative.
Whenever he spoke of something whose beauty had until then

remained hidden from me, of pine-forests or of hailstorms, of Notre-Dame Cathedral, of *Athalie* or of *Phèdre*, by some piece of imagery he would make their beauty explode into my consciousness. And so, realising that the universe contained innumerable elements which my feeble senses would be powerless to discern did he not bring them within my reach, I longed to have some opinion, some metaphor of his, upon everything in the world, and especially upon such things as I might some day have an opportunity of seeing for myself; and among these, more particularly still upon some of the historic buildings of France, upon certain seascapes, because the emphasis with which he referred to them in his books showed that he regarded them as rich in significance and beauty. But, alas, upon almost everything in the world his opinion was unknown to me. I had no doubt that it would differ entirely from my own, since his came down from an unknown sphere towards which I was striving to raise myself; convinced that my thoughts would have seemed pure foolishness to that perfected spirit, I had so completely obliterated them all that, if I happened to find in one of his books something which had already occurred to my own mind, my heart would swell as though some deity had, in his infinite bounty, restored it to me, had pronounced it to be beautiful and right. It happened now and then that a page of Bergotte would express precisely those ideas which I often used to write to my grandmother and my mother at night, when I was unable to sleep, so much so that this page of his had the appearance of a collection of epigraphs for me to set at the head of my letters. And so too, in later years, when I began to write a book of my own, and the quality of some of my sentences seemed so inadequate that I could not make up my mind to go on with the undertaking, I would find the equivalent in Bergotte. But it was only then, when I read them in his pages, that I could enjoy them; when it was I myself who composed them, in my anxiety that they should exactly reproduce what I had perceived in my mind's eye, and in my fear of their not turning out "true to life," how could I find time to ask myself whether what I was writing was pleasing! But in fact there was no other kind of prose, no other sort of ideas, that I really liked.

My feverish and unsatisfactory attempts were themselves a token of love, a love which brought me no pleasure but was nonetheless profound. And so, when I came suddenly upon similar phrases in the writings of another, that is to say stripped of their familiar accompaniment of scruples and repressions and self-tormentings, I was free to indulge to the full my own appetite for such things, like a cook who, for once having no dinner to prepare for other people, at last has the time to enjoy his food. When, one day, I came across in a book by Bergotte some joke about an old family servant which the writer's solemn and magnificent prose made even more comical, but which was in principle the same joke I had often made to my grandmother about Françoise, and when, another time, I discovered that he considered not unworthy of reflection in one of those mirrors of absolute truth which were his writings a remark similar to one which I had had occasion to make about our friend M. Legrandin (and moreover my remarks on Françoise and M. Legrandin were among those which I would most resolutely have sacrificed for Bergotte's sake, in the belief that he would find them quite without interest), then it was suddenly revealed to me that my own humble existence and the realms of the true were less widely separated than I had supposed, that at certain points they actually coincided, and in my new-found confidence and joy I had wept upon his printed page as in the arms of a long-lost father.

From his books I had formed an impression of Bergotte as a frail and disappointed old man, who had lost some of his children and had never got over the loss. And so I would read, or rather sing his sentences in my mind, with rather more *dolce*, rather more *lento* than he himself had perhaps intended, and his simplest phrase would strike my ears with something peculiarly gentle and loving in its intonation. More than anything else I cherished his philosophy, and had pledged myself to it in lifelong devotion. It made me impatient to reach the age when I should be eligible for the class at school called "Philosophy." But I did not wish to do anything else there but exist and be guided exclusively by the mind of Bergotte, and if I had been told then that the metaphysicians to whom I was actually to become attached there would resemble him in nothing, I should have been struck down by the despair of a young lover who has sworn lifelong fidelity, when a friend speaks to him of the other mistresses he will have in time to come.

One Sunday, while I was reading in the garden, I was interrupted by Swann, who had come to call upon my parents. "What are you reading? May I look? Why, it's Bergotte! Who has been telling you about him?"

I replied that Bloch was responsible.

"Oh, yes, that boy I saw here once, who looks so like the Bellini portrait of Mahomet II. It's an astonishing likeness; he has the same arched eyebrows and hooked nose and prominent cheekbones. When he has a little beard he'll be Mahomet himself. Anyhow, he has good taste, for Bergotte is a delightful soul." And seeing how much I seemed to admire Bergotte, Swann, who never spoke at all about the people he knew, made an exception in my favour and said: "I know him well. If you would like him to write a few words on the title-page of your book I could ask him for you."

I dared not accept such an offer, but bombarded Swann with questions about his friend. "Can you tell me, please, who is his favourite actor?"

"Actor? No, I can't say. But I do know this: there's not a man on the stage whom he thinks equal to Berma—he puts her above everyone. Have you seen her?"

"No, sir, my parents don't allow me to go to the theatre."

"That's a pity. You should insist. Berma in *Phèdre*, in the *Cid*; she's only an actress, if you like, but you know I don't believe very much in the 'hierarchy' of the arts." (As he spoke I noticed, what had often struck me before in his conversations with my grandmother's sisters, that whenever he spoke of serious matters, whenever he used an expression which seemed to imply a definite opinion upon some important subject, he would take care to isolate, to sterilise it by using a special intonation, mechanical and ironic, as though he had put the phrase or word between inverted commas, and was anxious to disclaim any personal responsibility for it; as who should

say "the '*hierarchy*,' don't you know, as silly people call it."
But then, if it was so absurd, why did he use the word?) A
moment later he went on: "Her acting will give you as noble an
inspiration as any masterpiece of art, as—oh, I don't know—"
and he laughed, "shall we say the Queens of Chartres?".
Until then I had supposed that this horror of having to give a
serious opinion was something Parisian and refined, in contrast to the provincial dogmatism of my grandmother's sisters;
and I imagined also that it was characteristic of the mental
attitude of the circle in which Swann moved, where, by a
natural reaction from the lyrical enthusiasms of earlier generations, an excessive importance was now given to precise and
petty facts, formerly regarded as vulgar, and anything in the
nature of "phrase-making" was proscribed. But now I found
myself slightly shocked by this attitude of Swann's. He appeared unwilling even to risk having an opinion, and to be
at his ease only when he could furnish, with meticulous
accuracy, some precise detail. But did he not realise that to
postulate that the accuracy of his information was of some
importance was tantamount to professing an opinion? I
thought again of the dinner that night when I had been so
unhappy because Mamma would not be coming up to my
room, and when he had dismissed the balls given by the
Princesse de Léon as being of no importance. And yet it was
to just that sort of amusement that he devoted his life. I found
all this contradictory. What other life did he set apart for
saying in all seriousness what he thought about things, for
formulating judgments which he would not put between
inverted commas, and for no longer indulging with punctilious politeness in occupations which at the same time he
professed to find absurd? I noticed, too, in the manner in
which Swann spoke to me of Bergotte, something which, to
do him justice, was not peculiar to himself, but was shared at
the time by all that writer's admirers, including my mother's
friend and Dr du Boulbon. Like Swann, they would say of
Bergotte: "He has a delightful mind, so individual, he has a
way of his own of saying things, which is a little far-fetched,
but so agreeable. You never need to look for the signature,
you can tell his work at once." But none of them would go

so far as to say "He's a great writer, he has great talent."
They did not even credit him with talent at all. They did not
do so, because they did not know. We are very slow to
recognise in the peculiar physiognomy of a new writer the
model which is labelled "great talent" in our museum of
general ideas. Simply because that physiognomy is new and
strange, we can find in it no resemblance to what we are
accustomed to call talent. We say rather originality, charm,
delicacy, strength; and then one day we realise that it is
precisely all this that adds up to talent.

"Are there any books in which Bergotte has written about
Berma?" I asked M. Swann.

"I think he has, in that little essay on Racine, but it must
be out of print. Still, perhaps there has been a second impression. I'll find out. In fact I can ask Bergotte himself all
you want to know next time he comes to dine with us. He
never misses a week, from one year's end to another. He's
my daughter's greatest friend. They go and look at old towns
and cathedrals and castles together."

As I was still completely ignorant of the social hierarchy,
the fact that my father found it impossible for us to see anything of Swann's wife and daughter had for a long time had
the effect, in making me imagine them as separated from us
by an enormous gulf, of enhancing their prestige in my eyes.
I was sorry that my mother did not dye her hair and redden
her lips, as I had heard our neighbour Mme Sazerat say that
Mme Swann did, to gratify not her husband but M. de Charlus;
and I felt that, to her, we must be an object of scorn, which
distressed me particularly on account of the daughter, such a
pretty little girl, as I had heard, of whom I used often to
dream, ascribing to her each time the same arbitrarily chosen
and enchanting features. But when, that day, I learned that Mlle
Swann was a creature living in such rare and fortunate circumstances, bathed, as in her natural element, in such a sea of
privilege that, if she should ask her parents whether anyone were coming to dinner, she would be answered by
those two syllables, radiant with light, by the name of that
golden guest who was to her no more than an old friend of
the family, Bergotte, that for her the intimate conversation

at table, corresponding to what my great-aunt's conversation was for me, would be the words of Bergotte on all those subjects which he had not been able to take up in his writings, and on which I should have liked to hear him pronounce his oracles, and that, above all, when she went to visit other towns, he would be walking by her side, unrecognised and glorious, like the gods who came down of old to dwell among mortals—then I realised both the rare worth of a creature such as Mlle Swann and, at the same time, how coarse and ignorant I should appear to her; and I felt so keenly how sweet and how impossible it would be for me to become her friend that I was filled at once with longing and despair. Henceforth, more often than not when I thought of her, I would see her standing before the porch of a cathedral, explaining to me what each of the statues meant, and, with a smile which was my highest commendation, presenting me as her friend to Bergotte. And invariably the charm of all the fancies which the thought of cathedrals used to inspire in me, the charm of the hills and valleys of the Ile-de-France and of the plains of Normandy, would be reflected in the picture I had formed in my mind's eye of Mlle Swann; nothing more remained but to know and to love her. The belief that a person has a share in an unknown life to which his or her love may win us admission is, of all the prerequisites of love, the one which it values most highly and which makes it set little store by all the rest. Even those women who claim to judge a man by his looks alone, see in those looks the emanation of a special way of life. That is why they fall in love with soldiers or with firemen; the uniform makes them less particular about the face; they feel they are embracing beneath the gleaming breastplate a heart different from the rest, more gallant, more adventurous, more tender; and so it is that a young king or a crown prince may make the most gratifying conquests in the countries that he visits, and yet lack entirely that regular and classic profile which would be indispensable, I dare say, for a stockbroker.

While I was reading in the garden, a thing my great-aunt would never have understood my doing save on a Sunday,

that being the day on which it is unlawful to indulge in any
serious occupation, and on which she herself would lay aside
her sewing (on a week-day she would have said, "What! still
amusing yourself with a book? It isn't Sunday, you know!"—
putting into the word "amusing" an implication of childishness and waste of time), my aunt Léonie would be gossiping
with Françoise until it was time for Eulalie to arrive. She
would tell her that she had just seen Mme Goupil go by
"without an umbrella, in the silk dress she had made for her
the other day at Châteaudun. If she has far to go before vespers,
she may get it properly soaked."

"Maybe, maybe" (which meant "maybe not"), was the
answer, for Françoise did not wish definitely to exclude the
possibility of a happier alternative.

"Heavens," said my aunt, slapping herself on the forehead,
"that reminds me I never heard if she got to church this morning
before the Elevation. I must remember to ask Eulalie ...
Françoise, just look at that black cloud behind the steeple,
and how poor the light is on the slates. You may be certain
it will rain before the day is out. It couldn't possibly go on
like that, it's been too hot. And the sooner the better, for until
the storm breaks my Vichy water won't 'go down,' " she
added, since, in her mind, the desire to accelerate the digestion
of her Vichy water was of infinitely greater importance than
her fear of seeing Mme Goupil's new dress ruined.

"Maybe, maybe."

"And you know that when it rains in the Square there's
none too much shelter." Suddenly my aunt turned pale.
"What, three o'clock!" she exclaimed. "But vespers will have
begun already, and I've forgotten my pepsin! Now I know
why that Vichy water has been lying on my stomach." And
pouncing on a prayer-book bound in purple velvet with gilt
clasps, out of which in her haste she let fall a shower of those
pictures bordered in a lace fringe of yellowish paper which
mark the pages of feast-days, my aunt, while she swallowed
her drops, began at full speed to mutter the words of the
sacred text, its meaning slightly clouded in her brain by the
uncertainty whether the pepsin, when taken so long after
the Vichy, would still be able to catch up with it and

"send it down." "Three o'clock! It's unbelievable how time
flies."

A little tap on the window-pane, as though something had
struck it, followed by a plentiful light falling sound, as of
grains of sand being sprinkled from a window overhead,
gradually spreading, intensifying, acquiring a regular rhythm,
becoming fluid, sonorous, musical, immeasurable, universal:
it was the rain.

"There, Françoise, what did I tell you? How it's coming
down! But I think I heard the bell at the garden gate: go along
and see who can be outside in this weather."

Françoise went and returned. "It's Mme Amédée" (my
grandmother). "She said she was going for a walk. And yet
it's raining hard."

"I'm not at all surprised," said my aunt, raising her eyes to
the heavens. "I've always said that she was not in the least
like other people. Well, I'm glad it's she and not myself who's
outside in all this."

"Mme Amédée is always the exact opposite of everyone
else," said Françoise, not unkindly, refraining until she should
be alone with the other servants from stating her belief that
my grandmother was "a bit off her head."

"There's Benediction over! Eulalie will never come now,"
sighed my aunt. "It will be the weather that's frightened her
away."

"But it's not five o'clock yet, Mme Octave, it's only half-
past four."

"Only half-past four! And here am I, obliged to draw back
the curtains just to get a tiny streak of daylight. At half-past
four! Only a week before the Rogation-days. Ah, my poor
Françoise, the good Lord must be sorely vexed with us. The
world is going too far these days. As my poor Octave used
to say, we have forgotten God too often, and He is taking his
revenge."

A bright flush animated my aunt's cheeks; it was Eulalie.
As ill luck would have it, scarcely had she been admitted to
the presence when Françoise reappeared and, with a smile
that was meant to indicate her full participation in the pleasure
which, she had no doubt, her tidings would give my aunt,

articulating each syllable so as to show that, in spite of her
having to translate them into indirect speech, she was repeating,
as a good servant should, the very words which the new
visitor had condescended to use, said: "His reverence the
Curé would be delighted, enchanted, if Mme Octave is not
resting just now, and could see him. His reverence don't
wish to disturb Mme Octave. His reverence is downstairs;
I told him to go into the parlour."

Had the truth been known, the Curé's visits gave my aunt
no such ecstatic pleasure as Françoise supposed, and the air of
jubilation with which she felt bound to illuminate her face
whenever she had to announce his arrival did not altogether
correspond to the sentiments of her invalid. The Curé (an
excellent man, with whom I now regret not having conversed
more often, for, even if he cared nothing for the arts, he knew
a great many etymologies), being in the habit of showing
distinguished visitors over his church (he had even planned
to compile a history of the Parish of Combray), used to weary
her with his endless commentaries which, incidentally, never
varied in the least degree. But when his visit synchronised
exactly with Eulalie's it became frankly distasteful to my aunt.
She would have preferred to make the most of Eulalie, and
not to have the whole of her circle about her at one time. But
she dared not send the Curé away, and had to content herself
with making a sign to Eulalie not to leave when he did, so
that she might have her to herself for a little after he had gone.

"What is this I have been hearing, Father, about a painter
setting up his easel in your church, and copying one of the
windows? Old as I am, I can safely say that I have never heard
of such a thing in all my life! What is the world coming to!
And the ugliest thing in the whole church, too."

"I will not go so far as to say that it's quite the ugliest, for
although there are certain things in Saint-Hilaire which are
well worth a visit, there are others that are very old now in
my poor basilica, the only one in all the diocese that has never
even been restored. God knows our porch is dirty and antiquated, but still it has a certain majesty. I'll even grant you
the Esther tapestries, which personally I wouldn't give a brass
farthing for, but which the experts place immediately after

the ones at Sens. I can quite see, too, that apart from certain
details which are—well, a trifle realistic, they show features
which testify to a genuine power of observation. But don't
talk to me about the windows. Is it common sense, I ask you,
to leave up windows which shut out all the daylight and even
confuse the eyes by throwing patches of colour, to which I
should be hard put to it to give a name, on to a floor in which
there are not two slabs on the same level and which they
refuse to renew for me because, if you please, those are the
tombstones of the Abbots of Combray and the Lords of
Guermantes, the old Counts, you know, of Brabant, direct
ancestors of the present Duc de Guermantes and of the
Duchess too since she was a Mademoiselle de Guermantes
who married her cousin?" (My grandmother, whose steadfast
refusal to take any interest in "persons" had ended in her
confusing all their names and titles, whenever anyone mentioned the Duchesse de Guermantes used to make out that
she must be related to Mme de Villeparisis. The whole family
would then burst out laughing; and she would attempt to
justify herself by harking back to some invitation to a christen-
ing or funeral: "I feel sure that there was a Guermantes in it
somewhere." And for once I would side with the others
against her, refusing to believe that there could be any connection between her school-friend and the descendant of
Geneviève de Brabant.)

"Look at Roussainville," the Curé went on. "It's nothing
more nowadays than a parish of tenant farmers, though in
olden times the place must have had a considerable importance
from its trade in felt hats and clocks. (I'm not certain, by the
way, of the etymology of Roussainville. I'm rather inclined
to think that the name was originally Rouville, from *Radulfi
villa*, analogous, don't you see, to Châteauroux, *Castrum
Radulfi*, but we'll talk about that some other time.) Anyway,
the church there has superb windows, almost all modern,
including that most imposing 'Entry of Louis-Philippe into
Combray' which would be more in keeping, surely, at Combray
itself and which is every bit as good, I understand, as the
famous windows at Chartres. Only yesterday I met Dr
Percepied's brother, who goes in for these things, and he told

me that he regarded it as a very fine piece of work. But, as I said to this artist, who, by the way, seems to be a most civil fellow, and is a regular virtuoso, it appears, with the brush, what on earth do you find so extraordinary in this window, which is if anything a little dingier than the rest?"

"I am sure that if you were to ask the Bishop," said my aunt in a resigned tone, for she had begun to feel that she was going to be "tired," "he would never refuse you a new window."

"You may depend upon it, Mme Octave," replied the Curé. "Why, it was his Lordship himself who started the outcry about the window, by proving that it represented Gilbert the Bad, a Lord of Guermantes and a direct descendant of Geneviève de Brabant who was a daughter of the House of Guermantes, receiving absolution from Saint Hilaire."

"But I don't see where Saint Hilaire comes in."

"Why yes, have you never noticed, in the corner of the window, a lady in a yellow robe? Well, that's Saint Hilaire, who is also known, you will remember, in certain parts of the country as Saint Illiers, Saint Hélier, and even, in the Jura, Saint Ylie. But these various corruptions of *Sanctus Hilarius* are by no means the most curious that have occurred in the names of the blessed. Take, for example, my good Eulalie, the case of your own patron, *Sancta Eulalia*; do you know what she has become in Burgundy? Saint Eloi, nothing more nor less! The lady has become a gentleman. Do you hear that, Eulalie—after you're dead they'll make a man of you!"

"His Reverence will always have his little joke."

"Gilbert's brother, Charles the Stammerer, was a pious prince, but, having early in life lost his father, Pepin the Mad, who died as a result of his mental infirmity, he wielded the supreme power with all the arrogance of a man who has not been subjected to discipline in his youth, so much so that, whenever he saw a man in a town whose face he didn't like, he would massacre the entire population. Gilbert, wishing to be avenged on Charles, caused the church at Combray to be burned down, the original church, that was, which Théodebert, when he and his court left the country residence he had near here, at Thiberzy (which is, of course, *Theodeberciacus*), to go

and fight the Burgundians, had promised to build over the
tomb of Saint Hilaire if the saint brought him victory. Nothing
remains of it now but the crypt, into which Théodore has
probably taken you, for Gilbert burned all the rest. Finally, he
defeated the unlucky Charles with the aid of William the
Conqueror," (the Curé pronounced it "Will'am"), "which is
why so many English still come to visit the place. But he
does not appear to have managed to win the affection of the
people of Combray, for they fell upon him as he was coming
out from mass, and cut off his head. Théodore has a little book
he lends people that tells the whole story.

"But what is unquestionably the most remarkable thing
about our church is the view from the belfry, which is full of
grandeur. Certainly in your case, since you are not very strong,
I should never recommend you to climb our ninety-seven
steps, just half the number they have in the famous cathedral
at Milan. It's quite tiring enough for the most active person,
especially as you have to bend double if you don't wish to
crack your skull, and you collect all the cobwebs off the staircase on your clothes. In any case you should be well wrapped
up," he went on, without noticing my aunt's indignation at
the mere suggestion that she could ever be capable of climbing
into his belfry, "for there's a strong breeze there once you
get to the top. Some people even assure me that they have
felt the chill of death up there. However, on Sundays there are
always clubs and societies who come, often from a long way off,
to admire our beautiful panorama, and they always go home
charmed. For instance, next Sunday, if the weather holds,
you'll be sure to find a lot of people there, for Rogation-tide.
No doubt about it, the view from up there is entrancing,
with what you might call vistas over the plain, which have
quite a special charm of their own. On a clear day you can see
as far as Verneuil. And then another thing; you can see at
the same time places which you normally see one without the
other, as, for instance, the course of the Vivonne and the
irrigation ditches at Saint-Assise-lès-Combray, which are separated by a screen of tall trees, or again, the various canals at
Jouy-le-Vicomte, which is *Gaudiacus vice comitis*, as of course
you know. Each time I've been to Jouy I've seen a bit of canal

in one place, and then I've turned a corner and seen another, but when I saw the second I could no longer see the first. I tried to put them together in my mind's eye; it was no good. But from the top of Saint-Hilaire it's quite another matter— a regular network in which the place is enclosed. Only you can't see any water; it's as though there were great clefts slicing up the town so neatly that it looks like a loaf of bread which still holds together after it has been cut up. To get it all quite perfect you would have to be in both places at once; up at the top of the steeple of Saint-Hilaire and down there at Jouy-le-Vicomte."

The Curé had so exhausted my aunt that no sooner had he gone than she was obliged to send Eulalie away.

"Here, my poor Eulalie," she said in a feeble voice, drawing a coin from a small purse which lay ready to her hand. "This is just something so that you won't forget me in your prayers."

"Oh, but, Mme Octave, I don't think I ought to; you know very well that I don't come here for that!" So Eulalie would answer, with the same hesitation and the same embarrassment, every Sunday as though it were the first, and with a look of vexation which delighted my aunt and never offended her, for if it happened that Eulalie, when she took the money, looked a little less peevish than usual, my aunt would remark afterwards, "I cannot think what has come over Eulalie; I gave her the same as I always give, and she did not look at all pleased."

"I don't think she has very much to complain of, all the same," Françoise would sigh grimly, for she had a tendency to regard as petty cash all that my aunt might give her for herself or her children, and as treasure riotously squandered on an ungrateful wretch the little coins slipped Sunday after Sunday into Eulalie's hand, but so discreetly that Françoise never managed to see them. It was not that she wanted for herself the money my aunt bestowed on Eulalie. She already enjoyed a sufficiency of all that my aunt possessed, in the knowledge that the wealth of the mistress automatically elevates and enhances the maid in the eyes of the world, and that she herself was renowned and glorified throughout Combray, Jouy-le-Vicomte, and other places, on account of

my aunt's many farms, her frequent and prolonged visits
from the Curé, and the astonishing number of bottles of Vichy
water which she consumed. Françoise was avaricious only
for my aunt; had she had control over my aunt's fortune (which
would have more than satisfied her highest ambition) she
would have guarded it from the assaults of strangers with a
maternal ferocity. She would, however, have seen no great
harm in what my aunt, whom she knew to be incurably
generous, allowed herself to give away, had she given only to
those who were already rich. Perhaps she felt that such persons,
not being actually in need of my aunt's presents, could not be
suspected of simulating affection for her on that account.
Besides, presents offered to persons of great wealth and position, such as Mme Sazerat, M. Swann, M. Legrandin and
Mme Goupil, to persons of the "same rank" as my aunt,
and who would naturally "mix with her," seemed to Françoise
to be included among the ornamental customs of that strange
and brilliant life led by rich people, who hunt and shoot and
give balls and pay each other visits, a life which she would
contemplate with an admiring smile. But it was by no means
the same thing if the beneficiaries of my aunt's generosity
were of the class whom Françoise would label "folk like me"
or "folk no better than me" and who were those she most
despised, unless they called her "Madame Françoise" and
considered themselves her inferiors. And when she saw that,
despite all her warnings, my aunt continued to do exactly as
she pleased, and to fling money away with both hands (or so
at least Françoise believed) on undeserving creatures, she
began to find that the presents she herself received from my
aunt were very small compared to the imaginary riches
squandered upon Eulalie. There was not, in the neighbourhood
of Combray, a farm of such prosperity and importance that
Françoise doubted Eulalie's ability to buy it, without thinking
twice, out of the capital which her visits to my aunt "brought
in." (It must be said that Eulalie had formed an exactly
similar estimate of the vast and secret hoards of Françoise.)
Every Sunday, after Eulalie had left, Françoise would utter
malevolent prophecies about her. She hated Eulalie, but was
at the same time afraid of her, and so felt bound, when

she was there, to show her a friendly face. She would make
up for it, however, after the other's departure; never, it is
true, alluding to her by name, but hinting at her in Sibylline
oracles or in maxims of a comprehensive character, like those
of Ecclesiastes, so worded that their special application could
not escape my aunt. After peering round the edge of the curtain
to see whether Eulalie had shut the front-door behind her,
"Flatterers know how to make themselves agreeable and to
feather their nests, but patience, one fine day the good Lord
will be avenged upon them!" she would declaim, with the
sidelong, insinuating glance of Joas thinking exclusively of
Athalia when he says that the

> prosperity
> Of wicked men runs like a torrent past,
> And soon is spent.

But when the Curé had come as well, and by his interminable
visit had drained my aunt's strength, Françoise would follow
Eulalie from the room, saying: "Mme Octave, I will leave you
to rest; you look really tired out."

And my aunt would answer her not a word, breathing a sigh
so faint that it seemed it must prove her last, and lying there
with closed eyes, as though already dead. But hardly had
Françoise arrived downstairs when four peals of a bell pulled
with the utmost violence reverberated through the house, and
my aunt, sitting bolt upright in her bed, would call out: "Has
Eulalie gone yet? Would you believe it; I forgot to ask her
whether Mme Goupil arrived in church before the Elevation.
Run after her, quick!"

But Françoise would return alone, having failed to overtake
Eulalie.

"It is most provoking," my aunt would say, shaking her
head. "The one important thing that I had to ask her."

In this way life went by for my aunt Léonie, always the same,
in the gentle uniformity of what she called, with a pretence of
deprecation but with a deep tenderness, her "little jog-trot."
Respected by all and sundry, not merely in her own house,
where every one of us, having learned the futility of recommending a healthier mode of life, had become gradually

resigned to its observance, but in the village as well, where, three streets away, a tradesman who had to hammer nails into a packing-case would send first to Françoise to make sure that my aunt was not "resting", this "jog-trot" was none the less brutally disturbed on one occasion that year. Like a fruit hidden among its leaves, which has grown and ripened unobserved and falls of its own accord, there came upon us one night the kitchen-maid's confinement. Her pains were unbearable, and, as there was no midwife in Combray, Françoise had to set off before dawn to fetch one from Thiberzy. My aunt was unable to rest owing to the cries of the girl, and as Françoise, though the distance was not great, was very late in returning, her services were greatly missed. And so, in the course of the morning, my mother said to me: "Run upstairs and see if your aunt wants anything."

I went into the first of her two rooms, and through the open door of the other saw my aunt lying on her side asleep; I could hear her snoring gently. I was about to slip away when the noise of my entry must have broken into her sleep and made it "change gear," as they say of motor-cars, for the music of her snore stopped for a second and began again on a lower note; then she awoke and half turned her face, which I could see for the first time; a kind of horror was imprinted on it; plainly she had just escaped from some terrifying dream. She could not see me from the position in which she was lying, and I stood there not knowing whether I ought to go forward or withdraw; but all at once she seemed to return to a sense of reality, and to grasp the falsehood of the visions that had terrified her; a smile of joy, of pious thanksgiving to God who is pleased to grant that life shall be less cruel than our dreams, feebly illumined her face, and, with the habit she had formed of speaking to herself half-aloud when she thought herself alone, she murmured: "God be praised! we have nothing to worry us here but the kitchen-maid's baby. And I've been dreaming that my poor Octave had come back to life and was trying to make me take a walk every day!" She stretched out a hand towards her rosary, which was lying on the small table, but sleep was once again overcoming her, and did not leave her the strength to reach it; she fell asleep,

her mind at rest, and I crept out of the room on tiptoe without
either her or anyone else ever knowing what I had seen and
heard.

When I say that, apart from such rare happenings as this
confinement, my aunt's daily routine never underwent any
variation, I do not include those which, repeated at regular
intervals and in identical form, did no more than print a sort
of uniform pattern upon the greater uniformity of her life.
Thus, for instance, every Saturday, as Françoise had to go in
the afternoon to market at Roussainville-le-Pin, the whole
household would have to have lunch an hour earlier. And my
aunt had so thoroughly acquired the habit of this weekly
exception to her general habits, that she clung to it as much as
to the rest. She was so well "routined" to it, as Françoise
would say, that if, on a Saturday, she had had to wait for her
lunch until the regular hour, it would have "upset" her as
much as if on an ordinary day she had had to put her lunch
forward to its Saturday hour. Incidentally this acceleration of
lunch gave Saturday, for all of us, an individual character,
kindly and rather attractive. At the moment when ordinarily
there is still an hour to be lived through before the meal-time
relaxation, we knew that in a few seconds we should see the
arrival of premature endives, a gratuitous omelette, an unmerited beefsteak. The recurrence of this asymmetrical Saturday was one of those minor events, intra-mural, localised,
almost civic, which, in uneventful lives and stable orders of
society, create a kind of national tie and become the favourite
theme for conversation, for pleasantries, for anecdotes which
can be embroidered as the narrator pleases; it would have
provided the ready-made kernel for a legendary cycle, had any
of us had an epic turn of mind. Early in the morning, before we
were dressed, without rhyme or reason, save for the pleasure
of proving the strength of our solidarity, we would call to one
another good-humouredly, cordially, patriotically, "Hurry up,
there's no time to waste; don't forget it's Saturday!" while
my aunt, conferring with Françoise and reflecting that the day
would be even longer than usual, would say, "You might
cook them a nice bit of veal, seeing that it's Saturday." If,
at half-past ten, someone absent-mindedly pulled out a watch

and said, "I say, an hour-and-a-half still before lunch,"
everyone else would be delighted to be able to retort at once:
"Why, what are you thinking about? Have you forgotten
that it's Saturday?" And a quarter of an hour later we would
still be laughing about it and reminding ourselves to go up
and tell aunt Léonie of this absurd mistake, to amuse her.
The very face of the sky appeared to undergo a change. After
lunch the sun, conscious that it was Saturday, would blaze
an hour longer in the zenith, and when someone, thinking
that we were late in starting for our walk, said, "What, only
two o'clock!" on registering the passage of the twin strokes
from the steeple of Saint-Hilaire (which as a rule met no one
at that hour upon the highways, deserted for the midday
meal or for the nap which follows it, or on the banks of the
bright and ever-flowing stream, which even the angler had
abandoned, and passed unaccompanied across the vacant sky,
where only a few loitering clouds remained to greet them)
the whole family would respond in chorus: "Why, you're
forgetting we had lunch an hour earlier; you know very well
it's Saturday."

The surprise of a "barbarian" (for so we termed everyone
who was not acquainted with Saturday's special customs) who
had called at eleven o'clock to speak to my father and had
found us at table, was an event which caused Françoise as
much merriment as anything that had ever happened in her
life. But if she found it amusing that the nonplussed visitor
should not have known beforehand that we had our lunch
an hour earlier on Saturdays, it was still more irresistibly
funny that my father himself (wholeheartedly as she sympa-
thised with the rigid chauvinism which prompted him)
should never have dreamed that the barbarian could fail to
be aware of the fact, and so had replied, with no further
enlightenment of the other's surprise at seeing us already in
the dining-room: "After all, it's Saturday!" On reaching this
point in the story, Françoise would pause to wipe the tears of
merriment from her eyes, and then, to add to her own enjoyment, would prolong the dialogue, inventing a further reply
for the visitor to whom the word "Saturday" had conveyed
nothing. And so far from our objecting to these interpolations,

we would feel that the story was not yet long enough, and would rally her with: "Oh, but surely he said something else. There was more to it than that, the first time you told it." My great-aunt herself would lay aside her needlework, and raise her head and look on at us over her glasses.

The day had yet another characteristic feature, namely, that during May we used to go out on Saturday evenings after dinner to the "Month of Mary" devotions.

As we were liable, there, to meet M. Vinteuil, who held very strict views on "the deplorable slovenliness of young people, which seems to be encouraged these days," my mother would first see that there was nothing out of order in my appearance, and then we would set out for the church. It was in the "Month of Mary" that I remember having first fallen in love with hawthorns. Not only were they in the church, where, holy ground as it was, we had all of us a right of entry, but arranged upon the altar itself, inseparable from the mysteries in whose celebration they participated, thrusting in among the tapers and the sacred vessels their serried branches, tied to one another horizontally in a stiff, festal scheme of decoration still further embellished by the festoons of leaves, over which were scattered in profusion, as over a bridal train, little clusters of buds of a dazzling whiteness. Though I dared not look at it save through my fingers, I could sense that this formal scheme was composed of living things, and that it was Nature herself who, by trimming the shape of the foliage, and by adding the crowning ornament of those snowy buds, had made the decorations worthy of what was at once a public rejoicing and a solemn mystery. Higher up on the altar, a flower had opened here and there with a careless grace, holding so unconcernedly, like a final, almost vaporous adornment, its bunch of stamens, slender as gossamer and entirely veiling each corolla, that in following, in trying to mimic to myself the action of their efflorescence, I imagined it as a swift and thoughtless movement of the head, with a provocative glance from her contracted pupils, by a young girl in white, insouciant and vivacious.

M. Vinteuil had come in with his daughter and had sat down beside us. He belonged to a good family, and had once been piano-teacher to my grandmother's sisters; so that when, after losing his wife and inheriting some property, he had retired to the neighbourhood of Combray, we used often to invite him to our house. But with his intense prudishness he had given up coming so as not to be obliged to meet Swann, who had made what he called "a most unsuitable marriage, as seems to be the fashion these days." My mother, on hearing that he composed, told him out of the kindness of her heart that, when she came to see him, he must play her something of his own. M. Vinteuil would have liked nothing better, but he carried politeness and consideration for others to such scrupulous lengths, always putting himself in their place, that he was afraid of boring them, or of appearing egotistical, if he carried out or even allowed them to suspect what were his own desires. On the day when my parents had gone to pay him a visit, I had accompanied them, but they had allowed me to remain outside, and as M. Vinteuil's house, Montjouvain, stood at the foot of a bushy hillock where I went to hide, I had found myself on a level with his drawing-room, upstairs, and only a few feet away from its window. When the servant came in to tell him that my parents had arrived, I had seen M. Vinteuil hurriedly place a sheet of music in a prominent position on the piano. But as soon as they entered the room he had snatched it away and put it in a corner. He was afraid, no doubt, of letting them suppose that he was glad to see them only because it gave him a chance of playing them some of his compositions. And every time that my mother, in the course of her visit, had returned to the subject he had hurriedly protested: "I can't think who put that on the piano; it's not the proper place for it at all," and had turned the conversation aside to other topics, precisely because they were of less interest to himself.

His one and only passion was for his daughter, and she, with her somewhat boyish appearance, looked so robust that it was hard to restrain a smile when one saw the precautions her father used to take for her health, with spare shawls always in readiness to wrap round her shoulders. My grandmother had drawn our attention to the gentle, delicate, almost timid expression which might often be caught flitting across the freckled face of this otherwise stolid child. Whenever she spoke, she heard her own words with the ears of those to whom she had addressed them, and became alarmed at the possibility of a misunderstanding, and one would see in clear outline, as though in a transparency, beneath the mannish face of the "good sort" that she was, the finer features of a tearful girl.

When, before turning to leave the church, I genuflected before the altar, I was suddenly aware of a bitter-sweet scent of almonds emanating from the hawthorn-blossom, and I then noticed on the flowers themselves little patches of a creamier colour, beneath which I imagined that this scent must lie concealed, as the taste of an almond cake lay beneath the burned parts, or of Mlle Vinteuil's cheeks beneath their freckles. Despite the motionless silence of the hawthorns, this inter-mittent odour came to me like the murmuring of an intense organic life with which the whole altar was quivering like a hedgerow explored by living antennae, of which I was re-minded by seeing some stamens, almost red in colour, which seemed to have kept the springtime virulence, the irritant power of stinging insects now transmuted into flowers.

On leaving the church we would stay chatting for a moment with M. Vinteuil in front of the porch. Boys would be chasing one another in the Square, and he would intervene, taking the side of the little ones and lecturing the big. If his daughter said in her gruff voice how glad she had been to see us, im-mediately it would seem as though a more sensitive sister within her had blushed at this thoughtless, schoolboyish utterance which might have made us think that she was angling for an invitation to the house. Her father would then arrange a cloak over her shoulders, they would clamber into a little dog-cart which she herself drove, and home they would both go to Montjouvain. As for ourselves, the next day being Sunday, with no need to be up and stirring before high mass, if it was a moonlight night and warm, my father, in his thirst for glory, instead of taking us home at once would lead us on a long walk round by the Calvary, which my mother's utter incapacity for taking her bearings, or even for knowing which road she might be on, made her regard as a triumph of his strategic genius. Sometimes we would go as far as the viaduct, whose long stone strides began at the railway station and to me typified all the wretchedness of exile beyond the last outposts of civilisation, because every year, as we came down from Paris, we were warned to take special care when we got to Combray not to miss the station, to be ready before the train stopped, since it would start again in two minutes and proceed across the viaduct out of the lands of Christendom, of which Combray, to me, represented the farthest limit. We would return by the Boulevard de la Gare, which contained the most attractive villas in the town. In each of their gardens the moonlight, copying the art of Hubert Robert, scattered its broken staircases of white marble, its fountains, its iron gates temptingly ajar. Its beams had swept away the telegraph office. All that was left of it was a column, half shattered but preserving the beauty of a ruin which endures for all time. I would by now be dragging my weary limbs and ready to drop with sleep; the balmy scent of the lime-trees seemed a reward that could be won only at the price of great fatigue and was not worth the effort. From gates far apart the watchdogs, awakened by our steps in the silence, would set up an antiphonal barking such as I still hear at times of an evening, and among which the Boulevard de la Gare (when the public gardens of Combray were constructed on its site) must have taken refuge, for wherever I may be, as soon as they begin their alternate challenge and response, I can see it again with its lime-trees, and its pavement glistening beneath the moon.

Suddenly my father would bring us to a standstill and ask my mother—"Where are we?" Exhausted by the walk but still proud of her husband, she would lovingly confess that she had not the least idea. He would shrug his shoulders and laugh. And then, as though he had produced it with his latchkey from his waistcoat pocket, he would point out to us, where it stood before our eyes, the back-gate of our own garden, which had come, hand-in-hand with the familiar corner of the Rue du Saint-Esprit, to greet us at the end of our wanderings over paths unknown. My mother would murmur admiringly "You really are wonderful!" And from that instant I did not have to take another step; the ground moved forward under my feet in that garden where for so long my actions had ceased to require any control, or even attention, from my will. Habit had come to take me in her arms and carry me all the way up to my bed like a little child.

Although Saturday, by beginning an hour earlier and by depriving her of the services of Françoise, passed more slowly than other days for my aunt, yet the moment it was past and a new week begun, she would look forward with impatience to its return, as something that embodied all the novelty and distraction which her frail and disordered body was still able to endure. This was not to say, however, that she did not long, at times, for some greater change, that she did not experience some of those exceptional moments when one thirsts for something other than what is, and when those who, through lack of energy or imagination, are unable to generate any motive power in themselves, cry out, as the clock strikes or the postman knocks, for something new, even if it is worse, some emotion, some sorrow; when the heartstrings, which contentment has silenced, like a harp laid by, yearn to be plucked and sounded again by some hand, however rough, even if it should break them; when the will, which has with such difficulty won the right to indulge without let or hindrance in its own desires and woes, would gladly fling the reins into the hands of imperious circumstance, however cruel. Of course, since my aunt's strength, which was completely drained by the slightest exertion, returned but drop by drop into the depths of her repose, the reservoir was very slow in filling, and months would go by before she reached that slight overflow which other people siphon off into activity of various kinds and which she was incapable of knowing or deciding how to use. And I have no doubt that then—just as a desire to have her potatoes served with béchamel sauce for a change would be formed, ultimately, from the pleasure she found in the daily reappearance of those mashed potatoes of which she never "tired"—she would extract from the accumulation of those monotonous days which she treasured so much a keen expectation of some domestic cataclysm, momentary in its duration but violent enough to compel her to put into effect, once for all, one of those changes which she knew would be

beneficial to her health but to which she could never make up
her mind without some such stimulus. She was genuinely
fond of us; she would have enjoyed the long luxury of weeping
for our untimely decease; coming at a moment when she felt
"well" and was not in a perspiration, the news that the house
was being destroyed by a fire in which all the rest of us had
already perished and which soon would leave not a single
stone standing upon another, but from which she herself would
still have plenty of time to escape without undue haste,
provided that she rose at once from her bed, must often have
haunted her dreams, as a prospect which combined with the
two minor advantages of letting her taste the full savour of
her affection for us in long years of mourning, and of causing
universal stupefaction in the village when she should sally
forth to conduct our obsequies, crushed but courageous,
moribund but erect, the paramount and priceless boon of
forcing her at the right moment, with no time to be lost, no
room for weakening hesitations, to go off and spend the summer at her charming farm of Mirougrain, where there was a
waterfall. Inasmuch as no such event had ever occurred,
though she must often have pondered its eventuality as she
lay alone absorbed in her interminable games of patience (and
though it would have plunged her in despair from the first
moment of its realisation, from the first of those little unforeseen contingencies, the first word of calamitous news,
whose accents can never afterwards be expunged from the
memory, everything that bears upon it the imprint of actual,
physical death, so terribly different from the logical abstraction
of its possibility) she would fall back from time to time, to
add an interest to her life, upon imaginary calamities which
she would follow up with passion. She would beguile herself
with a sudden pretence that Françoise had been robbing her,
that she had set a trap to make certain, and had caught her
betrayer red-handed; and being in the habit, when she made
up a game of cards by herself, of playing her own and her
adversary's hands at once, she would first stammer out
Françoise's awkward excuses, and then reply to them with
such a fiery indignation that any of us who happened to intrude
upon her at one of these moments would find her bathed in

perspiration, her eyes blazing, her false hair askew and exposing the baldness of her brows. Françoise must often, from the next room, have heard these mordant sarcasms levelled at herself, the mere framing of which in words would not have relieved my aunt's feelings sufficiently, had they been allowed to remain in a purely immaterial form, without the degree of substance and reality which she added to them by muttering them half-aloud. Sometimes, however, even these counterpane dramas would not satisfy my aunt; she must see her work staged. And so, on a Sunday, with all the doors mysteriously closed, she would confide to Eulalie her doubts of Françoise's integrity and her determination to be rid of her, and another time she would confide to Françoise her suspicions of the disloyalty of Eulalie, to whom the front-door would very soon be closed for good. A few days later she would be sick of her latest confidante and once more "as thick as thieves" with the traitor, but before the next performance, the two would yet again have changed roles. But the suspicions which Eulalie might occasionally arouse in her were no more than a flash in the pan that soon subsided for lack of fuel, since Eulalie was not living with her in the house. It was a very different matter in the case of Françoise, of whose presence under the same roof as herself my aunt was perpetually conscious, though for fear of catching cold were she to leave her bed, she would never dare go down to the kitchen to establish whether there were any grounds for her suspicions. Gradually her mind came to be exclusively occupied with trying to guess what Françoise might at any given moment be doing behind her back. She would detect a furtive look on Françoise's face, something contradictory in what she said, some desire which she appeared to be concealing. And she would show her that she was unmasked, with a single word, which made Françoise turn pale and which my aunt seemed to find a cruel satisfaction in driving deep into her unhappy servant's heart. And the very next Sunday a disclosure by Eulalie—like one of those discoveries that suddenly open up an unsuspected field of exploration for some new science that has got into something of a rut—proved to my aunt that her own worst suspicions fell a long way short of the appalling truth. "But Françoise ought to know that," said Eulalie, "now that you've given her a carriage."

"Now that I've given her a carriage!" gasped my aunt.

"Oh, I know nothing about it, I just thought, well, I saw her go by yesterday in a barouche, as proud as Lucifer, on her way to Roussainville market. I supposed that it must be Mme Octave who had given it to her."

And so by degrees Françoise and my aunt, the quarry and the hunter, had reached the point of constantly trying to forestall each other's ruses. My mother was afraid lest Françoise should develop a genuine hatred of my aunt, who did everything in her power to hurt her. However that might be, Françoise had come, more and more, to pay an infinitely scrupulous attention to my aunt's least word and gesture. When she had to ask her anything she would hesitate for a long time over how best to go about it. And when she had uttered her request, she would watch my aunt covertly, trying to guess from the expression on her face what she thought of it and how she would reply. And so it was that— whereas an artist who, reading the memoirs of the seventeenth century, and, wishing to bring himself nearer to the great Louis, considers that he is making progress in that direction by constructing a pedigree that traces his own descent from some historic family, or by engaging in correspondence with one of the reigning sovereigns of Europe, is actually turning his back on what he mistakenly seeks under identical and therefore moribund forms—an elderly provincial lady, by doing no more than yield wholeheartedly to her own ir- resistible eccentricities and a cruelty born of idleness, could see, without ever having given a thought to Louis XIV, the most trivial occupations of her daily life, her morning toilet, her lunch, her afternoon nap, assume, by virtue of their despotic singularity, something of the interest that was to be found in what Saint-Simon called the "mechanics" of life at Versailles; and was able, too, to persuade herself that her silences, a suggestion of good humour or of haughtiness on her features, would provide Françoise with matter for a mental commentary as tense with passion and terror as did the silence, the good humour or the haughtiness of the King when a courtier, or even his greatest nobles, had presented a petition to him in an avenue at Versailles.

One Sunday, when my aunt had received simultaneous visits from the Curé and from Eulalie, and had been left alone, afterwards, to rest, the whole family went upstairs to bid her good evening, and Mamma ventured to condole with her on the unlucky coincidence that always brought both visitors to her door at the same time.

"I hear that things worked out badly again to-day, Léonie," she said kindly, "you had all your friends here at once."

And my great-aunt interrupted with: "The more the merrier," for, since her daughter's illness, she felt herself in duty bound to cheer her up by always drawing her attention to the brighter side of things. But my father had begun to speak.

"I should like to take advantage," he said, "of the whole family's being here together to tell you a story, so as not to have to begin all over again to each of you separately. I'm afraid we are in M. Legrandin's bad books: he would hardly say 'How d'ye do' to me this morning."

I did not wait to hear the end of my father's story, for I had been with him myself after mass when we had met M. Legrandin; instead, I went downstairs to the kitchen to ask about the menu for our dinner, which was of fresh interest to me daily, like the news in a paper, and excited me as might the programme of a coming festivity.

As M. Legrandin had passed close by us on our way from church, walking by the side of a lady, the owner of a country house in the neighbourhood, whom we knew only by sight, my father had saluted him in a manner at once friendly and reserved, without stopping in his walk; M. Legrandin had barely acknowledged the courtesy, and then with an air of surprise, as though he had not recognised us, and with that distant look characteristic of people who do not wish to be agreeable and who, from the suddenly receding depths of their eyes, seem to have caught sight of you at the far end of an interminably straight road and at so great a distance that they content themselves with directing towards you an almost imperceptible movement of the head, commensurate with your doll-like dimensions.

Now, the lady who was walking with Legrandin was a
virtuous and highly respected person; there could be no
question of his being out for amorous adventure and embarrassed at being detected, and my father wondered how he
could possibly have displeased our friend.

"I should be all the more sorry to feel that he was vexed
with us," he said, "because among all those people in their
Sunday best there is something about him, with his little cut-
away coat and his soft neckties, so little 'dressed-up,' so
genuinely simple; an air of innocence, almost, which is really
attractive."

But the vote of the family council was unanimous, that my
father had imagined the whole thing, or that Legrandin, at
the moment in question, had been preoccupied in thinking
about something else. In any case my father's fears were
dispelled no later than the following evening. Returning
from a long walk, we saw Legrandin near the Pont-Vieux
(he was spending a few days more in Combray because of the
holidays). He came up to us with outstretched hand: "Do you
know, master booklover," he asked me, "this line of Paul
Desjardins?

Now are the woods all black, but still the sky is blue.

Isn't that a fine rendering of a moment like this? Perhaps
you have never read Paul Desjardins. Read him, my boy,
read him; in these days he is converted, they tell me, into a
preaching friar, but he used to have the most charming water-
colour touch—

Now are the woods all black, but still the sky is blue.

May you always see a blue sky overhead, my young friend;
and then, even when the time comes, as it has come for me
now, when the woods are all black, when night is fast falling,
you will be able to console yourself, as I do, by looking up at
the sky." He took a cigarette from his pocket and stood for a
long time with his eyes fixed on the horizon. "Good-bye,
friends!" he suddenly exclaimed, and left us.

At the hour when I usually went downstairs to find out
what there was for dinner, its preparation would already have

begun, and Françoise, a colonel with all the forces of nature
for her subalterns, as in the fairy-tales where giants hire
themselves out as scullions, would be stirring the coals,
putting the potatoes to steam, and, at the right moment,
finishing over the fire those culinary masterpieces which had
been first got ready in some of the great array of vessels,
triumphs of the potter's craft, which ranged from tubs and
boilers and cauldrons and fish kettles down to jars for game,
moulds for pastry, and tiny pannikins for cream, through an
entire collection of pots and pans of every shape and size.
I would stop by the table, where the kitchen-maid had shelled
them, to inspect the platoons of peas, drawn up in ranks and
numbered, like little green marbles, ready for a game; but
what most enraptured me were the asparagus, tinged with
ultramarine and pink which shaded off from their heads,
finely stippled in mauve and azure, through a series of imperceptible gradations to their white feet—still stained a little
by the soil of their garden-bed—with an iridescence that was
not of this world. I felt that these celestial hues indicated the
presence of exquisite creatures who had been pleased to assume
vegetable form and who, through the disguise of their firm,
comestible flesh, allowed me to discern in this radiance of
earliest dawn, these hinted rainbows, these blue evening
shades, that precious quality which I should recognise again
when, all night long after a dinner at which I had partaken of
them, they played (lyrical and coarse in their jesting as the
fairies in Shakespeare's *Dream*) at transforming my chamber
pot into a vase of aromatic perfume.

Poor Giotto's Charity, as Swann had named her, charged
by Françoise with the task of preparing them for the table,
would have them lying beside her in a basket, while she sat
there with a mournful air as though all the sorrows of the
world were heaped upon her; and the light crowns of azure
which capped the asparagus shoots above their pink jackets
were delicately outlined, star by star, as, in Giotto's fresco,
are the flowers encircling the brow or patterning the basket
of his Virtue at Padua. And meanwhile Françoise would be
turning on the spit one of those chickens such as she alone
knew how to roast, chickens which had wafted far abroad

from Combray the savour of her merits, and which, while she was serving them to us at table, would make the quality of sweetness predominate for the moment in my private conception of her character, the aroma of that cooked flesh which she knew how to make so unctuous and so tender seeming to me no more than the proper perfume of one of her many virtues.

But the day on which I went down to the kitchen while my father consulted the family council about our strange meeting with Legrandin was one of those days when Giotto's Charity, still very weak and ill after her recent confinement, had been unable to rise from her bed; Françoise, being without assistance, had fallen behind. When I went in, I saw her in the scullery which opened on to the back yard, in the process of killing a chicken which, by its desperate and quite natural resistance, accompanied by Françoise, beside herself with rage as she attempted to slit its throat beneath the ear, with shrill cries of "Filthy creature! Filthy creature!," made the saintly meekness and unction of our servant rather less prominent than it would do, next day at dinner, when it made its appearance in a skin gold-embroidered like a chasuble, and its precious juice was poured out drop by drop as from a pyx. When it was dead, Françoise collected its streaming blood, which did not, however, drown her rancour, for she gave vent to another burst of rage, and gazing down at the carcass of her enemy, uttered a final "Filthy creature!"

I crept out of the kitchen and upstairs, trembling all over; I could have prayed, then, for the instant dismissal of Françoise. But who would have baked me such hot rolls, made me such fragrant coffee, and even . . . roasted me such chickens? And, as it happened, everyone else had already had to make the same cowardly reckoning. For my aunt Léonie knew (though I was still in ignorance of this) that Françoise, who, for her own daughter or for her nephews, would have given her life without a murmur, showed a singular implacability in her dealings with the rest of the world. In spite of which my aunt had kept her, for, while conscious of her cruelty, she appreciated her services. I began gradually to realise that Françoise's kindness, her compunction, her numerous virtues, concealed many of these kitchen tragedies, just as history reveals to us that the reigns of the kings and queens who are portrayed as kneeling with their hands joined in prayer in the windows of churches were stained by oppression and bloodshed. I came to recognise that, apart from her own kinsfolk, the sufferings of humanity inspired in her a pity which increased in direct ratio to the distance separating the sufferers from herself. The tears that flowed from her in torrents when she read in a newspaper of the misfortunes of persons unknown to her were quickly stemmed once she had been able to form a more precise mental picture of the victims. One night, shortly after her confinement, the kitchen-maid was seized with the most appalling pains; Mamma heard her groans, and rose and awakened Françoise, who, quite unmoved, declared that all the outcry was mere malingering, that the girl wanted to "play the mistress." The doctor, who had been afraid of some such attack, had left a marker in a medical dictionary which we had, at the page on which the symptoms were described, and had told us to turn up this passage to discover the measures of "first aid" to be adopted. My mother sent Françoise to fetch the book, warning her not to let the marker drop out. An hour elapsed, and Françoise had not returned; my mother, supposing that she had gone back to bed, grew vexed, and told me to go myself to the library and fetch the volume. I did so, and there found Françoise who, in her curiosity to know what the marker indicated, had begun to read the clinical account of these after-pains, and was violently sobbing, now that it was a question of a prototype patient with whom she was unacquainted. At each painful symptom mentioned by the writer she would exclaim: "Oh, oh, Holy Virgin, is it possible that God wishes a wretched human creature to suffer so? Oh, the poor girl!"

But when I had called her, and she had returned to the bedside of Giotto's Charity, her tears at once ceased to flow; she could find no stimulus for that pleasant sensation of tenderness and pity with which she was familiar, having been moved to it often enough by the perusal of newspapers, nor any other pleasure of the same kind, in her boredom and

irritation at being dragged out of bed in the middle of the
night for the kitchen-maid; so that at the sight of those very
sufferings the printed account of which had moved her to
tears, she relapsed into ill-tempered mutterings, mingled with
bitter sarcasm, saying, when she thought that we were out
of earshot: "Well, she should have been careful not to do
what got her into this! She enjoyed it well enough, I dare say,
so she'd better not put on any airs now! All the same, he must
have been a godforsaken young fellow to go with the likes
of *her*. Dear, dear, it's just as they used to say in my poor
mother's day:

> Frogs and snails and puppy-dogs' tails,
>   And dirty sluts in plenty,
> Smell sweeter than roses in young men's noses
>   When the heart is one-and-twenty."

Although, when her grandson had a slight cold in his head,
she would set off at night, even if she were unwell, instead of
going to bed, to see whether he had everything he needed,
covering ten miles on foot before daybreak so as to be back
in time for work, this same love for her own people, and her
desire to establish the future greatness of her house on a solid
foundation, found expression, in her policy with regard to
the other servants, in one unvarying maxim, which was never
to let any of them set foot in my aunt's room; indeed she
showed a sort of pride in not allowing anyone else to come
near my aunt, preferring, when she herself was ill, to get out
of bed and to administer the Vichy water in person, rather
than to concede to the kitchen-maid the right of entry into
her mistress's presence. There is a species of hymenoptera
observed by Fabre, the burrowing wasp, which in order to
provide a supply of fresh meat for her offspring after her own
decease, calls in the science of anatomy to amplify the resources of her instinctive cruelty, and, having made a collection of weevils and spiders, proceeds with marvellous knowledge and skill to pierce the nerve-centre on which their
power of locomotion (but none of their other vital functions)
depends, so that the paralysed insect, beside which she lays
her eggs, will furnish the larvae, when hatched, with a docile,

inoffensive quarry, incapable either of flight or of resistance, but perfectly fresh for the larder: in the same way Françoise had adopted, to minister to her unfaltering resolution to render the house uninhabitable to any other servant, a series of stratagems so cunning and so pitiless that, many years later, we discovered that if we had been fed on asparagus day after day throughout that summer, it was because their smell gave the poor kitchen-maid who had to prepare them such violent attacks of asthma that she was finally obliged to leave my aunt's service.

Alas! we had definitely to alter our opinion of M. Legrandin. On one of the Sundays following our meeting with him on the Pont-Vieux, after which my father had been forced to confess himself mistaken, as mass drew to an end and, with the sun-shine and the noise of the outer world, something else invaded the church, an atmosphere so far from sacred that Mme Goupil, Mme Percepied (everyone, in fact, who not so long before, when I arrived a little late, had been sitting motionless, engrossed in their prayers, and who I might even have thought oblivious of my entry had not their feet moved slightly to push away the little kneeling-bench which was preventing me from getting to my chair) had begun to discuss with us out loud all manner of utterly mundane topics as though we were already outside in the Square, we saw Legrandin on the sun-baked threshold of the porch dominating the many-coloured tumult of the market, being introduced by the husband of the lady we had seen him with on the previous occasion to the wife of another large landed proprietor of the district. Legrandin's face wore an expression of extraordinary zeal and animation; he made a deep bow, with a subsidiary backward movement which brought his shoulders sharply up into a position behind their starting-point, a gesture in which he must have been trained by the husband of his sister, Mme de Cambremer. This rapid straightening-up caused a sort of tense muscular wave to ripple over Legrandin's rump, which I had not supposed to be so fleshy; I cannot say why, but this undulation of pure matter, this wholly carnal fluency devoid of spiritual significance, this wave lashed into a tempest by

an obsequious alacrity of the basest sort, awoke my mind
suddenly to the possibility of a Legrandin altogether different
from the one we knew. The lady gave him some message for
her coachman, and as he walked over to her carriage the
impression of shy and respectful happiness which the introduction had stamped upon his face still lingered there. Rapt
in a sort of dream, he smiled, then began to hurry back towards
the lady; as he was walking faster than usual, his shoulders
swayed backwards and forwards, right and left, in the most
absurd fashion; and altogether he looked, so utterly had he
abandoned himself to it, to the exclusion of all other considerations, as though he were the passive, wire-pulled
puppet of his own happiness. Meanwhile we were coming out
through the porch and were about to pass close beside him;
he was too well bred to turn his head away, but he fixed his
eyes, which had suddenly changed to those of a seer lost in
the profundity of his vision, on so distant a point of the
horizon that he could not see us and so had no need to acknowledge our presence. His face was as artless as ever above
his plain, single-breasted jacket, which looked as though
conscious of having been led astray and plunged willy-nilly
into surroundings of detested splendour. And a spotted bow-
tie, stirred by the breezes of the Square, continued to float in
front of Legrandin like the standard of his proud isolation
and his noble independence. When we reached the house my
mother discovered that the baker had forgotten to deliver the
cream tart and asked my father to go back with me and tell
them to send it up at once. Near the church we met Legrandin
coming towards us with the same lady, whom he was escorting
to her carriage. He brushed past us, and did not interrupt what
he was saying to her, but gave us, out of the corner of his
blue eye, a little sign which began and ended, so to speak,
inside his eyelids and which, as it did not involve the least
movement of his facial muscles, managed to pass quite unperceived by the lady; but, striving to compensate by the
intensity of his feelings for the somewhat restricted field in
which they had to find expression, he made that blue chink
which was set apart for us sparkle with all the zest of an
affability that went far beyond mere playfulness, almost

touched the border-line of roguery; he subtilised the refinements of good-fellowship into a wink of connivance, a hint, a hidden meaning, a secret understanding, all the mysteries of complicity, and finally elevated his assurances of friendship to the level of protestations of affection, even of a declaration of love, lighting up for us alone, with a secret and languid flame invisible to the chatelaine, an enamoured pupil in a countenance of ice.

Only the day before he had asked my parents to send me to dine with him on this same Sunday evening. "Come and bear your aged friend company," he had said to me. "Like the nosegay which a traveller sends us from some land to which we shall never return, come and let me breathe from the far country of your adolescence the scent of those spring flowers among which I also used to wander many years ago. Come with the primrose, the love-vine, the buttercup; come with the stone-crop, whereof are posies made, pledges of love, in the Balzacian flora, come with that flower of the Resurrection morning, the Easter daisy, come with the snowballs of the guelder-rose, which begin to perfume the alleys of your great-aunt's garden ere the last snows of Lent are melted from its soil. Come with the glorious silken raiment of the lily, apparel fit for Solomon, and with the polychrome hues of the pansies, but come, above all, with the spring breeze, still cooled by the last frosts of winter, wafting apart, for the two butterflies that have waited outside all morning, the closed portals of the first Jerusalem rose."

The question was raised at home whether, all things considered, I ought still to be sent to dine with M. Legrandin. But my grandmother refused to believe that he could have been impolite.

"You admit yourself that he appears there at church quite simply dressed and all that; he hardly looks like a man of fashion." She added that in any event, even if, assuming the worst, he had been intentionally rude, it was far better for us to pretend that we had noticed nothing. And indeed my father himself, though more annoyed than any of us by the attitude which Legrandin had adopted, may still have held in reserve a final uncertainty as to its true meaning. It was like

every attitude or action which reveals a man's underlying
character; they bear no relation to what he has previously
said, and we cannot confirm our suspicions by the culprit's
own testimony, for he will admit nothing; we are reduced to
the evidence of our own senses, and we ask ourselves, in the
face of this detached and incoherent fragment of recollection,
whether indeed our senses have not been the victims of a
hallucination; with the result that such attitudes, which are
alone of importance in indicating character, are the most apt
to leave us in perplexity.

I dined with Legrandin on the terrace of his house, by
moonlight. "There is a charming quality, is there not," he
said to me, "in this silence; for hearts that are wounded, as
mine is, a novelist whom you will read in time to come asserts
that there is no remedy but silence and shadow. And see you
this, my boy, there comes in all our lives a time, towards which
you still have far to go, when the weary eyes can endure but
one kind of light, the light which a fine evening like this
prepares for us in the stillroom of darkness, when the ears can
listen to no music save what the moonlight breathes through
the flute of silence."

I listened to M. Legrandin's words which always seemed to
me so pleasing; but I was preoccupied by the memory of a
lady whom I had seen recently for the first time and thinking,
now that I knew that Legrandin was on friendly terms with
several of the local aristocracy, that perhaps she also was
among his acquaintance, I summoned up all my courage and
said to him: "Tell me, sir, do you by any chance know the
lady . . . the ladies of Guermantes?"—glad, too, in pronouncing this name, to secure a sort of power over it, by the mere
act of drawing it up out of my day-dreams and giving it an
objective existence in the world of spoken things.

But, at the sound of the name Guermantes, I saw in the
middle of each of our friend's blue eyes a little brown dimple
appear, as though they had been stabbed by some invisible
pin-point, while the rest of the pupil reacted by secreting the
azure overflow. His fringed eyelids darkened and drooped.
His mouth, set in a bitter grimace, was the first to recover,
and smiled, while his eyes remained full of pain, like the

eyes of a handsome martyr whose body bristles with arrows.

"No, I don't know them," he said, but instead of vouchsafing so simple a piece of information, so very unremarkable a reply, in the natural conversational tone which would have been appropriate to it, he enunciated it with special emphasis on each word, leaning forward, nodding his head, with at once the vehemence which a man imparts, in order to be believed, to a highly improbable statement (as though the fact that he did not know the Guermantes could be due only to some strange accident of fortune) and the grandiloquence of a man who, finding himself unable to keep silence about what is to him a painful situation, chooses to proclaim it openly in order to convince his hearers that the confession he is making is one that causes him no embarrassment, is in fact easy, agreeable, spontaneous, that the situation itself—in this case the absence of relations with the Guermantes family—might very well have been not forced upon, but actually willed by him, might arise from some family tradition, some moral principle or mystical vow which expressly forbade his seeking their society.

"No," he went on, explaining by his words the tone in which they were uttered, "no, I don't know them, I've never wanted to; I've always made a point of preserving complete independence; at heart, you know, I'm a bit of a Jacobin. People are always coming to me about it, telling me I'm mistaken in not going to Guermantes, that I make myself seem ill-bred, uncivilised, an old bear. But that's not the sort of reputation that can frighten me; it's too true! In my heart of hearts I care for nothing in the world now but a few churches, two or three books and pictures, and the light of the moon when the fresh breeze of your youth wafts to my nostrils the scent of gardens whose flowers my old eyes can no longer distinguish."

I did not understand very clearly why, in order to refrain from going to the houses of people whom one did not know, it should be necessary to cling to one's independence, or how this could give one the appearance of a savage or a bear. But what I did understand was that Legrandin was not altogether truthful when he said that he cared only for churches, moonlight, and youth; he cared also, he cared a very great deal, for

people who lived in country houses, and in their presence was
so overcome by fear of incurring their displeasure that he
dared not let them see that he numbered among his friends
middle-class people, the sons of solicitors and stockbrokers,
preferring, if the truth must come to light, that it should do
so in his absence, a long way away, and "by default." In a
word, he was a snob. No doubt he would never have said any
of this in the poetical language which my family and I so
much enjoyed. And if I asked him, "Do you know the
Guermantes family?" Legrandin the talker would reply, "No,
I've never wished to know them." But unfortunately the
talker was now subordinated to another Legrandin, whom he
kept carefully hidden in his breast, whom he would never
consciously exhibit, because this other could tell compromising
stories about our own Legrandin and his snobbishness; and
this other Legrandin had replied to me already in that wounded
look, that twisted smile, the undue gravity of the tone of his
reply, in the thousand arrows by which our own Legrandin
had instantaneously been stabbed and prostrated like a St
Sebastian of snobbery: "Oh, how you hurt me! No, I don't
know the Guermantes family. Do not remind me of the great
sorrow of my life." And since this other, irrepressible, black-
mailing Legrandin, if he lacked our Legrandin's charming
vocabulary, showed an infinitely greater promptness in expressing himself, by means of what are called "reflexes,"
when Legrandin the talker attempted to silence him, he had
already spoken, and however much our friend deplored the
bad impression which the revelations of his *alter ego* must have
caused, he could do no more than endeavour to mitigate them.

This is not to say that M. Legrandin was anything but
sincere when he inveighed against snobs. He could not (from
his own knowledge, at least) be aware that he himself was one,
since it is only with the passions of others that we are ever
really familiar, and what we come to discover about our own
can only be learned from them. Upon ourselves they react only
indirectly, through our imagination, which substitutes for our
primary motives other, auxiliary motives, less stark and therefore more seemly. Never had Legrandin's snobbishness
prompted him to make a habit of visiting a duchess as such.

Instead, it would encourage his imagination to make that
duchess appear, in his eyes, endowed with all the graces. He
would gain acquaintance with the duchess, assuring himself
that he was yielding to the attractions of mind and heart
which the vile race of snobs could never understand. Only
his fellow-snobs knew that he was of their number, for, owing
to their inability to appreciate the intervening efforts of his
imagination, they saw in close juxtaposition the social activity
of Legrandin and its primary cause.

At home, meanwhile, we no longer had any illusions about
M. Legrandin, and our relations with him had become much
more distant. Mamma was greatly delighted whenever she
caught him red-handed in the sin which he never admitted to,
which he continued to call the unpardonable sin, snobbery.
As for my father, he found it difficult to take Legrandin's airs
in so light-hearted and detached a spirit; and when there was
talk, one year, of sending me to spend the summer holidays at
Balbec with my grandmother, he said: "I simply must tell
Legrandin that you're going to Balbec, to see whether he'll
offer to introduce you to his sister. He probably doesn't
remember telling us that she lived within a mile of the place."

My grandmother, who held that when one went to the
seaside one ought to be on the beach from morning to night
sniffing the salt breezes, and that one should not know anyone
there because visits and excursions are so much time filched
from the sea air, begged him on no account to speak to
Legrandin of our plans; for already, in her mind's eye, she
could see his sister, Mme de Cambremer, alighting from her
carriage at the door of our hotel just as we were on the point
of going out fishing, and obliging us to remain indoors to
entertain her. But Mamma laughed at her fears, thinking to
herself that the danger was not so threatening, and that
Legrandin would show no undue anxiety to put us in touch
with his sister. As it happened, there was no need for any of
us to introduce the subject of Balbec, for it was Legrandin
himself who, without the least suspicion that we had ever
had any intention of visiting those parts, walked into the trap
uninvited one evening when we met him strolling on the banks
of the Vivonne.

"There are tints in the clouds this evening, violets and blues, which are very beautiful, are they not, my friend?" he said to my father, "a blue, especially, more floral than aerial, a cineraria blue, which it is surprising to see in the sky. And that little pink cloud there, has it not also the tint of some flower, a carnation or hydrangea? Nowhere, perhaps, except on the shores of the Channel, where Normandy merges into Brittany, have I observed such copious examples of that sort of vegetable kingdom of the atmosphere. Down there, in that unspoiled country near Balbec, there is a charmingly quiet little bay where the sunsets of the Auge Valley, those red-and-gold sunsets (which, by the by, I am very far from despising) seem commonplace and insignificant; but in that moist and gentle atmosphere these celestial bouquets, pink and blue, will blossom all at once of an evening, incomparably lovely, and often lasting for hours before they fade. Others shed their flowers at once, and then it is lovelier still to see the sky strewn with their innumerable petals, sulphur or rose-pink. In that bay, which they call the Bay of Opal, the golden sands appear more charming still from being fastened, like fair Andromeda, to those terrible rocks of the surrounding coast, to that funereal shore, famed for the number of its wrecks, where every winter many a brave vessel falls victim to the perils of the sea. Balbec! the most ancient bone in the geological skeleton that underlies our soil, the true Ar-mor, the sea, the land's end, the accursed region which Anatole France—an enchanter whose works our young friend ought to read—has so well depicted, beneath its eternal fogs, as though it were indeed the land of the Cimmerians in the Odyssey. Balbec; yes, they are building hotels there now, superimposing them upon its ancient and charming soil which they are powerless to alter; how delightful it is to be able to make excursions into such primitive and beautiful regions only a step or two away!"

"Indeed! And do you know anyone at Balbec?" inquired my father. "As it happens, this young man is going to spend a couple of months there with his grandmother, and my wife too, perhaps."

Legrandin, taken unawares by the question at a moment

when he was looking directly at my father, was unable to avert his eyes, and so fastened them with steadily increasing intensity—smiling mournfully the while—upon the eyes of his questioner, with an air of friendliness and frankness and of not being afraid to look him in the face, until he seemed to have penetrated my father's skull as if it had become transparent, and to be seeing at that moment, far beyond and behind it, a brightly coloured cloud which provided him with a mental alibi and would enable him to establish that at the moment when he was asked whether he knew anyone at Balbec, he had been thinking of something else and so had not heard the question. As a rule such tactics make the questioner proceed to ask, "Why, what are you thinking about?" But my father, inquisitive, irritated and cruel, repeated: "Have you friends, then, in the neighbourhood, since you know Balbec so well?"

In a final and desperate effort, Legrandin's smiling gaze struggled to the extreme limits of tenderness, vagueness, candour and abstraction; but, feeling no doubt that there was nothing left for it now but to answer, he said to us: "I have friends wherever there are clusters of trees, stricken but not defeated, which have come together with touching perseverance to offer a common supplication to an inclement sky which has no mercy upon them."

"That is not quite what I meant," interrupted my father, as obstinate as the trees and as merciless as the sky. "I asked you, in case anything should happen to my mother-in-law and she wanted to feel that she was not all alone there in an out-of-the-way place, whether you knew anyone in the neighbourhood."

"There as elsewhere, I know everyone and I know no one," replied Legrandin, who did not give in so easily. "The places I know well, the people very slightly. But the places themselves seem like people, rare and wonderful people, of a delicate quality easily disillusioned by life. Perhaps it is a castle which you encounter upon the cliff's edge standing there by the path where it has halted to contemplate its sorrows beneath an evening sky, still roseate, in which the golden moon is climbing while the homeward-bound fishing-boats, cleaving the dappled waters, hoist its pennant at their mastheads and carry its colours. Or perhaps it is a simple dwelling-house that stands alone, plain and shy-looking but full of romance, hiding from every eye some imperishable secret of happiness and disenchantment. That land which knows not truth," he continued with Machiavellian subtlety, "that land of pure fiction makes bad reading for any boy, and is certainly not what I should choose or recommend for my young friend here, who is already so much inclined to melancholy—for a heart already predisposed to receive its impressions. Climates that breathe amorous secrets and futile regrets may suit a disillusioned old man like myself, but they must always prove fatal to a temperament that is still unformed. Believe me," he went on with emphasis, "the waters of that bay—more Breton than Norman—may exert a sedative influence, though even that is of questionable value, upon a heart which, like mine, is no longer intact, a heart for whose wounds there is no longer anything to compensate. But at your age, my boy, those waters are contra-indicated. ... Good night to you, neighbours," he added, moving away from us with that evasive abruptness to which we were accustomed; and then, turning towards us with a physicianly finger raised in warning, he resumed the consultation: "No Balbec before fifty!" he called out to us, "and even then it must depend on the state of the heart."

My father raised the subject again at our subsequent meetings, torturing him with questions, but it was labour in vain: like that scholarly swindler who devoted to the fabrication of forged palimpsests a wealth of skill and knowledge and industry the hundredth part of which would have sufficed to establish him in a more lucrative but honourable occupation, M. Legrandin, had we insisted further, would in the end have constructed a whole system of landscape ethics and a celestial geography of Lower Normandy sooner than admit to us that his own sister was living within a mile or two of Balbec, sooner than find himself obliged to offer us a letter of introduction, the prospect of which would never have inspired him with such terror had he been absolutely certain—as, from his knowledge of my grandmother's character, he really ought to have been—that we would never have dreamed of making use of it.

                 *   *   *

We used always to return from our walks in good time to pay aunt Léonie a visit before dinner. At the beginning of the season, when the days ended early, we would still be able to see, as we turned into the Rue du Saint-Esprit, a reflection of the setting sun in the windows of the house and a band of crimson beyond the timbers of the Calvary, which was mirrored further on in the pond; a fiery glow that, accompanied often by a sharp tang in the air, would associate itself in my mind with the glow of the fire over which, at that very moment, was roasting the chicken that was to furnish me, in place of the poetic pleasure of the walk, with the sensual pleasures of good feeding, warmth and rest. But in summer, when we came back to the house, the sun would not have set; and while we were upstairs paying our visit to aunt Léonie its rays, sinking until they lay along her window-sill, would be caught and held by the large inner curtains and the loops which tied them back to the wall, and then, split and ramified and filtered, encrusting with tiny flakes of gold the citron-wood of the chest-of-drawers, would illuminate the room with a delicate, slanting, woodland glow. But on some days, though very rarely, the chest-of-drawers would long since have shed its momentary incrustations, there would no longer, as we turned into the Rue du Saint-Esprit, be any reflection from the western sky lighting up the window-panes, and the pond beneath the Calvary would have lost its fiery glow, sometimes indeed had changed already to an opalescent pallor, while a long ribbon of moonlight, gradually broadening and splintered by every ripple upon the water's surface, would stretch across it from end to end. Then, as we drew near the house, we would see a figure standing upon the doorstep, and Mamma would say to me: "Good heavens! There's Françoise looking out for us; your aunt must be anxious; that means we're late."

And without wasting time by stopping to take off our things we would dash upstairs to my aunt Léonie's room to reassure her, to prove to her by our bodily presence that all her gloomy imaginings were false, that nothing had happened to us, but that we had gone the "Guermantes way," and when one took that walk, why, my aunt knew well enough that one could never be sure what time one would be home.

"There, Françoise," my aunt would say, "didn't I tell you that they must have gone the Guermantes way? Good gracious, they must be hungry! And your nice leg of mutton will be quite dried up now after all the hours it's been waiting. What a time to come in! Well, and so you went the Guermantes way?"

"But, Léonie, I supposed you knew," Mamma would answer. "I thought Françoise had seen us go out by the little gate through the kitchen-garden."

For there were, in the environs of Combray, two "ways" which we used to take for our walks, and they were so diametrically opposed that we would actually leave the house by a different door according to the way we had chosen: the way towards Méséglise-la-Vineuse, which we called also "Swann's way" because to get there one had to pass along the boundary of M. Swann's estate, and the "Guermantes way." Of Méséglise-la-Vineuse, to tell the truth, I never knew anything more than the "way," and some strangers who used to come over on Sundays to take the air in Combray, people whom, this time, neither my aunt herself nor any of us "knew from Adam," and whom we therefore assumed to be "people who must have come over from Méséglise." As for Guermantes, I was to know it well enough one day, but that day had still to come; and, during the whole of my boyhood, if Méséglise was to me something as inaccessible as the horizon, which remained hidden from sight, however far one went, by the folds of a landscape which no longer bore the least resemblance to the country round Combray, Guermantes, on the other hand, meant no more than the ultimate goal, ideal rather than real, of the "Guermantes way," a sort of abstract geographical term like the North Pole or the Equator or the Orient. And so to "take the Guermantes way" in order to get to Méséglise, or *vice versa*, would have seemed to me as nonsensical a proceeding as to turn to the east in order to reach the west. Since my father used always to speak of the "Méséglise way" as comprising the finest view of a plain that he knew anywhere, and of the "Guermantes way" as typical of river scenery, I had invested each of them, by conceiving them in this way as two distinct entities, with that cohesion, that unity which belong only to the figments of the mind; the smallest detail of either of them seemed to me a precious thing exemplifying the special excellence of the whole, while beside them, before one had reached the sacred soil of one or the other, the purely material paths amid which they were set down as the ideal view over a plain and the ideal river landscape, were no more worth the trouble of looking at than, to a keen play-goer and lover of dramatic art, are the little streets that run past the walls of a theatre. But above all I set between them, far more than the mere distance in miles that separated one from the other, the distance that there was between the two parts of my brain in which I used to think of them, one of those distances of the mind which not only keep things apart, but cut them off from one another and put them on different planes. And this distinction was rendered still more absolute because the habit we had of never going both ways on the same day, or in the course of the same walk, but the "Méséglise way" one time and the "Guermantes way" another, shut them off, so to speak, far apart from one another and unaware of each other's existence, in the airtight compartments of separate afternoons.

When we had decided to go the "Méséglise way" we would start (without undue haste, and even if the sky were clouded over, since the walk was not very long and did not take us too far from home), as though we were not going anywhere in particular, from the front-door of my aunt's house, which opened on to the Rue du Saint-Esprit. We would be greeted by the gunsmith, we would drop our letters into the box, we would tell Théodore, from Françoise, as we passed that she had run out of oil or coffee, and we would leave the town by the road which ran along the white fence of M. Swann's park. Before reaching it we would be met on our way by the scent of his lilac-trees, come out to welcome strangers. From amid the fresh little green hearts of their foliage they raised inquisitively over the fence of the park

their plumes of white or mauve blossom, which glowed, even
in the shade, with the sunlight in which they had bathed.
Some of them, half-concealed by the little tiled house known
as the Archers' Lodge in which Swann's keeper lived, overtopped its gothic gable with their pink minaret. The nymphs
of spring would have seemed coarse and vulgar in comparison
with these young houris, who retained in this French garden
the pure and vivid colouring of a Persian miniature. Despite
my desire to throw my arms about their pliant forms and to
draw down towards me the starry locks that crowned their
fragrant heads, we would pass them by without stopping,
for my parents had ceased to visit Tansonville since Swann's
marriage, and, so as not to appear to be looking into his park,
instead of taking the path which skirted his property and
then climbed straight up to the open fields, we took another
path which led in the same direction, but circuitously, and
brought us out beyond it.

One day my grandfather said to my father: "Don't you
remember Swann's telling us yesterday that his wife and
daughter had gone off to Rheims[6] and that he was taking the
opportunity of spending a day or two in Paris? We might go
along by the park, since the ladies are not at home; that will
make it a little shorter."

We stopped for a moment by the fence. Lilac-time was
nearly over; some of the trees still thrust aloft, in tall mauve
chandeliers, their delicate sprays of blossom, but in many
parts of the foliage which only a week before had been
drenched in their fragrant foam, there remained only a dry,
hollow, scentless froth, shrivelled and discoloured. My grandfather pointed out to my father in what respects the appearance
of the place was still the same, and how far it had altered since
the walk that he had taken with old M. Swann on the day of
his wife's death; and he seized the opportunity to tell us once
again the story of that walk.

In front of us a path bordered with nasturtiums ascended
in the full glare of the sun towards the house. But to our right
the park stretched across level ground. Overshadowed by the
tall trees which stood close around it, an ornamental pond
had been dug by Swann's parents; but, even in his most

artificial creations, nature is the material upon which man has to work; certain places persist in remaining surrounded by the vassals of their own especial sovereignty, and will flaunt their immemorial insignia in the middle of a park, just as they would have done far from any human interference, in a solitude which must everywhere return to engulf them, springing up out of the necessities of their exposed position and superimposed on the work of man's hands. And so it was that, at the foot of the path which led down to the artificial lake, there might be seen, in its two tiers woven of forget-me-nots and periwinkle flowers, a natural, delicate, blue garland encircling the water's luminous and shadowy brow, while the iris, flourishing its sword-blades in regal profusion, stretched out over agrimony and water-growing crowfoot the tattered fleurs-de-lis, violet and yellow, of its lacustrine sceptre.

The absence of Mlle Swann, which—since it preserved me from the terrible risk of seeing her appear on one of the paths, and of being identified and scorned by this privileged little girl who had Bergotte for a friend and used to go with him to visit cathedrals—made the exploration of Tansonville, now for the first time permissible, a matter of indifference to myself, seemed on the contrary to invest the property, in my grandfather's and my father's eyes, with an added attraction, a transient charm, and (like an entirely cloudless sky when one is going mountaineering) to make the day exceptionally propitious for a walk round it; I should have liked to see their reckoning proved false, to see, by a miracle, Mlle Swann appear with her father, so close to us that we should not have time to avoid her, and should therefore be obliged to make her acquaintance. And so, when I suddenly noticed a straw basket lying forgotten on the grass by the side of a fishing line whose float was bobbing in the water, I made every effort to keep my father and grandfather looking in another direction, away from this sign that she might, after all, be in residence. However, as Swann had told us that it was bad of him to go away just then as he had some people staying in the house, the line might equally belong to one of these guests. Not a footstep was to be heard on any of the paths. Quartering the

topmost branches of one of the tall trees, an invisible bird was
striving to make the day seem shorter, exploring with a long-
drawn note the solitude that pressed it on every side, but it
received at once so unanimous an answer, so powerful a
repercussion of silence and of immobility, that one felt it had
arrested for all eternity the moment which it had been trying
to make pass more quickly. The sunlight fell so implacably
from a motionless sky that one longed to escape its attentions,
and even the slumbering water, whose repose was perpetually disturbed by the insects that swarmed above its
surface, dreaming no doubt of some imaginary maelstrom,
intensified the uneasiness which the sight of that floating cork
had wrought in me by appearing to draw it at full speed across
the silent reaches of the reflected sky; now almost vertical,
it seemed on the point of plunging down out of sight, and I
had begun to wonder whether, setting aside the longing and
the terror that I had of making her acquaintance, it was not
actually my duty to warn Mlle Swann that the fish was biting—
when I was obliged to run after my father and grandfather who
were calling me, surprised that I had not followed them along
the little path leading up to the open fields into which they
had already turned. I found the whole path throbbing with
the fragrance of hawthorn-blossom. The hedge resembled a
series of chapels, whose walls were no longer visible under the
mountains of flowers that were heaped upon their altars; while
beneath them the sun cast a checkered light upon the ground,
as though it had just passed through a stained-glass window;
and their scent swept over me, as unctuous, as circumscribed
in its range, as though I had been standing before the Lady-
altar, and the flowers, themselves adorned also, held out each
its little bunch of glittering stamens with an absent-minded air,
delicate radiating veins in the flamboyant style like those
which, in the church, framed the stairway to the rood-loft or
the mullions of the windows and blossomed out into the
fleshy whiteness of strawberry-flowers. How simple and rustic
by comparison would seem the dog-roses which in a few
weeks' time would be climbing the same path in the heat of
the sun, dressed in the smooth silk of their blushing pink
bodices that dissolve in the first breath of wind.

But it was in vain that I lingered beside the hawthorns—breathing in their invisible and unchanging odour, trying to fix it in my mind (which did not know what to do with it), losing it, recapturing it, absorbing myself in the rhythm which disposed the flowers here and there with a youthful lightheartedness and at intervals as unexpected as certain intervals in music—they went on offering me the same charm in inexhaustible profusion, but without letting me delve any more deeply, like those melodies which one can play a hundred times in succession without coming any nearer to their secret. I turned away from them for a moment so as to be able to return to them afresh. My eyes travelled up the bank which rose steeply to the fields beyond the hedge, alighting on a stray poppy or a few laggard cornflowers which decorated the slope here and there like the border of a tapestry whereon may be glimpsed sporadically the rustic theme which will emerge triumphant in the panel itself; infrequent still, spaced out like the scattered houses which herald the approach of a village, they betokened to me the vast expanse of waving corn beneath the fleecy clouds, and the sight of a single poppy hoisting upon its slender rigging and holding against the breeze its scarlet ensign, over the buoy of rich black earth from which it sprang, made my heart beat like that of a traveller who glimpses on some low-lying ground a stranded boat which is being caulked and made sea-worthy, and cries out, although he has not yet caught sight of it, "The Sea!"

And then I returned to the hawthorns, and stood before them as one stands before those masterpieces which, one imagines, one will be better able to "take in" when one has looked away for a moment at something else; but in vain did I make a screen with my hands, the better to concentrate upon the flowers, the feeling they aroused in me remained obscure and vague, struggling and failing to free itself, to float across and become one with them. They themselves offered me no enlightenment, and I could not call upon any other flowers to satisfy this mysterious longing. And then, inspiring me with that rapture which we feel on seeing a work by our favourite painter quite different from those we already know, or, better still, when we are shown a painting of which we have hitherto seen no more than a pencilled sketch, or when a piece of music which we have heard only on the piano appears to us later clothed in all the colours of the orchestra, my grandfather called me to him, and, pointing to the Tansonville hedge, said to me: "You're fond of hawthorns; just look at this pink one—isn't it lovely?"

And it was indeed a hawthorn, but one whose blossom was pink, and lovelier even than the white. It, too, was in holiday attire—for one of those days which are the only true holidays, the holy days of religion, because they are not assigned by some arbitrary caprice, as secular holidays are, to days which are not specially ordained for them, which have nothing about them that is essentially festal—but it was attired even more richly than the rest, for the flowers which clung to its branches, one above another, so thickly as to leave no part of the tree undecorated, like the tassels wreathed about the crook of a rococo shepherdess, were every one of them "in colour," and consequently of a superior quality, by the aesthetic standards of Combray, if one was to judge by the scale of prices at the "stores" in the Square, or at Camus's, where the most expensive biscuits were those whose sugar was pink. For my own part, I set a higher value on cream cheese when it was pink, when I had been allowed to tinge it with crushed strawberries. And these flowers had chosen precisely one of those colours of some edible and delicious thing, or of some fond embellishment of a costume for a major feast, which, inasmuch as they make plain the reason for their superiority, are those whose beauty is most evident to the eyes of children, and for that reason must always seem more vivid and more natural than any other tints, even after the child's mind has realised that they offer no gratification to the appetite and have not been selected by the dressmaker. And indeed I had felt at once, as I had felt with the white blossom, but with even greater wonderment, that it was in no artificial manner, by no device of human fabrication, that the festal intention of these flowers was revealed, but that it was Nature herself who had spontaneously expressed it, with the simplicity of a woman from a village shop labouring at the decoration of a street altar for some procession, by overloading the bush with these little rosettes, almost too ravishing in colour, this rustic "pompadour." High up on the branches, like so many of those tiny rose-trees, their pots concealed in jackets of paper lace, whose slender shafts rose in a forest from the altar on major feast-days, a thousand buds were swelling and opening, paler in colour, but each disclosing as it burst, as at the bottom of a bowl of pink marble, its blood-red stain, and suggesting even more strongly than the full-blown flowers the special, irresistible quality of the thorn-bush which, wherever it budded, wherever it was about to blossom, could do so in ·pink alone. Embedded in the hedge, but as different from it as a young girl in festal attire among a crowd of dowdy women in everyday clothes who are staying at home, all ready for the "Month of Mary" of which it seemed already to form a part, it glowed there, smiling in its fresh pink garments, deliciously demure and Catholic.

The hedge afforded a glimpse, inside the park, of an alley bordered with jasmine, pansies, and verbenas, among which the stocks held open their fresh plump purses, of a pink as fragrant and as faded as old Spanish leather, while a long green hose, coiling across the gravel, sent up from its sprinkler a vertical and prismatic fan of multicoloured droplets. Suddenly I stood still, unable to move, as happens when we are faced with a vision that appeals not to our eyes only but requires a deeper kind of perception and takes possession of the whole of our being. A little girl with fair, reddish hair, who appeared to be returning from a walk, and held a spade in her hand, was looking at us, raising towards us a face powdered with pinkish freckles. Her black eyes gleamed, and since I did not at that time know, and indeed have never since learned, how to reduce a strong impression to its objective elements, since I had not, as they say, enough "power of observation" to isolate the notion of their colour, for a long time afterwards, whenever I thought of her, the memory of those bright eyes would at once present itself to me as a vivid azure, since her complexion was fair; so much so that, perhaps if her eyes had not been quite so black—which was what struck one most forcibly on first seeing her—I should not have been, as I was, so especially enamoured of their imagined blue.

I gazed at her, at first with that gaze which is not merely the messenger of the eyes, but at whose window all the senses assemble and lean out, petrified and anxious, a gaze eager to reach, touch, capture, bear off in triumph the body at which it is aimed, and the soul with the body; then (so frightened was I lest at any moment my grandfather and my father, catching sight of the girl, might tear me away from her by telling me to run on in front of them) with another, an unconsciously imploring look, whose object was to force her to pay attention to me, to see, to know me. She cast a glance forwards and sideways, so as to take stock of my grandfather and my father, and doubtless the impression she formed was that we were all ridiculous people, for she turned away with an indifferent and disdainful air, and stood sideways so as to spare her face the indignity of remaining within their field of vision; and while they, continuing to walk on without noticing her, overtook and passed me, she went on staring out of the corner of her eye in my direction, without any particular expression, without appearing to see me, but with a fixity and a half-hidden smile which I could only interpret, from the notions I had been vouchsafed of good breeding, as a mark of infinite contempt; and her hand, at the same time, sketched in the air an in-delicate gesture, for which, when it was addressed in public to a person whom one did not know, the little dictionary of manners which I carried in my mind supplied only one mean-ing, namely, a deliberate insult.

"Gilberte, come along; what are you doing?" called out in a piercing tone of authority a lady in white whom I had not seen until that moment, while, a little way beyond her, a gentleman in a suit of linen "ducks," whom I did not know either, stared at me with eyes which seemed to be starting from his head. The little girl's smile abruptly faded, and, seizing her spade, she made off without turning to look again in my direction, with an air of docility, inscrutable and sly.

Thus was wafted to my ears the name of Gilberte, bestowed on me like a talisman which might, perhaps, enable me some day to rediscover the girl that its syllables had just endowed with an identity, whereas the moment before she had been

merely an uncertain image. So it came to me, uttered across
the heads of the stocks and jasmines, pungent and cool as
the drops which fell from the green watering-pipe; impregnat-
ing and irradiating the zone of pure air through which it had
passed—and which it set apart and isolated—with the mystery
of the life of her whom its syllables designated to the happy
beings who lived and walked and travelled in her company;
unfolding beneath the arch of the pink hawthorn, at the
height of my shoulder, the quintessence of their familiarity—
so exquisitely painful to myself—with her and with the unknown world of her existence into which I should never
penetrate.

For a moment (as we moved away and my grandfather
murmured: "Poor Swann, what a life they are leading him—
sending him away so that she can be alone with her Charlus—
for it was he, I recognised him at once! And the child, too;
at her age, to be mixed up in all that!") the impression left
on me by the despotic tone in which Gilberte's mother had
spoken to her without her answering back, by exhibiting her
to me as being obliged to obey someone else, as not being
superior to the whole world, calmed my anguish somewhat,
revived some hope in me, and cooled the ardour of my love.
But very soon that love surged up again in me like a reaction
by which my humiliated heart sought to rise to Gilberte's level
or to bring her down to its own. I loved her; I was sorry not
to have had the time and the inspiration to insult her, to hurt
her, to force her to keep some memory of me. I thought her
so beautiful that I should have liked to be able to retrace my
steps so as to shake my fist at her and shout, "I think you're
hideous, grotesque; how I loathe you!" But I walked away,
carrying with me, then and for ever afterwards, as the first
illustration of a type of happiness rendered inaccessible to a
little boy of my kind by certain laws of nature which it was
impossible to transgress, the picture of a little girl with reddish
hair and a freckled skin, who held a spade in her hand and
smiled as she directed towards me a long, sly, expressionless
stare. And already the charm with which her name, like a
whiff of incense, had imbued that archway in the pink hawthorn through which she and I had together heard its sound,

was beginning to impregnate, to overlay, to perfume everything with which it had any association: her grandparents,
whom my own had had the unutterable good fortune to
know, the sublime profession of stockbroker, the melancholy
neighbourhood of the Champs-Elysées, where she lived in
Paris.

"Léonie," said my grandfather on our return, "I wish we
had had you with us this afternoon. You would never have
known Tansonville. If I had dared, I would have cut you a
branch of that pink hawthorn you used to like so much."
And so my grandfather told my aunt about our walk, either
to divert her, or because he had not yet given up hope of
persuading her to rise from her bed and to go out of doors.
For in earlier days she had been very fond of Tansonville,
and moreover Swann's visits had been the last that she had
continued to receive, at a time when she had already closed
her doors to all the world. And just as, when he now called to
inquire after her (she was the only person in our household
whom he still asked to see), she would send down to say that
she was tired at the moment and resting, but that she would be
happy to see him another time, so, this evening, she said to my
grandfather, "Yes, some day when the weather is fine I shall
go for a drive as far as the gate of the park." And in saying
this she was quite sincere. She would have liked to see Swann
and Tansonville again; but the mere wish to do so sufficed for
all that remained of her strength, which its fulfilment would
have more than exhausted. Sometimes a spell of fine weather
made her a little more energetic, and she would get up and
dress; but before she had reached the outer room she would
be tired again, and would insist on returning to her bed. The
process which had begun in her—and in her a little earlier
only than it must come to all of us—was the great renunciation
of old age as it prepared for death, wraps itself up in its
chrysalis, which may be observed at the end of lives that are
at all prolonged, even in old lovers who have lived for one
another, in old friends bound by the closest ties of mutual
sympathy, who, after a certain year, cease to make the necessary
journey or even to cross the street to see one another, cease to
correspond, and know that they will communicate no more in

this world. My aunt must have been perfectly well aware that she would never see Swann again, that she would never leave the house again, but this ultimate reclusion seemed to be made bearable to her by the very factor which, to our minds, ought to have made it more painful; namely, that this reclusion was forced upon her by the gradual diminution in her strength which she was able to measure daily and which, by making every action, every movement exhausting if not actually painful, gave to inaction, isolation and silence the blessed and restoring charm of repose.

My aunt did not go to see the pink hawthorn in the hedge, but at all hours of the day I would ask the rest of my family whether she was not going to do so, whether she used not, at one time, to go often to Tansonville, trying to make them speak of Mlle Swann's parents and grandparents, who appeared to me to be as great and glorious as gods. The name Swann had for me become almost mythological, and when I talked with my family I would grow sick with longing to hear them utter it; I dared not pronounce it myself, but I would draw them into the discussion of matters which led naturally to Gilberte and her family, in which she was involved, in speaking of which I would feel myself not too remotely exiled from her; and I would suddenly force my father (by pretending, for instance, to believe that my grandfather's appointment had been in our family before his day, or that the hedge with the pink hawthorn which my aunt Léonie wished to visit was on common land) to correct my assertions, to say, as though in opposition to me and of his own accord: "No, no, that appointment belonged to *Swann's* father, that hedge is part of *Swann's* park." And then I would be obliged to catch my breath, so suffocating was the pressure, upon that part of me where it was for ever inscribed, of that name which, at the moment when I heard it, seemed to me fuller, more portentous than any other, because it was heavy with the weight of all the occasions on which I had secretly uttered it in my mind. It caused me a pleasure which I was ashamed to have dared to demand from my parents, for so great was this pleasure that to have procured it for me must have caused them a good deal of effort, and with no recompense, since it was no pleasure for them. And so I would turn the conversation, out of tact, and out of scruple too. All the singular seductions with which I had invested the name Swann came back to me as soon as they uttered it. And then it seemed to me suddenly that my parents could not fail to experience the same emotions, that they must find themselves sharing my point of view, that they perceived in their turn, that they condoned, that they even embraced my visionary longings, and I was as wretched as though I had ravished and corrupted the innocence of their hearts.

That year my family fixed the day of our return to Paris rather earlier than usual. On the morning of our departure I had had my hair curled, to be ready to face the photographer, had had a new hat carefully set upon my head, and had been buttoned into a velvet jacket; a little later my mother, after searching everywhere for me, found me standing in tears on the steep little path near Tansonville, bidding farewell to my hawthorns, clasping their sharp branches in my arms and, like a princess in a tragedy oppressed by the weight of these vain ornaments, with no gratitude towards the importunate hand which, in curling all those ringlets, had been at pains to arrange my hair upon my forehead,[7] trampling underfoot the curl-papers which I had torn from my head, and my new hat with them. My mother was not at all moved by my tears, but she could not suppress a cry at the sight of my battered headgear and my ruined jacket. I did not, however, hear her. "Oh, my poor little hawthorns," I was assuring them through my sobs, "it isn't you who want to make me unhappy, to force me to leave you. *You*'ve never done me any harm. So I shall always love you." And, drying my eyes, I promised them that, when I grew up, I would never copy the foolish example of other men, but that even in Paris, on fine spring days, instead of paying calls and listening to silly talk, I would set off for the country to see the first hawthorn-trees in bloom.

Once in the fields, we never left them again during the rest of our Méséglise walk. They were perpetually traversed, as though by an invisible wanderer, by the wind which was to me the tutelary genius of Combray. Every year, on the day

of our arrival, in order to feel that I really was at Combray,
I would climb the hill to greet it as it swept through the
furrows and swept me along in its wake. One always had
the wind for companion when one went the "Méséglise way,"
on that gently undulating plain where for mile after mile it
met no rising ground. I knew that Mlle Swann used often to
go and spend a few days at Laon; for all that it was many miles
away, the distance was counterbalanced by the absence of any
intervening obstacle, and when, on hot afternoons, I saw a
breath of wind emerge from the farthest horizon, bowing the
heads of the corn in distant fields, pouring like a flood over all
that vast expanse, and finally come to rest, warm and rustling,
among the clover and sainfoin at my feet, that plain which was
common to us both seemed then to draw us together, to unite
us; I would imagine that the same breath of wind had passed
close to her, that it was some message from her that it was
whispering to me, without my being able to understand it,
and I would kiss it as it passed. On my left was a village called
Champieu (*Campus Pagani*, according to the Curé). On my
right I could see across the cornfields the two crocketed,
rustic spires of Saint-André-des-Champs, themselves as tapering, scaly, chequered, honeycombed, yellowing and friable as
two ears of wheat.

At regular intervals, amid the inimitable ornamentation of
their leaves, which can be mistaken for those of no other
fruit-tree, the apple-trees opened their broad petals of white
satin, or dangled the shy bunches of their blushing buds. It
was on the Méséglise way that I first noticed the circular
shadow which apple-trees cast upon the sunlit ground, and
also those impalpable threads of golden silk which the setting
sun weaves slantingly downwards from beneath their leaves,
and which I used to see my father slash through with his stick
without ever making them deviate.

Sometimes in the afternoon sky the moon would creep up,
white as a cloud, furtive, lustreless, suggesting an actress who
does not have to "come on" for a while, and watches the
rest of the company for a moment from the auditorium in
her ordinary clothes, keeping in the background, not wishing
to attract attention to herself. I enjoyed finding its image

reproduced in books and paintings, though these works of art
were very different—at least in my earlier years, before Bloch
had attuned my eyes and mind to more subtle harmonies—
from those in which the moon would seem fair to me to-day,
but in which I should not have recognised it then. It might,
for instance, be some novel by Saintine, some landscape by
Gleyre, in which it is silhouetted against the sky in the form
of a silver sickle, one of those works as naïvely unformed as
were my own impressions, and which it enraged my grandmother's sisters to see me admire. They held that one ought
to set before children, and that children showed their own
innate good taste in admiring, only such books and pictures
as they would continue to admire when their minds were
developed and mature. No doubt they regarded aesthetic
merits as material objects which an unclouded vision could
not fail to discern, without one's needing to nurture equivalents of them and let them slowly ripen in one's own heart.

It was along the Méséglise way, at Montjouvain, a house
built on the edge of a large pond against the side of a steep,
bushy hill, that M. Vinteuil lived. And so we used often to
meet his daughter driving her dogcart at full speed along the
road. After a certain year we never saw her alone, but always
accompanied by a friend, a girl older than herself with a bad
reputation in the neighbourhood, who one day installed herself permanently at Montjouvain. People said: "That poor
M. Vinteuil must be blinded by fatherly love not to see what
everyone is talking about—a man who is shocked by the
slightest loose word letting his daughter bring a woman like
that to live under his roof! He says that she is a most superior
woman, with a heart of gold, and that she would have shown
extraordinary musical talent if she had only been trained. He
may be sure it isn't music that she's teaching his daughter."
But M. Vinteuil assured them that it was, and indeed it is
remarkable how people never fail to arouse admiration for
their moral qualities in the relatives of those with whom they
are having carnal relations. Physical passion, so unjustly
decried, compels its victims to display every vestige that is
in them of kindness and self-abnegation, to such an extent
that they shine resplendent in the eyes of their immediate

entourage. Dr Percepied, whose hearty voice and bushy
eyebrows enabled him to play to his heart's content the role
of mischief-maker which his looks belied, without in the
least degree compromising his unassailable and quite unmerited reputation of being a kind-hearted old curmudgeon,
could make the Curé and everyone else laugh until they cried
by saying in a gruff voice: "What d'ye say to this, now? It
seems that she plays music with her friend, Mlle Vinteuil.
That surprises you, does it? I'm not so sure. It was Papa
Vinteuil who told me all about it yesterday. After all, she
has every right to be fond of music, that girl. I'm not one to
thwart the artistic vocation of a child; nor Vinteuil either, it
seems. And then he plays music too, with his daughter's
friend. Why, good lord, it must be a regular musical box, that
house! What are you laughing at? They play too much music,
those people, in my opinion. I met Papa Vinteuil the other
day, by the cemetery. It was all he could do to keep on his
feet."

Anyone who, like ourselves, had seen M. Vinteuil at that
time, avoiding people whom he knew, turning away as soon
as he caught sight of them, growing old within a few months,
brooding over his sorrows, becoming incapable of any effort
not directly aimed at promoting his daughter's happiness,
spending whole days beside his wife's grave, could hardly
have failed to realise that he was dying of a broken heart,
could hardly have supposed that he was unaware of the rumours
which were going about. He knew, perhaps he even believed,
what his neighbours were saying. There is probably no one,
however rigid his virtue, who is not liable to find himself,
by the complexity of circumstances, living at close quarters
with the very vice which he himself has been most outspoken
in condemning—without altogether recognising it beneath
the disguise of ambiguous behaviour which it assumes in his
presence: the strange remarks, the unaccountable attitude,
one evening, of a person whom he has a thousand reasons for
loving. But for a man of M. Vinteuil's sensibility it must have
been far more painful than for a hardened man of the world
to have to resign himself to one of those situations which are
wrongly supposed to be the monopoly of Bohemian circles;

for they occur whenever a vice which Nature herself has planted in the soul of a child—perhaps by no more than blending the virtues of its father and mother, as she might blend the colour of its eyes—needs to ensure for itself the room and the security necessary for its development. And yet however much M. Vinteuil may have known of his daughter's conduct it did not follow that his adoration of her grew any less. The facts of life do not penetrate to the sphere in which our beliefs are cherished; they did not engender those beliefs, and they are powerless to destroy them; they can inflict on them continual blows of contradiction and disproof without weakening them; and an avalanche of miseries and maladies succeeding one another without interruption in the bosom of a family will not make it lose faith in either the clemency of its God or the capacity of its physician. But when M. Vinteuil thought of his daughter and himself from the point of view of society, from the point of view of their reputation, when he attempted to place himself by her side in the rank which they occupied in the general estimation of their neighbours, then he was bound to give judgment, to utter his own and her social condemnation in precisely the same terms as the most hostile inhabitant of Combray; he saw himself and his daughter in the lowest depths, and his manners had of late been tinged with that humility, that respect for persons who ranked above him and to whom he now looked up (however far beneath him they might hitherto have been), that tendency to search for some means of rising again to their level, which is an almost mechanical result of any human downfall.

One day, when we were walking with Swann in one of the streets of Combray, M. Vinteuil, turning out of another street, found himself so suddenly face to face with us all that he had no time to escape; and Swann, with that condescending charity of a man of the world who, amid the dissolution of all his own moral prejudices, finds in another's shame merely a reason for treating him with a benevolence the expression of which serves to gratify all the more the self-esteem of the bestower because he feels that it is all the more precious to the recipient, conversed at great length with M. Vinteuil, with whom for a long time he had been barely on speaking terms, and invited him, before leaving us, to send his daughter over one day to play at Tansonville. It was an invitation which, two years earlier, would have incensed M. Vinteuil, but which now filled him with so much gratitude that he felt obliged to refrain from the indiscretion of accepting. Swann's friendly regard for his daughter seemed to him to be in itself so honourable, so precious a support that he felt it would perhaps be advisable not to make use of it, so as to have the wholly Platonic satisfaction of preserving it.

"What a charming man!" he said to us, after Swann had gone, with the same enthusiasm and veneration which make clever and pretty women of the middle classes fall victims to the charms of a duchess, however ugly and stupid. "What a charming man! What a pity that he should have made such a deplorable marriage!"

And then, so strong an element of hypocrisy is there in even the most sincere people, who lay aside the opinion they actually hold of a person while they are talking to him and express it as soon as he is no longer there, my family joined with M. Vinteuil in deploring Swann's marriage, invoking principles and conventions which (for the very reason that they were invoking them in common with him, as though they were all decent people of the same sort) they appeared to suggest were in no way infringed at Montjouvain. M. Vinteuil did not send his daughter to visit Swann, an omission which Swann was the first to regret. For whenever he met M. Vinteuil, he would remember afterwards that he had been meaning for a long time to ask him about someone of the same name, a relation of his, Swann supposed. And on this occasion he had made up his mind not to forget what he had to say to him when M. Vinteuil should appear with his daughter at Tansonville.

Since the "Méséglise way" was the shorter of the two that we used to take on our walks round Combray, and for that reason was reserved for days of uncertain weather, it followed that the climate of Méséglise was somewhat wet, and we would never lose sight of the fringe of Roussainville wood beneath whose dense thatch of leaves we could take shelter.

Often the sun would disappear behind a cloud, which impinged on its roundness and whose edge it gilded in return. The brightness though not the luminosity would be expunged from a landscape in which all life appeared to be suspended, while the little village of Roussainville carved its white gables in relief upon the sky with an overpowering precision and finish. A gust of wind put up a solitary crow, which flapped away and settled in the distance, while against a greying sky the woods on the horizon assumed a deeper tone of blue, as though painted in one of those monochromes that still decorate the overmantels of old houses.

But on other days the rain with which the barometer in the optician's window had threatened us would begin to fall. Its drops, like migrating birds which fly off in a body at a given moment, would come down out of the sky in serried ranks—never drifting apart, never wandering off on their own during their rapid course, but each one keeping its place and drawing its successor in its wake, so that the sky was more darkened than during the swallows' exodus. We would take refuge among the trees. And when it seemed that their flight was accomplished, a few last drops, feebler and slower than the rest, would still come down. But we would emerge from our shelter, for raindrops revel amidst foliage, and even when it was almost dry again underfoot, many a stray drop, lingering in the hollow of a leaf, would run down and hang glistening from the point of it until suddenly they splashed on to our upturned faces from the top of the branch.

Often, too, we would hurry to take shelter, huddled together cheek by jowl with its stony saints and patriarchs, under the porch of Saint-André-des-Champs. How French that church was! Over its door the saints, the chevalier kings with lilies in their hands, the wedding scenes and funerals were carved as they might have been in the mind of Françoise. The sculptor had also recorded certain anecdotes of Aristotle and Virgil, precisely as Françoise in her kitchen was wont to hold forth about St Louis as though she herself had known him, generally in order to depreciate, by contrast with him, my grandparents whom she considered less "righteous." One

could see that the notions which the mediaeval artist and the
mediaeval peasant (who had survived to cook for us in the
nineteenth century) had of classical and of early Christian
history, notions whose inaccuracy was atoned for by their
honest simplicity, were derived not from books, but from a
tradition at once ancient and direct, unbroken, oral, distorted,
unrecognisable, and alive. Another Combray personality whom
I could discern also, potential and presaged, in the Gothic
sculptures of Saint-André-des-Champs was young Théodore,
the assistant in Camus's shop. And, indeed, Françoise herself
was so well aware that she had in him a countryman and
contemporary that when my aunt was too ill for Françoise
to be able, unaided, to lift her in her bed or to carry her to
her chair, rather than let the kitchen-maid come upstairs and,
perhaps, "make an impression" on my aunt, she would send
out for Théodore. And this lad, who was rightly regarded as
a scapegrace, was so abounding in that spirit which had served
to decorate the porch of Saint-André-des-Champs, and particularly in the feelings of respect due, in Françoise's eyes,
to all "poor invalids," and above all to her own "poor mistress," that when he bent down to raise my aunt's head from
her pillow, he wore the same naïve and zealous mien as the
little angels in the bas-reliefs who throng, with tapers in their
hands, about the swooning Virgin, as though those carved
stone faces, naked and grey as trees in winter, were, like
them, asleep only, storing up life and waiting to flower again
in countless plebeian faces, reverent and cunning as the face of
Théodore, and glowing with the ruddy brilliance of ripe
apples.
    There, too, not affixed to the stone like the little angels,
but detached from the porch, of more than human stature,
erect upon her pedestal as upon a footstool that had been
placed there to save her feet from contact with the wet ground,
stood a saint with the full cheeks, the firm breasts swelling
out her draperies like clusters of ripe grapes inside a sack,
the narrow forehead, short and impudent nose, deep-set eyes,
and hardy, stolid, fearless demeanour of the country-women
of those parts. This similarity, which imparted to the statue
a kindliness that I had not looked to find in it, was corroborated

often by the arrival of some girl from the fields, come, like ourselves, for shelter beneath the porch, whose presence there —like the leaves of a climbing plant that have grown up beside some sculpted foliage—seemed deliberately intended to enable us, by confronting it with its type in nature, to form a critical estimate of the truth of the work of art. Before our eyes, in the distance, a promised or an accursed land, Roussainville, within whose walls I had never penetrated, Roussainville was now, when the rain had ceased for us, still being chastised like a village in the Old Testament by all the slings and arrows of the storm, which beat down obliquely upon the dwellings of its inhabitants, or else had already received the forgiveness of the Almighty, who had restored to it the light of his sun, which fell upon it in frayed, golden shafts, unequal in length like the rays of a monstrance.

Sometimes, when the weather had completely broken, we were obliged to go home and to remain shut up indoors. Here and there in the distance, in a landscape which in the failing light and saturated atmosphere resembled a seascape rather, a few solitary houses clinging to the lower slopes of a hill plunged in watery darkness shone out like little boats which have folded their sails and ride at anchor all night upon the sea. But what mattered rain or storm? In summer, bad weather is no more than a passing fit of superficial ill-temper on the part of the permanent, underlying fine weather which, in sharp contrast to the fluid and unstable fine weather of winter, having firmly established itself in the soil where it has materialised in dense masses of foliage on which the rain may drip without weakening the endurance of their deep-seated happiness, has hoisted for the entire season, in the very streets of the village, on the walls of its houses and its gardens, its silken banners, violet and white. Sitting in the little parlour, where I would pass the time until dinner with a book, I could hear the water dripping from our chestnut-trees, but I knew that the shower would merely burnish their leaves, and that they promised to remain there, like pledges of summer, all through the rainy night, ensuring the continuance of the fine weather; I knew that however much it rained, to-morrow, over the white fence of Tansonville, the little heart-shaped leaves would ripple, as numerous as ever; and it was without the least distress that I watched the poplar in the Rue des Perchamps praying for mercy, bowing in desperation before the storm; without the least distress that I heard, at the bottom of the garden, the last peals of thunder growling among the lilacs.

If the weather was bad all morning, my parents would abandon the idea of a walk, and I would remain at home. But, later on, I formed the habit of going out by myself on such days, and walking towards Méséglise-la-Vineuse, during that autumn when we had to come to Combray to settle my aunt Léonie's estate; for she had died at last, vindicating at one and the same time those who had insisted that her debilitating regimen would ultimately kill her and those who had always maintained that she suffered from a disease that was not imaginary but organic, by the visible proof of which the sceptics would be obliged to own themselves convinced, once she had succumbed to it; causing by her death no great grief save to one person alone, but to that one a grief that was savage in its violence. During the long fortnight of my aunt's last illness Françoise never left her for an instant, never undressed, allowed no one else to do anything for her, and did not leave her body until it was actually in its grave. Then at last we understood that the sort of terror in which Françoise had lived of my aunt's harsh words, her suspicions and her anger, had developed in her a feeling which we had mistaken for hatred and which was really veneration and love. Her true mistress, whose decisions had been impossible to foresee, whose ruses had been so difficult to foil, of whose good nature it had been so easy to take advantage, her sovereign, her mysterious and omnipotent monarch was no more. Compared with such a mistress we were of very little account. The time had long passed since, on first coming to spend our holidays at Combray, we had enjoyed as much prestige as my aunt in Françoise's eyes.

That autumn my parents, so preoccupied with all the legal formalities, the discussions with solicitors and tenants, that they had little time to make excursions, for which in any case the weather was unpropitious, began to let me go for walks

without them along the Méséglise way, wrapped up in a
huge Highland plaid which protected me from the rain, and
which I was all the more ready to throw over my shoulders
because I felt that the stripes of its gaudy tartan scandalised
Françoise, whom it was impossible to convince that the colour
of one's clothes had nothing whatever to do with one's
mourning for the dead, and to whom the grief which we had
shown on my aunt's death was wholly inadequate, since
we had not entertained the neighbours to a great funeral
banquet, and did not adopt a special tone when we spoke of
her, while I at times might be heard humming a tune. I am
sure that in a book—and to that extent my feelings were akin
to those of Françoise—such a conception of mourning, in the
manner of the *Chanson de Roland* and of the porch of Saint-
André-des-Champs, would have seemed most attractive. But
the moment Françoise herself was near me, some demon
would urge me to try to make her angry, and I would avail
myself of the slightest pretext to say to her that I regretted
my aunt's death because she had been a good woman in spite
of her absurdities, but not in the least because she was my
aunt; that she might have been my aunt and yet have seemed
to me so odious that her death would not have caused me a
moment's sorrow—statements which, in a book, would have
struck me as inept.

And if Françoise then, inspired like a poet with a flood of
confused reflections upon bereavement, grief and family
memories, pleaded her inability to rebut my theories, saying:
"I don't know how to *espress* myself," I would gloat over
her admission with an ironical and brutal common sense
worthy of Dr. Percepied; and if she went on: "All the same she
was kith and kindle; there's always the respect due to kindle,"
I would shrug my shoulders and say to myself: "It's really
very good of me to discuss the matter with an illiterate
old woman who makes such howlers," adopting, to deliver
judgment on Françoise, the mean and narrow outlook of the
pedant, whom those who are most contemptuous of him in
the impartiality of their own minds are only too prone to
emulate when they are obliged to play a part upon the vulgar
stage of life.

My walks, that autumn, were all the more delightful because
I used to take them after long hours spent over a book.
When I was tired of reading, after a whole morning in the
house, I would throw my plaid across my shoulders and set
out; my body, which in a long spell of enforced immobility
had stored up an accumulation of vital energy, now felt the
need, like a spinning-top wound up and let go, to expend
it in every direction. The walls of houses, the Tansonville
hedge, the trees of Roussainville wood, the bushes adjoining
Montjouvain, all must bear the blows of my walking-stick or
umbrella, must hear my shouts of happiness, these being
no more than expressions of the confused ideas which ex-
hilarated me, and which had not achieved the repose of enlightenment, preferring the pleasures of a lazy drift towards an
immediate outlet rather than submit to a slow and difficult
course of elucidation. Thus it is that most of our attempts to
translate our innermost feelings do no more than relieve us of
them by drawing them out in a blurred form which does not
help us to identify them. When I try to reckon up all that I
owe to the Méséglise way, all the humble discoveries of which
it was either the fortuitous setting or the direct inspiration and
cause, I am reminded that it was in that same autumn, on one
of those walks, near the bushy slope which overlooks Montjouvain, that I was struck for the first time by this discordance
between our impressions and their habitual expression. After
an hour of rain and wind, against which I had struggled
cheerfully, as I came to the edge of the Montjouvain pond,
beside a little hut with a tiled roof in which M. Vinteuil's
gardener kept his tools, the sun had just reappeared, and its
golden rays, washed clean by the shower, glittered anew in
the sky, on the trees, on the wall of the hut and the still wet
tiles of the roof, on the ridge of which a hen was strutting.
The wind tugged at the wild grass growing from cracks in
the wall and at the hen's downy feathers, which floated out
horizontally to their full extent with the unresisting submissiveness of light and lifeless things. The tiled roof cast
upon the pond, translucent again in the sunlight, a dappled
pink reflection which I had never observed before. And, seeing
upon the water, and on the surface of the wall, a pallid smile

responding to the smiling sky, I cried aloud in my enthusiasm, brandishing my furled umbrella: "Gosh, gosh, gosh, gosh!" But at the same time I felt that I was in duty bound not to content myself with these unilluminating words, but to endeavour to see more clearly into the sources of my rapture.

And it was at that moment, too—thanks to a peasant who went past, apparently in a bad enough humour already, but more so when he nearly got a poke in the face from my umbrella, and who replied somewhat coolly to my "Fine day, what! Good to be out walking!"—that I learned that identical emotions do not spring up simultaneously in the hearts of all men in accordance with a pre-established order. Later on, whenever a long spell of reading had put me in a mood for conversation, the friend to whom I was longing to talk would at that very moment have finished indulging himself in the delights of conversation, and wanted to be left to read undisturbed. And if I had just been thinking of my parents with affection, and forming resolutions of the kind most calculated to please them, they would have been using the same interval of time to discover some misdeed that I had already forgotten, and would begin to scold me severely as I was about to fling myself into their arms.

Sometimes to the exhilaration which I derived from being alone would be added an alternative feeling which I was unable to distinguish clearly from it, a feeling stimulated by the desire to see appear before my eyes a peasant-girl whom I might clasp in my arms. Springing up suddenly, and without giving me time to trace it accurately to its source among so many thoughts of a very different kind, the pleasure which accompanied this desire seemed only a degree superior to that which I derived from them. I found an additional merit in everything that was in my mind at that moment, in the pink reflection of the tiled roof, the grass growing out of the wall, the village of Roussainville into which I had long desired to penetrate, the trees of its wood and the steeple of its church, as a result of this fresh emotion which made them appear more desirable only because I thought it was they that had provoked it, and which seemed only to wish to bear me more swiftly towards them when it filled my sails with a potent, mysterious and propitious breeze. But if, for me, this desire that a woman should appear added something more exalting to the charms of nature, they in their turn enlarged what I might have found too restricted in the charms of the woman. It seemed to me that the beauty of the trees was hers also, and that her kisses would reveal to me the spirit of those horizons, of the village of Roussainville, of the books which I was reading that year; and, my imagination drawing strength from contact with my sensuality, my sensuality expanding through all the realms of my imagination, my desire no longer had any bounds. Moreover—just as in moments of musing contemplation of nature, the normal actions of the mind being suspended, and our abstract ideas of things set aside, we believe with the profoundest faith in the originality, in the individual existence of the place in which we may happen to be—the passing figure whom my desire evoked seemed to be not just any specimen of the genus "woman," but a necessary and natural product of this particular soil. For at that time everything that was not myself, the earth and the creatures upon it, seemed to me more precious, more important, endowed with a more real existence than they appear to full-grown men. And between the earth and its creatures I made no distinction. I had a desire for a peasant-girl from Méséglise or Roussainville, for a fisher-girl from Balbec, just as I had a desire for Balbec and Méséglise. The pleasure they might give me would have seemed less genuine, I should no longer have believed in it, if I had modified the conditions as I pleased. To meet a fisher-girl from Balbec or a peasant-girl from Méséglise in Paris would have been like receiving the present of a shell which I had never seen upon the beach, or of a fern which I had never found among the woods, would have stripped from the pleasure she might give me all those other pleasures amidst which my imagination had enwrapped her. But to wander thus among the woods of Roussainville without a peasant-girl to embrace was to see those woods and yet know nothing of their secret treasure, their deep-hidden beauty. That girl whom I invariably saw dappled with the shadows of their leaves was to me herself a plant of local growth, merely of a higher species than the rest, and one whose structure would enable me to

get closer than through them to the intimate savour of the
country. I could believe this all the more readily (and also
that the caresses by which she would bring that savour to my
senses would themselves be of a special kind, yielding a pleasure
which I could never derive from anyone else) since I was still,
and must for long remain, in that period of life when one has
not yet separated the fact of this sensual pleasure from the
various women in whose company one has tasted it, when one
has not yet reduced it to a general idea which makes one
regard them thenceforward as the interchangeable instruments
of a pleasure that is always the same. Indeed, that pleasure does
not even exist, isolated, distinct, formulated in the consciousness, as the ultimate aim for which one seeks a woman's
company, or as the cause of the preliminary perturbation that
one feels. Scarcely does one think of it as a pleasure in store
for one; rather does one call it *her* charm; for one does not
think of oneself, but only of escaping from oneself. Obscurely
awaited, immanent and concealed, it simply raises to such a
paroxysm, at the moment when at last it makes itself felt,
those other pleasures which we find in the tender glances, the
kisses, of the woman by our side, that it seems to us, more than
anything else, a sort of transport of gratitude for her kindness
of heart and for her touching predilection for us, which we
measure by the blessings and the happiness that she showers
upon us.

Alas, it was in vain that I implored the castle-keep of
Roussainville, that I begged it to send out to meet me some
daughter of its village, appealing to it as to the sole confidant of
my earliest desires when, at the top of our house in Combray,
in the little room that smelt of orris-root, I could see
nothing but its tower framed in the half-opened window
as, with the heroic misgivings of a traveller setting out on a
voyage of exploration or of a desperate wretch hesitating on the
verge of self-destruction, faint with emotion, I explored,
across the bounds of my own experience, an untrodden path
which for all I knew was deadly—until the moment when a
natural trail like that left by a snail smeared the leaves of the
flowering currant that drooped around me. In vain did I call
upon it now. In vain did I compress the whole landscape into

my field of vision, draining it with an exhaustive gaze which
sought to extract from it a female creature. I might go as far as
the porch of Saint-André-des-Champs: never did I find there
the peasant girl whom I should not have failed to meet had I
been with my grandfather and thus unable to engage her in
conversation. I would stare interminably at the trunk of a
distant tree, from behind which she would emerge and come
to me; I scanned the horizon, which remained as deserted as
before; night was falling; it was without hope now that I
concentrated my attention, as though to draw up from it the
creatures which it must conceal, upon that sterile soil, that
stale, exhausted earth, and it was no longer with exhilaration
but with sullen rage that I aimed blows at the trees of Roussainville wood, from among which no more living creatures
emerged than if they had been trees painted on the stretched
canvas background of a panorama, when, unable to resign
myself to returning home without having held in my arms the
woman I so greatly desired, I was yet obliged to retrace my
steps towards Combray, and to admit to myself that the
chance of her appearing in my path grew smaller every
moment. And if she had appeared, would I have dared to
speak to her? I felt that she would have regarded me as mad,
and I ceased to think of those desires which came to me on
my walks, but were never realised, as being shared by others,
or as having any existence outside myself. They seemed to
me now no more than the purely subjective, impotent, illusory
creations of my temperament. They no longer had any connection with nature, with the world of real things, which from
then onwards lost all its charm and significance, and meant no
more to my life than a purely conventional framework, what
the railway carriage on the bench of which a traveller is reading
to pass the time is to the fictional events of his novel.

It is perhaps from another impression which I received at
Montjouvain, some years later, an impression which at the
time remained obscure to me, that there arose, long afterwards, the notion I was to form of sadism. We shall see, in
due course, that for quite other reasons the memory of this
impression was to play an important part in my life. It was
during a spell of very hot weather; my parents, who had been

obliged to go away for the whole day, had told me that I
might stay out as late as I pleased; and having gone as far as
the Montjouvain pond, where I enjoyed seeing again the
reflection of the tiled roof of the hut, I had lain down in the
shade and fallen asleep among the bushes on the steep slope
overlooking the house, just where I had waited for my parents,
years before, one day when they had gone to call on M.
Vinteuil. It was almost dark when I awoke, and I was about
to get up and go away, but I saw Mlle Vinteuil (or thought,
at least, that I recognised her, for I had not seen her often at
Combray, and then only when she was still a child, whereas
she was now growing into a young woman), who had probably
just come in, standing in front of me, and only a few feet
away, in that room in which her father had entertained mine,
and which she had now made into a little sitting-room for
herself. The window was partly open; the lamp was lighted;
I could watch her every movement without her being able to
see me; but if I had moved away I would have made a rustling
sound among the bushes, she would have heard me, and she
might have thought that I had been hiding there in order to
spy upon her.

She was in deep mourning, for her father had recently
died. We had not gone to see her; my mother had not wished
it, by reason of a virtue which alone set limits to her benevolence—namely, modesty; but she pitied the girl from the
depths of her heart. My mother had not forgotten the sad
last years of M. Vinteuil's life, his complete absorption, first
in having to play mother and nursery-maid to his daughter,
and, later, in the suffering she had caused him; she could see
the tortured expression which was never absent from the old
man's face in those last years; she knew that he had finally
given up hope of finishing the task of copying out the whole
of his later work, the modest pieces, we imagined, of an old
piano-teacher, a retired village organist, which we assumed
were of little value in themselves, though we did not despise
them because they meant so much to him and had been the
chief motive of his life before he sacrificed them to his daughter;
pieces which, being mostly not even written down, but recorded only in his memory, while the rest were scribbled on

loose sheets of paper, and quite illegible, must now remain unknown for ever. My mother thought, too, of that other and still more cruel renunciation to which M. Vinteuil had been driven, that of a future of honourable and respected happiness for his daughter; when she called to mind all this utter and crushing misery that had come upon my aunts' old music-teacher, she was moved to very real grief, and shuddered to think of that other grief, so much more bitter, which Mlle Vinteuil must now be feeling, tinged with remorse at having virtually killed her father. "Poor M. Vinteuil," my mother would say, "he lived and died for his daughter, without getting his reward. Will he get it now, I wonder, and in what form? It can only come to him from her."

At the far end of Mlle Vinteuil's sitting-room, on the mantelpiece, stood a small photograph of her father which she went briskly to fetch, just as the sound of carriage wheels was heard from the road outside, then flung herself down on a sofa and drew towards her a little table on which she placed the photograph, as M. Vinteuil had placed beside him the piece of music which he would have liked to play to my parents. Presently her friend came into the room. Mlle Vinteuil greeted her without rising, clasping her hands behind her head and moving to one side of the sofa as though to make room for her. But no sooner had she done this than she evidently felt that she might seem to be imposing on her friend a posture which she might consider importunate. She thought that her friend would perhaps prefer to sit down at some distance from her, upon a chair; she felt that she had been indiscreet; her sensitive heart took fright; stretching herself out again over the whole of the sofa, she closed her eyes and began to yawn, as if to suggest that drowsiness was the sole reason for her recumbent position. Despite the brusque and hectoring familiarity with which she treated her companion, I could recognise in her the obsequious and reticent gestures and sudden scruples that had characterised her father. Presently she rose and came to the window, where she pretended to be trying to close the shutters and not succeeding.

"Leave them open," said her friend. "I'm hot."

"But it's too tiresome! People will see us," Mlle Vinteuil answered.

But then she must have guessed that her friend would think that she had uttered these words simply in order to provoke a reply in certain other words, which she did indeed wish to hear but, from discretion, would have preferred her friend to be the first to speak. And so her face, which I could not see very clearly, must have assumed the expression which my grandmother had once found so delightful, when she hastily went on: "When I say 'see us' I mean, of course, see us reading. It's so tiresome to think that whatever trivial little thing you do someone may be overlooking you."

With an instinctive rectitude and a gentility beyond her control, she refrained from uttering the premeditated words which she had felt to be indispensable for the full realisation of her desire. And perpetually, in the depths of her being, a shy and suppliant maiden entreated and reined back a rough and swaggering trooper.

"Oh, yes, it's so extremely likely that people are looking at us at this time of night in this densely populated district!" said her friend sarcastically. "And what if they are?" she went on, feeling bound to annotate with a fond and mischievous wink these words which she recited out of good-naturedness, as a text which she knew to be pleasing to Mlle Vinteuil, in a tone of studied cynicism. "And what if they are? All the better that they should see us."

Mlle Vinteuil shuddered and rose to her feet. Her sensitive and scrupulous heart was ignorant of the words that ought to flow spontaneously from her lips to match the scene for which her eager senses clamoured. She reached out as far as she could across the limitations of her true nature to find the language appropriate to the vicious young woman she longed to be thought, but the words which she imagined such a young woman might have uttered with sincerity sounded false on her own lips. And what little she allowed herself to say was said in a strained tone, in which her ingrained timidity paralysed her impulse towards audacity and was interlarded with: "You're sure you aren't cold? You aren't too hot? You don't want to sit and read by yourself? . . .

"Her ladyship's thoughts seem to be rather lubricious this evening," she concluded, doubtless repeating a phrase which she had heard used by her friend on some earlier occasion.

In the V-shaped opening of her crape bodice Mlle Vinteuil felt the sting of her friend's sudden kiss; she gave a little scream and broke away; and then they began to chase one another about the room, scrambling over the furniture, their wide sleeves fluttering like wings, clucking and squealing like a pair of amorous fowls. At last Mlle Vinteuil collapsed on to the sofa, with her friend lying on top of her. The latter now had her back turned to the little table on which the old music-master's portrait had been arranged. Mlle Vinteuil realised that her friend would not see it unless her attention were drawn to it, and so exclaimed, as if she herself had just noticed it for the first time: "Oh! there's my father's picture looking at us; I can't think who can have put it there; I'm sure I've told them a dozen times that it isn't the proper place for it."

I remembered the words that M. Vinteuil had used to my parents in apologising for an obtrusive sheet of music. This photograph was evidently in regular use for ritual profanations, for the friend replied in words which were clearly a liturgical response: "Let him stay there. He can't bother us any longer. D'you think he'd start whining, and wanting to put your overcoat on for you, if he saw you now with the window open, the ugly old monkey?"

To which Mlle Vinteuil replied in words of gentle reproach—"Come, come!"—which testified to the goodness of her nature, not that they were prompted by any resentment at hearing her father spoken of in this fashion (for that was evidently a feeling which she had trained herself, by a long course of sophistries, to keep in close subjection at such moments), but rather because they were a sort of curb which, in order not to appear selfish, she herself applied to the gratification which her friend was attempting to procure for her. It may well have been, too, that the smiling moderation with which she faced and answered these blasphemies, that this tender and hypocritical rebuke appeared to her frank and generous nature as a particularly shameful and seductive form of the wickedness she was striving to emulate. But she could not resist the attraction of being treated with tenderness by a woman who had shown herself so implacable towards the defenceless dead, and, springing on to her friend's lap she held out a chaste brow to be kissed precisely as a daughter would have done, with the exquisite sensation that they would thus, between them, inflict the last turn of the screw of cruelty by robbing M. Vinteuil, as though they were actually rifling his tomb, of the sacred rights of fatherhood. Her friend took Mlle Vinteuil's head between her hands and placed a kiss on her brow with a docility prompted by the real affection she had for her, as well as by the desire to bring what distraction she could into the dull and melancholy life of an orphan.

"Do you know what I should like to do to this old horror?" she said, taking up the photograph. And she murmured in Mlle Vinteuil's ear something that I could not distinguish.

"Oh! You wouldn't dare."

"Not dare to spit on it? On *that*?" said the friend with studied brutality.

I heard no more, for Mlle Vinteuil, with an air that was at once languid, awkward, bustling, sincere and rather sad, came to the window and drew the shutters close; but I knew now what was the reward that M. Vinteuil, in return for all the suffering that he had endured in his lifetime on account of his daughter, had received from her after his death.

And yet I have since reflected that if M. Vinteuil had been able to be present at this scene, he might still, in spite of everything, have continued to believe in his daughter's goodness of heart, and perhaps in so doing he would not have been altogether wrong. It was true that in Mlle Vinteuil's habits the appearance of evil was so absolute that it would have been hard to find it exhibited to such a degree of perfection save in a convinced sadist; it is behind the footlights of a Paris theatre and not under the homely lamp of an actual country house that one expects to see a girl encouraging a friend to spit upon the portrait of a father who has lived and died for her alone; and when we find in real life a desire for melodramatic effect, it is generally sadism that is responsible for it. It is possible that, without being in the least inclined towards sadism, a daughter might be guilty of equally cruel offences as those of Mlle Vinteuil against the memory and the wishes of her dead father, but she would not give them deliberate expression in an act so crude in its symbolism, so lacking in subtlety; the criminal element in her behaviour would be less evident to other people, and even to herself, since she would not admit to herself that she was doing wrong. But, appearances apart, in Mlle Vinteuil's soul, at least in the earlier stages, the evil element was probably not unmixed. A sadist of her kind is an artist in evil, which a wholly wicked person could not be, for in that case the evil would not have been external, it would have seemed quite natural to her, and would not even have been distinguishable from herself; and as for virtue, respect for the dead, filial affection, since she would never have practised the cult of these things, she would take no impious delight in profaning them. Sadists of Mlle Vinteuil's sort are creatures so purely sentimental, so naturally virtuous, that even sensual pleasure appears to them as something bad, the prerogative of the wicked. And when they allow themselves for a moment to enjoy it they endeavour to impersonate, to identify with, the wicked, and to make their partners do likewise, in order to gain the momentary illusion of having escaped beyond the control of their own gentle and scrupulous natures into the inhuman world of pleasure. And I could understand how she must have longed for such an escape when I saw how impossible it was for her to effect it. At the moment when she wished to be thought the very antithesis of her father, what she at once suggested to me were the mannerisms, in thought and speech, of the poor old piano-teacher. Far more than his photograph, what she really desecrated, what she subordinated to her pleasures though it remained between them and her and prevented her from any direct enjoyment of them, was the likeness between her face and his, his mother's blue eyes which he had handed down to her like a family jewel, those gestures of courtesy and kindness which interposed between her vice and herself a phraseology, a mentality which were not designed for vice and which prevented her from recognising it as something very different

from the numberless little social duties and courtesies to which
she must devote herself every day. It was not evil that gave
her the idea of pleasure, that seemed to her attractive; it was
pleasure, rather, that seemed evil. And as, each time she
indulged in it, it was accompanied by evil thoughts such as
ordinarily had no place in her virtuous mind, she came at
length to see in pleasure itself something diabolical, to identify
it with Evil. Perhaps Mlle Vinteuil felt that at heart her friend
was not altogether bad, nor really sincere when she gave vent
to those blasphemous utterances. At any rate, she had the
pleasure of receiving and returning those kisses, those smiles,
those glances, all feigned, perhaps, but akin in their base and
vicious mode of expression to those which would have been
evinced not by an ordinarily kind, suffering person but by a
cruel and wanton one. She could delude herself for a moment
into believing that she was indeed enjoying the pleasures
which, with so perverted an accomplice, a girl might enjoy
who really did harbour such barbarous feelings towards her
father's memory. Perhaps she would not have thought of
evil as a state so rare, so abnormal, so exotic, one in which it
was so refreshing to sojourn, had she been able to discern in
herself, as in everyone else, that indifference to the sufferings
one causes which, whatever other names one gives it, is the
most terrible and lasting form of cruelty.

If the "Méséglise way" was fairly easy, it was a very different
matter when we took the "Guermantes way," for that meant
a long walk, and we must first make sure of the weather.
When we seemed to have entered upon a spell of fine days;
when Françoise, in desperation that not a drop was falling
on the "poor crops," gazing up at the sky and seeing there
only an occasional white cloud floating upon its calm blue
surface, groaned aloud and exclaimed: "They look just like a
lot of dogfish swimming about and sticking up their snouts!
Ah, they never think of making it rain a little for the poor
labourers! And then when the corn is all ripe, down it will
come, pitter-patter all over the place, and think no more of
where it's falling than if it was the sea!"; when my father had
received the same favourable reply from the gardener and the

barometer several times in succession, then someone would say at dinner: "To-morrow, if the weather holds, we might go the Guermantes way." And off we would set, immediately after lunch, through the little garden gate into the Rue des Perchamps, narrow and bent at a sharp angle, dotted with clumps of grass among which two or three wasps would spend the day botanising, a street as quaint as its name, from which, I felt, its odd characteristics and cantankerous personality derived, a street for which one might search in vain through the Combray of to-day, for the village school now occupies its site. But in my dreams of Combray (like those architects, pupils of Viollet-le-Duc, who, fancying that they can detect, beneath a Renaissance rood-screen and an eighteenth-century altar, traces of a Romanesque choir, restore the whole church to the state in which it must have been in the twelfth century) I leave not a stone of the modern edifice standing, but pierce through it and "restore" the Rue des Perchamps. And for such reconstruction memory furnishes me with more detailed guidance than is generally at the disposal of restorers: the pictures which it has preserved—perhaps the last surviving in the world to-day, and soon to follow the rest into oblivion—of what Combray looked like in my childhood days; pictures which, because it was the old Combray that traced their outlines upon my mind before it vanished, are as moving—if I may compare a humble landscape with those glorious works, reproductions of which my grandmother was so fond of bestowing on me—as those old engravings of the *Last Supper* or that painting by Gentile Bellini, in which one sees, in a state in which they no longer exist, the masterpiece of Leonardo and the portico of Saint Mark's.

We would pass, in the Rue de l'Oiseau, in front of the old hostelry of the Oiseau Flesché, into whose great courtyard, once upon a time, would rumble the coaches of the Duchesses de Montpensier, de Guermantes and de Montmorency, when they had to come down to Combray for some litigation with their tenants, or to receive homage from them. We would come at length to the Mall, among whose tree-tops I could distinguish the steeple of Saint-Hilaire. And I should have liked to be able to sit down and spend the whole day there reading and listening to the bells, for it was so blissful and so quiet that, when an hour struck, you would have said not that it broke in upon the calm of the day, but that it relieved the day of its superfluity, and that the steeple, with the indolent, painstaking exactitude of a person who has nothing else to do, had simply—in order to squeeze out and let fall the few golden drops which had slowly and naturally accumulated in the hot sunlight—pressed, at a given moment, the distended surface of the silence.

The great charm of the Guermantes way was that we had beside us, almost all the time, the course of the Vivonne. We crossed it first, ten minutes after leaving the house, by a foot-bridge called the Pont-Vieux. And every year, when we arrived at Combray, on Easter Sunday, after the sermon, if the weather was fine, I would run there to see (amid all the disorder that prevails on the morning of a great festival, the sumptuous preparations for which make the everyday household utensils that they have not contrived to banish seem more sordid than usual) the river flowing past, sky-blue already between banks still black and bare, its only companions a clump of premature daffodils and early primroses, while here and there burned the blue flame of a violet, its stem drooping beneath the weight of the drop of perfume stored in its tiny horn. The Pont-Vieux led to a tow-path which at this point would be overhung in summer by the bluish foliage of a hazel tree, beneath which a fisherman in a straw hat seemed to have taken root. At Combray, where I could always detect the blacksmith or grocer's boy through the disguise of a verger's uniform or chorister's surplice, this fisherman was the only person whom I was never able to identify. He must have known my family, for he used to raise his hat when we passed; and then I would be just on the point of asking his name when someone would signal to me to be quiet or I would frighten the fish. We would follow the tow-path, which ran along the top of a steep bank several feet above the stream. The bank on the other side was lower, stretching in a series of broad meadows as far as the village and the distant railway-station. Over these were strewn the remains, half-buried in the long grass, of the castle of the old Counts of Combray, who, during the Middle Ages, had

had on this side the course of the Vivonne as a barrier against
attack from the Lords of Guermantes and Abbots of Martinville. Nothing was left now but a few barely visible stumps of
towers, hummocks upon the broad surface of the fields, and a
few broken battlements from which, in their day, the cross-
bowmen had hurled their missiles and the watchmen had
gazed out over Novepont, Clairefontaine, Martinville-le-Sec,
Bailleau-l'Exempt, fiefs all of them of Guermantes by which
Combray was hemmed in, but now razed to the level of the
grass and overrun by the boys from the lay brothers' school
who came there for study or recreation—a past that had almost
sunk into the ground, lying by the water's edge like an idler
taking the air, yet giving me much food for thought, making
the name of Combray connote to me not only the little town of
to-day but an historic city vastly different, gripping my imagination by the remote, incomprehensible features which it half-
concealed beneath a spangled veil of buttercups. For the
buttercups grew past numbering in this spot which they had
chosen for their games among the grass, standing singly, in
couples, in whole companies, yellow as the yolk of eggs, and
glowing with an added lustre, I felt, because, being powerless
to consummate with my palate the pleasure which the sight
of them never failed to give me, I would let it accumulate as
my eyes ranged over their golden expanse, until it became
potent enough to produce an effect of absolute, purposeless
beauty; and so it had been from my earliest childhood, when
from the tow-path I had stretched out my arms towards them
before I could even properly spell their charming name—a
name fit for the Prince in some fairy-tale—immigrants, perhaps, from Asia centuries ago, but naturalised now for ever in
the village, satisfied with their modest horizon, rejoicing in
the sunshine and the water's edge, faithful to their little glimpse
of the railway-station, yet keeping nonetheless like some of our
old paintings, in their plebeian simplicity, a poetic scintillation
from the golden East.

I enjoyed watching the glass jars which the village boys used
to lower into the Vivonne to catch minnows, and which,
filled by the stream, in which they in their turn were enclosed,
at once "containers" whose transparent sides were like

solidified water and "contents" plunged into a still larger
container of liquid, flowing crystal, conjured up an image of
coolness more delicious and more provoking than they would
have done standing upon a table laid for dinner, by showing
it as perpetually in flight between the impalpable water in
which my hands could not grasp it and the insoluble glass in
which my palate could not enjoy it. I made up my mind to
come there again with a fishing-line; meanwhile I procured
some bread from our picnic basket, and threw pellets of it
into the Vivonne which seemed to bring about a process of
super-saturation, for the water at once solidified round them
in oval clusters of emaciated tadpoles, which until then it
had no doubt been holding in solution, invisible and on the
verge of entering the stage of crystallisation.

Presently the course of the Vivonne became choked with
water-plants. At first they appeared singly—a lily, for instance,
which the current, across whose path it was unhappily placed,
would never leave at rest for a moment, so that, like a ferry-
boat mechanically propelled, it would drift over to one bank
only to return to the other, eternally repeating its double
journey. Thrust towards the bank, its stalk would uncoil,
lengthen, reach out, strain almost to breaking-point until the
current again caught it, its green moorings swung back over
their anchorage and brought the unhappy plant to what might
fitly be called its starting-point, since it was fated not to rest
there a moment before moving off once again. I would still
find it there, on one walk after another, always in the same
helpless state, suggesting certain victims of neurasthenia,
among whom my grandfather would have included my aunt
Léonie, who present year after year the unchanging spectacle
of their odd and unaccountable habits, which they constantly
imagine themselves to be on the point of shaking off but which
they always retain to the end; caught in the treadmill of their
own maladies and eccentricities, their futile endeavours to
escape serve only to actuate its mechanism, to keep in motion
the clockwork of their strange, ineluctable and baneful
dietetics. Such as these was the water-lily, and reminiscent also
of those wretches whose peculiar torments, repeated indefinitely throughout eternity, aroused the curiosity of Dante,

who would have inquired about them at greater length and in
fuller detail from the victims themselves had not Virgil,
striding on ahead, obliged him to hasten after him at full
speed, as I must hasten after my parents.

But further on the current slackened, at a point where the
stream ran through a property thrown open to the public by
its owner, who had made a hobby of aquatic gardening, so
that the little ponds into which the Vivonne was here diverted
were aflower with water-lilies. As the banks hereabouts were
thickly wooded, the heavy shade of the trees gave the water a
background which was ordinarily dark green, although sometimes, when we were coming home on a calm evening after a
stormy afternoon, I have seen in its depths a clear, crude blue
verging on violet, suggesting a floor of Japanese cloisonné.
Here and there on the surface, blushing like a strawberry,
floated a water-lily flower with a scarlet centre and white edges.
Farther on, the flowers were more numerous, paler, less
glossy, more thickly seeded, more tightly folded, and disposed,
by accident, in festoons so graceful that I would fancy I saw
floating upon the stream, as after the sad dismantling of some
Watteau *fête galante*, moss-roses in loosened garlands. Elsewhere a corner seemed to be reserved for the commoner
kinds of lily, of a neat pink or white like rocket-flowers,
washed clean like porcelain with housewifely care while, a
little farther again, others, pressed close together in a veritable
floating flower-bed, suggested garden pansies that had settled
here like butterflies and were fluttering their blue and burnished wings over the transparent depths of this watery
garden—this celestial garden, too, for it gave the flowers a
soil of a colour more precious, more moving than their own,
and, whether sparkling beneath the water-lilies in the afternoon in a kaleidoscope of silent, watchful and mobile contentment, or glowing, towards evening, like some distant haven,
with the roseate dreaminess of the setting sun, ceaselessly
changing yet remaining always in harmony, around the less
mutable colours of the flowers themselves, with all that is
most profound, most evanescent, most mysterious—all that
is infinite—in the passing hour, it seemed to have made them
blossom in the sky itself.

After leaving this park the Vivonne began to flow again more swiftly. How often have I watched, and longed to imitate when I should be free to live as I chose, a rower who had shipped his oars and lay flat on his back in the bottom of his boat, letting it drift with the current, seeing nothing but the sky gliding slowly by above him, his face aglow with a foretaste of happiness and peace!

We would sit down among the irises at the water's edge. In the holiday sky an idle cloud languorously dawdled. From time to time, oppressed by boredom, a carp would heave itself out of the water with an anxious gasp. It was time for our picnic. Before starting homewards we would sit there for a long time, eating fruit and bread and chocolate, on the grass over which came to us, faint, horizontal, but dense and metallic still, echoes of the bells of Saint-Hilaire, which had not melted into the air they had traversed for so long, and, ribbed by the successive palpitation of all their sound-waves, throbbed as they grazed the flowers at our feet.

Sometimes, at the water's edge and surrounded by trees, we would come upon a house of the kind called "pleasure houses," lonely and secluded, seeing nothing of the world save the river which bathed its feet. A young woman whose pensive face and elegant veils did not suggest a local origin, and who had doubtless come, in the popular phrase, "to bury herself" there, to taste the bitter sweetness of knowing that her name, and still more the name of him whose heart she had once held but had been unable to keep, were unknown there, stood framed in a window from which she had no outlook beyond the boat that was moored beside her door. She raised her eyes listlessly on hearing, through the trees that lined the bank, the voices of passers-by of whom, before they came in sight, she might be certain that never had they known, nor ever would know, the faithless lover, that nothing in their past lives bore his imprint, and nothing in their future would have occasion to receive it. One felt that in her renunciation of life she had deliberately abandoned those places in which she might at least have been able to see the man she loved, for others where he had never trod. And I watched her, returning from some walk along a path where she knew that he would not appear, drawing from her resigned hands long and uselessly elegant gloves.

Never, in the course of our walks along the "Guermantes way," were we able to penetrate as far as the source of the Vivonne, of which I had often thought and which had in my mind so abstract, so ideal an existence that I had been as surprised when someone told me that it was actually to be found in the same department, at a given number of miles from Combray, as I had been when I learned that there was another fixed point somewhere on the earth's surface, where, according to the ancients, opened the jaws of Hell. Nor could we ever get as far as that other goal which I so longed to reach, Guermantes itself. I knew that it was the residence of the Duc and Duchesse de Guermantes, I knew that they were real personages who did actually exist, but whenever I thought about them I pictured them either in tapestry, like the Comtesse de Guermantes in the "Coronation of Esther" which hung in our church, or else in iridescent colours, like Gilbert the Bad in the stained glass window where he changed from cabbage green, when I was dipping my fingers in the holy water stoup, to plum blue when I had reached our row of chairs, or again altogether impalpable, like the image of Geneviève de Brabant, ancestress of the Guermantes family, which the magic lantern sent wandering over the curtains of my room or flung aloft upon the ceiling—in short, invariably wrapped in the mystery of the Merovingian age and bathed, as in a sunset, in the amber light which glowed from the resounding syllable "antes." And if in spite of that they were for me, in their capacity as a duke and duchess, real people, though of an unfamiliar kind, this ducal personality of theirs was on the other hand enormously distended, immaterialised, so as to encircle and contain that Guermantes of which they were duke and duchess, all that sunlit "Guermantes way" of our walks, the course of the Vivonne, its water-lilies and its overshadowing trees, and an endless series of summer afternoons. And I knew that they bore not only the title of Duc and Duchesse de Guermantes, but that since the fourteenth century, when, after vain attempts to conquer its earlier lords in battle, they had allied themselves to them by marriage and so become Counts of Combray, the first citizens, consequently, of the place, and yet the only ones who did not reside in it—Comtes de Combray, possessing Combray, threading it on their string of names and titles, absorbing it in their personalities, and imbued, no doubt, with that strange and pious melancholy which was peculiar to Combray; proprietors of the town, though not of any particular house there; dwelling, presumably, outside, in the street, between heaven and earth, like that Gilbert de Guermantes of whom I could see, in the stained glass of the apse of Saint-Hilaire, only the reverse side in dull black lacquer, if I raised my eyes to look for him on my way to Camus's for a packet of salt.

And then it happened that, along the "Guermantes way," I sometimes passed beside well-watered little enclosures, over whose hedges rose clusters of dark blossom. I would stop, hoping to gain some precious addition to my experience, for I seemed to have before my eyes a fragment of that fluvial country which I had longed so much to see and know since coming upon a description of it by one of my favourite authors. And it was with that story-book land, with its imagined soil intersected by a hundred bubbling watercourses, that Guermantes, changing its aspect in my mind, became identified, after I heard Dr Percepied speak of the flowers and the charming rivulets and fountains that were to be seen there in the ducal park. I used to dream that Mme de Guermantes, taking a sudden capricious fancy to me, invited me there, that all day long she stood fishing for trout by my side. And when evening came, holding my hand in hers, as we passed by the little gardens of her vassals she would point out to me the flowers that leaned their red and purple spikes along the tops of the low walls, and would teach me all their names. She would make me tell her, too, all about the poems that I intended to compose. And these dreams reminded me that, since I wished some day to become a writer, it was high time to decide what sort of books I was going to write. But as soon as I asked myself the question, and tried to discover some subject to which I could impart a philosophical significance of infinite value, my mind would stop like a clock, my consciousness would be faced with a blank, I would feel either that I was

wholly devoid of talent or that perhaps some malady of the
brain was hindering its development. Sometimes I would
rely on my father to settle it all for me. He was so powerful,
in such high favour with people in office, that he made it
possible for us to transgress laws which Françoise had taught
me to regard as more ineluctable than the laws of life and
death, as when we were allowed to postpone for a year the
compulsory repointing of the walls of our house, alone among
all the houses in that part of Paris, or when he obtained permission from the Minister for Mme Sazerat's son, who had
been ordered to some watering-place, to take his baccalaureate
two months in advance, among the candidates whose surnames
began with "A," instead of having to wait his turn as an "S."
If I had fallen seriously ill, if I had been captured by brigands,
convinced that my father's understanding with the supreme
powers was too complete, that his letters of introduction to
the Almighty were too irresistible for my illness or captivity
to turn out to be anything but vain illusions, in which no
danger actually threatened me, I should have awaited with
perfect composure the inevitable hour of my return to comfortable realities, of my deliverance from bondage or restora-
tion to health; and perhaps this lack of genius, this black cavity
which gaped in my mind when I ransacked it for the theme of
my future writings, was itself no more than an insubstantial
illusion, and would vanish with the intervention of my father,
who must have agreed with the Government and with Provi-
dence that I should be the foremost writer of the day. But at
other times, while my parents were growing impatient at
seeing me loiter behind instead of following them, my present
life, instead of seeming an artificial creation of my father's
which he could modify as he chose, appeared, on the contrary,
to be comprised in a larger reality which had not been created
for my benefit, from whose judgments there was no appeal,
within which I had no friend or ally, and beyond which no
further possibilities lay concealed. It seemed to me then that I
existed in the same manner as all other men, that I must grow
old, that I must die like them, and that among them I was to
be distinguished merely as one of those who have no aptitude
for writing. And so, utterly despondent, I renounced literature

for ever, despite the encouragement Bloch had given me. This intimate, spontaneous feeling, this sense of the nullity of my intellect, prevailed against all the flattering words that might be lavished upon me, as a wicked man whose good deeds are praised by all is gnawed by secret remorse.

One day my mother said to me: "You're always talking about Mme de Guermantes. Well, Dr Percepied did a great deal for her when she was ill four years ago, and so she's coming to Combray for his daughter's wedding. You'll be able to see her in church." It was from Dr Percepied, as it happened, that I had heard most about Mme de Guermantes, and he had even shown us the number of an illustrated paper in which she was depicted in the costume she had worn at a fancy dress ball given by the Princesse de Léon.

Suddenly, during the nuptial mass, the verger, by moving to one side, enabled me to see in one of the chapels a fair-haired lady with a large nose, piercing blue eyes, a billowy scarf of mauve silk, glossy and new and bright, and a little pimple at the corner of her nose. And because on the surface of her face, which was red, as though she had been very hot, I could discern, diluted and barely perceptible, fragments of resemblance with the portrait that had been shown to me; because, more especially, the particular features which I remarked in this lady, if I attempted to catalogue them, formulated themselves in precisely the same terms—*a large nose*, *blue eyes*—as Dr Percepied had used when describing in my presence the Duchesse de Guermantes, I said to myself: "This lady is like the Duchesse de Guermantes." Now the chapel from which she was following the service was that of Gilbert the Bad, beneath the flat tombstones of which, yellowed and bulging like cells of honey in a comb, rested the bones of the old Counts of Brabant; and I remembered having heard it said that this chapel was reserved for the Guermantes family, whenever any of its members came to attend a ceremony at Combray; hence there was only one woman resembling the portrait of Mme de Guermantes who on that day, the very day on which she was expected to come there, could conceivably be sitting in that chapel: it was she! My disappointment was immense. It arose from my not having borne in mind, when I

thought of Mme de Guermantes, that I was picturing her to
myself in the colours of a tapestry or a stained-glass window,
as living in another century, as being of another substance
than the rest of the human race. Never had it occurred to me
that she might have a red face, a mauve scarf like Mme Sazerat;
and the oval curve of her cheeks reminded me so strongly of
people whom I had seen at home that the suspicion crossed
my mind (though it was immediately banished) that in her
causal principle, in the molecules of her physical composition,
this lady was perhaps not substantially the Duchesse de
Guermantes, but that her body, in ignorance of the name that
people had given it, belonged to a certain female type which
included also the wives of doctors and tradesmen. "So that's
Mme de Guermantes—that's all she is!" were the words underlying the attentive and astonished expression with which I
gazed upon this image which, naturally enough, bore no
resemblance to those that had so often, under the same title of
"Mme de Guermantes," appeared in my dreams, since it had
not, like the others, been formed arbitrarily by myself but had
leapt to my eyes for the first time only a moment ago, here in
church; an image which was not of the same nature, was not
colourable at will like those others that allowed themselves to
be impregnated with the amber hue of a sonorous syllable,
but was so real that everything, down to the fiery little spot
at the corner of her nose, attested to her subjection to the laws
of life, as, in a transformation scene on the stage, a crease in
the fairy's dress, a quivering of her tiny finger, betray the
physical presence of a living actress, whereas we were uncertain, till then, whether we were not looking merely at a
projection from a lantern.

But at the same time, I was endeavouring to apply to this
image, which the prominent nose, the piercing eyes pinned
down and fixed in my field of vision (perhaps because it was
they that had first struck it, that had made the first impression
on its surface, before I had had time to wonder whether the
woman who thus appeared before me might possibly be Mme
de Guermantes), to this fresh and unchanging image, the idea:
"It's Mme de Guermantes"; but I succeeded only in making
the idea pass between me and the image, as though they were

two discs moving in separate planes with a space between.
But this Mme de Guermantes of whom I had so often dreamed,
now that I could see that she had a real existence independent
of myself, acquired an even greater power over my imagination, which, paralysed for a moment by contact with a reality
so different from what it had expected, began to react and to
say to me: "Great and glorious before the days of Charlemagne,
the Guermantes had the right of life and death over their
vassals; the Duchesse de Guermantes descends from Geneviève
de Brabant. She does not know, nor would she consent to
know, any of the people who are here to-day."

And then—oh, marvellous independence of the human gaze,
tied to the human face by a cord so loose, so long, so elastic
that it can stray alone as far as it may choose—while Mme de
Guermantes sat in the chapel above the tombs of her dead
ancestors, her gaze wandered here and there, rose to the capitals
of the pillars, and even rested momentarily upon myself, like
a ray of sunlight straying down the nave, but a ray of sunlight
which, at the moment when I received its caress, appeared
conscious of where it fell. As for Mme de Guermantes herself,
since she remained motionless, sitting like a mother who affects
not to notice the mischievous impudence and the indiscreet
advances of her children when, in the course of their play,
they accost people whom she does not know, it was impossible
for me to determine whether, in the careless detachment of
her soul, she approved or condemned the vagrancy of her eyes.

I felt it to be important that she should not leave the church
before I had been able to look at her for long enough, reminding myself that for years past I had regarded the sight of her as
a thing eminently to be desired, and I kept my eyes fixed on
her, as though by gazing at her I should be able to carry away
and store up inside myself the memory of that prominent
nose, those red cheeks, of all those details which struck me as
so many precious, authentic and singular items of information
with regard to her face. And now that all the thoughts I
brought to bear upon it (especially, perhaps—a form of the
instinct of self-preservation with which we guard everything
that is best in ourselves—the familiar desire not to have been
disappointed) made me think it beautiful, and I set her once

again (since they were one and the same person, this lady
who sat before me and that Duchesse de Guermantes whom I
had hitherto conjured up in my imagination) apart from that
common run of humanity with which the actual sight of her
in the flesh had made me for a moment confound her, I grew
indignant when I heard people saying in the congregation
round me: "She's better looking than Mme Sazerat" or "than
Mlle Vinteuil," as though she was in any way comparable
with them. And my eyes resting upon her fair hair, her blue
eyes, the lines of her neck, and overlooking the features which
might have reminded me of the faces of other women, I
cried out within myself as I admired this deliberately unfinished
sketch: "How lovely she is! What true nobility! It is indeed a
proud Guermantes, the descendant of Geneviève de Brabant,
that I have before me!" And the attention which I focused on
her face succeeded in isolating it so completely that to-day,
when I call that marriage ceremony to mind, I find it impossible to visualise any single person who was present except
her, and the verger who answered me in the affirmative when
I inquired whether the lady was indeed Mme de Guermantes.
But I can see her still quite clearly, especially at the moment
when the procession filed into the sacristy, which was lit up
by the intermittent warm sunshine of a windy and rainy day
and in which Mme de Guermantes found herself in the midst
of all those Combray people whose names she did not even
know, but whose inferiority proclaimed her own supremacy
too loudly for her not to feel sincerely benevolent towards
them, and whom she might count on impressing even more
forcibly by virtue of her simplicity and graciousness. And so,
since she could not bring into play the deliberate glances,
charged with a definite meaning, which one directs towards
people one knows, but must allow her absent-minded thoughts
to flow continuously from her eyes in a stream of blue light
which she was powerless to contain, she was anxious not to
embarrass or to appear to be disdainful of those humbler
mortals whom it encountered on its way, on whom it was
constantly falling. I can still see, above her mauve scarf,
puffed and silky, the gentle astonishment in her eyes, to which
she had added, without daring to address it to anyone in

particular, but so that everyone might enjoy his share of it, a rather shy smile as of a sovereign lady who seems to be making an apology for her presence among the vassals whom she loves. This smile fell upon me, who had never taken my eyes off her. And remembering the glance which she had let fall upon me during mass, blue as a ray of sunlight that had penetrated the window of Gilbert the Bad, I said to myself: "She must have taken notice of me." I fancied that I had found favour in her eyes, that she would continue to think of me after she had left the church, and would perhaps feel sad that evening, at Guermantes, because of me. And at once I fell in love with her, for if it is sometimes enough to make us love a woman that she should look on us with contempt, as I supposed Mlle Swann to have done, and that we should think that she can never be ours, sometimes, too, it is enough that she should look on us kindly, as Mme de Guermantes was doing, and that we should think of her as almost ours already. Her eyes waxed blue as a periwinkle flower, impossible to pluck, yet dedicated by her to me; and the sun, bursting out again from behind a threatening cloud and darting the full force of its rays on to the Square and into the sacristy, shed a geranium glow over the red carpet laid down for the wedding, across which Mme de Guermantes was smilingly advancing, and covered its woollen texture with a nap of rosy velvet, a bloom of luminosity, that sort of tenderness, of solemn sweetness in the pomp of a joyful celebration, which characterise certain pages of *Lohengrin*, certain paintings by Carpaccio, and make us understand how Baudelaire was able to apply to the sound of the trumpet the epithet "delicious."

How often, after that day, in the course of my walks along the Guermantes way, and with what an intensified melancholy, did I reflect on my lack of qualification for a literary career, and abandon all hope of ever becoming a famous author. The regrets that I felt for this, as I lingered behind to muse awhile on my own, made me suffer so acutely that, in order to banish them, my mind of its own accord, by a sort of inhibition in the face of pain, ceased entirely to think of verse-making, of fiction, of the poetic future on which my lack of talent precluded me from counting. Then, quite independently of all these literary preoccupations and in no way connected with them, suddenly a roof, a gleam of sunlight on a stone, the smell of a path would make me stop still, to enjoy the special pleasure that each of them gave me, and also because they appeared to be concealing, beyond what my eyes could see, something which they invited me to come and take but which despite all my efforts I never managed to discover. Since I felt that this something was to be found in them, I would stand there motionless, looking, breathing, endeavouring to penetrate with my mind beyond the thing seen or smelt. And if I then had to hasten after my grandfather, to continue my walk, I would try to recapture them by closing my eyes; I would concentrate on recalling exactly the line of the roof, the colour of the stone, which, without my being able to understand why, had seemed to me to be bursting, ready to open, to yield up to me the secret treasure of which they were themselves no more than the lids. It was certainly not impressions of this kind that could restore the hope I had lost of succeeding one day in becoming an author and poet, for each of them was associated with some material object devoid of intellectual value and suggesting no abstract truth. But at least they gave me an unreasoning pleasure, the illusion of a sort of fecundity, and thereby distracted me from the tedium, from the sense of my own impotence which I had felt whenever I had sought a philosophic theme for some great literary work. But so arduous was the task imposed on my conscience by these impressions of form or scent or colour—to try to perceive what lay hidden beneath them—that I was not long in seeking an excuse which would allow me to relax so strenuous an effort and to spare myself the fatigue that it involved. As good luck would have it, my parents would call me; I felt that I did not, for the moment, enjoy the tranquillity necessary for the successful pursuit of my researches, and that it would be better to think no more of the matter until I reached home, and not to exhaust myself in the meantime to no purpose. And so I would concern myself no longer with the mystery that lay hidden in a shape or a perfume, quite at ease in my mind since I was taking it home with me, protected by its visible covering which I had imprinted on my mind and beneath which I

should find it still alive, like the fish which, on days when I
had been allowed to go out fishing, I used to carry back in my
basket, covered by a layer of grass which kept them cool and
fresh. Having reached home I would begin to think of something else, and so my mind would become littered (as my room
was with the flowers that I had gathered on my walks, or the
odds and ends that people had given me) with a mass of
disparate images—the play of sunlight on a stone, a roof, the
sound of a bell, the smell of fallen leaves—beneath which the
reality I once sensed, but never had the will-power to discover
and bring to light, has long since perished. Once, however,
when we had prolonged our walk far beyond its ordinary
limits, and so had been very glad to be overtaken half way
home, as afternoon darkened into evening, by Dr Percepied
who, driving by at full speed in his carriage, had seen and
recognised us, stopped, and made us jump in beside him, I
received an impression of this sort which I did not abandon
without getting to the bottom of it to some extent. I had been
set on the box beside the coachman, and we were going like
the wind because the doctor had still, before returning to
Combray, to call at Martinville-le-Sec to see a patient at whose
door it was agreed that we should wait for him. At a bend in
the road I experienced, suddenly, that special pleasure which
was unlike any other, on catching sight of the twin steeples of
Martinville, bathed in the setting sun and constantly changing
their position with the movement of the carriage and the
windings of the road, and then of a third steeple, that of
Vieuxvicq, which, although separated from them by a hill
and a valley, and rising from rather higher ground in the
distance, appeared none the less to be standing by their side.

In noticing and registering the shape of their spires, their
shifting lines, the sunny warmth of their surfaces, I felt that I
was not penetrating to the core of my impression, that
something more lay behind that mobility, that luminosity,
something which they seemed at once to contain and to
conceal.

The steeples appeared so distant, and we seemed to be
getting so little nearer them, that I was astonished when, a
few minutes later, we drew up outside the church of Martinville.

I did not know the reason for the pleasure I had felt on seeing them upon the horizon, and the business of trying to discover that reason seemed to me irksome; I wanted to store away in my mind those shifting, sunlit planes and, for the time being, to think of them no more. And it is probable that, had I done so, those two steeples would have gone to join the medley of trees and roofs and scents and sounds I had noticed and set apart because of the obscure pleasure they had given me which I had never fully explored. I got down from the box to talk to my parents while we waited for the doctor to reappear. Then it was time to set off again, and I resumed my seat, turning my head to look back once more at the steeples, of which, a little later, I caught a farewell glimpse at a turn in the road. The coachman, who seemed little inclined for conversation, having barely acknowledged my remarks, I was obliged, in default of other company, to fall back on my own, and to attempt to recapture the vision of my steeples. And presently their outlines and their sunlit surfaces, as though they had been a sort of rind, peeled away; something of what they had concealed from me became apparent; a thought came into my mind which had not existed for me a moment earlier, framing itself in words in my head; and the pleasure which the first sight of them had given me was so greatly enhanced that, overpowered by a sort of intoxication, I could no longer think of anything else. At that moment, as we were already some way from Martinville, turning my head I caught sight of them again, quite black this time, for the sun had meanwhile set. From time to time a turn in the road would sweep them out of sight; then they came into view for the last time, and finally I could see them no more.

Without admitting to myself that what lay hidden behind the steeples of Martinville must be something analogous to a pretty phrase, since it was in the form of words which gave me pleasure that it had appeared to me, I borrowed a pencil and some paper from the doctor, and in spite of the jolting of the carriage, to appease my conscience and to satisfy my enthusiasm, composed the following little fragment, which I have since discovered and now reproduce with only a slight revision here and there.

Alone, rising from the level of the plain, and seemingly lost in
that expanse of open country, the twin steeples of Martinville rose
towards the sky. Presently we saw three: springing into position
in front of them with a bold leap, a third, dilatory steeple, that of
Vieuxvicq, had come to join them. The minutes passed, we were
travelling fast, and yet the three steeples were always a long way
ahead of us, like three birds perched upon the plain, motionless
and conspicuous in the sunlight. Then the steeple of Vieuxvicq
drew aside, took its proper distance, and the steeples of Martinville
remained alone, gilded by the light of the setting sun which, even
at that distance, I could see playing and smiling upon their sloping
sides. We had been so long in approaching them that I was thinking
of the time that must still elapse before we could reach them when,
of a sudden, the carriage turned a corner and set us down at their
feet; and they had flung themselves so abruptly in our path that
we had barely time to stop before being dashed against the porch.

We resumed our journey. We had left Martinville some little
time, and the village, after accompanying us for a few seconds,
had already disappeared, when, lingering alone on the horizon to
watch our flight, its steeples and that of Vieuxvicq waved once
again their sun-bathed pinnacles in token of farewell. Sometimes
one would withdraw, so that the other two might watch us for a
moment still; then the road changed direction, they veered in the
evening light like three golden pivots, and vanished from my sight.
But a little later, when we were already close to Combray, the sun
having set meanwhile, I caught sight of them for the last time, far
away, and seeming no more now than three flowers painted upon
the sky above the low line of the fields. They made me think, too,
of three maidens in a legend, abandoned in a solitary place over
which night had begun to fall; and as we drew away from them at
a gallop, I could see them timidly seeking their way, and after some
awkward, stumbling movements of their noble silhouettes, drawing
close to one another, gliding one behind another, forming now
against the still rosy sky no more than a single dusky shape, charming and resigned, and so vanishing in the night.

I never thought again of this page, but at the moment when,
in the corner of the box-seat where the doctor's coachman was
in the habit of stowing in a hamper the poultry he had bought
at Martinville market, I had finished writing it, I was so filled
with happiness, I felt that it had so entirely relieved my mind
of its obsession with the steeples and the mystery which lay

behind them, that, as though I myself were a hen and had just laid an egg, I began to sing at the top of my voice.

All day long, during these walks, I had been able to muse upon the pleasure of being the friend of the Duchesse de Guermantes, of fishing for trout, of drifting in a boat on the Vivonne; and, greedy for happiness, I asked nothing more from life in such moments than that it should consist always of a series of joyous afternoons. But when, on our way home, I had caught sight of a farm on the left of the road, at some distance from two other farms which were themselves close together, from which, to return to Combray, we need only turn down an avenue of oaks bordered on one side by a series of orchard-closes planted at regular intervals with apple-trees which cast upon the ground, when they were lit by the setting sun, the Japanese stencil of their shadows, suddenly my heart would begin to pound, for I knew that in half an hour we should be at home, and that, as was the rule on days when we had taken the Guermantes way and dinner was in consequence served later than usual, I should be sent to bed as soon as I had swallowed my soup, and my mother, kept at table just as though there had been company to dinner, would not come upstairs to say good night to me in bed. The zone of melancholy which I then entered was as distinct from the zone in which I had been bounding with joy a moment before as, in certain skies, a band of pink is separated, as though by a line invisibly ruled, from a band of green or black. You may see a bird flying across the pink; it draws near the border-line, touches it, enters and is lost upon the black. I was now so remote from the longings by which I had just been absorbed—to go to Guermantes, to travel, to live a life of happiness—that their fulfilment would have afforded me no pleasure. How readily would I have sacrificed them all, just to be able to cry all night long in Mamma's arms! Quivering with emotion, I could not take my anguished eyes from my mother's face, which would not appear that evening in the bedroom where I could see myself already lying, and I wished only that I were lying dead. And this state would persist until the morrow, when, the rays of morning leaning their bars of light, like the rungs of the gardener's ladder, against the wall overgrown with nasturtiums,

which clambered up it as far as my window-sill, I would leap
out of bed to run down at once into the garden, with no
thought of the fact that evening must return, and with it the
hour when I must leave my mother. And so it was from the
Guermantes way that I learned to distinguish between these
states which reign alternately within me, during certain periods,
going so far as to divide each day between them, the one
returning to dispossess the other with the regularity of a fever:
contiguous, and yet so foreign to one another, so devoid of
means of communication, that I can no longer understand,
or even picture to myself, in one state what I have desired or
dreaded or accomplished in the other.

So the "Méséglise way" and the "Guermantes way" remain
for me linked with many of the little incidents of the life
which, of all the various lives we lead concurrently, is the
most episodic, the most full of vicissitudes; I mean the life
of the mind. Doubtless it progresses within us imperceptibly,
and we had for a long time been preparing for the discovery
of the truths which have changed its meaning and its aspect,
have opened new paths for us; but that preparation was
unconscious; and for us those truths date only from the day,
from the minute when they became apparent. The flowers
which played then among the grass, the water which rippled
past in the sunshine, the whole landscape which surrounded
their apparition still lingers around the memory of them with
its unconscious or unheeding countenance; and, certainly,
when they were contemplated at length by that humble passer-
by, by that dreaming child—as the face of a king is contemplated by a memorialist buried in the crowd—that piece of
nature, that corner of a garden could never suppose that it
would be thanks to him that they would be elected to survive
in all their most ephemeral details; and yet the scent of hawthorn which flits along the hedge from which, in a little while,
the dog-roses will have banished it, a sound of echoless
footsteps on a gravel path, a bubble formed against the side
of a water-plant by the current of the stream and instantaneously
bursting—all these my exaltation of mind has borne along with
it and kept alive through the succession of the years, while all
around them the paths have vanished and those who trod

them, and even the memory of those who trod them, are dead. Sometimes the fragment of landscape thus transported into the present will detach itself in such isolation from all associations that it floats uncertainly in my mind like a flowering Delos, and I am unable to say from what place, from what time—perhaps, quite simply, from what dream—it comes. But it is pre-eminently as the deepest layer of my mental soil, as the firm ground on which I still stand, that I regard the Méséglise and Guermantes ways. It is because I believed in things and in people while I walked along those paths that the things and the people they made known to me are the only ones that I still take seriously and that still bring me joy. Whether it is because the faith which creates has ceased to exist in me, or because reality takes shape in the memory alone, the flowers that people show me nowadays for the first time never seem to me to be true flowers. The Méséglise way with its lilacs, its hawthorns, its cornflowers, its poppies, its apple-trees, the Guermantes way with its river full of tadpoles, its water-lilies and its buttercups, constituted for me for all time the image of the landscape in which I should like to live, in which my principal requirements are that I may go fishing, drift idly in a boat, see the ruins of gothic fortifications, and find among the cornfields—like Saint-André-des-Champs—an old church, monumental, rustic, and golden as a haystack; and the cornflowers, the hawthorns, the apple-trees which I may still happen, when I travel, to encounter in the fields, because they are situated at the same depth, on the level of my past life, at once establish contact with my heart. And yet, because there is an element of individuality in places, if I were seized with a desire to revisit the Guermantes way, it would not be satisfied were I to be led to the banks of a river in which there were water-lilies as beautiful as, or even more beautiful than, those in the Vivonne, any more than on my return home in the evening—at the hour when there awakened in me that anguish which later transfers itself to the passion of love, and may even become its inseparable companion—I should have wished for a mother more beautiful and more intelligent than my own to come and say good night to me. No: just as the one thing necessary to send me to sleep contented—in that

untroubled peace which no mistress, in later years, has ever
been able to give me, since one has doubts of them even at
the moment when one believes in them, and never can possess
their hearts as I used to receive, in a kiss, my mother's heart,
whole and entire, without qualm or reservation, without the
smallest residue of an intention that was not for me alone—
was that it should be she who came to me, that it should be
her face that leaned over me, her face on which there was
something below the eye that was apparently a blemish, and
that I loved as much as all the rest—so what I want to see
again is the Guermantes way as I knew it, with the farm that
stood a little apart from the two neighbouring farms, huddled
side by side, at the entrance to the oak avenue; those meadows
in which, when they are burnished by the sun to the lumines-
cence of a pond, the leaves of the apple-trees are reflected;
that whole landscape whose individuality grips me sometimes
at night, in my dreams, with a power that is almost uncanny,
but of which I can discover no trace when I awake.

No doubt, by virtue of having permanently and indissolubly
united so many different impressions in my mind, simply
because they made me experience them at the same time, the
Méséglise and Guermantes ways left me exposed, in later life,
to much disillusionment and even to many mistakes. For often
I have wished to see a person again without realising that it
was simply because that person recalled to me a hedge of hawthorns in blossom, and I have been led to believe, and to make
someone else believe, in a renewal of affection, by what was
no more than an inclination to travel. But by the same token,
and by their persistence in those of my present-day impressions
to which they can still be linked, they give those impressions a
foundation, a depth, a dimension lacking from the rest. They
invest them, too, with a charm, a significance which is for me
alone. When, on a summer evening, the melodious sky growls
like a tawny lion, and everyone is complaining of the storm,
it is the memory of the Méséglise way that makes me stand
alone in ecstasy, inhaling, through the noise of the falling rain,
the lingering scent of invisible lilacs.

Thus would I often lie until morning, dreaming of the old days at Combray, of my melancholy and wakeful evenings there, of other days besides, the memory of which had been more recently restored to me by the taste—by what would have been called at Combray the "perfume"—of a cup of tea, and, by an association of memories, of a story which, many years after I had left the little place, had been told me of a love affair in which Swann had been involved before I was born, with a precision of detail which it is often easier to obtain for the lives of people who have been dead for centuries than for those of our own most intimate friends, an accuracy which it seems as impossible to attain as it seemed impossible to speak from one town to another, before we knew of the contrivance by which that impossibility has been overcome. All these memories, superimposed upon one another, now formed a single mass, but had not so far coalesced that I could not discern between them—between my oldest, my instinctive memories, and those others, inspired more recently by a taste or "perfume," and finally those which were actually the memories of another person from whom I had acquired them at second hand—if not real fissures, real geological faults, at least that veining, that variegation of colouring, which in certain rocks, in certain blocks of marble, points to differences of origin, age, and formation.

It is true that, when morning drew near, I would long have settled the brief uncertainty of my waking dream; I would know in what room I was actually lying, would have reconstructed it around me in the darkness, and—fixing my bearings by memory alone, or with the assistance of a feeble glimmer of light at the foot of which I placed the curtains and the window—would have reconstructed it complete and furnished, as an architect and an upholsterer might do, keeping the original plan of the doors and windows; would have replaced the mirrors and set the chest-of-drawers on its accustomed site. But scarcely had daylight itself—and no longer the gleam from a last, dying ember on a brass curtain-rod which I had mistaken for daylight—traced across the darkness, as with a stroke of chalk across a blackboard, its first white, correcting ray, than the window, with its curtains, would leave the frame of the doorway in which I had erroneously placed it, while, to make room for it, the writing-table, which my memory had clumsily installed where the window ought to be, would hurry off at full speed, thrusting before it the fireplace and sweeping aside the wall of the passage; a little courtyard would occupy the place where, a moment earlier, my dressing-room had lain, and the dwelling-place which I had built up for myself in the darkness would have gone to join all those other dwellings glimpsed in the whirlpool of awakening, put to flight by that pale sign traced above my window-curtains by the uplifted forefinger of dawn.

SWANN IN LOVE

To admit you to the "little nucleus," the "little group," the "little clan" at the Verdurins', one condition sufficed, but that one was indispensable: you must give tacit adherence to a Creed one of whose articles was that the young pianist whom Mme Verdurin had taken under her patronage that year and of whom she said "Really, it oughtn't to be allowed, to play Wagner as well as that!" licked both Planté and Rubinstein hollow, and that Dr Cottard was a more brilliant diagnostician than Potain. Each "new recruit" whom the Verdurins failed to persuade that the evenings spent by other people, in other houses than theirs, were as dull as ditch-water, saw himself banished forthwith. Women being in this respect more rebellious than men, more reluctant to lay aside all worldly curiosity and the desire to find out for themselves whether other salons might not sometimes be as entertaining, and the Verdurins feeling, moreover, that this critical spirit and this demon of frivolity might, by their contagion, prove fatal to the orthodoxy of the little church, they had been obliged to expel, one after another, all those of the "faithful" who were of the female sex.

Apart from the doctor's young wife, they were reduced almost exclusively that season (for all that Mme Verdurin herself was a thoroughly virtuous woman who came of a respectable middle-class family, excessively rich and wholly undistinguished, with which she had gradually and of her own accord severed all connection) to a young woman almost of the demi-monde, a Mme de Crécy, whom Mme Verdurin called by her Christian name, Odette, and pronounced a "love," and to the pianist's aunt, who looked as though she had, at one period, "answered the bell": ladies quite ignorant of society, who in their naïvety had so easily been led to believe that the Princesse de Sagan and the Duchesse de Guermantes were obliged to pay large sums of money to other

poor wretches in order to have anyone at their dinner-parties,
that if somebody had offered to procure them an invitation to
the house of either of those noblewomen, the ex-doorkeeper
and the woman of "easy virtue" would have contemptuously
declined.

The Verdurins never invited you to dinner; you had your
"place laid" there. There was never any programme for the
evening's entertainment. The young pianist would play, but
only if "the spirit moved him," for no one was forced to do
anything, and, as M. Verdurin used to say: "We're all friends
here. Liberty Hall, you know!"

If the pianist suggested playing the Ride of the Valkyries
or the Prelude to *Tristan*, Mme Verdurin would protest, not
because the music was displeasing to her, but, on the contrary, because it made too violent an impression on her. "Then
you want me to have one of my headaches? You know quite
well it's the same every time he plays that. I know what I'm in
for. To-morrow, when I want to get up—nothing doing!"
If he was not going to play they talked, and one of the friends
—usually the painter who was in favour there that year—would
"spin," as M. Verdurin put it, "a damned funny yarn that
made 'em all split with laughter," and especially Mme
Verdurin, who had such an inveterate habit of taking literally
the figurative descriptions of her emotions that Dr Cottard
(then a promising young practitioner) had once had to reset
her jaw, which she had dislocated from laughing too much.

Evening dress was barred, because you were all "good
pals" and didn't want to look like the "boring people" who
were to be avoided like the plague and only asked to the big
evenings, which were given as seldom as possible and then
only if it would amuse the painter or make the musician
better known. The rest of the time you were quite happy playing charades and having supper in fancy dress, and there
was no need to mingle any alien ingredient with the little
"clan."

But as the "good pals" came to take a more and more
prominent place in Mme Verdurin's life, the "bores," the
outcasts, grew to include everybody and everything that kept
her friends away from her, that made them sometimes plead

"previous engagements," the mother of one, the professional duties of another, the "little place in the country" or the ill-health of a third. If Dr Cottard felt bound to leave as soon as they rose from table, so as to go back to some patient who was seriously ill, "Who knows," Mme Verdurin would say, "it might do him far more good if you didn't go disturbing him again this evening; he'll have a good night without you; to-morrow morning you can go round early and you'll find him cured." From the beginning of December she was sick with anxiety at the thought that the "faithful" might "defect" on Christmas and New Year's Days. The pianist's aunt insisted that he must accompany her, on the latter, to a family dinner at her mother's.

"You don't suppose she'll die, your mother," exclaimed Mme Verdurin bitterly, "if you don't have dinner with her on New Year's Day, like people in the *provinces*!"

Her uneasiness was kindled again in Holy Week: "Now you, Doctor, you're a sensible, broad-minded man; you'll come of course on Good Friday, just like any other day?" she said to Cottard in the first year of the little "nucleus," in a loud and confident voice, as though there could be no doubt of his answer. But she trembled as she waited for it, for if he did not come she might find herself condemned to dine alone.

"I shall come on Good Friday—to say good-bye to you, for we're off to spend the holidays in Auvergne."

"In Auvergne? To be eaten alive by fleas and all sorts of creatures! A fine lot of good that will do you!" And after a solemn pause: "If you'd only told us, we would have tried to get up a party, and all gone there together in comfort."

And so, too, if one of the "faithful" had a friend, or one of the ladies a young man, who was liable, now and then, to make them miss an evening, the Verdurins, who were not in the least afraid of a woman's having a lover, provided that she had him in their company, loved him in their company and did not prefer him to their company, would say: "Very well, then, bring your friend along." And he would be engaged on probation, to see whether he was willing to have no secrets from Mme Verdurin, whether he was susceptible of being enrolled in the "little clan." If he failed to pass, the faithful one who had introduced him would be taken on one side, and would be tactfully assisted to break with the friend or lover or mistress. But if the test proved satisfactory, the newcomer would in turn be numbered among the "faithful." And so when, that year, the *demi-mondaine* told M. Verdurin that she had made the acquaintance of such a charming man, M. Swann, and hinted that he would very much like to be allowed to come, M. Verdurin carried the request at once to his wife. (He never formed an opinion on any subject until she had formed hers, it being his special function to carry out her wishes and those of the "faithful" generally, which he did with boundless ingenuity.)

"My dear, Mme de Crécy has something to say to you. She would like to bring one of her friends here, a M. Swann. What do you say?"

"Why, as if anybody could refuse anything to a little angel like that. Be quiet; no one asked your opinion. I tell you you're an angel."

"Just as you like," replied Odette, in an affected tone, and then added: "You know I'm not *fishing for compliments*."[8]

"Very well; bring your friend, if he's nice."

Now there was nothing whatsoever in common between the "little nucleus" and the society which Swann frequented, and true socialites would have thought it hardly worth while to occupy so exceptional a position in the fashionable world in order to end up with an introduction to the Verdurins. But Swann was so fond of women that, once he had got to know more or less all the women of the aristocracy and they had nothing more to teach him, he had ceased to regard those naturalisation papers, almost a patent of nobility, which the Faubourg Saint-Germain had bestowed upon him, save as a sort of negotiable bond, a letter of credit with no intrinsic value but which enabled him to improvise a status for himself in some out-of-the-way place in the country, or in some obscure quarter of Paris, where the good-looking daughter of a local squire or town clerk had taken his fancy. For at such times desire, or love, would revive in him a feeling of vanity from which he was now quite free in his everyday life (although it was doubtless this feeling which had originally prompted him towards the career as a man of fashion in which he had squandered his intellectual gifts on frivolous amusements and made use of his erudition in matters of art only to advise society ladies what pictures to buy and how to decorate their houses), which made him eager to shine, in the eyes of any unknown beauty he had fallen for, with an elegance which the name Swann did not in itself imply. And he was most eager when the unknown beauty was in humble circumstances. Just as it is not by other men of intelligence that an intelligent man is afraid of being thought a fool, so it is not by a nobleman but by an oaf that a man of fashion is afraid of finding his social value underrated. Three-quarters of the mental ingenuity and the mendacious boasting squandered ever since the world began by people who are only cheapened thereby, have been aimed at inferiors. And Swann, who behaved simply and casually with a duchess, would tremble for fear of being despised, and would instantly begin to pose, when in the presence of a housemaid.

Unlike so many people who, either from lack of energy or else from a resigned sense of the obligation laid upon them by their social grandeur to remain moored like house-boats to a particular point on the shore of life, abstain from the pleasures which are offered to them outside the wordly situation in which they remain confined until the day of their death, and are content, in the end, to describe as pleasures, for want of any better, those mediocre distractions, that just bearable tedium which it encompasses, Swann did not make an effort to find attractive the women with whom he spent his time, but sought to spend his time with women whom he had already found attractive. And as often as not they were women whose beauty was of a distinctly "common" type, for the physical qualities which he instinctively sought were the direct opposite of those he admired in the women painted or sculpted by his favourite masters. Depth of character, or a melancholy expression, would freeze his senses, which were, however, instantly aroused at the sight of healthy, abundant, rosy flesh.

If on his travels he met a family whom it would have been more correct for him to make no attempt to cultivate, but

among whom he glimpsed a woman possessed of a special
charm that was new to him, to remain on his "high horse"
and to stave off the desire she had kindled in him, to substitute
a different pleasure for the pleasure which he might have tasted
in her company by writing to invite one of his former mistresses
to come and join him, would have seemed to him as cowardly
an abdication in the face of life, as stupid a renunciation of a
new happiness as if, instead of visiting the country where he
was, he had shut himself up in his own rooms and looked at
views of Paris. He did not immure himself in the edifice of
his social relations, but had made of them, so as to be able to
set it up afresh upon new foundations wherever a woman
might take his fancy, one of those collapsible tents which
explorers carry about with them. Any part of it that was not
portable or could not be adapted to some fresh pleasure he
would have given away for nothing, however enviable it
might appear to others. How often had his credit with a
duchess, built up over the years by her desire to ingratiate
herself with him without having found an opportunity to do
so, been squandered in a moment by his calling upon her,
in an indiscreetly worded message, for a recommendation by
telegraph which would put him in touch at once with one of
her stewards whose daughter he had noticed in the country,
just as a starving man might barter a diamond for a crust of
bread. Indeed he would laugh about it afterwards, for there
was in his nature, redeemed by many rare refinements, an
element of caddishness. Then he belonged to that class of
intelligent men who have led a life of idleness, and who seek a
consolation and perhaps an excuse in the notion that their
idleness offers to their intelligence objects as worthy of interest
as any that might be offered by art or learning, the notion that
"Life" contains situations more interesting and more romantic
than all the romances ever written. So, at least, he affirmed,
and had no difficulty in persuading even the most sharp-witted
of his society friends, notably the Baron de Charlus, whom he
liked to entertain with accounts of the intriguing adventures
that had befallen him, such as when he had met a woman in
a train and taken her home with him, before discovering that
she was the sister of a reigning monarch in whose hands were

gathered at that moment all the threads of European politics, of which Swann was thus kept informed in the most delightful fashion, or when, by a complex freak of circumstance, it depended upon the choice which the Conclave was about to make whether he might or might not become the lover of somebody's cook.

It was not only the brilliant phalanx of virtuous dowagers, generals and academicians with whom he was most intimately associated that Swann so cynically compelled to serve him as panders. All his friends were accustomed to receive, from time to time, letters calling on them for a word of recommendation or introduction, with a diplomatic adroitness which, persisting throughout all his successive love affairs and varying pretexts, revealed, more glaringly than the clumsiest indiscretion, a permanent disposition and an identical quest. I used often to be told, many years later, when I began to take an interest in his character because of the similarities which, in wholly different respects, it offered to my own, how, when he used to write to my grandfather (who had not yet become my grandfather, for it was about the time of my birth that Swann's great love affair began, and it made a long interruption in his amatory practices), the latter, recognising his friend's handwriting on the envelope, would exclaim: "Here's Swann asking for something. On guard!" And, either from distrust or from the unconscious spirit of devilry which urges us to offer a thing only to those who do not want it, my grandparents would offer a blunt refusal to the most easily satisfied of his requests, as when he begged them to introduce him to a girl who dined with them every Sunday, and whom they were obliged, whenever Swann mentioned her, to pretend that they no longer saw, although they would be wondering all through the week whom they could invite with her, and often ended up with no one, sooner than get in touch with the man who would so gladly have accepted.

Occasionally a couple of my grandparents' acquaintance, who had been complaining for some time that they no longer saw Swann, would announce with satisfaction, and perhaps with a slight inclination to make my grandparents envious of them, that he had suddenly become as charming as he could

possibly be, and was never out of their house. My grandfather
would not want to shatter their pleasant illusion, but would
look at my grandmother as he hummed the air of:

> What is this mystery?
> I cannot understand it.

or of:

> Fugitive vision . . .

or of:

> In matters such as this
> 'Tis best to close one's eyes.

A few months later, if my grandfather asked Swann's new
friend: "What about Swann? Do you still see as much of him
as ever?" the other's face would fall: "Never mention his
name to me again!"

"But I thought you were such friends . . ."

He had been intimate in this way for several months with
some cousins of my grandmother, dining almost every evening
at their house. Suddenly, and without any warning, he ceased
to appear. They supposed him to be ill, and the lady of the
house was about to send to inquire for him when she found
in the pantry a letter in his hand, which her cook had left by
accident in the housekeeping book. In this he announced that
he was leaving Paris and would not be able to come to the
house again. The cook had been his mistress, and on breaking
off relations she was the only member of the household whom
he had thought it necessary to inform.

But when his mistress of the moment was a woman of rank,
or at least one whose birth was not so lowly nor her position
so irregular that he was unable to arrange for her reception in
"society," then for her sake he would return to it, but only to
the particular orbit in which she moved or into which he had
drawn her. "No good depending on Swann for this evening,"
people would say. "Don't you remember, it's his American's
night at the Opera?" He would secure invitations for her to
the most exclusive salons, to those houses where he himself
went regularly for weekly dinners or for poker; every evening,
after a slight wave imparted to his stiff red hair had tempered
with a certain softness the ardour of his bold green eyes, he

would select a flower for his buttonhole and set out to meet
his mistress at the house of one or other of the women of his
circle; and then, thinking of the affection and admiration which
the fashionable people, by whom he was so highly sought-after
and whom he would meet again there, would lavish on him
in the presence of the woman he loved, he would find a fresh
charm in that worldly existence which had begun to pall, but
whose substance, pervaded and warmly coloured by the bright
flame that now flickered in its midst, seemed to him beautiful
and rare since he had incorporated in it a new love.

But, whereas each of these liaisons, or each of these flirta-
tions, had been the realisation, more or less complete, of a
dream born of the sight of a face or a body which Swann had
spontaneously, without effort on his part, found attractive,
on the contrary when, one evening at the theatre, he was
introduced to Odette de Crécy by an old friend of his, who
had spoken of her as a ravishing creature with whom he might
possibly come to an understanding, but had made her out to
be harder of conquest than she actually was in order to appear
to have done him a bigger favour by the introduction, she
had struck Swann not, certainly, as being devoid of beauty,
but as endowed with a kind of beauty which left him indifferent, which aroused in him no desire, which gave him,
indeed, a sort of physical repulsion, as one of those women of
whom all of us can cite examples, different for each of us,
who are the converse of the type which our senses demand.
Her profile was too sharp, her skin too delicate, her cheekbones were too prominent, her features too tightly drawn,
to be attractive to him. Her eyes were beautiful, but so large
they seemed to droop beneath their own weight, strained the
rest of her face and always made her appear unwell or in a
bad mood. Some time after this introduction at the theatre
she had written to ask Swann whether she might see his
collections, which would very much interest her, "an ignorant
woman with a taste for beautiful things," adding that she
felt she would know him better when once she had seen him
in his "*home*,"[9] where she imagined him to be "so comfortable
with his tea and his books," though she had to admit that she
was surprised that he should live in a neighbourhood which

must be so depressing, and was "not nearly *smart* enough for
such a very *smart* man." And when he allowed her to come she
had said to him as she left how sorry she was to have stayed
so short a time in a house into which she was so glad to have
found her way at last, speaking of him as though he had
meant something more to her than the rest of the people she
knew, and appearing to establish between their two selves a
kind of romantic bond which had made him smile. But at the
time of life, tinged already with disenchantment, which Swann
was approaching, when a man can content himself with being
in love for the pleasure of loving without expecting too much
in return, this mutual sympathy, if it is no longer as in early
youth the goal towards which love inevitably tends, is nevertheless bound to it by so strong an association of ideas that it
may well become the cause of love if it manifests itself first.
In his younger days a man dreams of possessing the heart of
the woman whom he loves; later, the feeling that he possesses a
woman's heart may be enough to make him fall in love with
her. And so, at an age when it would appear—since one seeks
in love before everything else a subjective pleasure—that the
taste for a woman's beauty must play the largest part in it,
love may come into being, love of the most physical kind,
without any foundation in desire. At this time of life one has
already been wounded more than once by the darts of love;
it no longer evolves by itself, obeying its own incomprehensible
and fatal laws, before our passive and astonished hearts.
We come to its aid, we falsify it by memory and by suggestion.
Recognising one of its symptoms, we remember and recreate
the rest. Since we know its song, which is engraved on our
hearts in its entirety, there is no need for a woman to repeat
the opening strains—filled with the admiration which beauty
inspires—for us to remember what follows. And if she begins
in the middle—where hearts are joined and where it sings of
our existing, henceforward, for one another only—we are
well enough attuned to that music to be able to take it up
and follow our partner without hesitation at the appropriate
passage.

Odette de Crécy came again to see Swann; her visits grew
more frequent, and doubtless each visit revived the sense of

disappointment which he felt at the sight of a face whose
details he had somewhat forgotten in the interval, not remembering it as either so expressive or, in spite of her youth,
so faded; he used to regret, while she was talking to him, that
her really considerable beauty was not of the kind which he
spontaneously admired. It must be remarked that Odette's
face appeared thinner and sharper than it actually was, because
the forehead and the upper part of the cheeks, that smooth
and almost plane surface, were covered by the masses of hair
which women wore at that period drawn forward in a fringe,
raised in crimped waves and falling in stray locks over the
ears; while as for her figure—and she was admirably built—it
was impossible to make out its continuity (on account of the
fashion then prevailing, and in spite of her being one of the
best-dressed women in Paris) so much did the corsage, jutting
out as though over an imaginary stomach and ending in a
sharp point, beneath which bulged out the balloon of her
double skirts, give a woman the appearance of being composed
of different sections badly fitted together; to such an extent did
the frills, the flounces, the inner bodice follow quite independently, according to the whim of their designer or the
consistency of their material, the line which led them to the
bows, the festoons of lace, the fringes of dangling jet beads,
or carried them along the busk, but nowhere attached themselves to the living creature, who, according as the architecture
of these fripperies drew them towards or away from her own,
found herself either strait-laced to suffocation or else completely
buried.

But, after Odette had left him, Swann would think with a
smile of her telling how the time would drag until he allowed
her to come again; he remembered the anxious, timid way in
which she had once begged him that it might not be too long,
and the way she had gazed at him then, with a look of shy
entreaty which gave her a touching air beneath the bunches of
artificial pansies fastened in the front of her round bonnet of
white straw, tied with a ribbon of black velvet. "And won't
you," she had ventured, "come just once and have tea with
me?" He had pleaded pressure of work, an essay—which, in
reality, he had abandoned years ago—on Vermeer of Delft.

"I know that I'm quite useless," she had replied, "a pitiful creature like me beside a learned great man like you. I should be like the frog in the fable! And yet I should so much like to learn, to know things, to be initiated. What fun it would be to become a regular bookworm, to bury my nose in a lot of old papers!" she had added, with the self-satisfied air which an elegant woman adopts when she insists that her one desire is to undertake, without fear of soiling her fingers, some grubby task, such as cooking the dinner, "really getting down to it" herself. "You'll only laugh at me, but this painter who stops you from seeing me" (she meant Vermeer), "I've never even heard of him; is he alive still? Can I see any of his things in Paris, so as to have some idea of what's going on behind that great brow which works so hard, that head which I feel sure is always puzzling away about things; to be able to say 'There, that's what he's thinking about!' What a joy it would be to be able to help you with your work."

He had excused himself on the grounds of his fear of forming new friendships, which he gallantly described as his fear of being made unhappy. "You're afraid of affection? How odd that is, when I go about seeking nothing else, and would give my soul to find it!" she had said, so naturally and with such an air of conviction that he had been genuinely touched. "Some woman must have made you suffer. And you think that the rest are all like her. She can't have understood you: you're such an exceptional person. That's what I liked about you from the start; I felt that you weren't like everybody else."

"And then, besides, you too," he had said to her, "I know what women are; you must have a whole heap of things to do, and never any time to spare."

"I? Why, I never have anything to do. I'm always free, and I always will be free if you want me. At whatever hour of the day or night it may suit you to see me, just send for me, and I shall be only too delighted to come. Will you do that? Do you know what would be nice—if I were to introduce you to Mme Verdurin, where I go every evening. Just fancy our meeting there, and my thinking that it was a little for my sake that you had come."

And doubtless, in thus remembering their conversations, in

thinking about her thus when he was alone, he was simply turning over her image among those of countless other women in his romantic day-dreams; but if, thanks to some accidental circumstance (or even perhaps without that assistance, for the circumstance which presents itself at the moment when a mental state, hitherto latent, makes itself felt, may well have had no influence whatsoever upon that state), the image of Odette de Crécy came to absorb the whole of these day-dreams, if the memory of her could no longer be eliminated from them, then her bodily imperfections would no longer be of the least importance, nor would the conformity of her body, more or less than any other, to the requirements of Swann's taste, since, having become the body of the woman he loved, it must henceforth be the only one capable of causing him joy or anguish.

It so happened that my grandfather had known—which was more than could be said of any of their actual acquaintance —the family of these Verdurins. But he had entirely severed his connection with the "young Verdurin," as he called him, considering him more or less to have fallen—though without losing hold of his millions—among the riff-raff of Bohemia. One day he received a letter from Swann asking whether he could put him in touch with the Verdurins: "On guard! on guard!" my grandfather exclaimed as he read it, "I'm not at all surprised; Swann was bound to finish up like this. A nice lot of people! I cannot do what he asks, because in the first place I no longer know the gentleman in question. Besides, there must be a woman in it somewhere, and I never get mixed up in such matters. Ah, well, we shall see some fun if Swann begins running after the young Verdurins."

And on my grandfather's refusal to act as sponsor, it was Odette herself who had taken Swann to the house.

The Verdurins had had dining with them, on the day when Swann made his first appearance, Dr and Mme Cottard, the young pianist and his aunt, and the painter then in favour, and these were joined, in the course of the evening, by a few more of the "faithful."

Dr Cottard was never quite certain of the tone in which he ought to reply to any observation, or whether the speaker was jesting or in earnest. And so by way of precaution he would embellish all his facial expressions with the offer of a conditional, a provisional smile whose expectant subtlety would exonerate him from the charge of being a simpleton, if the remark addressed to him should turn out to have been facetious. But as he must also be prepared to face the alternative, he dared not allow this smile to assert itself positively on his features, and you would see there a perpetually flickering uncertainty, in which could be deciphered the question that he never dared to ask: "Do you really mean that?" He was no more confident of the manner in which he ought to conduct himself in the street, or indeed in life generally, than he was in a drawing-room; and he might be seen greeting passers-by, carriages, and anything that occurred with a knowing smile which absolved his subsequent behaviour of all impropriety, since it proved, if it should turn out unsuited to the occasion, that he was well aware of that, and that if he had assumed a smile, the jest was a secret of his own.

On all those points, however, where a plain question appeared to him to be permissible, the doctor was unsparing in his endeavours to cultivate the wilderness of his ignorance and uncertainty and to perfect his education.

So it was that, following the advice given him by a wise mother on his first coming up to the capital from his provincial home, he would never let pass either a figure of speech or a proper name that was new to him without an effort to secure the fullest information upon it.

As regards figures of speech, he was insatiable in his thirst for knowledge, for, often imagining them to have a more definite meaning than was actually the case, he would want to know what exactly was meant by those which he most frequently heard used: "devilish pretty," "blue blood," "a cat and dog life," "the day of reckoning," "the glass of fashion," "to give a free hand," "to be absolutely floored," and so forth; and in what particular circumstances he himself might make use of them in conversation. Failing these, he would adorn it with puns and other plays on words which he had learned by rote. As for unfamiliar names which were uttered in his hearing, he used merely to repeat them in a questioning tone, which he thought would suffice to procure him explanations for which he would not ostensibly be seeking.

Since he was completely lacking in the critical faculty on which he prided himself in everything, the refinement of good breeding which consists in assuring someone whom you are obliging, without expecting to be believed, that it is really you who are obliged to him, was wasted on Cottard, who took everything he heard in its literal sense. Blind though she was to his faults, Mme Verdurin was genuinely irritated, though she continued to regard him as brilliantly clever, when, after she had invited him to see and hear Sarah Bernhardt from a stage box, and had said politely: "It's so good of you to have come, Doctor, especially as I'm sure you must often have heard Sarah Bernhardt; and besides, I'm afraid we're rather too near the stage," the doctor, who had come into the box with a smile which waited before affirming itself or vanishing from his face until some authoritative person should enlighten him as to the merits of the spectacle, replied: "To be sure, we're far too near the stage, and one is beginning to get sick of Sarah Bernhardt. But you expressed a wish that I should come. And your wish is my command. I'm only too glad to be able to do you this little service. What would one not do to please you, you are so kind." And he went on, "Sarah Bernhardt—she's what they call the Golden Voice, isn't she? They say she sets the house on fire. That's an odd expression, ain't it?" in the hope of an enlightening commentary which, however, was not forthcoming.

"D'you know," Mme Verdurin had said to her husband, "I believe we're on the wrong tack when we belittle what we give to the Doctor. He's a scholar who lives in a world of his own; he has no idea what things are worth, and he accepts everything that we say as gospel."

"I never dared to mention it," M. Verdurin had answered, "but I've noticed the same thing myself." And on the following New Year's Day, instead of sending Dr Cottard a ruby that cost three thousand francs and pretending it was a mere trifle, M. Verdurin bought an artificial stone for three hundred, and let it be understood that it was something almost impossible to match.

When Mme Verdurin had announced that they were to see
M. Swann that evening, "Swann!" the doctor had exclaimed
in a tone rendered brutal by his astonishment, for the smallest
piece of news would always take him utterly unawares though
he imagined himself to be prepared for any eventuality. And
seeing that no one answered him, "Swann! Who on earth is
Swann?" he shouted, in a frenzy of anxiety which subsided as
soon as Mme Verdurin had explained, "Why, the friend
Odette told us about."

"Ah, good, good; that's all right, then," answered the
doctor, at once mollified. As for the painter, he was overjoyed at the prospect of Swann's appearing at the Verdurins',
because he supposed him to be in love with Odette, and was
always ready to encourage amorous liaisons. "Nothing amuses
me more than match-making," he confided to Cottard. "I've
brought off quite a few, even between women!"

In telling the Verdurins that Swann was extremely "smart,"
Odette had alarmed them with the prospect of another "bore."
When he arrived, however, he made an excellent impression,
an indirect cause of which, though they did not know it, was
his familiarity with the best society. He had, indeed, one of
the advantages which men who have lived and moved in
society enjoy over those, however intelligent, who have not,
namely that they no longer see it transfigured by the longing
or repulsion which it inspires, but regard it as of no importance. Their good nature, freed from all taint of snobbishness and from the fear of seeming too friendly, grown independent, in fact, has the ease, the grace of movement of a
trained gymnast each of whose supple limbs will carry out
precisely what is required without any clumsy participation
by the rest of his body. The simple and elementary gestures
of a man of the world as he courteously holds out his hand to
the unknown youth who is introduced to him, or bows discreetly to the ambassador to whom he is introduced, had
gradually pervaded the whole of Swann's social deportment
without his being conscious of it, so that in the company of
people from a lower social sphere, such as the Verdurins and
their friends, he displayed an instinctive alacrity, made amiable
overtures, from which in their view a "bore" would have

refrained. He showed a momentary coldness only on meeting Dr Cottard; for, seeing him wink at him with an ambiguous smile, before they had yet spoken to one another (a grimace which Cottard styled "letting 'em all come"), Swann supposed that the doctor recognised him from having met him already, probably in some haunt of pleasure, though these he himself very rarely visited, never having lived a life of debauchery. Regarding such an allusion as in bad taste, especially in front of Odette, whose opinion of himself it might easily alter for the worse, Swann assumed his most icy manner. But when he learned that a lady standing near him was Mme Cottard, he decided that so young a husband would not deliberately have hinted at amusements of that order in his wife's presence, and so ceased to interpret the doctor's expression in the sense which he had at first suspected. The painter at once invited Swann to visit his studio with Odette; Swann thought him very civil. "Perhaps you will be more highly favoured than I have been," said Mme Verdurin in a tone of mock resentment, "perhaps you'll be allowed to see Cottard's portrait" (which she had commissioned from the painter). "Take care, Master Biche," she reminded the painter, whom it was a time-honoured pleasantry to address as "Master," "to catch that nice look in his eyes, that witty little twinkle. You know what I want to have most of all is his smile; that's what I've asked you to paint—the portrait of his smile." And since the phrase struck her as noteworthy, she repeated it very loud, so as to make sure that as many as possible of her guests should hear it, and even made use of some vague pretext to draw the circle closer before she uttered it again. Swann begged to be introduced to everyone, even to an old friend of the Verdurins called Saniette, whose shyness, simplicity and good-nature had lost him most of the consideration he had earned for his skill in palaeography, his large fortune, and the distinguished family to which he belonged. When he spoke, his words came out in a burble which was delightful to hear because one felt that it indicated not so much a defect of speech as a quality of the soul, as it were a survival from the age of innocence which he had never wholly outgrown. All the consonants which he was unable to pronounce seemed like harsh utterances of

which his gentle lips were incapable. In asking to be introduced to M. Saniette, Swann gave Mme Verdurin the impression of reversing roles (so much so that she replied, with
emphasis on the distinction: "M. Swann, pray allow me to
introduce our friend Saniette to you") but aroused in Saniette
himself a warmth of devotion, which, however, the Verdurins
never disclosed to Swann, since Saniette rather irritated them,
and they did not feel inclined to provide him with friends.
On the other hand the Verdurins were extremely touched by
Swann's next request, for he felt that he must ask to meet the
pianist's aunt. She wore a black dress, as was her invariable
custom, for she believed that a woman always looked well in
black and that nothing could be more distinguished; but her
face was exceedingly red, as it always was for some time after
a meal. She bowed to Swann with deference, but drew herself
up again with great dignity. As she was entirely uneducated,
and was afraid of making mistakes in grammar and pronunciation, she used purposely to speak in an indistinct and garbling
manner, thinking that if she should make a slip it would be so
buried in the surrounding confusion that no one could be
certain whether she had actually made it or not; with the
result that her talk was a sort of continuous, blurred expectora-
tion, out of which would emerge, at rare intervals, the few
sounds and syllables of which she felt sure. Swann supposed
himself entitled to poke a little mild fun at her in conversation
with M. Verdurin, who, however, was rather put out.

"She's such an excellent woman!" he rejoined. "I grant you
that she's not exactly brilliant; but I assure you that she can
be most agreeable when you chat with her alone."

"I'm sure she can," Swann hastened to concede. "All I
meant was that she hardly struck me as 'distinguished,' " he
went on, isolating the epithet in the inverted commas of his
tone, "and that, on the whole, is something of a compliment."

"For instance," said M. Verdurin, "now this will surprise
you: she writes quite delightfully. You've never heard her
nephew play? It's admirable, eh, Doctor? Would you like me
to ask him to play something, M. Swann?"

"Why, it would be a joy . . ." Swann was beginning to reply,
when the doctor broke in derisively. Having once heard it

said, and never having forgotten, that in general conversation over-emphasis and the use of formal expressions were out of date, whenever he heard a solemn word used seriously, as the word "joy" had just been used by Swann, he felt that the speaker had been guilty of pomposity. And if, moreover, the word in question happened to occur also in what he called an old "tag," however common it might still be in current usage, the doctor jumped to the conclusion that the remark which was about to be made was ridiculous, and completed it ironically with the cliché he assumed the speaker was about to perpetrate, although in reality it had never entered his mind.

"A joy for ever!" he exclaimed mischievously, throwing up his arms in a grandiloquent gesture.

M. Verdurin could not help laughing.

"What are all those good people laughing at over there? There's no sign of brooding melancholy down in your corner," shouted Mme Verdurin. "You don't suppose I find it very amusing to be stuck up here by myself on the stool of repentance," she went on with mock peevishness, in a babyish tone of voice.

Mme Verdurin was seated on a high Swedish chair of waxed pinewood, which a violinist from that country had given her, and which she kept in her drawing-room although in appearance it suggested a work-stand and clashed with the really good antique furniture which she had besides; but she made a point of keeping on view the presents which her "faithful" were in the habit of making her from time to time, so that the donors might have the pleasure of seeing them there when they came to the house. She tried to persuade them to confine their tributes to flowers and sweets, which had at least the merit of mortality; but she never succeeded, and the house was gradually filled with a collection of foot-warmers, cushions, clocks, screens, barometers and vases, a constant repetition and a boundless incongruity of useless but indestructible objects.

From this lofty perch she would take a spirited part in the conversation of the "faithful," and would revel in all their "drollery;" but, since the accident to her jaw, she had abandoned the effort involved in wholehearted laughter, and

had substituted a kind of symbolical dumb-show which signified, without endangering or fatiguing her in any way, that
she was "splitting her sides." At the least witticism aimed by
a member of the circle against a "bore," or against a former
member who was now relegated to the limbo of "bores"—
and to the utter despair of M. Verdurin, who had always made
out that he was just as affable as his wife, but who, since his
laughter was the "real thing," was out of breath in a moment
and so was overtaken and vanquished by her device of a
feigned but continuous hilarity—she would utter a shrill cry,
shut tight her little bird-like eyes, which were beginning to
be clouded over by a cataract, and quickly, as though she had
only just time to avoid some indecent sight or to parry a
mortal blow, burying her face in her hands, which completely
engulfed it and hid it from view, would appear to be struggling
to suppress, to annihilate, a laugh which, had she succumbed
to it, must inevitably have left her inanimate. So, stupefied
with the gaiety of the "faithful," drunk with good-fellowship,
scandal and asseveration, Mme Verdurin, perched on her
high seat like a cage-bird whose biscuit has been steeped in
mulled wine, would sit aloft and sob with affability.

Meanwhile M. Verdurin, after first asking Swann's permission to light his pipe ("No ceremony here, you understand;
we're all pals!"), went and asked the young musician to sit
down at the piano.

"Leave him alone; don't bother him; he hasn't come here
to be tormented," cried Mme Verdurin. "I won't have him
tormented."

"But why on earth should it bother him?" rejoined M.
Verdurin. "I'm sure M. Swann has never heard the sonata in
F sharp which we discovered. He's going to play us the piano-
forte arrangement."

"No, no, no, not my sonata!" she screamed, "I don't want
to be made to cry until I get a cold in the head, and neuralgia
all down my face, like last time. Thanks very much, I don't
intend to repeat that performance. You're all so very kind
and considerate, it's easy to see that none of you will have to
stay in bed for a week."

This little scene, which was re-enacted as often as the

young pianist sat down to play, never failed to delight her friends as much as if they were witnessing it for the first time, as a proof of the seductive originality of the "Mistress" and of the acute sensitiveness of her musical "ear." Those nearest to her would attract the attention of the rest, who were smoking or playing cards at the other end of the room, by their cries of "Hear, hear!" which, as in Parliamentary debates, showed that something worth listening to was being said. And next day they would commiserate with those who had been prevented from coming that evening, assuring them that the scene had been even more amusing than usual.

"Well, all right, then," said M. Verdurin, "he can play just the *andante*."

"Just the *andante*! That really is a bit rich!" cried his wife. "As if it weren't precisely the *andante* that breaks every bone in my body. The Master is really too priceless! Just as though, in the Ninth, he said 'we'll just hear the *finale*,' or 'just the overture' of the *Mastersingers*."

The doctor, however, urged Mme Verdurin to let the pianist play, not because he supposed her to be feigning when she spoke of the distressing effects that music always had upon her—for he recognised certain neurasthenic symptoms therein—but from the habit, common to many doctors, of at once relaxing the strict letter of a prescription as soon as it jeopardises something they regard as more important, such as the success of a social gathering at which they are present, and of which the patient whom they urge for once to forget his dyspepsia or his flu is one of the essential ingredients.

"You won't be ill this time, you'll find," he told her, seeking at the same time to influence her with a hypnotic stare. "And if you are ill, we'll look after you."

"Will you really?" Mme Verdurin spoke as though, with so great a favour in store for her, there was nothing for it but to capitulate. Perhaps, too, by dint of saying that she was going to be ill, she had worked herself into a state in which she occasionally forgot that it was all a fabrication and adopted the attitude of a genuine invalid. And it may often be remarked that invalids, weary of having to make the infrequency of their attacks depend on their own prudence, like to persuade themselves that they can do everything that they enjoy, and that does them harm, with impunity, provided that they place themselves in the hands of a higher authority who, without putting them to the least inconvenience, can and will, by uttering a word or by administering a pill, set them once again on their feet.

Odette had gone to sit on a tapestry-covered settee near the piano, saying to Mme Verdurin, "I have my own little corner, haven't I?"

And Mme Verdurin, seeing Swann by himself on a chair, made him get up: "You're not at all comfortable there. Go along and sit by Odette. You can make room for M. Swann there, can't you, Odette?"

"What charming Beauvais!" said Swann politely, stopping to admire the settee before he sat down on it.

"Ah! I'm glad you appreciate my settee," replied Mme Verdurin, "and I warn you that if you expect ever to see another like it you may as well abandon the idea at once. They've never made anything else like it. And these little chairs, too, are perfect marvels. You can look at them in a moment. The emblems in each of the bronze mouldings correspond to the subject of the tapestry on the chair; you know, you'll have a great deal to enjoy if you want to look at them— I can promise you a delightful time, I assure you. Just look at the little friezes round the edges; here, look, the little vine on a red background in this one, the Bear and the Grapes. Isn't it well drawn? What do you say? I think they knew a thing or two about drawing! Doesn't it make your mouth water, that vine? My husband makes out that I'm not fond of fruit, because I eat less of them than he does. But not a bit of it, I'm greedier than any of you, but I have no need to fill my mouth with them when I can feed on them with my eyes. What are you all laughing at now, pray? Ask the doctor; he'll tell you that those grapes act on me like a regular purge. Some people go to Fontainebleau for cures; I take my own little Beauvais cure here. But, M. Swann, you mustn't run away without feeling the little bronze mouldings on the backs. Isn't it an exquisite patina? No, no, you must feel them properly, with your whole hand!"

"If Mme Verdurin is going to start fingering her bronzes," said the painter, "we shan't get any music to-night."

"Be quiet, you wretch! And yet we poor women," she went on, turning towards Swann, "are forbidden pleasures far less voluptuous than this. There is no flesh in the world to compare with it. None. When M. Verdurin did me the honour of being madly jealous . . . Come, you might at least be polite—don't say that you've never been jealous!"

"But, my dear, I've said absolutely nothing. Look here, Doctor, I call you as a witness. Did I utter a word?"

Swann had begun, out of politeness, to finger the bronzes, and did not like to stop.

"Come along; you can caress them later. Now it's you who are going to be caressed, caressed aurally. You'll like that, I think. Here's the young gentleman who will take charge of that."

After the pianist had played, Swann was even more affable towards him than towards any of the other guests, for the following reason:

The year before, at an evening party, he had heard a piece of music played on the piano and violin. At first he had appreciated only the material quality of the sounds which those instruments secreted. And it had been a source of keen pleasure when, below the delicate line of the violin-part, slender but robust, compact and commanding, he had suddenly become aware of the mass of the piano-part beginning to emerge in a sort of liquid rippling of sound, multiform but indivisible, smooth yet restless, like the deep blue tumult of the sea, silvered and charmed into a minor key by the moonlight. But then at a certain moment, without being able to distinguish any clear outline, or to give a name to what was pleasing him, suddenly enraptured, he had tried to grasp the phrase or harmony—he did not know which—that had just been played and that had opened and expanded his soul, as the fragrance of certain roses, wafted upon the moist air of evening, has the power of dilating one's nostrils. Perhaps it was owing to his ignorance of music that he had received so confused an impression, one of those that are nonetheless the only purely musical impressions, limited in their extent, entirely original, and irreducible to any other kind. An impression of this order, vanishing in an instant, is, so to speak, *sine materia*. Doubtless the notes which we hear at such moments tend, according to their pitch and volume, to spread out before our eyes over surfaces of varying dimensions, to trace arabesques, to give us the sensation of breadth or tenuity, stability or caprice. But the notes themselves have vanished before these sensations have developed sufficiently to escape submersion under those which the succeeding or even simultaneous notes have already begun to awaken in us. And this impression would continue to envelop in its liquidity, its ceaseless overlapping, the *motifs* which from time to time emerge, barely discernible, to plunge again and disappear and drown, recognised only by the particular kind of pleasure which they instil, impossible to describe, to recollect, to name, ineffable—did not our memory, like a labourer who toils at the laying down of firm foundations beneath the tumult of the waves, by fashioning for us facsimiles of those fugitive phrases, enable us to compare and to contrast them with those that follow. And so, scarcely had the exquisite sensation which Swann had experienced died away, before his memory had furnished him with an immediate transcript, sketchy, it is true, and provisional, which he had been able to glance at while the piece continued, so that, when the same impression suddenly returned, it was no longer impossible to grasp. He could picture to himself its extent, its symmetrical arrangement, its notation, its expressive value; he had before him something that was no longer pure music, but rather design, architecture, thought, and which allowed the actual music to be recalled. This time he had distinguished quite clearly a phrase which emerged for a few moments above the waves of sound. It had at once suggested to him a world of inexpressible delights, of whose existence, before hearing it, he had never dreamed, into which he felt that nothing else could initiate him; and he had been filled with love for it, as with a new and strange desire.

With a slow and rhythmical movement it led him first this way, then that, towards a state of happiness that was noble, unintelligible, and yet precise. And then suddenly, having reached a certain point from which he was preparing to follow

it, after a momentary pause, abruptly it changed direction, and
in a fresh movement, more rapid, fragile, melancholy, incessant, sweet, it bore him off with it towards new vistas.
Then it vanished. He hoped, with a passionate longing, that
he might find it again, a third time. And reappear it did,
though without speaking to him more clearly, bringing him,
indeed, a pleasure less profound. But when he returned home
he felt the need of it: he was like a man into whose life a woman
he has seen for a moment passing by has brought the image
of a new beauty which deepens his own sensibility, although
he does not even know her name or whether he will ever
see her again.

Indeed this passion for a phrase of music seemed, for a time,
to open up before Swann the possibility of a sort of rejuvenation. He had so long ceased to direct his life towards any ideal
goal, confining himself to the pursuit of ephemeral satisfactions, that he had come to believe, without ever admitting it
to himself in so many words, that he would remain in that
condition for the rest of his days. More than this, since his
mind no longer entertained any lofty ideas, he had ceased to
believe in (although he could not have expressly denied) their
reality. Thus he had grown into the habit of taking refuge in
trivial considerations, which enabled him to disregard matters
of fundamental importance. Just as he never stopped to ask
himself whether he would not have done better by not going
into society, but on the other hand knew for certain that if he
had accepted an invitation he must put in an appearance, and
that afterwards, if he did not actually call, he must at least leave
cards upon his hostess, so in his conversation he took care
never to express with any warmth a personal opinion about
anything, but instead would supply facts and details which
were valid enough in themselves and excused him from showing his real capacities. He would be extremely precise about
the recipe for a dish, the dates of a painter's birth and death,
and the titles of his works. Sometimes, in spite of himself,
he would let himself go so far as to express an opinion on a
work of art, or on someone's interpretation of life, but then
he would cloak his words in a tone of irony, as though he did
not altogether associate himself with what he was saying. But

now, like a confirmed invalid in whom, all of a sudden, a
change of air and surroundings, or a new course of treatment,
or sometimes an organic change in himself, spontaneous and
unaccountable, seems to have brought about such an improvement in his health that he begins to envisage the possibility,
hitherto beyond all hope, of starting to lead belatedly a wholly
different life, Swann found in himself, in the memory of the
phrase that he had heard, in certain other sonatas which he
had made people play to him to see whether he might not
perhaps discover his phrase therein, the presence of one of
those invisible realities in which he had ceased to believe and
to which, as though the music had had upon the moral barrenness from which he was suffering a sort of recreative influence,
he was conscious once again of the desire and almost the
strength to consecrate his life. But, never having managed to
find out whose work it was that he had heard played that
evening, he had been unable to procure a copy and had finally
forgotten the quest. He had indeed, in the course of that week,
encountered several of the people who had been at the party
with him, and had questioned them; but most of them had
either arrived after or left before the piece was played; some
had indeed been there at the time but had gone into another
room to talk, and those who had stayed to listen had no clearer
impression than the rest. As for his hosts, they knew that it
was a recent work which the musicians whom they had engaged for the evening had asked to be allowed to play; but, as
these last had gone away on tour, Swann could learn nothing
further. He had, of course, a number of musical friends, but,
vividly as he could recall the exquisite and inexpressible
pleasure which the little phrase had given him, and could see
in his mind's eye the forms that it had traced, he was quite
incapable of humming it to them. And so, at last, he ceased
to think of it.

But that night, at Mme Verdurin's, scarcely had the young
pianist begun to play than suddenly, after a high note sustained
through two whole bars, Swann sensed its approach, stealing
forth from beneath that long-drawn sonority, stretched like a
curtain of sound to veil the mystery of its incubation, and
recognised, secret, murmuring, detached, the airy and per-

fumed phrase that he had loved. And it was so peculiarly itself, it had so individual, so irreplaceable a charm, that Swann felt as though he had met, in a friend's drawing-room, a woman whom he had seen and admired in the street and had despaired of ever seeing again. Finally the phrase receded, diligently guiding its successors through the ramifications of its fragrance, leaving on Swann's features the reflection of its smile. But now, at last, he could ask the name of his fair unknown (and was told that it was the *andante* of Vinteuil's sonata for piano and violin); he held it safe, could have it again to himself, at home, as often as he wished, could study its language and acquire its secret.

And so, when the pianist had finished, Swann crossed the room and thanked him with a vivacity which delighted Mme Verdurin.

"Isn't he a charmer?" she asked Swann, "doesn't he just understand his sonata, the little wretch? You never dreamed, did you, that a piano could be made to express all that? Upon my word, you'd think it was everything but the piano! I'm caught out every time I hear it; I think I'm listening to an orchestra. Though it's better, really, than an orchestra, more complete."

The young pianist bowed as he answered, smiling and underlining each of his words as though he were making an epigram: "You are most generous to me."

And while Mme Verdurin was saying to her husband, "Run and fetch him a glass of orangeade; he's earned it," Swann began to tell Odette how he had fallen in love with that little phrase. When their hostess, who was some way off, called out, "Well! It looks to me as though someone was saying nice things to you, Odette!" she replied, "Yes, very nice," and he found her simplicity delightful. Then he asked for information about this Vinteuil: what else he had done, at what period in his life he had composed the sonata, and what meaning the little phrase could have had for him—that was what Swann wanted most to know.

But none of these people who professed to admire this musician (when Swann had said that the sonata was really beautiful Mme Verdurin had exclaimed, "Of course it's

beautiful! But you don't dare to confess that you don't know
Vinteuil's sonata; you have no right not to know it!"—and
the painter had added, "Ah, yes, it's a very fine bit of work,
isn't it? Not, of course, if you want something 'obvious,'
something 'popular,' but, I mean to say, it makes a very great
impression on us artists"), none of them seemed ever to have
asked himself these questions, for none of them was able to
answer them.

Even to one or two particular remarks made by Swann about
his favourite phrase: "D'you know, that's a funny thing; I
had never noticed it. I may as well tell you that I don't much
care about peering at things through a microscope, and pricking myself on pin-points of difference. No, we don't waste
time splitting hairs in this house," Mme Verdurin replied,
while Dr Cottard gazed at her with open-mouthed admiration
and studious zeal as she skipped lightly from one stepping-
stone to another of her stock of ready-made phrases. Both he,
however, and Mme Cottard, with a kind of common sense
which is shared by many people of humble origin, were
careful not to express an opinion, or to pretend to admire a
piece of music which they confessed to each other, once they
were back at home, that they no more understood than they
could understand the art of "Master" Biche. Inasmuch as the
public cannot recognise the charm, the beauty, even the outlines of nature save in the stereotyped impressions of an art
which they have gradually assimilated, while an original artist
starts by rejecting those stereotypes, so M. and Mme Cottard,
typical, in this respect, of the public, were incapable of finding,
either in Vinteuil's sonata or in Biche's portraits, what constituted for them harmony in music or beauty in painting. It
appeared to them, when the pianist played his sonata, as
though he were striking at random from the piano a medley
of notes which bore no relation to the musical forms to which
they themselves were accustomed, and that the painter simply
flung the colours at random on his canvases. When, in one of
these, they were able to distinguish a human form, they always
found it coarsened and vulgarised (that is to say lacking in
the elegance of the school of painting through whose spectacles
they were in the habit of seeing even the real, living people

who passed them in the street) and devoid of truth, as though M. Biche had not known how the human shoulder was constructed, or that a woman's hair was not ordinarily purple.

However, when the "faithful" were scattered out of earshot, the doctor felt that the opportunity was too good to be missed, and so (while Mme Verdurin was adding a final word of commendation of Vinteuil's sonata), like a would-be swimmer who jumps into the water so as to learn, but chooses a moment when there are not too many people looking on: "Yes, indeed; he's what they call a musician *di primo cartello!*" he exclaimed with sudden determination.

Swann discovered no more than that the recent appearance of Vinteuil's sonata had caused a great stir among the most advanced school of musicians, but that it was still unknown to the general public.

"I know someone called Vinteuil," said Swann, thinking of the old piano-teacher at Combray who had taught my grandmother's sisters.

"Perhaps he's the man," cried Mme Verdurin.

"Oh, no, if you'd ever set eyes on him you wouldn't entertain the idea."

"Then to entertain the idea is to affirm it?" the doctor suggested.

"But it may well be some relation," Swann went on. "That would be bad enough; but, after all, there's no reason why a genius shouldn't have a cousin who's a silly old fool. And if that should be so, I swear there's no known or unknown form of torture I wouldn't undergo to get the old fool to introduce me to the man who composed the sonata; starting with the torture of the old fool's company, which would be ghastly."

The painter understood that Vinteuil was seriously ill at the moment, and that Dr Potain despaired of his life.

"What!" cried Mme Verdurin, "Do people still call in Potain?"

"Ah! Mme Verdurin," Cottard simpered, "you forget that you are speaking of one of my colleagues—I should say one of my masters."

The painter had heard it said that Vinteuil was threatened

with the loss of his reason. And he insisted that signs of this could be detected in certain passages in the sonata. This remark did not strike Swann as ridiculous; but it disturbed him, for, since a work of pure music contains none of the logical sequences whose deformation, in spoken or written language, is a proof of insanity, so insanity diagnosed in a sonata seemed to him as mysterious a thing as the insanity of a dog or a horse, although instances may be observed of these.

"Don't speak to me about your masters; you know ten times as much as he does!" Mme Verdurin answered Dr Cottard, in the tone of a woman who has the courage of her convictions and is quite ready to stand up to anyone who disagrees with her. "At least you don't kill your patients!"

"But, Madame, he is in the Academy," replied the doctor with heavy irony. "If a patient prefers to die at the hands of one of the princes of science. . . . It's much smarter to be able to say, 'Yes, I have Potain.' "

"Oh, indeed! Smarter, is it?" said Mme Verdurin. "So there are fashions, nowadays, in illness, are there? I didn't know that. . . . Oh, you do make me laugh!" she screamed suddenly, burying her face in her hands. "And here was I, poor thing, talking quite seriously and never realising that you were pulling my leg."

As for M. Verdurin, finding it rather a strain to raise a laugh for so little, he was content with puffing out a cloud of smoke from his pipe, reflecting sadly that he could never hope to keep pace with his wife in her Atalanta-flights across the field of mirth.

"D'you know, we like your friend very much," said Mme Verdurin when Odette was bidding her good night. "He's so unaffected, quite charming. If they're all like that, the friends you want to introduce to us, by all means bring them."

M. Verdurin remarked that Swann had failed, all the same, to appreciate the pianist's aunt.

"I dare say he felt a little out of his depth, poor man," suggested Mme Verdurin. "You can't expect him to have caught the tone of the house already, like Cottard, who has been one of our little clan now for years. The first time doesn't count; it's just for breaking the ice. Odette, it's agreed that he's to join us to-morrow at the Châtelet. Perhaps you might call for him?"

"No, he doesn't want that."

"Oh, very well; just as you like. Provided he doesn't fail us at the last moment."

Greatly to Mme Verdurin's surprise, he never failed them. He would go to meet them no matter where, sometimes at restaurants on the outskirts of Paris which were little frequented as yet, since the season had not yet begun, more often at the theatre, of which Mme Verdurin was particularly fond. One evening at her house he heard her remark how useful it would be to have a special pass for first nights and gala performances, and what a nuisance it had been not having one on the day of Gambetta's funeral. Swann, who never spoke of his brilliant connections, but only of those not highly thought of in the Faubourg Saint-Germain whom he would have considered it snobbish to conceal, and among whom he had come to include his connections in the official world, broke in: "I'll see to that. You shall have it in time for the *Danicheff* revival. I happen to be lunching with the Prefect of Police to-morrow at the Elysée."

"What's that? The Elysée?" Dr Cottard roared in a voice of thunder.

"Yes, at M. Grévy's," replied Swann, a little embarrassed at the effect which his announcement had produced.

"Are you often taken like that?" the painter asked Cottard with mock-seriousness.

As a rule, once an explanation had been given, Cottard would say: "Ah, good, good; that's all right, then," after which he would show not the least trace of emotion. But this time Swann's last words, instead of the usual calming effect, had that of raising to fever-pitch his astonishment at the discovery that a man with whom he himself was actually sitting at table, a man who had no official position, no honours or distinction of any sort, was on visiting terms with the Head of State.

"What's that you say? M. Grévy? You know M. Grévy?" he demanded of Swann, in the stupid and incredulous tone of a constable on duty at the palace who, when a stranger asks to see the President of the Republic, realising at once "the sort of man he is dealing with," as the newspapers say, assures the poor lunatic that he will be admitted at once, and directs him to the reception ward of the police infirmary.

"I know him slightly; we have some friends in common" (Swann dared not add that one of these friends was the Prince of Wales). "Besides, he is very free with his invitations, and I assure you his luncheon-parties are not the least bit amusing. They're very simple affairs, too, you know—never more than eight at table," he went on, trying desperately to cut out everything that seemed to show off his relations with the President in a light too dazzling for the doctor's eyes.

Whereupon Cottard, at once conforming in his mind to the literal interpretation of what Swann was saying, decided that invitations from M. Grévy were very little sought after, were sent out, in fact, into the highways and byways. And from that moment he was no longer surprised to hear that Swann, or anyone else, was "always at the Elysée"; he even felt a little sorry for a man who had to go to luncheon-parties which he himself admitted were a bore.

"Ah, good, good; that's quite all right, then," he said, in the tone of a suspicious customs official who, after hearing your explanations, stamps your passport and lets you proceed on your journey without troubling to examine your luggage.

"I can well believe you don't find them amusing, those luncheons. Indeed, it's very good of you to go to them," said Mme Verdurin, who regarded the President of the Republic as a "bore" to be especially dreaded, since he had at his disposal means of seduction, and even of compulsion, which, if employed to captivate her "faithful," might easily make them default. "It seems he's as deaf as a post and eats with his fingers."

"Upon my word! Then it can't be much fun for you, going there." A note of pity sounded in the doctor's voice; and then struck by the number—only eight at table—"Are these luncheons what you would describe as 'intimate'?" he inquired briskly, not so much out of idle curiosity as from linguistic zeal.

But so great was the prestige of the President of the Republic in the eyes of Dr Cottard that neither the modesty of Swann nor the malevolence of Mme Verdurin could wholly efface it, and he never sat down to dinner with the Verdurins without asking anxiously, "D'you think we shall see M. Swann here this evening? He's a personal friend of M. Grévy's. I suppose that means he's what you'd call a 'gentleman'?" He even went to the length of offering Swann a card of invitation to the Dental Exhibition.

"This will let you in, and anyone you take with you," he explained, "but dogs are not admitted. I'm just warning you, you understand, because some friends of mine went there once without knowing, and bitterly regretted it."

As for M. Verdurin, he did not fail to observe the distressing effect upon his wife of the discovery that Swann had influential friends of whom he had never spoken.

If no arrangement had been made to go out, it was at the Verdurins' that Swann would find the "little nucleus" assembled, but he never appeared there except in the evenings, and rarely accepted their invitations to dinner, in spite of Odette's entreaties.

"I could dine with you alone somewhere, if you'd rather," she suggested.

"But what about Mme Verdurin?"

"Oh, that's quite simple. I need only say that my dress wasn't ready, or that my cab came late. There's always some excuse."

"How sweet of you."

But Swann told himself that if he could make Odette feel (by consenting to meet her only after dinner) that there were other pleasures which he preferred to that of her company, then the desire that she felt for his would be all the longer in reaching the point of satiety. Besides, as he infinitely preferred to Odette's style of beauty that of a young seamstress, as fresh and plump as a rose, with whom he was smitten, he preferred to spend the first part of the evening with her, knowing that he was sure to see Odette later on. It was for the same reason that he never allowed Odette to call for him at his house, to take him on to the Verdurins'. The little seamstress would wait for him at a street corner which Rémi,

his coachman, knew; she would jump in beside him, and
remain in his arms until the carriage drew up at the Verdurins'.
He would enter the drawing-room; and there, while Mme
Verdurin, pointing to the roses which he had sent her that
morning, said: "I'm furious with you," and sent him to the
place kept for him beside Odette, the pianist would play to
them—for their two selves—the little phrase by Vinteuil
which was, so to speak, the national anthem of their love.
He would begin with the sustained tremolos of the violin
part which for several bars were heard alone, filling the whole
foreground; until suddenly they seemed to draw aside, and—as
in those interiors by Pieter de Hooch which are deepened by
the narrow frame of a half-opened door, in the far distance, of
a different colour, velvety with the radiance of some intervening light—the little phrase appeared, dancing, pastoral,
interpolated, episodic, belonging to another world. It rippled
past, simple and immortal, scattering on every side the bounties
of its grace, with the same ineffable smile; but Swann thought
that he could now discern in it some disenchantment. It
seemed to be aware how vain, how hollow was the happiness
to which it showed the way. In its airy grace there was the
sense of something over and done with, like the mood of
philosophic detachment which follows an outburst of vain
regret. But all this mattered little to him; he contemplated the
little phrase less in its own light—in what it might express to
a musician who knew nothing of the existence of him and
Odette when he had composed it, and to all those who would
hear it in centuries to come—than as a pledge, a token of
his love, which made even the Verdurins and their young
pianist think of Odette at the same time as himself—which
bound her to him by a lasting tie; so much so that (whimsically
entreated by Odette) he had abandoned the idea of getting
some professional to play over to him the whole sonata, of
which he still knew no more than this one passage. "Why
do you want the rest?" she had asked him. "Our little bit;
that's all we need." Indeed, agonised by the reflection, as it
floated by, so near and yet so infinitely remote, that while it
was addressed to them it did not know them, he almost regretted that it had a meaning of its own, an intrinsic and un-

alterable beauty, extraneous to themselves, just as in the jewels
given to us, or even in the letters written to us by a woman
we love, we find fault with the "water" of the stone, or with
the words of the message, because they are not fashioned
exclusively from the essence of a transient liaison and a particular
person.

Often it would happen that he had stayed so long with the
young seamstress before going to the Verdurins' that, as
soon as the little phrase had been rendered by the pianist,
Swann realised that it was almost time for Odette to go home.
He used to take her back as far as the door of her little house
in the Rue La Pérouse, behind the Arc de Triomphe. And it
was perhaps on this account, and so as not to demand the
monopoly of her favours, that he sacrificed the pleasure (not
so essential to his well-being) of seeing her earlier in the
evening, of arriving with her at the Verdurins', to the exercise
of this other privilege which she accorded him of their leaving
together; a privilege he valued all the more because it gave
him the feeling that no one else would see her, no one would
thrust himself between them, no one could prevent him from
remaining with her in spirit, after he had left her for the night.

And so, night after night, she would return home in Swann's
carriage. Once, after she had got down, and while he stood at
the gate murmuring "Till to-morrow, then," she turned im-
pulsively from him, plucked a last lingering chrysanthemum
from the little garden in front of the house, and gave it to
him before he left. He held it pressed to his lips during the
drive home, and when in due course the flower withered, he
put it away carefully in a drawer of his desk.

But he never went into her house. Twice only, in the daytime, had he done so, to take part in the ceremony—of such
vital importance in her life—of "afternoon tea." The loneliness
and emptiness of those short streets (consisting almost entirely
of low-roofed houses, self-contained but not detached, their
monotony interrupted here and there by the dark intrusion
of some sinister workshop, at once an historical witness to
and a sordid survival from the days when the district was
still one of ill repute), the snow which still clung to the
garden-beds and the branches of the trees, the unkemptness of

the season, the proximity of nature, had all combined to add
an element of mystery to the warmth, the flowers, the luxury
which he had found inside.

From the ground floor, somewhat raised above street level,
leaving on the left Odette's bedroom, which looked out to the
back over another little street running parallel with her own,
he had climbed a staircase that went straight up between dark
painted walls hung with Oriental draperies, strings of Turkish
beads, and a huge Japanese lantern suspended by a silken
cord (which last, however, so that her visitors should not be
deprived of the latest comforts of Western civilisation, was
lighted by a gas-jet inside), to the two drawing-rooms, large
and small. These were entered through a narrow vestibule,
the wall of which, chequered with the lozenges of a wooden
trellis such as you see on garden walls, only gilded, was lined
from end to end by a long rectangular box in which bloomed,
as in a hothouse, a row of large chrysanthemums, at that time
still uncommon though by no means so large as the mammoth
specimens which horticulturists have since succeeded in producing. Swann was irritated, as a rule, by the sight of these
flowers, which had then been fashionable in Paris for about a
year, but it had pleased him, on this occasion, to see the
gloom of the vestibule shot with rays of pink and gold and
white by the fragrant petals of these ephemeral stars, which
kindle their cold fires in the murky atmosphere of winter
afternoons. Odette had received him in a pink silk dressing-
gown, which left her neck and arms bare. She had made him
sit down beside her in one of the many mysterious little
alcoves which had been contrived in the various recesses of
the room, sheltered by enormous palms growing out of pots
of Chinese porcelain, or by screens upon which were fastened
photographs and fans and bows of ribbon. She had said at
once, "You're not comfortable there; wait a minute, I'll
arrange things for you," and with a little simpering laugh
which implied that some special invention of her own was
being brought into play, she had installed behind his head
and beneath his feet great cushions of Japanese silk which she
pummelled and buffeted as though to prove that she was
prodigal of these riches, regardless of their value. But when her

footman came into the room bringing, one after another, the innumerable lamps which (contained, mostly, in porcelain vases) burned singly or in pairs upon the different pieces of furniture as upon so many altars, rekindling in the twilight, already almost nocturnal, of this winter afternoon the glow of a sunset more lasting, more roseate, more human—filling, perhaps, with romantic wonder the thoughts of some solitary lover wandering in the street below and brought to a standstill before the mystery of the human presence which those lighted windows at once revealed and screened from sight—she had kept a sharp eye on the servant, to see that he set them down in their appointed places. She felt that if he were to put even one of them where it ought not to be the general effect of her drawing-room would be destroyed, and her portrait, which rested upon a sloping easel draped with plush, inadequately lit. And so she followed the man's clumsy movements with feverish impatience, scolding him severely when he passed too close to a pair of jardinières, which she made a point of always cleaning herself for fear that they might be damaged, and went across to examine now to make sure he had not chipped them. She found something "quaint" in the shape of each of her Chinese ornaments, and also in her orchids, the cattleyas especially—these being, with chrysanthemums, her favourite flowers, because they had the supreme merit of not looking like flowers, but of being made, apparently, of silk or satin. "This one looks just as though it had been cut out of the lining of my cloak," she said to Swann, pointing to an orchid, with a shade of respect in her voice for so "chic" a flower, for this elegant, unexpected sister whom nature had bestowed upon her, so far removed from her in the scale of existence, and yet so delicate, so refined, so much more worthy than many real women of admission to her drawing-room. As she drew his attention, now to the fiery-tongued dragons painted on a bowl or stitched on a screen, now to a fleshy cluster of orchids, now to a dromedary of inlaid silver-work with ruby eyes which kept company, upon her mantel-piece, with a toad carved in jade, she would pretend now to be shrinking from the ferocity of the monsters or laughing at their absurdity, now blushing at the indecency of the flowers, now

carried away by an irresistible desire to run across and kiss the
toad and dromedary, calling them "darlings." And these
affectations were in sharp contrast to the sincerity of some of
her attitudes, notably her devotion to Our Lady of Laghet,
who had once, when Odette was living at Nice, cured her
of a mortal illness, and whose medal, in gold, she always
carried on her person, attributing to it unlimited powers. She
poured out Swann's tea, inquired "Lemon or cream?" and,
on his answering "Cream, please," said to him with a laugh:
"A cloud!" And as he pronounced it excellent, "You see, I
know just how you like it." This tea had indeed seemed to
Swann, just as it seemed to her, something precious, and love
has such a need to find some justification for itself, some
guarantee of duration, in pleasures which without it would
have no existence and must cease with its passing, that when
he left her at seven o'clock to go and dress for the evening,
all the way home in his brougham, unable to repress the
happiness with which the afternoon's adventure had filled
him, he kept repeating to himself: "How nice it would be to
have a little woman like that in whose house one could always
be certain of finding, what one never can be certain of finding,
a really good cup of tea." An hour or so later he received a
note from Odette, and at once recognised that large handwriting in which an affectation of British stiffness imposed an
apparent discipline upon ill-formed characters, suggestive,
perhaps, to less biassed eyes than his, of an untidiness of
mind, a fragmentary education, a want of sincerity and will-
power. Swann had left his cigarette-case at her house. "If
only," she wrote, "you had also forgotten your heart! I
should never have let you have that back."

More important, perhaps, was a second visit which he paid
her a little later. On his way to the house, as always when he
knew that they were to meet, he formed a picture of her in
his mind; and the necessity, if he was to find any beauty in
her face, of concentrating on the fresh and rosy cheekbones
to the exclusion of the rest of her cheeks which were so often
drawn and sallow, and sometimes mottled with little red spots,
distressed him as proving that the ideal is unattainable and
happiness mediocre. He was bringing her an engraving which

she had asked to see. She was not very well, and received him
in a dressing-gown of mauve *crêpe de Chine*, drawing its richly
embroidered material over her bosom like a cloak. Standing
there beside him, her loosened hair flowing down her cheeks,
bending one knee in a slightly balletic pose in order to be able
to lean without effort over the picture at which she was gazing,
her head on one side, with those great eyes of hers which
seemed so tired and sullen when there was nothing to animate
her, she struck Swann by her resemblance to the figure of
Zipporah, Jethro's daughter, which is to be seen in one of
the Sistine frescoes. He had always found a peculiar fascination in tracing in the paintings of the old masters not merely
the general characteristics of the people whom he encountered
in his daily life, but rather what seems least susceptible of
generalisation, the individual features of men and women
whom he knew: as, for instance, in a bust of the Doge Loredan
by Antonio Rizzo, the prominent cheekbones, the slanting
eyebrows, in short, a speaking likeness to his own coachman
Rémi; in the colouring of a Ghirlandaio, the nose of M. de
Palancy; in a portrait by Tintoretto, the invasion of the cheek
by an outcrop of whisker, the broken nose, the penetrating
stare, the swollen eyelids of Dr du Boulbon. Perhaps, having
always regretted, in his heart, that he had confined his attention to the social side of life, had talked, always, rather than
acted, he imagined a sort of indulgence bestowed upon him
by those great artists in the fact that they also had regarded
with pleasure and had introduced into their works such types
of physiognomy as give those works the strongest possible
certificate of reality and truth to life, a modern, almost a
topical savour; perhaps, also, he had so far succumbed to the
prevailing frivolity of the world of fashion that he felt the
need to find in an old masterpiece some such anticipatory and
rejuvenating allusion to personalities of to-day. Perhaps, on
the other hand, he had retained enough of the artistic temperament to be able to find a genuine satisfaction in watching these
individual characteristics take on a more general significance
when he saw them, uprooted and disembodied, in the resemblance between an historic portrait and a modern original
whom it was not intended to represent. However that might

be—and perhaps because the abundance of impressions which he had been receiving for some time past, even though they had come to him rather through the channel of his appreciation of music, had enriched his appetite for painting as well— it was with an unusual intensity of pleasure, a pleasure destined to have a lasting effect upon him, that Swann remarked Odette's resemblance to the Zipporah of that Alessandro de Mariano to whom one shrinks from giving his more popular surname, Botticelli, now that it suggests not so much the actual work of the Master as that false and banal conception of it which has of late obtained common currency. He no longer based his estimate of the merit of Odette's face on the doubtful quality of her cheeks and the purely fleshy softness which he supposed would greet his lips there should he ever hazard a kiss, but regarded it rather as a skein of beautiful, delicate lines which his eyes unravelled, following their curves and convolutions, relating the rhythm of the neck to the effusion of the hair and the droop of the eyelids, as though in a portrait of her in which her type was made clearly intelligible.

He stood gazing at her; traces of the old fresco were apparent in her face and her body, and these he tried incessantly to recapture thereafter, both when he was with Odette and when he was only thinking of her in her absence; and, although his admiration for the Florentine masterpiece was doubtless based upon his discovery that it had been reproduced in her, the similarity enhanced her beauty also, and made her more precious. Swann reproached himself with his failure, hitherto, to estimate at her true worth a creature whom the great Sandro would have adored, and was gratified that his pleasure in seeing Odette should have found a justification in his own aesthetic culture. He told himself that in associating the thought of Odette with his dreams of ideal happiness he had not resigned himself to a stopgap as inadequate as he had hitherto supposed, since she satisfied his most refined predilections in matters of art. He failed to observe that this quality would not naturally avail to bring Odette into the category of women whom he found desirable, since, as it happened, his desires had always run counter to his aesthetic taste. The words "Florentine painting" were invaluable to Swann. They enabled him, like

a title, to introduce the image of Odette into a world of dreams
and fancies which, until then, she had been debarred from
entering, and where she assumed a new and nobler form. And
whereas the mere sight of her in the flesh, by perpetually
reviving his misgivings as to the quality of her face, her body,
the whole of her beauty, cooled the ardour of his love, those
misgivings were swept away and that love confirmed now that
he could re-erect his estimate of her on the sure foundations
of aesthetic principle; while the kiss, the physical possession
which would have seemed natural and but moderately attractive had they been granted him by a creature of somewhat
blemished flesh and sluggish blood, coming, as they now came,
to crown his adoration of a masterpiece in a gallery, must, it
seemed, prove supernaturally delicious.

And when he was tempted to regret that, for months past,
he had done nothing but see Odette, he would assure himself
that he was not unreasonable in giving up much of his time to
an inestimably precious work of art, cast for once in a new,
a different, an especially delectable metal, in an unmatched
exemplar which he would contemplate at one moment with
the humble, spiritual, disinterested mind of an artist, at
another with the pride, the selfishness, the sensual thrill of a
collector.

He placed on his study table, as if it were a photograph of
Odette, a reproduction of Jethro's daughter. He would gaze
in admiration at the large eyes, the delicate features in which
the imperfection of the skin might be surmised, the marvellous
locks of hair that fell along the tired cheeks; and, adapting to
the idea of a living woman what he had until then felt to be
beautiful on aesthetic grounds, he converted it into a series of
physical merits which he was gratified to find assembled in
the person of one whom he might ultimately possess. The
vague feeling of sympathy which attracts one to a work of art,
now that he knew the original in flesh and blood of Jethro's
daughter, became a desire which more than compensated,
thenceforward, for the desire which Odette's physical charms
had at first failed to inspire in him. When he had sat for a long
time gazing at the Botticelli, he would think of his own living
Botticelli, who seemed even lovelier still, and as he drew

towards him the photograph of Zipporah he would imagine that he was holding Odette against his heart.

It was not only Odette's lassitude, however, that he must take pains to circumvent; it was also, not infrequently, his own. Feeling that, since Odette had had every facility for seeing him, she seemed no longer to have very much to say to him, he was afraid lest the manner—at once trivial, monotonous, and seemingly unalterable—which she now adopted when they were together should ultimately destroy in him that romantic hope, which alone had aroused and sustained his love, that a day might come when she would declare her passion. And so, in an attempt to revitalise Odette's too fixed and unvarying attitude towards him, of which he was afraid of growing weary, he would write to her, suddenly, a letter full of feigned disappointment and simulated anger, which he sent off so that it should reach her before dinner. He knew that she would be alarmed, and that she would reply, and he hoped that, when the fear of losing him clutched at her heart, it would force from her words such as he had never yet heard her utter; and indeed, it was by this device that he had won from her the most affectionate letters she had so far written him. One of them, which she had sent round to him at midday from the Maison Dorée (it was the day of the Paris-Murcie Fête given for the victims of the recent floods in Murcia) began: "My dear, my hand trembles so that I can scarcely write," and had been put in the same drawer as the withered chrysanthemum. Or else, if she had not had time to write to him, when he arrived at the Verdurins' she would come running up to him with an "I've something to say to you!" and he would gaze curiously at the revelation in her face and speech of what she had hitherto kept concealed from him of her heart.

Even before he reached the Verdurins' door, when he caught sight of the great lamp-lit spaces of the drawing-room windows, whose shutters were never closed, he would begin to melt at the thought of the charming creature he would see as he entered the room, basking in that golden light. Here and there the figures of the guests stood out in silhouette, slender and black, between lamp and window, like those little pictures which one sees at regular intervals round a translucent lamp-shade, the other panels of which are simply naked light. He would try to distinguish Odette's silhouette. And then, when he was once inside, without his being aware of it, his eyes would sparkle suddenly with such radiant happiness that M. Verdurin said to the painter: "Hm. Seems to be warming up." And indeed her presence gave the house what none of the other houses that he visited seemed to possess: a sort of nervous system, a sensory network which ramified into each of its rooms and sent a constant stimulus to his heart.

Thus the simple and regular manifestations of this social organism, the "little clan," automatically provided Swann with a daily rendezvous with Odette, and enabled him to feign indifference to the prospect of seeing her, or even a desire not to see her; in doing which he incurred no very great risk since, even though he had written to her during the day, he would of necessity see her in the evening and accompany her home.

But one evening, when, depressed by the thought of that inevitable dark drive together, he had taken his young seamstress all the way to the Bois, so as to delay as long as possible the moment of his appearance at the Verdurins', he arrived at the house so late that Odette, supposing that he did not intend to come, had already left. Seeing the room bare of her, Swann felt a sudden stab at the heart; he trembled at the thought of being deprived of a pleasure whose intensity he was able for the first time to gauge, having always, hitherto, had that certainty of finding it whenever he wished which (as in the case of all our pleasures) reduced if it did not altogether blind him to its dimensions.

"Did you notice the face he pulled when he saw that she wasn't here?" M. Verdurin asked his wife. "I think we may say that he's hooked."

"The face he pulled?" exploded Dr Cottard who, having left the house for a moment to visit a patient, had just returned to fetch his wife and did not know whom they were discussing.

"D'you mean to say you didn't meet him on the doorstep— the loveliest of Swanns?"

"No. M. Swann has been here?"

"Just for a moment. We had a glimpse of a Swann tremendously agitated. In a state of nerves. You see, Odette had left."

"You mean to say that she has gone the 'whole hog' with him; that she has 'burned her boats'?" inquired the doctor, cautiously trying out the meaning of these phrases.

"Why, of course not, there's absolutely nothing in it; in fact, between you and me, I think she's making a great mistake, and behaving like a silly little fool, which is what she is, in fact."

"Come, come, come!" said M. Verdurin, "How on earth do you know that there's 'nothing in it'? We haven't been there to see, have we now?"

"She would have told me," answered Mme Verdurin with dignity. "I may say that she tells me everything. As she has no one else at present, I told her that she ought to sleep with him. She makes out that she can't, that she did in fact have a crush on him at first, but he's always shy with her, and that makes her shy with him. Besides, she doesn't care for him in that way, she says; it's an ideal love, 'Platonic,' you know; she's afraid of rubbing the bloom off—oh, I don't know half the things she says, how should I? And yet it's just what she needs."

"I beg to differ from you," M. Verdurin courteously interrupted. "I don't entirely care for the gentleman. I feel he puts on airs."

Mme Verdurin's whole body stiffened, and her eyes stared blankly as though she had suddenly been turned into a statue; a device which enabled her to appear not to have caught the sound of that unutterable phrase which seemed to imply that it was possible for people to "put on airs" in their house, in other words consider themselves "superior" to them.

"Anyhow, if there's nothing in it, I don't suppose it's because our friend believes she's *virtuous*," M. Verdurin went on sarcastically. "And yet, you never know; he seems to think she's intelligent. I don't know whether you heard the way he lectured her the other evening about Vinteuil's sonata. I'm devoted to Odette, but really—to expound theories of aesthetics to her—the man must be a prize idiot."

"Look here, I won't have you saying nasty things about Odette," broke in Mme Verdurin in her "little girl" manner. "She's sweet."

"But that doesn't prevent her from being sweet. We're not saying anything nasty about her, only that she isn't exactly the embodiment of virtue or intellect. After all," he turned to the painter, "does it matter so very much whether she's virtuous or not? She might be a great deal less charming if she were."

On the landing Swann had run into the Verdurins' butler, who had been somewhere else a moment earlier when he arrived, and who had been asked by Odette to tell Swann in case he still turned up (but that was at least an hour ago) that she would probably stop for a cup of chocolate at Prévost's on her way home. Swann set off at once for Prévost's, but every few yards his carriage was held up by others, or by people crossing the street, loathsome obstacles that he would gladly have crushed beneath his wheels, were it not that a policeman fumbling with a note-book would delay him even longer than the actual passage of the pedestrian. He counted the minutes feverishly, adding a few seconds to each so as to be quite certain that he had not given himself short measure and so, possibly, exaggerated whatever chance there might actually be of his arriving at Prévost's in time, and of finding her still there. And then, in a moment of illumination, like a man in a fever who awakes from sleep and is conscious of the absurdity of the dream-shapes among which his mind has been wandering without any clear distinction between himself and them, Swann suddenly perceived how foreign to his nature were the thoughts which had been revolving in his mind ever since he had heard at the Verdurins' that Odette had left, how novel the heartache from which he was suffering, but of which he was only now conscious, as though he had just woken up. What! all this agitation simply because he would not see Odette till to-morrow, exactly what he had been hoping, not an hour before, as he drove towards Mme Verdurin's. He was obliged to acknowledge that now, as he sat in that same carriage and drove to Prévost's, he was no longer the same man, was no longer alone even—that a new person was there beside him, adhering to him, amalgamated with him, a person whom he might, perhaps, be unable to shake off, whom he might have to treat with circumspection, like a master or an illness. And yet, from the moment he had begun to feel that another, a fresh personality was thus conjoined with his own, life had seemed somehow more interesting.

He gave scarcely a thought to the likelihood that this possible meeting at Prévost's (the tension of waiting for which so ravished and stripped bare the intervening moments that he could find nothing, not one idea, not one memory in his mind behind which his troubled spirit might take shelter and repose) would after all, should it take place, be much the same as all their meetings, of no great significance. As on every other evening, once he was in Odette's company, casting furtive glances at her changeable face and instantly withdrawing his eyes lest she should read in them the first signs of desire and no longer believe in his indifference, he would cease to be able even to think of her, so busy would he be in the search for pretexts which would enable him not to leave her immediately and to ensure, without betraying his concern, that he would find her again next evening at the Verdurins'; pretexts, that is to say, which would enable him to prolong for the time being, and to renew for one day more, the disappointment and the torture engendered by the vain presence of this woman whom he pursued yet never dared embrace.

She was not at Prévost's; he must search for her, then, in every restaurant along the boulevards. To save time, while he went in one direction, he sent in the other his coachman Rémi (Rizzo's Doge Loredan) for whom he presently—after a fruitless search—found himself waiting at the spot where the carriage was to meet him. It did not appear, and Swann tantalised himself with alternate pictures of the approaching moment, as one in which Rémi would say to him: "Sir, the lady is there," or as one in which Rémi would say to him: "Sir, the lady was not in any of the cafés." And so he saw the remainder of the evening stretching out in front of him, single and yet alternative, preceded either by the meeting with Odette which would put an end to his agony, or by the abandonment of all hope of finding her that evening, the acceptance of the necessity of returning home without having seen her.

The coachman returned; but, as he drew up opposite him, Swann asked, not "Did you find the lady?" but "Remind me, to-morrow, to order in some more firewood. I'm sure we must be running short." Perhaps he had persuaded himself that, if Rémi had at last found Odette in some café where she was waiting for him, then the baleful alternative was already obliterated by the realisation, begun already in his mind, of the happy one, and that there was no need for him to hasten towards the attainment of a joy already captured and held in a safe place, which would not escape his grasp again. But it was also from the force of inertia; there was in his soul that want of adaptability that afflicts the bodies of certain people who, when the moment comes to avoid a collision, to snatch their clothes out of reach of a flame, or to perform any other such necessary movement, take their time, begin by remaining for a moment in their original position, as though seeking to find in it a fulcrum, a springboard, a source of momentum. And no doubt, if the coachman had interrupted him with, "I have found the lady," he would have answered, "Oh, yes, of course; that's what I told you to do. I'd quite forgotten," and would have continued to discuss his supply of firewood, so as to hide from his servant the emotion he had felt, and to give himself time to break away from the thraldom of his anxieties and devote himself to happiness.

The coachman came back, however, with the report that he could not find her anywhere, and added the advice, as an old and privileged servant: "I think, sir, that all we can do now is to go home."

But the air of indifference which Swann could so lightly assume when Rémi uttered his final, unalterable response, fell from him like a cast-off cloak when he saw Rémi attempt to make him abandon hope and retire from the quest.

"Certainly not!" he exclaimed. "We must find the lady. It's most important. She would be extremely put out—it's a business matter—and vexed with me if she didn't see me."

"But I don't see how the lady can be vexed," answered

Rémi, "since it was she who left without waiting for you, sir, and said she was going to Prévost's, and then wasn't there."

Meanwhile the restaurants were closing and their lights began to go out. Under the trees of the boulevards there were still a few people strolling to and fro, barely distinguishable in the gathering darkness. From time to time the shadowy figure of a woman gliding up to Swann, murmuring a few words in his ear, asking him to take her home, would make him start. Anxiously he clutched at all these dim forms, as though, among the phantoms of the dead, in the realms of darkness, he had been searching for a lost Eurydice.

Among all the modes by which love is brought into being, among all the agents which disseminate that blessed bane, there are few so efficacious as this gust of feverish agitation that sweeps over us from time to time. For then the die is cast, the person whose company we enjoy at that moment is the person we shall henceforward love. It is not even necessary for that person to have attracted us, up till then, more than or even as much as others. All that was needed was that our predilection should become exclusive. And that condition is fulfilled when—in this moment of deprivation—the quest for the pleasures we enjoyed in his or her company is suddenly replaced by an anxious, torturing need, whose object is the person alone, an absurd, irrational need which the laws of this world make it impossible to satisfy and difficult to assuage—the insensate, agonising need to possess exclusively.

Swann made Rémi drive him to such restaurants as were still open; it was only the hypothesis of a happy outcome that he had envisaged with calm; now he no longer concealed his agitation, the price he set upon their meeting, and promised in case of success to reward his coachman, as though, by inspiring in him a will to succeed which would reinforce his own, he could bring it to pass, by a miracle, that Odette—assuming that she had long since gone home to bed—might yet be found seated in some restaurant on the boulevards. He pursued the search as far as the Maison Dorée, burst twice into Tortoni's and, still without seeing her, had just emerged from the Café Anglais and was striding, wild-eyed, towards his carriage, which was waiting for him at the corner of the Boulevard des Italiens, when he collided with a person coming in the opposite direction: it was Odette. She explained, later, that there had been no room at Prévost's, that she had gone, instead, to sup at the Maison Dorée, in an alcove where he must have failed to see her, and that she was going back to her carriage.

She had so little expected to see him that she started back in alarm. As for him, he had ransacked the streets of Paris not because he supposed it possible that he should find her, but because it was too painful for him to abandon the attempt. But this happiness which his reason had never ceased to regard as unattainable, that evening at least, now seemed doubly real; for, since he himself had contributed nothing to it by anticipating probabilities, it remained external to himself; there was no need for him to think it into existence—it was from itself that there emanated, it was itself that projected towards him, that truth whose radiance dispelled like a bad dream the loneliness he had so dreaded, that truth on which his happy musings now dwelt unthinkingly. So will a traveller, arriving in glorious weather at the Mediterranean shore, no longer certain of the existence of the lands he has left behind, let his eyes be dazzled by the radiance streaming towards him from the luminous and unfading azure of the sea.

He climbed after her into the carriage which she had kept waiting, and ordered his own to follow.

She was holding in her hand a bunch of cattleyas, and Swann could see, beneath the film of lace that covered her head, more of the same flowers fastened to a swansdown plume. She was dressed, beneath her cloak, in a flowing gown of black velvet, caught up on one side to reveal a large triangle of white silk skirt, and with a yoke, also of white silk, in the cleft of the low-necked bodice, in which were fastened a few more cattleyas. She had scarcely recovered from the shock which the sight of Swann had given her, when some obstacle made the horse start to one side. They were thrown forward in their seats; she uttered a cry, and fell back quivering and breathless.

"It's all right," he assured her, "don't be frightened." And he slipped his arm round her shoulder, supporting her body against his own. Then he went on: "Whatever you do, don't

utter a word; just make a sign, yes or no, or you'll be out of
breath again. You won't mind if I straighten the flowers on
your bodice? The jolt has disarranged them. I'm afraid of their
dropping out, so I'd just like to fasten them a little more
securely."

She was not used to being made so much fuss of by men,
and she smiled as she answered: "No, not at all; I don't mind
in the least."

But he, daunted a little by her answer, and also, perhaps, to
bear out the pretence that he had been sincere in adopting the
stratagem, or even because he was already beginning to believe
that he had been, exclaimed, "No, no, you mustn't speak.
You'll get out of breath again. You can easily answer in signs;
I shall understand. Really and truly now, you don't mind my
doing this? Look, there's a little—I think it must be pollen,
spilt over your dress. Do you mind if I brush it off with my
hand? That's not too hard? I'm not hurting you, am I? Perhaps I'm tickling you a bit? I don't want to touch the velvet in
case I crease it. But you see, I really had to fasten the flowers;
they would have fallen out if I hadn't. Like that, now; if I just
tuck them a little farther down. . . . Seriously, I'm not annoying
you, am I? And if I just sniff them to see whether they've really
got no scent? I don't believe I ever smelt any before. May I?
Tell the truth, now."

Still smiling, she shrugged her shoulders ever so slightly, as
who should say, "You're quite mad; you know very well that
I like it."

He ran his other hand upwards along Odette's cheek; she
gazed at him fixedly, with that languishing and solemn air
which marks the women of the Florentine master in whose
faces he had found a resemblance with hers; swimming at the
brink of the eyelids, her brilliant eyes, wide and slender like
theirs, seemed on the verge of welling out like two great tears.
She bent her neck, as all their necks may be seen to bend,
in the pagan scenes as well as in the religious pictures. And in
an attitude that was doubtless habitual to her, one which she
knew to be appropriate to such moments and was careful not to
forget to assume, she seemed to need all her strength to hold
her face back, as though some invisible force were drawing it

towards Swann's. And it was Swann who, before she allowed it, as though in spite of herself, to fall upon his lips, held it back for a moment longer, at a little distance, between his hands. He had wanted to leave time for his mind to catch up with him, to recognise the dream which it had so long cherished and to assist at its realisation, like a relative invited as a spectator when a prize is given to a child of whom she has been especially fond. Perhaps, too, he was fixing upon the face of an Odette not yet possessed, nor even kissed by him, which he was seeing for the last time, the comprehensive gaze with which, on the day of his departure, a traveller hopes to bear away with him in memory a landscape he is leaving forever.

But he was so shy in approaching her that, after this evening which had begun by his arranging her cattleyas and had ended in her complete surrender, whether from fear of offending her, or from reluctance to appear retrospectively to have lied, or perhaps because he lacked the audacity to formulate a more urgent requirement than this (which could always be repeated, since it had not annoyed her on the first occasion), he resorted to the same pretext on the following days. If she had cattleyas pinned to her bodice, he would say: "It's most unfortunate; the cattleyas don't need tucking in this evening; they've not been disturbed as they were the other night. I think, though, that this one isn't quite straight. May I see if they have more scent than the others?" Or else, if she had none: "Oh! no cattleyas this evening; then there's no chance of my indulging in my little rearrangements." So that for some time there was no change in the procedure which he had followed on that first evening, starting with fumblings with fingers and lips at Odette's bosom, and it was thus that his caresses still began. And long afterwards, when the rearrangement (or, rather, the ritual pretence of a rearrangement) of her cattleyas had quite fallen into desuetude, the metaphor "Do a cattleya," transmuted into a simple verb which they would employ without thinking when they wished to refer to the act of physical possession (in which, paradoxically, the possessor possesses nothing), survived to commemorate in their vocabulary the long forgotten custom from which it sprang. And perhaps this particular manner of saying "to make love" did not mean

exactly the same thing as its synonyms. However jaded we may
be about women, however much we may regard the possession
of the most divergent types as a repetitive and predictable
experience, it none the less becomes a fresh and stimulating
pleasure if the women concerned are—or are thought by us to
be—so difficult as to oblige us to make it spring from some
unrehearsed incident in our relations with them, as had
originally been for Swann the arrangement of the cattleyas. He
tremblingly hoped, that evening (but Odette, he told himself,
if she was deceived by his stratagem, could not guess his
intention), that it was the possession of this woman that would
emerge for him from their large mauve petals; and the pleasure
which he had already felt and which Odette tolerated, he
thought, perhaps only because she had not recognised it,
seemed to him for that reason—as it might have seemed to
the first man when he enjoyed it amid the flowers of the earthly
paradise—a pleasure which had never before existed, which he
was striving now to create, a pleasure—as the special name he
gave it was to certify—entirely individual and new.

Now, every evening, when he had taken her home, he had
to go in with her; and often she would come out again in her
dressing-gown and escort him to his carriage, and would kiss
him in front of his coachman, saying: "What do I care what
other people think?" And on evenings when he did not go to
the Verdurins' (which happened occasionally now that he had
opportunities of seeing Odette elsewhere), when—more and
more rarely—he went into society, she would ask him to come
to her on his way home, however late he might be. It was
spring, and the nights were clear and frosty. Coming away
from a party, he would climb into his victoria, spread a rug
over his knees, tell the friends who were leaving at the same
time and who wanted him to join them, that he couldn't, that
he wasn't going in their direction; and the coachman would
set off at a fast trot without further orders, knowing where he
had to go. His friends would be left wondering, and indeed
Swann was no longer the same man. No one ever received a
letter from him now demanding an introduction to a woman.
He had ceased to pay any attention to women, and kept away
from the places in which they were ordinarily to be met. In a

restaurant, or in the country, his attitude was the opposite of the one by which, only yesterday, his friends would have recognised him, and which had seemed inevitably and permanently his. To such an extent does passion manifest itself in us as a temporary and distinct character which not only takes the place of our normal character but obliterates the invariable signs by which it has hitherto been discernible! What was invariable now was that wherever Swann might be, he never failed to go on afterwards to Odette. The interval of space separating her from him was one which he must traverse as inevitably as though it were the irresistible and rapid slope of life itself. Truth to tell, as often as not, when he had stayed late at a party, he would have preferred to return home at once, without going so far out of his way, and to postpone their meeting until the morrow; but the very fact of his putting himself to such inconvenience at an abnormal hour in order to visit her, while he guessed that his friends, as he left them, were saying to one another: "He's tied hand and foot; there must certainly be a woman somewhere who insists on his going to her at all hours," made him feel that he was leading the life of the class of men whose existence is coloured by a love-affair, and in whom the perpetual sacrifice they make of their comfort and of their practical interests engenders a sort of inner charm. Then, though he may not consciously have taken this into consideration, the certainty that she was waiting for him, that she was not elsewhere with others, that he would see her before he went home, drew the sting from that anguish, forgotten but latent and ever ready to be reawakened, which he had felt on the evening when Odette had left the Verdurins' before his arrival, an anguish the present assuagement of which was so agreeable that it might almost be called happiness. Perhaps it was to that hour of anguish that he owed the importance which Odette had since assumed in his life. Other people as a rule mean so little to us that, when we have invested one of them with the power to cause us so much suffering or happiness, that person seems at once to belong to a different universe, is surrounded with poetry, makes of one's life a sort of stirring arena in which he or she will be more or less close to one. Swann could not ask himself with equanimity what Odette

would mean to him in the years that were to come. Sometimes,
as he looked up from his victoria on those fine and frosty nights
and saw the bright moonbeams fall between his eyes and the
deserted street, he would think of that other face, gleaming and
faintly roseate like the moon's, which had, one day, risen on
the horizon of his mind, and since then had shed upon the
world the mysterious light in which he saw it bathed. If he
arrived after the hour at which Odette sent her servants to
bed, before ringing the bell at the gate of her little garden he
would go round first into the other street, over which, on the
ground-floor, among the windows (all exactly alike, but
darkened) of the adjoining houses, shone the solitary lighted
window of her room. He would rap on the pane, and she would
hear the signal, and answer, before going to meet him at the
front door. He would find, lying open on the piano, some of
her favourite music, the *Valse des Roses*, the *Pauvre Fou* of
Tagliafico (which, according to the instructions embodied in
her will, was to be played at her funeral); but he would ask her,
instead, to give him the little phrase from Vinteuil's sonata. It
was true that Odette played vilely, but often the most memorable impression of a piece of music is one that has arisen out
of a jumble of wrong notes struck by unskilful fingers upon a
tuneless piano. The little phrase continued to be associated in
Swann's mind with his love for Odette. He was well aware
that his love was something that did not correspond to anything outside itself, verifiable by others besides him; he realised
that Odette's qualities were not such as to justify his setting so
high a value on the hours he spent in her company. And
often, when the cold government of reason stood unchallenged in his mind, he would readily have ceased to sacrifice so
many of his intellectual and social interests to this imaginary
pleasure. But the little phrase, as soon as it struck his ear, had
the power to liberate in him the space that was needed to contain it; the proportions of Swann's soul were altered; a margin
was left for an enjoyment that corresponded no more than
his love for Odette to any external object and yet was not, like
his enjoyment of that love, purely individual, but assumed for
him a sort of reality superior to that of concrete things. This
thirst for an unknown delight was awakened in him by the

little phrase, but without bringing him any precise gratification to assuage it. With the result that those parts of Swann's
soul in which the little phrase had obliterated all concern for
material interests, those human considerations which affect all
men alike, were left vacant by it, blank pages on which he was
at liberty to inscribe the name of Odette. Moreover, in so far as
Odette's affection might seem a little abrupt and disappointing,
the little phrase would come to supplement it, to blend with
it its own mysterious essence. Watching Swann's face while
he listened to the phrase, one would have said that he was inhaling an anaesthetic which allowed him to breathe more
freely. And the pleasure which the music gave him, which was
shortly to create in him a real need, was in fact akin at such
moments to the pleasure which he would have derived from
experimenting with perfumes, from entering into contact with
a world for which we men were not made, which appears to us
formless because our eyes cannot perceive it, meaningless because it eludes our understanding, to which we may attain by
way of one sense only. There was a deep repose, a mysterious refreshment for Swann,—whose eyes, although delicate
interpreters of painting, whose mind, although an acute observer of manners, must bear for ever the indelible imprint of
the barrenness of his life,—in feeling himself transformed into
a creature estranged from humanity, blinded, deprived of his
logical faculty, almost a fantastic unicorn, a chimaera-like
creature conscious of the world through his hearing alone. And
since he sought in the little phrase for a meaning to which his
intelligence could not descend, with what a strange frenzy of
intoxication did he strip bare his innermost soul of the whole
armour of reason and make it pass unattended through the
dark filter of sound! He began to realise how much that was
painful, perhaps even how much secret and unappeased sorrow
underlay the sweetness of the phrase; and yet to him it brought
no suffering. What matter though the phrase repeated that love
is frail and fleeting, when his love was so strong! He played
with the melancholy which the music diffused, he felt it stealing
over him, but like a caress which only deepened and sweetened
his sense of his own happiness. He would make Odette play
it over to him again and again, ten, twenty times on end,

insisting that, as she did so, she must never stop kissing him. Every kiss provokes another. Ah, in those earliest days of love how naturally the kisses spring into life! So closely, in their profusion, do they crowd together that lovers would find it as hard to count the kisses exchanged in an hour as to count the flowers in a meadow in May. Then she would pretend to stop, saying: "How do you expect me to play when you keep on holding me? I can't do everything at once. Make up your mind what you want: am I to play the phrase or do you want to play with me?" and he would get angry, and she would burst out laughing, a laugh that was soon transformed and descended upon him in a shower of kisses. Or else she would look at him sulkily, and he would see once again a face worthy to figure in Botticelli's "Life of Moses"; he would place it there, giving to Odette's neck the necessary inclination; and when he had finished her portrait in tempera, in the fifteenth century, on the wall of the Sistine, the idea that she was none the less in the room with him still, by the piano, at that very moment, ready to be kissed and enjoyed, the idea of her material existence, would sweep over him with so violent an intoxication that, with eyes starting from his head and jaws tensed as though to devour her, he would fling himself upon this Botticelli maiden and kiss and bite her cheeks. And then, once he had left her, not without returning to kiss her again because he had forgotten to take away with him the memory of some detail of her fragrance or of her features, as he drove home in his victoria he blessed Odette for allowing him these daily visits which could not, he felt, bring any great joy to her, but which, by keeping him immune from the fever of jealousy—by removing from him any possibility of a fresh outbreak of the heart-sickness which had afflicted him on the evening when he had failed to find her at the Verdurins'—would help him to arrive, without any recurrence of those crises of which the first had been so painful that it must also be the last, at the end of this strange period of his life, of these hours, enchanted almost, like those in which he drove through Paris by moonlight. And, noticing as he drove home that the moon had now changed its position relatively to his own and was almost touching the horizon, feeling that his love, too, was obedient to these immutable

natural laws, he asked himself whether this period upon which
he had entered would last much longer, whether presently his
mind's eye would cease to behold that beloved face save as
occupying a distant and diminished position, and on the verge
of ceasing to shed on him the radiance of its charm. For Swann
was once more finding in things, since he had fallen in love,
the charm that he had found when, in his adolescence, he had
fancied himself an artist; with this difference, that the charm
that lay in them now was conferred by Odette alone. He felt
the inspirations of his youth, which had been dissipated by a
frivolous life, stirring again in him, but they all bore now the
reflection, the stamp of a particular being; and during the long
hours which he now found a subtle pleasure in spending at
home, alone with his convalescent soul, he became gradually
himself again, but himself in thraldom to another.

He went to her only in the evenings, and knew nothing of
how she spent her time during the day, any more than of her
past; so little, indeed, that he had not even the tiny, initial clue
which, by allowing us to imagine what we do not know, stimu-
lates a desire for knowledge. And so he never asked himself
what she might be doing, or what her life had been. Only he
smiled sometimes at the thought of how, some years earlier,
when he did not yet know her, people had spoken to him of a
woman who, if he remembered rightly, must certainly have
been Odette, as of a "tart," a "kept" woman, one of those
women to whom he still attributed (having lived but little in
their company) the wilful, fundamentally perverse character
with which they had so long been endowed by the imagination
of certain novelists. He told himself that as often as not one
has only to take the opposite view to the reputation created
by the world in order to judge a person accurately, when with
such a character he contrasted that of Odette, so kind, so
simple, so enthusiastic in the pursuit of ideals, so incapable,
almost, of not telling the truth that, when he had once begged
her, so that they might dine together alone, to write to Mme
Verdurin saying that she was unwell, the next day he had seen
her, face to face with Mme Verdurin who asked whether she
had recovered, blushing, stammering and in spite of herself
revealing in every feature how painful, what a torture it was to

her to act a lie and, as in her answer she multiplied the fictitious details of her alleged indisposition, seeming to ask
forgiveness, by her suppliant look and her stricken accents, for
the obvious falsehood of her words.

On certain days, however, though these were rare, she
would call upon him in the afternoon, interrupting his musings
or the essay on Vermeer to which he had latterly returned. His
servant would come in to say that Mme de Crécy was in the
small drawing-room. He would go and join her, and when he
opened the door, on Odette's rosy face, as soon as she caught
sight of Swann, would appear—changing the curve of her lips,
the look in her eyes, the moulding of her cheeks—an all-
absorbing smile. Once he was alone he would see that smile
again, and also her smile of the day before, and another with
which she had greeted him sometime else, and the smile which
had been her answer, in the carriage that night, when he had
asked her whether she objected to his rearranging her cattleyas; and the life of Odette at all other times, since he knew
nothing of it, appeared to him, with its neutral and colourless
background, like those sheets of sketches by Watteau upon
which one sees here, there, at every corner and at various
angles, traced in three colours upon the buff paper, innumerable smiles. But once in a while, illuminating a chink of that
existence which Swann still saw as a complete blank, even if his
mind assured him that it was not, because he was unable to
visualise it, some friend who knew them both and, suspecting
that they were in love, would not have dared to tell him anything about her that was of the least importance, would describe how he had glimpsed Odette that very morning walking
up the Rue Abbattucci, in a cape trimmed with skunk, a
Rembrandt hat, and a bunch of violets in her bosom. Swann
would be bowled over by this simple sketch because it suddenly made him realise that Odette had an existence that was
not wholly subordinated to his own; he longed to know whom
she had been seeking to impress by this costume in which he
had never seen her, and he made up his mind to ask her where
she had been going at that intercepted moment, as though, in
all the colourless life of his mistress—a life almost non-existent,
since it was invisible to him—there had been but a single inci-

dent apart from all those smiles directed towards himself: namely, her walking abroad beneath a Rembrandt hat, with a bunch of violets in her bosom.

Except when he asked her for Vinteuil's little phrase instead of the *Valse des Roses*, Swann made no effort to induce her to play the things that he himself preferred, or, in literature any more than in music, to correct the manifold errors of her taste. He fully realised that she was not intelligent. When she said how much she would like him to tell her about the great poets, she had imagined that she would immediately get to know whole pages of romantic and heroic verse, in the style of the Vicomte de Borelli, only even more moving. As for Vermeer of Delft, she asked whether he had been made to suffer by a woman, if it was a woman who had inspired him, and once Swann had told her that no one knew, she had lost all interest in that painter. She would often say: "Poetry, you know—well, of course, there'd be nothing like it if it was all true, if the poets really believed what they say. But as often as not you'll find there's no one so mean and calculating as those fellows. I know something about it: I had a friend, once, who was in love with a poet of sorts. In his verses he never spoke of anything but love and the sky and the stars. Oh! she was properly taken in! He had more than three hundred thousand francs out of her before he'd finished."

If, then, Swann tried to show her what artistic beauty consisted in, how one ought to appreciate poetry or painting, after a minute or two she would cease to listen, saying: "Yes . . . I never thought it would be like that." And he felt that her disappointment was so great that he preferred to lie to her, assuring her that what he had said was nothing, that he had only touched the surface, that he had no time to go into it all properly, that there was more in it than that. Then she would interrupt sharply: "More in it? What? . . . Do tell me!", but he did not tell her, knowing how feeble it would appear to her, how different from what she had expected, less sensational and less touching, and fearing lest, disillusioned with art, she might at the same time be disillusioned with love.

With the result that she found Swann inferior, intellectually, to what she had supposed. "You're always so reserved; I can't make you out." She was more impressed by his indifference to money, by his kindness to everyone, by his courtesy and tact. And indeed it happens, often enough, to greater men than Swann, to a scientist or an artist, when he is not misunderstood by the people among whom he lives, that the feeling on their part which proves that they have been convinced of the superiority of his intellect is not their admiration for his ideas—for these are beyond them—but their respect for his kindness. Swann's position in society also inspired Odette with respect, but she had no desire that he should attempt to secure invitations for herself. Perhaps she felt that such attempts would be bound to fail; perhaps she even feared that, merely by speaking of her to his friends, he might provoke disclosures of an unwelcome kind. At all events she had made him promise never to mention her name. Her reason for not wishing to go into society was, she had told him, a quarrel she had once had with a friend who had avenged herself subsequently by speaking ill of her. "But surely," Swann objected, "not everyone knew your friend." "Yes, but don't you see, it spreads like wildfire; people are so horrid." Swann found this story frankly incomprehensible; on the other hand, he knew that such generalisations as "People are so horrid," and "A word of scandal spreads like wildfire," were generally accepted as true; there must be cases to which they were applicable. Could Odette's be one of these? He teased himself with the question, though not for long, for he too was subject to that mental torpor that had so weighed upon his father, whenever he was faced by a difficult problem. In any event, that world of society which so frightened Odette did not, perhaps, inspire her with any great longings, since it was too far removed from the world she knew for her to be able to form any clear conception of it. At the same time, while in certain aspects she had retained a genuine simplicity (she had, for instance, kept up a friendship with a little dressmaker, now retired from business, up whose steep and dark and fetid staircase she clambered almost every day), she still thirsted to be in the fashion, though her idea of it was not altogether the same as that of society people. For the latter, it emanates from a comparatively small number of individuals, who pro-

ject it to a considerable distance—more and more faintly the
further one is from their intimate centre—within the circle
of their friends and the friends of their friends, whose names
form a sort of tabulated index. People "in society" know this
index by heart; they are gifted in such matters with an erudition from which they have extracted a sort of taste, of tact, so
automatic in its operation that Swann, for example, without
needing to draw upon his knowledge of the world, if he read in
a newspaper the names of the people who had been at a dinner-
party, could tell at once its exact degree of smartness, just
as a man of letters, simply by reading a sentence, can estimate exactly the literary merit of its author. But Odette was
one of those persons (an extremely numerous category, whatever the fashionable world may think, and to be found in every
class of society) who do not share these notions, but imagine
smartness to be something quite other, which assumes different
aspects according to the circle to which they themselves
belong, but has the special characteristic—common alike to
the fashion of which Odette dreamed and to that before
which Mme Cottard bowed—of being directly accessible to
all. The other kind, the smartness of society people, is, it
must be admitted, accessible also; but there is a time-lag.
Odette would say of someone: "He only goes to really smart
places."

And if Swann asked her what she meant by that, she would
answer with a touch of contempt: "Smart places! Why, good
heavens, just fancy, at your age, having to be told what the
smart places are in Paris! Well, on Sunday mornings there's
the Avenue de l'Impératrice, and round the lake at five o'clock,
and on Thursdays, the Eden-Théâtre, and the Races on Fridays;
then there are the balls . . ."

"What balls?"

"Why, silly, the balls people give in Paris; the smart ones,
I mean. For instance, Herbinger, you know who I mean, the
fellow who's in one of the jobbers' offices. Yes, of course you
must know him, he's one of the best-known men in Paris,
that great big fair-haired boy who wears such swagger clothes
—always has a flower in his buttonhole and a light-coloured
overcoat with a stripe down the back. He goes about with that

old frump, takes her to all the first-nights. Well, he gave a ball the other night, and all the smart people in Paris were there. I should have loved to go! But you had to show your invitation at the door, and I couldn't get one anywhere. Still, I'm just as glad, now, that I didn't go; I should have been killed in the crush, and seen nothing. It's really just to be able to say you've been to Herbinger's ball. You know what a braggart I am! However, you may be quite certain that half the people who tell you they were there are lying. . . . But I'm surprised you weren't there, a regular 'tip-topper' like you."

Swann made no attempt, however, to modify this conception of fashionable life; feeling that his own came no nearer to the truth, was just as fatuous and trivial, he saw no point in imparting it to his mistress, with the result that, after a few months, she ceased to take any interest in the people to whose houses he went, except as a means of obtaining tickets for the paddock at race-meetings or first-nights at the theatre. She hoped that he would continue to cultivate such profitable acquaintances, but in other respects she was inclined to regard them as anything but smart, ever since she had passed the Marquise de Villeparisis in the street, wearing a black woollen dress and a bonnet with strings.

"But she looks like a lavatory attendant, like an old charwoman, darling! A marquise, her! Goodness knows I'm not a marquise, but you'd have to pay me a lot of money before you'd get me to go round Paris rigged out like that!"

Nor could she understand Swann's continuing to live in his house on the Quai d'Orléans, which, though she dared not tell him so, she considered unworthy of him.

It was true that she claimed to be fond of "antiques," and used to assume a rapturous and knowing air when she confessed how she loved to spend the whole day "rummaging" in curio shops, hunting for "bric-à-brac" and "period" things. Although it was a point of honour to which she obstinately clung, as though obeying some old family precept, that she should never answer questions or "account for" how she spent her days, she spoke to Swann once about a friend to whose house she had been invited, and had found that everything in it was "of the period." Swann could not get her to tell him what "period" it was. But after thinking the matter over she replied that it was "mediaeval"; by which she meant that the walls were panelled. Some time later she spoke to him again of her friend, and added, in the hesitant tone and with the knowing air one adopts in referring to a person one has met at dinner the night before and of whom one had never heard until then, but whom one's hosts seemed to regard as someone so celebrated and important that one hopes that one's listener will know who is meant and be duly impressed: "Her dining-room ... is ... eighteenth century!" She herself had thought it hideous, all bare, as though the house were still unfinished; women looked frightful in it, and it would never become the fashion. She mentioned it again, a third time, when she showed Swann a card with the name and address of the man who had designed the dining-room, and whom she wanted to send for when she had enough money, to see whether he couldn't do one for her too; not one like that, of course, but one of the sort she used to dream of and which unfortunately her little house wasn't large enough to contain, with tall sideboards, Renaissance furniture and fireplaces like the château at Blois. It was on this occasion that she blurted out to Swann what she really thought of his abode on the Quai d'Orléans; he having ventured the criticism that her friend had indulged, not in the Louis XVI style, for although that was not, of course, done, still it might be made charming, but in the "sham-antique."

"You wouldn't have her live like you among a lot of broken-down chairs and threadbare carpets!" she exclaimed, the innate respectability of the bourgeois housewife getting the better of the acquired dilettantism of the courtesan.

People who enjoyed picking up antiques, who liked poetry, despised sordid calculations of profit and loss, and nourished ideals of honour and love, she placed in a class by themselves, superior to the rest of humanity. There was no need actually to have those tastes, as long as one proclaimed them; when a man had told her at dinner that he loved to wander about and get his hands covered with dust in old furniture shops, that he would never be really appreciated in this commercial age since he was not interested in its concerns, and that he belonged

to another generation altogether, she would come home saying: "Why, he's an adorable creature, so sensitive, I had no
idea," and she would conceive for him an immediate bond of
friendship. But on the other hand, men who, like Swann, had
these tastes but did not speak of them, left her cold. She was
obliged, of course, to admit that Swann was not interested in
money, but she would add sulkily: "It's not the same thing,
you see, with him," and, as a matter of fact, what appealed to
her imagination was not the practice of disinterestedness, but
its vocabulary.

Feeling that, often, he could not give her in reality the
pleasures of which she dreamed, he tried at least to ensure that
she should be happy in his company, tried not to counteract
those vulgar ideas, that bad taste which she displayed on every
possible occasion, and which in fact he loved, as he could not
help loving everything that came from her, which enchanted
him even, for were they not so many characteristic features by
virtue of which the essence of this woman revealed itself to
him? And so, when she was in a happy mood because she was
going to see the *Reine Topaze*,[10] or when her expression grew
serious, worried, petulant because she was afraid of missing
the flower-show, or merely of not being in time for tea, with
muffins and toast, at the Rue Royale tea-rooms, where she believed that regular attendance was indispensable in order to
set the seal upon a woman's certificate of elegance, Swann,
enraptured as we all are at times by the naturalness of a child
or the verisimilitude of a portrait which appears to be on the
point of speaking, would feel so distinctly the soul of his
mistress rising to the surface of her face that he could not refrain from touching it with his lips. "Ah, so little Odette wants
us to take her to the flower-show, does she? She wants to be
admired, does she? Very well, we'll take her there, we can but
obey her wishes." As Swann was a little short-sighted, he had
to resign himself to wearing spectacles at home when working,
while to face the world he adopted a monocle as being less
disfiguring. The first time that she saw it in his eye, she could
not contain her joy: "I really do think—for a man, that is to
say—it's tremendously smart! How nice you look with it!
Every inch a gentleman. All you want now is a title!" she

concluded with a tinge of regret. He liked Odette to say these
things, just as if he had been in love with a Breton girl, he
would have enjoyed seeing her in her coif and hearing her say
that she believed in ghosts. Always until then, as is common
among men whose taste for the arts develops independently
of their sensuality, a weird disparity had existed between the
satisfactions which he would accord to both simultaneously;
yielding to the seductions of more and more rarefied works of
art in the company of more and more vulgar women, taking a
little servant-girl to a screened box at the theatre for the performance of a decadent piece he particularly wanted to see,
or to an exhibition of impressionist painting, convinced, moreover, that a cultivated "society" woman would have understood them no better, but would not have managed to remain
so prettily silent. But, now that he was in love with Odette,
all this was changed; to share her sympathies, to strive to be
one with her in spirit, was a task so attractive that he tried to
find enjoyment in the things that she liked, and did find a
pleasure, not only in imitating her habits but in adopting her
opinions, which was all the deeper because, as those habits
and opinions had no roots in his own intelligence, they reminded him only of his love, for the sake of which he had
preferred them to his own. If he went again to *Serge Panine*, if
he looked out for opportunities of going to see Olivier Métra
conduct,[11] it was for the pleasure of being initiated into every
one of Odette's ideas and fancies, of feeling that he had an
equal share in all her tastes. This charm, which her favourite
plays and pictures and places possessed, of drawing him closer
to her, struck him as being more mysterious than the intrinsic
charm of more beautiful things and places with which she had
no connection. Besides, having allowed the intellectual beliefs
of his youth to languish, and his man-of-the-world scepticism
having permeated them without his being aware of it, he felt
(or at least he had felt for so long that he had fallen into the
habit of saying) that the objects we admire have no absolute
value in themselves, that the whole thing is a matter of period
and class, is no more than a series of fashions, the most vulgar
of which are worth just as much as those which are regarded
as the most refined. And as he considered that the importance

Odette attached to receiving an invitation to a private view
was not in itself any more ridiculous than the pleasure he himself had at one time felt in lunching with the Prince of Wales,
so he did not think that the admiration she professed for
Monte-Carlo or for the Righi was any more unreasonable than
his own liking for Holland (which she imagined to be ugly)
and for Versailles (which bored her to tears). And so he denied
himself the pleasure of visiting those places, delighted to be
able to tell himself that it was for her sake, that he wished only
to feel, to enjoy things with her.

Like everything else that formed part of Odette's environment, and was no more, in a sense, than the means whereby
he might see and talk to her more often, he enjoyed the society
of the Verdurins. There, since at the heart of all their entertainments, dinners, musical evenings, games, suppers in fancy
dress, excursions to the country, theatre outings, even the
infrequent "gala evenings" when they entertained the "bores,"
there was the presence of Odette, the sight of Odette, conversation with Odette, an inestimable boon which the Verdurins bestowed on Swann by inviting him to their house,
he was happier in the little "nucleus" than anywhere else, and
tried to find some genuine merit in each of its members,
imagining that this would lead him to frequent their society
from choice for the rest of his life. Not daring to tell himself,
lest he should doubt the truth of the suggestion, that he would
always love Odette, at least in supposing that he would go on
visiting the Verdurins (a proposition which, *a priori*, raised
fewer fundamental objections on the part of his intelligence)
he saw himself in the future continuing to meet Odette every
evening; that did not, perhaps, come quite to the same thing
as loving her for ever, but for the moment, while he loved her,
to feel that he would not eventually cease to see her was all
that he asked. "What a charming atmosphere!" he said to himself. "How entirely genuine is the life these people lead! How
much more intelligent, more artistic, they are than the people
one knows! And Mme Verdurin, in spite of a few trifling
exaggerations which are rather absurd, what a sincere love of
painting and music she has, what a passion for works of art,
what anxiety to give pleasure to artists! Her ideas about some

of the people one knows are not quite right, but then their ideas about artistic circles are altogether wrong! Possibly I make no great intellectual demands in conversation, but I'm perfectly happy talking to Cottard, although he does trot out those idiotic puns. And as for the painter, if he is rather disagreeably pretentious when he tries to shock, still he has one of the finest brains that I've ever come across. Besides, what is most important, one feels quite free there, one does what one likes without constraint or fuss. What a flow of good humour there is every day in that drawing-room! No question about it, with a few rare exceptions I never want to go anywhere else again. It will become more and more of a habit, and I shall spend the rest of my life among them."

And as the qualities which he supposed to be intrinsic to the Verdurins were no more than the superficial reflection of pleasures which he had enjoyed in their society through his love for Odette, those qualities became more serious, more profound, more vital, when those pleasures were too. Since Mme Verdurin often gave Swann what alone could constitute his happiness—since, on an evening when he felt anxious because Odette had talked rather more to one of the party than to another, and, irritated by this, would not take the initiative of asking her whether she was coming home with him, Mme Verdurin brought peace and joy to his troubled spirit by saying spontaneously: "Odette, you'll see M. Swann home, won't you?"; and since, when the summer holidays were impending and he had asked himself uneasily whether Odette might not leave Paris without him, whether he would still be able to see her every day, Mme Verdurin had invited them both to spend the summer with her in the country—Swann, unconsciously allowing gratitude and self-interest to infiltrate his intelligence and to influence his ideas, went so far as to proclaim that Mme Verdurin was "a great and noble soul." Should one of his old fellow-students from the Ecole du Louvre speak to him of some delightful or eminent people he had come across, "I'd a hundred times rather have the Verdurins" he would reply. And, with a solemnity of diction that was new in him: "They are magnanimous creatures, and magnanimity is, after all, the one thing that matters, the one thing that gives us distinction here on earth. You see, there are only two classes of people, the magnanimous, and the rest; and I have reached an age when one has to take sides, to decide once and for all whom one is going to like and dislike, to stick to the people one likes, and, to make up for the time one has wasted with the others, never to leave them again as long as one lives. And so," he went on, with the slight thrill of emotion which a man feels when, even without being fully aware of it, he says something not because it is true but because he enjoys saying it, and listens to his own voice uttering the words as though they came from someone else, "the die is now cast. I have elected to love none but magnanimous souls, and to live only in an atmosphere of magnanimity. You ask me whether Mme Verdurin is really intelligent. I can assure you that she has given me proofs of a nobility of heart, of a loftiness of soul, to which no one could possibly attain without a corresponding loftiness of mind. Without question, she has a profound understanding of art. But it is not, perhaps, in that that she is most admirable; every little action, ingeniously, exquisitely kind, which she has performed for my sake, every thoughtful attention, every little gesture, quite domestic and yet quite sublime, reveals a more profound comprehension of existence than all your text-books of philosophy."

He might have reminded himself that there were various old friends of his family who were just as simple as the Verdurins, companions of his youth who were just as fond of art, that he knew other "great-hearted" people, and that nevertheless, since he had opted in favour of simplicity, the arts, and magnanimity, he had entirely ceased to see them. But these people did not know Odette, and, if they had known her, would never have thought of introducing her to him.

And so, in the whole of the Verdurin circle, there was probably not a single one of the "faithful" who loved them, or believed that he loved them, as dearly as did Swann. And yet, when M. Verdurin had said that he did not take to Swann, he had not only expressed his own sentiments, he had divined those of his wife. Doubtless Swann had too exclusive an affection for Odette, of which he had neglected to make Mme Verdurin his regular confidante; doubtless the very discretion with which he availed himself of the Verdurins' hospitality, often refraining from coming to dine with them for a reason which they never suspected and in place of which they saw only an anxiety on his part not to have to decline an invitation to the house of some "bore" or other, and doubtless, too, despite all the precautions which he had taken to keep it from them, the gradual discovery which they were making of his brilliant position in society—doubtless all this contributed to their growing irritation with Swann. But the real, the fundamental reason was quite different. The fact was that they had very quickly sensed in him a locked door, a reserved, impenetrable chamber in which he still professed silently to himself that the Princesse de Sagan was not grotesque and that Cottard's jokes were not amusing, in a word, for all that he never deviated from his affability or revolted against their dogmas, an impermeability to those dogmas, a resistance to complete conversion, the like of which they had never come across in anyone before. They would have forgiven him for associating with "bores" (to whom, as it happened, in his heart of hearts he infinitely preferred the Verdurins and all the little "nucleus") had he consented to set a good example by openly renouncing those "bores" in the presence of the "faithful." But that was an abjuration which they realised they were powerless to extort from him.

How different he was from a "newcomer" whom Odette had asked them to invite, although she herself had met him only a few times, and on whom they were building great hopes— the Comte de Forcheville! (It turned out that he was Saniette's brother-in-law, a discovery which filled all the faithful with amazement: the manners of the old palaeographer were so humble that they had always supposed him to be socially inferior to themselves, and had never expected to learn that he came from a rich and relatively aristocratic background.) Of course, Forcheville was a colossal snob, which Swann was not; of course he would never dream of placing, as Swann now did, the Verdurin circle above all others. But he lacked that natural refinement which prevented Swann from associating himself with the more obviously false accusations that Mme Verdurin levelled at people he knew. As for the vulgar and

pretentious tirades in which the painter sometimes indulged,
the commercial traveller's pleasantries which Cottard used to
hazard, and for which Swann, who liked both men sincerely,
could easily find excuses without having either the heart or the
hypocrisy to applaud them, Forcheville by contrast was of an
intellectual calibre to be dumbfounded, awestruck by the first
(without in the least understanding them) and to revel in the
second. And as it happened, the very first dinner at the Verdurins' at which Forcheville was present threw a glaring light
upon all these differences, brought out his qualities and precipitated Swann's fall from grace.

There was at this dinner, besides the usual party, a professor
from the Sorbonne, one Brichot, who had met M. and Mme
Verdurin at a watering-place somewhere and who, if his university duties and scholarly labours had not left him with very
little time to spare, would gladly have come to them more
often. For he had the sort of curiosity and superstitious wor-
ship of life which, combined with a certain scepticism with
regard to the object of their studies, earns for some intelligent
men of whatever profession, doctors who do not believe in
medicine, schoolmasters who do not believe in Latin exercises,
the reputation of having broad, brilliant and indeed superior
minds. He affected, when at Mme Verdurin's, to choose his
illustrations from among the most topical subjects of the day
when he spoke of philosophy or history, principally because
he regarded those sciences as no more than a preparation for
life, and imagined that he was seeing put into practice by the
"little clan" what hitherto he had known only from books, and
perhaps also because, having had instilled into him as a boy,
and having unconsciously preserved, a reverence for certain
subjects, he thought that he was casting aside the scholar's
gown when he ventured to treat those subjects with a conversational licence which in fact seemed daring to him only because the folds of the gown still clung.

Early in the course of the dinner, when M. de Forcheville,
seated on the right of Mme Verdurin who in the "newcomer's"
honour had taken great pains with her toilet, observed to her:
"Quite original, that white dress," the doctor, who had never
taken his eyes off him so curious was he to learn the nature and

attributes of what he called a "de," and who was on the look-
out for an opportunity of attracting his attention and coming
into closer contact with him, caught in its flight the adjective
"*blanche*" and, his eyes still glued to his plate, snapped out,
"*Blanche?* Blanche of Castile?" then, without moving his head,
shot a furtive glance to right and left of him, smiling uncertainly. While Swann, by the painful and futile effort which he
made to smile, showed that he thought the pun absurd,
Forcheville had shown at one and the same time that he could
appreciate its subtlety and that he was a man of the world, by
keeping within its proper limits a mirth the spontaneity of
which had charmed Mme Verdurin.

"What do you make of a scientist like that?" she asked
Forcheville. "You can't talk seriously to him for two minutes
on end. Is that the sort of thing you tell them at your hospital?"
she went on, turning to the doctor. "They must have some
pretty lively times there, if that's the case. I can see that I shall
have to get taken in as a patient!"

"I think I heard the Doctor speak of that old termagant,
Blanche of Castile, if I may so express myself. Am I not right,
Madame?" Brichot appealed to Mme Verdurin, who, swooning
with merriment, her eyes tightly closed, had buried her face in
her hands, from behind which muffled screams could be heard.

"Good gracious, Madame, I would not dream of shocking
the reverent-minded, if there are any such around this table,
sub rosa . . . I recognise, moreover, that our ineffable and
Athenian—oh, how infinitely Athenian—republic is capable of
honouring, in the person of that obscurantist old she-Capet,
the first of our strong-arm chiefs of police. Yes, indeed, my
dear host, yes indeed, yes indeed!" he repeated in his ringing
voice, which sounded a separate note for each syllable, in reply
to a protest from M. Verdurin. "The Chronicle of Saint Denis,
and the authenticity of its information is beyond question,
leaves us no room for doubt on that point. No one could be
more fitly chosen as patron by a secularised proletariat than
that mother of a saint, to whom, incidentally, she gave a
pretty rough time, according to Suger and other great St
Bernards of the sort; for with her everyone got hauled over
the coals."

"Who is that gentleman?" Forcheville asked Mme Verdurin.
"He seems first-rate."

"What! Do you mean to say you don't know the famous
Brichot? Why, he's celebrated all over Euope."

"Oh, that's Bréchot, is it?" exclaimed Forcheville, who had
not quite caught the name. "You must tell me all about him,"
he went on, fastening a pair of goggle eyes on the celebrity.
"It's always interesting to dine with prominent people. But, I
say, you ask one to very select parties here. No dull evenings
in this house, I'm sure."

"Well, you know what it is really," said Mme Verdurin
modestly, "they feel at ease here. They can talk about whatever
they like, and the conversation goes off like fireworks. Now
Brichot, this evening, is nothing. I've seen him, don't you
know, when he's been in my house, simply dazzling; you'd
want to go on your knees to him. Well, anywhere else he's not
the same man, he's not in the least witty, you have to drag the
words out of him, he's even boring."

"That's strange," remarked Forcheville with fitting astonishment.

A sort of wit like Brichot's would have been regarded as
out-and-out stupidity by the people among whom Swann had
spent his early life, for all that it is quite compatible with real
intelligence. And the intelligence of the Professor's vigorous
and well-nourished brain might easily have been envied by
many of the people in society who seemed witty enough to
Swann. But these last had so thoroughly inculcated into him
their likes and dislikes, at least in everything that pertained to
social life, including that adjunct to social life which belongs,
strictly speaking, to the domain of intelligence, namely, conversation, that Swann could not but find Brichot's pleasantries
pedantic, vulgar and nauseating. He was shocked, too, being
accustomed to good manners, by the rude, almost barrack-
room tone the pugnacious academic adopted no matter to
whom he was speaking. Finally, perhaps, he had lost some
of his tolerance that evening when he saw the cordiality
displayed by Mme Verdurin towards this Forcheville fellow
whom it had been Odette's unaccountable idea to bring to
the house. Somewhat embarrassed vis-à-vis Swann, she

asked him on her arrival: "What do you think of my guest?"

And he, suddenly realising for the first time that Forcheville, whom he had known for years, could actually attract a woman and was quite a good-looking man, replied: "Unspeakable!" It did not occur to him to be jealous of Odette, but he did not feel quite so happy as usual, and when Brichot, having begun to tell them the story of Blanche of Castile's mother who, according to him, "had been with Henry Plantagenet for years before they were married," tried to prompt Swann to beg him to continue the story by interjecting "Isn't that so, M. Swann?" in the martial accents people use in order to put themselves on a level with a country bumpkin or to put the fear of God into a trooper, Swann cut his story short, to the intense fury of their hostess, by begging to be excused for taking so little interest in Blanche of Castile, as he had something that he wished to ask the painter. The latter, it appeared, had been that afternoon to an exhibition of the work of another artist, also a friend of Mme Verdurin, who had recently died, and Swann wished to find out from him (for he valued his discrimination) whether there had really been anything more in these last works than the virtuosity which had struck people so forcibly in his earlier exhibitions.

"From that point of view it was remarkable, but it did not seem to me to be a form of art which you could call 'elevated,' " said Swann with a smile.

"Elevated . . . to the purple," interrupted Cottard, raising his arms with mock solemnity. The whole table burst out laughing.

"What did I tell you?" said Mme Verdurin to Forcheville. "It's simply impossible to be serious with him. When you least expect it, out he comes with some piece of foolery."

But she observed that Swann alone had not unbent. For one thing he was none too pleased with Cottard for having secured a laugh at his expense in front of Forcheville. But the painter, instead of replying in a way that might have interested Swann, as he would probably have done had they been alone together, preferred to win the easy admiration of the rest with a witty dissertation on the talent of the deceased master.

"I went up to one of them," he began, "just to see how it was done. I stuck my nose into it. Well, it's just not true! Impossible to say whether it was done with glue, with soap, with sealing-wax, with sunshine, with leaven, with caca!"

"And one makes twelve!" shouted the doctor, but just too late, for no one saw the point of his interruption.

"It looks as though it was done with nothing at all," resumed the painter. "No more chance of discovering the trick than there is in the 'Night Watch' or the 'Female Regents,' and technically it's even better than Rembrandt or Hals. It's all there—but really, I swear it."

Then, just as singers who have reached the highest note in their compass continue in a head voice, *piano*, he proceeded to murmur, laughing the while, as if, after all, there had been something irresistibly absurd in the sheer beauty of the painting: "It smells good, it makes your head whirl; it takes your breath away; you feel ticklish all over—and not the faintest clue to how it's done. The man's a sorcerer; the thing's a conjuring-trick, a miracle," bursting into outright laughter, "it's almost dishonest!" And stopping, solemnly raising his head, pitching his voice on a *basso profundo* note which he struggled to bring into harmony, he concluded, "And it's so sincere!"

Except at the moment when he had called it "better than the 'Night Watch,'" a blasphemy which had called forth an instant protest from Mme Verdurin, who regarded the "Night Watch" as the supreme masterpiece of the universe (conjointly with the "Ninth" and the "Winged Victory"), and at the word "caca," which had made Forcheville throw a sweeping glance round the table to see whether it was "all right," before he allowed his lips to curve in a prudish and conciliatory smile, all the guests (save Swann) had kept their fascinated and adoring eyes fixed upon the painter.

"I do so love him when he gets carried away like that!" cried Mme Verdurin the moment he had finished, enraptured that the table-talk should have proved so entertaining on the very night that Forcheville was dining with them for the first time. "Hallo, you!" she turned to her husband, "What's the matter with you, sitting there gaping like a great animal? You know he talks well. Anybody would think it was the first time he had ever listened to you," she added to the painter. "If you had only seen him while you were speaking; he was just drinking it all in. And to-morrow he'll tell us everything you said, without missing out a word."

"No, really, I'm not joking!" protested the painter, enchanted by the success of his speech. "You all look as if you thought I was pulling your legs, that it's all eyewash. I'll take you to see the show, and then you can say whether I've been exaggerating; I'll bet you anything you like, you'll come away even more enthusiastic than I am!"

"But we don't suppose for a moment that you're exaggerating. We only want you to go on with your dinner, and my husband too. Give M. Biche some more sole, can't you see his has got cold? We're not in any hurry; you're dashing round as if the house was on fire. Wait a little; don't serve the salad just yet."

Mme Cottard, who was a modest woman and spoke but seldom, was not however lacking in self-assurance when a happy inspiration put the right word in her mouth. She felt that it would be well received, and this gave her confidence, but what she did with it was with the object not so much of shining herself as of helping her husband on in his career. And so she did not allow the word "salad," which Mme Verdurin had just uttered, to pass unchallenged.

"It's not a Japanese salad, is it?" she said in a loud undertone, turning towards Odette.

And then, in her joy and confusion at the aptness and daring of making so discreet and yet so unmistakable an allusion to the new and brilliantly successful play by Dumas, she broke into a charming, girlish laugh, not very loud, but so irresistible that it was some time before she could control it.

"Who is that lady? She seems devilish clever," said Forcheville.

"No, it is not. But we'll make one for you if you'll all come to dinner on Friday."

"You will think me dreadfully provincial," said Mme Cottard to Swann, "but I haven't yet seen this famous *Francillon* that everybody's talking about. The Doctor has been (I remember now, he told me he had the great pleasure of spending

the evening with you) and I must confess I didn't think it very
sensible for him to spend money on seats in order to see it
again with me. Of course an evening at the Théâtre-Français
is never really wasted; the acting's so good there always; but
we have some very nice friends" (Mme Cottard rarely uttered
a proper name, but restricted herself to "some friends of ours"
or "one of my friends," as being more "distinguished,"
speaking in an affected tone and with the self-importance of a
person who need give names only when she chooses) "who
often have a box, and are kind enough to take us to all the new
pieces that are worth going to, and so I'm certain to see
Francillon sooner or later, and then I shall know what to think.
But I do feel such a fool about it, I must confess, for wherever
I go I naturally find everybody talking about that wretched
Japanese salad. In fact one's beginning to get just a little
tired of hearing about it," she went on, seeing that Swann
seemed less interested than she had hoped in so burning a topic.
"I must admit, though, that it provides an excuse for some
quite amusing notions. I've got a friend, now, who is most
original, though she's a very pretty woman, very popular in
society, very sought-after, and she tells me that she got her
cook to make one of these Japanese salads, putting in everything that young M. Dumas says you're to in the play. Then
she asked a few friends to come and taste it. I was not among
the favoured few, I'm sorry to say. But she told us all about it
at her next 'at home'; it seems it was quite horrible, she
made us all laugh till we cried. But of course it's all in the
telling," Mme Cottard added, seeing that Swann still looked
grave.

And imagining that it was perhaps because he had not liked
Francillon: "Well, I daresay I shall be disappointed with it, after
all. I don't suppose it's as good as the piece Mme de Crécy
worships, *Serge Panine*. There's a play, if you like; really deep,
makes you think! But just fancy giving a recipe for a salad
on the stage of the Théâtre-Français! Now, *Serge Panine*!
But then, it's like everything that comes from the pen of
M. Georges Ohnet, it's always so well written. I wonder if
you know the *Maître des Forges*, which I like even better than
Serge Panine."

"Forgive me," said Swann with polite irony, "but I must confess that my want of admiration is almost equally divided between those masterpieces."

'Really, and what don't you like about them? Are you sure you aren't prejudiced? Perhaps you think he's a little too sad. Well, well, what I always say is, one should never argue about plays or novels. Everyone has his own way of looking at things, and what you find detestable may be just what I like best."

She was interrupted by Forcheville addressing Swann. While Mme Cottard was discussing *Francillon*, Forcheville had been expressing to Mme Verdurin his admiration for what he called the painter's "little speech": "Your friend has such a flow of language, such a memory!" he said to her when the painter had come to a standstill. "I've seldom come across anything like it. He'd make a first-rate preacher. By Jove, I wish I was like that. What with him and M. Bréchot you've got a couple of real characters, though as regards the gift of the gab, I'm not so sure that this one doesn't knock a few spots off the Professor. It comes more naturally with him, it's less studied. Although now and then he does use some words that are a bit realistic, but that's quite the thing nowadays. Anyhow, it's not often I've seen a man hold the floor as cleverly as that— 'hold the spittoon' as we used to say in the regiment, where, by the way, we had a man he rather reminds me of. You could take anything you liked—I don't know what—this glass, say, and he'd rattle on about it for hours; no, not this glass, that's a silly thing to say, but something like the battle of Waterloo, or anything of that sort, he'd spin you such a yarn you simply wouldn't believe it. Why, Swann was in the same regiment; he must have known him."

"Do you see much of M. Swann?" asked Mme Verdurin.

"Oh dear, no!" he answered, and then, thinking that if he made himself pleasant to Swann he might find favour with Odette, he decided to take this opportunity of flattering him by speaking of his fashionable friends, but to do so as a man of the world himself, in a tone of good-natured criticism, and not as though he were congratulating Swann upon some un-expected success. "Isn't that so, Swann? I never see anything

of you, do I?—But then, where on earth is one to see him?
The fellow spends all his time ensconced with the La Trémoïlles, the Laumes and all that lot!" The imputation would
have been false at any time, and was all the more so now that
for at least a year Swann scarcely went anywhere except to the
Verdurins'. But the mere name of a person whom the Verdurins did not know was greeted by them with a disapproving silence. M. Verdurin, dreading the painful impression
which the names of these "bores," especially when flung at
her in this tactless fashion in front of all the "faithful," were
bound to make on his wife, cast a covert glance at her, instinct
with anxious solicitude. He saw then that in her determination
not to take cognizance of, not to have been affected by the news
which had just been imparted to her, not merely to remain
dumb, but to have been deaf as well, as we pretend to be when
a friend who has offended us attempts to slip into his conversation some excuse which we might appear to be accepting if we
heard it without protesting, or when someone utters the name
of an enemy the very mention of whom in our presence is forbidden, Mme Verdurin, so that her silence should have the
appearance not of consent but of the unconscious silence of
inanimate objects, had suddenly emptied her face of all life, of
all mobility; her domed forehead was no more than an exquisite
piece of sculpture in the round, which the name of those La
Trémoïlles with whom Swann was always "ensconced" had
failed to penetrate; her nose, just perceptibly wrinkled in a
frown, exposed to view two dark cavities that seemed modelled
from life. You would have said that her half-opened lips were
just about to speak. She was no more than a wax cast, a plaster
mask, a maquette for a monument, a bust for the Palace of
Industry, in front of which the public would most certainly
gather and marvel to see how the sculptor, in expressing the
unchallengeable dignity of the Verdurins as opposed to that of
the La Trémoïlles or Laumes, whose equals (if not indeed their
betters) they were, and the equals and betters of all other
"bores" upon the face of the earth, had contrived to impart an
almost papal majesty to the whiteness and rigidity of the stone.
But the marble at last came to life and let it be understood that
it didn't do to be at all squeamish if one went to that house,

since the wife was always drunk and the husband so uneducated that he called a corridor a "collidor"!

"You'd need to pay me a lot of money before I'd let any
of that lot set foot inside my house," Mme Verdurin concluded,
gazing imperially down on Swann.

She could scarcely have expected him to capitulate so completely as to echo the holy simplicity of the pianist's aunt, who
at once exclaimed: "To think of that, now! What surprises me
is that they can get anybody to go near them. I'm sure I should
be afraid; one can't be too careful. How can people be so common as to go running after them?" But he might at least have
replied, like Forcheville: "Gad, she's a duchess; there are still
plenty of people who are impressed by that sort of thing,"
which would at least have permitted Mme Verdurin the retort,
"And a lot of good may it do them!" Instead of which, Swann
merely smiled, in a manner which intimated that he could not,
of course, take such an outrageous statement seriously. M.
Verdurin, who was still casting furtive glances at his wife, saw
with regret and understood only too well that she was now inflamed with the passion of a Grand Inquisitor who has failed
to stamp out heresy; and so, in the hope of bringing Swann
round to a recantation (for the courage of one's opinions is
always a form of calculating cowardice in the eyes of the
"other side"), challenged him: "Tell us frankly, now, what you
think of them yourself. We shan't repeat it to them, you may
be sure."

To which Swann answered: "Why, I'm not in the least
afraid of the Duchess (if it's the La Trémoïlles you're speaking
of). I can assure you that everyone likes going to her house. I
wouldn't go so far as to say that she's at all 'profound' " (he
pronounced "profound" as if it was a ridiculous word, for his
speech kept the traces of certain mental habits which the recent
change in his life, a rejuvenation illustrated by his passion for
music, had inclined him temporarily to discard, so that at times
he would actually state his views with considerable warmth)
"but I'm quite sincere when I say that she's intelligent, while
her husband is positively a man of letters. They're charming
people."

Whereupon Mme Verdurin, realising that this one infidel

would prevent her "little nucleus" from achieving complete
unanimity, was unable to restrain herself, in her fury at the
obstinacy of this wretch who could not see what anguish his
words were causing her, from screaming at him from the
depths of her tortured heart: "You may think so if you wish,
but at least you needn't say so to us."

"It all depends on what you call intelligence." Forcheville
felt that it was his turn to be brilliant. "Come now, Swann, tell
us what you mean by intelligence."

"There," cried Odette, "that's the sort of big subject I'm
always asking him to talk to me about, and he never will."

"Oh, but . . ." protested Swann.

"Oh, but nonsense!" said Odette.

"A water-butt?" asked the doctor.

"In your opinion," pursued Forcheville, "does intelligence
mean the gift cf the gab—you know, glib society talk?"

"Finish your sweet, so that they can take your plate away,"
said Mme Verdurin sourly to Saniette, who was lost in thought
and had stopped eating. And then, perhaps a little ashamed of
her rudeness, "It doesn't matter, you can take your time about
it. I only reminded you because of the others, you know; it
keeps the servants back."

"There is," began Brichot, hammering out each syllable, "a
rather curious definition of intelligence by that gentle old
anarchist Fénelon . . ."

"Just listen to this!" Mme Verdurin rallied Forcheville and
the doctor. "He's going to give us Fénelon's definition of
intelligence. Most interesting. It's not often you get a chance
of hearing that!"

But Brichot was keeping Fénelon's definition until Swann
had given his. Swann remained silent, and, by this fresh act
of recreancy, spoiled the brilliant dialectical contest which
Mme Verdurin was rejoicing at being able to offer to Forcheville.

"You see, it's just the same as with me!" said Odette
peevishly. "I'm not at all sorry to see that I'm not the only one
he doesn't find quite up to his level."

"Are these de La Trémouailles whom Mme Verdurin has
shown us to be so undesirable," inquired Brichot, articulating

vigorously, "descended from the couple whom that worthy old snob Mme de Sévigné said she was delighted to know because it was so good for her peasants? True, the Marquise had another reason, which in her case probably came first, for she was a thorough journalist at heart, and always on the look-out for "copy." And in the journal which she used to send regularly to her daughter, it was Mme de La Trémouaille, kept well-informed through all her grand connections, who supplied the foreign politics."

"No, no, I don't think they're the same family," hazarded Mme Verdurin.

Saniette, who ever since he had surrendered his untouched plate to the butler had been plunged once more in silent meditation, emerged finally to tell them, with a nervous laugh, the story of a dinner he had once had with the Duc de La Trémoïlle, from which it transpired that the Duke did not know that George Sand was the pseudonym of a woman. Swann, who was fond of Saniette, felt bound to supply him with a few facts illustrative of the Duke's culture proving that such ignorance on his part was literally impossible; but suddenly he stopped short, realising that Saniette needed no proof, but knew already that the story was untrue for the simple reason that he had just invented it. The worthy man suffered acutely from the Verdurins' always finding him so boring; and as he was conscious of having been more than ordinarily dull this evening, he had made up his mind that he would succeed in being amusing at least once before the end of dinner. He capitulated so quickly, looked so wretched at the sight of his castle in ruins, and replied in so craven a tone to Swann, appealing to him not to persist in a refutation which was now superfluous—"All right; all right; anyhow, even if I'm mistaken it's not a crime, I hope"—that Swann longed to be able to console him by insisting that the story was indubitably true and exquisitely funny. The doctor, who had been listening, had an idea that it was the right moment to interject "*Se non è vero*," but he was not quite certain of the words, and was afraid of getting them wrong.

After dinner, Forcheville went up to the doctor.

"She can't have been at all bad looking, Mme Verdurin; and

besides, she's a woman you can really talk to, which is the main thing. Of course she's getting a bit broad in the beam. But Mme de Crécy! There's a little woman who knows what's what, all right. Upon my word and soul, you can see at a glance she's got her wits about her, that girl. We're speaking of Mme de Crécy," he explained, as M. Verdurin joined them, his pipe in his mouth. "I should say that, as a specimen of the female form . . ."

"I'd rather have it in my bed than a slap with a wet fish," the words came tumbling from Cottard, who had for some time been waiting in vain for Forcheville to pause for breath so that he might get in this hoary old joke for which there might not be another cue if the conversation should take a different turn and which he now produced with that excessive spontaneity and confidence that seeks to cover up the coldness and the anxiety inseparable from a prepared recitation. Forcheville knew and saw the joke, and was thoroughly amused. As for M. Verdurin, he was unsparing of his merriment, having recently discovered a way of expressing it by a convention that was different from his wife's but equally simple and obvious. Scarcely had he begun the movement of head and shoulders of a man "shaking with laughter" than he would begin at once to cough, as though, in laughing too violently, he had swallowed a mouthful of pipe-smoke. And by keeping the pipe firmly in his mouth he could prolong indefinitely the dumb-show of suffocation and hilarity. Thus he and Mme Verdurin (who, at the other side of the room, where the painter was telling her a story, was shutting her eyes preparatory to flinging her face into her hands) resembled two masks in a theatre each representing Comedy in a different way.

M. Verdurin had been wiser than he knew in not taking his pipe out of his mouth, for Cottard, having occasion to leave the room for a moment, murmured a witty euphemism which he had recently acquired and repeated now whenever he had to go to the place in question: "I must just go and see the Duc d'Aumale for a minute," so drolly that M. Verdurin's cough began all over again.

"Do take your pipe out of your mouth. Can't you see that you'll choke if you try to bottle up your laughter like that," counselled Mme Verdurin as she came round with a tray of liqueurs.

"What a delightful man your husband is; he's devilish witty," declared Forcheville to Mme Cottard. "Thank you, thank you, an old soldier like me can never say no to a drink."

"M. de Forcheville thinks Odette charming," M. Verdurin told his wife.

"Ah, as a matter of fact she'd like to have lunch with you one day. We must arrange it, but don't on any account let Swann hear about it. He spoils everything, don't you know. I don't mean to say that you're not to come to dinner too, of course; we hope to see you very often. Now that the warm weather's coming, we're going to dine out of doors whenever we can. It won't bore you will it, a quiet little dinner now and then in the Bois? Splendid, splendid, it will be so nice. . . .

"I say, aren't you going to do any work this evening?" she screamed suddenly to the young pianist, seeing an opportunity for displaying, before a "newcomer" of Forcheville's importance, at once her unfailing wit and her despotic power over the "faithful."

"M. de Forcheville has been saying dreadful things about you," Mme Cottard told her husband as he reappeared in the room. And he, still following up the idea of Forcheville's noble birth, which had obsessed him all through dinner, said to him: "I'm treating a Baroness just now, Baroness Putbus. Weren't there some Putbuses in the Crusades? Anyhow they've got a lake in Pomerania that's ten times the size of the Place de la Concorde. I'm treating her for rheumatoid arthritis; she's a charming woman. Mme Verdurin knows her too, I believe."

Which enabled Forcheville, a moment later, finding himself alone again with Mme Cottard, to complete his favourable verdict on her husband with: "He's an interesting man, too; you can see that he knows a few people. Gad! they do get to know a lot of things, those doctors."

"I'm going to play the phrase from the sonata for M. Swann," said the pianist.

"What the devil's that? Not the sonata-snake, I hope!" shouted M. de Forcheville, hoping to create an effect.

But Dr Cottard, who had never heard this pun, missed the point of it, and imagined that M. de Forcheville had made a mistake. He dashed in boldly to correct him: "No, no. The word isn't *serpent-à-sonates*, it's *serpent-à-sonnettes!*" he explained in a tone at once zealous, impatient, and triumphant.[12]

Forcheville explained the joke to him. The doctor blushed.

"You'll admit it's not bad, eh, Doctor?"

"Oh! I've known it for ages."

Then they were silent; beneath the restless tremolos of the violin part which protected it with their throbbing *sostenuto* two octaves above it—and as in a mountainous country, behind the seeming immobility of a vertiginous waterfall, one descries, two hundred feet below, the tiny form of a woman walking in the valley—the little phrase had just appeared, distant, graceful, protected by the long, gradual unfurling of its transparent, incessant and sonorous curtain. And Swann, in his heart of hearts, turned to it as to a confidant of his love, as to a friend of Odette who would surely tell her to pay no attention to this Forcheville.

"Ah! you've come too late!" Mme Verdurin greeted one of the faithful whose invitation had been only "to look in after dinner." "We've been having a simply incomparable Brichot! You never heard such eloquence! But he's gone. Isn't that so, M. Swann? I believe it's the first time you've met him," she went on, to emphasise the fact that it was to her that Swann owed the introduction. "Wasn't he delicious, our Brichot?"

Swann bowed politely.

"No? You weren't interested?" she asked dryly.

"Oh, but I assure you, I was quite enthralled. He's perhaps a little too peremptory, a little too jovial for my taste. I should like to see him a little less confident at times, a little more tolerant, but one feels that he knows a great deal, and on the whole he seems a very sound fellow."

The party broke up very late. Cottard's first words to his wife were: "I've rarely seen Mme Verdurin in such form as she was to-night."

"What exactly is your Mme Verdurin? A bit of a demirep, eh?" said Forcheville to the painter, to whom he had offered a lift.

Odette watched his departure with regret; she dared not refuse to let Swann take her home, but she was moody and irritable in the carriage, and when he asked whether he might come in, replied, "I suppose so," with an impatient shrug of her shoulders.

When all the guests had gone, Mme Verdurin said to her husband: "Did you notice the way Swann laughed, such an idiotic laugh, when we spoke about Mme La Trémoïlle?"

She had remarked, more than once, how Swann and Forcheville suppressed the particle "de" before that lady's name. Never doubting that it was done on purpose, to show that they were not afraid of a title, she had made up her mind to imitate their arrogance, but had not quite grasped what grammatical form it ought to take. And so, the natural corruptness of her speech overcoming her implacable republicanism, she still said instinctively "the de La Trémoïlles," or rather (by an abbreviation sanctified by usage in music hall lyrics and cartoon captions, where the 'de' is elided), "the d'La Trémoïlles," but redeemed herself by saying "Madame La Trémoïlle.—The *Duchess*, as Swann calls her," she added ironically, with a smile which proved that she was merely quoting and would not, herself, accept the least responsibility for a classification so puerile and absurd.

"I don't mind saying that I thought him extremely stupid."

M. Verdurin took it up: "He's not sincere. He's a crafty customer, always sitting on the fence, always trying to run with the hare and hunt with the hounds. What a difference between him and Forcheville. There at least you have a man who tells you straight out what he thinks. Either you agree with him or you don't. Not like the other fellow, who's never definitely fish or fowl. Did you notice, by the way, that Odette seemed all out for Forcheville, and I don't blame her, either. And besides, if Swann wants to come the man of fashion over us, the champion of distressed duchesses, at any rate the other man has got a title—he's always Comte de Forcheville," he concluded with an air of discrimination, as though, familiar with every page of the history of that dignity, he were making a scrupulously exact estimate of its value in relation to others of the sort.

"I may tell you," Mme Verdurin went on, "that he saw fit
to utter some venomous and quite absurd insinuations against
Brichot. Naturally, once he saw that Brichot was popular
in this house, it was a way of hitting back at us, of spoiling
our party. I know his sort, the dear, good friend of the family
who runs you down behind your back."

"Didn't I say so?" retorted her husband. "He's simply a
failure, one of those small-minded individuals who are envious of anything that's at all big."

In reality there was not one of the "faithful" who was not
infinitely more malicious than Swann; but they all took the
precaution of tempering their calumnies with obvious pleasantries, with little sparks of emotion and cordiality; while the
slightest reservation on Swann's part, undraped in any such
conventional formula as "Of course, I don't mean to be unkind," to which he would not have deigned to stoop, appeared
to them a deliberate act of treachery. There are certain original
and distinguished authors in whom the least outspokenness is
thought shocking because they have not begun by flattering
the tastes of the public and serving up to it the commonplaces
to which it is accustomed; it was by the same process that
Swann infuriated M. Verdurin. In his case as in theirs it was the
novelty of his language which led his audience to suspect the
blackness of his designs.

Swann was still unconscious of the disgrace that threatened
him at the Verdurins', and continued to regard all their absurdities in the most rosy light, through the admiring eyes of love.

As a rule he met Odette only in the evenings; he was afraid
of her growing tired of him if he visited her during the day as
well, but, being reluctant to forfeit the place that he held in
her thoughts, he was constantly looking out for opportunities
of claiming her attention in ways that would not be displeasing
to her. If, in a florist's or a jeweller's window, a plant or an
ornament caught his eye, he would at once think of sending
them to Odette, imagining that the pleasure which the casual
sight of them had given him would instinctively be felt also by
her, and would increase her affection for him; and he would
order them to be taken at once to the Rue La Pérouse, so as to
accelerate the moment when, as she received an offering from

him, he might feel himself somehow transported into her presence. He was particularly anxious, always, that she should receive these presents before she went out for the evening, so that her gratitude towards him might give additional tenderness to her welcome when he arrived at the Verdurins', might even—for all he knew—if the shopkeeper made haste, bring him a letter from her before dinner, or herself in person upon his doorstep, come on a little supplementary visit of thanks. As in an earlier phase, when he had tested the reactions of chagrin on Odette's nature, he now sought by those of gratitude to elicit from her intimate scraps of feeling which she had not yet revealed to him.

Often she was plagued with money troubles, and under pressure from a creditor would appeal to him for assistance. He was pleased by this, as he was pleased by anything that might impress Odette with his love for her, or merely with his influence, with the extent to which he could be of use to her. If anyone had said to him at the beginning, "It's your position that attracts her," or at this stage, "It's your money that she's really in love with," he would probably not have believed the suggestion; nor, on the other hand, would he have been greatly distressed by the thought that people supposed her to be attached to him—that people felt them to be united—by ties so binding as those of snobbishness or wealth. But even if he had believed it to be true, it might not have caused him any suffering to discover that Odette's love for him was based on a foundation more lasting than the charms or the qualities which she might see in him: namely, self-interest, a self-interest which would postpone for ever the fatal day when she might be tempted to bring their relations to an end. For the moment, by heaping presents on her, by doing her all manner of favours, he could fall back on advantages extraneous to his person, or to his intellect, as a relief from the endless, killing effort to make himself attractive to her. And the pleasure of being a lover, of living by love alone, the reality of which he was sometimes inclined to doubt, was enhanced in his eyes, as a dilettante of intangible sensations, by the price he was paying for it—as one sees people who are doubtful whether the sight of the sea and the sound of its waves are really

enjoyable become convinced that they are—and convinced
also of the rare quality and absolute detachment of their own
taste—when they have agreed to pay several pounds a day for
a room in an hotel from which that sight and that sound
may be enjoyed.

One day, when reflections of this sort had brought him
back to the memory of the time when someone had spoken to
him of Odette as of a "kept woman," and he was amusing
himself once again with contrasting that strange personifica-
tion, the "kept woman"—an iridescent mixture of unknown
and demoniacal qualities embroidered, as in some fantasy of
Gustave Moreau, with poison-dripping flowers interwoven
with precious jewels—with the Odette on whose face he had
seen the same expressions of pity for a sufferer, revolt against
an act of injustice, gratitude for an act of kindness, which he
had seen in earlier days on his own mother's face and on the
faces of his friends, the Odette whose conversation so frequently turned on the things that he himself knew better than
anyone, his collections, his room, his old servant, the banker
who kept all his securities, it happened that the thought of the
banker reminded him that he must call on him shortly to draw
some money. The fact was that if, during the current month,
he were to come less liberally to the aid of Odette in her financial difficulties than in the month before, when he had
given her five thousand francs, if he refrained from offering
her a diamond necklace for which she longed, he would be
allowing her admiration for his generosity, her heart-warming
gratitude, to decline, and would even run the risk of giving
her to believe that his love for her (as she saw its visible
manifestations grow smaller) had itself diminished. And then,
suddenly, he wondered whether that was not precisely what was
implied by "keeping" a woman (as if, in fact, that notion of
"keeping" could be derived from elements not at all mysterious
or perverse but belonging to the intimate routine of his daily
life, such as that thousand-franc note, a familiar and domestic
object, torn in places and stuck together again, which his valet,
after paying the household accounts and the rent, had locked
up in a drawer in the old writing-desk whence he had extracted
it to send it, with four others, to Odette) and whether it

might not be possible to apply to Odette, since he had known her (for he never suspected for a moment that she could ever have taken money from anyone before him), that title, which he had believed so wholly inapplicable to her, of "kept woman." He could not explore the idea further, for a sudden access of that mental lethargy which was, with him, congenital, intermittent and providential, happened at that moment to extinguish every particle of light in his brain, as instantaneously as, at a later period, when electric lighting had been everywhere installed, it became possible to cut off the supply of light from a house. His mind fumbled for a moment in the darkness, he took off his spectacles, wiped the glasses, drew his hand across his eyes, and only saw light again when he found himself face to face with a wholly different idea, to wit, that he must endeavour, in the coming month, to send Odette six or seven thousand francs instead of five because of the surprise and pleasure it would cause her.

In the evening, when he did not stay at home until it was time to meet Odette at the Verdurins', or rather at one of the open-air restaurants which they patronised in the Bois and especially at Saint-Cloud, he would go to dine in one of those fashionable houses in which at one time he had been a constant guest. He did not wish to lose touch with people who, for all that he knew, might some day be of use to Odette, and thanks to whom he was often, in the meantime, able to procure for her some privilege or pleasure. Besides, his long inurement to luxury and high society had given him a need as well as a contempt for them, with the result that by the time he had come to regard the humblest lodgings as precisely on a par with the most princely mansions, his senses were so thoroughly accustomed to the latter that he could not enter the former without a feeling of acute discomfort. He had the same regard—to a degree of identity which they would never have suspected—for the little families with small incomes who asked him to dances in their flats ("straight upstairs to the fifth floor, and the door on the left") as for the Princesse de Parme who gave the most splendid parties in Paris; but he did not have the feeling of being actually at a party when he found himself herded with the fathers of families in the bedroom of the lady of the house, while the spectacle of wash-hand-stands covered over with towels, and of beds converted into cloak-rooms, with a mass of hats and greatcoats sprawling over their counterpanes, gave him the same stifling sensation that, nowadays, people who have been used for half a lifetime to electric light derive from a smoking lamp or a candle that needs to be snuffed.

If he was dining out, he would order his carriage for half-past seven. While he changed his clothes, he would be thinking all the time about Odette, and in this way was never alone, for the constant thought of Odette gave the moments during which he was separated from her the same peculiar charm as those in which she was at his side. He would get into his car-riage and drive off, but he knew that this thought had jumped in after him and had settled down on his lap, like a pet animal which he might take everywhere, and would keep with him at the dinner-table unbeknownst to his fellow-guests. He would stroke and fondle it, warm himself with it, and, over-come with a sort of languor, would give way to a slight shuddering which contracted his throat and nostrils—a new experience, this,—as he fastened the bunch of columbines in his buttonhole. He had for some time been feeling depressed and unwell, especially since Odette had introduced Forcheville to the Verdurins, and he would have liked to go away for a while to rest in the country. But he could never summon up the courage to leave Paris, even for a day, while Odette was there. The air was warm; it was beautiful spring weather. And for all that he was driving through a city of stone to immure himself in a house without grass or garden, what was incessantly before his eyes was a park which he owned near Combray, where, at four in the afternoon, before coming to the asparagus-bed, thanks to the breeze that was wafted across the fields from Méséglise, one could enjoy the fragrant cool-ness of the air beneath an arbour in the garden as much as by the edge of the pond fringed with forget-me-nots and iris, and where, when he sat down to dinner, the table ran riot with the roses and the flowering currant trained and twined by his gardener's skilful hand.

After dinner, if he had an early appointment in the Bois or at

Saint-Cloud, he would rise from table and leave the house so abruptly—especially if it threatened to rain, and thus to scatter the "faithful" before their normal time—that on one occasion the Princesse des Laumes (at whose house dinner had been so late that Swann had left before the coffee was served to join the Verdurins on the Island in the Bois) observed: "Really, if Swann were thirty years older and had bladder trouble, there might be some excuse for his running away like that. I must say it's pretty cool of him."

He persuaded himself that the charm of spring which he could not go down to Combray to enjoy might at least be found on the Ile des Cygnes or at Saint-Cloud. But as he could think only of Odette, he did not even know whether he had smelt the fragrance of the young leaves, or if the moon had been shining. He would be greeted by the little phrase from the sonata, played in the garden on the restaurant piano. If there was no piano in the garden, the Verdurins would have taken immense pains to have one brought down either from one of the rooms or from the dining-room. Not that Swann was now restored to favour; far from it. But the idea of arranging an ingenious form of entertainment for someone, even for some-one they disliked, would stimulate them, during the time spent in its preparation, to a momentary sense of cordiality and affection. From time to time he would remind himself that another fine spring evening was drawing to a close, and would force himself to notice the trees and the sky. But the state of agitation into which Odette's presence never failed to throw him, added to a feverish ailment which had persisted for some time now, robbed him of that calm and well-being which are the indispensable background to the impressions we derive from nature.

One evening, when Swann had consented to dine with the Verdurins, and had mentioned during dinner that he had to attend next day the annual banquet of an old comrades' associa-tion, Odette had exclaimed across the table, in front of Forche-ville, who was now one of the "faithful," in front of the painter, in front of Cottard:

"Yes, I know you have your banquet to-morrow; I shan't see you, then, till I get home; don't be too late."

And although Swann had never yet taken serious offence at
Odette's friendship for one or other of the "faithful," he felt
an exquisite pleasure on hearing her thus avow in front of
them all, with that calm immodesty, the fact that they saw each
other regularly every evening, his privileged position in her
house and the preference for him which it implied. It was true
that Swann had often reflected that Odette was in no way a
remarkable woman, and there was nothing especially flattering
in seeing the supremacy he wielded over someone so inferior
to himself proclaimed to all the "faithful"; but since he had
observed that to many other men besides himself Odette
seemed a fascinating and desirable woman, the attraction which
her body held for them had aroused in him a painful longing to
secure the absolute mastery of even the tiniest particles of her
heart. And he had begun to attach an incalculable value to those
moments spent in her house in the evenings, when he held her
upon his knee, made her tell him what she thought about this
or that, and counted over the only possessions on earth to
which he still clung. And so, drawing her aside after this
dinner, he took care to thank her effusively, seeking to indicate
to her by the extent of his gratitude the corresponding in-
intensity of the pleasures which it was in her power to bestow
on him, the supreme pleasure being to guarantee him im-
munity, for so long as his love should last and he remain vulnerable, from the assaults of jealousy.

When he came away from his banquet, the next evening, it
was pouring with rain, and he had nothing but his victoria. A
friend offered to take him home in a closed carriage, and as
Odette, by the fact of her having invited him to come, had
given him an assurance that she was expecting no one else, he
could have gone home to bed with a quiet mind and an untroubled heart, rather than set off thus in the rain. But perhaps, if she saw that he seemed not to adhere to his resolution
to spend the late evening always, without exception, in her
company, she might not bother to keep it free for him on the
one occasion when he particularly desired it.

It was after eleven when he reached her door, and as he
made his apology for having been unable to come away earlier,
she complained that it was indeed very late, that the storm had

made her feel unwell and her head ached, and warned him that she would not let him stay more than half an hour, that at midnight she would send him away; a little while later she felt tired and wished to sleep.

"No cattleya, then, to-night?" he asked, "and I've been so looking forward to a nice little cattleya."

She seemed peevish and on edge, and replied: "No, dear, no cattleya to-night. Can't you see I'm not well?"

"It might have done you good, but I won't bother you."

She asked him to put out the light before he went; he drew the curtains round her bed and left. But, when he was back in his own house, the idea suddenly struck him that perhaps Odette was expecting someone else that evening, that she had merely pretended to be tired, so that she had asked him to put the light out only so that he should suppose that she was going to sleep, that the moment he had left the house she had put it on again and had opened her door to the man who was to spend the night with her. He looked at his watch. It was about an hour and a half since he had left her. He went out, took a cab, and stopped it close to her house, in a little street running at right angles to that other street which lay at the back of her house and along which he used sometimes to go, to tap upon her bedroom window, for her to let him in. He left his cab; the streets were deserted and dark; he walked a few yards and came out almost opposite her house. Amid the glimmering blackness of the row of windows in which the lights had long since been put out, he saw one, and only one, from which percolated—between the slats of its shutters, closed like a wine-press over its mysterious golden juice—the light that filled the room within, a light which on so many other evenings, as soon as he saw it from afar as he turned into the street, had rejoiced his heart with its message: "She is there—expecting you," and which now tortured him, saying: "She is there with the man she was expecting." He must know who; he tiptoed along the wall until he reached the window, but between the slanting bars of the shutters he could see nothing, could only hear, in the silence of the night, the murmur of conversation.

Certainly he suffered as he watched that light, in whose

golden atmosphere, behind the closed sash, stirred the unseen
and detested pair, as he listened to that murmur which revealed the presence of the man who had crept in after his own
departure, the perfidy of Odette, and the pleasures which she
was at that moment enjoying with the stranger. And yet he
was not sorry he had come; the torment which had forced him
to leave his own house had become less acute now that it had
become less vague, now that Odette's other life, of which he
had had, at that first moment, a sudden helpless suspicion, was
definitely there, in the full glare of the lamp-light, almost within
his grasp, an unwitting prisoner in that room into which,
when he chose, he would force his way to seize it unawares;
or rather he would knock on the shutters, as he often did when
he came very late, and by that signal Odette would at least
learn that he knew, that he had seen the light and had heard
the voices, and he himself, who a moment ago had been picturing her as laughing with the other at his illusions, now it
was he who saw them, confident in their error, tricked by
none other than himself, whom they believed to be far away
but who was there, in person, there with a plan, there with
the knowledge that he was going, in another minute, to knock
on the shutter. And perhaps the almost pleasurable sensation
he felt at that moment was something more than the assuagement of a doubt, and of a pain: was an intellectual pleasure. If,
since he had fallen in love, things had recovered a little of the
delightful interest that they had had for him long ago—though
only in so far as they were illuminated by the thought or the
memory of Odette—now it was another of the faculties of his
studious youth that his jealousy revived, the passion for truth,
but for a truth which, too, was interposed between himself and
his mistress, receiving its light from her alone, a private and
personal truth the sole object of which (an infinitely precious
object, and one almost disinterested in its beauty) was Odette's
life, her actions, her environment, her plans, her past. At every
other period in his life, the little everyday activities of another
person had always seemed meaningless to Swann; if gossip
about such things was repeated to him, he would dismiss it
as insignificant, and while he listened it was only the lowest, the
most commonplace part of his mind that was engaged; these

were the moments when he felt at his most inglorious. But in this strange phase of love the personality of another person becomes so enlarged, so deepened, that the curiosity which he now felt stirring inside him with regard to the smallest details of a woman's daily life, was the same thirst for knowledge with which he had once studied history. And all manner of actions from which hitherto he would have recoiled in shame, such as spying, to-night, outside a window, to-morrow perhaps, for all he knew, putting adroitly provocative questions to casual witnesses, bribing servants, listening at doors, seemed to him now to be precisely on a level with the deciphering of manuscripts, the weighing of evidence, the interpretation of old monuments—so many different methods of scientific investigation with a genuine intellectual value and legitimately employable in the search for truth.

On the point of knocking on the shutters, he felt a pang of shame at the thought that Odette would now know that he had suspected her, that he had returned, that he had posted himself outside her window. She had often told him what a horror she had of jealous men, of lovers who spied. What he was about to do was singularly inept, and she would detest him for ever after, whereas now, for the moment, for so long as he refrained from knocking, even in the act of infidelity, perhaps she loved him still. How often the prospect of future happiness is thus sacrificed to one's impatient insistence upon an immediate gratification! But his desire to know the truth was stronger, and seemed to him nobler. He knew that the reality of certain circumstances which he would have given his life to be able to reconstruct accurately and in full, was to be read behind that window, streaked with bars of light, as within the illuminated, golden boards of one of those precious manuscripts by whose artistic wealth itself the scholar who consults them cannot remain unmoved. He felt a voluptuous pleasure in learning the truth which he passionately sought in that unique, ephemeral and precious transcript, on that translucent page, so warm, so beautiful. And moreover, the advantage which he felt—which he so desperately wanted to feel —that he had over them lay perhaps not so much in knowing as in being able to show them that he knew. He raised himself on tiptoe. He knocked. They had not heard; he knocked again, louder, and the conversation ceased. A man's voice—he strained his ears to distinguish whose, among such of Odette's friends as he knew, it might be—asked:

"Who's there?"

He could not be certain of the voice. He knocked once again. The window first, then the shutters were thrown open. It was too late, now, to draw back, and since she was about to know all, in order not to seem too miserable, too jealous and inquisitive, he called out in a cheerful, casual tone of voice:

"Please don't bother; I just happened to be passing, and saw the light. I wanted to know if you were feeling better."

He looked up. Two old gentlemen stood facing him at the window, one of them with a lamp in his hand; and beyond them he could see into the room, a room that he had never seen before. Having fallen into the habit, when he came late to Odette, of identifying her window by the fact that it was the only one still lit up in a row of windows otherwise all alike, he had been misled this time by the light, and had knocked at the window beyond hers, which belonged to the adjoining house. He made what apology he could and hurried home, glad that the satisfaction of his curiosity had preserved their love intact, and that, having feigned for so long a sort of indifference towards Odette, he had not now, by his jealousy, given her the proof that he loved her too much, which, between a pair of lovers, forever dispenses the recipient from the obligation to love enough.

He never spoke to her of this misadventure, and ceased even to think of it himself. But now and then his thoughts in their wandering course would come upon this memory where it lay unobserved, would startle it into life, thrust it forward into his consciousness, and leave him aching with a sharp, deeprooted pain. As though it were a bodily pain, Swann's mind was powerless to alleviate it; but at least, in the case of bodily pain, since it is independent of the mind, the mind can dwell upon it, can note that it has diminished, that it has momentarily ceased. But in this case the mind, merely by recalling the pain, created it afresh. To determine not to think of it was to think of it still, to suffer from it still. And when, in conversa-

tion with his friends, he forgot about it, suddenly a word
casually uttered would make him change countenance like a
wounded man when a clumsy hand has touched his aching limb.
When he came away from Odette he was happy, he felt calm,
he recalled her smiles, of gentle mockery when speaking of
this or that other person, of tenderness for himself; he recalled
the gravity of her head which she seemed to have lifted from
its axis to let it droop and fall, as though in spite of herself,
upon his lips, as she had done on the first evening in the carriage, the languishing looks she had given him as she lay in
his arms, nestling her head against her shoulder as though
shrinking from the cold.

But then at once his jealousy, as though it were the shadow
of his love, presented him with the complement, with the converse of that new smile with which she had greeted him that
very evening—and which now, perversely, mocked Swann
and shone with love for another—of that droop of the head,
now sinking on to other lips, of all the marks of affection
(now given to another) that she had shown to him. And all the
voluptuous memories which he bore away from her house
were, so to speak, but so many sketches, rough plans like those
which a decorator submits to one, enabling Swann to form an
idea of the various attitudes, aflame or faint with passion, which
she might adopt for others. With the result that he came to
regret every pleasure that he tasted in her company, every
new caress of which he had been so imprudent as to point out
to her the delights, every fresh charm that he found in her,
for he knew that, a moment later, they would go to enrich the
collection of instruments in his secret torture-chamber.

A fresh turn was given to the screw when Swann recalled a
sudden expression which he had intercepted, a few days
earlier, and for the first time, in Odette's eyes. It was after
dinner at the Verdurins'. Whether it was because Forcheville,
aware that Saniette, his brother-in-law, was not in favour with
them, had decided to make a butt of him and to shine at his
expense, or because he had been annoyed by some awkward
remark which Saniette had made to him, although it had
passed unnoticed by the rest of the party who knew nothing of
whatever offensive allusion it might quite unintentionally

have concealed, or possibly because he had been for some time
looking for an opportunity of securing the expulsion from the
house of a fellow-guest who knew rather too much about him,
and whom he knew to be so sensitive that he himself could not
help feeling embarrassed at times merely by his presence in the
room, Forcheville replied to Saniette's tactless utterance with
such a volley of abuse, going out of his way to insult him,
emboldened, the louder he shouted, by the fear, the pain, the
entreaties of his victim, that the poor creature, after asking
Mme Verdurin whether he should stay and receiving no
answer, had left the house in stammering confusion, and with
tears in his eyes. Odette had watched this scene impassively,
but when the door had closed behind Saniette, she had forced
the normal expression of her face down, so to speak, by several
pegs, in order to bring herself on to the same level of baseness
as Forcheville, her eyes had sparkled with a malicious smile of
congratulation upon his audacity, of ironical pity for the poor
wretch who had been its victim, she had darted at him a look
of complicity in the crime which so clearly implied: "That's
finished him off, or I'm very much mistaken. Did you see how
pathetic he looked? He was actually crying," that Forcheville,
when his eyes met hers, sobering instantaneously from the
anger, or simulated anger, with which he was still flushed,
smiled as he explained: "He need only have made himself
pleasant and he'd have been here still; a good dressing-down
does a man no harm, at any age."

One day when Swann had gone out early in the afternoon
to pay a call, and had failed to find the person he wished to see,
it occurred to him to go to see Odette instead, at an hour when,
although he never called on her then as a rule, he knew that she
was always at home resting or writing letters until tea-time,
and would enjoy seeing her for a moment without disturbing
her. The porter told him that he believed Odette to be in;
Swann rang the bell, thought he heard the sound of footsteps,
but no one came to the door. Anxious and irritated, he went
round to the other little street at the back of her house and
stood beneath her bedroom window: the curtains were drawn
and he could see nothing; he knocked loudly upon the pane,
and called out; no one opened. He could see that the neigh-

bours were staring at him. He turned away, thinking that after
all he had perhaps been mistaken in believing that he heard
footsteps; but he remained so preoccupied with the suspicion
that he could not think of anything else. After waiting for
an hour, he returned. He found her at home; she told him
that she had been in the house when he rang, but had been
asleep; the bell had awakened her, she had guessed that it must
be Swann, and had run to meet him, but he had already gone.
She had, of course, heard him knocking at the window. Swann
could at once detect in this story one of those fragments of
literal truth which liars, when caught off guard, console themselves by introducing into the composition of the falsehood
which they have to invent, thinking that it can be safely incorporated and will lend the whole story an air of verisimilitude. It was true that when Odette had just done something
she did not wish to disclose, she would take pains to bury it
deep down inside herself. But as soon as she found herself
face to face with the man to whom she was obliged to lie, she
became uneasy, all her ideas melted like wax before a flame,
her inventive and her reasoning faculties were paralysed, she
might ransack her brain but could find only a void; yet she
must say something, and there lay within her reach precisely
the fact which she had wished to conceal and which, being the
truth, was the one thing that had remained. She broke off
from it a tiny fragment, of no importance in itself, assuring
herself that, after all, it was the best thing to do, since it was a
verifiable detail and less dangerous, therefore, than a fictitious
one. "At any rate, that's true," she said to herself, "which is
something to the good. He may make inquiries, and he'll see
that it's true, so at least it won't be that that gives me away."
But she was wrong; it *was* what gave her away; she had failed
to realise that this fragmentary detail of the truth had sharp
edges which could not be made to fit in, except with those contiguous fragments of the truth from which she had arbitrarily
detached it, edges which, whatever the fictitious details in which
she might embed it, would continue to show, by their overlapping angles and by the gaps she had forgotten to fill in,
that its proper place was elsewhere.

"She admits that she heard me ring and then knock, that

she knew it was me, and that she wanted to see me," Swann
thought to himself. "But that doesn't fit in with the fact that
she didn't let me in."

He did not, however, draw her attention to this inconsis-
tency, for he thought that if left to herself Odette might perhaps produce some falsehood which would give him a faint
indication of the truth. She went on speaking, and he did not
interrupt her, but gathered up, with an eager and sorrowful
piety, the words that fell from her lips, feeling (and rightly
feeling, since she was hiding the truth behind them as she
spoke) that, like the sacred veil, they retained a vague imprint,
traced a faint outline, of that infinitely precious and, alas,
undiscoverable reality—what she had been doing that afternoon at three o'clock when he had called—of which he would
never possess any more than these falsifications, illegible and
divine traces, and which would exist henceforward only in the
secretive memory of this woman who could contemplate it in
utter ignorance of its value but would never yield it up to him.
Of course it occurred to him from time to time that Odette's
daily activities were not in themselves passionately interesting,
and that such relations as she might have with other men did
not exhale naturally, universally and for every rational being
a spirit of morbid gloom capable of infecting with fever or of
inciting to suicide. He realised at such moments that that
interest, that gloom, existed in him alone, like a disease, and
that once he was cured of this disease, the actions of Odette,
the kisses that she might have bestowed, would become once
again as innocuous as those of countless other women. But the
consciousness that the painful curiosity which he now brought
to them had its origin only in himself was not enough to make
Swann decide that it was unreasonable to regard that curiosity
as important and to take every possible step to satisfy it. The
fact was that Swann had reached an age whose philosophy—
encouraged, in his case, by the current philosophy of the day,
as well as by that of the circle in which he had spent much of
his life, the group that surrounded the Princesse des Laumes,
where it was agreed that intelligence was in direct ratio to the
degree of scepticism and nothing was considered real and
incontestable except the individual tastes of each person—

is no longer that of youth, but a positive, almost a medical philosophy, the philosophy of men who, instead of exteriorising the objects of their aspirations, endeavour to extract from the accumulation of the years already spent a fixed residue of habits and passions which they can regard as characteristic and permanent, and with which they will deliberately arrange, before anything else, that the kind of existence they choose to adopt shall not prove inharmonious. Swann deemed it wise to make allowance in his life for the suffering which he derived from not knowing what Odette had done, just as he made allowance for the impetus which a damp climate always gave to his eczema; to anticipate in his budget the expenditure of a considerable sum on procuring, with regard to the daily occupations of Odette, information the lack of which would make him unhappy, just as he reserved a margin for the gratification of other tastes from which he knew that pleasure was to be expected (at least, before he had fallen in love), such as his taste for collecting or for good cooking.

When he proposed to take leave of Odette and return home, she begged him to stay a little longer and even detained him forcibly, seizing him by the arm as he was opening the door to go. But he paid no heed to this, for among the multiplicity of gestures, remarks, little incidents that go to make up a conversation, it is inevitable that we should pass (without noticing anything that attracts our attention) close by those that hide a truth for which our suspicions are blindly searching, whereas we stop to examine others beneath which nothing lies concealed. She kept on saying: "What a dreadful pity—you never come in the afternoon, and the one time you do come I miss you." He knew very well that she was not sufficiently in love with him to be so keenly distressed merely at having missed his visit, but since she was good-natured, anxious to make him happy, and often grieved when she had offended him, he found it quite natural that she should be sorry on this occasion for having deprived him of the pleasure of spending an hour in her company, which was so very great, if not for her, at any rate for him. All the same, it was a matter of so little importance that her air of unrelieved sorrow began at length to astonish him. She reminded him, even more than usual, of the faces of some of the women created by the painter of the "Primavera." She had at this moment their downcast, heart-broken expression, which seems ready to succumb beneath the burden of a grief too heavy to be borne when they are merely allowing the Infant Jesus to play with a pomegranate or watching Moses pour water into a trough. He had seen the same sorrow once before on her face, but when, he could no longer say. Then, suddenly, he remembered: it was when Odette had lied in apologising to Mme Verdurin on the evening after the dinner from which she had stayed away on a pretext of illness, but really so that she might be alone with Swann. Surely, even had she been the most scrupulous of women, she could hardly have felt remorse for so innocent a lie. But the lies which Odette ordinarily told were less inno-cent, and served to prevent discoveries which might have involved her in the most terrible difficulties with one or another of her friends. And so when she lied, smitten with fear, feeling herself to be but feebly armed for her defence, unconfident of success, she felt like weeping from sheer ex-haustion, as children weep sometimes when they have not slept. Moreover she knew that her lie was usually wounding to the man to whom she was telling it, and that she might find herself at his mercy if she told it badly. Therefore she felt at once humble and guilty in his presence. And when she had to tell an insignificant social lie its hazardous associations, and the memories which it recalled, would leave her weak with a sense of exhaustion and penitent with a consciousness of wrongdoing.

What depressing lie was she now concocting for Swann's benefit, to give her that doleful expression, that plaintive voice, which seemed to falter beneath the effort she was forc-ing herself to make, and to plead for mercy? He had an idea that it was not merely the truth about what had occurred that afternoon that she was endeavouring to hide from him, but something more immediate, something, possibly, that had not yet happened, that was imminent, and that would throw light upon that earlier event. At that moment, he heard the front-door bell ring. Odette went on talking, but her words dwindled

into an inarticulate moan. Her regret at not having seen
Swann that afternoon, at not having opened the door to him,
had become a veritable cry of despair.

He could hear the front door being closed, and the sound
of a carriage, as though someone were going away—probably
the person whom Swann must on no account meet—after
being told that Odette was not at home. And then, when he
reflected that merely by coming at an hour when he was not
in the habit of coming he had managed to disturb so many
arrangements of which she did not wish him to know, he
was overcome with a feeling of despondency that amounted
almost to anguish. But since he was in love with Odette, since
he was in the habit of turning all his thoughts towards her, the
pity with which he might have been inspired for himself he
felt for her instead, and he murmured: "Poor darling!" When
finally he left her, she took up several letters which were lying
on the table, and asked him to post them for her. He took
them away with him, and having reached home realised that
they were still in his pocket. He walked back to the post-
office, took the letters out of his pocket, and, before dropping
each of them into the box, scanned its address. They were all
to tradesmen, except one which was to Forcheville. He kept
it in his hand. "If I saw what was in this," he argued, "I should
know what she calls him, how she talks to him, whether there
really is anything between them. Perhaps indeed by not looking
inside I'm behaving shoddily towards Odette, since it's the
only way I can rid myself of a suspicion which is perhaps
slanderous to her, which must in any case cause her suffering,
and which can never possibly be set at rest once the letter is
posted."

He left the post-office and went home, but he had kept this
last letter with him. He lit a candle and held up close to its
flame the envelope which he had not dared to open. At first
he could distinguish nothing, but the envelope was thin, and
by pressing it down on to the stiff card which it enclosed he
was able, through the transparent paper, to read the concluding words. They consisted of a stiffly formal ending. If,
instead of its being he who was looking at a letter addressed
to Forcheville, it had been Forcheville who had read a letter

addressed to Swann, he would have found words in it of an altogether more affectionate kind! He took a firm hold of the card which was sliding to and fro, the envelope being too large for it, and then, by moving it with his finger and thumb, brought one line after another beneath the part of the envelope where the paper was not doubled, through which alone it was possible to read.

In spite of these manoeuvres he could not make it out clearly. Not that it mattered, for he had seen enough to assure himself that the letter was about some trifling incident which had no connection with amorous relations; it was something to do with an uncle of Odette's. Swann had read quite plainly at the beginning of the line: "I was right," but did not understand what Odette had been right in doing, until suddenly a word which he had not been able at first to decipher came to light and made the whole sentence intelligible: "I was right to open the door; it was my uncle." To open the door! So Forcheville had been there when Swann rang the bell, and she had sent him away, hence the sound that he had heard.

After that he read the whole letter. At the end she apologised for having treated Forcheville with so little ceremony, and reminded him that he had left his cigarette-case at her house, precisely what she had written to Swann after one of his first visits. But to Swann she had added: "If only you had forgotten your heart! I should never have let you have that back." To Forcheville nothing of that sort: no allusion that might suggest any intrigue between them. And, really, he was obliged to admit that in all this Forcheville had been worse treated than himself, since Odette was writing to him to assure him that the visitor had been her uncle. From which it followed that he, Swann, was the man to whom she attached importance and for whose sake she had sent the other away. And yet, if there was nothing between Odette and Forcheville, why not have opened the door at once, why have said, "I was right to open the door; it was my uncle." If she was doing nothing wrong at that moment, how could Forcheville possibly have accounted for her not opening the door? For some time Swann stood there, disconsolate, bewildered and yet happy, gazing at this envelope which Odette had handed to him without a qualm, so absolute was her trust in his honour, but through the transparent screen of which had been disclosed to him, together with the secret history of an incident which he had despaired of ever being able to learn, a fragment of Odette's life, like a luminous section cut out of the unknown. Then his jealousy rejoiced at the discovery, as though that jealousy had an independent existence, fiercely egotistical, gluttonous of everything that would feed its vitality, even at the expense of Swann himself. Now it had something to feed on, and Swann could begin to worry every day about the visits Odette received about five o'clock, could seek to discover where Forcheville had been at that hour. For Swann's affection for Odette still preserved the form which had been imposed on it from the beginning by his ignorance of how she spent her days and by the mental lethargy which prevented him from supplementing that ignorance by imagination. He was not jealous, at first, of the whole of Odette's life, but of those moments only in which an incident, which he had perhaps misinterpreted, had led him to suppose that Odette might have played him false. His jealousy, like an octopus which throws out a first, then a second, and finally a third tentacle, fastened itself firmly to that particular moment, five o'clock in the afternoon, then to another, then to another again. But Swann was incapable of inventing his sufferings. They were only the memory, the perpetuation of a suffering that had come to him from without.

From without, however, everything brought him fresh suffering. He decided to separate Odette from Forcheville by taking her away for a few days to the south. But he imagined that she was coveted by every male person in the hotel, and that she coveted them in return. And so he who in former days, on journeys, used always to seek out new people and crowded places, might now be seen morosely shunning human society as if it had cruelly injured him. And how could he not have turned misanthrope, when in every man he saw a potential lover for Odette? And thus his jealousy did even more than the happy, sensual feeling he had originally experienced for Odette had done to alter Swann's character, completely changing, in the eyes of the world, even the outward signs by which that character had been intelligible.

A month after the evening on which he had intercepted and
read Odette's letter to Forcheville, Swann went to a dinner
which the Verdurins were giving in the Bois. As the party was
breaking up he noticed a series of confabulations between
Mme Verdurin and several of her guests, and thought he heard
the pianist being reminded to come next day to a party at
Chatou, to which he, Swann, had not been invited.

The Verdurins had spoken only in whispers, and in vague
terms, but the painter, perhaps without thinking, exclaimed
aloud: "There must be no lights of any sort, and he must play
the Moonlight Sonata in the dark."

Mme Verdurin, seeing that Swann was within earshot,
assumed an expression in which the two-fold desire to silence
the speaker and to preserve an air of innocence in the eyes of
the listener is neutralised into an intense vacuity wherein the
motionless sign of intelligent complicity is concealed beneath
an ingenuous smile, an expression which, common to everyone who has noticed a gaffe, instantaneously reveals it, if not
to its perpetrator, at any rate to its victim. Odette seemed
suddenly to be in despair, as though she had given up the
struggle against the crushing difficulties of life, and Swann
anxiously counted the minutes that still separated him from
the point at which, after leaving the restaurant, while he drove
her home, he would be able to ask her for an explanation,
make her promise either that she would not go to Chatou next
day or that she would procure an invitation for him also, and
to lull to rest in her arms the anguish that tormented him. At
last the carriages were ordered. Mme Verdurin said to Swann:
"Good-bye, then. We shall see you soon, I hope," trying, by
the friendliness of her manner and the constraint of her smile,
to prevent him from noticing that she was not saying, as she
would always have said hitherto: "To-morrow, then, at Chatou,
and at my house the day after."

M. and Mme Verdurin invited Forcheville into their carriage. Swann's was drawn up behind it, and he waited for
theirs to start before helping Odette into his.

"Odette, we'll take you," said Mme Verdurin, "we've kept
a little corner for you, beside M. de Forcheville."

"Yes, Mme Verdurin," said Odette meekly.

"What! I thought I was to take you home," cried Swann, flinging discretion to the wind, for the carriage-door hung open, the seconds were running out, and he could not, in his present state, go home without her.

"But Mme Verdurin has asked me . . ."

"Come, you can quite well go home alone; we've left her with you quite often enough," said Mme Verdurin.

"But I had something important to say to Mme de Crécy."

"Very well, you can write it to her instead."

"Good-bye," said Odette, holding out her hand.

He tried hard to smile, but looked utterly dejected.

"Did you see the airs Swann is pleased to put on with us?" Mme Verdurin asked her husband when they had reached home. "I was afraid he was going to eat me, simply because we offered to take Odette back. It's positively indecent! Why doesn't he say straight out that we keep a bawdy-house? I can't conceive how Odette can stand such manners. He literally seems to be saying, 'You belong to me!' I shall tell Odette exactly what I think about it all, and I hope she'll have the sense to understand me."

A moment later she added, inarticulate with rage: "No, but, don't you agree, the filthy creature . . ." unwittingly using, perhaps in obedience to the same obscure need to justify herself—like Françoise at Combray, when the chicken refused to die—the very words which the last convulsions of an inoffensive animal in its death throes wring from the peasant who is engaged in taking its life.

And when Mme Verdurin's carriage had moved on and Swann's took its place, his coachman, catching sight of his face, asked whether he was unwell, or had heard some bad news.

Swann dismissed him; he wanted to walk, and returned home on foot through the Bois, talking to himself, aloud, in the same slightly artificial tone he used to adopt when enumerating the charms of the "little nucleus" and extolling the magnanimity of the Verdurins. But just as the conversation, the smiles, the kisses of Odette became as odious to him as he had once found them pleasing, if they were addressed to others, so the Verdurins' salon, which, not an hour before, had still

seemed to him amusing, inspired with a genuine feeling for
art and even with a sort of moral nobility, exhibited to him all
its absurdities, its foolishness, its ignominy, now that it was
another than himself whom Odette was going to meet there,
to love there without restraint.

He pictured to himself with disgust the party next evening
at Chatou. "Imagine going to Chatou, of all places! Like a lot
of drapers after shutting up shop! Upon my word, these people
are really sublime in their bourgeois mediocrity, they can't be
real, they must all have come out of a Labiche comedy!"

The Cottards would be there; possibly Brichot. "Could anything be more grotesque than the lives of these nonentities,
hanging on to one another like that. They'd imagine they were
utterly lost, upon my soul they would, if they didn't all meet
again to-morrow at *Chatou*!" Alas! there would also be the
painter, the painter who enjoyed match-making, who would
invite Forcheville to come with Odette to his studio. He could
see Odette in a dress far too smart for a country outing,
"because she's so vulgar, and, poor little thing, such an absolute fool!"

He could hear the jokes that Mme Verdurin would make
after dinner, jokes which, whoever the "bore" might be at
whom they were aimed, had always amused him because he
could watch Odette laughing at them, laughing with him, her
laughter almost a part of his. Now he felt that it was possibly
at him that they would make Odette laugh. "What fetid
humour!" he exclaimed, twisting his mouth into an expression
of disgust so violent that he could feel the muscles of his
throat stiffen against his collar. "How in God's name can a
creature made in his image find anything to laugh at in those
nauseating witticisms? The least sensitive nose must turn away
in horror from such stale exhalations. It's really impossible to
believe that a human being can fail to understand that, in
allowing herself to smile at the expense of a fellow-creature
who has loyally held out his hand to her, she is sinking into a
mire from which it will be impossible, with the best will in the
world, ever to rescue her. I inhabit a plane so infinitely far
above the sewers in which these filthy vermin sprawl and crawl
and bawl their cheap obscenities, that I cannot possibly be

spattered by the witticisms of a Verdurin!" he shouted, tossing up his head and proudly throwing back his shoulders. "God knows I've honestly tried to pull Odette out of that quagmire, and to teach her to breathe a nobler and a purer air. But human patience has its limits, and mine is at an end," he concluded, as though this sacred mission to tear Odette away from an atmosphere of sarcasms dated from longer than a few minutes ago, as though he had not undertaken it only since it had occurred to him that those sarcasms might perhaps be directed at himself, and might have the effect of detaching Odette from him.

He could see the pianist sitting down to play the Moonlight Sonata, and the grimaces of Mme Verdurin in terrified anticipation of the wrecking of her nerves by Beethoven's music. "Idiot, liar!" he shouted, "and a creature like that imagines that she loves *Art*!" She would say to Odette, after deftly insinuating a few words of praise for Forcheville, as she had so often done for him: "You can make room for M. de Forcheville, there, can't you, Odette?" . . . " 'In the dark!' (he remembered the painter's words), filthy old procuress!" "Procuress" was the name he applied also to the music which would invite them to sit in silence, to dream together, to gaze into each other's eyes, to feel for each other's hands. He felt that there was much to be said, after all, for a sternly censorious attitude towards the arts, such as Plato adopted, and Bossuet, and the old school of education in France.

In a word, the life they led at the Verdurins', which he had so often described as "the true life", seemed to him now the worst of all, and their "little nucleus" the lowest of the low. "It really is," he said, "beneath the lowest rung of the social ladder, the nethermost circle of Dante. No doubt about it, the august words of the Florentine refer to the Verdurins! When you come to think of it, surely people 'in society' (with whom one may find fault now and then but who are after all a very different matter from that riffraff) show a profound sagacity in refusing to know them, or even to soil the tips of their fingers with them. What a sound intuition there is in that '*Noli me tangere*' of the Faubourg Saint-Germain."

He had long since emerged from the paths and avenues of

the Bois, had almost reached his own house, and still, having
not yet shaken off the intoxication of his misery and pain and
the inspired insincerity which the counterfeit tones and artificial
sonority of his own voice raised to ever more exhilarating
heights, he continued to perorate aloud in the silence of the
night: "Society people have their failings, as no one knows
better than I; but there are certain things they simply wouldn't
stoop to. So-and-so" (a fashionable woman whom he had
known) "was far from being perfect, but she did after all have
a fundamental decency, a sense of honour in her dealings
which would have made her incapable, whatever happened,
of any sort of treachery and which puts a vast gulf between
her and an old hag like Verdurin. Verdurin! What a name!
Oh, it must be said that they're perfect specimens of their
disgusting kind! Thank God, it was high time that I stopped
condescending to promiscuous intercourse with such infamy,
such dung."

But, just as the virtues which he had still attributed to the
Verdurins an hour or so earlier would not have sufficed, even
if the Verdurins had actually possessed them, if they had not
also encouraged and protected his love, to excite Swann to
that state of intoxication in which he waxed tender over their
magnanimity—an intoxication which, even when disseminated
through the medium of other persons, could have come to him
from Odette alone—so the immorality (had it really existed)
which he now found in the Verdurins would have been
powerless, if they had not invited Odette with Forcheville and
without him, to unleash his indignation and make him ful-
minate against their "infamy." And doubtless Swann's voice was
more perspicacious than Swann himself when it refused to
utter those words full of disgust with the Verdurins and their
circle, and of joy at having shaken himself free of it, save in an
artificial and rhetorical tone and as though they had been
chosen rather to appease his anger than to express his thoughts.
The latter, in fact, while he abandoned himself to his invective, were probably, though he did not realise it, occupied with
a wholly different matter, for having reached home, no sooner
had he closed the front-door behind him than he suddenly
struck his forehead, and reopening it, dashed out again

exclaiming, in a voice which, this time, was quite natural: "I think I've found a way of getting invited to the dinner at Chatou to-morrow!" But it must have been a bad way, for Swann was not invited. Dr Cottard, who, having been summoned to attend a serious case in the country, had not seen the Verdurins for some days and had been prevented from appearing at Chatou, said on the evening after this dinner, as he sat down to table at their house: "But aren't we going to see M. Swann this evening? He's quite what you might call a personal friend of . . ."

"I sincerely trust we shan't!" cried Mme Verdurin. "Heaven preserve us from him; he's too deadly for words, a stupid, ill-bred boor."

On hearing these words Cottard exhibited an intense astonishment blended with entire submission, as though in the face of a scientific truth which contradicted everything that he had previously believed but was supported by an irresistible weight of evidence; and bowing his head over his plate with timorous emotion, he simply replied: "Oh—oh—oh—oh—oh!" traversing, in an orderly withdrawal of his forces into the depths of his being, along a descending scale, the whole compass of his voice. After which there was no more talk of Swann at the Verdurins'.

And so that drawing-room which had brought Swann and Odette together became an obstacle in the way of their meeting. She no longer said to him, as in the early days of their love: "We shall meet, anyhow, to-morrow evening; there's a supper-party at the Verdurins," but "We shan't be able to meet to-morrow evening; there's a supper-party at the Verdurins." Or else the Verdurins were taking her to the Opéra-Comique, to see *Une Nuit de Cléopâtre*, and Swann could read in her eyes that terror lest he should ask her not to go, which not long since he could not have refrained from greeting with a kiss as it flitted across the face of his mistress, but which now exasperated him. "Yet it's not really anger," he assured himself, "that I feel when I see how she longs to run away and scratch around in that dunghill of cacophony. It's disappointment, not of course for myself but for her; I'm disappointed to

find that, after living for more than six months in daily contact
with me, she hasn't changed enough to be able spontaneously
to reject Victor Massé—above all, that she hasn't yet reached
the stage of understanding that there are evenings when anyone with the least delicacy of feeling should be willing to forgo
a pleasure when asked to do so. She ought to have the sense to
say 'I won't go,' if only from policy, since it is by her answer
that the quality of her heart will be judged once and for all."
And having persuaded himself that it was solely, after all, in
order that he might arrive at a favourable estimate of Odette's
spiritual worth that he wished her to stay at home with him that
evening instead of going to the Opéra-Comique, he adopted
the same line of reasoning with her, with the same degree
of insincerity as he had used with himself, or even a degree
more, for in her case he was yielding also to the desire to
capture her through her own self-esteem.

"I swear to you," he told her, shortly before she was to
leave for the theatre, "that, in asking you not to go, I should
hope, were I a selfish man, for nothing so much as that you
should refuse, for I have a thousand other things to do this
evening and I shall feel trapped myself, and rather annoyed, if,
after all, you tell me you're not going. But my occupations,
my pleasures are not everything; I must think of you too. A day
may come when, seeing me irrevocably sundered from you,
you will be entitled to reproach me for not having warned you
at the decisive hour in which I felt that I was about to pass
judgment on you, one of those stern judgments which love
cannot long resist. You see, your *Nuit de Cléopâtre* (what a
title!) has no bearing on the point. What I must know is
whether you are indeed one of those creatures in the lowest
grade of mentality and even of charm, one of those contemptible creatures who are incapable of forgoing a pleasure.
And if you are such, how could anyone love you, for you are
not even a person, a clearly defined entity, imperfect but at
least perfectible. You are a formless water that will trickle
down any slope that offers itself, a fish devoid of memory,
incapable of thought, which all its life long in its aquarium
will continue to dash itself a hundred times a day against the
glass wall, always mistaking it for water. Do you realise that

your answer will have the effect—I won't say of making me cease loving you immediately, of course, but of making you less attractive in my eyes when I realise that you are not a person, that you are beneath everything in the world and incapable of raising yourself one inch higher. Obviously, I should have preferred to ask you as a matter of little or no importance to give up your *Nuit de Cléopâtre* (since you compel me to sully my lips with so abject a name) in the hope that you would go to it none the less. But, having decided to make such an issue of it, to draw such drastic consequences from your reply, I considered it more honourable to give you due warning."

Meanwhile, Odette had shown signs of increasing emotion and uncertainty. Although the meaning of this speech was beyond her, she grasped that it was to be included in the category of "harangues" and scenes of reproach or supplication, which her familiarity with the ways of men enabled her, without paying any heed to the words that were uttered, to conclude that they would not make unless they were in love, and that since they were in love, it was unnecessary to obey them, as they would only be more in love later on. And so she would have heard Swann out with the utmost tranquillity had she not noticed that it was growing late, and that if he went on talking much longer she would "never", as she told him with a fond smile, obstinate if slightly abashed, "get there in time for the Overture."

On other occasions he told her that the one thing that would make him cease to love her more than anything else would be her refusal to abandon the habit of lying. "Even from the point of view of coquetry, pure and simple," he said to her, "can't you see how much of your attraction you throw away when you stoop to lying? Think how many faults you might redeem by a frank admission! You really are far less intelligent than I supposed!" In vain, however, did Swann expound to her thus all the reasons that she had for not lying; they might have succeeded in overthrowing a general system of mendacity, but Odette had no such system; she was simply content, whenever she wished Swann to remain in ignorance of anything she had done, not to tell him of it. So that lying was for her an expedient of a specific order, and the only thing that could make her decide whether she should avail herself of it or confess the truth was a reason that was also of a specific or contingent order, namely the chance of Swann's discovering that she had not told him the truth.

Physically, she was going through a bad phase; she was putting on weight, and the expressive, sorrowful charm, the surprised, wistful expression of old seemed to have vanished with her first youth. So that she had become most precious to Swann as it were just at the moment when he found her distinctly less good-looking. He would gaze at her searchingly, trying to recapture the charm which he had once seen in her, and no longer finding it. And yet the knowledge that within this new chrysalis it was still Odette who lurked, still the same fleeting, sly, elusive will, was enough to keep Swann seeking as passionately as ever to capture her. Then he would look at photographs of her taken two years before, and would remember how exquisite she had been. And that would console him a little for all the agony he suffered on her account.

When the Verdurins took her off to Saint-Germain, or to Chatou, or to Meulan, as often as not, if the weather was fine, they would decide to stay the night and return next day. Mme Verdurin would endeavour to set at rest the scruples of the pianist, whose aunt had remained in Paris: "She'll be only too glad to be rid of you for a day. Why on earth should she be anxious, when she knows you're with us? Anyhow, I'll take full responsibility."

If this attempt failed, M. Verdurin would set off across country to find a telegraph office or a messenger, after first finding out which of the "faithful" had someone they must notify. But Odette would thank him and assure him that she had no message for anyone, for she had told Swann once and for all that she could not possibly send messages to him, in front of all those people, without compromising herself. Sometimes she would be absent for several days on end, when the Verdurins took her to see the tombs at Dreux, or to Compiègne, on the painter's advice, to watch the sunsets in the forest—after which they went on to the Château of Pierrefonds.

"To think that she could visit really historic buildings with me, who have spent ten years in the study of architecture, who am constantly bombarded by people who really count to take them to Beauvais or Saint-Loup-de-Naud, and refuse to take anyone but her; and instead of that she trundles off with the most abject brutes to go into ecstasies over the petrified excretions of Louis-Philippe and Viollet-le-Duc! One hardly needs much knowledge of art, I should say, to do that; surely, even without a particularly refined sense of smell, one doesn't deliberately choose to spend a holiday in the latrines so as to be within range of their fragrant exhalations."

But when she had set off for Dreux or Pierrefonds—alas, without allowing him to turn up there, as though by chance, for that, she said, "would create a deplorable impression"— he would plunge into the most intoxicating romance in the lover's library, the railway time-table, from which he learned the ways of joining her there in the afternoon, in the evening, even that very morning. The ways? More than that, the authority, the right to join her. For after all, the time-table, and the trains themselves, were not meant for dogs. If the public was informed, by means of the printed word, that at eight o'clock in the morning a train left for Pierrefonds which arrived there at ten, that could only be because going to Pierrefonds was a lawful act, for which permission from Odette would be superfluous; an act, moreover, which might be performed from a motive altogether different from the desire to see Odette, since persons who had never even heard of her performed it daily, and in such numbers as justified the labour and expense of stoking the engines.

All things considered, she could not really prevent him from going to Pierrefonds if he felt inclined to do so. And as it happened, he did feel so inclined, and had he not known Odette, would certainly have gone. For a long time past he had wanted to form a more definite impression of Viollet-le-Duc's work as a restorer. And the weather being what it was, he felt an overwhelming desire to go for a walk in the forest of Compiègne.

It really was bad luck that she had forbidden him access to the one spot that tempted him to-day. To-day! Why, if he went there in defiance of her prohibition, he would be able to see her that very day! But whereas, if she had met at Pierrefonds someone who did not matter to her, she would have hailed him with obvious pleasure: "What, you here?" and would have invited him to come and see her at the hotel where she was staying with the Verdurins, if on the other hand it was himself, Swann, that she ran into, she would be offended, would complain that she was being followed, would love him less in consequence, might even turn away in anger when she caught sight of him. "So, I'm not allowed to travel any more!" she would say to him on her return, whereas in fact it was he who was not allowed to travel!

At one moment he had had the idea, in order to be able to visit Compiègne and Pierrefonds without letting it be supposed that his object was to meet Odette, of securing an invitation from one of his friends, the Marquis de Forestelle, who had a country house in that neighbourhood. The latter, whom he apprised of his plan without disclosing its ulterior purpose, was beside himself with joy and astonishment at Swann's consenting at last, after fifteen years, to come down and visit his property, and since he did not (he had told him) wish to stay there, promising at least to spend some days going for walks and excursions with him. Swann imagined himself already down there with M. de Forestelle. Even before he saw Odette, even if he did not succeed in seeing her there, what a joy it would be to set foot on that soil, where not knowing the exact spot in which, at any moment, she was to be found, he would feel all around him the thrilling possibility of her sudden apparition: in the courtyard of the Château, now beautiful in his eyes since it was on her account that he had gone to visit it; in all the streets of the town, which struck him as romantic; down every ride of the forest, roseate with the deep and tender glow of sunset;—innumerable and alternative sanctuaries, in which, in the uncertain ubiquity of his hopes, his happy, vagabond and divided heart would simultaneously take refuge. "We mustn't on any account," he would warn M. de Forestelle, "run across Odette and the Verdurins. I've just heard that they're at Pierrefonds, of all places, to-day. One has plenty of time to see them in Paris; it would hardly be worth while

coming down here if one couldn't go a yard without meeting
them." And his host would fail to understand why, once they
were there, Swann would change his plans twenty times in an
hour, inspect the dining-rooms of all the hotels in Compiègne
without being able to make up his mind to settle down in any
of them, although they had seen no trace anywhere of the
Verdurins, seeming to be in search of what he claimed to be
most anxious to avoid, and would in fact avoid the moment he
found it, for if he had come upon the little "group" he would
have hastened away at once with studied indifference, satisfied
that he had seen Odette and she him, especially that she had
seen him not bothering his head about her. But no; she would
guess at once that it was for her sake that he was there. And
when M. de Forestelle came to fetch him, and it was time to
start, he excused himself: "No, I'm afraid I can't go to Pierrefonds to-day. You see, Odette is there." And Swann was happy
in spite of everything to feel that if he, alone among mortals,
had not the right to go to Pierrefonds that day, it was because
he was in fact, for Odette, someone different from all other
mortals, her lover, and because that restriction imposed for
him alone on the universal right to freedom of movement was
but one of the many forms of the slavery, the love that was
so dear to him. Decidedly, it was better not to risk a quarrel
with her, to be patient, to wait for her return. He spent his
days poring over a map of the forest of Compiègne as though
it had been that of the "Pays du Tendre,"[13] and surrounded
himself with photographs of the Château of Pierrefonds. When
the day dawned on which it was possible that she might
return, he opened the time-table again, calculated what train
she must have taken, and, should she have postponed her departure, what trains were still left for her to take. He did not
leave the house for fear of missing a telegram, did not go to
bed in case, having come by the last train, she decided to
surprise him with a midnight visit. Yes! The front-door bell
rang. There seemed some delay in opening the door, he wanted
to awaken the porter, he leaned out of the window to shout
to Odette if it was she, for in spite of the orders which he had
gone downstairs a dozen times to deliver in person, they were
quite capable of telling her that he was not at home. It was

only a servant coming in. He noticed the incessant rumble of passing carriages, to which he had never paid any attention before. He could hear them, one after another, a long way off, coming nearer, passing his door without stopping, and bearing away into the distance a message which was not for him. He waited all night, to no purpose, for the Verdurins had decided to return early, and Odette had been in Paris since midday. It had not occurred to her to tell him, and not knowing what to do with herself she had spent the evening alone at a theatre, had long since gone home to bed, and was peacefully asleep.

As a matter of fact, she had not even given him a thought. And such moments as these, in which she forgot Swann's very existence, were more useful to Odette, did more to bind him to her, than all her coquetry. For in this way Swann was kept in that state of painful agitation which had already been powerful enough to cause his love to blossom, on the night when he had failed to find Odette at the Verdurins' and had hunted for her all evening. And he did not have (as I had at Combray in my childhood) happy days in which to forget the sufferings that would return with the night. For his days were spent without Odette; and there were times when he told himself that to allow so pretty a woman to go out by herself in Paris was just as rash as to leave a case filled with jewels in the middle of the street. Then he would rail against all the passers-by, as though they were so many pickpockets. But their faces— a collective and formless mass—escaped the grasp of his imagination, and failed to feed the flame of his jealousy. The effort exhausted Swann's brain, until, putting his hand over his eyes, he cried out: "Heaven help me!" as people, after lashing themselves into an intellectual frenzy in their endeavours to master the problem of the reality of the external world or the immortality of the soul, afford relief to their weary brains by an unreasoning act of faith. But the thought of his absent mistress was incessantly, indissolubly blended with all the simplest actions of Swann's daily life—when he took his meals, opened his letters, went for a walk or to bed—by the very sadness he felt at having to perform those actions without her; like those initials of Philibert the Fair which, in the church of

Brou, because of her grief and longing for him, Margaret of Austria intertwined everywhere with her own. On some days, instead of staying at home, he would go for luncheon to a restaurant not far off to which he had once been attracted by the excellence of its cookery, but to which he now went only for one of those reasons, at once mystical and absurd, which people call "romantic"; because this restaurant (which, by the way, still exists) bore the same name as the street in which Odette lived: La Pérouse.

Sometimes, when she had been away on a short visit somewhere, several days would elapse before she thought of letting him know that she had returned to Paris. And then she would say quite simply, without taking (as she would once have taken) the precaution of covering herself, just in case, with a little fragment borrowed from the truth, that she had at that very moment arrived by the morning train. These words were mendacious; at least for Odette they were mendacious, insubstantial, lacking (what they would have had if true) a basis of support in her memory of her actual arrival at the station; she was even prevented from forming a mental picture of them as she uttered them, by the contradictory picture of whatever quite different thing she had been doing at the moment when she pretended to have been alighting from the train. In Swann's mind, however, these words, meeting no opposition, settled and hardened until they assumed the indestructibility of a truth so indubitable that, if some friend happened to tell him that he had come by the same train and had not seen Odette, Swann was convinced that it was the friend who had mistaken the day or the hour, since his version did not agree with the words uttered by Odette. These words would have appeared to him false only if he had suspected beforehand that they were going to be. For him to be believe that she was lying, an anticipatory suspicion was indispensable. It was also, however, sufficient. Given that, everything Odette said appeared to him suspect. If she mentioned a name, it was obviously that of one of her lovers, and once this supposition had taken shape, he would spend weeks tormenting himself. On one occasion he even approached a firm of "inquiry agents" to find out the address and the occupation of the

unknown rival who would give him no peace until he could be
proved to have gone abroad, and who (he ultimately learned)
was an uncle of Odette who had been dead for twenty years.

Although she would not allow him as a rule to meet her in
public, saying that people would talk, it happened occasionally
that, at an evening party to which he and she had both been
invited—at Forcheville's, at the painter's, or at a charity ball
given in one of the Ministries—he found himself in the same
room with her. He could see her, but dared not stay for fear
of annoying her by seeming to be spying upon the pleasures she
enjoyed in other company, pleasures which—as he drove home
in utter loneliness, and went to bed as miserable as I was to be
some years later on the evenings when he came to dine with
us at Combray—seemed to him limitless since he had not seen
the end of them. And once or twice he experienced on such
evenings the sort of happiness which one would be inclined
(did it not originate in so violent a reaction from an anxiety
abruptly terminated) to call peaceful, since it consists in a paci-
fying of the mind. On one occasion he had looked in for a
moment at a party in the painter's studio, and was preparing
to go home, leaving behind him Odette transformed into a
brilliant stranger, surrounded by men to whom her glances
and her gaiety, which were not for him, seemed to hint at
some voluptuous pleasures to be enjoyed there or elsewhere
(possibly at the Bal des Incohérents, to which he trembled to
think that she might be going on afterwards) which caused
Swann more jealousy than the carnal act itself, since he found it
more difficult to imagine; he was already at the door when he
heard himself called back in these words (which, by cutting off
from the party that possible ending which had so appalled
him, made it seem innocent in retrospect, made Odette's return
home a thing no longer inconceivable and terrible, but tender
and familiar, a thing that would stay beside him, like a part of
his daily life, in his carriage, and stripped Odette herself of the
excess of brilliance and gaiety in her appearance, showed that
it was only a disguise which she had assumed for a moment,
for its own sake and not with a view to any mysterious pleasures, and of which she had already wearied)—in these words
which Odette tossed at him as he was crossing the threshold:

"Can't you wait a minute for me? I'm just going; we'll drive back together and you can take me home."

It was true that on one occasion Forcheville had asked to be driven home at the same time, but when, on reaching Odette's door, he had begged to be allowed to come in too, she had replied, pointing to Swann: "Ah! That depends on this gentleman. You must ask him. Very well, you may come in just for a minute, if you insist, but you mustn't stay long, because I warn you, he likes to sit and talk quietly with me, and he's not at all pleased if I have visitors when he's here. Oh, if you only knew the creature as I know him! Isn't that so, my love, no one really knows you well except me?"

And Swann was perhaps even more touched by the spectacle of her addressing to him thus, in front of Forcheville, not only these tender words of predilection, but also certain criticisms, such as: "I feel sure you haven't written yet to your friends about dining with them on Sunday. You needn't go if you don't want to, but you might at least be polite," or, "Now, have you left your essay on Vermeer here so that you can do a little more of it to-morrow? What a lazy-bones! I'm going to make you work, I can tell you," which proved that Odette kept herself in touch with his social engagements and his literary work, that they had indeed a life in common. And as she spoke she gave him a smile that told him she was entirely his.

At such moments as these, while she was making them some orangeade, suddenly, just as when an ill-adjusted reflector begins by casting huge, fantastic shadows on an object on the wall which then contract and merge into it, all the terrible and shifting ideas which he had formed about Odette melted away and vanished into the charming creature who stood there before his eyes. He had the sudden suspicion that this hour spent in Odette's house, in the lamp-light, was perhaps, after all, not an artificial hour, invented for his special use (with the object of concealing that frightening and delicious thing which was incessantly in his thoughts without his ever being able to form a satisfactory impression of it, an hour of Odette's real life, of her life when he was not there), with theatrical properties and pasteboard fruits, but was perhaps a genuine hour of

Odette's life; that if he himself had not been there she would have pulled forward the same armchair for Forcheville, would have poured out for him, not some unknown brew, but precisely this same orangeade; that the world inhabited by Odette was not that other fearful and supernatural world in which he spent his time placing her—and which existed, perhaps, only in his imagination—but the real world, exhaling no special atmosphere of gloom, comprising that table at which he might sit down presently and write, this drink which he was now being permitted to taste, all these objects which he contemplated with as much curiosity and admiration as gratitude— for if, in absorbing his dreams, they had delivered him from them, they themselves in return had been enriched by them, they showed him the palpable realisation of his fancies, and they impressed themselves upon his mind, took shape and grew solid before his eyes, at the same time as they soothed his troubled heart. Ah, if fate had allowed him to share a single dwelling with Odette, so that in her house he should be in his own, if, when asking the servant what there was for lunch, it had been Odette's menu that he had been given in reply, if, when Odette wished to go for a morning walk in the Avenue du Bois de Boulogne, his duty as a good husband had obliged him, though he had no desire to go out, to accompany her, carrying her overcoat when she was too warm, and in the evening, after dinner, if she wished to stay at home in deshabille, if he had been forced to stay beside her, to do what she asked; then how completely would all the trivial details of Swann's life which seemed to him now so melancholy have taken on, for the very reason that they would at the same time have formed part of Odette's life—like this lamp, this orangeade, this armchair, which had absorbed so much of his dreams, which materialised so much of his longing—a sort of superabundant sweetness and a mysterious density!

And yet he was inclined to suspect that the state for which he so longed was a calm, a peace, which would not have been a propitious atmosphere for his love. When Odette ceased to be for him a creature always absent, regretted, imagined, when the feeling that he had for her was no longer the same mysterious turmoil that was wrought in him by the phrase from the sonata, but affection and gratitude, when normal relations that would put an end to his melancholy madness were established between them—then, no doubt, the actions of Odette's daily life would appear to him as being of little intrinsic interest—as he had several times already felt that they might be, on the day, for instance, when he had read through its envelope her letter to Forcheville. Examining his complaint with as much scientific detachment as if he had inoculated himself with it in order to study its effects, he told himself that, when he was cured of it, what Odette might or might not do would be a matter of indifference to him. But the truth was that in the depths of his morbid condition he feared death itself no more than such a recovery, which would in fact amount to the death of all that he now was.

After these quiet evenings, Swann's suspicions would be temporarily lulled; he would bless the name of Odette, and next day, in the morning would order the finest jewels to be sent to her, because her kindnesses to him overnight had excited either his gratitude, or the desire to see them repeated, or a paroxysm of love for her which had need of some such outlet.

But at other times, his anguish would again take hold of him; he would imagine that Odette was Forcheville's mistress, and that when they had both sat watching him from the depths of the Verdurins' landau in the Bois on the evening before the party at Chatou to which he had not been invited, while he implored her in vain, with that look of despair on his face which even his coachman had noticed, to come home with him, and then turned away, solitary and crushed, she must have glanced at Forcheville, as she drew his attention to him, saying "Look how furious he is!" with the same expression, sparkling, malicious, sidelong and sly, as on the evening when Forcheville had driven Saniette from the Verdurins'.

At such times Swann detested her. "But I've been a fool, too," he would argue. "I'm paying for other men's pleasures with my money. All the same, she'd better take care, and not push her luck, because I might very well stop giving her anything at all. At any rate, we'd better knock off supplementary favours for the time being. To think that only yesterday, when she said she would like to go to Bayreuth for the season, I was

such an ass as to offer to take one of those nice little castles the
King of Bavaria has in the neighbourhood for the two of us.
However she didn't seem particularly keen; she hasn't said
yes or no yet. Let's hope she'll refuse. Good God! Think of
listening to Wagner for a whole fortnight with a woman who
takes about as much interest in music as a tone-deaf newt—
that would be fun!" And his hatred, like his love, needing to
manifest itself in action, he took pleasure in urging his evil
imaginings further and further, because, thanks to the perfidies
of which he accused Odette, he detested her still more, and
would be able, if it turned out—as he tried to convince himself
—that she was indeed guilty of them, to take the opportunity
of punishing her, and of venting his mounting rage on her.
Thus he went so far as to suppose that he was about to receive
a letter from her in which she would ask him for money to
take the castle near Bayreuth, but with the warning that he
was not to come there himself, as she had promised to invite
Forcheville and the Verdurins. How he would have loved
it if she had had the audacity to do this! How he would have
enjoyed refusing, drawing up the vindictive reply, the terms of
which he amused himself by selecting and declaiming aloud,
though he had actually received such a letter!

The very next day, he did. She wrote that the Verdurins and
their friends had expressed a desire to attend these performances
of Wagner, and that, if he would be so good as to send her the
money, she would at last have the pleasure, after going so often
to their house, of entertaining the Verdurins in hers. Of him
she said not a word; it was to be taken for granted that their
presence would be a bar to his.

Then he had the pleasure of sending round to her that an-
nihilating answer, every word of which he had carefully rehearsed overnight without venturing to hope that it could ever
be used. Alas! he felt only too certain that with the money she
had, or could easily procure, she would be able all the same
to take a house at Bayreuth, since she wished to do so, she who
was incapable of distinguishing between Bach and Clapisson.
Let her take it, then: at least she would have to live in it more
frugally. No chance (as there would have been if he had replied
by sending her several thousand-franc notes) of organising

each evening in some castle those exquisite little suppers after which she might perhaps indulge the whim (which, it was possible, had never yet seized her) of falling into the arms of Forcheville. At any rate it would not be he, Swann, who paid for this loathsome expedition! Ah! if he could only manage to prevent it, if she could sprain her ankle before setting out, if the driver of the carriage which was to take her to the station would consent (at no matter what price) to smuggle her to some place where she could be kept for a time in seclusion—that perfidious woman, her eyes glittering with a smile of complicity for Forcheville, that Odette had become for Swann in the last forty-eight hours!

But she was never that for very long. After a few days the shining, crafty eyes lost their brightness and their duplicity, the picture of a hateful Odette saying to Forcheville "Look how furious he is!" began to fade and dissolve. Then gradually the face of the other Odette would reappear and rise before him, softly radiant—that Odette who also turned with a smile to Forcheville, but with a smile in which there was nothing but tenderness for Swann, when she said: "You mustn't stay long, because this gentleman doesn't much like my having visitors when he's here. Oh! if you only knew the creature as I know him!"—that same smile with which she used to thank Swann for some instance of his courtesy which she prized so highly, for some advice for which she had asked him in one of those moments of crisis when she would turn to him alone.

And thinking of this other Odette, he would ask himself what could have induced him to write that outrageous letter, of which, probably, until then she would never have supposed him capable, a letter which must have brought him down from the high, from the supreme place which by his generosity, by his loyalty, he had won for himself in her esteem. He would become less dear to her, since it was for those qualities, which she found neither in Forcheville nor in any other, that she loved him. It was for them that Odette so often showed him a reciprocal warmth which counted for less than nothing in his moments of jealousy, because it was not a sign of reciprocal desire, was indeed a proof rather of affection than of love, but the importance of which he began once more to feel in proportion as the spontaneous relaxation of his suspicions, often accelerated by the distraction brought to him by reading about art or by the conversation of a friend, rendered his passion less exacting of reciprocities.

Now that, after this swing of the pendulum, Odette had naturally returned to the place from which Swann's jealousy had momentarily driven her, to the angle from which he found her charming, he pictured her to himself as full of tenderness, with a look of consent in her eyes, and so beautiful that he could not refrain from proffering her his lips as though she had actually been in the room for him to kiss; and he felt as strong a sense of gratitude towards her for that bewitching, kindly glance as if it had been real, as if it had not been merely his imagination that had portrayed it in order to satisfy his desire.

What distress he must have caused her! Certainly he could find valid reasons for his resentment, but they would not have been sufficient to make him feel that resentment if he had not loved her so passionately. Had he not nourished equally serious grievances against other women, to whom he would none the less willingly render a service to-day, feeling no anger towards them because he no longer loved them? If the day ever came when he found himself in the same state of indifference with regard to Odette, he would then understand that it was his jealousy alone which had led him to find something heinous, unpardonable, in this desire of hers (which was after all so natural, springing from a childlike ingenuousness and also from a certain delicacy in her nature) to be able in her turn, since the opportunity had arisen, to repay the Verdurins for their hospitality, and to play the hostess in a house of her own.

He returned to this other point of view, which was the opposite of the one based on his love and jealousy and to which he resorted at times by a sort of intellectual equity and in order to make allowance for the various probabilities, and tried to judge Odette as though he had not been in love with her, as though she were like any other woman, as though her life (as soon as he was no longer present) had not been different, woven secretly behind his back, hatched against him.

Why should he think that she would enjoy out there with

Forcheville or with other men intoxicating pleasures which she
had never experienced with him, and which his jealousy alone
had fabricated out of nothing? At Bayreuth, as in Paris, if it
should happen that Forcheville thought of him at all, it would
only be as of someone who counted for a great deal in Odette's
life, someone for whom he was obliged to make way when they
met at her house. If Forcheville and she gloated at the idea of
being there together in spite of him, it was he who would have
engineered it by striving in vain to prevent her from going,
whereas if he had approved of her plan, which for that matter
was quite defensible, she would have had the appearance of
being there on his advice, she would have felt that she had been
sent there, housed there by him, would have been beholden to
him for the pleasure which she derived from entertaining those
people who had so often entertained her.

And if—instead of letting her go off on bad terms with him,
without having seen him again—he were to send her this
money, if he were to encourage her to undertake this journey
and go out of his way to make it agreeable for her, she would
come running to him, happy and grateful, and he would have
the joy of seeing her which he had not known for nearly a
week and which nothing else could replace. For once Swann
could picture her to himself without revulsion, could see once
again the friendliness in her smile, once the desire to tear her
away from every rival was no longer imposed by his jealousy
upon his love, that love became once again, more than anything,
a taste for the sensations which Odette's person gave him, for
the pleasure he took in admiring as a spectacle, or in examining
as a phenomenon, the dawn of one of her glances, the formation of one of her smiles, the emission of a particular vocal
cadence. And this pleasure, different from every other, had in the
end created in him a need of her, which she alone by her presence or by her letters could assuage, almost as disinterested,
almost as artistic, as perverse, as another need which characterised this new period in Swann's life, when the sereness, the
depression of the preceding years had been followed by a sort
of spiritual overflowing, without his knowing to what he
owed this unlooked-for enrichment of his inner life, any more
than a person in delicate health who from a certain moment

grows stronger, puts on flesh, and seems for a time to be on the
road to a complete recovery. This other need, which developed independently of the visible, material world, was the
need to listen to music and improve his knowledge of it.

And so, through the chemical action of his malady, after he
had created jealousy out of his love, he began again to manu-
facture tenderness and pity for Odette. She had become once
more the old Odette, charming and kind. He was full of remorse for having treated her harshly. He wished her to come
to him, and, before she came, he wished to have already procured for her some pleasure, so as to watch her gratitude
taking shape in her face and moulding her smile.

And consequently Odette, certain of seeing him come to her
after a few days, as tender and submissive as before, to plead
with her for a reconciliation, became inured, was no longer
afraid of displeasing him or even of making him angry, and
refused him, whenever it suited her, the favours by which he
set most store.

Perhaps she did not realise how sincere he had been with
her during their quarrel, when he had told her that he would
not send her any money and would do everything he could to
hurt her. Perhaps she did not realise, either, how sincere he
was, if not with her, at any rate with himself, on other occasions when, for the sake of the future of their relationship, to
show Odette that he was capable of doing without her, that a
rupture was still possible between them, he decided to wait
some time before going to see her again.

Sometimes it would be after several days during which she
had caused him no fresh anxiety; and since he knew that he
was likely to derive no very great pleasure from his impending
visits, but more probably some annoyance which would put
an end to his present state of calm, he would write to her saying
that he was very busy, and would not be able to see her on
any of the days that he had suggested. Meanwhile, a letter
from her, crossing his, asked him to postpone one of those very
meetings. He wondered why; his suspicions, his anguish,
again took hold of him. He could no longer abide, in the new
state of agitation into which he found himself plunged, by the
arrangements which he had made in his preceding state of com-

parative calm; he would hurry round to her, and would insist upon seeing her on each of the following days. And even if she had not written first, if she merely acknowledged his letter, agreeing to his request for a brief separation, it was enough to make him unable to rest without seeing her. For, contrary to his calculations, Odette's acquiescence had entirely changed his attitude. Like everyone who possesses something precious, in order to know what would happen if he ceased for a moment to possess it, he had detached the precious object from his mind, leaving, as he thought, everything else in the same state as when it was there. But the absence of one part from a whole is not only that, it is not simply a partial lack, it is a derangement of all the other parts, a new state which it was impossible to foresee in the old.

But at other times—when Odette was on the point of going away for a holiday—it was after some trifling quarrel for which he had chosen the pretext that he resolved not to write to her and not to see her until her return, thus giving the appearance (and expecting the reward) of a serious rupture, which she would perhaps regard as final, to a separation the greater part of which was the inevitable consequence of her proposed journey, which he was merely allowing to start a little sooner than it must. At once he could imagine Odette puzzled, anxious, distressed at having received neither visit nor letter from him, and this picture of her, by calming his jealousy, made it easy for him to break himself of the habit of seeing her. At moments, no doubt, in the furthest recesses of his mind where his determination had thrust it away thanks to the long interval of the three weeks' separation which he had accepted, it was with pleasure that he considered the idea that he would see Odette again on her return; but it was also with so little impatience that he began to wonder whether he would not readily consent to the doubling of the period of so easy an abstinence. It had lasted, so far, but three days, a much shorter time than he had often spent without seeing Odette, and without having, as on this occasion, premeditated it. And yet, suddenly, some minor vexation or physical ailment—by inciting him to regard the present moment as an exceptional one, outside the rules, one in which common wisdom would

allow him to take advantage of the soothing effects of a pleasure and, until there was some purpose in a resumption of
effort, to give his will a rest—suspended the operation of the
latter, which ceased to exert its inhibitive control; or, without
that even, the thought of something he had forgotten to ask
Odette, such as whether she had decided in what colour she
would have her carriage repainted, or, with regard to some investment, whether they were "ordinary" or "preference"
shares that she wished him to buy (for it was all very well to
show her that he could live without seeing her, but if, after
that, the carriage had to be painted over again, or if the shares
produced no dividend, a lot of good it would have done him),
—and suddenly, like a stretched piece of elastic which is let
go, or the air in a pneumatic machine which is ripped open,
the idea of seeing her again sprang back from the distant
depths in which it lay dormant into the field of the present and
of immediate possibilities.

It sprang back thus without meeting any further resistance,
so irresistible, in fact, that Swann had found it far less painful
to watch the fortnight he was to spend separated from Odette
creeping by day after day than to wait the ten minutes it took
his coachman to bring round the carriage which was to take
him to her, minutes which he spent in transports of impatience
and joy, in which he recaptured a thousand times over, to
lavish on it all the wealth of his affection, that idea of meeting
her again which, by so abrupt a reversal, at a moment when
he supposed it so remote, was once more present and on the
very surface of his consciousness. The fact was that his idea
no longer found as an obstacle in its course the desire to
resist it without further delay, a desire which had ceased to
have any place in Swann's mind since, having proved to himself—or so at least he believed—that he was so easily capable of
resisting it, he no longer saw any danger in postponing a plan
of separation which he was now certain of being able to put
into operation whenever he wished. Furthermore, this idea of
seeing her again came back to him adorned with a novelty, a
seductiveness, armed with a virulence, which long habit had
dulled but which had been retempered during this privation,
not of three days but of a fortnight (for a period of abstinence

may be calculated, by anticipation, as having lasted already until the final date assigned to it), and had converted what had been until then a pleasure in store which could easily be sacrificed into an unlooked-for happiness which he was powerless to resist. Finally, the idea returned to him embellished by his ignorance of what Odette might have thought, might perhaps have done, on finding that he had given no sign of life, with the result that what he was going now to find was the entrancing revelation of an almost unknown Odette.

But she, just as she had supposed that his refusal to send her money was only a sham, saw nothing but a pretext in the questions he was now coming to ask her, about the repainting of her carriage or the purchase of shares. For she could not reconstruct the several phases of these crises through which he was passing, and the notion she had formed of them omitted any attempt to understand their mechanism, but looked only to what she knew beforehand, their necessary, never-failing and always identical termination. An incomplete notion (though possibly all the more profound in consequence), if one were to judge it from the point of view of Swann, who would doubtless have considered himself misunderstood by Odette, just as a drug-addict or a consumptive, each persuaded that he has been held back, one by some outside event at the moment when he was about to shake himself free of his inveterate habit, the other by an accidental indisposition at the moment when he was about to be finally cured, feels himself to be misunderstood by the doctor who does not attach the same importance to these alleged contingencies, mere disguises, according to him, assumed, so as to make themselves felt once more, by the vice of the one and the morbid state of the other, which in reality have never ceased to weigh heavily and incurably upon the patients while they were nursing their dreams of reformation or health. And, as a matter of fact, Swann's love had reached the stage at which the boldest of physicians or (in the case of certain affections) of surgeons ask themselves whether to deprive a patient of his vice or to rid him of his malady is still reasonable or indeed possible.

Certainly, of the extent of this love Swann had no direct awareness. When he sought to measure it, it happened sometimes that he found it diminished, shrunk almost to nothing; for instance, the lack of enthusiasm, amounting almost to distaste, which, in the days before he was in love with Odette, he had felt for her expressive features, her faded complexion, returned on certain days. "Really, I'm making distinct headway," he would tell himself next day. "Looking at things quite honestly, I can't say I got much pleasure last night from being in bed with her. It's an odd thing, but I actually thought her ugly." And certainly he was sincere, but his love extended a long way beyond the province of physical desire. Odette's person, indeed, no longer held any great place in it. When his eyes fell upon the photograph of Odette on his table, or when she came to see him, he had difficulty in identifying her face, either in the flesh or on the pasteboard, with the painful and continuous anxiety which dwelt in his mind. He would say to himself, almost with astonishment, "It's she!" as though suddenly we were to be shown in a detached, externalised form one of our own maladies, and we found it bore no resemblance to what we are suffering. "She"—he tried to ask himself what that meant; for it is a point of resemblance between love and death, far more striking than those which are usually pointed out, that they make us probe deeper, in the fear that its reality may elude us, into the mystery of personality. And this malady which Swann's love had become had so proliferated, was so closely interwoven with all his habits, with all his actions, with his thoughts, his health, his sleep, his life, even with what he hoped for after his death, was so utterly inseparable from him, that it would have been impossible to eradicate it without almost entirely destroying him; as surgeons say, his love was no longer operable.

By this love Swann had been so far detached from all other interests that when by chance he reappeared in society, reminding himself that his social relations, like a beautifully wrought setting (although she would not have been able to form any very exact estimate of its worth), might restore something of his own prestige in Odette's eyes (as indeed they might have done had they not been cheapened by his love itself, which for Odette depreciated everything that it touched by seeming to proclaim such things less precious), he would feel there, side by side with his distress at being in places and among people she did not know, the same detached pleasure as he would have derived from a novel or a painting in which were depicted the amusements of a leisured class; just as, at home, he used to enjoy the thought of the smooth efficiency of his household, the elegance of his wardrobe and of his servants' liveries, the soundness of his investments, with the same relish as when he read in Saint-Simon, who was one of his favourite authors, of the mechanics of daily life at Versailles, what Mme de Maintenon ate and drank, or the shrewd avarice and great pomp of Lulli. And to the small extent to which this detachment was not absolute, the reason for this new pleasure which Swann was tasting was that he could take refuge for a moment in those few and distant parts of himself which had remained more or less extraneous to his love and to his pain. In this respect the personality which my great-aunt attributed to him as "young Swann," as distinct from the more individual personality of Charles Swann, was the one in which he was now happiest. Once, wishing to send the Princesse de Parme some fruit for her birthday (and because she could often be of use indirectly to Odette, by letting her have seats for galas and jubilees and the like) and not being quite sure how to order it, he had entrusted the task to a cousin of his mother who, delighted to do an errand for him, had written to him, when sending him the account, to say that she had not ordered all the fruit from the same place, but the grapes from Crapote, whose speciality they were, the strawberries from Jauret, the pears from Chevet, who always had the best, and so on, "every fruit inspected and examined, one by one, by myself." And in the sequel, by the cordiality with which the Princess thanked him, he had been able to judge of the flavour of the strawberries and of the ripeness of the pears. But, most of all, that "every fruit inspected and examined, one by one, by myself" had brought balm to his sufferings by carrying his mind off to a region which he rarely visited, although it was his by right as the heir to a rich, upper-middle-class family in which had been handed down from generation to generation the knowledge of the "right places" and the art of placing an order.

Indeed, he had too long forgotten that he was "young Swann" not to feel, when he assumed the role again for a moment, a keener pleasure than those he might have felt at other times but which had palled; and if the friendliness of the bourgeoisie, for whom he had never been anything else than "young Swann," was less animated than that of the aristocracy (though more flattering, for all that, since with them it is always inseparable from respect), no letter from a royal personage, whatever princely entertainment it offered, could ever be so agreeable to Swann as a letter inviting him to be a witness, or merely to be present, at a wedding in the family of some old friends of his parents, some of whom had "kept up" with him—like my grandfather, who, the year before these events, had invited him to my mother's wedding—while others barely knew him by sight, but considered themselves in duty bound to show civility to the son, to the worthy successor, of the late M. Swann.

But, by virtue of his intimacy, already time-honoured, with so many of its members, the nobility was in a certain sense also a part of his house, his domestic establishment, and his family. He felt, when his mind dwelt upon his brilliant connections, the same external support, the same solid comfort as when he looked at the fine estates, the fine silver, the fine table-linen which had come to him from his own family. And the thought that, if he were struck down by a sudden illness and confined to the house, the people whom his valet would instinctively run to fetch would be the Duc de Chartres, the Prince de Reuss, the Duc de Luxembourg and the Baron de Charlus, brought him the same consolation as our old Françoise derived from the knowledge that she would one day be buried in her own fine sheets, marked with her name, not darned at all (or so exquisitely darned that it merely enhanced one's idea of the skill and patience of the seamstress), a shroud from the constant image of which in her mind's eye she drew a certain satisfactory sense, if not actually of wealth and prosperity, at any rate of self-esteem. But most of all,—since in every one of his actions and thoughts which had reference to Odette, Swann was constantly obsessed and influenced by the unavowed feeling that he was, perhaps not less dear, but less welcome to her than anyone, even the most tedious of the Verdurin "faithful,"—when he betook himself to a world in which he was the paragon of taste, a man whom no pains were spared to attract, whom people were genuinely sorry not to see, he began once again to believe in the existence of a happier life, almost to feel an appetite for it, as an invalid may feel who has been bedridden for months, on a strict diet, when he picks up a newspaper and reads the account of an official banquet or an advertisement for a cruise round Sicily.

If he was obliged to make excuses to his society friends for not visiting them, it was precisely for visiting her that he sought to excuse himself to Odette. Even so, he paid for his visits (asking himself at the end of the month, should he have overtaxed her patience and gone rather often to see her, whether it would be enough if he sent her four thousand francs), and for each one found a pretext, a present that he had to bring her, a piece of information which she required, M. de Charlus whom he had met actually going to her house and who had insisted on Swann's accompanying him. And, failing an excuse, he would ask M. de Charlus to go round to her house and say to her, as though spontaneously, in the course of conversation, that he had just remembered something he had to say to Swann, and would she please send a message to Swann asking him to come to her then and there; but as a rule Swann waited at home in vain, and M. de Charlus informed him later in the evening that his ruse had not proved successful. With the result that, if she was now frequently away from Paris, even when she was there he scarcely saw her, and she who, when she was in love with him, used to say "I'm always free" and "What do I care what other people think?" now, whenever he wanted to see her, appealed to the proprieties or pleaded some engagement. When he spoke of going to a charity entertainment, or a private view, or a first-night at which she was to be present, she would complain that he wished to advertise their liaison, that he was treating her like a whore. Things came to such a pitch that, in an effort to avoid being debarred from meeting her anywhere, Swann, remembering that she knew and was deeply attached to my great-uncle Adolphe, whose friend he himself had also been, went to see him in his little flat in the Rue de Bellechasse, to ask him to use his influence with Odette. Since she invariably adopted a poetical tone when she spoke to Swann about my uncle, saying: "Ah, yes, he's not in the least like you; it's such an exquisite thing, a great, a beautiful thing, his friendship for me. He's not the sort of man who would have so little consideration for me as to let himself be seen with me everywhere in public," this was embarrassing for Swann, who did not know quite to what rhetorical pitch he should screw himself up in speaking of Odette to my uncle. He began by alluding to her *a priori* excellence, her axiomatic and seraphic super-humanity, the inspiration of her transcendental, inexpressible virtues. "I should like to speak to you about her," he went on. "You know what an incomparably superior woman, what an adorable creature, what an angel Odette is. But you know, also, what life is in Paris. Not everyone knows Odette in the light in which you and I have been privileged to know her. And so there are people who think I'm behaving rather foolishly; she won't even allow me to meet her out of doors, at the theatre. Now you, in whom she has such enormous confidence, couldn't you say a few words for me to her, just to assure her that she exaggerates the harm which my greeting her in public might do her?"

My uncle advised Swann not to see Odette for some days, after which she would love him all the more, and advised Odette to let Swann meet her whenever and as often as he pleased. A few days later Odette told Swann that she had just had a rude awakening, on discovering that my uncle was the same as other men: he had tried to take her by force. She calmed Swann down when he wanted to rush out to challenge my uncle to a duel, but he refused to shake hands with him when they met again. He regretted this rupture all the more because he had hoped, if he had met my uncle Adolphe again a few times and had contrived to talk things over with him in strict confidence, to be able to get him to throw light on certain rumours with regard to the life that Odette had formerly led in Nice. For my uncle Adolphe used to spend the winter there, and Swann thought that it might indeed have been there that he had first known Odette. The few words which someone had let fall in his hearing about a man who, it appeared, had been Odette's lover, had left Swann dumbfounded. But the very things which, before knowing them, he would have regarded as the most terrible to learn and the most impossible to believe, were, once he knew them, absorbed forever into the general mass of his gloom; he accepted them, he could no longer have understood their not existing. Only, each one of them added a new and indelible touch to the picture he had formed of his mistress. At one point indeed he was given to understand that this moral laxity of which he would never have suspected Odette was fairly well known, and that at Baden or Nice, when she used to go to spend several months in one or the other place, she had enjoyed a sort of amorous notoriety. He thought of getting in touch with one or two pleasure-seekers and interrogating them; but they were aware that he knew Odette, and besides, he was afraid of putting the thought of her into their heads, of setting them once more upon her track. But he, to whom nothing could have seemed more tedious hitherto than all that pertained to the cosmopolitan life of Baden or of Nice, having learned that Odette had perhaps once led a gay life in those pleasure-cities, although he could never find out whether it had been solely to satisfy a need for money which, thanks to him, she no longer felt, or from some capricious instinct which might at any moment revive in her, now leaned in impotent, blind, dizzy anguish over the bottomless abyss in which those early years of MacMahon's Presidency had been engulfed, years during which one spent the winter on the Promenade des Anglais, the summer beneath the limes of Baden, and he would find in them a painful but magnificent profundity, such as a poet might have lent them; indeed he would have devoted to the reconstruction of the petty details of social life on the Côte d'Azur in those days, if it could have helped him to understand something of Odette's smile and the look in her eyes—candid and simple though they were—as much passion as the aesthete who ransacks the extant documents of fifteenth-century Florence in order to penetrate further into the soul of the Primavera, the fair Vanna or the Venus of Botticelli.

Often he would sit, without saying a word, gazing at her

dreamily, and she would say: "You do look sad!" It was not
very long since he had switched from the idea that she was a
really good person, comparable to the nicest he had known,
to that of her being a kept woman; conversely, it had happened
to him since to revert from the Odette de Crécy who was perhaps too well known to the roisterers, the ladies' men of
Nice and Baden, to this face whose expression was often so
gentle and sweet, to this nature so eminently human. He would
ask himself: "What does it mean, after all, if everyone at Nice
knows who Odette de Crécy is? Reputations of that sort,
even when they're true, are always based upon other people's
ideas"; he would reflect that this legend—even if it was
authentic—was something extraneous to Odette, was not
an innate, pernicious and ineradicable part of her personality;
that the creature who might have been led astray was a woman
with frank eyes, a heart full of pity for the sufferings of others,
a docile body which he had clasped in his arms and explored
with his hands, a woman whom he might one day come to
possess absolutely, if he succeeded in making himself indispensable to her.

She would sit there, often tired, her face momentarily
drained of that eager, febrile preoccupation with the unknown
things that made Swann suffer; she would push back her hair
with both hands, and her forehead, her whole face, would seem
to grow larger; then, suddenly, some ordinary human thought,
some kindly sentiment such as are to be found in all individuals when, in a moment of rest or reclusion, they are free to
express their true selves, would flash from her eyes like a
ray of gold. And immediately the whole of her face would
light up like a grey landscape swathed in clouds which are
suddenly swept aside, leaving it transfigured by the setting
sun. The life which occupied Odette at such times, even the
future which she seemed to be dreamily contemplating,
Swann could have shared with her; no evil disturbance seemed
to have left its residue there. Rare though they became, those
moments did not occur in vain. By the process of memory,
Swann joined the fragments together, abolished the intervals
between them, cast, as in molten gold, the image of an Odette
compact of kindness and tranquillity, for whom (as we shall

see in the second part of this story) he was later to make sacrifices which the other Odette would never have won from him. But how rare those moments were, and how seldom he now saw her! Even in the case of their evening meetings, she would never tell him until the last minute whether she would be able to see him, for, counting on his being always free, she wished first to be certain that no-one else would propose coming round. She would plead that she was obliged to wait for an answer that was of the very greatest importance to her, and if, even after she had allowed Swann to come, any of her friends asked her, half-way through the evening, to join them at some theatre or at supper afterwards, she would jump for joy and dress with all speed. As her toilet progressed, every movement she made brought Swann nearer to the moment when he would have to part from her, when she would fly off with irresistible zest; and when at length she was ready, and, peering into her mirror for the last time with eyes tense and bright with anxiety to look well, added a touch of lipstick, fixed a stray lock of hair over her brow, and called for her cloak of sky-blue silk with golden tassels, Swann looked so wretched that she would be unable to restrain a gesture of impatience as she flung at him: "So that's how you thank me for keeping you here till the last minute! And I thought I was being so nice to you. Well, I shall know better another time!" Sometimes, at the risk of annoying her, he made up his mind that he would find out where she had gone, and even dreamed of an alliance with Forcheville, who might perhaps have been able to enlighten him. In any case, when he knew with whom she was spending the evening, he was usually able to discover, among all his innumerable acquaintance, someone who knew—if only indirectly—the man in question, and could easily obtain this or that piece of information about him. And while he was writing to one of his friends, asking him to try to clear up some point or other, he would feel a sense of relief on ceasing to vex himself with questions to which there was no answer and transferring to someone else the strain of interrogation. It is true that Swann was no better off for such information as he did receive. To know a thing does not always enable us to prevent it, but at least the things we know we do hold, if not in our hands, at any rate in our minds, where we can dispose of them as we choose, and this gives us the illusion of a sort of power over them. He was quite happy whenever M. de Charlus was with Odette. He knew that between M. de Charlus and her nothing untoward could ever happen, that when M. de Charlus went out with her, it was out of friendship for him, and that he would make no difficulty about telling him everything she had done. Sometimes she had declared so emphatically to Swann that it was impossible for her to see him on a particular evening, she seemed to be looking forward so keenly to some outing, that Swann felt it really important that M. de Charlus should be free to accompany her. Next day, without daring to put too many questions to M. de Charlus, he would force him, by appearing not quite to understand his first answers, to give him more, after each of which he would feel increasingly relieved, for he very soon learned that Odette had spent her evening in the most innocent of dissipations.

"But what do you mean, my dear Mémé, I don't quite understand. . . . You didn't go straight from her house to the Musée Grévin? Surely you went somewhere else first? No? How very funny! You've no idea how much you amuse me, my dear Mémé. But what an odd idea of hers to go on to the Chat Noir afterwards. It was her idea, I suppose? No? Yours? How strange. But after all, it wasn't such a bad idea; she must have known dozens of people there? No? She never spoke to a soul? How extraordinary! Then you sat there like that, just you and she, all by yourselves? I can just picture you. What a nice fellow you are, my dear Mémé. I'm exceedingly fond of you."

Swann was relieved. So often had it happened to him, when chatting with chance acquaintances to whom he was hardly listening, to hear certain detached sentences (as, for instance, "I saw Mme de Crécy yesterday with a man I didn't know"), sentences which dropped into his heart and turned at once into a solid state, grew hard as stalagmites, and seared and tore him as they lay there, irremovable, that the words "She didn't know a soul, she never spoke to a soul" were, by way of contrast, like a soothing balm. How freely they coursed through him, how fluid they were, how vaporous, how easy to breathe! And yet, a moment later, he was telling himself that Odette must find him very dull if those were the pleasures she preferred to his company. And their very insignificance, though it reassured him, pained him as if her enjoyment of them had been an act of treachery.

Even when he could not discover where she had gone, it would have sufficed him, to alleviate the anguish which he then felt, and against which Odette's presence, the joy of being with her, was the sole specific (a specific which in the long run served to aggravate the disease, but at least brought temporary relief to his sufferings), it would have sufficed him, if only Odette had allowed it, to remain in her house while she was out, to wait for her there until the hour of her return, into whose stillness and peace would have flowed and dissolved those intervening hours which some sorcery, some evil spell had made him imagine as somehow different from the rest. But she would not; he had to return home; he forced himself, on the way, to form various plans, ceased to think of Odette; he even succeeded, while he undressed, in turning over some quite happy ideas in his mind; and it was with a light heart, buoyed with the anticipation of going to see some favourite work of art the next day, that he got into bed and turned out the light; but no sooner, in preparing himself for sleep, did he relax the self-control of which he was not even conscious so habitual had it become, than an icy shudder convulsed him and he began to sob. He did not even wish to know why, but wiped his eyes and said to himself with a smile: "This is delightful; I'm getting neurotic." After which he felt a profound lassitude at the thought that, next day, he must begin afresh his attempts to find out what Odette had been doing, must use all his influence to contrive to see her. This compulsion to an activity without respite, without variety, without results, was so cruel a scourge that one day, noticing a swelling on his stomach, he felt genuinely happy at the thought that he had, perhaps, a tumour which would prove fatal, that he need no longer concern himself with anything, that illness was going to govern his life, to make a plaything of him, until the not-distant end. And indeed if, at this period, it often happened that, without admitting it to himself, he longed for death, it was in order to

escape not so much from the acuity of his sufferings as from
the monotony of his struggle.

And yet he would have liked to live until the time came
when he no longer loved her, when she would have no reason
for lying to him, when at length he might learn from her
whether, on the day when he had gone to see her in the afternoon, she had or had not been in bed with Forcheville. Often
for several days on end the suspicion that she was in love with
someone else would distract his mind from the question of
Forcheville, making it almost immaterial to him, like those
new developments in a continuous state of ill-health which
seem momentarily to have delivered us from their predecessors. There were even days when he was not tormented by any
suspicion. He fancied that he was cured. But next morning,
when he awoke, he felt in the same place the same pain, the
sensation of which, the day before, he had as it were diluted in
the stream of different daytime impressions. But it had not
stirred from its place. Indeed, it was the sharpness of this pain
that had awakened him.

Since Odette never gave him any information as to those
vastly important matters which took up so much of her time
every day (although he had lived long enough to know that
such matters are never anything else than pleasures), he could
not sustain for any length of time the effort of imagining
them; his brain would become a void; then he would draw a
finger over his tired eyelids as he might have wiped his eyeglass, and would cease altogether to think. There emerged,
however, from this terra incognita, certain landmarks which reappeared from time to time, vaguely connected by Odette with
some obligation towards distant relatives or old friends who,
inasmuch as they were the only people whom she was in the
habit of mentioning as preventing her from seeing him, seemed
to Swann to compose the necessary, unalterable setting of her
life. Because of the tone in which she referred from time to
time to "the day when I go with my friend to the races," if,
having suddenly felt unwell and thought, "Perhaps Odette
would be kind enough to come and see me," he remembered
that it was one of those very days, he would say to himself:
"Oh, no! There's no point in asking her to come. I should have

thought of it before, this is the day when she goes with her
friend to the races. We must confine ourselves to what's
possible; no use wasting time proposing things that are *ipso
facto* unacceptable." And the duty incumbent upon Odette
of going to the races, to which Swann thus gave way, seemed
to him to be not merely ineluctable in itself, but the mark of
necessity with which it was stamped seemed to make plausible
and legitimate everything that was even remotely connected
with it. If, having acknowledged a greeting from a passer-by
in the street which had aroused Swann's jealousy, Odette replied to his questions by associating the stranger with one of
the two or three paramount duties of which she had often
spoken to him—if, for instance, she said: "That's a gentleman
who was in my friend's box at the races the other day"—
this explanation would set Swann's suspicions at rest; it was,
after all, inevitable that this friend should have other guests
than Odette in her box at the races, though he had never sought
to form or succeeded in forming any coherent impression of
them. Ah, how he would have loved to know her, the friend
who went to the races! If only she would invite him there with
Odette. How readily he would have sacrificed all his grand
connections for no matter what person who was in the habit
of seeing Odette, even if she were a manicurist or a shop
assistant! He would have put himself out for her, taken more
trouble than he would have done for a queen. Would they not
have supplied him, from their store of knowledge of the life of
Odette, with the one effective anodyne for his pain? With
what joy would he have hastened to spend his days with one
or other of those humble folk with whom Odette kept up
friendly relations, either with some ulterior motive or from
genuine simplicity of nature! How willingly would he have
taken up residence for ever in the attic of some sordid but
enviable house where Odette went but never took him and
where, if he had lived with the little retired dressmaker, whose
lover he would readily have pretended to be, he would have
been visited by Odette almost daily! In those almost plebeian
districts, what a modest existence, abject even, but happy,
nourished by tranquillity and peace of mind, he would have
consented to lead indefinitely!

It sometimes happened, again, that when, after meeting Swann, she saw some man approaching whom he did not know, he could distinguish upon Odette's face that look of dismay which she had worn on the day when he had come to her while Forcheville was there. But this was rare; for on the days when, in spite of all that she had to do, and of her dread of what people might think, she did actually manage to see Swann, what predominated in her attitude now was self-assurance; a striking contrast, perhaps an unconscious revenge for, or a natural reaction from, the timorous emotion which, in the early days of their friendship, she had felt in his presence, and even in his absence, when she began a letter to him with the words: "My dear, my hand trembles so that I can scarcely write" (so, at least, she pretended, and a little of that emotion must have been sincere, or she would not have wanted to feign more). She had been attracted to Swann then. We do not tremble except for ourselves, or for those whom we love. When our happiness is no longer in their hands, how calm, how relaxed, how bold we become in their presence! In speaking to him, in writing to him now, she no longer employed those words by which she had sought to give herself the illusion that he belonged to her, creating opportunities for saying "my" and "mine" when she referred to him—"You are my very own; it is the perfume of our friendship, I shall keep it"—for speaking to him of the future, of death itself, as of a single adventure which they would share. In those early days, whatever he might say to her she would answer admiringly: "You know, you'll never be like other people!"—she would gaze at that long face and slightly bald head, of which people who knew of his successes with women used to think: "He's not conventionally good-looking, if you like, but he has style: that toupee, that eyeglass, that smile!"—and, with more curiosity perhaps to know him as he really was than desire to become his mistress, she would sigh: "If only I knew what was in that head of yours!"

But now, whatever he said, she would answer in a tone that was sometimes irritable, sometimes indulgent: "Ah! won't you ever be like other people!" And gazing at that face which was only a little aged by his recent anxieties (though people now thought of it, by the same mental process which enables one to discover the meaning of a piece of symphonic music of which one has read the programme, or the resemblance of a child whose family one knows: "He's not positively ugly, if you like, but he's really rather absurd: that eyeglass, that toupee, that smile!"—adumbrating in their suggestible imaginations the invisible boundary which separates, at a few months' interval, the face of a successful lover from that of a cuckold), she would say: "Oh, I do wish I could change you, put some sense into that head of yours."

Always ready to believe in the truth of what he hoped, if Odette's way of behaving to him left the slightest room for doubt, he would fling himself greedily upon her words: "You can if you like," he would say to her.

And he tried to explain to her that to comfort him, to guide him, to make him work, would be a noble task, to which numbers of other women asked for nothing better than to be allowed to devote themselves, though it is only fair to add that in those other women's hands the noble task would have seemed to Swann a tactless and intolerable usurpation of his freedom. "If she didn't love me just a little," he told himself, "she wouldn't want to change me. And to change me, she will have to see me more often." Thus he saw her very reproaches as proofs of her interest, perhaps of her love; and indeed she now gave him so few that he was obliged to regard as such the various prohibitions which she imposed on him from time to time. One day she announced that she did not care for his coachman, who, she thought, might be setting Swann against her, and anyhow did not show the promptness and deference to Swann's orders which she would have liked to see. She felt that he wanted to hear her say: "Don't take him again when you come to me," just as he might have wanted her to kiss him. So, being in a good mood, she said it: and he was touched. That evening, talking to M. de Charlus, with whom he had the consolation of being able to speak of her openly (for the most trivial remarks that he uttered now, even to people who had never heard of her, always somehow related to Odette), he said to him: "I believe, all the same, that she loves me. She's so nice to me, and she certainly takes an interest in what I do."

And if, when he was setting off for her house, climbing into his carriage with a friend whom he was to drop somewhere on the way, his friend said: "Hullo! that isn't Loredan on the box?" with what melancholy joy Swann would answer him:

"Oh! Good heavens, no! I can tell you, I daren't take Loredan when I go to the Rue La Pérouse. Odette doesn't like me to take Loredan, she doesn't think he treats me properly. What on earth is one to do? Women, you know, women. My dear fellow, she'd be furious. Oh, lord, yes; if I took Rémi there I should never hear the last of it!"

This new manner, indifferent, offhand, irritable, which Odette now adopted with Swann, undoubtedly made him suffer; but he did not realise how much he suffered; since it was only gradually, day by day, that Odette had cooled towards him, it was only by directly contrasting what she was to-day with what she had been at first that he could have measured the extent of the change that had taken place. But this change was his deep, secret wound, which tormented him day and night, and whenever he felt that his thoughts were straying too near it, he would quickly turn them into another channel for fear of suffering too much. He might say to himself in an abstract way: "There was a time when Odette loved me more," but he never formed any definite picture of that time. Just as he had in his study a chest of drawers which he contrived never to look at, which he made a detour to avoid whenever he went in or out of the room, because in one of its drawers he had locked away the chrysanthemum which she had given him on one of those first evenings when he had taken her home in his carriage, and the letters in which she said: "If only you had forgotten your heart also. I should never have let you have that back," and "At whatever hour of the day or night you may need me, just send me a word, and dispose of me as you please," so there was a place in his heart where he would never allow his thoughts to trespass, forcing them, if need be, into a long divagation so that they should not have to pass within reach of it; the place in which lingered his memory of happier days.

But his meticulous prudence was defeated one evening when he had gone out to a party.

It was at the Marquise de Saint-Euverte's, the last, for that season, of the evenings on which she invited people to listen to the musicians who would serve, later on, for her charity concerts. Swann, who had intended to go to each of the previous evenings in turn but never succeeded in making up his mind, received, while he was dressing for this one, a visit from the Baron de Charlus, who came with an offer to accompany him to the party, if this would help him to feel a little less bored and unhappy when he got there. Swann thanked him and said:

"You can't conceive how glad I should be of your company. But the greatest pleasure you can give me is to go instead to see Odette. You know what an excellent influence you have over her. I don't suppose she'll be going anywhere this evening before she goes to see her old dressmaker, and I'm sure she'd be delighted if you accompanied her there. In any case, you'll find her at home before then. Try to entertain her, and also to give her a little sound advice. If you could arrange something for to-morrow that would please her, something we could all three do together. . . . Try to put out a feeler, too, for the summer; see if there's anything she wants to do, a cruise that the three of us might take, or something. I don't expect to see her to-night myself; still, if she'd like me to come, or if you find a loophole, you've only to send me a word at Mme de Saint-Euverte's up till midnight, and afterwards here. Thank you for all your kindness—you know how fond I am of you."

The Baron promised to do as Swann wished as soon as he had deposited him at the door of the Saint-Euverte house, where Swann arrived soothed by the thought that M. de Charlus would be spending the evening at the Rue La Pérouse, but in a state of melancholy indifference to everything that did not concern Odette, and in particular to the details of fashionable life, a state which invested them with the charm that is to be found in anything which, being no longer an object of our desire, appears to us in its own guise. On alighting from his carriage, in the foreground of that fictitious summary of their domestic existence which hostesses are pleased to offer to their guests on ceremonial occasions, and in which they show a great regard for accuracy of costume and setting, Swann was

delighted to see the heirs and successors of Balzac's "tigers"—
now "grooms"—who normally followed their mistress on her
daily drive, now hatted and booted and posted outside in the
roadway in front of the house, or in front of the stables, like
gardeners drawn up for inspection beside their flower-beds.
The tendency he had always had to look for analogies between
living people and the portraits in galleries reasserted itself
here, but in a more positive and more general form; it was
society as a whole, now that he was detached from it, which
presented itself to him as a series of pictures. In the hall, which
in the old days, when he was still a regular attender at such
functions, he would have entered swathed in his overcoat to
emerge from it in his tails, without noticing what had happened during the few moments he had spent there, his mind
having been either still at the party which he had just left or
already at the party into which he was about to be ushered,
he now noticed for the first time, roused by the unexpected
arrival of so belated a guest, the scattered pack of tall, magnificent, idle footmen who were drowsing here and there upon
benches and chests and who, pointing their noble greyhound
profiles, now rose to their feet and gathered in a circle round
about him.

One of them, of a particularly ferocious aspect, and not
unlike the headsman in certain Renaissance pictures which
represent executions, tortures and the like, advanced upon him
with an implacable air to take his "things." But the harshness
of his steely glare was compensated by the softness of his cotton
gloves, so that, as he approached Swann, he seemed to be
exhibiting at once an utter contempt for his person and the most
tender regard for his hat. He took it with a care to which the
precision of his movements imparted something that was almost over-fastidious, and with a delicacy that was rendered
almost touching by the evidence of his splendid strength. Then
he passed it to one of his satellites, a timid novice who expressed the panic that overpowered him by casting furious
glances in every direction, and displayed all the dumb agitation of a wild animal in the first hours of its captivity.

A few feet away, a strapping great fellow in livery stood
musing, motionless, statuesque, useless, like that purely

decorative warrior whom one sees in the most tumultuous of
Mantegna's paintings, lost in thought, leaning upon his shield,
while the people around him are rushing about slaughtering one
another; detached from the group of his companions who were
thronging about Swann, he seemed as determined to remain
aloof from that scene, which he followed vaguely with his
cruel, glaucous eyes, as if it had been the Massacre of the
Innocents or the Martyrdom of St James. He seemed precisely to have sprung from that vanished race—if, indeed, it
ever existed, save in the reredos of San Zeno and the frescoes
of the Eremitani, where Swann had come in contact with it,
and where it still dreams—fruit of the impregnation of a classical statue by one of the Master's Paduan models or an
Albrecht Dürer Saxon. And the locks of his reddish hair,
crinkled by nature but glued to his head by brilliantine, were
treated broadly as they are in that Greek sculpture which the
Mantuan painter never ceased to study, and which, if in its
creator's purpose it represents but man, manages at least to
extract from man's simple outlines such a variety of richness,
borrowed, as it were, from the whole of animate nature, that
a head of hair, by the glossy undulation and beak-like points of
its curls, or in the superimposition of the florid triple diadem
of its tresses, can suggest at once a bunch of seaweed, a brood
of fledgling doves, a bed of hyacinths and a coil of snakes.
    Others again, no less colossal, were disposed upon the steps
of a monumental staircase for which their decorative presence
and marmorean immobility might have earned, like the one
in the Palace of the Doges, the name "Staircase of the Giants,"
and on which Swann now set foot, saddened by the thought
that Odette had never climbed it. Ah, with what joy by contrast would he have raced up the dark, evil-smelling, break-
neck flights to the little dressmaker's, in whose attic he would
so gladly have paid the price of a weekly stage-box at the Opera
for the right to spend the evening there when Odette came,
and other days too, for the privilege of talking about her, of
living among people whom she was in the habit of seeing
when he was not there, and who on that account seemed to
be possessed of some part of his mistress's life that was more
real, more inaccessible and more mysterious than anything that

he knew. Whereas upon that pestilential but longed-for staircase to the old dressmaker's, since there was no other, no
service stair in the building, one saw in the evening outside
every door an empty, unwashed milk-can set out upon the
door-mat in readiness for the morning round, on the splendid
but despised staircase which Swann was now climbing, on
either side of him, at different levels, before each anfractuosity
made in its walls by the window of the porter's lodge or the
entrance to a set of rooms, representing the departments of
indoor service which they controlled and doing homage for
them to the guests, a concierge, a major-domo, a steward
(worthy men who spent the rest of the week in semi-indepen-
dence in their own domains, dined there by themselves like
small shop-keepers, and might to-morrow lapse to the bourgeois service of some successful doctor or industrial magnate),
scrupulous in observing to the letter all the instructions they
had been given before being allowed to don the brilliant
livery which they wore only at rare intervals and in which they
did not feel altogether at their ease, stood each in the arcade of
his doorway with a pompous splendour tempered by democratic good-fellowship, like saints in their niches, while a
gigantic usher, dressed Swiss Guard fashion like the beadle in a
church, struck the floor with his staff as each fresh arrival
passed him. Coming to the top of the staircase, up which he
had been followed by a servant with a pallid countenance and
a small pigtail clubbed at the back of his head, like a Goya
sacristan or a tabellion in an old play, Swann passed in front
of a desk at which lackeys seated like notaries before their
massive register rose solemnly to their feet and inscribed his
name. He next crossed a little hall which—like certain rooms
that are arranged by their owners to serve as the setting for a
single work of art (from which they take their name), and,
in their studied bareness, contain nothing else—displayed at
its entrance, like some priceless effigy by Benvenuto Cellini
of an armed watchman, a young footman, his body slightly
bent forward, rearing above his crimson gorget an even more
crimson face from which gushed torrents of fire, timidity and
zeal, who, as he pierced with his impetuous, vigilant, desperate
gaze the Aubusson tapestries screening the door of the room

in which the music was being given, appeared, with a soldierly
impassiveness or a supernatural faith—an allegory of alarums,
incarnation of alertness, commemoration of the call to arms—
to be watching, angel or sentinel, from the tower of a castle or
cathedral, for the approach of the enemy or for the hour of
Judgment. Swann had now only to enter the concert-room,
the doors of which were thrown open to him by an usher
loaded with chains, who bowed low before him as though
tendering to him the keys of a conquered city. But he thought
of the house in which at that very moment he might have been
if Odette had only permitted it, and the remembered glimpse
of an empty milk-can upon a door-mat wrung his heart.

Swann speedily recovered his sense of the general ugliness
of the human male when, on the other side of the tapestry
curtain, the spectacle of the servants gave place to that of the
guests. But even this ugliness of faces which of course were
mostly familiar to him seemed something new now that their
features—instead of being to him symbols of practical utility in
the identification of this or that person who until then had
represented merely so many pleasures to be pursued, boredoms
to be avoided, or courtesies to be acknowledged—rested in
the autonomy of their lines, measurable by aesthetic co-ordi-
nates alone. And in these men by whom Swann now found
himself surrounded there was nothing, down to the monocles
which many of them wore (and which previously would at
the most have enabled Swann to say that so-and-so wore a
monocle) that, no longer restricted to the general connota-
tion of a habit, the same in all of them, did not now strike
him with a sense of individuality in each. Perhaps because he
regarded General de Froberville and the Marquis de Bréauté,
who were talking to each other just inside the door, simply as
two figures in a picture, whereas they were the old and useful
friends who had put him up for the Jockey Club and had supported him in duels, the General's monocle, stuck between
his eyelids like a shell-splinter in his vulgar, scarred and over-
bearing face, in the middle of a forehead which it dominated
like the single eye of the Cyclops, appeared to Swann as a
monstrous wound which it might have been glorious to receive
but which it was indecent to expose, while that which M. de

Bréauté sported, as a festive badge, with his pearl-grey gloves, his crush hat and white tie, substituting it for the familiar pair of glasses (as Swann himself did) when he went to society functions, bore, glued to its other side, like a specimen prepared on a slide for the microscope, an infinitesimal gaze that swarmed with affability and never ceased to twinkle at the loftiness of the ceilings, the delightfulness of the entertainment, the interestingness of the programmes and the excellence of the refreshments.

"Hallo, you here! Why, it's ages since we've seen you," the General greeted Swann and, noticing his drawn features and concluding that it was perhaps a serious illness that had kept him away, added: "You're looking well, old man!" while M. de Bréauté exclaimed: "My dear fellow, what on earth are you doing here?" to a society novelist who had just fitted into the angle of eyebrow and cheek a monocle that was his sole instrument of psychological investigation and remorseless analysis, and who now replied with an air of mystery and self-importance, rolling the "r": "I am observing!"

The Marquis de Forestelle's monocle was minute and rimless, and, by enforcing an incessant and painful contraction of the eye in which it was embedded like a superfluous cartilage the presence of which is inexplicable and its substance unimaginable, gave to his face a melancholy refinement, and led women to suppose him capable of suffering greatly from the pangs of love. But that of M. de Saint-Candé, encircled, like Saturn, with an enormous ring, was the centre of gravity of a face which adjusted itself constantly in relation to it, a face whose quivering red nose and swollen sarcastic lips endeavoured by their grimaces to keep up with the running fire of wit that sparkled in the polished disk, and saw itself preferred to the most handsome looks in the world by snobbish and depraved young women whom it set dreaming of artificial charms and a refinement of sensual bliss. Meanwhile, behind him, M. de Palancy, who with his huge carp's head and goggling eyes moved slowly through the festive gathering, periodically unclenching his mandibles as though in search of his orientation, had the air of carrying about upon his person only an accidental and perhaps purely symbolical fragment of the glass wall of his aquarium, a part intended to suggest the whole, which recalled to Swann, a fervent admirer of Giotto's Vices and Virtues at Padua, that figure representing Injustice by whose side a leafy bough evokes the idea of the forests that enshroud his secret lair.

Swann had gone forward into the room at Mme de Saint-Euverte's insistence, and in order to listen to an air from *Orfeo* which was being rendered on the flute, had taken up a position in a corner from which, unfortunately, his horizon was bounded by two ladies of mature years seated side by side, the Marquise de Cambremer and the Vicomtesse de Franquetot, who, because they were cousins, spent their time at parties wandering through the room each clutching her bag and followed by her daughter, hunting for one another like people at a railway station, and could never be at rest until they had reserved two adjacent chairs by marking them with their fans or handkerchiefs—Mme de Cambremer, since she knew scarcely anyone, being all the more glad of a companion, while Mme de Franquetot, who, on the contrary, was extremely well-connected, thought it elegant and original to show all her fine friends that she preferred to their company that of an obscure country cousin with whom she had childhood memories in common. Filled with melancholy irony, Swann watched them as they listened to the pianoforte intermezzo (Liszt's "Saint Francis preaching to the birds") which had succeeded the flute and followed the virtuoso in his dizzy flight, Mme de Franquetot anxiously, her eyes starting from her head as though the keys over which his fingers skipped with such agility were a series of trapezes from any one of which he might come crashing a hundred feet to the ground, stealing now and then a glance of astonishment and unbelief at her companion, as who should say: "It isn't possible, I'd never have believed that a human being could do that!", Mme de Cambremer, as a woman who had received a sound musical education, beating time with her head, transformed for the nonce into the pendulum of a metronome, the sweep and rapidity of whose oscillations from one shoulder to the other (performed with that look of wild abandonment in her eye which a sufferer shows when he has lost control of himself and

is no longer able to master his pain, saying merely "I can't
help it") so increased that at every moment her diamond
earrings caught in the trimming of her bodice, and she was
obliged to straighten the bunch of black grapes which she had
in her hair, though without any interruption of her constantly
accelerated motion. On the other side (and a little way in front)
of Mme de Franquetot was the Marquise de Gallardon, absorbed in her favourite subject of meditation, namely her
kinship with the Guermantes family, from which she derived
both publicly and in private a good deal of glory not un-
mingled with shame, the most brilliant ornaments of that
house remaining somewhat aloof from her, perhaps because
she was boring, or because she was disagreeable, or because she
came of an inferior branch of the family, or very possibly for
no reason at all. When she found herself seated next to someone whom she did not know, as she was at this moment next
to Mme de Franquetot, she suffered acutely from the feeling
that her own consciousness of her Guermantes connection
could not be made externally manifest in visible characters
like those which, in the mosaics in Byzantine churches, placed
one beneath another, inscribe in a vertical column by the side
of some holy personage the words which he is supposed to be
uttering. At this moment she was pondering the fact that she
had never received an invitation, or even a call, from her young
cousin the Princesse des Laumes during the six years that had
elapsed since the latter's marriage. The thought filled her with
anger, but also with pride; for, by dint of telling everyone who
expressed surprise at never seeing her at Mme des Laumes's
that it was because of the risk of meeting the Princesse Mathilde
there—a degradation which her own ultra-Legitimist family
would never have forgiven her—she had come to believe that
this actually was the reason for her not visiting her young
cousin. She remembered, it is true, that she had several times
inquired of Mme des Laumes how they might contrive to
meet, but she remembered it only confusedly and, besides,
more than neutralised this slightly humiliating reminiscence by
murmuring, "After all, it isn't for me to take the first step; I'm
at least twenty years older than she is." And fortified by these
unspoken words she flung her shoulders proudly back until

they seemed to part company with her bust, while her head, which lay almost horizontally upon them, was reminiscent of the "detachable" head of a pheasant which is brought to the table regally adorned with its feathers. Not that she in the least resembled a pheasant, having been endowed by nature with a squat, dumpy and masculine figure; but successive mortifications had given her a backward tilt, such as one may observe in trees which have taken root on the edge of a precipice and are forced to grow backwards to preserve their balance. Since she was obliged, in order to console herself for not being quite the equal of the rest of the Guermantes clan, to repeat to herself incessantly that it was owing to the uncompromising rigidity of her principles and pride that she saw so little of them, the constant iteration had ended up by remoulding her body and giving her a sort of presence which was accepted by bourgeois ladies as a sign of breeding, and even kindled at times a momentary spark in the jaded eyes of old clubmen. Had anyone subjected Mme de Gallardon's conversation to that form of analysis which by noting the relative frequency of its several terms enables one to discover the key to a coded text, they would at once have remarked that no expression, not even the commonest, occurred in it nearly so often as "at my cousins the Guermantes'," "at my aunt Guermantes's," "Elzéar de Guermantes's health," "my cousin Guermantes's box." If anyone spoke to her of a distinguished personage, she would reply that, although she was not personally acquainted with him, she had seen him hundreds of times at her aunt Guermantes's, but she would utter this reply in so icy a tone, in such a hollow voice, that it was clear that if she did not know the celebrity personally it was by virtue of all the stubborn and ineradicable principles against which her shoulders leaned, as against one of those ladders on which gymnastic instructors make us stretch in order to develop the expansion of our chests.

As it happened, the Princesse des Laumes, whom no one would have expected to appear at Mme de Saint-Euverte's, had just arrived there. To show that she did not wish to flaunt her superior rank in a salon to which she had come only out of condescension, she had sidled in with her arms pressed close to her sides, even when there was no crowd to be squeezed through and no one attempting to get past her, staying purposely at the back, with the air of being in her proper place, like a king who stands in the queue at the doors of a theatre where the management have not been warned of his coming; and, restricting her gaze—so as not to seem to be advertising her presence and claiming the consideration that was her due—to the study of a pattern in the carpet or her own skirt, she stood there on the spot which had struck her as the most modest (and from which, as she very well knew, a rapturous exclamation from Mme de Saint-Euverte would extricate her as soon as her presence there was noticed), next to Mme de Cambremer, whom she did not know. She observed the dumbshow by which her neighbour was expressing her passion for music, but she refrained from imitating it. This was not to say that, having for once consented to spend a few minutes in Mme de Saint-Euverte's house, the Princesse des Laumes would not have wished (so that the courtesy she was doing her hostess might, so to speak, "count double") to show herself as friendly and obliging as possible. But she had a natural horror of what she called "exaggerating," and always made a point of letting people see that she "had no desire" to indulge in displays of emotion that were not in keeping with the tone of the circle in which she moved, although on the other hand such displays could not help but make an impression upon her, by virtue of that spirit of imitation, akin to timidity, which is developed in the most self-confident persons by contact with an unfamiliar environment, even though it be inferior to their own. She began to ask herself whether these gesticulations might not, perhaps, be a necessary concomitant of the piece of music that was being played—a piece which did not quite come within the scope of the music she was used to hearing—whether to abstain from them might not be evidence of incomprehension as regards the music and of discourtesy towards the lady of the house; with the result that, in order to express by a compromise both of her contradictory inclinations in turn, at one moment she would confine herself to straightening her shoulder-straps or feeling in her golden hair for the little balls of coral or of pink enamel, frosted with

tiny diamonds, which formed its simple but charming ornament, scrutinising her impassioned neighbour with cold curiosity the while, and at the next would beat time for a few bars
with her fan, but, so as not to forfeit her independence, against
the rhythm. The pianist having finished the Liszt intermezzo
and begun a prelude by Chopin, Mme de Cambremer turned
to Mme de Franquetot with a fond smile of knowing satisfaction and allusion to the past. She had learned in her girlhood
to fondle and cherish those long sinuous phrases of Chopin,
so free, so flexible, so tactile, which begin by reaching out and
exploring far outside and away from the direction in which they
started, far beyond the point which one might have expected
their notes to reach, and which divert themselves in those
byways of fantasy only to return more deliberately—with a
more premeditated reprise, with more precision, as on a crystal
bowl that reverberates to the point of making you cry out—to
strike at your heart.

Brought up in a provincial household with few connections,
hardly ever invited to a ball, she had revelled, in the solitude
of her old manor-house, in setting the pace, now slow, now
breathlessly whirling, for all those imaginary waltzing couples,
in picking them off like flowers, leaving the ball-room for a
moment to listen to the wind sighing among the pine-trees on
the shore of the lake, and seeing all of a sudden advancing
towards her, more different from anything one has ever
dreamed of than earthly lovers are, a slender young man
with a slightly sing-song voice, strange and out of tune, in
white gloves. But nowadays the old-fashioned beauty of this
music seemed to have become a trifle stale. Having forfeited,
some years back, the esteem of the connoisseurs, it had lost
its distinction and its charm, and even those whose taste was
frankly bad had ceased to find in it more than a moderate
pleasure to which they hardly liked to confess. Mme de
Cambremer cast a furtive glance behind her. She knew
that her young daughter-in-law (full of respect for her new
family, except as regards the things of the mind, upon which,
having "got as far" as Harmony and the Greek alphabet, she
was specially enlightened) despised Chopin, and felt quite ill
when she heard him played. But finding herself free from the

scrutiny of this Wagnerian, who was sitting at some distance in a group of her own contemporaries, Mme de Cambremer let herself drift upon a stream of exquisite sensations. The Princesse des Laumes felt them too. Though without any natural gift for music, she had had lessons some fifteen years earlier from a piano-teacher of the Faubourg Saint-Germain, a woman of genius who towards the end of her life had been reduced to penury and had returned, at seventy, to instruct the daughters and granddaughters of her old pupils. This lady was now dead. But her method, her beautiful tone, came to life now and then beneath the fingers of her pupils, even of those who had become in other respects quite mediocre, had given up music, and hardly ever opened a piano. Thus Mme des Laumes could wave her head to and fro with complete conviction, with a just appreciation of the manner in which the pianist was rendering this prelude, since she knew it by heart. The closing notes of the phrase that he had begun sounded already on her lips. And she murmured "How *ch*arming it is!" with a double *ch* at the beginning of the word which was a mark of refinement and by which she felt her lips so romantically crinkled, like the petals of a beautiful, budding flower, that she instinctively brought her eyes into harmony with them, illuminating them for a moment with a vague and sentimental gaze. Meanwhile Mme de Gallardon was saying to herself how annoying it was that she had so few opportunities of meeting the Princesse des Laumes, for she meant to teach her a lesson by not acknowledging her greeting. She did not know that her cousin was in the room. A movement of Mme Franquetot's head disclosed the Princess. At once Mme de Gallardon dashed towards her, disturbing everybody; although determined to preserve a distant and glacial manner which should remind everyone present that she had no desire to be on friendly terms with a person in whose house one might find oneself cheek by jowl with the Princesse Mathilde, and to whom it was not for her to make advances since she was not "of her generation," she felt bound to modify this air of dignity and reserve by some non-committal remark which would justify her overture and force the Princess to engage in conversation; and so, when she reached her cousin, Mme de

Gallardon, with a stern countenance and one hand thrust out as though she were trying to "force" a card, said to her: "How is your husband?" in the same anxious tone that she would have used if the Prince had been seriously ill. The Princess, breaking into a laugh which was characteristic of her and was intended at once to draw attention to the fact that she was making fun of someone and also to enhance her beauty by concentrating her features around her animated lips and sparkling eyes, answered: "Why, he's never been better in his life!" And she went on laughing.

Whereupon Mme de Gallardon drew herself up and, putting on an even chillier expression, though still apparently concerned about the Prince's health, said to her cousin:

"Oriane" (at once Mme des Laumes looked with amused astonishment towards an invisible third person, whom she seemed to call to witness that she had never authorised Mme de Gallardon to use her Christian name), "I should be so pleased if you would look in for a moment to-morrow evening, to hear a clarinet quintet by Mozart. I should like to have your opinion of it."

She seemed not so much to be issuing an invitation as to be asking a favour, and to want the Princess's opinion of the Mozart quintet just as though it had been a dish invented by a new cook, whose talent it was most important that an epicure should come to judge.

"But I know that quintet quite well. I can tell you now— that I adore it."

"You know my husband isn't at all well—his liver . . . He would so much like to see you," Mme de Gallardon went on, making it now a charitable obligation for the Princess to appear at her party.

The Princess never liked to tell people that she would not go to their houses. Every day she would write to express her regret at having been kept away—by the sudden arrival of her husband's mother, by an invitation from her brother-in-law, by the Opera, by some excursion to the country—from some party to which she would never have dreamed of going. In this way she gave many people the satisfaction of feeling that she was on intimate terms with them, that she would gladly have come to their houses, and that she had been prevented from doing so only by some princely obstacle which they were flattered to find competing with their own humble entertainment. And then, as she belonged to that witty Guermantes set in which there survived something of the mental briskness, stripped of all commonplace phrases and conventional sentiments, which goes back to Mérimée and has found its final expression in the plays of Meilhac and Halévy, she adapted it even for the purposes of her social relations, transposed it into the form of politeness which she favoured and which endeavoured to be positive and precise, to approximate itself to the plain truth. She would never develop at any length to a hostess the expression of her anxiety to be present at her party; she thought it more amiable to put to her a few little facts on which it would depend whether or not it was possible for her to come.

"Listen, and I'll explain," she said to Mme de Gallardon. "To-morrow evening I must go to a friend of mine who has been pestering me to fix a day for ages. If she takes us to the theatre afterwards, with the best will in the world there'll be no possibility of my coming to you; but if we just stay in the house, since I know there won't be anyone else there, I shall be able to slip away."

"Tell me, have you seen your friend M. Swann?"

"No! my beloved Charles! I never knew he was here. I must catch his eye."

"It's odd that he should come to old Saint-Euverte's," Mme de Gallardon went on. "Oh, I know he's very clever," meaning by that "very cunning," "but that makes no difference —the idea of a Jew in the house of a sister and sister-in-law of Archbishops!"

"I'm ashamed to confess that I'm not in the least shocked," said the Princesse des Laumes.

"I know he's a convert and all that, and even his parents and grandparents before him. But they do say that the converted ones remain more attached to their religion than the practising ones, that it's all just a pretence; is that true, d'you think?"

"I can throw no light at all on the matter."

The pianist, who was "down" to play two pieces by Chopin,

after finishing the Prelude had at once attacked a Polonaise. But once Mme de Gallardon had informed her cousin that Swann was in the room, Chopin himself might have risen from the grave and played all his works in turn without Mme des Laumes paying him the slightest attention. She belonged to that half of the human race in whom the curiosity the other half feels about the people it does not know is replaced by an interest in the people it does. As with many women of the Faubourg Saint-Germain, the presence in any room in which she might find herself of another member of her set, even though she had nothing in particular to say to him, monopolised her attention to the exclusion of everything else. From that moment, in the hope that Swann would catch sight of her, the Princess spent her whole time (like a tame white mouse when a lump of sugar is put down before its nose and then taken away) turning her face, which was filled with countless signs of complicity, none of them with the least relevance to the sentiment underlying Chopin's music, in the direction where Swann was standing and, if he moved, diverting accordingly the course of her magnetic smile.

"Oriane, don't be angry with me," resumed Mme de Gallardon, who could never restrain herself from sacrificing her highest social ambitions, and the hope that she might one day dazzle the world, to the immediate, obscure and private satisfaction of saying something disagreeable, "people do say about your M. Swann that he's the sort of man one can't have in one's house; is that true?"

"Why, you of all people ought to know that it's true," replied the Princesse des Laumes, "since you must have asked him a hundred times, and he's never been to your house once."

And leaving her cousin mortified, she burst out laughing again, scandalising everyone who was trying to listen to the music, but attracting the attention of Mme de Saint-Euverte, who had stayed, out of politeness, near the piano, and now caught sight of the Princess for the first time. Mme de Saint-Euverte was all the more delighted to see Mme des Laumes as she imagined her to be still at Guermantes, looking after her sick father-in-law.

"My dear Princess, you here?"

"Yes, I tucked myself away in a corner, and I've been hearing such lovely things."

"What, you've been here for quite a time?"

"Oh, yes, a very long time which seemed very short, long only because I couldn't see you."

Mme de Saint-Euverte offered her own chair to the Princess, who declined it, saying:

"Oh, please, no! Why should you? I don't mind in the least where I sit." And deliberately picking out, the better to display the simplicity of a really great lady, a low seat without a back: "There now, that pouf, that's all I need. It will make me keep my back straight. Oh! good heavens, I'm making a noise again; they'll be telling you to have me chucked out."

Meanwhile, the pianist having redoubled his speed, the musical excitement was at its height, a servant was handing refreshments round on a salver, and was making the spoons rattle, and, as happened every week, Mme de Saint-Euverte was making unavailing signs to him to go away. A recent bride, who had been told that a young woman ought never to appear bored, was smiling vigorously, trying to catch her hostess's eye so as to flash her a look of gratitude for having "thought of her" in connection with so delightful an entertainment. However, although she remained calmer than Mme de Franquetot, it was not without some uneasiness that she followed the flying fingers, the object of her concern being not the pianist but the piano, on which a lighted candle, jumping at each *fortissimo*, threatened, if not to set its shade on fire, at least to spill wax upon the rosewood. At last she could contain herself no longer, and, running up the two steps of the platform on which the piano stood, flung herself on the candle to adjust its sconce. But scarcely had her hand come within reach of it when, on a final chord, the piece came to an end and the pianist rose to his feet. Nevertheless the bold initiative shown by this young woman and the brief promiscuity between her and the instrumentalist which resulted from it, produced a generally favourable impression.

"Did you see what that girl did just now, Princess?" asked General de Froberville, who had come up to Mme des Laumes as her hostess left her for a moment. "Odd, wasn't it? Is she one of the performers?"

"No, she's a little Mme de Cambremer," replied the Princess without thinking, and then added hurriedly: "I'm only repeating what I've heard—I haven't the faintest notion who she is; someone behind me said that they were neighbours of Mme de Saint-Euverte in the country, but I don't believe anyone knows them, really. They must be 'country cousins'! By the way, I don't know whether you're particularly familiar with the brilliant society which we see before us, because I've no idea who all these astonishing people can be. What do you suppose they do with themselves when they're not at Mme de Saint-Euverte's parties? She must have ordered them along with the musicians and the chairs and the food. 'Universal providers,' you know. You must admit they're rather splendid, General. But can she really have the heart to hire the same 'supers' every week? It isn't possible!"

"Oh, but Cambremer is quite a good name—old, too," protested the General.

"I see no objection to its being old," the Princess answered dryly, "but whatever else it is it's not *euphonious*," she went on, isolating the word euphonious as though between inverted commas, a little affectation to which the Guermantes set were addicted.

"You think not, eh! She's a regular little peach, though," said the General, whose eyes never strayed from Mme de Cambremer. "Don't you agree with me, Princess?"

"She thrusts herself forward too much. I think, in so young a woman, that's not very nice—for I don't suppose she's my generation," replied Mme des Laumes (this expression being common, it appeared, to Gallardon and Guermantes). And then, seeing that M. de Froberville was still gazing at Mme de Cambremer, she added, half out of malice towards the latter, half out of amiability towards the General: "Not very nice . . . for her husband! I'm sorry I don't know her, since you've set your heart on her—I might have introduced you to her," said the Princess, who, if she had known the young woman, would probably have done nothing of the sort. "And now I must say good night, because one of my friends is having a birthday party, and I must go and wish her many happy returns," she explained in a tone of modest sincerity, reducing the fashionable gathering to which she was going to the simple proportions of a ceremony which would be boring in the extreme but which it was obligatory and touching to attend. "Besides, I must pick up Basin who while I've been here has gone to see those friends of his—you know them too I believe, —who are called after a bridge—oh, yes, the Iénas."

"It was a victory before it was a bridge, Princess," said the General. "I mean to say, to an old soldier like me," he went on, wiping his monocle and replacing it, as though he were laying a fresh dressing on the raw wound beneath, while the Princess instinctively looked away, "that Empire nobility, well of course it's not the same thing, but, after all, taking it for what it is, it's very fine of its kind—they were people who really did fight like heroes."

"But I have the deepest respect for heroes," the Princess assented with a faint trace of irony. "If I don't go with Basin to see this Princess d'Iéna, it isn't at all because of that, it's simply because I don't know them. Basin knows them, and is deeply attached to them. Oh, no, it's not what you think, it's not a flirtation. I've no reason to object. Besides, what good has it ever done when I have objected," she added in a melancholy voice, for the whole world knew that, ever since the day when the Prince des Laumes had married his ravishing cousin, he had been consistently unfaithful to her. "Anyhow, it isn't that at all. They're people he has known for a long time, he takes advantage of them, and that suits me down to the ground. In any case, what he's told me about their house is quite enough. Can you imagine it, all their furniture is 'Empire'!"

"But, my dear Princess, that's only natural; it belonged to their grandparents."

"I don't say it didn't, but that doesn't make it any less ugly. I quite understand that people can't always have nice things, but at least they needn't have things that are merely grotesque. I'm sorry, but I can think of nothing more pretentious and bourgeois than that hideous style—cabinets with swans' heads, like baths!"

"But I believe, all the same, that they've got some fine

things; why, they must have that famous mosaic table on which the Treaty of . . ."

"Oh, I don't deny they may have things that are interesting enough from the historic point of view. But things like that can't ever be beautiful . . . because they're simply horrible! I've got things like that myself, that came to Basin from the Montesquious. Only, they're up in the attics at Guermantes, where nobody ever sees them. But in any case that's not the point, I would rush round to see them with Basin, I'd even go to see them among all their sphinxes and brasses if I knew them, but—I don't know them! D'you know, I was always taught when I was a little girl that it wasn't polite to call on people one didn't know." She assumed a tone of childish gravity. "And so I'm just doing what I was taught to do. Can't you see those good people, with a totally strange woman bursting into their house? Why, I might get a most hostile reception."

And she coquettishly enhanced the charm of the smile which that supposition had brought to her lips, by giving to her blue eyes, which were fixed on the General, a gentle, dreamy expression.

"My dear Princess, you know that they'd be simply wild with joy."

"No, why?" she inquired with the utmost vivacity, either to give the impression of being unaware that it would be because she was one of the first ladies in France, or in order to have the pleasure of hearing the General tell her so. "Why? How can you tell? Perhaps they might find it extremely disagreeable. I don't know, but if they're anything like me, I find it quite boring enough to see the people I do know, and I'm sure if I had to see people I didn't know as well, even if they had 'fought like heroes,' I should go stark mad. Besides, except when it's an old friend like you, whom one knows quite apart from that, I'm not sure that heroism takes one very far in society. It's often quite boring enough to have to give a dinner-party, but if one had to offer one's arm to Spartacus to go into dinner . . . Really, no, it would never be Vercingetorix I should send for to make a fourteenth. I feel sure I should keep him for really big 'crushes.' And as I never give any . . ."

"Ah! Princess, it's easy to see you're not a Guermantes for

nothing. You have your share of it, all right, the 'wit of the Guermantes'!"

"But people always talk about the wit of *the* Guermantes in the plural. I never could make out why. Do you really know any *others* who have it?" she rallied him, with a rippling flow of laughter, her features concentrated, yoked to the service of her animation, her eyes sparkling, blazing with a radiant sunshine of gaiety which could be kindled only by such observations— even if the Princess had to make them herself—as were in praise of her wit or of her beauty. "Look, there's Swann talking to your Cambremer; over there, beside old mother Saint-Euverte, don't you see him? Ask him to introduce you. But hurry up, he seems to be just going!"

"Did you notice how dreadfully ill he's looking?" asked the General.

"My precious Charles? Ah, he's coming at last. I was beginning to think he didn't want to see me!"

Swann was extremely fond of the Princesse des Laumes, and the sight of her reminded him of Guermantes, the estate next to Combray, and all that country which he so dearly loved and had ceased to visit in order not to be separated from Odette. Slipping into the manner, half-artistic, half-amorous, with which he could always manage to amuse the Princess—a manner which came to him quite naturally whenever he dipped for a moment into the old social atmosphere—and wishing also to express in words, for his own satisfaction, the longing that he felt for the country:

"Ah!" he began in a declamatory tone, so as to be audible at once to Mme de Saint-Euverte, to whom he was speaking, and to Mme des Laumes, for whom he was speaking, "Behold our charming Princess! Look, she has come up on purpose from Guermantes to hear Saint Francis preach to the birds, and has only just had time, like a dear little titmouse, to go and pick a few little hips and haws and put them in her hair; there are even some drops of dew upon them still, a little of the hoar-frost which must be making the Duchess shiver. It's very pretty indeed, my dear Princess."

"What! The Princess came up on purpose from Guermantes? But that's too wonderful! I never knew; I'm quite overcome," Mme de Saint-Euverte protested with quaint simplicity, being but little accustomed to Swann's form of wit. And then, examining the Princess's headdress, "Why, you're quite right; it is copied from . . . what shall I say, not chestnuts, no,—oh, it's a delightful idea, but how can the Princess have known what was going to be on my programme? The musicians didn't tell me, even."

Swann, who was accustomed, when he was with a woman whom he had kept up the habit of addressing in terms of gallantry, to pay her delicate compliments which most society people were incapable of understanding, did not condescend to explain to Mme de Saint-Euverte that he had been speaking metaphorically. As for the Princess, she was in fits of laughter, both because Swann's wit was highly appreciated by her set, and because she could never hear a compliment addressed to herself without finding it exquisitely subtle and irresistibly amusing.

"Well, I'm delighted, Charles, if my little hips and haws meet with your approval. But tell me, why did you pay your respects to that Cambremer person, are you also her neighbour in the country?"

Mme de Saint-Euverte, seeing that the Princess seemed quite happy talking to Swann, had drifted away.

"But you are yourself, Princess!"

"I! Why, they must have 'countries' everywhere, those people! Don't I wish I had!"

"No, not the Cambremers; her own people. She was a Legrandin, and used to come to Combray. I don't know whether you're aware that you are Comtesse de Combray, and and that the Chapter owes you a due."

"I don't know what the Chapter owes me, but I do know that I'm touched for a hundred francs every year by the Curé, which is a due that I could do very well without. But surely these Cambremers have rather a startling name. It ends just in time, but it ends badly!" she said with a laugh.[14]

"It begins no better." Swann took the point.

"Yes; that double abbreviation!"

"Someone very angry and very proper who didn't dare to finish the first word."

"But since he couldn't stop himself beginning the second, he'd have done better to finish the first and be done with it. I must say our jokes are in really charming taste, my dear Charles . . . but how tiresome it is that I never see you now," she went on in a winning tone, "I do so love talking to you. Just imagine, I couldn't even have made that idiot Froberville see that there was anything funny about the name Cambremer. Do you agree that life is a dreadful business. It's only when I see you that I stop feeling bored."

Which was probably not true. But Swann and the Princess had a similar way of looking at the little things of life, the effect —if not the cause—of which was a close analogy between their modes of expression and even of pronunciation. This similarity was not immediately striking because no two things could have been more unlike than their voices. But if one took the trouble to imagine Swann's utterances divested of the sonority that enwrapped them, of the moustache from under which they emerged, one realised that they were the same phrases, the same inflexions, that they had the "tone" of the Guermantes set. On important matters, Swann and the Princess had not an idea in common. But since Swann had become so melancholy, and was always in that tremulous condition which precedes the onset of tears, he felt the same need to speak about his grief as a murderer to speak about his crime. And when he heard the Princess say that life was a dreadful business, it gave him a feeling of solace as if she had spoken to him of Odette.

"Yes, life is a dreadful business! We must meet more often, my dear Princess. What is so nice about you is that you're not cheerful. We might spend an evening together."

"By all means. Why not come down to Guermantes? My mother-in-law would be wild with joy. It's supposed to be very ugly down there, but I must say I find the neighbourhood not at all unattractive; I have a horror of 'picturesque spots'."

"Yes, I know, it's delightful!" replied Swann. "It's almost too beautiful, too alive for me just at present; it's a country to be happy in. It's perhaps because I've lived there, but things there speak to me so. As soon as a breath of wind gets up, and the cornfields begin to stir, I feel that someone is going to appear suddenly, that I'm going to hear some news; and those little houses by the water's edge ... I should be quite wretched!"

"Oh! my dear Charles, look out, there's that appalling Rampillon woman; she's seen me; please hide me. Remind me what it was that happened to her; I get so confused; she's just married off her daughter, or her lover (I never can remember) —perhaps both—to each other! Oh, no, I remember now, she's been dropped by her prince ... Pretend to be talking to me, so that the poor old Berenice shan't come and invite me to dinner. Anyhow, I'm going. Listen, my dearest Charles, now that I've seen you for once, won't you let me carry you off and take you to the Princesse de Parme's? She'd be so pleased to see you, and Basin too, for that matter—he's meeting me there. If one didn't get news of you, sometimes, from Mémé ... Imagine, I never see you at all now!"

Swann declined. Having told M. de Charlus that on leaving Mme de Saint-Euverte's he would go straight home, he did not care to run the risk, by going on now to the Princesse de Parme's, of missing a message which he had all the time been hoping to see brought in to him by one of the footmen during the party, and which he might perhaps find with his own porter when he got home.

"Poor Swann," said Mme des Laumes that night to her husband, "he's as charming as ever, but he does look so dreadfully unhappy. You'll see for yourself, as he has promised to dine with us one of these days. I do feel it's absurd that a man of his intelligence should let himself suffer for a woman of that sort, and one who isn't even interesting, for they tell me she's an absolute idiot!" she added with the wisdom invariably shown by people who, not being in love themselves, feel that a clever man should only be unhappy about a person who is worth his while; which is rather like being astonished that anyone should condescend to die of cholera at the bidding of so insignificant a creature as the comma bacillus.

Swann wanted to go home, but just as he was making his escape, General de Froberville caught him and asked for an introduction to Mme de Cambremer, and he was obliged to go back into the room with him to look for her.

"I say, Swann, I'd rather be married to that little woman than slaughtered by savages, what do you say?"

The words "slaughtered by savages" pierced Swann's aching heart; and at once he felt the need to continue the conversation. "Ah!" he began, "some fine lives have been lost in that way ... There was, you remember, that navigator whose remains Dumont d'Urville brought back, La Pérouse . . ." (and he was at once happy again, as though he had named Odette). "He was a fine character, and interests me very much, does La Pérouse," he added with a melancholy air.

"Oh, yes, of course, La Pérouse," said the General. "It's quite a well-known name. There's a street called that."

"Do you know anyone in the Rue La Pérouse?" asked Swann excitedly.

"Only Mme de Chanlivault, the sister of that good fellow Chaussepierre. She gave a most amusing theatre-party the other evening. That'll be a really elegant salon one of these days, you'll see!"

"Oh, so she lives in the Rue La Pérouse. It's attractive, a delightful street, so gloomy."

"Not at all. You can't have been in it for a long time; it isn't gloomy now; they're beginning to build all round there."

When Swann did finally introduce M. de Froberville to the young Mme de Cambremer, since it was the first time she had heard the General's name she offered him the smile of joy and surprise with which she would have greeted him if no one had ever uttered any other; for, not knowing any of the friends of her new family, whenever someone was presented to her she assumed that he must be one of them, and thinking that she was showing evidence of tact by appearing to have heard "such a lot about him" since her marriage, she would hold out her hand with a hesitant air that was meant as a proof at once of the inculcated reserve which she had to overcome and of the spontaneous friendliness which successfully overcame it. And so her parents-in-law, whom she still regarded as the most eminent people in France, declared that she was an angel; all the more so because they preferred to appear, in marrying their son to her, to have yielded to the attraction rather of her natural charm than of her considerable fortune.

"It's easy to see that you're a musician heart and soul, Madame," said the General, alluding to the incident of the candle.

Meanwhile the concert had begun again, and Swann saw that he could not now go before the end of the new number. He suffered greatly from being shut up among all these people whose stupidity and absurdities struck him all the more painfully since, being ignorant of his love and incapable, had they known of it, of taking any interest or of doing more than smile at it as at some childish nonsense or deplore it as an act of folly, they made it appear to him in the aspect of a subjective state which existed for himself alone, whose reality there was nothing external to confirm; he suffered above all, to the point where even the sound of the instruments made him want to cry out, from having to prolong his exile in this place to which Odette would never come, in which no one, nothing was aware of her existence, from which she was entirely absent.

But suddenly it was as though she had entered, and this apparition was so agonisingly painful that his hand clutched at his heart. The violin had risen to a series of high notes on which it rested as though awaiting something, holding on to them in a prolonged expectancy, in the exaltation of already seeing the object of its expectation approaching, and with a desperate effort to last out until its arrival, to welcome it before itself expiring, to keep the way open for a moment longer, with all its remaining strength, so that the stranger might pass, as one holds a door open that would otherwise automatically close. And before Swann had had time to understand what was happening and to say to himself: "It's the little phrase from Vinteuil's sonata—I mustn't listen!", all his memories of the days when Odette had been in love with him, which he had succeeded until that moment in keeping invisible in the depths of his being, deceived by this sudden reflection of a season of love whose sun, they supposed, had dawned again, had awakened from their slumber, had taken wing and risen to sing maddeningly in his ears, without pity for his present desolation, the forgotten strains of happiness.

In place of the abstract expressions "the time when I was

happy," "the time when I was loved," which he had often used before then without suffering too much since his intelligence had not embodied in them anything of the past save fictitious extracts which preserved none of the reality, he now recovered everything that had fixed unalterably the specific, volatile essence of that lost happiness; he could see it all: the snowy, curled petals of the chrysanthemum which she had tossed after him into his carriage, which he had kept pressed to his lips—the address "Maison Dorée" embossed on the note-paper on which he had read "My hand trembles so as I write to you"—the contraction of her eyebrows when she said pleadingly: "You won't leave it too long before getting in touch with me?"; he could smell the heated iron of the barber whom he used to have singe his hair while Loredan went to fetch the little seamstress; could feel the showers which fell so often that spring, the ice-cold homeward drive in his victoria, by moonlight; all the network of mental habits, of seasonal impressions, of sensory reactions, which had extended over a series of weeks its uniform meshes in which his body found itself inextricably caught. At that time he had been satisfying a sensual curiosity in discovering the pleasures of those who live for love alone. He had supposed that he could stop there, that he would not be obliged to learn their sorrows also; yet how small a thing the actual charm of Odette was now in comparison with the fearsome terror which extended it like a cloudy halo all around her, the immense anguish of not knowing at every hour of the day and night what she had been doing, of not possessing her wholly, always and everywhere! Alas, he recalled the accents in which she had exclaimed: "But I can see you at any time; I'm always free!"—she who was never free now; he remembered the interest, the curiosity she had shown in his life, her passionate desire that he should do her the favour —which it was he who had dreaded at that time as a possibly tedious waste of his time and disturbance of his arrangements— of granting her access to his study; how she had been obliged to beg him to let her take him to the Verdurins'; and, when he allowed her to come to him once a month, how she had had to repeat to him time and again, before he let himself be swayed, what a joy it would be to see each other daily, a custom for which she longed when to him it seemed only a tiresome distraction, which she had then grown tired of and finally broken while for him it had become so irresistible and painful a need. Little had he suspected how truly he spoke, when at their third meeting, as she repeated: "But why don't you let me come to you oftener?" he had told her, laughing, and in a vein of gallantry, that it was for fear of forming a hopeless passion. Now, alas, it still happened at times that she wrote to him from a restaurant or hotel, on paper which bore a printed address, but printed in letters of fire that seared his heart. "It's written from the Hôtel Vouillemont. What on earth can she have gone there for? With whom? What happened there?" He remembered the gas-jets being extinguished along the Boulevard des Italiens when he had met her against all expectations among the errant shades on that night which had seemed to him almost supernatural and which indeed—a night from a period when he had not even to ask himself whether he would be annoying her by looking for her and finding her, so certain was he that she knew no greater happiness than to see him and to let him take her home—belonged to a mysterious world to which one never may return again once its doors are closed. And Swann could distinguish, standing motionless before that scene of remembered happiness, a wretched figure who filled him with such pity, because he did not at first recognise who it was, that he had to lower his eyes lest anyone should observe that they were filled with tears. It was himself.

When he had realised this, his pity ceased; he was jealous, now, of that other self whom she had loved, he was jealous of those men of whom he had so often said, without suffering too much: "Perhaps she loves them," now that he had exchanged the vague idea of loving, in which there is no love, for the petals of the chrysanthemum and the "letter-heading" of the Maison d'Or, which were full of it. And then, his anguish becoming too intense, he drew his hand across his forehead, let the monocle drop from his eye, and wiped its glass. And doubtless, if he had caught sight of himself at that moment, he would have added, to the collection of those which he had already identified, this monocle which he removed like an importunate, worrying thought and from whose misty

surface, with his handkerchief, he sought to obliterate his
cares.

There are in the music of the violin—if one does not see the
instrument itself, and so cannot relate what one hears to its
form, which modifies the tone—accents so closely akin to those
of certain contralto voices that one has the illusion that a singer
has taken her place amid the orchestra. One raises one's eyes,
and sees only the wooden case, delicate as a Chinese box, but,
at moments, one is still tricked by the siren's deceiving call; at
times, too, one thinks one is listening to a captive genie, struggling in the darkness of the sapient, quivering and enchanted
box, like a devil immersed in a stoup of holy water; sometimes,
again, it is in the air, at large, like a pure and supernatural
being that unfolds its invisible message as it goes by.

As though the musicians were not nearly so much playing
the little phrase as performing the rites on which it insisted
before it would consent to appear, and proceeding to utter the
incantations necessary to procure, and to prolong for a few
moments, the miracle of its apparition, Swann, who was no
more able to see it than if it had belonged to a world of ultra-
violet light, and who experienced something like the refreshing
sense of a metamorphosis in the momentary blindness with
which he was struck as he approached it, Swann felt its presence like that of a protective goddess, a confidante of his love,
who, in order to be able to come to him through the crowd
and to draw him aside to speak to him, had disguised herself
in this sweeping cloak of sound. And as she passed, light,
soothing, murmurous as the perfume of a flower, telling him
what she had to say, every word of which he closely scanned,
regretful to see them fly away so fast, he made involuntarily
with his lips the motion of kissing, as it went by him, the
harmonious, fleeting form. He felt that he was no longer in
exile and alone since she, who addressed herself to him, was
whispering to him of Odette. For he had no longer, as of old,
the impression that Odette and he were unknown to the little
phrase. Had it not often been the witness of their joys? True
that, as often, it had warned him of their frailty. And indeed,
whereas in that earlier time he had divined an element of
suffering in its smile, in its limpid, disenchanted tones,

tonight he found there rather the grace of a resignation that was almost gay. Of those sorrows which the little phrase fore-shadowed to him then, which, without being affected by them himself, he had seen it carry past him, smiling, on its sinuous and rapid course, of those sorrows which had now become his own, without his having any hope of being ever delivered from them, it seemed to say to him, as once it had said of his happi-ness: "What does it all matter? It means nothing." And Swann's thoughts were borne for the first time on a wave of pity and tenderness towards Vinteuil, towards that unknown, exalted brother who must also have suffered so greatly. What could his life have been? From the depths of what well of sorrow could he have drawn that god-like strength, that unlimited power of creation?

When it was the little phrase that spoke to him of the vanity of his sufferings, Swann found a solace in that very wisdom which, but a little while back, had seemed to him intolerable when he fancied he could read it on the faces of indifferent strangers who regarded his love as an insignificant aberration. For the little phrase, unlike them, whatever opinion it might hold on the transience of these states of the soul, saw in them something not, as all these people did, less serious than the events of everyday life, but, on the contrary, so far superior to it as to be alone worth while expressing. It was the charms of an intimate sadness that it sought to imitate, to re-create, and their very essence, for all that it consists in being incom-municable and in appearing trivial to everyone save him who experiences them, had been captured and made visible by the little phrase. So much so that it caused their value to be ac-knowledged, their divine sweetness savoured, by all those same onlookers, if they were at all musical—who then would fail to recognise them in real life, in every individual love that came into being beneath their eyes. Doubtless the form in which it had codified those charms could not be resolved into rational discourse. But ever since, more than a year before, discovering to him many of the riches of his own soul, the love of music had, for a time at least, been born in him, Swann had re-garded musical *motifs* as actual ideas, of another world, of another order, ideas veiled in shadow, unknown, impenetrable to the human mind, but none the less perfectly distinct from one another, unequal among themselves in value and significance. When, after that first evening at the Verdurins', he had had the little phrase played over to him again, and had sought to disentangle from his confused impressions how it was that, like a perfume or a caress, it swept over and enveloped him, he had observed that it was to the closeness of the intervals between the five notes which composed it and to the constant repetition of two of them that was due that impression of a frigid and withdrawn sweetness; but in reality he knew that he was basing this conclusion not upon the phrase itself, but merely upon certain equivalents, substituted (for his mind's convenience) for the mysterious entity of which he had become aware, before ever he knew the Verdurins, at that earlier party when for the first time he had heard the sonata played. He knew that the very memory of the piano falsified still further the perspective in which he saw the elements of music, that the field open to the musician is not a miserable stave of seven notes, but an immeasurable keyboard (still almost entirely unknown) on which, here and there only, separated by the thick darkness of its unexplored tracts, some few among the millions of keys of tenderness, of passion, of courage, of serenity, which compose it, each one differing from all the rest as one universe differs from another, have been discovered by a few great artists who do us the service, when they awaken in us the emotion corresponding to the theme they have discovered, of showing us what richness, what variety lies hidden, unknown to us, in that vast, unfathomed and forbidding night of our soul which we take to be an impenetrable void. Vinteuil had been one of those musicians. In his little phrase, although it might present a clouded surface to the eye of reason, one sensed a content so solid, so consistent, so explicit, to which it gave so new, so original a force, that those who had once heard it preserved the memory of it on an equal footing with the ideas of the intellect. Swann referred back to it as to a conception of love and happiness whose distinctive character he recognised at once as he would that of the *Princesse de Clèves*, or of *René*, should either of those titles occur to him. Even when he was not thinking of the little phrase, it

existed latent in his mind on the same footing as certain other
notions without material equivalent, such as our notions of
light, of sound, of perspective, of physical pleasure, the rich
possessions wherewith our inner temple is diversified and
adorned. Perhaps we shall lose them, perhaps they will be
obliterated, if we return to nothingness. But so long as we are
alive, we can no more bring ourselves to a state in which we
shall not have known them than we can with regard to any
material object, than we can, for example, doubt the luminosity
of a lamp that has just been lit, in view of the changed aspect of
everything in the room, from which even the memory of the
darkness has vanished. In that way Vinteuil's phrase, like some
theme, say, in *Tristan*, which represents to us also a certain
emotional accretion, had espoused our mortal state, had endued
a vesture of humanity that was peculiarly affecting. Its destiny
was linked to the future, to the reality of the human soul, of
which it was one of the most special and distinctive ornaments.
Perhaps it is not-being that is the true state, and all our dream
of life is inexistent; but, if so, we feel that these phrases of
music, these conceptions which exist in relation to our dream,
must be nothing either. We shall perish, but we have as
hostages these divine captives who will follow and share our
fate. And death in their company is somehow less bitter, less
inglorious, perhaps even less probable.

So Swann was not mistaken in believing that the phrase of
the sonata really did exist. Human as it was from this point of
view, it yet belonged to an order of supernatural beings
whom we have never seen, but whom, in spite of that, we
recognise and acclaim with rapture when some explorer of the
unseen contrives to coax one forth, to bring it down, from that
divine world to which he has access, to shine for a brief
moment in the firmament of ours. This was what Vinteuil had
done with the little phrase. Swann felt that the composer had
been content (with the musical instruments at his disposal) to
unveil it, to make it visible, following and respecting its outlines with a hand so loving, so prudent, so delicate and so sure
that the sound altered at every moment, softening and blurr-
ing to indicate a shadow, springing back into life when it must
follow the curve of some bolder projection. And one proof

that Swann was not mistaken when he believed in the real existence of this phrase, was that anyone with the least discernment would at once have detected the imposture had Vinteuil, endowed with less power to see and to render its forms, sought to dissemble, by adding a counterfeit touch here and there, the flaws in his vision or the deficiencies of his hand.

The phrase had disappeared. Swann knew that it would come again at the end of the last movement, after a long passage which Mme Verdurin's pianist always "skipped." There were in this passage some admirable ideas which Swann had not distinguished on first hearing the sonata and which he now perceived, as if, in the cloak-room of his memory, they had divested themselves of the uniform disguise of their novelty. Swann listened to all the scattered themes which would enter into the composition of the phrase, as its premisses enter into the inevitable conclusion of a syllogism; he was assisting at the mystery of its birth. "An audacity," he exclaimed to himself, "as inspired, perhaps, as that of a Lavoisier or an Ampère—the audacity of a Vinteuil experimenting, discovering the secret laws that govern an unknown force, driving, across a region unexplored, towards the one possible goal, the invisible team in which he has placed his trust and which he may never discern!" How beautiful the dialogue which Swann now heard between piano and violin, at the beginning of the last passage! The suppression of human speech, so far from letting fancy reign there uncontrolled (as one might have thought), had eliminated it altogether; never was spoken language so inexorably determined, never had it known questions so pertinent, such irrefutable replies. At first the piano complained alone, like a bird deserted by its mate; the violin heard and answered it, as from a neighbouring tree. It was as at the beginning of the world, as if there were as yet only the two of them on the earth, or rather in this world closed to all the rest, so fashioned by the logic of its creator that in it there should never be any but themselves: the world of this sonata. Was it a bird, was it the soul, as yet not fully formed, of the little phrase, was it a fairy—that being invisibly lamenting, whose plaint the piano heard and tenderly repeated? Its cries were so sudden that the violinist must snatch up his bow and

race to catch them as they came. Marvellous bird! The violinist
seemed to wish to charm, to tame, to capture it. Already it
had passed into his soul, already the little phrase which it
evoked shook like a medium's the body of the violinist,
"possessed" indeed. Swann knew that the phrase was going to
speak to him once again. And his personality was now so
divided that the strain of waiting for the imminent moment
when he would find himself face to face with it again shook
him with one of those sobs which a beautiful line of poetry or a
sad piece of news will wring from us, not when we are alone,
but when we impart them to friends in whom we see ourselves
reflected like a third person whose probable emotion affects
them too. It reappeared, but this time to remain poised in the
air, and to sport there for a moment only, as though immobile,
and shortly to expire. And so Swann lost nothing of the precious
time for which it lingered. It was still there, like an iridescent
bubble that floats for a while unbroken. As a rainbow whose
brightness is fading seems to subside, then soars again and,
before it is extinguished, shines forth with greater splendour
than it has ever shown; so to the two colours which the little
phrase had hitherto allowed to appear it added others now,
chords shot with every hue in the prism, and made them sing.
Swann dared not move, and would have liked to compel all
the other people in the room to remain still also, as if the
slightest movement might imperil the magic presence, supernatural, delicious, frail, that was so soon to vanish. But no one,
as it happened, dreamed of speaking. The ineffable utterance
of one solitary man, absent, perhaps dead (Swann did not
know whether Vinteuil was still alive), breathed out above the
rites of those two hierophants, sufficed to arrest the attention
of three hundred minds, and made of that platform on which a
soul was thus called into being one of the noblest altars on
which a supernatural ceremony could be performed. So that
when the phrase had unravelled itself at last, and only its fragmentary echoes floated among the subsequent themes which had
already taken its place, if Swann at first was irritated to see the
Comtesse de Monteriender, famed for her imbecilities, lean
over towards him to confide her impressions to him before
even the sonata had come to an end, he could not refrain from

smiling, and perhaps also found an underlying sense, which she herself was incapable of perceiving, in the words that she used. Dazzled by the virtuosity of the performers, the Comtesse exclaimed to Swann: "It's astonishing! I've never seen anything to beat it . . ." But a scrupulous regard for accuracy making her correct her first assertion, she added the reservation: "anything to beat it . . . since the table-turning!"

From that evening onwards, Swann understood that the feeling which Odette had once had for him would never revive, that his hopes of happiness would not be realised now. And on the days on which she happened to be once more kind and affectionate towards him, had shown him some thoughtful attention, he recorded these deceptive signs of a change of feeling on her part with the fond and sceptical solicitude, the desperate joy of people who, nursing a friend in the last days of an incurable illness, relate as facts of infinitely precious insignificance: "Yesterday he went through his accounts himself, and actually corrected a mistake we had made in adding them up; he ate an egg to-day and seemed quite to enjoy it, and if he digests it properly we shall try him with a cutlet to-morrow,"— although they themselves know that these things are meaningless on the eve of an inevitable death. No doubt Swann was assured that if he had now been living at a distance from Odette he would gradually have lost interest in her, so that he would have been glad to learn that she was leaving Paris for ever; he would have had the heart to remain there; but he hadn't the heart to go.

He had often thought of going. Now that he was once again at work upon his essay on Vermeer, he needed to return, for a few days at least, to The Hague, to Dresden, to Brunswick. He was convinced that a picture of "Diana and her Companions" which had been acquired by the Mauritshuis at the Goldschmidt sale as a Nicholas Maes was in reality a Vermeer. And he would have liked to be able to examine the picture on the spot, in order to buttress his conviction. But to leave Paris while Odette was there, and even when she was not there—for in strange places where our sensations have not been numbed by habit, we revive, we resharpen an old pain—was for him so cruel a project that he felt capable of entertaining it

incessantly in his mind only because he knew he was determined
never to put it into effect. But it sometimes happened that,
while he was asleep, the intention to travel would reawaken
in him (without his remembering that it was out of the question) and would actually take place. One night he dreamed that
he was going away for a year; leaning from the window of the
train towards a young man on the platform who wept as he
bade him farewell, he was trying to persuade this young man
to come away also. The train began to move, he awoke in
alarm, and remembered that he was not going away, that he
would see Odette that evening, and the next day and almost
every day. And then, being still deeply affected by his dream,
he thanked heaven for those special circumstances which made
him independent, thanks to which he could remain close to
Odette, and could even succeed in getting her to allow him to
see her sometimes; and, recapitulating all his advantages: his
social position—his wealth, from which she stood too often in
need of assistance not to shrink from the prospect of a definite
rupture (having even, so people said, an ulterior plan of getting
him to marry her),—his friendship with M. de Charlus, which,
it was true, had never won him any very great favour from
Odette, but which gave him the consolatory feeling that she
was always hearing complimentary things said about him by
this friend in common for whom she had so great an esteem,—
and even his intelligence, which was exclusively occupied in
devising each day a fresh scheme which would make his presence, if not agreeable, at any rate necessary to Odette—remembering all this, he thought of what might have become of
him if these advantages had been lacking; it struck him that
if, like so many other men, he had been poor, humble,
deprived, forced to accept any work that might be offered
to him, or tied down by parents or by a wife, he might have
been obliged to part from Odette, that that dream, the terror
of which was still so recent, might well have been true; and
he said to himself: "People don't know when they're happy.
One is never as unhappy as one thinks." But he reflected that
this existence had already lasted for several years, that all he
could now hope for was that it would last for ever, that he
would sacrifice his work, his pleasures, his friends, in fact the

whole of his life to the daily expectation of a meeting which, if it occurred, could bring him no happiness; and he asked himself whether he was not mistaken, whether the circumstances that had favoured his liaison and had prevented its final rupture had not done a disservice to his career, whether the outcome to be desired might not have been that as to which he rejoiced that it had happened only in a dream—his own departure; and he said to himself that people did not know when they were unhappy, that one is never as happy as one thinks.

Sometimes he hoped that she would die, painlessly, in some accident, since she was out of doors, in the streets, crossing busy thoroughfares, from morning to night. And as she always returned safe and sound, he marvelled at the strength and the suppleness of the human body, which was able continually to hold at bay, to outwit all the perils that beset it (which to Swann seemed innumerable since his own secret desire had strewn them in her path), and so allowed mankind to abandon itself, day after day, and almost with impunity, to its career of mendacity, to the pursuit of pleasure. And Swann felt a very cordial sympathy with the sultan Mahomet II whose portrait by Bellini he admired, who, on finding that he had fallen madly in love with one of his wives, stabbed her to death in order, as his Venetian biographer artlessly relates, to recover his peace of mind. Then he would be ashamed of thinking thus only of himself, and his own sufferings would seem to deserve no pity now that he himself held Odette's very life so cheap.

Unable to cut himself off from her irrevocably, if at least he had seen her continuously and without separations his anguish would ultimately have been assuaged, and his love, perhaps, have died. And since she did not wish to leave Paris for ever, he hoped that she would never leave it. As he knew that her one prolonged absence, every year, was in August and September, at least he had abundant opportunity, several months in advance, to dissolve the bitter thought of it in all the Time to come which he stored up inside himself in anticipation, and which, composed of days identical with those of the present, flowed through his mind, transparent and cold, nourishing his sadness but without causing him any intolerable pain. But that

inner future, that colourless, free-flowing stream, was suddenly
convulsed by a single remark from Odette which, penetrating
Swann's defences, immobilised it like a block of ice, congealed
its fluidity, froze it altogether; and Swann felt himself suddenly
filled with an enormous and infrangible mass which pressed on
the inner walls of his being until it almost burst asunder; for
Odette had said to him casually, observing him with a malicious
smile: "Forcheville's going on a fine trip at Whitsun. He's
going to Egypt!" and Swann had at once understood this to
mean: "I'm going to Egypt at Whitsun with Forcheville." And
in fact, if, a few days later, Swann said to her: "About that trip
you told me you were going to take with Forcheville," she
would answer carelessly: "Yes, my dear boy, we're starting on
the 19th; we'll send you a view of the Pyramids." Then he was
determined to know whether she was Forcheville's mistress, to
ask her point-blank, to insist upon her telling him. He knew
that, superstitious as she was, there were some perjuries which
she would not commit, and besides, the fear, which had hitherto restrained his curiosity, of making Odette angry if he questioned her, of making her hate him, had ceased to exist now
that he had lost all hope of ever being loved by her.

One day he received an anonymous letter telling him that
Odette had been the mistress of countless men (several of
whom it named, among them Forcheville, M. de Bréauté and
the painter) and women, and that she frequented houses of ill-
fame. He was tormented by the discovery that there was to be
numbered among his friends a creature capable of sending him
such a letter (for certain details betrayed in the writer a
familiarity with his private life). He wondered who it could be.
But he had never had any suspicion with regard to the unknown actions of other people, those which had no visible
connection with what they said. And when he pondered
whether it was beneath the ostensible character of M. de
Charlus, or of M. des Laumes, or of M. d'Orsan that he must
seek the uncharted region in which this ignoble action had had
its birth, since none of these men had ever, in conversation
with Swann, given any indication of approving of anonymous letters, and since everything they had ever said to him
implied that they strongly disapproved, he saw no reason for

associating this infamy with the character of any one of them
rather than the others. M. de Charlus was somewhat inclined
to eccentricity, but he was fundamentally good and kind; M.
des Laumes was a trifle hard, but sound and straightforward.
As for M. d'Orsan, Swann had never met anyone who, even
in the most depressing circumstances, would approach him
with more heartfelt words, in a more tactful and judicious
manner. So much so that he was unable to understand the
rather indelicate role commonly attributed to M. d'Orsan in
his relations with a certain wealthy woman, and whenever he
thought of him he was obliged to set that evil reputation on
one side, as being irreconcilable with so many unmistakable
proofs of his fastidiousness. For a moment Swann felt that his
mind was becoming clouded, and he thought of something
else so as to recover a little light, until he had the strength
to return to these reflections. But then, having been unable
to suspect anyone, he was forced to suspect everyone. After
all, though M. de Charlus was fond of him, was extremely
good-hearted, he was also a neurotic; to-morrow, perhaps, he
would burst into tears on hearing that Swann was ill, and to-
day, from jealousy, or anger, or carried away by a sudden
whim, he might have wished to do him harm. Really, that kind
of man was the worst of all. The Prince des Laumes was certainly far less devoted to Swann than was M. de Charlus. But
for that very reason he did not suffer from the same sus-
ceptibilities with regard to him; and besides, his was a nature
which, though no doubt cold, was as incapable of base as of
magnanimous actions. Swann regretted not having formed
attachments only to such people. Then he reflected that what
prevents men from doing harm to their neighbours is fellow-
feeling, that he could only, in the last resort, answer for men
whose natures were analogous to his own, as was, so far as
the heart went, that of M. de Charlus. The mere thought of
causing Swann so much distress would have revolted him.
But with an insensitive man, of another order of humanity, as
was the Prince des Laumes, how was one to foresee the actions
to which he might be led by the promptings of a different
nature? To have a kind heart was everything, and M. de
Charlus had one. M. d'Orsan was not lacking in heart either,

and his relations with Swann—cordial if not intimate, arising from the pleasure which, holding the same views about everything, they found in talking together—were more restful than the overwrought affection of M. de Charlus, capable of being led into acts of passion, good or evil. If there was anyone by whom Swann had always felt himself understood and discriminatingly liked, it was M. d'Orsan. Yes, but what of the disreputable life he led? Swann regretted that he had never taken any notice of those rumours, had often admitted jestingly that he had never felt so keen a sense of sympathy and respect as in the company of a scoundrel. "It's not for nothing," he now assured himself, "that whenever people pass judgment on their fellows, it's always on their actions. It's only what we do that counts, and not at all what we say or what we think. Charlus and des Laumes may have this or that fault, but they are men of honour. Orsan may not have these faults, but he's not a man of honour. He may have acted dishonourably once again." Then Swann suspected Rémi, who, it was true, could only have inspired the letter, but he now felt himself for a moment to be on the right track. To begin with, Loredan had reasons for bearing a grudge against Odette. And then, how could one not suppose that servants, living in a situation inferior to our own, adding to our wealth and our weaknesses imaginary riches and vices for which they envy and despise us, must inevitably be led to act in a manner abhorrent to people of our own class? He also suspected my grandfather. Every time Swann had asked a favour of him, had he not invariably refused? Besides, with his ideas of middle-class respectability, he might have thought that he was acting for Swann's good. He went on to suspect Bergotte, the painter, the Verdurins, pausing for a moment to admire once again the wisdom of society people in refusing to mix with those artistic circles in which such things were possible, perhaps even openly avowed as good jokes; but then he recalled the traits of honesty that were to be observed in those Bohemians and contrasted them with the life of expedients, often bordering on fraudulence, to which the want of money, the craving for luxury, the corrupting influence of their pleasures often drove members of the aristocracy.

In a word, this anonymous letter proved that he knew a human being capable of the most infamous conduct, but he could see no more reason why that infamy should lurk in the unfathomed depths of the character of the man with the warm heart rather than the cold, the artist rather than the bourgeois, the noble rather than the flunkey. What criterion ought one to adopt to judge one's fellows? After all, there was not a single person he knew who might not, in certain circumstances, prove capable of a shameful action. Must he then cease to see them all? His mind grew clouded; he drew his hands two or three times across his brow, wiped his glasses with his handkerchief, and remembering that, after all, men as good as himself frequented the society of M. de Charlus, the Prince des Laumes and the rest, he persuaded himself that this meant, if not that they were incapable of infamy, at least it was a necessity in human life, to which everyone must submit, to frequent the society of people who were perhaps not incapable of such actions. And he continued to shake hands with all the friends whom he had suspected, with the purely formal reservation that each one of them had possibly sought to drive him to despair.

As for the actual contents of the letter, they did not disturb him since not one of the charges formulated against Odette had the slightest verisimilitude. Like many other men, Swann had a naturally lazy mind and lacked imagination. He knew perfectly well as a general truth that human life is full of contrasts, but in the case of each individual human being he imagined all that part of his or her life with which he was not familiar as being identical with the part with which he was. He imagined what was kept secret from him in the light of what was revealed. At such times as he spent with Odette, if their conversation turned upon an indelicate act committed or an indelicate sentiment expressed by some third person, she would condemn them by virtue of the same moral principles which Swann had always heard expressed by his own parents and to which he himself had remained faithful; and then she would arrange her flowers, would sip her tea, would inquire about Swann's work. So Swann extended those attitudes to fill the rest of her life, and reconstructed those actions when he wished to form a picture of the moments in which he and she were apart. If anyone had portrayed her to him as she was, or rather as she had been for so long, with himself, but had substituted some other man, he would have been distressed, for such a portrait would have struck him as lifelike. But to suppose that she went to procuresses, that she indulged in orgies with other women, that she led the crapulous existence of the most abject, the most contemptible of mortals—what an insane aberration, for the realisation of which, thank heaven, the remembered chrysanthemums, the daily cups of tea, the virtuous indignation left neither time nor place! However, from time to time he gave Odette to understand that people maliciously kept him informed of everything that she did; and making opportune use of some detail—insignificant but true—which he had accidentally learned, as though it were the sole fragment which he had involuntarily let slip of a complete reconstruction of her daily life which he carried secretly in his mind, he led her to suppose that he was perfectly informed upon matters which in reality he neither knew nor even suspected, for if he often adjured Odette never to swerve from the truth, that was only, whether he realised it or not, in order that Odette should tell him everything that she did. No doubt, as he used to assure Odette, he loved sincerity, but only as he might love a pimp who could keep him in touch with the daily life of his mistress. Thus his love of sincerity, not being disinterested, had not improved his character. The truth which he cherished was the truth which Odette would tell him; but he himself, in order to extract that truth from her, was not afraid to have recourse to falsehood, that very falsehood which he never ceased to depict to Odette as leading every human creature down to utter degradation. In a word, he lied as much as did Odette because, more unhappy than she, he was no less egotistical. And she, when she heard him repeating thus to her the things that she had done, would stare at him with a look of distrust and, at all hazards, of indignation, so as not to appear to be humiliated and to be blushing for her actions.

One day, during the longest period of calm through which he had yet been able to exist without being overtaken by an

access of jealousy, he had accepted an invitation to spend the
evening at the theatre with the Princesse des Laumes. Having
opened his newspaper to find out what was being played, the
sight of the title—*Les Filles de Marbre*, by Théodore Barrière—
struck him so cruel a blow that he recoiled instinctively and
turned his head away. Lit up as though by a row of footlights,
in the new surroundings in which it now appeared, the word
"marble," which he had lost the power to distinguish, so accustomed was he to see it passing in print beneath his eyes,
had suddenly become visible again, and had at once brought
back to his mind the story which Odette had told him long ago
of a visit which she had paid to the Salon at the Palais de l'Industrie with Mme Verdurin, who had said to her, "Take care,
now! I know how to melt you, all right. You're not made of
marble." Odette had assured him that it was only a joke, and
he had attached no importance to it at the time. But he had
had more confidence in her then than he had now. And the
anonymous letter referred explicitly to relations of that sort.
Without daring to lift his eyes towards the newspaper, he
opened it, turned the page so as not to see again the words
Filles de Marbre, and began to read mechanically the news from
the provinces. There had been a storm in the Channel, and
damage was reported from Dieppe, Cabourg, Beuzeval. . . .
Suddenly he recoiled again in horror.

The name Beuzeval had reminded him of another place in
the same area, Beuzeville, which carried also, bound to it by a
hyphen, a second name, to wit Bréauté, which he had often
seen on maps, but without ever previously remarking that it
was the same as that of his friend M. de Bréauté, whom the
anonymous letter accused of having been Odette's lover. After
all, in the case of M. de Bréauté, there was nothing improbable
in the charge; but so far as Mme Verdurin was concerned, it
was a sheer impossibility. From the fact that Odette occasionally told a lie there was no reason to conclude that she
never told the truth, and in those remarks she had exchanged
with Mme Verdurin and which she herself had repeated to
Swann, he had recognised the meaningless and dangerous
jokes which, from inexperience of life and ignorance of vice,
are often made by women whose very innocence is revealed

thereby and who—as for instance Odette—are least likely to cherish impassioned feelings for another of their sex. Whereas the indignation with which she had rejected the suspicions which for a moment she had unintentionally aroused in his mind by her story fitted in with everything that he knew of the tastes and the temperament of his mistress. But now, by one of those inspirations of jealousy analogous to the inspiration which reveals to a poet or a philosopher, who has nothing, so far, to go on but an odd pair of rhymes or a detached observation, the idea or the natural law which will give him the power he needs, Swann recalled for the first time an observation which Odette had made to him at least two years before: "Oh, Mme Verdurin, she won't hear of anyone just now but me. I'm a 'love,' if you please, and she kisses me, and wants me to go with her everywhere, and call her by her Christian name." So far from seeing at the time in this observation any connection with the absurd remarks intended to simulate vice which Odette had reported to him, he had welcomed them as a proof of Mme Verdurin's warm-hearted and generous friendship. But now this memory of her affection for Odette had coalesced suddenly with the memory of her unseemly conversation. He could no longer separate them in his mind, and he saw them assimilated in reality, the affection imparting a certain seriousness and importance to the pleasantries which, in return, robbed the affection of its innocence. He went to see Odette. He sat down at a distance from her. He did not dare to embrace her, not knowing whether it would be affection or anger that a kiss would provoke, either in her or in himself. He sat there silent, watching their love expire. Suddenly he made up his mind.

"Odette, my darling," he began, "I know I'm being simply odious, but I must ask you a few questions. You remember the idea I once had about you and Mme Verdurin? Tell me, was it true? Have you, with her or anyone else, ever?"

She shook her head, pursing her lips, a sign which people commonly employ to signify that they are not going, because it would bore them to go, when someone has asked, "Are you coming to watch the procession go by?", or "Will you be at the review?". But this shake of the head thus normally applied to an event that has yet to come, imparts for that reason an element of uncertainty to the denial of an event that is past. Furthermore, it suggests reasons of personal propriety only, rather than of disapprobation or moral impossibility. When he saw Odette thus signal to him that the insinuation was false, Swann realised that it was quite possibly true.

"I've told you, no. You know quite well," she added, seeming angry and uncomfortable.

"Yes, I know, but are you quite sure? Don't say to me, 'You know quite well'; say, 'I have never done anything of that sort with any woman.'"

She repeated his words like a lesson learned by rote, in a sarcastic tone, and as though she hoped thereby to be rid of him: "I have never done anything of that sort with any woman.'"

"Can you swear to me on the medal of Our Lady of Laghet?"

Swann knew that Odette would never perjure herself on that.

"Oh, you do make me so miserable," she cried, with a jerk of her body as though to shake herself free of the constraint of his question. "Haven't you had enough? What's the matter with you to-day? You seem determined to make me hate you. I wanted to be friends with you again, for us to have a nice time together, like the old days; and this is all the thanks I get!"

However, he would not let her go but sat there like a surgeon waiting for a spasm to subside that has interrupted his operation but will not make him abandon it.

"You're quite wrong to suppose that I'd bear you the least ill-will in the world, Odette," he said to her with a persuasive and deceitful gentleness. "I never speak to you except of what I already know, and I always know a great deal more than I say. But you alone can mitigate by your confession what makes me hate you so long as it has been reported to me only by other people. My anger with you has nothing to do with your actions—I can and do forgive you everything because I love you—but with your untruthfulness, the ridiculous untruthfulness which makes you persist in denying things which I know to be true. How can you expect me to go on loving you when I see you maintain, when I hear you swear to me a thing

which I know to be false? Odette, don't prolong this moment
which is agony for us both. If you want to, you can end it in a
second, you'll be free of it for ever. Tell me, on your medal,
yes or no, whether you have ever done these things."

"How on earth do I know?" she exclaimed angrily. "Perhaps I have, ever so long ago, when I didn't know what I was
doing, perhaps two or three times."

Swann had prepared himself for every possibility. Reality
must therefore be something that bears no relation to possibilities, any more than the stab of a knife in one's body bears
to the gradual movement of the clouds overhead, since those
words, "two or three times," carved as it were a cross upon
the living tissues of his heart. Strange indeed that those
words, "two or three times," nothing more than words, words
uttered in the air, at a distance, could so lacerate a man's heart,
as if they had actually pierced it, could make a man ill, like a
poison he has drunk. Instinctively Swann thought of the remark he had heard at Mme de Saint-Euverte's: "I've never seen
anything to beat it since the table-turning." The agony that he
now suffered in no way resembled what he had supposed. Not
only because, even in his moments of most complete distrust,
he had rarely imagined such an extremity of evil, but because,
even when he did try to imagine this thing, it remained vague,
uncertain, was not clothed in the particular horror which had
sprung from the words "perhaps two or three times," was not
armed with that specific cruelty, as different from anything that
he had known as a disease by which one is struck down for the
first time. And yet this Odette from whom all this evil sprang
was no less dear to him, was, on the contrary, more precious, as
if, in proportion as his sufferings increased, the price of the
sedative, of the antidote which this woman alone possessed, increased at the same time. He wanted to devote more care to her,
as one tends a disease which one has suddenly discovered to be
more serious. He wanted the horrible things which, she had
told him, she had done "two or three times," not to happen
again. To ensure that, he must watch over Odette. People
often say that, by pointing out to a man the faults of his mistress, you succeed only in strengthening his attachment to her,
because he does not believe you; yet how much more if he

does! But, Swann asked himself, how could he manage to protect her? He might perhaps be able to preserve her from the
contamination of a particular woman, but there were hundreds
of others; and he realised what madness had come over him
when, on the evening when he had failed to find Odette at the
Verdurins', he had begun to desire the possession—as if that
were ever possible—of another person. Happily for Swann,
beneath the mass of new sufferings which had entered his soul
like an invading horde, there lay a natural foundation, older,
more placid, and silently industrious, like the cells of an injured organ which at once set to work to repair the damaged
tissues, or the muscles of a paralysed limb which tend to recover
their former movements. These older, more autochthonous
inhabitants of his soul absorbed all Swann's strength, for a
while, in that obscure task of reparation which gives one an illusory sense of repose during convalescence, or after an operation. This time it was not so much—as it ordinarily was—in
Swann's brain that this slackening of tension due to exhaustion
took effect, it was rather in his heart. But all the things in life
that have once existed tend to recur, and like a dying animal
stirred once more by the throes of a convulsion which seemed
to have ended, upon Swann's heart, spared for a moment only,
the same agony returned of its own accord to trace the same
cross. He remembered those moonlit evenings, when, leaning
back in the victoria that was taking him to the Rue La Pérouse,
he would wallow voluptuously in the emotions of a man in
love, oblivious of the poisoned fruit that such emotions must
inevitably bear. But all those thoughts lasted for no more than
a second, the time that it took him to press his hand to his
heart, to draw breath again and to contrive to smile, in order to
hide his torment. Already he had begun to put further questions. For his jealousy, which had taken more pains than any
enemy would have done to strike him this savage blow, to
make him forcibly acquainted with the most cruel suffering he
had ever known, his jealousy was not satisfied that he had yet
suffered enough, and sought to expose him to an even deeper
wound. Thus, like an evil deity, his jealousy inspired Swann,
driving him on towards his ruin. It was not his fault, but
Odette's alone, if at first his torment was not exacerbated.

"My darling," he began again, "it's all over now. Was it with anyone I know?"

"No, I swear it wasn't. Besides, I think I exaggerated, I never really went as far as that."

He smiled, and went on: "Just as you like. It doesn't really matter, but it's a pity that you can't give me the name. If I were able to form an idea of the person it would prevent my ever thinking of her again. I say it for your sake, because then I shouldn't bother you any more about it. It's so calming to be able to form a clear picture of things in one's mind. What is really terrible is what one can't imagine. But you've been so sweet to me; I don't want to tire you. I do thank you with all my heart for all the good that you've done me. I've quite finished now. Only one word more: how long ago?"

"Oh, Charles, can't you see you're killing me? It's all so long ago. I've never given it a thought. Anyone would think you were positively trying to put those ideas into my head again. A lot of good that would do you!" she concluded, with unconscious stupidity but intentional malice.

"Oh, I only wanted to know whether it had been since I've known you. It's only natural. Did it happen here? You can't give me any particular evening, so that I can remind myself what I was doing at the time? You must realise that it's not possible that you don't remember with whom, Odette, my love."

"But I don't know; really, I don't. I think it was in the Bois, one evening when you came to meet us on the Island. You'd been dining with the Princesse des Laumes," she added, happy to be able to furnish him with a precise detail which testified to her veracity. "There was a woman at the next table whom I hadn't seen for ages. She said to me, 'Come round behind the rock, there, and look at the moonlight on the water!' At first I just yawned, and said, 'No, I'm too tired, and I'm quite happy where I am, thank you.' She assured me there'd never been any moonlight to touch it. 'I've heard that tale before,' I said to her. I knew quite well what she was after."

Odette narrated this episode almost with a smile, either because it appeared to her to be quite natural, or because she thought she was thereby minimising its importance, or else so as not to appear humiliated. But, catching sight of Swann's face, she changed her tone:

"You're a fiend! You enjoy torturing me, making me tell you lies, just so that you'll leave me in peace."

This second blow was even more terrible for Swann than the first. Never had he supposed it to have been so recent an event, hidden from his eyes that had been too innocent to discern it, not in a past which he had never known, but in the course of evenings which he so well remembered, which he had lived through with Odette, of which he had supposed himself to have such an intimate, such an exhaustive knowledge, and which now assumed, retrospectively, an aspect of ugliness and deceit. In the midst of them, suddenly, a gaping chasm had opened: that moment on the island in the Bois de Boulogne. Without being intelligent, Odette had the charm of naturalness. She had recounted, she had acted the little scene with such simplicity that Swann, as he gasped for breath, could vividly see it: Odette yawning, the "rock, there," . . . He could hear her answer—alas, how gaily—"I've heard that tale before!" He felt that she would tell him nothing more that evening, that no further revelation was to be expected for the present. He was silent for a time, then said to her:

"My poor darling, you must forgive me; I know I've distressed you, but it's all over now; I won't think of it any more."

But she saw that his eyes remained fixed upon the things that he did not know, and on that past era of their love, monotonous and soothing in his memory because it was vague, and now rent, as with a gaping wound, by that moment on the Island in the Bois, by moonlight, after his dinner with the Princesse des Laumes. But he was so imbued with the habit of finding life interesting—of marvelling at the strange discoveries that there are to be made in it—that even while he was suffering so acutely that he did not believe he could bear such agony much longer, he was saying to himself: "Life is really astonishing, and holds some fine surprises; it appears that vice is far more common than one has been led to believe. Here is a woman I trusted, who seems so simple, so straightforward, who, in any case, even allowing that her morals are not strict, seemed quite normal and healthy in her tastes and inclinations. On the basis of a most improbable accusation, I question her, and the little that she admits reveals far more than I could ever have suspected." But he could not confine himself to these detached observations. He sought to form an exact estimate of the significance of what she had just told him, in order to decide whether she had done these things often and was likely to do them again. He repeated her words to himself: "I knew quite well what she was after." "Two or three times." "I've heard that tale before." But they did not reappear in his memory unarmed; each of them still held its knife, with which it stabbed him anew. For a long time, like a sick man who cannot restrain himself from attempting every minute to make the movement that he knows will hurt him, he kept on murmuring to himself: "I'm quite happy where I am, thank you," "I've heard that tale before," but the pain was so intense that he was obliged to stop. He was amazed to find that acts which he had always hitherto judged so lightly, had dismissed, indeed, with a laugh, should have become as serious to him as a disease which may prove fatal. He knew any number of women whom he could ask to keep an eye on Odette, but how was he to expect them to adjust themselves to his new point of view, and not to look at the matter from the one which for so long had been his own, which had always guided him in sexual matters; not to say to him with a laugh: "You jealous monster, wanting to rob other people of their pleasure!" By what trap-door suddenly lowered had he (who had never had hitherto from his love for Odette any but the most refined pleasures) been precipitated into this new circle of hell from which he could not see how he was ever to escape. Poor Odette! He did not hold it against her. She was only half to blame. Had he not been told that it was her own mother who had sold her, when she was still hardly more than a child, at Nice, to a wealthy Englishman? But what an agonising truth was now contained for him in those lines of Alfred de Vigny's *Journal d'un Poète* which he had previously read without emotion: "When one feels oneself smitten by love for a woman, one should say to oneself, 'Who are the people around her? What kind of life has she led?' All one's future happiness lies in the answer." Swann was

astonished that such simple sentences, spelt over in his mind,
as "I've heard that tale before" or "I knew quite well what she
was after," could cause him so much pain. But he realised that
what he thought of as simple sentences were in fact the components of the framework which still enclosed, and could
inflict on him again, the anguish he had felt while Odette was
telling her story. For it was indeed the same anguish that he
now was feeling anew. For all that he now knew—for all that,
as time went on, he might even have partly forgotten and forgiven—whenever he repeated her words his old anguish refashioned him as he had been before Odette had spoken:
ignorant, trustful; his merciless jealousy placed him once
again, so that he might be pierced by Odette's admission, in
the position of a man who does not yet know; and after several
months this old story would still shatter him like a sudden
revelation. He marvelled at the terrible recreative power of his
memory. It was only by the weakening of that generative
force, whose fecundity diminishes with age, that he could hope
for a relaxation of his torments. But, as soon as the power of
any one of Odette's remarks to make Swann suffer seemed to
be nearly exhausted, lo and behold another, one of those to
which he had hitherto paid little attention, almost a new observation, came to reinforce the others and to strike at him with
undiminished force. The memory of the evening on which he
had dined with the Princesse des Laumes was painful to him,
but it was no more than the centre, the core of his pain, which
radiated vaguely round about it, overflowing into all the preceding and following days. And on whatever point in it his
memory sought to linger, it was the whole of that season, during which the Verdurins had so often gone to dine on the
Island in the Bois, that racked him. So violently that by slow
degrees the curiosity which his jealousy aroused in him was
neutralised by his fear of the fresh tortures he would be in-
flicting upon himself were he to satisfy it. He recognised that
the entire period of Odette's life which had elapsed before she
first met him, a period of which he had never sought to form
a picture in his mind, was not the featureless abstraction which
he could vaguely see, but had consisted of so many definite,
dated years, each crowded with concrete incidents. But were

he to learn more of them, he feared lest that past of hers, colourless, fluid and supportable, might assume a tangible and monstrous form, an individual and diabolical countenance. And he continued to refrain from seeking to visualise it, no longer from laziness of mind, but from fear of suffering. He hoped that, some day, he might be able to hear the Island in the Bois or the Princesse des Laumes mentioned without feeling any twinge of the old heartache; and meanwhile he thought it imprudent to provoke Odette into furnishing him with new facts, the names of more places and different circumstances which, when his malady was still scarcely healed, would revive it again in another form.

But, often enough, the things that he did know, that he dreaded, now, to learn, were revealed to him by Odette herself, spontaneously and unwittingly; for the gap which her vices made between her actual life and the comparatively innocent life which Swann had believed, and often still believed his mistress to lead, was far wider than she knew. A vicious person, always affecting the same air of virtue before people whom he is anxious to keep from having any suspicion of his vices, has no gauge at hand from which to ascertain how far those vices, whose continuous growth is imperceptible to himself, have gradually segregated him from the normal ways of life. In the course of their cohabitation, in Odette's mind, side by side with the memory of those of her actions which she concealed from Swann, others were gradually coloured, infected by them, without her being able to detect anything strange in them, without their causing any jarring note in the particular surroundings which they occupied in her inner world; but if she related them to Swann, he was shattered by the revelation of the way of life to which they pointed. One day he was trying—without hurting Odette—to discover from her whether she had ever had any dealings with procuresses. He was, as a matter of fact, convinced that she had not; the anonymous letter had put the idea into his mind, but in a mechanical way; it had met with no credence there, but for all that had remained, and Swann, wishing to be rid of the purely material but none the less burdensome presence of the suspicion, hoped that Odette would now extirpate it for ever.

"Oh, no! . . . Not that they don't pester me," she added
with a smile of self-satisfied vanity, quite unaware that it
could not appear justifiable to Swann. "There was one of
them waited more than two hours for me yesterday—offered
me any money I asked. It seems there's an ambassador who
said to her, 'I'll kill myself if you don't bring her to me'—
meaning me! They told her I'd gone out, but she waited and
waited, and in the end I had to go and speak to her myself
before she'd go away. I wish you could have seen the way I
went for her; my maid could hear me from the next room and
told me I was shouting at the top of my voice: 'But haven't
I told you I don't want to! It's just the way I feel. I should
hope I'm still free to do as I please! If I needed the money, I
could understand . . .' The porter has orders not to let her in
again; he's to tell her I'm out of town. Oh, I wish I could have
had you hidden somewhere in the room while I was talking to
her. I know you'd have been pleased, my darling. There's some
good in your little Odette, you see, after all, though people
do say such dreadful things about her."

Besides, her very admissions—when she made any—of faults
which she supposed him to have discovered, served Swann as
a starting-point for new doubts rather than putting an end to the
old. For her admissions never exactly coincided with his
doubts. In vain might Odette expurgate her confession of all
its essentials, there would remain in the accessories something
which Swann had never yet imagined, which crushed him
anew, and would enable him to alter the terms of the problem
of his jealousy. And these admissions he could never forget.
His soul carried them along, cast them aside, then cradled
them again in its bosom, like corpses in a river. And they
poisoned it.

She spoke to him once of a visit that Forcheville had paid
her on the day of the Paris-Murcie Fête. "What! you knew
him as long ago as that? Oh, yes, of course you did," he corrected himself, so as not to show that he had been ignorant of
the fact. And suddenly he began to tremble at the thought that,
on the day of the Paris-Murcie Fête, when he had received
from her the letter which he had so carefully preserved, she
had perhaps been having lunch with Forcheville at the Maison

d'Or. She swore that she had not. "Still, the Maison d'Or reminds me of something or other which I knew at the time wasn't true," he pursued, hoping to frighten her. "Yes, that I hadn't been there at all that evening when I told you I had just come from there, and you'd been looking for me at Prévost's," she replied (judging by his manner that he knew) with a firmness that was based not so much on cynicism as on timidity, a fear of offending Swann which her own self-respect made her anxious to conceal, and a desire to show him that she could be perfectly frank if she chose. And so she struck with all the precision and force of a headsman wielding his axe, and yet could not be charged with cruelty since she was quite unconscious of hurting him; she even laughed, though perhaps, it is true, chiefly in order not to appear chastened or embarrassed. "It's quite true, I hadn't been to the Maison Dorée. I was coming away from Forcheville's. I really had been to Prévost's—I didn't make that up—and he met me there and asked me to come in and look at his prints. But someone else came to see him. I told you I'd come from the Maison d'Or because I was afraid you might be angry with me. It was rather nice of me, really, don't you see? Even if I did wrong, at least I'm telling you all about it now, aren't I? What would I have to gain by not telling you that I lunched with him on the day of the Paris-Murcie Fête, if it was true? Especially as at the time we didn't know one another quite so well as we do now, did we, darling?"

He smiled back at her with the sudden, craven weakness of the shattered creature which these crushing words had made of him. So, even in the months of which he had never dared to think again because they had been too happy, in those months when she had loved him, she was already lying to him! Besides that moment (that first evening on which they had "done a cattleya") when she had told him that she was coming from the Maison Dorée, how many others must there have been, each of them also concealing a falsehood of which Swann had had no suspicion. He recalled how she had said to him once: "I need only tell Mme Verdurin that my dress wasn't ready, or that my cab came late. There's always some excuse." From himself too, probably, many a time when she had glibly uttered

such words as explain a delay or justify an alteration of the
hour fixed for a meeting, they must have hidden, without his
having the least inkling of it at the time, an appointment she
had with some other man, some man to whom she had said:
"I need only tell Swann that my dress wasn't ready, or that my
cab came late. There's always some excuse." And beneath all
his most tender memories, beneath the simplest words that
Odette had spoken to him in those early days, words which
he had believed as though they were gospel, beneath the daily
actions which she had recounted to him, beneath the most
ordinary places, her dressmaker's flat, the Avenue du Bois,
the race-course, he could feel (dissembled by virtue of that
temporal superfluity which, even in days that have been most
circumstantially accounted for, still leaves a margin of room
that may serve as a hiding place for certain unconfessed actions), he could feel the insinuation of a possible undercurrent
of falsehood which rendered ignoble all that had remained
most precious to him (his happiest evenings, the Rue La
Pérouse itself, which Odette must constantly have been leaving
at other hours than those of which she told him) everywhere
disseminating something of the shadowy horror that had
gripped him when he had heard her admission with regard to
the Maison Dorée, and, like the obscene creatures in the
"Desolation of Nineveh," shattering stone by stone the whole
edifice of his past. . . . If, now, he turned away whenever his
memory repeated the cruel name of the Maison Dorée, it was
because that name recalled to him no longer, as, but recently,
at Mme de Saint-Euverte's party, a happiness which he had
long since lost, but a misfortune of which he had just become
aware. Then it happened with the Maison Dorée as it had happened with the Island in the Bois, that gradually its name
ceased to trouble him. For what we suppose to be our love or
our jealousy is never a single, continuous and indivisible
passion. It is composed of an infinity of successive loves,
of different jealousies, each of which is ephemeral, although by
their uninterrupted multiplicity they give us the impression of
continuity, the illusion of unity. The life of Swann's love, the
fidelity of his jealousy, were formed of the death, the infidelity,
of innumerable desires, innumerable doubts, all of which

had Odette for their object. If he had remained for any length of time without seeing her, those that died would not have been replaced by others. But the presence of Odette continued to sow in Swann's heart alternate seeds of love and suspicion.

On certain evenings she would suddenly resume towards him an amenity of which she would warn him sternly that he must take immediate advantage, under penalty of not seeing it repeated for years to come; he must instantly accompany her home, to "do a cattleya," and the desire which she claimed to have for him was so sudden, so inexplicable, so imperious, the caresses which she lavished on him were so demonstrative and so unwonted, that this brutal and improbable fondness made Swann just as unhappy as any lie or unkindness. One evening when he had thus, in obedience to her command, gone home with her, and she was interspersing her kisses with passionate words, in strange contrast to her habitual coldness, he suddenly thought he heard a sound; he rose, searched everywhere and found nobody, but hadn't the heart to return to his place by her side; whereupon, in the height of fury, she broke a vase and said to him: "One can never do anything right with you!" And he was left uncertain whether she had not actually had some man concealed in the room, whose jealousy she had wished to exacerbate or his senses to inflame.

Sometimes he repaired to brothels in the hope of learning something about Odette, although he dared not mention her name. "I have a little thing you're sure to like," the "manageress" would greet him, and he would stay for an hour or so chatting gloomily to some poor girl who sat there astonished that he went no further. One of them, who was quite young and very pretty, said to him once: "Of course, what I'd like would be to find a real friend—then he might be quite certain I'd never go with any other men again."

"Really, do you think it possible for a woman to be touched by a man's loving her, and never to be unfaithful to him?" asked Swann anxiously.

"Why, of course! It all depends on people's characters!"

Swann could not help saying to these girls the sort of things that would have delighted the Princesse des Laumes. To the

one who was in search of a friend he said with a smile: "But
how nice, you've put on blue eyes to go with your sash."

"And you too, you've got blue cuffs on."

"What a charming conversation we're having for a place of
this sort! I'm not boring you, am I; or keeping you?"

"No, I'm not in a hurry. If you'd have bored me I'd have said
so. But I like hearing you talk."

"I'm very flattered. . . . Aren't we having a nice chat?" he
asked the "manageress", who had just looked in.

"Why, yes, that's just what I was saying to myself, how
good they're being! But there it is! People come to my house
now just to talk. The Prince was telling me only the other day
that it's far nicer here than at home with his wife. It seems
that, nowadays, all the society ladies are so flighty; a real
scandal, I call it. But I'll leave you in peace now," she ended
discreetly, and left Swann with the girl who had the blue eyes.
But presently he rose and said good-bye to her. She had ceased
to interest him. She did not know Odette.

The painter having been ill, Dr Cottard recommended a
sea-voyage. Several of the "faithful" spoke of accompanying
him. The Verdurins could not face the prospect of being left
alone in Paris, so first of all hired and finally purchased a
yacht; thus Odette went on frequent cruises. Whenever she had
been away for any length of time, Swann would feel that he was
beginning to detach himself from her, but as though this moral
distance were proportionate to the physical distance between
them, whenever he heard that Odette had returned to Paris,
he could not rest without seeing her. Once, when they had
gone away ostensibly for a month only, either they succumbed
to a series of temptations, or else M. Verdurin had cunningly
arranged everything beforehand to please his wife, and disclosed his plans to the "faithful" only as time went on; at all
events, from Algiers they flitted to Tunis; then to Italy, Greece,
Constantinople, Asia Minor. They had been absent for nearly
a year, and Swann felt perfectly at ease and almost happy.
Although Mme Verdurin had endeavoured to persuade the
pianist and Dr Cottard that their respective aunt and patients
had no need of them, and that in any event it was most rash to
allow Mme Cottard to return to Paris which, so M. Verdurin

affirmed, was in the throes of revolution, she was obliged to grant them their liberty at Constantinople. And the painter came home with them. One day, shortly after the return of these four travellers, Swann, seeing an omnibus for the Luxembourg approaching and having some business there, had jumped on it and found himself sitting opposite Mme Cottard, who was paying a round of visits to people whose "day" it was, in full fig, with a plume in her hat, a silk dress, a muff, an umbrella-sunshade, a card-case, and a pair of white gloves fresh from the cleaners. Clothed in these regalia, she would, in fine weather, go on foot from one house to another in the same neighbourhood, but when she had to proceed to another district, would make use of a transfer-ticket on the omnibus. For the first minute or two, until the natural amiability of the woman broke through the starched surface of the doctor's-wife, not being certain, moreover, whether she ought to talk to Swann about the Verdurins, she proceeded to hold forth, in her slow, awkward and soft-spoken voice, which every now and then was completely drowned by the rattling of the omnibus, on topics selected from those which she had picked up and would repeat in each of the score of houses up the stairs of which she clambered in the course of an afternoon.

"I needn't ask you, M. Swann, whether a man so much in the swim as yourself has been to the Mirlitons to see the portrait by Machard which the whole of Paris is rushing to see. Well and what do you think of it? Whose camp are you in, those who approve or those who don't? It's the same in every house in Paris now, no one talks about anything else but Machard's portrait. You aren't smart, you aren't really cultured, you aren't up-to-date unless you give an opinion on Machard's portrait."

Swann having replied that he had not seen this portrait, Mme Cottard was afraid that she might have hurt his feelings by obliging him to confess the omission.

"Oh, that's quite all right! At least you admit it frankly. You don't consider yourself disgraced because you haven't seen Machard's portrait. I find that most commendable. Well now, I have seen it. Opinion is divided, you know, there are some people who find it a bit over-finical, like whipped cream, they

say; but I think it's just ideal. Of course, she's not a bit like
the blue and yellow ladies of our friend Biche. But I must tell
you quite frankly (you'll think me dreadfully old-fashioned,
but I always say just what I think), that I don't understand his
work. I can quite see the good points in his portrait of my
husband, oh, dear me, yes, and it's certainly less odd than most
of what he does, but even then he had to give the poor man a
blue moustache! But Machard! Just listen to this now, the husband of the friend I'm on my way to see at this very moment
(which has given me the very great pleasure of your company),
has promised her that if he is elected to the Academy (he's one
of the Doctor's colleagues) he'll get Machard to paint her
portrait. *There's* something to look forward to! I have another
friend who insists that she'd rather have Leloir. I'm only a
wretched Philistine, and for all I know Leloir may be technically superior to Machard. But I do think that the most
important thing about a portrait, especially when it's going to
cost ten thousand francs, is that it should be like, and a pleasant likeness if you know what I mean."

Having exhausted this topic, to which she had been inspired
by the loftiness of her plume, the monogram on her card-case,
the little number inked inside each of her gloves by the
cleaner, and the embarrassment of speaking to Swann about
the Verdurins, Mme Cottard, seeing that they had still a long
way to go before they would reach the corner of the Rue
Bonaparte where the conductor was to set her down, listened
to the promptings of her heart, which counselled other words
than these.

"Your ears must have been burning," she ventured, "while
we were on the yacht with Mme Verdurin. We talked about
you all the time."

Swann was genuinely astonished, for he supposed that his
name was never uttered in the Verdurins' presence.

"You see," Mme Cottard went on, "Mme de Crécy was
there; need I say more? Wherever Odette is, it's never long
before she begins talking about you. And you can imagine
that it's never unfavourably. What, you don't believe me!" she
went on, noticing that Swann looked sceptical.

And, carried away by the sincerity of her conviction, without

putting any sly meaning into the word, which she used purely
in the sense in which one employs it to speak of the affection
that unites a pair of friends: "Why, she *adores* you! No, indeed,
I'm sure it would never do to say anything against you
when she was about; one would soon be put in one's place!
Whatever we might be doing, if we were looking at a picture,
for instance, she would say, 'If only we had him here, he's
the man who could tell us whether it's genuine or not.
There's no one like him for that.' And all day long she would
be saying, 'What can he be doing just now? I do hope he's
doing a little work! It's too dreadful that a fellow with
such gifts as he has should be so lazy.' (Forgive me, won't
you.) 'I can see him this very moment; he's thinking of us,
he's wondering where we are.' Indeed, she made a remark
which I found absolutely charming. M. Verdurin asked her,
'How in the world can you see what he's doing, when he's
a thousand miles away?' And Odette answered, 'Nothing is
impossible to the eye of a friend.' No, I assure you, I'm not
saying it just to flatter you; you have a true friend in her, such
as one doesn't often find. I can tell you, besides, that if
you don't know it you're the only one who doesn't. Mme
Verdurin told me as much herself on our last day with them
(one talks freely, don't you know, before a parting), 'I don't
say that Odette isn't fond of us, but anything that we may say
to her counts for very little beside what Swann might say.'
Oh, mercy, there's the conductor stopping for me. Here I've
been chatting away to you, and would have gone right past the
Rue Bonaparte and never noticed. . . . Will you be so very kind
as to tell me if my plume is straight?"

And Mme Cottard withdrew from her muff, to offer it to
Swann, a white-gloved hand from which there floated, together with a transfer-ticket, a vision of high life that pervaded
the omnibus, blended with the fragrance of newly cleaned
kid. And Swann felt himself overflowing with affection towards her, as well as towards Mme Verdurin (and almost
towards Odette, for the feeling that he now entertained for
her, being no longer tinged with pain, could scarcely be
described, now, as love) as from the platform of the omnibus
he followed her with fond eyes as she gallantly threaded her

way along the Rue Bonaparte, her plume erect, her skirt held
up in one hand, while in the other she clasped her umbrella
and her card-case with its monogram exposed to view, her
muff dancing up and down in front of her as she went.

To counterbalance the morbid feelings that Swann cherished
for Odette, Mme Cottard, a wiser physician, in this case, than
ever her husband would have been, had grafted on to them
others more normal, feelings of gratitude, of friendship,
which in Swann's mind would make Odette seem more human
(more like other women, since other women could inspire the
same feelings in him), would hasten her final transformation
back into the Odette, loved with an undisturbed affection,
who had taken him home one evening after a revel at the
painter's to drink a glass of orangeade with Forcheville, the
Odette with whom Swann had glimpsed the possibility of
living in happiness.

In the past, having often thought with terror that a day
must come when he would cease to be in love with Odette,
he had determined to keep a sharp look-out, and as soon as he
felt that love was beginning to leave him, to cling to it and
hold it back. But now, to the diminution of his love there corresponded a simultaneous diminution in his desire to remain
in love. For a man cannot change, that is to say become another
person, while continuing to obey the dictates of the self which
he has ceased to be. Occasionally the name glimpsed in a
newspaper, of one of the men whom he supposed to have been
Odette's lovers, reawakened his jealousy. But it was very
mild, and, inasmuch as it proved to him that he had not completely emerged from that period in which he had so greatly
suffered—but in which he had also known so voluptuous a
way of feeling—and that the hazards of the road ahead might
still enable him to catch an occasional furtive, distant glimpse
of its beauties, this jealousy gave him, if anything, an agreeable
thrill, as, to the sad Parisian who is leaving Venice behind him
to return to France, a last mosquito proves that Italy and summer are still not too remote. But, as a rule, with this particular
period of his life from which he was emerging, when he made
an effort, if not to remain in it, at least to obtain a clear view
of it while he still could, he discovered that already it was too

late; he would have liked to glimpse, as though it were a landscape that was about to disappear, that love from which he had departed; but it is so difficult to enter into a state of duality and to present to oneself the lifelike spectacle of a feeling one has ceased to possess, that very soon, the clouds gathering in his brain, he could see nothing at all, abandoned the attempt, took the glasses from his nose and wiped them; and he told himself that he would do better to rest for a little, that there would be time enough later on, and settled back into his corner with the incuriosity, the torpor of the drowsy traveller who pulls his hat down over his eyes to get some sleep in the railway-carriage that is drawing him, he feels, faster and faster out of the country in which he has lived for so long and which he had vowed not to allow to slip away from him without looking out to bid it a last farewell. Indeed, like the same traveller if he does not awake until he has crossed the frontier and is back in France, when Swann chanced to alight, close at hand, on proof that Forcheville had been Odette's lover, he realised that it caused him no pain, that love was now far behind, and he regretted that he had had no warning of the moment when he had emerged from it for ever. And just as, before kissing Odette for the first time, he had sought to imprint upon his memory the face that for so long had been familiar before it was altered by the additional memory of their kiss, so he could have wished—in thought at least—to have been able to bid farewell, while she still existed, to the Odette who had aroused his love and jealousy, to the Odette who had caused him to suffer, and whom now he would never see again.

He was mistaken. He was destined to see her once again, a few weeks later. It was while he was asleep, in the twilight of a dream. He was walking with Mme Verdurin, Dr Cottard, a young man in a fez whom he failed to identify, the painter, Odette, Napoleon III and my grandfather, along a path which followed the line of the coast, and overhung the sea, now at a great height, now by a few feet only, so that they were continually going up and down. Those of the party who had reached the downward slope were no longer visible to those who were still climbing; what little daylight yet remained was failing, and it seemed as though they were about to be shrouded

in darkness. From time to time the waves dashed against the
edge, and Swann could feel on his cheek a shower of freezing
spray. Odette told him to wipe it off, but he could not, and felt
confused and helpless in her company, as well as because he was
in his nightshirt. He hoped that, in the darkness, this might pass
unnoticed; Mme Verdurin, however, fixed her astonished gaze
upon him for an endless moment, during which he saw her
face change shape, her nose grow longer, while beneath it
there sprouted a heavy moustache. He turned round to look at
Odette; her cheeks were pale, with little red spots, her features
drawn and ringed with shadows; but she looked back at him
with eyes welling with affection, ready to detach themselves like
tears and to fall upon his face, and he felt that he loved her so
much that he would have liked to carry her off with him at
once. Suddenly Odette turned her wrist, glanced at a tiny
watch, and said: "I must go." She took leave of everyone in
the same formal manner, without taking Swann aside, without
telling him where they were to meet that evening, or next day.
He dared not ask; he would have liked to follow her, but he
was obliged, without turning back in her direction, to answer
with a smile some question from Mme Verdurin; but his heart
was frantically beating, he felt that he now hated Odette, he
would gladly have gouged out those eyes which a moment ago
he had loved so much, have crushed those flaccid cheeks. He
continued to climb with Mme Verdurin, that is to say to draw
further away with each step from Odette, who was going
downhill in the other direction. A second passed and it was
many hours since she had left them. The painter remarked to
Swann that Napoleon III had slipped away immediately after
Odette. "They had obviously arranged it between them," he
added. "They must have met at the foot of the cliff, but they
didn't want to say good-bye together because of appearances.
She is his mistress." The strange young man burst into tears.
Swann tried to console him. "After all, she's quite right," he
said to the young man, drying his eyes for him and taking off
the fez to make him feel more at ease. "I've advised her to do
it dozens of times. Why be so distressed? He was obviously
the man to understand her." So Swann reasoned with himself, for the young man whom he had failed at first to identify

was himself too; like certain novelists, he had distributed his own personality between two characters, the one who was dreaming the dream, and another whom he saw in front of him sporting a fez.

As for Napoleon III, it was to Forcheville that some vague association of ideas, then a certain modification of the baron's usual physiognomy, and lastly the broad ribbon of the Legion of Honour across his breast, had made Swann give that name; in reality, and in everything that the person who appeared in his dream represented and recalled to him, it was indeed Forcheville. For, from an incomplete and changing set of images, Swann in his sleep drew false deductions, enjoying at the same time, momentarily, such a creative power that he was able to reproduce himself by a simple act of division, like certain lower organisms; with the warmth that he felt in his own palm he modelled the hollow of a strange hand which he thought he was clasping, and out of feelings and impressions of which he was not yet conscious he brought about sudden vicissitudes which, by a chain of logical sequences, would produce, at specific points in his dream, the person required to receive his love or to startle him awake. In an instant night grew black about him; a tocsin sounded, people ran past him, escaping from their blazing houses; he could hear the thunder of the surging waves, and also of his own heart, which with equal violence was anxiously beating in his breast. Suddenly the speed of these palpitations redoubled, he felt an inexplicable pain and nausea. A peasant, dreadfully burned, flung at him as he passed: "Come and ask Charlus where Odette spent the night with her friend. He used to go about with her in the past, and she tells him everything. It was they who started the fire." It was his valet, come to awaken him, and saying:—

"Sir, it's eight o'clock, and the barber is here. I've told him to call again in an hour."

But these words, as they plunged through the waves of sleep in which Swann was submerged, did not reach his consciousness without undergoing that refraction which turns a ray of light in the depths of water into another sun; just as, a moment earlier, the sound of the door-bell, swelling in the depths of his abyss of sleep into the clangour of a tocsin, had

engendered the episode of the fire. Meanwhile, the scenery of
his dream-stage scattered into dust, he opened his eyes, and
heard for the last time the boom of a wave in the sea, now
distant. He touched his cheek. It was dry. And yet he remembered the sting of the cold spray, and the taste of salt on
his lips. He rose and dressed himself. He had made the barber
come early because he had written the day before to my grandfather to say that he was going to Combray that afternoon,
having learned that Mme de Cambremer—Mlle Legrandin
that had been—was spending a few days there. The association
in his memory of her young and charming face with a countryside he had not visited for so long offered him a combined
attraction which had made him decide at last to leave Paris
for a while. As the different circumstances that bring us into
contact with certain people do not coincide with the period
in which we are in love with them, but, overlapping it, may
occur before love has begun, and may be repeated after it has
ended, the earliest appearances in our lives of a person who is
destined to take our fancy later on assume retrospectively in
our eyes a certain value as an indication, a warning, a presage.
It was in this fashion that Swann had often reverted in his
mind to the image of Odette encountered in the theatre on that
first evening when he had no thought of ever seeing her again
—and that he now recalled the party at Mme de Saint-Euverte's
at which he had introduced General de Froberville to Mme
de Cambremer. So manifold are our interests in life that it is
not uncommon, on the self-same occasion, for the foundations
of a happiness which does not yet exist to be laid down simultaneously with the aggravation of a grief from which we are
still suffering. And doubtless this could have occurred to Swann
elsewhere than at Mme de Saint-Euverte's. Who indeed can
say whether, in the event of his having gone elsewhere that
evening, other happinesses, other griefs might not have come
to him, which later would have appeared to him to have been
inevitable? But what did seem to him to have been inevitable
was what had indeed taken place, and he was not far short of
seeing something providential in the fact that he had decided
to go to Mme de Saint-Euverte's that evening, because his
mind, anxious to admire the richness of invention that life

shows, and incapable of facing a difficult problem for any
length of time, such as deciding what was most to be wished
for, came to the conclusion that the sufferings through which
he had passed that evening, and the pleasures, as yet unsuspected, which were already germinating there—the exact
balance between which was too difficult to establish—were
linked by a sort of concatenation of necessity.

But while, an hour after his awakening, he was giving
instructions to the barber to see that his stiffly brushed hair
should not become disarranged on the journey, he thought
of his dream again, and saw once again, as he had felt them
close beside him, Odette's pallid complexion, her too thin
cheeks, her drawn features, her tired eyes, all the things which
—in the course of those successive bursts of affection which
had made of his enduring love for Odette a long oblivion of
the first impression that he had formed of her—he had ceased
to notice since the early days of their intimacy, days to which
doubtless, while he slept, his memory had returned to seek
their exact sensation. And with the old, intermittent caddishness which reappeared in him when he was no longer
unhappy and his moral standards dropped accordingly, he
exclaimed to himself: "To think that I've wasted years of my
life, that I've longed to die, that I've experienced my greatest
love, for a woman who didn't appeal to me, who wasn't even
my type!"

PLACE-NAMES:
THE NAME

AMONG the rooms which used most commonly to take shape in my mind during my long nights of sleeplessness, there was none that differed more utterly from the rooms at Combray, thickly powdered with the motes of an atmosphere granular, pollinated, edible and devout, than my room in the Grand Hôtel de la Plage, at Balbec, the ripolin-painted walls of which enclosed, like the polished sides of a bathing-pool in which the water glows blue, a finer air, pure, azure-tinted, saline. The Bavarian upholsterer who had been entrusted with the furnishing of this hotel had varied his scheme of decoration in different rooms, and in that which I found myself occupying had set against the walls, on three sides of it, a series of low book-cases with glass fronts, in which, according to where they stood, by a law of nature which he had not perhaps foreseen, was reflected this or that section of the ever-changing view of the sea, so that the walls were lined with a frieze of sea-scapes, interrupted only by the polished mahogany of the actual shelves. So much so that the whole room had the appearance of one of those model bedrooms which are to be seen in exhibitions of modern housing, decorated with works of art calculated by their designer to gladden the eyes of whoever may ultimately sleep therein, the subjects being in keeping with the locality and surroundings of the houses for which the rooms are planned.

And yet nothing could have differed more utterly, either, from the real Balbec than that other Balbec of which I had often dreamed, on stormy days, when the wind was so strong that Françoise, as she took me to the Champs-Elysées, would advise me not to walk too close to the walls or I might have my head knocked off by a falling slate, and would recount to me, with many a groan, the terrible disasters and shipwrecks that were reported in the newspaper. I longed for nothing more than to behold a stormy sea, less as a mighty spectacle than as a momentary revelation of the true life of nature; or rather there were for me no mighty spectacles save those which I knew to be not artificially composed for my entertainment, but necessary and unalterable,—the beauty of landscapes or of great works of art. I was curious and eager to know only what I believed to be more real than myself, what had for me the supreme merit of showing me a fragment of the mind of a great genius, or of the force or the grace of nature as it appeared when left entirely to itself, without human interference. Just as the beautiful sound of her voice, reproduced by itself on the gramophone, would never console one for the loss of one's mother, so a mechanical imitation of a storm would have left me as cold as did the illuminated fountains at the Exhibition. I required also, if the storm was to be absolutely genuine, that the shore from which I watched it should be a natural shore, not an embankment recently constructed by a municipality. Besides, nature, by virtue of all the feelings that it aroused in me, seemed to me the thing most diametrically opposed to the mechanical inventions of mankind. The less it bore their imprint, the more room it offered for the expansion of my heart. And, as it happened, I had preserved the name of Balbec, which Legrandin had cited to us, as that of a sea-side place in the very midst of "that funereal coast, famed for the number of its wrecks, swathed, for six months of the year, in a shroud of fog and flying foam from the waves."

"You still feel there beneath your feet," he had told me, "far more than at Finistère itself (and even though hotels are now being superimposed upon it, without power, however, to modify that oldest ossature of the earth) you feel there that you are actually at the land's end of France, of Europe, of the Old World. And it is the ultimate encampment of the fishermen, the heirs of all the fishermen who have lived since the world's beginning, facing the everlasting kingdom of the sea-fogs and shadows of the night."

One day when, at Combray, I had spoken of this seaside resort of Balbec in the presence of M. Swann, hoping to learn from him whether it was the best point to select for seeing the most violent storms, he had replied: "Yes indeed I know Balbec! The church there, built in the twelfth and thirteenth centuries, and still half Romanesque, is perhaps the most curious example to be found of our Norman Gothic, and so singular that one is tempted to describe it as Persian in its inspiration."

And that region which, until then, had seemed to me to be nothing else than a part of immemorial nature, that had remained contemporaneous with the great phenomena of geology—and as remote from human history as the Ocean itself or the Great Bear, with its wild race of fishermen for whom no more than for their whales had there been any Middle Ages—it had been a great joy to me to see it suddenly take its place in the order of the centuries, with a stored consciousness of the Romanesque epoch, and to know that the Gothic trefoil had come to diversify those wild rocks too at the appointed time, like those frail but hardy plants which in the Polar regions, when spring returns, scatter their stars about the eternal snows. And if Gothic art brought to those places and people an identification which otherwise they lacked, they too conferred one upon it in return. I tried to picture how those fishermen had lived, the timid and undreamt-of experiment in social relations which they had attempted there, clustered upon a promontory of the shores of Hell, at the foot of the cliffs of death; and Gothic art seemed to me a more living thing now that, detached from the towns in which until then I had always imagined it, I could see how, in a particular instance, upon a reef of savage rocks, it had taken root and grown until it flowered in a tapering spire. I was taken to see reproductions of the most famous of the statues at Balbec—the shaggy, snub-nosed Apostles, the Virgin from the porch—and I could scarcely breathe for joy at the thought that I might myself, one day, see them stand out in relief against the eternal briny fog. Thereafter, on delightful, stormy February nights, the wind—breathing into my heart, which it shook no less violently than the chimney of my bedroom, the project of a visit to Balbec—blended in me the desire for Gothic architecture as well as for a storm upon the sea.

I should have liked to take, the very next day, the fine, generous 1.22 train, whose hour of departure I could never read without a palpitating heart on the railway company's bills or in advertisements for circular tours: it seemed to me to cut, at a precise point in every afternoon, a delectable groove, a mysterious mark, from which the diverted hours still led, of course, towards evening, towards to-morrow morning, but an evening and morning which one would behold, not in Paris, but in one of those towns through which the train passed and among which it allowed one to choose; for it stopped at Bayeux, at Coutances, at Vitré, at Questambert, at Pontorson, at Balbec, at Lannion, at Lamballe, at Benodet, at Pont-Aven, at Quimperlé, and progressed magnificently overloaded with proffered names among which I did not know the one to choose, so impossible was it to sacrifice any. But even without waiting till next day, I could, by dressing with all speed, leave Paris that very evening, should my parents permit, and arrive at Balbec as dawn spread westward over the raging sea, from whose driven foam I would seek shelter in that church in the Persian style. But at the approach of the Easter holidays, when my parents had promised to let me spend them for once in the North of Italy, suddenly, in place of those dreams of tempests by which I had been entirely possessed, not wishing to see anything but waves dashing in from all sides, mounting ever higher, upon the wildest of coasts, beside churches as rugged and precipitous as cliffs, in whose towers the sea-birds would be wailing, suddenly, effacing them, taking away all their charm, excluding them because they were its opposite and could only have weakened its effect, was substituted in me the converse dream of the most colourful of springs, not the spring of Combray, which still pricked sharply with all the needle-points of the winter's frost, but that which already covered the meadows of Fiesole with lilies and anemones, and gave Florence a dazzling golden background like those in Fra Angelico's pictures. From that moment onwards, only sun-light, perfumes, colours, seemed to me of any worth; for this alternation of images had effected a change of front in my desire, and—as abrupt as those that occur sometimes in music —a complete change of key in my sensibility. Then it came about that a simple atmospheric variation was sufficient to provoke in me that modulation, without there being any need for me to await the return of a season. For often in one we find

a day that has strayed from another, that makes us live in that
other, evokes at once and makes us long for its particular
pleasures, and interrupts the dreams that we were in process
of weaving, by inserting out of its turn, too early or too late,
this leaf torn from another chapter in the interpolated calendar
of Happiness. But soon, in the same way as those natural
phenomena from which our comfort or our health can derive
but an accidental and all too modest benefit until the day
when science takes control of them and, producing them at
will, places in our hands the power to order their appearance,
free from the tutelage and independent of the mandate of
chance, so the production of these dreams of the Atlantic and
of Italy ceased to depend exclusively upon the changes of the
seasons and of the weather. I need only, to make them reappear, pronounce the names Balbec, Venice, Florence, within
whose syllables had gradually accumulated the longing inspired in me by the places for which they stood. Even in
spring, to come upon the name Balbec in a book sufficed to
awaken in me the desire for storms at sea and for Norman
Gothic; even on a stormy day the name Florence or Venice
would awaken the desire for sunshine, for lilies, for the Palace
of the Doges and for Santa Maria del Fiore.

But if these names thus permanently absorbed the image I
had formed of these towns, it was only by transforming that
image, by subordinating its reappearance in me to their own
special laws; and in consequence of this they made it more
beautiful, but at the same time more different from anything
that the towns of Normandy or Tuscany could in reality be,
and, by increasing the arbitrary delights of my imagination,
aggravated the disenchantment that was in store for me when
I set out upon my travels. They magnified the idea that I had
formed of certain places on the surface of the globe, making
them more special and in consequence more real. I did not then
represent to myself cities, landscapes, historical monuments, as
more or less attractive pictures, cut out here and there of a
substance that was common to them all, but looked on each of
them as on an unknown thing, different in essence from all
the rest, a thing for which my soul thirsted and which it would
profit from knowing. How much more individual still was the

character they assumed from being designated by names, names that were for themselves alone, proper names such as people have! Words present to us a little picture of things, clear and familiar, like the pictures hung on the walls of schoolrooms to give children an illustration of what is meant by a carpenter's bench, a bird, an anthill, things chosen as typical of everything else of the same sort. But names present to us—of persons, and of towns which they accustom us to regard as individual, as unique, like persons—a confused picture, which draws from them, from the brightness or darkness of their tone, the colour in which it is uniformly painted, like one of those posters, entirely blue or entirely red, in which, on account of the limitations imposed by the process used in their reproduction or by a whim on the designer's part, not only the sky and the sea are blue or red, but the ships and the church and the people in the streets. The name of Parma, one of the towns that I most longed to visit after reading the *Chartreuse*, seeming to me compact, smooth, violet-tinted and soft, if anyone were to speak of such or such a house in Parma in which I should be lodged, he would give me the pleasure of thinking that I was to inhabit a dwelling that was compact, smooth, violet-tinted and soft, that bore no relation to the houses in any other town in Italy, since I could imagine it only by the aid of that heavy first syllable of the name of Parma, in which no breath of air stirs, and of all that I had made it assume of Stendhalian sweetness and the reflected hue of violets. And when I thought of Florence it was of a town miraculously scented and flower-like, since it was called the City of the Lilies, and its cathedral, Our Lady of the Flower. As for Balbec, it was one of those names in which, as on an old piece of Norman pottery that still keeps the colour of the earth from which it was fashioned, one sees depicted still the representation of some long-abolished custom, of some feudal right, of the former status of some locality, of an obsolete way of pronouncing the language which had shaped and wedded its incongruous syllables and which I never doubted that I should find spoken there even by the inn-keeper who would serve me coffee on my arrival, taking me down to watch the turbulent sea in front of the church, and to whom I would ascribe the disputatious, solemn and mediaeval aspect of some character in an old romance.

If my health had grown stronger and my parents allowed me, if not actually to go down to stay at Balbec, at least to take, just once, in order to become acquainted with the architecture and landscapes of Normandy or of Brittany, that 1.22 train into which I had so often clambered in imagination, I should have wished to stop, for preference, at the most beautiful of its towns; but in vain did I compare and contrast them—how to choose, any more than between individual persons who are not interchangeable, between Bayeux, so lofty in its noble coronet of russet lacework, whose pinnacle was illumined by the old gold of its second syllable; Vitré, whose acute accent barred its ancient glass with wooden lozenges; gentle Lamballe, whose whiteness ranged from egg-shell yellow to pearl grey; Coutances, a Norman cathedral which its final consonants, rich and yellowing, crowned with a tower of butter; Lannion with the rumbling noise, in the silence of its village street, of a coach with a fly buzzing after it; Questambert, Pontorson, ridiculous and naïve, white feathers and yellow beaks strewn along the road to those well-watered and poetic spots; Benodet, a name scarcely moored that the river seemed to be striving to drag down into the tangle of its algae; Pont-Aven, pink-white flash of the wing of a lightly posed coif, tremulously reflected in the greenish waters of a canal; Quimperlé, more firmly anchored, ever since the Middle Ages, among its babbling rivulets threading their pearls in a grey iridescence like the pattern made, through the cobwebs on a church window, by rays of sunlight changed into blunted points of tarnished silver?

These images were false for another reason also—namely, that they were necessarily much simplified. Doubtless whatever it was that my imagination aspired to, that my senses took in only incompletely and without any immediate pleasure, I had committed to the safe custody of names; doubtless, because I had accumulated there a store of dreams, those names now magnetised my desires; but names themselves are not very comprehensive; the most that I could do was to include in each of them two or three of the principal "curiosities" of the town, which would lie there side by side, without intermediary; in the name of Balbec, as in the magnifying glasses set in those penholders which one buys at sea-side places, I could distinguish waves surging round a church built in the Persian style. Perhaps, indeed, the enforced simplicity of these images was one of the reasons for the hold that they had over me. When my father had decided, one year, that we should go for the Easter holidays to Florence and Venice, not finding room to introduce into the name of Florence the elements that ordinarily constitute a town, I was obliged to evolve a supernatural city from the impregnation by certain vernal scents of what I supposed to be, in its essentials, the genius of Giotto. At most —and because one cannot make a name extend much further in time than in space—like some of Giotto's paintings themselves which show us at two separate moments the same person engaged in different actions, here lying in his bed, there getting ready to mount his horse, the name of Florence was divided into two compartments. In one, beneath an architectural canopy, I gazed at a fresco over which was partly drawn a curtain of morning sunlight, dusty, oblique and gradually spreading; in the other (for, since I thought of names not as an inaccessible ideal but as a real and enveloping atmosphere into which I was about to plunge, the life not yet lived, the life, intact and pure, which I enclosed in them gave to the most material pleasures, to the simplest scenes, the same attraction that they have in the works of the Primitives), I moved swiftly —the quicker to arrive at the lunch-table that was spread for me with fruit and a flask of Chianti—across a Ponte Vecchio heaped with jonquils, narcissi and anemones. That (even though I was still in Paris) was what I saw, and not what was actually round about me. Even from the simplest, the most realistic point of view, the countries which we long for occupy, at any given moment, a far larger place in our actual life than the country in which we happen to be. Doubtless, if, at that time, I had paid more attention to what was in my mind when I pronounced the words "going to Florence, to Parma, to Pisa, to Venice," I should have realised that what I saw was in no sense a town, but something as different from anything that I knew, something as delicious, as might be, for a human race whose whole existence had passed in a series of late winter afternoons, that inconceivable marvel, a morning in spring. These images, unreal, fixed, always alike, filling all my nights and days, differentiated this period in my life from those which had gone before it (and might easily have been confused with it by an observer who saw things only from without, that is to say who saw nothing), as in an opera a melodic theme introduces a novel atmosphere which one could never have suspected if one had done no more than read the libretto, still less if one had remained outside the theatre counting only the minutes as they passed. And besides, even from the point of view of mere quantity, in our lives the days are not all equal. To get through each day, natures that are at all highly strung, as was mine, are equipped, like motor-cars, with different gears. There are mountainous, arduous days, up which one takes an infinite time to climb, and downward-sloping days which one can descend at full tilt, singing as one goes. During this month—in which I turned over and over in my mind, like a tune of which one never tires, these visions of Florence, Venice, Pisa, of which the desire that they excited in me retained something as profoundly personal as if it had been love, love for a person—I never ceased to believe that they corresponded to a reality independent of myself, and they made me conscious of as glorious a hope as could have been cherished by a Christian in the primitive age of faith on the eve of his entry into Paradise. Thus, without my paying any heed to the contradiction that there was in my wishing to look at and to touch with the organs of my senses what had been elaborated by the spell of my dreams and not perceived by my senses at all—though all the more tempting to them, in consequence, more different from anything that they knew—it was that which recalled to me the reality of these visions that most inflamed my desire, by seeming to offer the promise that it would be gratified. And for all that the motive force of my exaltation was a longing for aesthetic enjoyments, the guide-books ministered even more to it than books on aesthetics, and, more again than the guide-books, the railway time-tables. What moved me was the thought that this Florence which I could see, so near and yet inaccessible, in my imagination, if the journey which separated it from me, in myself, was not a viable one, could yet be reached circuitously were I to take the plain, terrestrial route. True, when I repeated to myself, giving thus a special value to what I was going to see, that Venice was the "School of Giorgione, the home of Titian, the most complete museum of the domestic architecture of the Middle Ages," I felt happy. But I was happier still when, out on an errand and walking briskly on account of the weather, which, after several days of a precocious spring, had relapsed into winter (like the weather we invariably found awaiting us at Combray in Holy Week), —seeing on the boulevards that the chestnut-trees, though plunged in a glacial atmosphere that soaked through them like water, were none the less beginning, punctual guests, arrayed already for the party and admitting no discouragement, to shape and chisel and curve in its frozen lumps the irrepressible verdure whose steady growth the abortive power of the cold might hinder but could not succeed in restraining—I reflected that already the Ponte Vecchio was heaped high with an abundance of hyacinths and anemones, and that the spring sunshine was already tingeing the waters of the Grand Canal with so deep an azure and such noble emeralds that when they washed against the foot of a Titian painting they could vie with it in the richness of their colouring. I could no longer contain myself for joy when my father, in the intervals of tapping the barometer and complaining of the cold, began to look out which were the best trains, and when I understood that by making one's way after luncheon into the coal-grimed laboratory, the wizard's cell that undertook to contrive a complete transmutation of its surroundings, one could wake up next morning in the city of marble and gold, "its walls embellished with jasper and its streets paved with emeralds." So that it and the City of the Lilies were not just artificial scenes which I could set up at will in front of my imagination, but existed at a certain distance from Paris which must inevitably be traversed if I wished to see them, at a particular place on the earth's surface and at no other—in a word, were entirely real. They became even more real to me when my father, by saying, "Well, you can stay in Venice from the 20th to the 29th, and reach Florence on Easter morning," made

them both emerge, no longer only from the abstraction of
Space, but from that imaginary Time in which we place not
one journey at a time but others simultaneously, without too
much agitation since they are only possibilities—that Time
which reconstructs itself so effectively that one can spend it
again in one town after one has already spent it in another—
and assigned to them some of those actual, calendar days which
are the certificates of authenticity of the objects on which they
are spent, for these unique days are consumed by being used,
they do not return, one cannot live them again here when one
has lived them there. I felt that it was towards the week that
would begin with the Monday on which the laundress was to
bring back the white waistcoat I had stained with ink that they
were hastening to absorb themselves, on emerging from that
ideal Time in which they did not yet exist—those two queens
of cities of which I was soon to be able, by the most thrilling
kind of geometry, to inscribe the domes and towers on a
page of my own life. But I was still only on the way to the
supreme pinnacle of happiness; I reached it finally (for not until
then did the revelation burst upon me that on the clattering
streets, reddened by the light reflected from Giorgione's frescoes, it was not, as I had continued to imagine despite so many
admonitions, men "majestic and terrible as the sea, bearing
armour that gleamed with bronze beneath the folds of their
blood-red cloaks" who would be walking in Venice next week,
on Easter eve, but that I myself might be the minute personage
whom, in an enlarged photograph of St. Mark's that had been
lent to me, the illustrator had portrayed, in a bowler hat, in
front of the portico) when I heard my father say: "It must be
pretty cold, still, on the Grand Canal; you'd do well, just in
case, to pack your winter greatcoat and your thick suit." At
these words I was raised to a sort of ecstasy; I felt myself—
something I had until then deemed impossible—to be penetrating indeed between those "rocks of amethyst, like a reef
in the Indian Ocean"; by a supreme muscular effort, far in
excess of my real strength, divesting myself, as of a shell that
served no purpose, of the air in my own room which surrounded me, I replaced it by an equal quantity of Venetian air,
that marine atmosphere, indescribable and peculiar as the

atmosphere of dreams, which my imagination had secreted in the name of Venice; I felt myself undergoing a miraculous disincarnation, which was at once accompanied by that vague desire to vomit which one feels when one has developed a very sore throat; and I had to be put to bed with a fever so persistent that the doctor declared not only that a visit now to Florence and Venice was absolutely out of the question, but that, even when I had completely recovered, I must for at least a year give up all idea of travelling and be kept from anything that was liable to excite me.

And alas, he also imposed a formal ban on my being allowed to go to the theatre to hear Berma. The sublime artist whose genius Bergotte had proclaimed might, by introducing me to something else that was perhaps as important and beautiful, have consoled me for not having been to Florence and Venice, for not going to Balbec. My parents had to be content with sending me every day to the Champs-Elysées, in the custody of a person who would see that I did not tire myself; this person being none other than Françoise, who had entered our service after the death of my aunt Léonie. Going to the Champs-Elysées I found unendurable. If only Bergotte had described the place in one of his books, I should no doubt have longed to get to know it, like so many things else of which a simulacrum had first found its way into my imagination. This breathed life into them, gave them a personality, and I sought then to rediscover them in reality; but in this public garden there was nothing that attached itself to my dreams.

One day, as I was bored with our usual place beside the roundabout, Françoise had taken me for an excursion—across the frontier guarded at regular intervals by the little bastions of the barley-sugar women—into those neighbouring but foreign regions where the faces of the passers-by were strange, where the goat-carriage went past; then she had gone back to collect her things from her chair that stood with its back to a shrubbery of laurels. While I waited for her I was pacing the broad lawn of meagre, close-cropped, sun-baked grass, dominated, at its far end, by a statue rising from a fountain, in front of which a little girl with reddish hair was playing battledore and shuttlecock, when from the path another little girl, who was putting on her coat and covering up her racquet, called out sharply: "Good-bye, Gilberte, I'm going home now; don't forget we're coming to you this evening, after dinner." The name Gilberte passed close by me, evoking all the more forcefully the girl whom it labelled in that it did not merely refer to her, as one speaks of someone in his absence, but was directly addressed to her; it passed thus close by me, in action so to speak, with a force that increased with the curve of its trajectory and the proximity of its target;—carrying in its wake, I could feel, the knowledge, the impressions concerning her to whom it was addressed that belonged not to me but to the friend who called it out, everything that, as she uttered the words, she recalled, or at least possessed in her memory, of their daily intimacy, of the visits that they paid to each other, of that unknown existence which was all the more inaccessible, all the more painful to me from being, conversely, so familiar, so tractable to this happy girl who let it brush past me without my being able to penetrate it, who flung it on the air with a light-hearted cry;—wafting through the air the exquisite emanation which it had distilled, by touching them with the utmost precision, from certain invisible points in Mlle Swann's life, from the evening to come, just as it would be, after dinner, at her home;—forming, on its celestial passage through the midst of the children and their nursemaids, a little cloud, delicately coloured, resembling one of those clouds that, billowing over a Poussin landscape, reflect minutely, like a cloud in the opera teeming with chariots and horses, some apparition of the life of the gods;—casting, finally, on that ragged grass, at the spot where it was at one and the same time a scrap of withered lawn and a moment in the afternoon of the fair battledore player (who continued to launch and retrieve her shuttlecock until a governess with a blue feather in her hat had called her away) a marvellous little band of light, the colour of heliotrope, impalpable as a reflection and superimposed like a carpet on which I could not help but drag my lingering, nostalgic and desecrating feet, while Françoise shouted: "Come on, button up your coat and let's clear off home!" and I remarked for the first time how common her speech was, and that she had, alas, no blue feather in her hat.

But would *she* come back to the Champs-Elysées? Next day she was not there; but I saw her on the following days, and spent all my time revolving round the spot where she played with her friends, to such effect that once, when they found that there were not enough of them to make up a prisoner's base, she sent one of them to ask me if I cared to complete their side, and from that day I played with her whenever she came. But this did not happen every day; there were days when she was prevented from coming by her lessons, by her catechism, by a tea-party, by the whole of that life, separated from my own, which twice only, condensed into the name Gilberte, I had felt pass so painfully close to me, in the hawthorn lane near Combray and on the grass of the Champs-Elysées. On such days she would tell us in advance that we would not be seeing her; if it was because of her lessons, she would say: "It's too tiresome, I shan't be able to come to-morrow; you'll all be enjoying yourselves here without me," with an air of regret which to some extent consoled me; if, on the other hand, she had been invited to a party, and I, not knowing this, asked her whether she was coming to play with us, she would reply: "I should jolly well hope not! I hope Mamma will let me go to my friend's." But on these days I did at least know that I would not see her, whereas on others, without any warning, her mother would take her shopping, and next day she would say: "Oh, yes! I went out with Mamma," as though it had been the most natural thing in the world, and not the greatest possible misfortune for someone else. There were also the days of bad weather on which her governess, afraid on her own account of the rain, would not bring Gilberte to the Champs-Elysées.

And so, if the sky was overcast, from early morning I would not cease to examine it, observing all the omens. If I saw the lady opposite putting on her hat beside her window, I would say to myself: "That lady is going out; so it must be weather in which one can go out. Why shouldn't Gilberte do the same as that lady?" But the weather would cloud over. My mother would say that it might clear again, that one burst of sunshine would be enough, but that more probably it would rain; and if

it rained, what was the use of going to the Champs-Elysées?
And so, from lunch-time onwards, my anxious eyes never left
the unsettled, clouded sky. It remained dark. The balcony in
front of the window was grey. Suddenly, on its sullen stone,
I would not exactly see a less leaden colour, but I would feel
as it were a striving towards a less leaden colour, the pulsation
of a hesitant ray that struggled to discharge its light. A moment later, the balcony was as pale and luminous as a pool
at dawn, and a thousand shadows from the iron-work of its
balustrade had alighted on it. A breath of wind would disperse
them, and the stone darkened again, but, as though they had
been tamed, they would return; imperceptibly the stone
whitened once more, and as in one of those uninterrupted
crescendos which, in music, at the end of an overture, carry
a single note to the supreme fortissimo by making it pass
rapidly through all the intermediate stages, I would see it reach
that fixed, unalterable gold of fine days, on which the clear-cut
shadow of the wrought iron of the balustrade was outlined in
black like some capricious vegetation, with a delicacy in the
delineation of its smallest details that seemed to indicate a
deliberate application, an artist's satisfaction, and with so much
relief, so velvety a bloom in the restfulness of its dark, feli-
citous masses that in truth those broad and leafy reflections on
that lake of sunshine seemed aware that they were pledges of
tranquillity and happiness.

Brief, fading ivy, climbing, fugitive flora!—the most colourless, the most depressing, to many minds, of all that creep on
walls or decorate windows; to me the dearest of them all ever
since the day when it appeared upon our balcony, like the very
shadow of the presence of Gilberte, who was perhaps already
in the Champs-Elysées, and as soon as I arrived there would
greet me with: "Let's begin at once; you're on my side"; frail,
swept away by a breath, but at the same time in harmony, not
with the season, but with the hour; promise of that immediate
happiness which the day will deny or fulfil, and thereby of the
one paramount immediate happiness, the happiness of love;
softer, warmer upon the stone even than moss; robust, a ray
of sunlight sufficing for it to spring into life and blossom into
joy, even in the heart of winter.

And even on those days when all other vegetation had disappeared, when the fine green hide which covered the trunks of the old trees was hidden beneath the snow, and, though the latter had ceased to fall, the sky was still too overcast for me to hope that Gilberte would venture out, then suddenly—inspiring my mother to say: "Look, it's quite fine now; I think you might perhaps try going to the Champs-Elysées after all"—on the mantle of snow that swathed the balcony, the sun would appear and weave a tracery of golden threads and black shadows. On one such day we found no one, or only a solitary little girl on the point of departure, who assured me that Gilberte was not coming. The chairs, deserted by the imposing but shivering assembly of governesses, stood empty. Alone, beside the lawn, sat a lady of uncertain age who came in all weathers, dressed always in an identical style, splendid and sombre, to make whose acquaintance I would at that time have sacrificed, had it lain in my power, all the greatest advantages and privileges of my future life. For Gilberte went up to greet her every day; she used to ask Gilberte for news of her "adorable mother"; and it struck me that, if I had known her, I should have been for Gilberte someone wholly different, someone who knew people in her parents' world. While her grandchildren played together at a little distance, she would sit and read the *Journal des Débats*, which she called "My old *Débats*," and with aristocratic affectation would say, speaking of the policeman or the woman who let the chairs, "My old friend the policeman," or "The chair-keeper and I, who are old friends."

Françoise found it too cold to stand about, so we walked to the Pont de la Concorde to see the Seine frozen over, which everyone, even children, approached fearlessly, as though it were an enormous whale, stranded, defenceless, and about to be cut up. We returned to the Champs-Elysées; I was growing sick with misery between the motionless roundabout and the white lawn, caught in the black network of the paths from which the snow had been cleared, while the statue that surmounted it held in its hand a long pendent icicle which seemed to explain its gesture. The old lady herself, having folded up her *Débats*, asked a passing nursemaid the time, thanking her

with "How very good of you!" then begged the road-sweeper
to tell her grandchildren to come, as she felt cold, adding: "A
thousand thanks. I am sorry to give you so much trouble!"
Suddenly the sky was rent in two; between the punch-and-
judy and the horses, against the opening horizon, I had just
seen, like a miraculous sign, Mademoiselle's blue feather. And
now Gilberte was running at full speed towards me, sparkling
and rosy beneath a cap trimmed with fur, animated by the cold,
her lateness and the desire for a game; shortly before she
reached me, she slid along the ice and, either to keep her
balance, or because it appeared to her graceful, or else pretending that she was on skates, it was with outstretched arms
that she smilingly advanced, as though to embrace me.
"Bravo! bravo! that's splendid; 'topping,' I should say, like
you—'sporting,' I suppose I ought to say, only I'm a hundred-
and-one, a woman of the old school," exclaimed the old lady,
uttering, on behalf of the voiceless Champs-Elysées, their
thanks to Gilberte for having come without letting herself be
frightened away by the weather. "You are like me, faithful at
all costs to our old Champs-Elysées. We're two brave souls!
You wouldn't believe me, I dare say, if I told you that I love
them, even like this. This snow (I know you'll laugh at me), it
makes me think of ermine!" And the old lady began to laugh
herself.

The first of these days—to which the snow, a symbol of the
powers that could deprive me of the sight of Gilberte, imparted the sadness of a day of separation, almost the aspect of
a day of departure, because it changed the outward form and
almost forbade the use of the customary scene of our only
encounters, now altered, covered, as it were, in dust-sheets—
that day, none the less, marked a stage in the progress of my
love, for it was like a first sorrow that we shared together.
There were only our two selves of our little company, and to
be thus alone with her was not merely like a beginning of
intimacy, but also on her part—as though she had come there
solely to please me in such weather—it seemed to me as touching as if, on one of those days when she had been invited to a
party, she had given it up in order to come to join me in the
Champs-Elysées; I acquired more confidence in the vitality, in

the future of a friendship which could remain so enduring amid the torpor, the solitude, the decay of our surroundings; and while she stuffed snowballs down my neck, I smiled lovingly at what seemed to me at once a predilection that she showed for me in thus tolerating me as her travelling companion in this new and wintry land, and a sort of loyalty which she cherished for me through evil times. Presently, one after another, like shyly hopping sparrows, her friends arrived, black against the snow. We got ready to play and, since this day which had begun so sadly was destined to end in joy, as I went up, before the game started, to the friend with the sharp voice whom I had heard the first day calling Gilberte by name, she said to me: "No, no, I'm sure you'd much rather be in Gilberte's camp; besides, look, she's signalling to you." She was in fact summoning me to cross the snowy lawn to her camp, to "take the field," which the sun, by casting over it a rosy gleam, the metallic lustre of old and worn brocades, had turned into a Field of the Cloth of Gold.

This day which I had so dreaded was, as it happened, one of the few on which I was not unduly wretched.

For, although I now no longer thought of anything save not to let a single day pass without seeing Gilberte (so much so that once, when my grandmother had not come home by dinner-time, I could not resist the instinctive reflection that if she had been run over in the street and killed, I should not for some time be allowed to play in the Champs-Elysées; when one is in love one has no love left for anyone) yet those moments which I spent in her company, for which I had waited so impatiently all night and morning, for which I had quivered with excitement, to which I would have sacrificed everything else in the world, were by no means happy moments; and well did I know it, for they were the only moments in my life on which I concentrated a scrupulous, unflagging attention, and yet could not discover in them one atom of pleasure.

All the time I was away from Gilberte, I felt the need to see her, because, constantly trying to picture her in my mind, I ended up by being unable to do so, and by no longer knowing precisely what my love represented. Besides, she had never yet told me that she loved me. Far from it: she had often

boasted that she knew other boys whom she preferred to myself, that I was a good companion, with whom she was always
willing to play, although I was too absent-minded, not attentive enough to the game; indeed, she had often shown signs of
apparent coldness towards me which might have shaken my
faith that I was for her a person different from the rest, had
that faith been founded upon a love that Gilberte felt for me
and not, as was the case, upon the love I felt for her, which
strengthened its resistance to the assaults of doubt by making
it depend entirely on the manner in which I was obliged by
an internal compulsion to think of Gilberte. But I myself had
not yet ventured to declare my feelings towards her. True, on
every page of my exercise-books I wrote out, in endless repetition, her name and address, but at the sight of those vague
lines which I traced without her thinking of me any the more
on that account, which made her take up so much apparent
space around me without her being any the more involved in
my life, I felt discouraged, because they spoke to me, not of
Gilberte, who would never so much as see them, but of my
own desire, which they seemed to show me in its true colours,
as something purely personal, unreal, tedious and ineffectual.
The important thing was that we should see each other,
Gilberte and I, and should have an opportunity of making a
mutual avowal of our love which, until then, would not officially (so to speak) have begun. Doubtless the various reasons
which made me so impatient to see her would have appeared
less urgent to a grown man. As life goes on, we acquire such
adroitness in the cultivation of our pleasures, that we content
ourselves with the pleasure we derive from thinking of a
woman, as I thought of Gilberte, without troubling ourselves
to ascertain whether the image corresponds to the reality,
and also with the pleasure of loving her without needing to
be sure that she loves us too; or again that we renounce the
pleasure of confessing our inclination for her, so as to preserve and enhance her inclination for us, like those Japanese
gardeners who, to obtain one perfect blossom, will sacrifice
several others. But at the period when I was in love with Gilberte, I still believed that Love did really exist outside ourselves; that, allowing us at the most to surmount the obstacles

in our way, it offered its blessings in an order to which we were not free to make the least alteration; it seemed to me that if I had, on my own initiative, substituted for the sweetness of avowal a pretence of indifference, I should not only have been depriving myself of one of the joys for which I most longed, but fabricating, quite arbitrarily, a love that was artificial and valueless, that bore no relation to the true one, whose mysterious and fore-ordained ways I should thus have ceased to follow.

But when I arrived in the Champs-Elysées,—and, as at first sight it appeared, was in a position to confront my love, so as to make it undergo the necessary modifications, with its living cause, independent of myself—as soon as I was in the presence of that Gilberte Swann on the sight of whom I had counted to revive the images that my tired memory could no longer recapture, of that Gilberte Swann with whom I had played the day before, and whom I had just been prompted to greet and recognise by a blind instinct like that which, when we are walking, sets one foot before the other without giving us time to think what we are doing, then at once it became as though she and the little girl who was the object of my dreams had been two different people. If, for instance, I had retained in my memory overnight two fiery eyes above plump and rosy cheeks, Gilberte's face would now offer me with overpowering insistence something that I distinctly had not remembered, a certain sharp tapering of the nose which, instantaneously associating itself with certain other features, assumed the importance of those characteristics which in natural history define a species, and transformed her into a little girl of the kind that have pointed noses. While I was getting ready to take advantage of this longed-for moment to effect, on the basis of the image of Gilberte which I had prepared beforehand but which had now gone from my head, the adjustment that would enable me, during the long hours I must spend alone, to be certain that it was indeed her that I had in mind, that it was indeed my love for her that I was gradually putting together as one composes a book, she passed me a ball; and, like the idealist philosopher whose body takes account of the external world in the reality of which his intellect declines to

believe, the same self which had made me greet her before I
had identified her now urged me to seize the ball that she
handed to me (as though she were a companion with whom I
had come to play, and not a sister-soul with whom I had come
to be united), made me, out of decorum, address a thousand and
one polite and trivial remarks to her until the time came when
she had to go, and so prevented me either from keeping a
silence during which I might at last have laid hands once more
on the urgent truant image, or from uttering the words which
might have brought about the decisive progress in the course
of our love the hope of which I was always obliged to postpone until the following afternoon.

It did, however, make some progress. One day, we had
gone with Gilberte to the stall of our own special vendor,
who was always particularly nice to us, since it was to her that
M. Swann used to send for his gingerbread, of which, for
reasons of health (he suffered from ethnic eczema and from
the constipation of the prophets), he consumed a great deal,
and Gilberte pointed out to me with a laugh two little boys
who were like the little artist and the little naturalist in the
children's story-books. For one of them would not have a red
stick of barley sugar because he preferred the purple, while
the other, with tears in his eyes, refused a plum which his
nurse was buying for him because, as he finally explained in
passionate tones: "I want the other plum; it's got a worm in it!"
I purchased two ha'penny marbles. With admiring eyes I
gazed at the agate marbles, luminous and imprisoned in a
bowl apart, which seemed precious to me because they were
as fair and smiling as little girls, and because they cost six-
pence each. Gilberte, who was given a great deal more pocket
money than I ever had, asked me which I thought the prettiest.
They had the transparency and mellowness of life itself. I
would not have had her sacrifice a single one of them. I should
have liked her to be able to buy them, to liberate them all.
Still, I pointed out one that had the same colour as her eyes.
Gilberte took it, turned it round until it shone with a ray of
gold, fondled it, paid its ransom, but at once handed me her
captive, saying: "Here, it's for you. Keep it as a souvenir."
Another time, being still obsessed by the desire to hear

Berma in classic drama, I had asked her whether she had a copy of a booklet in which Bergotte spoke of Racine, and which was now out of print. She had asked me to let her know the exact title of it, and that evening I had sent her an express letter, writing on its envelope the name, Gilberte Swann, which I had so often traced in my exercise-book. The next day she brought me the booklet, for which she had instituted a search, in a parcel tied with mauve ribbon and sealed with white wax. "You see, it's what you asked me for," she said, taking from her muff the express letter that I had sent her. But in the address on the pneumatic message[15]—which, only yesterday, was nothing, was merely a *petit bleu* that I had written, and which, after a messenger had delivered it to Gilberte's porter and a servant had taken it up to her room, had become that priceless thing, one of the *petits bleus* that she had received in the course of the day—I had difficulty in recognising the futile, straggling lines of my own handwriting beneath the circles stamped on it at the post-office, the inscriptions added in pencil by a postman, signs of effectual realisation, seals of the external world, violet bands symbolical of life itself, which for the first time came to espouse, to maintain, to lift, to gladden my dream.

And there was another day when she said to me: "You know, you may call me 'Gilberte.' In any case, I'm going to call you by your first name. It's too silly not to." Yet she continued for a while to address me by the more formal "*vous*," and when I drew her attention to this, she smiled and, composing, constructing a phrase like those that are put into the grammar-books of foreign languages with no other object than to teach us to make use of a new word, ended it with my Christian name. Recalling, some time later, what I had felt at the time, I distinguished the impression of having been held for a moment in her mouth, myself, naked, without any of the social attributes which belonged equally to her other play-mates and, when she used my surname, to my parents, accessories of which her lips—by the effort she made, a little after her father's manner, to articulate the words to which she wished to give a special emphasis—had the air of stripping, of divesting me, like the skin from a fruit of which one can swallow only

the pulp, while her glance, adapting itself to the same new
degree of intimacy as her speech, fell on me also more directly
and testified to the consciousness, the pleasure, even the
gratitude that it felt by accompanying itself with a smile.

But at the actual moment I was unable to appreciate the
value of these new pleasures. They were given, not by the
little girl whom I loved to the "me" who loved her, but by
the other, the one with whom I used to play, to that other
"me" who possessed neither the memory of the true Gilberte,
nor the inalienably committed heart which alone could have
known the value of a happiness which it alone had desired.
Even after I had returned home I did not savour these pleasures, since every day the necessity which made me hope that
on the morrow I should arrive at a clear, calm, happy contemplation of Gilberte, that she would at last confess her love for
me, explaining why she had been obliged hitherto to conceal
it from me, that same necessity forced me to regard the past
as of no account, to look ahead of me only, to consider the
small favours she had granted me not in themselves and as if
they were self-sufficient, but as fresh rungs of the ladder on
which I might set my feet, which would enable me to advance
one step further towards the final attainment of that happiness
which I had not yet encountered.

If at times she showed me these marks of affection, she
pained me also by seeming not to be pleased to see me, and
this happened often on the very days on which I had most
counted for the realisation of my hopes. I was sure that Gilberte was coming to the Champs-Elysées, and I felt an elation
which seemed merely the anticipation of a great happiness
when—going into the drawing-room in the morning to kiss
Mamma, who was already dressed to go out, the coils of her
black hair elaborately built up, and her beautiful plump white
hands fragrant still with soap—I had been apprised, on seeing
a column of dust standing up by itself in the air above the
piano, and on hearing a barrel-organ playing beneath the
window *En revenant de la revue,* that the winter had received,
until nightfall, an unexpected, radiant visit from a day of
spring. While we sat at lunch, the lady opposite, by opening her window, had sent packing in the twinkling of an eye

from beside my chair—sweeping at one bound across the whole width of our dining-room—a sunbeam which had settled down there for its midday rest and returned to continue it a moment later. At school, during the one o'clock lesson, the sun made me sick with impatience and boredom as it trailed a golden glow across my desk, like an invitation to festivities at which I could not myself arrive before three o'clock, until the moment when Françoise came to fetch me at the school-gate and we made our way towards the Champs-Elysées through streets bejewelled with sunlight, dense with people, over which the balconies, detached by the sun and made vaporous, seemed to float in front of the houses like clouds of gold. Alas! in the Champs-Elysées I found no Gilberte; she had not yet arrived. Motionless on the lawn nurtured by the invisible sun which, here and there, kindled to a flame the point of a blade of grass, while the pigeons that had alighted upon it had the appearance of ancient sculptures which the gardener's pick had heaved to the surface of a hallowed soil, I stood with my eyes fixed on the horizon, expecting at every moment to see Gilberte's form, following that of her governess, appearing from behind the statue that seemed to be holding out the glistening child it carried to receive the sun's benediction. The old lady who read the *Débats* was sitting on her chair, in her invariable place, and had just accosted a park attendant with a friendly wave of her hand as she exclaimed "What a lovely day!" And when the chair-keeper came up to collect her fee, with an infinity of simpering affectations she folded the ticket away inside her glove, as though it had been a posy of flowers for which she had sought, in gratitude to the donor, the most becoming place upon her person. When she had found it, she performed a circular movement with her neck, straightened her boa, and fastened upon the collector, as she showed her the edge of a yellow paper that stuck out over her bare wrist, the bewitching smile with which a woman says to a young man, pointing to her bosom: "You see I'm wearing your roses!"

I dragged Françoise, in the hope of meeting Gilberte half-way, as far as the Arc de Triomphe; we did not meet her, and I was returning towards the lawn convinced, now, that she

was not coming, when, in front of the roundabout, the little
girl with the sharp voice flung herself upon me: "Quick, quick,
Gilberte's been here a quarter of an hour. She's going soon.
We've been waiting for you to make up a prisoner's base."

While I had been going up the Avenue des Champs-Elysées,
Gilberte had arrived by the Rue Boissy-d'Anglas, Mademoiselle having taken advantage of the fine weather to do some
shopping for her; and M. Swann was coming to fetch his
daughter. And so it was my fault; I ought not to have strayed
from the lawn; for one never knew for certain from what
direction Gilberte would appear, and whether she would be
early or late, and this perpetual tension succeeded in making
more thrilling not only the entire Champs-Elysées and the
whole span of the afternoon, like a vast expanse of space and
time on every point and at every moment of which it was
possible that Gilberte's form might appear, but also that
form itself, since behind that form I felt that there lay concealed the reason why it had flashed into my presence at four
o'clock instead of at half-past two, crowned with a party hat
instead of a playtime beret, in front of the Ambassadeurs and
not between the two puppet-shows, I divined one of those
occupations in which I might not follow Gilberte and which
forced her to go out or stay at home, I was in contact with the
mystery of her unknown life. It was this mystery, too, that
troubled me when, running at the sharp-voiced girl's bidding
to begin our game without further delay, I saw Gilberte, so
brusque and informal with us, making a curtsey to the old
lady of the *Débats* (who acknowledged it with "What a lovely
sun! You'd think there was a fire burning") and speaking to
her with a shy smile, with an air of constraint which called to
my mind the other little girl that Gilberte must be when at
home with her parents, or with friends of her parents or paying calls, in the whole of that other existence of hers which
eluded me. But of that existence no one gave me so strong an
impression as did M. Swann, who came a little later to fetch
his daughter. For he and Mme Swann—inasmuch as their
daughter lived with them, and her lessons, her games, her
friendships depended upon them—contained for me, like
Gilberte, perhaps even more than Gilberte, as befitted gods

with an all-powerful control over her, in whom it must have had its source, an undefined, an inaccessible quality of melancholy charm. Everything that concerned them was the object of so constant a preoccupation on my part that the days on which, as on this day, M. Swann (whom I had seen so often in the past without his having aroused my curiosity, when he was still on good terms with my parents) came to fetch Gilberte from the Champs-Elysées, once the violent throbbing of my heart provoked by the appearance of his grey hat and hooded cape had subsided, the sight of him still impressed me as might that of an historic personage about whom one has just been reading a series of books and the minutest details of whose life and person intrigue us. His relations with the Comte de Paris, which, when I heard them discussed at Combray, had left me indifferent, became now in my eyes something to be marvelled at, as if no one else had ever known the House of Orleans; they made him stand out vividly against the vulgar background of pedestrians of different classes who encumbered that particular path in the Champs-Elysées, in the midst of whom I admired his condescending to figure without claiming any special deference, which as it happened none of them dreamed of paying him, so profound was the incognito in which he was wrapped.

He responded politely to the salutations of Gilberte's playmates, even to mine, for all that he was no longer on good terms with my family, but without appearing to know me. (This reminded me that he had seen me quite often in the country; a memory which I had retained, but kept out of sight, because, since I had seen Gilberte again, Swann had become to me pre-eminently her father, and no longer the Combray Swann; since the ideas to which I now connected his name were different from the ideas in the system of which it was formerly comprised, ideas which I no longer utilised when I had occasion to think of him, he had become a new, another person; nevertheless, I attached him by an artificial, secondary and transversal thread to our former guest; and since nothing had henceforth any value for me except so far as my love might profit by it, it was with a spasm of shame and of regret at not being able to erase them that I recalled the years in

which, in the eyes of this same Swann who was at this moment
before me in the Champs-Elysées and to whom, fortunately,
Gilberte had perhaps not mentioned my name, I had so often,
in the evenings, made myself ridiculous by sending to ask
Mamma to come upstairs to my room to say good-night to
me, while she was drinking coffee with him and my father
and my grandparents at the table in the garden.) He told Gilberte that she had his permission to play one game, that he
could wait for a quarter of an hour; and, sitting down just
like anyone else on an iron chair, paid for his ticket with that
hand which Philippe VII had so often held in his, while we
began our game upon the lawn, scattering the pigeons whose
beautiful, iridescent bodies (shaped like hearts and, as it were,
the lilacs of the feathered kingdom) took refuge as in so many
sanctuaries, one on the great stone basin, to which its beak,
as it disappeared below the rim, imparted the gesture and assigned the purpose of offering in abundance the fruit or grain
at which it appeared to be pecking, another on the head of the
statue, which it seemed to crown with one of those enamelled
objects whose polychrome varies the monotony of the stone
in certain classical works, and with an attribute which, when
the goddess bears it, earns her a particular epithet and makes
of her, as a different Christian name makes of a mortal, a new
divinity.

On one of these sunny days which had failed to fulfil my
hopes, I could not conceal my disappointment from Gilberte.

"I had so many things to ask you," I said to her; "I thought
that to-day was going to mean so much in our friendship. And
no sooner have you come than you go away! Try to come early
to-morrow, so that I can talk to you."

Her face lit up and she jumped for joy as she answered:
"To-morrow, you may depend upon it, my dear boy, I shan't
be coming. I've got a big tea-party. The day after to-morrow
I'm going to a friend's house to watch the arrival of King
Theodosius from the window—won't that be splendid?—and
the day after that I'm going to *Michel Strogoff*, and then it will
soon be Christmas and the New Year holidays! Perhaps they'll
take me to the Riviera—wouldn't that be nice? though I should
miss the Christmas-tree here. Anyhow, if I do stay in Paris, I

shan't be coming here, because I shall be out paying calls with Mamma. Good-bye—there's Papa calling me."

I returned home with Françoise through the streets that were still gay with sunshine, as on the evening of a holiday when the merriment is over. I could scarcely drag my legs along.

"I'm not surprised," said Françoise, "it's not the right weather for the time of year; it's much too warm. Oh dear, oh dear, to think of all the poor sick people there must be everywhere. It's like as if everything's topsy-turvy up there too."

I repeated to myself, stifling my sobs, the words in which Gilberte had given utterance to her joy at the prospect of not coming back for a long time to the Champs-Elysées. But already the charm with which, by the mere act of thinking, my mind was filled as soon as it thought of her, and the special, unique position, however painful, in which I was inevitably placed in relation to Gilberte by the inner constraint of a mental habit, had begun to lend a romantic aura even to that mark of her indifference, and in the midst of my tears my lips shaped themselves into a smile which was simply the timid adumbration of a kiss. And when the time came for the postman to arrive I said to myself, that evening as on every other: "I'm going to get a letter from Gilberte; she's going to tell me at last that she has never ceased to love me, and explain to me the mysterious reason why she has been forced to conceal it from me until now, to pretend to be able to be happy without seeing me, the reason why she has assumed the form of the other Gilberte who is simply a playmate."

Every evening I would beguile myself by imagining this letter, believing that I was actually reading it, reciting each of its sentences in turn. Suddenly I would stop in alarm. I had realised that if I was to receive a letter from Gilberte, it could not, in any case, be this letter, since it was I myself who had just composed it. And from then on I would strive to divert my thoughts from the words which I should have liked her to write to me, for fear that, by voicing them, I should be excluding just those words,—the dearest, the most desired—from the field of possibilities. Even if, by some improbable coincidence, it had been precisely the letter of my invention that Gilberte addressed to me of her own accord, recognising my own work

in it I should not have had the impression that I was receiving
something that had not originated from me, something real,
something new, a happiness external to my mind, independent
of my will, a true gift of love.

Meanwhile, I re-read a page which, although it had not been
written to me by Gilberte, at least came to me from her, that
page of Bergotte's on the beauty of the old myths whence
Racine drew his inspiration, which (with the agate marble) I
always kept close at hand. I was touched by my friend's kindness in having procured the book for me; and as everyone
needs to find reasons for his passion, to the extent of being glad
to recognise in the loved one qualities which (he has learned
from literature or conversation) are worthy of love, to the
extent of assimilating them by imitation and making them
additional reasons for his love, even though these qualities are
diametrically opposed to those his love would have sought
after as long as it was spontaneous—as Swann, before my day,
had sought to establish the aesthetic basis of Odette's beauty—
I, who had at first loved Gilberte, from Combray onwards, on
account of all the unknown element in her life in which I
longed to be immersed, reincarnated, discarding my own as a
thing of no account, I thought now, as of an inestimable
privilege, that of this too familiar, despised life of mine
Gilberte might one day become the humble servant, the kindly
and comforting collaborator, who in the evenings, helping me
in my work, would collate for me the texts of rare pamphlets.
As for Bergotte, that infinitely wise, almost divine old man,
because of whom I had first loved Gilberte, before I had even
seen her, now it was above all for Gilberte's sake that I loved
him. With as much pleasure as the pages that he had written
about Racine I studied the wrapper, folded under the great
white seals of wax tied with festoons of mauve ribbon, in
which she had brought them to me. I kissed the agate marble,
which was the better part of my love's heart, the part that was
not frivolous but faithful, and which, for all that it was
adorned with the mysterious charm of Gilberte's life, dwelt
close beside me, inhabited my room, shared my bed. But the
beauty of that stone, and the beauty also of those pages of Bergotte which I was glad to associate with the idea of my love

for Gilberte, as if, in the moments when it seemed no more than a void, they gave it a kind of consistency, were, I perceived, anterior to that love and in no way resembled it; their elements had been determined by the writer's talent or the laws of mineralogy before ever Gilberte had known me; nothing in book or stone would have been different if Gilberte had not loved me, and nothing, consequently, authorised me to read in them a message of happiness. And while my love, incessantly waiting for the morrow to bring the avowal of Gilberte's for me, destroyed, unravelled every evening the ill-done work of the day, in some shadowed part of my being an unknown seamstress refused to abandon the discarded threads, but collected and rearranged them, without any thought of pleasing me or of toiling for my happiness, in the different order which she gave to all her handiwork. Showing no special interest in my love, not beginning by deciding that I was loved, she gathered together those of Gilberte's actions that had seemed to me inexplicable and her faults which I had excused. Then, one and all, they took on a meaning. It seemed to tell me, this new arrangement, that when I saw Gilberte, instead of coming to the Champs-Elysées, going to a party, or going shopping with her governess, or preparing for an absence that would extend over the New Year holidays, I was wrong in thinking: "It's because she's frivolous or docile." For she would have ceased to be either if she had loved me, and if she had been forced to obey, it would have been with the same despair in her heart that I felt on the days when I did not see her. It showed me further, this new arrangement, that I ought after all to know what it was to love, since I loved Gilberte; it drew my attention to the constant anxiety that I had to shine in her eyes, by reason of which I tried to persuade my mother to buy Françoise a waterproof coat and a hat with a blue feather, or, better still, to stop sending me to the Champs-Elysées in the company of a servant with whom I blushed to be seen (to which my mother replied that I was unjust to Françoise, that she was an excellent woman and devoted to us all), and also that exclusive need to see Gilberte, the result of which was that, months in advance, I could think of nothing else but how to find out when she would be leaving Paris and where she was

going, feeling that the most attractive country in the world
would be a place of exile if she was not to be there, and asking
only to be allowed to stay for ever in Paris so long as I might
see her in the Champs-Elysées; and it had little difficulty in
making me see that neither my anxiety nor my need could be
justified by anything in Gilberte's conduct. She, on the contrary, appreciated her governess, without troubling herself over
what I might choose to think about her. It seemed quite
natural to her not to come to the Champs-Elysées if she had to
go shopping with Mademoiselle, delightful if she had to go
out with her mother. And even supposing that she had allowed
me to spend my holidays in the same place as herself, when it
came to choosing that place she would consider her parents'
wishes, and the various amusements of which she had been
told, and not at all that it should be the place to which my
family were proposing to send me. When she assured me (as
she sometimes did) that she liked me less than some other of her
friends, less than she had liked me the day before, because by
my clumsiness I had made her side lose a game, I would ask
her forgiveness, would beg her to tell me what I must do in
order that she should begin to like me again as much as, or
more than anyone else; I wanted her to tell me that that was
already the case, I besought her as though she were capable of
modifying her affection for me as she or I chose, in order to
please me, simply by the words she would utter, as my good or
bad conduct should deserve. Did I not then know that what I
felt for her depended neither upon her actions nor upon my will?

It showed me finally, the new arrangement devised by the
invisible seamstress, that, if we find ourselves hoping that the
actions of a person who has hitherto caused us pain may prove
not to have been sincere, they shed in their wake a light which
our hopes are powerless to extinguish and to which we must
address ourselves, rather than to our hopes, if we are to know
what will be that person's actions on the morrow.

My love listened to these new counsels; they persuaded it
that the morrow would not be different from all the days that
had gone before; that Gilberte's feeling for me, too long
established now to be capable of alteration, was indifference;
that in my friendship with Gilberte, it was I alone who loved.

"It's true," my love answered, "there is nothing more to be made of that friendship. It will not alter now." And so, as from the very next day (or from the next public holiday, if there was one in the offing, or an anniversary, or the New Year, perhaps—one of those days which are not like other days, on which time starts afresh, casting aside the heritage of the past, declining its legacy of sorrows) I would ask Gilberte to terminate our old friendship and to join me in laying the foundations of a new one.

* * *

I always had within reach a plan of Paris which, because I could see on it the street in which M. and Mme Swann lived, seemed to me to contain a secret treasure. And for pure pleasure, as well as from a sort of chivalrous loyalty, on no matter what pretext I would utter the name of that street until my father, not being, like my mother and grandmother, apprised of my love, would ask me: "But why are you always talking about that street? There's nothing wonderful about it. It's a very agreeable street to live in because it's only a few minutes' walk from the Bois, but there are a dozen other streets to which the same applies."

I went out of my way to find occasions for my parents to pronounce Swann's name. In my own mind, of course, I never ceased to murmur it; but I needed also to hear its exquisite sound, to have others play to me that music the voiceless rendering of which did not suffice me. Moreover, the name Swann, with which I had for so long been familiar, had now become for me (as happens with certain aphasiacs in the case of the most ordinary words) a new name. It was for ever present in my mind, which could not, however, grow accustomed to it. I analysed it, I spelt it; its orthography came to me as a surprise. And together with its familiarity it had simultaneously lost its innocence. The pleasure that I derived from the sound of it I felt to be so sinful that it seemed to me as though the others read my thoughts and changed the conversation if I tried to guide it in that direction. I fell back on subjects which still concerned Gilberte, I repeated over and over again the same words, and although I knew that they were only words—words uttered in her absence, which she could not hear, words without virtue in themselves, repeating what were facts but powerless to modify them—it seemed to me none the less that by dint of thus manipulating, stirring up everything that had reference to Gilberte, I might perhaps elicit from it something that would bring me happiness. I told my parents again that Gilberte was fond of her governess, as if that proposition, voiced for the hundredth time, would at last have the effect of making Gilberte suddenly burst into the room, come to live with us for ever. I had already sung the praises of the old lady who read the *Débats* (I had hinted to my parents that she was an ambassadress, if not actually a Highness) and I continued to descant on her beauty, her splendour, her nobility, until the day I mentioned that, from what I had heard Gilberte call her, she appeared to be a Mme Blatin.

"Oh, now I know who you mean," exclaimed my mother, while I felt myself blushing with shame. "On guard! on guard! —as your poor grandfather would have said. So she's the one you find so beautiful! Why, she's perfectly horrible, and always has been. She's the widow of a bailiff. Don't you remember, when you were little, all the trouble I used to go to in order to avoid her at your gym lessons, where she was always trying to get hold of me—I didn't know the woman, of course—to tell me that you were 'much too beautiful for a boy.' She has always had a mania for getting to know people, and she really must be a sort of maniac, as I've always thought, if she does in fact know Mme Swann. For even if she does come from a very common background, I've never heard anything against her morals. But she must always be forcing herself upon strangers. She really is a horrible woman, frightfully vulgar, and an affected old humbug besides."

As for Swann, in order to try to resemble him, I spent all my time at table pulling my nose and rubbing my eyes. My father would exclaim: "The child's a perfect idiot, he'll make himself quite hideous." More than anything else I should have liked to be as bald as Swann. He seemed to me a being so extraordinary that I found it miraculous that people of my acquaintance knew him too and in the course of the day might run into him. And once my mother, while she was telling us, as she did every evening at dinner, where she had been and what she had done that afternoon, merely by the words: "By the way, guess whom I saw in the Trois Quartiers—at the umbrella counter—Swann!" brought forth in the midst of her narrative (an arid desert to me) a mystic blossom. What a melancholy pleasure to learn that Swann, that very afternoon, his supernatural form silhouetted against the crowd, had gone to buy an umbrella. Among the events of the day, great and small, but all equally insignificant, that one alone aroused in me those peculiar vibrations by which my love for Gilberte was perpetually stirred. My father complained that I took no interest in anything because I did not listen while he was speaking of the political consequences that might follow the visit of King Theodosius, at the moment in France as the nation's guest and (it was claimed) ally. But how I longed, on the other hand, to know whether Swann had been wearing his hooded cape!

"Did you speak to him?" I asked.

"Why, of course I did," answered my mother, who always seemed afraid lest, were she to admit that we were not on the best of terms with Swann, people would seek to reconcile us more than she cared for, in view of the existence of Mme Swann, whom she did not wish to know. "It was he who came up and spoke to me. I hadn't seen him."

"Then you haven't quarrelled?"

"Quarrelled? What on earth makes you think we've quarrelled?" she briskly parried, as though I had cast doubt on the fiction of her friendly relations with Swann, and tried to bring about a reconciliation.

"He might be cross with you for never asking him here."

"One isn't obliged to ask everyone to one's house, you know. Has he ever asked me to his? I don't know his wife."

"But he often used to come at Combray."

"Yes, I know he used to come at Combray, and now, in Paris, he has other things to do, and so have I. But I can promise you, we didn't look in the least like people who had quarrelled. We were kept waiting there for some time, while they brought him his parcel. He asked after you; he told me you played with his daughter," my mother went on, dazzling me with the stupendous revelation that I existed in Swann's mind; even more, that I existed in so complete, so material a form that when I stood before him, trembling with love, in the Champs-Elysées, he had known my name, and who my mother was, and had been able to bring together around my capacity as his daughter's playmate certain facts with regard to my grandparents and their connections, the place where we lived, and certain details of our past life which were perhaps unknown even to me. But my mother did not seem to have discovered a particular charm in that counter at the Trois Quartiers where she had represented to Swann, at the moment when he caught sight of her, a definite person with whom he had sufficient memories in common to impel him to go up to her and greet her.

Nor did either she or my father seem to find, in speaking of Swann's family, or the title of honorary stockbroker, a pleasure that surpassed all others. My imagination had isolated and hallowed in social Paris a certain family, just as it had set apart in structural Paris a certain house, whose entrance it had sculpted and its windows bejewelled. But these ornaments I alone had eyes to see. Just as my father and mother regarded the house in which Swann lived as identical with the other houses built at the same period in the neighbourhood of the Bois, so Swann's family seemed to them to be in the same category as many other families of stockbrokers. They judged it more or less favourably according to the degree to which it shared in merits that were common to the rest of the universe, and saw nothing unique in it. On the contrary, what they appreciated in it they found in equal if not superior degree elsewhere. And so, after admitting that the house was in a good position, they would go on to speak of some other house that was in a better, but had nothing to do with Gilberte, or of financiers who were a cut above her grandfather; and if they had appeared for a moment to be of my opinion, that was through a misunderstanding which was very soon dispelled. For in order to distinguish in everything that surrounded Gilberte an indefinable quality analogous in the world of the emotions to what in the world of colours is called infra-red, my parents would have needed that supplementary sense with which love had temporarily endowed me.

On the days when Gilberte had warned me that she would not be coming to the Champs-Elysées, I tried to arrange my walks so that I should be brought into some kind of contact with her. Sometimes I would take Françoise on a pilgrimage to the house in which the Swanns lived, making her repeat to me unendingly all that she had learned from the governess with regard to Mme Swann. "It seems she's got great faith in medals. She wouldn't think of starting on a journey if she'd heard an owl hoot, or a sort of tick-tock in the wall, or if she'd seen a cat at midnight, or if the furniture had creaked. Oh yes! she's a most religious lady, she is!" I was so madly in love with Gilberte that if, on our way, I caught sight of their old butler taking the dog out, my emotion would bring me to a standstill and I would gaze at his white whiskers with eyes filled with passion. Françoise would say: "What's wrong with you now, child?"

Then we would continue on our way until we reached their gateway, where a porter, different from every other porter in the world and saturated, down to the very braid on his livery, with the same melancholy charm that I had felt to be latent in the name of Gilberte, looked as though he knew that I was one of those whose natural unworthiness would for ever prohibit from penetrating into the mysteries of the life which it was his duty to guard and upon which the ground-floor windows appeared conscious of being protectingly closed, with far less resemblance, between the nobly sweeping arches of their muslin curtains, to any other windows in the world than to Gilberte's glancing eyes. On other days we would go along the boulevards, and I would take up a position at the corner of the Rue Duphot, along which I had heard that Swann was often to be seen passing on his way to his dentist; and my imagination so far differentiated Gilberte's father from the rest of humanity, his presence in the midst of the real world introduced into it such an element of wonder, that even before we reached the Madeleine I would be trembling with emotion at the thought that I was approaching a street from which that supernatural apparition might at any moment burst upon me unawares.

But most often of all—on days when I was not to see

Gilberte—as I had heard that Mme Swann went for a walk or a drive almost every day in the Allée des Acacias, round the big lake, and in the Allée de la Reine Marguerite, I would lead Françoise to the Bois de Boulogne. It was to me like one of those zoological gardens in which one sees assembled together a variety of flora and contrasted landscapes, where from a hill one passes to a grotto, a meadow, rocks, a stream, a pit, another hill, a marsh, but knows that they are there only to enable the hippopotamus, zebra, crocodile, rabbit, bear and heron to disport themselves in a natural or a picturesque setting; it, the Bois, equally complex, uniting a multitude of little worlds, distinct and separate—alternating a plantation of redwood trees and American oaks, like an experimental forest in Virginia, with a fir-wood by the edge of the lake, or a grove from which would suddenly emerge, in her raiment of soft fur, with the large, appealing eyes of a dumb animal, a hastening walker—was the Garden of Woman; and like the myrtle-alley in the *Aeneid*, planted for their delight with trees of one kind only, the Allée des Acacias was thronged with the famous beauties of the day. As, from a long way off, the sight of the jutting crag from which it dives into the pool thrills with joy the children who know that they are going to see the seal, so, long before I reached the acacias, their fragrance which, radiating all around, made one aware of the approach and the singularity of a vegetable personality at once powerful and soft, then, as I drew near, the glimpsed summit of their lightly tossing foliage, in its easy grace, its coquettish outline, its delicate fabric, on which hundreds of flowers had swooped, like winged and throbbing colonies of precious insects, and finally their name itself, feminine, indolent, dulcet, made my heart beat, but with a social longing, like those waltzes which remind us only of the names of the fair dancers, called aloud as they enter the ballroom. I had been told that I should see in the alley certain women of fashion, who, in spite of their not all having husbands, were habitually mentioned in conjunction with Mme Swann, but most often by their professional names—their new names, when they had any, being but a sort of incognito, a veil which those who wished to speak of them were careful to draw aside in order to make themselves understood. Thinking that Beauty—in the order of feminine elegance—was governed by occult laws into the knowledge of which they had been initiated, and that they had the power to realise it, I accepted in advance like a revelation the appearance of their clothes, of their carriages and horses, of countless details in which I placed my faith as in an inner soul which gave the cohesion of a work of art to that ephemeral and shifting pageant. But it was Mme Swann whom I wished to see, and I waited for her to go past, as thrilled as though she were Gilberte, whose parents, impregnated, like everything that surrounded her, with her own special charm, excited in me as keen a passion as she did herself, indeed a still more painful agitation (since their point of contact with her was that intimate, that internal part of her life from which I was excluded), and furthermore (for I very soon learned, as we shall see in due course, that they did not like my playing with her) that feeling of veneration which we always have for those who hold, and exercise without restraint, the power to do us harm.

I assigned the first place in the order of aesthetic merit and of social grandeur to simplicity, when I saw Mme Swann on foot, in a "polonaise" of plain cloth, a little toque on her head trimmed with a pheasant's wing, a bunch of violets in her bosom, hastening along the Allée des Acacias as if it had been merely the shortest way back to her house, and acknowledging with a wink the greetings of the gentlemen in carriages who, recognising her figure at a distance, raised their hats to her and said to one another that there was never anyone so well turned out as she. But instead of simplicity it was to ostentation that I must assign the first place if, after I had compelled Françoise, who was worn out and complained that her feet were "killing" her, to stroll up and down with me for another hour, I saw at length emerging from the Porte Dauphine—figuring for me a royal dignity, the passage of a sovereign, an impression such as no real queen has ever since been able to give me, because my notion of their power has been less vague, more founded upon experience—borne along by the flight of a pair of fiery horses, slender and shapely as one sees them in the drawings of Constantin Guys, carrying on its box an enormous coachman furred like a cossack, and by his side a

diminutive groom like Toby, "the late Beaudenord's tiger," I
saw—or rather I felt its outlines engraved upon my heart by
a clean and poignant wound—a matchless victoria, built rather
high, and hinting, through the extreme modernity of its appointments, at the forms of an earlier day, in the depths of
which Mme Swann negligently reclined, her hair, now blonde
with one grey lock, encircled with a narrow band of flowers,
usually violets, from which floated down long veils, a lilac
parasol in her hand, on her lips an ambiguous smile in which I
read only the benign condescension of Majesty, though it was
pre-eminently the provocative smile of the courtesan, which
she graciously bestowed upon the men who greeted her. This
smile was in reality saying, to one: "Oh yes, I remember very
well; it was wonderful!" to another: "How I should have loved
to! It was bad luck!" to a third: "Yes, if you like! I must just
follow in the procession for a moment, then as soon as I can
I'll break away." When strangers passed a lazy smile still played
about her lips, as though in expectation or remembrance of
some friend, which made people say: "What a lovely woman!"
And for certain men only she had a sour, strained, shy, cold
smile which meant: "Yes, you old goat, I know that you've got
a tongue like a viper, that you can't keep quiet for a moment.
But do you suppose that I care what you say?" Coquelin
passed, holding forth among a group of listening friends, and
with a sweeping wave of his hand bade a theatrical good day
to the people in the carriages. But I thought only of Mme
Swann, and pretended not to have seen her yet, for I knew
that when she reached the pigeon-shooting ground she would
tell her coachmen to "break away" and to stop the carriage, so
that she might come back on foot. And on days when I felt
that I had the courage to pass close by her I would drag
Françoise off in that direction; until the moment came when I
saw Mme Swann, trailing behind her the long train of her lilac
skirt, dressed, as the populace imagine queens to be dressed,
in rich finery such as no other woman wore, occasionally looking down at the handle of her parasol, and paying scant attention to the passers-by, as though her sole object was to take
exercise, without thinking that she was being observed and
that every head was turned towards her. Sometimes, however,

when she had looked back to call her dog, she would cast, almost imperceptibly, a sweeping glance round about her.

Even those who did not know her were warned by something exceptional, something exorbitant about her—or perhaps by a telepathic suggestion such as would move an ignorant audience to a frenzy of applause at moments when Berma was being "sublime"—that she must be someone well known. They would ask one another, "Who is she?", or sometimes would interrogate a passing stranger, or would make a mental note of how she was dressed as an indication for some better-informed friend who would at once enlighten them. Another pair of strollers, half-stopping in their walk, would say to each other:

"You know who that is? Mme Swann! That conveys nothing to you? Odette de Crécy, then?"

"Odette de Crécy! Why, I thought as much. Those great, sad eyes . . . But I say, you know, she can't be as young as she was once, eh? I remember I slept with her on the day Mac-Mahon resigned."

"I shouldn't remind her of it, if I were you. She's now Mme Swann, the wife of a gentleman in the Jockey Club, a friend of the Prince of Wales. But she still looks superb."

"Oh, but you should have known her then. Gad, she was lovely! She lived in a very odd little house with a lot of Chinese stuff. I remember we were bothered all the time by the newsboys shouting outside; in the end she made me get up and go."

Without hearing these reflections, I could feel all about her the indistinct murmur of fame. My heart throbbed with impatience when I thought that a few seconds must still elapse before all these people, among whom I was dismayed not to find a certain mulatto banker by whom I felt I was despised, would see the unknown youth, to whom they had not as yet paid the slightest attention, salute (without knowing her, it was true, but I felt that I was authorised to do so because my parents knew her husband and I was her daughter's playmate) this woman whose reputation for beauty, misconduct and elegance was universal. But I was now close to Mme Swann, and I doffed my hat to her with so lavish, so prolonged a gesture that she could not repress a smile. People laughed. As for

her, she had never seen me with Gilberte, she did not know
my name, but I was for her—like one of the keepers in the
Bois, or the boatman, or the ducks on the lake to which she
threw scraps of bread—one of the minor personages, familiar,
nameless, as devoid of individual character as a stage-hand in a
theatre, of her daily walks in the Bois.

On certain days when I had missed her in the Allée des
Acacias I would sometimes meet her in the Allée de la Reine
Marguerite, where women went who wanted to be alone, or to
appear to want to be alone; she would not be alone for long,
being soon overtaken by some friend, often in a grey "topper,"
whom I did not know, and who would talk to her for some
time, while their two carriages crawled behind.

*   *   *

That sense of the complexity of the Bois de Boulogne
which makes it an artificial place and, in the zoological or
mythological sense of the word, a Garden, came to me again
this year as I crossed it on my way to Trianon, on one of those
mornings early in November when, in Paris, if we stay indoors, being so near and yet excluded from the transformation
scene of autumn, which is drawing so rapidly to a close without our witnessing it, we feel a veritable fever of yearning
for the fallen leaves that can go so far as to keep us awake at
night. Into my closed room they had been drifting already for
a month, summoned there by my desire to see them, slipping
between my thoughts and the object, whatever it might be,
upon which I was trying to concentrate them, whirling in front
of me like those brown spots that sometimes, whatever we may
be looking at, will seem to be dancing or swimming before our
eyes. And on that morning, no longer hearing the splash of
the rain as on the preceding days, seeing the smile of fine
weather at the corners of my drawn curtains, as at the corners
of closed lips betraying the secret of their happiness, I had
felt that I might be able to look at those yellow leaves with the
light shining through them, in their supreme beauty; and being
no more able to restrain myself from going to see the trees
than, in my childhood days, when the wind howled in the
chimney, I had been able to resist the longing to visit the sea,

I had risen and left the house to go to Trianon via the Bois de Boulogne. It was the hour and the season in which the Bois seems, perhaps, most multiform, not only because it is the most subdivided, but because it is subdivided in a different way. Even in the unwooded parts, where the horizon is large, here and there against the background of a dark and distant mass of trees, now leafless or still keeping their summer foliage unchanged, a double row of orange-red chestnuts seemed, as in a picture just begun, to be the only thing painted so far by an artist who had not yet laid any colour on the rest, and to be offering their cloister, in full daylight, for the casual exercise of the human figures that would be added to the picture later on.

Farther off, at a place where the trees were still all green, one alone, small, stunted, lopped, but stubborn in its resistance, was tossing in the breeze an ugly mane of red. Elsewhere, again, might be seen the first awakening of this Maytime of the leaves, and those of an ampelopsis, a smiling miracle like a red hawthorn flowering in winter, had that very morning all "come out," so to speak, in blossom. And the Bois had the temporary, unfinished, artificial look of a nursery garden or a park in which, either for some botanic purpose or in preparation for a festival, there have been embedded among the trees of commoner growth which have not yet been transplanted elsewhere, a few rare specimens, with fantastic foliage, which seem to be clearing all round themselves an empty space, making room, giving air, diffusing light. Thus it was the time of year at which the Bois de Boulogne displays more separate characteristics, assembles more distinct elements in a composite whole than at any other. It was also the time of day. In places where the trees still kept their leaves, they seemed to have undergone an alteration of their substance from the point at which they were touched by the sun's light, still, at this hour in the morning, almost horizontal, as it would be again, a few hours later, at the moment when in the gathering dusk it flames up like a lamp, projects afar over the leaves a warm and artificial glow, and sets ablaze the few topmost boughs of a tree that itself remains unchanged, a sombre incombustible candelabrum beneath its flaming crest. At one point it thickened the leaves of the chestnut-trees as it were like bricks, and, like a piece of yellow Persian masonry patterned in blue, cemented them crudely against the sky; at another, it detached them from the sky, towards which they stretched out their curling, golden fingers. Half-way up the trunk of a tree draped with Virginia creeper, it had grafted and brought to blossom, too dazzling to be clearly distinguished, an enormous bouquet as of red flowers, perhaps a new variety of carnation. The different parts of the Bois, so easily confounded in summer in the density and monotony of their universal green, were now clearly divided. Open spaces made visible the approach to almost every one of them, or else a splendid mass of foliage stood out before it like an oriflamme. One could make out, as on a coloured map, Armenonville, the Pré Catelan, Madrid, the Race Course and the shore of the lake. Here and there would appear some meaningless erection, a sham grotto, a mill for which the trees made room by standing aside from it, or which was borne upon the soft green platform of a grassy lawn. One sensed that the Bois was not only a wood, that it existed for a purpose alien to the life of its trees; the exhilaration that I felt was due not only to admiration of the autumn tints but to an obscure desire—wellspring of a joy which the heart feels at first without being conscious of its cause, without understanding that it results from no external impulse. Thus I gazed at the trees with an unsatisfied longing that went beyond them and, without my knowledge, directed itself towards that masterpiece of the fair walkers which the trees enshrine for a few hours each day. I walked towards the Allée des Acacias. I passed through groves in which the morning light, breaking them into new sections, lopped and trimmed the trees, united different trunks in marriage, made nosegays of their branches. It would skilfully draw towards it a pair of trees; making deft use of the sharp chisel of light and shade, it would cut away from each of them half of its trunks and branches, and, weaving together the two halves that remained, would make of them either a single pillar of shade, defined by the surrounding sunlight, or a single luminous phantom whose artificial, quivering contour was encompassed in a network of inky shadows. When a ray of sunshine gilded the highest branches,

they seemed, soaked and still dripping with a sparkling moisture, to have emerged alone from the liquid, emerald-green
atmosphere in which the whole grove was plunged as though
beneath the sea. For the trees continued to live by their own
vitality, which, when they had no longer any leaves, gleamed
more brightly still on the nap of green velvet that carpeted their
trunks, or in the white enamel of the globes of mistletoe that
were scattered among the topmost boughs of the poplars,
rounded like the sun and moon in Michelangelo's "Creation."
But, forced for so many years now, by a sort of grafting process, to share in the life of feminine humanity, they called to my
mind the figure of the dryad, the fair worldling, swiftly walking, brightly coloured, whom they shelter with their branches
as she passes beneath them, obliging her to acknowledge, as
they themselves acknowledge, the power of the season; they
recalled to me the happy days of my unquestioning youth,
when I would hasten eagerly to the spots where masterpieces
of female elegance would be incarnate for a few moments beneath the unconscious, accommodating boughs. But the beauty
for which the firs and acacias of the Bois de Boulogne made me
long, more disquieting in that respect than the chestnuts and
lilacs of Trianon which I was about to see, was not fixed
somewhere outside myself in the relics of an historical period,
in works of art, in a little temple of love at whose door was
piled an oblation of autumn leaves ribbed with gold. I reached
the shore of the lake; I walked on as far as the pigeon-shooting
ground. The idea of perfection which I had within me I had
bestowed, in that other time, upon the height of a victoria,
upon the raking thinness of those horses, frenzied and light as
wasps on the wing, with bloodshot eyes like the cruel steeds
of Diomed, which now, smitten by a desire to see again what
I had once loved, as ardent as the desire that had driven me
many years before along the same paths, I wished to see anew
before my eyes at the moment when Mme Swann's enormous
coachman, supervised by a groom no bigger than his fist and
as infantile as St George in the picture, endeavoured to
curb the ardour of the quivering steel-tipped pinions with
which they thundered over the ground. Alas! there was nothing now but motor-cars driven each by a moustached mechanic,

with a tall footman towering by his side. I wished to hold before my bodily eyes, to see whether they were indeed as charming as they appeared to the eyes of memory, little women's hats, so low-crowned as to seem no more than garlands. All the hats now were immense, covered with all manner of fruits and flowers and birds. In place of the beautiful dresses in which Mme Swann walked like a queen, Graeco-Saxon tunics, pleated à la Tanagra, or sometimes in the Directoire style, accentuated Liberty chiffons sprinkled with flowers like wallpaper. On the heads of the gentlemen who might have been strolling with Mme Swann in the Allée de la Reine Marguerite, I no longer found the grey "toppers" of old, nor indeed any other kind of hat. They went out bare-headed. And seeing all these new components of the spectacle, I had no longer a belief to infuse into them to give them consistency, unity and life; they passed before me in a desultory, haphazard, meaningless fashion, containing in themselves no beauty which my eyes might have tried, as in the old days, to re-create. They were just women, in whose elegance I had no faith, and whose clothes seemed to me unimportant. But when a belief vanishes, there survives it—more and more vigorously so as to cloak the absence of the power, now lost to us, of imparting reality to new things—a fetishistic attachment to the old things which it did once animate, as if it was in them and not in ourselves that the divine spark resided, and as if our present incredulity had a contingent cause—the death of the gods.

How horrible! I exclaimed to myself. Can anyone find these motor-cars as elegant as the old carriage-and-pair? I dare say I am too old now—but I was not intended for a world in which women shackle themselves in garments that are not even made of cloth. To what purpose shall I walk among these trees if there is nothing left now of the assembly that used to gather beneath this delicate tracery of reddening leaves, if vulgarity and folly have supplanted the exquisite thing that their branches once framed. How horrible! My consolation is to think of the women whom I knew in the past, now that there is no elegance left. But how could the people who watch these dreadful creatures hobble by beneath hats on which have been heaped the spoils of aviary or kitchen-garden, how could they even imagine the charm that there was in the sight of Mme Swann in a simple mauve bonnet or a little hat with a single iris sticking up out of it? Could I even have made them understand the emotion that I used to feel on winter mornings, when I met Mme Swann on foot, in an otter-skin coat, with a woollen cap from which stuck out two blade-like partridge-feathers, but enveloped also in the artificial warmth of her own house, which was suggested by nothing more than the bunch of violets crushed into her bosom, whose flowering, vivid and blue against the grey sky, the freezing air, the naked boughs, had the same charming effect of using the season and the weather merely as a setting, and of living actually in a human atmosphere, in the atmosphere of this woman, as had, in the vases and jardinières of her drawing-room, beside the blazing fire, in front of the silk-covered settee, the flowers that looked out through closed windows at the falling snow? But it would not have sufficed me that the costumes alone should still have been the same as those in distant years. Because of the solidarity that binds together the different parts of a general impression that our memory keeps in a balanced whole of which we are not permitted to subtract or to decline any fraction, I should have liked to be able to pass the rest of the day with one of those women, over a cup of tea, in an apartment with dark-painted walls (as Mme Swann's were still in the year after that in which the first part of this story ends) against which would glow the orange flame, the red combustion, the pink and white flickering of her chrysanthemums in the twilight of a November evening, in moments similar to those in which (as we shall see) I had not managed to discover the pleasures for which I longed. But now, even though they had led to nothing, those moments struck me as having been charming enough in themselves. I wanted to find them again as I remembered them. Alas! there was nothing now but flats decorated in the Louis XVI style, all white, with a sprinkling of blue hydrangeas. Moreover, people did not return to Paris, now, until much later. Mme Swann would have written to me from a country house to say that she would not be in town before February, long after the chrysanthemum season, had I asked her to reconstruct for me the elements of that memory which I felt to belong to a particular distant year, a particular vintage towards which it was forbidden me to ascend again the fatal slope, the elements of that longing which had itself become as inaccessible as the pleasure that it had once vainly pursued. And I should have required also that they should be the same women, those whose costume interested me because, at the time when I still had faith, my imagination had individualised them and had provided each of them with a legend. Alas! in the acacia-avenue—the myrtle-alley—I did see some of them again, grown old, no more now than grim spectres of what they had once been, wandering, desperately searching for heaven knew what, through the Virgilian groves. They had long since fled, and still I stood vainly questioning the deserted paths. The sun had gone. Nature was resuming its reign over the Bois, from which had vanished all trace of the idea that it was the Elysian Garden of Woman; above the gimcrack wind-mill the real sky was grey; the wind wrinkled the surface of the Grand Lac in little wavelets, like a real lake; large birds flew swiftly over the Bois, as over a real wood, and with shrill cries perched, one after another, on the great oaks which, beneath their Druidical crown, and with Dodonian majesty, seemed to proclaim the inhuman emptiness of this abandoned forest, and helped me to understand how paradoxical it is to seek in reality for the pictures that are stored in one's memory, which must inevitably lose the charm that comes to them from memory itself and from their not being apprehended by the senses. The reality that I had known no longer existed. It sufficed that Mme Swann did not appear, in the same attire and at the same moment, for the whole avenue to be altered. The places we have known do not belong only to the world of space on which we map them for our own convenience. None of them was ever more than a thin slice, held between the contiguous impressions that composed our life at that time; the memory of a particular image is but regret for a particular moment; and houses, roads, avenues are as fugitive, alas, as the years.

WITHIN A
BUDDING GROVE

MADAME SWANN
AT HOME

My mother, when it was a question of our having M. de Norpois to dinner for the first time, having expressed her regret that Professor Cottard was away from home and that she herself had quite ceased to see anything of Swann, since either of these might have helped to entertain the ex-ambassador, my father replied that so eminent a guest, so distinguished a man of science as Cottard could never be out of place at a dinner-table, but that Swann, with his ostentation, his habit of crying aloud from the house-tops the name of everyone he knew, however slightly, was a vulgar show-off whom the Marquis de Norpois would be sure to dismiss as—to use his own epithet—a "pestilent" fellow. Now, this attitude on my father's part may be felt to require a few words of explanation, inasmuch as some of us, no doubt, remember a Cottard of distinct mediocrity and a Swann by whom modesty and discretion, in all his social relations, were carried to the utmost refinement of delicacy. But in his case what had happened was that, to the original "young Swann" and also to the Swann of the Jockey Club, our old friend had added a new personality (which was not to be his last), that of Odette's husband. Adapting to the humble ambitions of that lady the instinct, the desire, the industry which he had always had, he had laboriously constructed for himself, a long way beneath the old, a new position more appropriate to the companion who was to share it with him. In this new position he revealed himself a different man. Since (while continuing to meet his own personal friends by himself, not wishing to impose Odette on them unless they expressly asked to be introduced to her) it was a second life that he had begun to lead, in common with his wife, among a new set of people, it would have been understandable if, in order to gauge the social importance of these new acquaintances and thereby the degree of self-esteem that might be derived from entertaining them, he had used, as a standard of comparison, not the brilliant society in which he himself had moved before his marriage, but former connections of Odette's. But, even when one knew that it was with uncouth functionaries and tainted women, the ornaments of ministerial ball-rooms, that he now wished to associate, it was still astonishing to hear him, who in the old days, and even still, would so gracefully refrain from mentioning an invitation to Twickenham or to Buckingham Palace, proclaim with quite unnecessary emphasis that the wife of some Assistant Under-Secretary for Something had returned Mme Swann's call. It will perhaps be objected here that what this really implied was that the simplicity of the fashionable Swann had been simply a more refined form of vanity, and that, like certain other Jews, my parents' old friend had contrived to illustrate in turn all the successive stages through which those of his race had passed, from the most naïve snobbery and the crudest vulgarity to the most exquisite good manners. But the chief reason—and one which is applicable to humanity as a whole—was that our virtues themselves are not free and floating qualities over which we retain a permanent control and power of disposal; they come to be so closely linked in our minds with the actions in conjunction with which we have made it our duty to exercise them that if we come to engage in an activity of a different kind, it catches us off guard and without the slightest awareness that it might involve the application of those same virtues. Swann, in his solicitude for these new connections and in the pride with which he referred to them, was like those great artists—modest or generous by nature—who, if in their declining years they take to cooking or to gardening, display a childlike gratification at the compliments that are paid to their dishes or their borders, and will not allow any of the criticism which they readily accept when it is applied to their real achievements; or who, while giving away a canvas for nothing, cannot conceal their annoyance if they lose a couple of francs at dominoes.

As for Professor Cottard, we shall meet him again and can study him at our leisure, much later in the course of our story, with the "Mistress," Mme Verdurin, in her country house la Raspelière. For the present, the following observations must suffice: first of all, whereas in the case of Swann the alteration may indeed be surprising, since it had been accomplished and yet was not suspected by me when I used to see Gilberte's father in the Champs-Elysées, where in any case, as he never spoke to me, he could not very well boast to me of his political connections (it is true that if he had done so, I might not at once have discerned his vanity, for the idea that one has long held of a person is apt to stop one's eyes and ears; my mother, for three whole years, had no more noticed the rouge with which one of her nieces used to paint her lips than if it had been invisibly dissolved in some liquid; until one day a streak too much, or else some other cause, brought about the phenomenon known as super-saturation; all the paint that had hitherto passed unperceived now crystallised, and my mother, in the face of this sudden riot of colour, declared, in the best Combray manner, that it was a perfect scandal, and almost severed relations with her niece); in the case of Cottard, on the other hand, the period when we saw him in attendance at Swann's first meetings with the Verdurins was already fairly remote; and honours, offices and titles come with the passage of the years. Secondly, a man may be illiterate, and make stupid puns, and yet have a special gift which no amount of general culture can replace—such as the gift of a great strategist or physician. And so it was not merely as an obscure practitioner, who had attained in course of time to European celebrity, that the rest of his profession regarded Cottard. The most intelligent of the younger doctors used to assert—for a year or two at least, for fashions change, being themselves begotten of the desire for change—that if they themselves ever fell ill Cottard was the only one of the leading men to whom they would entrust their lives. No doubt they preferred the company of certain others who were better read, more artistic, with whom they could discuss Nietzsche and Wagner. When there was a musical party at Mme Cottard's, on the evenings when—in the hope that it might one day make him Dean of the Faculty—she entertained the colleagues and pupils of her husband, the latter, instead of listening, preferred to play cards in another room. But everyone praised the quickness, the penetration, the unerring judgment of his diagnoses. Thirdly, in considering the general impression which Professor Cottard must have made on a man like my father, we must bear in mind that the character which a man exhibits in the latter half of his life is not always, though it often is, his original character developed or withered, attenuated or enlarged; it is sometimes the exact reverse, like a garment that has been turned. Except from the Verdurins, who were infatuated with him, Cottard's hesitating manner, his excessive shyness and affability had, in his young days, called down upon him endless taunts and sneers. What charitable friend counselled that glacial air? The importance of his professional standing made it all the more easy for him to adopt. Wherever he went, save at the Verdurins', where he instinctively became himself again, he would assume a repellent coldness, remain deliberately silent, adopt a peremptory tone when he was obliged to speak, and never fail to say the most disagreeable things. He had every opportunity of rehearsing this new attitude before his patients, who, seeing him for the first time, were not in a position to make comparisons, and would have been greatly surprised to learn that he was not at all a rude man by nature. Impassiveness was what he strove to attain, and even while visiting his hospital wards, when he allowed himself to utter one of those puns which left everyone, from the house physician to the most junior student, helpless with laughter, he would always make it without moving a muscle of his face, which was itself no longer recognisable now that he had shaved off his beard and moustache.

Who, finally, was the Marquis de Norpois? He had been Minister Plenipotentiary before the War, and was actually an ambassador on the Sixteenth of May;[16] in spite of which, and to the general astonishment, he had since been several times chosen to represent France on special missions—even as Controller of the Public Debt in Egypt, where, thanks to his considerable financial skill, he had rendered important services—by Radical cabinets under which a simple bourgeois reactionary would have declined to serve, and in whose eyes M. de Norpois, in view of his past, his connexions and his opinions, ought presumably to have been suspect. But these advanced ministers seemed to be aware that, in making such an appointment, they were showing how broadminded they were when the higher interests of France were at stake, were raising themselves above the general run of politicians to the extent that the *Journal des Débats* itself referred to them as "statesmen," and were reaping direct advantage from the prestige that attaches to an aristocratic name and the dramatic interest always aroused by an unexpected appointment. And they knew also that, in calling upon M. de Norpois, they could reap these advantages without having to fear any want of political loyalty on his part, a fault against which his noble birth not only need not put them on their guard but offered a positive guarantee. And in this calculation the Government of the Republic was not mistaken. In the first place, because an aristocrat of a certain type, brought up from his cradle to regard his name as an innate asset of which no accident can deprive him (and of whose value his peers, or those of even nobler birth, can form a fairly exact estimate), knows that he can dispense with the efforts (since they can in no way enhance his position) in which, without any appreciable result, so many public men of the middle class spend themselves to profess only orthodox opinions and associate only with "right-thinking" people. Anxious, on the other hand, to enhance his own importance in the eyes of the princely or ducal families which take immediate precedence of his own, he knows that he can do so only by complementing his name with something that it lacked, something that will give it priority over other names heraldically its equals: such as political influence, a literary or an artistic reputation, or a large fortune. And so what he saves by ignoring the ineffectual squires who are sought after by his bourgeois colleagues, but of his sterile friendship with whom a prince would think nothing, he will lavish on the politicians who (freemasons, or worse, though they be) can advance him in diplomacy or support him in elections, and on the artists or scientists whose patronage can help him to "break into" the branches in which they are predominant, on anyone, in fact, who is in a position to confer a fresh distinction or to help "bring off" a rich marriage.

But in the case of M. de Norpois there was above all the fact that, in the course of a long career in diplomacy, he had become imbued with that negative, methodical, conservative spirit, a "governmental mind," which is common to all governments and, under every government, particularly inspires its foreign service. He had imbibed, during that career, an aversion, a dread, a contempt for the methods of procedure, more or less revolutionary and at the very least improper, which are those of an Opposition. Save in the case of a few illiterates—high or low, it makes no matter—by whom no difference in quality is perceptible, what brings men together is not a community of views but a consanguinity of minds. An Academician of the Legouvé type, an upholder of the classics, would have applauded Maxime Ducamp's or Mézière's eulogy of Victor Hugo with more fervour than that of Boileau by Claudel. A common nationalism suffices to endear Barrès to his electors, who scarcely distinguish between him and M. Georges Berry, but not to those of his brother Academicians who, with the same political opinions but a different type of mind, will be more partial even to enemies such as M. Ribot and M. Deschanel, with whom, in turn, the most loyal Monarchists feel themselves more at home than with Maurras or Léon Daudet, who nevertheless also desire the King's return. Sparing of his words, not only from a professional habit of prudence and reserve, but because words themselves have more value, present more subtleties of definition to men whose efforts, protracted over a decade, to bring two countries to an understanding are condensed, translated—in a speech or in a protocol—into a single adjective, colourless in all appearance, but to them pregnant with a world of meaning, M. de Norpois was considered very stiff, on the Commission, where he sat next to my father, whom everyone else congratulated on the astonishing way in which the ex-ambassador unbent to him. My father was himself more astonished than anyone. For, being generally somewhat unsociable, he was not used to being sought after outside the circle of his intimates, and frankly admitted it. He realised that these overtures on the part of the diplomat were a reflection of the completely individual standpoint which each of us adopts for himself in making his choice of friends, and from which all a man's intellectual qualities or his sensibility will be a far less potent recommenda-

tion to someone who is bored or irritated by him than the
frankness and gaiety of another man whom many would
consider vapid, frivolous and null. "De Norpois has asked
me to dinner again; it's quite extraordinary; everyone on
the Commission is amazed, as he has no personal relations
with anyone else. I'm sure he's going to tell me some more
fascinating things about the 'Seventy war." My father knew
that M. de Norpois had warned, had perhaps been alone in
warning the Emperor of the growing strength and bellicose
designs of Prussia, and that Bismarck rated his intelligence most
highly. Only the other day, at the Opera, during the gala
performance given for King Theodosius, the newspapers
had all drawn attention to the long conversation which that
monarch had had with M. de Norpois. "I must ask him whether
the King's visit had any real significance," my father went on,
for he was keenly interested in foreign policy. "I know old
Norpois keeps very close as a rule, but when he's with me he
opens out quite charmingly."

As for my mother, perhaps the Ambassador had not the
type of mind towards which she felt herself most attracted.
And it must be said that his conversation furnished so exhaustive a glossary of the superannuated forms of speech peculiar
to a certain profession, class and period—a period which,
for that profession and that class, might be said not to have
altogether passed away—that I sometimes regret not having
kept a literal record simply of the things that I heard him say.
I should thus have obtained an effect of old-fashioned usage
by the same process and at as little expense as that actor at
the Palais-Royal who, when asked where on earth he managed
to find his astounding hats, answered, "I do not find my hats.
I keep them." In a word, I suppose that my mother considered M. de Norpois a trifle "out-of-date," which was by
no means a fault in her eyes, so far as manners were concerned,
but attracted her less in the realm, not, in this instance, of
ideas—for those of M. de Norpois were extremely modern—
but of idiom. She felt, however, that she was paying a delicate
compliment to her husband when she spoke admiringly of
the diplomat who had shown so remarkable a predilection for
him. By reinforcing in my father's mind the good opinion that

he already had of M. de Norpois, and so inducing him to form
a good opinion of himself also, she knew that she was carrying
out that wifely duty which consisted in making life pleasant
and comfortable for her husband, just as when she saw to it
that his dinner was perfectly cooked and served in silence.
And as she was incapable of deceiving my father, she compelled herself to admire the Ambassador in order to be able
to praise him with sincerity. In any event she could naturally
appreciate his air of kindliness, his somewhat antiquated
courtesy (so ceremonious that when, as he was walking along
the street, his tall figure rigidly erect, he caught sight of my
mother driving past, before raising his hat to her he would fling
away the cigar that he had just lighted), his conversation, so
elaborately circumspect, in which he referred as seldom as
possible to himself and always considered what might interest
the person to whom he was speaking, and his promptness in
answering a letter, which was so astonishing that whenever my
father, just after posting one himself to M. de Norpois, saw
his handwriting on an envelope, his first impulse was always
one of annoyance that their letters must unfortunately have
crossed: it was as though he enjoyed at the post office the
special and luxurious privilege of supplementary deliveries and
collections at all hours of the day and night. My mother marvelled at his being so punctilious although so busy, so friendly
although so much in demand, never realising that "although,"
with such people, is invariably an unrecognised "because,"
and that (just as old men are always wonderful for their age,
and kings extraordinarily simple, and country cousins astonishingly well-informed) it was the same system of habits that
enabled M. de Norpois to meet so many social demands and
to be so methodical in answering letters, to go everywhere and
to be so friendly when he came to us. Moreover she made the
mistake which everyone makes who is unduly modest; she
rated everything that concerned herself below, and consequently outside, the range of other people's duties and engagements. The letter which it seemed to her so meritorious in my
father's friend to have written us promptly, since in the course
of the day he must have had so many letters to write, she
excepted from that great number of letters of which it was only

one; in the same way she did not consider that dining with us was, for M. de Norpois, merely one of the innumerable activities of his social life: she never guessed that the Ambassador had trained himself, long ago, to look upon dining-out as part of his diplomatic functions, and to display, at table, an inveterate charm which it would have been too much to have expected him specially to discard when he came to dine with us.

The evening on which M. de Norpois first appeared at our table, in a year when I still went to play in the Champs-Elysées, has remained fixed in my memory because the afternoon of the same day was that upon which I at last went to a matinée to see Berma in *Phèdre*, and also because in talking to M. de Norpois I realised suddenly, and in a new and different way, how completely the feelings aroused in me by all that concerned Gilberte Swann and her parents differed from those which the same family inspired in everyone else.

It was no doubt the dejection into which I was plunged by the approach of the New Year holidays during which, as she herself had informed me, I was to see nothing of Gilberte, that prompted my mother to suggest one day, in the hope of distracting my mind: "If you're still longing to see Berma, I think your father might perhaps allow you to go; your grandmother can take you."

But it was because M. de Norpois had told him that he ought to let me see Berma, that it was an experience for a young man to remember in later life, that my father, who had hitherto been so resolutely opposed to my going and wasting my time, with the added risk of my falling ill again, on what he used to shock my grandmother by calling "futilities," was now not far from regarding this outing recommended by the Ambassador as vaguely forming part of a sum of precious formulae for success in a brilliant career. My grandmother, who, in renouncing on my behalf the benefit which, according to her, I should have derived from hearing Berma, had made a considerable sacrifice in the interests of my health, was surprised to find that this last had become of no account at a mere word from M. de Norpois. Reposing the unconquerable hopes of her rationalist spirit in the strict course of fresh air and early hours which had been prescribed for me, she now deplored as something disastrous the infringement of these rules that I was about to commit, and in anguished tones exclaimed "How frivolous you are!" to my father, who replied angrily "What! So now it's you who don't want him to go! It's really a bit much, after your telling us all day and every day that it would be so good for him."

M. de Norpois had also brought about a change in my father's plans in a matter of far greater importance to myself. My father had always wanted me to be a diplomat, and I could not endure the thought that, even if I were to remain for some years attached to the Ministry, I might run the risk of being sent later on as ambassador to capitals in which there would be no Gilberte. I should have preferred to return to the literary career that I had planned for myself and then abandoned years before during my wanderings along the Guermantes way. But my father had steadily opposed my devoting myself to litera-ture, which he regarded as vastly inferior to diplomacy, refus-ing even to dignify it with the title of career, until the day when M. de Norpois, who had little love for the more recent genera-tions of diplomatic officials, assured him that it was quite possible, as a writer, to attract as much attention, to receive as much consideration, to exercise as much influence as in the ambassadorial world, and at the same time to preserve more independence.

"Well, well, I should never have believed it—old Norpois doesn't at all disapprove of the idea of your taking up writing," my father had reported. And as he had a certain amount of influence himself, he imagined that there was nothing that could not be "arranged," no problem for which a happy solu-tion might not be found in the conversation of people who "counted." "I shall bring him back to dinner, one of these days, from the Commission. You must talk to him a bit, so that he can get some idea of your calibre. Write something good that you can show him; he's a great friend of the editor of the *Deux-Mondes*; he'll get you in there; he'll fix it all, the cunning old fox; and, upon my soul, he seems to think that diplomacy, nowadays! . . ."

My happiness at the prospect of not being separated from

Gilberte made me desirous, but not capable, of writing something good which could be shown to M. de Norpois. After a few laboured pages, the tedium of it made the pen drop from my fingers, and I wept with rage at the thought that I should never have any talent, that I was not "gifted," that I could not even take advantage of the chance that M. de Norpois's coming visit offered me of spending the rest of my life in Paris. The recollection that I was to be taken to see Berma alone distracted me from my grief. But just as I wished to see storms only on those coasts where they raged with most violence, so I should not have cared to see the great actress except in one of those classic parts in which Swann had told me that she touched the sublime. For when it is in the hope of making a priceless discovery that we desire to receive certain impressions from nature or from works of art, we have qualms lest our soul imbibe inferior impressions which might lead us to form a false estimate of the value of Beauty. Berma in *Andromaque*, in *Les Caprices de Marianne*, in *Phèdre*, was one of those famous spectacles which my imagination had long desired. I should enjoy the same rapture as on the day when a gondola would deposit me at the foot of the Titian of the Frari or the Carpaccios of San Giorgio dei Schiavoni, were I ever to hear Berma recite the lines beginning,

> On dit qu'un prompt départ vous éloigne de nous,
> Seigneur . . .

I was familiar with them from the simple reproduction in black and white which was given of them upon the printed page; but my heart beat furiously at the thought—as of the realisation of a long-planned voyage—that I should see them at length bathed and brought to life in the atmosphere and sunshine of the golden voice. A Carpaccio in Venice, Berma in *Phèdre*, masterpieces of pictorial or dramatic art which the glamour, the dignity attaching to them made so vividly alive for me, that is to say so indivisible, that if I had been to see Carpaccios in one of the galleries of the Louvre, or Berma in some piece of which I had never heard, I should not have experienced the same delicious amazement at finding myself at last, with wide-open eyes, before the unique and inconceivable

object of so many thousand dreams. Then, expecting as I did
from Berma's playing the revelation of certain aspects of
nobility and tragic grief, it seemed to me that whatever greatness, whatever truth there might be in her playing must be enhanced if the actress superimposed it upon a work of real value,
instead of what would, after all, be but embroidering a pattern
of truth and beauty upon a commonplace and vulgar web.

Finally, if I went to see Berma in a new play, it would not
be easy for me to assess her art and her diction, since I should
be unable to discriminate between a text which was not already
familiar to me and what she added to it by her vocal inflexions
and gestures, an addition which would seem to me to be an
integral part of it; whereas the old plays, the classics which I
knew by heart, presented themselves to me as vast and empty
walls, reserved and made ready for my inspection, on which I
should be able to appreciate without restriction the devices
by which Berma would cover them, as with frescoes, with the
perpetually fresh discoveries of her inspiration. Unfortunately,
for some years now, since she had abandoned the serious stage
to throw in her lot with a commercial theatre where she was the
"star," she had ceased to appear in classic parts, and in vain
did I scan the hoardings, they never advertised any but the
newest pieces, written specially for her by authors in fashion
at the moment. When, one morning, searching through the
column of theatre advertisements to find the afternoon performances for the week of the New Year holidays, I saw there
for the first time—at the foot of the bill, after some probably
insignificant curtain-raiser, whose title was opaque to me
because it contained all the particulars of a plot I did not know
—two acts of *Phèdre* with Mme Berma, and, on the following
afternoons, *Le Demi-Monde* and *Les Caprices de Marianne*,
names which, like that of *Phèdre*, were for me transparent, filled
with light only, so familiar were those works to me, illuminated to their very depths by the revealing smile of art. They
seemed to me to invest with a fresh nobility Mme Berma herself when I read in the newspapers, after the programme of
these performances, that it was she who had decided to show
herself once more to the public in some of her early creations.
She was conscious, then, that certain roles have an interest

which survives the novelty of their first production or the
success of a revival; she regarded them, when interpreted by
herself, as museum pieces which it might be instructive to set
once more before the eyes of the generation which had admired
her in them long ago, or of the one which had never yet seen
her in them. In thus advertising, in the middle of a column
of plays intended only to while away an evening, this *Phèdre*,
whose title was no bigger than any of the rest, nor set in
different type, she added to it, as it were, the unspoken comment of a hostess who, on introducing you to her other guests
before going in to dinner, casually mentions amid the string of
names which are the names of guests and nothing more, and
without any change of tone:—"M. Anatole France."

The doctor who was attending me—the same who had forbidden me to travel—advised my parents not to let me go to
the theatre; I should only be ill again afterwards, perhaps for
weeks, and in the long run derive more pain than pleasure from
the experience. The fear of this might have availed to stop me,
if what I had anticipated from such a spectacle had been only a
pleasure which a subsequent pain could offset and annul. But
what I demanded from this performance—as from the visit
to Balbec and the visit to Venice for which I had so intensely
longed—was something quite different from pleasure: verities
pertaining to a world more real than that in which I lived,
which, once acquired, could never be taken from me again by
any trivial incident—even though it were to cause me bodily
suffering—of my otiose existence. At most, the pleasure which
I might experience during the performance appeared to me as
the perhaps necessary form of the perception of these truths;
and I hoped only that the predicted ailments would not begin
until the play was finished, so that this pleasure should not be
in any way compromised or spoiled. I implored my parents,
who, after the doctor's visit, were no longer inclined to let me
go to *Phèdre*. I recited to myself all day long the speech
beginning,

On dit qu'un prompt départ vous éloigne de nous . . .

trying out every inflexion and intonation that could be put
into it, the better to appreciate the unexpected way which

Berma would have found of uttering the lines. Concealed, like the Holy of Holies, beneath the veil that screened her from my gaze and behind which I invested her from one moment to the next with a fresh aspect, according to whichever of the words of Bergotte (in the booklet that Gilberte had found for me) came to my mind—"plastic nobility," "Christian austerity" or "Jansenist pallor," "Princess of Troezen and of Cleves," "Mycenean drama," "delphic symbol," "solar myth"—, the goddess of beauty whom Berma's acting was to reveal to me was enthroned, night and day, upon an altar perpetually lit, in the sanctuary of my mind—on whose behalf my stern and fickle parents were to decide whether or not it was to enshrine, and for all time, the perfections of the Deity unveiled in that same spot where her invisible form now reigned. And with my eyes fastened on that inconceivable image, I strove from morning to night to overcome the barriers which my family were putting in my way. But when these had at last fallen, when my mother—although this *matinée* was actually to coincide with the meeting of the Commission from which my father had promised to bring M. de Norpois home to dinner—had said to me, "Very well, we don't want to make you unhappy—if you think you will enjoy it so very much, you must go," when this visit to the theatre, hitherto forbidden and unattainable, depended now on myself alone, then for the first time, being no longer troubled by the wish that it might cease to be impossible, I wondered whether it was desirable, whether there were not other reasons than my parents' prohibition which should have made me abandon it. In the first place, whereas I had hated them for their cruelty, their consent made them now so dear to me that the thought of causing them pain stabbed me also with a pain through which the purpose of life now appeared to me as the pursuit not of truth but of loving-kindness, and life itself seemed good or evil only in so far as my parents were happy or sad. "I would rather not go, if it distresses you," I told my mother, who, on the contrary, strove hard to expel from my mind any lurking fear that she might regret my going, since that, she said, would spoil the pleasure which I should otherwise derive from *Phèdre* and in consideration of which she and my father

had reversed their earlier decision. But then this sort of obligation to find pleasure in the performance seemed to me very
burdensome. Besides, if I returned home ill, should I be well
again in time to be able to go to the Champs-Elysées as soon
as the holidays were over and Gilberte returned? Against all
these arguments I set, in order to decide which course I should
take, the idea, invisible there behind its veil, of Berma's perfection. I placed on one side of the scales "Making Mamma
unhappy," "risking not being able to go to the Champs-
Elysées," and on the other, "Jansenist pallor," solar myth,"
until the words themselves grew dark and clouded in my
mind's vision, ceased to say anything to me, lost all their force;
and gradually my hesitations became so painful that if I had
now opted for the theatre it would have been only in order
to bring them to an end and be delivered from them once
and for all. It would have been to fix a term to my sufferings,
and no longer in the expectation of an intellectual benediction,
yielding to the attractions of perfection, that I would have
allowed myself to be led, not now to the Wise Goddess, but to
the stern, implacable Divinity, faceless and unnamed, who had
been surreptitiously substituted for her behind her veil. But
suddenly everything was altered. My desire to go and see
Berma received a fresh stimulus which enabled me to await the
coming of the *matinée* with impatience and with joy. Having
gone to take up my daily station, as excruciating, of late, as
that of a stylite, in front of the column on which the playbills
were displayed, I had seen there, still moist and wrinkled, the
complete bill of *Phèdre*, which had just been pasted up for the
first time (and on which, I must confess, the rest of the cast
furnished no additional attraction which could help me to
decide). But it gave to one of the goals between which my
indecision wavered a form at once more concrete and—
inasmuch as the bill bore the date not of the day on which I
was reading it but that on which the performance would take
place, and the very hour at which the curtain would rise—
almost imminent, already well on the way to its realisation, so
that I jumped for joy before the column at the thought that on
that day, and at that hour precisely, I should be sitting there in
my seat, ready to hear the voice of Berma; and for fear lest my

parents might not now be in time to secure two good seats for
my grandmother and myself, I raced back to the house,
whipped on by the magic words which had now taken the
place in my mind of "Jansenist pallor" and "solar myth":
"Ladies will not be admitted to the stalls in hats. The doors
will be closed at two o'clock."

Alas! that first *matinée* was to prove a bitter disappointment.
My father offered to drop my grandmother and me at the
theatre, on his way to the Commission. Before leaving the
house he said to my mother: "Try and have a good dinner for
us to-night; you remember I'm bringing de Norpois back with
me." My mother had not forgotten. And ever since the day
before, Françoise, rejoicing in the opportunity to devote herself to that art of cooking at which she was so gifted, stimulated, moreover, by the prospect of a new guest, and knowing
that she would have to compose, by methods known to her
alone, a dish of *boeuf à la gelée*, had been living in the efferves-
cence of creation; since she attached the utmost importance to
the intrinsic quality of the materials which were to enter into
the fabric of her work, she had gone herself to the Halles to
procure the best cuts of rump-steak, shin of beef, calves'-feet,
just as Michelangelo spent eight months in the mountains of
Carrara choosing the most perfect blocks of marble for the
monument of Julius II. Françoise expended on these comings
and goings so much ardour that Mamma, at the sight of her
flaming cheeks, was alarmed lest our old servant should fall
ill from overwork, like the sculptor of the Tombs of the
Medici in the quarries of Pietrasanta. And overnight Françoise
had sent to be cooked in the baker's oven protected with bread-
crumbs, like a block of pink marble packed in sawdust, what
she called a "Nev'-York ham." Believing the language to be
less rich in words than it is, and her own ears untrustworthy,
the first time she had heard someone mention York ham she
had thought, no doubt,—feeling it to be hardly conceivable
that the dictionary could be so prodigal as to include at once
a "York" and a "New York"—that she had misheard, and
that the ham was really called by the name already familiar to
her. And so, ever since, the word York was preceded in her
ears, or before her eyes when she read it in an advertisement,

by the affix "New" which she pronounced "Nev'." And it
was with the utmost conviction that she would say to her
kitchen-maid: "Go and get me some ham from Olida's.
Madame told me especially that it must be Nev'-York."

On that particular day, if Françoise was consumed by the
burning certainty of creative genius, my lot was the cruel
anxiety of the seeker after truth. No doubt, so long as I had
not yet heard Berma speak, I still felt some pleasure. I felt it
in the little square that lay in front of the theatre, in which, in
two hours' time, the bare boughs of the chestnut trees would
gleam with a metallic lustre as the lighted gas-lamps showed up
every detail of their structure; and before the ticket attendants,
whose selection, advancement and ultimate fate depended
upon the great artist—for she alone held power in this ad-
ministration at the head of which ephemeral and purely
nominal managers followed one after the other in an obscure
succession—who took our tickets without even glancing at
us, so preoccupied were they in seeing that all Mme Berma's
instructions had been duly transmitted to the new members
of the staff, that it was clearly understood that the hired applause must never sound for her, that the windows must all
be kept open so long as she was not on the stage and every
door closed tight the moment she appeared, that a bowl of hot
water must be concealed somewhere close to her to make the
dust settle. And, indeed, at any moment now her carriage,
drawn by a pair of horses with flowing manes, would be
stopping outside the theatre, she would alight from it muffled
in furs, and, crossly acknowledging people's salutes, would
send one of her attendants to find out whether a stage box had
been kept for her friends, what the temperature was "in front,"
who were in the other boxes, how the programme sellers were
turned out; theatre and audience being to her no more than
a second, outer cloak which she would put on, and the medium,
the more or less "good" conductor, through which her talent
would have to pass. I was happy, too, in the theatre itself;
since I had made the discovery that—contrary to the notion so
long entertained by my childish imagination—there was but
one stage for everybody, I had supposed that I should be prevented from seeing it properly by the presence of the other

spectators, as one is when in the thick of a crowd; now I
registered the fact that, on the contrary, thanks to an arrangement which is, as it were, symbolical of all spectatorship,
everyone feels himself to be the centre of the theatre; which
explained to me why, when Françoise had been sent once to
see some melodrama from the top gallery, she had assured us
on her return that her seat had been the best in the house, and
that instead of finding herself too far from the stage she had
been positively frightened by the mysterious and living proximity of the curtain. My pleasure increased further when I
began to distinguish behind this lowered curtain such obscure
noises as one hears through the shell of an egg before the
chicken emerges, sounds which presently grew louder and
suddenly, from that world which, impenetrable to our eyes,
yet scrutinised us with its own, addressed themselves indubitably to us in the imperious form of three consecutive thumps
as thrilling as any signals from the planet Mars. And—once
this curtain had risen,—when on the stage a writing-table and
a fireplace, in no way out of the ordinary, had indicated that
the persons who were about to enter would be, not actors
come to recite as I had once seen some of them do at an
evening party, but real people, just living their lives at home,
on whom I was thus able to spy without their seeing me, my
pleasure still endured. It was broken by a momentary uneasiness: just as I was pricking up my ears in readiness before the
piece began, two men appeared on the stage obviously furious
with one another since they were talking so loud that in this
auditorium where there were at least a thousand people one
could hear every word, whereas in quite a small *café* one is
obliged to ask the waiter what two individuals who appear to
be quarrelling are saying; but at that moment, while I sat
astonished to find that the audience was listening to them
without protest, submerged as it was in a unanimous silence
upon which presently a little wave of laughter broke here and
there, that these insolent fellows were the actors, and that
the short piece known as "the curtain-raiser" had now begun.
It was followed by an interval so long that the audience,
having returned to their seats, grew impatient and began to
stamp their feet. I was terrified at this; for just as in the report

of a criminal trial, when I read that some noble-minded person was coming, in defiance of his own interests, to testify on behalf of an innocent man, I was always afraid that they would not be nice enough to him, would not show enough gratitude, would not recompense him lavishly, and that he, in disgust, would then range himself on the side of injustice, so now, assimilating genius with virtue, I was afraid lest Berma, vexed by the bad behaviour of so ill-bred an audience—in which, on the contrary, I should have liked her to recognise with gratification a few celebrities to whose judgment she would be bound to attach importance—should express her displeasure and disdain by acting badly. And I looked round imploringly at these stamping brutes, who were about to shatter, in their insensate rage, the rare and fragile impression which I had come to seek. The last moments of my pleasure were during the opening scenes of the *Phèdre*. The heroine herself does not appear in these first scenes of the second act; and yet, as soon as the curtain rose, and another curtain, of red velvet this time, was drawn aside (a curtain which was used to halve the depth of the stage in all the plays in which the star appeared), an actress entered from the back who had the face and voice which, I had been told, were those of Berma. The cast must therefore have been changed; all the trouble that I had taken in studying the part of the wife of Theseus was wasted. But a second actress now responded to the first. I must have been mistaken in supposing that the first was Berma, for the second resembled her even more closely and, more than the other, had her diction. Both of them, moreover, embellished their roles with noble gestures—which I could clearly distinguish, and could appreciate in their relation to the text, while they raised and let fall the folds of their beautiful robes—and also with skilful changes of tone, now passionate, now ironical, which made me understand the significance of lines that I had read to myself at home without paying sufficient attention to what they really meant. But all of a sudden, in the cleft of the red curtain that veiled her sanctuary, as in a frame, a woman appeared, and instantly, from the fear that seized me, far more anxious than Berma's own fear could be, lest someone should upset her by opening a window, or drown one of her

lines by rustling a programme, or annoy her by applauding
the others and by not applauding her enough, from the way in
which, from that moment, more absolutely than Berma herself,
I considered theatre, audience, play and my own body only
as an acoustic medium of no importance save in the degree to
which it was favourable to the inflexions of that voice, I
realised that the two actresses whom I had been admiring for
some minutes bore not the least resemblance to her whom I
had come to hear. But at the same time all my pleasure had
ceased; in vain did I strain towards Berma eyes, ears, mind, so
as not to let one morsel escape me of the reasons which she
would give me for admiring her, I did not succeed in glean-
ing a single one. I could not even, as I could with her companions, distinguish in her diction and in her playing intelligent
modulations or beautiful gestures. I listened to her as though I
were reading *Phèdre*, or as though Phaedra herself had at that
moment uttered the words that I was hearing, without its
appearing that Berma's talent had added anything at all to
them. I could have wished—in order to be able to explore them
fully, to try to discover what it was in them that was beautiful—
to arrest, to immobilise for a time before my senses every
inflexion of the artist's voice, every expression of her features;
at least I did attempt, by dint of mental agility, by having,
before a line came, my attention ready and tuned to catch
it, not to waste upon preparations any morsel of the precious
time that each word, each gesture occupied, and, thanks to
the intensity of my observation, to contrive to penetrate as far
into them as if I had had whole hours to spend upon them
by myself. But how short their duration was! Scarcely had a
sound been received by my ear than it was displaced there
by another. In one scene, where Berma stands motionless
for a moment, her arm raised to the level of her face, bathed,
by some artifice of lighting, in a greenish glow, before a
back-cloth painted to represent the sea, the whole house broke
out in applause; but already the actress had moved, and the
tableau that I should have liked to study existed no longer.
I told my grandmother that I could not see very well, and
she handed me her glasses. But when one believes in the reality
of things, making them visible by artificial means is not quite

the same as feeling that they are close at hand. I thought that it was no longer Berma but her image that I was seeing in the magnifying lenses. I put the glasses down. But perhaps the image that my eye received of her, diminished by distance, was no more exact; which of the two Bermas was the real one? As for her declaration to Hippolyte, I had greatly counted on that, since, to judge by the ingenious significance which her companions were disclosing to me every moment in less beautiful passages, she would certainly render it with modulations more surprising than any which, when reading the play at home, I had contrived to imagine; but she did not attain even to the heights which Œnone or Aricie would naturally have reached, she planed down into a uniform chant the whole of a speech in which there were mingled together contrasts so striking that the least intelligent of actresses, even the pupils of an academy, could not have missed their effect; besides which, she delivered it so rapidly that it was only when she had come to the last line that my mind became aware of the deliberate monotony which she had imposed on it throughout.

Then at last I felt my first impulse of admiration, which was provoked by the frenzied applause of the audience. I mingled my own with theirs, endeavouring to prolong it so that Berma, in her gratitude, should surpass herself, and I be certain of having heard her on one of her great days. A curious thing, by the way, was that the moment when this storm of enthusiasm broke loose was, as I afterwards learned, that in which Berma has one of her finest inspirations. It would appear that certain transcendent realities emit all around them a sort of radiation to which the crowd is sensitive. Thus it is that when any great event occurs, when on a distant frontier an army is in jeopardy, or defeated, or victorious, the vague and conflicting reports from which an educated man can derive little enlightenment stimulate in the crowd an emotion which surprises him and in which, once the experts have informed him of the actual military situation, he recognises the popular perception of that "aura" which surrounds momentous happenings and which may be visible hundreds of miles away. One learns of a victory either after the event, when the war is over, or at once, from the hilarious joy of one's hall porter. One discovers the touch of genius in Berma's acting either a week after one has heard her, from a review, or else on the spot, from the thundering acclamation of the stalls. But this immediate recognition by the crowd being mingled with a hundred others, all erroneous, the applause came most often at wrong moments, apart from the fact that it was mechanically produced by the effect of the applause that had gone before, just as in a storm, once the sea is sufficiently disturbed, it will continue to swell even after the wind has begun to subside. No matter; the more I applauded, the better, it seemed to me, did Berma act. "I say," a fairly ordinary-looking woman sitting next to me was saying, "she fairly gives it you, she does; you'd think she'd do herself an injury, the way she runs about. I call that acting, don't you?" And happy to find these reasons for Berma's superiority, though not without a suspicion that they no more accounted for it than a peasant's gawping exclamation—"That's a good bit of work. It's all gold, look! Fine, ain't it?"—would for that of the Gioconda or Benvenuto's Perseus, I greedily imbibed the rough wine of this popular enthusiasm. Nevertheless, when the curtain had fallen for the last time, I was disappointed that the pleasure for which I had so longed had not been greater, but at the same time I felt the need to prolong it, not to relinquish for ever, by leaving the auditorium, this strange life of the theatre which for a few hours had been mine, and from which I should have torn myself away as though I were being dragged into exile by going straight home, had I not hoped there to learn a great deal more about Berma from her admirer M. de Norpois, to whom I was indebted already for having been permitted to go to *Phèdre*.

I was introduced to him before dinner by my father, who summoned me into his study for the purpose. As I entered, the Ambassador rose, held out his hand, bowed his tall figure and fixed his blue eyes attentively on my face. As the foreign visitors who used to be presented to him, in the days when he still represented France abroad, were all more or less (even the famous singers) persons of note, with regard to whom he therefore knew that he would be able to say later on, when he heard their names mentioned in Paris or in Petersburg, that he remembered perfectly the evening he had spent with them in Munich or Sofia, he had formed the habit of impressing upon them, by his affability, the pleasure he felt in making their acquaintance; but in addition to this, being convinced that in the life of foreign capitals, in contact at once with all the interesting personalities that passed through them and with the manners and customs of the native populations, one acquired a deeper insight than could be gleaned from books into the history, the geography, the traditions of the different nations, and into the intellectual trends of Europe, he would exercise upon each newcomer his keen power of observation, so as to decide at once with what manner of man he had to deal. It was some time since the Government had entrusted him with a post abroad, but as soon as anyone was introduced to him, his eyes, as though they had not yet received notification of their master's retirement, began their fruitful observation, while by his whole attitude he endeavoured to convey that the stranger's name was not unknown to him. And so, while speaking to me kindly and with the air of self-importance of a man who is conscious of the vastness of his experience, he never ceased to examine me with a sagacious curiosity for his own profit, as though I had been some exotic custom, some historic and instructive monument or some star on tour. And in this way he gave proof, in his attitude towards me, at once of the majestic benevolence of the sage Mentor and of the zealous curiosity of the young Anacharsis.

He offered me absolutely no opening to the *Revue des Deux-Mondes*, but put a number of questions to me about my life and my studies, and about my tastes which I heard thus spoken of for the first time as though it might be a reasonable thing to obey their promptings, whereas hitherto I had always supposed it to be my duty to suppress them. Since they inclined me towards literature, he did not dissuade me from it; on the contrary, he spoke of it with deference, as of some venerable and charming personage whose select circle, in Rome or at Dresden, one remembers with pleasure and regrets only that one's multifarious duties in life enable one to revisit so seldom. He appeared to envy me, with an almost rakish smile, the delightful hours which, more fortunate than himself and more free, I should be able to spend with such a mistress. But the very terms that he employed showed me Literature as something entirely different from the image that I had formed of it at Combray, and I realised that I had been doubly right in renouncing it. Until now, I had concluded only that I had no gift for writing; now M. de Norpois took away from me even the desire to write. I wanted to express to him what had been my dreams; trembling with emotion, I was painfully anxious that all the words I uttered would be the sincerest possible equivalent of what I had felt and had never yet attempted to formulate; which is to say that my words were very unclear. Perhaps from a professional habit, perhaps by virtue of the calm that is acquired by every important personage whose advice is commonly sought, and who, knowing that he will keep the control of the conversation in his own hands, allows his interlocutor to fret, to struggle, to toil to his heart's content, perhaps also to show off the character of his face (Greek, according to himself, despite his sweeping whiskers), M. de Norpois, while anything was being expounded to him, would preserve a facial immobility as absolute as if you had been addressing some ancient—and deaf—bust in a museum. Until suddenly, falling upon you like an auctioneer's hammer or a Delphic oracle, the Ambassador's voice, as he replied to you, would be all the more striking in that nothing in his face had allowed you to guess what sort of impression you had made on him, or what opinion he was about to express.

"Precisely," he suddenly began, as though the case were now heard and judged, after having allowed me to stammer incoherently beneath those motionless eyes which never for an instant left my face; "a friend of mine has a son whose case, *mutatis mutandis*, is very much like yours." He adopted in speaking of our common predisposition the same reassuring tone as if it had been a predisposition not for literature but for rheumatism, and he had wished to assure me that it would not necessarily prove fatal. "He too chose to leave the Quai d'Orsay, although the way had been paved for him there by his father, and without caring what people might say, he settled down to write. And certainly, he's had no reason to regret it. He published two years ago—of course, he's much

older than you—a book about the Sense of the Infinite on the
western shore of Lake Victoria Nyanza, and this year he has
brought out a short treatise, less weighty but written with a
lively, not to say cutting pen, on the Repeating Rifle in the
Bulgarian Army; and these have put him quite in a class by
himself. He's already gone pretty far, and he's not the sort of
man to stop half way. I happen to know that (without any
suggestion, of course, of his standing for election) his name
has been mentioned several times in conversation, and not at
all unfavourably, at the Academy of Moral Sciences. And so,
though one can't say yet, of course, that he's exactly at the
pinnacle, he has fought his way by sheer merit to a very fine
position indeed, and success—which doesn't always come only
to the pushers and the muddlers, the mountebanks and the
humbugs—success has crowned his efforts."

My father, seeing me already, in a few years' time, an
Academician, exuded a satisfaction which M. de Norpois
raised to the highest pitch when, after a momentary hesitation
during which he appeared to be calculating the possible consequences of his act, he handed me his card and said: "Why not
go and see him yourself? Tell him I sent you. He may be able
to give you some good advice," plunging me by these words
into as painful a state of anxiety as if he had told me that I was
to embark next day as cabin-boy on board a wind-jammer.

My aunt Léonie had bequeathed to me, together with a
multiplicity of objects and furniture which were something of
an embarrassment, almost all her liquid assets—revealing thus
after her death an affection for me which I had little suspected
in her lifetime. My father, who was trustee of this estate until
I came of age, now consulted M. de Norpois with regard to
a number of investments. He recommended certain stocks
bearing a low rate of interest, which he considered particularly
sound, notably English consols and Russian four per cents.
"With absolutely first-class securities such as those," said M.
de Norpois, "even if your income from them is nothing very
great, you may be certain of never losing any of your capital."
My father then gave him a rough indication of what else he
had bought. M. de Norpois gave a just perceptible smile of
congratulation; like all capitalists, he regarded wealth as an

enviable thing, but thought it more delicate to compliment
people upon their possessions only by an inconspicuous sign
of intelligent sympathy; at the same time, as he was himself
colossally rich, he thought it in good taste to seem to regard as
considerable the inferior incomes of his friends, with, however, a happy and comforting reference to the superiority of
his own. On the other hand, he did not hesitate to congratulate
my father on the "composition" of his portfolio, selected
"with so sure, so delicate, so fine a taste." It was as though he
attributed to the relative values of shares, and even to shares
themselves, something akin to aesthetic merit. Of one, comparatively recent and still little known, which my father mentioned, M. de Norpois, like the people who have always read
the books of which you imagined you alone had ever heard,
said at once, "Ah, yes, I used to amuse myself watching it for
a time; it was not uninteresting," with the retrospective smile
of a regular subscriber who has read the latest novel already, in
monthly instalments, in his magazine. "It wouldn't be at all a
bad idea to apply for some of this new issue. It's distinctly
attractive; they're offering it at a most tempting discount."
But when he came to some of the older investments, my father,
who could not remember their exact names, which it was easy
to confuse with others of the same kind, opened a drawer and
showed the securities themselves to the Ambassador. The sight
of them enchanted me. They were ornamented with cathedral
spires and allegorical figures, like some of the old romantic
editions that I had pored over as a child. All the products of
one period resemble one another; the artists who illustrate the
poetry of their generation are the same artists who are employed by the big financial houses. And nothing reminds me
more strongly of the instalments of *Notre-Dame de Paris* and of
various works of Gérard de Nerval, that used to hang outside
the grocer's door at Combray, than does, in its rectangular and
flowery border, supported by recumbent river-gods, a "personal share" in the Water Company.

The contempt which my father had for my kind of intelligence was so far tempered by affection that, in practice,
his attitude towards everything I did was one of blind indulgence. And so he had no qualm about sending me to fetch a

little prose poem which I had made up years before at Combray on coming home from a walk. I had written it in a state of exaltation which must, I felt certain, communicate itself to everyone who read it. But it was not destined to captivate M. de Norpois, for he handed it back to me without a word.

My mother, who was full of respect for all my father's occupations, came in now to ask timidly whether dinner might be served. She was afraid to interrupt a conversation in which she herself could have no part. And indeed my father was continually reminding the Marquis of some useful measure which they had decided to support at the next meeting of the Commission, speaking in the peculiar tone always adopted in a strange environment by a pair of colleagues—akin, in this respect, to a pair of schoolfellows—whose professional routine has furnished them with a common fund of memories to which others have no access and to which they apologise for referring in their presence.

But the absolute control over his facial muscles to which M. de Norpois had attained allowed him to listen without seeming to hear a word. At length my father became uneasy: "I had thought," he ventured, after an endless preamble, "of asking the advice of the Commission . . ." Then from the face of the noble virtuoso, who had maintained the passivity of an orchestral player whose moment has not yet come, there emerged with an even delivery, on a sharp note, and as though they were no more than the completion (but scored for a different voice) of the phrase that my father had begun, the words: "of which you will not hesitate, of course, to call a meeting, more especially as the members are all known to you personally and can easily make themselves available." It was not in itself a very remarkable ending. But the immobility that had preceded it made it detach itself with the crystal clarity, the almost mischievous unexpectedness of those phrases with which the piano, silent until then, takes over, at a given moment, from the cello to which one has just been listening, in a Mozart concerto.

"Well, did you enjoy your *matinée?*" asked my father as we moved to the dining-room, hoping to draw me out and with the idea that my enthusiasm would give M. de Norpois a good opinion of me. "He has just been to see Berma. You remember we talked about it the other day," he went on, turning towards the diplomat, in the same tone of retrospective, technical and mysterious allusiveness as if he had been referring to a meeting of the Commission.

"You must have been enchanted, especially if you had never seen her before. Your father was alarmed at the possible repercussions that this little jaunt might have upon your health, which is none too good, I am told, none too robust. But I soon set his mind at rest. Theatres to-day are not what they were even twenty years ago. You have more or less comfortable seats now, and a certain amount of ventilation, although we have still a long way to go before we come up to the standard of Germany or England, who in that respect as in many others are immeasurably ahead of us. I have never seen Mme Berma in *Phèdre*, but I have always heard that she is excellent in the part. You were charmed with her, of course?"

M. de Norpois, a man a thousand times more intelligent than myself, must know that hidden truth which I had failed to extract from Berma's playing, and would reveal it to me; in answering his question I would ask him to let me know in what that truth consisted; and he would thereby justify me in the longing that I had felt to see and hear the actress. I had only a moment; I must take advantage of it and bring my cross examination to bear upon the essential points. But what were they? Fastening my whole attention upon my own so confused impressions, with no thought of winning the admiration of M. de Norpois but only that of learning from him the truth that I had still to discover, I made no attempt to substitute ready-made phrases for the words that failed me but stood there stammering until finally, in the hope of provoking him into declaring what was so admirable about Berma, I confessed that I had been disappointed.

"What's that?" cried my father, annoyed at the bad impression which this admission of my failure to appreciate the performance must make on M. de Norpois, "How can you possibly say that you didn't enjoy it? Why, your grandmother has been telling us that you sat there hanging on every word that Berma uttered, with your eyes starting out of your head;

that everyone else in the theatre seemed quite bored beside you."

"Oh, yes, I listened as hard as I could, trying to find out what it was that was supposed to be so wonderful about her. Of course, she's frightfully good and all that . . ."

"If she is 'frightfully good,' what more do you want?"

"One of the things that have undoubtedly contributed to the success of Mme Berma," said M. de Norpois, turning with application towards my mother, so as not to leave her out of the conversation, and in conscientious fulfilment of his duty of politeness to the lady of the house, "is the perfect taste that she shows in her choice of roles, which always assures her of complete success, and success of the right sort. She hardly ever appears in anything trivial. Look how she has thrown herself into the part of Phèdre. And then, she brings the same good taste to the choice of her costumes, and to her acting. In spite of her frequent and lucrative tours in England and America, the vulgarity—I will not say of John Bull, which would be unjust, at any rate as regards the England of the Victorian era—but of Uncle Sam has not infected her. No loud colours, no rant. And then that admirable voice, which serves her so well and upon which she plays so ravishingly—I should almost be tempted to describe it as a musical instrument!"

My interest in Berma's acting had continued to grow ever since the fall of the curtain because it was no longer compressed within the limits of reality; but I felt the need to find explanations for it; moreover it had been concentrated with equal intensity, while Berma was on the stage, upon everything that she offered, in the indivisibility of a living whole, to my eyes and ears; it had made no attempt to separate or discriminate; accordingly it welcomed the discovery of a reasonable cause for itself in these tributes paid to the simplicity, to the good taste of the actress, it drew them to itself by its power of absorption, seized upon them as the optimism of a drunken man seizes upon the actions of his neighbour, in each of which he finds an excuse for maudlin emotion. "It's true!" I told myself, "what a beautiful voice, what an absence of shrillness, what simple costumes, what intelligence to have chosen Phèdre! No, I have not been disappointed!"

The cold spiced beef with carrots made its appearance,

couched by the Michelangelo of our kitchen upon enormous crystals of aspic, like transparent blocks of quartz.

"You have a first-rate cook, Madame," said M. de Norpois, "and that is no small matter. I myself, who have had, when abroad, to maintain a certain style in housekeeping, I know how difficult it often is to find a perfect chef. This is a positive banquet that you have set before us!"

And indeed Françoise, in the excitement of her ambition to make a success, for so distinguished a guest, of a dinner the preparation of which had been sown with difficulties worthy of her powers, had put herself out as she no longer did when we were alone, and had recaptured her incomparable Combray manner.

"That is a thing you don't get in a chophouse, not even in the best of them: a spiced beef in which the aspic doesn't taste of glue and the beef has caught the flavour of the carrots. It's admirable! Allow me to come again," he went on, making a sign to show that he wanted more of the aspic. "I should be interested to see how your chef managed a dish of quite a different kind; I should like, for instance, to see him tackle a *bœuf Stroganoff*."

To add his own contribution to the pleasures of the repast, M. de Norpois entertained us with a number of the stories with which he was in the habit of regaling his diplomatic colleagues, quoting now some ludicrous period uttered by a politician notorious for long sentences packed with incoherent images, now some lapidary epigram of a diplomat sparkling with attic salt. But, to tell the truth, the criterion which for him set the two kinds of sentence apart in no way resembled that which I was in the habit of applying to literature. Most of the finer shades escaped me; the words which he recited with derision seemed to me not to differ very greatly from those which he found remarkable. He belonged to the class of men who, had we come to discuss the books I liked, would have said: "So you understand that, do you? I must confess that I don't; I'm not initiated," but I could have retaliated in kind, for I did not grasp the wit or folly, the eloquence or pomposity which he found in a retort or in a speech, and the absence of any perceptible reason for this being good and that bad made that sort of literature seem more mysterious, more obscure to me than any other. All that I grasped was that to repeat what everybody else was thinking was, in politics, the mark not of an inferior but of a superior mind. When M. de Norpois used certain expressions which were common currency in the newspapers, and uttered them with emphasis, one felt that they became an official pronouncement by the mere fact of his having employed them, and a pronouncement which would provoke widespread comment.

My mother was counting greatly upon the pineapple and truffle salad. But the Ambassador, after fastening for a moment on the confection the penetrating gaze of a trained observer, ate it with the inscrutable discretion of a diplomat, without disclosing his opinion. My mother insisted on his taking some more, which he did, but saying only, in place of the compliment for which she was hoping: "I obey, Madame, for I can see that it is, on your part, a positive ukase."

"We saw in the papers that you had a long talk with King Theodosius," my father ventured.

"Why, yes, the King, who has a wonderful memory for faces, was kind enough to remember, when he noticed me in the stalls, that I had had the honour to meet him on several occasions at the Court of Bavaria, at a time when he had never dreamed of his oriental throne—to which, as you know, he was summoned by a European Congress, and indeed had grave doubts about accepting, regarding that particular sovereignty as unworthy of his race, the noblest, heraldically speaking, in the whole of Europe. An aide-de-camp came down to bid me pay my respects to His Majesty, whose command I hastened, naturally, to obey."

"And I trust you are satisfied with the results of his visit?"

"Enchanted! One was justified in feeling some apprehension as to the manner in which a sovereign who is still so young would handle such an awkward situation, particularly at this highly delicate juncture. For my own part, I had complete confidence in the King's political sense. But I must confess that he far surpassed my expectations. The speech that he made at the Elysée, which, according to information that has come to me from a most authoritative source, was composed from

beginning to end by the King himself, was fully deserving of
the interest that it has aroused in all quarters. It was simply
masterly; a trifle daring, I quite admit, but it was an audacity
which, after all, was fully justified by the event. Traditional
diplomacy is all very well in its way, but in practice it has made
his country and ours live in a hermetically sealed atmosphere
in which it was no longer possible to breathe. Very well! There
is one method of letting in fresh air, obviously not a method
that one could officially recommend, but one which King
Theodosius could allow himself to adopt—and that is to
break the windows. Which he accordingly did, with a spontaneous good humour that delighted everybody, and also with
an aptness in his choice of words in which one could at once
detect the race of scholarly princes from whom he is descended
through his mother. There can be no question that when he
spoke of the 'affinities' that bind his country to France, the
expression, unusual though it be in the vocabulary of the
chancelleries, was a singularly happy one. You see that literary
ability is no drawback, even in diplomacy, even upon a
throne," he added, turning to me. "The community of interests had long been apparent, I quite admit, and relations
between the two powers were excellent. Still, it needed saying.
The word was awaited; it was chosen with marvellous aptitude; you have seen the effect it had. For my part, I thoroughly
applaud it."

"Your friend M. de Vaugoubert will be pleased, after preparing for the agreement all these years."

"All the more so in that His Majesty, who is quite in-
corrigible in some ways, had taken care to spring it on him as
a surprise. And it did come as a complete surprise, incidentally, to everyone concerned, beginning with the Foreign
Minister himself, who—I have heard—did not find it at all
to his liking. It appears that when someone spoke to him
about it he replied pretty sharply, and loud enough to be over-
heard by people in the vicinity: 'I was neither consulted nor
informed,' indicating clearly that he declined to accept any
responsibility in the matter. I must own that the incident
has caused a great furore, and I should not go so far as to
deny," he went on with a mischievous smile, "that certain of

my colleagues, who are only too inclined to take the line of least resistance, may have been shaken from their habitual repose. As for Vaugoubert, you are aware that he has been bitterly attacked for his policy of bringing that country into closer relations with France, and this must have been more than ordinarily painful to him since he is a sensitive and tender-hearted man. I can amply testify to that, since, for all that he is considerably my junior, I have had many dealings with him, we are friends of long standing and I know him intimately. Besides, who could help knowing him? His is a heart of crystal. Indeed, that is the one fault to be found with him; it is not necessary for the heart of a diplomat to be as transparent as his. Nevertheless there is talk of his being sent to Rome, which would be a splendid promotion, but a pretty big plum to swallow. Between ourselves, I fancy that Vaugoubert, utterly devoid of ambition as he is, would be extremely pleased, and would by no means ask for that cup to pass from him. For all we know, he may do wonders down there; he is the chosen candidate of the Consulta, and for my part I can see him perfectly well, with his artistic leanings, in the setting of the Farnese Palace and the Caracci Gallery. You would suppose that at least it was impossible for anyone to hate him; but there is a whole camarilla collected round King Theodosius which is more or less pledged to the Wilhelmstrasse, whose suggestions it slavishly follows, and which did everything in its power to spike his guns. Not only did Vaugoubert have to face these backstairs intrigues, he also had to endure the insults of a gang of paid hacks who later on, being like every hireling journalist the most arrant cowards, were the first to cry quits, but in the interval did not shrink from hurling at our representative the most fatuous accusations that the wit of irresponsible fools could invent. For a month and more Vaugoubert's enemies danced around him howling for his scalp" (M. de Norpois detached this word with sharp emphasis). "But forewarned is forearmed; he treated their insults with the contempt they deserved," he added even more forcibly, and with so fierce a glare in his eye that for a moment we forgot our food. "In the words of a fine Arab proverb, 'The dogs may bark; the caravan moves on!' "

After launching this quotation M. de Norpois paused and examined our faces, to see what effect it had had upon us. The effect was great, the proverb being familiar to us already. It had taken the place, that year, among the men of consequence, of "He who sows the wind shall reap the whirlwind," which was sorely in need of a rest, not having the perennial freshness of "Working for the King of Prussia." For the culture of these eminent men was an alternating one, usually triennial. Of course, the use of quotations such as these, with which M. de Norpois excelled in sprinkling his articles in the *Revue*, was in no way essential to their appearing sound and well-informed. Even without the ornament which the quotations supplied, it sufficed that M. de Norpois should write at a suitable point (as he never failed to do): "The Court of St. James was not the last to be sensible of the peril," or "Feeling ran high on the Singers' Bridge, where the selfish but skilful policy of the Dual Monarchy was being followed with anxious eyes," or "A cry of alarm sounded from Montecitorio," or yet again, "That perpetual double dealing which is so characteristic of the Ballplatz."[17] By these expressions the lay reader had at once recognised and acknowledged the career diplomat. But what had made people say that he was something more than that, that he was endowed with a superior culture, had been his judicious use of quotations, the perfect example of which, at that date, was still: "Give me a good policy and I will give you good finances, *to quote the favourite words of Baron Louis*": for we had not yet imported from the Far East: "Victory is on the side that can hold out a quarter of an hour longer than the other, *as the Japanese say*." This reputation as a literary man, combined with a positive genius for intrigue which he concealed beneath a mask of indifference, had secured the election of M. de Norpois to the Académie des Sciences Morales. And there were some who even thought that he would not be out of place in the Académie Française, on the famous day when, wishing to indicate that it was only by strengthening the Russian Alliance that we could hope to arrive at an understanding with Great Britain, he had not hesitated to write: "Let it be clearly understood in the Quai d'Orsay, let it be taught henceforward in all the manuals of geography, which

appear to be incomplete in this respect, let his certificate of
graduation be remorselessly withheld from every candidate
who has not learned to say, 'If all roads lead to Rome, nevertheless the way from Paris to London runs of necessity through
St. Petersburg.' "

"In short," M. de Norpois went on, addressing my father,
"Vaugoubert has brought off a considerable triumph, and
one that even surpassed his expectations. He expected, you
understand, a formal toast (which, after the storm-clouds of
recent years, would have been already an achievement) but
nothing more. Several persons who had the honour to be
present have assured me that it is impossible merely from
reading the speech to form any conception of the effect that it
produced when articulated with marvellous clearness of
diction by the King, who is a master of the art of public speaking and underlined in passing every delicate intention, every
subtle courtesy. In this connection, one of my informants
told me a little anecdote which brings out once again that
frank, boyish charm by which King Theodosius has won so
many hearts. I am assured that, precisely at that word
'affinities,' which was, on the whole, the great innovation of
the speech, and one that, you will see, will be the talk of the
chancelleries for years to come, His Majesty, anticipating the
delight of our ambassador, who would see it as the just con-
summation of his efforts—of his dreams, one might almost
say—and, in a word, his marshal's baton, made a half turn
towards Vaugoubert and fixing upon him the arresting gaze
so characteristic of the Oettingens, brought out that admirably
chosen word 'affinities,' a veritable brain-wave, in a tone which
made it plain to all his hearers that it was employed of set
purpose and with full knowledge of its implications. It appears
that Vaugoubert found some difficulty in mastering his emotion, and I must confess that, to a certain extent, I can well
understand it. Indeed, a person worthy of absolute credence
confided to me that the King came up to Vaugoubert after the
dinner, when His Majesty was holding informal court, and
was heard to say, 'Well, are you satisfied with your pupil, my
dear Marquis?' "

"One thing, however," M. de Norpois concluded, "is

certain; and that is that a speech of such a nature has done more than twenty years of negotiation towards bringing the two countries together, uniting their 'affinities,' to borrow the picturesque expression of Theodosius II. It is no more than a word, if you like, but look what success it has had, how the whole of the European press is repeating it, what interest it has aroused, what a new note it has struck. Besides, it is entirely in keeping with the young sovereign's style. I will not go so far as to say that he lights upon a diamond of that water every day. But it is very seldom that, in his prepared speeches, or better still in the spontaneous flow of his conversation, he does not reveal his character—I was on the point of saying 'does not affix his signature'—by the use of some incisive word. I myself am quite free from any suspicion of partiality in this respect since I am opposed to all innovations in terminology. Nine times out of ten they are most dangerous."

"Yes, I was thinking only the other day that the recent telegram from the Emperor of Germany could not be much to your liking," said my father.

M. de Norpois raised his eyes to heaven, as who should say, "Oh, that fellow!" before he replied: "In the first place, it is an act of ingratitude. It is more than a crime, it's a blunder, and one of a crassness which I can describe only as pyramidal! Indeed, unless someone puts a check on his activities, the man who got rid of Bismarck is quite capable of repudiating by degrees the whole of the Bismarckian policy; after which it will be a leap in the dark."

"My husband tells me, Monsieur, that you may perhaps take him to Spain one summer. I'm delighted for his sake."

"Why yes, it's an idea that greatly appeals to me. I should very much like to make this journey with you, my dear fellow. And you, Madame, have you decided yet how you are going to spend your holidays?"

"I shall perhaps go with my son to Balbec, but I'm not certain."

"Ah! Balbec is quite charming. I was down that way a few years ago. They are beginning to build some very attractive little villas there; I think you'll like the place. But may I ask what made you choose Balbec?"

"My son is very anxious to visit some of the churches in that neighbourhood, and Balbec church in particular. I was a little afraid that the tiring journey there and the discomfort of staying in the place might be too much for his health. But I hear that they have just opened an excellent hotel, in which he will be able to get all the comfort that he requires."

"Indeed! I must make a note of that for a certain person who will not turn up her nose at a comfortable hotel."

"The church at Balbec is very beautiful, is it not, Monsieur?" I inquired, repressing my sorrow at learning that one of the attractions of Balbec consisted in its pretty little villas.

"No, it's not bad; but it cannot be compared for a moment with such positive jewels in stone as the cathedrals of Rheims and Chartres, or with what is to my mind the pearl among them all, the Sainte-Chapelle here in Paris."

"But Balbec church is partly Romanesque, is it not?"

"Why, yes, it is in the Romanesque style, which is to say very cold and lifeless, with not the slightest hint of the grace, the fantasy of the later Gothic builders, who worked their stone as if it had been so much lace. Balbec church is well worth a visit if one is in the neighbourhood; it is decidedly quaint. On a wet day, when you have nothing better to do, you might look inside; you'll see the tomb of Tourville."[18]

"Tell me, were you at the Foreign Ministry dinner last night?" asked my father. "I couldn't go."

"No," M. de Norpois smiled, "I must confess that I renounced it for a party of a very different sort. I was dining with a lady of whom you may possibly have heard, the beautiful Mme Swann."

My mother repressed a shudder of apprehension, for, being more rapid in perception than my father, she grew alarmed on his account over things which only began to vex him a moment later. Whatever might cause him annoyance was first noticed by her, just as bad news of France is always known abroad sooner than among ourselves. But being curious to know what sort of people the Swanns might entertain, she inquired of M. de Norpois as to whom he had met there.

"Why, my dear lady, it is a house which (or so it struck me) is especially attractive to gentlemen. There were several

married men there last night, but their wives were all, as it
happened, unwell, and so had not come with them," replied
the Ambassador with a slyness veiled by good-humour, casting round the table a glance the gentleness and discretion of
which appeared to be tempering while in reality intensifying
its malice.

"In all fairness," he went on, "I must add that women do
go to the house, but women who belong rather—what shall I
say—to the Republican world than to Swann's" (he pronounced
it "Svann's") "circle. Who knows? Perhaps it will turn into a
political or a literary salon some day. Anyhow, they appear to
be quite content as they are. Indeed, I feel that Swann adver-
tises his contentment just a trifle too blatantly. He told us the
names of all the people who had asked him and his wife out
for the next week, people whose friendship there is no reason
to be proud of, with a want of reserve, of taste, almost of tact,
which I was astonished to remark in so refined a man. He
kept on repeating, 'We haven't a free evening!' as though that
was a thing to boast of, positively like a *parvenu*, and he is
certainly not that. For Swann had always plenty of friends,
women as well as men, and without seeming over-bold, without the least wish to appear indiscreet, I think I may safely
say that not all of them, of course, nor even the majority of
them, but one at least, who is a lady of the very highest rank,
would perhaps not have shown herself inexorably averse from
the idea of entering into relations with Mme Swann, in which
case it is safe to assume that more than one sheep of the social
flock would have followed her lead. But it seems that there
has been no indication of any approach on Swann's part in
that direction . . . What do I see? A Nesselrode pudding! As
well! I declare I shall need a course at Carlsbad after such a
Lucullus-feast as this . . . Possibly Swann felt that there would
be too much resistance to overcome. The marriage—so
much is certain—was not well received. There has been some
talk of his wife's having money, but that's the grossest fallacy.
At all events, the whole affair has been looked upon with dis-
favour. And then, Swann has an aunt who is excessively rich
and in an admirable position socially, married to a man who,
financially speaking, is a power in the land. Not only did she

refuse to meet Mme Swann, she conducted an out-and-out campaign to force her friends and acquaintance to do the same. I don't mean to say that any well-bred Parisian has shown actual incivility to Mme Swann. . . . No! A hundred times no! Quite apart from her husband's being eminently a man to take up the gauntlet. At all events, the odd thing is to see the alacrity with which Swann, who knows so many of the most select people, cultivates a society of which the best that can be said is that it is extremely mixed. I myself, who knew him in the old days, must admit that I felt more astonished than amused at seeing a man so well-bred as he, so much at home in the most exclusive circles, effusively thanking the Principal Private Secretary to the Minister of Posts for coming to their house, and asking him whether Mme Swann might *take the liberty* of calling upon his wife. He must feel like a fish out of water, don't you know; obviously, it's quite a different world. All the same, I don't think Swann is unhappy. It's true that for some years before the marriage she was always trying to blackmail him in a rather disgraceful way; she would take the child away whenever Swann refused her anything. Poor Swann, who is as ingenuous as he is in other ways discerning, believed every time that the child's disappearance was a coincidence, and declined to face the facts. Apart from that, she made such continual scenes that everyone expected that, as soon as she achieved her object and was safely married, nothing could possibly restrain her and that their life would be a hell on earth. Instead of which, just the opposite has happened. People are inclined to laugh at the way Swann speaks of his wife; it's become a standing joke. Of course one hardly expected that, more or less aware of being . . . (you know Molière's word),[19] he would go and proclaim it *urbi et orbi*; all the same, people find it a little excessive when he says that she's an excellent wife. And yet that is not so far from the truth as people imagine. In her own way—which is not, perhaps, what all husbands would choose, but then, between you and me, I find it difficult to believe that Swann, who has known her for a long time and is far from being an utter fool, did not know what to expect—there can be no denying that she does seem to have a certain regard for him. I don't say she isn't flighty, and Swann himself is not noted for his constancy, if one is to believe the charitable tongues which, as you may suppose, continue to wag. But she is grateful to him for what he has done for her, and, contrary to the fears that were generally expressed, her temper seems to have become angelic."

This alteration was perhaps not so extraordinary as M. de Norpois professed to find it. Odette had not believed that Swann would ever consent to marry her; each time she made the tendentious announcement that some man about town had just married his mistress she had seen him stiffen into a glacial silence, or at the most, if she challenged him directly by asking: "Don't you think it's very good and very right, what he's done for a woman who sacrificed all her youth to him?" had heard him answer dryly: "But I don't say that there's anything wrong in it. Everyone does as he thinks fit." She came very near, indeed, to believing that (as he used to threaten in moments of anger) he would leave her altogether, for she had heard it said, not long since, by a woman sculptor, that "You can't be surprised at anything men do, they're such cads," and impressed by the profundity of this pessimistic maxim she had appropriated it for herself, and repeated it on every possible occasion with a despondent air that seemed to imply: "After all, it's not at all impossible; it would be just my luck." Meanwhile all the virtue had gone from the optimistic maxim which had hitherto guided Odette through life: "You can do anything with men when they're in love with you, they're such idiots!" a doctrine which was expressed on her face by the same flicker of the eyelids that might have accompanied such words as: "Don't be frightened; he won't break anything." While she waited, Odette was tormented by the thought of what such and such a friend of hers, who had been married by a man who had not lived with her for nearly so long as she herself had lived with Swann, and had no child by him, and who was now relatively esteemed, invited to balls at the Elysée and so forth, must think of Swann's behaviour. A consultant more discerning than M. de Norpois would doubtless have been able to diagnose that it was this feeling of shame and humiliation that had embittered Odette, that the infernal temper she displayed was not an essential part of her nature, was not an incurable disease, and so would easily have foretold what had indeed come to pass, namely that a new regimen, that of matrimony, would put an end with almost magic swiftness to those painful incidents, of daily occurrence but in no sense organic. Almost everyone was surprised at the marriage, and that in itself is surprising. No doubt very few people understand the purely subjective nature of the phenomenon that we call love, or how it creates, so to speak, a supplementary person, distinct from the person whom the world knows by the same name, a person most of whose constituent elements are derived from ourselves. And so there are very few who can regard as natural the enormous proportions that a person comes to assume in our eyes who is not the same as the person that they see. It would seem, none the less, that so far as Odette was concerned people could have taken into account the fact that if, indeed, she had never entirely understood Swann's mentality, at least she was acquainted with the titles and with all the details of his studies, so much so that the name of Vermeer was as familiar to her as that of her own dressmaker; while as for Swann himself, she knew intimately those traits of character of which the rest of the world is ignorant or which it scoffs at, and of which only a mistress or a sister possesses the true and cherished image; and so strongly are we attached to such idiosyncrasies, even to those of them which we are most anxious to correct, that it is because a woman comes in time to acquire an indulgent, an affectionately mocking familiarity with them, such as we ourselves or our relatives have, that love affairs of long standing have something of the sweetness and strength of family affection. The bonds that unite us to another human being are sanctified when he or she adopts the same point of view as ourselves in judging one of our imperfections. And among these special traits there were others, besides, which belonged as much to Swann's intellect as to his character, but which nevertheless, because they had their roots in the latter, Odette had been able more easily to discern. She complained that when Swann turned author, when he published his essays, these characteristics were not to be found in them to the same extent as in his letters or in his conversation, where they abounded. She urged him to give them a more prominent place. She wanted this because it was these things that she herself most liked in him, but since she liked them because they were the things most typical of him, she was perhaps not wrong in wishing that they might be found in his writings. Perhaps also she thought that his work, if endowed with more vitality, so that it ultimately brought him success, might enable her also to form what at the Verdurins' she had been taught to value above everything else in the world—a salon.

Among the people to whom this sort of marriage appeared ridiculous, people who in their own case would ask themselves, "What will M. de Guermantes think, what will Bréauté say, when I marry Mlle de Montmorency?", among the people who cherished that sort of social ideal, would have figured, twenty years earlier, Swann himself, the Swann who had taken endless pains to get himself elected to the Jockey Club and had reckoned at that time on making a brilliant marriage which, by consolidating his position, would have made him one of the most prominent figures in Paris. However, the visions which such a marriage suggests to the mind of the interested party need, like all visions, if they are not to fade away and be altogether lost, to receive sustenance from without. Your most ardent longing is to humiliate the man who has insulted you. But if you never hear of him any more, having removed to some other place, your enemy will come to have no longer the slightest importance to you. If for twenty years one has lost sight of all the people on whose account one would have liked to be elected to the Jockey Club or the Institute, the prospect of becoming a member of one or other of those establishments will have ceased to tempt one. Now, fully as much as retirement, ill-health or religious conversion, a protracted love affair will substitute fresh visions for the old. There was no renunciation on Swann's part, when he married Odette, of his social ambitions, for from those ambitions Odette had long ago, in the spiritual sense of the word, detached him. Besides, had he not been so detached, his marriage would have been all the more creditable. It is because they entail the sacrifice of a more or less advantageous position to a purely private happiness that, as a general rule, ignominious marriages are the most estimable of all. (One cannot very well include among ignominious marriages those that are made for money, there being no instance on record of a couple, of whom the wife or else the husband has thus sold himself, who have not sooner or later been admitted into society, if only by tradition, and on the strength of so many precedents, and so as not to have, as it were, one law for the rich and another for the poor.) Perhaps, on the other hand, the artistic, if not the perverse side of Swann's nature would in any event have derived a certain pleasure from coupling himself, in one of those crossings of species such as Mendelians practise and mythology records, with a creature of a different race, arch-duchess or prostitute—from contracting a royal alliance or marrying beneath him. There had been but one person in all the world whose opinion he took into consideration whenever he thought of his possible marriage with Odette; this was, and from no snobbish motive, the Duchesse de Guermantes—with whom Odette, on the contrary, was but little concerned, thinking only of those people whose position was immediately above her own rather than in so vague an empyrean. But when Swann in his daydreams saw Odette as already his wife he invariably pictured to himself the moment when he would take her—her, and above all his daughter—to call upon the Princesse des Laumes (who was shortly, on the death of her father-in-law, to become Duchesse de Guermantes). He had no desire to introduce them anywhere else, but his heart would soften as he imagined—articulating to himself their actual words—all the things that the Duchess would say of him to Odette, and Odette to the Duchess, the affection that she would show for Gilberte, spoiling her, making him proud of his child. He enacted to himself the scene of this introduction with the same precision in each of its imaginary details that people show when they consider how they would spend, supposing they were to win it, a lottery prize the amount of which they have arbitrarily determined. In so far as a mental picture which accompanies one of our resolutions may be said to motivate it, so it might be said that if Swann married Odette it was in order to introduce her, together with Gilberte, without anyone else being present, without, if need be, anyone else ever coming to know of it, to the Duchesse de Guermantes. We shall see how this sole social ambition that he had entertained for his wife and daughter was precisely the one whose realisation proved to be forbidden him, by a veto so absolute that Swann died in the belief that the Duchess could never come to know them. We shall see too that, on the contrary, the Duchesse de Guermantes did strike up a friendship with Odette and Gilberte after Swann's death. And doubtless he would have been wiser— in so far as he could attach such importance to so small a matter—not to have formed too dark a picture of the future in this connexion, but to have consoled himself with the hope that the desired meeting might indeed take place when he was no longer there to enjoy it. The laborious process of causation which sooner or later will bring about every possible effect, including, consequently, those which one had believed to be least possible, naturally slow at times, is rendered slower still by our desire (which in seeking to accelerate only obstructs it), by our very existence, and comes to fruition only when we have ceased to desire, and sometimes ceased to live. Was not Swann conscious of this from his own experience, and was there not already in his lifetime—as it were a prefiguration of what was to happen after his death—a posthumous happiness in this marriage with Odette whom he had passionately loved—even if she had not attracted him at first sight—whom he had married when he no longer loved her, when the person who, in Swann, had so longed to live and so despaired of living all his life with Odette, when that person was dead?

I began to talk about the Comte de Paris, to ask whether he was not one of Swann's friends, for I was afraid lest the conversation should drift away from him. "Why, yes!" replied M. de Norpois, turning towards me and fixing upon my modest person the azure gaze in which there floated, as in their vital element, his immense capacity for work and his power of assimilation. "And upon my word," he added, once more addressing my father, "I do not think that I shall be overstepping the bounds of the respect which I have always professed for the Prince (without, however, maintaining any personal relations with him, which would inevitably com-

promise my position, unofficial though it may now be) if I tell
you of a little episode which is not unintriguing. No more
than four years ago, at a small railway station in one of the
countries of Central Europe, the Prince happened to set eyes
on Mme Swann. Naturally, none of his circle ventured to ask
His Royal Highness what he thought of her. That would not
have been seemly. But when her name came up by chance in
conversation, by certain signs—barely perceptible, if you like,
but quite unmistakable—the Prince appeared willing enough
to let it be understood that his impression of her had on the
whole been far from unfavourable."

"But there could have been no possibility, surely, of her
being presented to the Comte de Paris?" inquired my father.

"Well, we don't know; with princes one never does know,"
replied M. de Norpois. "The most exalted, those who know
best how to secure what is due to them, are as often as not the
last to let themselves be embarrassed by the decrees of popular
opinion, even by those for which there is most justification,
especially when it is a question of their rewarding a personal
attachment to themselves. And it is certain that the Comte de
Paris has always most graciously acknowledged the devotion
of Swann, who is moreover a man of wit if ever there was one."

"And what was your own impression, Your Excellency?"
my mother asked, from politeness as well as from curiosity.

All the vigour of an old connoisseur broke through the
habitual moderation of his speech as he answered: "Quite
excellent!"

And knowing that the admission that a strong impression
has been made on one by a woman takes its place, provided
that one makes it in a playful tone, in a certain form of the art
of conversation that is highly appreciated, he broke into a
little laugh that lasted for several moments, moistening the
old diplomat's blue eyes and making his nostrils, with their
network of tiny scarlet veins, quiver. "She is altogether
charming!"

"Was there a writer of the name of Bergotte at this dinner,
Monsieur?" I asked timidly, still trying to keep the conversation to the subject of the Swanns.

"Yes, Bergotte was there," replied M. de Norpois, inclining

his head courteously towards me, as though in his desire to be
agreeable to my father he attached to everything connected
with him a genuine importance, even to the questions of a
boy of my age who was not accustomed to see such politeness
shown to him by persons of his. "Do you know him?" he
went on, fastening on me that clear gaze the penetration of
which had won the admiration of Bismarck.

"My son does not know him, but he admires his work
immensely," my mother explained.

"Good heavens!" exclaimed M. de Norpois, inspiring me
with doubts of my own intelligence far graver than those that
ordinarily tormented me, when I saw that what I valued a
thousand times more than myself, what I regarded as the most
exalted thing in the world, was for him at the bottom of the
scale of admiration, "I do not share your son's point of view.
Bergotte is what I call a flute-player: one must admit that he
plays very agreeably, although with a great deal of mannerism, of affectation. But when all is said, there's no more to it
than that, and that is not much. Nowhere does one find in his
flaccid works what one might call structure. No action—or
very little—but above all no range. His books fail at the foundation, or rather they have no foundation at all. At a time like
the present, when the ever-increasing complexity of life leaves
one scarcely a moment for reading, when the map of Europe
has undergone radical alterations and is on the eve, perhaps,
of undergoing others more drastic still, when so many new
and threatening problems are arising on every side, you will
allow me to suggest that one is entitled to ask that a writer
should be something more than a clever fellow who lulls us
into forgetting, amid otiose and byzantine discussions of the
merits of pure form, that we may be overwhelmed at any
moment by a double tide of barbarians, those from without
and those from within our borders. I am aware that this is to
blaspheme against the sacrosanct school of what these gentlemen term 'Art for Art's sake,' but at this period of history
there are tasks more urgent than the manipulation of words in
a harmonious manner. I don't deny that Bergotte's manner
can be quite seductive at times, but taken as a whole, it is all
very precious, very thin, and altogether lacking in virility. I

can now understand more easily, when I bear in mind your
altogether excessive regard for Bergotte, the few lines that
you showed me just now, which it would be ungracious of me
not to overlook, since you yourself told me in all simplicity
that they were merely a childish scribble." (I had indeed said
so, but I did not mean a word of it.) "For every sin there is
forgiveness, and especially for the sins of youth. After all,
others as well as yourself have such sins upon their conscience,
and you are not the only one who has believed himself a poet
in his idle moments. But one can see in what you showed me
the unfortunate influence of Bergotte. You will not, of course,
be surprised when I say that it had none of his qualities, since
he is a past-master in the art—entirely superficial by the by—
of handling a certain style of which, at your age, you cannot
have acquired even the rudiments. But already there is the
same fault, that nonsense of stringing together fine-sounding
words and only afterwards troubling about what they mean.
That is putting the cart before the horse. Even in Bergotte's
books, all those Chinese puzzles of form, all those subtleties of
a deliquescent mandarin seem to me to be quite futile. Given a
few fireworks let off prettily enough by an author, and up goes
the shout of masterpiece. Masterpieces are not so common as
all that! Bergotte cannot place to his credit—does not carry in
his baggage, if I may use the expression—a single novel that
is at all lofty in its conception, one of those books which one
keeps in a special corner of one's library. I cannot think of
one such in the whole of his work. But that does not mean
that, in his case, the work is not infinitely superior to the
author. Ah! there's a man who justifies the wit who insisted
that one ought never to know an author except through his
books. It would be impossible to imagine an individual who
corresponded less to his—more pretentious, more pompous,
more ill-bred. Vulgar at times, at others talking like a book,
and not even like one of his own, but like a boring book,
which his, to do them justice, are not—such is your Bergotte.
He has the most confused and convoluted mind, what our
forebears called sesquipedalian, and he makes the things that
he says even more unpleasing by the manner in which he says
them. I forget for the moment whether it is Loménie or

Sainte-Beuve who tells us that Vigny repelled people by the same failing. But Bergotte has never given us a *Cinq-Mars*, or a *Cachet rouge*, certain pages of which are veritable anthology pieces."

Shattered by what M. de Norpois had just said to me with regard to the fragment which I had submitted to him, and remembering at the same time the difficulties that I experienced when I attempted to write an essay or merely to devote myself to serious thought, I felt conscious once again of my intellectual nullity and told myself that I was not cut out for the literary life. Doubtless in the old days at Combray certain impressions of a very humble order, or a few pages of Bergotte, had plunged me into a state of reverie which had appeared to me to be of great value. But this state was what my prose poem reflected; there could be no doubt that M. de Norpois had at once grasped and seen through the fallacy of what I had thought to be beautiful simply through a deceptive mirage, since the Ambassador had not been taken in by it. He had shown me, on the contrary, what an infinitely unimportant place was mine when I was judged from outside, objectively, by the best-disposed and most intelligent of experts. I felt dismayed, diminished; and my mind, like a fluid which is without dimensions save those of the vessel that is provided for it, just as it had expanded in the past to fill the vast capacity of genius, contracted now, was entirely contained within the straitened mediocrity in which M. de Norpois had of a sudden enclosed and sealed it.

"Our first introduction—I speak of Bergotte and myself," he resumed, turning to my father, "was somewhat beset with thorns (which is, after all, only another way of saying that it was excessively prickly). Bergotte—some years ago, now— paid a visit to Vienna while I was Ambassador there; he was introduced to me by the Princess Metternich, came and wrote his name in the Embassy book, and made it known that he wished to be invited. Now, being when abroad the representative of France, to which he has after all done some honour by his writings, to a certain extent (let us say, to be precise, to a very slight extent), I was prepared to set aside the unfavourable opinion that I hold of his private life. But he was not travelling alone, and moreover he let it be understood that he was not to be invited without his companion. I trust that I am no more of a prude than most men, and, being a bachelor, I was perhaps in a position to throw open the doors of the Embassy a little wider than if I had been married and the father of a family. Nevertheless, I confess that there are depths of ignominy to which I refuse to accommodate myself and which are made more repulsive still by the tone, more than just moral, but frankly moralising, that Bergotte adopts in his books, where one finds nothing but perpetual and, between ourselves, somewhat wearisome analyses, painful scruples, morbid remorse, and, for the merest peccadilloes, veritable homilies (one knows what they're worth), while all the time he is showing such frivolity and cynicism in his private life. To cut a long story short, I avoided answering, the Princess returned to the charge, but with no greater success. So that I do not suppose that I appear exactly in the odour of sanctity to the gentleman, and I am not sure how far he appreciated Swann's kindness in inviting him and myself on the same evening. Unless of course it was he who asked for the invitation. One can never tell, for really he is not normal. Indeed that is his sole excuse."

"And was Mme Swann's daughter at the dinner?" I asked M. de Norpois, taking advantage, to put this question, of a moment in which, as we all moved towards the drawing-room, I could more easily conceal my emotion than would have been possible at table, where I was held fast in the glare of the lamplight.

M. de Norpois appeared to be trying for a moment to remember:

"Ah, yes, you mean a young person of fourteen or fifteen? Yes, of course, I remember now that she was introduced to me before dinner as the daughter of our Amphitryon. I'm afraid that I saw little of her; she retired to bed early. Or else she went out to see some friends—I forget which. But I can see that you are very intimate with the Swann household."

"I play with Mlle Swann in the Champs-Elysées, and she's delightful."

"Oh! so that's it? But I assure you, I too thought her

charming. I must confess to you, however, that I do not
believe that she will ever come anywhere near her mother, if
I may say as much without hurting your feelings."

"I prefer Mlle Swann's face, but I admire her mother,
too, enormously. I go for walks in the Bois simply in the hope
of seeing her pass."

"Ah! But I must tell them that; they will be highly flattered."

While he was uttering these words, and for a few seconds
after he had uttered them, M. de Norpois was still in the same
position as anyone else who, hearing me speak of Swann as an
intelligent man, of his family as respectable stockbrokers, of
his house as a fine house, imagined that I would speak just as
readily of another man equally intelligent, of other stockbrokers equally respectable, of another house equally fine;
it was the moment in which a sane man who is talking to a
lunatic has not yet perceived that he is a lunatic. M. de Norpois
knew that there is nothing unnatural in the pleasure one
derives from looking at pretty women, that it is good manners,
when someone speaks to you of a pretty woman with any
warmth, to pretend to think that he is in love with her, and to
promise to further his designs. But in saying that he would
speak of me to Gilberte and her mother (which would enable me, like an Olympian deity who has taken on the fluidity
of a breath of wind, or rather the aspect of the old greybeard
whose form Minerva borrows, to insinuate myself, unseen,
into Mme Swann's drawing-room, to attract her attention, to
occupy her thoughts, to arouse her gratitude for my admiration, to appear before her as the friend of an important person,
to seem to her worthy to be invited by her in the future and
to enter into the intimate life of her family), this important
person who was going to use on my behalf the great influence
which he must have with Mme Swann inspired in me suddenly
an affection so compelling that I had difficulty in restraining
myself from kissing his soft, white, wrinkled hands, which
looked as though they had been left lying too long in water.
I almost made as if to do so, in an impulsive movement which
I believed that I alone had noticed. For it is difficult for any
of us to calculate exactly the extent to which our words or
gestures are apparent to others. Partly from the fear of exag-

gerating our own importance, and also because we enlarge to
enormous proportions the field over which the impressions
formed by other people in the course of their lives are obliged
to extend, we imagine that the incidentals of our speech and
of our postures scarcely penetrate the consciousness, still less
remain in the memory of those with whom we converse. It
is, no doubt, to a supposition of this sort that criminals yield
when they "touch up" the wording of a statement already
made, thinking that the new variant cannot be confronted
with any existing version. But it is quite possible that, even
with respect to the millennial existence of the human race, the
philosophy of the journalist, according to which everything
is doomed to oblivion, is less true than a contrary philosophy
which would predict the conservation of everything. In the
same newspaper in which the moralist of the leader column
says to us of an event, of a work of art, *a fortiori* of a singer
who has enjoyed her "crowded hour": "Who will remember
this in ten years' time?", does not the report of the Académie
des Inscriptions overleaf speak often of a fact in itself of
smaller importance, of a poem of little merit, which dates from
the epoch of the Pharaohs and is still known in its entirety?
Perhaps this does not quite hold true for the brief life of a
human being. And yet, some years later, in a house in which
M. de Norpois, who was also a guest there, seemed to me the
most solid support that I could hope to find, because he was
a friend of my father, indulgent, inclined to wish us all well,
and moreover, by profession and upbringing trained to discretion, when, after the Ambassador had gone, I was told that
he had alluded to an evening long ago when he had "seen the
moment in which I was about to kiss his hand," not only did
I blush to the roots of my hair but I was stupefied to learn how
different from what I might have believed was not only the
manner in which M. de Norpois spoke of me but also the
composition of his memory. This piece of gossip enlightened
me as to the incalculable proportions of absence and presence
of mind, of recollection and forgetfulness, of which the human
mind is composed; and I was as marvellously surprised as on
the day on which I read for the first time, in one of Maspero's
books, that there existed a precise list of the sportsmen whom

Assurbanipal used to invite to his hunts a thousand years before the birth of Christ.

"Oh, Monsieur," I assured M. de Norpois, when he told me that he would inform Gilberte and her mother how much I admired them, "if you would do that, if you would speak of me to Mme Swann my whole life would not be long enough to prove my gratitude, and that life would be all at your service. But I feel bound to point out to you that I do not know Mme Swann, and that I have never been introduced to her."

I had added these last words from a scruple of conscience, and so as not to appear to be boasting of an acquaintance which I did not possess. But as I uttered them I sensed that they were already superfluous, for from the beginning of my speech of thanks, with its chilling ardour, I had seen flitting across the face of the Ambassador an expression of hesitation and displeasure, and in his eyes that vertical, narrow, slanting look (like, in the drawing of a solid body in perspective, the receding line of one of its surfaces), that look which one addresses to the invisible interlocutor whom one has within oneself at the moment when one is telling him something that one's other interlocutor, the person to whom one has been talking up till then—myself, in this instance—is not meant to hear. I realised in a flash that the words I had pronounced, which, feeble as they were when measured against the flood of gratitude that was coursing through me, had seemed to me bound to touch M. de Norpois and to confirm his decision upon an intervention which would have given him so little trouble and me so much joy, were perhaps (out of all those that could have been chosen with diabolical malice by persons anxious to do me harm) the only ones that could result in his abandoning his intention. Indeed, on hearing them, in the same way as when a stranger with whom we have been pleasantly exchanging impressions which we might have supposed to be similar about passers-by whom we agreed in regarding as vulgar, reveals suddenly the pathological abyss that divides him from us by adding carelessly as he feels his pocket: "What a pity I haven't got my revolver with me; I could have picked off the lot of them," M. de Norpois, who knew that nothing was less costly or more simple than to be commended to Mme

Swann and taken to her house, and saw that to me, on the contrary, such favours bore so high a price and must consequently
be very difficult to obtain, thought that the desire I had expressed, though ostensibly normal, must cloak some different
motive, some suspect intention, some prior transgression, on
account of which, in the certainty of displeasing Mme Swann,
no one had hitherto been willing to undertake the responsibility for conveying a message to her from me. And I realised
that this mission was one he would never discharge, that
he might see Mme Swann daily, for years to come, without
ever mentioning my name. He did indeed ask her, a few days
later, for some information which I required, and charged my
father to convey it to me. But he had not thought fit to tell her
on whose behalf he was inquiring. So she would never discover that I knew M. de Norpois and that I so longed to be
asked to her house; and this was perhaps a lesser misfortune
than I supposed. For the second of these discoveries would
probably not have added much to the efficacy of the first,
which was in any event dubious: for Odette, the idea of her own
life and of her own home awakened no mysterious uneasiness,
and a person who knew her, who came to her house, did not
seem to her a fabulous creature such as he seemed to me who
would have flung a stone through Swann's windows if I could
have written upon it that I knew M. de Norpois; I was convinced that such a message, even when transmitted in so
brutal a fashion, would have given me far more prestige in the
eyes of the lady of the house than it would have prejudiced
her against me. But even if I had been capable of understanding
that the mission which M. de Norpois did not perform must
have remained futile, indeed that it might have damaged my
credit with the Swanns, I should not have had the courage, had
he proved himself willing, to relieve the Ambassador of it
and to renounce the pleasure—however fatal its consequences
might prove—of feeling that my name and my person were
thus brought for a moment into Gilberte's presence, into her
unknown life and home.

     After M. de Norpois had gone my father cast an eye over
the evening paper, and I thought once more of Berma. The
pleasure which I had experienced in listening to her required

all the more to be reinforced in that it had fallen far short of what I had promised myself; and so it at once assimilated everything that was capable of giving it nourishment, for instance those merits which M. de Norpois had ascribed to her and which my mind had imbibed at a single draught, like a dry lawn when water is poured on it. Then my father handed me the newspaper, pointing out to me a paragraph which ran more or less as follows:—

The performance of *Phèdre*, given this afternoon before an enthusiastic audience which included the foremost representatives of the artistic and critical world, was for Mme Berma, who played the heroine, the occasion of a triumph as brilliant as any that she has known in the course of her phenomenal career. We shall return at greater length to this performance, which is indeed an event in the history of the stage; suffice it to say here, that the best qualified judges were unanimous in declaring that this interpretation shed an entirely new light on the role of Phèdre, which is one of the finest and most complex of Racine's creations, and that it constituted the purest and most exalted manifestation of dramatic art which it has been the privilege of our generation to witness.

As soon as my mind had conceived this new idea of "the purest and most exalted manifestation of dramatic art," it, the idea, sped to join the imperfect pleasure which I had felt in the theatre, adding to it a little of what it lacked, and the combination formed something so exalting that I exclaimed to myself: "What a great artist!" It will doubtless be argued that I was not absolutely sincere. But let us bear in mind, rather, the countless writers who, dissatisfied with the passage they have just written, read some eulogy of the genius of Chateaubriand, or evoke the spirit of some great artist whose equal they aspire to be, humming to themselves, for instance, a phrase of Beethoven the melancholy of which they compare with what they have been trying to express in their prose, and become so imbued with this idea of genius that they add it to their own productions when they return to them, no longer see them in the light in which they appeared at first, and, hazarding an act of faith in the value of their work, say to themselves: "After all!" without taking into account that, into the total which determines their ultimate satisfaction, they have intro-

duced the memory of marvellous pages of Chateaubriand
which they assimilate to their own but which, after all, they
did not write; let us bear in mind the numberless men who
believe in the love of a mistress who has done nothing but
betray them; all those, too, who are sustained by the alternative
hopes, on the one hand of an incomprehensible survival after
death, when they think, inconsolable husbands, of the wives
whom they have lost but have not ceased to love, or, artists, of
the posthumous glory which they may thus enjoy, and on the
other of a reassuring void, when their thoughts turn to the misdeeds that otherwise they must expiate after their death; let us
bear in mind also the travellers who come home enraptured by
the over-all splendour of a journey from which day by day they
experienced nothing but tedium; and let us then declare
whether, in the communal life that is led by our ideas in the
enclosure of our minds, there is a single one of those that
makes us most happy which has not first sought, like a real
parasite, and won from an alien but neighbouring idea the
greater part of the strength that it originally lacked.

My mother appeared none too pleased that my father no
longer thought of a diplomatic career for me. I fancy that,
anxious above all else that a definite rule of life should
discipline the vagaries of my nervous system, what she regretted was not so much seeing me abandon diplomacy as the
prospect of my devoting myself to literature. "Don't worry,"
my father told her, "the main thing is that a man should find
pleasure in his work. He's no longer a child. He knows pretty
well now what he likes, it's very unlikely that he will change,
and he's quite capable of deciding for himself what will make
him happy in life."

That evening, as I waited for the time to arrive when, thanks
to the freedom of choice which they allowed me, I should or
should not begin to be happy in life, my father's words caused
me great uneasiness. His unexpected kindnesses, when they
occurred, had always made me long to kiss his glowing cheeks
above his beard, and if I did not yield to the impulse, it was
simply because I was afraid of annoying him. Now, as an
author becomes alarmed when he sees the fruits of his own
meditations, which do not appear to him to be of great value

since he does not separate them from himself, oblige a publisher to choose a brand of paper, to employ a type-face finer, perhaps, than they deserve, I asked myself whether my desire to write was of sufficient importance to justify my father in dispensing so much generosity. But apart from that, in speaking of my inclinations as no longer liable to change, and of what was destined to make my life happy, he aroused in me two very painful suspicions. The first was that (at a time when, every day, I regarded myself as standing upon the threshold of a life which was still intact and would not enter upon its course until the following morning) my existence had already begun, and that, furthermore, what was yet to follow would not differ to any extent from what had gone before. The second suspicion, which was really no more than a variant of the first, was that I was not situated somewhere outside Time, but was subject to its laws, just like those characters in novels who, for that reason, used to plunge me into such gloom when I read of their lives, down at Combray, in the fastness of my hooded wicker chair. In theory one is aware that the earth revolves, but in practice one does not perceive it, the ground upon which one treads seems not to move, and one can rest assured. So it is with Time in one's life. And to make its flight perceptible novelists are obliged, by wildly accelerating the beat of the pendulum, to transport the reader in a couple of minutes over ten, or twenty, or even thirty years. At the top of one page we have left a lover full of hope; at the foot of the next we meet him again, a bowed old man of eighty, painfully dragging himself on his daily walk around the courtyard of a hospital, scarcely replying to what is said to him, oblivious of the past. In saying of me, "He's no longer a child," "His tastes won't change now," and so forth, my father had suddenly made me conscious of myself in Time, and caused me the same kind of depression as if I had been, not yet the enfeebled old pensioner, but one of those heroes of whom the author, in a tone of indifference which is particularly galling, says to us at the end of a book: "He very seldom comes up from the country now. He has finally decided to end his days there."

Meanwhile my father, in order to forestall any criticism that we might feel tempted to make of our guest, said to my mother: "Upon my word, old Norpois was a bit 'stuffy,' as you call it, this evening, wasn't he? When he said that it wouldn't have been 'seemly' to ask the Comte de Paris a question, I was quite afraid you would burst out laughing."

"Not at all!" answered my mother. "I was delighted to see a man of his standing and his age with that sort of simplicity, which is really a sign of decency and good breeding."

"I dare say. But that doesn't prevent him from having a shrewd and discerning mind—as I know very well since I see him on the Commission, remember, where he's very different from what he was here," exclaimed my father, who was glad to see that Mamma appreciated M. de Norpois, and anxious to persuade her that he was even better than she supposed, because a cordial nature exaggerates a friend's qualities with as much pleasure as a mischievous one finds in depreciating them. "What was it that he said, again—'With princes one never does know' . . .?"

"Yes, that was it. I noticed it at the time; it was very shrewd. You can see that he has a profound experience of life."

"It's extraordinary that he should have dined with the Swanns, and that he seems to have found quite respectable people there, government officials. How on earth can Mme Swann have managed to get hold of them?"

"Did you notice the malicious way he said: 'It is a house which is especially attractive to gentlemen!'?"

And each of them attempted to reproduce the manner in which M. de Norpois had uttered these words, as they might have attempted to capture some intonation of Bressant's voice or of Thiron's in *L'Aventurière* or in *Le Gendre de M. Poirier*. But of all his sayings there was none so keenly relished as one was by Françoise, who, years afterwards, could not "keep a straight face" if we reminded her that she had been described by the Ambassador as "a first-rate chef," a compliment which my mother had gone in person to transmit to her, like a War Minister passing on the congratulations of a visiting sovereign after reviewing the troops. I had, as it happened, preceded my mother to the kitchen. For I had extorted from Françoise, who though a pacifist was cruel, a promise that she would

cause no undue suffering to the rabbit which she had to kill,
and I had had no report yet of its death. Françoise assured me
that it had passed away as peacefully as could be desired, and
very swiftly. "I've never seen a beast like it; it died without
saying a blessed word; you would have thought it was dumb."
Being but little versed in the language of beasts, I suggested
that rabbits perhaps did not squeal like chickens. "Just wait
till you see," said Françoise, filled with contempt for my ignorance, "if rabbits don't squeal every bit as much as chickens.
Why, their voices are even louder."

Françoise received the compliments of M. de Norpois with
the proud simplicity, the joyful and (if only momentarily)
intelligent expression of an artist when someone speaks to him
of his art. My mother had sent her when she first came to us
to several of the big restaurants to see how the cooking there
was done. I had the same pleasure, that evening, in hearing her
dismiss the most famous of them as mere cookshops, that I had
had long ago when I learned with regard to theatrical artists
that the hierarchy of their merits did not at all correspond to
that of their reputations. "The Ambassador," my mother told
her, "assured me that he knows nowhere where one can get
cold beef and soufflés as good as yours." Françoise, with an air
of modesty and of paying just homage to the truth, agreed,
but seemed not at all impressed by the title "Ambassador";
she said of M. de Norpois, with the friendliness due to a man
who had taken her for a chef: "He's a good old soul, like me."
She had indeed hoped to catch sight of him as he arrived, but
knowing that Mamma hated people lurking behind doors and
at windows, and thinking that she would get to know from
the other servants or from the porter that she had been
keeping watch (for Françoise saw everywhere nothing but
"jealousies" and "tale-bearings," which played the same
baleful and perennial role in her imagination as, for certain
other people, the intrigues of the Jesuits or the Jews), she had
contented herself with a peep from the kitchen window, "so
as not to have words with Madame," and from her momentary
glimpses of M. de Norpois had "thought it was Monsieur
Legrandin," because of what she called his "agility" and in
spite of their having not a single point in common.

"Well then," inquired my mother, "and how do you explain that nobody else can make an aspic as well as you—when you choose?" "I really couldn't say how that becomes about," replied Françoise, who had established no very clear line of demarcation between the verb "to come," in certain of its meanings, and the verb "to become." She was speaking the truth, moreover, if only in part, being scarcely more capable— or desirous—of revealing the mystery which ensured the superiority of her aspics or her creams than a well-dressed woman the secrets of her toilettes or a great singer those of her voice. Their explanations tell us little; it was the same with the recipes of our cook. "They do it in too much of a hurry," she went on, alluding to the great restaurants, "and then it's not all done together. You want the beef to become like a sponge, then it will drink up all the juice to the last drop. Still, there was one of those cafés where I thought they did know a little bit about cooking. I don't say it was altogether my aspic, but it was very nicely done, and the *soufflés* had plenty of cream."

"Do you mean Henry's?" asked my father (who had now joined us), for he greatly enjoyed that restaurant in the Place Gaillon where he went regularly to regimental dinners. "Oh, dear no!" said Françoise with a mildness which cloaked a profound contempt. "I meant a little restaurant. At that Henry's it's all very good, sure enough, but it's not a restaurant, it's more like a—soup-kitchen." "Weber's, then?" "Oh, no, Monsieur, I meant a good restaurant. Weber's, that's in the Rue Royale; that's not a restaurant, it's a brasserie. I don't know that the food they give you there is even served. I think they don't even have any table-cloths; they just shove it down in front of you like that, with a take it or leave it." "Ciro's?" Françoise smiled. "Oh! there I should say the main dishes are ladies of the world." (*Monde* meant for Françoise the *demi-monde*.) "Lord! they need them to fetch the boys in."

We could see that, with all her air of simplicity, Françoise was for the celebrities of her profession a more ferocious "colleague" than the most jealous, the most self-infatuated of actresses. We felt, all the same, that she had a proper feeling for her art and a respect for tradition, for she added:

"No, I mean a restaurant where it looked like they kept a
very good little family table. It's a place of some consequence, too. Plenty of custom there. Oh, they raked in the
coppers, there, all right." (Françoise, being thrifty, reckoned
in coppers, where your plunger would reckon in gold.)
"Madame knows the place well enough, down there to the
right along the main boulevards, a little way back." The
restaurant of which she spoke with this blend of pride
and good-humoured tolerance was, it turned out, the Café
Anglais.

When New Year's Day came, I first of all paid a round of
family visits with Mamma who, so as not to tire me, had
planned them beforehand (with the aid of an itinerary drawn
up by my father) according to district rather than degree of
kinship. But no sooner had we entered the drawing-room of
the distant cousin whose claim to being visited first was that
her house was at no distance from ours, than my mother was
horrified to see standing there, his present of *marrons glacés* or
déguisés in his hand, the bosom friend of the most sensitive of
all my uncles, to whom he would at once go and report that
we had not begun our round with him. And this uncle would
certainly be hurt; he would have thought it quite natural that
we should go from the Madeleine to the Jardin des Plantes,
where he lived, before stopping at Saint-Augustin, on our way
to the Rue de l'Ecole de Médecine.

Our visits ended (my grandmother had dispensed us from
the duty of calling on her, since we were to dine there that
evening), I ran all the way to the Champs-Elysées to give to
our own special stall-keeper, with instructions to hand it over
to the person who came to her several times a week from the
Swanns to buy gingerbread, the letter which, on the day when
my beloved had caused me so much pain, I had decided to send
her at the New Year, and in which I told her that our old friendship was vanishing with the old year, that I would now forget
my grievances and disappointments, and that, from this first
day of January, it was a new friendship that we were going to
build, so solid that nothing could destroy it, so wonderful that
I hoped Gilberte would go out of her way to preserve it in
all its beauty and to warn me in time, as I promised to warn

her, should either of us detect the least sign of a peril that might endanger it.

On the way home Françoise made me stop at the corner of the Rue Royale, before an open-air stall from which she selected for her own stock of presents photographs of Pius IX and Raspail, while for myself I purchased one of Berma. The wholesale admiration which that artist excited gave an air of slight impoverishment to this one face that she had to respond with, immutable and precarious like the garments of people who have none "spare," this face on which she must continually expose to view only the tiny dimple upon her upper lip, the arch of her eyebrows, and a few other physical characteristics, always the same, which, after all, were at the mercy of a burn or a blow. This face, moreover, would not in itself have seemed to me beautiful, but it gave me the idea and consequently the desire to kiss it, by reason of all the kisses that it must have sustained and for which, from its page in the album, it seemed still to be appealing with that coquettishly tender gaze, that artfully ingenuous smile. For Berma must indeed have felt for many young men those desires which she confessed under cover of the character of Phèdre, desires which everything, even the glamour of her name which enhanced her beauty and prolonged her youth, must make it so easy for her to appease. Night was falling; I stopped before a column of playbills, on which was posted the performance in which she was to appear on January 1. A moist and gentle breeze was blowing. It was a weather with which I was familiar; I suddenly had a feeling and a presentiment that New Year's Day was not a day different from the rest, that it was not the first day of a new world in which I might, by a chance that was still intact, have made Gilberte's acquaintance anew as at the time of the Creation, as though the past did not yet exist, as though, together with the lessons I could have drawn from them for my future guidance, the disappointments which she had sometimes brought me had been obliterated; a new world in which nothing should subsist from the old—save one thing, my desire that Gilberte should love me. I realised that if my heart hoped for such a regeneration all around it of a universe that had not satisfied it before, it was because it,

my heart, had not altered, and I told myself that there was no
reason to suppose that Gilberte's had altered either; I felt that
this new friendship was the same, just as there is no boundary
ditch between their fore-runners and those new years which
our desire, without being able to reach and so to modify them,
invests, unknown to themselves, with a different name. For
all that I might dedicate this new year to Gilberte, and, as
one superimposes a religion on the blind laws of nature, endeavour to stamp New Year's Day with the particular image
that I had formed of it, it was in vain. I felt that it was not
aware that people called it New Year's Day, that it was passing
in a wintry dusk in a manner that was not new to me: in the
gentle breeze that blew around the column of playbills, I
had recognised, had sensed the reappearance of, the eternal
common substance, the familiar moisture, the unheeding
fluidity of the old days and years.

I returned home. I had just spent the New Year's Day of
old men, who differ on that day from their juniors, not because
people have ceased to give them presents but because they
themselves have ceased to believe in the New Year. Presents
I had indeed received, but not that present which alone could
bring me pleasure, namely a line from Gilberte. I was nevertheless still young, since I had been able to write her one, by
means of which I hoped, in telling her of my solitary dreams
of love and longing, to arouse similar dreams in her. The sadness of men who have grown old lies in their no longer even
thinking of writing such letters, the futility of which their
experience has shown.

When I was in bed, the noises of the street, unduly prolonged on this festive evening, kept me awake. I thought of
all the people who would end the night in pleasure, of the
lover, the troop of debauchees perhaps, who would be going
to meet Berma at the stage-door after the performance that I
had seen announced for this evening. I was not even able,
to calm the agitation which this idea engendered in me during
my sleepless night, to assure myself that Berma was not, perhaps, thinking about love, since the lines that she recited,
which she had long and carefully rehearsed, reminded her at
every moment that love is an exquisite thing, as of course she

already knew, and knew so well that she displayed its familiar pangs—only enriched with a new violence and an unsuspected sweetness—to her astonished audience, each member of which had felt them for himself. I lighted my candle again, to look at her face once more. At the thought that it was no doubt at that very moment being caressed by those men whom I could not prevent from giving to Berma and receiving from her joys superhuman but vague, I felt an emotion more cruel than voluptuous, a longing that was presently intensified by the sound of the horn, as one hears it on the nights of the mid-Lent festival and often of other public holidays, which, because it then lacks all poetry, is more saddening, coming from a tavern, than "at evening, in the depths of the woods." At that moment, a message from Gilberte would perhaps not have been what I wanted. Our desires cut across one another, and in this confused existence it is rare for happiness to coincide with the desire that clamoured for it.

I continued to go to the Champs-Elysées on fine days, along streets whose elegant pink houses seemed to be washed (because exhibitions of water-colours were then the height of fashion) in a lightly floating atmosphere. It would be untrue to say that in those days the palaces of Gabriel struck me as being of greater beauty than, or even of another period from, the neighbouring houses. I found more style and should have supposed more antiquity if not in the Palais de l'Industrie at any rate in the Trocadéro. Plunged in a restless sleep, my adolescence embraced in one uniform vision the whole of the quarter through which it guided it, and I had never dreamed that there could be an eighteenth-century building in the Rue Royale, just as I should have been astonished to learn that the Porte Saint-Martin and the Porte Saint-Denis, those glories of the age of Louis XIV, were not contemporary with the most recently built tenements in the sordid districts that bore their names. Once only one of Gabriel's palaces made me stop for more than a moment; this was because, night having fallen, its columns, dematerialised by the moonlight, had the appearance of having been cut out in pasteboard, and by reminding me of a set from the operetta *Orphée aux Enfers*, gave me for the first time an impression of beauty.

Meanwhile Gilberte never came to the Champs-Elysées. And yet it was imperative that I should see her, for I could not so much as remember her face. The questing, anxious, exacting way that we have of looking at the person we love, our eagerness for the word which will give us or take from us the hope of an appointment for the morrow, and, until that word is uttered, our alternate if not simultaneous imaginings of joy and despair, all this makes our attention in the presence of the beloved too tremulous to be able to carry away a very clear impression of her. Perhaps, also, that activity of all the senses at once which yet endeavours to discover with the eyes alone what lies beyond them is over-indulgent to the myriad forms, to the different savours, to the movements of the living person whom as a rule, when we are not in love, we immobilise. Whereas the beloved model does not stay still; and our mental photographs of it are always blurred. I no longer really knew how Gilberte's features were composed, save in the heavenly moments when she unfolded them to me: I could remember nothing but her smile. And being unable to visualise that beloved face, despite every effort that I might make to recapture it, I was disgusted to find, etched on my memory with a maddening precision of detail, the meaningless, emphatic faces of the roundabout man and the barley-sugar woman; just as those who have lost a loved one whom they never see again in sleep, are enraged at meeting incessantly in their dreams any number of insupportable people whom it is quite enough to have known in the waking world. In their inability to form an image of the object of their grief they are almost led to accuse themselves of feeling no grief. And I was not far from believing that, since I could not recall Gilberte's features, I had forgotten Gilberte herself, and no longer loved her.

At last she returned to play there almost every day, setting before me fresh pleasures to desire, to demand of her for the morrow, in this sense indeed making my love for her each day a new love. But an incident was to change once again, and abruptly, the manner in which, at about two o'clock every afternoon, the problem of my love confronted me. Had M. Swann intercepted the letter that I had written to his daughter, or was Gilberte merely confessing to me long after the event, and so that I should be more prudent in future, a state of affairs already long established? As I was telling her how greatly I admired her father and mother, she assumed that vague air, full of reticence and secrecy, which she invariably wore when one spoke to her of what she was going to do, her walks, drives, visits, then suddenly said to me: "You know, they can't stand you!" and, slipping from me like the water-sprite that she was, burst out laughing. Often her laughter, out of harmony with her words, seemed, as music seems, to be tracing an invisible surface on another plane. M. and Mme Swann did not require Gilberte to give up playing with me, but they would have been just as well pleased, she thought, if we had never begun. They did not look upon our relations with a kindly eye, believed me to be a person of low moral standard and imagined that I could only be a bad influence on their daughter. This type of unscrupulous youth whom Swann thought I resembled, I pictured to myself as detesting the parents of the girl he loves, flattering them to their faces but, when he is alone with her, making fun of them, urging her on to disobey them and, when once he has completed his conquest, preventing them even from seeing her. With these characteristics (though they are never those under which the basest of scoundrels recognises himself) how vehemently did my heart contrast the sentiments by which it was animated with regard to Swann, so passionate, on the contrary, that I had no doubt that had he had an inkling of them he would have repented of his judgment of me as of a judicial error. All that I felt towards him I made bold to express to him in a long letter which I entrusted to Gilberte with the request that she deliver it to him. She agreed to do so. Alas! he must have seen in me an even greater impostor than I had feared; he must have suspected the sentiments which I had supposed myself to be portraying, in sixteen pages, with such conviction and truth: in short, the letter that I wrote to him, as ardent and as sincere as the words that I had uttered to M. de Norpois, met with no more success. Gilberte told me next day, after taking me aside behind a clump of laurels, on a little path where we sat down on a couple of chairs, that as he read my letter, which she had now brought

back to me, her father had shrugged his shoulders and said:
"All this means nothing; it only goes to prove how right I
was." I who knew the purity of my intentions, the goodness of
my soul, was furious that my words should not even have
impinged upon the surface of Swann's ridiculous error. For
it was an error; of that I had then no doubt. I felt that I had
described with such accuracy certain irrefutable characteristics of my generous sentiments that, if Swann had not at once
recognised their authenticity, had not come to ask my forgiveness and to admit that he had been mistaken, it must be
because he himself had never experienced these noble sentiments, and this would make him incapable of understanding
their existence in other people.

But perhaps it was simply that Swann knew that nobility
is often no more than the inner aspect which our egotistical
feelings assume when we have not yet named and classified
them. Perhaps he had recognised in the regard that I expressed
for him simply an effect—and the strongest possible proof—of
my love for Gilberte, by which—and not by my secondary
veneration for himself—my subsequent actions would be
inevitably controlled. I was unable to share his predictions,
since I had not succeeded in abstracting my love from myself,
in fitting it into the common experience of humanity and
computing, experimentally, its consequences; I was in despair.
I was obliged to leave Gilberte for a moment; Françoise had
called me. I had to accompany her into a little pavilion covered
in a green trellis, not unlike one of the disused toll-houses of
old Paris, in which had recently been installed what in England
they call a lavatory but in France, by an ill-informed piece of
Anglomania, "water-closets." The old, damp walls of the
entrance, where I stood waiting for Françoise, emitted a cool,
fusty smell which, relieving me at once of the anxieties that
Swann's words, as reported by Gilberte, had just awakened in
me, filled me with a pleasure of a different kind from other
pleasures, which leave one more unstable, incapable of grasping them, of possessing them, a pleasure that was solid and
consistent, on which I could lean for support, delicious, soothing, rich with a truth that was lasting, unexplained and sure.
I should have liked, as, long ago, in my walks along the

Guermantes way, to endeavour to penetrate the charm of this
impression which had seized hold of me, and, remaining there
motionless, to explore this antiquated emanation which invited
me not to enjoy the pleasure which it was offering me only as
a bonus, but to descend into the underlying reality which it
had not yet disclosed to me. But the keeper of the establishment, an elderly dame with painted cheeks and an auburn
wig, began to talk to me. Françoise thought her "a proper
lady." Her young "missy" had married what Françoise called
"a young man of family," which meant that he differed more,
in her eyes, from a workman than, in Saint-Simon's, a duke did
from a man "risen from the dregs of the people." No doubt the
keeper, before entering upon her tenancy, had suffered set-
backs. But Françoise was positive that she was a "marquise,"
and belonged to the Saint-Ferréol family. This "marquise"
now warned me not to stand outside in the cold, and even
opened one of her doors for me, saying: "Won't you go inside
for a minute? Look, here's a nice clean one, and I shan't
charge *you* anything." Perhaps she made this offer simply in
the spirit in which the young ladies at Gouache's, when we
went in there to order something, used to offer me one of the
sweets which they kept on the counter under glass bells, and
which, alas, Mamma would never allow me to accept; perhaps,
less innocently, like the old florist whom Mamma used to have
in to replenish her flower-stands, who rolled languishing eyes
at me as she handed me a rose. In any event, if the "marquise"
had a weakness for little boys, when she threw open to them
the hypogean doors of those cubicles of stone in which men
crouch like sphinxes, she must have been moved to that
generosity less by the hope of corrupting them than by the
pleasure which all of us feel in displaying a needless prodigality to those whom we love, for I never saw her with any
other visitor except an old park-keeper.

A moment later I said good-bye to the "marquise," and
went out accompanied by Françoise, whom I left to return
to Gilberte. I caught sight of her at once, on a chair, behind
the clump of laurels. She was there so as not to be seen by her
friends: they were playing hide-and-seek. I went and sat down
beside her. She had on a flat cap which came low over her eyes,

giving her the same "underhand," brooding, sly look which I
had remarked in her that first time at Combray. I asked her if
there was not some way for me to have it out with her father
face to face. Gilberte said that she had suggested that to him,
but that he had thought it pointless. "Here," she went on,
"don't go away without your letter. I must run along to the
others, as they haven't found me."

Had Swann appeared on the scene then before I had recovered this letter by the sincerity of which I felt that he had
been so unreasonable in not letting himself be convinced,
perhaps he would have seen that it was he who had been in
the right. For, approaching Gilberte, who, leaning back in
her chair, told me to take the letter but did not hold it out to
me, I felt myself so irresistibly attracted by her body that I said
to her: "I say, why don't you try to stop me from getting it;
we'll see who's the stronger."

She thrust it behind her back; I put my arms round her neck,
raising the plaits of hair which she wore over her shoulders,
either because she was still of an age for it or because her
mother chose to make her look a child for a little longer so
as to make herself seem younger; and we wrestled, locked together. I tried to pull her towards me, and she resisted; her
cheeks, inflamed by the effort, were as red and round as two
cherries; she laughed as though I were tickling her; I held her
gripped between my legs like a young tree which I was trying
to climb; and, in the middle of my gymnastics, when I was
already out of breath with the muscular exercise and the
heat of the game, I felt, like a few drops of sweat wrung
from me by the effort, my pleasure express itself in a form
which I could not even pause for a moment to analyse; immediately I snatched the letter from her. Whereupon Gilberte
said good-naturedly: "You know, if you like, we might go on
wrestling a bit longer."

Perhaps she was dimly conscious that my game had another
object than the one I had avowed, but too dimly to have been
able to see that I had attained it. And I who was afraid that she
had noticed (and a slight movement of recoil and constraint
as of offended modesty which she made and checked a moment
later made me think that my fear had not been unfounded)

agreed to go on wrestling, lest she should suppose that I had indeed had no other object in view than the one after which I wished only to sit quietly by her side.

On my way home I perceived, I suddenly recalled the impression, concealed from me until then, of which, without letting me distinguish or recognise it, the cold and almost sooty smell of the trellised pavilion had reminded me. It was that of my uncle Adolphe's little sitting-room at Combray, which had indeed exhaled the same odour of humidity. But I could not understand, and I postponed until later the attempt to discover why the recollection of so trivial an impression had filled me with such happiness. Meanwhile it struck me that I did indeed deserve the contempt of M. de Norpois: I had preferred hitherto to all other writers one whom he styled a mere "flute-player," and a positive rapture had been conveyed to me, not by some important idea, but by a musty smell.

For some time past, in certain households, the name of the Champs-Elysées, if a visitor mentioned it, would be greeted by the mothers with that baleful air which they reserve for a physician of established reputation whom they claim to have seen make too many false diagnoses to have any faith left in him; people insisted that these gardens were not good for children, that they knew of more than one sore throat, more than one case of measles and any number of feverish chills for which they must be held responsible. Without venturing openly to doubt the maternal affection of Mamma, who continued to let me play there, several of her friends deplored her inability to see what was as plain as daylight.

Neurotic subjects are perhaps less addicted than any, despite the time-honoured phrase, to "listening to their insides": they hear so many things going on inside themselves by which they realise later that they were wrong to let themselves be alarmed, that they end by paying no attention to any of them. Their nervous systems have so often cried out to them for help, as though with some serious malady, when it was simply going to start snowing or they were going to move house, that they have acquired the habit of paying no more heed to these warnings than a soldier who in the heat of battle perceives them so little that he is capable, although dying, of carrying on for some days still the life of a man in perfect health. One morning, bearing within me all my habitual ailments, from whose constant internal circulation I kept my mind turned as resolutely away as from the circulation of my blood, I came running blithely into the dining-room where my parents were already at table, and—having assured myself, as usual, that to feel cold may mean not that one ought to warm oneself but that, for instance, one has received a scolding, and not to feel hungry that it is going to rain and not that one ought not to eat anything—had taken my place between them when in the act of swallowing the first mouthful of a particularly tempting cutlet, a nausea and dizziness brought me to a halt, the feverish reaction of an illness that had already begun, the symptoms of which had been masked and retarded by the ice of my indifference, but which obstinately refused the nourishment that I was not in a fit state to absorb. Then, at the same moment, the thought that I would be prevented from going out if I was seen to be unwell gave me, as the instinct of self-preservation gives a wounded man, the strength to crawl to my own room, where I found that I had a temperature of 104, and then to get ready to go to the Champs-Elysées. Through the languid and vulnerable shell which encased them, my eager thoughts were urging me towards, were clamouring for the soothing delight of a game of prisoner's base with Gilberte, and an hour later, barely able to keep on my feet, but happy in being by her side, I had still the strength to enjoy it.

Françoise, on our return, declared that I had been "taken bad," that I must have caught a "hot and cold," while the doctor, who was called in at once, declared that he "preferred" the "severity," the "virulence" of the rise in temperature which accompanied my congestion of the lungs, and would be no more than "a flash in the pan," to other symptoms, more "insidious" and "latent." For some time now I had been liable to fits of breathlessness, and our doctor, braving the disapproval of my grandmother, who saw me already dying a drunkard's death, had recommended me to take, as well as the caffeine which had been prescribed to help me to breathe, beer, champagne or brandy when I felt an attack coming. These attacks would subside, he said, in the "euphoria" brought on by the alcohol. I was often obliged, so that my grandmother should allow it to be given to me, instead of disguising, almost to make a display of my state of suffocation. On the other hand, as soon as I felt it coming, never being quite certain what proportions it would assume, I would grow distressed at the thought of my grandmother's anxiety, of which I was far more afraid than of my own sufferings. But at the same time my body, either because it was too weak to keep those sufferings secret, or because it feared lest, in their ignorance of the imminent attack, people might demand of me some exertion which it would have found impossible or dangerous, gave me the need to warn my grandmother of my symptoms with a precision into which I put a sort of physiological punctiliousness. If I observed in myself a disturbing symptom which I had not previously discerned, my body was in distress so long as I had not communicated it to my grandmother. If she pretended to take no notice, it made me insist. Sometimes I went too far; and that beloved face, which was no longer able always to control its emotion as in the past, would betray an expression of pity, a painful contraction. Then my heart was wrung by the sight of her grief; as if my kisses had the power to expel that grief, as if my affection could give my grandmother as much joy as my recovery, I flung myself into her arms. And its scruples being at the same time calmed by the certainty that she was now aware of the discomfort that I felt, my body offered no opposition to my reassuring her. I protested that this discomfort was not really painful, that I was in no sense to be pitied, that she might be quite sure that I was now happy; my body had wished to secure exactly the amount of pity that it deserved, and, provided that someone knew that it "had a pain" in its right side, it could see no harm in my declaring that this pain was of no consequence and was not an obstacle to my happiness; for my body did not pride itself on its philosophy; that was outside its province. Almost every day during my convalescence I had some of these fits of suffocation. One evening, after my grandmother had left me comparatively well, she returned to my room very late and, seeing me struggling for breath, "Oh, my poor boy," she exclaimed, her face quivering with sympathy, "you must be in dreadful pain." She left me at once; I heard the street door open, and in a little while she came back with some brandy which she had gone out to buy since there was none in the house. Presently I began to feel better. My grandmother, who was rather flushed, seemed somehow embarrassed, and her eyes had a look of weariness and dejection.

"I shall leave you alone now, and let you take advantage of this improvement," she said, rising suddenly to go. I detained her, however, for a kiss, and could feel on her cold cheek something moist, but did not know whether it was the dampness of the night air through which she had just passed. Next day, she did not come to my room until the evening, having had, she told me, to go out. I considered that this showed a surprising indifference to my well-being, and I had to restrain myself in order not to reproach her with it.

My suffocations having persisted long after any congestion remained that could account for them, my parents brought in Professor Cottard. It is not enough that a physician who is called in to treat cases of this sort should be learned. Confronted with symptoms which may be those of three or four different complaints, it is in the long run his flair, his instinctive judgment, that must decide with which, despite the more or less similar appearance of them all, he has to deal. This mysterious gift does not imply any superiority in the other departments of the intellect, and a person of the utmost vulgarity, who admires the worst pictures, the worst music, who is without the slightest intellectual curiosity, may perfectly well possess it. In my case, what was physically evident might well have been caused by nervous spasms, by incipient tuberculosis, by asthma, by a toxi-alimentary dyspnoea with renal insufficiency, by chronic bronchitis, or by a complex state into which more than one of these factors entered. Now, nervous spasms required to be treated firmly, and discouraged, tuberculosis with infinite care and the sort of "feeding-up" which would have been bad for an arthritic condition such as asthma and might indeed have been dangerous in a case of toxi-alimentary dyspnoea, this last calling for a strict diet which, in turn, would be fatal to a tubercular patient. But Cottard's hesitations were brief and his prescriptions imperious: "Purges, violent and drastic purges; milk for some days, nothing but milk. No meat. No alcohol." My mother murmured that I needed, all the same, to be "built up," that I was already very nervy, that drenching me like a horse and restricting my diet would make me worse. I could see in Cottard's eyes, as anxious as if he was afraid of missing a train, that he was wondering whether he had not succumbed to his natural gentleness. He was trying to think whether he had remembered to put on his mask of coldness, as one looks for a mirror to see whether one has forgotten to tie one's tie. In his uncertainty, and in order to compensate just in case, he replied brutally: "I am not in the habit of repeating my prescriptions. Give me a pen. Now remember, milk! Later on, when we've got the breathlessness and the agrypnia under control, I'm prepared to let you take a little clear soup, and then a little broth, but always with milk; *au lait!* You'll enjoy that, since Spain is all the rage just now; *olé, olé!*" (His pupils knew this joke well, for he made it at the hospital whenever he had to put a heart or liver case on a milk diet.) "After that, you'll gradually return to your normal life. But whenever there's any coughing or choking—purges, injections, bed, milk!" He listened with icy calm, and without replying, to my mother's final objections, and as he left us without having condescended to explain the reasons for this course of treatment, my parents concluded that it had no bearing on my case, and would weaken me to no purpose, and so they did not make me try it. Naturally they sought to conceal their disobedience from the Professor, and to make sure of it avoided all the houses in which they might have run across him. Then, as my health deteriorated, they decided to make me follow Cottard's prescriptions to the letter; in three days my "rattle" and cough had ceased, I could breathe freely. Whereupon we realised that Cottard, while finding, as he told us later on, that I was distinctly asthmatic, and above all "batty," had discerned that what was really the matter with me at the moment was tox-aemia, and that by loosening my liver and washing out my kidneys he would clear my bronchial tubes and thus give me back my breath, my sleep and my strength. And we realised that this imbecile was a great physician.

At last I was able to get up. But there was talk of my no longer being allowed to go to the Champs-Elysées. The reason given was that the air there was bad; but I felt sure that this was only a pretext so that I should no longer be able to see Mlle Swann, and I forced myself to repeat the name of Gilberte all the time, like the native tongue which peoples in captivity endeavour to preserve among themselves so as not to forget the land that they will never see again.

Sometimes my mother would stroke my forehead, saying: "So little boys don't tell Mamma their troubles any more?" And Françoise used to come up to me every day and say: "What a face, to be sure! If you could just see yourself! Anyone would think there was a corpse in the house." It is true that, if I had simply had a cold in the head, Françoise would have assumed the same funereal air. These lamentations pertained rather to her "class" than to the state of my health. I could not at the time distinguish whether this pessimism was due to sorrow or to satisfaction. I decided provisionally that it was social and professional.

One day, after the postman had called, my mother laid a letter upon my bed. I opened it carelessly, since it could not bear the one signature that would have made me happy, the name of Gilberte, with whom I had no relations outside the Champs-Elysées. But there, at the foot of the page, which was embossed with a silver seal representing a helmeted head above a scroll with the device *Per viam rectam*, beneath a letter written in a large and flowing hand in which almost every phrase appeared to be underlined, simply because the crosses of the "t"s ran not across but over them, and so drew a line beneath the corresponding letters of the word above, it was precisely Gilberte's signature that I saw. But because I knew this to be impossible in a letter addressed to me, the sight of it unaccompanied by any belief in it gave me no pleasure. For a moment it merely gave an impression of unreality to everything around me. With dizzy speed the improbable signature danced about my bed, the fireplace, the four walls. I saw everything reel, as one does when one falls from a horse, and I asked myself whether there was not an existence altogether different from the one I knew, in direct contradic-

tion to it, but itself the real one, which, being suddenly
revealed to me, filled me with that hesitation which sculptors,
in representing the Last Judgment, have given to the awakening dead who find themselves at the gates of the next world.
"My dear friend," said the letter, "I hear that you have been
very ill and have given up going to the Champs-Elysées. I
hardly ever go there either because there has been such an
enormous lot of illness. But my friends come to tea here every
Monday and Friday. Mamma asks me to tell you that it will
be a great pleasure to us all if you will come too as soon as
you are well again, and we can have some more nice talks
here as we did in the Champs-Elysées. Good-bye, my dear
friend; I hope that your parents will allow you to come to tea
very often. With all my kindest regards. GILBERTE."

While I was reading these words, my nervous system
received, with admirable promptitude, the news that a great
happiness had befallen me. But my mind, that is to say myself,
in other words the party principally concerned, was still
unaware of it. Happiness, happiness through Gilberte, was a
thing I had never ceased to think of, a thing wholly in my
mind—as Leonardo said of painting, *cosa mentale*. Now, a
sheet of paper covered with writing is not a thing that the
mind assimilates at once. But as soon as I had finished reading
the letter, I thought of it, it became an object of reverie, it too
became *cosa mentale*, and I loved it so much now that every
few minutes I had to re-read it and kiss it. Then at last I was
conscious of my happiness.

Life is strewn with these miracles for which people who
love can always hope. It is possible that this one had been
artificially brought about by my mother who, seeing that for
some time past I had lost all interest in life, may have suggested to Gilberte to write to me, just as, when I first went
sea-bathing, in order to make me enjoy diving which I hated
because it took away my breath, she used secretly to hand to
my bathing instructor marvellous boxes made of shells, and
branches of coral, which I believed that I myself discovered
lying at the bottom of the sea. However, with every occurrence
in life and its contrasting situations that relates to love, it is
best to make no attempt to understand, since in so far as these

are as inexorable as they are unlooked-for, they appear to be governed by magic rather than by rational laws. When a multi-millionaire—who for all his millions is a charming man—sent packing by a poor and unattractive woman with whom he has been living, calls to his aid, in his despair, all the resources of wealth and brings every worldly influence to bear without succeeding in making her take him back, it is wiser for him, in the face of the implacable obstinacy of his mistress, to suppose that Fate intends to crush him and to make him die of an affection of the heart rather than to seek any logical explanation. These obstacles against which lovers have to contend and which their imagination, over-excited by suffering, seeks in vain to analyse, are to be found, as often as not, in some peculiar characteristic of the woman whom they cannot win back—in her stupidity, in the influence acquired over her and the fears suggested to her by people whom the lover does not know, in the kind of pleasures which at that moment she demands of life, pleasures which neither her lover nor her lover's wealth can procure for her. In any event, the lover is not in the best position to discover the nature of these obstacles which the woman's guile conceals from him and his own judgment, distorted by love, prevents him from estimating exactly. They may be compared with those tumours which the doctor succeeds in reducing, but without having traced them to their source. Like them these obstacles remain mysterious but are temporary. Only they last, as a rule, longer than love itself. And as the latter is not a disinterested passion, the lover who no longer loves does not seek to know why the woman, neither rich nor virtuous, with whom he was in love refused obstinately for years to let him continue to keep her.

Now the same mystery which often veils from our eyes the reason for a catastrophe envelops just as frequently, when love is in question, the suddenness of certain happy solutions, such as had been brought to me by Gilberte's letter. Happy, or at least seemingly happy, for there are few that can really be happy when we are dealing with a sentiment of such a kind that any satisfaction we can give it does no more, as a rule, than dislodge some pain. And yet sometimes a respite is granted us, and we have for a little while the illusion of being healed.

As regards this letter, at the foot of which Françoise refused to recognise Gilberte's name because the elaborate capital "G" leaning against the undotted "i" looked more like an "A," while the final syllable was indefinitely prolonged by a waving flourish, if we persist in looking for a rational explanation of the sudden change of feeling towards me which it reflected, and which made me so radiantly happy, we may perhaps find that I was to some extent indebted for it to an incident which I should have supposed, on the contrary, to be calculated to ruin me for ever in the eyes of the Swann family. A short while back, Bloch had come to see me at a time when Professor Cottard, who, now that I was following his prescriptions, had again been called in, happened to be in my room. As his examination was over and he was sitting with me simply as a visitor because my parents had invited him to stay to dinner, Bloch was allowed to come in. While we were all talking, Bloch having mentioned that he had been told by a lady with whom he had been dining the day before, and who was a great friend of Mme Swann's, that the latter was very fond of me, I should have liked to reply that he was most certainly mistaken, and to establish the fact (from the same scruple of conscience that had made me proclaim it to M. de Norpois, and for fear that Mme Swann might take me for a liar) that I did not know her and had never spoken to her. But I did not have the heart to correct Bloch's mistake, because I realised that it was deliberate, and that, if he had made up something that Mme Swann could not possibly have said, it was simply to let us know (what he considered flattering to himself, and was not true either) that he had been dining with one of that lady's friends. And thus it came about that whereas M. de Norpois, on learning that I did not know but would very much like to know Mme Swann, had taken good care to avoid speaking to her about me, Cottard, who was her doctor, having gathered from what he had heard Bloch say that she knew me quite well and thought highly of me, concluded that to remark, when next he saw her, that I was a charming young fellow and a great friend of his could not be of the smallest use to me and would be advantageous to himself, two reasons which induced him to speak of me to Odette whenever an opportunity arose.

Thus at length I came to know that house from which was wafted even on to the staircase the scent that Mme Swann used, but which was more redolent still of the peculiar, disturbing charm that emanated from the life of Gilberte. The implacable concierge, transformed into a benevolent Eumenid, adopted the habit, when I asked him if I might go upstairs, of indicating to me, by raising his cap with a propitious hand, that he granted my prayer. Those windows which, seen from outside, used to interpose between me and the treasures within, which were not destined for me, a polished, distant and superficial stare, which seemed to me the very stare of the Swanns themselves, it fell to my lot, when in the warm weather I had spent a whole afternoon with Gilberte in her room, to open myself so as to let in a little air and even to lean out of beside her, if it was her mother's "at home" day, to watch the visitors arrive who would often look up as they stepped out of their carriages and greet me with a wave of the hand, taking me for some nephew of their hostess. At such moments Gilberte's plaits used to brush my cheek. They seemed to me, in the fineness of their grain, at once natural and supernatural, and in the strength of their skilfully woven tracery, a matchless work of art in the composition of which had been used the very grass of Paradise. To a section of them, however infinitesimal, what celestial herbarium would I not have given as a reliquary? But since I never hoped to obtain an actual fragment of those plaits, if at least I had been able to have a photograph of them, how far more precious than one of a sheet of flowers drawn by Leonardo! To acquire one, I stooped to servilities, with friends of the Swanns and even with photographers, which not only failed to procure for me what I wanted, but tied me for life to a number of extremely boring people.

Gilberte's parents, who for so long had prevented me from seeing her, now—when I entered the dark hall in which hovered perpetually, more formidable and more to be desired than, at Versailles, the apparition of the King, the possibility

of my encountering them, in which too, invariably, after
bumping into an enormous seven-branched hat-stand, like the
Candlestick in Holy Writ, I would begin bowing profusely
to a footman, seated among the skirts of his long grey coat
upon the wood chest, whom in the dim light I had mistaken
for Mme Swann—Gilberte's parents, if one of them happened
to be passing at the moment of my arrival, so far from seeming
annoyed would come and shake hands with me with a smile,
and say: "How d'ye do?" (which they both pronounced in
the same clipped way, which, as may be imagined, I made it
my incessant and delightful task to imitate when I was back
at home). "Does Gilberte know you're here? She does?
Then I'll leave you to her."

Better still, the tea-parties themselves to which Gilberte
invited her friends, parties which for so long had seemed to
me the most insurmountable of the barriers heaped up between
her and myself, became now an opportunity for bringing us
together of which she would inform me in a few lines written
(because I was still a comparative stranger) on writing-paper
that was always different. Once it was adorned with a poodle
embossed in blue, above a humorous inscription in English
with an exclamation mark after it; another time it would be
engraved with an anchor, or with the initials G. S. pre-
posterously elongated in a rectangle which ran from top to
bottom of the page, or else with the name Gilberte, now traced
across one corner in letters of gold which imitated her signature and ended with a flourish, beneath an open umbrella
printed in black, now enclosed in a monogram in the shape of a
Chinaman's hat which contained all the letters of the name in
capitals without its being possible to make out a single one of
them. Finally, as the series of different writing-papers which
Gilberte possessed, numerous though it was, was not unlimited, after a certain number of weeks I saw reappear the
sheet that bore (like the first letter she had written me) the
motto *Per viam rectam*, and over it the helmeted head set in a
medallion of tarnished silver. And each of them was chosen
for one day rather than another by virtue of a certain ritual, as
I then supposed, but more probably, I now think, because she
tried to remember which of them she had already used, so as

never to send the same one twice to any of her correspondents, of those at least whom she took special pains to please, save at the longest possible intervals. As, on account of the different times of their lessons, some of the friends whom Gilberte used to invite to her parties were obliged to leave just as the rest were arriving, while I was still on the stairs I could hear emanating from the hall a murmur of voices which, such was the emotion aroused in me by the imposing ceremony in which I was to take part, suddenly broke the bonds that connected me with my previous life long before I had reached the landing, so that I did not even remember that I was to take off my muffler as soon as I felt too hot and to keep an eye on the clock so as not to be late in getting home. That staircase, too, all of wood as they were built about that time in certain apartment houses in that Henri II style which had for so long been Odette's ideal though she was shortly to abandon it, and furnished with a placard, to which there was no equivalent at home, on which one read the words: "NOTICE. Please do not use the lift when going downstairs," seemed to me a thing so marvellous that I told my parents that it was an antique staircase brought from ever so far away by M. Swann. My regard for the truth was so great that I should not have hesitated to give them this information even if I had known it to be false, for it alone could enable them to feel for the dignity of the Swanns' staircase the same respect that I felt myself—just as when one is talking to some ignorant person who cannot understand what constitutes the genius of a great doctor, it is well not to admit that he does not know how to cure a cold in the head. But since I was extremely unobservant, and since, as a general rule, I never knew either the name or the nature of the things I came across and could understand only that when they were connected with the Swanns they must be extraordinary, it did not seem absolutely certain to me that in notifying my parents of the artistic value and remote origin of the staircase I was guilty of a falsehood. It did not seem certain; but it must have seemed probable, for I felt myself turn very red when my father interrupted me with: "I know those houses. I've been in one of them. They're all alike; Swann just has several floors in one; it was Berlier built them all." He added that he had thought of taking a flat in one of them, but that he had changed his mind, finding that they were not conveniently arranged, and that the landings were too dark. So he said; but I felt instinctively that I must make the sacrifices necessary to the glory of the Swanns and to my own happiness, and by an internal decree, in spite of what I had just heard, I banished for ever from my mind, as a good Catholic banishes Renan's *Vie de Jésus*, the corrupting thought that their house was just an ordinary flat in which we ourselves might have been living.

Meanwhile, on those tea-party days, pulling myself up the staircase step by step, reason and memory already cast off like outer garments, and myself no more now than the sport of the basest reflexes, I would arrive in the zone in which the scent of Mme Swann greeted my nostrils. I could already visualise the majesty of the chocolate cake, encircled by plates heaped with biscuits, and by tiny napkins of patterned grey damask, as required by convention but peculiar to the Swanns. But this ordered and unalterable design seemed, like Kant's necessary universe, to depend on a supreme act of free will. For when we were all together in Gilberte's little sitting-room, suddenly she would look at the clock and exclaim:

"I say! It's getting a long time since luncheon, and we aren't having dinner till eight. I feel as if I could eat something. What do you say?"

And she would usher us into the dining-room, as sombre as the interior of an Asiatic temple painted by Rembrandt, in which an architectural cake, as urbane and familiar as it was imposing, seemed to be enthroned there on the off-chance as on any other day, in case the fancy seized Gilberte to discrown it of its chocolate battlements and to hew down the steep brown slopes of its ramparts, baked in the oven like the bastions of the palace of Darius. Better still, in proceeding to the demolition of that Ninevite pastry, Gilberte did not consider only her own hunger; she inquired also after mine, while she extracted for me from the crumbling monument a whole glazed slab jewelled with scarlet fruits, in the oriental style. She would even ask me what time my parents dined, as if I still knew, as if the agitation which overwhelmed me had allowed the sensation of satiety or of hunger, the notion of dinner or the image of my family, to persist in my empty memory and paralysed stomach. Alas, its paralysis was but momentary. A time would come when I should have to digest the cakes that I took without noticing them. But that time was still remote. Meanwhile Gilberte was making "my" tea. I would go on drinking it indefinitely, although a single cup would keep me awake for twenty-four hours. As a consequence of which my mother used always to say: "What a nuisance it is; this child can never go to the Swanns' without coming home ill." But was I aware even, when I was at the Swann's, that it was tea that I was drinking? Had I known, I should have drunk it just the same, for even supposing that I had recovered for a moment the sense of the present, that would not have restored to me the memory of the past or the apprehension of the future. My imagination was incapable of reaching to the distant time in which I might have the idea of going to bed and the need to sleep.

Gilberte's girl friends were not all plunged in that state of intoxication in which it is impossible to make any decisions. Some of them even refused tea! Then Gilberte would say, using a phrase that was very popular that year: "I can see I'm not having much of a success with my tea!" And to eradicate even more completely any notion of ceremony, she would disarrange the chairs that were drawn up round the table, saying: "It's just like a wedding breakfast. Goodness, how stupid servants are!"

She would nibble away, perched sideways upon a cross-legged seat placed at an angle to the table. And then, just as though she could have had all those cakes at her disposal without having asked her mother's permission, when Mme Swann, whose "day" coincided as a rule with Gilberte's tea-parties, having shown one of her visitors to the door, came sweeping in a moment later, dressed sometimes in blue velvet, more often in a black satin gown draped with white lace, she would say with an air of astonishment: "I say, that looks good, what you've got there. It makes me quite hungry to see you all eating cake."

"But, Mamma, do! We invite you," Gilberte would answer.

"Thank you, no, my precious; what would my visitors say? I've still got Mme Trombert and Mme Cottard and Mme Bontemps. You know dear Mme Bontemps never pays very short visits, and she has only just come. What would all those good people say if I didn't go back to them? If no one else calls, I'll come back and have a chat with you (which will be far more amusing) after they've all gone. I really think I've earned a little rest. I've had forty-five different people to-day, and forty-two of them have told me about Gérôme's picture! But you must come along one of these days," she turned to me, "and take 'your' tea with Gilberte. She'll make it for you just as you like it, as you have it in your own little 'den'," she added as she rushed off to her visitors and as if it had been something as familiar to me as my own habits (such as the habit I might have had of drinking tea, had I ever done so; as for my "den," I was uncertain whether I had one or not) that I had come to seek in this mysterious world. "When can you come? To-morrow? We'll make you some toast that's every bit as good as you get at Colombin's. No? You are horrid!"—for, since she too had begun to form a salon, she was adopting Mme Verdurin's mannerisms, and notably her tone of simpering autocracy. "Toast" being as unfamiliar to me as "Colombin's," this further promise could not have added to my temptation. It will appear stranger, now that everyone uses such expressions—perhaps even at Combray— that I had not at first understood who Mme Swann was speaking of when I heard her sing the praises of our old "nurse." I did not know any English; I soon gathered, however, that the word was intended to denote Françoise. Having been so terrified in the Champs-Elysées of the bad impression that she must make, I now learned from Mme Swann that it was all the things that Gilberte had told them about my "nurse" that had attracted her husband and her to me. "One feels that she is so devoted to you, that she must be so nice!" (At once my opinion of Françoise was diametrically changed. Conversely, to have a governess equipped with a waterproof and a feather in her hat no longer appeared quite so essential.) Finally I learned from some words which Mme Swann let fall with regard to Mme Blatin (whose good nature she acknowledged but whose visits she dreaded) that personal relations with that lady would have been of less value to me than I had supposed, and would not in any way have improved my standing with the Swanns.

If I had now begun to explore with tremors of reverence and joy the enchanted domain which, against all expectations, had opened to me its hitherto impenetrable approaches, this was still only in my capacity as a friend of Gilberte. The realm into which I was admitted was itself contained within another, more mysterious still, in which Swann and his wife led their supernatural existence and towards which they made their way, after shaking my hand, when they crossed the hall at the same moment as myself but in the other direction. But soon I was to penetrate also to the heart of the Sanctuary. For instance, Gilberte might be out when I called, but M. or Mme Swann was at home. They would ask who had rung, and on being told that it was I, would send out to ask me to come in for a moment and talk to them, desiring me to use in one way or another, with this or that object in view, my influence over their daughter. I remembered the letter, so complete and so persuasive, which I had written to Swann only the other day, and which he had not deigned even to acknowledge. I marvelled at the impotence of the mind, the reason and the heart to effect the least conversion, to solve a single one of those difficulties which subsequently life, without one's so much as knowing how it went about it, so easily unravels. My new position as the friend of Gilberte, endowed with an excellent influence over her, now enabled me to enjoy the same favours as if, having had as a companion at some school where I was always at the top of my class the son of a king, I had owed to that accident the right of informal entry into the palace and to audiences in the throne-room. Swann, with an infinite benevolence and as though he were not over-burdened with glorious occupations, would take me into his library and there allow me for an hour on end to respond in stammered monosyllables, timid silences broken by brief and incoherent bursts of courage, to observations of which my excitement prevented me from understanding a single word; would show me works of art and books which he thought likely to interest me, things as to which I had no doubt that they infinitely surpassed in beauty anything that the Louvre or the Bibliothèque Nationale possessed, but at which I found it impossible to look. At such moments I should have been delighted if Swann's butler had demanded from me my watch, my tie-pin, my boots, and made me sign a deed acknowledging him as my heir; in the admirable words of a popular expression of which, as of the most famous epics, we do not know the author, although, like these epics, and with all deference to Wolf and his theory,[20] it most certainly had one (one of those inventive and modest souls such as we come across every year, who light upon such gems as "putting a name to a face," though their own names they never reveal), *I did not know what I was doing.* The most I was capable of was astonishment, when my visit was at all prolonged, at the nullity of achievement, at the utter incon- clusiveness of those hours spent in the enchanted dwelling. But my disappointment arose neither from the inadequacy of the works of art that were shown to me nor from the im- possibility of fixing upon them my distracted gaze. For it was not the intrinsic beauty of the objects themselves that made it miraculous for me to be sitting in Swann's library, it was the attachment to those objects—which might have been the ugliest in the world—of the particular feeling, melancholy and voluptuous, which I had for so many years located in that room and which still impregnated it; similarly the multitude of mirrors, of silver-backed brushes, of altars to Saint Anthony of Padua carved and painted by the most eminent artists, her friends, counted for nothing in the feeling of my own un- worthiness and of her regal benevolence which was aroused in me when Mme Swann received me for a moment in her bedroom, in which three beautiful and impressive creatures, her first, second and third lady's-maids, smilingly prepared for her the most marvellous toilettes, and towards which, on the order conveyed to me by the footman in knee-breeches that Madame wished to say a few words to me, I would make my way along the tortuous path of a corridor perfumed for the whole of its length with the precious essences which ceaselessly wafted from her dressing-room their fragrant exhalations.

When Mme Swann had returned to her visitors, we could still hear her talking and laughing, for even with only two people in the room, and as though she had to cope with all the "chums" at once, she would raise her voice, ejaculate her words, as she had so often in the "little clan" heard the "Mistress" do, at the moments when she "led the conversation." The expressions which we have recently borrowed from other people being those which, for a time at least, we are fondest of using, Mme Swann used to select sometimes those which she had learned from distinguished people whom her husband had not been able to avoid introducing to her (it was from them that she derived the mannerism which consists in suppressing the article or demonstrative pronoun before an adjective qualifying a person's name), sometimes others more vulgar (such as "He's a mere nothing!"—the favourite expression of one of her friends), and tried to place them in all the stories which, from a habit formed in the "little clan," she loved to tell. She would follow these up automatically with, "I do love that story!" or "Do admit, it's a very *good* story!" which came to her, through her husband, from the Guermantes whom she did not know.

Mme Swann had left the dining-room, but her husband, having just returned home, would make his appearance among us in turn. "Do you know if your mother is alone, Gilberte?" "No, Papa, she still has some visitors." "What, still? At seven o'clock! It's appalling. The poor woman must be absolutely dead. It's odious." (At home I had always heard the first syllable of this word pronounced with a long "o," like "ode," but M. and Mme Swann made it short, as in "odd.") "Just think of it; ever since two o'clock this afternoon!" he went on, turning to me. "And Camille tells me that between four and five he let in at least a dozen people. Did I say a dozen? I believe he told me fourteen. No, a dozen; I don't remember. When I came home I had quite forgotten it was her 'day,' and when I saw all those carriages outside the door I thought there must be a wedding in the house. And just now, while I've been in the library for a short while, the bell has never stopped ringing; upon my word, it's given me quite a headache. And are there a lot of them in there still?" "No; only two." "Who

are they, do you know?" "Mme Cottard and Mme Bontemps."
"Oh! the wife of the Chief Secretary to the Minister of Public
Works." "I know her husband works in some Ministry or
other, but I don't know what as," Gilberte would say in
a babyish manner.

"What's that? You silly child, you talk as if you were two
years old. What do you mean: 'works in some Ministry or
other' indeed! He's nothing less than Chief Secretary, head
of the whole show, and what's more—what on earth am I
thinking of? Upon my word, I'm getting as stupid as yourself:
he isn't the Chief Secretary, he's the Permanent Secretary."

"How should I know? Is that supposed to mean a lot, being
Permanent Secretary?" answered Gilberte, who never let slip
an opportunity of displaying her own indifference to anything
that gave her parents cause for vanity. (She may, of course,
have considered that she only enhanced the brilliance of such
an acquaintance by not seeming to attach any undue importance to it.)

"I should think it did 'mean a lot!' " exclaimed Swann, who
preferred to this modesty, which might have left me in doubt,
a more explicit parlance. "Why it means simply that he's the
first man after the Minister. In fact, he's more important than
the Minister, because it's he who does all the work. Besides,
it appears that he's immensely able, a man quite of the first
rank, a most distinguished individual. He's an Officer of the
Legion of Honour. A delightful man, and very good-looking
too."

(This man's wife, incidentally, had married him against
everyone's wishes and advice because he was a "charming
creature." He had, what may be sufficient to constitute a
rare and delicate whole, a fair, silky beard, good features, a
nasal voice, bad breath, and a glass eye.)

"I may tell you," he added, turning to me, "that I'm greatly
amused to see that lot serving in the present government,
because they are Bontemps of the Bontemps-Chenut family,
typical of the old-fashioned bourgeoisie, reactionary, clerical,
tremendously straitlaced. Your grandfather knew quite well,
at least by name and by sight, old Chenut, the father, who
never tipped cabmen more than a sou, though he was a rich

man for those days, and the Baron Bréau-Chenut. All their
money went in the Union Générale smash—you're too young
to remember that, of course—and, gad! they've had to get it
back as best they could."

"He's the uncle of a girl who used to come to my lessons,
in a class a long way below mine, the famous 'Albertine.'
She's certain to be dreadfully 'fast' when she's older, but just
now she's the queerest-looking specimen."

"She is amazing, this daughter of mine. She knows everyone."

"I don't know her. I only used to see her about, and hear
them calling 'Albertine' here and 'Albertine' there. But I do
know Mme Bontemps, and I don't like her much either."

"You are quite wrong; she's charming, pretty, intelligent.
She's even quite witty. I shall go in and say how d'ye do to
her, and ask her if her husband thinks we're going to have a
war, and whether we can rely on King Theodosius. He's
bound to know, don't you think, since he's in the counsels of
the gods."

It was not thus that Swann used to talk in days gone by; but
which of us cannot call to mind some quite unpretentious
royal princess who has let herself be carried off by a footman,
and then, ten years later, trying to get back into society and
sensing that people are not very willing to call on her, spontaneously adopts the language of all the old bores, and, when
a fashionable duchess is mentioned, can be heard to say:
"She came to see me only yesterday," or "I live a very quiet
life"? Thus it is superfluous to make a study of social mores,
since we can deduce them from psychological laws.

The Swanns shared this failing of people who are not
much sought after; a visit, an invitation, a mere friendly word
from anyone at all prominent was for them an event to which
they felt the need to give full publicity. If bad luck would
have it that the Verdurins were in London when Odette gave
a rather smart dinner-party, it would be arranged for some
common friend to cable a report to them across the Channel.
The Swanns were incapable even of keeping to themselves the
complimentary letters and telegrams received by Odette. They
spoke of them to their friends, passed them from hand to

hand. Thus the Swanns' drawing-room was reminiscent of a seaside hotel where telegrams are posted up on a board.

Moreover, people who had known the old Swann not merely outside society, as I had, but in society, in that Guermantes set which, with certain concessions to Highnesses and Duchesses, was infinitely exacting in the matter of wit and charm, from which banishment was sternly decreed for men of real eminence whom its members found boring or vulgar,— such people might have been astonished to observe that the old Swann had ceased not only to be discreet when he spoke of his acquaintance, but particular when it came to choosing it. How was it that Mme Bontemps, so common, so ill-natured, failed to exasperate him? How could he possibly describe her as attractive? The memory of the Guermantes set must, one would suppose, have prevented him; in fact it encouraged him. There was certainly among the Guermantes, as compared with the great majority of groups in society, a degree of taste, even refined taste, but also a snobbishness from which there arose the possibility of a momentary interruption in the exercise of that taste. In the case of someone who was not indispensable to their circle, of a Minister of Foreign Affairs, a slightly pompous Republican, or an Academician who talked too much, their taste would be brought to bear heavily against him; Swann would condole with Mme de Guermantes on having had to sit next to such people at dinner at one of the embassies; and they would a thousand times rather have a man of fashion, that is to say a man of the Guermantes kind, good for nothing, but endowed with the wit of the Guermantes, someone who belonged to the same clique. Only, a Grand Duchess, a Princess of the Blood, should she dine often with Mme de Guermantes, would soon find herself enrolled in that clique also, without having any right to be there, without being at all so endowed. But with the naïvety of society people, from the moment they had her in their houses they went out of their way to find her agreeable, since they were unable to say to themselves that it was because she was agreeable that they invited her. Swann, coming to the rescue of Mme de Guermantes, would say to her after the Highness had gone: "After all, she's not such a bad sort; really, she has quite a sense of humour. I don't suppose for a moment she has mastered the *Critique of Pure Reason*; still, she's not unpleasant." "Oh, I do so entirely agree with you!" the Duchess would reply. "Besides, she was a little shy: you'll see that she can be charming." "She is certainly a great deal less boring than Mme X——" (the wife of the talkative Academician, who was in fact a remarkable woman) "who quotes twenty volumes at you." "Oh, but there's no comparison." The faculty of saying such things as these, and of saying them sincerely, Swann had acquired from the Duchess, and had never lost. He made use of it now with reference to the people who came to his house. He went out of his way to discern and to admire in them the qualities that every human being will display if we examine him with a prejudice in his favour and not with the distaste of the nice-minded; he extolled the merits of Mme Bontemps as he had once extolled those of the Princesse de Parme, who must have been excluded from the Guermantes set if there had not been privileged terms of admission for certain Highnesses, and if, when they too presented themselves for election, the only consideration had been wit and a certain charm. We have seen already, moreover, that Swann had always an inclination (which he was now putting into practice merely in a more lasting fashion) to exchange his social position for another which, in certain circumstances, might suit him better. It is only people incapable of dissecting what at first sight appears indivisible in their perception who believe that one's position is an integral part of one's person. One and the same man, taken at successive points in his life, will be found to breathe, on different rungs of the social ladder, in atmospheres that do not of necessity become more and more refined; whenever, in any period of our existence, we form or re-form associations with a certain circle, and feel cherished and at ease in it, we begin quite naturally to cling to it by putting down human roots.

Where Mme Bontemps was concerned, I believe also that Swann, in speaking of her with so much emphasis, was not sorry to think that my parents would hear that she had been to see his wife. To tell the truth, in our house the names of the people whom Mme Swann was gradually getting to

know aroused more curiosity than admiration. At the name of
Mme Trombert, my mother exclaimed: "Ah! there's a new
recruit who will bring in others." And as though she found a
similarity between the somewhat summary, rapid, and violent
manner in which Mme Swann conquered her new connections
and a colonial expedition, Mamma went on to observe:
"Now that the Tromberts have been subdued, the neighbouring tribes will soon surrender." If she had passed Mme Swann
in the street, she would tell us when she came home: "I saw
Mme Swann in all her war-paint; she must have been embarking on some triumphant offensive against the Massachu-
toes, or the Singhalese, or the Tromberts." And so with all the
new people whom I told her that I had seen in that somewhat
composite and artificial society, to which they had often been
brought with some difficulty and from widely different worlds,
Mamma would at once divine their origin, and, speaking of
them as of trophies dearly bought, would say: "Brought back
from the expedition against the so-and-so!"

As for Mme Cottard, my father was astonished that Mme
Swann could see anything to be gained from inviting so
utterly undistinguished a woman to her house, and said: "In
spite of the Professor's position, I must say that I cannot
understand it." Mamma, on the other hand, understood very
well; she knew that a great deal of the pleasure which a woman
finds in entering a class of society different from that in which
she has previously lived would be lacking if she had no means of
keeping her old associates informed of those others, relatively
more brilliant, with whom she has replaced them. For this,
she requires an eye-witness who may be allowed to penetrate
this new, delicious world (as a buzzing, browsing insect bores
its way into a flower) and will then, so it is hoped, as the course
of her visits may carry her, spread abroad the tidings, the
latent germ of envy and of wonder. Mme Cottard, who might
have been created on purpose to fulfil this role, belonged to
that special category in a visiting list which Mamma (who
inherited certain facets of her father's turn of mind) used to call
"Go tell the Spartans" people. Besides—apart from another
reason which did not come to our knowledge until many
years later—Mme Swann, in inviting this good-natured,

reserved and modest friend to her "at homes," had no need to fear lest she might be introducing into her drawing-room a traitor or a rival. She knew what a vast number of bourgeois calyxes that busy worker, armed with her plume and card-case, could visit in a single afternoon. She knew her power of pollination, and, basing her calculations upon the law of probability, was justified in thinking that almost certainly some intimate of the Verdurins would be bound to hear, within two or three days, how the Governor of Paris had left cards upon her, or that M. Verdurin himself would be told how M. Le Hault de Pressagny, the President of the Horse Show, had taken them, Swann and herself, to the King Theodosius gala; she imagined the Verdurins to be informed of these two events, both so flattering to herself, and of these alone, because the particular manifestations in which we en-visage and pursue fame are but few in number, through the deficiency of our own minds, which are incapable of imagining at one and the same time all the forms which we none the less hope—on the whole—that fame will not fail simultaneously to assume for our benefit.

Mme Swann had, however, met with no success outside what was called the "official world." Elegant women did not go to her house. It was not the presence there of Republican "notables" that frightened them away. In the days of my early childhood, everything that pertained to conservative society was worldly, and no respectable salon would ever have opened its doors to a Republican. The people who lived in such an atmosphere imagined that the impossibility of ever inviting an "opportunist"—still, more a "horrid radical"—was some-thing that would endure for ever, like oil-lamps and horse-drawn omnibuses. But, like a kaleidoscope which is every now and then given a turn, society arranges successively in different orders elements which one would have supposed immutable, and composes a new pattern. Before I had made my first Communion, right-minded ladies had had the stupefying experience of meeting an elegant Jewess while paying a social call. These new arrangements of the kaleidoscope are pro-duced by what a philosopher would call a "change of criterion." The Dreyfus case brought about another, at a

period rather later than that in which I began to go to Mme
Swann's, and the kaleidoscope once more reversed its coloured
lozenges. Everything Jewish, even the elegant lady herself,
went down, and various obscure nationalists rose to take its
place. The most brilliant salon in Paris was that of an ultra-
Catholic Austrian prince. If instead of the Dreyfus case there
had come a war with Germany, the pattern of the kaleidoscope
would have taken a turn in the other direction. The Jews
having shown, to the general astonishment, that they were
patriots, would have kept their position, and no one would
any longer have cared to go, or even to admit that he had
ever gone any longer to the Austrian prince's. None of this
alters the fact, however, that whenever society is momentarily
stationary, the people who live in it imagine that no further
change will occur, just as, in spite of having witnessed the
birth of the telephone, they decline to believe in the aeroplane. Meanwhile the philosophers of journalism are at work
castigating the preceding epoch, and not only the kind of
pleasures in which it indulged, which seem to them to be the
last word in corruption, but even the work of its artists and
philosophers, which have no longer the least value in their eyes,
as though they were indissolubly linked to the successive
moods of fashionable frivolity. The one thing that does not
change is that at any and every time it appears that there have
been "great changes." At the time when I went to Mme
Swann's the Dreyfus storm had not yet broken, and some of the
more prominent Jews were extremely powerful—none more
so than Sir Rufus Israels, whose wife, Lady Israels, was
Swann's aunt. She herself had no intimate connections as
distinguished as those of her nephew, who, since he did not
care for her, had never much cultivated her society, although
he was presumed to be her heir. But she was the only one of
Swann's relations who had any idea of his social position, the
others having always remained in the state of ignorance, in that
respect, which had long been our own. When one of the members of a family emigrates into "high society"—which to him
appears a feat without parallel until after the lapse of a decade
he observes that it has been performed in other ways and for
different reasons by more than one young man whom he

knew as a boy—he draws round about himself a zone of shadow, a *terra incognita*, which is clearly visible in its minutest details to all those who inhabit it but is darkest night, pure nothingness, to those who do not penetrate it but touch its fringe without the least suspicion of its existence in their midst. There being no news agency to furnish Swann's cousins with intelligence of the people with whom he consorted, it was (before his appalling marriage, of course) with a smile of condescension that they would tell one another over family dinner-tables that they had spent a "virtuous" Sunday in going to see "cousin Charles," whom (regarding him as a "poor relation" who was inclined to envy their prosperity) they used wittily to name, playing upon the title of Balzac's novel, "Le Cousin Bête." Lady Israels, however, was letter-perfect in the names and quality of the people who lavished upon Swann a friendship of which she was frankly jealous. Her husband's family, which was roughly the equivalent of the Rothschilds, had for several generations managed the affairs of the Orleans princes. Lady Israels, being immensely rich, exercised a wide influence, and had employed it so as to ensure that no one whom she knew should be "at home" to Odette. One alone had disobeyed her, in secret, the Comtesse de Marsantes. And then, as ill luck would have it, Odette having gone to call upon Mme de Marsantes, Lady Israels had entered the room almost at her heels. Mme de Marsantes was on tenterhooks.* With the cowardice of those who are nevertheless in a position to act as they choose, she did not address a single word to Odette, who thus found little encouragement to pursue any further an incursion into a world which was not in any case the one into which she wished to be received. In her complete detachment from the Faubourg Saint-Germain, Odette continued to be the illiterate courtesan, utterly different from those bourgeois snobs, "well up" in all the minutest points of genealogy, who endeavour to quench by reading old memoirs their thirst for the aristocratic connections with which real life has omitted to provide them. And Swann, for his part, continued no doubt to be the lover in whose eyes all these peculiarities of an old mistress seem lovable or at least inoffensive, for I often heard his wife perpetuate veritable

social heresies without his attempting to correct them, whether
from lingering affection, lack of esteem, or weariness of the
effort to improve her. It was perhaps also another form of the
simplicity which for so long had misled us at Combray,
and which now had the effect that, while he continued to
know, on his own account at least, very grand people, he had
no wish for them to appear to be regarded as of any importance
in conversation in his wife's drawing-room. They had, indeed,
less importance than ever for Swann, the centre of gravity of
his life having shifted. In any case, Odette's ignorance in
social matters was such that if the name of the Princesse de
Guermantes were mentioned in conversation after that of
the Duchess, her cousin, "Those ones are princes, are they?"
she would exclaim; "So they've gone up a step?" Were anyone to say "the Prince," in speaking of the Duc de Chartres,
she would put him right: "The Duke, you mean; he's Duc de
Chartres, not Prince." As for the Duc d'Orléans, son of the
Comte de Paris: "That's funny; the son is higher than the
father!" she would remark, adding, for she was afflicted with
Anglomania, "Those *Royalties* are so dreadfully confusing!"—
while to someone who asked her from what province the
Guermantes family came she would reply: "From the Aisne."

But so far as Odette was concerned, Swann was quite blind,
not merely to these deficiencies in her education but to the
general mediocrity of her intelligence. More than that; whenever Odette told a silly story Swann would sit listening to his
wife with a complacency, a merriment, almost an admiration
in which some vestige of desire for her must have played a
part; while in the same conversation, anything subtle or even
profound that he himself might say would be listened to by
Odette with an habitual lack of interest, rather curtly, with
impatience, and would at times be sharply contradicted. And
we may conclude that this subservience of refinement to
vulgarity is the rule in many households, when we think,
conversely, of all the superior women who yield to the
blandishments of a boor, merciless in his censure of their most
delicate utterances, while they themselves, with the infinite
indulgence of love, are enraptured by the feeblest of his witticisms. To return to the reasons which prevented Odette, at

this period, from gaining admittance to the Faubourg Saint-Germain, it must be observed that the latest turn of the social kaleidoscope had been actuated by a series of scandals. Women to whose houses one had been going with perfect confidence had been discovered to be common prostitutes or British spies. For some time thereafter one expected people to be (such at least was one's intention) staid and solidly based. Odette represented exactly what one had just severed relations with, only, incidentally, to renew them at once (for men, their natures not altering overnight, seek in every new order a continuance of the old), though seeking it under another form which would allow one to be taken in, and to believe that it was no longer the same society as before the crisis. However, the "exposed" women of that society and Odette were too closely alike. Society people are very short-sighted; at the moment when they cease to have any relations with the Jewish ladies they know, while they are wondering how they are to fill the gap thus made in their lives, they perceive, thrust into it as by the windfall of a night of storm, a new lady, also Jewish; but by virtue of her novelty she is not associated in their minds with her predecessors, with what they are convinced that they must abjure. She does not ask that they shall respect her God. They take her up. There was no question of anti-semitism at the time when I used first to visit Odette. But she resembled what people wished for a time to avoid.

As for Swann himself, he still often called on some of his former acquaintances, who, of course, belonged to the very highest society. And yet when he spoke to us of the people whom he had just been to see I noticed that, among those whom he had known in the old days, the choice that he made was dictated by the same kind of taste, partly artistic, partly historic, that inspired him as a collector. And remarking that it was often some Bohemian noblewoman who interested him because she had been the mistress of Liszt or because one of Balzac's novels had been dedicated to her grandmother (as he would purchase a drawing if Chateaubriand had written about it), I conceived a suspicion that we had, at Combray, replaced one error, that of regarding Swann as a rich bourgeois who did not go into society, by another, when we supposed him to be one of

the smartest men in Paris. To be a friend of the Comte de
Paris means nothing at all. Is not the world full of such
"friends of princes," who would not be received in any house
that was at all "exclusive?" Princes know themselves to be
princes, and are not snobs; besides, they believe themselves to
be so far above everything that is not of their blood royal that
noblemen and commoners appear, in the depths beneath
them, to be practically on a level.

But Swann was not content with seeking in society, and
fastening on the names which the past has inscribed on its
roll and which are still to be read there, a simple artistic and
literary pleasure; he indulged in the slightly vulgar diversion
of arranging as it were social nosegays by grouping heterogeneous elements, by bringing together people taken at random
here, there and everywhere. These amusing (to Swann) sociological experiments did not always provoke an identical
reaction from all his wife's friends. "I'm thinking of asking the
Cottards to meet the Duchesse de Vendôme," he would say
to Mme Bontemps with a laugh, in the zestful tone of an
epicure who has thought of and intends to try substituting
cayenne pepper for cloves in a sauce. But this plan, which
might indeed appear agreeable to the Cottards, was calculated
to infuriate Mme Bontemps. She herself had recently been
introduced by the Swanns to the Duchesse de Vendôme, and
had found this as agreeable as it seemed to her natural. The
thought of being able to boast about it at the Cottards' had
been by no means the least savoury ingredient of her pleasure.
But like those persons recently decorated who, their investi-
ture once accomplished, would like to see the fountain of
honour turned off at the main, Mme Bontemps would have
preferred that, after herself, no one else in her own circle
should be made known to the Princess. She inwardly cursed
the depraved taste which caused Swann, in order to gratify a
wretched aesthetic whim, to destroy at one swoop the
dazzling impression she had made on the Cottards when she
told them about the Duchesse de Vendôme. How was she
even to dare to announce to her husband that the Professor
and his wife were in their turn to partake of this pleasure of
which she had boasted to him as though it were unique. If

only the Cottards could be made to know that they were being invited not seriously but for the amusement of their host! It is true that the Bontemps had been invited for the same reason, but Swann, having acquired from the aristocracy that eternal Donjuanism which, in treating with two women of no importance, makes each of them believe that it is she alone who is seriously loved, had spoken to Mme Bontemps of the Duchesse de Vendôme as of a person with whom it was essential for her to dine. "Yes, we're having the Princess here with the Cottards," said Mme Swann a few weeks later. "My husband thinks that we might get something quite amusing out of the conjunction." For if she had retained from the "little nucleus" certain habits dear to Mme Verdurin, such as that of shouting things aloud so as to be heard by all the faithful, she made use, at the same time, of certain expressions, such as "conjunction," which were dear to the Guermantes circle, of which she was thus undergoing the attraction, unconsciously and at a distance, as the sea is swayed by the moon, though without being drawn perceptibly closer to it. "Yes, the Cottards and the Duchesse de Vendôme. Don't you think that might be rather fun?" asked Swann.

"I think they'll be exceedingly ill-assorted, and it can only lead to a lot of bother. People oughtn't to play with fire, is what I say," snapped Mme Bontemps, furious. She and her husband, and also the Prince d'Agrigente, were, as it happened, invited to this dinner, which Mme Bontemps and Cottard had each two alternative ways of describing, according to whom they were addressing. To some Mme Bontemps for her part, and Cottard for his, would say casually, when asked who else had been of the party: "Only the Prince d'Agrigente; it was very intimate." But there were others who might, alas, be better informed (once, indeed, someone had challenged Cottard with: "But weren't the Bontemps there too?" "Oh, I forgot them," Cottard had blushingly admitted to the tactless questioner whom he ever afterwards classified among the slanderers and mischiefmakers). For these the Bontemps and the Cottards had each adopted, without any mutual arrangement, a version the framework of which was identical for both parties, their own names being interchanged. "Let me see," Cottard would say, "there were our host and hostess, the Duc and Duchesse de Vendôme—" (with a self-satisfied smile) "Professor and Mme Cottard, the Prince d'Agrigente, and, upon my soul, heaven only knows how they got there, for they were like fish out of water, M. and Mme Bontemps!" Mme Bontemps would recite exactly the same "piece," only it was M. and Mme Bontemps who were named with self-satisfied emphasis between the Duchesse de Vendôme and the Prince d'Agrigente, while the "also rans," whom she wound up by accusing of having invited themselves, and who completely spoiled the picture, were the Cottards.

When he had been paying social calls Swann would often come home with little time to spare before dinner. At that point in the evening, around six o'clock, when in the old days he used to feel so wretched, he no longer asked himself what Odette might be about, and was hardly at all concerned to hear that she had people with her or had gone out. He recalled at times that he had once, years ago, tried to read through its envelope a letter addressed by Odette to Forcheville. But this memory was not pleasing to him, and rather than plumb the depths of shame that he felt in it he preferred to indulge in a little grimace, twisting up the corners of his mouth and adding, if need be, a shake of the head which signified "What do I care about it?" True, he considered now that the hypothesis on which he had often dwelt at that time, according to which it was his jealous imagination alone that blackened what was in reality the innocent life of Odette—that this hypothesis (which after all was beneficent, since, so long as his amorous malady had lasted, it had diminished his sufferings by making them seem imaginary) was not the correct one, that it was his jealousy that had seen things in the correct light, and that if Odette had loved him more than he supposed, she had also deceived him more. Formerly, while his sufferings were still keen, he had vowed that, as soon as he had ceased to love Odette and was no longer afraid either of vexing her or of making her believe that he loved her too much, he would give himself the satisfaction of elucidating with her, simply from his love of truth and as a point of historical interest, whether or not Forcheville had been in bed with her that day when he had rung her bell and rapped on her window in vain, and she had written to Forcheville that it was an uncle of hers who had called. But this so interesting problem, which he was only waiting for his jealousy to subside before clearing up, had precisely lost all interest in Swann's eyes when he had ceased to be jealous. Not immediately, however. Long after he had ceased to feel any jealousy with regard to Odette, the memory of that day, that afternoon spent knocking vainly at the little house in the Rue La Pérouse, had continued to torment him. It was as though his jealousy, not dissimilar in that respect from those maladies which appear to have their seat, their centre of contagion, less in certain persons than in certain places, in certain houses, had had for its object not so much Odette herself as that day, that hour in the irrevocable past when Swann had knocked at every entrance to her house in turn, as though that day, that hour alone had caught and pre-served a few last fragments of the amorous personality which had once been Swann's, that there alone could he now recap-ture them. For a long time now it had been a matter of indiffer-ence to him whether Odette had been, or was being, unfaithful to him. And yet he had continued for some years to seek out old servants of hers, to such an extent had the painful curiosity persisted in him to know whether on that day, so long ago, at six o'clock, Odette had been in bed with Forcheville. Then that curiosity itself had disappeared, without, however, his abandoning his investigations. He went on trying to discover what no longer interested him, because his old self, though it had shrivelled to extreme decrepitude, still acted mechanically, in accordance with preoccupations so utterly abandoned that Swann could not now succeed even in picturing to himself that anguish—so compelling once that he had been unable to imagine that he would ever be delivered from it, that only the death of the woman he loved (though death, as will be shown later on in this story by a cruel corroboration, in no way diminishes the sufferings caused by jealousy) seemed to him capable of smoothing the path of his life which then seemed impassably obstructed.

But to bring to light, some day, those passages in the life of Odette to which he had owed his sufferings had not been

Swann's only ambition; he had also resolved to avenge himself for his sufferings when, being no longer in love with Odette, he should no longer be afraid of her; and the opportunity of gratifying this second ambition had now presented itself, for Swann was in love with another woman, a woman who gave him no grounds for jealousy but none the less made him jealous, because he was no longer capable of altering his mode of loving, and it was the mode he had employed with Odette that must serve him now for another. To make Swann's jealousy revive it was not necessary for this woman to be unfaithful; it sufficed that for some reason or other she should have been away from him, at a party for instance, and should have appeared to enjoy herself. That was enough to re-awaken in him the old anguish, that lamentable and contradictory excrescence of his love, which alienated Swann from what it was in fact a sort of need to attain (the real feelings this young woman had for him, the hidden longing that absorbed her days, the secret places of her heart), for between Swann and the woman whom he loved this anguish piled up an unyielding mass of previous suspicions, having their cause in Odette, or in some other perhaps who had preceded Odette, which allowed the ageing lover to know his mistress of to-day only through the old, collective spectre of the "woman who aroused his jealousy" in which he had arbitrarily embodied his new love. Often, however, Swann would accuse his jealousy of making him believe in imaginary infidelities; but then he would remember that he had given Odette the benefit of the same argument, and wrongly. And so everything that the young woman whom he loved did in the hours when he was not with her ceased to appear innocent. But whereas at that other time he had made a vow that if ever he ceased to love the woman who, though he did not then know it, was to be his future wife, he would show her an implacable indifference that would at last be sincere, in order to avenge his pride that had so long been humiliated, now that he could enforce those reprisals without risk to himself (for what harm could it do him to be taken at his word and deprived of those intimate moments with Odette that had once been so necessary to him?), he no longer wished to do so; with his love had vanished the desire to show that he no longer loved. And he who, when he was suffering at the hands of Odette, so longed to let her see one day that he had fallen for another, now that he was in a position to do so took infinite precautions lest his wife should suspect the existence of this new love.

It was not only in those tea-parties, on account of which I had formerly had the sorrow of seeing Gilberte leave me and go home earlier than usual, that I was henceforth to take part, but the excursions she made with her mother which, by preventing her from coming to the Champs-Elysées, had deprived me of her on those days when I loitered alone upon the lawn in front of the roundabout—in these also M. and Mme Swann now included me: I had a seat in their landau, and indeed it was me that they asked if I would rather go to the theatre, to a dancing lesson at the house of one of Gilberte's friends, to some social gathering given by a friend of Mme Swann's (what the latter called "a little *meeting*") or to visit the tombs at Saint-Denis.

On the days when I was to go out with the Swanns I would arrive at their house in time for what Mme Swann called "le lunch." As one was not expected before half-past twelve, while my parents in those days had their meal at a quarter past eleven, it was not until they had risen from table that I made my way towards that sumptuous quarter, deserted enough at any time, but more particularly at that hour, when everyone had gone home. Even on frosty days in winter if the weather was fine, tightening every few minutes the knot of a gorgeous Charvet tie and looking to see that my patent-leather boots were not getting dirty, I would wander up and down the avenues, waiting until twenty-seven minutes past the hour. I could see from afar in the Swanns' little garden-plot the sunlight glittering like hoar-frost from the bare-boughed trees. It is true that the garden boasted only two. The unusual hour presented the scene in a new light. These pleasures of nature (intensified by the suppression of habit and indeed by my physical hunger), were infused by the thrilling prospect of sitting down to lunch with Mme Swann. It did not diminish them, but dominated and subdued them, made of them social accessories; so that if, at this hour when ordinarily I did not notice them, I seemed now to be discovering the fine weather, the cold, the wintry sunlight, it was all as a sort of preface to the creamed eggs, as a patina, a cool pink glaze applied to the decoration of that mystic chapel which was the habitation of Mme Swann, and in the heart of which there was by contrast so much warmth, so many scents and flowers.

At half-past twelve I would finally make up my mind to enter the house which, like an immense Christmas stocking, seemed ready to bestow upon me supernatural delights. (The French name "Noël" was, by the way, unknown to Mme Swann and Gilberte, who had substituted for it the English "Christmas," and would speak of nothing but "Christmas pudding," what people had given them as "Christmas presents," of going away—the thought of which maddened me with grief—"for Christmas." Even at home I should have thought it degrading to use the word "Noël," and always said "Christmas," which my father considered extremely silly.)

I encountered no one at first but a footman who, after leading me through several large drawing-rooms, showed me into one that was quite small, empty, its windows beginning to dream already in the blue light of afternoon. I was left alone there in the company of orchids, roses and violets, which, like people waiting beside you who do not know you, preserved a silence which their individuality as living things made all the more striking, and warmed themselves in the heat of a glowing coal fire, preciously ensconced behind a crystal screen, in a basin of white marble over which it spilled from time to time its dangerous rubies.

I had sat down, but rose hurriedly on hearing the door open; it was only another footman, and then a third, and the slender result that their vainly alarming entrances and exits achieved was to put a little more coal on the fire or water in the vases. They departed, and I found myself alone again, once that door was shut which Mme Swann was surely soon to open. Of a truth, I should have been less ill at ease in a magician's cave than in this little waiting-room where the fire appeared to me to be performing alchemical transmutations as in Klingsor's laboratory. Footsteps sounded afresh, but I did not get up; it was sure to be yet another footman. It was M. Swann. "What! all by yourself? What is one to do? That poor wife of mine has never been able to remember what time means! Ten minutes to one. She gets later every day. And as you'll see, she will come sailing in without the least hurry, and imagine she's in heaps of time." And since he was still subject to neuritis, and was becoming a trifle ridiculous, the fact of possessing so unpunctual a wife, who came in so late from the Bois, forgot everything at her dressmaker's and was never in time for lunch, made Swann anxious for his digestion but flattered his self-esteem.

He would show me his latest acquisitions and explain to me the interesting points about them, but my emotion, added to the unfamiliarity of being still unfed at this hour, stirred my mind while leaving it void, so that while I was capable of speech I was incapable of hearing. In any event, as far as the works of art in Swann's possession were concerned, it was enough for me that they were contained in his house, formed a part there of the delicious hour that preceded luncheon. The Gioconda herself might have appeared there without giving me any more pleasure than one of Mme Swann's indoor gowns, or her scent bottles.

I continued to wait, alone, or with Swann and often Gilberte, who came in to keep us company. The arrival of Mme Swann, prepared for me by all those majestic apparitions, must, I felt, be something truly immense. I strained my ears to catch the slightest sound. But one never finds a cathedral, a wave in a storm, a dancer's leap in the air quite as high as one has been expecting; after those liveried footmen, suggesting the chorus whose processional entry upon the stage leads up to and at the same time diminishes the final appearance of the queen, Mme Swann, creeping furtively in, in a little otter-skin coat, her veil lowered to cover a nose pink-tipped by the cold, did not fulfil the promises lavished upon my imagination during my vigil.

But if she had stayed at home all morning, when she arrived in the drawing-room she would be clad in a brightly-coloured *crêpe-de-Chine* housecoat which seemed to me more exquisite than any of her dresses.

Sometimes the Swanns decided to remain in the house all afternoon, and then, as we had lunched so late, very soon I would see, beyond the garden-wall, the sun setting on that day which had seemed to me bound to be different from other days; and in vain might the servants bring in lamps of every size and shape, burning each upon the consecrated altar of a console, a wall-bracket, a corner-cupboard, an occasional table, as though for the celebration of some strange and secret rite, nothing extraordinary transpired in the conversation, and I went home disappointed, as one often is in one's childhood after midnight mass.

But that disappointment was scarcely more than spiritual. I was radiant with happiness in this house where Gilberte, when she was not yet with us, was about to appear and would bestow on me in a moment, and for hours to come, her speech, her smiling and attentive gaze as I had glimpsed it for the first time at Combray. At the most I was a trifle jealous when I saw her so often disappear into vast rooms above, reached by an interior staircase. Obliged myself to remain in the drawing-room, like a man in love with an actress who is confined to his stall and wonders anxiously what is going on behind the scenes, in the green-room, I put to Swann some artfully veiled questions with regard to this other part of the house, but in a tone from which I could not succeed in banishing a slight uneasiness. He explained to me that the room to which Gilberte had gone was the linen-room, offered to show it to me himself, and promised me that whenever Gilberte had occasion to go there again he would insist on her taking me with her. By these last words and the relief which they brought me, Swann at once abolished for me one of those terrifying inner perspectives at the end of which a woman with whom we are in love appears so remote. At that moment I felt for him an affection which I believed to be deeper than my affection for Gilberte. For he, his daughter's master, was giving her to me, whereas she withheld herself at times; I had not the same direct control over her as I had indirectly through Swann. Besides, it was she whom I loved and whom I could not therefore see without that anxiety, without that desire for something more, which destroys in us, in the presence of the person we love, the sensation of loving. As a rule, however, we did not stay indoors but went out. Sometimes, before going to dress, Mme Swann would sit down at the piano. Her lovely hands emerging from the pink, or white, or, often, vividly coloured sleeves of her *crêpe-de-Chine* housecoat, drooped over the keys with that same melancholy which was in her eyes but was not in her heart. It was on one of those days that she happened to play for me the passage in Vinteuil's sonata that contained the little phrase of which Swann had been so fond. But often one hears nothing when one listens for the first time to a piece of music that is at all complicated. And yet when, later on, this sonata had been played to me two or three times I found that I knew it perfectly well. And so it is not wrong to speak of hearing a thing for the first time. If one had indeed, as one supposes, received no impression from the first hearing, the second, the third would be equally "first hearings" and there would be no reason why one should understand it any better after the tenth. Probably what is wanting, the first time, is not comprehension but memory. For our memory, relatively to the complexity of the impressions which it has to face while we are listening, is infinitesimal, as brief as the memory of a man who in his sleep thinks of a thousand things and at once forgets them, or as that of a man in his second childhood who cannot recall a minute afterwards what one has just said to him. Of these multiple impressions our memory is not capable of furnishing us with an immediate picture. But that picture gradually takes shape in the memory, and, with regard to works we have heard more than once, we are like the schoolboy who has read several times over before going to sleep a lesson which he supposed himself not to know, and finds that he can repeat it by heart next morning. But I had not, until then, heard a note of the sonata, and where Swann and his wife could make out a distinct phrase, it was as far beyond the range of my perception as a name which one endeavours to recall and in place of which one discovers only a void, a void from which, an hour later, when one is not thinking about them, will spring of their own accord, at one bound, the syllables that one has solicited in vain. And not only does one not grasp at once and remember works that are truly rare, but even within those works (as happened to me in the case of Vinteuil's sonata) it is the least precious parts that one at first perceives. So much so that I was mistaken not only in thinking that this work held nothing further in store for me (so that for a long time I made no effort to hear it again) from the moment Mme Swann had played me its most famous passage (I was in this respect as stupid as people are who expect to feel no astonishment when they stand in Venice before the façade of Saint Mark's, because photography has already acquainted them with the outline of its domes); far more than that, even when I had heard the sonata from beginning to end, it remained almost wholly invisible to me, like a monument of which distance or a haze allows us to catch but a faint and fragmentary glimpse. Hence the melancholy inseparable from one's knowledge of such works, as of everything that takes place in time. When the least obvious beauties of Vinteuil's sonata were revealed to me, already, borne by the force of habit beyond the grasp of my sensibility, those that I had from the first distinguished and preferred in it were beginning to escape, to elude me. Since I was able to enjoy everything that this sonata had to give me only in a succession of hearings, I never possessed it in its entirety: it was like life itself. But, less disappointing than life, great works of art do not begin by giving us the best of themselves. In a work such as Vinteuil's sonata the beauties that one discovers soonest are also those of which one tires most quickly, and for the same reason, no doubt—namely, that they are less different from what one already knows. But when those first impressions have receded, there remains for our enjoyment some passage whose structure, too new and strange to offer anything but confusion to our mind, had made it indistinguishable and so preserved intact; and this, which we had passed every day without knowing it, which had held itself in reserve for us, which by the sheer power of its beauty had become invisible and remained unknown, this comes to us last of all. But we shall also relinquish it last. And we shall love it longer than the rest because we have taken longer to get to love it. The time, moreover, that a person requires—as I required in the case of this sonata—to penetrate a work of any depth is merely an epitome, a symbol, one might say, of the years, the centuries even, that must elapse before the public can begin to cherish a masterpiece that is really new. So that the man of genius, to spare himself the ignorant contempt of the world, may say to himself that, since one's contemporaries are incapable of the nececessary detachment, works written for posterity should be read by posterity alone, like certain pictures which one cannot appreciate when one stands too close to them. But in reality any such cowardly precaution to avoid false judgments is doomed to failure; they are unavoidable. The reason why a work of genius is not easily admired from the first is that the man who has created it is extraordinary, that few other men resemble him. It is his work itself that, by fertilising the rare minds capable of understanding it, will make them increase and multiply. It was Beethoven's quartets themselves (the Twelfth, Thirteenth, Fourteenth and Fifteenth) that devoted half a century to forming, fashioning and enlarging the audience for Beethoven's quartets, thus marking, like every great work of art, an advance if not in the quality of artists at least in the community of minds, largely composed to-day of what was not to be found when the work first appeared, that is to say of persons capable of appreciating it. What is called posterity is the posterity of the work of art. It is essential that the work (leaving out of account, for simplicity's sake, the contingency that several men of genius may at the same time be working along parallel lines to create a more instructed public in the future, from which other men of genius will benefit) should create its own posterity. For if the work were held in reserve, were revealed only to posterity, that audience, for that particular work, would be not posterity but a group of contemporaries who were merely living half-a-century later in time. And so it is essential that the artist (and this is what Vinteuil had done), if he wishes his work to be free to follow its own course, should launch it, there where there is sufficient depth, boldly into the distant future. And yet, if leaving out of account this time to come, the true perspective in which to appreciate a work of art, is the mistake made by bad judges, taking it into account is at times a dangerous precaution of good ones. No doubt it is easy to imagine, by an illusion similar to that which makes everything on the horizon appear equidistant, that all the revolutions which have hitherto occurred in painting or in music did at least respect certain rules, whereas that which immediately confronts us, be it impressionism, the pursuit of dissonance, an exclusive use of the Chinese scale, cubism, futurism or what you will, differs outrageously from all that has occurred before. This is because everything that went before we are apt to regard as a whole, forgetting that a long process of assimilation has converted it into a substance that is varied of course but, taken as a whole, homogeneous, in which Hugo is juxtaposed with Molière. Let us try to imagine the shocking disparities we should find, if we did not take account of the future and the changes that it must bring, in a horoscope of our own riper years cast for us in our youth. Only horoscopes are not always accurate, and the necessity, when judging a work of art, of including the temporal factor in the sum total of its beauty introduces into our judgment something as conjectural, and consequently as barren of interest, as any prophecy the non-fulfilment of which will in no way imply any inadequacy on the prophet's part, for the power to summon possibilities into existence or to exclude them from it is not necessarily within the competence of genius; one may have had genius and yet not have believed in the future of railways or of flight, or, although a brilliant psychologist, in the infidelity of a mistress or of a friend whose treachery persons far less gifted would have foreseen.

If I did not understand the sonata, I was enchanted to hear Mme Swann play. Her touch appeared to me (like her wrapper, like the scent of her staircase, like her coats, like her chrysanthemums) to form part of an individual and mysterious whole, in a world infinitely superior to that in which reason is capable of analysing talent. "Isn't it beautiful, that Vinteuil sonata?" Swann asked me. "The moment when night is falling among the trees, when the arpeggios of the violin call down a cooling dew upon the earth. You must admit it's lovely; it shows all the static side of moonlight, which is the essential part. It's not surprising that a course of radiant heat such as my wife is taking should act on the muscles, since moonlight can prevent the leaves from stirring. That's what is expressed so well in that little phrase, the Bois de Boulogne plunged in a cataleptic trance. By the sea it's even more striking, because you have there the faint response of the waves, which, of course, you can hear quite distinctly since nothing else can move. In Paris it's the other way round: at most, you may notice unfamiliar lights among the old buildings, the sky lit up as though by a colourless and harmless conflagration, a sort of vast news item of which you get a hint here and there. But in Vinteuil's little phrase, and in the whole sonata for that matter, it's not like that; the scene is laid in the Bois; in the *gruppetto* you can distinctly hear a voice saying: 'I can almost see to read the paper!' "

These words of Swann's might have distorted, later on, my impression of the sonata, music being too little exclusive to dismiss absolutely what other people suggest that we should find in it. But I understood from other remarks he made that this nocturnal foliage was simply that beneath whose shade, in many a restaurant on the outskirts of Paris, he had listened on so many evenings to the little phrase. In place of the profound meaning that he had so often sought in it, what it now recalled to Swann were the leafy boughs, ordered, wreathed, painted round about it (which it gave him the desire to see again because it seemed to him to be their inner, their hidden self, as it were their soul), was the whole of one spring season which he had not been able to enjoy at the time, not having had—feverish and sad as he then was—the requisite physical and mental well-being, and which (as one puts by for an invalid the dainties that he has not been able to eat) it had kept for him. The charm that he had been made to feel by certain evenings in the Bois, a charm of which Vinteuil's sonata served to remind him, he could not have recaptured by questioning Odette, although she, as well as the little phrase, had been his companion there. But Odette had been merely by his side, not (as the phrase had been) within him, and so had seen nothing—nor would have, had she been a thousand times as comprehending—of that vision which for none of us (or at least I was long under the impression that this rule admitted of no exception) can be externalised. "It's rather a charming thought, don't you think," Swann continued, "that sound can reflect, like water, like a mirror. And it's curious, too, that Vinteuil's phrase now shows me only the things to which I paid no attention then. Of my troubles, my loves of those days, it recalls nothing, it has swapped things around." "Charles, I don't think that's very polite to me, what you're saying." "Not polite? Really, you women are superb! I was simply trying to explain to this young man that what the music shows—to me, at least—is not 'the triumph of the Will' or 'In Tune with the Infinite,' but shall we say old Verdurin in his frock coat in the palmhouse in the Zoological Gardens. Hundreds of times, without my leaving this room, the little phrase has carried me off to dine with it at Armenonville. Gad, it's less boring, anyhow, than having to go there with Mme de Cambremer."

Mme Swann laughed. "That is a lady who's supposed to have been violently in love with Charles," she explained, in the same tone in which, shortly before, when we were speaking of Vermeer of Delft, of whose existence I had been surprised to find her informed, she had replied to me: "I ought to explain that Monsieur Swann was very much taken up with that painter at the time he was courting me. Isn't that so, Charles dear?" "You're not to start saying things about Mme de Cambremer," Swann checked her, secretly flattered. "But I'm only repeating what I've been told. Besides, it seems that she's extremely clever; I don't know her myself. I believe she's very *pushing*, which surprises me rather in a clever woman. But everyone says that she was quite mad about you; there's nothing wounding in that." Swann remained silent as a deaf-mute, which was a sort of confirmation, and a proof of his self-complacency.

"Since what I'm playing reminds you of the Zoo," his wife went on, with a playful pretence of being offended, "we might drive this boy there this afternoon if it would amuse him. The weather's lovely now, and you can recapture your fond impressions! Which reminds me, talking of the Zoo, do you know, this young man thought that we were devotedly attached to a person whom I cut as a matter of fact whenever

I possibly can, Mme Blatin. I think it's rather humiliating for
us that she should be taken for a friend of ours. Just fancy,
dear Dr Cottard, who never says a harsh word about anyone,
declares that she's positively repellent." "A frightful woman!
The one thing to be said for her is that she's exactly like Savonarola. She's the very image of that portrait of Savonarola by
Fra Bartolommeo."

This mania of Swann's for finding likenesses to people in
pictures was defensible, for even what we call individual
expression is—as we so painfully discover when we are in
love and would like to believe in the unique reality of the
beloved—something diffused and general, which can be found
existing at different periods. But if one had listened to Swann,
the retinues of the Magi, already so anachronistic when Benozzo Gozzoli introduced in their midst various Medicis, would
have been even more so, since they would have included the
portraits of a whole crowd of men, contemporaries not of
Gozzoli but of Swann, subsequent, that is to say, not only by
fifteen centuries to the Nativity but by four more to the
painter himself. There was not missing from those cortèges,
according to Swann, a single living Parisian of note, any more
than there was from that act in one of Sardou's plays, in
which, out of friendship for the author and for the leading
lady, and also because it was the fashion, all the notabilities of
Paris, famous doctors, politicians, barristers, amused themselves, each on a different evening, by "walking on."

"But what has she got to do with the Zoo?" "Everything!"
"What? You don't suggest that she's got a sky-blue behind,
like the monkeys?" "Charles, you really are too dreadful! I
was thinking of what the Singhalese said to her. Do tell him,
Charles, it really is a gem." "Oh, it's too silly. You know Mme
Blatin loves accosting people, in a tone which she thinks
friendly, but which is really condescending." "What our good
friends on the Thames call *patronising*," interrupted Odette.
"Exactly. Well, she went the other day to the Zoo, where they
have some blackamoors—Singhalese I think I heard my wife
say—she is much 'better up' in ethnology than I am." "Now,
Charles, you're not to make fun of poor me." "I'm not making
fun, I assure you. Well, to continue, she went up to one of

these black fellows with 'Good morning, nigger!'...."
"She's a nothing!" Mme Swann interjected. "Anyhow, this
classification seems to have displeased the black. 'Me nigger,'
he said angrily to Mme Blatin, 'me nigger; you old cow!' " "I
do think that's so delightful! I adore that story. Don't you
think it's a good one. Can't you see old Blatin standing there:
'Me nigger; you old cow?' "

I expressed an intense desire to go there and see these
Singhalese, one of whom had called Mme Blatin an old cow.
They did not interest me in the least. But I reflected that on
the way to the Zoo, and again on our way home, we should
pass through the Allée des Acacias in which I used to gaze so
admiringly at Mme Swann, and that perhaps Coquelin's
mulatto friend, to whom I had never managed to exhibit
myself in the act of saluting her, would see me there, seated at
her side, as the victoria swept by.

During those minutes in which Gilberte, having gone to
"get ready," was not in the room with us, M. and Mme Swann
would take delight in revealing to me all the rare virtues of
their child. And everything that I myself observed seemed to
prove the truth of what they said. I remarked that, as her
mother had told me, she had not only for her friends but for
the servants, for the poor, the most delicate attentions, carefully thought out, a desire to give pleasure, a fear of causing
displeasure, expressed in all sorts of little things over which she
often took a great deal of trouble. She had done a piece of
needlework for our stall-keeper in the Champs-Elysées, and
went out in the snow to give it to her with her own hands,
so as not to lose a day. "You have no idea how kind-hearted
she is, since she never lets it be seen," her father assured me.
Young as she was, she appeared far more sensible already than
her parents. When Swann boasted of his wife's grand friends
Gilberte would turn away and remain silent, but without any
appearance of reproaching him, for it seemed inconceivable
to her that her father could be the object of the slightest criticism. One day, when I had spoken to her of Mlle Vinteuil, she
said to me:

"I never want to know her, for a very good reason, and
that is that she was not nice to her father, from what one hears,

and made him very unhappy. You can't understand that any more than I, can you? I'm sure you could no more live without your papa than I could, which is quite natural after all. How can one ever forget a person one has loved all one's life?"

And once when she was being particularly loving with Swann, and I mentioned this to her when he was out of the room:

"Yes, poor Papa, it's the anniversary of his father's death round about now. You can understand what he must be feeling. You do understand, don't you—you and I feel the same about things like that. So I just try to be a little less naughty than usual." "But he doesn't ever think you naughty. He thinks you're quite perfect." "Poor Papa, that's because he's far too good himself."

But her parents were not content with singing the praises of Gilberte—that same Gilberte who, even before I had set eyes on her, used to appear to me standing in front of a church, in a landscape of the Ile-de-France, and later, awakening in me not dreams now but memories, was embowered always in a hedge of pink hawthorn, in the little lane that I took when I was going the Méséglise way. Once when I had asked Mme Swann (making an effort to assume the indifferent tone of a friend of the family, curious to know the preferences of a child) which among all her playmates Gilberte liked the best, Mme Swann replied: "But you ought to know a great deal better than I do, since you're in her confidence, the great favourite, the *crack*, as the English say."

Doubtless, in such perfect coincidences as this, when reality folds back and overlays what we have long dreamed of, it completely hides it from us, merges with it, like two equal superimposed figures which appear to be one, whereas, to give our happiness its full meaning, we would rather preserve for all those separate points of our desire, at the very moment in which we succeed in touching them—and to be quite certain that it is indeed they—the distinction of being intangible. And our thoughts cannot even reconstruct the old state in order to compare it with the new, for it has no longer a clear field: the acquaintance we have made, the memory of those first, unhoped-for moments, the talk we have heard, are there now

to block the passage of our consciousness, and as they control
the outlets of our memory far more than those of our imagination, they react more forcibly upon our past, which we are no
longer able to visualise without taking them into account,
than upon the form, still unshaped, of our future. For years I
had believed that the notion of going to Mme Swann's was a
vague, chimerical dream to which I should never attain;
after I had spent a quarter of an hour in her drawing-room, it
was the time when I did not yet know her that had become
chimerical and vague like a possibility which the realisation
of an alternative possibility has destroyed. How could I ever
dream again of her dining-room as of an inconceivable place,
when I could not make the least movement in my mind without crossing the path of that inextinguishable ray cast backwards ad infinitum, into my own most distant past, by the
lobster *à l'Américaine* which I had just been eating. And Swann
must have observed in his own case a similar phenomenon:
for this house in which he now entertained me might be
regarded as the place into which had flowed, to merge and
coincide, not only the ideal dwelling that my imagination had
constructed, but another still, which his jealous love, as inventive as any fantasy of mine, had so often depicted to him,
that dwelling common to Odette and himself which had
appeared to him so inaccessible once, on an evening when
Odette had taken him home with Forcheville to drink orangeade with her; and what had flowed in to be absorbed, for him,
in the walls and furniture of the dining-room in which we now
sat down to lunch was that unhoped-for paradise in which,
in the old days, he could not without a pang imagine that he
would one day be saying to *their* butler the very words, "Is
Madame ready yet?" which I now heard him utter with a
touch of impatience mingled with self-satisfaction. No more,
probably, than Swann himself could I succeed in knowing my
own happiness, and when Gilberte herself once broke out:
"Who would ever have said that the little girl you watched
playing prisoners' base, without daring to speak to her, would
one day be your greatest friend whose home you could go to
whenever you liked?", she spoke of a change which I could
verify only by observing it from without, finding no trace

of it within myself, for it was composed of two separate states which I could not, without their ceasing to be distinct from one another, succeed in imagining at one and the same time.

And yet this house, because it had been so passionately desired by Swann, must have kept for him some of its sweetness, if I was to judge by myself for whom it had not lost all its mystery. That singular charm in which I had for so long supposed the life of the Swanns to be bathed had not been entirely exorcised from their house on my being admitted to it: I had made it draw back, overwhelmed as it was by the sight of the stranger, the pariah that I had been, to whom now Mme Swann graciously pushed forward an exquisite, hostile and scandalised armchair for him to sit in; but all around me in my memory, I can perceive it still. Is it because, on the days when M. and Mme Swann invited me to lunch, to go out afterwards with them and Gilberte, I imprinted with my gaze—while I sat waiting for them alone—on the carpet, the sofas, the tables, the screens, the pictures, the idea engraved upon my mind that Mme Swann, or her husband, or Gilberte was about to enter? Is it because those objects have dwelt ever since in my memory side by side with the Swanns, and have gradually acquired something of their identity? Is it because, knowing that they spent their existence among these things, I made of them all as it were emblems of the life and habits of the Swanns from which I had too long been excluded for them not to continue to appear strange to me, even when I was allowed the privilege of sharing in them? However it may be, whenever I think of that drawing-room which Swann (not that the criticism implied on his part any intention to find fault with his wife's taste) found so amorphous—because, while it was still conceived in the style, half conservatory half studio, which had been that of the rooms in which he had first known Odette, she had none the less begun to replace in this jumble a number of the Chinese ornaments which she now felt to be rather sham, a trifle dowdy, by a swarm of little chairs and stools and things draped in old Louis XVI silks; not to mention the works of art brought by Swann himself from his house on the Quai d'Orléans—it has kept in my memory, that

composite, heterogeneous room, a cohesion, a unity, an individual charm that are not to be found even in the most complete, the least spoiled of the collections that the past has
bequeathed to us, or the most modern, alive and stamped
with the imprint of a living personality; for we alone, by our
belief that they have an existence of their own, can give to
certain things we see a soul which they afterwards keep and
which they develop in our minds. All the ideas that I had
formed of the hours, different from those that exist for other
men, passed by the Swanns in that house which was to their
everyday life what the body is to the soul, and whose singularity it must have expressed, all those ideas were distributed, amalgamated—equally disturbing and indefinable
throughout—in the arrangement of the furniture, the thickness of the carpets, the position of the windows, the ministra-
tions of the servants. When, after lunch, we went to drink our
coffee in the sunshine of the great bay window of the drawing-
room, as Mme Swann was asking me how many lumps of
sugar I took, it was not only the silk-covered stool which she
pushed towards me that exuded, together with the agonising
charm that I had long ago discerned—first among the pink
hawthorn and then beside the clump of laurels—in the name
of Gilberte, the hostility that her parents had shown to me
and which this little piece of furniture seemed to have so well
understood and shared that I felt myself unworthy and found
myself almost reluctant to set my feet on its defenceless
cushion; a personality, a soul was latent there which linked it
secretly to the afternoon light, so different from any other
light in the gulf which spread beneath our feet its sparkling
tide of gold out of which the bluish sofas and vaporous
tapestries emerged like enchanted islands; and there was nothing, not even the painting by Rubens that hung above the
chimneypiece, that was not endowed with the same quality
and almost the same intensity of charm as the laced boots of
M. Swann and the hooded cape the like of which I had so
dearly longed to wear, whereas Odette would now beg her
husband to go and put on another, so as to appear smarter,
whenever I did them the honour of driving out with them.
She too went away to dress—not heeding my protestations

that no "outdoor" clothes could be nearly so becoming as the marvellous garment of *crêpe-de-Chine* or silk, old rose, cherry-coloured, Tiepolo pink, white, mauve, green, red or yellow, plain or patterned, in which Mme Swann had sat down to lunch and which she was now going to take off. When I told her that she ought to go out in that costume, she laughed, either in mockery of my ignorance or from delight in my compliment. She apologised for having so many housecoats, explaining that they were the only kind of dress in which she felt comfortable, and left us to go and array herself in one of those regal toilettes which imposed their majesty on all beholders, and yet among which I was sometimes summoned to decide which I would prefer her to put on.

In the Zoo, how proud I was, when we had left the carriage, to be walking by the side of Mme Swann! As she strolled negligently along, letting her cloak stream in the air behind her, I kept eyeing her with an admiring gaze to which she coquettishly responded in a lingering smile. And now, were we to meet one or other of Gilberte's friends, boy or girl, who greeted us from afar, it was my turn to be looked upon by them as one of those happy creatures whose lot I had envied, one of those friends of Gilberte who knew her family and had a share in that other part of her life, the part which was not spent in the Champs-Elysées.

Often upon the paths of the Bois or the Zoo we would be greeted by some distinguished lady who was a friend of Swann's, whom sometimes he had not at first seen and who would be pointed out to him by his wife: "Charles! Don't you see Mme de Montmorency?" And Swann, with that amicable smile bred of a long and intimate friendship, would none the less doff his hat with a sweeping gesture, and with a grace peculiarly his own. Sometimes the lady would stop, glad of an opportunity to show Mme Swann a courtesy which would set no tiresome precedent, of which they all knew that she would never take advantage, so thoroughly had Swann trained her in reserve. She had none the less acquired all the manners of polite society, and however elegant, however stately the lady might be, Mme Swann was invariably a match for her; halting for a moment before the friend whom her husband had recognised and was addressing, she would introduce us, Gilberte and myself, with so much ease of manner, would remain so free, so relaxed in her affability, that it would have been hard to say, looking at them both, which of the two was the aristocrat.

The day on which we went to inspect the Singhalese, on our way home we saw coming in our direction, and followed by two others who seemed to be acting as her escort, an elderly but still handsome lady enveloped in a dark overcoat and wearing a little bonnet tied beneath her chin with a pair of ribbons. "Ah! here's someone who will interest you!" said Swann. The old lady, who was now within a few yards of us, smiled at us with a caressing sweetness. Swann doffed his hat. Mme Swann swept to the ground in a curtsey and made as if to kiss the hand of the lady, who, standing there like a Winterhalter portrait, drew her up again and kissed her cheek. "Come, come, will you put your hat on, you!" she scolded Swann in a thick and almost growling voice, speaking like an old and familiar friend. "I'm going to present you to Her Imperial Highness," Mme Swann whispered.

Swann drew me aside for a moment while his wife talked to the Princess about the weather and the animals recently added to the Zoo. "That is the Princesse Mathilde," he told me, "you know who I mean, the friend of Flaubert, Sainte-Beuve, Dumas. Just fancy, she's the niece of Napoleon I. She had offers of marriage from Napoleon III and the Emperor of Russia. Isn't that interesting? Talk to her a little. But I hope she won't keep us standing here for an hour! ... I met Taine the other day," he went on, addressing the Princess, "and he told me Your Highness was vexed with him." "He's behaved like a perfect peeg!" she said gruffly, pronouncing the word *cochon* as though she referred to Joan of Arc's contemporary, Bishop Cauchon. "After his article on the Emperor I left my card on him with p. p. c. on it."[21]

I felt the surprise that one feels on opening the correspondence of that Duchesse d'Orléans who was by birth a Princess Palatine. And indeed Princesse Mathilde, animated by sentiments so entirely French, expressed them with a straightforward bluntness that recalled the Germany of an older generation, and was inherited, doubtless, from her Württemberger mother. This somewhat rough and almost masculine frankness she softened, as soon as she began to smile, with an Italian languor. And the whole person was clothed in an outfit so typically Second Empire that—for all that the Princess wore it simply and solely, no doubt, from attachment to the fashions that she had loved when she was young—she seemed to have deliberately planned to avoid the slightest discrepancy in historic colour, and to be satisfying the expectations of those who looked to her to evoke the memory of another age. I whispered to Swann to ask her whether she had known Musset. "Very slightly, Monsieur," was the answer, given in a tone which seemed to feign annoyance at the question, and of course it was by way of a joke that she called Swann Monsieur, since they were intimate friends. "I had him to dine once. I had invited him for seven o'clock. At half-past seven, as he had not appeared, we sat down to dinner. He arrived at eight, bowed to me, took his seat, never opened his lips, and went off after dinner without letting me hear the sound of his voice. Of course he was dead drunk. That hardly encouraged me to make another attempt." We were standing a little way off, Swann and I. "I hope this little audience is not going to last much longer," he muttered, "the soles of my feet are hurting. I can't think why my wife keeps on making conversation. When we get home it will be she who complains of being tired, and she knows I simply cannot go on standing like this."

For Mme Swann, who had had the news from Mme Bontemps, was in the process of telling the Princess that the Government, having at last begun to realise the depth of its shoddiness, had decided to send her an invitation to be present on the platform in a few days' time, when the Tsar Nicholas was to visit the Invalides. But the Princess who, in spite of appearances, in spite of the character of her entourage, which consisted mainly of artists and literary people, had remained at heart and showed herself, whenever she had to take action, the niece of Napoleon, replied: "Yes, Madame, I received it this morning and I sent it back to the Minister, who must have had it by now. I told him that I had no need of an invitation to go to the Invalides. If the Government desires my presence there, it will not be on the platform but in our vault, where the Emperor's tomb is. I have no need of a card to admit me there. I have my own keys. I go in and out when I choose. The Government has only to let me know whether it wishes me to be present or not. But if I do go to the Invalides, it will be down below or nowhere at all."

At that moment we were saluted, Mme Swann and I, by a young man who greeted her without stopping, and whom I was not aware that she knew; it was Bloch. When I asked her about him, she told me that he had been introduced to her by Mme Bontemps, and that he was employed in the Minister's secretariat, which was news to me. At all events, she could not have seen him often—or perhaps she had not cared to utter the name Bloch, hardly "smart" enough for her liking, for she told me that he was called M. Moreul. I assured her that she was mistaken, that his name was Bloch.

The Princess gathered up the train that flowed out behind her, and Mme Swann gazed at it with admiring eyes. "Yes, at it happens, it's a fur that the Emperor of Russia sent me," she explained, "and as I've just been to see him I put it on to show him that I'd managed to have it made up as a coat." "I hear that Prince Louis has joined the Russian Army; the Princess will be very sad at losing him," went on Mme Swann, not noticing her husband's signs of impatience. "He *would* go and do that! As I said to him, 'Just because there's been a soldier in the family there's no need to follow suit,'" replied the Princess, alluding with this abrupt simplicity to Napoleon the Great.

But Swann could hold out no longer: "Ma'am, it is I that am going to play the Royal Highness and ask your permission to retire; but you see, my wife hasn't been too well, and I don't like her to stand around for too long." Mme Swann curtseyed again, and the Princess conferred upon us all a celestial smile, which she seemed to have summoned out of the past, from among the graces of her girlhood, from the evenings at Compiègne, a smile which stole, sweet and unbroken, over her hitherto surly face. Then she went on her way, followed by the two ladies in waiting, who had confined themselves, in the manner of interpreters, of children's or invalids' nurses, to punctuating our conversation with meaningless remarks and superfluous explanations. "You should go and write your name in her book one day this week," Mme Swann counselled me. "One doesn't leave cards upon these 'Royalties,' as the English call them, but she will invite you to her house if you put your name down."

Sometimes in those last days of winter, before proceeding on our expedition we would go into one of the small picture-shows that were beginning to open and where Swann, as a collector of note, was greeted with special deference by the dealers in whose galleries they were held. And in that still wintry weather the old longing to set out for the South of France and Venice would be re-awakened in me by those rooms in which a springtime, already well advanced, and a blazing sun cast violet shadows upon the roseate Alpilles and gave the intense transparency of emeralds to the Grand Canal. If the weather was bad, we would go to a concert or a theatre, and afterwards to one of the fashionable tea-rooms. There, whenever Mme Swann had anything to say to me which she did not wish the people at the next table or even the waiters who brought our tea to understand, she would say it in English, as though that had been a secret language known to our two selves alone. As it happened everyone in the place knew English —I alone had not yet learned the language, and was obliged to say so to Mme Swann in order that she might cease to make, about the people who were drinking tea or serving us with it, remarks which I guessed to be uncomplimentary without either my understanding or the person referred to missing a single word.

Once, in connection with a matinée at the theatre, Gilberte gave me a great surprise. It was precisely the day of which she had spoken to me in advance, on which fell the anniversary of her grandfather's death. We were to go, she and I, with her governess, to hear selections from an opera, and Gilberte had dressed with a view to attending this performance, wearing the air of indifference with which she was in the habit of treating whatever we might be going to do, saying that it might be anything in the world, no matter what, provided that it amused me and had her parents' approval. Before lunch, her mother drew us aside to tell her that her father was vexed at the thought of our going to a concert on that particular day. This seemed to be only natural. Gilberte remained impassive, but grew pale with an anger which she was unable to conceal, and uttered not a word. When M. Swann joined us his wife took him to the other end of the room and said something in his ear. He called Gilberte, and they went together into the next room. We could hear their raised voices. Yet I could not bring myself to believe that Gilberte, so submissive, so loving, so thoughtful, would resist her father's appeal, on such a day and for so trifling a matter. At length Swann reappeared with her, saying: "You heard what I said. Now do as you like."

Gilberte's features remained contracted in a frown throughout luncheon, after which she retired to her room. Then suddenly, without hesitating and as though she had never at any point hesitated over her course of action: "Two o'clock!" she exclaimed, "You know the concert begins at half-past." And she told her governess to make haste.

"But," I reminded her, "won't your father be cross with you?"

"Not the least little bit!"

"Surely he was afraid it would look odd, because of the anniversary."

"What do I care what people think? I think it's perfectly absurd to worry about other people in matters of sentiment. We feel things for ourselves, not for the public. Mademoiselle has very few pleasures, and she's been looking forward to going to this concert. I'm not going to deprive her of it just to satisfy public opinion."

"But, Gilberte," I protested, taking her by the arm, "it's not to satisfy public opinion, it's to please your father."

"You're not going to start scolding me, I hope," she said sharply, plucking her arm away.

A favour still more precious than their taking me with them to the Zoo, the Swanns did not exclude me even from their friendship with Bergotte, which had been at the root of the

attraction that I had found in them when, before I had even
seen Gilberte, I reflected that her intimacy with that godlike
elder would have made her, for me, the most enthralling of
friends, had not the disdain that I was bound to inspire in her
forbidden me to hope that she would ever take me, in his
company, to visit the towns that he loved. And then, one day,
Mme Swann invited me to a big luncheon-party. I did not
know who the guests were to be. On my arrival I was dis-
concerted, as I crossed the hall, by an alarming incident. Mme
Swann seldom missed an opportunity of adopting any of
those customs which are thought fashionable for a season,
and then, failing to "catch on," are presently abandoned (as,
for instance, many years before, she had had her *hansom cab*,
or had printed in English upon a card inviting people to
luncheon the words *To meet*, followed by the name of
some more or less important personage). Often enough these
usages implied nothing mysterious and required no initiation.
For instance, a minor innovation of those days, imported from
England: Odette had made her husband have some visiting
cards printed on which the name Charles Swann was preceded
by "Mr." After the first visit that I paid her, Mme Swann
had left at my door one of these "pasteboards," as she called
them. No one had ever left a card on me before, and I felt at
once so much pride, emotion and gratitude that, scraping
together all the money I possessed, I ordered a superb basket
of camellias and sent it round to Mme Swann. I implored my
father to go and leave a card on her, but first, quickly, to have
some printed on which his name should bear the prefix "Mr."
He complied with neither of my requests. I was in despair for
some days, and then asked myself whether he might not after
all have been right. But this use of "Mr," if it meant nothing,
was at least intelligible. Not so with another that was revealed
to me on the occasion of this luncheon-party, but revealed
without any indication of its purport. At the moment when I
was about to step from the hall into the drawing-room, the
butler handed me a thin, oblong envelope upon which my
name was inscribed. In my surprise I thanked him; but I eyed
the envelope with misgivings. I no more knew what I was
expected to do with it than a foreigner knows what to do with

one of those little utensils that they lay in his place at a Chinese banquet. Noticing that it was gummed down, I was afraid of appearing indiscreet were I to open it then and there, and so I thrust it into my pocket with a knowing air. Mme Swann had written to me a few days before, asking me to come to "a small, informal luncheon." There were, however, sixteen people, among whom I never suspected for a moment that I was to find Bergotte. Mme Swann, who had already "named" me, as she called it, to several of her guests, suddenly, after my name, in the same tone that she had used in uttering it (and as though we were merely two of the guests at her luncheon who ought to each feel equally flattered on meeting the other), pronounced that of the gentle Bard with the snowy locks. The name Bergotte made me start, like the sound of a revolver fired at me point blank, but instinctively, to keep my countenance, I bowed: there, in front of me, like one of those conjurers whom we see standing whole and unharmed, in their frock coats, in the smoke of a pistol shot out of which a pigeon had just fluttered, my greeting was returned by a youngish, uncouth, thickset and myopic little man, with a red nose curled like a snail-shell and a goatee beard. I was cruelly disappointed, for what had just vanished in the dust of the explosion was not only the languorous old man, of whom no vestige now remained, but also the beauty of an immense work which I had contrived to enshrine in the frail and hallowed organism that I had constructed, like a temple, expressly for it, but for which no room was to be found in the squat figure, packed tight with blood-vessels, bones, glands, sinews, of the little man with the snub nose and black beard who stood before me. The whole of the Bergotte whom I had slowly and delicately elaborated for myself, drop by drop, like a stalactite, out of the transparent beauty of his books, ceased (I could see at once) to be of any possible use, the moment I was obliged to include in him the snail-shell nose and to utilise the goatee beard —just as we must reject as worthless the solution we have found for a problem the terms of which we had not read in full and so failed to observe that the total must amount to a specified figure. The nose and beard were elements similarly ineluctable, and all the more aggravating in that, while forcing me to

reconstruct entirely the personage of Bergotte, they seemed
further to imply, to produce, to secrete incessantly a certain
quality of mind, alert and self-satisfied, which was not fair, for
such a mind had no connexion whatever with the sort of
intelligence that was diffused throughout those books, so
intimately familiar to me, which were permeated by a gentle
and godlike wisdom. Starting from them, I should never have
arrived at that snail-shell nose; but starting from the nose,
which did not appear to be in the slightest degree ashamed of
itself, but stood out alone there like a grotesque ornament
fastened on his face, I found myself proceeding in a totally
different direction from the work of Bergotte, and must arrive,
it would seem, at the mentality of a busy and preoccupied
engineer, of the sort who when you accost them in the street
think it correct to say: "Thanks, and you?" before you have
actually inquired of them how they are, or else, if you assure
them that you have been delighted to make their acquaintance,
respond with an abbreviation which they imagine to be smart,
intelligent and up-to-date, inasmuch as it avoids any waste of
precious time on vain formalities: "Same here!" Names, no
doubt, are whimsical draughtsmen, giving us of people as
well as of places sketches so unlike the reality that we often
experience a kind of stupor when we have before our eyes, in
place of the imagined, the visible world (which, for that matter,
is not the real world, our senses being little more endowed than
our imagination with the art of portraiture—so little, indeed,
that the final and approximately lifelike pictures which we
manage to obtain of reality are at least as different from the
visible world as that was from the imagined). But in Bergotte's
case, my preconceived idea of him from his name troubled me
far less than my familiarity with his work, to which I was
obliged to attach, as to the cord of a balloon, the man with
the goatee beard, without knowing whether it would still
have the strength to raise him from the ground. It seemed clear,
however, that it really was he who had written the books that
I had so loved, for Mme Swann having thought it incumbent
upon her to tell him of my admiration for one of these, he
showed no surprise that she should have mentioned this to him
rather than to any other guest, and did not seem to regard it as

due to a misapprehension, but, swelling out the frock coat
which he had put on in honour of all these distinguished guests
with a body avid for the coming meal, while his mind was
completely occupied by other, more important realities, it was
only as at some finished episode in his life, and as though one
had alluded to a costume as the Duc de Guise which he had
worn, one season, at a fancy dress ball, that he smiled as he
bore his mind back to the idea of his books; which at once
began to fall in my estimation (bringing down with them the
whole value of Beauty, of the world, of life itself), until they
seemed to have been merely the casual recreation of a man
with a goatee beard. I told myself that he must have taken
pains over them, but that, if he had lived on an island surrounded by beds of pearl-oysters, he would instead have
devoted himself with equal success to the pearling trade. His
work no longer appeared to me so inevitable. And then I
asked myself whether originality did indeed prove that great
writers are gods, ruling each over a kingdom that is his alone,
or whether there is not an element of sham in it all, whether
the differences between one man's books and another's were not
the result of their respective labours rather than the expression
of a radical and essential difference between diverse personalities.

Meanwhile we had taken our places at table. By the side
of my plate I found a carnation, the stalk of which was wrapped
in silver paper. It embarrassed me less than the envelope that
had been handed to me in the hall, which, however, I had
completely forgotten. Its use, strange as it was to me, seemed
to me more intelligible when I saw all the male guests take up
the similar carnations that were lying by their plates and slip
them into their buttonholes. I did as they had done, with the
air of naturalness that a free-thinker assumes in church when
he is not familiar with the Mass but rises when everyone else
rises and kneels a moment after everyone else is on his knees.
Another usage, equally strange to me but less ephemeral, disquieted me more. On the other side of my plate was a smaller
plate, on which was heaped a blackish substance which I did not
then know to be caviare. I was ignorant of what was to be
done with it but firmly determined not to let it enter my mouth.

Bergotte was sitting not far from me and I could hear quite clearly everything that he said. I understood then the impression that M. de Norpois had formed of him. He had indeed a peculiar "organ"; there is nothing that so alters the material qualities of the voice as the presence of thought behind what is being said: the resonance of the diphthongs, the energy of the labials are profoundly affected—as is the diction. His seemed to me to differ entirely from his way of writing, and even the things that he said from those with which he filled his books. But the voice issues from a mask behind which it is not powerful enough to make us recognise at first sight a face which we have seen uncovered in the speaker's literary style. At certain points in the conversation when Bergotte was in the habit of talking in a manner which not only M. de Norpois would have thought affected or unpleasant, it was a long time before I discovered an exact correspondence with the parts of his books in which his form became so poetic and so musical. At those points he could see in what he was saying a plastic beauty independent of whatever his sentences might mean, and as human speech reflects the human soul, though without expressing it as does literary style, Bergotte appeared almost to be talking nonsense, intoning certain words and, if he were pursuing, beneath them, a single image, stringing them together uninterruptedly on one continuous note, with a wearisome monotony. So that a pretentious, turgid and monotonous delivery was a sign of the rare aesthetic value of what he was saying, and an effect, in his conversation, of the same power which, in his books, produced that harmonious flow of imagery. I had had all the more difficulty in discovering this at first since what he said at such moments, precisely because it was the authentic utterance of Bergotte, did not appear to be typical Bergotte. It was a profusion of precise ideas, not included in that "Bergotte manner" which so many essayists had appropriated to themselves; and this dissimilarity was probably but another aspect—seen in a blurred way through the stream of conversation, like an image seen through smoked glass—of the fact that when one read a page of Bergotte it was never what would have been written by any of those lifeless imitators who, nevertheless, in newspapers and in books, adorned their prose with so many "Bergottish" images and ideas. This difference in style arose from the fact that what was meant by "Bergottism" was, first and foremost, a priceless element of truth hidden in the heart of each thing, whence it was extracted by that great writer by virtue of his genius, and that this extraction, rather than the perpetration of "Bergottisms," was the aim of the gentle Bard. Though, it must be added, he continued to perpetrate them in spite of himself because he was Bergotte, and so in this sense every fresh beauty in his work was the little drop of Bergotte buried at the heart of a thing and which he had distilled from it. But if, for that reason, each of those beauties was related to all the rest and had a "family likeness," yet each remained separate and individual, as was the act of discovery that had brought it to the light of day; new, and consequently different from what was known as the Bergotte manner, which was a loose synthesis of all the "Bergottisms" already thought up and written down by him, with no indication by which men who lacked genius might foresee what would be his next discovery. So it is with all great writers: the beauty of their sentences is as unforeseeable as is that of a woman whom we have never seen; it is creative, because it is applied to an external object which they have thought of—as opposed to thinking about themselves—and to which they have not yet given expression. An author of memoirs of our time, wishing to write without too obviously seeming to be writing like Saint-Simon, might at a pinch give us the first line of his portrait of Villars: "He was a rather tall man, dark . . . with an alert, open, expressive physiognomy," but what law of determinism could bring him to the discovery of Saint-Simon's next line, which begins with "and, to tell the truth, a trifle mad"? The true variety is in this abundance of real and unexpected elements, in the branch loaded with blue flowers which shoots up, against all reason, from the spring hedgerow that seemed already overcharged with blossoms, whereas the purely formal imitation of variety (and one might advance the same argument for all the other qualities of style) is but a barren uniformity, that is to say the very antithesis of variety, and cannot, in the work of imitators, give the illusion or recall the memory of it save to a reader who has not acquired the sense of it from the masters themselves.

And so—just as Bergotte's way of speaking would no doubt have charmed the listener if he himself had been merely an amateur reciting imitation Bergotte, whereas it was attached to the thought of Bergotte, at work and in action, by vital links which the ear did not at once distinguish—so it was because Bergotte applied that thought with precision to the reality which pleased him that his language had in it something down-to-earth, something over-nourishing, which disappointed those who expected to hear him speak only of the "eternal torrent of forms" and of the "mysterious tremors of beauty." Moreover the quality, always rare and new, of what he wrote was expressed in his conversation by so subtle a manner of approaching a question, ignoring every aspect of it that was already familiar, that he appeared to be seizing hold of an unimportant detail, to be off the point, to be indulging in paradox, so that his ideas seemed as often as not to be confused, for each of us sees clarity only in those ideas which have the same degree of confusion as his own. Besides, as all novelty depends upon the prior elimination of the stereotyped attitude to which we had grown accustomed, and which seemed to us to be reality itself, any new form of conversation, like all original painting and music, must always appear complicated and exhausting. It is based on figures of speech with which we are not familiar, the speaker appears to us to be talking entirely in metaphors; and this wearies us, and gives us the impression of a want of truth. (After all, the old forms of speech must also in their time have been images difficult to follow, when the listener was not yet cognisant of the universe which they depicted. But for a long time it has been taken to be the real universe, and is instinctively relied upon.) So when Bergotte—and his figures appear simple enough to-day—said of Cottard that he was a mannikin in a bottle, always trying to rise to the surface, and of Brichot that "for him even more than for Mme Swann the arrangement of his hair was a matter for anxious deliberation, because, in his twofold preoccupation with his profile and his reputation, he had always to make sure that it was so brushed as to give him the air at

once of a lion and of a philosopher," people immediately felt
the strain, and sought a foothold upon something which they
called more concrete, meaning by that more usual. It was
indeed to the writer whom I admired that the unrecognisable
words issuing from the mask I had before my eyes must be
attributed, and yet they could not have been inserted among
his books like pieces in a jigsaw puzzle, they were on another
plane and required a transposition by means of which, one day,
when I was repeating to myself certain phrases that I had
heard Bergotte use, I discovered in them the whole framework
of his written style, the different elements of which I was able
to recognise and to name in this spoken discourse which had
struck me as being so different.

From a more subsidiary point of view the special way, a
little too meticulous, too intense, that he had of pronouncing
certain words, certain adjectives which constantly recurred in
his conversation and which he never uttered without a certain
emphasis, giving to each of their syllables a separate force and
intoning the last (as for instance the word *visage* which he
always used in preference to *figure* and enriched with a number
of superfluous v's and s's and g's, which seemed all to explode
from his outstretched palm at such moments) corresponded
exactly to the fine passages where, in his prose, he brought
out those favourite words, preceded by a sort of pause and
composed in such a way in the metrical whole of the sentence
that the reader was obliged, if he was not to make a false
quantity, to give to each of them its full value. And yet one
did not find in Bergotte's speech a certain luminosity which in
his books, as in those of some other writers, often modified in the
written sentence the appearance of its words. This was doubtless because that light issues from so profound a depth that its
rays do not penetrate to our spoken words in the hours in
which, thrown open to others by the act of conversation, we
are to a certain extent closed to ourselves. In this respect,
there was more modulation, more stress in his books than in
his talk: stress independent of beauty of style, which the
author himself has possibly not perceived, since it is not
separable from his most intimate personality. It was this
stress which, at the moments when, in his books, Bergotte

was entirely natural, gave a rhythm to the words—often at such times quite insignificant—that he wrote. This stress is not marked on the printed page, there is nothing there to indicate it, and yet it imposes itself of its own accord on the writer's sentences, one cannot pronounce them in any other way, it is what was most ephemeral and at the same time most profound in the writer, and it is what will bear witness to his true nature, what will ultimately say whether, despite all the asperities he expressed, he was gentle, or despite all his sensualities, sentimental.

Certain pecularities of elocution, faint traces of which were to be found in Bergotte's conversation, were not exclusively his own; for when, later on, I came to know his brothers and sisters I found those peculiarities much more pronounced in them. There was something abrupt and harsh in the closing words of a cheerful sentence, something faint and dying at the end of a sad one. Swann, who had known the Master as a boy, told me that in those days one used to hear on his lips, just as much as on his brothers' and sisters', those family inflexions, shouts of violent merriment interspersed with murmurings of a long-drawn melancholy, and that in the room in which they all played together he used to perform his part, better than any of them, in their symphonies, alternately deafening and subdued. However characteristic it may be, the sound that escapes from a person's lips is fugitive and does not survive him. But it was not so with the pronunciation of the Bergotte family. For if it is difficult ever to understand, even in the *Meistersinger*, how an artist can invent music by listening to the twittering of birds, yet Bergotte had transposed and perpetuated in his prose that manner of dwelling on words which repeat themselves in shouts of joy or fall drop by drop in melancholy sighs. There are in his books just such closing phrases where the accumulated sonorities are prolonged (as in the last chords of the overture of an opera which cannot bring itself to a close and repeats several times over its final cadence before the conductor finally lays down his baton), in which, later on, I was to find a musical equivalent for those phonetic "brasses" of the Bergotte family. But in his own case, from the moment when he transferred them to his books, he ceased instinctively to make use of them in his speech. From the day on which he had begun to write—and thus all the more markedly later, when I first knew him—his voice had abandoned this orchestration for ever.

These young Bergottes—the future writer and his brothers and sisters—were doubtless in no way superior, far from it, to other young people, more refined, more intellectual than themselves, who found the Bergottes rather noisy, not to say a trifle vulgar, irritating in their witticisms which characterised the tone, at once pretentious and asinine, of the household. But genius, and even great talent, springs less from seeds of intellect and social refinement superior to those of other people than from the faculty of transforming and transposing them. To heat a liquid with an electric lamp requires not the strongest lamp possible, but one of which the current can cease to illuminate, can be diverted so as to give heat instead of light. To mount the skies it is not necessary to have the most powerful of motors, one must have a motor which, instead of continuing to run along the earth's surface, intersecting with a vertical line the horizontal which it began by following, is capable of converting its speed into lifting power. Similarly, the men who produce works of genius are not those who live in the most delicate atmosphere, whose conversation is the most brilliant or their culture the most extensive, but those who have had the power, ceasing suddenly to live only for themselves, to transform their personality into a sort of mirror, in such a way that their life, however mediocre it may be socially and even, in a sense, intellectually, is reflected by it, genius consisting in reflecting power and not in the intrinsic quality of the scene reflected. The day on which the young Bergotte succeeded in showing to the world of his readers the tasteless household in which he had spent his childhood, and the not very amusing conversations between himself and his brothers, was the day on which he rose above the friends of his family, more intellectual and more distinguished than himself; they in their fine Rolls Royces might return home expressing due contempt for the vulgarity of the Bergottes; but he, in his modest machine which had at last "taken off," soared above their heads.

There were other characteristics of his elocution which he shared not with the members of his family, but with certain contemporary writers. Younger men who were beginning to repudiate him and disclaimed any intellectual affinity with him nevertheless displayed it willy-nilly by employing the same adverbs, the same prepositions that he incessantly repeated, by constructing their sentences in the same way, speaking in the same quiescent, lingering tone, in reaction against the eloquent and facile language of an earlier generation. Perhaps these young men—we shall come across some of whom this may be said—had never known Bergotte. But his way of thinking, inoculated into them, had led them to those alterations of syntax and accentuation which bear a necessary relation to originality of mind. A relation which, incidentally, requires to be traced. Thus Bergotte, if he owed nothing to anyone in his manner of writing, derived his manner of speaking from one of his early associates, a marvellous talker to whose spell he had succumbed, whom he imitated unwittingly in his conversation, but who himself, being less gifted, had never written any really outstanding book. So that if one had been in quest of originality in speech, Bergotte must have been labelled a disciple, a second-hand writer, whereas, influenced by his friend only in the domain of conversation, he had been original and creative in his writings. Doubtless again to distinguish himself from the previous generation, too fond as it had been of abstractions, of weighty commonplaces, when Bergotte wished to speak favourably of a book, what he would emphasise, what he would quote with approval would always be some scene that furnished the reader with an image, some picture that had no rational meaning. "Ah, yes!" he would exclaim, "it's good! There's a little girl in an orange shawl. It's excellent!" or again, "Oh yes, there's a passage in which there's a regiment marching along the street; yes, it's good!" As for style, he was not altogether of his time (and remained quite exclusively French, abominating Tolstoy, George Eliot, Ibsen and Dostoievsky), for the word that always came to his lips when he wished to praise the style of any writer was "mellow." "Yes, you know I like Chateaubriand better in *Atala* than in *Rancé*; it seems to me to be mellower."

He said the word like a doctor who, when his patient assures him that milk will give him indigestion, answers, "But, you know, it's quite mellow." And it is true that there was in Bergotte's style a kind of harmony similar to that for which the ancients used to praise certain of their orators in terms which we now find hard to understand, accustomed as we are to our own modern tongues in which effects of that kind are not sought.

He would say also, with a shy smile, of pages of his own for which someone had expressed admiration: "I think it's more or less true, more or less accurate; it may be of some value perhaps," but he would say this simply from modesty, as a woman to whom one has said that her dress or her daughter is beautiful replies, "It's comfortable," or "She's a good girl." But the instinct of the maker, the builder, was too deeply implanted in Bergotte for him not to be aware that the sole proof that he had built both usefully and truthfully lay in the pleasure that his work had given, to himself first of all and afterwards to his readers. Only, many years later, when he no longer had any talent, whenever he wrote anything with which he was not satisfied, in order not to have to suppress it, as he ought to have done, in order to be able to publish it, he would repeat, but to himself this time: "After all, it's more or less accurate, it must be of some value to my country." So that the phrase murmured long ago among his admirers by the crafty voice of modesty came in the end to be whispered in the secrecy of his heart by the uneasy tongue of pride. And the same words which had served Bergotte as a superfluous excuse for the excellence of his early works became as it were an ineffective consolation to him for the mediocrity of the last.

A kind of austerity of taste which he had, a kind of determination to write nothing of which he could not say that it was "mellow," which had made people for so many years regard him as a sterile and precious artist, a chiseller of exquisite trifles, was on the contrary the secret of his strength, for habit forms the style of the writer just as much as the character of the man, and the author who has more than once been content to attain, in the expression of his thoughts, to a certain kind of attractiveness, in so doing lays down unalterably the boundaries of his talent, just as, in succumbing too often to pleasure, to laziness, to the fear of being put to trouble, one traces for oneself, on a character which it will finally be impossible to retouch, the lineaments of one's vices and the limits of one's virtue.

If, however, despite all the similarities which I was to perceive later on between the writer and the man, I had not at first sight, in Mme Swann's drawing-room, believed that this could be Bergotte, the author of so many divine books, who stood before me, perhaps I was not altogether wrong, for he himself did not, in the strict sense of the word, "believe" it either. He did not believe it since he showed some alacrity in ingratiating himself with fashionable people (though he was not a snob), and with literary men and journalists who were vastly inferior to himself. Of course he had long since learned, from the suffrage of his readers, that he had genius, compared to which social position and official rank were as nothing. He had learned that he had genius, but he did not believe it since he continued to simulate deference towards mediocre writers in order to succeed, shortly, in becoming an Academician, when the Academy and the Faubourg Saint-Germain have no more to do with that part of the Eternal Mind which is the author of the works of Bergotte than with the law of causality or the idea of God. That also he knew, but as a kleptomaniac knows, without profiting by the knowledge, that it is wrong to steal. And the man with the goatee beard and snail-shell nose knew and used all the tricks of the gentleman who pockets your spoons, in his efforts to reach the coveted academic chair, or some duchess or other who could command several votes at the election, but to do so in a way that ensured that no one who would consider the pursuit of such a goal a vice in him would see what he was doing. He was only half-successful; one could hear, alternating with the speech of the true Bergotte, that of the other, selfish and ambitious Bergotte who talked only of his powerful, rich or noble friends in order to enhance himself, he who in his books, when he was really himself, had so well portrayed the charm, pure as a mountain spring, of the poor.

As for those other vices to which M. de Norpois had alluded, that almost incestuous love affair, which was made still worse, people said, by a want of delicacy in the matter of money, if they contradicted in a shocking manner the trend of his latest novels, filled with such a painfully scrupulous concern for what was right and good that the most innocent pleasures of their heroes were poisoned by it, and that even for the reader himself it exhaled a sense of anguish in the light of which even the quietest of lives seemed scarcely bearable, those vices did not necessarily prove, supposing that they were fairly imputed to Bergotte, that his literature was a lie and all his sensitiveness mere play-acting. Just as in pathology certain conditions similar in appearance are due, some to an excess, others to an insufficiency of blood pressure, of glandular secretion and so forth, there may be vice arising from hypersensitiveness just as much as from the lack of it. Perhaps it is only in really vicious lives that the problem of morality can arise in all its disquieting strength. And to this problem the artist offers a solution in the terms not of his own personal life but of what is for him his true life, a general, a literary solution. As the great Doctors of the Church began often, while remaining good, by experiencing the sins of all mankind, out of which they drew their own personal sanctity, so great artists often, while being wicked, make use of their vices in order to arrive at a conception of the moral law that is binding upon us all. It is the vices (or merely the weaknesses and follies) of the circle in which they live, the meaningless conversation, the frivolous or shocking lives of their daughters, the infidelity of their wives, or their own misdeeds that writers have most often castigated in their books, without, however, thinking to alter their way of life or improve the tone of their household. But this contrast had never before been so striking as it was in Bergotte's time, because, on the one hand, in proportion as society grew more corrupt, notions of morality became increasingly refined, and on the other hand the public became a great deal more conversant than it had ever been before with the private lives of literary men; and on certain evenings in the theatre people would point out the author whom I had so greatly admired at Combray, sitting at the back of a box the very composition of which seemed an oddly humorous or poignant comment on, an impudent denial of, the thesis which he had just been maintaining in his latest book. Nothing that this or that casual informant might tell me was of much use in helping me to settle the question of the goodness or wickedness of Bergotte. An intimate friend would furnish proofs of his hardheartedness; then a stranger would cite some instance (touching, since it had evidently been destined to remain hidden) of his real depth of feeling. He had behaved cruelly to his wife. But, in a village inn where he had gone to spend the night, he had sat up with a poor woman who had tried to drown herself, and when he was obliged to go had left a large sum of money with the landlord, so that he should not turn the poor creature out but see that she got proper attention. Perhaps the more the great writer developed in Bergotte at the expense of the little man with the beard, the more his own personal life was drowned in the flood of all the lives that he imagined, until he no longer felt himself obliged to perform certain practical duties, for which he had substituted the duty of imagining those other lives. But at the same time, because he imagined the feelings of others as completely as if they had been his own, whenever the occasion arose for him to have to deal with an unfortunate person, at least in a transitory way, he would do so not from his own personal standpoint but that of the sufferer himself, a standpoint from which he would have been horrified by the language of those who continue to think of their own petty concerns in the presence of another's grief. With the result that he gave rise everywhere to justifiable rancour and to undying gratitude.

Above all, he was a man who in his heart of hearts only really loved certain images and (like a miniature set in the floor of a casket) composing and painting them in words. For a trifle that someone had sent him, if that trifle gave him the opportunity of weaving a few images round it, he would be prodigal in the expression of his gratitude, while showing none whatever for an expensive present. And if he had had to plead before a tribunal, he would inevitably have chosen his words not for the effect that they might have on the judge but with an eye to certain images which the judge would certainly never have perceived.

That first day on which I met him with Gilberte's parents, I mentioned to Bergotte that I had recently been to see Berma in *Phèdre*; and he told me that in the scene in which she stood with her arm raised to the level of her shoulder—one of those very scenes that had been greeted with such applause—she had managed to suggest with great nobility of art certain classical figures which quite possibly she had never even seen, a Hesperid carved in the same attitude upon a metope at Olympia, and also the beautiful primitive virgins on the Erechtheum.

"It may be sheer divination, and yet I fancy that she goes to museums. It would be interesting to 'register' that." ("Register" was one of those regular Bergotte expressions, and one which various young men who had never met him had caught from him, speaking like him by some sort of telepathic suggestion.)

"Do you mean the Caryatids?" asked Swann.

"No, no," said Bergotte, "except in the scene where she confesses her passion to Œnone, where she moves her hand exactly like Hegeso on the stele in the Ceramicus, it's a far more primitive art that she evokes. I was referring to the Korai of the old Erechtheum, and I admit that there is perhaps nothing quite so remote from the art of Racine, but there are so many things already in *Phèdre*, . . . that one more . . . Oh, and then, yes, she's really charming, that little sixth-century Phaedra, the rigidity of the arm, the lock of hair 'frozen into marble,' yes, you know, it's wonderful of her to have discovered all that. There is a great deal more antiquity in it than in most of the books they're labelling 'antique' this year."

Since Bergotte had in one of his books addressed a famous invocation to these archaic statues, the words that he was now uttering were quite intelligible to me, and gave me a fresh reason for taking an interest in Berma's acting. I tried to picture her again in my mind, as she had looked in that scene in which I remembered that she had raised her arm to the level of her shoulder. And I said to myself: "There we have the Hesperid of Olympia; there we have the sister of those adorable suppliants on the Acropolis; there indeed is nobility in art!" But in order for these thoughts to enhance for me the

beauty of Berma's gesture, Bergotte would have had to put
them into my head before the performance. Then, while that
attitude of the actress actually existed in flesh and blood before my eyes, at that moment when the thing that is happening still has the plenitude of reality, I might have tried to
extract from it the idea of archaic sculpture. But all that I
retained of Berma in that scene was a memory which was no
longer susceptible of modification; as meagre as an image
devoid of those deep layers of the present in which one can
delve and genuinely discover something new, an image on
which one cannot retrospectively impose an interpretation
that is not subject to verification and objective sanction.

At this point Mme Swann chipped into the conversation,
asking me whether Gilberte had remembered to give me what
Bergotte had written about *Phèdre*, and adding, "My daughter
is such a scatter-brain!" Bergotte smiled modestly and protested that they were only a few pages of no importance.
"But it's absolute delightful, that little booklet, that little
'tract' of yours," Mme Swann assured him, to show that she
was a good hostess, to give the impression that she had read
Bergotte's essay, and also because she liked not merely to flatter
Bergotte, but to pick and choose from what he wrote, to
influence him. And it must be admitted that she did inspire him,
though not in the way that she supposed. But when all is said
there are, between what constituted the elegance of Mme
Swann's drawing-room and a whole aspect of Bergotte's
work, connections such that each of them may serve, among
elderly men to-day, as a commentary upon the other.

I let myself go in telling him what my impressions had been.
Often Bergotte disagreed, but he allowed me to go on talking.
I told him that I had liked the green light which was turned on
when Phèdre raised her arm. "Ah! the designer will be glad
to hear that; he's a real artist, and I shall tell him you liked it,
because he is very proud of that effect. I must say, myself, that
I don't care for it much, it bathes everything in a sort of sea-
green glow, little Phèdre standing there looks too like a branch
of coral on the floor of an aquarium. You will tell me, of
course, that it brings out the cosmic aspect of the play. That's
quite true. All the same, it would be more appropriate if the

scene were laid in the Court of Neptune. Oh yes, I know the
Vengeance of Neptune does come into the play. I don't suggest
for a moment that we should think only of Port-Royal, but
after all Racine isn't telling us a story about love among the
sea-urchins. Still, it's what my friend wanted, and it's very well
done, right or wrong, and really quite pretty. Yes, so you liked
it, did you; you understood what he was after. We feel the
same about it, don't we, really: it's a bit crazy, what he's done,
you agree with me, but on the whole it's very clever." And
when Bergotte's opinion was thus contrary to mine, he in no
way reduced me to silence, to the impossibility of framing any
reply, as M. de Norpois would have done. This does not prove
that Bergotte's opinions were less valid than the Ambassador's;
far from it. A powerful idea communicates some of its power
to the man who contradicts it. Partaking of the universal
community of minds, it infiltrates, grafts itself on to, the
mind of him whom it refutes, among other contiguous ideas,
with the aid of which, counter-attacking, he complements and
corrects it; so that the final verdict is always to some extent
the work of both parties to a discussion. It is to ideas which
are not, strictly speaking, ideas at all, to ideas which, based on
nothing, can find no foothold, no fraternal echo in the mind
of the adversary, that the latter, grappling as it were with thin
air, can find no word to say in answer. The arguments of M.
de Norpois (in the matter of art) were unanswerable simply
because they were devoid of reality.

Since Bergotte did not sweep aside my objections, I confessed to him that they had been treated with contempt by
M. de Norpois. "But he's an old goose!" was the answer. "He
keeps on pecking at you because he imagines all the time that
you're a piece of cake, or a slice of cuttle-fish." "What, you
know Norpois?" asked Swann. "He's as dull as a wet Sunday,"
interrupted his wife, who had great faith in Bergotte's judgment, and was no doubt afraid that M. de Norpois might have
spoken ill of her to us. "I tried to make him talk after dinner; I
don't know if it's his age or his digestion, but I found him too
sticky for words. I really thought I should have to 'dope' him."
"Yes, isn't he?" Bergotte chimed in. "You see, he has to keep
his mouth shut half the time so as not to use up all the stock of

inanities that keep his shirt-front starched and his waistcoat white."

"I think that Bergotte and my wife are both very hard on him," came from Swann, who took the "line," in his own house, of being a plain, sensible man. "I quite see that Norpois cannot interest you very much, but from another point of view," (for Swann made a hobby of collecting scraps of "real life") "he is quite remarkable, quite a remarkable instance of a 'lover.' When he was Counsellor in Rome," he went on, after making sure that Gilberte could not hear him, "he had a mistress here in Paris with whom he was madly in love, and he found time to make the double journey twice a week to see her for a couple of hours. She was, as it happens, a most intelligent woman, and remarkably beautiful then; she's a dowager now. And he has had any number of others since. I'm sure I should have gone stark mad if the woman I was in love with lived in Paris and I had to be in Rome. Highly-strung people ought always to love, as the lower orders say, 'beneath' them, so that their women have a material inducement to be at their disposal."

As he spoke, Swann realised that I might be applying this maxim to himself and Odette, and as, even among superior people, at the moment when they seem to be soaring with you above the plane of life, their personal pride is still basely human, he was overcome with profound irritation towards me. But it manifested itself only in the uneasiness of his glance. He said nothing to me at the time. Not that this need surprise us. When Racine (according to a story that is in fact apocryphal though its substance may be found recurring every day in Parisian life) made an allusion to Scarron in front of Louis XIV, the most powerful monarch on earth said nothing to the poet that evening. It was on the following day that he fell from grace.

But since a theory requires to be stated as a whole, Swann, after this momentary irritation, and after wiping his eyeglass, completed his thought in these words, words which were to assume later on in my memory the importance of a prophetic warning which I had not had the sense to heed: "The danger of that kind of love, however, is that the woman's subjection calms the man's jealousy for a time but also makes it more exacting. After a while he will force his mistress to live like one of those prisoners whose cells are kept lighted day and night to prevent their escaping. And that generally ends in trouble."

I reverted to M. de Norpois. "You must never trust him; he has the most wicked tongue," said Mme Swann in a tone which seemed to me to indicate that M. de Norpois had spoken ill of her, especially as Swann looked across at his wife with an air of rebuke, as though to stop her before she went too far.

Meanwhile Gilberte, who had twice been told to go and get ready to go out, remained listening to our conversation, sitting between her mother and her father, her head resting affectionately against the latter's shoulder. Nothing, at first sight, could be in greater contrast to Mme Swann, who was dark, than this child with her red hair and golden skin. But after a while one saw in Gilberte many of the features—for instance, the nose cut short with a sharp, unerring decision by the invisible sculptor whose chisel repeats its work upon successive generations—the expression, the movements of her mother; to take an illustration from another art, she recalled a portrait that was as yet a poor likeness of Mme Swann, whom the painter, from some colourist's whim, had posed in a partial disguise, dressed to go out to a party in Venetian "character." And since not only was she wearing a fair wig, but every atom of darkness had been evicted from her flesh which, stripped of its brown veils, seemed more naked, covered simply in rays shed by an internal sun, this "make-up" was not just superficial but incarnate: Gilberte had the air of embodying some fabulous animal or of having assumed a mythological fancy dress. This reddish skin was so exactly that of her father that nature seemed to have had, when Gilberte was being created, to solve the problem of how to reconstruct Mme Swann piecemeal, without any material at its disposal save the skin of M. Swann. And nature had utilised this to perfection, like a master carver who makes a point of leaving the grain, the knots of his wood in evidence. On Gilberte's face, at the corner of a perfect reproduction of Odette's nose, the skin was raised so as to preserve intact M. Swann's two moles. It was a new variety of Mme

Swann that was thus obtained, growing there by her side like a white lilac-tree beside a purple. At the same time it would be wrong to imagine the line of demarcation between these two likenesses as absolutely clear-cut. Now and then, when Gilberte smiled, one could distinguish the oval of her father's cheek upon her mother's face, as though they had been put together to see what would result from the blend; this oval took shape as an embryo forms; it lengthened obliquely, swelled, and a moment later had disappeared. In Gilberte's eyes there was the frank and honest gaze of her father; this was how she had looked at me when she gave me the agate marble and said "Keep it as a souvenir of our friendship." But were one to question Gilberte about what she had been doing, then one saw in those same eyes the embarrassment, the uncertainty, the prevarication, the misery that Odette used in the old days to betray, when Swann asked her where she had been and she gave him one of those lying answers which in those days drove the lover to despair and now made him abruptly change the conversation as an incurious and prudent husband. Often, in the Champs-Elysées, I was disturbed to see this look in Gilberte's eyes. But as a rule my fears were unfounded. For in her, a purely physical survival of her mother, this look (if no other) had ceased to have any meaning. It was when she had been to her classes, when she must go home for some lesson, that Gilberte's pupils executed that movement which, in the past, in Odette's eyes, had been caused by the fear of disclosing that she had opened the door that day to one of her lovers, or was at that moment in a hurry to get to some assignation. Thus did one see the two natures of M. and Mme Swann ripple and flow and overlap one upon the other in the body of this Mélusine.

It is, of course, common knowledge that a child takes after both its father and its mother. And yet the distribution of the qualities and defects which it inherits is so oddly planned that, of two good qualities which seemed inseparable in one of the parents, only one will be found in the child, and allied to the very fault in the other parent which seemed most irreconcilable with it. Indeed, the embodiment of a good moral quality in an incompatible physical blemish is often one of the laws of

filial resemblance. Of two sisters, one will combine with the
proud bearing of her father the mean little soul of her mother;
the other, abundantly endowed with the paternal intelligence,
will present it to the world in the aspect which her mother has
made familiar; her mother's shapeless nose and scraggy bosom
and even her voice have become the bodily vestment of gifts
which one had learned to recognise beneath a superb presence.
With the result that of each of the sisters one can say with equal
justification that it is she who takes more after one or other of
her parents. It is true that Gilberte was an only child, but there
were, at the least, two Gilbertes. The two natures, her father's
and her mother's, did more than just blend themselves in her;
they disputed the possession of her—and even that would be
not entirely accurate since it would give the impression that a
third Gilberte was in the meantime suffering from being the
prey of the two others. Whereas Gilberte was alternately one
and then the other, and at any given moment only one of the
two, that is to say incapable, when she was not being good, of
suffering accordingly, the better Gilberte being unable at the
time, on account of her momentary absence, to detect the
other's lapse from virtue. And so the less good of the two was
free to enjoy pleasures of an ignoble kind. When the other
spoke to you with her father's heart she held broad and
generous views, and you would have liked to engage with her
upon a fine and beneficent enterprise; you told her so, but,
just as your arrangements were being completed, her mother's
heart would already have claimed its turn, and hers was the
voice that answered; and you would be disappointed and
vexed—almost baffled, as though by the substitution of one
person for another—by a mean remark, a sly snigger, in which
Gilberte would take delight, since they sprang from what she
herself at that moment was. Indeed, the disparity was at times
so great between the two Gilbertes that you asked yourself,
though without finding an answer, what on earth you could
have said or done to her to find her now so different. When she
herself had suggested meeting you somewhere, not only would
she fail to appear and would offer no excuse afterwards, but,
whatever the influence might have been that had made her
change her mind, she would appear so different that you might

well have supposed that, taken in by a resemblance such as forms the plot of the *Menaechmi*, you were now talking to a different person from the one who had so sweetly expressed a desire to see you, had she not shown signs of an ill-humour which revealed that she felt herself to be in the wrong and wished to avoid entering into explanations.

"Now then, run along and get ready; you're keeping us waiting," her mother reminded her.

"I'm so happy here with my little Papa; I want to stay just for a minute," replied Gilberte, burying her head beneath the arm of her father, who passed his fingers lovingly through her fair hair.

Swann was one of those men who, having lived for a long time amid the illusions of love, have seen the blessings they have brought to numberless women increase the happiness of those women without exciting in them any gratitude, any tenderness towards their benefactors; but who believe that in their children they can feel an affection which, being incarnate in their own name, will enable them to survive after their death. When there should no longer be any Charles Swann, there would still be a Mlle Swann, or a Mme X, *née* Swann, who would continue to love the vanished father. Indeed, to love him too well perhaps, Swann may have been thinking, for he acknowledged Gilberte's caress with a "You're a good girl," in the tone softened by uneasiness to which, when we think of the future, we are prompted by the too passionate affection of a person who is destined to survive us. To conceal his emotion, he joined in our talk about Berma. He pointed out to me, but in a detached, bored tone, as though he wished to remain somehow detached from what he was saying, with what intelligence, with what an astonishing fitness the actress said to Œnone, "You knew it!" He was right. That intonation at least had a validity that was really intelligible, and might thereby have satisfied my desire to find incontestable reasons for admiring Berma. But it was because of its very clarity that it did not in the least satisfy me. Her intonation was so ingenious, so definite in intention and meaning, that it seemed to exist by itself, so that any intelligent actress might have acquired it. It was a fine idea; but whoever else might express it as fully must possess it equally. It remained to Berma's credit that she had discovered it, but can one use the word "discover" when the object in question is something that would not be different if one had been given it, something that does not belong essentially to one's own nature since someone else may afterwards reproduce it?

"Upon my soul, your presence among us does raise the tone of the conversation!" Swann observed to me, as though to excuse himself to Bergotte; for he had formed the habit, in the Guermantes set, of entertaining great artists as if they were just ordinary friends whom one seeks only to provide with the opportunity to eat the dishes or play the games they like, or, in the country, indulge in whatever form of sport they please. "It seems to me that we're talking a great deal about *art*," he went on. "But it's so nice, I do love it!" said Mme Swann, throwing me a look of gratitude, from good nature as well as because she had not abandoned her old aspirations towards intellectual conversation. After this it was to others of the party, and principally to Gilberte, that Bergotte addressed himself. I had told him everything that I felt with a freedom which had astonished me and which was due to the fact that, having acquired with him, years before (in the course of all those hours of solitary reading, in which he was to me merely the better part of myself), the habit of sincerity, of frankness, of confidence, I found him less intimidating than a person with whom I was talking for the first time. And yet, for the same reason, I was very uneasy about the impression that I must have been making on him, the contempt that I had supposed he would feel for my ideas dating not from that afternoon but from the already distant time in which I had begun to read his books in our garden at Combray. I ought perhaps to have reminded myself nevertheless that since it was in all sincerity, abandoning myself to the train of my thoughts, that I had felt on the one hand so intensely in sympathy with the work of Bergotte and on the other hand, in the theatre, a disappointment the reasons for which I did not know, those two instinctive impulses could not be so very different from one another, but must be obedient to the same laws; and that that mind of Bergotte's which I had loved in his books could not be entirely alien and

hostile to my disappointment and to my inability to express it.
For my intelligence must be one—perhaps indeed there exists
but a single intelligence of which everyone is a co-tenant, an
intelligence towards which each of us from out of his own
separate body turns his eyes, as in a theatre where, if everyone
has his own separate seat, there is on the other hand but a
single stage. Doubtless the ideas which I was tempted to seek
to disentangle were not those which Bergotte usually explored
in his books. But if it was one and the same intelligence which
we had, he and I, at our disposal, he must, when he heard
me express those ideas, be reminded of them, cherish them,
smile upon them, keeping probably, in spite of what I
supposed, before his mind's eye, quite a different part of his
intelligence than that of which an excerpt had passed into his
books, an excerpt upon which I had based my notion of his
whole mental universe. Just as priests, having the widest experience of the human heart, are best able to pardon the sins
which they do not themselves commit, so genius, having the
widest experience of the human intelligence, can best understand the ideas most directly in opposition to those which form
the foundation of its own works. I ought to have told myself
all this (though in fact it is none too consoling a thought, for
the benevolent condescension of great minds has as a corollary
the incomprehension and hostility of small; and one derives
far less happiness from the amiability of a great writer, which
one can find after all in his books, than suffering from the
hostility of a woman whom one did not choose for her intelligence but cannot help loving). I ought to have told myself
all this, but I did not; I was convinced that I had appeared a
fool to Bergotte, when Gilberte whispered in my ear:

"You can't think how overjoyed I am, because you've made
a conquest of my great friend Bergotte. He's been telling
Mamma that he found you extremely intelligent."

"Where are we going?" I asked her.

"Oh, wherever you like. You know it's all the same to me."

But since the incident that had occurred on the anniversary
of her grandfather's death I had begun to wonder whether
Gilberte's character was not other than I had supposed,
whether that indifference to what was to be done, that docility,

that calm, that gentle and constant submissiveness did not indeed conceal passionate longings which her pride would not allow her to reveal and which she disclosed only by her sudden resistance whenever by any chance they were thwarted.

As Bergotte lived in the same neighbourhood as my parents, we left the house together. In the carriage he spoke to me of my health: "Our friends were telling me that you had been ill. I'm very sorry. And yet, after all, I'm not too sorry, because I can see quite well that you are able to enjoy the pleasures of the mind, and they are probably what means most to you, as to everyone who has known them."

Alas, how little I felt that what he was saying applied to me, whom all reasoning, however exalted it might be, left cold, who was happy only in moments of pure idleness, when I was comfortable and well. I felt how purely material was everything that I desired in life, and how easily I could dispense with the intellect. As I made no distinction among my pleasures between those that came to me from different sources, of varying depth and permanence, I thought, when the moment came to answer him, that I should have liked an existence in which I was on intimate terms with the Duchesse de Guermantes and often came across, as in the old toll-house in the Champs-Elysées, a fusty coolness that would remind me of Combray. And in this ideal existence which I dared not confide to him, the pleasures of the mind found no place.

"No, Monsieur, the pleasures of the mind count for very little with me; it is not them that I seek after; indeed I don't even know that I have ever tasted them."

"You really think not?" he replied. "Well, you know, after all, that must be what you like best—at least that's my guess, that's what I think."

He did not convince me, of course, and yet I already felt happier, less constricted. After what M. de Norpois had said to me, I had regarded my moments of day-dreaming, of enthusiasm, of self-confidence as purely subjective and false. But according to Bergotte, who appeared to understand my case, it seemed that it was quite the contrary, that the symptom I ought to disregard was, in fact, my doubts, my disgust with myself. Moreover, what he had said about M. de Norpois took

most of the sting out of a sentence from which I had supposed
that no appeal was possible.

"Are you being properly looked after?" Bergotte asked me.
"Who is treating you?" I told him that I had seen, and should
probably go on seeing, Cottard. "But that's not at all the sort of
man you want!" he told me. "I know nothing about him as a
doctor. But I've met him at Mme Swann's. The man's an
imbecile. Even supposing that that doesn't prevent his being
a good doctor, which I hesitate to believe, it does prevent his
being a good doctor for artists, for intelligent people. People like
you must have suitable doctors, I would almost go so far as
to say treatment and medicines specially adapted to themselves.
Cottard will bore you, and that alone will prevent his treatment
from having any effect. Besides, the proper course of treatment
cannot possibly be the same for you as for any Tom, Dick or
Harry. Nine tenths of the ills from which intelligent people
suffer spring from their intellect. They need at least a doctor
who understands *that* disease. How do you expect Cottard to
be able to treat you? He has made allowances for the difficulty
of digesting sauces, for gastric trouble, but he has made no
allowance for the effect of reading Shakespeare. So that his
calculations are inaccurate in your case, the balance is upset;
you see, always the little bottle-imp bobbing up again. He will
find that you have a distended stomach; he has no need to
examine you for it, since he has it already in his eye. You can
see it there, reflected in his glasses."

This manner of speaking tired me greatly. I said to myself
with the stupidity of common sense: "There's no more a distended stomach reflected in Professor Cottard's glasses than
there are inanities stored behind M. de Norpois's white waistcoat."

"I should recommend you, instead," went on Bergotte,
"to consult Dr du Boulbon, who is an extremely intelligent
man." "He's a great admirer of your books," I replied.

I saw that Bergotte knew this, and I concluded that kindred
spirits soon come together, that one has few really "unknown
friends." What Bergotte had said to me with respect to Cottard
impressed me, while running contrary to everything that I
myself believed. I was in no way disturbed at finding my doc-

tor a bore; what I expected of him was that, thanks to an art
whose laws escaped me, he should pronounce on the subject
of my health an infallible oracle after consultation of my en-
trails. And I did not at all require that, with the aid of an
intelligence in which I could compete with him, he should
seek to understand mine, which I pictured to myself merely as
a means, of no importance in itself, of trying to attain to certain
external verities. I very much doubted whether intelligent
people required a different form of hygiene from imbeciles,
and I was quite prepared to submit myself to the latter.

"I'll tell you who does need a good doctor, and that's our
friend Swann," said Bergotte. And on my asking whether he
was ill, "Well, don't you see, he's typical of the man who has
married a whore, and has to pocket a dozen insults a day from
women who refuse to meet his wife or men who have slept
with her. Just look, one day when you're there, at the way
he lifts his eyebrows when he comes in, to see who's in the
room."

The malice with which Bergotte spoke thus to a stranger of
the friends in whose house he had for so long been received as
a welcome guest was as new to me as the almost tender tone
he invariably adopted towards them in their presence. Certainly a person like my great-aunt, for instance, would have
been incapable of treating any of us to the blandishments
which I had heard Bergotte lavishing upon Swann. Even to
the people whom she liked, she enjoyed saying disagreeable
things. But behind their backs she would never have uttered a
word to which they might not have listened. There was nothing less like the social "world" than our society at Combray.
The Swanns' was already a step on the way to it, towards its
inconstant waters. If they had not yet reached the open sea,
they were certainly in the estuary. "This is all between ourselves," said Bergotte as he left me outside my own door. A
few years later I should have answered: "I never repeat things."
That is the ritual phrase of society people, from which the
slanderer always derives a false reassurance. It is what I would
have said then and there to Bergotte—for one does not invent
everything one says, especially when one is acting merely as
a social being—but I did not yet know the formula. What my

great-aunt, on the other hand, would have said on a similar
occasion was: "If you don't wish it to be repeated, why do you
say it?" That is the answer of the unsociable, of the dissenter.
I was nothing of that sort: I bowed my head in silence.

Men of letters who were in my eyes persons of considerable
importance had to intrigue for years before they succeeded in
forming with Bergotte relations which remained always dimly
literary and never emerged beyond the four walls of his study,
whereas I had now been installed among the friends of the
great writer, straight off and without any effort, like someone
who, instead of standing in a queue for hours in order to
secure a bad seat in a theatre, is shown in at once to the best,
having entered by a door that is closed to the public. If Swann
had thus opened such a door to me, it was doubtless because,
just as a king finds himself naturally inviting his children's
friends into the royal box, or on board the royal yacht, so
Gilberte's parents received their daughter's friends among all
the precious things that they had in their house and the even
more precious intimacies that were enshrined there. But at the
time I thought, and perhaps was right in thinking, that this
friendliness on Swann's part was aimed indirectly at my
parents. I seemed to remember having heard once at Combray
that he had suggested to them that, in view of my admiration
for Bergotte, he should take me to dine with him, and that my
parents had declined, saying that I was too young and too
highly-strung to "go out." My parents doubtless represented
to certain other people (precisely those who seemed to me the
most wonderful) something quite different from what they
were to me, so that, just as when the lady in pink had paid my
father a tribute of which he had shown himself so unworthy,
I should have wished them to understand what an inestimable
present I had just received and, to show their gratitude to that
generous and courteous Swann who had offered it to me, or to
them rather, without seeming any more conscious of its value
than the charming Mage with the arched nose and fair hair in
Luini's fresco, to whom, it was said, Swann had at one time
been thought to bear a striking resemblance.

Unfortunately, this favour that Swann had done me, which,
on returning home, before I had even taken off my greatcoat,

I reported to my parents in the hope that it would awaken in their hearts an emotion equal to my own and would determine them upon some immense and decisive gesture towards the Swanns, did not appear to be greatly appreciated by them. "Swann introduced you to Bergotte? An excellent acquaintance, a charming relationship!" exclaimed my father sarcastically: "That really does crown it all!" Alas, when I went on to say that Bergotte was by no means inclined to admire M. de Norpois:

"I dare say!" retorted my father. "That simply proves that he's a false and evil-minded fellow. My poor boy, you never had much common sense, but I'm sorry to see that you've fallen among people who will send you off the rails altogether."

Already the mere fact of my associating with the Swanns had far from delighted my parents. This introduction to Bergotte seemed to them a fatal but natural consequence of an original mistake, namely their own weakness, which my grandfather would have called a "want of circumspection." I felt that in order to put the finishing touch to their ill humour, it only remained for me to tell them that this perverse fellow who did not appreciate M. de Norpois had found me extremely intelligent. For I had observed that whenever my father decided that anyone, one of my school friends for instance, was going astray—as I was at that moment—if that person had the approval of somebody whom my father did not respect, he would see in this testimony the confirmation of his own stern judgment. The evil merely seemed to him the greater. Already I could hear him exclaiming, "Of course, it all hangs together," an expression that terrified me by the vagueness and vastness of the reforms the introduction of which into my quiet life it seemed to threaten. But since, even if I did not tell them what Bergotte had said of me, nothing could anyhow efface the impression my parents had already formed, that it should be made slightly worse mattered little. Besides, they seemed to me so unfair, so completely mistaken, that not only had I no hope, I had scarcely any desire to bring them to a more equitable point of view. However, sensing, as the words were passing my lips, how alarmed my parents would be at the thought that

I had found favour in the sight of a person who dismissed clever men as fools, who had earned the contempt of all decent people, and praise from whom, since it seemed to me a thing to be desired, would only encourage me in wrongdoing, it was in faltering tones and with a slightly shamefaced air that I reached the coda: "He told the Swanns that he had found me extremely intelligent." Just as a poisoned dog in a field flings itself without knowing why at the grass which is precisely the antidote to the toxin that he has swallowed, so I, without in the least suspecting it, had said the one thing in the world that was capable of overcoming in my parents this prejudice with respect to Bergotte, a prejudice which all the best arguments that I could have put forward, all the tributes that I could have paid him, must have proved powerless to defeat. Instantly the situation changed.

"Oh! he said that he found you intelligent," repeated my mother. "I'm glad to hear that, because he's a man of talent."

"What! he said that, did he?" my father joined in ... "I don't for a moment deny his literary distinction, before which the whole world bows; only it's a pity that he should lead that disreputable existence to which old Norpois made a guarded allusion," he went on, not seeing that against the sovereign virtue of the magic words which I had just pronounced, the depravity of Bergotte's morals was scarcely more capable of holding out any longer than the falsity of his judgment.

"But, my dear," Mamma interrupted, "we've no proof that it's true. People say all sorts of things. Besides, M. de Norpois may have the most perfect manners in the world, but he's not always very good-natured, especially about people who are not exactly his sort."

"That's quite true; I've noticed it myself," my father admitted.

"And then, too, a great deal ought to be forgiven Bergotte since he thinks well of my little son," Mamma went on, stroking my hair and fastening upon me a long and pensive gaze.

My mother had not in fact awaited this verdict from Bergotte before telling me that I might ask Gilberte to tea whenever I had friends coming. But I dared not do so for two

reasons. The first was that at Gilberte's nothing else but tea
was ever served. Whereas at home Mamma insisted on there
being hot chocolate as well. I was afraid that Gilberte might
regard this as "common" and so conceive a great contempt for
us. The other reason was a formal difficulty, a question of
procedure which I could never succeed in settling. When I
arrived at Mme Swann's she used to ask me: "And how is your
mother?"

I had made several overtures to Mamma to find out whether
she would do the same when Gilberte came to us, a point which
seemed to me more serious than, at the Court of Louis XIV,
the use of "Monseigneur." But Mamma would not hear of it
for a moment.

"Certainly not. I do not know Mme Swann."

"But neither does she know you."

"I never said she did, but we're not obliged to behave in
exactly the same way about everything. I shall find other ways
of being nice to Gilberte than Mme Swann does with you."

But I remained unconvinced, and preferred not to invite
Gilberte.

Leaving my parents, I went upstairs to change my clothes
and on emptying my pockets came suddenly upon the envelope
which the Swann's butler had handed me before showing me
into the drawing-room. I was now alone. I opened it; inside
was a card on which was indicated the name of the lady whom
I ought to have "taken in" to luncheon.

It was about this period that Bloch overthrew my conception
of the world and opened for me fresh possibilities of happiness
(which, as it happened, were to change later on into possibilities
of suffering), by assuring me that, contrary to all that I had
believed at the time of my walks along the Méséglise way,
women never asked for anything better than to make love. He
added to this service a second, the value of which I was not to
appreciate until much later: it was he who took me for the first
time into a house of assignation. He had indeed told me that
there were any number of pretty women whom one might
enjoy. But I could see them only in a vague outline for which
those houses were to enable me to substitute actual human
features. So that if I owed to Bloch—for his "good tidings"

that happiness and the enjoyment of beauty were not inaccessible things that we have made a meaningless sacrifice in renouncing forever—a debt of gratitude of the same kind as that we owe to an optimistic physician or philosopher who has given us reason to hope for longevity in this world and not to be entirely cut off from it when we shall have passed into another, the houses of assignation which I frequented some years later—by furnishing me with samples of happiness, by allowing me to add to the beauty of women that element which we are powerless to invent, which is something more than a mere summary of former beauties, that present indeed divine, the only one that we cannot bestow upon ourselves, before which all the logical creations of our intellect pale, and which we can seek from reality alone: an individual charm— deserved to be ranked by me with those other benefactors more recent in origin but of comparable utility (before finding which we used to imagine without any warmth the seductive charms of Mantegna, of Wagner, of Siena, on the basis of our knowledge of other painters, other composers, other cities): namely illustrated editions of the Old Masters, symphony concerts, and guidebooks to historic towns. But the house to which Bloch took me (and which he himself in fact had long ceased to visit) was of too inferior a grade and its personnel too mediocre and too little varied to be able to satisfy my old or to stimulate new curiosities. The mistress of this house knew none of the women with whom one asked her to negotiate, and was always suggesting others whom one did not want. She boasted to me of one in particular, of whom, with a smile full of promise (as though this was a great rarity and a special treat), she would say: "She's Jewish. How about that?" (It was doubtless for this reason that she called her Rachel.) And with an inane affectation of excitement which she hoped would prove contagious, and which ended in a hoarse gurgle, almost of sensual satisfaction: "Think of that, my boy, a Jewess! Wouldn't that be thrilling? Rrrr!" This Rachel, of whom I caught a glimpse without her seeing me, was dark, not pretty, but intelligent-looking, and would pass the tip of her tongue over her lips as she smiled with a look of boundless impertinence at the customers who were introduced to her and whom I could hear making conversation. Her thin and narrow face was framed with curly black hair, irregular as though outlined in pen-strokes upon a wash-drawing in Indian ink. Every evening I promised the madame, who offered her to me with a special insistence, boasting of her superior intelligence and her education, that I would not fail to come some day on purpose to make the acquaintance of Rachel, whom I had nicknamed "Rachel when from the Lord."[22] But the first evening I had heard her say to the madame as she was leaving the house: "That's settled then. I shall be free to-morrow, so if you have anyone you won't forget to send for me."

And these words had prevented me from recognising her as a person because they had made me classify her at once in a general category of women whose habit, common to all of them, was to come there in the evening to see whether there might not be a louis or two to be earned. She would simply vary her formula, saying indifferently: "If you need me" or "If you need anybody."

The madame, who was not familiar with Halévy's opera, did not know why I always called the girl "Rachel when from the Lord." But failure to understand a joke has never yet made anyone find it less amusing, and it was always with a whole-hearted laugh that she would say to me:

"Then there's nothing doing to-night? When am I going to fix you up with 'Rachel when from the Lord'? How do you say that: 'Rachel when from the Lord'? Oh, that's a nice one, that is. I'm going to make a match of you two. You won't regret it, you'll see."

Once I nearly made up my mind, but she had "gone to press," another time she was in the hands of the "hairdresser," an old gentleman who never did anything to the women except pour oil on their loosened hair and then comb it. And I grew tired of waiting, even though several of the humbler denizens of the place (so-called working girls, though they always seemed to be out of work), had come to make tea for me and to hold long conversations to which, despite the gravity of the subjects discussed, the partial or total nudity of my interlocutors gave an attractive simplicity. I ceased moreover to go to this house because, anxious to present a token of my good-will to the

woman who kept it and was in need of furniture, I had given
her a few pieces—notably a big sofa—which I had inherited
from my aunt Léonie. I used never to see them, for want of
space had prevented my parents from taking them in at home,
and they were stored in a warehouse. But as soon as I saw
them again in the house where these women were putting them
to their own uses, all the virtues that pervaded my aunt's
room at Combray at once appeared to me, tortured by the
cruel contact to which I had abandoned them in their de-
fencelessness! Had I outraged the dead, I would not have
suffered such remorse. I returned no more to visit their new
mistress, for they seemed to me to be alive and to be appealing
to me, like those apparently inanimate objects in a Persian
fairy-tale, in which imprisoned human souls are undergoing
martyrdom and pleading for deliverance. Besides, as our
memory does not as a rule present things to us in their chronological sequence but as it were by a reflection in which the order
of the parts is reversed, I remembered only long afterwards that
it was upon that same sofa that, many years before, I had
tasted for the first time the delights of love with one of my
girl cousins, with whom I had not known where to go until
she somewhat rashly suggested our taking advantage of a
moment in which Aunt Léonie had left her room.
    A whole lot more of my aunt Léonie's things, and notably
a magnificent set of old silver plate, I sold, against my parents'
advice, so as to have more money to spend, and to be able to
send more flowers to Mme Swann who would greet me, after
receiving an immense basket of orchids, with: "If I were your
father, I should have you up before the magistrate for this."
How could I suppose that one day I might particularly regret
the loss of my silver plate, and rank certain other pleasures
more highly than that (which might perhaps have shrunk to
nothing) of paying courtesies to Gilberte's parents. Similarly,
it was with Gilberte in my mind, and in order not to be separated from her, that I had decided not to enter upon a career of
diplomacy abroad. It is always thus, impelled by a state of
mind which is destined not to last, that we make our irrevocable decisions. I could scarcely imagine that that strange substance which was housed in Gilberte, and which radiated from

her parents and her home, leaving me indifferent to all things else, could be liberated, could migrate into another person. Unquestionably the same substance, and yet one that would have a wholly different effect on me. For the same sickness evolves; and a delicious poison can no longer be taken with the same impunity when, with the passing of the years, the heart's resistance has diminished.

My parents meanwhile would have liked to see the intelligence that Bergotte had discerned in me made manifest in some outstanding piece of work. When I still did not know the Swanns I thought that I was prevented from working by the state of agitation into which I was thrown by the impossibility of seeing Gilberte when I chose. But now that their door stood open to me, scarcely had I sat down at my desk than I would get up and hurry round to them. And after I had left them and was back at home, my isolation was apparent only, my mind was powerless to swim against the stream of words on which I had allowed myself mechanically to be borne for hours on end. Sitting alone, I continued to fashion remarks such as might have pleased or amused the Swanns, and to make this pastime more entertaining I myself took the parts of those absent players, putting to myself fictitious questions so chosen that my brilliant epigrams served simply as apt repartee. Though conducted in silence, this exercise was none the less a conversation and not a meditation, my solitude a mental social round in which it was not I myself but imaginary interlocutors who controlled my choice of words, and in which, as I formulated, instead of the thoughts that I believed to be true, those that came easily to my mind and involved no retrogression from the outside inwards, I experienced the sort of pleasure, entirely passive, which sitting still affords to anyone who is burdened with a sluggish digestion.

Had I been less firmly resolved upon settling down definitively to work, I should perhaps have made an effort to begin at once. But since my resolution was explicit, since within twenty-four hours, in the empty frame of the following day where everything was so well arranged because I myself was not yet in it, my good intentions would be realised without difficulty, it was better not to start on an evening when I felt ill-prepared. The following days were not, alas, to prove more propitious. But I was reasonable. It would have been puerile, on the part of one who had waited now for years, not to put up with a postponement of two or three days. Confident that by the day after to-morrow I should have written several pages, I said not a word more to my parents of my decision; I preferred to remain patient for a few hours and then to bring to a convinced and comforted grandmother a sample of work that was already under way. Unfortunately the next day was not that vast, extraneous expanse of time to which I had feverishly looked forward. When it drew to a close, my laziness and my painful struggle to overcome certain internal obstacles had simply lasted twenty-four hours longer. And at the end of several days, my plans not having matured, I had no longer the same hope that they would be realised at once, and hence no longer the heart to subordinate everything else to their realisation: I began again to stay up late, having no longer, to oblige me to go to bed early one evening, the certain hope of seeing my work begun next morning. I needed, before I could recover my creative energy, a few days of relaxation, and the only time my grandmother ventured, in a gentle and disillusioned tone, to frame the reproach: "Well, this famous work, don't we even speak about it any more?", I resented her intrusion, convinced that in her inability to see that my decision was irrevocably made, she had further and perhaps for a long time postponed its execution by the shock which her denial of justice had administered to my nerves and under the impact of which I should be disinclined to begin my work. She felt that her scepticism had stumbled blindly against a genuine intention. She apologised, kissing me: "I'm sorry, I shan't say another word," and, so that I should not be discouraged, assured me that as soon as I was quite well again, the work would come of its own accord to boot.

Besides, I said to myself, in spending all my time with the Swanns, am I not doing exactly what Bergotte does? To my parents it seemed almost as though, idle as I was, I was leading, since it was spent in the same salon as a great writer, the life most favourable to the growth of talent. And yet the assumption that anyone can be dispensed from having to create that talent for himself, from within himself, and can acquire it from someone else, is as erroneous as to suppose that a man can keep himself in good health (in spite of neglecting all the rules of hygiene and of indulging in the worst excesses) merely by dining out often in the company of a physician. The person, incidentally, who was most completely taken in by this illusion which misled me as well as my parents, was Mme Swann. When I explained to her that I was unable to come, that I must stay at home and work, she looked as though she felt that I was making a great fuss about nothing, that I was being rather stupidly pretentious:

"After all, Bergotte's coming. Do you mean you don't think what he writes is any good? It will be even better very soon," she went on, "because he's sharper and pithier in newspaper articles than in his books, where he's apt to pad a bit. I've arranged that in future he's to do the *leaders* in the *Figaro*. He'll be distinctly *the right man in the right place* there." And finally she added: "Do come! He'll tell you better than anyone what you ought to do."

And so, just as one invites a gentleman ranker with his colonel, it was in the interests of my career, and as though masterpieces arose out of "getting to know" people, that she told me not to fail to come to dinner next day with Bergotte.

Thus, no more from the Swanns than from my parents, that is to say from those who, at different times, had seemed bound to resist it, was there any further opposition to that delectable existence in which I might see Gilberte as often as I chose, with enchantment if not with peace of mind. There can be no peace of mind in love, since what one has obtained is never anything but a new starting-point for further desires. So long as I had been unable to go to her house, with my eyes fixed upon that inaccessible happiness, I could not even imagine the fresh grounds for anxiety that lay in wait for me there. Once the resistance of her parents was broken, and the problem solved at last, it began to set itself anew, each time in different terms. In this sense it was indeed a new friendship that began each day. Each evening, on arriving home, I reminded myself that I had things to say to Gilberte of prime importance, things upon which our whole friendship hung, and these things were never the same. But at least I was happy, and no further threat arose to endanger my happiness. One was to appear, alas, from a quarter in which I had never detected any peril, namely from Gilberte and myself. And yet I should have been tormented by what, on the contrary, reassured me, by what I mistook for happiness. We are, when we love, in an abnormal state, capable of giving at once to the most apparently simple accident, an accident which may at any moment occur, a seriousness which in itself it would not entail. What makes us so happy is the presence in our hearts of an unstable element which we contrive perpetually to maintain and of which we cease almost to be aware so long as it is not displaced. In reality, there is in love a permanent strain of suffering which happiness neutralises, makes potential only, postpones, but which may at any moment become, what it would long since have been had we not obtained what we wanted, excrutiating.

On several occasions I sensed that Gilberte was anxious to put off my visits. It is true that when I was at all anxious to see her I had only to get myself invited by her parents who were increasingly persuaded of my excellent influence over her. "Thanks to them," I thought, "my love is in no danger; seeing that I have them on my side, I can set my mind at rest since they have complete authority over Gilberte." Until, alas, detecting certain signs of impatience which she betrayed when her father asked me to the house almost against her will, I wondered whether what I had regarded as a protection for my happiness was not in fact the secret reason why that happiness could not last.

The last time I came to see Gilberte, it was raining; she had been asked to a dancing lesson in the house of some people whom she knew too slightly to be able to take me there with her. In view of the dampness of the air I had taken rather more caffeine than usual. Perhaps on account of the weather, perhaps because she had some objection to the house in which this party was being given, Mme Swann, as her daughter was about to leave, called her back in the sharpest of tones: "Gilberte!" and pointed to me, to indicate that I had come there to see her and that she ought to stay with me. This "Gilberte!" had been uttered, or shouted rather, with the best of intentions towards myself, but from the way in which Gilberte shrugged her shoulders as she took off her outdoor clothes I divined that her mother had unwittingly hastened a process, which until then it might perhaps have been possible to arrest, which was gradually drawing my beloved away from me. "One doesn't have to go out dancing every day," Odette told her daughter, with a sagacity acquired no doubt in earlier days from Swann. Then, becoming once more Odette, she began to speak to her daughter in English. At once it was as though a wall had sprung up to hide from me a part of Gilberte's life, as though an evil genius had spirited her far away. In a language that we know, we have substituted for the opacity of sounds the transparency of ideas. But a language which we do not know is a fortress sealed, within whose walls the one we love is free to play us false, while we, standing outside, desperately keyed up in our impotence, can see, can prevent nothing. So this conversation in English, at which a month earlier I should merely have smiled, interspersed with a few proper names in French which served only to intensify and pinpoint my anxieties, and conducted within a few feet of me by two motionless persons, was as painful to me, left me as much abandoned and alone, as the forcible abduction of my companion. At length Mme Swann left us. That day, perhaps from resentment against me, the involuntary cause of her not going out to enjoy herself, perhaps also because, guessing her to be angry with me, I was pre-emptively colder than usual with her, Gilberte's face, divested of every sign of joy, bleak, bare, ravaged, seemed all afternoon to be harbouring a melancholy regret for the pas-de-quatre which my arrival had prevented her from going to dance, and to be defying every living creature, beginning with myself, to understand the subtle reasons that had induced in her a sentimental attachment to the boston. She confined herself to exchanging with me now and again, on the weather, the increasing violence of the rain, the fastness of the clock, a conversation punctuated with silences and monosyllables, in which I myself persisted, with a sort of desperate rage, in destroying those moments which we might have devoted to friendship and happiness. And on

each of our remarks a sort of transcendent harshness was conferred by the paroxysm of their stupefying insignificance,
which at the same time consoled me, for it prevented Gilberte
from being taken in by the banality of my observations and the
indifference of my tone. In vain did I say: "I thought the other
day that the clock was slow, if anything," she clearly understood me to mean: "How nasty you are!" Obstinately as I
might protract, over the whole length of that rain-sodden
afternoon, the dull cloud of words through which no fitful
ray shone, I knew that my coldness was not so unalterably
fixed as I pretended, and that Gilberte must be fully aware that
if, after already saying it to her three times, I had hazarded a
fourth repetition of the statement that the evenings were
drawing in, I should have had difficulty in restraining myself
from bursting into tears. When she was like this, when no
smile filled her eyes or opened up her face, I cannot describe
the devastating monotony that stamped her melancholy eyes
and sullen features. Her face, grown almost ugly, reminded
me then of those dreary beaches where the sea, ebbing far out,
wearies one with its faint shimmering, everywhere the same,
encircled by an immutable low horizon. At length, seeing
no sign in Gilberte of the happy change for which I had been
waiting now for some hours, I told her that she was not being
nice. "It's you who are not being nice," was her answer.
"Yes I am!" I wondered what I could have done, and,
finding no answer, put the question to her. "Naturally, you
think yourself nice!" she said to me with a laugh, and went on
laughing. Whereupon I felt how agonising it was for me not
to be able to attain to that other, more elusive plane of her
mind which her laughter reflected. It seemed, that laughter, to
mean: "No, no, I'm not going to be taken in by anything that
you say, I know you're mad about me, but that leaves me
neither hot nor cold, for I don't care a rap for you." But I told
myself that, after all, laughter was not a language so well defined that I could be certain of understanding what this laugh
really meant. And Gilberte's words were affectionate. "But
how am I not being nice," I asked her, "tell me—I'll do anything you want." "No; that wouldn't be any good. I can't
explain." For a moment I was afraid that she thought that I

did not love her, and this was for me a fresh agony, no less acute, but one that required a different dialectic. "If you knew how much you were hurting me you would tell me." But this pain which, had she doubted my love, must have rejoiced her, seemed instead to irritate her the more. Then, realising my mistake, making up my mind to pay no more attention to what she had said, letting her (without believing her) assure me: "I really did love you; you'll see one day" (that day on which the guilty are convinced that their innocence will be made clear, and which, for some mysterious reason, never happens to be the day on which their evidence is taken), I suddenly had the courage to resolve never to see her again, and without telling her yet since she would not have believed me.

Grief that is caused by a person one loves can be bitter, even when it is interspersed with preoccupations, occupations, pleasures in which that person is not involved and from which our attention is diverted only now and again to return to the beloved. But when such a grief has its birth—as was the case with mine—at a moment when the happiness of seeing that person fills us to the exclusion of all else, the sharp depression that then affects our spirits, hitherto sunny, sustained and calm, lets loose in us a raging storm against which we feel we may not be capable of struggling to the end. The storm that was blowing in my heart was so violent that I made my way home battered and bruised, feeling that I could recover my breath only by retracing my steps, by returning, upon whatever pretext, into Gilberte's presence. But she would have said to herself: "Back again! Evidently I can do what I like with him: he'll come back every time, and the more wretched he is when he leaves me the more docile he'll be." Besides, I was irresistibly drawn towards her by my thoughts, and those alternative orientations, that wild spinning of my inner compass, persisted after I had reached home, and expressed themselves in the mutually contradictory letters to Gilberte which I began to draft.

I was about to pass through one of those difficult crises which we generally find that we have to face at various stages in life, and which, for all that there has been no change in our character, in our nature (that nature which itself creates our loves, and almost creates the women we love, down to their very faults), we do not face in the same way on each occasion, that is to say at every age. At such moments our life is divided, and so to speak distributed over a pair of scales, in two counterpoised pans which between them contain it all. In one there is our desire not to displease, not to appear too humble to the person whom we love without being able to understand, but whom we find it more astute at times to appear almost to disregard, so that she shall not have that sense of her own indispensability which may turn her from us; in the other scale there is a feeling of pain—and one that is not localised and partial only—which cannot be assuaged unless, abandoning every thought of pleasing the woman and of making her believe that we can do without her, we go to her at once. If we withdraw from the pan that holds our pride a small quantity of the will-power which we have weakly allowed to wither with age, if we add to the pan that holds our suffering a physical pain which we have acquired and have allowed to get worse, then, instead of the brave solution that would have carried the day at twenty, it is the other, grown too heavy and insufficiently counter-balanced, that pulls us down at fifty. All the more because situations, while repeating themselves, tend to alter, and there is every likelihood that, in middle life or in old age, we shall have had the fatal self-indulgence of complicating our love by an intrusion of habit which adolescence, detained by too many other duties, less free to choose, knows nothing of.

I had just written Gilberte a letter in which I allowed the tempest of my fury to thunder, not however without throwing her the lifebuoy of a few words disposed as though by accident on the page, by clinging to which my beloved might be brought to a reconciliation. A moment later, the wind having changed, they were phrases full of love that I addressed to her, chosen for the sweetness of certain forlorn expressions, those "nevermores" so touching to those who pen them, so wearisome to her who will have to read them, whether she believes them to be false and translates "nevermore" by "this very evening, if you want me," or believes them to be true and so to be breaking the news to her of one of those final separa-

tions to which we are so utterly indifferent when the person
concerned is one with whom we are not in love. But since we
are incapable, while we are in love, of acting as fit predecessors of the person whom we shall presently have become and
who will be in love no longer, how are we to imagine the
actual state of mind of a woman whom, even when we are
conscious that we are of no account to her, we have perpetually
represented in our musings as uttering, in order to lull us into
a happy dream or to console us for a great sorrow, the same
words that she would use if she loved us. Faced with the
thoughts, the actions of a woman whom we love, we are as
completely at a loss as the world's first natural philosophers
must have been, face to face with the phenomena of nature,
before their science had been elaborated and had cast a ray of
light over the unknown. Or, worse still, we are like a person in
whose mind the law of causality barely exists, a person who
would be incapable, therefore, of establishing a connexion
between one phenomenon and another and to whose eyes the
spectacle of the world would appear as unstable as a dream. Of
course I made efforts to emerge from this incoherence, to find
reasons for things. I tried even to be "objective" and, to that
end, to bear in mind the disproportion that existed between the
importance which Gilberte had in my eyes and that, not only
which I had in hers, but which she herself had in the eyes of
other people, a disproportion which, had I failed to remark it,
might have caused me to mistake mere friendliness on her part
for a passionate avowal, and a grotesque and debasing display
on mine for the simple and amiable impulse that directs us
towards a pretty face. But I was afraid also of falling into the
opposite excess, whereby I should have seen in Gilberte's un-
punctuality in keeping an appointment, merely on a bad-
tempered impulse, an irremediable hostility. I tried to discover
between these two perspectives, equally distorting, a third
which would enable me to see things as they really were; the
calculations I was obliged to make with that object helped to
take my mind off my sufferings; and whether in obedience to
the laws of arithmetic or because I had made them give me the
answer that I desired, I made up my mind to go round to the
Swanns' next day, happy, but happy in the same way as people

who, having long been tormented by the thought of a journey which they have not wished to make, go no further than the station and then return home to unpack their boxes. And since, while one is hesitating, the mere idea of a possible decision (unless one has rendered that idea sterile by deciding that one will make no decision) develops, like a seed in the ground, the lineaments, the minutiae, of the emotions that would spring from the performance of the action, I told myself that it had been quite absurd of me to go to as much trouble, in planning never to see Gilberte again, as if I had really had to put this plan into effect and that since, on the contrary, I was to end by returning to her side, I might have spared myself all those painful velleities and acceptances.

But this resumption of friendly relations lasted only so long as it took me to reach the Swanns'; not because their butler, who was really fond of me, told me that Gilberte had gone out (a statement the truth of which was confirmed to me, as it happened, the same evening, by people who had seen her somewhere), but because of the manner in which he said it: "Sir, the young lady is not at home; I can assure you, sir, that I am speaking the truth. If you wish to make any inquiries I can fetch the young lady's maid. You know very well, sir, that I would do everything in my power to oblige you, and that if the young lady was at home I would take you to her at once." These words being of the only kind that is really important, that is to say involuntary, the kind that gives us a sort of X-ray photograph of the unimaginable reality which would be wholly concealed beneath a prepared speech, proved that in Gilberte's household there was an impression that she found me importunate; and so, scarcely had the man uttered them than they had aroused in me a hatred of which I preferred to make him rather than Gilberte the victim; he drew upon his own head all the angry feelings that I might have had for my beloved; relieved of them thanks to his words, my love subsisted alone; but his words had at the same time shown me that I must cease for the present to attempt to see Gilberte. She would be certain to write to me to apologise. In spite of which, I should not return at once to see her, so as to prove to her that I was capable of living without her. Besides, once

I had received her letter, Gilberte's society was a thing with which I could more easily dispense for a time, since I should be certain of finding her ready to receive me whenever I chose. All that I needed in order to support less gloomily the pain of a voluntary separation was to feel that my heart was rid of the terrible uncertainty as to whether we were not irreconcilably sundered, whether she had not become engaged, left Paris, been taken away by force. The days that followed resembled the first week of that previous New Year which I had had to spend without Gilberte. But when that week had dragged to its end, for one thing my beloved would be coming again to the Champs-Elysées, I should be seeing her as before, of that I had been sure; for another thing, I had known with no less certainty that so long as the New Year holidays lasted there was no point in my going to the Champs-Elysées, which meant that during that miserable week, which was already ancient history, I had endured my wretchedness with a quiet mind because it was mixed with neither fear nor hope. Now, on the other hand, it was the latter of these which, almost as much as fear, made my suffering intolerable.

Not having had a letter from Gilberte that evening, I had attributed this to her negligence, to her other occupations, and I did not doubt that I should find one from her in the morning's post. This I awaited, every day, with a throbbing of the heart that subsided, leaving me utterly prostrate, when I found in it only letters from people who were not Gilberte, or else nothing at all, which was no worse, the proofs of another's friendship making all the more cruel those of her indifference. I transferred my hopes to the afternoon post. Even between the times at which letters were delivered I dared not leave the house, for she might be sending hers by a messenger. Then, the time coming at last when neither the postman nor a footman from the Swanns' could possibly appear that night, I had to postpone till the morrow my hope of being reassured, and thus, because I believed that my sufferings were not destined to last, I was obliged, so to speak, incessantly to renew them. My disappointment was perhaps the same, but instead of just uniformly prolonging, as formerly it had, an initial emotion, it began again several times daily, starting each time with an emotion so frequently renewed that it ended—it, so purely physical, so instantaneous a state—by becoming stabilised, so that the strain of waiting having hardly time to subside before a fresh reason for waiting supervened, there was no longer a single minute in the day during which I was not in that state of anxiety which it is so difficult to bear even for an hour. Thus my suffering was infinitely more cruel than in those former New Year holidays, because this time there was in me, instead of the acceptance, pure and simple, of that suffering, the hope, at every moment, of seeing it come to an end.

And yet I did ultimately arrive at this acceptance: then I realised that it must be final, and I renounced Gilberte for ever, in the interests of my love itself and because I hoped above all that she would not retain a contemptuous memory of me. Indeed, from that moment, so that she should not be led to suppose any sort of lover's spite on my part, when she made appointments for me to see her I used often to accept them and then, at the last moment, write to her to say that I could not come, but with the same protestations of disappointment as I should have made to someone whom I had not wished to see. These expressions of regret, which we reserve as a rule for people who do not matter, would do more, I imagined, to persuade Gilberte of my indifference than would the tone of indifference which we affect only towards those we love. When, better than by mere words, by a course of action indefinitely repeated, I should have proved to her that I had no inclination to see her, perhaps she would discover once again an inclination to see me. Alas! I was doomed to failure; to attempt, by ceasing to see her, to reawaken in her that inclination to see me was to lose her for ever; first of all because, when it began to revive, if I wished it to last I must not give way to it at once; besides, the most agonising hours would then have passed; it was at this very moment that she was indispensable to me, and I should have liked to be able to warn her that what presently she would assuage, by seeing me again, would be a grief so far diminished as to be no longer (as now it would still be), in order to put an end to it, a motive for surrender, reconciliation and further meetings. And later on, when I should at last be able safely to confess to Gilberte (so much would her

feeling for me have regained its strength) my feeling for her,
the latter, not having been able to resist the strain of so long a
separation, would have ceased to exist; I should have become
indifferent to Gilberte. I knew this, but I could not explain it
to her; she would have assumed that if I was claiming that I
would cease to love her if I remained for too long without
seeing her, that was solely to persuade her to summon me back
to her at once. In the meantime, what made it easier for me to
sentence myself to this separation was the fact that (in order to
make it quite clear to her that despite my protestations to the
contrary it was my own free will and not any extraneous
obstacle, not the state of my health, that prevented me from
seeing her), whenever I knew beforehand that Gilberte would
not be in the house, was going out somewhere with a friend
and would not be home for dinner, I went to see Mme Swann,
who had once more become to me what she had been at the
time when I had such difficulty in seeing her daughter and (on
days when the latter was not coming to the Champs-Elysées)
used to repair to the Allée des Acacias. In this way I should
hear about Gilberte, and could be certain that she would in
due course hear about me, and in terms which would show her
that I was not hankering after her. And I found, as all those who
suffer find, that my melancholy situation might have been
worse. For, being free at any time to enter the house in which
Gilberte lived, I constantly reminded myself, for all that I was
firmly resolved to make no use of that privilege, that if ever
my pain grew too sharp there was a way of making it cease.
I was not unhappy, save only from day to day. And even that is
an exaggeration. How many times an hour (but now without
that anxious expectancy which had strained my every nerve
in the first weeks after our quarrel, before I had gone again to
the Swanns') did I not recite to myself the words of the letter
which, one day soon, Gilberte would surely send, would
perhaps even bring to me herself! The perpetual vision of that
imagined happiness helped me to endure the destruction of
my real happiness. With women who do not love us, as with
the "dear departed," the knowledge that there is no hope left
does not prevent us from continuing to wait. We live in expectancy, constantly on the alert; the mother whose son has

gone to sea on some perilous voyage of discovery sees him in imagination every moment, long after the fact of his having perished has been established, striding into the room, saved by a miracle and in the best of health. And this expectancy, according to the strength of her memory and the resistance of her bodily organs, either helps her on her journey through the years, at the end of which she will be able to endure the knowledge that her son is no more, to forget gradually and to survive his loss—or else it kills her.

At the same time, my grief found consolation in the idea that my love must profit by it. Every visit that I paid to Mme Swann without seeing Gilberte was painful to me, but I felt that it correspondingly enhanced the idea that Gilberte had of me. Besides, if I always took care, before going to see Mme Swann, to ensure that her daughter was absent, this arose not only from my determination to break with her, but no less perhaps from the hope of reconciliation which overlay my intention to renounce her (very few of such intentions are absolute, at least in a continuous form, in this human soul of ours, one of whose laws, confirmed by the unlooked-for wealth of illustration that memory supplies, is intermittence), and hid from me something of its cruelty. I knew how chimerical was this hope. I was like a pauper who moistens his dry crust with fewer tears if he assures himself that at any moment a total stranger is perhaps going to leave him his entire fortune. We are all of us obliged, if we are to make reality endurable, to nurse a few little follies in ourselves. And my hope remained more intact—while at the same time our separation became more ineluctable—if I refrained from meeting Gilberte. If I had found myself face to face with her in her mother's drawing-room, we might perhaps have exchanged irrevocable words which would have rendered our breach final, killed my hope and, at the same time, by creating a fresh anxiety, reawakened my love and made resignation harder.

Long before my break with her daughter, Mme Swann had said to me: "It's all very well your coming to see Gilberte but I should like you to come sometimes for my sake, not to my 'kettle-drums,' which would bore you because there's such a crowd, but on the other days, when you will always find me at home if you come fairly late." So that I might be thought, when I came to see her, to be belatedly complying with a wish that she had expressed in the past. And very late in the afternoon, when it was already dark, almost at the hour at which my parents would be sitting down to dinner, I would set out to pay Mme Swann a visit during the course of which I knew that I should not see Gilberte and yet should be thinking only of her. In that quarter, then looked upon as remote, of a Paris darker than it is to-day, where even in the centre there was no electric light in the public thoroughfares and very little in private houses, the lamps of a drawing-room situated on the ground floor or a low mezzanine (as were the rooms in which Mme Swann generally received her visitors) were enough to lighten the street and to make the passer-by raise his eyes and connect with the glow from the windows, as with its apparent though veiled cause, the presence outside the door of a string of smart broughams. This passer-by was led to believe, not without a certain excitement, that a modification had been effected in this mysterious cause, when he saw one of the carriages begin to move; but it was merely a coachman who, afraid that his horses might catch cold, started them now and again on a brisk walk, all the more impressive because the rubber-tired wheels gave the sound of their hooves a background of silence from which it stood out more distinct and more explicit.

The "winter-garden," of which in those days the passer-by generally caught a glimpse, in whatever street he might be walking, if the drawing-room did not stand too high above the pavement, is to be seen to-day only in photogravures in the gift-books of P. J. Stahl, where, in contrast to the infrequent floral decorations of the Louis XIV drawing-rooms now in fashion—a single rose or a Japanese iris in a long-necked vase of crystal into which it would be impossible to squeeze a second—it seems, because of the profusion of indoor plants which people had then, and of the absolute lack of stylisation in their arrangement, as though it must have responded in the ladies whose houses it adorned to some lively and delightful passion for botany rather than to any cold concern for lifeless decoration. It suggested to one, only on a larger scale, in the

houses of those days, those tiny, portable hothouses laid out on
New Year's morning beneath the lighted lamp—for the
children were always too impatient to wait for daylight—
among all the other New Year presents but the loveliest of
them all, consoling them, with its real plants which they could
tend as they grew, for the bareness of the winter soil; and even
more than those little houses themselves, those winter gardens
were like the hothouse that the children could see there at the
same time, portrayed in a delightful book, another New Year
present and one which, for all that it was given not to them
but to Mlle Lili, the heroine of the story, enchanted them to
such a pitch that even now, when they are almost old men and
women, they ask themselves whether, in those fortunate years,
winter was not the loveliest of the seasons. And finally, beyond
the winter-garden, through the various kinds of arborescence
which from the street made the lighted window appear like
the glass front of one of those children's playthings, pictured or
real, the passer-by, drawing himself up on tiptoe, would generally observe a man in a frock coat, a gardenia or a carnation
in his buttonhole, standing before a seated lady, both vaguely
outlined like two intaglios cut in a topaz, in the depths of the
drawing-room atmosphere clouded by the samovar—then a
recent importation—with steam which may escape from it still
to-day, but to which, if it does, we have grown so accustomed
now that no one notices it. Mme Swann attached great importance to her "tea"; she thought that she showed her originality
and expressed her charm when she said to a man: "You'll find
me at home any day, fairly late; come to tea," and so would
accompany with a sweet and subtle smile these words which
she pronounced with a fleeting trace of an English accent,
and which her listener duly noted, bowing solemnly in acknowledgment, as though the invitation had been something
important and uncommon which commanded deference and
required attention. There was another reason, apart from those
given already, for the flowers' having more than a merely
ornamental significance in Mme Swann's drawing-room, and
this reason pertained not to the period but, in some degree,
to the life that Odette had formerly led. A great courtesan,
such as she had been, lives largely for her lovers, that is to

say at home, which means that she comes in time to live for
her home. The things that one sees in the house of a "respectable" woman, things which may of course appear to her also
to be of importance, are those which are in any event of the
utmost importance to the courtesan. The culminating point
of her day is not the moment in which she dresses herself for
society, but that in which she undresses herself for a man. She
must be as elegant in her dressing-gown, in her night-dress,
as in her outdoor attire. Other women display their jewels,
but she lives in the intimacy of her pearls. This kind of existence imposes on her the obligation, and ends by giving her
the taste, for a luxury which is secret, that is to say which
comes near to being disinterested. Mme Swann extended this
to include her flowers. There was always beside her chair an
immense crystal bowl filled to the brim with Parma violets or
with long white daisy-petals floating in the water, which seemed
to testify, in the eyes of the arriving guest, to some favourite
occupation now interrupted, as would also have been the cup
of tea which Mme Swann might have been drinking there alone
for her own pleasure; an occupation more intimate still and
more mysterious, so much so that one wanted to apologise on
seeing the flowers exposed there by her side, as one would
have apologised for looking at the title of the still open book
which would have revealed to one Odette's recent reading and
hence perhaps her present thoughts. And even more than the
book, the flowers were living things; one was embarrassed,
when one entered the room to pay Mme Swann a visit, to
discover that she was not alone, or if one came home with her,
not to find the room empty, so enigmatic a place, intimately associated with hours in the life of their mistress of which one
knew nothing, did those flowers assume, those flowers which
had not been arranged for Odette's visitors but, as it were,
forgotten there by her, had held and would hold with her
again intimate talks which one was afraid of disturbing, the
secret of which one tried in vain to read by staring at the
washed-out, liquid, mauve and dissolute colour of the Parma
violets. From the end of October Odette would begin to come
home with the utmost punctuality for tea (which was still
known at that time as "five-o'clock tea") having once heard it

said, and being fond of repeating, that if Mme Verdurin had been able to form a salon it was because people were always certain of finding her at home at the same hour. She imagined that she herself had one also, of the same kind, but freer, *senza rigore* as she liked to say. She saw herself figuring thus as a sort of Lespinasse, and believed that she had founded a rival salon by taking from the du Deffand of the little group several of her most attractive men, notably Swann himself, who had followed her in her secession and into her retirement, according to a version for which one can understand that she had succeeded in gaining credit among newcomers who were ignorant of the past, though without convincing herself. But certain favourite roles are played by us so often before the public and rehearsed so carefully when we are alone that we find it easier to refer to their fictitious testimony than to that of a reality which we have almost entirely forgotten. On days when Mme Swann had not left the house, one found her in a *crêpe-de-Chine* dressing-gown, white as the first snows of winter, or, it might be, in one of those long pleated chiffon garments, which looked like nothing so much as a shower of pink or white petals, and would be regarded to-day as highly inappropriate for winter—though quite wrongly, for these light fabrics and soft colours gave to a woman—in the stifling warmth of the drawing-rooms of those days, with their heavily curtained doors, rooms of which the most elegant thing that the society novelists of the time could find to say was that they were "exquisitely padded"—the same air of coolness that they gave to the roses which were able to stay in the room there beside her, despite the winter, in the glowing flesh tints of their nudity, as though it were already spring. Because of the muffling of all sound by the carpets, and of her withdrawal into a cosy recess, the lady of the house, not being apprised of your entry as she is to-day, would continue to read almost until you were standing before her chair, which enhanced still further that sense of the romantic, that charm as of detecting a secret, which we can recapture to-day in the memory of those gowns, already out of fashion even then, which Mme Swann was perhaps alone in not having discarded, and which give us the feeling that the woman who wore them must have been the heroine of a novel because most of us have scarcely set eyes on them outside the pages of certain of Henry Gréville's novels. Odette had now in her drawing-room, at the beginning of winter, chrysanthemums of enormous size and of a variety of colours such as Swann, in the old days, certainly never saw in her drawing-room in the Rue La Pérouse. My admiration for them—when I went to pay Mme Swann one of those melancholy visits during which, prompted by my sorrow, I discovered in her all the mysterious poetry of her character as the mother of that Gilberte to whom she would say next day: "Your friend came to see me yesterday"—sprang, no doubt, from my sense that, pale pink like the Louis XIV silk that covered her chairs, snow-white like her *crêpe-de-Chine* dressing-gown, or of a metallic red like her samovar, they superimposed upon the decoration of the room another, a supplementary scheme of decoration, as rich and as delicate in its colouring, but one that was alive and would last for a few days only. But I was touched to find that these chrysanthemums appeared not so much ephemeral as relatively durable compared with the tones, equally pink or equally coppery, which the setting sun so gorgeously displays amid the mists of a November afternoon, and which, after seeing them fading from the sky before I had entered the house, I found again inside, prolonged, transposed in the flaming palette of the flowers. Like the fires caught and fixed by a great colourist from the impermanence of the atmosphere and the sun, so that they should enter and adorn a human dwelling, they invited me, those chrysanthemums, to put away all my sorrows and to taste with a greedy rapture during that "tea-time" hour the all-too-fleeting pleasures of November, whose intimate and mysterious splendour they set ablaze all around me. Alas, it was not in the conversations which I heard that I could hope to attain to that splendour; they had little in common with it. Even with Mme Cottard, and although it was growing late, Mme Swann would assume her most caressing manner to say: "Oh, no, it's quite early really; you mustn't look at the clock; that's not the right time; it's stopped; you can't possibly have anything very urgent to do," as she pressed a final tartlet upon the Professor's wife, who was gripping her card-case in readiness for flight.

"One simply can't tear oneself away from this house," observed Mme Bontemps to Mme Swann, while Mme Cottard, in her astonishment at hearing her own thought put into words, exclaimed: "Why, that's just what I always say to myself, in my common-sensical little way, in my heart of hearts!" winning the approval of the gentlemen from the Jockey Club, who had been profuse in their salutations, as though overwhelmed by such an honour, when Mme Swann had introduced them to this graceless little bourgeois woman, who, when confronted with Odette's brilliant friends, remained on her guard, if not on what she herself called "the defensive," for she always used stately language to describe the simplest things.

"I should never have suspected it," was Mme Swann's comment, "three Wednesdays running you've let me down." "That's quite true, Odette; it's *simply ages*, *it's an eternity* since I saw you last. You see I plead guilty; but I must tell you," she went on with a vague and prudish air (for although a doctor's wife she would never have dared to speak without periphrasis of rheumatism or of a chill on the kidneys), "that I have a lot of little *troubles*. As we all have, I dare say. And besides that I've had a crisis among my masculine staff. Without being more imbued than most with a sense of my own authority, I've been obliged, just to make an example you know, to give my Vatel notice;[23] I believe he was looking out anyhow for a more remunerative place. But his departure nearly brought about the resignation of the entire Ministry. My own maid refused to stay in the house a moment longer; oh, we have had some Homeric scenes. However I held fast to the helm through thick and thin; the whole affair's been a perfect object lesson, which won't be lost on me, I can tell you. I'm afraid I'm boring you with all these stories about servants, but you know as well as I do what a business it is when one is obliged to set about rearranging one's household."

"Aren't we to see anything of your delicious daughter?" she wound up. "No, my delicious daughter is dining with a friend," replied Mme Swann, and then, turning to me: "I believe she's written to you, asking you to come and see her to-morrow. And your *babies*?" she went on to Mme Cottard.

I breathed a sigh of relief. These words of Mme Swann's,

which proved to me that I could see Gilberte whenever I chose, gave me precisely the comfort which I had come to seek, and which at that time made my visits to Mme Swann so necessary. "No, I'm afraid not; I shall write her a note this evening. Besides, Gilberte and I can no longer see one another," I added, pretending to attribute our separation to some mysterious cause, which gave me a further illusion of love, sustained as well by the affectionate way in which I spoke of Gilberte and she of me.

"You know she's simply devoted to you," said Mme Swann. "Really, you won't come to-morrow?"

Suddenly I was filled with elation; the thought had just struck me—"After all, why not, since it's her own mother who suggests it?" But at once I relapsed into my gloom. I was afraid lest Gilberte, on seeing me, might think that my indifference of late had been feigned, and it seemed wiser to prolong our separation. During these asides Mme Bontemps had been complaining of the insufferable dullness of politicians' wives, for she affected to find everyone too deadly or too stupid for words, and to deplore her husband's official position.

"Do you mean to say you can shake hands with fifty doctors' wives, like that, one after the other?" she exclaimed to Mme Cottard, who, on the contrary, was full of benevolence towards everybody, and determined to do her duty in every respect. "Ah! you're a woman of virtue! As for me, at the Ministry, of course I have my obligations. Well, it's more than I can stand. You know what those officials' wives are like, it's all I can do not to put my tongue out at them. And my niece Albertine is just like me. You've no idea how insolent she is, that child. Last week, during my 'at home,' I had the wife of the Under Secretary of State for Finance, who told us that she knew nothing at all about cooking. 'But surely, ma'am,' my niece chipped in with her most winning smile, 'you ought to know all about it, since your father was a scullion.'"

"Oh, I do love that story; I think it's simply exquisite!" cried Mme Swann. "But certainly for the Doctor's consultation days you should make a point of having a little *home*, with your flowers and books and all your pretty things," she urged Mme Cottard.

"Straight out like that! Slap-bang, right in the face! She made no bones about it, I can tell you! And she didn't give me a word of warning, the little minx; she's as cunning as a monkey. You're lucky to be able to hold yourself back; I do envy people who can hide what's in their minds." "But I've no need to do that, Mme Bontemps, I'm not so hard to please," Mme Cottard gently expostulated. "For one thing, I'm not in such a privileged position as you," she went on, slightly raising her voice as was her custom, as though to underline the remark, whenever she slipped into the conversation one of those delicate courtesies, those skilful flatteries which won her the admiration and assisted the career of her husband. "And besides I'm only too glad to do anything that can be of use to the Professor."

"But, my dear, it isn't what one's glad to do; it's what one is able to do! I expect you're not highly-strung. Do you know, whenever I see the War Minister's wife grimacing, I start imitating her at once. It's a dreadful thing to have a temperament like mine."

"Ah, yes," said Mme Cottard, "I've heard that she had a twitch. My husband knows someone else who occupies a very high position, and it's only natural, when these gentlemen get talking together . . ."

"And then you know, it's just the same with the Head of Protocol, who's a hunchback. He has only to be in my house five minutes before my fingers are itching to stroke his hump. I can't help it. My husband says I'll cost him his place. What if I do! Pooh to the Ministry! Yes, pooh to the Ministry! I should like to have that printed as a motto on my notepaper. I can see I'm shocking you; you're so good, but I must say there's nothing amuses me like a little devilry now and then. Life would be dreadfully monotonous without it."

And she went on talking about the Ministry all the time, as though it had been Mount Olympus. To change the subject, Mme Swann turned to Mme Cottard: "But you're looking very elegant to-day. Redfern *fecit*?"

"No, you know I always swear by Rauthnitz. Besides, it's only an old thing I've had done up."

"Well, well! it's really smart!"

"Guess how much. . . . No, change the first figure!"

"You don't say so! Why, it's dirt cheap, it's a gift! Three times that at least, I was told."

"That's how history comes to be written," concluded the doctor's wife. And pointing to a neck-ribbon which had been a present from Mme Swann: "Look, Odette! Do you recognise it?"

Through the gap between a pair of curtains a head peeped with ceremonious deference, making a playful pretence of being afraid of disturbing the party: it was Swann. "Odette, the Prince d'Agrigente is with me in my study and wants to know if he may pay his respects to you. What am I to tell him?" "Why, that I shall be delighted," Odette replied, secretly flattered but without losing anything of the composure which came to her all the more easily since she had always, even as a cocotte, been accustomed to entertain men of fashion. Swann disappeared to deliver the message, to return presently with the Prince, unless in the meantime Mme Verdurin had arrived.

When he married Odette Swann had insisted on her ceasing to frequent the little clan. (He had several good reasons for this stipulation, and even if he had had none, would have made it none the less in obedience to a law of ingratitude which admits of no exception and proves that every "go-between" is either lacking in foresight or else singularly disinterested.) He had conceded only that Odette might exchange visits with Mme Verdurin once a year, and even this seemed excessive to some of the "faithful," indignant at the insult offered to the "Mistress" who for so many years had treated Odette and even Swann himself as the spoiled children of her house. For if it contained false brethren who defaulted on certain evenings in order that they might secretly accept an invitation from Odette, ready, in the event of discovery, with the excuse that they were curious to meet Bergotte (although the Mistress assured them that he never went to the Swanns' and was totally devoid of talent—in spite of which she made the most strenuous efforts, to quote one of her favourite expressions, to "attract" him), the little group had its "die-hards" too. And these—though ignorant of those refinements of convention

which often dissuade people from the extreme attitude one
would like to see them adopt in order to annoy someone else—
would have wished Mme Verdurin but had never managed to
prevail upon her to sever all relations with Odette and thus
deprive her of the satisfaction of saying with a laugh: "We
seldom go to the Mistress's now, since the Schism. It was all
very well while my husband was still a bachelor, but when one
is married, you know, it isn't always so easy. . . . If you must
know, M. Swann can't abide old Ma Verdurin, and he wouldn't
much like the idea of my going there regularly as I used to.
And I, as a dutiful spouse, don't you see . . .?" Swann would
accompany his wife to their annual evening there but would
take care not to be in the room when Mme Verdurin came to
call on Odette. And so, if the Mistress was in the drawing-
room, the Prince d'Agrigente would enter it alone. Alone,
too, he was presented to her by Odette, who preferred that
Mme Verdurin should be left in ignorance of the names of her
humbler guests and, seeing more than one strange face in
the room, might be led to believe that she was mixing with the
cream of the aristocracy, a device which proved so successful
that Mme Verdurin said to her husband that evening with profound contempt: "Charming people, her friends! I met all the
flower of Reaction!"

Odette was living, with respect to Mme Verdurin, under a
converse illusion. Not that the latter's salon had even begun,
at that time, to develop into what we shall one day see it
become. Mme Verdurin had not yet reached the period
of incubation in which one dispenses with the big parties
where the few brilliant specimens recently acquired would be
lost in the crowd, and prefers to wait until the generative force
of the ten just men whom one has succeeded in attracting shall
have multiplied those ten seventy-fold. As Odette was not to
be long now in doing, Mme Verdurin did indeed entertain the
idea of "Society" as her final objective, but her zone of attack
was as yet so restricted, and moreover so remote from that
by way of which Odette stood some chance of arriving at an
identical goal, of breaking through, that the latter remained in
total ignorance of the strategic plans which the Mistress was
elaborating. And it was with the most perfect sincerity that

Odette, when anyone spoke to her of Mme Verdurin as a snob, would answer, laughing: "Oh, no, quite the opposite! For one thing, she hasn't the basis for it: she doesn't know anyone. And then, to do her justice, I must say that she seems quite content with things as they are. No, what she likes are her Wednesdays, good talkers." And in her hearts of hearts she envied Mme Verdurin (for all that she did not despair of having herself, in so eminent a school, succeeded in acquiring them) those arts to which the Mistress attached such paramount importance, although they did no more than discriminate between shades of the non-existent, sculpture the void, and were, strictly speaking, the Arts of Nonentity: to wit those, in the lady of a house, of knowing how to "bring people together," how to "group," to "draw out," to "keep in the background," to act as a "connecting link."

At all events Mme Swann's friends were impressed when they saw in her house a lady of whom they were accustomed to think only as in her own, in an inseparable setting of guests, in the midst of her little group which they were astonished to behold thus evoked, summarised, compressed into a single armchair in the bodily form of the Mistress, the hostess turned visitor, muffled in her cloak with its grebe trimming, as fluffy as the white furs that carpeted that drawing-room, embowered in which Mme Verdurin was a drawing-room in herself. The more timid among the women thought it prudent to retire, and using the plural, as people do when they mean to hint to the rest of the room that it is wiser not to tire a convalescent who is out of bed for the first time, "Odette," they murmured, "we're going to leave you." They envied Mme Cottard, whom the Mistress called by her Christian name.

"Can I drop you anywhere?" Mme Verdurin asked her, unable to bear the thought that one of the faithful was going to remain behind instead of following her from the room.

"Oh, but this lady has been so very kind as to say she'll take me," replied Mme Cottard, not wishing to appear to be forgetting, when approached by a more illustrious personage, that she had accepted the offer which Mme Bontemps had made to drive her home behind her cockaded coachman. "I must say that I'm always specially grateful to the friends who are so kind as to take me with them in their vehicles. It's a regular godsend to me who have no Automedon."

"Especially," broke in the Mistress, who felt that she must say something, since she knew Mme Bontemps slightly and had just invited her to her Wednesdays, "as at Mme de Crécy's house you're not very near home. Oh, good gracious, I shall never get into the habit of saying Mme Swann!" It was a recognised joke in the little clan, among those who were not over-endowed with wit, to pretend that they could never grow used to saying "Mme Swann": "I've been so accustomed to saying Mme de Crécy that I nearly went wrong again!" Only Mme Verdurin, when she spoke to Odette, was not content with the nearly, but went wrong on purpose.

"Don't you feel afraid, Odette, living out in the wilds like this? I'm sure I shouldn't feel at all comfortable, coming home after dark. Besides, it's so damp. It can't be at all good for your husband's eczema. You haven't rats in the house, I hope!" "Oh, dear no. What a horrid idea!" "That's a good thing; I was told you had. I'm glad to know it's not true, because I have a perfect horror of the creatures, and I should never have come to see you again. Good-bye, my dear child, we shall meet again soon; you know what a pleasure it is to me to see you. You don't know how to arrange chrysanthemums," she added as she prepared to leave the room, Mme Swann having risen to escort her. "They are Japanese flowers; you must arrange them the same way as the Japanese."

"I do not agree with Mme Verdurin, although she is the fount of wisdom to me in all things! There's no one like you, Odette, for finding such lovely chrysanthemums, or chrysanthema rather, for it seems that's what we ought to call them now," declared Mme Cottard as soon as the Mistress had shut the door behind her.

"Dear Mme Verdurin is not always very kind about other people's flowers," said Odette sweetly. "Whom do you go to, Odette," asked Mme Cottard, to forestall any further criticism of the Mistress. "Lemaître? I must confess, the other day in Lemaître's window I saw a lovely pink shrub which made me commit the wildest extravagance." But modesty forbade her to give any more precise details as to the price of the shrub, and she said merely that the Professor, "and you know, he's not at all a quick-tempered man," had "flown off the handle" and told her that she "didn't know the value of money."

"No, no, I've no regular florist except Debac." "Me too," said Mme Cottard, "but I confess that I forsake him now and then for Lachaume." "Oh, you're unfaithful to him with Lachaume, are you? I must tell him that," replied Odette, always anxious to show her wit, and to lead the conversation in her own house, where she felt more at her ease than in the little clan. "Besides, Lachaume is really becoming too dear; his prices are quite excessive, don't you know; I find his prices indecent!" she added, laughing.

Meanwhile Mme Bontemps, who had been heard a hundred times to declare that nothing would induce her to go to the Verdurins', delighted at being asked to the famous Wednesdays, was working out how she could manage to attend as many of them as possible. She was not aware that Mme Verdurin liked people not to miss a single one; moreover she was one of those people whose company is but little sought after who, when a hostess invites them to a series of "at homes," instead of going to her house without more ado— like those who know that it is always a pleasure to see them— whenever they have a moment to spare and feel inclined to go out, deny themselves for example the first evening and the third, imagining that their absence will be noticed, and save themselves up for the second and fourth, unless it should happen that, having heard from a trustworthy source that the third is to be a particularly brilliant party, they reverse the original order, assuring their hostess that "most unfortunately, we had another engagement last week." So Mme Bontemps was calculating how many Wednesdays there could still be left before Easter, and by what means she might manage to secure an extra one and yet not appear to be thrusting herself upon her hostess. She relied upon Mme Cottard, whom she would have with her in the carriage going home, to give her a few hints.

"Oh, Mme Bontemps, I see you getting up to go; it's very bad of you to give the signal for flight like that! You owe me some compensation for not turning up last Thursday. . . .

Come, sit down again, just for a minute. You can't possibly
be going anywhere else before dinner. Really, you won't let
yourself be tempted?" went on Mme Swann, and, as she held
out a plate of cakes, "You know, they're not at all bad, these
little horrors. They may not be much to look at, but just you
taste one and you'll see."

"On the contrary, they look quite delicious," broke in Mme
Cottard. "In your house, Odette, one is never short of victuals.
I have no need to ask to see the trade-mark; I know you get
everything from Rebattet. I must say that I am more eclectic.
For sweets and cakes and so forth I repair, as often as not, to
Bourbonneux. But I agree that they simply don't know what
an ice means. Rebattet for everything iced, and syrups and
sorbets; they're past masters. As my husband would say, they're
the *ne plus ultra*."

"Oh, but these are home-made. You won't, really?" "I
shan't be able to eat a scrap of dinner," pleaded Mme Bontemps, "but I'll sit down again for a moment. You know, I
adore talking to a clever woman like you."

"You'll think me highly indiscreet, Odette, but I should so
like to know what you thought of the hat Mme Trombert had
on. I know, of course, that big hats are the fashion just now.
All the same, wasn't it just the least little bit exaggerated? And
compared to the hat she came to see me in the other day, the
one she was wearing just now was microscopic!" "Oh no,
I'm not at all clever," said Odette, thinking that this sounded
well. "I am a perfect simpleton, I believe everything people
say, and worry myself to death over the least thing." And she
insinuated that she had, just at first, suffered terribly from
having married a man like Swann who had a separate life of
his own and was unfaithful to her.

Meanwhile the Prince d'Agrigente, having caught the words
"I'm not at all clever," thought it incumbent on him to protest,
but unfortunately lacked the gift of repartee. "Fiddlesticks!"
cried Mme Bontemps, "not clever, you!" "That's just what I
was saying to myself—'What do I hear?', " the Prince clutched
at this straw. "My ears must have played me false!"

"No, I assure you," went on Odette, "I'm really just an
ordinary woman, very easily shocked, full of prejudices, living

in my own little groove and dreadfully ignorant." And then, in case he had any news of the Baron de Charlus, "Have you seen our dear Baronet?" she asked him.

"You, ignorant!" cried Mme Bontemps. "Then I wonder what you'd say of the official world, all those wives of Excellencies who can talk of nothing but their frocks. . . . Just imagine, not more than a week ago I happened to mention *Lohengrin* to the Education Minister's wife. She stared at me and said '*Lohengrin?* Oh, yes, the new review at the Folies-Bergère. I hear it's a perfect scream!' Well, I ask you! When people say things like that it makes your blood boil. I could have hit her. Because I have a bit of a temper of my own. What do you say, Monsieur," she added, turning to me, "was I not right?"

"But still," said Mme Cottard, "it's forgivable to be a little off the mark when you're asked a thing like that point blank, without any warning. I know something about it, because Mme Verdurin also has a habit of putting a pistol to your head."

"Speaking of Mme Verdurin," Mme Bontemps asked Mme Cottard, "do you know who will be there on Wednesday? Oh, I've just remembered that we've accepted an invitation for next Wednesday. You wouldn't care to dine with us on Wednesday week? We could go on together to Mme Verdurin's. I should never dare to go there by myself. I don't know why it is, that great lady always terrifies me."

"I'll tell you what it is," replied Mme Cottard, "that frightens you about Mme Verdurin: it's her voice. But you see everyone can't have such a charming voice as Mme Swann. Once you've found your tongue, as the Mistress says, the ice will soon be broken. For she's a very easy person, really, to get on with. But I can quite understand what you feel; it's never pleasant to find oneself for the first time in strange surroundings."

"Won't you dine with us, too?" said Mme Bontemps to Mme Swann. "After dinner we could all go to the Verdurins together, 'do a Verdurin'; and even if it means that the Mistress will glare at me and never ask me to the house again, once we are there we'll just sit by ourselves and have a quiet

talk, I'm sure that's what I should like best." But this assertion
can hardly have been quite truthful, for Mme Bontemps went
on to ask: "Who do you think will be there on Wednesday
week? What will be happening? There won't be too big a
crowd, I hope!"

"I certainly shan't be there," said Odette. "We'll just put
in a brief appearance on the last Wednesday of all. If you don't
mind waiting till then . . ." But Mme Bontemps did not
appear to be tempted by the proposal.

Granted that the intellectual distinction of a salon and its
elegance are generally in inverse rather than direct ratio, one
must suppose, since Swann found Mme Bontemps agreeable,
that any forfeiture of position once accepted has the consequence
of making people less particular with regard to those among
whom they have resigned themselves to move, less particular
with regard to their intelligence as to everything else about
them. And if this is true, men, like nations, must see their
culture and even their language disappear with their independence. One of the effects of this indulgence is to aggravate
the tendency people have after a certain age to derive pleasure
from words that are a homage to their own turn of mind, to
their weaknesses, and an encouragement to them to yield to
them; that is the age at which a great artist prefers to the company of original minds that of pupils who have nothing in
common with him save the letter of his doctrine, who listen
to him and offer incense; at which a man or woman of distinction who lives exclusively for love will think the most
intelligent person in a gathering the one who, however
inferior, has shown by some remark that he can understand
and approve an existence devoted to gallantry, and has thus
pleasantly flattered the voluptuous instincts of the lover or
mistress; it was the age, too, at which Swann, inasmuch as he
had become the husband of Odette, enjoyed hearing Mme
Bontemps say how silly it was to have nobody in one's house
but duchesses (concluding from that, contrary to what he
would have done in the old days at the Verdurins', that she
was a good creature, extremely witty and not at all a snob) and
telling her stories which made her "die laughing," because she
had not heard them before and moreover "saw the point" of

them at once, since she enjoyed flattering and exchanging jokes.

"So the Doctor is not mad about flowers, like you?" Mme Swann asked Mme Cottard.

"Oh, well, you know, my husband is a sage; he practises moderation in all things. Wait, though, he does have one passion."

Her eye aflame with malice, joy, curiosity, "And what is that, pray?" inquired Mme Bontemps.

Artlessly Mme Cottard replied: "Reading." "Oh, that's a very restful passion in a husband!" cried Mme Bontemps, suppressing a diabolical laugh.

"When the Doctor gets a book in his hands, you know!"

"Well, that needn't alarm you much . . ."

"But it does, for his eyesight. I must go now and look after him, Odette, and I shall come back at the very first opportunity and knock at your door. Talking of eyesight, have you heard that the new house Mme Verdurin has just bought is to be lighted by electricity? I didn't get that from my own little secret service, you know, but from quite a different source; it was the electrician himself, Mildé, who told me. You see, I quote my authorities! Even the bedrooms, he says, are to have electric lamps with shades which will filter the light. It's obviously a charming luxury for those who can afford it. But it seems that our contemporaries must absolutely have the newest thing if it's the only one of its kind in the world. Just fancy, the sister-in-law of a friend of mine has had the telephone installed in her house! She can order things from tradesmen without having to go out! I confess that I've indulged in the most bare-faced intrigues to get permission to go there one day, just to speak into the instrument. It's very tempting, but rather in a friend's house than at home. I don't think I should like to have the telephone in my establishment. Once the first excitement is over, it must be a real headache. Now, Odette, I must be off; you're not to keep Mme Bontemps any longer, she's looking after me. I must absolutely tear myself away: a nice way you're making me behave—I shall be getting home after my husband!"

And for myself also it was time to return home, before I had tasted those wintry delights of which the chrysanthemums had seemed to me to be the brilliant envelope. These pleasures had not appeared, and yet Mme Swann did not look as though she expected anything more. She allowed the servants to carry away the tea-things, as who should say "Time, please, gentlemen!" And finally she said to me: "Really, must you go? Well then, *good-bye!*" I felt that I might have stayed there without encountering those unknown pleasures, and that my sadness was not the only cause of my having to forgo them. Were they to be found, then, situated not upon that beaten track of hours which leads one always so rapidly to the moment of departure, but rather upon some unknown by-road along which I ought to have digressed? At least the object of my visit had been attained; Gilberte would know that I had come to her parents' house when she was not at home, and that I had, as Mme Cottard had incessantly assured me, "made a complete conquest, first shot, of Mme Verdurin" (whom, she added, she had never seen "make so much" of anyone: "You and she must be soulmates"). She would know that I had spoken of her as was fitting, with affection, but that I had not that incapacity for living without our seeing one another which I believed to be at the root of the boredom that she had shown at our last meetings. I had told Mme Swann that I could not be with Gilberte any more. I had said this as though I had finally decided not to see her again. And the letter which I was going to send Gilberte would be framed on those lines. Only to myself, to fortify my courage, I proposed no more than a final, concentrated effort, lasting a few days only. I said to myself: "This is the last time that I shall refuse an invitation to meet her; I shall accept the next one." To make our separation less difficult to realise, I did not picture it to myself as final. But I knew very well that it would be.

The first of January was exceptionally painful to me that winter. So, no doubt, is everything that marks a date and an anniversary, when we are unhappy. But if our unhappiness is due to the loss of someone dear to us, our suffering consists merely in an unusually vivid comparison of the present with the past. Added to this, in my case, was the unformulated hope that Gilberte, having wished to leave me to take the first steps towards a reconciliation, and discovering that I had not taken them, had been waiting only for the excuse of New Year's Day to write to me, saying: "What is the matter? I'm mad about you, so come and have it out frankly, I can't live without seeing you." As the last days of the old year went by, such a letter began to seem probable. It was, perhaps, nothing of the sort, but to make us believe that such a thing is probable the desire, the need that we have for it suffices. The soldier is convinced that a certain interval of time, capable of being indefinitely prolonged, will be allowed him before the bullet finds him, the thief before he is caught, men in general before they have to die. That is the amulet which preserves people— and sometimes peoples—not from danger but from the fear of danger, in reality from the belief in danger, which in certain cases allows them to brave it without actually needing to be brave. It is confidence of this sort, and with as little foundation, that sustains the lover who is counting on a reconciliation, on a letter. For me to cease to expect a reconciliation, it would have sufficed that I should have ceased to wish for one. However indifferent to us we may know the beloved to be, we attribute to her a series of thoughts (though their sum-total be indifference), the intention to express those thoughts, a complication of her inner life in which one is the object of her antipathy, perhaps, but also of her constant attention. But to imagine what was going on in Gilberte's mind I should have required simply the power to anticipate on that New Year's Day what I should feel on the first day of any of the following years, when the attention or the silence or the affection or the coldness of Gilberte would pass almost unnoticed by me and I should not dream, should not even be able to dream, of seeking a solution to problems which would have ceased to perplex me. When we are in love, our love is too big a thing for us to be able altogether to contain it within ourselves. It radiates towards the loved one, finds there a surface which arrests it, forcing it to return to its starting-point, and it is this repercussion of our own feeling which we call the other's feelings and which charms us more then than on its outward journey because we do not recognise it as having originated in ourselves.

New Year's Day went by, hour after hour, without bringing

me that letter from Gilberte. And as I received a few others containing greetings belated or retarded by the congestion of the mails at that season, on the third and fourth of January I still hoped, but more and more faintly. On the days that followed, I wept a great deal. True, this was due to the fact that, having been less sincere than I thought in my renunciation of Gilberte, I had clung to the hope of a letter from her in the New Year. And seeing that hope exhausted before I had had time to shelter myself behind another, I suffered like an invalid who has emptied his phial of morphia without having another within his reach. But perhaps also in my case—and these two explanations are not mutually exclusive, for a single feeling is often made up of contrary elements—the hope that I entertained of ultimately receiving a letter had brought to my mind's eye once again the image of Gilberte, had reawakened the emotions which the expectation of finding myself in her presence, the sight of her, her behaviour towards me, had aroused in me before. The immediate possibility of a reconciliation had suppressed in me that faculty the immense importance of which we are apt to overlook: the faculty of resignation. Neurasthenics find it impossible to believe the friends who assure them that they will gradually recover their peace of mind if they will stay in bed and receive no letters, read no newspapers. They imagine that such a regime will only exasperate their twitching nerves. And similarly lovers, contemplating it from within a contrary state of mind, not having yet begun to put it to the test, are unable to believe in the healing power of renunciation.

Because of the violence of my heart-beats, my doses of caffeine were reduced; the palpitations ceased. Whereupon I asked myself whether it was not to some extent the drug that had been responsible for the anguish I had felt when I had fallen out with Gilberte, an anguish which I had attributed, whenever it recurred, to the pain of not seeing her any more or of running the risk of seeing her only when she was a prey to the same ill-humour. But if this drug had been at the root of the sufferings which my imagination must in that case have interpreted wrongly (not that there would be anything extraordinary in that, seeing that, for lovers, the most acute

mental suffering often has its origin in the physical presence of
the woman with whom they are living), it had been, in that
sense, like the philtre which, long after they have absorbed it,
continues to bind Tristan to Isolde. For the physical improvement which the reduction of my caffeine effected almost at
once did not arrest the evolution of that grief which my
absorption of the toxin had perhaps, if not created, at any rate
contrived to render more acute.

Only, as the middle of the month of January approached,
once my hopes of a New Year letter had been disappointed,
once the additional pang that had come with their disappointment had been assuaged, it was my old sorrow, that of "before
the holidays," which began again. What was perhaps the most
cruel thing about it was that I myself was its architect, unconscious, wilful, merciless and patient. The one thing that
mattered to me was my relationship with Gilberte, and it was
I who was labouring to make it impossible by gradually
creating out of this prolonged separation from my beloved,
not indeed her indifference, but what would come to the same
thing in the end, my own. It was to a slow and painful suicide
of that self which loved Gilberte that I was goading myself
with untiring energy, with a clear sense not only of what I
was doing in the present but of what must result from it in
the future: I knew not only that after a certain time I should
cease to love Gilberte, but also that she herself would regret it
and that the attempts which she would then make to see me
would be as vain as those that she was making now, no longer
because I loved her too much but because I should certainly
be in love with some other woman whom I should continue
to desire, to wait for, through hours of which I should not
dare to divert a single particle of a second to Gilberte who
would be nothing to me then. And no doubt at that very
moment in which (since I was determined not to see her again,
barring a formal request for a reconciliation, a complete
declaration of love on her part, neither of which was in the
least degree likely to be forthcoming) I had already lost Gilberte, and loved her more than ever since I could feel all that
she was to me better than in the previous year when, spending
all my afternoons in her company, or as many as I chose, I

believed that no peril threatened our friendship,—no doubt at that moment the idea that I should one day entertain identical feelings for another was odious to me, for that idea deprived me, not only of Gilberte, but of my love and my suffering: my love, my suffering, in which through my tears I was attempting to grasp precisely what Gilberte was, and yet was obliged to recognise that they did not pertain exclusively to her but would, sooner or later, be some other woman's fate. So that—or such, at least, was my way of thinking then—we are always detached from our fellow-creatures: when we love, we sense that our love does not bear a name, that it may spring up again in the future, could have sprung up already in the past, for another person rather than this one; and during the time when we are not in love, if we resign ourselves philosophically to love's inconsistencies and contradictions, it is because we do not at that moment feel the love which we speak about so freely, and hence do not know it, knowledge in these matters being intermittent and not outlasting the actual presence of the sentiment. Of course there would still have been time to warn Gilberte that that future in which I should no longer love her, which my suffering helped me to divine although my imagination was not yet able to form a clear picture of it, would gradually take shape, that its coming was, if not imminent, at least inevitable, if she herself did not come to my rescue and nip my future indifference in the bud. How often was I not on the point of writing, or of going to Gilberte to tell her: "Take care. My mind is made up. This is my final attempt. I am seeing you now for the last time. Soon I shall love you no longer!" But to what end? By what right could I reproach her for an indifference which, without considering myself guilty on that account, I myself manifested towards everything that was not Gilberte? The last time! To me, that appeared as something of immense significance, because I loved Gilberte. On her it would doubtless have made just as much impression as those letters in which our friends ask whether they may pay us a visit before they finally leave the country, requests which, like those made by tiresome women who are in love with us, we decline because we have pleasures of our own in prospect. The time which we have at our disposal every day is elastic; the passions that we feel expand it, those that we inspire contract it; and habit fills up what remains.

Besides, what good would it have done if I had spoken to Gilberte? She would not have heard me. We imagine always when we speak that it is our own ears, our own mind, that are listening. My words would have come to her only in a distorted form, as though they had had to pass through the moving curtain of a waterfall before they reached my beloved, unrecognisable, sounding false and absurd, having no longer any kind of meaning. The truth which one puts into one's words does not carve out a direct path for itself, is not irresistibly self-evident. A considerable time must elapse before a truth of the same order can take shape in them. Then the political opponent who, despite every argument, every proof, condemns the votary of the rival doctrine as a traitor, himself comes to share the hated conviction, in which he who once sought in vain to disseminate it no longer believes. Then the masterpiece of literature whose excellence seemed self-evident to the admirers who read it aloud, while to those who listened it presented only a senseless or commonplace image, will by those too be proclaimed a masterpiece, but too late for the author to learn of their conversion. Similarly, in love, the barriers, do what he may, cannot be broken down from without by the despairing lover; it is when he no longer cares about them that suddenly, as the result of an effort directed from elsewhere, accomplished within the heart of the one who did not love, those barriers which he has charged in vain will fall to no avail. If I had come to Gilberte to tell her of my future indifference and the means of preventing it, she would have assumed that my love for her, the need that I had of her, were even greater than she had supposed, and her reluctance to see me would thereby have been increased. And it is all too true, moreover, that it was that love for her which helped me, by the disparate states of mind which it successively produced in me, to foresee, more clearly than she herself could, the end of that love. And yet some such warning I might perhaps have addressed, by letter or by word of mouth, to Gilberte, after a long enough interval, which would render her, it is true, less indispensable to me, but might also have proved to her that she was not so indispensable. Unfortunately certain well or ill intentioned persons spoke of me to her in a fashion which must have led her to think that they were doing so at my request. Whenever I thus learned that Cottard, my own mother, even M. de Norpois had by a few ill-chosen words nullified the whole sacrifice that I had just been making, wasted all the advantage of my reserve by wrongly making me appear to have emerged from it, I had a double grievance. In the first place I now had to date from that day only my laborious and fruitful abstention which these tiresome people had, unknown to me, interrupted and consequently brought to nothing. But in addition I should now have less pleasure in seeing Gilberte, who would think of me no longer as containing myself in dignified resignation, but as plotting in the dark for an interview which she had scorned to grant me. I cursed all this idle chatter of people who so often, without any intention either of hurting us or of doing us a service, for no reason, for talking's sake, sometimes because we ourselves have not been able to refrain from talking in their presence and because they are indiscreet (as we ourselves are), do us, at a crucial moment, so much harm. It is true that in the baleful task of destroying our love they are far from playing a part comparable to that played by two persons who are in the habit, one from excess of goodwill and the other from excess of ill-will, of undoing everything at the moment when everything is on the point of being settled. But against these two persons we bear no such grudge as against the inopportune Cottards of this world, for one of them is the person whom we love and the other is ourself.

Meanwhile, since almost every time I went to see her Mme Swann would invite me to come to tea with her daughter and tell me to reply to the latter direct, I was constantly writing to Gilberte, and in this correspondence I did not choose the expressions which might, I felt, have won her over, but sought only to carve out the easiest channel for the flow of my tears. For regret, like desire, seeks not to analyse but to gratify itself. When one begins to love, one spends one's time, not in getting to know what one's love really is, but in arranging for to-morrow's rendezvous. When one renounces love one seeks not to know one's grief but to offer to the person who is its cause the expression of it which seems most moving. One says the things which one feels the need to say, and which the other will not understand: one speaks for oneself alone. I wrote: "I had thought that it would not be possible. Alas, I see now that it is not so difficult." I said also: "I shall probably never see you again," and said it while continuing to avoid showing a coldness which she might think feigned, and the words, as I wrote them, made me weep because I felt that they expressed not what I should have liked to believe but what was probably going to happen. For at the next request for a meeting which she would convey to me I should have again, as I had now, the courage not to yield, and, with one refusal after another, I should gradually come to the moment when, by virtue of not having seen her again, I should no longer wish to see her. I wept, but I found courage enough to sacrifice, I savoured the melancholy pleasure of sacrificing, the happiness of being with her to the possibility of being pleasing in her eyes one day—a day, alas, when being pleasing in her eyes would be immaterial to me. Even the supposition, improbable though it was, that at this moment, as she had claimed during the last visit that I had paid her, she loved me, that what I took for the boredom which one feels in the company of a person of whom one has grown tired had been due only to a jealous susceptibility, to a feigned indifference analogous to my own, only rendered my decision less painful. It seemed to me that in years to come, when we had forgotten one another, when I should be able to look back and tell her that this letter which I was now in the course of writing to her had not been for one moment sincere, she would answer: "What, you really did love me, did you? If you only knew how I waited for that letter, how I longed for us to meet, how I cried when I read it." The thought, while I was writing it, immediately on my return from her mother's house, that I was perhaps consummating that very misunderstanding, that thought, by its very sadness, by the pleasure of imagining that I was loved by Gilberte, gave me the impulse to continue my letter.

If, at the moment of leaving Mme Swann, when her tea-party ended, I was thinking of what I was going to write to her

daughter, Mme Cottard, as she departed, had been filled with
thoughts of a wholly different kind. On her little "tour of
inspection" she had not failed to congratulate Mme Swann on
the new "pieces," the recent "acquisitions" which caught the
eye in her drawing-room. She could also see among them
some, though only a very few, of the things that Odette had
had in the old days in the Rue La Pérouse, for instance her
animals carved in precious stones, her mascots.

For since Mme Swann had picked up from a friend whose
opinion she valued the word "trashy"—which had opened to
her new horizons because it denoted precisely those things
which a few years earlier she had considered "smart"—all
those things had, one after another, followed into retirement
the gilded trellis that had served as background to her
chrysanthemums, innumerable bonbonnières from Giroux's,
and the coroneted note-paper (not to mention the coins of
gilt pasteboard littered about on the mantelpieces, which,
even before she had come to know Swann, a man of taste had
advised her to jettison). Moreover in the artistic disorder, the
studio-like jumble of the rooms, whose walls were still painted
in sombre colours which made them as different as possible
from the white-enamelled drawing-rooms Mme Swann was to
favour a little later, the Far East was retreating more and more
before the invading forces of the eighteenth century; and the
cushions which, to make me "comfortable," Mme Swann
heaped up and buffeted into position behind my back were
sprinkled with Louis XV garlands and not, as of old, with
Chinese dragons. In the room in which she was usually to be
found, and of which she would say, "Yes, I like this room; I
use it a great deal. I couldn't live with a lot of hostile, pompous
things; this is where I do my work" (though she never stated
precisely at what she was working, whether a picture, or
perhaps a book, for the hobby of writing was beginning to
become common among women who liked to "do something,"
not to be quite useless), she was surrounded by Dresden
pieces (having a fancy for that sort of porcelain, which she
pronounced with an English accent, saying in any connexion:
"How pretty that is; it reminds me of Dresden flowers"),
and dreaded for them even more than in the old days for her

grotesque figures and her vases the ignorant handling of her servants who were made to expiate the anxiety that they had caused her by submitting to outbursts of rage at which Swann, the most courteous and considerate of masters, looked on without being shocked. Not that the clear perception of certain weaknesses in those we love in any way diminishes our affection for them; rather that affection makes us find those weaknesses charming. Nowadays it was rarely in Japanese kimonos that Odette received her intimates, but rather in the bright and billowing silk of a Watteau housecoat whose flowering foam she would make as though to rub gently over her bosom, and in which she basked, lolled, disported herself with such an air of well-being, of cool freshness, taking such deep breaths, that she seemed to look on these garments not as something decorative, a mere setting for herself, but as necessary, in the same way as her "tub" or her daily "constitutional," to satisfy the requirements of her physiognomy and the niceties of hygiene. She used often to say that she would go without bread rather than give up art and cleanliness, and that the burning of the "Gioconda" would distress her infinitely more than the destruction, by the same element, of the "millions" of people she knew. Theories which seemed paradoxical to her friends, but made them regard her as a superior woman, and earned her a weekly visit from the Belgian Minister, so that in the little world of which she was the sun everyone would have been greatly astonished to learn that elsewhere—at the Verdurins', for instance—she was reckoned a fool. It was this vivacity of mind that made Mme Swann prefer men's society to women's. But when she criticised the latter it was always from the courtesan's standpoint, singling out the blemishes that might lower them in the esteem of men, thick ankles, a bad complexion, inability to spell, hairy legs, foul breath, pencilled eyebrows. But towards a woman who had shown her kindness or indulgence in the past she was more lenient, especially if this woman was now in trouble. She would defend her warmly, saying: "People are not fair to her. I assure you, she's quite a nice woman really."

It was not only the furniture of Odette's drawing-room, it was Odette herself whom Mme Cottard and all those who had frequented the society of Mme de Crécy would have found it difficult, if they had not seen her for some little time, to recognise. She seemed to be so much younger. No doubt this was partly because she had put on a little weight, was in better health, seemed at once calmer, cooler, more restful, and also because the new way in which she braided her hair gave more breadth to a face which was animated by an application of pink powder, and into which her eyes and profile, formerly too prominent, seemed now to have been reabsorbed. But another reason for this change lay in the fact that, having reached the turning-point of life, Odette had at length discovered, or invented, a physiognomy of her own, an unalterable "character," a "style of beauty," and on her uncoordinated features—which for so long, exposed to the dangerous and futile vagaries of the flesh, putting on momentarily years, a sort of fleeting old age, as a result of the slightest fatigue, had composed for her somehow or other, according to her mood and her state of health, a dishevelled, changeable, formless, charming face—had now set this fixed type, as it were an immortal youthfulness.

Swann had in his room, instead of the handsome photographs that were now taken of his wife, in all of which the same enigmatic and winning expression enabled one to recognise, whatever dress and hat she was wearing, her triumphant face and figure, a little daguerreotype of her, quite plain, taken long before the appearance of this new type, from which the youthfulness and beauty of Odette, which she had not yet discovered when it was taken, appeared to be missing. But doubtless Swann, having remained constant, or having reverted, to a different conception of her, enjoyed in the frail young woman with pensive eyes and tired features, caught in a pose between stillness and motion, a more Botticellian charm. For he still liked to see his wife as a Botticelli figure. Odette, who on the contrary sought not to bring out but to compensate for, to cover and conceal the points about her looks that did not please her, what might perhaps to an artist express her "character" but in her woman's eyes were blemishes, would not have that painter mentioned in her presence. Swann had a wonderful scarf of oriental silk, blue and

pink, which he had bought because it was exactly that worn
by the Virgin in the *Magnificat*. But Mme Swann refused to
wear it. Once only she allowed her husband to order her a
dress covered all over with daisies, cornflowers, forget-me-
nots and bluebells, like that of the Primavera. And sometimes
in the evening, when she was tired, he would quietly draw
my attention to the way in which she was giving, quite unconsciously, to her pensive hands the uncontrolled, almost
distraught movement of the Virgin who dips her pen into the
inkpot that the angel holds out to her, before writing upon the
sacred page on which is already traced the word "*Magnificat.*"
But he added: "Whatever you do, don't say anything about it
to her; if she knew she was doing it, she would change her pose
at once."

Save at these moments of involuntary relaxation in which
Swann sought to recapture the melancholy Botticellian droop,
Odette's body seemed now to be cut out in a single silhouette
wholly confined within a "line" which, following the contours of the woman, had abandoned the ups and downs, the
ins and outs, the reticulations, the elaborate dispersions of the
fashions of former days, but also, where it was her anatomy
that went wrong by making unnecessary digressions within or
without the ideal form traced for it, was able to rectify, by a
bold stroke, the errors of nature, to make good, along a whole
section of its course, the lapses of the flesh as well as of the
material. The pads, the preposterous "bustle" had disappeared,
as well as those tailed bodices which, overlapping the skirt
and stiffened by rods of whalebone, had so long amplified
Odette with an artificial stomach and had given her the appearance of being composed of several disparate pieces which
there was no individuality to bind together. The vertical fall
of the fringes, the curve of the ruches had made way for the
inflexion of a body which made silk palpitate as a siren stirs the
waves and gave to cambric a human expression, now that it
had been liberated, like an organic and living form, from the
long chaos and nebulous envelopment of fashions at last dethroned. But Mme Swann had chosen, had contrived to preserve some vestiges of certain of these, in the very midst of
those that had supplanted them. When, in the evening, finding

myself unable to work and knowing that Gilberte had gone to
the theatre with friends, I paid a surprise visit to her parents,
I used often to find Mme Swann in an elegant dishabille the
skirt of which, of one of those rich dark colours, blood-red or
orange, which seemed to have a special meaning because they
were no longer in fashion, was crossed diagonally, though not
concealed, by a broad band of black lace which recalled the
flounces of an earlier day. When, on a still chilly afternoon in
spring, she had taken me (before my break with her daughter)
to the Zoo, under her jacket, which she opened or buttoned up
according as the exercise made her feel warm, the dog-toothed
edging of her blouse suggested a glimpse of the lapel of some
non-existent waistcoat such as she had been accustomed to
wear some years earlier, when she had liked their edges to
have the same slight indentations; and her scarf—of that same
"tartan" to which she had remained faithful, but whose tones
she had so far softened, red becoming pink and blue lilac, that
one might almost have taken it for one of those pigeon's-
breast taffetas which were the latest novelty—was knotted in
such a way under her chin, without one's being able to make
out where it was fastened, that one was irresistibly reminded of
those bonnet-strings which were now no longer worn. She
need only "hold out" like this for a little longer and young
men attempting to understand her theory of dress would say:
"Mme Swann is quite a period in herself, isn't she?" As in a
fine literary style which superimposes different forms but is
strengthened by a tradition that lies concealed behind them,
so in Mme Swann's attire those half-tinted memories of waist-
coats or of ringlets, sometimes a tendency, at once repressed,
towards the "all aboard," or even a distant and vague allusion
to the "follow-me-lad," kept alive beneath the concrete form
the unfinished likeness of other, older forms which one would
not have been able to find effectively reproduced by the
milliner or the dressmaker, but about which one's thoughts
incessantly hovered, and enveloped Mme Swann in a sort of
nobility—perhaps because the very uselessness of these fripperies made them seem designed to serve some more than
utilitarian purpose, perhaps because of the traces they preserved of vanished years, or else because of a vestimentary

personality peculiar to this woman, which gave to the most dissimilar of her costumes a distinct family likeness. One felt that she did not dress simply for the comfort or the adornment of her body; she was surrounded by her garments as by the delicate and spiritualised machinery of a whole civilisation.

When Gilberte, who, as a rule, gave her tea-parties on the days when her mother was "at home," had for some reason to go out and I was therefore free to attend Mme Swann's "kettle-drum," I would find her dressed in one or other of her beautiful dresses, some of which were of taffeta, others of grosgrain, or of velvet, or of *crêpe-de-Chine*, or satin or silk, dresses which, not being loose like the gowns she generally wore in the house but pulled together as though she were just going out in them, gave to her stay-at-home laziness on those afternoons something alert and energetic. And no doubt the bold simplicity of their cut was singularly appropriate to her figure and to her movements, which her sleeves appeared to be symbolising in colours that varied from day to day: one felt that there was a sudden determination in the blue velvet, an easy-going good humour in the white taffeta, and that a sort of supreme discretion full of dignity in her way of holding out her arm had, in order to become visible, put on the appearance, dazzling with the smile of one who had made great sacrifices, of the black *crêpe-de-Chine*. But at the same time, to these animated dresses the complication of their trimmings, none of which had any practical utility or served any visible purpose, added something detached, pensive, secret, in harmony with the melancholy which Mme Swann still retained, at least in the shadows under her eyes and the drooping arches of her hands. Beneath the profusion of sapphire charms, enamelled four-leaf clovers, silver medals, gold medallions, turquoise amulets, ruby chains and topaz chestnuts there would be on the dress itself some design carried out in colour which pursued across the surface of an inserted panel a preconceived existence of its own, some row of little satin buttons which buttoned nothing and could not be unbuttoned, a strip of braid that sought to please the eye with the minuteness, the discretion of a delicate reminder; and these, as well as the jewels, gave the impression—having otherwise no possible

justification—of disclosing a secret intention, being a pledge of
affection, keeping a secret, ministering to a superstition,
commemorating a recovery from sickness, a granted wish, a
love affair or a philopena. And now and then in the blue
velvet of the bodice a hint of "slashes," in the Henri II style,
or in the gown of black satin a slight swelling which, if it was
in the sleeves, just below the shoulders, made one think of the
"leg of mutton" sleeves of 1830, or if, on the other hand, it
was beneath the skirt, of Louis XV "panniers," gave the dress
a just perceptible air of being a "fancy dress" costume and at
all events, by insinuating beneath the life of the present day a
vague reminiscence of the past, blended with the person of
Mme Swann the charm of certain heroines of history or romance. And if I were to draw her attention to this: "I don't
play golf," she would answer, "like so many of my friends.
So I should have no excuse for going about in *sweaters* as they
do."

In the confusion of her drawing-room, on her way from
showing out one visitor, or with a plateful of cakes to "tempt"
another, Mme Swann as she passed by me would take me aside
for a moment: "I've been specially charged by Gilberte to
invite you to luncheon the day after to-morrow. As I wasn't
sure of seeing you here, I was going to write to you if you
hadn't come." I continued to resist. And this resistance was
costing me gradually less and less, because, however much we
may love the poison that is destroying us, when necessity
has deprived us of it for some time past, we cannot help
attaching a certain value to the peace of mind which we had
ceased to know, to the absence of emotion and suffering. If
we are not altogether sincere in telling ourselves that we never
wish to see the one we love again, we would not be a whit
more sincere in saying that we do. For no doubt we can endure
her absence only by promising ourselves that it will not be
for long, and thinking of the day when we shall see her again,
but at the same time we feel how much less painful are those
daily recurring dreams of an imminent and constantly postponed meeting than would be an interview which might be
followed by a spasm of jealousy, with the result that the news
that we are shortly to see her would create a disagreeable

turmoil in our mind. What we now put off from day to day
is no longer the end of the intolerable anxiety caused by separation, it is the dreaded renewal of emotions which can lead to
nothing. How infinitely we prefer to any such interview the
docile memory which we can supplement at will with dreams
in which she who in reality does not love us seems, on the
contrary, to be making protestations of her love, when we are
all alone! How infinitely we prefer that memory which, by
blending gradually with it a great deal of what we desire, we
can contrive to make as sweet as we choose, to the deferred
interview in which we would have to deal with a person to
whom we could no longer dictate at will the words that we
want to hear on her lips, but from whom we can expect to
meet with new coldness, unforeseen aggressions! We know,
all of us, when we no longer love, that forgetfulness, or even
a vague memory, does not cause us so much suffering as an ill-
starred love. It was the reposeful tranquillity of such forgetfulness that in anticipation I preferred, without acknowledging it
to myself.

Moreover, however painful such a course of psychical detachment and isolation may be, it grows steadily less so for
another reason, namely that it weakens while it is in process
of healing that fixed obsession which is a state of love. Mine
was still strong enough for me to wish to recapture my old
position in Gilberte's estimation, which in view of my voluntary abstention must, it seemed to me, be steadily increasing,
so that each of those calm and melancholy days on which I did
not see her, coming one after the other without interruption,
continuing too without prescription (unless some busy-body
were to meddle in my affairs), was a day not lost but gained.
Gained to no purpose, perhaps, for presently I might be pronounced cured. Resignation, modulating our habits, allows
certain elements of our strength to be indefinitely increased.
Those—so wretchedly inadequate—that I had had to support
my grief, on the first evening of my rupture with Gilberte, had
since multiplied to an incalculable power. Only, the tendency
of everything that exists to prolong its own existence is sometimes interrupted by sudden impulses to which we allow
ourselves to surrender with all the fewer qualms because we

know for how many days, for how many months even, we
have been able, and might still be able to abstain. And often
it is when the purse in which we hoard our savings is nearly
full that we suddenly empty it, it is without waiting for the
result of our treatment and when we have succeeded in growing accustomed to it that we abandon it. And so, one day,
when Mme Swann repeated her familiar words about the
pleasure it would be to Gilberte to see me, thus putting the
happiness of which I had now for so long been depriving myself as it were within arm's reach, I was stupefied by the realisation that it was still possible for me to enjoy it; and I could
hardly wait until next day; for I had made up my mind to
pay a surprise visit to Gilberte before her dinner.

What helped me to remain patient throughout the long day
that followed was a little plan that I made. As soon as everything was forgotten, as soon as I was reconciled with Gilberte,
I no longer wished to visit her save as a lover. Every day she
would receive from me the finest flowers that grew. And if
Mme Swann, although she had no right to be too severe a
mother, should forbid my making a daily offering of flowers, I
should find other gifts, more precious and less frequent. My
parents did not give me enough money for me to be able to
buy expensive things. I thought of a big vase of old Chinese
porcelain which had been left to me by Aunt Léonie, and of
which Mamma prophesied daily that Françoise would come to
her and say "Oh, it's all come to pieces!" and that would be
the end of it. Would it not be wiser, in that case, to part with
it, to sell it so as to be able to give Gilberte all the pleasure I
could. I felt sure that I could easily get a thousand francs for
it. I had it wrapped up; I had grown so used to it that I had
ceased altogether to notice it: parting with it had at least the
advantage of making me realise what it was like. I took it
with me on my way to the Swanns', and, giving the driver their
address, told him to go by the Champs-Elysées, at one end of
which was the shop of a big dealer in oriental objects whom my
father knew. Greatly to my surprise he offered me there and
then not one thousand but ten thousand francs for the vase.
I took the notes with rapture: every day, for a whole year, I
could smother Gilberte in roses and lilac. When I left the shop

and got back into the carriage the driver (naturally enough, since the Swanns lived out by the Bois) instead of taking the ordinary way began to drive along the Avenue des Champs-Elysées. He had just passed the corner of the Rue de Berri when, in the failing light, I thought I saw, close to the Swanns' house but going in the other direction, away from it, Gilberte, who was walking slowly, though with a firm step, by the side of a young man with whom she was conversing and whose face I could not distinguish. I stood up in the cab, meaning to tell the driver to stop; then hesitated. The strolling couple were already some way away, and the two parallel lines which their leisurely progress was quietly drawing were on the verge of disappearing in the Elysian gloom. A moment later, I had reached Gilberte's door. I was received by Mme Swann. "Oh! she will be sorry!" was my greeting, "I can't think why she isn't in. But she was complaining of the heat just now after a lesson, and said she might go out for a breath of fresh air with one of her girl friends." "I thought I saw her in the Avenue des Champs-Elysées." "Oh, I don't think it can have been her. Anyhow, don't mention it to her father; he doesn't approve of her going out at this time of night. Must you go? *Good-bye*." I left her, told my driver to go back the same way, but found no trace of the two walkers. Where had they been? What were they saying to one another in the darkness with that confidential air?

I returned home, despairingly clutching my windfall of ten thousand francs, which would have enabled me to arrange so many pleasant surprises for that Gilberte whom now I had made up my mind never to see again. No doubt my call at the dealer's had brought me happiness by allowing me to hope that in future, whenever I saw my beloved, she would be pleased with me and grateful. But if I had not called there, if the carriage had not taken the Avenue des Champs-Elysées, I should not have seen Gilberte with that young man. Thus a single action may have two contradictory effects, and the misfortune that it engenders cancel the good fortune it had brought one. What had happened to me was the opposite of what so frequently occurs. We desire some pleasure, and the material means of obtaining it are lacking. "It is sad,"

La Bruyère tells us, "to love without an ample fortune." There is nothing for it but to try to eradicate little by little our desire for that pleasure. In my case, however, the material means had been forthcoming, but at the same moment, if not by a logical effect, at any rate as a fortuitous consequence of that initial success, my pleasure had been snatched from me. As, for that matter, it seems as though it must always be. As a rule, however, not on the same evening as we have acquired what makes it possible. Usually, we continue to struggle and hope for a little longer. But happiness can never be achieved. If we succeed in overcoming the force of circumstances, nature at once shifts the battle-ground, placing it within ourselves, and effects a gradual change in our hearts until they desire something other than what they are about to possess. And if the change of fortune has been so rapid that our hearts have not had time to change, nature does not on that account despair of conquering us, in a manner more gradual, it is true, more subtle, but no less efficacious. It is then at the last moment that the possession of our happiness is wrested from us, or rather it is that very possession which nature, with diabolical cunning, uses to destroy our happiness. Having failed in everything related to the sphere of life and action, it is a final impossibility, the psychological impossibility of happiness, that nature creates. The phenomenon of happiness either fails to appear, or at once gives rise to the bitterest reactions.

I put my ten thousand francs in a drawer. But they were no longer of any use to me. I ran through them, as it happened, even more rapidly than if I had sent flowers every day to Gilberte, for when evening came I was always too wretched to stay at home and went to drown my sorrows in the arms of women whom I did not love. As for seeking to give any sort of pleasure to Gilberte, I no longer thought of that; to visit her house again now could only give me pain. Even the sight of Gilberte, which would have been so exquisite a pleasure only yesterday, would no longer have sufficed me. For I should have been anxious all the time that I was not actually with her. That is how a woman, by every fresh torture that she inflicts on us, often quite unwittingly, increases her power over us and at the same time our demands upon her. With each injury that she does us, she encircles us more and more completely, redoubles our chains, but also those which hitherto we had thought adequate to bind her in order to keep our minds at rest. Only yesterday, had I not been afraid of annoying Gilberte, I should have been content to ask for no more than occasional meetings, which now would no longer have sufficed me and for which I should now have substituted quite different terms. For in this respect love is not like war; after each battle we renew the fight with keener ardour, which we never cease to intensify the more thoroughly we are defeated, provided always that we are still in a position to give battle. This was not my case with regard to Gilberte. Hence I preferred at first not to return to her mother's house. I continued, it is true, to assure myself that Gilberte did not love me, that I had known this for some time, that I could see her again if I chose, and, if I did not choose, forget her in the long run. But these ideas, like a remedy which has no effect upon certain complaints, had no power whatsoever to obliterate those two parallel lines which I kept on seeing, traced by Gilberte and the young man as they slowly disappeared along the Avenue des Champs-Elysées. This was a new malady, which like the rest would gradually lose its force, a fresh image which would one day present itself to my mind's eye completely purged of every noxious element that it now contained, like those deadly poisons which one can handle without danger, or like a crumb of dynamite which one can use to light one's cigarette without fear of an explosion. Meanwhile there was in me another force which strove with all its might to overpower that unwholesome force which still showed me, without alteration, the figure of Gilberte walking in the dusk: to meet and to break the shock of the renewed assaults of memory, I had, toiling effectively in the opposite direction, imagination. The first of these two forces did indeed continue to show me that couple walking in the Champs-Elysées, and offered me other disagreeable pictures drawn from the past, as for instance Gilberte shrugging her shoulders when her mother asked her to stay and entertain me. But the second force, working upon the canvas of my hopes, outlined a future far more attractively developed than this meagre past which

was on the whole so restricted. For one minute in which I saw
Gilberte's sullen face, how many were there in which I devised
steps she might take with a view to our reconciliation, perhaps
even to our engagement! It is true that this force, which
my imagination was focusing upon the future, it drew, after
all, from the past. As my vexation at Gilberte's having
shrugged her shoulders gradually faded, the memory of her
charm, a memory that made me wish for her to return to me,
would diminish too. But I was still a long way from such a
death of the past. I was still in love with her, even though I
believed that I detested her. Whenever anyone told me that I was
looking well, or was nicely dressed, I wished that she could
have been there to see me. I was irritated by the desire that
many people showed about this time to ask me to their houses,
and refused all their invitations. There was a scene at home
because I did not accompany my father to an official dinner at
which the Bontemps were to be present with their niece
Albertine, a young girl still hardly more than a child. So it is
that the different periods of our lives overlap one another. We
scornfully decline, because of one whom we love and who will
some day be of so little account, to see another who is of no
account to-day, whom we shall love to-morrow, whom we
might perhaps, had we consented to see her now, have loved
a little sooner and who would thus have put an end to our
present sufferings, bringing others, it is true, in their place.
Mine were steadily growing less. I was amazed to observe
deep down inside me, one sentiment one day, another the
next, generally inspired by some hope or some fear relative to
Gilberte. To the Gilberte whom I carried within me. I ought
to have reminded myself that the other, the real Gilberte, was
perhaps entirely different from mine, knew nothing of the
regrets that I ascribed to her, thought probably much less about
me, not merely than I thought about her but than I made her
think about me when I was closeted alone with my fictitious
Gilberte, wondering what really were her feelings towards me,
and imagining her thus, her attention as constantly directed
towards myself.

During those periods in which grief and bitterness of spirit,
though steadily diminishing, still persist, a distinction must

be drawn between the pain which comes to us from the constant thought of the beloved herself and that which is revived by certain memories, some cruel remark, some verb used in a letter that we have had from her. Pending the description, in the context of another and later love affair, of the various forms that pain can assume, suffice it to say that, of these two kinds, the former is infinitely the less cruel. That is because our conception of the person, still living within us, is there adorned with the halo with which we are bound before long to invest her, and is imprinted if not with the frequent solace of hope, at any rate with the tranquillity of a permanent sadness. (It must also be observed that the image of a person who makes us suffer counts for little in those complications which aggravate the unhappiness of love, prolong it and prevent our recovery, just as in certain maladies the cause is out of proportion to the fever which follows it and the slowness of the process of convalescence.) But if the idea of the person we love is reflected in the light of an intelligence that is on the whole optimistic, the same is not true of those particular memories, those cruel remarks, that hostile letter (I received only one that could be so described from Gilberte); it is as though the person herself dwelt in those fragments, however limited, multiplied to a power which she is far from possessing in the habitual image we form of her as a whole. Because the letter has not—as the image of the loved one has— been contemplated by us in the melancholy calm of regret; we have read it, devoured it in the fearful anguish with which we were wrung by an unforeseen misfortune. Sorrows of this sort come to us in another way—from without—and it is by way of the most cruel suffering that they have penetrated to our hearts. The picture of the beloved in our minds which we believe to be old, original, authentic, has in reality been refashioned by us many times over. The cruel memory, on the other hand, is not contemporaneous with the restored picture, it is of another age, it is one of the rare witnesses to a monstrous past. But inasmuch as this past continues to exist, save in ourselves who have been pleased to substitute for it a miraculous golden age, a paradise in which all mankind shall be reconciled, those memories, those letters carry us back to reality, and cannot but make us feel, by the sudden pang they give us, what a long way we have been borne from that reality by the baseless hopes engendered by our daily expectation. Not that the said reality is bound always to remain the same, though that does indeed happen at times. There are in our lives any number of women whom we have never sought to see again, and who have quite naturally responded to our in no way calculated silence with a silence as profound. Only in their case, since we never loved them, we have never counted the years spent apart from them, and this instance, which would invalidate our whole argument, we are inclined to forget when we consider the healing effect of isolation, just as people who believe in presentiments forget all the occasions on which their own have not "come true."

But after a time, absence may prove efficacious. The desire, the appetite for seeing us again may after all be reborn in the heart which at present contemns us. Only, we must allow time. But our demands as far as time is concerned are no less exorbitant than those which the heart requires in order to change. For one thing, time is the very thing that we are least willing to allow, for our suffering is acute and we are anxious to see it brought to an end. And then, too, the time which the other heart will need in order to change will have been spent by our own heart in changing itself too, so that when the goal we had set ourselves becomes attainable it will have ceased to be our goal. Besides, the very idea that it will be attainable, that there is no happiness that, when it has ceased to be a happiness for us, we cannot ultimately attain, contains an element, but only an element, of truth. It falls to us when we have grown indifferent to it. But the very fact of our indifference will have made us less exacting, and enabled us in retrospect to feel convinced that it would have delighted us had it come at a time when perhaps it would have seemed to us miserably inadequate. One is not very particular, nor a very good judge, about things which no longer matter to one. The friendly overtures of a person whom we no longer love, overtures which in our indifference strike us as excessive, would perhaps have fallen a long way short of satisfying our love. Those tender words, that offer to meet us, we think only of the

pleasure which they would have given us, and not of all those
other words and meetings by which we should have wished
to see them immediately followed, and which by this greed of
ours we might perhaps have prevented from ever happening.
So that we can never be certain that the happiness which
comes to us too late, when we can no longer enjoy it, when we
are no longer in love, is altogether the same as that same
happiness the lack of which made us at one time so unhappy.
There is only one person who could decide this—our then
self; it is no longer with us, and were it to reappear, no doubt
our happiness—identical or not—would vanish.

Pending these belated fulfilments of a dream about which I
should by then have ceased to care, by dint of inventing, as
in the days when I still hardly knew Gilberte, words or letters
in which she implored my forgiveness, swore that she had
never loved anyone but myself and besought me to marry her,
a series of pleasant images incessantly renewed came by degrees
to hold a larger place in my mind than the vision of Gilberte
and the young man, which had nothing now to feed upon. At
this point I should perhaps have resumed my visits to Mme
Swann but for a dream I had in which one of my friends, who
was not, however, one that I could identify, behaved with the
utmost treachery towards me and appeared to believe that I
had been treacherous to him. Abruptly awakened by the pain
which this dream had caused me, and finding that it persisted
after I was awake, I turned my thoughts back to the dream,
racked my brains to remember who the friend was that I had
seen in my sleep and whose name—a Spanish name—was no
longer distinct. Combining Joseph's part with Pharaoh's, I set
to work to interpret my dream. I knew that in many cases it is
a mistake to pay too much attention to the appearance of the
people one saw in one's dream, who may perhaps have been
disguised or have exchanged faces, like those mutilated saints
in cathedrals which ignorant archaeologists have restored,
fitting the head of one to the body of another and jumbling all
their attributes and names. Those that people bear in a dream
are apt to mislead us. The person whom we love is to be
recognised only by the intensity of the pain that we suffer.
From mine I learned that, transformed while I was asleep into

a young man, the person whose recent betrayal still hurt me was Gilberte. I remembered then that, the last time I had seen her, on the day when her mother had forbidden her to go out to a dancing-lesson, she had, whether in sincerity or in pretence, declined, laughing in a strange manner, to believe in the genuineness of my feelings for her. And by association this memory brought back to me another. Long before that, it was Swann who had not wished to believe in my sincerity, or that I was a suitable friend for Gilberte. In vain had I written to him, Gilberte had brought back my letter and had returned it to me with the same incomprehensible laugh. She had not returned it to me at once: I remembered now the whole of that scene behind the clump of laurels. One becomes moral as soon as one is unhappy. Gilberte's present antipathy for me seemed to me a punishment meted out to me by life for my conduct that afternoon. One thinks one can escape such punishments because one is careful when crossing the street, and avoids obvious dangers. But there are others that take effect within us. The accident comes from the direction one least expected, from inside, from the heart. Gilberte's words: "If you like, we might go on wrestling," made me shudder. I imagined her behaving like that, at home perhaps, in the linen-room, with the young man whom I had seen escorting her along the Avenue des Champs-Elysées. And so, just as much as to believe (as I had a little time back) that I was calmly established in a state of happiness, it had been foolish in me, now that I had abandoned all thought of happiness, to take it for granted that at least I had become and would be able to remain calm. For, so long as our heart keeps enshrined with any permanence the image of another person, it is not only our happiness that may at any moment be destroyed; when that happiness has vanished, when we have suffered and then succeeded in anaesthetising our sufferings, the thing then that is as elusive, as precarious as ever our happiness was, is calm. Mine returned to me in the end, for the cloud which, affecting one's spirits, one's desires, has entered one's mind under cover of a dream, will also in course of time dissolve: permanence and stability being assured to nothing in this world, not even to grief. Besides, those who suffer through love are, as we say of certain invalids, their own physicians. Since consolation can come to them only from the person who is the cause of their grief, and since their grief is an emanation from that person, it is in their grief itself that they must in the end find a remedy: which it will disclose to them at a given moment, for the longer they turn it over in their minds, this grief will continue to show them fresh aspects of the loved, the regretted person, at one moment so intensely hateful that one has no longer the slightest desire to see her since before finding enjoyment in her company one would have to make her suffer, at another so sweet and gentle that one gives her credit for the virtue one attributes to her, and finds in it a fresh reason for hope. But even though the anguish that had re-awakened in me did at length subside, I no longer wished—except rarely— to visit Mme Swann. In the first place because, in those who love and have been forsaken, the state of incessant—even if unconfessed—expectancy in which they live undergoes a spontaneous transformation, and, while to all appearances unchanged, substitutes for its original state a second that is precisely the opposite. The first was the consequence, the reflection of the painful incidents which had upset us. Expectation of what may happen is mingled with fear, all the more since we desire at that moment, should we hear nothing new from the loved one, to act ourselves, and are none too confident of the success of a step which, once we have taken it, we may find it impossible to follow up. But presently, without our having noticed any change, expectation, which still endures, is sustained, we discover, no longer by our recollection of the painful past but by anticipation of an imaginary future. From then on, it is almost pleasant. Besides, the first state, by continuing for some time, has accustomed us to living in expectation. The pain we felt during those last meetings survives in us still, but is already lulled to sleep. We are in no hurry to arouse it, especially as we do not see very clearly what to ask for now. The possession of a little more of the woman we love would only make more necessary to us the part that we do not possess, which would inevitably remain, in spite of everything, since our requirements are begotten of our satisfactions, an irreducible quantity.

Another, final reason came later on to reinforce this, and to make me discontinue altogether my visits to Mme Swann. This reason, slow in revealing itself, was not that I had yet forgotten Gilberte but that I must make every effort to forget her as speedily as possible. No doubt, now that the keen edge of my suffering was dulled, my visits to Mme Swann had become once again, for the residue of my sadness, the sedative and distraction which had been so precious to me at first. But the reason for the efficacy of the former was the drawback of the latter, namely that with these visits the memory of Gilberte was intimately blended. The distraction would be of no avail to me unless it set up, in opposition to a feeling no longer nourished by Gilberte's presence, thoughts, interests, passions in which Gilberte had no part. These states of consciousness to which the person whom we love remains a stranger then occupy a place which, however small it may be at first, is always that much reconquered from the love that had been in unchallenged possession of our whole soul. We must seek to encourage these thoughts, to make them grow, while the sentiment which is no more now than a memory dwindles, so that the new elements introduced into the mind contest with that sentiment, wrest from it an ever-increasing portion of our soul, until at last the victory is complete. I realised that this was the only way in which my love could be killed, and I was still young enough and brave enough to undertake the attempt, to subject myself to that most cruel grief which springs from the certainty that, however long it may take us, we shall succeed in the end. The reason I now gave in my letters to Gilberte for refusing to see her was an allusion to some mysterious misunderstanding, wholly fictitious, which was supposed to have arisen between her and myself, and as to which I had hoped at first that Gilberte would demand an explanation. But, in fact, never, even in the most insignificant relations in life, does a request for enlightenment come from a correspondent who knows that an obscure, untruthful, incriminating sentence has been introduced on purpose, so that he shall protest against it; he is only too happy to feel thereby that he possesses—and to keep in his own hands—the initiative in the matter. All the more so is this true in our more tender relations, in which love is endowed with so much eloquence, indifference with so little curiosity. Gilberte never having questioned or sought to learn about this misunderstanding, it became for me a real entity, to which I referred anew in every letter. And there is in these baseless situations, in the affectation of coldness, a sort of fascination which tempts one to persevere in them. By dint of writing: "Now that our hearts are sundered," so that Gilberte might answer: "But they're not. Do let's talk it over," I had gradually come to believe that they were. By constantly repeating, "Life may have changed for us, but it will never destroy the feeling that we had for one another," in the hope of at last hearing the answer: "But there has been no change, the feeling is stronger now than it ever was," I was living with the idea that life had indeed changed, that we should keep the memory of the feeling which no longer existed, as certain neurotics, from having at first pretended to be ill, end by becoming chronic invalids. Now, whenever I had to write to Gilberte, I brought my mind back to this imagined change, which, being now tacitly admitted by the silence which she preserved with regard to it in her replies, would in future subsist between us. Then Gilberte ceased to confine herself to preterition. She too adopted my point of view; and, as in the speeches at official banquets, when the Head of State who is being entertained adopts more or less the same expressions as have just been used by the Head of State who is entertaining him, whenever I wrote to Gilberte: "Life may have parted us, but the memory of the days when we knew one another will endure," she never failed to respond: "Life may have parted us, but it cannot make us forget those happy hours which will always be dear to us both" (though we should have found it hard to say why or how "Life" had parted us, or what change had occurred). My sufferings were no longer excessive. And yet, one day when I was telling her in a letter that I had heard of the death of our old barley-sugar woman in the Champs-Elysées, as I wrote the words: "I felt that this would grieve you; in me it awakened a host of memories," I could not restrain myself from bursting into tears when I saw that I was speaking in the past tense, as though it were of some dead friend, now almost forgotten, of that love of which in

spite of myself I had never ceased to think as something still
alive, or at least capable of reviving. Nothing could have been
more tender than this correspondence between friends who
did not wish to see one another any more. Gilberte's letters to
me had all the delicacy of those which I used to write to people
who did not matter to me, and showed me the same apparent
marks of affection, which it was so soothing for me to receive
from her.

But, as time went on, every refusal to see her grieved me
less. And as she became less dear to me, my painful memories
were no longer strong enough to destroy by their incessant
return the growing pleasure which I found in thinking of
Florence or of Venice. I regretted, at such moments, that I
had abandoned the idea of diplomacy and had condemned
myself to a sedentary existence, in order not to be separated
from a girl whom I should never see again and had already
almost forgotten. We construct our lives for one person, and
when at length it is ready to receive her that person does not
come; presently she is dead to us, and we live on, prisoners
within the walls which were intended only for her. If Venice
seemed to my parents to be too far away and its climate too
treacherous for me, it would be at least quite easy and not too
tiring to go and settle down at Balbec. But to do that I should
have had to leave Paris, to forgo those visits thanks to which,
infrequent as they were, I might sometimes hear Mme Swann
talk to me about her daughter. Besides, I was beginning to find
in them various pleasures in which Gilberte had no part.

When spring arrived, and with it the cold weather, during
an icy Lent and the hailstorms of Holy Week, as Mme Swann
declared that it was freezing in her house, I used often to see
her entertaining her guests in her furs, her shivering hands and
shoulders buried beneath the gleaming white carpets of an immense rectangular muff and a cape, both of ermine, which she
had not taken off on coming in from her drive, and which
suggested the last patches of the snows of winter, more persistent than the rest, which neither the heat of the fire nor the
advancing season had succeeded in melting. And the all-
embracing truth about these glacial but already flowering weeks
was suggested to me in this drawing-room, which soon I

should be entering no more, by other more intoxicating forms
of whiteness, that for example of the guelder-roses clustering,
at the summits of their tall bare stalks, like the rectilinear
trees in pre-Raphaelite paintings, their balls of blossom, divided
yet composite, white as annunciating angels and exhaling a
fragrance as of lemons. For the mistress of Tansonville knew
that April, even an ice-bound April, is not barren of flowers,
that winter, spring, summer are not held apart by barriers as
hermetic as might be supposed by the town-dweller who, until
the first hot day, imagines the world as containing nothing but
houses that stand naked in the rain. That Mme Swann was
content with the consignments furnished by her Combray
gardener, that she did not, through the medium of her own
"regular" florist, fill the gaps in an inadequate display with
borrowings from a precocious Mediterranean shore, I do not
for a moment suggest, nor did it worry me at the time. It was
enough to fill me with longing for country scenes that, over-
hanging the loose snowdrifts of the muff in which Mme Swann
kept her hands, the guelder-rose snow-balls (which served
very possibly in the mind of my hostess no other purpose than
to compose, on the advice of Bergotte, a "Symphony in
White" with her furniture and her garments) should remind
me that the Good Friday music in *Parsifal* symbolises a
natural miracle which one could see performed every year if
one had the sense to look for it, and, assisted by the acid and
heady perfume of other kinds of blossom which, although their
names were unknown to me, had brought me so often to a
standstill on my walks round Combray, should make Mme
Swann's drawing-room as virginal, as candidly in blossom
without the least trace of verdure, as overladen with genuine
scents of flowers, as was the little lane by Tansonville.

But it was still too much for me that these memories should
be revived. There was a risk of their fostering what little remained of my love for Gilberte. And so, though I no longer
felt the least distress during these visits to Mme Swann, I
spaced them out even more and endeavoured to see as little of
her as possible. At most, since I continued not to go out of
Paris, I allowed myself an occasional walk with her. The fine
weather had come at last, and the sun was hot. As I knew that

before luncheon Mme Swann used to go out every day for an
hour's stroll in the Avenue du Bois, near the Etoile—a spot
which at that time, because of the people who used to collect
there to gaze at the "swells" whom they knew only by name,
was known as the "Down-and-outs Club"—I persuaded my
parents, on Sunday (for on weekdays I was busy all morning)
to let me postpone my lunch until long after theirs, until a
quarter past one, and go for a walk before it. During that
month of May I never missed a Sunday, Gilberte having gone
to stay with friends in the country. I used to arrive at the
Arc-de-Triomphe about noon. I kept watch at the entrance to
the Avenue, never taking my eyes off the corner of the side-
street along which Mme Swann, who had only a few yards to
walk, would come from her house. Since by this time many of
the people who had been strolling there were going home to
lunch, those who remained were few in number and, for the
most part, fashionably dressed. Suddenly, on the gravelled
path, unhurrying, cool, luxuriant, Mme Swann would appear,
blossoming out in a costume which was never twice the same
but which I remember as being typically mauve; then she
would hoist and unfurl at the end of its long stalk, just at the
moment when her radiance was at its zenith, the silken banner
of a wide parasol of a shade that matched the showering petals
of her dress. A whole troop of people escorted her; Swann
himself, four or five clubmen who had been to call upon her
that morning or whom she had met in the street: and their
black or grey agglomeration, obedient to her every gesture,
performing the almost mechanical movements of a lifeless
setting in which Odette was framed, gave to this woman, in
whose eyes alone was there any intensity, the air of looking out
in front of her, from among all those men, as from a window
behind which she had taken her stand, and made her loom
there, frail but fearless, in the nudity of her delicate colours,
like the apparition of a creature of a different species, of an
unknown race, and of almost martial power, by virtue of which
she seemed by herself a match for all her multiple escort.
Smiling, rejoicing in the fine weather, in the sunshine which
had not yet become trying, with the air of calm assurance
of a creator who has accomplished his task and takes no

thought for anything besides, certain that her clothes—even
though the vulgar herd should fail to appreciate them—were
the most elegant of all, wearing them for herself and for her
friends, naturally, without exaggerated attention to them but
also without absolute detachment, not preventing the little
bows of ribbon on her bodice and skirt from floating buoyantly
upon the air before her like creatures of whose presence she
was not unaware and whom she indulgently permitted to disport themselves in accordance with their own rhythm, provided that they followed where she led, and even upon her
mauve parasol, which, as often as not, she still held closed
when she appeared on the scene, letting fall now and then, as
though upon a bunch of Parma violets, her happy gaze, so
kindly that, when it was fastened no longer upon her friends
but on some inanimate object, still seemed to smile. She thus
reserved, kept open for her wardrobe, this interval of elegance
of which the men with whom she was on the most familiar
terms respected both the extent and the necessity, not without
a certain deference, as of profane visitors to a shrine, an
admission of their own ignorance, and over which they
acknowledged (as to an invalid over the special precautions that
he has to take, or a mother over the bringing up of her children)
their friend's competence and jurisdiction. No less than by the
court which encircled her and seemed not to observe the
passers-by, Mme Swann, by the belatedness of her appearance,
evoked those rooms in which she had spent so long, so leisurely
a morning and to which she must presently return for luncheon; she seemed to indicate their proximity by the sauntering
ease of her progress, like the stroll one takes up and down
one's own garden; of those rooms one would have said that
she carried about her still the cool, the indoor shade. But for
that very reason the sight of her made me feel the more strongly
a sensation of open air and warmth—all the more so because,
already persuaded as I was that, by virtue of the liturgy and
ritual in which Mme Swann was so profoundly versed, her
clothes were connected with the season and the hour by a
bond both necessary and unique, the flowers on the flexible
straw brim of her hat, the ribbons on her dress, seemed to me
to spring from the month of May even more naturally than

the flowers of garden or woodland; and to learn what latest
change there was in weather or season, I did not raise my eyes
higher than to her parasol, open and outstretched like another,
a nearer sky, round, clement, mobile and blue. For these rites,
sovereign though they were, subjugated their glory (and,
consequently, Mme Swann her own) in condescending obedience to the day, the spring, the sun, none of which struck
me as being sufficiently flattered that so elegant a woman had
deigned not to ignore their existence, and had chosen on their
account a dress of a brighter, thinner fabric, suggesting to me,
by a splaying at the collar and sleeves, the moist warmness of
the throat and wrists that they exposed,—in a word, had taken
for them all the pains of a great lady who, having gaily condescended to pay a visit to common folk in the country, and
whom everyone, even the most plebeian, knows, yet makes a
point of donning for the occasion suitably pastoral attire. On
her arrival I would greet Mme Swann, and she would stop
me and say (in English) *"Good morning"* with a smile. We would
walk a little way together. And I realised that it was for
herself that she obeyed these canons in accordance with which
she dressed, as though yielding to a superior wisdom of
which she herself was the high priestess: for if it should happen
that, feeling too warm, she threw open or even took off altogether and gave me to carry the jacket which she had intended to keep buttoned up, I would discover in the blouse
beneath it a thousand details of execution which had had every
chance of remaining unobserved, like those parts of an orchestral score to which the composer has devoted infinite labour
although they may never reach the ears of the public: or, in the
sleeves of the jacket that lay folded across my arm I would see,
and would lengthily gaze at, for my own pleasure or from
affection for its wearer, some exquisite detail, a deliciously
tinted strap, a lining of mauve satinette which, ordinarily concealed from every eye, was yet just as delicately fashioned as
the outer parts, like those Gothic carvings on a cathedral, hidden on the inside of a balustrade eighty feet from the ground,
as perfect as the bas-reliefs over the main porch, and yet never
seen by any living man until, happening to pass that way upon
his travels, an artist obtains leave to climb up there among

them, to stroll in the open air, overlooking the whole town, between the soaring towers.

What enhanced this impression that Mme Swann walked in the Avenue du Bois as though along the paths of her own garden, was—for people ignorant of her habit of taking a "constitutional,"—the fact that she had come there on foot, without any carriage following, she whom, once May had begun, they were accustomed to see, behind the most brilliant "turn-out," the smartest liveries in Paris, indolently and majestically seated, like a goddess, in the balmy open air of an immense victoria on eight springs. On foot, Mme Swann had the appearance—especially when her step was slowed by the heat of the sun—of having yielded to curiosity, of committing an elegant breach of the rules of protocol, like those crowned heads who, without consulting anyone, accompanied by the slightly scandalised admiration of a suite which dares not venture any criticism, step out of their boxes during a gala performance and visit the lobby of the theatre, mingling for a moment or two with the rest of the audience. So between Mme Swann and themselves the crowd felt that there existed those barriers of a certain kind of opulence which seem to them the most insurmountable of all. The Faubourg Saint-Germain may have its barriers too, but these are less "meaningful" to the eyes and imagination of the "down-and-out." These latter, in the presence of an aristocratic lady who is simpler, more easily mistaken for an ordinary middle-class woman, less remote from the people, will not feel the same sense of inequality, almost of unworthiness, as they do before a Mme Swann. Of course women of this sort are not themselves dazzled, as the crowd are, by the splendour in which they are surrounded; they have ceased to pay any attention to it, but only because they have grown used to it, that is to say have come to look upon it more and more as natural and necessary, to judge their fellow creatures according as they are more or less initiated into these luxurious ways: so that (the grandeur which they allow themselves to display or discover in others being wholly material, easily verified, slowly acquired, the lack of it hard to compensate) if such women place a passer-by in the lowest rank, it is by the same process that has made them

appear to him as in the highest, that is to say instinctively, at
first sight, and without possibility of appeal. Perhaps that social
class which included in those days women like Lady Israels,
who mixed with the women of the aristocracy, and Mme
Swann, who was to get to know them later on, that intermediate class, inferior to the Faubourg Saint-Germain, since
it courted the latter, but superior to everything that was not of
the Faubourg Saint-Germain, possessing this peculiarity that,
while already detached from the world of the merely rich, it
was riches still that it represented, but riches that had become
ductile, obedient to a conscious artistic purpose, malleable
gold, chased with a poetic design and taught to smile; perhaps
that class—in the same form, at least, and with the same charm
—exists no longer. In any event, the women who were its
members would not satisfy to-day what was the primary condition on which they reigned, since with advancing age they
have lost—almost all of them—their beauty. Whereas it was
from the glorious zenith of her ripe and still so fragrant
summer as much as from the pinnacle of her noble wealth that
Mme Swann, majestic, smiling, benign, advancing along the
Avenue du Bois, saw, like Hypatia, worlds revolving beneath
the slow tread of her feet. Young men as they passed looked at
her anxiously, not knowing whether their vague acquaintance
with her (especially since, having been introduced only once,
at the most, to Swann, they were afraid that he might not
remember them) was sufficient excuse for their venturing to
doff their hats. And they trembled to think of the consequences as they made up their minds to do so, wondering
whether this audaciously provocative and sacrilegious gesture,
challenging the inviolable supremacy of a caste, would not let
loose the catastrophic forces of nature or bring down upon
them the vengeance of a jealous god. It provoked only, like
the winding of a piece of clockwork, a series of gesticulations
from little, bowing figures, who were none other than Odette's
escort, beginning with Swann himself, who raised his tall hat
lined in green leather with a smiling courtesy which he had
acquired in the Faubourg Saint-Germain but to which was
no longer wedded the indifference that he would at one time
have shown. Its place was now taken (for he had been to some

extent permeated by Odette's prejudices) at once by irritation
at having to acknowledge the salute of a person who was none
too well dressed and by satisfaction at his wife's knowing so
many people, a mixed sensation to which he gave expression
by saying to the smart friends who walked by his side: "What,
another one! Upon my word, I can't imagine where my wife
picks all these fellows up!" Meanwhile, having acknowledged
with a nod the greeting of some terrified young man who
had already passed out of sight though his heart was still
beating furiously, Mme Swann turned to me: "Then it's all
over?" she said. "You aren't ever coming to see Gilberte
again? I'm glad you make an exception of me, and are not
going to *drop* me completely. I like seeing you, but I also liked
the influence you had over my daughter. I'm sure she's very
sorry about it, too. However, I mustn't bully you, or you'll
make up your mind at once that you never want to set eyes on
me again." "Odette, there's Sagan saying good-day to you,"
Swann pointed out to his wife. And there indeed was the
Prince, as in some grand finale at the theatre or the circus or in
an old painting, wheeling his horse round so as to face her,
and doffing his hat with a sweeping theatrical and, as it were,
allegorical flourish in which he displayed all the chivalrous
courtesy of the great nobleman bowing in token of respect
for Womanhood, even if it was embodied in a woman whom it
was impossible for his mother or his sister to know. And in
fact at every turn, recognised in the depths of the liquid transparency and of the luminous glaze of the shadow which her
parasol cast over her, Mme Swann received the salutations of
the last belated horsemen, who passed as though filmed at the
gallop in the blinding glare of the Avenue, clubmen whose
names, those of celebrities for the public—Antoine de Castel-
lane, Adalbert de Montmorency and the rest—were for Mme
Swann the familiar names of friends. And as the average span
of life, the relative longevity of our memories of poetical
sensations is much greater than that of our memories of what
the heart has suffered, now that the sorrows that I once felt
on Gilberte's account have long since faded and vanished, there
has survived them the pleasure that I still derive—whenever I
close my eyes and read, as it were upon the face of a sundial,

the minutes that are recorded between a quarter past twelve and one o'clock in the month of May—from seeing myself once again strolling and talking thus with Mme Swann, beneath her parasol, as though in the coloured shade of a wistaria bower.

PLACE-NAMES:
THE PLACE

I HAD arrived at a state of almost complete indifference to Gilberte when, two years later, I went with my grandmother to Balbec. When I succumbed to the attraction of a new face, when it was with the help of some other girl that I hoped to discover the Gothic cathedrals, the palaces and gardens of Italy, I said to myself sadly that this love of ours, in so far as it is a love for one particular creature, is not perhaps a very real thing, since, though associations of pleasant or painful musings can attach it for a time to a woman to the extent of making us believe that it has been inspired by her in a logically necessary way, if on the other hand we detach ourselves deliberately or unconsciously from those associations, this love, as though it were in fact spontaneous and sprang from ourselves alone, will revive in order to bestow itself on another woman. At the time, however, of my departure for Balbec, and during the earlier part of my stay there, my indifference was still only intermittent. Often, our life being so careless of chronology, interpolating so many anachronisms into the sequence of our days, I found myself living in those—far older days than yesterday or last week—when I still loved Gilberte. And then no longer seeing her became suddenly painful, as it would have been at that time. The self that had loved her, which another self had already almost entirely supplanted, would reappear, stimulated far more often by a trivial than by an important event. For instance, if I may anticipate for a moment my arrival in Normandy, I heard someone who passed me on the sea-front at Balbec refer to "the head of the Ministry of Posts and his family." Now, since I as yet knew nothing of the influence which that family was to have on my life, this remark ought to have passed unheeded; instead, it gave me at once an acute twinge, which a self that had for the most part long since been outgrown in me felt at being parted from Gilberte. For I had never given another thought to a conversation which Gilberte had had with her father in my hearing, in which allusion was made to the Secretary to the Ministry of Posts and his family. Now the memories of love are no exception to the general laws of memory, which in turn are governed by the still more general laws of Habit. And as Habit weakens everything, what best reminds us of a person is precisely what we had forgotten (because it was of no importance, and we therefore left it in full possession of its strength). That is why the better part of our memories exists outside us, in a blatter of rain, in the smell of an unaired room or of the first crackling brushwood fire in a cold grate: wherever, in short, we happen upon what our mind, having no use for it, had rejected, the last treasure that the past has in store, the richest, that which, when all our flow of tears seems to have dried at the source, can make us weep again. Outside us? Within us, rather, but hidden from our eyes in an oblivion more or less prolonged. It is thanks to this oblivion alone that we can from time to time recover the person that we were, place ourselves in relation to things as he was placed, suffer anew because we are no longer ourselves but he, and because he loved what now leaves us indifferent. In the broad daylight of our habitual memory the images of the past turn gradually pale and fade out of sight, nothing remains of them, we shall never recapture it. Or rather we should never recapture it had not a few words (such as this "head of the Ministry of Posts") been carefully locked away in oblivion, just as an author deposits in the National Library a copy of a book which might otherwise become unobtainable.

But this pain and this recrudescence of my love for Gilberte lasted no longer than such things last in a dream, and this time, on the contrary, because at Balbec the old Habit was no longer there to keep them alive. And if these effects of Habit appear to be incompatible, that is because Habit is bound by a diversity of laws. In Paris I had grown more and more indifferent to Gilberte, thanks to Habit. The change of habit, that is to say the temporary cessation of Habit, completed Habit's work when I set out for Balbec. It weakens, but it stabilises; it leads to disintegration but it makes the scattered elements last indefinitely. Day after day, for years past, I had modelled my state of mind as best I could upon that of the day before. At Balbec a strange bed, to the side of which a tray was brought in the morning that differed from my Paris breakfast tray, could no longer sustain the thoughts upon which my love for Gilberte had fed: there are cases (fairly rare, it is true) where, one's days being paralysed by a sedentary life, the best way to gain time is to change one's place of residence. My journey to Balbec was like the first outing of a convalescent who needed only that to convince him that he was cured.

The journey was one that would now no doubt be made by motor-car, with a view to making it more agreeable. We shall see that, accomplished in such a way, it would even be in a sense more real, since one would be following more closely, in a more intimate contiguity, the various gradations by which the surface of the earth is diversified. But after all the specific attraction of a journey lies not in our being able to alight at places on the way and to stop altogether as soon as we grow tired, but in its making the difference between departure and arrival not as imperceptible but as intense as possible, so that we are conscious of it in its totality, intact, as it existed in us when our imagination bore us from the place in which we were living right to the very heart of a place we longed to see, in a single sweep which seemed miraculous to us not so much because it covered a certain distance as because it united two distinct individualities of the world, took us from one name to another name, and which is schematised (better than in a form of locomotion in which, since one can disembark where one chooses, there can scarcely be said to be any point of arrival) by the mysterious operation performed in those peculiar places, railway stations, which scarcely form part of the surrounding town but contain the essence of its personality just as upon their sign-boards they bear its painted name.

But in this respect as in every other, our age is infected with a mania for showing things only in the environment that properly belongs to them, thereby suppressing the essential thing, the act of the mind which isolated them from that environment. A picture is nowadays "presented" in the midst of furniture, ornaments, hangings of the same period, stale settings which the hostess who but yesterday was so crassly

ignorant but who now spends her time in archives and libraries
excels at composing in the houses of to-day, and in the midst
of which the masterpiece we contemplate as we dine does not
give us the exhilarating delight that we can expect from it
only in a public gallery, which symbolises far better, by its
bareness and by the absence of all irritating detail, those
innermost spaces into which the artist withdrew to create
it.

Unhappily those marvellous places, railway stations, from
which one sets out for a remote destination, are tragic places
also, for if in them the miracle is accomplished whereby scenes
which hitherto have had no existence save in our minds are
about to become the scenes among which we shall be living,
for that very reason we must, as we emerge from the waiting-
room, abandon any thought of presently finding ourselves once
more in the familiar room which but a moment ago still
housed us. We must lay aside all hope of going home to sleep
in our own bed, once we have decided to penetrate into the
pestiferous cavern through which we gain access to the
mystery, into one of those vast, glass-roofed sheds, like that of
Saint-Lazare into which I went to find the train for Balbec,
and which extended over the eviscerated city one of those
bleak and boundless ·skies, heavy with an accumulation of
dramatic menace, like certain skies painted with an almost
Parisian modernity by Mantegna or Veronese, beneath which
only some terrible and solemn act could be in process, such
as a departure by train or the erection of the Cross.

So long as I had been content to look out from the warmth
of my own bed in Paris at the Persian church of Balbec,
shrouded in driving sleet, no sort of objection to this journey
had been offered by my body. Its objections began only when
it realised that it would be of the party, and that on the evening
of my arrival I should be shown to "my" room which would
be unknown to it. Its revolt was all the more profound
in that on the very eve of my departure I learned that my
mother would not be coming with us, my father, who would
be kept busy at the Ministry until it was time for him to set off
for Spain with M. de Norpois, having preferred to take a
house in the neighbourhood of Paris. On the other hand, the

contemplation of Balbec seemed to me none the less desirable because I must purchase it at the price of a discomfort which, on the contrary, seemed to me to symbolise and to guarantee the reality of the impression which I was going there to seek, an impression which no allegedly equivalent spectacle, no "panorama" which I might have gone to see without being thereby precluded from returning home to sleep in my own bed, could possibly have replaced. It was not for the first time that I felt that those who love and those who enjoy are not always the same. I believed that I hankered after Balbec just as much as the doctor who was treating me and who said to me on the morning of our departure, surprised to see me looking so unhappy: "I don't mind telling you that if I could only manage a week to go down and get a blow by the sea, I shouldn't have to be asked twice. You'll be having races, regattas and I don't know what all!" But I had already learned the lesson—long before I was taken to see Berma—that, whatever it might be that I loved, it would never be attained, save at the end of a long and painful pursuit, in the course of which I should have first to sacrifice my pleasure to that paramount good instead of seeking it therein.

My grandmother, naturally enough, looked upon our exodus from a somewhat different point of view, and (anxious as ever that the presents which were made me should take some artistic form) had planned, in order to offer me a "print" of this journey that was at least partly "old," for us to repeat, partly by rail and partly by road, the itinerary that Mme de Sévigné had followed when she went from Paris to "L'Orient" by way of Chaulnes and "the Pont-Audemer." But my grandmother had been obliged to abandon this project at the instance of my father, who knew, whenever she organised any expedition with a view to extracting from it the utmost intellectual benefit that it was capable of yielding, what a tale there would be to tell of missed trains, lost luggage, sore throats and broken rules. She was free at least to rejoice in the thought that never, when the time came for us to sally forth to the beach, would we be exposed to the risk of being kept indoors by the sudden appearance of what her beloved Sévigné calls a "beast of a coachload," since we should know not a soul at Balbec,

Legrandin having refrained from offering us a letter of introduction to his sister. (This abstention had not been so well
appreciated by my aunts Céline and Flora, who, having known
that lady as a girl and always hitherto referred to her, to commemorate this early intimacy, as "Renée de Cambremer," and
having had from her and still possessing a number of those
little presents which continue to ornament a room or a conversation but to which the present reality no longer corresponds, imagined themselves to be avenging the insult by
never uttering the name of her daughter again, when they
called upon Mme Legrandin senior, confining themselves to
mutual congratulations, once they were safely out of the
house, such as: "I made no reference to you know whom. I
think it went home!")

And so we were simply to leave Paris by that 1.22 train
which I had too often beguiled myself by looking up in
the railway time-table, where it never failed to give me the
emotion, almost the illusion of departure, not to feel that
I already knew it. As the delineation in our minds of the
features of any form of happiness depends more on the nature
of the longings that it inspires in us than on the accuracy of the
information which we have about it, I felt that I already knew
this happiness in all its details, and had no doubt that I should
feel in my compartment a special delight as the day began to
cool, should contemplate this or that view as the train approached one or another station; so much so that this train,
which always brought to my mind's eye the images of the same
towns which I swathed in the light of those post-meridian
hours through which it sped, seemed to me to be different
from every other train; and I had ended—as we are apt to do
with a person whom we have never seen but whose friendship
we like to believe that we have won—by giving a distinct and
unalterable cast of countenance to the fair, artistic traveller
who would thus have taken me with him upon his journey,
and to whom I should bid farewell beneath the Cathedral of
Saint-Lô before he disappeared towards the setting sun.

As my grandmother could not bring herself to go "purely
and simply" to Balbec, she was to break the journey half-way,
staying the night with one of her friends, from whose house I

was to proceed the same evening, so as not to be in the way there and also in order that I might arrive by daylight and see Balbec church, which, we had learned, was at some distance from Balbec-Plage, and which I might not have a chance to visit later on, when I had begun my course of bathing. And perhaps it was less painful for me to feel that the admirable goal of my journey stood between me and that cruel first night on which I should have to enter a new habitation and consent to dwell there. But I had had first to leave the old; my mother had arranged to "move in" that very afternoon at Saint-Cloud, and had made, or pretended to make, all the arrangements for going there directly after she had seen us off at the station, without having to call again at our own house, to which she was afraid that I might otherwise feel impelled to return with her at the last moment, instead of going to Balbec. In fact, on the pretext of having so much to see to in the house which she had just taken and of being pressed for time, but in reality so as to spare me the cruel ordeal of a long-drawn parting, she had decided not to wait with us until the moment of the train's departure when, concealed amidst comings and goings and preparations that involve no final commitment, a separation suddenly looms up, impossible to endure when it is no longer possible to avoid, concentrated in its entirety in one enormous instant of impotent and supreme lucidity.

For the first time I began to feel that it was possible that my mother might live another kind of life, without me, otherwise than for me. She was going to live on her own with my father, whose existence it may have seemed to her that my ill-health, my nervous excitability, made somewhat complicated and gloomy. This separation made me all the more wretched because I told myself that for my mother it was probably the outcome of the successive disappointments which I had caused her, of which she had never said a word to me but which had made her realise the difficulty of our taking our holidays together; and perhaps also a preliminary trial for a form of existence to which she was beginning, now, to resign herself for the future, as the years crept on for my father and herself, an existence in which I should see less of her, in which (a thing that not even in my nightmares had yet been revealed

to me) she would already have become something of a stranger
to me, a lady who might be seen going home by herself to a
house in which I should not be, asking the concierge whether
there was a letter for her from me.

I could scarcely answer the porter who offered to take my
bag. My mother tried to comfort me by the methods which
seemed to her most efficacious. Thinking it useless to appear
not to notice my unhappiness, she gently teased me about it:
"Well, and what would Balbec church say if it knew that
people pulled long faces like that when they were going to see
it? Surely this is not the enraptured traveller Ruskin speaks of.
In any case I shall know if you have risen to the occasion, even
when we're miles apart I shall still be with my little man. You
shall have a letter to-morrow from your Mamma."

"My dear," said my grandmother, "I picture you like Mme
de Sévigné, your eyes glued to the map, and never losing sight
of us for an instant."

Then Mamma sought to distract me by asking what I
thought of having for dinner and drawing my attention to
Françoise, whom she complimented on a hat and coat which
she did not recognise, although they had horrified her long
ago when she first saw them, new, upon my great-aunt, the
one with an immense bird towering over it, the other decorated
with a hideous pattern and jet beads. But the cloak having
grown too shabby to wear, Françoise had had it turned,
exposing an "inside" of plain cloth and quite a good colour.
As for the bird, it had long since come to grief and been discarded. And just as it is disturbing, sometimes, to find the
effects which the most conscious artists have to strive for in a
folk-song or on the wall of some peasant's cottage where above
the door, at precisely the right spot in the composition, blooms
a white or yellow rose—so with the velvet band, the loop of
ribbon that would have delighted one in a portrait by Chardin
or Whistler, which Françoise had set with simple but unerring
taste upon the hat, which was now charming.

To take a parallel from an earlier age, the modesty and
integrity which often gave an air of nobility to the face of our
old servant having extended also to the clothes which, as a
discreet but by no means servile woman, who knew how to

hold her own and to keep her place, she had put on for the
journey so as to be fit to be seen in our company without at the
same time seeming or wishing to make herself conspicuous,
Françoise, in the faded cherry-coloured cloth of her coat and
the discreet nap of her fur collar, brought to mind one of those
miniatures of Anne of Brittany painted in Books of Hours by
an old master, in which everything is so exactly in the right
place, the sense of the whole is so evenly distributed throughout the parts, that the rich and obsolete singularity of the costume expresses the same pious gravity as the eyes, the lips and
the hands.

Of thought, in relation to Françoise, one could hardly speak.
She knew nothing, in that absolute sense in which to know
nothing means to understand nothing, save the rare truths to
which the heart is capable of directly attaining. The vast world
of ideas did not exist for her. But when one studied the clearness of her gaze, the delicate lines of the nose and the lips, all
those signs lacking from so many cultivated people in whom
they would have signified a supreme distinction, the noble detachment of a rare mind, one was disquieted, as one is by the
frank, intelligent eyes of a dog, to which nevertheless one
knows that all our human conceptions are alien, and one might
have been led to wonder whether there may not be, among
those other humbler brethren, the peasants, individuals who
are as it were the élite of the world of the simple-minded, or
rather who, condemned by an unjust fate to live among the
simple-minded, deprived of enlightenment and yet more
naturally, more essentially akin to the chosen spirits than most
educated people, are members as it were, dispersed, strayed,
robbed of their heritage of reason, of the sacred family, kinsfolk, left behind in infancy, of the loftiest minds, in whom—
as is apparent from the unmistakable light in their eyes, although it is applied to nothing—there has been lacking, to
endow them with talent, only the gift of knowledge.

My mother, seeing that I was having difficulty in keeping
back my tears, said to me: " 'Regulus was in the habit, when
things looked grave. . . .' Besides, it isn't very nice for your
Mamma! What does Mme de Sévigné say? Your grandmother
will tell you: 'I shall be obliged to draw upon all the courage

that you lack.' " And remembering that affection for another distracts one's attention from selfish griefs, she endeavoured to beguile me by telling me that she expected the removal to Saint-Cloud to go without a hitch, that she was pleased with the cab, which she had kept waiting, that the driver seemed civil and the seats comfortable. I made an effort to smile at these trifles, and bowed my head with an air of acquiescence and contentment. But they helped me only to picture to myself the more accurately Mamma's imminent departure, and it was with a heavy heart that I gazed at her as though she were already torn from me, beneath that wide-brimmed straw hat which she had bought to wear in the country, in a flimsy dress which she had put on in view of the long drive through the sweltering midday heat; hat and dress making her someone else, someone who belonged already to the Villa Montretout, in which I should not see her.

To prevent the suffocating fits which the journey might bring on, the doctor had advised me to take a stiff dose of beer or brandy at the moment of departure, so as to begin the journey in a state of what he called "euphoria," in which the nervous system is for a time less vulnerable. I had not yet made up my mind whether to do this, but I wished at least that my grandmother should acknowledge that, if I did so decide, I should have wisdom and authority on my side. I spoke about it therefore as if my hesitation were concerned only with where I should go for my drink, to the platform buffet or to the bar on the train. But immediately, at the air of reproach which my grandmother's face assumed, an air of not wishing even to entertain such an idea for a moment, "What!" I cried, suddenly resolving upon this action of going to get a drink, the performance of which became necessary as a proof of my independence since the verbal announcement of it had not succeeded in passing unchallenged, "What! You know how ill I am, you know what the doctor ordered, and you treat me like this!"

When I had explained to my grandmother how unwell I felt, her distress, her kindness were so apparent as she replied, "Run along then, quickly; get yourself some beer or a liqueur if it will do you good," that I flung myself upon her and smothered her with kisses. And if after that I went and drank a great deal too much in the bar of the train it was because I felt that otherwise I should have too violent an attack, which was what would distress her most. When at the first stop I clambered back into our compartment I told my grandmother how pleased I was to be going to Balbec, that I felt that everything would go off splendidly, that after all I should soon grow used to being without Mamma, that the train was most comfortable, the barman and the attendants so friendly that I should like to make the journey often so as to have the opportunity of seeing them again. My grandmother, however, did not appear to be quite so overjoyed at all these good tidings. She answered, without looking me in the face: "Why don't you try to get a little sleep?" and turned her eyes to the window, the blind of which, though we had lowered it, did not completely cover the glass, so that the sun could shed on the polished oak of the door and the cloth of the seat (like a far more persuasive advertisement for a life shared with nature than those hung high up on the wall of the compartment by the railway company, representing landscapes whose names I could not make out from where I sat) the same warm and slumbrous light which drowsed in the forest glades.

But when my grandmother thought that my eyes were shut I could see her now and again, from behind her spotted veil, steal a glance at me, then withdraw it, then look back again, like a person trying to make himself perform some exercise that hurts him in order to get into the habit.

Thereupon I spoke to her, but that did not seem to please her. And yet to myself the sound of my own voice was agreeable, as were the most imperceptible, the innermost movements of my body. And so I endeavoured to prolong them. I allowed each of my inflexions to linger lazily upon the words, I felt each glance from my eyes pause pleasurably on the spot where it came to rest and remain there beyond its normal time. "Now, now, sit still and rest," said my grandmother. "If you can't manage to sleep, read something." And she handed me a volume of Mme de Sévigné which I opened, while she buried herself in the *Mémoires de Madame de Beausergent*.[24] She never travelled anywhere without a volume of each. They were her two favourite authors. Unwilling to move my head for the moment, and experiencing the greatest pleasure from maintaining a position once I was in it, I sat holding the volume of Mme de Sévigné without looking at it, without even lowering my eyes, which were confronted with nothing but the blue window-blind. But the contemplation of this blind appeared to me an admirable thing, and I should not have troubled to answer anyone who might have sought to distract me from contemplating it. The blue of this blind seemed to me, not perhaps by its beauty but by its intense vividness, to efface so completely all the colours that had passed before my eyes from the day of my birth up to the moment when I had gulped down the last of my drink and it had begun to take effect, that compared with this blue they were as drab, as null, as the darkness in which he has lived must be in retrospect to a man born blind whom a subsequent operation has at length enabled to see and to distinguish colours. An old ticket-collector came to ask for our tickets. I was charmed by the silvery gleam that shone from the metal buttons of his tunic. I wanted to ask him to sit down beside us. But he passed on to the next carriage, and I thought with longing of the life led by railwaymen for whom, since they spent all their time on the line, hardly a day could pass without their seeing this old collector. The pleasure that I found in staring at the blind, and in feeling that my mouth was half-open, began at length to diminish. I became more mobile; I shifted in my seat; I opened the book that my grandmother had given me and turned its pages casually, reading whatever caught my eye. And as I read I felt my admiration for Mme de Sévigné grow.

One must not be taken in by purely formal characteristics, idioms of the period or social conventions, the effect of which is that certain people believe that they have caught the Sévigné manner when they have said: "Acquaint me, my dear," or "That count struck me as being a man of parts," or "Haymaking is the sweetest thing in the world." Mme de Simiane imagines already that she is being like her grandmother because she can write: "M. de la Boulie is bearing wonderfully, sir, and is in excellent condition to hear the news of his death," or "Oh, my dear Marquis, how your letter enchanted me! What can I do but answer it?" or "Meseems, sir, that you owe me a letter, and I owe you some boxes of bergamot. I discharge my debt to the number of eight; others shall follow. . . . Never has the soil borne so many—evidently for your gratification." And she writes in this style also her letter on bleeding, on lemons and so forth, supposing it to be typical of the letters of Mme de Sévigné. But my grandmother, who had come to the latter from within, from love of her family and of nature, had taught me to enjoy the real beauties of her correspondence, which are altogether different. They were soon to strike me all the more forcibly inasmuch as Mme de Sévigné is a great artist of the same family as a painter whom I was to meet at Balbec and who had such a profound influence on my way of seeing things. I realised at Balbec that it was in the same way as he that she presented things to her readers, in the order of our perception of them, instead of first explaining them in relation to their several causes. But already that afternoon in the railway carriage, on re-reading that letter in which the moonlight appears —"I could not resist the temptation: I put on all my bonnets and cloaks, though there is no need of them, I walk along this mall, where the air is as sweet as that of my chamber; I find a thousand phantasms, *monks white and black, nuns grey and white, linen cast here and there on the ground, men enshrouded upright against the tree-trunks*"—I was enraptured by what, a little later, I should have described (for does not she draw landscapes in the same way as he draws characters?) as the Dostoievsky side of Mme de Sévigné's Letters.

When, that evening, after having accompanied my grandmother to her destination and spent some hours in her friend's house, I had returned by myself to the train, at any rate I found nothing to distress me in the night which followed; this was because I did not have to spend it imprisoned in a room whose somnolence would have kept me awake; I was surrounded by the soothing activity of all those movements of the train which kept me company, offered to stay and talk to me if I could not sleep, lulled me with their sounds which I combined—like the chime of the Combray bells—now in one rhythm, now in another (hearing as the whim took me first four equal semi-quavers, then one semi-quaver furiously dashing against a crotchet); they neutralised the centrifugal force of my insomnia by exerting on it contrary pressures which kept me in equilibrium and on which my immobility and presently my drowsiness seemed to be borne with the same sense of relaxation that I should have felt had I been resting under the protecting vigilance of powerful forces in the heart of nature and of life, had I been able for a moment to metamorphose myself into a fish that sleeps in the sea, carried along in its slumber by the currents and the waves, or an eagle outstretched upon the buoyant air of the storm.

Sunrise is a necessary concomitant of long railway journeys, just as are hard-boiled eggs, illustrated papers, packs of cards, rivers upon which boats strain but make no progress. At a certain moment, when I was counting over the thoughts that had filled my mind during the preceding minutes, so as to discover whether I had just been asleep or not (and when the very uncertainty which made me ask myself the question was about to furnish me with an affirmative answer), in the pale square of the window, above a small black wood, I saw some ragged clouds whose fleecy edges were of a fixed, dead pink, not liable to change, like the colour that dyes the feathers of a wing that has assimilated it or a pastel on which it has been deposited by the artist's whim. But I felt that, unlike them, this colour was neither inertia nor caprice, but necessity and life. Presently there gathered behind it reserves of light. It brightened; the sky turned to a glowing pink which I strove, glueing my eyes to the window, to see more clearly, for I felt that it was related somehow to the most intimate life of Nature, but, the course of the line altering, the train turned, the morning scene gave place in the frame of the window to a nocturnal village, its roofs still blue with moonlight, its pond encrusted with the opalescent sheen of night, beneath a firmament still spangled with all its stars, and I was lamenting the loss of my strip of pink sky when I caught sight of it anew, but red this time, in the opposite window which it left at a second bend in the line; so that I spent my time running from one window to the other to reassemble, to collect on a single canvas the intermittent, antipodean fragments of my fine, scarlet, ever-changing morning, and to obtain a comprehensive view and a continuous picture of it.

The scenery became hilly and steep, and the train stopped at a little station between two mountains. Far down the gorge, on the edge of a hurrying stream, one could see only a solitary watch-house, embedded in the water which ran past on a level with its windows. If a person can be the product of a soil to the extent of embodying for us the quintessence of its peculiar charm, more even than the peasant girl whom I had so desperately longed to see appear when I wandered by myself along the Méséglise way, in the woods of Roussainville, such a person must have been the tall girl whom I now saw emerge from the house and, climbing a path lighted by the first slanting rays of the sun, come towards the station carrying a jar of milk. In her valley from which the rest of the world was hidden by these heights, she must never see anyone save in these trains which stopped for a moment only. She passed down the line of windows, offering coffee and milk to a few awakened passengers. Flushed with the glow of morning, her face was rosier than the sky. I felt on seeing her that desire to live which is reborn in us whenever we become conscious anew of beauty and of happiness. We invariably forget that these are individual qualities, and, mentally substituting for them a conventional type at which we arrive by striking a sort of mean among the different faces that have taken our fancy, among the pleasures we have known, we are left with mere abstract images which are lifeless and insipid because they lack precisely that element of novelty, different from anything we have known, that element which is peculiar to beauty and to happiness. And we deliver on life a pessimistic judgment which we suppose to be accurate, for we believed that we were taking happiness and beauty into account, whereas in fact we left them out and replaced them by syntheses in which there is not a single atom of either. So it is that a well-read man will at once begin to yawn with boredom when one speaks to him of a new "good book," because he imagines a sort of composite of all the good books that he has read, whereas a good book is something special, something unforeseeable, and is made up not of the sum of all previous masterpieces but of something which the most thorough assimilation of every one of them would not enable him to discover, since it exists not in their sum but beyond it. Once he has become acquainted with this new work, the well-read man, however jaded his palate, feels his interest awaken in the reality which it depicts. So, completely unrelated to the models of beauty which I was wont to conjure up in my mind when I was by myself, this handsome girl gave me at once the taste for a certain happiness (the sole form, always different, in which we may acquire a taste for happiness), for a happiness that would be realised by my staying and living there by her side. But in this again the temporary cessation of Habit played a great part. I was giving the milk-girl the benefit of the fact that it was the whole of my being, fit to taste the keenest joys, which confronted her. As a rule it is with our being reduced to a minimum that we live; most of our faculties lie dormant because they can rely upon Habit, which knows what there is to be done and has no need of their services. But on this morning of travel, the interruption of the routine of my existence, the unfamiliar place and time, had made their presence indispensable. My habits, which were sedentary and not matutinal, for once were missing, and all my faculties came hurrying to take their place, vying with one another in their zeal, rising, each of them, like waves, to the same unaccustomed level, from the basest to the most exalted, from breath, appetite, the circulation of my blood to receptivity and imagination. I cannot say whether, in making me believe that this girl was unlike the rest of women, the rugged charm of the locality added to her own, but she was equal to it. Life would have seemed an exquisite thing to me if only I had been free to spend it, hour after hour, with her, to go with her to the stream, to the cow, to the train, to be always at her side, to feel that I was known to her, had my place in her thoughts. She would have initiated me into the delights of country life and of early hours of the day. I signalled to her to bring me some of her coffee. I felt the need to be noticed by her. She did not see me; I called to her. Above her tall figure, the complexion of her face was so burnished and so glowing that it was as if one were seeing her through a lighted window. She retraced her steps. I could not take my eyes from her face which

grew larger as she approached, like a sun which it was somehow possible to stare at and which was coming nearer and
nearer, letting itself be seen at close quarters, dazzling you
with its blaze of red and gold. She fastened on me her penetrating gaze, but doors were being closed and the train had
begun to move. I saw her leave the station and go down the
hill to her home; it was broad daylight now; I was speeding
away from the dawn. Whether my exaltation had been produced by this girl or had on the other hand been responsible
for most of the pleasure that I had found in her presence, in
either event she was so closely associated with it that my desire
to see her again was above all a mental desire not to allow this
state of excitement to perish utterly, not to be separated for
ever from the person who, however unwittingly, had participated in it. It was not only that this state was a pleasant one.
It was above all that (just as increased tension upon a string
or the accelerated vibration of a nerve produces a different
sound or colour) it gave another tonality to all that I saw,
introduced me as an actor upon the stage of an unknown and
infinitely more interesting universe; that handsome girl whom
I still could see, as the train gathered speed, was like part of a
life other than the life I knew, separated from it by a clear
boundary, in which the sensations aroused in me by things
were no longer the same, from which to emerge now would
be, as it were, to die to myself. To have the consolation of feeling that I had at least an attachment to this new life, it would
suffice that I should live near enough to the little station to be
able to come to it every morning for a cup of coffee from the
girl. But alas, she must be for ever absent from the other life
towards which I was being borne with ever increasing speed,
a life which I could resign myself to accept only by weaving
plans that would enable me to take the same train again some
day and to stop at the same station, a project which had the
further advantage of providing food for the selfish, active,
practical, mechanical, indolent, centrifugal tendency which is
that of the human mind, for it turns all too readily aside from
the effort which is required to analyse and probe, in a general
and disinterested manner, an agreeable impression which we
have received. And since, at the same time, we wish to

continue to think of that impression, the mind prefers to imagine
it in the future tense, to continue to bring about the circumstances which may make it recur—which, while giving us no
clue as to the real nature of the thing, saves us the trouble of
recreating it within ourselves and allows us to hope that we
may receive it afresh from without.

Certain names of towns, Vézelay or Chartres, Bourges or
Beauvais, serve to designate, by abbreviation, their principal
churches. This partial acceptation comes at length—if the
names in question are those of places that we do not yet know
—to mould the name as a whole which henceforth, whenever
we wish to introduce into it the idea of the town—the town
which we have never seen—will impose on it the same carved
outlines, in the same style, will make of it a sort of vast cathedral. It was, however, in a railway-station, above the door of
a refreshment-room in white letters on a blue panel, that I read
the name—almost Persian in style—of Balbec. I strode buoyantly through the station and across the avenue that led up to
it, and asked the way to the shore, so as to see nothing in the
place but its church and the sea. People seemed not to understand what I meant. Old Balbec, Balbec-en-Terre, at which I
had arrived, had neither beach nor harbour. True, it was indeed
in the sea that the fishermen, according to the legend, had
found the miraculous Christ of which a window in the church
that stood a few yards from where I now was recorded the
discovery; it was indeed from cliffs battered by the waves that
the stone of its nave and towers had been quarried. But this
sea, which for those reasons I had imagined as coming to
expire at the foot of the window, was twelve miles away and
more, at Balbec-Plage, and, rising beside its cupola, that steeple
which, because I had read that it was itself a rugged Norman
cliff round which the winds howled and the sea-birds wheeled,
I had always pictured to myself as receiving at its base the last
dying foam of the uplifted waves, stood on a square which was
the junction of two tramway routes, opposite a café which bore,
in letters of gold, the legend "Billiards," against a background
of houses with the roofs of which no upstanding mast was
blended. And the church—impinging on my attention at the
same time as the café, the passing stranger of whom I had had

to ask my way, the station to which presently I should have to return—merged with all the rest, seemed an accident, a by-product of this summer afternoon, in which the mellow and distended dome against the sky was like a fruit of which the same light that bathed the chimneys of the houses ripened the pink, glowing, luscious skin. But I wished only to consider the eternal significance of the carvings when I recognised the Apostles, of which I had seen casts in the Trocadéro museum, and which on either side of the Virgin, before the deep bay of the porch, were awaiting me as though to do me honour. With their benign, blunt, mild faces and bowed shoulders they seemed to be advancing upon me with an air of welcome, singing the Alleluia of a fine day. But it was evident that their expression was as unchanging as that of a corpse, and altered only if one walked round them. I said to myself: "Here I am: this is the Church of Balbec. This square, which looks as though it were conscious of its glory, is the only place in the world that possesses Balbec Church. All that I have seen so far have been photographs of this church—and of these famous Apostles, this Virgin of the Porch, mere casts only. Now it is the church itself, the statue itself, they, the only ones—this is something far greater."

It was also something less, perhaps. As a young man on the day of an examination or of a duel feels the question that he has been asked, the shot that he has fired, to be very insignificant when he thinks of the reserves of knowledge and of valour that he would like to have displayed, so my mind, which had lifted the Virgin of the Porch far above the reproductions that I had had before my eyes, invulnerable to the vicissitudes which might threaten them, intact even if they were destroyed, ideal, endowed with a universal value, was astonished to see the statue which it had carved a thousand times, reduced now to its own stone semblance, occupying, in relation to the reach of my arm, a place in which it had for rivals an election poster and the point of my stick, fettered to the Square, inseparable from the opening of the main street, powerless to hide from the gaze of the café and of the omnibus office, receiving on its face half of the ray of the setting sun (and presently, in a few hours' time, of the light of the street lamp) of which the savings bank received the other half, affected simultaneously with that branch office of a loan society by the smells from the pastry-cook's oven, subjected to the tyranny of the Particular to such a point that, if I had chosen to scribble my name upon that stone, it was she, the illustrious Virgin whom until then I had endowed with a general existence and an intangible beauty, the Virgin of Balbec, the unique (which meant, alas, the only one), who, on her body coated with the same soot as defiled the neighbouring houses, would have displayed—powerless to rid herself of them—to all the admiring strangers come there to gaze upon her, the marks of my piece of chalk and the letters of my name, and it was she, finally, the immortal work of art so long desired, whom I found transformed, as was the church itself, into a little old woman in stone whose height I could measure and whose wrinkles I could count. But time was passing; I must return to the station, where I was to wait for my grandmother and Françoise, so that we should all go on to Balbec-Plage together. I reminded myself of what I had read about Balbec, of Swann's saying: "It's exquisite; as beautiful as Siena." And casting the blame for my disappointment upon various accidental causes, such as the state of my health, my exhaustion after the journey, my incapacity for looking at things properly, I endeavoured to console myself with the thought that other towns still remained intact for me, that I might soon, perhaps, be making my way, as into a shower of pearls, into the cool babbling murmur of watery Quimperlé, or traversing the roseate glow in which verdant Pont-Aven was bathed; but as for Balbec, no sooner had I set foot in it than it was as though I had broken open a name which ought to have been kept hermetically closed, and into which, seizing at once the opportunity that I had imprudently given them, expelling all the images that had lived in it until then, a tramway, a café, people crossing the square, the branch of the savings bank, irresistibly propelled by some external pressure, by a pneumatic force, had come surging into the interior of those two syllables which, closing over them, now let them frame the porch of the Persian church and would henceforth never cease to contain them.

I found my grandmother in the little train of the local railway which was to take us to Balbec-Plage, but found her alone—for she had had the idea of sending Françoise on ahead of her, so that everything should be ready before we arrived, but having given her the wrong instructions, had succeeded only in sending her off in the wrong direction, so that Françoise at that moment was being carried down all unsuspectingly at full speed to Nantes, and would probably wake up next morning at Bordeaux. No sooner had I taken my seat in the carriage, which was filled with the fleeting light of sunset and with the lingering heat of the afternoon (the former enabling me, alas, to see written clearly upon my grandmother's face how much the latter had tired her), than she began: "Well, and Balbec?" with a smile so brightly illuminated by her expectation of the great pleasure which she supposed me to have experienced that I dared not at once confess to her my disappointment. Besides, the impression which my mind had been seeking occupied it steadily less as the place to which my body would have to become accustomed drew nearer. At the end—still more than an hour away—of this journey I was trying to form a picture of the manager of the hotel at Balbec, for whom I, at that moment, did not exist, and I should have liked to be presenting myself to him in more impressive company than that of my grandmother, who would be certain to ask for a reduction of his terms. He appeared to me to be endowed with an indubitable haughtiness, but its contours were very vague.

Every few minutes the little train brought us to a standstill at one of the stations which came before Balbec-Plage, stations the mere names of which (Incarville, Marcouville, Doville, Pont-à-Couleuvre, Arambouville, Saint-Mars-le-Vieux, Hermonville, Maineville) seemed to me outlandish, whereas if I had come upon them in a book I should at once have been struck by their affinity to the names of certain places in the neighbourhood of Combray. But to the ear of a musician two themes, substantially composed of the same notes, will present no similarity whatever if they differ in the colour of their harmony and orchestration. In the same way, nothing could have reminded me less than these dreary names, redolent of sand, of space too airy and empty, and of salt, out of which the

suffix "ville" emerged like "fly" in "butterfly"—nothing
could have reminded me less of those other names, Roussainville or Martinville, which, because I had heard them pronounced so often by my great-aunt at table, in the dining-room,
had acquired a certain sombre charm in which were blended
perhaps extracts of the flavour of "preserves," the smell of the
log fire and of the pages of one of Bergotte's books, or the
colour of the sandstone front of the house opposite, and which
even to-day, when they rise like a gaseous bubble from the
depths of my memory, preserve their own specific virtue
through all the successive layers of different environments
which they must traverse before reaching the surface.

Overlooking the distant sea from the crests of their dunes
or already settling down for the night at the foot of hills of a
harsh green and a disagreeable shape, like that of the sofa in
one's bedroom in an hotel at which one has just arrived, each
composed of a cluster of villas whose line was extended to include a tennis court and occasionally a casino over which a
flag flapped in the freshening, hollow, uneasy wind, they were
a series of little watering-places which now showed me for the
first time their denizens, but showed them only through their
habitual exterior—tennis players in white hats, the station-
master living there on the spot among his tamarisks and roses,
a lady in a straw "boater" who, following the everyday routine
of an existence which I should never know, was calling to her
dog which had stopped to examine something in the road
before going in to her bungalow where the lamp was already
lighted—and which with these strangely ordinary and disdainfully familiar sights cruelly stung my unconsidered eyes
and stabbed my homesick heart. But how much more were my
sufferings increased when we had finally landed in the hall of
the Grand Hotel at Balbec, and I stood there in front of the
monumental staircase of imitation marble, while my grandmother, regardless of the growing hostility and contempt
of the strangers among whom we were about to live, discussed
"terms" with the manager, a pot-bellied figure with a face and
a voice alike covered with scars (left by the excision of countless pustules from the one, and from the other of the divers
accents acquired from an alien ancestry and a cosmopolitan

upbringing), a smart dinner-jacket, and the air of a psychologist who, whenever the "omnibus" discharged a fresh load, invariably took the grandees for haggling skinflints and the flashy crooks for grandees! Forgetting, doubtless, that he himself was not drawing five hundred francs a month, he had a profound contempt for people to whom five hundred francs —or, as he preferred to put it, "twenty-five louis"—was "a lot of money," and regarded them as belonging to a race of pariahs for whom the Grand Hotel was certainly not intended. It is true that even within its walls there were people who did not pay very much and yet had not forfeited the manager's esteem, provided that he was assured that they were watching their expenditure not from poverty so much as from avarice. For this could in no way lower their standing, since it is a vice and may consequently be found at every grade in the social hierarchy. Social position was the one thing by which the manager was impressed—social position, or rather the signs which seemed to him to imply that it was exalted, such as not taking one's hat off when one came into the hall, wearing knickerbockers or an overcoat with a waist, and taking a cigar with a band of purple and gold out of a crushed morocco case—to none of which advantages could I, alas, lay claim. He would also adorn his business conversation with choice expressions, to which, as a rule, he gave the wrong meaning.

While I heard my grandmother, who betrayed no sign of annoyance at his listening to her with his hat on his head and whistling through his teeth, ask him in an artificial tone of voice "And what are . . . your charges? . . . Oh! far too high for my little budget," waiting on a bench, I took refuge in the innermost depths of my being, strove to migrate to a plane of eternal thoughts, to leave nothing of myself, nothing living, on the surface of my body—anaesthetised like those of certain animals, which, by inhibition, feign death when they are wounded—so as not to suffer too keenly in this place, my total unfamiliarity with which was impressed upon me all the more forcibly by the familiarity with it that seemed to be evinced at the same moment by a smartly dressed lady to whom the manager showed his respect by taking liberties with the little dog that followed her across the hall, the young "blood" with a feather in his hat who came in asking if there were "any letters," all these people for whom climbing those imitation marble stairs meant going home. And at the same time the triple stare of Minos, Æacus and Rhadamanthus (into which I plunged my naked soul as into an unknown element where there was nothing now to protect it) was bent sternly upon me by a group of gentlemen who, though little versed perhaps in the art of receiving, yet bore the title "reception clerks," while beyond them again, behind a glass partition, were people sitting in a reading-room for the description of which I should have had to borrow from Dante alternately the colours in which he paints Paradise and Hell, according as I was thinking of the happiness of the elect who had the right to sit and read there undisturbed, or of the terror which my grandmother would have inspired in me if, in her insensibility to this sort of impression, she had asked me to go in there and wait for her by myself.

My sense of loneliness was further increased a moment later. When I had confessed to my grandmother that I did not feel well, that I thought that we should be obliged to return to Paris, she had offered no protest, saying merely that she was going out to buy a few things which would be equally useful whether we left or stayed (and which, I afterwards learned, were all intended for me, Françoise having gone off with certain articles which I might need). While I waited for her I had taken a turn through the streets, which were packed with a crowd of people who imparted to them a sort of indoor warmth, and in which the hairdresser's shop and the pastry-cook's were still open, the latter filled with customers eating ices opposite the statue of Duguay-Trouin. This crowd gave me just about as much pleasure as a photograph of it in one of the "illustrateds" might give a patient who was turning its pages in the surgeon's waiting-room. I was astonished to find that there were people so different from myself that this stroll through the town had actually been recommended to me by the manager as a diversion, and also that the torture chamber which a new place of residence is could appear to some people a "delightful abode," to quote the hotel prospectus, which might perhaps exaggerate but was none the less addressed to a whole army of clients to whose tastes it must appeal. True, it invoked, to make them come to the Grand Hotel, Balbec, not only the "exquisite fare" and the "magical view across the Casino gardens," but also the "ordinances of Her Majesty Queen Fashion, which no one may violate with impunity without being taken for a philistine, a charge that no well-bred man would willingly incur."

The need that I now felt for my grandmother was enhanced by my fear that I had shattered another of her illusions. She must be feeling discouraged, feeling that if I could not stand the fatigue of this journey there was no hope that any change of air could ever do me good. I decided to return to the hotel and to wait for her there; the manager himself came forward and pressed a button, whereupon a personage whose acquaintance I had not yet made, known as "lift" (who at the highest point in the building, where the lantern would be in a Norman church, was installed like a photographer behind his curtain or an organist in his loft) began to descend towards me with the agility of a domestic, industrious and captive squirrel. Then, gliding upwards again along a steel pillar, he bore me aloft in his wake towards the dome of this temple of Mammon. On each floor, on either side of a narrow communicating stair, a range of shadowy galleries opened out fanwise, along one of which came a chambermaid carrying a bolster. I applied to her face, which was blurred in the twilight, the mask of my most impassioned dreams, but read in her eyes as they turned towards me the horror of my own nonentity. Meanwhile, to dissipate, in the course of this interminable ascent, the mortal anguish which I felt in traversing in silence the mystery of this chiaroscuro so devoid of poetry, lighted by a single vertical line of little windows which were those of the solitary water-closet on each landing, I addressed a few words to the young organist, artificer of my journey and my partner in captivity, who continued to manipulate the registers of his instrument and to finger the stops. I apologised for taking up so much room, for giving him so much trouble, and asked whether I was not obstructing him in the practice of an art in regard to which, in order to flatter the virtuoso, more than displaying curiosity, I confessed my strong attachment. But he vouchsafed no answer, whether from astonishment at my words, preoccupation with his work, regard for etiquette, hardness of hearing, respect for holy ground, fear of danger, slowness of understanding, or the manager's orders.

There is perhaps nothing that gives us so strong an impression of the reality of the external world as the difference in the position, relative to ourselves, of even a quite unimportant person before we have met him and after. I was the same man who had taken, that afternoon, the little train from Balbec to the coast; I carried in my body the same consciousness. But on that consciousness, in the place where at six o'clock there had been, together with the impossibility of forming any idea of the manager, the Grand Hotel or its staff, a vague and timorous anticipation of the moment at which I should reach my destination, were to be found now the pustules excised from the face of the cosmopolitan manager (he was, in fact, a naturalised Monegasque, although—as he himself put it, for he was always using expressions which he thought distinguished without noticing that they were incorrect—"of Rumanian originality"), his action in ringing for the lift, the lift-boy himself, a whole frieze of puppet-show characters issuing from that Pandora's box which was the Grand Hotel, undeniable, irremovable, and, like everything that is realised, jejune. But at least this change which I had done nothing to bring about proved to me that something had happened which was external to myself—however devoid of interest that thing might be in itself—and I was like a traveller who, having had the sun in his face when he started, concludes that he has been for so many hours on the road when he finds the sun behind him. I was half dead with exhaustion, I was burning with fever; I would gladly have gone to bed, but I had no night-things. I should have liked at least to lie down for a little while on the bed, but to what purpose, since I should not have been able to procure any rest for that mass of sensations which is for each of us his conscious if not his physical body, and since the unfamiliar objects which encircled that body, forcing it to place its perceptions on the permanent footing of a vigilant defensive, would have kept my sight, my hearing, all my senses in a position as cramped and uncomfortable (even if I had stretched out my legs) as that of Cardinal La Balue in the cage in which he could neither stand nor sit? It is our noticing them that puts things in a room, our growing used to them that takes them away again and clears a space for us. Space there was none for me in my bedroom (mine in name only) at Balbec; it was full of things which did not know me, which flung back at me the distrustful glance I cast at them, and, without taking any heed of my existence, showed that I was interrupting the humdrum course of theirs. The clock—whereas at home I heard mine tick only a few seconds in a week, when I was coming out of some profound meditation—continued without a moment's interruption to utter, in an unknown tongue, a series of observations which must have been most uncomplimentary to myself, for the violet curtains listened to them without replying, but in an attitude such as people adopt who shrug their shoulders to indicate that the sight of a third person irritates them. They gave to this room with its lofty ceiling a quasi-historical character which might have made it a suitable place for the assassination of the Duc de Guise, and afterwards for parties of tourists personally conducted by one of Messrs. Thomas Cook and Son's guides, but for me to sleep in—no. I was tormented by the presence of some little bookcases with glass fronts which ran along the walls, but especially by a large cheval-glass which stood across one corner and before the departure of which I felt there could be no possibility of rest for me there. I kept raising my eyes—which the things in my room in Paris disturbed no more than did my eyelids themselves, for they were merely extensions of my organs, an enlargement of myself—towards the high ceiling of this belvedere planted upon the summit of the hotel which my grandmother had chosen for me; and deep down in that region more intimate than that in which we see and hear, in that region where we experience the quality of smells, almost in the very heart of my inmost self, the scent of flowering grasses next launched its offensive against my last feeble line of trenches, an offensive against which I opposed, not without exhausting myself still further, the futile and unremitting riposte of an alarmed sniffling. Having no world, no room, no body now that was not menaced by the enemies thronging round me, penetrated to the very bones by fever, I was alone, and longed to die. Then my grandmother came in, and to the expansion of my constricted heart there opened at once an infinity of space.

She was wearing a loose cambric dressing-gown which she put on at home whenever any of us was ill (because she felt more comfortable in it, she used to say, for she always ascribed selfish motives to her actions), and which was, for tending us, for watching by our beds, her servant's smock, her nurse's uniform, her nun's habit. But whereas the attentions of servants, nurses and nuns, their kindness to us, the merits we find in them and the gratitude we owe them, increase the impression we have of being, in their eyes, someone else, of feeling that we are alone, keeping in our own hands the control over our thoughts, our will to live, I knew, when I was with my grandmother, that however great the misery that there was in me, it would be received by her with a pity still more vast, that everything that was mine, my cares, my wishes, would be buttressed, in my grandmother, by a desire to preserve and enhance my life that was altogether stronger than was my own; and my thoughts were continued and extended in her without undergoing the slightest deflection, since they passed from my mind into hers without any change of atmosphere or of personality. And—like a man who tries to fasten his tie in front of a glass and forgets that the end which he sees reflected is not on the side to which he raises his hand, or like a dog that chases along the ground the dancing shadow of an insect in the air— misled by her appearance in the body as we are apt to be in this world where we have no direct perception of people's souls, I threw myself into the arms of my grandmother and pressed my lips to her face as though I were thus gaining access to that immense heart which she opened to me. And when I felt my mouth glued to her cheeks, to her brow, I drew from them something so beneficial, so nourishing, that I remained as motionless, as solemn, as calmly gluttonous as a babe at the breast.

Afterwards I gazed inexhaustibly at her large face, outlined like a beautiful cloud, glowing and serene, behind which I could discern the radiance of her tender love. And everything that received, in however slight a degree, any share of her

sensations, everything that could be said to belong in any
way to her was at once so spiritualised, so sanctified that with
outstretched hands I smoothed her beautiful hair, still hardly
grey, with as much respect, precaution and gentleness as if I
had actually been caressing her goodness. She found such
pleasure in taking any trouble that saved me one, and in a
moment of immobility and rest for my weary limbs something
so exquisite, that when, having seen that she wished to help me
undress and go to bed, I made as though to stop her and to
undress myself, with an imploring gaze she arrested my hands
as they fumbled with the top buttons of my jacket and my boots.
  "Oh, do let me!" she begged. "It's such a joy for your
Granny. And be sure you knock on the wall if you want anything in the night. My bed is just on the other side, and the
partition is quite thin. Just give a knock now, as soon as
you're in bed, so that we shall know where we are."
  And, sure enough, that evening I gave three knocks—a
signal which, a week later, when I was ill, I repeated every
morning for several days, because my grandmother wanted me
to have some milk early. Then, when I thought that I could
hear her stirring—so that she should not be kept waiting but
might, the moment she had brought me the milk, go to sleep
again—I would venture three little taps, timidly, faintly, but
for all that distinctly, for if I was afraid of disturbing her in
case I had been mistaken and she was still asleep, neither did I
wish her to lie awake listening for a summons which she had
not at once caught and which I should not have the heart
to repeat. And scarcely had I given my taps than I heard
three others, in a different tone from mine, stamped with a
calm authority, repeated twice over so that there should be
no mistake, and saying to me plainly: "Don't get agitated; I've
heard you; I shall be with you in a minute!" and shortly afterwards my grandmother would appear. I would explain to her
that I had been afraid she would not hear me, or might think
that it was someone in the room beyond who was tapping; at
which she would smile: "Mistake my poor pet's knocking for
anyone else's! Why, Granny could tell it a mile away! Do you
suppose there's anyone else in the world who's such a silly-
billy, with such febrile little knuckles, so afraid of waking me

up and of not making me understand? Even if it just gave the tiniest scratch, Granny could tell her mouse's sound at once, especially such a poor miserable little mouse as mine is. I could hear it just now, trying to make up its mind, and rustling the bedclothes, and going through all its tricks."

She would push open the shutters, and where a wing of the hotel jutted out at right angles to my window, the sun would already have settled on the roof, like a slater who is up betimes, and starts early and works quietly so as not to rouse the sleeping town whose stillness makes him seem more agile. She would tell me what time it was, what sort of day it would be, that it was not worth while my getting up and coming to the window, that there was a mist over the sea, whether the baker's shop had opened yet, what the vehicle was that I could hear passing—that whole trifling curtain-raiser, that insignificant *introit* of a new day which no one attends, a little scrap of life which was only for our two selves, but which I should have no hesitation in evoking, later on, to Françoise or even to strangers, speaking of the fog "which you could have cut with a knife" at six o'clock that morning, with the ostentation of one who was boasting not of a piece of knowledge that he had acquired but of a mark of affection shown to himself alone; sweet morning moment which opened like a symphony with the rhythmical dialogue of my three taps, to which the thin wall of my bedroom, steeped in love and joy, grown melodious, incorporeal, singing like the angelic choir, responded with three other taps, eagerly awaited, repeated once and again, in which it contrived to waft to me the soul of my grandmother, whole and perfect, and the promise of her coming, with the swiftness of an annunciation and a musical fidelity. But on this first night after our arrival, when my grandmother had left me, I began again to suffer as I had suffered the day before, in Paris, at the moment of leaving home. Perhaps this fear that I had—and that is shared by so many others—of sleeping in a strange room, perhaps this fear is only the most humble, obscure, organic, almost unconscious form of that great and desperate resistance put up by the things that constitute the better part of our present life against our mentally acknowledging the possibility of a future in which they are to have no part; a

resistance which was at the root of the horror that I had so
often been made to feel by the thought that my parents would
die some day, that the stern necessity of life might oblige me to
live far from Gilberte, or simply to settle permanently in a
place where I should never see any of my old friends; a
resistance which was also at the root of the difficulty that I
found in imagining my own death, or a survival such as Bergotte used to promise to mankind in his books, a survival in
which I should not be allowed to take with me my memories,
my frailties, my character, which did not easily resign themselves to the idea of ceasing to be, and desired for me neither
extinction nor an eternity in which they would have no part.

When Swann had said to me in Paris one day when I felt
particularly unwell: "You ought to go off to one of those
glorious islands in the Pacific; you'd never come back again if
you did," I should have liked to answer: "But then I shall never
see your daughter again, I shall be living among people and
things she has never seen." And yet my reason, my better
judgment whispered: "What difference can that make, since
you won't be distressed by it? When M. Swann tells you that
you won't come back he means by that that you won't want
to come back, and if you don't want to that is because you'll
be happier out there." For my reason was aware that Habit—
Habit which was even now setting to work to make me like
this unfamiliar lodging, to change the position of the mirror,
the shade of the curtains, to stop the clock—undertakes as well
to make dear to us the companions whom at first we disliked,
to give another appearance to their faces, to make the sound of
their voices attractive, to modify the inclinations of their
hearts. It is true that these new friendships for places and people
are based upon forgetfulness of the old; my reason precisely
thought that I could envisage without dread the prospect of a
life in which I should be for ever separated from people all
memory of whom I should lose, and it was by way of consolation that it offered my heart a promise of oblivion which in fact
succeeded only in sharpening the edge of its despair. Not that
the heart, too, is not bound in time, when separation is complete, to feel the analgesic effect of habit; but until then it will
continue to suffer. And our dread of a future in which we must

forgo the sight of faces and the sound of voices which we love and from which today we derive our dearest joy, this dread, far from being dissipated, is intensified, if to the pain of such a privation we feel that there will be added what seems to us now in anticipation more painful still: not to feel it as a pain at all—to remain indifferent; for then our old self would have changed, it would then be not merely the charm of our family, our mistress, our friends that had ceased to environ us, but our affection for them would have been so completely eradicated from our hearts, of which to-day it is so conspicuous an element, that we should be able to enjoy a life apart from them, the very thought of which to-day makes us recoil in horror; so that it would be in a real sense the death of the self, a death followed, it is true, by resurrection, but in a different self, to the love of which the elements of the old self that are condemned to die cannot bring themselves to aspire. It is they—even the meanest of them, such as our obscure attachments to the dimensions, to the atmosphere of a bed-room—that take fright and refuse, in acts of rebellion which we must recognise to be a secret, partial, tangible and true aspect of our resistance to death, of the long, desperate, daily resistance to the fragmentary and continuous death that insinuates itself throughout the whole course of our life, detaching from us at each moment a shred of ourself, dead matter on which new cells will multiply and grow. And for a neurotic nature such as mine—one, that is to say, in which the intermediaries, the nerves, perform their functions badly, fail to arrest on its way to the consciousness, allow indeed to reach it, distinct, exhausting, innumerable and distressing, the plaints of the most humble elements of the self which are about to disappear—the anxiety and alarm which I felt as I lay beneath that strange and too lofty ceiling were but the protest of an affection that survived in me for a ceiling that was familiar and low. Doubtless this affection too would disappear, another having taken its place (when death, and then another life, had, in the guise of Habit, performed their double task); but until its annihilation, every night it would suffer afresh, and on this first night especially, confronted with an irreversible future in which there would no longer be any

place for it, it rose in revolt, it tortured me with the sound
of its lamentations whenever my straining eyes, powerless to
turn from what was wounding them, endeavoured to fasten
themselves upon that inaccessible ceiling.

But next morning!—after a servant had come to call me
and to bring me hot water, and while I was washing and dressing myself and trying in vain to find the things that I needed
in my trunk, from which I extracted, pell-mell, only a lot of
things that were of no use whatever, what a joy it was to me,
thinking already of the pleasure of lunch and a walk along the
shore, to see in the window, and in all the glass fronts of
the bookcases, as in the portholes of a ship's cabin, the open
sea, naked, unshadowed, and yet with half of its expanse in
shadow, bounded by a thin, fluctuating line, and to follow with
my eyes the waves that leapt up one behind another like
jumpers on a trampoline. Every other moment, holding in my
hand the stiff starched towel with the name of the hotel printed
upon it, with which I was making futile efforts to dry myself, I
returned to the window to have another look at that vast,
dazzling, mountainous amphitheatre, and at the snowy crests of
its emerald waves, here and there polished and translucent,
which with a placid violence and a leonine frown, to which the
sun added a faceless smile, allowed their crumbling slopes to
topple down at last. It was at this window that I was later to
take up my position every morning, as at the window of a
stage-coach in which one has slept, to see whether, during the
night, a longed-for mountain range has come nearer or receded—only here it was those hills of the sea which, before
they come dancing back towards us, are apt to withdraw so
far that often it was only at the end of a long, sandy plain that
I would distinguish, far off, their first undulations in a transparent, vaporous, bluish distance, like the glaciers that one
sees in the backgrounds of the Tuscan Primitives. On other
mornings it was quite close at hand that the sun laughed upon
those waters of a green as tender as that preserved in Alpine
pastures (among mountains on which the sun displays himself
here and there like a giant who may at any moment come leap-
ing gaily down their craggy sides) less by the moisture of the
soil than by the liquid mobility of the light. Moreover, in that

breach which the shore and the waves open up in the midst of
the rest of the world for the passage or the accumulation of
light, it is above all the light, according to the direction from
which it comes and along which our eyes follow it, it is the
light that displaces and situates the undulations of the sea.
Diversity of lighting modifies no less the orientation of a place,
erects no less before our eyes new goals which it inspires in us
the yearning to attain, than would a distance in space actually
traversed in the course of a long journey. When, in the morning, the sun came from behind the hotel, disclosing to me the
sands bathed in light as far as the first bastions of the sea, it
seemed to be showing me another side of the picture, and to be
inviting me to pursue, along the winding path of its rays, a
motionless but varied journey amid all the fairest scenes of the
diversified landscape of the hours. And on this first morning,
it pointed out to me far off, with a jovial finger, those blue
peaks of the sea which bear no name on any map, until, dizzy
with its sublime excursion over the thundering and chaotic
surface of their crests and avalanches, it came to take shelter
from the wind in my bedroom, lolling across the unmade bed
and scattering its riches over the splashed surface of the basin-
stand and into my open trunk, where, by its very splendour and
misplaced luxury, it added still further to the general impression of disorder. Alas for that sea-wind: an hour later, in the
big dining-room—while we were having lunch, and from the
leathern gourd of a lemon were sprinkling a few golden drops
on to a pair of soles which presently left on our plates the
plumes of their picked skeletons, curled like stiff feathers and
resonant as citherns,—it seemed to my grandmother a cruel
deprivation not to be able to feel its life-giving breath on her
cheek, on account of the glass partition, transparent but closed,
which, like the front of a glass case in a museum, separated us
from the beach while allowing us to look out upon its whole
expanse, and into which the sky fitted so completely that its
azure had the effect of being the colour of the windows and its
white clouds so many flaws in the glass. Imagining that I was
"sitting on the mole" or at rest in the "boudoir" of which
Baudelaire speaks, I wondered whether his "sun's rays upon
the sea" were not—a very different thing from the evening

ray, simple and superficial as a tremulous golden shaft—just what at that moment was scorching the sea topaz-yellow, fermenting it, turning it pale and milky like beer, frothy like milk, while now and then there hovered over it great blue shadows which, for his own amusement, some god seemed to be shifting to and fro by moving a mirror in the sky. Unfortunately, it was not only in its outlook that this dining-room at Balbec—bare-walled, filled with a sunlight green as the water in a pond, while a few feet away from it the high tide and broad daylight erected as though before the gates of the heavenly city an indestructible and mobile rampart of emerald and gold—differed from our dining-room at Combray which gave on to the houses across the street. At Combray, since we were known to everyone, I took heed of no one. In seaside life one does not know one's neighbours. I was not yet old enough, and was still too sensitive to have outgrown the desire to find favour in the sight of other people and to possess their hearts. Nor had I acquired the more noble indifference which a man of the world would have felt towards the people who were eating in the dining-room or the boys and girls who strolled past the window, with whom I was pained by the thought that I should never be allowed to go on expeditions, though not so pained as if my grandmother, contemptuous of social formalities and concerned only with my health, had gone to them with the request, humiliating for me, that they should consent to allow me to accompany them. Whether they were returning to some villa beyond my ken, or had emerged from one, racquet in hand, on their way to a tennis court, or were riding horses whose hooves trampled my heart, I gazed at them with a passionate curiosity, in that blinding light of the beach by which social distinctions are altered, I followed all their movements through the transparency of that great bay of glass which allowed so much light to flood the room. But it intercepted the wind, and this was a defect in the eyes of my grandmother, who, unable to endure the thought that I was losing the benefit of an hour in the open air, surreptitiously opened a pane and at once sent flying, together with the menus, the newspapers, veils and hats of all the people at the other tables, while she herself, fortified by the celestial draught, remained calm and smiling like Saint Blandina amid the torrent of invective which, increasing my sense of isolation and misery, those contemptuous, dishevelled, furious visitors combined to pour on us.

To a certain extent—and this, at Balbec, gave to the population, as a rule monotonously rich and cosmopolitan, of that sort of "grand" hotel a quite distinctive local character—they were composed of eminent persons from the departmental capitals of that region of France, a senior judge from Caen, a leader of the Cherbourg bar, a notary public from Le Mans, who annually, when the holidays came round, starting from the various points over which, throughout the working year, they were scattered like snipers on a battlefield or draughtsmen upon a board, concentrated their forces in this hotel. They always reserved the same rooms, and with their wives, who had pretensions to aristocracy, formed a little group which was joined by a leading barrister and a leading doctor from Paris, who on the day of their departure would say to the others: "Oh, yes, of course; you don't go by our train. You're privileged, you'll be home in time for lunch."

"Privileged, you say? You who live in the capital, in Paris, while I have to live in a wretched county town of a hundred thousand souls (it's true we managed to muster a hundred and two thousand at the last census, but what is that compared to your two and a half millions?), going back, too, to asphalt streets and all the bustle and gaiety of Paris life."

They said this with a rustic burring of their 'r's, without acrimony, for they were leading lights each in his own province, who could like others have gone to Paris had they chosen —the senior judge from Caen had several times been offered a seat on the Court of Appeal—but had preferred to stay where they were, from love of their native towns, or of obscurity, or of fame, or because they were reactionaries, and enjoyed being on friendly terms with the country houses of the neighbourhood. Besides, several of them were not going back at once to their county towns.

For—inasmuch as the Bay of Balbec was a little world apart in the midst of the great, a basketful of the seasons in which good days and bad, and the successive months, were clustered in a ring, so that not only on days when one could make out Rivebelle, which was a sign of storm, could one see the sunlight on the houses there while Balbec was plunged in darkness, but later on, when the cold weather had reached Balbec, one could be certain of finding on that opposite shore two or three supplementary months of warmth—those of the regular visitors to the Grand Hotel whose holidays began late or lasted long gave orders, when the rains and the mists came and autumn was in the air, for their boxes to be packed and loaded on to a boat, and set sail across the bay to find the summer again at Rivebelle or Costedor. This little group in the Balbec hotel looked at each new arrival with suspicion, and, while affecting to take not the least interest in him, hastened, all of them, to interrogate their friend the head waiter about him. For it was the same head waiter—Aimé—who returned every year for the season, and kept their tables for them; and their lady-wives, having heard that his wife was "expecting," would sit after meals working each at one of the "tiny garments," stopping only to put up their glasses and stare at my grandmother and myself because we were eating hard-boiled eggs in salad, which was considered common and was "not done" in the best society of Alençon. They affected an attitude of contemptuous irony with regard to a Frenchman who was called "His Majesty" and who had indeed proclaimed himself king of a small island in the South Seas peopled only by a few savages. He was staying in the hotel with his pretty mistress, whom, as she crossed the beach to bathe, the little boys would greet with "Long live the Queen!" because she would reward them with a shower of small silver. The judge and the barrister went so far as to pretend not to see her, and if any of their friends happened to look at her, felt bound to warn him that she was only a little shop-girl.

"But I was told that at Ostend they used the royal bathing-hut."

"Well, and why not? It's on hire for twenty francs. You can take it yourself, if you care for that sort of thing. Anyhow, I know for a fact that the fellow asked for an audience with the King, who sent back word that he wasn't interested in pantomime princes."

"Really, that's interesting! What queer people there are in the world, to be sure!"

And no doubt all this was true; but it was also from resentment of the thought that, to many of their fellow-visitors, they were themselves simply solid middle-class citizens who did not know this king and queen who were so prodigal with their small change, that the notary, the judge, the barrister, when what they were pleased to call the "Carnival" went by, felt so much annoyance and expressed aloud an indignation that was quite understood by their friend the head waiter who, obliged to show proper civility to these generous if not authentic sovereigns, would nevertheless, as he took their orders, glance across the room at his old patrons and give them a meaningful wink. Perhaps there was also something of the same resentment at being erroneously supposed to be less "smart" and unable to explain that they were more, at the bottom of the "Fine specimen!" with which they referred to a young toff, the consumptive and dissipated son of an industrial magnate, who appeared every day in a new suit of clothes with an orchid in his buttonhole, drank champagne at luncheon, and then went off to the Casino, pale, impassive, a smile of complete indifference on his lips, to throw away at the baccarat table enormous sums "which he could ill afford to lose," as the notary said with a knowing air to the senior judge, whose wife had it "on good authority" that this "decadent" young man was bringing his parents' grey hair in sorrow to the grave.

Furthermore, the barrister and his friends were inexhaustibly sarcastic on the subject of a wealthy old lady of title, because she never moved anywhere without taking her whole household with her. Whenever the wives of the notary and the judge saw her in the dining-room at meal-times, they put up their lorgnettes and gave her an insolent scrutiny, as meticulous and distrustful as if she had been some dish with a pretentious name but a suspicious appearance which, after the adverse result of a systematic study, is sent away with a lofty wave of the hand and a grimace of disgust.

No doubt by this behaviour they meant only to show that, if there were things in the world which they themselves lacked

—in this instance, certain prerogatives which the old lady enjoyed, and the privilege of her acquaintance—it was not because they could not, but because they did not choose to acquire them. But they had ended up by convincing themselves that this really was what they felt; and the suppression of all desire for, of all curiosity about, ways of life which are unfamiliar, of all hope of endearing oneself to new people, for which, in these women, had been substituted a feigned contempt, a spurious jubilation, had the disagreeable effect of obliging them to label their discontent satisfaction and to lie everlastingly to themselves, two reasons why they were unhappy. But everyone else in the hotel was no doubt behaving in a similar fashion, though under different forms, and sacrificing, if not to self-esteem, at any rate to certain inculcated principles or mental habits, the disturbing thrill of being involved in an unfamiliar way of life. Of course the microcosm in which the old lady isolated herself was not poisoned with virulent rancour, as was the group in which the wives of the notary and the judge sat sneering with rage. It was indeed embalmed with a delicate and old-world fragrance which, however, was no less artificial. For at heart the old lady would probably have discovered, in attracting, in attaching to herself (and, in doing so, renewing herself) the mysterious sympathy of new people, a charm which is altogether lacking from the pleasure that is to be derived from mixing only with the people of one's own world, and reminding oneself that, this being the best of all possible worlds, the ill-informed contempt of "outsiders" may be disregarded. Perhaps she felt that if she arrived *incognito* at the Grand Hotel, Balbec, she would, in her black woollen dress and old-fashioned bonnet, bring a smile to the lips of some old reprobate, who from the depths of his rocking chair would glance up and murmur, "What a scarecrow!" or, still worse, to those of some worthy man who had, like the judge, kept between his pepper-and-salt whiskers a fresh complexion and a pair of sparkling eyes such as she liked to see, and who would at once bring the magnifying lens of the conjugal glasses to bear upon so quaint a phenomenon; and perhaps it was in unconscious apprehension of those first few minutes which one knows will be brief but which are

none the less dreaded—like one's first header into the sea—
that this lady sent a servant down in advance to inform the
hotel of the personality and habits of his mistress, and, cutting
short the manager's greetings with an abruptness in which
there was more shyness than pride, made straight for her room,
where her own curtains, replacing those that draped the hotel
windows, her own screens and photographs, set up so effectively
between her and the outside world, to which otherwise she
would have had to adapt herself, the barrier of her private life
and habits, that it was her home (in the cocoon of which she
had remained) that travelled rather than herself.

Thenceforward, having placed, between herself on the one
hand and the hotel staff and the tradesmen on the other, her
own servants who bore instead of her the shock of contact
with all this strange humanity and kept up the familiar atmosphere around their mistress, having set her prejudices between
herself and the other visitors, indifferent whether or not she
gave offence to people whom her friends would not have had
in their houses, it was in her own world that she continued to
live, by correspondence with her friends, by memories, by her
intimate awareness of her own position, the quality of her
manners, the adroitness of her courtesy. And every day,
when she came downstairs to go for a drive in her own carriage, the lady's-maid who came after her carrying her wraps,
and the footman who preceded her, seemed like sentries who,
at the gate of an embassy, flying the flag of the country to
which she belonged, assured to her upon foreign soil the
privilege of extra-territoriality. She did not leave her room
until the middle of the afternoon on the day after our arrival,
so that we did not see her in the dining-room, into which the
manager, since we were newcomers, conducted us at the lunch
hour, taking us under his wing, as a corporal takes a squad of
recruits to the master-tailor to have them fitted; we did however see a moment later a country squire and his daughter, of
an obscure but very ancient Breton family, M. and Mlle de
Stermaria, whose table had been allotted to us in the belief
that they had gone out and would not be back until the evening. Having come to Balbec only to see various country
magnates whom they knew in that neighbourhood, they spent

in the hotel dining-room, what with the invitations they accepted and the visits they paid, only such time as was strictly unavoidable. It was their haughtiness that preserved them intact from all human sympathy, from arousing the least interest in the strangers seated round about them, among whom M. de Stermaria kept up the glacial, preoccupied, distant, stiff, punctilious and ill-intentioned air that we assume in a railway refreshment-room in the midst of fellow-passengers whom we have never seen before and will never see again, and with whom we can conceive of no other relations than to defend from their onslaught our "portion" of cold chicken and our corner seat in the train. No sooner had we begun our lunch than we were asked to leave the table on the instructions of M. de Stermaria who had just arrived and, without the faintest attempt at an apology to us, requested the head waiter in our hearing to "see that such a mistake did not occur again," for it was repugnant to him that "people whom he did not know" should have taken his table.

And certainly the feeling which impelled a young actress (better known in fact for her smart clothes, her wit, her collection of German porcelain, than for the occasional parts that she had played at the Odéon), her lover, an immensely rich young man for whose sake she had acquired her culture, and two sprigs of the aristocracy at that time much in the public eye, to form an exclusive group, to travel only together, to come down to luncheon—when at Balbec—very late, after everyone else had finished, to spend the whole day in their sitting-room playing cards, reflected no sort of ill-will towards the rest of us but simply the requirements of the taste that they had formed for a certain type of witty conversation, for certain refinements of good living, which made them find pleasure in spending their time, in taking their meals, only by themselves, and would have rendered intolerable a life in common with people who had not been initiated into their mysteries. Even at a dinner-table or a card table, each of them had to be certain that in the diner or partner who sat opposite to him there were, latent and in abeyance, a certain brand of knowledge which would enable him to identify the rubbish which so many houses in Paris boast of as genuine mediaeval or Renaissance

"pieces" and, whatever the subject of discussion, criteria
common to them all wherewith to distinguish the good from
the bad. No doubt by now, at such moments, it was merely by
some rare and amusing interjection flung into the general
silence of meal or game, or by the new and charming frock
which the young actress had put on for lunch or for poker,
that the special kind of existence in which these four friends
desired everywhere to remain plunged was made apparent.
But by engulfing them thus in a system of habits which they
knew by heart it sufficed to protect them from the mystery of
the life that was going on all round them. All the long afternoon, the sea was suspended there before their eyes only as a
canvas of attractive colouring might hang on the wall of a
wealthy bachelor's flat, and it was only in the intervals between "hands" that one of the players, finding nothing better to
do, raised his eyes to it to seek some indication of the weather
or the time, and to remind the others that tea was ready. And
at night they did not dine in the hotel, where, hidden springs of
electricity flooding the great dining-room with light, it became as it were an immense and wonderful aquarium against
whose glass wall the working population of Balbec, the
fishermen and also the tradesmen's families, clustering invisibly in the outer darkness, pressed their faces to watch
the luxurious life of its occupants gently floating upon the
golden eddies within, a thing as extraordinary to the poor as
the life of strange fishes or molluscs (an important social
question, this: whether the glass wall will always protect the
banquets of these weird and wonderful creatures, or whether
the obscure folk who watch them hungrily out of the night
will not break in some day to gather them from their aquarium
and devour them). Meanwhile, perhaps, amid the dumbfounded stationary crowd out there in the dark, there may
have been some writer, some student of human ichthyology,
who, as he watched the jaws of old feminine monstrosities
close over a mouthful of submerged food, was amusing himself by classifying them by race, by innate characteristics, as
well as by those acquired characteristics which bring it about
that an old Serbian lady whose buccal appendage is that of a
great sea-fish, because from her earliest years she has moved

in the fresh waters of the Faubourg Saint-Germain, eats her salad for all the world like a La Rochefoucauld.

At that hour the three young men in dinner-jackets could be observed waiting for the young woman, who was as usual late but presently, wearing a dress that was almost always different and one of a series of scarves chosen to gratify some special taste in her lover, after having rung for the lift from her landing, would emerge from it like a doll coming out of its box. And then all four, finding that the international phenomenon of the "de luxe" hotel, having taken root at Balbec, had blossomed there in material luxury rather than in food that was fit to eat, climbed into a carriage and went off to dine a mile away in a little restaurant of repute where they held endless discussions with the cook about the composition of the menu and the cooking of its various dishes. During their drive, the road bordered with apple-trees that led out of Balbec was no more to them than the distance that must be traversed—barely distinguishable in the darkness from that which separated their homes in Paris from the Café Anglais or the Tour d'Argent—before they arrived at the fashionable little restaurant where, while the rich young man's friends envied him because he had such a smartly dressed mistress, the latter's scarves hung before the little company a sort of fragrant, flowing veil, but one that kept it apart from the outer world.

Alas for my peace of mind, I had none of the detachment that all these people showed. To many of them I gave constant thought; I should have liked not to pass unobserved by a man with a receding forehead and eyes that dodged between the blinkers of his prejudices and his upbringing, the grandee of the district, who was none other than the brother-in-law of Legrandin. He came every now and then to see somebody at Balbec, and on Sundays, by reason of the weekly garden-party that his wife and he gave, robbed the hotel of a large number of its occupants, because one or two of them were invited to these entertainments and the others, so as not to appear not to have been invited, chose that day for an expedition to some distant spot. He had had, as it happened, an exceedingly bad reception at the hotel on the first day of the

season, when the staff, freshly imported from the Riviera, did
not yet know who or what he was. Not only was he not wearing white flannels, but, with old-fashioned French courtesy
and in his ignorance of the ways of grand hotels, on coming
into the hall in which there were ladies sitting, he had taken
off his hat at the door, with the result that the manager had
not so much as raised a finger to his own in acknowledgment,
concluding that this must be someone of the most humble
extraction, what he called "sprung from the ordinary." The
notary's wife alone had felt attracted to the stranger, who
exhaled all the starched vulgarity of the really respectable, and
she had declared, with the unerring discernment and the indisputable authority of a person for whom the highest society
of Le Mans held no secrets, that one could see at a glance that
one was in the presence of a gentleman of great distinction, of
perfect breeding, a striking contrast to the sort of people one
usually saw at Balbec, whom she condemned as impossible to
know so long as she did not know them. This favourable
judgment which she had pronounced on Legrandin's brother-
in-law was based perhaps on the spiritless appearance of a
man about whom there was nothing to intimidate anyone;
perhaps also she had recognised in this gentleman farmer with
the look of a sacristan the Masonic signs of her own inveterate
clericalism.

For all that I knew that the young men who went past the
hotel every day on horseback were the sons of the shady
proprietor of a fancy goods shop whom my father would never
have dreamed of knowing, the glamour of "seaside life"
exalted them in my eyes to equestrian statues of demi-gods,
and the best thing that I could hope for was that they would
never allow their proud gaze to fall upon the wretched boy
who was myself, who left the hotel dining-room only to sit
humbly upon the sands. I should have been glad to arouse
some response even from the adventurer who had been king
of a desert island in the South Seas, even from the young consumptive, of whom I liked to think that he concealed beneath
his insolent exterior a shy and tender heart, which might
perhaps have lavished on me, and on me alone, the treasures
of its affection. Besides (contrary to what is usually said about

travelling acquaintances) since being seen in certain company can invest us, in a watering-place to which we shall return another year, with a coefficient that has no equivalent in real social life, there is nothing that, far from keeping resolutely at a distance, we cultivate with such assiduity after our return to Paris as the friendships that we have formed by the sea. I was concerned about the impression I might make on all these temporary or local celebrities whom my tendency to put myself in the place of other people and to re-create their state of mind made me place not in their true rank, that which they would have occupied in Paris for instance and which would have been quite low, but in that which they must imagine to be theirs and which indeed was theirs at Balbec, where the want of a common denominator gave them a sort of relative superiority and unwonted interest. Alas, none of these people's contempt was so painful to me as that of M. de Stermaria.

For I had noticed his daughter the moment she came into the room, her pretty face, her pallid, almost bluish complexion, the distinctiveness in the carriage of her tall figure, in her gait, which suggested to me, with reason, her heredity, her aristocratic upbringing, all the more vividly because I knew her name—like those expressive themes invented by musicians of genius which paint in splendid colours the glow of fire, the rush of water, the peace of fields and woods, to audiences who, having glanced through the programme in advance, have their imaginations trained in the right direction. "Pedigree," by adding to Mlle de Stermaria's charms the idea of their origin, made them more intelligible, more complete. It made them more desirable also, advertising their inaccessibility as a high price enhances the value of a thing that has already taken our fancy. And its stock of heredity gave to her complexion, in which so many selected juices had been blended, the savour of an exotic fruit or of a famous vintage.

Now, chance had suddenly put into our hands, my grandmother's and mine, the means of acquiring instantaneous prestige in the eyes of all the other occupants of the hotel. For on that first afternoon, at the moment when the old lady came downstairs from her room, producing, thanks to the footman who preceded her and the maid who came running

after her with a book and a rug that she had forgotten, a
marked effect upon all who beheld her and arousing in each of
them a curiosity from which it was evident that none was so
little immune as M. de Stermaria, the manager leaned across
to my grandmother and out of kindness (as one might point
out the Shah or Queen Ranavalo to an obscure onlooker who
could obviously have no sort of connexion with such mighty
potentates, but might all the same be interested to know that
he had been standing within a few feet of one) whispered in
her ear, "The Marquise de Villeparisis!" while at the same
moment the old lady, catching sight of my grandmother, could
not repress a start of pleased surprise.

It may be imagined that the sudden appearance, in the guise
of a little old woman, of the most powerful of fairies would
not have given me more pleasure, destitute as I was of any
means of access to Mlle de Stermaria, in a strange place where
I knew no one: no one, that is to say, for any practical purpose.
Aesthetically, the number of human types is so restricted that
we must constantly, wherever we may be, have the pleasure of
seeing people we know, even without looking for them in the
works of the old masters, like Swann. Thus it happened that in
the first few days of our visit to Balbec I had succeeded in
encountering Legrandin, Swann's hall porter, and Mme Swann
herself, transformed into a waiter, a foreign visitor whom I
never saw again, and a bathing superintendent. And a sort of
magnetisation attracts and retains so inseparably, one beside
another, certain characteristics of physiognomy and mentality,
that when Nature thus introduces a person into a new body she
does not mutilate him unduly. Legrandin turned waiter kept
intact his stature, the outline of his nose, part of his chin;
Mme Swann, in the masculine gender and the calling of a bathing superintendent, had been accompanied not only by her
familiar features but even by certain mannerisms of speech.
Only she could be of little if any more use to me, standing upon
the beach there in the red sash of her office, and hoisting at the
first gust of wind the flag which forbade us to bathe (for these
superintendents are prudent men, seldom knowing how to
swim), than she would have been in that fresco of the *Life of
Moses* in which Swann had long ago identified her in the person

of Jethro's Daughter. Whereas this Mme de Villeparisis was her real self; she had not been the victim of a magic spell which had robbed her of her power, but was capable, on the contrary, of putting at the disposal of mine a spell which would multiply it a hundredfold, and thanks to which, as though I had been swept through the air on the wings of a fabulous bird, I was about to cross in a few moments the infinitely wide social gulf which separated me—at least at Balbec—from Mlle de Stermaria.

Unfortunately, if there was one person in the world who, more than anyone else, lived shut up in a little world of her own, it was my grandmother. She would not even have despised me, she would simply not have understood what I meant, if she had known that I attached importance to the opinions, that I felt an interest in the persons, of people the very existence of whom she never noticed and of whom, when the time came to leave Balbec, she would not remember the names. I dared not confess to her that if these same people had seen her talking to Mme de Villeparisis, I should have been immensely gratified, because I felt that the Marquise enjoyed some prestige in the hotel and that her friendship would have given us status in the eyes of Mlle de Stermaria. Not that my grandmother's friend represented to me, in any sense of the word, a member of the aristocracy: I was too accustomed to her name, which had been familiar to my ears before my mind had begun to consider it, when as a child I had heard it uttered in conversation at home; while her title added to it only a touch of quaintness, as some uncommon Christian name would have done, or as in the names of streets, among which we can see nothing more noble in the Rue Lord Byron, in the plebeian and even squalid Rue Rochechouart, or in the Rue de Gramont than in the Rue Léonce-Reynaud or the Rue Hippolyte-Lebas. Mme de Villeparisis no more made me think of a person who belonged to a special social world than did her cousin MacMahon, whom I did not clearly distinguish from M. Carnot, likewise President of the Republic, or from Raspail, whose photograph Françoise had bought with that of Pius IX. It was one of my grandmother's principles that, when away from home, one should cease to have any social intercourse, that one did not go to the seaside to meet people, having plenty of time for that sort of thing in Paris, that they would make one waste in polite exchanges, in pointless conversation, the precious time which ought all to be spent in the open air, beside the waves; and finding it convenient to assume that this view was shared by everyone else, and that it authorised, between old friends whom chance brought face to face in the same hotel, the fiction of a mutual *incognito*, on hearing her friend's name from the manager she merely looked the other way and pretended not to see Mme de Villeparisis, who, realising that my grandmother did not want to be recognised, likewise gazed into space. She went past, and I was left in my isolation like a shipwrecked mariner who has seen a vessel apparently approaching, which has then vanished under the horizon.

She, too, had her meals in the dining-room, but at the other end of it. She knew none of the people who were staying in the hotel or who came there to call, not even M. de Cambremer; indeed, I noticed that he gave her no greeting one day when, with his wife, he had accepted an invitation to lunch with the barrister, who, intoxicated with the honour of having the nobleman at his table, avoided his habitual friends and confined himself to a distant twitch of the eyelid, so as to draw their attention to this historic event but so discreetly that his signal could not be interpreted as an invitation to join the party.

"Well, I hope you've done yourself proud, I hope you feel smart enough," the judge's wife said to him that evening.

"Smart? Why should I?" asked the barrister, concealing his rapture in an exaggerated astonishment. "Because of my guests, do you mean?" he went on, feeling that it was impossible to keep up the farce any longer. "But what is there smart about having a few friends to lunch? After all, they must feed somewhere!"

"Of course it's smart! They were the *de* Cambremers, weren't they? I recognised them at once. She's a Marquise. And quite genuine, too. Not through the females."

"Oh, she's a very simple soul, she's charming, no standoffishness about her. I thought you were coming to join us. I was making signals to you . . . I would have introduced you!" he asserted, tempering with a hint of irony the vast generosity of the offer, like Ahasuerus when he says to Esther: "Of all my Kingdom must I give you half!"

"No, no, no, no! We lie hidden, like the modest violet."

"But you were quite wrong, I assure you," replied the barrister, emboldened now that the danger point was passed. "They weren't going to eat you. I say, aren't we going to have our little game of bezique?"

"Why, of course! We didn't dare suggest it, now that you go about entertaining marquises."

"Oh, get along with you; there's nothing so very wonderful about them. Why, I'm dining there to-morrow. Would you care to go instead of me? I mean it. Honestly, I'd just as soon stay here."

"No, no! I should be removed from the bench as a reactionary," cried the senior judge, laughing till the tears came to his eyes at his own joke. "But you go to Féterne too, don't you?" he went on, turning to the notary.

"Oh, I go there on Sundays—in one door and out the other. But they don't come and have lunch with me like the Leader."

M. de Stermaria was not at Balbec that day, to the barrister's great regret. But he managed to say a word in season to the head waiter:

"Aimé, you can tell M. de Stermaria that he's not the only nobleman you've had in here. You saw the gentleman who was with me to-day at lunch? Eh? A small moustache, looked like a military man. Well, that was the Marquis de Cambremer!"

"Was it indeed? I'm not surprised to hear it."

"That will show him that he's not the only man who's got a title. That'll teach him! It's not a bad thing to take 'em down a peg or two, those noblemen. I say, Aimé, don't say anything to him unless you want to. I mean to say, it's no business of mine; besides, they know each other already."

And next day M. de Stermaria, who remembered that the barrister had once represented one of his friends, came up and introduced himself.

"Our friends in common, the de Cambremers, were anxious that we should meet, the days didn't fit—I don't know quite what went wrong," said the barrister, who, like most liars, imagined that other people do not take the trouble to investigate an unimportant detail which, for all that, may be sufficient (if chance puts you in possession of the humble facts of the case, and they contradict it) to show the liar in his true colours and to inspire a lasting mistrust.

As usual, but more easily now that her father had left her to talk to the barrister, I was gazing at Mlle de Stermaria. No less than the bold and always graceful distinctiveness of her attitudes, as when, leaning her elbows on the table, she raised her glass in both hands over her fore-arms, the dry flame of a glance at once extinguished, the ingrained, congenital hardness that one could sense, ill-concealed by her own personal inflexions, in the depths of her voice, and that had shocked my grandmother, a sort of atavistic ratchet to which she returned as soon as, in a glance or an intonation, she had finished expressing her own thoughts—all this brought the thoughts of the observer back to the long line of ancestors who had bequeathed to her that inadequacy of human sympathy, those gaps in her sensibility, a lack of fullness in the stuff of which she was made. But from a certain look which flooded for a moment the wells—instantly dry again—of her eyes, a look in which one sensed that almost humble docility which the predominance of a taste for sensual pleasures gives to the proudest of women, who will soon come to recognise but one form of personal magic, that which any man will enjoy in her eyes who can make her feel those pleasures, an actor or a mountebank for whom, perhaps, she will one day leave her husband, and from a certain pink tinge, warm and sensual, which flushed her pallid cheeks, like the colour that stained the hearts of the white water-lilies in the Vivonne, I thought I could discern that she might readily have consented to my coming to seek in her the savour of that life of poetry and romance which she led in Brittany, a life to which, whether from over-familiarity or from innate superiority, or from disgust at the penury or the avarice of her family, she seemed to attach no great value, but which, for all that, she held enclosed in her body. In the meagre stock of will-power that had been transmitted to her, and gave her expression a hint of weakness, she would not perhaps have found the strength to resist. And, crowned by a feather that was a trifle old-fashioned and pretentious, the grey felt hat which she invariably wore at meals made her all the more attractive to me, not because it was in harmony with her silver and rose complexion, but because, by making me suppose her to be poor, it brought her closer to me. Obliged by her father's presence to adopt a conventional attitude, but already bringing to the perception and classification of the people who passed before her eyes other principles than his, perhaps she saw in me not my humble rank, but the right sex and age. If one day M. de Stermaria had gone out leaving her behind, if, above all, Mme de Villeparisis, by coming to sit at our table, had given her an opinion of me which might have emboldened me to approach her, perhaps then we might have contrived to exchange a few words, to arrange a meeting, to form a closer tie. And for a whole month during which she would be left alone without her parents in her romantic Breton castle, we should perhaps have been able to wander by ourselves at evening, she and I together in the twilight through which the pink flowers of the bell heather would glow more softly above the darkening water, beneath oak trees beaten and stunted by the pounding of the waves. Together we should have roamed that island impregnated with so intense a charm for me because it had enclosed the everyday life of Mlle de Stermaria and was reflected in the memory of her eyes. For it seemed to me that I should truly have possessed her only there, when I had traversed those regions which enveloped her in so many memories—a veil which my desire longed to tear aside, one of those veils which nature interposes between woman and her pursuers (with the same intention as when, for all of us, she places the act of reproduction between ourselves and our keenest pleasure, and for insects, places before the nectar the pollen which they must carry away with them) in order that, tricked by the illusion of possessing her thus more completely, they may be forced to occupy first the scenes among which she lives and which, of more service to their imagination than sensual pleasure can be, yet would not without that pleasure have sufficed to attract them.

But I was obliged to take my eyes from Mlle de Stermaria, for already, considering no doubt that making the acquaintance of an important person was an odd, brief act which was sufficient in itself and, to bring out all the interest that was latent in it, required only a handshake and a penetrating stare, without either immediate conversation or any subsequent relations, her father had taken leave of the barrister and returned to sit down facing her, rubbing his hands like a man who has just made a valuable acquisition. As for the barrister, once the first emotion of this interview had subsided, he could be heard, as on other days, addressing the head waiter every other minute: "But I'm not a king, Aimé; go and attend to the king! I say, Chief, those little trout don't look at all bad, do they? We must ask Aimé to let us have some. Aimé, that little fish you have over there looks to me highly commendable: will you bring us some, please, Aimé, and don't be sparing with it."

He repeated the name "Aimé" all the time, with the result than when he had anyone to dinner the guest would remark "I can see you're quite at home in this place," and would feel himself obliged to keep on saying "Aimé" also, from that tendency, combining elements of timidity, vulgarity and silliness, which many people have to believe that it is smart and witty to imitate slavishly the people in whose company they happen to be. The barrister repeated the name incessantly, but with a smile, for he wanted to exhibit at one and the same time his good relations with the head waiter and his own superior station. And the head waiter, whenever he caught the sound of his own name, smiled too, as though touched and at the same time proud, showing that he was conscious of the honour and could appreciate the joke.

Terrifying as I always found these meals, in that vast restaurant, generally full, of the Grand Hotel, they became even more terrifying when there arrived for a few days the proprietor (or he may have been only the general manager, appointed by a board of directors) not only of this "palace" but of seven or eight more besides, situated at all the four corners of France, in each of which, shuttling from one to the other, he would spend a week now and again. Then, just after dinner had begun, there appeared every evening at the entrance to the dining-room this small man with the white hair and a red nose, astonishingly neat and impassive, who was known, it appeared, as well in London as at Monte Carlo, as one of the leading hoteliers in Europe. Once when I had gone out for a moment at the beginning of dinner, as I came in again I passed close by him, and he bowed to me, no doubt to acknowledge that he was my host, but with a coldness in which I could not distinguish whether it was attributable to the reserve of a man who could never forget what he was, or to his contempt for a customer of so little importance. To those, on the other hand, whose importance was considerable, the general manager would bow with quite as much coldness but more deeply, lowering his eyelids with a sort of bashful respect, as though he had found himself confronted, at a funeral, with the father of the deceased or with the Blessed Sacrament. Except for these icy and infrequent salutations, he made not the slightest movement, as if to show that his glittering eyes, which appeared to be starting out of his head, saw everything, controlled everything, ensured for the "Dinner at the Grand Hotel" perfection in every detail as well an overall harmony. He felt, evidently, that he was more than the producer, more than the conductor, nothing less than the generalissimo. Having decided that a contemplation raised to the maximum degree of intensity would suffice to assure him that everything was in readiness, that no mistake had been made which could lead to disaster, and enable him at last to assume his responsibilities, he abstained not merely from any gesture but even from moving his eyes, which, petrified by the intensity of their gaze, took in and directed operations as a whole. I felt that even the movements of my spoon did not escape him, and were he to vanish after the soup, for the whole of dinner, the inspection he had held would have taken away my appetite. His own was exceedingly good, as one could see at luncheon, which he took like an ordinary guest of the hotel at the same hour as everyone else in the public dining-room. His table had this peculiarity only, that by his side, while he was eating, the other manager, the resident one, remained standing all the time making conversation. For, being subordinate to the general manager, he was anxious to please a man of whom he lived in constant fear. My own fear of him diminished during these luncheons, for being then lost in the crowd of visitors he would exercise the discretion of a general sitting in a restaurant where there are also private soldiers, in not seeming to take any notice of them. Nevertheless when the porter, from the midst of his cluster of bell-hops, announced to me: "He leaves to-morrow morning for Dinard. Then he's going down to Biarritz, and after that to Cannes," I began to breathe more freely.

My life in the hotel was rendered not only gloomy because I had made no friends there but uncomfortable because Françoise had made many. It might be thought that they would have made things easier for us in various respects. Quite the contrary. The proletariat, if they succeeded only with great difficulty in being treated as people she knew by Françoise, and could not succeed at all unless they fulfilled certain exacting conditions of politeness towards her, were, on the other hand, once they had reached that point, the only people who mattered to her. Her time-honoured code taught her that she was in no way beholden to the friends of her employers, that she might, if she was busy, shut the door without ceremony in the face of a lady who had come to call on my grandmother. But towards her own acquaintance, that is to say the select handful of the lower orders whom she admitted to her fastidious friendship, her actions were regulated by the most subtle and most stringent of protocols. Thus Françoise, having made the acquaintance of the man in the coffee-shop and of a young lady's-maid who did dressmaking for a Belgian lady, no longer went upstairs immediately after lunch to get my grandmother's things ready, but came an hour later, because the coffee-man had wanted to make her a cup of coffee or a *tisane* in his shop, or the maid had invited her to go and watch her sew, and to refuse either of them would have been impossible, one of those things that were not done. Moreover, particular regard was due to the little sewing-maid, who was an orphan and had been brought up by strangers to whom she still went occasionally for a few days' holiday. Her situation aroused Françoise's pity, and also her benevolent contempt. She who had a family, a little house that had come to her from her parents, with a field in which her brother kept a few cows, could not regard so uprooted a creature as her equal. And since this girl hoped, on Assumption Day, to be allowed to pay her benefactors a visit, Françoise kept on repeating: "She does make me laugh! She says, 'I hope to be going home for the Assumption.' Home, says she! It isn't just that it's not her own place, it's people as took her in from nowhere, and the creature says 'home' just as if it really was her home. Poor thing! What a misery it must be, not to know what it is to have a home." Still, if Françoise had associated only with the ladies'-maids brought to the hotel by other visitors, who fed with her in the "service" quarters and, seeing her grand lace cap and her fine profile, took her perhaps for some lady of noble birth, whom "reduced circumstances" or a personal attachment had driven to serve as companion to my grandmother, if in a word Françoise had known only people who did not belong to the hotel, no great harm would have been done, since she could not have prevented them from being of some service to us, for the simple reason that in no circumstances, even without her knowledge, would it have been possible for them to be of service to us at all. But she had formed connexions also with one of the wine waiters, with a man in the kitchen, and with the head chambermaid of our landing. And the result of this in our everyday life was that Françoise—who on the day of her arrival, when she still did not know anyone, would set all the bells jangling for the slightest thing, at hours when my grandmother and I would never have dared to ring, and if we offered some gentle admonition would answer: "Well, we're paying enough for it, aren't we?" as though it were she herself that would have to pay— now that she had made friends with a personage in the kitchen, which had appeared to us to augur well for our future comfort, were my grandmother or I to complain of cold feet, Françoise, even at an hour that was quite normal, dared not ring, assuring us that it would give offence because they would have to relight the boilers, or because it would interrupt the servants' dinner and they would be annoyed. And she ended with a formula that, in spite of the dubious way in which she pronounced it, was none the less clear and put us plainly in the wrong: "The fact is ..." We did not insist, for fear of bringing upon ourselves another, far more serious: "It's a matter ...!" So that what it amounted to was that we could no longer have any hot water because Françoise had become a friend of the person who heated it.

In the end we too made a social connexion, in spite of but through my grandmother, for she and Mme de Villeparisis collided one morning in a doorway and were obliged to accost each other, not without having first exchanged gestures of surprise and hesitation, performed movements of withdrawal and uncertainty, and finally broken into protestations of joy and greeting, as in certain scenes in Molière where two actors who have been delivering long soliloquies each on his own account, a few feet apart, are supposed not yet to have seen each other, and then suddenly catching sight of each other, cannot believe their eyes, break off what they are saying, and then simultaneously find their tongues again (the chorus meanwhile having kept the dialogue going) and fall into each other's arms. Mme de Villeparisis tactfully made as if to leave my grandmother to herself after the first greetings, but my grandmother insisted on staying to talk to her until lunch-time, being anxious to discover how her friend managed to get her letters earlier than we got ours, and to get such nice grilled dishes (for Mme de Villeparisis, who took a keen interest in her food, had the poorest opinion of the hotel kitchen which served us with meals that my grandmother, still quoting Mme de Sévigné, described as "of a sumptuousness to make you die of hunger"). And the Marquise formed the habit of coming every day, while waiting to be served, to sit down for a moment at our table in the dining-room, insisting that we should not rise from our chairs or in any way put ourselves out. At the most we would occasionally linger, after finishing our lunch, to chat to her, at that sordid moment when the knives are left littering the tablecloth among crumpled napkins. For my own part, in order to preserve (so that I might be able to enjoy Balbec) the idea that I was on the uttermost promontory of the earth, I compelled myself to look farther afield, to notice only the sea, to seek in it the effects described by Baudelaire and to let my gaze fall upon our table only on days when there was set on it some gigantic fish, some marine monster, which unlike the knives and forks was contemporary with the primitive epochs in which the Ocean first began to teem with life, at the time of the Cimmerians, a fish whose body with its numberless vertebrae, its blue and pink veins, had been constructed by nature, but according to an architectural plan, like a polychrome cathedral of the deep.

As a barber, seeing an officer whom he is accustomed to shave with special deference and care recognise a customer who has just entered the shop and stop for a moment to talk to him, rejoices in the thought that these are two men of the same social order, and cannot help smiling as he goes to fetch the bowl of soap, for he knows that in his establishment, to the vulgar routine of a mere barber's-shop are being added social, not to say aristocratic pleasures, so Aimé, seeing that Mme de Villeparisis had found in us old friends, went to fetch our finger-bowls with the proudly modest and knowingly discreet smile of a hostess who knows when to leave her guests to themselves. He suggested also a pleased and loving father who watches silently over the happy pair who have plighted their troth at his hospitable board. Besides, it was enough merely to utter the name of a person of title for Aimé to appear pleased, unlike Françoise, in whose presence you could not mention Count So-and-so without her face darkening and her speech becoming dry and curt, which meant that she cherished the aristocracy not less than Aimé but more. But then Françoise had that quality which in others she condemned as the worst possible fault: she was proud. She was not of that amenable and good-natured race to which Aimé belonged. They feel and they exhibit an intense delight when you tell them a piece of news which may be more or less sensational but is at any rate new, and not to be found in the papers. Françoise would refuse to appear surprised. You might have announced in her hearing that the Archduke Rudolf—not that she had the least suspicion of his having ever existed—was not, as was generally supposed, dead, but "alive and kicking," and she would have answered only "Yes," as though she had known it all the time. It may, however, have been that if, even from our own lips, from us

whom she so meekly called her masters and who had so nearly
succeeded in taming her, she could not hear the name of a
nobleman without having to restrain an impulse of anger, this
was because the family from which she had sprung occupied
in its own village a comfortable and independent position,
unlikely to be disturbed in the consideration which it enjoyed
save by those same nobles in whose households, meanwhile,
from his boyhood, an Aimé would have been domiciled as a
servant, if not actually brought up by their charity. Hence, for
Françoise, Mme de Villeparisis had to make amends for being
noble. But (in France, at any rate) that is precisely the talent,
in fact the sole occupation of the aristocracy. Françoise, following the common tendency of servants, who pick up incessantly
from the conversation of their masters with other people
fragmentary observations from which they are apt to draw
erroneous conclusions—as humans do with respect to the
habits of animals—was constantly discovering that somebody
had "snubbed" us, a conclusion to which she was easily led
not so much, perhaps, by her extravagant love for us as by the
delight that she took in being disagreeable to us. But having
once established, without possibility of error, the endless
consideration and kindness shown to us, and shown to herself
also, by Mme de Villeparisis, Françoise forgave her for being
a marquise, and, as she had never ceased to admire her for
being one, preferred her thenceforward to all our other friends.
It must be added that no one else took the trouble to be so
continually nice to us. Whenever my grandmother remarked
on a book that Mme de Villeparisis was reading, or said she
had been admiring the fruit which someone had just sent to
our friend, within an hour the footman would come to our
rooms with book or fruit. And the next time we saw her, in
response to our thanks she would simply say, as though trying
to find an excuse for her present in some special use to which
it might be put: "It's nothing wonderful, but the newspapers
come so late here; one must have something to read," or "It's
always wiser to have fruit one can be quite certain of, at the
seaside."

"But I don't believe I've ever seen you eating oysters," she
said to us one day (increasing the sense of disgust which I felt

at that moment, for the living flesh of oysters revolted me even more than the viscosity of the stranded jelly-fish defiled on the Balbec beach for me). "They're quite delicious down here! Oh, let me tell my maid to fetch your letters when she goes for mine. What, your daughter writes to you *every day?* But what on earth can you find to say to each other?"

My grandmother was silent, but it may be assumed that her silence was due to disdain, for she used to repeat, when she wrote to Mamma, the words of Mme de Sévigné: "As soon as I have received a letter, I want another at once; I sigh for nothing else. There are few who are worthy to understand what I feel." And I was afraid that she might apply to Mme de Villeparisis the conclusion: "I seek out those who are of this chosen few, and I avoid the rest." She fell back upon praise of the fruit which Mme de Villeparisis had sent us the day before. And it had indeed been so fine that the manager, in spite of the jealousy aroused by our neglect of his official offerings, had said to me: "I am like you; I am sweeter for fruit than any other kind of dessert." My grandmother told her friend that she had enjoyed them all the more because the fruit which we got in the hotel was generally horrid. "I cannot," she went on, "say with Mme de Sévigné that if we should take a sudden fancy for bad fruit we should be obliged to order it from Paris." "Oh yes, of course, you read Mme de Sévigné. I've seen you with her letters ever since the day you came." (She forgot that she had never officially seen my grandmother in the hotel before meeting her in that doorway.) "Don't you find it rather exaggerated, her constant anxiety about her daughter? She refers to it too often to be really sincere. She's not very natural." My grandmother felt that any discussion would be futile, and so as not to be obliged to speak of the things she loved to a person incapable of understanding them, concealed the *Mémoires de Madame de Beausergent* by laying her bag upon them.

Were she to encounter Françoise at the moment (which Françoise called "the noon") when, wearing her fine cap and surrounded with every mark of respect, she was coming downstairs to "feed with the service," Mme Villeparisis would stop her to ask after us. And Françoise, when transmitting to us the

Marquise's message: "She said to me, 'You'll be sure and bid them good day,' she said," would counterfeit the voice of Mme de Villeparisis, whose exact words she imagined herself to be quoting textually, whereas in fact she was distorting them no less than Plato distorts the words of Socrates or St John the words of Jesus. Françoise was naturally deeply touched by these attentions. Only she did not believe my grandmother, but supposed that she must be lying in the interests of class (the rich always supporting one another) when she assured us that Mme de Villeparisis had been lovely as a young woman. It was true that of this loveliness only the faintest trace remained, from which no one—unless he happened to be a great deal more of an artist than Françoise—would have been able to reconstitute her ruined beauty. For in order to understand how beautiful an elderly woman may once have been one must not only study but interpret every line of her face.

"I must remember some time to ask her whether I'm not right, after all, in thinking that there's some connexion with the Guermantes," said my grandmother, to my great indignation. How could I be expected to believe in a common origin uniting two names which had entered my consciousness, one through the low and shameful gate of experience, the other by the golden gate of imagination?

We had several times, in the last few days, seen driving past us in a stately equipage, tall, red-haired, handsome, with a rather prominent nose, the Princesse de Luxembourg, who was staying in the neighbourhood for a few weeks. Her carriage had stopped outside the hotel, a footman had come in and spoken to the manager, had gone back to the carriage and had reappeared with the most amazing armful of fruit (which combined a variety of seasons in a single basket, like the bay itself) with a card: "La Princesse de Luxembourg," on which were scrawled a few words in pencil. For what princely traveller, sojourning here *incognito*, could they be intended, those plums, glaucous, luminous and spherical as was at that moment the circumfluent sea, those transparent grapes clustering on the shrivelled wood, like a fine day in autumn, those pears of a heavenly ultramarine? For it could not be on my grandmother's friend that the Princess had meant to pay a call.

And yet on the following evening Mme de Villeparisis sent us the bunch of grapes, cool, liquid, golden, and plums and pears which we remembered too, though the plums had changed, like the sea at our dinner-hour, to a dull purple, and in the ultramarine of the pears there floated the shapes of a few pink clouds.

A few days later we met Mme de Villeparisis as we came away from the symphony concert that was given every morning on the beach. Convinced that the music that I heard there (the Prelude to *Lohengrin*, the Overture to *Tannhäuser* and suchlike) expressed the loftiest of truths, I tried to raise myself in so far as I could in order to reach and grasp them, I drew from myself, in order to understand them, and put back into them all that was best and most profound in my own nature at that time. But, as we came out of the concert, and, on our way back to the hotel, had stopped for a moment on the front, my grandmother and I, to exchange a few words with Mme de Villeparisis who told us that she had ordered some *croque-monsieurs* and a dish of creamed eggs for us at the hotel, I saw, in the distance, coming in our direction, the Princesse de Luxembourg, half leaning upon a parasol in such a way as to impart to her tall and wonderful form that slight inclination, to make it trace that arabesque, so dear to the women who had been beautiful under the Empire and knew how, with drooping shoulders, arched backs, concave hips and taut legs, to make their bodies float as softly as a silken scarf about the rigid armature of an invisible shaft which might be supposed to have transfixed it. She went out every morning for a stroll on the beach almost at the time when everyone else, after bathing, was coming home to lunch, and as hers was not until half past one she did not return to her villa until long after the hungry bathers had left the scorching beach a desert. Mme de Villeparisis introduced my grandmother and was about to introduce me, but had first to ask me my name, which she could not remember. She had perhaps never known it, or if she had must have forgotten years ago to whom my grandmother had married her daughter. The name appeared to make a sharp impression on Mme de Villeparisis. Meanwhile the Princesse de Luxembourg had offered us her hand and from

time to time, while she chatted to the Marquise, turned to
bestow a kindly glance on my grandmother and myself, with
that embryonic kiss which we put into our smiles when they
are addressed to a baby out with its "Nana." Indeed, in
her anxiety not to appear to be enthroned in a higher sphere
than ours, she had probably miscalculated the distance, for by
an error in adjustment her eyes became infused with such
benevolence that I foresaw the moment when she would put out
her hand and stroke us like two lovable beasts who had poked
our heads out at her through the bars of our cage in the Zoo.
And immediately, as it happened, this idea of caged animals
and the Bois de Boulogne received striking confirmation. It
was the time of day when the beach is crowded by itinerant and
clamorous vendors, hawking cakes and sweets and biscuits.
Not knowing quite what to do to show her affection for us,
the Princess hailed the next one to come by; he had nothing
left but a loaf of rye bread, of the kind one throws to the
ducks. The Princess took it and said to me: "For your grandmother." And yet it was to me that she held it out, saying with
a friendly smile, "You shall give it to her yourself," thinking
that my pleasure would thus be more complete if there were
no intermediary between myself and the animals. Other vendors came up, and she stuffed my pockets with everything that
they had, tied up in packets, comfits, sponge-cakes, sugar-
sticks. "You will eat some yourself," she told me, "and give
some to your grandmother," and she had the vendors paid
by the little negro page, dressed in red satin, who followed her
everywhere and was a nine days' wonder on the beach. Then
she said good-bye to Mme de Villeparisis and held out her
hand to us with the intention of treating us in the same way as
she treated her friend, as people whom she knew, and of bringing herself within our reach. But this time she must have
reckoned our level as not quite so low in the scale of creation,
for her equality with us was indicated by the Princess to my
grandmother by that tender and maternal smile which one
bestows upon a little boy when one says good-bye to him as
though to a grown-up person. By a miraculous stride in evolution, my grandmother was no longer a duck or an antelope,
but had already become what Mme Swann would have called

a *"baby."* Finally, having taken leave of us all, the Princess resumed her stroll along the sunlit esplanade, curving and inflecting her splendid form, which, like a serpent coiled about a wand, twined itself round the white parasol patterned in blue which she carried unopened in her hand. She was my first Royalty—I say my first, for the Princesse Mathilde was not at all royal in her ways. The second, as we shall see in due course, was to astonish me no less by her graciousness. One aspect of the benevolence of the nobility, kindly intermediaries between commoners and kings, was revealed to me next day when Mme de Villeparisis reported: "She thought you quite charming. She is a woman of the soundest judgment, the warmest heart. Not like so many queens and highnesses. She has real merit." And Mme de Villeparisis added in a tone of conviction, and quite thrilled to be able to say it to us: "I think she would be delighted to see you again."

But on that previous morning, after we had parted from the Princesse de Luxembourg, Mme de Villeparisis said a thing which impressed me far more and was not prompted merely by friendly feeling.

"Are you," she had asked me, "the son of the Permanent Secretary at the Ministry? Indeed! I'm told your father is a most charming man. He is having a splendid holiday just now."

A few days earlier we had heard, in a letter from Mamma, that my father and his travelling-companion M. de Norpois had lost their luggage.

"It has been found, or rather it was never really lost. I can tell you what happened," explained Mme de Villeparisis, who, without our knowing how, seemed to be far better informed than ourselves about my father's travels. "I think your father is now planning to come home earlier, next week, in fact, as he will probably give up the idea of going to Algeciras. But he's anxious to spend a day longer in Toledo, since he's an admirer of a pupil of Titian—I forget the name—whose work can only be seen properly there."

And I wondered by what strange accident, in the impartial telescope through which Mme de Villeparisis considered, from a safe distance, the minuscule, perfunctory, vague agitation of the host of people whom she knew, there had come to be inserted at the spot through which she observed my father a fragment of glass of prodigious magnifying power which made her see in such high relief and in the fullest detail everything that was agreeable about him, the contingencies that obliged him to return home, his difficulties with the customs, his admiration for El Greco, and, altering the scale of her vision, showed her this one man, so large among all the rest so small, like that Jupiter to whom Gustave Moreau, when he portrayed him by the side of a weak mortal, gave a superhuman stature.

My grandmother bade Mme de Villeparisis good-bye, so that we might stay and imbibe the fresh air for a little while longer outside the hotel, until they signalled to us through the glazed partition that our lunch was ready. There were sounds of uproar. The young mistress of the King of the Cannibal Island had been down to bathe and was now coming back to the hotel.

"Really and truly, it's a perfect plague, it's enough to make one decide to emigrate!" cried the barrister in a towering rage as he crossed her path.

Meanwhile the notary's wife was following the bogus queen with eyes that seemed ready to start from their sockets.

"I can't tell you how angry Mme Blandais makes me when she stares at those people like that," said the barrister to the judge, "I feel I want to slap her. That's just the way to make the wretches appear important, which is of course the very thing they want. Do ask her husband to tell her what a fool she's making of herself. I swear I won't go out with them again if they stop and gape at those masqueraders."

As to the coming of the Princesse de Luxembourg, whose carriage, on the day she had left the fruit, had drawn up outside the hotel, it had not passed unobserved by the little group of wives, the notary's, the barrister's and the judge's, who had already for some time past been extremely anxious to know whether that Mme de Villeparisis whom everyone treated with so much respect—which all these ladies were burning to hear that she did not deserve—was a genuine marquise and not an adventuress. Whenever Mme de Villeparisis passed through the hall the judge's wife, who scented irregularities everywhere, would lift her nose from her needlework and stare at the intruder in a way that made her friends die with laughter.

"Oh, well, you know," she proudly explained, "I always begin by believing the worst. I will never admit that a woman is properly married until she has shown me her birth certificate and her marriage lines. But never fear—just wait till I've finished my little investigation."

And so day after day the ladies would come together and laughingly ask: "Any news?"

But on the evening of the Princesse de Luxembourg's call the judge's wife laid a finger on her lips.

"I've discovered something."

"Oh, isn't Mme Poncin simply wonderful? I never saw . . . But do tell us! What's happened?"

"Just listen to this. A woman with yellow hair and six inches of paint on her face and a carriage which reeked of harlot a mile away—which only a creature like that would dare to have—came here to-day to call on the so-called Marquise!"

"Oh-yow-yow! Tut-tut-tut-tut. Did you ever! Why, it must be the woman we saw—you remember, Leader—we said at the time we didn't at all like the look of her, but we didn't know that it was the 'Marquise' she'd come to see. A woman with a nigger-boy, you mean?"

"That's the one."

"You don't say! Do you happen to know her name?"

"Yes, I made a mistake on purpose. I picked up her card. She *trades* under the name of the 'Princesse de Luxembourg'! Wasn't I right to have my doubts about her? It's a nice thing to have to fraternise with a Baronne d'Ange like that?"[25]

The barrister quoted Mathurin Régnier's *Macette* to the judge.

It must not, however, be supposed that this misunderstanding was merely temporary, like those that occur in the second act of a farce to be cleared up before the final curtain. Mme de Luxembourg, a niece of the King of England and of the Emperor of Austria, and Mme de Villeparisis, when one called to take the other for a drive, always appeared like two "old trots" of the kind one has always such difficulty in avoid-

ing at a watering-place. Nine tenths of the men of the Faubourg Saint-Germain appear to a large section of the middle
classes as crapulous paupers (which, individually, they not
infrequently are) whom no respectable person would dream of
asking to dinner. The middle classes pitch their standards in this
respect too high, for the failings of these men would never
prevent their being received with every mark of esteem in
houses which they themselves will never enter. And so fondly
do the aristocracy imagine that the middle classes know this
that they affect a simplicity in speaking of themselves, a dis-
paragement of friends of theirs who are particularly "on their
beam ends," that compounds the misunderstanding. If, by
chance, a man of the fashionable world has dealings with the
petty bourgeoisie because, having more money than he knows
what to do with, he finds himself elected chairman of all
sorts of important financial concerns, his business associates
who at last see a nobleman worthy to be ranked with the professional classes, would take their oaths that such a man would
not consort with the Marquis ruined by gambling whom the
said business associates assume to be all the more destitute of
friends the more friendly he makes himself. And they cannot
get over their surprise when the duke who is Chairman of the
Board of Directors of the colossal undertaking arranges a
marriage for his son with the daughter of that very marquis,
who may be a gambler but who bears the oldest name in
France, just as a sovereign would sooner see his son marry
the daughter of a dethroned king than that of a president still
in office. In other words, the two worlds have as fanciful
a view of one another as the inhabitants of the resort situated at
one end of Balbec Bay have of the resort at the other end: from
Rivebelle you can just see Marcouville l'Orgueilleuse; but
even that is deceptive, for you imagine that you are seen from
Marcouville, where, as a matter of fact, the splendours of
Rivebelle are almost wholly invisible.

The Balbec doctor, called in to cope with a sudden feverish
attack, gave the opinion that I ought not to stay out all day on
the beach in the blazing sun during the hot weather, and wrote
out various prescriptions for me. My grandmother took these
with a show of respect in which I could at once discern her

firm resolve to ignore them all, but did pay attention to the advice on the matter of hygienics, and accepted an offer from Mme de Villeparisis to take us for drives in her carriage. After this I would spend the mornings going to and fro between my own room and my grandmother's. Hers did not look out directly on the sea, as mine did, but was open on three of its four sides—on to a strip of the esplanade, a court-yard, and a view of the country inland—and was furnished differently from mine, with armchairs embroidered with metallic filigree and pink flowers from which the cool and pleasant odour that greeted one on entering seemed to ema-nate. And at that hour when the sun's rays, drawn from different exposures and, as it were, from different hours of the day, broke the angles of the wall, projected on to the chest of drawers, side by side with a reflection of the beach, a festal altar as variegated as a bank of field-flowers, hung on the fourth wall the folded, quivering, warm wings of a radiance ready at any moment to resume its flight, warmed like a bath a square of provincial carpet before the window overlooking the courtyard which the sun festooned and patterned like a climbing vine, and added to the charm and complexity of the room's furniture by seeming to pluck and scatter the petals of the silken flowers on the chairs and to make their silver threads stand out from the fabric, this room in which I lingered for a moment before going to get ready for our drive suggested a prism in which the colours of the light that shone outside were broken up, a hive in which the sweet juices of the day which I was about to taste were distilled, scattered, intoxicating and visible, a garden of hope which dissolved in a quivering haze of silver threads and rose petals. But before all this I had drawn back my own curtains, impatient to know what Sea it was that was playing that morning by the shore, like a Nereid. For none of those Seas ever stayed with us longer than a day. The next day there would be another, which some-times resembled its predecessor. But I never saw the same one twice.

There were some that were of so rare a beauty that my pleasure on catching sight of them was enhanced by surprise. By what privilege, on one morning rather than another, did the window on being uncurtained disclose to my wondering eyes the nymph Glauconome, whose lazy beauty, gently breathing, had the transparency of a vaporous emerald through which I could see teeming the ponderable elements that coloured it? She made the sun join in her play, with a smile attenuated by an invisible haze which was no more than a space kept vacant about her translucent surface, which, thus curtailed, was rendered more striking, like those goddesses whom the sculptor carves in relief upon a block of marble the rest of which he leaves unchiselled. So, in her matchless colour, she invited us out over those rough terrestrial roads, from which, sitting with Mme de Villeparisis in her barouche, we should glimpse, all day long and without ever reaching it, the coolness of her soft palpitation.

Mme de Villeparisis used to order her carriage early, so that we should have time to reach Saint-Mars-le-Vêtu, or the rocks of Quetteholme, or some other goal which, for a somewhat lumbering vehicle, was far enough off to require the whole day. In my joy at the thought of the long drive we were going to take I would hum some tune that I had heard recently as I strolled up and down until Mme de Villeparisis was ready. If it was Sunday, hers would not be the only carriage drawn up outside the hotel; several hired cabs would be waiting there, not only for the people who had been invited to Féterne by Mme de Cambremer, but for those who, rather than stay at home all day like children in disgrace, declared that Sunday was always quite impossible at Balbec and set off immediately after lunch to hide themselves in some neighbouring watering-place or to visit one of the "sights" of the neighbourhood. And indeed whenever (which was often) Mme Blandais was asked if she had been to the Cambremers', she would answer emphatically: "No, we went to the Falls of the Bec," as though that were the sole reason for her not having spent the day at Féterne. And the barrister would charitably remark: "I envy you. I wish I had gone there instead. They must be well worth seeing."

Beside the row of carriages, in front of the porch in which I stood waiting, was planted, like some shrub of a rare species, a young page who attracted the eye no less by the unusual and harmonious colouring of his hair than by his plant-like epidermis. Inside, in the hall, corresponding to the narthex, or Church of the Catechumens in a primitive basilica, through which the persons who were not staying in the hotel were entitled to pass, the comrades of the "outside" page did not indeed work much harder than he but did at least execute certain movements. It is probable that in the early morning they helped with the cleaning. But in the afternoon they stood there only like a chorus who, even when there is nothing for them to do, remain upon the stage in order to strengthen the representation. The General Manager, the same who had so terrified me, reckoned on increasing their number considerably next year, for he had "big ideas." And this prospect greatly afflicted the manager of the hotel, who found that all these boys were simply "busybodies," by which he meant that they got in the visitors' way and were of no use to anyone. But between lunch and dinner at least, between the exits and entrances of the visitors, they did fill an otherwise empty stage, like those pupils of Mme de Maintenon who, in the garb of young Israelites, carry on the action whenever Esther or Joad "goes off." But the outside page, with his delicate tints, his slender, fragile frame, in proximity to whom I stood waiting for the Marquise to come down, preserved an immobility mixed with a certain melancholy, for his elder brothers had left the hotel for more brilliant careers elsewhere, and he felt isolated upon this alien soil. At last Mme de Villeparisis appeared. To stand by her carriage and to help her into it ought perhaps to have been part of the young page's duties. But he knew that a person who brings her own servants to an hotel expects them to wait on her and is not as a rule lavish with her tips, and that the same was true also of the nobility of the old Faubourg Saint-Germain. Mme de Villeparisis belonged to both these categories. The arborescent page concluded therefore that he could expect nothing from her, and leaving her own maid and footman to pack her and her belongings into the carriage, he continued to dream sadly of the enviable lot of his brothers and preserved his vegetable immobility.

We would set off; some time after rounding the railway station, we came into a country road which soon became as

familiar to me as the roads round Combray, from the bend
where it took off between charming orchards to the turning
at which we left it where there were tilled fields on either side.
Among these we could see here and there an apple-tree,
stripped it was true of its blossom and bearing no more than a
fringe of pistils, but sufficient even so to enchant me since I
could imagine, seeing those inimitable leaves, how their broad
expanse, like the ceremonial carpet spread for a wedding that
was now over, had been only recently swept by the white
satin train of their blushing flowers.

How often in Paris, during the month of May of the following year, was I to bring home a branch of apple-blossom from
the florist and afterwards to spend the night in company with its
flowers in which bloomed the same creamy essence that still
powdered with its froth the burgeoning leaves and between
whose white corollas it seemed almost as though it had been the
florist who, from generosity towards me, from a taste for invention too and as an effective contrast, had added on either side the
supplement of a becoming pink bud: I sat gazing at them, I
grouped them in the light of my lamp—for so long that I was
often still there when the dawn brought to their whiteness the
same flush with which it must at that moment have been tingeing
their sisters on the Balbec road—and I sought to carry them
back in my imagination to that roadside, to multiply them, to
spread them out within the frame prepared for them, on the
canvas already primed, of those fields and orchards whose
outline I knew by heart, which I so longed to see, which
one day I must see, again, at the moment when, with the
exquisite fervour of genius, spring covers their canvas with its
colours.

Before getting into the carriage, I had composed the seascape which I was going to look out for, which I hoped to see
with Baudelaire's "radiant sun" upon it, and which at Balbec I
could distinguish only in too fragmentary a form, broken by so
many vulgar adjuncts that had no place in my dream—
bathers, cabins, pleasure yachts. But when, Mme de Villeparisis's carriage having reached the top of a hill, I caught a
glimpse of the sea through the leafy boughs of the trees, then
no doubt at such a distance those temporal details which had

set it apart, as it were, from nature and history disappeared,
and I could try to persuade myself as I looked down upon its
waters that they were the same which Leconte de Lisle describes for us in his *Orestie*, where "like a flight of birds of
prey, before the dawn of day" the long-haired warriors of heroic
Hellas "with oars an hundred thousand sweep the huge resounding deep." But on the other hand I was no longer near
enough to the sea, which seemed to me not alive but congealed, I no longer felt any power beneath its colours, spread
like those of a picture between the leaves, through which it
appeared as insubstantial as the sky and only of an intenser blue.

Mme de Villeparisis, seeing that I was fond of churches,
promised me that we should visit several of them, and especially the church at Carqueville "quite buried in all its old
ivy," as she said with a gesture of her hand which seemed
tastefully to be clothing the absent façade in an invisible and
delicate screen of foliage. Mme de Villeparisis would often,
with this little descriptive gesture, find just the right word to
define the charm and distinctiveness of an historic building,
always avoiding technical terms, but incapable of concealing
her thorough understanding of the things to which she referred. She appeared to seek an excuse for this erudition in the
fact that one of her father's country houses, the one in which
she had lived as a girl, was situated in a region where there
were churches similar in style to those round Balbec, so that
it would have been shameful if she had not acquired a taste for
architecture, this house being, incidentally, one of the finest
examples of that of the Renaissance. But as it was also a regular
museum, as moreover Chopin and Liszt had played there,
Lamartine recited poetry, all the most famous artists for fully a
century written thoughts, dashed off melodies, made sketches
in the family album, Mme de Villeparisis ascribed, whether
from delicacy, good breeding, true modesty or want of
speculative intelligence, only this purely material origin to her
acquaintance with all the arts, and had seemingly come to
regard painting, music, literature, and philosophy as the
appanage of a young lady brought up on the most aristocratic
lines in an historic building that was classified and starred. One
got the impression that for her there were no other pictures

than those that have been inherited. She was pleased that my
grandmother liked a necklace which she wore, and which
hung over her dress. It appeared in the portrait of an ancestress of hers, by Titian, which had never left the family.
So that one could be certain of its being genuine. She would not
hear a word about pictures bought, heaven knew where, by a
Croesus; she was persuaded in advance that they were fakes,
and had no desire to see them. We knew that she herself
painted flowers in water-colour, and my grandmother, who
had heard these praised, spoke to her of them. Mme de Villeparisis modestly changed the subject, but without showing
any more surprise or pleasure than would an artist of established reputation to whom compliments mean nothing. She
said merely that it was a delightful pastime because, even if
the flowers that sprang from the brush were nothing wonderful, at least the work made you live in the company of real
flowers, of the beauty of which, especially when you were
obliged to study them closely in order to draw them, you
could never grow tired. But at Balbec Mme de Villeparisis
was giving herself a holiday, in order to rest her eyes.

We were astonished, my grandmother and I, to find how
much more "liberal" she was than even the majority of the
middle class. She did not understand how anyone could be
scandalised by the expulsion of the Jesuits, saying that it had
always been done, even under the Monarchy, in Spain even.
She defended the Republic, reproaching it for its anti-clerical-
ism only to this extent: "I should find it just as bad to be
prevented from going to mass when I wanted to, as to be
forced to go to it when I didn't!" and even startled us with
such remarks as: "Oh! the aristocracy in these days, what does
it amount to?" or, "To my mind, a man who doesn't work
doesn't count!"—perhaps only because she sensed how much
they gained in spice and piquancy, how memorable they became, on her lips.

When we heard these advanced opinions—though never so
far advanced as to amount to socialism, which Mme de Villeparisis held in abhorrence—expressed so frequently and with
so much frankness precisely by one of those people in consideration of whose intelligence our scrupulous and timid

impartiality would refuse to condemn outright the ideas of conservatives, we came very near, my grandmother and I, to believing that in the pleasant companion of our drives was to be found the measure and the pattern of truth in all things. We took her word for it when she pronounced judgment on her Titians, the colonnade of her country house, the conversational talent of Louis-Philippe. But—like those learned people who hold us spellbound when we get them on to Egyptian painting or Etruscan inscriptions, and yet talk so tritely about modern work that we wonder whether we have not overestimated the interest of the sciences in which they are versed since they do not betray therein the mediocrity of mind which they must have brought to those studies just as much as to their fatuous essays on Baudelaire—Mme de Villeparisis, questioned by me about Chateaubriand, about Balzac, about Victor Hugo, each of whom in his day had been the guest of her parents and had been glimpsed by her, smiled at my reverence, told amusing anecdotes about them such as she had just been telling us about dukes and statesmen, and severely criticised those writers precisely because they had been lacking in that modesty, that self-effacement, that sober art which is satisfied with a single precise stroke and does not over-emphasise, which avoids above all else the absurdity of grandiloquence, in that aptness, those qualities of moderation, of judgment and simplicity to which she had been taught that real greatness aspired and attained. It was evident that she had no hesitation in placing above them men who might after all, perhaps, by virtue of those qualities, have had the advantage of a Balzac, a Hugo, a Vigny in a drawing-room, an academy, a cabinet council, men like Molé, Fontanes, Vitrolles, Bersot, Pasquier, Lebrun, Salvandy or Daru.

"Like those novels of Stendhal which you seem to admire. You would have given him a great surprise, I assure you, if you had spoken to him in that tone. My father, who used to meet him at M. Mérimée's—now he was a man of talent, if you like—often told me that Beyle (that was his real name) was appallingly vulgar, but quite good company at dinner, and not in the least conceited about his books. Why, you must have seen for yourself how he just shrugged his shoulders at the absurdly extravagant compliments of M. de Balzac. There at least he showed that he knew how to behave like a gentleman."

She possessed the autographs of all these great men, and seemed, presuming on the personal relations which her family had had with them, to think that her judgment of them must be better founded than that of young people who, like myself, had had no opportunity of meeting them. "I think I have a right to speak about them, since they used to come to my father's house; and as M. Sainte-Beuve, who was a most intelligent man, used to say, in forming an estimate you must take the word of people who saw them close to and were able to judge more exactly their real worth."

Sometimes, as the carriage laboured up a steep road through ploughlands, making the fields more real, adding to them a mark of authenticity like the precious floweret with which certain of the old masters used to sign their pictures, a few hesitant cornflowers, like those of Combray, would follow in our wake. Presently the horses outdistanced them, but a little way on we would glimpse another which while awaiting us had pricked up its azure star in front of us in the grass. Some made so bold as to come and plant themselves by the side of the road, and a whole constellation began to take shape, what with my distant memories and these domesticated flowers.

We began to go down the hill; and then we would meet, climbing it on foot, on a bicycle, in a cart or carriage, one of those creatures—flowers of a fine day but unlike the flowers of the field, for each of them secretes something that is not to be found in another and that will prevent us from gratifying with any of her peers the desire she has aroused in us—a farm-girl driving her cow or reclining on the back of a waggon, a shopkeeper's daughter taking the air, a fashionable young lady erect on the back seat of a landau, facing her parents. Certainly Bloch had been the means of opening a new era and had altered the value of life for me on the day when he had told me that the dreams which I had entertained on my solitary walks along the Méséglise way, when I hoped that some peasant girl might pass whom I could take in my arms, were not a mere fantasy which corresponded to nothing outside myself but that all the girls one met, whether villagers or "young ladies," were alike ready and willing to give heed to such yearnings. And even if I were fated, now that I was ill and did not go out by myself, never to be able to make love to them, I was happy all the same, like a child born in a prison or a hospital who, having long supposed that the human organism was capable of digesting only dry bread and "physic," has learned suddenly that peaches, apricots and grapes are not simply part of the decoration of the country scene but delicious and easily assimilated food. Even if his gaoler or his nurse does not allow him to pluck those tempting fruits, still the world seems to him a better place and existence in it more clement. For a desire seems to us more attractive, we repose on it with more confidence, when we know that outside ourselves there is a reality which conforms to it, even if, for us, it is not to be realised. And we think more joyfully of a life in which (on condition that we eliminate for a moment from our mind the tiny obstacle, accidental and special, which prevents us personally from doing so) we can imagine ourselves to be assuaging that desire. As to the pretty girls who went past, from the day on which I had first known that their cheeks could be kissed, I had became curious about their souls. And the universe had appeared to me more interesting.

Mme de Villeparisis's carriage moved fast. I scarcely had time to see the girl who was coming in our direction; and yet— since the beauty of human beings is not like the beauty of things, and we feel that it is that of a unique creature, endowed with consciousness and free-will—as soon as her individuality, a soul still vague, a will unknown to me, presented a tiny picture of itself, enormously reduced but complete, in the depths of her indifferent eyes, at once, by a mysterious response of the pollen ready in me for the pistils that should receive it, I felt surging through me the embryo, equally vague, equally minute, of the desire not to let this girl pass without forcing her mind to become aware of my person, without preventing her desires from wandering to someone else, without insinuating myself into her dreams and taking possession of her heart. Meanwhile our carriage had moved on; the pretty girl was already behind us; and as she had—of me—none of those notions which constitute a person in one's mind, her eyes, which had barely seen me, had forgotten me already. Was it because I had caught but a momentary glimpse of her that I had found her so attractive? It may have been. In the first place, the impossibility of stopping when we meet a woman, the risk of not meeting her again another day, give her at once the same charm as a place derives from the illness or poverty that prevents us from visiting it, or the lustreless days which remain to us to live from the battle in which we shall doubtless fall. So that, if there were no such thing as habit, life must appear delightful to those of us who are continually under the threat of death—that is to say, to all mankind. Then, if our imagination is set going by the desire for what we cannot possess, its flight is not limited by a reality perceived in these casual encounters in which the charms of the passing stranger are generally in direct ratio to the swiftness of our passage. If night is falling and the carriage is moving fast, whether in town or country, there is not a single torso, disfigured like an antique marble by the speed that tears us away and the dusk that blurs it, that does not aim at our heart, from every crossing, from the lighted interior of every shop, the arrows of Beauty, that Beauty of which we are sometimes tempted to ask ourselves whether it is, in this world, anything more than the complementary part that is added to a fragmentary and fugitive stranger by our imagination, overstimulated by regret.

Had I been free to get down from the carriage and to speak to the girl whom we were passing, I might perhaps have been disillusioned by some blemish on her skin which from the carriage I had not distinguished. (Whereupon any attempt to penetrate into her life would have seemed suddenly impossible. For beauty is a sequence of hypotheses which ugliness cuts short when it bars the way that we could already see opening into the unknown.) Perhaps a single word which she might have uttered, or a smile, would have furnished me with an unexpected key or clue with which to read the expression on her face, to interpret her bearing, which would at once have become commonplace. It is possible, for I have never in real life met any girls so desirable as on days when I was with some solemn person from whom, despite the myriad pretexts that I invented, I could not tear myself away: some years after the one in the course of which I went for the first time to Balbec, as I was driving through Paris with a friend of my father, and had caught sight of a woman walking quickly along the dark street, I felt that it was unreasonable to forfeit, for a purely conventional scruple, my share of happiness in what may very well be the only life there is, and jumping from the carriage without a word of apology I went in search of the stranger, lost her at the junction of two streets, caught up with her again in a third, and arrived at last, breathless, beneath a street lamp, face to face with old Mme Verdurin whom I had been carefully avoiding for years, and who, in her delight and surprise, exclaimed: "But how very nice of you to have run all this way just to say how d'ye do to me!"

That year at Balbec, on the occasion of such encounters, I would assure my grandmother and Mme de Villeparisis that I had so severe a headache that the best thing for me would be to go home alone on foot. But they would never let me get out of the carriage. And I must add the pretty girl (far harder to find again than an historic monument, for she was nameless and had the power of locomotion) to the collection of all those whom I promised myself that I would examine more closely at a later date. One of them, however, happened to pass more than once before my eyes in circumstances which allowed me to believe that I should be able to get to know her as fully as I wished. This was a milk-girl who came from a farm with an additional supply of cream for the hotel. I fancied that she had recognised me also; and she did indeed look at me with an attentiveness which was perhaps due only to the surprise which my attentiveness caused her. And next day, a day on which I had been resting all morning, when Françoise came in about noon to draw my curtains, she handed me a letter which had been left for me downstairs. I knew no one at Balbec. I had no doubt that the letter was from the milk-girl. Alas, it was only from Bergotte who, as he happened to be passing, had tried to see me, but on hearing that I was asleep had scribbled a few charming lines for which the lift-boy had addressed an envelope which I had supposed to have been written by the milk-girl. I was bitterly disappointed, and the thought that it was more difficult and more flattering to get a letter from Bergotte did not in the least console me for this particular letter's not being from her. As for the girl, I never came across her again, any more than I came across those whom I had seen only from Mme de Villeparisis's carriage. Seeing and then losing them all thus increased the state of agitation in which I was living, and I found a certain wisdom in the philosophers who recommend us to set a limit to our desires (if, that is, they refer to our desire for people, for that is the only kind that leads to anxiety, having for its object something unknown but conscious. To suppose that philosophy could be referring to the desire for wealth would be too absurd.) At the same time I was inclined to regard this wisdom as incomplete, for I told myself that these encounters made me find even more beautiful a world which thus caused to grow along all the country roads flowers at once rare and common, fleeting treasures of the day, windfalls of the drive, of which the contingent circumstances that might not, perhaps, recur had alone prevented me from taking advantage, and which gave a new zest to life.

But perhaps in hoping that, one day, with greater freedom, I should be able to find similar girls on other roads, I was already beginning to falsify and corrupt what is exclusively individual in the desire to live in the company of a woman whom one has found attractive, and by the mere fact that I admitted the possibility of bringing it about artificially, I had implicitly acknowledged its illusoriness.

On the day when Mme de Villeparisis took us to Carqueville to see the ivy-covered church of which she had spoken to us and which, built upon rising ground, dominated both the village and the river that flowed beneath it with its little mediaeval bridge, my grandmother, thinking that I would like to be left alone to study the building at my leisure, suggested to her friend that they should go on and wait for me at the pastry-cook's, in the village square which was clearly visible from where we were and beneath its mellow patina seemed like another part of a wholly ancient object. It was agreed that I should join them there later. In the mass of verdure in front of which I was left standing I was obliged, in order to recognise a church, to make a mental effort which involved my grasping more intensely the idea "Church." In fact, as happens to schoolboys who gather more fully the meaning of a sentence when they are made, by translating or by paraphrasing it, to divest it of the forms to which they are accustomed, I was obliged perpetually to refer back to this idea of "Church," which as a rule I scarcely needed when I stood beneath steeples that were recognisable in themselves, in order not to forget, here that the arch of this clump of ivy was that of a Gothic window, there that the salience of the leaves was due to the carved relief of a capital. Then came a breath of wind, sending a tremor through the mobile porch, which was traversed by eddies flickering and spreading like light; the leaves unfurled against one another; and, quivering, the arboreal façade bore away with it the undulant, rustling, fugitive pillars.

As I came away from the church I saw by the old bridge a cluster of girls from the village who, probably because it was Sunday, were standing about in their best clothes, hailing the boys who went past. One of them, a tall girl not so well dressed as the others but seeming to enjoy some ascendancy over them—for she scarcely answered when they spoke to her —with a more serious and a more self-willed air, was sitting on the parapet of the bridge with her feet hanging down, and holding on her lap a bowl full of fish which she had presumably just caught. She had a tanned complexion, soft eyes but with a look of contempt for her surroundings, and a small nose, delicately and attractively modelled. My eyes alighted upon her skin; and my lips, at a pinch, might have believed that they had followed my eyes. But it was not only to her body that I should have liked to attain; it was also the person that lived inside it, and with which there is but one form of contact, namely to attract its attention, but one sort of penetration, to awaken an idea in it.

And this inner being of the handsome fisher-girl seemed to be still closed to me; I was doubtful whether I had entered it, even after I had seen my own image furtively reflected in the twin mirrors of her gaze, following an index of refraction that was as unknown to me as if I had been placed in the field of vision of a doe. But just as it would not have sufficed that my lips should find pleasure in hers without giving pleasure to them too, so I could have wished that the idea of me which entered this being and took hold in it should bring me not merely her attention but her admiration, her desire, and should compel her to keep me in her memory until the day when I should be able to meet her again. Meanwhile I could see, within a stone's-throw, the square in which Mme de Ville-parisis's carriage must be waiting for me. I had not a moment to lose; and already I could feel that the girls were beginning to laugh at the sight of me standing there before them. I had a five-franc piece in my pocket. I drew it out, and, before ex-plaining to the girl the errand on which I proposed to send her, in order to have a better chance of her listening to me I held the coin for a moment before her eyes.

"Since you seem to belong to the place," I said to her, "I wonder if you would be so good as to take a message for me. I want you to go to a pastry-cook's—which is apparently in a square, but I don't know where that is—where there is a car-riage waiting for me. One moment! To make quite sure, will you ask if the carriage belongs to the Marquise de Villeparisis? But you can't miss it; it's a carriage and pair."

That was what I wished her to know, so that she should regard me as someone of importance. But when I had uttered the words "Marquise" and "carriage and pair," suddenly I had a sense of enormous assuagement. I felt that the fisher-girl would remember me, and together with my fear of not being able to see her again, a part of my desire to do so evaporated too. It seemed to me that I had succeeded in touching her person with invisible lips, and that I had pleased her. And this forcible appropriation of her mind, this immaterial possession, had robbed her of mystery as much as physical possession would have done . . .

We came down towards Hudimesnil; and suddenly I was overwhelmed with a profound happiness which I had not felt since Combray, a happiness analogous to that which had been given me by—among other things—the steeples of Martinville. But this time it remained incomplete. I had just seen, standing a little way back from the hog's-back road along which we were travelling, three trees which probably marked the entry to a covered driveway and formed a pattern which I was not seeing for the first time. I could not succeed in re-constructing the place from which they had been as it were detached, but I felt that it had been familiar to me once; so that, my mind having wavered between some distant year and the present moment, Balbec and its surroundings began to dissolve and I wondered whether the whole of this drive were not a make-believe, Balbec a place to which I had never gone save in imagination, Mme de Villeparisis a character in a story and the three old trees the reality which one recaptures on raising one's eyes from the book which one has been reading and which describes an environment into which one has come to believe that one has been bodily transported.

I looked at the three trees; I could see them plainly, but my mind felt that they were concealing something which it could not grasp, as when an object is placed out of our reach, so that our fingers, stretched out at arm's-length, can only touch for a moment its outer surface, without managing to take hold of anything. Then we rest for a little while before thrusting out our arm with renewed momentum, and trying to reach an inch or two further. But if my mind was thus to collect itself, to gather momentum, I should have to be alone. What would I not have given to be able to draw aside as I used to do on those walks along the Guermantes way, when I detached myself from my parents! I felt indeed that I ought to do so. I recognised that kind of pleasure which requires, it is true, a certain effort on the part of the mind, but in comparison with which the attractions of the indolence which inclines us to renounce that pleasure seem very slight. That pleasure, the object of which I could only dimly feel, which I must create for myself, I experienced only on rare occasions, but on each of these it seemed to me that the things that had happened in the meantime were of little importance, and that in attaching myself to the reality of that pleasure alone could I at length begin to lead a true life. I put my hand for a moment across my eyes, so as to be able to shut them without Mme de Ville-parisis's noticing. I sat there thinking of nothing, then with my thoughts collected, compressed and strengthened I sprang further forward in the direction of the trees, or rather in that inner direction at the end of which I could see them inside myself. I felt again behind them the same object, known to me and yet vague, which I could not bring nearer. And yet all three of them, as the carriage moved on, I could see coming towards me. Where had I looked at them before? There was no place near Combray where an avenue opened off the road like that. Nor was there room for the site which they recalled to me in the scenery of the place in Germany where I had gone one year with my grandmother to take the waters. Was I to suppose, then, that they came from years already so remote in my life that the landscape which surrounded them had been entirely obliterated from my memory and that, like the pages which, with a sudden thrill, we recognise in a book that we imagined we had never read, they alone survived from the forgotten book of my earliest childhood? Were they not rather to be numbered among those dream landscapes, always the same, at least for me in whom their strange aspect was only the objectivation in my sleeping mind of the effort I made while awake either to penetrate the mystery of a place beneath the outward appearance of which I was dimly conscious of there being something more, as had so often happened to me on the Guermantes way, or to try to put mystery back into a place which I had longed to know and which, from the day when I had come to know it, had seemed to me to be wholly superficial, like Balbec? Or were they merely an image freshly extracted from a dream of the night before, but already so worn, so faded that it seemed to me to come from somewhere far more distant? Or had I indeed never seen them before, and did they conceal beneath their surface, like certain trees on tufts of grass that I had seen beside the Guermantes way, a meaning as obscure, as hard to grasp, as is a distant past, so that, whereas they were inviting me to probe a new thought, I imagined that I had to identify an old memory? Or again, were they concealing no hidden thought, and was it simply visual fatigue that made me see them double in time as one sometimes sees double in space? I could not tell. And meanwhile they were coming towards me; perhaps some fabulous apparition, a ring of witches or of Norns who would propound their oracles to me. I chose rather to believe that they were phantoms of the past, dear companions of my childhood, vanished friends who were invoking our common memories. Like ghosts they seemed to be appealing to me to take them with me, to bring them back to life. In their simple and passionate gesticulation I could discern the helpless anguish of a beloved person who has lost the power of speech, and feels that he will never be able to say to us what he wishes to say and we can never guess. Presently, at a cross-roads, the carriage left them. It was bearing me away from what alone I believed to be true, what would have made me truly happy; it was like my life.

I watched the trees gradually recede, waving their despairing arms, seeming to say to me: "What you fail to learn from us to-day, you will never know. If you allow us to drop back into the hollow of this road from which we sought to raise ourselves up to you, a whole part of yourself which we were bringing to you will vanish forever into thin air." And indeed if, in the course of time, I did discover the kind of pleasure and disquiet which I had just felt once again, and if one evening—too late, but then for all time—I fastened myself to it, of those trees themselves I was never to know what they had been trying to give me nor where else I had seen them. And when, the road having forked and the carriage with it, I turned my back on them and ceased to see them, while Mme de Villeparisis asked me what I was dreaming about, I was as wretched as if I had just lost a friend, had died to myself, had broken faith with the dead or repudiated a god.

It was time to be thinking of home. Mme de Villeparisis, who had a certain feeling for nature, colder than that of my grandmother but capable of recognising, even outside museums and noblemen's houses, the simple and majestic beauty of certain old and venerable things, told her coachman to take us back by the old Balbec road, a road little used but planted with old elm-trees which we thought magnificent.

Once we had got to know this road, for a change we would return—unless we had taken it on the outward journey—by another which ran through the woods of Chantereine and

Canteloup. The invisibility of the numberless birds that took up one another's song close beside us in the trees gave me the same sense of being at rest that one has when one shuts one's eyes. Chained to my flap-seat like Prometheus on his rock, I listened to my Oceanides. And whenever I caught a glimpse of one of those birds as it flitted from one leaf to another, there was so little apparent connexion between it and the songs I heard that I could not believe I was beholding their cause in that little body, fluttering, startled and inscrutable.

This road was like many others of the same kind which are to be found in France, climbing on a fairly steep gradient and then gradually descending over a long stretch. At that particular moment, I found no great attraction in it; I was only glad to be going home. But it became for me later on a frequent source of joy by remaining in my memory as a lodestone to which all the similar roads that I was to take, on walks or drives or journeys, would at once attach themselves without breach of continuity and would be able, thanks to it, to communicate immediately with my heart. For as soon as the carriage or the motor-car turned into one of these roads that seemed to be the continuation of the road along which I had driven with Mme de Villeparisis, what I found my present consciousness immediately dwelling upon, as upon the most recent event in my past, would be (all the intervening years being quietly obliterated) the impressions that I had had on those bright summer afternoons and evenings, driving in the neighbourhood of Balbec, when the leaves smelt good, the mist was rising from the ground, and beyond the nearby village one could see through the trees the sun setting as though it had been some place further along the road, distant and forested, which we should not have time to reach that evening. Linked up with those I was experiencing now in another place, on a similar road, surrounded by all the incidental sensations of breathing fresh air, of curiosity, indolence, appetite, gaiety which were common to them both, and excluding all others, these impressions would be reinforced, would take on the consistency of a particular type of pleasure, and almost of a framework of existence which, as it happened, I rarely had the luck to come across, but in which these awakened memories introduced, amid the reality that my senses could perceive, a large enough element of evoked, dreamed, unseizable reality to give me, among these regions through which I was passing, more than an aesthetic feeling, a fleeting but exalted ambition to stay and live there forever. How often since then, at a mere whiff of green leaves, has not being seated on a folding-seat opposite Mme de Villeparisis, meeting the Princesse de Luxembourg who waved a greeting to her from her own carriage, coming back to dinner at the Grand Hotel, appeared to me as one of those ineffable moments of happiness which neither the present nor the future can restore to us and which we taste only once in a lifetime!

Often dusk would have fallen before we reached the hotel. Shyly I would quote to Mme de Villeparisis, pointing to the moon in the sky, some memorable expression of Chateaubriand or Vigny or Victor Hugo: "She shed all around her that ancient secret of melancholy" or "Weeping like Diana by the brink of her streams" or "The shadows nuptial, solemn and august."

"And you think that good, do you?" she would ask, "inspired, as you call it. I must confess that I am always surprised to see people taking things seriously nowadays which the friends of those gentlemen, while giving them full credit for their qualities, were the first to laugh at. People weren't so free then with the word 'genius' as they are now, when if you say to a writer that he has talent he takes it as an insult. You quote me a fine phrase of M. de Chateaubriand's about moonlight. You shall see that I have my own reasons for being resistant to it. M. de Chateaubriand used often to come to see my father. He was quite a pleasant person when you were alone with him, because then he was simple and amusing, but the moment he had an audience he would begin to pose, and then he became absurd. Once, in my father's presence, he claimed that he had flung his resignation in the King's face, and that he had controlled the voting in the Conclave, forgetting that he had asked my father to beg the King to take him back, and that my father had heard him make the most idiotic forecasts of the Papal election. You ought to have heard M. de Blacas on that famous Conclave; he was a very different kind of man from M. de Chateaubriand. As to his fine phrases about the moon, they became part of our regular programme for entertaining our guests. Whenever the moon was shining, if there was anyone staying with us for the first time he would be told to take M. de Chateaubriand for a stroll after dinner. When they came in, my father would take his guest aside and say: 'Well, and was M. de Chateaubriand very eloquent?'— 'Oh, yes.' 'He talked to you about the moonlight.'—'Yes, how did you know?'—'One moment, didn't he say——' and then my father would quote the phrase. 'He did; but how in the world . . .?'—'And he spoke to you of the moonlight on the Roman Campagna?'—'But, my dear sir, you're a magician.' My father was no magician, but M. de Chateaubriand had the same little speech about the moon which he served up every time."

At the mention of Vigny she laughed: "The man who said: 'I am the Comte Alfred de Vigny!' One is either a count or one isn't; it is not of the slightest importance."

And then perhaps she discovered that it was, after all, of some slight importance, for she went on: "For one thing I'm by no means sure that he was, and in any case he was of very inferior stock, that gentleman who speaks in his verses of his 'esquire's crest.' In such charming taste, is it not, and so interesting to his readers! Like Musset, a plain Paris cit, who laid so much stress on 'The golden falcon that surmounts my helm.' As if you would ever hear a real gentleman say a thing like that! At least Musset had some talent as a poet. But except for *Cinq-Mars*, I've never been able to read a thing by M. de Vigny. I get so bored that the book falls from my hands. M. Molé, who had all the wit and tact that were wanting in M. de Vigny, put him properly in his place when he welcomed him to the Academy. What, you don't know the speech? It's a masterpiece of irony and impertinence."

She found fault with Balzac, whom she was surprised to find her nephews admiring, for having presumed to describe a society "in which he was never received" and of which his descriptions were wildly improbable. As for Victor Hugo, she told us that M. de Bouillon, her father, who had friends among the young Romantics thanks to whom he had attended the first performance of *Hernani*, had been unable to sit through it, so ridiculous had he found the verse of that gifted but extravagant writer who had acquired the title of "major poet" only by virtue of having struck a bargain, and as a reward for the not disinterested indulgence that he showed towards the dangerous aberrations of the socialists.

We had now come in sight of the hotel, with its lights, so hostile that first evening on our arrival, now protective and kind, speaking to us of home. And when the carriage drew up outside the door, the porter, the bell-hops, the lift-boy, attentive, clumsy, vaguely uneasy at our lateness, massed on the steps to receive us, were numbered, now that they had grown familiar, among those beings who change so many times in the course of our lives, as we ourselves change, but in whom, when they are for the time being the mirror of our habits, we find comfort in the feeling that we are being faithfully and amicably reflected. We prefer them to friends whom we have not seen for some time, for they contain more of what we are at present. Only the outside page, exposed to the sun all day, had been taken indoors for protection from the cold night air and swaddled in thick woollen garments which, combined with the orange effulgence of his locks and the curiously red bloom of his cheeks, made one, seeing him there in the glassed-in hall, think of a hot-house plant muffled up for protection from the frost. We got out of the carriage with the help of a great many more servants than were required, but they were conscious of the importance of the scene and each felt obliged to take some part in it. I was always very hungry. And so, often, in order not to keep dinner waiting, I would not go upstairs to the room which had succeeded in becoming so really mine that to catch sight of its long violet curtains and low bookcases was to find myself alone again with that self of which things, like people, gave me a reflected image; and we would all wait together in the hall until the head waiter came to tell us that our dinner was ready. This gave us another opportunity of listening to Mme de Villeparisis.

"But you must be tired of us by now," my grandmother would protest.

"Not at all! Why, I'm delighted, what could be nicer?" replied her friend with a winning smile, drawing out, almost intoning her words in a way that contrasted markedly with her customary simplicity of speech.

And indeed at such moments as this she was not natural; her mind reverted to her early training, to the aristocratic manner in which a great lady is supposed to show commoners that she is glad to be with them, that she is not at all arrogant. And her one and only failure in true politeness lay in this excess of politeness—which it was easy to identify as one of those professional "wrinkles" of a lady of the Faubourg Saint-Germain, who, always seeing in her humbler friends the latent discontent that she must one day arouse in their bosoms, greedily seizes every possible opportunity to establish in advance, in the ledger in which she keeps her social account with them, a credit balance which will enable her presently to enter on the debit side the dinner or reception to which she will not invite them. And so, having long ago taken effect in her once and for all, and oblivious of the fact that now both the circumstances and the people concerned were different, that in Paris she would wish to see us often at her house, the spirit of her caste was urging Mme de Villeparisis on with feverish ardour, as if the time that was allowed her for being amiable to us was limited, to step up, while we were at Balbec, her gifts of roses and melons, loans of books, drives in her carriage and verbal effusions. And for that reason, quite as much as the dazzling splendour of the beach, the many-coloured flamboyance and subaqueous light of the rooms, as much even as the riding-lessons by which tradesmen's sons were deified like Alexander of Macedon, the daily kindnesses shown us by Mme de Villeparisis, and also the unaccustomed, momentary, holiday ease with which my grandmother accepted them, have remained in my memory as typical of life at the seaside.

"Give them your coats to take upstairs."

My grandmother handed them to the manager, and because he had been so nice to me I was distressed by this want of consideration, which seemed to pain him.

"I think you've hurt his feelings," said the Marquise. "He probably fancies himself too great a gentleman to carry your wraps. I remember so well the Duc de Nemours, when I was still quite little, coming to see my father who was living then on the top floor of the Hôtel Bouillon, with a fat parcel under his arm, and letters and newspapers. I can see the Prince now, in his blue coat, framed in our doorway, which had such pretty panelling—I think it was Bagard who used to do it—you know those fine laths that they used to cut, so supple that the joiner would twist them sometimes into little shells and flowers, like the ribbons round a nosegay. 'Here you are, Cyrus,' he said to my father, 'look what your porter's given me to bring you. He said to me: Since you're going up to see the Count, it's not worth my while climbing all those stairs; but take care you don't break the string.'—Now that you've got rid of your things, why don't you sit down," she said to my grandmother, taking her by the hand. "Here, take this chair."

"Oh, if you don't mind, not that one! It's too small for two, and too big for me by myself. I shouldn't feel comfortable."

"You remind me, for it was exactly like this one, of an armchair I had for many years until at last I couldn't keep it any longer because it had been given to my mother by the unfortunate Duchesse de Praslin. My mother, though she was the simplest person in the world, really, had ideas that belonged to another generation, which even in those days I could scarcely understand; and at first she had not been at all willing to let herself be introduced to Mme de Praslin, who had been plain Mlle Sebastiani, while she, because she was a Duchess, felt that it was not for her to be introduced to my mother. And really, you know," Mme de Villeparisis went on, forgetting that she herself did not understand these fine shades of distinction, "even if she had just been Mme de Choiseul, there was a good deal to be said for her claim. The Choiseuls are everything you could want; they spring from a sister of Louis the Fat; they were real sovereigns down in Bassigny. I admit that we beat them in marriages and in distinction, but the seniority is pretty much the same. This little matter of precedence gave rise to several comic incidents, such as a luncheon party which was kept waiting a whole hour or more before one of these ladies could make up her mind to let herself be introduced to the other. In spite of which they became great friends, and she gave my mother a chair like this one, in which people always refused to sit, as you've just done, until one day my mother heard a carriage drive into the courtyard. She asked a young servant who it was. 'The Duchesse de La Rochefoucauld, ma'am.' 'Very well, say that I am at home.' A quarter of an hour passed; no one came. 'What about the Duchesse de La Rochefoucauld?' my mother asked, 'where is she?' 'She's on the stairs, ma'am, getting her breath,' said the young servant, who had not been long up from the country, where my mother had the excellent habit of getting all her servants. Often she had seen them born. That's the only way to get really good ones. And they're the rarest of luxuries. And sure enough the Duchesse de La Rochefoucauld had the greatest difficulty in getting upstairs, for she was an enormous woman, so enormous, indeed, that when she did come into the room my mother was quite at a loss for a moment to know where to put her. And then the seat that Mme de Praslin had given her caught her eye. 'Won't you sit down?' she said, bringing it forward. And the Duchess filled it from side to side. She was quite a pleasant woman, for all her . . . imposingness. 'She still creates a certain effect when she comes in,' one of our friends said once. 'She certainly creates an effect when she goes out,' said my mother, who was rather more free in her speech than would be thought proper nowadays. Even in Mme de La Rochefoucauld's own drawing-room people didn't hesitate to make fun of her to her face (and she was always the first to laugh at it) over her ample proportions. 'But are you all alone?' my mother once asked M. de La Rochefoucauld, when she had come to pay a call on the Duchess, and being met at the door by him had not seen his wife who was in an alcove at the other end of the room. 'Is Mme de La Rochefoucauld not at home? I don't see her.'— 'How charming of you!' replied the Duke, who had about the worst judgment of any man I have ever known, but was not altogether lacking in humour."

After dinner, when I had gone upstairs with my grandmother, I said to her that the qualities which attracted us in Mme de Villeparisis, her tact, her shrewdness, her discretion, her self-effacement, were not perhaps of very great value since those who possessed them in the highest degree were merely people like Molé and Loménie, and that if the want of them can make everyday social relations disagreeable yet it did not prevent from becoming Chateaubriand, Vigny, Hugo, Balzac conceited fellows who had no judgment, at whom it was easy to mock, like Bloch.... But at the name of Bloch, my grandmother expostulated. And she proceeded to sing the praises of Mme de Villeparisis. As we are told that it is the preservation of the species which guides our individual preferences in love and, so that the child may be constituted in the most normal fashion, sends fat men in pursuit of lean women and *vice versa*, so in some dim way it was the requirements of my happiness, threatened by my disordered nerves, by my morbid tendency to melancholy and solitude, that made her allot the highest place to the qualities of balance and judgment, peculiar not only to Mme de Villeparisis but to a society in which I might find distraction and assuagement—a society similar to the one in which our ancestors saw the minds of a Doudan, a M. de Rémusat flourish, not to mention a Beausergent, a Joubert, a Sévigné, a type of mind that invests life with more happiness, with greater dignity than the converse refinements which had led a Baudelaire, a Poe, a Verlaine, a Rimbaud to sufferings, to a disrepute such as my grandmother did not wish for her daughter's child. I interrupted her with a kiss and asked her if she had noticed such and such a remark Mme de Villeparisis had made which seemed to point to a woman who thought more of her noble birth than she was prepared to admit. In this way I used to submit my impressions of life to my grandmother, for I was never certain what degree of respect was due to anyone until she had pointed it out to me. Every evening I would come to her with the mental sketches that I had made during the day of all those non-existent people who were not her.

Once I said to her: "I couldn't live without you."

"But you mustn't speak like that," she replied in a troubled voice. "We must be a bit pluckier than that. Otherwise, what would become of you if I went away on a journey? But I hope that you would be quite sensible and quite happy."

"I could manage to be sensible if you went away for a few days, but I should count the hours."

"But if I were to go away for months . . ." (at the mere thought my heart turned over) ". . . for years . . . for . . ."
We both fell silent. We dared not look one another in the face. And yet I was suffering more keenly from her anguish than from my own. And so I walked across to the window and said to her distinctly, with averted eyes: "You know what a creature of habit I am. For the first few days after I've been separated from the people I love best, I'm miserable. But though I go on loving them just as much, I get used to their absence, my life becomes calm and smooth. I could stand being parted from them for months, for years . . ."
I was obliged to stop speaking and look straight out of the window. My grandmother left the room for a moment. But next day I began to talk to her about philosophy, and, speaking in the most casual tone but at the same time taking care that my grandmother should pay attention to my words, I remarked what a curious thing it was that, according to the latest scientific discoveries, the materialist position appeared to be crumbling, and what was again most likely was the immortality of souls and their future reunion.
Mme de Villeparisis gave us warning that presently she would not be able to see so much of us. A young nephew who was preparing for Saumur, and was meanwhile stationed in the neighbourhood, at Doncières, was coming to spend a few weeks' leave with her, and she would be devoting most of her time to him. In the course of our drives together she had spoken highly of his intelligence and above all his kind-heartedness, and already I imagined that he would take a liking to me, that I should be his best friend; and when, before his arrival, his aunt gave my grandmother to understand that he had unfortunately fallen into the clutches of an appalling woman with whom he was infatuated and who would never let him go, since I was persuaded that that sort of love was doomed to end in mental derangement, crime and suicide, thinking how short a time was reserved for our friendship, already so great in my heart although I had not yet set eyes on him, I wept for that friendship and for the misfortunes that were in store for it, as we weep for someone we love when we learn that he is seriously ill and that his days are numbered.

One afternoon of scorching heat I was in the dining-room of
the hotel, plunged in semi-darkness to shield it from the sun,
which gilded the drawn curtains through the gaps between
which twinkled the blue of the sea, when along the central
gangway leading from the beach to the road I saw approaching, tall, slim, bare-necked, his head held proudly erect,
a young man with searching eyes whose skin was as fair and
his hair as golden as if they had absorbed all the rays of the sun.
Dressed in a suit of soft, whitish material such as I could never
have believed that any man would have the audacity to wear,
the thinness of which suggested no less vividly than the coolness of the dining-room the heat and brightness of the glorious
day outside, he was walking fast. His penetrating eyes, from
one of which a monocle kept dropping, were the colour of the
sea. Everyone looked at him with interest as he passed,
knowing that this young Marquis de Saint-Loup-en-Bray was
famed for his elegance. All the newspapers had described the
suit in which he had recently acted as second to the young
Duc d'Uzès in a duel. One felt that the distinctive quality of
his hair, his eyes, his skin, his bearing, which would have
marked him out in a crowd like a precious vein of opal,
azure-shot and luminous, embedded in a mass of coarser substance, must correspond to a life different from that led by other
men. So that when, before the attachment which Mme de Villeparisis had been deploring, the prettiest women in society had
disputed the possession of him, his presence, at a watering-place
for instance, in the company of the beauty of the season to whom
he was paying court, not only brought her into the limelight, but
attracted every eye fully as much to himself. Because of his
"tone," because he had the insolent manner of a young
"blood," above all because of his extraordinary good looks,
some even thought him effeminate-looking, though without
holding it against him since they knew how virile he was and
how passionately fond of women. This was the nephew about
whom Mme de Villeparisis had spoken to us. I was delighted
at the thought that I was going to enjoy his company for some
weeks, and confident that he would bestow on me all his
affection. He strode rapidly across the whole width of the hotel,
seeming to be in pursuit of his monocle, which kept darting

away in front of him like a butterfly. He was coming from the
beach, and the sea which filled the lower half of the glass
front of the hall made a background against which he stood
out full-length, as in certain portraits whose painters attempt,
without in any way falsifying the most accurate observation of
contemporary life, but by choosing for their sitter an appropriate setting—a polo ground, golf links, a race-course, the
bridge of a yacht—to furnish a modern equivalent of those
canvases on which the old masters used to present the human
figure in the foreground of a landscape. A carriage and pair
awaited him at the door; and, while his monocle resumed
its gambollings on the sunlit road, with the elegance and
mastery which a great pianist contrives to display in the
simplest stroke of execution, where it did not seem possible
that he could reveal his superiority to a performer of the second
class, Mme de Villeparisis's nephew, taking the reins that were
handed him by the coachman, sat down beside him and, while
opening a letter which the manager of the hotel brought out
to him, started up his horses.

How disappointed I was on the days that followed, when,
each time that I met him outside or in the hotel—his head
erect, perpetually balancing the movements of his limbs
round the fugitive and dancing monocle which seemed to be
their centre of gravity—I was forced to acknowledge that he
had evidently no desire to make our acquaintance, and saw
that he did not bow to us although he must have known that
we were friends of his aunt. And calling to mind the friendliness that Mme de Villeparisis, and before her M. de Norpois,
had shown me, I thought that perhaps they were only mock
aristocrats and that there must be a secret article in the laws
that govern the nobility which allowed women, perhaps, and
certain diplomats to discard, in their relations with commoners,
for a reason which was beyond me, the haughtiness which
must, on the other hand, be pitilessly maintained by a young
marquis. My intelligence might have told me the opposite.
But the characteristic feature of the ridiculous age I was
going through—awkward indeed but by no means infertile—
is that we do not consult our intelligence and that the most
trivial attributes of other people seem to us to form an in-

separable part of their personality. In a world thronged with monsters and with gods, we know little peace of mind. There is hardly a single action we perform in that phase which we would not give anything, in later life, to be able to annul. Whereas what we ought to regret is that we no longer possess the spontaneity which made us perform them. In later life we look at things in a more practical way, in full conformity with the rest of society, but adolescence is the only period in which we learn anything.

This insolence which I surmised in M. de Saint-Loup, and all that it implied of innate hardness, received confirmation from his attitude whenever he passed us, his body as inflexibly erect as ever, his head held as high, his gaze as impassive, not to say as implacable, devoid of that vague respect which one has for the rights of other people, even if they do not know one's aunt, in accordance with which I did not behave in quite the same way towards an old lady as towards a gas lamp. These frigid manners were as far removed from the charming letters which, only a few days before, I had still imagined him writing to me to express his regard as, from the enthusiasm of the Chamber and of the populace which he has pictured himself rousing by an imperishable speech, is the humble, dull, obscure position of the dreamer who, after rehearsing it thus by himself, for himself, aloud, finds himself, once the imaginary applause has died away, just the same Tom, Dick or Harry as before. When Mme de Villeparisis, doubtless in an attempt to counteract the bad impression that had been made on us by an exterior indicative of an arrogant and unfriendly nature, spoke to us again of the inexhaustible kindness of her great-nephew (he was the son of one of her nieces, and a little older than myself), I marvelled how the gentry, with an utter disregard of truth, ascribe tenderness of heart to people whose hearts are in reality so hard and dry, provided only that they behave with common courtesy to the brilliant members of their own set. Mme de Villeparisis herself confirmed, though indirectly, my diagnosis, which was already a conviction, of the essential points of her nephew's character one day when I met them both coming along a path so narrow that she could not do otherwise than introduce me to him. He seemed not to hear that a person's name was being announced to him; not a muscle of his face moved; his eyes, in which there shone not the faintest gleam of human sympathy, showed merely, in the insensibility, in the inanity of their gaze an exaggeration failing which there would have been nothing to distinguish them from lifeless mirrors. Then, fastening on me those hard eyes as though he wished to examine me before returning my salute, with an abrupt gesture which seemed to be due rather to a reflex action of his muscles than to an exercise of will, keeping between himself and me the greatest possible interval, he stretched his arm out to its full extension and, at the end of it, offered me his hand. I supposed that it must mean, at the very least, a duel when, next day, he sent me his card. But he spoke to me when we met only of literature, and declared after a long talk that he would like immensely to spend several hours with me every day. He had not only, in this encounter, given proof of an ardent zest for the things of the mind; he had shown a regard for me which was little in keeping with his greeting of the day before. After I had seen him repeat the same process every time some-one was introduced to him, I realised that it was simply a social usage peculiar to his branch of the family, to which his mother, who had seen to it that he should be perfectly brought up, had moulded his limbs; he went through those motions without thinking about them any more than he thought about his beautiful clothes or hair; they were a thing devoid of the moral significance which I had at first ascribed to them, a thing purely acquired, like that other habit that he had of at once demanding an introduction to the family of anyone he knew, which had become so instinctive in him that, seeing me again the day after our meeting, he bore down on me and without further ado asked to be introduced to my grand-mother who was with me, with the same feverish haste as if the request had been due to some instinct of self-preservation, like the act of warding off a blow or of shutting one's eyes to avoid a stream of boiling water, without the protection of which it would have been dangerous to remain a moment longer.

The first rites of exorcism once performed, as a wicked fairy discards her preliminary guise and endues all the most enchanting graces, I saw this disdainful creature become the most friendly, the most considerate young man that I had ever met. "Right," I said to myself, "I've been mistaken about him once already. I was the victim of a mirage. But I've got over the first only to fall for a second, for he must be a dyed-in-the-wool grandee who's trying to hide it." As a matter of fact it was not long before all the exquisite breeding, all the friendliness of Saint-Loup were indeed to let me see another person, but one very different from what I had suspected.

This young man who had the air of a disdainful aristocrat and sportsman had in fact no respect or curiosity except for the things of the mind, and especially those modern manifestations of literature and art which seemed so ridiculous to his aunt; he was imbued, moreover, with what she called "socialistic spoutings," was filled with the most profound contempt for his caste, and spent long hours in the study of Nietzsche and Proudhon. He was one of those "intellectuals" easily moved to admiration, who shut themselves up in a book and are interested only in the higher thought. Indeed in Saint-Loup the expression of this highly abstract tendency, which removed him so far from my customary preoccupations, while it seemed to me touching, also annoyed me a little. I may say that when I fully realised who his father had been, on days when I had been reading memoirs rich in anecdotes of that famous Comte de Marsantes in whom were embodied the special graces of a generation already remote, my mind full of speculations, and anxious to obtain fuller details of the life that M. de Marsantes had led, I was infuriated that Robert de Saint-Loup, instead of being content to be the son of his father, instead of being able to guide me through the old-fashioned romance which his father's existence had been, had raised himself up to the heights of Nietzsche and Proudhon. His father would not have shared my regret. He had been himself a man of intelligence, who had transcended the narrow confines of his life as a man of the world. He had hardly had time to know his son, but had hoped that he would prove a better man than himself. And I dare say that, unlike the rest of the family, he would have admired his son, would have rejoiced at his abandoning what had been his own small diversions for austere meditations, and without saying a word, in his modesty as a nobleman of wit, would have read in secret his son's favourite authors in order to appreciate how far Robert was superior to himself.

There was, however, this rather painful consideration: that if M. de Marsantes, with his extremely open mind, would have appreciated a son so different from himself, Robert de Saint-Loup, because he was one of those people who believe that merit is attached only to certain forms of art and of life, had an affectionate but slightly contemptuous memory of a father who had spent all his time hunting and racing, who yawned at Wagner and raved over Offenbach. Saint-Loup was not intelligent enough to understand that intellectual worth has nothing to do with adhesion to any one aesthetic formula, and regarded the "intellectuality" of M. de Marsantes with much the same sort of scorn as might have been felt for Boieldieu or Labiche by sons of Boieldieu or Labiche who had become adherents of the most extreme symbolist literature and the most complicated music. "I scarcely knew my father," he used to say. "He seems to have been a charming man. His tragedy was the deplorable age in which he lived. To have been born in the Faubourg Saint-Germain and to have to live in the days of *La Belle Hélène* would be enough to wreck any existence. Perhaps if he'd been some little shopkeeper mad about the *Ring* he'd have turned out quite different. Indeed they tell me that he was fond of literature. But it's impossible to know, because literature to him meant only the most antiquated stuff." And in my own case, if I found Saint-Loup a trifle earnest, he could not understand why I was not more earnest still. Never judging anything except by its intellectual weightiness, never perceiving the magic appeal to the imagination that I found in things which he condemned as frivolous, he was astonished that I—to whom he imagined himself to be so utterly inferior—could take any interest in them.

From the first Saint-Loup made a conquest of my grandmother, not only by the incessant kindness which he went out of his way to show to us both, but by the naturalness which he put into it as into everything else. For naturalness—doubtless because through the artifice of man it allows a feeling of nature to permeate—was the quality which my grandmother preferred to all others, whether in gardens, where she did not like there to be, as in our Combray garden, too formal flower-beds, or in cooking, where she detested those dressed-up dishes in which you can hardly detect the foodstuffs that have gone to make them, or in piano-playing, which she did not like to be too finicking, too polished, having indeed had a special weakness for the discords, the wrong notes of Rubinstein. This naturalness she found and appreciated even in the clothes that Saint-Loup wore, of a loose elegance, with nothing "swagger" or "dressed-up" about them, no stiffness or starch. She appreciated this rich young man still more highly for the free and careless way that he had of living in luxury without "smelling of money," without giving himself airs; she even discovered the charm of this naturalness in the incapacity which Saint-Loup had kept—though as a rule it is outgrown with childhood, at the same time as certain physiological peculiarities of that age—for preventing his face from at once reflecting every emotion. Something, for instance, that he wanted to have but had not expected, if only a compliment, induced in him a pleasure so quick, so glowing, so volatile, so expansive that it was impossible for him to contain and to conceal it; a grin of delight seized irresistible hold of his face, the too delicate skin of his cheeks allowed a bright red glow to shine through them, his eyes sparkled with confusion and joy; and my grandmother was infinitely touched by this charming show of innocence and frankness, which indeed in Saint-Loup—at any rate at the time of our first friendship—was not misleading. But I have known another person, and there are many such, in whom the physiological sincerity of that fleeting blush in no way excluded moral duplicity; as often as not it proves nothing more than the intensity with which pleasure may be felt—to the extent of disarming them and forcing them publicly to confess it—by natures capable of the vilest treachery. But where my grandmother especially adored Saint-Loup's naturalness was in his way of confessing without the slightest reservation his affection for me, to give expression to which he

found words than which she herself, she told me, could not
have thought of any more appropriate, more truly loving,
words to which "Sévigné and Beausergent" might have set
their signatures. He was not afraid to make fun of my weaknesses—which he had discerned with a shrewdness that made
her smile—but as she herself would have done, affectionately,
at the same time extolling my good qualities with a warmth,
an impulsive freedom that showed no sign of the reserve, the
coldness by means of which young men of his age are apt to
suppose that they give themselves importance. And he
evinced, in anticipating my every discomfort, however slight,
in covering my legs if the day had turned cold without my
noticing it, in arranging (without telling me) to stay later with
me in the evening if he thought I was sad or gloomy, a vigilance which, from the point of view of my health, for which a
more hardening discipline would perhaps have been better,
my grandmother found almost excessive, though as a proof of
his affection for me she was deeply touched by it.

It was promptly settled between us that he and I were to be
great friends for ever, and he would say "our friendship"
as though he were speaking of some important and delightful
thing which had an existence independent of ourselves, and
which he soon called—apart from his love for his mistress—
the great joy of his life. These words filled me with a sort of
melancholy and I was at a loss for an answer, for I felt when I
was with him, when I was talking to him—and no doubt it
would have been the same with anyone else—none of that
happiness which it was possible for me to experience when I
was by myself. Alone, at times, I felt surging from the depths
of my being one or other of those impressions which gave me a
delicious sense of well-being. But as soon as I was with
someone else, as soon as I was talking to a friend, my mind as
it were faced about, it was towards this interlocutor and not
towards myself that it directed its thoughts, and when they
followed this outward course they brought me no pleasure.
Once I had left Saint-Loup, I managed, with the help of
words, to put some sort of order into the confused minutes
that I had spent with him; I told myself that I had a good
friend, that a good friend was a rare thing, and I savoured,

when I felt myself surrounded by assets that were difficult to acquire, what was precisely the opposite of the pleasure that was natural to me, the opposite of the pleasure of having extracted from myself and brought to light something that was hidden in my inner darkness. If I had spent two or three hours in conversation with Saint-Loup and he had expressed his admiration of what I had said to him, I felt a sort of remorse, or regret, or weariness at not having remained alone and settled down to work at last. But I told myself that one is not intelligent for oneself alone, that the greatest of men have wanted to be appreciated, that hours in which I had built up a lofty idea of myself in my friend's mind could not be considered wasted. I had no difficulty in persuading myself that I ought to be happy in consequence, and I hoped all the more keenly that this happiness might never be taken from me because I had not actually felt it. We fear more than the loss of anything else the disappearance of possessions that have remained outside ourselves, because our hearts have not taken possession of them. I felt that I was capable of exemplifying the virtues of friendship better than most people (because I should always place the good of my friends before those personal interests to which other people are devoted but which did not count for me), but not of finding happiness in a feeling which, instead of increasing the differences that there were between my nature and those of other people—as there are between all of us—would eliminate them. On the other hand there were moments when my mind distinguished in Saint-Loup a personality more generalised than his own, that of the "nobleman," which like an indwelling spirit moved his limbs, ordered his gestures and his actions; then, at such moments, although in his company, I was alone, as I should have been in front of a landscape the harmony of which I could understand. He was no more then than an object the properties of which, in my musings, I sought to explore. The discovery in him of this pre-existent, this immemorial being, this aristocrat who was precisely what Robert aspired not to be, gave me intense joy, but a joy of the mind rather than the feelings. In the moral and physical agility which gave so much grace to his kindnesses, in the ease with

which he offered my grandmother his carriage and helped her
into it, in the alacrity with which he sprang from the box
when he was afraid that I might be cold, to spread his own
cloak over my shoulders, I sensed not only the inherited
litheness of the mighty hunters who had been for generations
the ancestors of this young man who had no pretensions except to intellectuality, their scorn of wealth which, subsisting
in him side by side with his enjoyment of it simply because it
enabled him to entertain his friends more lavishly, made him so
carelessly shower his riches at their feet; I sensed in it above all
the certainty or the illusion in the minds of those great lords of
being "better than other people," thanks to which they had
not been able to hand down to Saint-Loup that anxiety to
show that one is "just as good as the next man," that dread of
seeming too assiduous of which he was indeed wholly innocent and which mars with so much stiffness and awkwardness
the most sincere plebeian civility. Sometimes I reproached
myself for thus taking pleasure in considering my friend as
a work of art, that is to say in regarding the play of all the
parts of his being as harmoniously ordered by a general idea
from which they depended but of which he was unaware and
which consequently added nothing to his own qualities, to
that personal value, intellectual and moral, which he prized
so highly.

And yet that idea was to a certain extent their determining
cause. It was because he was a gentleman that that mental
activity, those socialist aspirations, which made him seek the
company of arrogant and ill-dressed young students, con-
noted in him something really pure and disinterested which
was not to be found in them. Looking upon himself as the heir
of an ignorant and selfish caste, he was sincerely anxious that
they should forgive in him that aristocratic origin which they,
on the contrary, found irresistibly attractive and on account
of which they sought his acquaintance while simulating
coldness and indeed insolence towards him. He was thus led to
make advances to people from whom my parents, faithful to
the sociological theories of Combray, would have been
stupefied at his not turning away in disgust. One day when we
were sitting on the sands, Saint-Loup and I, we heard issuing

from a canvas tent against which we were leaning a torrent of
imprecation against the swarm of Jews that infested Balbec.
"You can't go a yard without meeting them," said the voice.
"I am not in principle irremediably hostile to the Jewish
race, but here there is a plethora of them. You hear nothing
but, 'I thay, Apraham, I've chust theen Chacop.' You would
think you were in the Rue d'Aboukir." The man who thus
inveighed against Israel emerged at last from the tent, and we
raised our eyes to behold this anti-semite. It was my old
friend Bloch. Saint-Loup at once asked me to remind him that
they had met each other at the *concours général*, when Bloch had
carried off the prize of honour, and since then at a people's
university course.[26]

At the most I may have smiled now and then, to discover in
Robert the marks of his Jesuit schooling in the embarrassment which the fear of hurting people's feelings at once
provoked in him whenever one of his intellectual friends made
a social error or did something silly to which Saint-Loup
himself attached no importance but felt that the other would
have blushed if anybody had noticed it. And it was Robert
who used to blush as though he were the guilty party, for
instance on the day when Bloch, after promising to come and
see him at the hotel, went on: "As I cannot endure to be kept
waiting among all the false splendour of these great cara-
vanserais, and the Hungarian band would make me ill, you
must tell the 'lighft-boy' to make them shut up, and to let
you know at once."

Personally, I was not particularly anxious that Bloch should
come to the hotel. He was at Balbec, not by himself, unfortunately, but with his sisters, and they in turn had innumerable
relatives and friends staying there. Now this Jewish colony was
more picturesque than pleasing. Balbec was in this respect
like such countries as Russia or Rumania, where the geography books teach us that the Jewish population does not
enjoy the same esteem and has not reached the same stage of
assimilation as, for instance, in Paris. Always together, with no
admixture of any other element, when the cousins and uncles
of Bloch or their co-religionists male or female repaired to the
Casino, the ladies to dance, the gentlemen branching off

towards the baccarat-tables, they formed a solid troop, homogeneous within itself, and utterly dissimilar to the people who watched them go by and found them there again every year without ever exchanging a word or a greeting, whether these were the Cambremer set, or the presiding judge's little group, professional or "business" people, or even simple corn-chandlers from Paris, whose daughters, handsome, proud, mocking and French as the statues at Rheims, would not care to mix with that horde of ill-bred sluts who carried their zeal for "seaside fashions" so far as to be always apparently on their way home from shrimping or out to dance the tango. As for the men, despite the brilliance of their dinner-jackets and patent-leather shoes, the exaggeration of their type made one think of the so-called "bright ideas" of those painters who, having to illustrate the Gospels or the Arabian Nights, consider the country in which the scenes are laid, and give to St Peter or to Ali-Baba the identical features of the heaviest "punter" at the Balbec tables. Bloch introduced his sisters, who, though he silenced their chatter with the utmost rudeness, screamed with laughter at the mildest sallies of this brother who was their blindly worshipped idol. Although it is probable that this set of people contained, like every other, perhaps more than any other, plenty of attractions, qualities and virtues, in order to experience these one would first have had to penetrate it. But it was not popular, could sense this, and saw in it the mark of an anti-semitism to which it presented a bold front in a compact and closed phalanx into which, as it happened, no one ever dreamed of trying to force his way.

As regards the word "lighft," I had all the less reason to be surprised at Bloch's pronunciation in that, a few days before, when he had asked me why I had come to Balbec (although it seemed to him perfectly natural that he himself should be there) and whether it had been "in the hope of making grand friends," and I had explained to him that this visit was a fulfilment of one of my earliest longings, though one not so deep as my longing to see Venice, he had replied: "Yes, of course, to sip iced drinks with the pretty ladies, while pretending to read the *Stones of Venighce* by Lord John Ruskin, a dreary bore, in fact one of the most tedious old prosers you could find." Thus Bloch evidently thought that in England not only were all the inhabitants of the male sex called "Lord," but the letter "i" was invariably pronounced "igh." As for Saint-Loup, this mistake in pronunciation seemed to him all the more venial inasmuch as he saw in it pre-eminently a want of those almost "society" notions which my new friend despised as fully as he was versed in them. But the fear lest Bloch, discovering one day that one says "Venice" and that Ruskin was not a lord, should retrospectively imagine that Robert had thought him ridiculous, made the latter feel as guilty as if he had been found wanting in the indulgence with which, as we have seen, he overflowed, so that the blush which would doubtless one day dye the cheek of Bloch on the discovery of his error, Robert already, by anticipation and reversibility, could feel mounting to his own. For he assumed that Bloch attached more importance than he to this mistake—an assumption which Bloch confirmed some days later, when he heard me pronounce the word "lift," by breaking in with: "Oh, one says 'lift,' does one?" And then, in a dry and lofty tone: "Not that it's of the slightest importance." A phrase that is like a reflex action, the same in all proud and susceptible men, in the gravest circumstances as well as in the most trivial, betraying there as clearly as on this occasion how important the thing in question seems to him who declares that it is of no importance; a tragic phrase at times, the first to escape (and then how heart-breakingly) the lips of any man who is at all proud from whom we have just removed the last hope to which he still clung by refusing to do him a service: "Oh, well, it's not of the slightest importance; I shall make some other arrangement": the other arrangement which it is not of the slightest importance that he should be driven to adopt being sometimes suicide.

Thereupon Bloch made me the prettiest speeches. He was certainly anxious to be on the best of terms with me. And yet he asked me: "Is it because you've taken a fancy to the minor aristocracy that you run after de Saint-Loup-en-Bray? You must be suffering from a severe attack of snobbery. Tell me, are you a snob? I think so, what?" Not that his desire to be friendly had suddenly changed. But what is called in not too correct language "ill breeding" was his defect, therefore the defect which he was bound to overlook, and *a fortiori* the defect by which he did not believe that other people could be shocked.

In the human race, the frequency of the virtues that are identical in us all is not more wonderful than the multiplicity of the defects that are peculiar to each one of us. Undoubtedly, it is not common sense that is "the commonest thing in the world"; it is human kindness. In the most distant, the most desolate corners of the earth, we marvel to see it blossom of its own accord, as in a remote valley a poppy like all the poppies in the rest of the world, which it has never seen as it has never known anything but the wind that occasionally stirs the folds of its lonely scarlet cloak. Even if this human kindness, paralysed by self-interest, is not put into practice, it exists none the less, and whenever there is no selfish motive to restrain it, for example when reading a novel or a newspaper, it will blossom, even in the heart of one who, cold-blooded in real life, has retained a tender heart as a lover of serial romances, and turn towards the weak, the just and the persecuted. But the variety of our defects is no less remarkable than the similarity of our virtues. The most perfect person in the world has a certain defect which shocks us or makes us angry. One man is of rare intelligence, sees everything from the loftiest viewpoint, never speaks ill of anyone, but will pocket and forget letters of supreme importance which he himself asked you to let him post for you, and so make you miss a vital engagement without offering you any excuse, with a smile, because he prides himself upon never knowing the time. Another is so refined, so gentle, so delicate in his conduct that he never says anything to you about yourself that you would not be glad to hear, but you feel that he suppresses, that he keeps buried in his heart, where they turn sour, other, quite different opinions, and the pleasure that he derives from seeing you is so dear to him that he will let you faint with exhaustion sooner than leave you to yourself. A third has more sincerity, but carries it so far that he feels bound to let you know, when you have pleaded the state of your health as an excuse for not

having been to see him, that you were seen going to the theatre
and were reported to be looking well, or else that he has not
been able to take full advantage of the step you took on his
behalf, which in any case three other people had already
offered to take, so that he is only moderately indebted to
you. In similar circumstances the previous friend would have
pretended not to know that you had gone to the theatre, or
that other people could have done him the same service. But
this last friend feels himself obliged to repeat or to reveal to
somebody the very thing that is most likely to give offence; is
delighted with his own frankness and tells you, emphatically:
"I am like that." While others infuriate you by their exaggerated curiosity, or by a want of curiosity so absolute that
you can speak to them of the most sensational happenings
without their knowing what it is all about; and others again
take months to answer you if your letter has been about
something that concerns yourself and not them, or else, if they
write that they are coming to ask you for something and you
dare not leave the house for fear of missing them, do not
appear, but leave you in suspense for weeks because, not
having received from you the answer which their letter did not
in the least call for, they have concluded that you must be cross
with them. And others, considering their own wishes and not
yours, talk to you without letting you get a word in if they are
in good spirits and want to see you, however urgent the work
you may have in hand, but if they feel exhausted by the weather
or out of humour, you cannot drag a word out of them, they
greet your efforts with an inert languor and no more take the
trouble to reply, even in monosyllables, to what you say to
them than if they had not heard you. Each of our friends has
his defects, to such an extent that to continue to love him we
are obliged to console ourselves for them—by thinking of his
talent, his kindness, his affection—or rather by ignoring them,
for which we need to deploy all our good will. Unfortunately
our obliging obstinacy in refusing to see the defect in our friend
is surpassed by the obstinacy with which he persists in that
defect, from his own blindness to it or the blindness that he
attributes to other people. For he does not notice it himself
or imagines that it is not noticed. Since the risk of giving

offence arises principally from the difficulty of appreciating what does and what does not pass unnoticed, we ought at least, from prudence, never to speak of ourselves, because that is a subject on which we may be sure that other people's views are never in accordance with our own. If, when we discover the true lives of other people, the real world beneath the world of appearance, we get as many surprises as on visiting a house of plain exterior which inside is full of hidden treasures, torture-chambers or skeletons, we are no less surprised if, in place of the image that we have of ourselves as a result of all the things that people have said to us, we learn from the way they speak of us in our absence what an entirely different image they have been carrying in their minds of us and of our lives. So that whenever we have spoken about ourselves, we may be sure that our inoffensive and prudent words, listened to with apparent politeness and hypocritical approbation, have given rise afterwards to the most exasperated or the most mirthful, but in either case the least favourable comments. At the very least we run the risk of irritating people by the disproportion between our idea of ourselves and the words that we use, a disproportion which as a rule makes people's talk about themselves as ludicrous as the performances of those self-styled music-lovers who when they feel the need to hum a favourite tune compensate for the inadequacy of their inarticulate murmurings by a strenuous mimicry and an air of admiration which is hardly justified by what they let us hear. And to the bad habit of speaking about oneself and one's defects there must be added, as part of the same thing, that habit of denouncing in other people defects precisely analogous to one's own. For it is always of those defects that one speaks, as though it were a way of speaking of oneself indirectly, and adding to the pleasure of absolving oneself the pleasure of confession. Moreover it seems that our attention, always attracted by what is characteristic of ourselves, notices it more than anything else in other people. One short-sighted man says of another: "But he can scarcely open his eyes!"; a consumptive has his doubts as to the pulmonary integrity of the most robust; an unwashed man speaks only of the baths that other people do not take; an evil-smelling man

insists that other people smell; a cuckold sees cuckolds everywhere, a light woman light women, a snob snobs. Then, too,
every vice, like every profession, requires and develops a
special knowledge which we are never loath to display. The
invert sniffs out inverts; the tailor asked out to dine has
hardly begun to talk to you before he has already appraised the
cloth of your coat, which his fingers are itching to feel; and if
after a few words of conversation you were to ask a dentist
what he really thought of you, he would tell you how many
of your teeth wanted filling. To him nothing appears more
important, or to you, who have noticed his, more absurd. And
it is not only when we speak of ourselves that we imagine
other people to be blind; we behave as though they were.
Each one of us has a special god in attendance who hides from
him or promises him the concealment of his defect from other
people, just as he closes the eyes and nostrils of people who do
not wash to the streaks of dirt which they carry in their ears
and the smell of sweat that emanates from their armpits, and
assures them that they can with impunity carry both of these
about a world that will notice nothing. And those who wear
artificial pearls, or give them as presents, imagine that people
will take them to be genuine.

Bloch was ill-bred, neurotic and snobbish, and since he
belonged to a family of little repute, had to support, as on the
floor of the ocean, the incalculable pressures imposed on him
not only by the Christians at the surface but by all the intervening layers of Jewish castes superior to his own, each of
them crushing with its contempt the one that was immediately beneath it. To pierce his way through to the open air by
raising himself from Jewish family to Jewish family would
have taken Bloch many thousands of years. It was better to
seek an outlet in another direction.

When Bloch spoke to me of the attack of snobbery from
which I must be suffering, and bade me confess that I was a
snob, I might well have replied: "If I were, I shouldn't be
going about with you." I said merely that he was not being
very polite. Then he wanted to apologise, but in the way that
is typical of the ill-bred man who is only too happy, in re-
tracting his words, to find an opportunity to aggravate his

offence. "Forgive me," he would now say to me whenever we met, "I've distressed you, tormented you, I've been wantonly mischievous. And yet—man in general and your friend in particular is so singular an animal—you cannot imagine the affection that I, I who tease you so cruelly, have for you. It brings me often, when I think of you, to the verge of tears." And he gave an audible sob.

What astonished me more in Bloch than his bad manners was to find how the quality of his conversation varied. This youth, so hard to please that of authors who were at the height of their fame he would say: "He's a dismal fool; he's a sheer imbecile," would every now and then recount with immense gusto anecdotes that were simply not funny or would instance as a "really remarkable person" someone who was completely insignificant. This double scale of measuring the wit, the worth, the interest of people continued to puzzle me until I was introduced to M. Bloch, senior.

I had not supposed that we should ever be allowed to meet him, for Bloch junior had spoken ill of me to Saint-Loup and of Saint-Loup to me. In particular, he had said to Robert that I was (still) a frightful snob. "Yes, really, he's thrilled to know M. LLLLegrandin." This trick of Bloch's of isolating a word was a sign at once of irony and literature. Saint-Loup, who had never heard the name Legrandin, was bewildered: "But who is he?" "Oh, he's a *very distinguished* person," Bloch replied with a laugh, thrusting his hands into his pockets as though for warmth, convinced that he was at that moment engaged in contemplation of the picturesque aspect of an extraordinary country gentleman compared to whom those of Barbey d'Aurevilly were as nothing. He consoled himself for his inability to portray M. Legrandin by giving him a string of capital L's and smacking his lips over the name as over a wine of the finest vintage. But these subjective enjoyments remained hidden from other people. If he spoke ill of me to Saint-Loup he made up for it by speaking no less ill of Saint-Loup to me. We had each of us learned these slanders in detail the very next day, not that we had repeated them to each other, a thing which would have seemed to us very wrong but to Bloch appeared so natural and almost inevitable that in his natural anxiety, in the certainty moreover that he would be telling us only what each of us was bound sooner or later to learn, he preferred to anticipate the disclosure and, taking Saint-Loup aside, admitted that he had spoken ill of him, on purpose, so that it might be repeated to him, swore to him "by Zeus Kronion, binder of oaths" that he loved him dearly, that he would lay down his life for him, and wiped away a tear. The same day, he contrived to see me alone, made his confession, declared that he had acted in my interest, because he felt that a certain kind of social intercourse was fatal to me and that I was "worthy of better things." Then, clasping me by the hand with the sentimentality of a drunkard, although his drunkenness was purely nervous: "Believe me," he said, "and may the black Ker seize me this instant and bear me across the portals of Hades, hateful to men, if yesterday, when I thought of you, of Combray, of my boundless affection for you, of afternoon hours in class which you do not even remember, I did not lie awake sobbing all night long. Yes, all night long, I swear it, and alas, I know—for I know the human soul— you will not believe me." I did indeed "not believe" him, and to these words which I felt he was making up on the spur of the moment and developing as he went on, his swearing "by Ker" added no great weight, the Hellenic cult being in Bloch purely literary. Besides, whenever he began to get emotional over a falsehood and wanted one to share his emotion, he would say "I swear it," more for the hysterical pleasure of lying than to make one think that he was speaking the truth. I did not believe what he was saying, but I bore him no ill-will on that account, for I had inherited from my mother and grandmother their incapacity for rancour even against far worse offenders, and their habit of never condemning anyone.

Besides, Bloch was not altogether a bad fellow: he was capable of being extremely nice. And now that the race of Combray, the race from which sprang creatures as absolutely unspoiled as my grandmother and my mother, seems almost extinct, since I no longer have much choice save between decent brutes, frank and insensitive, the mere sound of whose voices shows at once that they take absolutely no interest in your life—and another kind of men who so long as they are

with you understand you, cherish you, grow sentimental to
the point of tears, then make up for it a few hours later with
some cruel joke at your expense, but come back to you, always
just as understanding, as charming, as in tune with you for
the moment, I think that it is of this latter sort that I prefer,
if not the moral worth, at any rate the society.

"You cannot imagine my grief when I think of you," Bloch
went on. "Actually, I suppose it's a rather Jewish side of my
nature coming out," he added ironically, contracting his
pupils as though measuring out under the microscope an infinitesimal quantity of "Jewish blood," as a French nobleman
might (but never would) have said who among his exclusively
Christian ancestry nevertheless numbered Samuel Bernard,
or further back still, the Blessed Virgin from whom, it is
said, the Lévy family claim descent. "I rather like," he continued, "to take into account the element in my feelings (slight
though it is) which may be ascribed to my Jewish origin." He
made this statement because it seemed to him at once clever
and courageous to speak the truth about his race, a truth
which at the same time he managed to water down to a remarkable extent, like misers who decide to discharge their
debts but cannot bring themselves to pay more than half of
them. This kind of deceit which consists in having the boldness to proclaim the truth, but only after mixing with it an
ample measure of lies which falsify it, is commoner than people
think, and even among those who do not habitually practise
it certain crises in life, especially those in which a love affair
is involved, give them occasion to indulge in it.

All these confidential diatribes by Bloch to Saint-Loup
against me and to me against Saint-Loup ended in an invitation
to dinner. I am by no means sure that he did not first make an
attempt to secure Saint-Loup by himself. It would have been
so like Bloch to do so that probably he did; but if so, success
did not crown his effort, for it was to myself and Saint-Loup
both that he said one day: "Dear master, and you, O horseman
beloved of Ares, de Saint-Loup-en-Bray, tamer of horses,
since I have encountered you by the shore of Amphitrite, resounding with foam, hard by the tents of the swift-shipped
Meniers, will both of you come to dinner one day this week

with my illustrious sire, of blameless heart?" He proffered this invitation because he desired to attach himself more closely to Saint-Loup who would, he hoped, secure him the right of entry into aristocratic circles. Formed by me, for myself, this ambition would have seemed to Bloch the mark of the most hideous snobbery, quite in keeping with the opinion that he already held of a whole side of my nature which he did not regard—or at least had not hitherto regarded—as the most important side; but the same ambition in himself seemed to him the proof of a finely developed curiosity in a mind anxious to carry out certain social explorations from which he might perhaps glean some literary benefit. M. Bloch senior, when his son had told him that he was going to bring one of his friends in to dinner, and had in a sarcastic but self-satisfied tone enunciated the name and title of that friend: "The Marquis de Saint-Loup-en-Bray," had been thrown into great commotion. "The Marquis de Saint-Loup-en-Bray! I'll be jiggered!" he had exclaimed, using the oath which was with him the strongest indication of social deference. And he gazed at a son capable of having formed such an acquaintance with an admiring look which seemed to say: "He really is astounding. Can this prodigy be indeed a child of mine!" which gave my friend as much pleasure as if his monthly allowance had been increased by fifty francs. For Bloch was not in his element at home and felt that his father treated him like a black sheep because of his inveterate admiration for Leconte de Lisle, Heredia and other "Bohemians." But to have got to know Saint-Loup-en-Bray, whose father had been chairman of the Suez Canal board ("I'll be jiggered!") was an indisputable "score." What a pity that they had left the stereoscope in Paris for fear of its being broken on the journey. M. Bloch senior alone had the skill, or at least the right, to manipulate it. He did so, moreover, on rare occasions only, and then to good purpose, on evenings when there was a full-dress affair, with hired waiters. So that from these stereoscope sessions there emanated, for those who were present, as it were a special distinction, a privileged position, and for the master of the house who gave them, a prestige such as talent confers on a man—which could not have been greater had the pictures been taken by M. Bloch himself and the machine his own invention. "You weren't invited to Solomon's yesterday?" one of the family would ask another. "No! I wasn't one of the elect. What was on?" "Oh, a great how-d'ye-do, the stereoscope, the whole box of tricks!" "Indeed! If they had the stereoscope I'm sorry I wasn't there; they say Solomon is quite amazing when he works it."

"Ah, well," said M. Bloch now to his son, "it's a mistake to let him have everything at once. Now he'll have something else to look forward to."

He had actually thought, in his paternal affection and in the hope of touching his son's heart, of sending for the instrument. But it was not "physically possible" in the time, or rather they had thought it would not be; for we were obliged to put off the dinner because Saint-Loup could not leave the hotel, where he was expecting an uncle who was coming to spend a few days with Mme de Villeparisis. Since he was greatly addicted to physical culture, and especially to long walks, it was largely on foot, spending the night in wayside farms, that this uncle was to make the journey from the country house in which he was staying, and the precise moment of his arrival at Balbec was somewhat uncertain. Indeed Saint-Loup, afraid to stir out of doors, even entrusted me with the duty of taking to Incarville, where the nearest telegraph-office was, the messages that he sent every day to his mistress. The uncle in question was called Palamède, a Christian name that had come down to him from his ancestors the Princes of Sicily. And later on, when I found, in the course of my historical reading, belonging to this or that Podestà or Prince of the Church, the same Christian name, a fine Renaissance medal—some said a genuine antique—that had always remained in the family, having passed from generation to generation, from the Vatican cabinet to the uncle of my friend, I felt the pleasure that is reserved for those who, unable from lack of means to start a medal collection or a picture gallery, look out for old names (names of localities, instructive and picturesque as an old map, a bird's-eye view, a sign-board or a return of customs; baptismal names whose fine French endings echo the defect of speech, the intonation of an ethnic vulgarity, the corrupt pronunciation whereby our ancestors made Latin and Saxon words undergo lasting mutilations which in due course became the august law-givers of our grammar books) and, in short, by drawing upon these collections of ancient sonorities, give themselves concerts like the people who acquire viole da gamba and viole d'amore to perform the music of the past on old instruments. Saint-Loup told me that even in the most exclusive aristocratic society his uncle Palamède stood out as being particularly unapproachable, scornful, obsessed with his nobility, forming with his brother's wife and a few other chosen spirits what was known as the Phoenix Club. Even there his insolence was so dreaded that it had happened more than once that society people who had been anxious to meet him and had applied to his own brother for an introduction had met with a refusal: "Really, you mustn't ask me to introduce you to my brother Palamède. Even if my wife and the whole lot of us put ourselves to the task it would be no good. Or else you'd run the risk of his being rude to you, and I shouldn't like that." At the Jockey Club he had, with a few of his friends, marked a list of two hundred members whom they would never allow to be introduced to them. And in the Comte de Paris's circle he was known by the nickname of "The Prince" because of his elegance and his pride.

Saint-Loup told me about his uncle's early life, now long since past. Every day he used to take women to a bachelor establishment which he shared with two of his friends, as good-looking as himself, on account of which they were known as "the three Graces."

"One day, a man who is now one of the brightest luminaries of the Faubourg Saint-Germain, as Balzac would have said, but who at a rather unfortunate stage of his early life displayed bizarre tastes, asked my uncle to let him come to this place. But no sooner had he arrived than it was not to the ladies but to my uncle Palamède that he began to make overtures. My uncle pretended not to understand, and took his two friends aside on some pretext or other. They reappeared on the scene, seized the offender, stripped him, thrashed him till he bled, and then in ten degrees of frost kicked him outside where he was found more dead than alive; so much so that the police started an inquiry which the poor devil had the greatest difficulty in getting them to abandon. My uncle would never go in for such drastic methods now—in fact you can't imagine the number of working men he takes under his wing, only to be repaid quite often with the basest ingratitude —though he's so haughty with society people. It may be a servant who has looked after him in a hotel, for whom he will find a place in Paris, or a farm-labourer whom he will pay to have taught a trade. It's a really rather nice side of his character, in contrast to his social side." For Saint-Loup belonged to that type of young men of fashion, situated at an altitude at which it has been possible to cultivate such expressions as "what is really rather nice about him," "his nicer side," precious seeds which produce very rapidly a way of looking at things in which one counts oneself as nothing and the "people" as everything; the exact opposite, in a word, of plebeian pride. "I'm told it was quite extraordinary to what extent he set the tone, to what extent he laid down the law for the whole of society when he was a young man. As far as he was concerned, in any circumstance he did whatever seemed most agreeable or most convenient to himself, but immediately it was imitated by all the snobs. If he felt thirsty at the theatre, and had a drink brought to him in his box, a week later the little sitting-rooms behind all the boxes would be filled with refreshments. One wet summer when he had a touch of rheumatism, he ordered an overcoat of a loose but warm vicuna wool, which is used only for travelling rugs, and insisted on the usual blue and orange stripes. The big tailors at once received orders from all the customers for blue and orange overcoats of rough wool. If for some reason he wanted to remove every aspect of ceremony from a dinner in a country house where he was spending the day, and to underline the distinction had come without evening clothes and sat down to table in the suit he had been wearing that afternoon, it became the fashion not to dress for dinner in the country. If instead of taking a spoon to eat a pudding he used a fork, or a special implement of his own invention which he had had made for him by a silversmith, or his fingers, it was no longer permissible to eat it in any other way. He wanted once to hear some Beethoven quartets again (for with all his preposterous ideas he is far from being a fool and has great gifts) and arranged for some musicians to come and play them to him and a few friends once a week. The ultra-fashionable thing that season was to give quite small parties with chamber music. I should say he's not done at all badly out of life. With his looks, he must have had any number of women! I couldn't tell you exactly which, because he's very discreet. But I do know that he was thoroughly unfaithful to my poor aunt. Which doesn't mean that he wasn't always perfectly charming to her, that she didn't adore him, and that he didn't go on mourning her for years. When he's in Paris, he still goes to the cemetery nearly every day."

The morning after Robert had told me all these things about his uncle while waiting for him (as it happened in vain), as I was passing the Casino alone on my way back to the hotel, I had the sensation of being watched by somebody who was not far off. I turned my head and saw a man of about forty, very tall and rather stout, with a very black moustache, who, nervously slapping the leg of his trousers with a switch, was staring at me, his eyes dilated with extreme attentiveness. From time to time these eyes were shot through by a look of restless activity such as the sight of a person they do not know excites only in men in whom, for whatever reason, it inspires thoughts that would not occur to anyone else—madmen, for instance, or spies. He darted a final glance at me that was at once bold, prudent, rapid and profound, like a last shot which one fires at an enemy as one turns to flee, and, after first looking all round him, suddenly adopting an absent and lofty air, with an abrupt revolution of his whole person he turned towards a playbill in the reading of which he became absorbed, while he hummed a tune and fingered the moss-rose in his buttonhole. He drew from his pocket a note-book in which he appeared to be taking down the title of the performance that was announced, looked at his watch two or three times, pulled down over his eyes a black straw hat the brim of which he extended with his hand held out over it like an eye-shade, as though to see whether someone was coming at last, made the perfunctory gesture of annoyance by which people mean to show that they have waited long enough, although they never

make it when they are really waiting, then pushing back his
hat and exposing a scalp cropped close except at the sides
where he allowed a pair of waved "pigeon's-wings" to grow
quite long, he emitted the loud panting breath that people
exhale not when they are too hot but when they wish it to
be thought that they are too hot. He gave me the impression
of a hotel crook who, having been watching my grandmother
and myself for some days, and planning to rob us, had just
discovered that I had caught him in the act of spying on me.
Perhaps he was only seeking by his new attitude to express
abstractedness and detachment in order to put me off the
scent, but it was with an exaggeration so aggressive that his
object appeared to be—at least as much as the dissipating of
the suspicions he might have aroused in me—to avenge a
humiliation which I must unwittingly have inflicted on him,
to give me the idea not so much that he had not seen me as
that I was an object of too little importance to attract his
attention. He threw back his shoulders with an air of bravado,
pursed his lips, twisted his moustache, and adjusted his
face into an expression that was at once indifferent, harsh, and
almost insulting. So much so that I took him at one moment
for a thief and at another for a lunatic. And yet his scrupulously
ordered attire was far more sober and far more simple than
that of any of the summer visitors I saw at Balbec, and reassured me as to my own suit, so often humiliated by the usual
dazzling whiteness of their holiday garb. But my grandmother
was coming towards me, we took a turn together, and I was
waiting for her, an hour later, outside the hotel into which
she had gone for a moment, when I saw emerge from it Mme
de Villeparisis with Robert de Saint-Loup and the stranger
who had stared at me so intently outside the Casino. Swift as a
lightning-flash his look shot through me, just as at the moment
when I had first noticed him, and returned, as though he had
not seen me, to hover, slightly lowered, before his eyes,
deadened, like the neutral look which feigns to see nothing
without and is incapable of reporting anything to the mind
within, the look which expresses merely the satisfaction of
feeling round it the eyelids which it keeps apart with its
beatific roundness, the devout and sanctimonious look that we

see on the faces of certain hypocrites, the smug look on those of certain fools. I saw that he had changed his clothes. The suit he was wearing was darker even than the other; and no doubt true elegance lies nearer to simplicity than false; but there was something more: from close at hand one felt that if colour was almost entirely absent from these garments it was not because he who had banished it from them was indifferent to it but rather because for some reason he forbade himself the enjoyment of it. And the sobriety which they displayed seemed to be of the kind that comes from obedience to a rule of diet rather than from lack of appetite. A dark green thread harmonised, in the stuff of his trousers, with the stripe on his socks, with a refinement which betrayed the vivacity of a taste that was everywhere else subdued, to which this single concession had been made out of tolerance, while a spot of red on his tie was imperceptible, like a liberty which one dares not take.

"How are you? Let me introduce my nephew, the Baron de Guermantes," Mme de Villeparisis said to me, while the stranger, without looking at me, muttering a vague "Charmed!" which he followed with a "H'm, h'm, h'm," to make his affability seem somehow forced, and crooking his little finger, forefinger and thumb, held out to me his middle and ring fingers, destitute of rings, which I clasped through his suede glove; then, without lifting his eyes to my face, he turned towards Mme de Villeparisis.

"Good gracious, I shall be forgetting my own name next!" she exclaimed with a laugh. "Here am I calling you Baron de Guermantes. Let me introduce the Baron de Charlus. But after all, it's not a very serious mistake," she went on, "for you're a thorough Guermantes whatever else you are."

By this time my grandmother had reappeared, and we all set out together. Saint-Loup's uncle declined to honour me not only with a word but with so much as a look in my direction. If he stared strangers out of countenance (and during this short excursion he two or three times hurled his terrible and searching scrutiny like a sounding lead at insignificant people of the most humble extraction who happened to pass), on the other hand he never for a moment, if I was to judge by myself, looked at persons whom he knew—as a detective on a secret mission might except his personal friends from his professional vigilance. Leaving my grandmother, Mme de Villeparisis and him to talk to one another, I fell behind with Saint-Loup.

"Tell me, am I right in thinking I heard Mme de Villeparisis say just now to your uncle that he was a Guermantes?"

"Of course he is: Palamède de Guermantes."

"Not the same Guermantes who have a place near Combray, and claim descent from Geneviève de Brabant?"

"Most certainly: my uncle, who is the very last word in heraldry and all that sort of thing, would tell you that our 'cry,' our war-cry, that is to say, which was changed afterwards to 'Passavant' was originally 'Combraysis,'" he said, smiling so as not to appear to be priding himself on this prerogative of a "cry," which only the quasi-royal houses, the great chiefs of feudal bands, enjoyed. "It's his brother who has the place now."

So she was related, and very closely, to the Guermantes, this Mme de Villeparisis who had for so long been for me the lady who had given me a duck filled with chocolates when I was small, more remote then from the Guermantes way than if she had been shut up somewhere on the Méséglise way, less brilliant, less highly placed by me than was the Combray optician, and who now suddenly went through one of those fantastic rises in value, parallel to the no less unforeseen depreciations of other objects in our possession, which—rise and fall alike—introduce in our youth, and in those periods of our life in which a trace of youth persists, changes as numerous as the Metamorphoses of Ovid.*

"Haven't they got the busts of all the old lords of Guermantes down there?"

"Yes, and a lovely sight they are!" Saint-Loup was ironical. "Between you and me, I look on all that sort of thing as rather a joke. But what they have got at Guermantes, which is a little more interesting, is quite a touching portrait of my aunt by Carrière. It's as fine as Whistler or Velasquez," went on Saint-Loup, who in his neophyte zeal was not always very exact about degrees of greatness. "There are also some stunning pictures by Gustave Moreau. My aunt is the niece of your friend Mme de Villeparisis; she was brought up by her, and married her cousin, who was a nephew, too, of my aunt Villeparisis, the present Duc de Guermantes."

"Then what is your uncle?"

"He bears the title of Baron de Charlus. Strictly, when my great-uncle died, my uncle Palamède ought to have taken the title of Prince des Laumes, which was that of his brother before he became Duc de Guermantes—in that family they change their names as often as their shirts. But my uncle has peculiar ideas about all that sort of thing. And as he feels that people are rather apt to overdo the Italian Prince and Grandee of Spain business nowadays, and although he had half-a-dozen princely titles to choose from, he has remained Baron de Charlus, as a protest, and with an apparent simplicity which really covers a good deal of pride. 'In these days,' he says, 'everybody is a prince; one really must have something to distinguish one; I shall call myself Prince when I wish to travel incognito.' According to him there is no older title than the Charlus barony; to prove to you that it's earlier than the Montmorency title, though they used to claim, quite wrongly, to be the premier barons of France when they were only premier in the Ile-de-France, where their fief was, my uncle will hold forth to you for hours on end and enjoy doing so because, although he's a most intelligent man, really gifted, he regards that sort of thing as quite a live topic of conversation." Saint-Loup smiled again. "But as I'm not like him, you mustn't ask me to talk pedigrees. I know nothing more deadly, more outdated; really, life's too short."

I now recognised in the hard look which had made me turn round outside the Casino the same that I had seen fixed on me at Tansonville at the moment when Mme Swann had called Gilberte away.

"Wasn't Mme Swann one of the numerous mistresses you told me your uncle M. de Charlus had had?"

"Good lord, no! That is to say, my uncle's a great friend of Swann, and has always stood up for him. But no one has ever suggested that he was his wife's lover. You would cause the utmost astonishment in Parisian society if people thought you believed that."

I dared not reply that it would have caused even greater astonishment in Combray society if people had thought that I did not believe it.

My grandmother was delighted with M. de Charlus. No doubt he attached an extreme importance to all questions of birth and social position, and my grandmother had remarked this, but without any trace of that severity which as a rule embodies a secret envy and irritation, at seeing another person enjoy advantages which one would like but cannot oneself possess. Since, on the contrary, my grandmother, content with her lot and not for a moment regretting that she did not move in a more brilliant sphere, employed only her intellect in observing the eccentricities of M. de Charlus, she spoke of Saint-Loup's uncle with that detached, smiling, almost affectionate benevolence with which we reward the object of our disinterested observation for the pleasure that it has given us, all the more so because this time the object was a person whose pretensions, if not legitimate at any rate picturesque, made him stand out in fairly vivid contrast to the people whom she generally had occasion to see. But it was above all in consideration of his intelligence and sensibility, qualities which it was easy to see that M. de Charlus, unlike so many of the society people whom Saint-Loup derided, possessed in a marked degree, that my grandmother had so readily forgiven him his aristocratic prejudice. And yet this prejudice had not been sacrificed by the uncle, as it had been by the nephew, to higher qualities. Rather, M. de Charlus had reconciled it with them. Possessing, by virtue of his descent from the Ducs de Nemours and the Princes de Lamballe, documents, furniture, tapestries, portraits painted for his ancestors by Raphael, Velasquez, Boucher, justified in saying that he was "visiting" a museum and a matchless library when he was merely going over his family mementoes, he still placed the whole heritage of the aristocracy in the high position from which Saint-Loup had toppled it. Perhaps also, being less ideological than Saint-Loup, less satisfied with words, a more realistic observer of men, he did not care to neglect an essential element of prestige in their eyes which, if it gave certain disinterested pleasures to his imagination, could often be a powerfully effective aid to his utilitarian activities. No agreement can ever be reached between men of his sort and those who obey an inner ideal which drives them to rid themselves of such advantages so that they may seek only to realise that ideal, resembling in that respect the painters and writers who renounce their virtuosity, the artistic people who modernise themselves, the warrior people who initiate universal disarmament, the absolute governments which turn democratic and repeal their harsh laws, though as often as not the sequel fails to reward their noble efforts; for the artists lose their talent, the nations their age-old predominance; pacifism often breeds wars and tolerance criminality. If Saint-Loup's strivings towards sincerity and emancipation could not but be regarded as extremely noble, to judge by their visible result, one could still be thankful that they had failed to bear fruit in M. de Charlus, who had transferred to his own home much of the admirable furniture from the Hôtel Guermantes instead of replacing it, like his nephew, with Art Nouveau furniture, pieces by Lebourg or Guillaumin. It was none the less true that M. de Charlus's ideal was highly artificial, and, if the epithet can be applied to the word ideal, as much social as artistic. In certain women of great beauty and rare culture whose ancestresses, two centuries earlier, had shared in all the glory and grace of the old order, he found a distinction which made him capable of taking pleasure in their society alone, and doubtless his admiration for them was sincere, but countless reminiscences, historical and artistic, evoked by their names played a considerable part in it, just as memories of classical antiquity are one of the reasons for the pleasure which a literary man finds in reading an ode by Horace that is perhaps inferior to poems of our own day which would leave him cold. Any of these women by the side of a pretty commoner was for him what an old picture is to a contemporary canvas representing a procession or a wedding—one of those old pictures the history of which we know, from the Pope or King who ordered them, through the hands of the eminent persons whose acquisition of them, by gift, purchase, conquest or inheritance, recalls to us some event or at least some alliance of historic interest, and consequently some knowledge that we ourselves have acquired, gives it new meaning, increases our sense of the richness of the possessions of our memory or of our erudition. M. de Charlus was thankful that a prejudice similar to his own, by preventing these few great ladies from mixing with women whose blood was less pure, presented them for his veneration intact, in their unadulterated nobility, like some eighteenth-century façade supported on its flat columns of pink marble, in which the passage of time has wrought no change.

M. de Charlus extolled the true "nobility" of mind and heart which characterised these women, playing upon the word in a double sense by which he himself was taken in, and in which lay the falsehood of this bastard conception, of this medley of aristocracy, generosity and art, but also its seductiveness, dangerous to people like my grandmother, to whom the less refined but more innocent prejudice of a noble-man who cared only about quarterings and took no thought for anything besides would have appeared too silly for words, whereas she was defenceless as soon as a thing presented itself under the externals of an intellectual superiority, so much so, indeed, that she regarded princes as enviable above all other men because they were able to have a La Bruyère or a Fénelon as their tutors.

Outside the Grand Hotel the three Guermantes left us; they were going to luncheon with the Princesse de Luxembourg. While my grandmother was saying good-bye to Mme de Villeparisis and Saint-Loup to my grandmother, M. de Charlus, who up till then had not addressed a single word to me, drew back from the group and arriving at my side, said to me: "I shall be taking tea this evening after dinner in my aunt Villeparisis's room. I hope that you will give me the pleasure of seeing you there with your grandmother." With which he re-joined the Marquise.

Although it was Sunday, there were no more carriages waiting outside the hotel now than at the beginning of the season. The notary's wife, in particular, had decided that it was not worth the expense of hiring one every time simply because she was not going to the Cambremers', and simply stayed in her room.

"Is Mme Blandais not well?" her husband was asked. "We haven't seen her all morning."

"She has a slight headache—the heat, you know, this thundery weather. The least thing upsets her. But I expect you'll see her this evening. I've told her she ought to come down. It can do her nothing but good."

I had supposed that in thus inviting us to take tea with his aunt, whom I never doubted that he would have warned of our coming, M. de Charlus wished to make amends for the impoliteness which he had shown me during our walk that morning. But when, on our entering Mme de Villeparisis's room, I attempted to greet her nephew, for all that I walked right round him while in shrill accents he was telling a somewhat spiteful story about one of his relatives, I could not succeed in catching his eye. I decided to say "Good evening" to him, and fairly loud, to warn him of my presence; but I realised that he had observed it, for before ever a word had passed my lips, just as I was beginning to bow to him, I saw his two fingers held out for me to shake without his having turned to look at me or paused in his story. He had evidently seen me, without letting it appear that he had, and I noticed then that his eyes, which were never fixed on the person to whom he was speaking, strayed perpetually in all directions, like those of certain frightened animals, or those of street hawkers who, while delivering their patter and displaying their illicit merchandise, keep a sharp look-out, though without turning their heads, on the different points of the horizon from which the police may appear at any moment. At the same time I was a little surprised to find that Mme de Villeparisis, while glad to see us, did not seem to have been expecting us, and I was still more surprised to hear M. de Charlus say to my grandmother: "Ah! what a capital idea of yours to come and pay us a visit! Charming of them, is it not, my dear aunt?" No doubt he had noticed his aunt's surprise at our entry and thought, as a man accustomed to set the tone, that it would be enough to transform that surprise into joy were he to show that he himself felt it, that it was indeed the feeling which our arrival there ought to prompt. In which he calculated wisely; for Mme de Villeparisis, who had a high opinion of her nephew and knew

how difficult it was to please him, appeared suddenly to have
found new attractions in my grandmother and welcomed her
with open arms. But I failed to understand how M. de Charlus
could, in the space of a few hours, have forgotten the invitation—so curt but apparently so intentional, so premeditated—
which he had addressed to me that same morning, or why he
called a "capital idea" on my grandmother's part an idea that
had been entirely his own. With a regard for accuracy which I
retained until I had reached the age at which I realised that it
is not by questioning him that one learns the truth of what
another man has had in his mind, and that the risk of a misunderstanding which will probably pass unobserved is less
than that which may come from a purblind insistence: "But,
Monsieur," I reminded him, "you remember, surely, that it
was you who asked me if we would come round this evening?"
Not a sound, not a movement betrayed that M. de Charles had
so much as heard my question. Seeing which, I repeated it, like
diplomats or like young men after a misunderstanding who
endeavour, with untiring and unrewarded zeal, to obtain an
explanation which their adversary is determined not to give
them. Still M. de Charlus answered me not a word. I seemed
to see hovering upon his lips the smile of those who from a
great height pass judgment on the character and breeding of
their inferiors.

Since he refused all explanation, I tried to provide one for
myself, but succeeded only in hesitating between several,
none of which might have been the right one. Perhaps he did
not remember, or perhaps it was I who had failed to understand what he had said to me that morning. . . . More probably,
in his pride, he did not wish to appear to have sought the company of people he despised, and preferred to cast upon them the
responsibility for their intrusion. But then, if he despised us, why
had he been so anxious that we should come, or rather that
my grandmother should come, for of the two of us it was to
her alone that he spoke that evening, and never once to me?
Talking with the utmost animation to her, as also to Mme de
Villeparisis, hiding, so to speak, behind them as though he
were seated at the back of a theatre-box, he merely turned
from them every now and then the searching gaze of his

penetrating eyes and fastened it on my face, with the same
gravity, the same air of preoccupation, as if it had been a
manuscript difficult to decipher.

No doubt, had it not been for those eyes, M. de Charlus's face
would have been similar to the faces of many good-looking
men. And when Saint-Loup, speaking to me of various other
Guermantes, said on a later occasion: "Gad, they've got that
thoroughbred air, that look of being noblemen to their
finger-tips, that uncle Palamède has," confirming my suspicion that a thoroughbred air and aristocratic distinction were
not something mysterious and new but consisted in elements
which I had recognised without difficulty and without receiving any particular impression from them, I was to feel
that another of my illusions had been shattered. But however
much M. de Charlus tried to seal hermetically the expression
on that face, to which a light coating of powder lent a faintly
theatrical aspect, the eyes were like two crevices, two loop-
holes which alone he had failed to stop, and through which,
according to one's position in relation to him, one suddenly
felt oneself in the path of some hidden weapon which seemed to
bode no good, even to him who, without being altogether
master of it, carried it within himself in a state of precarious
equilibrium and always on the verge of explosion; and the
circumspect and unceasingly restless expression of those eyes,
with all the signs of exhaustion which the heavy pouches beneath them stamped upon his face, however carefully he
might compose and regulate it, made one think of some
incognito, some disguise assumed by a powerful man in danger,
or merely by a dangerous—but tragic—individual. I should
have liked to divine what was this secret which other men did
not carry in their breasts and which had already made M. de
Charlus's stare seem to me so enigmatic when I had seen him
that morning outside the Casino. But with what I now knew
of his family I could no longer believe that it was that of a
thief, nor, after what I had heard of his conversation, of a
madman. If he was so cold towards me, while making himself
so agreeable to my grandmother, this did not perhaps arise
from any personal antipathy, for in general, to the extent that
he was kindly disposed towards women, of whose faults he

spoke without, as a rule, departing from the utmost tolerance,
he displayed towards men, and especially young men, a
hatred so violent as to suggest that of certain misogynists
for women. Of two or three "gigolos," relatives or intimate
friends of Saint-Loup, who happened to mention their names,
M. de Charlus remarked with an almost ferocious expression
in sharp contrast to his usual coldness: "Young scum!"
I gathered that the particular fault which he found in the
young men of the day was their effeminacy. "They're nothing
but women," he said with scorn. But what life would not
have appeared effeminate beside that which he expected a
man to lead, and never found energetic or virile enough? (He
himself, when he walked across country, after long hours on
the road would plunge his heated body into frozen streams.)
He would not even concede that a man should wear a single
ring.

But this obsession with virility did not prevent his having
also the most delicate sensibilities. When Mme de Villeparisis
asked him to describe to my grandmother some country
house in which Mme de Sévigné had stayed, adding that she
could not help feeling that there was something rather "literary" about that lady's distress at being parted from "that
tiresome Mme de Grignan":

"On the contrary," he retorted, "I can think of nothing
more genuine. Besides, it was a time in which feelings of that
sort were thoroughly understood. The inhabitant of La
Fontaine's Monomotapa, running round to see his friend who
had appeared to him in a dream looking rather sad, the pigeon
finding that the greatest of evils is the absence of the other
pigeon, seem to you perhaps, my dear aunt, as exaggerated as
Mme de Sévigné's impatience for the moment when she will
be alone with her daughter. It's so beautiful, what she says
when she leaves her: 'This parting gives a pain to my soul which
I feel like an ache in my body. In absence one is liberal with the
hours. One anticipates a time for which one is longing.' "

My grandmother was delighted to hear the Letters thus
spoken of, exactly as she would have spoken of them herself.
She was astonished that a man could understand them so well.
She found in M. de Charlus a delicacy, a sensibility that were

quite feminine. We said to each other afterwards, when we were by ourselves and discussed him together, that he must have come under the strong influence of a woman—his mother, or in later life his daughter if he had any children. "A mistress, perhaps," I thought to myself, remembering the influence which Saint-Loup's seemed to have had over him and which enabled me to realise the degree to which men can be refined by the women with whom they live.

"Once she was with her daughter, she had probably nothing to say to her," put in Mme de Villeparisis.

"Most certainly she had: if it was only what she calls 'things so slight that nobody else would notice them but you and I.' And anyhow she was with her. And La Bruyère tells us that that is everything: 'To be with the people one loves, to speak to them, not to speak to them, it is all the same.' He is right: that is the only true happiness," added M. de Charlus in a mournful voice, "and alas, life is so ill arranged that one very rarely experiences it. Mme de Sévigné was after all less to be pitied than most of us. She spent a great part of her life with the person whom she loved."

"You forget that it wasn't 'love' in her case, since it was her daughter."

"But what matters in life is not whom or what one loves," he went on, in a judicial, peremptory, almost cutting tone, "it is the fact of loving. What Mme de Sévigné felt for her daughter has a far better claim to rank with the passion that Racine described in *Andromaque* or *Phèdre* than the commonplace relations young Sévigné had with his mistresses. It's the same with a mystic's love for his God. The hard and fast lines with which we circumscribe love arise solely from our complete ignorance of life."

"You think all that of *Andromaque* and *Phèdre*, do you?" Saint-Loup asked his uncle in a faintly contemptuous tone.

"There is more truth in a single tragedy of Racine than in all the dramatic works of Monsieur Victor Hugo," replied M. de Charlus.

"Society people really are appalling," Saint-Loup murmured in my ear. "Say what you like, to prefer Racine to Victor is a bit thick!" He was genuinely distressed by his

uncle's words, but the satisfaction of saying "say what you
like" and better still "a bit thick" consoled him.

In these reflexions upon the sadness of having to live apart
from those one loves (which were to lead my grandmother to
say to me that Mme de Villeparisis's nephew understood
certain things a great deal better than his aunt, and moreover
had something about him that set him far above the average
clubman) M. de Charlus not only revealed a refinement of
feeling such as men rarely show; his voice itself, like certain
contralto voices in which the middle register has not been
sufficiently cultivated, so that when they sing it sounds like an
alternating duet between a young man and a woman, mounted,
when he expressed these delicate sentiments, to its higher
notes, took on an unexpected sweetness and seemed to embody
choirs of betrothed maidens, of sisters, pouring out their fond
feelings. But the bevy of young girls whom M. de Charlus in
his horror of every kind of effeminacy would have been so
distressed to learn that he gave the impression of sheltering
thus within his voice did not confine themselves to the interpretation, the modulation of sentimental ditties. Often while
M. de Charlus was talking one could hear their laughter, the
shrill, fresh laughter of school-girls or coquettes quizzing their
companions with all the archness and malice of clever tongues
and pretty wits.

He told us about a house that had belonged to his family,
in which Marie-Antoinette had slept, with a park laid out by
Le Nôtre, which now belonged to the Israels, the wealthy
financiers, who had bought it. "Israel—at least that is the name
these people go by, though it seems to me a generic, an ethnic
term rather than a proper name. One cannot tell; possibly
people of that sort do not have names, and are designated
only by the collective title of the tribe to which they belong.
It is of no importance! To have been the abode of the Guermantes and to belong to the Israels! ! !" His voice rose. "It reminds me of a room in the Château of Blois where the caretaker
who was showing me round said to me: 'This is where Mary
Stuart used to say her prayers. I use it to keep my brooms in.'
Naturally I wish to know no more of this house that has disgraced itself, any more than of my cousin Clara de Chimay

who has left her husband. But I keep a photograph of the house, taken when it was still unspoiled, just as I keep one of the Princess before her large eyes had learned to gaze on anyone but my cousin. A photograph acquires something of the dignity which it ordinarily lacks when it ceases to be a reproduction of reality and shows us things that no longer exist. I could give you a copy, since you are interested in that style of architecture," he said to my grandmother. At that moment, noticing that the embroidered handkerchief which he had in his pocket was exhibiting its coloured border, he thrust it sharply down out of sight with the scandalised air of a prudish but far from innocent lady concealing attractions which, by an excess of scrupulosity, she regards as indecent.

"Would you believe it?" he went on. "The first thing these people did was to destroy Le Nôtre's park, which is as bad as slashing a picture by Poussin. For that alone, these Israels ought to be in prison. It is true," he added with a smile, after a moment's silence, "that there are probably plenty of other reasons why they should be there! In any case, you can imagine the effect of an English garden with that architecture."

"But the house is in the same style as the Petit Trianon," said Mme de Villeparisis, "and Marie-Antoinette had an English garden laid out there."

"Which, after all, ruins Gabriel's façade," replied M. de Charlus. "Obviously, it would be an act of vandalism now to destroy the Hameau. But whatever may be the spirit of the age, I beg leave to doubt whether, in that respect, a whim of Mme Israel has the same justification as the memory of the Queen."

Meanwhile my grandmother had been making signs to me to go up to bed, in spite of the urgent appeals of Saint-Loup who, to my utter shame, had alluded in front of M. de Charlus to the depression which used often to come upon me at night before I went to sleep, and which his uncle must regard as betokening a sad want of virility. I lingered a few moments still, then went upstairs, and was greatly surprised when, a little later, having heard a knock at my bedroom door and asked who was there, I heard the voice of M. de Charlus saying dryly: "It is Charlus. May I come in, Monsieur? Monsieur," he continued in the same tone as soon as he had shut the door, "my nephew was saying just now that you were apt to be a little upset at night before going to sleep, and also that you were an admirer of Bergotte's books. As I had one here in my luggage which you probably do not know, I have brought it to you to while away these moments during which you are unhappy."

I thanked M. de Charlus warmly and told him that I had been afraid that what Saint-Loup had said to him about my distress at the approach of night would have made me appear in his eyes even more stupid than I was.

"Not at all," he answered in a gentler voice. "You have not, perhaps, any personal merit—I've no idea, so few people have! But for a time at least you have youth, and that is always an attraction. Besides, Monsieur, the greatest folly of all is to mock or to condemn in others what one does not happen to feel oneself. I love the night, and you tell me that you are afraid of it. I love the scent of roses, and I have a friend whom it throws into a fever. Do you suppose that for that reason I consider him inferior to me? I try to understand everything and I take care to condemn nothing. In short, you must not be too sorry for yourself; I do not say that these moods of depression are not painful, I know how much one can suffer from things which others would not understand. But at least you have placed your affection wisely in your grandmother. You see a great deal of her. And besides, it is a legitimate affection, I mean one that is repaid. There are so many of which that cannot be said!"

He walked up and down the room, looking at one thing, picking up another. I had the impression that he had something to tell me, and could not find the right words to express it.

"I have another volume of Bergotte here. I will have it fetched for you," he went on, and rang the bell. Presently a page came. "Go and find me your head waiter. He is the only person here who is capable of performing an errand intelligently," said M. de Charlus stiffly. "Monsieur Aimé, sir?" asked the page. "I cannot tell you his name. Ah yes, I remember now, I did hear him called Aimé. Run along, I'm in a hurry."

"He won't be a minute, sir, I saw him downstairs just now," said the page, anxious to appear efficient. A few minutes went by. The page returned. "Sir, M. Aimé has gone to bed. But I can take a message." "No, you must get him out of bed." "But I can't do that, sir; he doesn't sleep here." "Then you can leave us alone."

"But, Monsieur," I said when the page had gone, "you are too kind; one volume of Bergotte will be quite enough."

"That is just what I was thinking, after all." M. de Charlus continued to walk up and down the room. Several minutes passed in this way, then after a few moments' hesitation and several false starts, he swung sharply round and, in his earlier biting tone of voice, flung at me: "Good night, Monsieur!" and left the room.

After all the lofty sentiments which I had heard him express that evening, next day, which was the day of his departure, on the beach in the morning, as I was on my way down to bathe, when M. de Charlus came across to tell me that my grandmother was waiting for me to join her as soon as I left the water, I was greatly surprised to hear him say, pinching my neck as he spoke with a familiarity and a laugh that were frankly vulgar: "But he doesn't care a fig for his old grandmother, does he, eh? Little rascal!"

"What, Monsieur! I adore her!"

"Monsieur," he said stepping back a pace, and with a glacial air, "you are still young; you should profit by your youth to learn two things: first, to refrain from expressing sentiments that are too natural not to be taken for granted; and secondly not to rush into speech in reply to things that are said to you before you have penetrated their meaning. If you had taken this precaution a moment ago you would have saved yourself the appearance of speaking at cross-purposes like a deaf man, thereby adding a second absurdity to that of having anchors embroidered on your bathing-dress. I have lent you a book by Bergotte which I require. See that it is brought to me within the next hour by that head waiter with the absurd and in-appropriate name, who, I suppose, is not in bed at this time of day. You make me realise that I was premature in speaking to you last night of the charms of youth. I should have done

you a greater service had I pointed out to you its thoughtlessness, its inconsequence, and its want of comprehension. I hope,
Monsieur, that this little douche will be no less salutary to you
than your bathe. But don't let me keep you standing: you may
catch cold. Good day, Monsieur."

No doubt he felt remorse for this speech, for some time
later I received—in a morocco binding on the front of which
was inlaid a panel of tooled leather representing in demi-relief
a spray of forget-me-nots—the book which he had lent me,
and which I had sent back to him, not by Aimé who was
apparently "off duty," but by the lift-boy.

M. de Charlus having gone, Robert and I were free at last
to dine with Bloch. And I realised during this little party that
the stories too readily admitted by our friend as funny were
favourite stories of M. Bloch senior, and that the son's "really
remarkable person" was always one of his father's friends
whom he had so classified. There are a certain number of people
whom we admire in our childhood, a father who is wittier
than the rest of the family, a teacher who acquires credit in our
eyes from the philosophy he reveals to us, a schoolfellow more
advanced than we are (which was what Bloch had been to me)
who despises the Musset of the *Espoir en Dieu* when we still
admire it, and when we have reached Leconte or Claudel will
be raving only about

> A Saint-Blaise, à la Zuecca
> Vous étiez, vous étiez bien aise ...

to which he will add:

> Padoue est un fort bel endroit
> Où de très grands docteurs en droit. ...
> Mais j'aime mieux la polenta. ...
> Passe dans son domino noir
>   La Toppatelle.

and of all the *Nuits* will remember only:

> Au Havre, devant l'Atlantique,
> A Venise, à l'affreux Lido,
> Où vient sur l'herbe d'un tombeau
> Mourir la pâle Adriatique.

So, whenever we confidently admire anyone, we collect from him and quote with admiration sayings vastly inferior to the sort which, left to our own judgment, we would sternly reject, just as the writer of a novel puts into it, on the pretext that they are true, "witticisms" and characters which in the living context are like a dead weight, make a dull impact. Saint-Simon's portraits, composed by himself evidently without any self-admiration, are admirable, whereas the strokes of wit of the clever people he knew which he cites as being delightful are frankly mediocre when they have not become meaningless. He would have scorned to invent what he reports as so acute or so colourful when said by Mme Cornuel or Louis XIV, a point which is to be remarked also in many other writers, and is capable of various interpretations, of which it is enough to note but one for the present: namely, that in the state of mind in which we "observe" we are a long way below the level to which we rise when we create.

There was, then, embedded in my friend Bloch, a father Bloch who lagged forty years behind his son and told preposterous stories at which he laughed as loudly, inside my friend's being, as did the real, visible, authentic Bloch senior, since to the laugh which the latter emitted, not without several times repeating the last word so that his audience might taste the full flavour of the story, was added the braying laugh with which the son never failed, at table, to greet his father's anecdotes. Thus it came about that after saying the most intelligent things Bloch junior, manifesting the portion that he had inherited from his family, would tell us for the thirtieth time some of the gems which Bloch senior brought out only (together with his swallow-tail coat) on the solemn occasions on which Bloch junior brought someone to the house on whom it was worth while making an impression: one of his masters, a "chum" who had taken all the prizes, or, this evening, Saint-Loup and myself. For instance: "A military critic of great insight, who had brilliantly worked out, supporting them with infallible proofs, the reasons for which, in the Russo-Japanese war, the Japanese must inevitably be beaten and the Russians victorious," or else: "He is an eminent gentleman who passes for a great financier in political

circles and for a great politician in financial circles." These
stories were interchangeable with one about the Baron de
Rothschild and one about Sir Rufus Israels, who were
brought into the conversation in an equivocal manner
which might let it be supposed that M. Bloch knew them
personally.

I myself was taken in, and from the way in which M. Bloch
spoke of Bergotte I assumed that he too was an old friend.
In fact, all the famous people M. Bloch claimed to know he knew
only "without actually knowing them," from having seen them
at a distance in the theatre or in the street. He imagined, moreover, that his own appearance, his name, his personality were not
unknown to them, and that when they caught sight of him
they had often to repress a furtive inclination to greet him.
People in society, because they know men of talent in the
flesh, because they have them to dinner in their houses, do not
on that account understand them any better. But when one
has lived to some extent in society, the silliness of its inhabitants makes one too anxious to live, suppose too high a
standard of intelligence, in the obscure circles in which people
know only "without actually knowing." I was to discover this
when I introduced the topic of Bergotte.

M. Bloch was not alone in being a social success at home.
My friend was even more so with his sisters, whom he continually twitted in hectoring tones, burying his face in his
plate, and making them laugh until they cried. They had
adopted their brother's language, and spoke it fluently, as if it
had been obligatory and the only form of speech that intelligent people could use. When we arrived, the eldest
sister said to one of the younger ones: "Go, tell our sage father
and our venerable mother!" "Whelps," said Bloch, "I present
to you the cavalier Saint-Loup, hurler of javelins, who is
come for a few days from Doncières to the dwellings of
polished stone, fruitful in horses." And, since he was as
vulgar as he was literate, his speech ended as a rule in some
pleasantry of a less Homeric kind: "Come, draw closer your
pepla with the fair clasps. What's all this fandangle? Does
your mother know you're out?" And the misses Bloch collapsed in a tempest of laughter. I told their brother how much

pleasure he had given me by recommending me to read
Bergotte, whose books I had loved.

M. Bloch senior, who knew Bergotte only by sight, and
Bergotte's life only from what was common gossip, had a
manner quite as indirect of making the acquaintance of his
books, by the help of judgments that were by way of being
literary. He lived in the world of approximations, where
people salute in a void and criticise in error, a world where
assurance, far from being tempered by ignorance and inaccuracy, is increased thereby. It is the propitious miracle of
self-esteem that, since few of us can have brilliant connections
or profound attainments, those to whom they are denied still
believe themselves to be the best endowed of men, because the
optics of our social perspective make every grade of society
seem the best to him who occupies it and who regards as less
favoured than himself, ill-endowed, to be pitied, the greater
men whom he names and calumniates without knowing them,
judges and despises without understanding them. Even in
cases where the multiplication of his modest personal advantages by self-esteem would not suffice to assure a man the
share of happiness, superior to that accorded to others, which
is essential to him, envy is always there to make up the balance.
It is true that if envy finds expression in scornful phrases, we
must translate "I have no wish to know him" by "I have no
means of knowing him." That is the intellectual meaning. But
the emotional meaning is indeed, "I have no wish to know him."
The speaker knows that it is not true, but he does not, all the
same, say it simply to deceive; he says it because it is what he
feels, and that is sufficient to bridge the gulf, that is to say to
make him happy.

Self-centredness thus enabling every human being to see the
universe spread out in descending tiers beneath himself who
is its lord, M. Bloch afforded himself the luxury of being a
pitiless one when in the morning, as he drank his chocolate,
seeing Bergotte's signature at the foot of an article in the newspaper which he had scarcely opened, he disdainfully granted
him a hearing which was soon cut short, pronounced sentence
upon him, and gave himself the comforting pleasure of repeating after every mouthful of the scalding brew: "That

fellow Bergotte has become unreadable. My word, what a
bore the brute can be. I really must stop my subscription. It's
all so tortured and involved—bread and butter rubbish!" And
he helped himself to another slice.

This illusory importance of M. Bloch senior did, however,
extend some little way beyond the radius of his own perceptions. In the first place his children regarded him as a
superior person. Children have always a tendency either to
depreciate or to exalt their parents, and to a good son his
father is always the best of fathers, quite apart from any
objective reasons there may be for admiring him. Now, such
reasons were not altogether lacking in the case of M. Bloch,
who was an educated man, shrewd, affectionate towards his
family. In his most intimate circle they were all the more
proud of him because if, in "society," people are judged, in
accordance with a standard scale which is incidentally absurd
and a series of false but fixed rules, by comparison with the
aggregate of all the other fashionable people, in the sub-
divisions of middle-class life on the other hand, dinner parties
and family reunions turn upon certain people who are pronounced agreeable and amusing but who in "society" would
not survive a second evening. Moreover in this social environment where the artificial values of the aristocracy do not exist,
their place is taken by even more stupid distinctions. Thus it
was that in his family circle, and even to a fairly remote degree
of consanguinity, an alleged similarity in his way of wearing
his moustache and in the bridge of his nose led to M. Bloch's
being called "the Duc d'Aumale's double." (In the world
of club bell-hops, is not the one who wears his cap on one
side and his tunic tightly buttoned so as to give himself the
appearance, he imagines, of a foreign officer, also a personage of
a sort to his colleagues?)

The resemblance was of the faintest, but it seemed almost to
confer a title. Whenever he was mentioned, it was always:
"Bloch? Which one? The Duc d'Aumale?" as people say
"Princesse Murat? Which one? The Queen (of Naples)?" And
together with certain other minor indications it combined to
give him, in the eyes of the cousinhood, an acknowledged
claim to distinction. Not going to the lengths of having a car-

riage of his own, M. Bloch used on special occasions to hire an
open victoria with a pair of horses from the Company, and
would drive through the Bois de Boulogne, reclining indolently, two fingers on his temple, two others under his
chin, and if people who did not know him concluded that he
was an "old humbug," they were convinced in the family that
in point of elegance Uncle Solomon could have taught Gramont-
Caderousse a thing or two. He was one of those people who
when they die, because for years they have shared a table in a
restaurant on the boulevard with its editor, are described in
the social column of the *Radical* as "well known Paris figures."
M. Bloch told Saint-Loup and me that Bergotte knew so well
why he, M. Bloch, always cut him that as soon as he caught
sight of him, at the theatre or in the club, he avoided his eye.
Saint-Loup blushed, for it occurred to him that this club
could not be the Jockey, of which his father had been president.
On the other hand it must be a fairly exclusive club, for M.
Bloch had said that Bergotte would never have got into it if
he had come up now. So it was not without the fear that he
might be "underrating his adversary" that Saint-Loup asked
whether the club in question were that of the Rue Royale,
which was considered "degrading" by his own family, and to
which he knew that certain Jews were admitted. "No," replied
M. Bloch in a tone at once careless, proud and ashamed, "it is
a small club, but far more agreeable: the Ganaches. We're
very strict there, don't you know." "Isn't Sir Rufus Israels
the president?" Bloch junior asked his father, so as to give
him the opportunity for a glorious lie, unaware that the
financier had not the same eminence in Saint-Loup's eyes
as in his. The fact of the matter was that the Ganaches club
boasted not Sir Rufus Israels but one of his staff. But as this
man was on the best of terms with his employer, he had at his
disposal a stock of the financier's cards, and would give one
to M. Bloch whenever he wished to travel on a line of which
Sir Rufus was a director, so that old Bloch was able to say:
"I'm just going round to the Club to ask for a letter of introduction from Sir Rufus." And the card enabled him to dazzle
the guards on the trains.
The misses Bloch were more interested in Bergotte and,

reverting to him rather than pursue the subject of the Ganaches, the youngest asked her brother, in the most serious tone imaginable, for she believed that there existed, for the designation of men of talent, no other terms than those which he was in the habit of using.

"Is he a really amazing cove, this Bergotte? Is he in the category of the great johnnies, chaps like Villiers and Catulle?"

"I've met him several times at dress rehearsals," said M. Nissim Bernard. "He is an uncouth creature, a sort of Schlemihl."

There was nothing very serious in this allusion to Chamisso's story, but the epithet "Schlemihl" formed part of that dialect, half-German, half-Jewish, which delighted M. Bloch in the family circle, but struck him as vulgar and out of place in front of strangers. And so he cast a reproving glance at his uncle.

"He has talent," said Bloch.

"Ah!" said his sister gravely, as though to imply that in that case there was some excuse for me.

"All writers have talent," said M. Bloch scornfully.

"In fact it appears," went on his son, raising his fork and screwing up his eyes with an air of diabolical irony, "that he is going to put up for the Academy."

"Go on. He hasn't enough to show them," replied his father, who seemed not to have for the Academy the same contempt as his son and daughters. "He hasn't the necessary calibre."

"Besides, the Academy is a salon, and Bergotte has no polish," declared the uncle (from whom Mme Bloch had expectations), a mild and inoffensive person whose surname, Bernard, might perhaps by itself have quickened my grandfather's powers of diagnosis, but would have appeared too little in harmony with a face which looked as if it had been brought back from Darius's palace and restored by Mme Dieulafoy, had not his first name, Nissim, chosen by some collector desirous of giving a crowning touch of orientalism to this figure from Susa, set hovering above it the pinions of an androcephalous bull from Khorsabad. But M. Bloch never stopped insulting his uncle, either because he was inflamed

PLACE-NAMES: THE PLACE 831

by the unresisting good-humour of his butt, or because, the
rent of the villa being paid by M. Nissim Bernard, the bene-
ficiary wished to show that he retained his independence and
above all scorned to seek by flattery to make sure of the rich
inheritance to come.

"Of course, whenever there's a chance of saying something
pompous and stupid, one can be quite certain that you won't
miss it. You'd be the first to lick his boots if he were in the
room!" shouted M. Bloch, while M. Nissim Bernard in sorrow
lowered over his plate the ringleted beard of King Sargon. (My
schoolfriend, since he had begun to grow a beard, which also
was blue-black and crimped, looked very like his great- uncle).

What most hurt the old man was being treated so rudely in
front of his manservant. He murmured an unintelligible
sentence of which all that could be made out was: "When the
meschores are in the room." "Meschores," in the Bible, means
"the servant of God." In the family circle the Blochs used the
word to refer to the servants, and were always delighted by it,
because their certainty of not being understood either by
Christians or by the servants themselves enhanced in M.
Nissim Bernard and M. Bloch their twofold distinction of
being "masters" and at the same time "Jews." But this latter
source of satisfaction became a source of displeasure when
there was "company." At such times M. Bloch, hearing his
uncle say "meschores," felt that he was over-exposing his
oriental side, just as a harlot who has invited some of her sisters
to meet her respectable friends is annoyed if they allude to
their profession or use objectionable words. Hence, far from
being mollified by his uncle's plea, M. Bloch, beside himself
with rage, could contain himself no longer. He let no opportunity pass of scarifying the wretched old man.

"What! Are you the son of the Marquis de Marsantes? Why,
I knew him very well," said M. Nissim Bernard to Saint-
Loup. I supposed that he meant the word "knew" in the
sense in which Bloch's father had said that he knew Bergotte,
namely by sight. But he went on: "Your father was a great
friend of mine." Meanwhile, Bloch had turned very red, his
father was looking intensely cross, and the misses Bloch were
choking with suppressed laughter. The fact was that in M.

Nissim Bernard the love of ostentation, which in M. Bloch and his children was held in check, had engendered the habit of perpetual lying. For instance, if he was staying in an hotel, M. Nissim Bernard, as M. Bloch equally might have done, would have his newspapers brought to him by his valet in the dining-room in the middle of lunch, when everybody was there, so that they should see that he travelled with a valet. But to the people with whom he made friends in the hotel the uncle used to say, what the nephew would never have said, that he was a senator. For all that he was certain that they would sooner or later discover that the title was usurped, he could not, at the critical moment, resist the temptation to assume it. M. Bloch suffered acutely from his uncle's lies and from all the embarrassments that they caused him. "Don't pay any attention to him, he's a terrible old yarn-spinner," he whispered to Saint-Loup, whose interest was whetted all the more, for he was curious to explore the psychology of liars. "A greater liar even than the Ithacan Odysseus, albeit Athene called him the greatest liar among mortals," his son completed the indictment. "Well, upon my word!" cried M. Nissim Bernard, "If I'd known that I was going to sit down to dinner with my old friend's son! Why, I have a photograph still of your father at home in Paris, and any number of letters from him. He used always to call me 'uncle,' nobody ever knew why. He was a charming man, sparkling. I remember so well a dinner I gave at Nice: there was Sardou, Labiche, Augier" . . . "Molière, Racine, Corneille," M. Bloch added sarcastically, while his son completed the list of guests with "Plautus, Menander, Kalidasa." M. Nissim Bernard, cut to the quick, stopped short in his reminiscence, and, ascetically depriving himself of a great pleasure, remained silent until the end of dinner.

"Saint-Loup with helm of bronze," said Bloch, "have a piece more of this duck with thighs heavy with fat, over which the illustrious sacrificer of birds has poured numerous libations of red wine."

As a rule, after bringing out from his store for one of his son's distinguished fellow-students his anecdotes of Sir Rufus Israels and others, M. Bloch, feeling that he had succeeded in

touching and melting his son's heart, would withdraw, in order
not to "demean" himself in the eyes of a "schoolkid." If, however, there was an absolutely compelling reason, as for instance
on the night when his son won his fellowship, M. Bloch would
add to the usual string of anecdotes the following ironical
reflexion which he ordinarily reserved for his own personal
friends and which the young Bloch was extremely proud to
see produced for his: "The Government have acted un-
pardonably. They have forgotten to consult M. Coquelin! M.
Coquelin has let it be known that he is displeased." (M.
Bloch prided himself on being a reactionary, and contemptuous
of theatrical people.)

But the misses Bloch and their brother blushed to the tips
of their ears, so impressed were they when Bloch senior, to
show that he could be regal to the last in his entertainment of
his son's two "chums," gave the order for champagne to be
served, and announced casually that, as a "treat" for us, he
had taken three stalls for the performance which a company from the Opéra-Comique was giving that evening at the
Casino. He was sorry that he had not been able to get a box.
They had all been taken. In any case, he had often been in the
boxes, and really one saw and heard better in the stalls. However, if the failing of his son, that is to say the failing which his
son believed to be invisible to other people, was coarseness,
the father's was avarice. And so it was in a decanter that we
were served, under the name of champagne, with a light
sparkling wine, while under that of orchestra stalls he had
taken three in the pit, which cost half as much, miraculously
persuaded by the divine intervention of his failing that neither
at table nor in the theatre (where the boxes were all empty)
would the difference be noticed. When M. Bloch had invited
us to moisten our lips in the flat glasses which his son dignified with the style and title of "craters with deeply hollowed
flanks," he showed us a picture to which he was so much
attached that he always brought it with him to Balbec. He told
us that it was a Rubens. Saint-Loup asked innocently if it was
signed. M. Bloch replied, blushing, that he had had the signature cut off to make it fit the frame, but that it made no difference, as he had no intention of selling the picture. Then he

hurriedly bade us good-night, in order to bury himself in the
Journal Officiel, back numbers of which littered the house and
which, he informed us, he was obliged to read carefully on
account of his "parliamentary position," as to the precise
nature of which he gave us no enlightenment.

"I shall take a muffler," said Bloch, "for Zephyrus and
Boreas are vying with each other over the fish-teeming sea,
and should we but tarry a little after the show is over, we shall
not be home before the first flush of Eos, the rosy-fingered.*
By the way," he asked Saint-Loup when we were outside
(and I trembled, for I realised at once that it was of M. de
Charlus that Bloch spoke in tones of sarcasm), "who was that
splendid old card dressed in black that I saw you walking
with the day before yesterday on the beach?"

"That was my uncle," replied Saint-Loup, somewhat
ruffled.

Unfortunately, a "floater" was far from seeming to Bloch
a thing to be avoided. He shook with laughter. "Heartiest
congratulations. I ought to have guessed: he has a lot of style,
and the most priceless dial of an old dotard of the highest
lineage."

"You are absolutely mistaken: he's an extremely clever
man," retorted Saint-Loup, now furious.

"I'm sorry about that; it makes him less complete. All the
same, I should very much like to know him, for I flatter myself
I could write some highly adequate pieces about old buffers
like that. He's killing when you see him go by. But I should
disregard the caricaturable aspect of his mug, which really is
hardly worthy of an artist enamoured of the plastic beauty of
phrases, although (you'll forgive me) it had me doubled up for
quite a while with joyous laughter, and I should bring out
the aristocratic side of your uncle, who on the whole makes a
tip-top impression, and when one has finished laughing, does
strike one with his considerable sense of style. But," he went
on, addressing me this time, "there is something in a completely
different connexion about which I have been meaning to
question you, and every time we are together, some god,
some blessed denizen of Olympus, makes me completely
forget to ask for a piece of information which might before

now have been and is sure some day to be of the greatest use to me. Tell me, who was the lovely lady I saw you with in the Zoological Gardens accompanied by a gentleman whom I seem to know by sight and a girl with long hair?"

It had been quite plain to me at the time that Mme Swann did not remember Bloch's name, since she had referred to him by another, and had described my friend as being on the staff of some Ministry, as to which I had never since then thought of finding out whether he had joined it. But how came it that Bloch, who, according to what she then told me, had got himself introduced to her, was ignorant of her name? I was so astonished that I paused for a moment before answering.

"Whoever she is," he went on, "hearty congratulations. You can't have been bored with her. I picked her up a few days before that on the Zone railway, where, speaking of zones, she was so kind as to undo hers for the benefit of your humble servant. I've never had such a time in my life, and we were just going to make arrangements to meet again when somebody she knew had the bad taste to get in at the last station but one."

My continued silence did not appear to please Bloch. "I was hoping," he said, "thanks to you, to learn her address, so as to go there several times a week to taste in her arms the delights of Eros, dear to the gods; but I do not insist since you seem pledged to discretion with respect to a professional who gave herself to me three times running, and in the most rarefied manner, between Paris and the Point-du-Jour. I'm bound to see her again some night."

I called upon Bloch after this dinner; he returned my call, but I was out and he was seen asking for me by Françoise, who, as it happened, although he had visited us at Combray, had never set eyes on him before. So that she knew only that one of "the gentlemen" I knew had looked in to see me, she did not know "with what effect," dressed in a nondescript way which had not made any particular impression upon her. Now though I knew quite well that certain of Françoise's social ideas must for ever remain impenetrable to me, based as they were, perhaps, partly upon confusions between words and names which she had once and for all time mistaken for one another, I could not refrain, for all that I had long since abandoned the quest for enlightenment in such cases, from seeking—though in vain—to discover what could be the immense significance that the name of Bloch had for Françoise. For no sooner had I mentioned to her that the young man whom she had seen was M. Bloch than she took several paces backwards so great were her stupor and disappointment. "What! Is that M. Bloch?" she cried, thunderstruck, as if so portentous a personage ought to have been endowed with an appearance which "made you realise" as soon as you saw him that you were in the presence of one of the great ones of the earth; and, like someone who has discovered that an historical character is not "up to" the level of his reputation, she repeated in an awed tone of voice, in which I could detect the latent seeds of a universal scepticism: "So that's M. Bloch! Well, really, you would never think it, to look at him." She seemed also to bear me a grudge, as if I had always "overdone" the praise of Bloch to her. At the same time she was kind enough to add: "Well, he may be M. Bloch, and all that, but at least Monsieur can say he's every bit as good."

She had presently, with respect to Saint-Loup, whom she worshipped, a disillusionment of a different kind and of shorter duration: she discovered that he was a Republican. For although, when speaking for instance of the Queen of Portugal, she would say with that disrespect which is, among the people, the supreme form of respect: "Amélie, Philippe's sister," Françoise was a Royalist. But above all a marquis, a marquis who had dazzled her at first sight, and who was for the Republic, seemed no longer real. And it aroused in her the same ill-humour as if I had given her a box which she had believed to be made of gold, and had thanked me for it effusively, and then a jeweller had revealed to her that it was only plated. She at once withdrew her esteem from Saint-Loup, but soon afterwards restored it to him, having reflected that he could not, being the Marquis de Saint-Loup, be a Republican, that he was just pretending, out of self-interest, for with the Government we had it might be a great advantage to him. From that moment her coldness towards him and her resentment towards me ceased. And when she spoke of Saint-

Loup she said: "He's a hypocrite," with a broad and kindly smile which made it clear that she "considered" him again just as much as when she first knew him, and that she had forgiven him.

In fact, Saint-Loup was obviously sincere and disinterested, and it was this intense moral purity which, not being able to find entire satisfaction in a selfish emotion such as love, and at the same time failing to find in him that sense (which existed in me, for instance) of the impossibility of finding one's spiritual nourishment elsewhere than in oneself, rendered him truly capable (to the extent that I was incapable) of friendship.

Françoise was no less mistaken about Saint-Loup when she said that he "just pretended" not to look down on the common people: you had only to see him when he was in a temper with his groom. It had indeed sometimes happened that Robert would scold his groom with a certain amount of brutality, which was proof in him of a sense not so much of the difference as of the equality between the classes. "But," he said when I reproached him for having treated the man rather harshly, "why should I go out of my way to speak politely to him? Isn't he my equal? Isn't he just as near to me as any of my uncles and cousins? You seem to think I ought to treat him with respect, as an inferior. You talk like an aristocrat!" he added scornfully.

And indeed if there was a class to which he showed himself prejudiced and hostile, it was the aristocracy, so much so that he found it as hard to believe in the superior qualities of a man of the world as he found it easy to believe in those of a man of the people. When I mentioned the Princesse de Luxembourg, whom I had met with his aunt:

"An old trout," was his comment. "Like all that lot. She's a sort of cousin of mine, by the way."

Having a strong prejudice against the people who frequented it, he went rarely into "society," and the contemptuous or hostile attitude which he adopted towards it served to intensify, among all his closest relatives, the painful impression made by his liaison with a woman of the theatre, a liaison which, they declared, would be his ruin, blaming it specially

for having bred in him that spirit of denigration, that rebel-
liousness, for having "led him astray," until it was only a
matter of time before he dropped out altogether. And so,
many easy-going men of the Faubourg Saint-Germain were
without compunction when they spoke of Robert's mistress.
"Whores do their job," they would say, "they're as good as
anybody else. But not that one! We can't forgive her. She has
done too much harm to a fellow we're fond of." Of course,
he was not the first to be thus ensnared. But the others amused
themselves like men of the world, continued to think like
men of the world about politics and everything else. Whereas
Saint-Loup's family found him "soured." They failed to
realise that for many young men of fashion who would otherwise remain uncultivated mentally, rough in their friendships,
without gentleness or taste, it is very often their mistresses
who are their real masters, and liaisons of this sort the only
school of ethics in which they are initiated into a superior
culture, where they learn the value of disinterested relations.
Even among the lower orders (who in point of coarseness so
often remind us of high society) the woman, more sensitive,
more fastidious, more leisured, is driven by curiosity to adopt
certain refinements, respects certain beauties of sentiment and
of art which, though she may not understand them, she nevertheless places above what has seemed most desirable to the
man, above money or position. Now whether it be the mistress
of a young blood (such as Saint-Loup) or a young workman
(electricians, for instance, must now be included in our truest
order of Chivalry) her lover has too much admiration and
respect for her not to extend them also to what she herself
respects and admires; and for him the scale of values is thereby
overturned. Her very sex makes her weak; she suffers from
nervous troubles, inexplicable things which in a man, or even
in another woman—a woman whose nephew or cousin he
was—would bring a smile to the lips of this robust young man.
But he cannot bear to see the woman he loves suffer. The
young nobleman who, like Saint-Loup, has a mistress acquires
the habit, when he takes her out to dine, of carrying in his
pocket the valerian "drops" which she may need, of ordering
the waiter, firmly and with no hint of sarcasm, to see that he

shuts the doors quietly and does not put any damp moss on the
table, so as to spare his companion those little ailments which
he himself has never felt, which compose for him an occult
world in whose reality she has taught him to believe, ailments
for which he now feels sympathy without needing to understand them, for which he will still feel sympathy when women
other than she are the sufferers. Saint-Loup's mistress— as the
first monks of the Middle Ages taught Christendom—had
taught him to be kind to animals, for which she had a passion,
never going anywhere without her dog, her canaries, her
parrots; Saint-Loup looked after them with motherly devotion
and regarded those who were unkind to animals as brutes.
At the same time an actress, or so-called actress, like the woman
who was living with him—whether she was intelligent or not,
and as to that I had no knowledge—by making him find society
women boring, and look upon having to go out to a party as a
painful duty, had saved him from snobbishness and cured him
of frivolity. Thanks to her, social relations filled a smaller
place in the life of her young lover, but whereas, if he had
been simply a man about town, vanity or self-interest would
have dictated his choice of friends as rudeness would have
characterised his treatment of them, his mistress had taught
him to bring nobility and refinement into his friendships.
With her feminine instinct, with a keener appreciation of
certain qualities of sensibility in men which her lover might
perhaps, without her guidance, have misunderstood and
mocked, she had always been quick to distinguish from among
the rest of Saint-Loup's friends the one who had a real affection for him, and to make that one her favourite. She knew
how to persuade him to feel grateful to that friend, to show
his gratitude, to notice what things gave his friend pleasure
and what pain. And presently Saint-Loup, without any more
need for her to prompt him, began to think of these things by
himself, and at Balbec, where she was not with him, for me
whom she had never seen, whom he had perhaps not yet so
much as mentioned in his letters to her, of his own accord
would pull up the window of a carriage in which I was sitting,
take out of the room the flowers that made me feel unwell, and
when he had to say good-bye to several people at once would

contrive to do so before it was actually time for him to go, so as to be left alone and last with me, to make that distinction between them and me, to treat me differently from the rest. His mistress had opened his mind to the invisible, had brought an element of seriousness into his life, of delicacy into his heart, but all this escaped his sorrowing family who repeated: "That creature will be the death of him, and meanwhile she's doing what she can to disgrace him."

It is true that he had already drawn from her all the good that she was capable of doing him; and that she now caused him only incessant suffering, for she had taken an intense dislike to him and tormented him in every possible way. She had begun, one fine day, to regard him as stupid and absurd because the friends that she had among the younger writers and actors had assured her that he was, and she duly repeated what they had said with that passion, that lack of reserve which we show whenever we receive from without, and adopt as our own, opinions or customs of which we previously knew nothing. She readily professed, like her actor friends, that between Saint-Loup and herself there was an unbridgeable gulf, because they were of a different breed, because she was an intellectual and he, whatever he might claim, by birth an enemy of the intellect. This view of him seemed to her profound, and she sought confirmation of it in the most insignificant words, the most trivial actions of her lover. But when the same friends had further convinced her that she was destroying the great promise she had shown in company so ill-suited to her, that her lover's influence would finally rub off on her, that by living with him she was ruining her future as an artist, to her contempt for Saint-Loup was added the sort of hatred that she would have felt for him if he had insisted upon inoculating her with a deadly germ. She saw him as seldom as possible, at the same time postponing a definite rupture, which seemed to me a highly improbable event. Saint-Loup made such sacrifices for her that unless she was ravishingly beautiful (but he had always refused to show me her photograph, saying: "For one thing, she's not a beauty, and besides she always takes badly. They're only some snapshots that I took myself with my Kodak; they would give you a false impression of her") it seemed unlikely that she would find another man prepared to do the same. I never reflected that a fancy to make a name for oneself even when one has no talent, that the admiration, no more than the privately expressed admiration of people by whom one is impressed, can (although it may not perhaps have been the case with Saint-Loup's mistress), even for a little prostitute, be motives more determining than the pleasure of making money. Without quite understanding what was going on in his mistress's mind, Saint-Loup did not believe her to be completely sincere either in her unfair reproaches or in her promises of undying love, but nevertheless at certain moments had the feeling that she would break with him whenever she could, and accordingly, impelled no doubt by an instinctive desire to preserve his love that was perhaps more clear-sighted than he was himself, and incidentally bringing into play a practical capacity for business which was compatible in him with the loftiest and blindest impulses of the heart, had refused to settle any capital on her, had borrowed an enormous sum so that she should want nothing, but made it over to her only from day to day. And no doubt, assuming that she really did think of leaving him, she was calmly waiting until she had "feathered her nest", a process which, with the money given her by Saint-Loup, would not perhaps take very long, but would all the same be an extra lease of time to prolong the happiness of my new friend—or his misery.

This dramatic period of their liaison—which had now reached its most acute, its cruellest state for Saint-Loup, for she had forbidden him to remain in Paris, where his presence exasperated her, and had forced him to spend his leave at Balbec, within easy reach of his regiment—had begun one evening at the house of one of his aunts, on whom he had prevailed to allow his mistress to come there, before a large party, to recite some fragments of a symbolist play in which she had once appeared in an avant-garde theatre, and for which she had brought him to share the admiration that she herself professed.

But when she appeared in the room, with a large lily in her hand, and wearing a costume copied from the *Ancilla Domini* which she had persuaded Saint-Loup was an absolute "vision of beauty," her entrance had been greeted, in that assemblage of clubmen and duchesses, with smiles which the monotonous tone of her sing-song, the oddity of certain words and their frequent repetition, had changed into fits of giggles, stifled at first but presently so uncontrollable that the wretched reciter had been unable to go on. Next day Saint-Loup's aunt had been universally censured for having allowed so grotesque an actress to appear in her drawing-room. A well-known duke made no bones about telling her that she had only herself to blame if she found herself criticised. "Damn it all, people really don't come to see 'turns' like that! If the woman had talent, even; but she has none and never will have any. 'Pon my soul, Paris is not so stupid as people make out. Society does not consist exclusively of imbeciles. This little lady evidently believed that she was going to take Paris by surprise. But Paris is not so easily surprised as all that, and there are still some things that they can't make us swallow."

As for the actress, she left the house with Saint-Loup, exclaiming: "What do you mean by letting me in for those old hens, those uneducated bitches, those dirty corner-boys? I don't mind telling you, there wasn't a man in the room who hadn't leered at me or tried to paw me, and it was because I wouldn't look at them that they were out to get their revenge."

Words which had changed Robert's antipathy for society people into a horror that was altogether more profound and distressing, and was provoked in him most of all by those who least deserved it, devoted kinsmen who, on behalf of the family, had sought to persuade his mistress to break with him, a move which she represented to him as inspired by their passion for her. Robert, although he had at once ceased to see them, used to imagine when he was separated from his mistress as he was now, that they or others like them were profiting by his absence to return to the charge and had possibly enjoyed her favours. And when he spoke of the lechers who betrayed their friends, who sought to corrupt women, tried to make them come to houses of assignation, his whole face radiated suffering and hatred.

"I'd kill them with less compunction than I'd kill a dog,

which is at least a decent, honest and faithful beast. They're the ones who deserve the guillotine if you like, far more than poor wretches who've been led into crime by poverty and by the cruelty of the rich."

He spent the greater part of his time sending letters and telegrams to his mistress. Every time that, while still preventing him from returning to Paris, she found an excuse to quarrel with him by post, I read the news at once on his tormented face. Since she never told him in what way he was at fault, he suspected that she did not know herself, and had simply had enough of him; but he nevertheless longed for an explanation and would write to her: "Tell me what I've done wrong. I'm quite ready to acknowledge my faults," the grief that overpowered him having the effect of persuading him that he had behaved badly.

But she kept him waiting indefinitely for answers which, when they came, were utterly meaningless. And so it was almost always with a furrowed brow and often empty-handed that I would see Saint-Loup returning from the post office, where, alone in all the hotel, he and Françoise went to fetch or to hand in letters, he from a lover's impatience, she with a servant's mistrust of others. (His telegrams obliged him to make a much longer journey.)

When, some days after our dinner with the Blochs, my grandmother told me with a joyful air that Saint-Loup had just asked her whether she would like him to take a photograph of her before he left Balbec, and when I saw that she had put on her nicest dress for the purpose and was hesitating between various hats, I felt a little annoyed at this childishness, which surprised me on her part. I even wondered whether I had not been mistaken in my grandmother, whether I did not put her on too lofty a pedestal, whether she was as unconcerned about her person as I had always supposed, whether she was entirely innocent of the weakness which I had always thought most alien to her, namely vanity.

Unfortunately, the displeasure that was aroused in me by the prospect of this photographic session, and more particularly by the delight with which my grandmother appeared to be looking forward to it, was sufficiently apparent for Françoise to notice it and to do her best, unintentionally, to increase it by making me a sentimental, gushing speech by which I refused to appear moved.

"Oh, Monsieur, my poor Madame will be so pleased at having her likeness taken. She's going to wear the hat that her old Françoise has trimmed for her: you must let her."

I persuaded myself that it was not cruel of me to mock Françoise's sensibility, by reminding myself that my mother and grandmother, my models in all things, often did the same. But my grandmother, noticing that I seemed put out, said that if her sitting for her photograph offended me in any way she would give up the idea. I would not hear of it. I assured her that I saw no harm in it, and let her adorn herself, but, thinking to show how shrewd and forceful I was, added a few sarcastic and wounding words calculated to neutralise the pleasure which she seemed to find in being photographed, with the result that, if I was obliged to see my grandmother's magnificent hat, I succeeded at least in driving from her face that joyful expression which ought to have made me happy. Alas, it too often happens, while the people we love best are still alive, that such expressions appear to us as the exasperating manifestation of some petty whim rather than as the precious form of the happiness which we should dearly like to procure for them. My ill-humour arose more particularly from the fact that, during that week, my grandmother had appeared to be avoiding me, and I had not been able to have her to myself for a moment, either by night or day. When I came back in the afternoon to be alone with her for a little I was told that she was not in the hotel; or else she would shut herself up with Françoise for endless confabulations which I was not permitted to interrupt. And when, after being out all evening with Saint-Loup, I had been thinking on the way home of the moment at which I should be able to go to my grandmother and embrace her, I waited in vain for her to give the three little knocks on the party wall which would tell me to go in and say good night to her. At length I would go to bed, a little resentful of her for depriving me, with an indifference so new and strange in her, of a joy on which I had counted so much, and I would lie there for a while, my heart throbbing as in my childhood, listening to the wall which remained silent, until I cried myself to sleep.

That day, as for some days past, Saint-Loup had been obliged to go to Doncières, where, until he returned there for good, he would be on duty now until late every afternoon. I was sorry that he was not at Balbec. I had seen some young women, who at a distance had seemed to me lovely, alighting from carriages and entering either the ballroom of the Casino or the ice-cream shop. I was going through one of those phases of youth, devoid of any particular love, as it were in abeyance, in which at all times and in all places—as a lover the woman by whose charms he is smitten—we desire, we seek, we see Beauty. Let but a single flash of reality—the glimpse of a woman from afar or from behind—enable us to project the image of Beauty before our eyes, and we imagine that we have recognised it, our hearts beat, and we will always remain half-persuaded that it was She, provided that the woman has vanished: it is only if we manage to overtake her that we realise our mistake.

Moreover, as I was becoming more and more unwell, I was inclined to overrate the simplest pleasures because of the very difficulty of attaining them. I seemed to see charming women all round me, because I was too tired, if it was on the beach, too shy if it was in the Casino or at a pastry-cook's, to go anywhere near them. And yet, if I was soon to die, I should have liked to know beforehand what the prettiest girls that life had to offer looked like at close quarters, in reality, even if it should be another than myself or no one at all who was to take advantage of that offer (I did not, in fact, realise that a desire for possession underlay my curiosity). I should have had the courage to enter the ballroom if Saint-Loup had been with me. Left by myself, I was simply hanging about in front of the Grand Hotel until it was time for me to join my grand-mother, when, still almost at the far end of the esplanade, along which they projected a striking patch of colour, I saw five or six young girls as different in appearance and manner from all the people one was accustomed to see at Balbec as would have been a flock of gulls arriving from God knows where and performing with measured tread upon the sands— the dawdlers flapping their wings to catch up with the rest— a parade the purpose of which seems as obscure to the human bathers whom they do not appear to see as it is clearly determined in their own birdish minds.

One of these unknown girls was pushing a bicycle in front of her; two others carried golf-clubs; and their attire generally was in striking contrast to that of the other girls at Balbec, some of whom, it was true, went in for sports, but without adopting a special outfit.

It was the hour at which ladies and gentlemen came out every day for a stroll along the front, exposed to the merciless fire of the lorgnette fastened upon them, as if they had each borne some disfigurement which she felt it her duty to inspect in its minutest details, by the senior judge's wife, proudly seated there with her back to the band-stand, in the middle of that dread line of chairs on which presently they too, actors turned critics, would come and establish themselves, to scrutinise in their turn the passing crowds. All these people who paced up and down the esplanade, reeling and lurching as heavily as if it had been the deck of a ship (for they could not lift a leg without at the same time waving their arms, turning their heads and eyes, squaring their shoulders, compensating by a balancing movement on one side for the movement they had just made on the other, and puffing out their faces), pretending not to see, so as to let it be thought that they were not interested in them, but covertly eyeing, for fear of running into them, the people who were walking beside or coming towards them, did in fact bump into them, became entangled with them, because each was mutually the object of the same secret attention veiled beneath the same apparent disdain— love, and consequently fear, of the crowd being one of the most powerful motives in all human beings, whether they seek to please other people or to impress them, or to show that they despise them; and in the case of the solitary, even if his seclusion is absolute and lifelong it is often based on a deranged love of the crowd which so far overrides every other feeling that, unable to win the admiration of his hall-porter, of the passers-by, of the cabman he hails when he goes out, he prefers not to be seen by them at all, and with that object abandons every activity that would oblige him to go out of doors.

In the midst of all these people, some of whom were pursuing a train of thought, but then betrayed its instability by a fitfulness of gesture, an aberrancy of gaze as inharmonious as the circumspect titubation of their neighbours, the girls whom I had noticed, with the control of gesture that comes from the perfect suppleness of one's own body and a sincere contempt for the rest of humanity, were advancing straight ahead, without hesitation or stiffness, performing exactly the movements that they wished to perform, each of their limbs completely independent of the others, the rest of the body preserving that immobility which is so noticeable in good waltzers. They were now quite near me. Although each was of a type absolutely different from the others, they all had beauty; but to tell the truth I had seen them for so short a time, and without venturing to look hard at them, that I had not yet individualised any of them. Except for one, whose straight nose and dark complexion singled her out from the rest, like the Arabian king in a Renaissance picture of the Epiphany, they were known to me only by a pair of hard, obstinate and mocking eyes, for instance, or by cheeks whose pinkness had a coppery tint reminiscent of geraniums; and even these features I had not yet indissolubly attached to any one of these girls rather than to another; and when (according to the order in which the group met the eye, marvellous because the most different aspects were juxtaposed, because all the colour scales were combined in it, but confused as a piece of music in which I was unable to isolate and identify at the moment of their passage the successive phrases, no sooner distinguished than forgotten) I saw a pallid oval, black eyes, green eyes, emerge, I did not know if these were the same that had already charmed me a moment ago, I could not relate them to any one girl whom I had set apart from the rest and identified. And this want, in my vision, of the demarcations which I should presently establish between them permeated the group with a sort of shimmering harmony, the continuous transmutation of a fluid, collective and mobile beauty.

It was not perhaps mere chance in life that, in forming this group of friends, had chosen them all so beautiful; perhaps these girls (whose demeanour was enough to reveal their bold, hard and frivolous natures), extremely aware of everything that was ludicrous or ugly, incapable of yielding to an intellectual or moral attraction, had naturally felt a certain repulsion for all those among the companions of their own age in whom a pensive or sensitive disposition was betrayed by shyness, awkwardness, constraint, by what they would regard as antipathetic, and from such had held aloof; while attaching themselves, conversely, to others to whom they were drawn by a certain blend of grace, suppleness and physical elegance, the only form in which they were able to picture a straightforward and attractive character and the promise of pleasant hours in one another's company. Perhaps, too, the class to which they belonged, a class which I should not have found it easy to define, was at that point in its evolution when, thanks either to its growing wealth and leisure, or to new sporting habits, now prevalent even among certain elements of the working class, and a physical culture to which had not yet been added the culture of the mind, a social group comparable to the smooth and prolific schools of sculpture which have not yet gone in for tortured expression, produces naturally, and in abundance, fine bodies, fine legs, fine hips, wholesome, serene faces, with an air of agility and guile. And were they not noble and calm models of human beauty that I beheld there, outlined against the sea, like statues exposed to the sunlight on a Grecian shore?

Just as if, within their little band, which progressed along the esplanade like a luminous comet, they had decided that the surrounding crowd was composed of beings of another race not even whose sufferings could awaken in them any sense of fellowship, they appeared not to see them, forced those who had stopped to talk to step aside, as though from the path of a machine which had been set going by itself and which could not be expected to avoid pedestrians; and if some terrified or furious old gentleman whose existence they did not even acknowledge and whose contact they spurned took precipitate and ludicrous flight, they merely looked at one another and laughed. They had, for whatever did not form part of their group, no affectation of contempt; their genuine contempt was sufficient. But they could not set eyes on an obstacle without amusing themselves by clearing it, either in a running jump or with both feet together, because they were all brimming over with the exuberance that youth so urgently needs to expend that even when it is unhappy or unwell, obedient rather to the necessities of age than to the mood of the day, it can never let pass an opportunity to jump or to slide without indulging in it conscientiously, interrupting and interspersing even the slowest walk—as Chopin his most melancholy phrase—with graceful deviations in which caprice is blended with virtuosity. The wife of an elderly banker, after hesitating between various possible exposures for her husband, had settled him in a deck-chair facing the esplanade, sheltered from wind and sun by the bandstand. Having seen him comfortably installed there, she had gone to buy a newspaper which she would read aloud to him by way of diversion, one of her little absences which she never prolonged for more than five minutes, which seemed to her quite long enough but which she repeated at fairly frequent intervals so that this old husband on whom she lavished an attention that she took care to conceal should have the impression that he was still quite alive and like other people and was in no need of protection. The platform of the band-stand provided, above his head, a natural and tempting springboard across which, without a moment's hesitation, the eldest of the little band began to run; she jumped over the terrified old man, whose yachting cap was brushed by her nimble feet, to the great delight of the other girls, especially of a pair of green eyes in a doll-like face, which expressed, for that bold act, an admiration and a merriment in which I seemed to discern a trace of shyness, a shamefaced and blustering shyness which did not exist in the others. "Oh, the poor old boy, I feel sorry for him; he looks half dead," said a girl in a rasping voice, with more sarcasm than sympathy. They walked on a little way, then stopped for a moment in the middle of the road, oblivious of the fact that they were impeding the passage of other people, in an agglomerate that was at once irregular in shape, compact, weird and shrill, like an assembly of birds before taking flight; then they resumed their leisurely stroll along the esplanade, against the background of the sea.

By this time their charming features had ceased to be indistinct and jumbled. I had dealt them like cards into so many heaps to compose (failing their names, of which I was still ignorant): the tall one who had jumped over the old banker; the little one silhouetted against the horizon of sea with her plump and rosy cheeks and green eyes; the one with the straight nose and dark complexion who stood out among the rest; another, with a face as white as an egg in which a tiny nose described an arc of a circle like a chicken's beak—a face such as one sometimes sees in the very young; yet another, also tall, wearing a hooded cape (which gave her so shabby an appearance and so contradicted the elegance of the figure beneath that the explanation which suggested itself was that this girl must have parents of high position who valued their self-esteem so far above the visitors to Balbec and the sartorial elegance of their own children that it was a matter of the utmost indifference to them that their daughter should stroll on the front dressed in a way which humbler people would have considered too modest); a girl with brilliant, laughing eyes and plump, matt cheeks, a black polo-cap crammed on her head, who was pushing a bicycle with such an uninhibited swing of the hips, and using slang terms so typically of the gutter and shouted so loud when I passed her (although among her expressions I caught that tiresome phrase "living one's own life") that, abandoning the hypothesis which her friend's hooded cape had prompted me to formulate, I concluded instead that all these girls belonged to the population which frequents the racing-tracks, and must be the very juvenile mistresses of professional cyclists. In any event, none of my suppositions embraced the possibility of their being virtuous. At first sight—in the way in which they looked at one another and laughed, in the insistent stare of the one with the matt complexion—I had grasped that they were not. Besides, my grandmother had always watched over me with a delicacy too tremulous for me not to believe that the sum total of the things one ought not to do is indivisible and that girls who are lacking in respect for their elders would not suddenly be stopped short by scruples at the prospect of pleasures more tempting than that of jumping over an octogenarian.

Though they were now separately identifiable, still the interplay of their eyes, animated with self-assurance and the spirit of comradeship and lit up from one moment to the next either by the interest or the insolent indifference which shone from each of them according to whether her glance was directed at her friends or at passers-by, together with the consciousness of knowing one another intimately enough always to go about together in an exclusive "gang," established between their independent and separate bodies, as they slowly advanced, an invisible but harmonious bond, like a single warm shadow, a single atmosphere, making of them a whole as homogeneous in its parts as it was different from the crowd through which their procession gradually wound.

For an instant, as I passed the dark one with the plump cheeks who was wheeling a bicycle, I caught her smiling, sidelong glance, aimed from the centre of that inhuman world which enclosed the life of this little tribe, an inaccessible, unknown world wherein the idea of what I was could certainly never penetrate or find a place. Wholly occupied with what her companions were saying, had she seen me—this young girl in the polo-cap pulled down very low over her forehead—at the moment in which the dark ray emanating from her eyes had fallen on me? If she had seen me, what could I have represented to her? From the depths of what universe did she discern me? It would have been as difficult for me to say as, when certain distinguishing features in a neighbouring planet are made visible thanks to the telescope, it is to conclude therefrom that human beings inhabit it, and that they can see us, and to guess what ideas the sight of us can have aroused in their minds.

If we thought that the eyes of such a girl were merely two glittering sequins of mica, we should not be athirst to know her and to unite her life to ours. But we sense that what shines in those reflecting discs is not due solely to their material compo-

sition; that it is the dark shadows, unknown to us, of the
ideas that that person cherishes about the people and places
she knows—the turf of race-courses, the sand of cycling tracks
over which, pedalling on past fields and woods, she would have
drawn me after her, that little peri, more seductive to me than
she of the Persian paradise—the shadows, too, of the home to
which she will presently return, of the plans that she is forming
or that others have formed for her; and above all that it is
she, with her desires, her sympathies, her revulsions, her
obscure and incessant will. I knew that I should never possess
this young cyclist if I did not possess also what was in her
eyes. And it was consequently her whole life that filled me with
desire; a sorrowful desire because I felt that it was not to be
fulfilled, but an exhilarating one because, what had hitherto been
my life having ceased of a sudden to be my whole life, being
no more now than a small part of the space stretching out before me which I was burning to cover and which was composed
of the lives of these girls, it offered me that prolongation, that
possible multiplication of oneself, which is happiness. And no
doubt the fact that we had, these girls and I, not one habit—
as we had not one idea—in common must make it more difficult for me to make friends with them and to win their regard.
But perhaps, also, it was thanks to those differences, to my
consciousness that not a single element that I knew or possessed entered into the composition of the nature and actions
of these girls, that satiety had been succeeded in me by a thirst
—akin to that with which a parched land burns—for a life
which my soul, because it had never until now received one
drop of it, would absorb all the more greedily, in long draughts,
with a more perfect imbibition.

I had looked so closely at the dark cyclist with the bright
eyes that she seemed to notice my attention, and said to the
tallest of the girls something that I could not hear but that
made her laugh. Truth to tell, this dark-haired one was not the
one who attracted me most, simply because she was dark and
because (since the day on which, from the little path by
Tansonville, I had seen Gilberte) a girl with reddish hair and a
golden skin had remained for me the inaccessible ideal. But
had I not loved Gilberte herself principally because she had

appeared to me haloed with that aureole of being the friend of Bergotte, of going to look at cathedrals with him? And in the same way could I not rejoice at having seen this dark girl look at me (which made me hope that it would be easier for me to get to know her first), for she would introduce me to the pitiless one who had jumped over the old man's head, to the cruel one who had said "I feel sorry for the poor old boy," to all these girls in turn of whom she enjoyed the prestige of being the inseparable companion? And yet the supposition that I might some day be the friend of one or other of these girls, that these eyes, whose incomprehensible gaze struck me from time to time and played unwittingly upon me like an effect of sunlight on a wall, might ever, by some miraculous alchemy, allow the idea of my existence, some affection for my person, to interpenetrate their ineffable particles, that I myself might some day take my place among them in the evolution of their course by the sea's edge—that supposition appeared to me to contain within it a contradiction as insoluble as if, standing before some Attic frieze or a fresco representing a procession, I had believed it possible for me, the spectator, to take my place, beloved of them, among the divine participants.

Was, then, the happiness of knowing these girls unattainable? Certainly it would not have been the first of its kind that I had renounced. I had only to recall the numberless strangers whom, even at Balbec, the carriage bowling away from them at full speed had forced me for ever to abandon. And indeed the pleasure I derived from the little band, as noble as if it had been composed of Hellenic virgins, arose from the fact that it had something of the fleetingness of the passing figures on the road. This evanescence of persons who are not known to us, who force us to put out from the harbour of life in which the women whose society we frequent have all, in course of time, laid bare their blemishes, urges us into that state of pursuit in which there is no longer anything to stem the tide of imagination. To strip our pleasures of imagination is to reduce them to their own dimensions, that is to say to nothing. Offered me by one of those procuresses whose good offices, as has been seen, I by no means always scorned, withdrawn from the element which gave them so many subtle nuances, such enigmatic vagueness, these girls would have enchanted me less. We need imagination, awakened by the uncertainty of being unable to attain its object, to create a goal which hides the other goal from us, and by substituting for sensual pleasures the idea of penetrating another life, prevents us from recognising that pleasure, from tasting its true savour, from restricting it to its own range. We need, between us and the fish which, if we saw it for the first time cooked and served on a table, would not appear worth the endless shifts and wiles required to catch it, the intervention, during our afternoons with the rod, of the rippling eddy to whose surface come flashing, without our quite knowing what we intend to do with them, the bright gleam of flesh, the hint of a form, in the fluidity of a transparent and mobile azure.

These girls benefited also by that alteration of social proportions characteristic of seaside life. All the advantages which, in our ordinary environment, extend and enhance us, we there find to have become invisible, in fact eliminated; while on the other hand the people whom we suppose, without reason, to enjoy similar advantages appear to us amplified to artificial dimensions. This made it easier for unknown women in general, and to-day for these girls in particular, to acquire an enormous importance in my eyes, and impossible to make them aware of such importance as I might myself possess.

But if the parade of the little band could be said to be but an excerpt from the endless flight of passing women, which had always disturbed me, that flight was here reduced to a movement so slow as to approach immobility. And the very fact that, in a phase so far from rapid, faces no longer swept away in a whirlwind, but calm and distinct, still seemed to me beautiful, prevented me from thinking, as I had so often thought when Mme de Villeparisis's carriage bore me away, that at closer quarters, if I had stopped for a moment, certain details, a pock-marked skin, a flaw in the nostrils, a gawping expression, a grimace of a smile, an ugly figure, might have been substituted, in the face and body of the woman, for those that I had doubtless imagined; for no more than a pretty outline, the glimpse of a fresh complexion, had sufficed for me to add, in entire good faith, a ravishing shoulder, a delicious glance of which I carried in my mind for ever a memory or a preconceived idea, these rapid decipherings of a person whom we momentarily glimpse exposing us thus to the same errors as those too rapid readings in which, on the basis of a single syllable and without waiting to identify the rest, we replace the word that is in the text by a wholly different word with which our memory supplies us. It could not be so with me now. I had looked at their faces long and carefully; I had seen each of them, not from every angle and rarely in full face, but all the same in two or three aspects different enough to enable me to make the necessary correction or verification to "prove" the difficult suppositions of line and colour that are hazarded at first sight, and to see subsist in them, through successive expressions, something unalterably material. I could say to myself with conviction that neither in Paris nor at Balbec, on the most favourable assumption of what, even if I had been able to stop and talk to them, the passing women who had caught my eye would have been like, had there ever been any whose appearance, followed by their disappearance without my having got to know them, had left me with more regret than would these, had given me the idea that their friendship could be so intoxicating. Never, among actresses or peasants or convent girls, had I seen anything so beautiful, impregnated with so much that was unknown, so inestimably precious, so apparently inaccessible. They were, of the unknown and potential happiness of life, an illustration so delicious and in so perfect a state that it was almost for intellectual reasons that I was sick with despair at the thought of being unable to sample, in unique conditions which left no room for any possibility of error, all that is most mysterious in the beauty which we desire, and which we console ourselves for never possessing by demanding pleasure—as Swann had always refused to do before Odette's day—from women whom we have not desired, so that we die without ever having known what that other pleasure was. It might well be, of course, that it was not in reality an unknown pleasure, that on close inspection its mystery would dissolve, that it was no more than a projection, a mirage of desire. But in that case I had only to blame the compulsion of a law of nature,—which if it applied to these girls would apply to all—and not the imperfection of the object. For it was the one that I would have chosen above all others, convinced as I was, with a botanist's satisfaction, that it was not possible to find gathered together rarer specimens than these young flowers that at this moment before my eyes were breaking the line of the sea with their slender hedge, like a bower of Pennsylvania roses adorning a cliffside garden, between whose blooms is contained the whole tract of ocean crossed by some steamer, so slow in gliding along the blue, horizontal line that stretches from one stem to the next that an idle butterfly, dawdling in the cup of a flower which the ship's hull has long since passed, can wait, before flying off in time to arrive before it, until nothing but the tiniest chink of blue still separates the prow from the first petal of the flower towards which it is steering.

I went indoors because I was to dine at Rivebelle with Robert, and my grandmother insisted that on those evenings, before going out, I must lie down for an hour on my bed, a rest which the Balbec doctor presently ordered me to extend to all other evenings too.

As it happened, there was no need, when one went indoors, to leave the esplanade and to enter the hotel by the hall, that is to say from the back. By virtue of an alteration of the clock which reminded me of those Saturdays when, at Combray, we used to have lunch an hour earlier, now with summer at the full the days had become so long that the sun was still high in the heavens, as though it were only tea-time, when the tables were being laid for dinner in the Grand Hotel. And so the great sliding windows remained open on to the esplanade. I had only to step across a low wooden sill to find myself in the dining-room, through which I walked to take the lift.

As I passed the reception desk I addressed a smile to the manager, and without the slightest twinge of distaste collected one in return from a face which, since I had been at Balbec, my comprehensive study had impregnated and transformed like a natural history specimen. His features had become familiar to me, charged with a meaning that was of no importance but none the less intelligible like a script which one can read, and had ceased in any way to resemble those strange and repellent characteristics which his face had presented to me on that first day, when I had seen before me a personage now forgotten, or, if I succeeded in recalling him, unrecognisable, difficult to identify with this insignificant and polite individual of which the other was but a caricature, a hideous and rapid sketch. Without either the shyness or the sadness of the evening of my arrival, I rang for the lift attendant, who no longer stood in silence while I rose by his side as in a mobile thoracic cage propelled upwards along its ascending pillar, but repeated to me:

"There aren't the people now as there was a month back. They're beginning to go now; the days are drawing in." He said this not because there was any truth in it but because, having an engagement, presently, on a warmer part of the coast, he would have liked us all to leave as soon as possible so that the hotel could be shut up and he have a few days to himself before "rejoining" his new place. "Rejoin" and "new" were not, as it happened, incompatible terms, since, for the lift-boy, "rejoin" was the usual form of the verb "to join." The only thing that surprised me was that he condescended to say "place," for he belonged to that modern proletariat which seeks to eliminate from its speech every trace of a career in service. And a moment later indeed he informed me that in the "situation" which he was about to "rejoin," he would have a smarter "tunic" and a better "salary," the words "livery" and "wages" sounding to him obsolete and unseemly. And since, by an absurd contradiction, the vocabulary has survived the conception of inequality among the "masters," I was always failing to understand what the lift-boy said. For instance, the only thing that interested me was to know whether my grandmother was in the hotel. Now, forestalling my questions, the lift-boy would say to me: "That lady has just come out of your rooms." I was invariably taken in; I supposed that he meant my grandmother. "No, that lady who I think is an employee of yours." Since, in the traditional vocabulary of the upper classes which ought indeed to be done away with, a cook is not called an employee, I thought for a moment: "But he must have made a mistake. We don't own a factory; we haven't any employees." Suddenly I remembered that the title of "employee," like the wearing of a moustache among waiters, is a sop to their self-esteem given to servants, and realised that this lady who had just gone out must be Françoise (probably on a visit to the coffee-maker, or to watch the Belgian lady's maid at her sewing), though even this sop did not satisfy the lift-boy, for he would say quite naturally, speaking pityingly of his own class, "the working man" or "the small man," using the same singular form as Racine when he speaks of "the poor man." But as a rule, for my zeal and timidity of the first evening were now things of the past, I no longer spoke to the lift-boy. It was he now who stood there and received no answer during the short journey on which he threaded his way through the hotel, which, hollowed out inside like a toy, deployed around us, floor by floor, the ramifications of its corridors in the depths of which the light grew velvety, lost its tone, blurred the communicating doors or the steps of the service stairs which it transformed into that amber haze, unsubstantial and mysterious as a twilight, in which Rembrandt picks out here and there a window-sill or a well-head. And on each landing a golden light reflected from the carpet indicated the setting sun and the lavatory window.

I wondered whether the girls I had just seen lived at Balbec, and who they could be. When our desire is thus concentrated upon a little tribe of humanity which it singles out from the rest, everything that can be associated with that tribe becomes a spring of emotion and then of reflexion. I had heard a lady say on the esplanade: "She's a friend of the Simonet girl" with that self-important air of inside knowledge, as who should say: "He's the inseparable companion of young La Rochefoucauld." And immediately she had detected on the face of the person to whom she gave this information a curiosity to see more of the favoured person who was "a friend of the Simonet girl." A privilege, obviously, that did not appear to be granted to all the world. For aristocracy is a relative thing. And there are plenty of out-of-the-way places where the son of an upholsterer is the arbiter of fashion and reigns over a court like any young Prince of Wales. I have often since then sought to recall how it first sounded to me there on the beach, that name of Simonet, still uncertain in its form, which I had not clearly distinguished, and also in its significance, its designation of such and such a person as opposed to another; instinct, in short, with that vagueness and novelty which we find so moving in the sequel, when a name whose letters are every moment engraved more deeply on our hearts by our incessant thought of them has become (though this was not to happen to me with the name of the "Simonet girl" until several years had passed) the first coherent sound that comes to our lips, whether on waking from sleep or on recovering from a fainting fit, even before the idea of what time it is or of where we are, almost before the word "I," as though the person whom it names were more "us" than we are ourselves, and as though after a brief spell of unconsciousness the phase that is the first to dissolve were that in which we were not thinking of her. I do not know why I said to myself from the first that the name Simonet must be that of one of the band of girls; from that moment I never ceased to wonder how I could get to know the Simonet family, get to know them, moreover, through people whom they would consider superior to themselves (which ought not to be difficult if they were only common little wenches) so that they might not form a disdainful idea of me. For one cannot have a perfect knowledge, one cannot effect the complete absorption of a person who disdains one, so long as one has not overcome that disdain. And since, whenever the idea of women who are so different from us penetrates our minds, unless we are able to forget it or the competition of other ideas eliminates it, we know no rest until we have converted these aliens into something that is compatible with ourselves, the mind being in this respect endowed with the same kind of reaction and activity as our physical organism, which cannot abide the infusion of any foreign body into its veins without at once striving to digest and assimilate it. The Simonet girl must be the prettiest of them all—she who, I felt moreover, might yet become my mistress, for she was the only one who, two or three times half-turning her head, had appeared to take cognisance of my fixed stare. I asked the lift-boy whether he knew of any people at Balbec called Simonet. Not liking to admit that there was anything he did not know, he replied that he seemed to have heard the name somewhere. When we reached the top floor I asked him to send me up the latest list of visitors.

I stepped out of the lift, but instead of going to my room I made my way further along the corridor, for before my arrival the valet in charge of the landing, despite his horror of draughts, had opened the window at the end, which instead of looking out to the sea faced the hill and valley inland, but never allowed them to be seen because its panes, which were made of clouded glass, were generally closed. I made a brief halt in front of it, time enough just to pay my devotions to the view which for once it revealed beyond the hill immediately behind the hotel, a view that contained only a single house situated at some distance, to which the perspective and the evening light, while preserving its mass, gave a gem-like precision and a velvet casing, as though to one of those architectural works in miniature, tiny temples or chapels wrought in gold and enamel, which serve as reliquaries and are exposed only on rare and solemn days for the veneration of the faithful. But this moment of adoration had already lasted too long, for the valet, who carried in one hand a bunch of keys and with the other saluted me by touching his sacristan's skull cap, though without raising it on account of the pure, cool evening air, came and drew together, like those of a shrine, the two sides of the window, and so shut off the minute edifice, the glistening relic from my adoring gaze.

I went into my room. Gradually, as the season advanced, the picture that I found there in my window changed. At first it was broad daylight, and dark only if the weather was bad: and then, in the greenish glass which it distended with the curve of its rounded waves, the sea, set between the iron uprights of my casement window like a piece of stained glass in its leads, ravelled out over all the deep rocky border of the bay little plumed triangles of motionless foam etched with the delicacy of a feather or a downy breast from Pisanello's pencil, and fixed in that white, unvarying, creamy enamel which is used to depict fallen snow in Gallé's glass.

Presently the days grew shorter and at the moment when I entered the room the violet sky seemed branded with the stiff, geometrical, fleeting, effulgent figure of the sun (like the representation of some miraculous sign, of some mystical apparition) lowering over the sea on the edge of the horizon like a sacred picture over a high altar, while the different parts of the western sky exposed in the glass fronts of the low mahogany bookcases that ran along the walls, which I carried back in my mind to the marvellous painting from which they had been detached, seemed like those different scenes executed long ago for a confraternity by some old master on a reliquary, whose separate panels are now exhibited side by side in a gallery, so that the visitor's imagination alone can restore them to their place on the predella of the reredos.

A few weeks later, when I went upstairs, the sun had already set. Like the one that I used to see at Combray, behind the Calvary, when I came home from a walk and was getting ready to go down to the kitchen before dinner, a band of red sky above the sea, compact and clear-cut as a layer of aspic over meat, then, a little later, over a sea already cold and steel-blue like a grey mullet, a sky of the same pink as the salmon that we should presently be ordering at Rivebelle, reawakened my pleasure in dressing to go out to dinner. Close to the shore, patches of vapour, soot-black but with the burnish and consistency of agate, visibly solid and palpable, were trying to rise one above another over the sea in ever wider tiers, so that the highest of them, poised on top of the twisted column and overreaching the centre of gravity of those which had hitherto supported them, seemed on the point of bringing down in ruin this lofty structure already half-way up the sky, and precipitating it into the sea. The sight of a ship receding like a nocturnal traveller gave me the same impression that I had had in the train of being set free from the necessity of sleep and from confinement in a bedroom. Not that I felt myself a prisoner in the room in which I now was, since in another hour I should be leaving it to drive away in a carriage. I threw myself down on the bed; and, just as if I had been lying in a berth on board one of those steamers which I could see quite near me and which at night it would be strange to see stealing slowly through the darkness, like shadowy and silent but unsleeping swans, I was surrounded on all sides by pictures of the sea.

But as often as not they were, indeed, only pictures; I forgot
that below their coloured expanse lay the sad desolation of the
beach, swept by the restless evening breeze whose breath I had
so anxiously felt on my arrival at Balbec; besides, even in my
room, being wholly taken up with thoughts of the girls I had
seen go by, I was no longer in a sufficiently calm or disinterested state of mind to receive any really profound impression
of beauty. The anticipation of dinner at Rivebelle made my
mood more frivolous still, and my mind, dwelling at such
moments upon the surface of the body which I was about to
dress up in order to try to appear as pleasing as possible to the
feminine eyes which would scrutinise me in the well-lit restaurant, was incapable of putting any depth behind the colour of
things. And if, beneath my window, the soft, unwearying
flight of swifts and swallows had not arisen like a playing
fountain, like living fireworks, joining the intervals between
their soaring rockets with the motionless white streaming lines
of long horizontal wakes—without the charming miracle of
this natural and local phenomenon which brought into touch
with reality the scenes that I had before my eyes—I might
easily have believed that they were no more than a selection,
made afresh every day, of paintings which were shown quite
arbitrarily in the place in which I happened to be and without
having any necessary connexion with that place. At one time
it was an exhibition of Japanese colour-prints: beside the neat
disc of sun, red and round as the moon, a yellow cloud seemed
a lake against which black swords were outlined like the trees
upon its shore, while a bar of a tender pink which I had never
seen since my first paint-box swelled out like a river on either
bank of which boats seemed to be waiting high and dry for
someone to push them down and set them afloat. And with
the contemptuous, bored and frivolous glance of an amateur
or a woman hurrying through a picture gallery between two
social engagements, I would say to myself: "Curious sunset,
this; it's different from what they usually are but after all I've
seen them just as delicate, just as remarkable as this." I had
more pleasure on evenings when a ship, absorbed and liquefied
by the horizon, appeared so much the same colour as its background, as in an Impressionist picture, that it seemed to be

also of the same substance, as though its hull and the rigging in which it tapered into a slender filigree had simply been cut out from the vaporous blue of the sky. Sometimes the ocean filled almost the whole of my window, raised as it was by a band of sky edged at the top only by a line that was of the same blue as the sea, so that I supposed it to be still sea, and the change in colour due only to some effect of lighting. Another day the sea was painted only in the lower part of the window, all the rest of which was filled with so many clouds, packed one against another in horizontal bands, that its panes seemed, by some premeditation or predilection on the part of the artist, to be presenting a "Cloud Study," while the fronts of the various bookcases showing similar clouds but in another part of the horizon and differently coloured by the light, appeared to be offering as it were the repetition—dear to certain contemporary masters—of one and the same effect caught at different hours but able now in the immobility of art to be seen all together in a single room, drawn in pastel and mounted under glass. And sometimes to a sky and sea uniformly grey a touch of pink would be added with an exquisite delicacy, while a little butterfly that had gone to sleep at the foot of the window seemed to be appending with its wings at the corner of this "Harmony in Grey and Pink" in the Whistler manner the favourite signature of the Chelsea master. Then even the pink would vanish; there was nothing now left to look at. I would get to my feet and, before lying down again, close the inner curtains. Above them I could see from my bed the ray of light that still remained, growing steadily fainter and thinner, but it was without any feeling of sadness, without any regret for its passing, that I thus allowed the hour at which as a rule I was seated at table to die above the curtains, for I knew that this day was of another kind from ordinary days, longer, like those arctic days which night interrupts for a few minutes only; I knew that from the chrysalis of this twilight, by a radiant metamorphosis, the dazzling light of the Rivebelle restaurant was preparing to emerge. I said to myself: "It's time"; I stretched myself on the bed, and rose, and finished dressing; and I found a charm in these idle moments, relieved of every material burden, in which, while the others were

dining down below, I was employing the forces accumulated
during the inactivity of this late evening hour only in drying
my washed body, in putting on a dinner jacket, in tying my
tie, in making all those gestures which were already dictated
by the anticipated pleasure of seeing again some woman whom
I had noticed at Rivebelle last time, who had seemed to be
watching me, had perhaps left the table for a moment only in
the hope that I would follow her; it was with joy that I embellished myself with all these allurements so as to give myself,
fresh, alert and whole-hearted, a new life, free, without cares,
in which I would lean my hesitations upon the calm strength of
Saint-Loup and would choose, from among the different
species of animated nature and the produce of every land,
those which, composing the unfamiliar dishes that my companion would at once order, might have tempted my appetite
or my imagination.

And then at the end of the season came the days when I
could no longer go straight in from the front through the
dining-room; its windows stood open no more, for it was night
now outside and the swarm of poor folk and curious idlers,
attracted by the blaze of light which was beyond their reach,
hung in black clusters, chilled by the north wind, on the luminous sliding walls of that buzzing hive of glass.

There was a knock at my door; it was Aimé who had come
upstairs in person with the latest list of visitors.

Aimé could not go away without telling me that Dreyfus
was guilty a thousand times over. "It will all come out," he
assured me, "not this year, but next. It was a gentleman who's
very thick with the General Staff who told me. I asked him if
they wouldn't decide to bring it all to light at once, before the
year is out. He laid down his cigarette," Aimé went on, acting
the scene for my benefit, and shaking his head and his forefinger as his informant had done, as much as to say: "We
mustn't be too impatient."—" 'Not this year, Aimé,' he said
to me, putting his hand on my shoulder, 'It isn't possible. But
next Easter, yes!' " And Aimé tapped me gently on the
shoulder, saying, "You see, I'm showing you exactly what he
did," whether because he was flattered at this act of familiarity
by a distinguished person or so that I might better appreciate,

with a full knowledge of the facts, the weight of the argument and our grounds for hope.

It was not without a slight pang that on the first page of the list I caught sight of the words "Simonet and family." I had in me a store of old dream-memories dating from my childhood, in which all the tenderness that existed in my heart but, being felt by my heart, was not distinguishable from it, was wafted to me by a being as different as possible from myself. Once again I fashioned such a being, utilising for the purpose the name Simonet and the memory of the harmony that had reigned between the young bodies which I had seen deployed on the beach in a sportive procession worthy of Greek art or of Giotto. I did not know which of these girls was Mlle Simonet, if indeed any of them was so named, but I did know that I was loved by Mlle Simonet and that with Saint-Loup's help I was going to try to get to know her. Unfortunately, having on that condition only obtained an extension of his leave, he was obliged to report for duty every day at Doncières: but to make him commit a breach of his military obligations I had felt that I might count, more even than on his friendship for myself, on that same curiosity as a human naturalist which I myself had so often felt—even without having seen the person mentioned, and simply on hearing it said that there was a pretty cashier at a fruiterer's—to become acquainted with a new variety of feminine beauty. But I had been wrong in hoping to excite that curiosity in Saint-Loup by speaking to him of my band of girls. For it had been and would remain paralysed in him by his love for the actress whose lover he was. And even if he had felt it lightly stirring within him he would have repressed it, from an almost superstitious belief that on his own fidelity might depend that of his mistress. And so it was without any promise from him that he would take an active interest in my girls that we set off to dine at Rivebelle.

On the first few occasions, when we arrived there, the sun would just have set, but it was light still; in the garden outside the restaurant, where the lamps had not yet been lighted, the heat of the day was falling and settling, as though in a vase along the sides of which the transparent, dusky jelly of the air

seemed of such consistency that a tall rose-tree, fastened against
the dim wall which it veined with pink, looked like the arborescence that one sees at the heart of an onyx. Presently it was
after nightfall when we alighted from the carriage, often indeed
when we started from Balbec if the weather was bad and we had
put off sending for the carriage in the hope of a lull. But on
those days it was with no sense of gloom that I listened to the
wind howling, for I knew that it did not mean the abandonment of my plans, imprisonment in my bedroom, I knew that
in the great dining-room of the restaurant which we would
enter to the sound of the music of the gipsy band, the innumerable lamps would triumph easily over the darkness and
the cold, by applying to them their broad cauteries of molten
gold, and I climbed light-heartedly after Saint-Loup into the
closed carriage which stood waiting for us in the rain.

For some time past the words of Bergotte, when he pronounced himself positive that, in spite of all I might say, I
had been created to enjoy pre-eminently the pleasures of the
mind, had restored to me, with regard to what I might succeed
in achieving later on, a hope that was disappointed afresh
every day by the boredom I felt on settling down before a
writing-table to start work on a critical essay or a novel. "After
all," I said to myself, "perhaps the pleasure one feels in writing
it is not the infallible test of the literary value of a page;
perhaps it is only a secondary state which is often superadded,
but the want of which can have no prejudicial effect on it.
Perhaps some of the greatest masterpieces were written while
yawning." My grandmother set my doubts at rest by telling
me that I should be able to work, and to enjoy working, as
soon as I was well. And, our doctor having thought it only
prudent to warn me of the grave risks to which my state of
health might expose me, and having outlined all the hygienic
precautions that I ought to take to avoid any accident, I
subordinated all my pleasures to an object which I judged to
be infinitely more important than them, that of becoming
strong enough to be able to bring into being the work which
I had, possibly, within me, and had been exercising over
myself, ever since I had come to Balbec, a scrupulous and
constant control. Nothing would have induced me to touch

the cup of coffee which would have robbed me of the night's sleep that was necessary if I was not to be tired next day. But when we arrived at Rivebelle, immediately—what with the excitement of a new pleasure, and finding myself in that different zone into which the exceptional introduces us after having cut the thread, patiently spun throughout so many days, that was guiding us towards wisdom—as though there were never to be any such thing as to-morrow, nor any lofty aims to be realised, all that precise machinery of prudent hygiene which had been working to safeguard them vanished. A waiter was offering to take my coat, whereupon Saint-Loup asked: "You're sure you won't be cold? Perhaps you'd better keep it: it's not very warm in here."

"No, no," I assured him, and perhaps I did not feel the cold; but however that might be, I no longer knew the fear of falling ill, the necessity of not dying, the importance of work. I gave up my coat; we entered the dining-room to the sound of some warlike march played by the gipsy band, we advanced between two rows of tables laid for dinner as along an easy path of glory, and, feeling a happy glow imparted to our bodies by the rhythms of the band which conferred on us these military honours, this unmerited triumph, we concealed it beneath a grave and frozen mien, beneath a languid, casual gait, so as not to be like those music-hall "mashers" who, wedding a ribald verse to a patriotic air, come running on to the stage with the martial countenance of a victorious general.

From that moment I was a new man, who was no longer my grandmother's grandson and would remember her only when it was time to get up and go, but the brother, for the time being, of the waiters who were going to bring us our dinner.

The dose of beer, and *a fortiori* of champagne, which at Balbec I should not have ventured to take in a week, albeit to my calm and lucid consciousness the savour of those beverages represented a pleasure clearly appreciable if easily sacrificed, I now imbibed at a sitting, adding to it a few drops of port which I was too bemused to be able to taste, and I gave the violinist who had just been playing the two louis which I had been saving up for the last month with a view to buying something, I could not remember what. Several of the waiters, let

loose among the tables, were flying along at full speed, each
carrying on his outstretched palm a dish which it seemed to be
the object of this kind of race not to let fall. And in fact the
chocolate *soufflés* arrived at their destination unspilled, the
potatoes *à l'anglaise*, in spite of the gallop that must have given
them a shaking, arranged as at the start round the Pauillac
lamb. I noticed one of these waiters, very tall, plumed with
superb black locks, his face dyed in a tint that suggested certain
species of rare birds rather than a human being, who, running
without pause (and, one would have said, without purpose)
from one end of the room to the other, recalled one of those
macaws which fill the big aviaries in zoological gardens with
their gorgeous colouring and incomprehensible agitation.
Presently the spectacle settled down, in my eyes at least, into
an order at once more noble and more calm. All this dizzy
activity became fixed in a quiet harmony. I looked at the round
tables whose innumerable assemblage filled the restaurant
like so many planets, as the latter are represented in old allegorical pictures. Moreover, there seemed to be some irresistible
force of attraction at work among these divers stars, and at
each table the diners had eyes only for the tables at which they
were not sitting, with the possible exception of some wealthy
amphitryon who, having managed to secure a famous author,
was endeavouring to extract from him, thanks to the magic
properties of the turning-table, a few insignificant remarks at
which the ladies marvelled. The harmony of these astral tables
did not prevent the incessant revolution of the countless
waiters who, because instead of being seated like the diners
they were on their feet, performed their gyrations in a more
exalted sphere. No doubt they were running, one to fetch the
hors d'œuvre, another to change the wine or to bring clean
glasses. But despite these special reasons, their perpetual
course among the round tables yielded, after a time, to the
observer the law of its dizzy but ordered circulation. Seated
behind a bank of flowers, two horrible cashiers, busy with
endless calculations, seemed two witches occupied in fore-
casting by astrological signs the disasters that might from time
to time occur in this celestial vault fashioned according to the
scientific conceptions of the Middle Ages.

And I rather pitied all the diners because I felt that for them the round tables were not planets and that they had not cut through the scheme of things in such a way as to be delivered from the bondage of habitual appearances and enabled to perceive analogies. They thought that they were dining with this or that person, that the dinner would cost roughly so much, and that to-morrow they would begin all over again. And they appeared absolutely indifferent to the progress through their midst of a train of young waiters who, having probably at that moment no urgent duty, advanced processionally bearing rolls of bread in baskets. Some of these, the youngest, stunned by the cuffs which the head waiters administered to them as they passed, fixed melancholy eyes upon a distant dream and were consoled only if some visitor from the Balbec hotel in which they had once been employed, recognising them, said a few words to them, telling them in person to take away the champagne which was not fit to drink, an order that filled them with pride.

I could hear the twanging of my nerves, in which there was a sense of well-being independent of the external objects that might have produced it, and which the least shifting of my body or of my attention was enough to make me feel, just as to a closed eye a slight compression gives the sensation of colour. I had already drunk a good deal of port, and if I now asked for more it was not so much with a view to the well-being which the additional glasses would bring me as an effect of the well-being produced by the glasses that had gone before. I allowed the music itself to guide my pleasure from note to note, and, meekly following, it rested on each in turn. If, like one of those chemical industries by means of which compounds are produced in large quantities which in a state of nature are encountered only by accident and very rarely, this restaurant at Rivebelle assembled at one and the same moment more women to tempt me with beckoning vistas of happiness than I should have come across in the course of walks or travels in a whole year, at the same time this music that greeted our ears,—arrangements of waltzes, of German operettas, of music-hall songs, all of them quite new to me— was itself like an ethereal pleasure-dome superimposed upon the other and more intoxicating still. For these tunes, each as individual as a woman, did not reserve, as she would have done, for some privileged person the voluptuous secret which they contained: they offered it to me, ogled me, came up to me with lewd or provocative movements, accosted me, caressed me as if I had suddenly become more seductive, more powerful, richer. Certainly I found in these tunes an element of cruelty; because any such thing as a disinterested feeling for beauty, a gleam of intelligence, was unknown to them; for them physical pleasure alone existed. And they are the most merciless of hells, the most gateless and imprisoning for the jealous wretch to whom they present that pleasure—that pleasure which the woman he loves is enjoying with another— as the only thing that exists in the world for her who is all the world to him. But while I was humming softly to myself the notes of this tune and returning its kiss, the pleasure peculiar to itself which it made me feel became so dear to me that I would have left my father and mother to follow it through the singular world which it constructed in the invisible, in lines alternately filled with languor and vivacity. Although such a pleasure as this is not calculated to enhance the value of the person to whom it comes, for it is perceived by him alone, and although whenever, in the course of our lives, we have failed to attract a woman who has caught sight of us, she did not know whether at that moment we possessed this inward and subjective felicity which, consequently, could in no way have altered the judgment that she passed on us, I felt myself more powerful, almost irresistible. It seemed to me that my love was no longer something unattractive, at which people might smile, but had precisely the touching beauty, the seductiveness, of this music, itself comparable to a congenial atmosphere in which she whom I loved and I were to meet, suddenly grown intimate.

This restaurant was not frequented solely by women of easy virtue, but also by people of the very best society, who came there for afternoon tea or gave big dinner-parties there. The tea-parties were held in a long gallery, glazed and narrow, shaped like a funnel, which led from the entrance hall to the dining-room and was bounded on one side by the garden, from which it was separated (save for a few stone pillars) only by its wall of glass which opened here and there. The result of which, apart from ubiquitous draughts, was sudden and intermittent bursts of sunshine, a dazzling and changeable light that made it almost impossible to see the tea-drinkers, so that when they were installed there, at tables crowded pair after pair the whole way along the narrow gully, shimmering and sparkling with every movement they made in drinking their tea or in greeting one another, it resembled a giant fish-tank or bow-net in which a fisherman has collected all his glittering catch, which, half out of water and bathed in sun-light, coruscate before one's eyes in an ever-changing iri-descence.

A few hours later, during dinner, which, naturally, was served in the dining-room, the lights would be turned on, even when it was still quite light out of doors, so that one saw before one's eyes, in the garden, among summer-houses glim-mering in the twilight like pale spectres of evening, arbours whose glaucous verdure was pierced by the last rays of the setting sun and which, from the lamp-lit room in which one was dining, appeared through the glass no longer—as one would have said of the ladies drinking tea in the afternoon along the blue and gold corridor—caught in a glittering and dripping net, but like the vegetation of a pale and green aquarium of gigantic size lit by a supernatural light. People began to rise from the table; and if each party, while their dinner lasted, although they spent the whole time examining, recognising, naming the party at the next table, had been held in perfect cohesion about their own, the magnetic force that had kept them gravitating round their host of the evening lost its power at the moment when they repaired for coffee to the same corridor that had been used for the tea-parties; so that it often happened that in its passage from place to place some party on the march dropped one or more of its human cor-puscles who, having come under the irresistible attraction of the rival party, detached themselves for a moment from their own, in which their places were taken by ladies or gentlemen who had come across to speak to friends before hurrying off with an "I really must get back to my host Monsieur X . . ."

And for the moment one was reminded of two separate bouquets that had exchanged a few of their flowers. Then the corridor too began to empty. Often, since even after dinner there might still be a little light left outside, this long corridor was left unlighted, and, skirted by the trees that overhung it on the other side of the glass, it suggested a pleached alley in a wooded and shady garden. Sometimes, in the gloom, a fair diner would be lingering there. As I passed through it one evening on my way out I saw, sitting among a group of strangers, the beautiful Princesse de Luxembourg. I raised my hat without stopping. She recognised me, and nodded to me with a smile; in the air, far above her salutation, but emanating from the movement, rose melodiously a few words addressed to myself, which must have been a somewhat amplified good-evening, intended not to stop me but simply to complete the gesture, to make it a spoken greeting. But her words remained so indistinct and the sound which was all that I caught was prolonged so sweetly and seemed to me so musical that it was as if, among the dim branches of the trees, a nightingale had begun to sing.

If it so happened that, to finish the evening with a party of his friends whom we had met, Saint-Loup decided to go on to the Casino of a neighbouring resort, and, taking them with him, put me in a carriage by myself, I would urge the driver to go as fast as he possibly could, so that the minutes might pass less slowly which I must spend without having anyone at hand to dispense me from the obligation to provide my own sensibility—reversing the engine, so to speak, and emerging from the passivity in which I was caught and held as in a mesh —with those modifications which, since my arrival at Rivebelle, I had been receiving from other people. The risk of collision with a carriage coming the other way along those lanes where there was barely room for one and it was dark as pitch; the instability of the surface, crumbling in many places, at the cliff's edge; the proximity of its vertical drop to the sea— none of these things exerted on me the slight stimulus that would have been required to bring the vision and the fear of danger within the orbit of my reason. For just as it is not the desire to become famous but the habit of being industrious that enables us to produce a finished work, so it is not the activity of the present moment but wise reflexions from the past that help us to safeguard the future. But if already, before this point, on my arrival at Rivebelle, I had flung irretrievably away from me those crutches of reason and self-control which help our infirmity to follow the right road, if I now found myself the victim of a sort of moral ataxia, the alcohol that I had drunk, in stretching my nerves exceptionally, had given to the present moment a quality, a charm, which did not have the effect of making me more competent or indeed more resolute to defend it; for in making me prefer it a thousand times to the rest of my life, my exaltation isolated it therefrom; I was enclosed in the present, like heroes and drunkards; momentarily eclipsed, my past no longer projected before me that shadow of itself which we call our future; placing the goal of my life no longer in the realisation of the dreams of the past, but in the felicity of the present moment, I could see no further than it. So that, by a contradiction which was only apparent, it was at the very moment in which I was experiencing an exceptional pleasure, in which I felt that my life might yet be happy, in which it should have become more precious in my sight, it was at this very moment that, delivered from the anxieties which it had hitherto inspired in me, I unhesitatingly abandoned it to the risk of an accident. But after all, I was doing no more than concentrate in a single evening the carelessness that, for most men, is diluted throughout their whole existence, in which every day they face unnecessarily the dangers of a sea-voyage, of a trip in an aeroplane or motor-car, when there is waiting for them at home the person whom their death would shatter, or when the book whose eventual publication is the sole reason for their existence is still stored in the fragile receptacle of their brain. And so too in the Rivebelle restaurant, on evenings when we stayed there after dinner, if anyone had come in with the intention of killing me, since I no longer saw, save in a distance too remote to have any reality, my grandmother, my life to come, the books I might write, since I now clung body and soul to the scent of the woman at the next table, to the politeness of the waiters, to the contours of the waltz that the band was playing, since I was glued to the sensation of the moment, with no extension beyond its limits, nor any object other than not to be separated from it, I should have died in and with that sensation, I should have let myself be slaughtered without offering any resistance, without a movement, a bee drugged with tobacco smoke that had ceased to take any thought for preserving the accumulation of its labours and the hopes of its hive.

I ought here to add that this insignificance into which the most serious matters relapsed, by contrast with the violence of my exaltation, came in the end to include Mlle Simonet and her friends. The enterprise of knowing them seemed to me easy now but a matter of indifference, for my immediate sensation, thanks to its extraordinary intensity, to the joy that its slightest modifications, its mere continuity provoked, alone had any importance for me; all the rest, parents, work, pleasures, girls at Balbec, weighed no more than a flake of foam in a strong wind that will not let it find a resting place, existed no longer save in relation to this internal power: inebriation brings about for an hour or two a state of subjective idealism, pure phenomenalism; everything is reduced to appearances and exists only as a function of our sublime self. This is not to say that a genuine love, if we have one, cannot subsist in such a state. But we feel so unmistakably, as though in a new atmosphere, that unknown pressures have altered the dimensions of that love, that we can no longer consider it in the old way. It is indeed still there, but somehow displaced, no longer weighing upon us, satisfied by the sensation which the present affords it, a sensation that is sufficient for us, since for what is not the here and now we take no thought. Unfortunately the coefficient which thus alters our values alters them only during that hour of intoxication. The people who were no longer of any importance, whom we scattered with our breath like soap-bubbles, will to-morrow resume their density; we shall have to try afresh to settle down to work which had ceased to have any meaning. A more serious matter still, these mathematics of the morrow, the same as those of yesterday, in whose problems we shall find ourselves inexorably involved, govern us even during those hours, and we alone are unconscious of their rule. If there is a hostile or virtuous woman in our vicinity, that question so difficult an hour ago—to know whether we should succeed in finding favour with her—seems to us now a million times easier of solution without having become easier in any respect, for it is only in our eyes, in our own inward eyes, that we have altered. And she is as displeased with us at this moment for having taken a liberty with her as we shall be with ourselves next day at the thought of having given a hundred francs to the bell-hop, and for the same reason, which in our case has merely been delayed, namely the absence of intoxication.

I knew none of the women who were at Rivebelle and who, because they were part and parcel of my intoxication just as its reflections are part and parcel of a mirror, appeared to me a thousand times more desirable than the less and less existent Mlle Simonet. One of them, young, fair, alone, with a sad expression on a face framed in a straw hat trimmed with field-flowers, gazed at me for a moment with a dreamy air and struck me as being attractive. Then it was the turn of another, and of a third; finally of a dark one with glowing cheeks. Almost all of them were known, if not to myself, to Saint-Loup.

He had, in fact, before he made the acquaintance of his present mistress, lived so much in the restricted world of amorous adventure that of all the women who were dining on those evenings at Rivebelle, where many of them had appeared quite by chance, having come to the coast some to join their lovers, others in the hope of finding lovers, there was scarcely one that he did not know from having spent— he himself, or one or other of his friends—at least one night with her. He did not greet them if they were with men, and they, although they looked more at him than at anyone else because the indifference which he was known to feel towards every woman who was not his actress gave him in their eyes a special glamour, appeared not to know him. But you could hear them whispering: "That's young Saint-Loup. It seems he's still quite gone on that tart of his. It's true love! What a handsome fellow he is! I think he's just wonderful. And what style! Some women have all the luck, don't they? And he's so nice in every way. I saw a lot of him when I was with d'Orléans. They were quite inseparable, those two. He was going the pace in those days. But he's given it all up now, she can't complain. Ah! she can certainly consider herself lucky. I wonder what in the world he sees in her. He must be a bit of a chump, when all's said and done. She's got feet like boats, whiskers like an American, and her undies are filthy. I can tell you, a little shop-girl would be ashamed to be seen in her knickers. Do just look at his eyes a moment: you'd go to hell for a man like that. Hush, don't say a word; he's seen me; look, he's smiling. Oh, he knew me all right. Just you mention my name to him, and see what he says!" Between these women and him I caught a glance of mutual understanding. I should have liked him to introduce me to them, so that I might ask them for assignations which they would grant me, even if I was unable to keep them. For otherwise each of their faces would remain for all time devoid, in my memory, of that part of itself—just as though it had been hidden by a veil—which varies in every woman, which we cannot imagine in any woman until we have actually seen it in her, and which appears only in the look she gives us that acquiesces in our desire and promises that it shall be satisfied. And yet, even thus reduced, their faces meant far more to me than those of women whom I knew to be virtuous, and did not seem to me to be flat, like theirs, with nothing behind them, fashioned in one piece with no depth or solidity. It was not, of course, for me what it must be for Saint-Loup who, by an act of memory, beneath the indifference, transparent to him, of the motionless features which affected not to know him, or beneath the dull formality of the greeting that might equally well have been addressed to anyone else, could recall, could see, dishevelled locks, a swooning mouth, a pair of half-closed eyes, a whole silent picture like those that painters, to deceive the bulk of their visitors, drape with a decent covering. For me, who felt that nothing of my personality had penetrated the surface of any one of these women, or would be borne by her upon the unknown ways which she would tread through life, these faces remained sealed. But it was enough for me to know that they did open in order for them to seem to me to be more precious than I should have thought them had they been only handsome medals instead of lockets within which memories of love were hidden. As for Robert, scarcely able to keep his seat at table, concealing beneath a courtier's smile his warrior's thirst for action—when I looked at him closely I could see to what extent the vigorous bone structure of his triangular face must have been modelled on that of his ancestors, a face designed rather for an ardent bowman than for a sensitive man of letters. Beneath the delicate skin the bold construction, the feudal architecture were apparent. His head reminded one of those old castle keeps on which the disused battlements are still to be seen, although inside they have been converted into libraries.

On the way back to Balbec, of this or that charmer to whom he had introduced me I would repeat to myself without a moment's interruption, and yet almost unconsciously: "What a delightful woman!" as one sings a refrain. True, these words were prompted rather by over-excitement than by any lasting judgment. It was nevertheless true that if I had had a thousand francs on me and if there had still been a jeweller's shop open at that hour, I should have bought the lady a ring. When the successive hours of our lives unfold as though on too widely disparate planes, we find that we give away too much of ourselves to all sorts of people who next day will not interest us in the least. But we feel that we are still responsible for what we said to them overnight, and that we must honour our promises.

Since, on those evenings, I came back late, it was a pleasure to be reunited, in a room no longer hostile, with the bed in which, on the day of my arrival, I had supposed that it would always be impossible for me to find any rest, whereas now my weary limbs longed for its support; so that, one after the other, my thighs, my hips and my shoulders sought to adhere at every point to the sheets that covered its mattress, as if my fatigue, like a sculptor, had wished to take a cast of an entire human body. But I could not get to sleep; I sensed the approach of morning; peace of mind, health of body were no longer mine. In my distress it seemed to me that I should never recapture them. I should have had to sleep for a long time if I were to find them again. But then, had I begun to doze, I must in any event be awakened in a couple of hours by the symphony

concert on the beach. Suddenly I fell asleep, plunged into
that deep slumber in which vistas are opened to us of a return
to childhood, the recapture of past years, and forgotten feelings, of disincarnation, the transmigration of souls, the evoking
of the dead, the illusions of madness, retrogression towards the
most elementary of the natural kingdoms (for we say that we
often see animals in our dreams, but we forget that almost
always we are ourselves animals therein, deprived of that
reasoning power which projects upon things the light of
certainty; on the contrary we bring to bear on the spectacle of
life only a dubious vision, extinguished anew every moment by
oblivion, the former reality fading before that which follows
it as one projection of a magic lantern fades before the next
as we change the slide), all those mysteries which we imagine
ourselves not to know and into which we are in reality initiated
almost every night, as into the other great mystery of extinction and resurrection. Rendered more vagabond by the
difficulty of digesting my Rivebelle dinner, the successive and
flickering illumination of shadowy zones of my past made of
me a person for whom the supreme happiness would have been
to meet Legrandin, with whom I had just been talking in my
dream.

And then, even my own life was entirely hidden from me by
a new scene, like the "drop" lowered right at the front of the
stage before which, while the scene shifters are busy behind,
actors appear in an interim "turn." The turn in which I was
now playing a part was in the manner of an Oriental fairy-
tale; I retained no knowledge of my past or of myself, on
account of the extreme proximity of this interposed scenery;
I was merely a character receiving the bastinado and undergoing various punishments for a crime the nature of which I
could not make out, though it was actually that of having
drunk too much port. Suddenly I awoke and discovered that,
thanks to a long sleep, I had not heard a note of the concert.
It was already afternoon; I verified this by my watch after
several efforts to sit up in bed, efforts fruitless at first and
interrupted by backward falls on to my pillow, brief falls of
the kind that are a sequel of sleep as of other forms of intoxication, whether due to wine or to convalescence; in any case,

even before I had looked at the time, I was certain that it was past midday. Last night I had been nothing more than an empty vessel, weightless, and (since one must have been lying down in order to be able to sit up, and have been asleep to be able to keep silent) had been unable to refrain from moving about and talking, no longer had any stability, any centre of gravity; I had been set in motion and it seemed that I might have continued on my dreary course until I reached the moon. But if, while I slept, my eyes had not seen the time, my body had nevertheless contrived to calculate it, had measured the hours not on a dial superficially decorated with figures, but by the steadily growing weight of all my replenished forces which, like a powerful clock, it had allowed, notch by notch, to descend from my brain into the rest of my body where they now accumulated as far as the top of my knees the unimpaired abundance of their store. If it is true that the sea was once upon a time our native element, in which we must plunge our blood to recover our strength, it is the same with the oblivion, the mental nothingness of sleep; we seem then to absent ourselves for a few hours from time, but the forces which have gathered in that interval without being expended measure it by their quantity as accurately as the pendulum of the clock or the crumbling hillocks of the hourglass. Moreover, one does not emerge more easily from such a sleep than from a prolonged spell of wakefulness, so strongly does everything tend to persist; and if it is true that certain narcotics make us sleep, to have slept for a long time is an even more potent narcotic, after which we have great difficulty in making ourselves wake up. Like a sailor who sees plainly the quay where he can moor his boat, still tossed by the waves, I had every intention of looking at the time and of getting up, but my body was constantly cast back upon the tide of sleep; the landing was difficult, and before I attained a position in which I could reach my watch and confront its time with that indicated by the wealth of accumulated materials which my exhausted limbs had at their disposal, I fell back two or three times more upon my pillow.

At length I could reach and read it: "two o'clock in the afternoon!" I rang; but at once I plunged back into a sleep

which this time must have lasted infinitely longer if I was to
judge by the refreshment, the vision of an immense night out-
lived, which I experienced on awakening. And yet, since my
awakening was caused by the entry of Françoise, and since
her entry had been prompted by my ringing the bell, this
second sleep which, it seemed to me, must have been longer
than the other and had brought me so much well-being and
forgetfulness, could not have lasted for more than half a
minute.

My grandmother opened the door of my bedroom, and I
asked her countless questions about the Legrandin family.

It is not enough to say that I had returned to tranquillity
and health, for it was more than a mere interval of space that
had divided them from me the day before; I had had all night
long to struggle against a contrary tide, and then I not only
found myself again in their presence, but they had once more
entered into me. At certain definite and still somewhat painful
points beneath the surface of my empty head which would one
day be broken, letting my ideas dissolve forever, those ideas
had once again taken their proper place and resumed that
existence by which hitherto, alas, they had failed to profit.

Once again I had escaped from the impossibility of sleeping,
from the deluge, the shipwreck of my nervous storms. I no
longer feared the threats that had loomed over me the evening
before, when I was deprived of rest. A new life was opening
before me; without making a single movement, for I was still
shattered, although quite alert and well, I savoured my weariness with a light heart; it had isolated and broken the bones of
my legs and arms, which I could feel assembled before me,
ready to come together again, and which I would rebuild
merely by singing, like the architect in the fable.[27]

Suddenly I remembered the fair girl with the sad expression
whom I had seen at Rivebelle and who had looked at me for a
moment. Many others, in the course of the evening, had seemed
to me attractive; now she alone arose from the depths of my
memory. I felt that she had noticed me, and expected one of
the Rivebelle waiters to come to me with a whispered message
from her. Saint-Loup did not know her and believed that she
was respectable. It would be very difficult to see her, to see her

constantly. But I was prepared to make any sacrifice: I thought now only of her. Philosophy distinguishes often between free and necessary acts. Perhaps there is none to the necessity of which we are more completely subjected than that which, by virtue of a climbing power held in check during the act itself, brings back (once our mind is at rest) a memory until then levelled down with all the rest by the oppressive force of bemusement and makes it spring to the surface because unknown to us it contained more than any of the others a charm of which we do not become aware until the following day. And perhaps, too, there is no act so free, for it is still unprompted by habit, by that sort of mental obsession which, in matters of love, encourages the invariable reappearance of the image of one particular person.

That day, as it happened, was the day after the one on which I had seen the beautiful procession of young girls advancing along the sea-front. I questioned a number of the visitors in the hotel about them, people who came almost every year to Balbec. They could tell me nothing. Later on, a photograph showed me why. Who could now have recognised in them, scarcely and yet quite definitely beyond the age at which one changes so completely, an amorphous, delicious mass, still utterly childish, of little girls who, only a few years back, might have been seen sitting in a ring on the sand round a tent: a sort of vague, white constellation in which one would have distinguished a pair of eyes that sparkled more than the rest, a mischievous face, flaxen hair, only to lose them again and to confound them almost at once in the indistinct and milky nebula.

No doubt, in those earlier years that were still so comparatively recent, it was not, as it had been yesterday when they appeared for the first time before me, the impression of the group but the group itself that had been lacking in clearness. Then those children, still mere babies, had been at that elementary stage in their development when personality has not yet stamped its seal on each face. Like those primitive organisms in which the individual barely exists by itself, is constituted by the polypary rather than by each of the polyps that compose it, they were still pressed one against another. Sometimes one pushed her neighbour over, and then a giggle, which seemed the sole manifestation of their personal life, convulsed them all together, obliterating, merging those imprecise and grinning faces in the congealment of a single cluster, scintillating and tremulous. In an old photograph of themselves, which they were one day to give me, and which I have kept ever since, their childish troupe already presents the same number of participants as, later, their feminine procession; one can sense from it that their presence must even then have made on the beach an unusual impression which forced itself on the attention, but one cannot recognise them individually save by a process of reasoning, making allowances for all the transformations possible during girlhood, up to the point at which these reconstituted forms would begin to encroach upon another individuality which must be identified also, and whose handsome face, owing to the concomitance of a tall build and curly hair, may quite possibly have been, long ago, that wizened and impish little grin which the photograph album presents to us; and the distance traversed in a short interval of time by the physical characteristics of each of these girls making of them a criterion too vague to be of any use, and moreover what they had in common and, so to speak, collectively, being therefore very pronounced, it sometimes happened that even their most intimate friends mistook one for another in this photograph, so much so that the question could in the last resort be settled only by some detail of costume which one of them was certain to have worn to the exclusion of the others. Since those days, so different from the day on which I had just seen them strolling along the front, so different and yet so close in time, they still gave way to fits of laughter, as I had observed the previous afternoon, but to laughter of a kind that was no longer the intermittent and almost automatic laughter of childhood, a spasmodic explosion which, in those days, had continually sent their heads dipping out of the circle, as the clusters of minnows in the Vivonne used to scatter and vanish only to gather again a moment later; each of their physiognomies was now mistress of itself, their eyes were fixed on the goal they were pursuing; and it

had taken, yesterday, the tremulous uncertainty of my first
impression to make me confuse vaguely (as their childish
hilarity and the old photograph had confused) the spores, now
individualised and disjoined, of the pale madrepore.

Doubtless often enough before, when pretty girls went by, I
had promised myself that I would see them again. As a rule,
people thus seen do not appear a second time; moreover our
memory, which speedily forgets their existence, would find
it difficult to recall their features; our eyes would not recognise
them, perhaps, and in the meantime we have seen others go
by, whom we shall not see again either. But at other times,
and this was what was to happen with the pert little band at
Balbec, chance brings them back insistently before our eyes.
Chance seems to us then a good and useful thing, for we
discern in it as it were the rudiments of organisation, of an
attempt to arrange our lives; and it makes it easy, inevitable,
and sometimes—after interruptions that have made us hope
that we may cease to remember—painful for us to retain in our
minds images for the possession of which we shall come in
time to believe that we were predestined, and which but for
chance we should from the very first have managed to forget,
like so many others, so easily.

Presently Saint-Loup's visit drew to an end. I had not seen
those girls again on the beach. He was too little at Balbec in
the afternoons to have time to pay attention to them and
attempt, in my interest, to make their acquaintance. In the
evenings he was freer, and continued to take me regularly
to Rivebelle. There are, in such restaurants, as there are in
public gardens and railway trains, people enclosed in a quite
ordinary appearance, whose names astonish us when, having
happened to ask, we discover that they are not the mere inoffensive strangers whom we supposed but no less than the
Minister or the Duke of whom we have so often heard. Two
or three times already, in the Rivebelle restaurant, when everyone else was getting ready to leave, Saint-Loup and I had seen
a man of large stature, very muscular, with regular features
and a grizzled beard, come in and sit down at a table, where his
pensive gaze remained fixed with concentrated attention upon
the void. One evening, on our asking the landlord who this

obscure, solitary and belated diner was, "What!" he exclaimed, "do you mean to say you don't know the famous painter Elstir?" Swann had once mentioned his name to me, I had entirely forgotten in what connexion; but the omission of a particular memory, like that of part of a sentence when we are reading, leads sometimes not to uncertainty but to the birth of a premature certainty. "He's a friend of Swann's, and a very well-known artist, extremely good," I told Saint-Loup. Immediately the thought swept through us both like a thrill of emotion, that Elstir was a great artist, a celebrated man, and that, confounding us with the rest of the diners, he had no suspicion of the ecstasy into which we were plunged by the idea of his talent. Doubtless, his unconsciousness of our admiration and of our acquaintance with Swann would not have troubled us had we not been at the seaside. But since we were still at an age when enthusiasm cannot keep silence, and had been transported into a life where anonymity is suffocating, we wrote a letter, signed with both our names, in which we revealed to Elstir in the two diners seated within a few feet of him two passionate admirers of his talent, two friends of his great friend Swann, and asked to be allowed to pay our homage to him in person. A waiter undertook to convey this missive to the celebrity.

A celebrity Elstir was perhaps not yet at this period quite to the extent claimed by the landlord, though he was to reach the height of his fame within a very few years. But he had been one of the first to frequent this restaurant when it was still only a sort of farmhouse, and had brought to it a whole colony of artists (who had all, as it happened, migrated elsewhere as soon as the farm, where they used to feed in the open air under a lean-to roof, had become a fashionable centre; Elstir himself had returned to Rivebelle this evening on account of the temporary absence of his wife, with whom he lived not far away). But great talent, even when its existence is not yet recognised, will inevitably provoke a few quirks of admiration, such as the landlord had managed to detect in the questions asked by more than one English lady visitor, athirst for information as to the life led by Elstir, or in the number of letters that he received from abroad. Then the landlord had

further remarked that Elstir did not like to be disturbed when
he was working, that he would rise in the middle of the night
and take a young model down to the sea-shore to pose for
him, nude, if the moon was shining, and had told himself that
so much labour was not in vain, nor the admiration of the
tourist unjustified, when he had recognised in one of Elstir's
pictures a wooden cross which stood by the roadside on the
way into Rivebelle.

"That's it all right," he would repeat with stupefaction,
"there are all the four beams! Oh, he does take a lot of trouble!"

And he did not know whether a little *Sunrise over the Sea*
which Elstir had given him might not be worth a fortune.

We watched him read our letter, put it in his pocket, finish
his dinner, begin to ask for his things, get up to go; and we
were so convinced that we had offended him by our overture
that we would now have hoped (as keenly as at first we had
dreaded) to make our escape without his noticing us. What did
not cross our minds for a single instant was a consideration
which should have seemed to us of cardinal importance,
namely that our enthusiasm for Elstir, on the sincerity of which
we would not have allowed the least doubt to be cast, which we
could indeed have confirmed with the evidence of our bated
breath, our desire to do no matter what that was difficult or
heroic for the great man, was not, as we imagined it to be,
admiration, since neither of us had ever seen anything that he
had painted; our feeling might have as its object the hollow
idea of a "great artist," but not a body of work which was
unknown to us. It was, at most, admiration in the abstract, the
nervous envelope, the sentimental framework of an admiration
without content, that is to say a thing as indissolubly attached
to boyhood as are certain organs which no longer exist in the
adult man; we were still boys. Elstir meanwhile was approaching the door when suddenly he turned and came towards us.
I was overcome by a delicious thrill of terror such as I could
not have felt a few years later, because, as age diminishes the
capacity, familiarity with the world meanwhile destroys in us
any inclination, to provoke such strange encounters, to feel that
kind of emotion.

In the course of the few words that Elstir came to say to us, sitting down at our table, he never replied to me on the several occasions on which I spoke to him of Swann. I began to think that he did not know him. He nevertheless asked me to come and see him at his Balbec studio, an invitation which he did not extend to Saint-Loup, and which I had earned, as I might not, perhaps, from Swann's recommendation had Elstir been a friend of his (for the part played by disinterested motives is greater than we are inclined to think in people's lives), by a few words which made him think that I was devoted to the arts. He lavished on me a friendliness which was as far above that of Saint-Loup as the latter's was above the affability of a shopkeeper. Compared with that of a great artist, the friendliness of a great nobleman, however charming it may be, seems like play-acting, like simulation. Saint-Loup sought to please; Elstir loved to give, to give himself. Everything that he possessed, ideas, works, and the rest which he counted for far less, he would have given gladly to anyone who understood him. But, for lack of congenial company, he lived in an unsociable isolation which fashionable people called pose and ill-breeding, the authorities a recalcitrant spirit, his neighbours madness, his family selfishness and pride.

And no doubt at first he had thought with pleasure, even in his solitude, that, thanks to his work, he was addressing from a distance, was imbuing with a loftier idea of himself, those who had misunderstood or offended him. Perhaps, in those days, he lived alone not from indifference but from love of his fellows, and, just as I had renounced Gilberte in order to appear to her again one day in more attractive colours, dedicated his work to certain people as a sort of new approach to them whereby, without actually seeing him, they would be brought to love him, admire him, talk about him; a renunciation is not always total from the start, when we decide upon it in our original frame of mind and before it has reacted upon us, whether it be the renunciation of an invalid, a monk, an artist or a hero. But if he had wished to produce with certain people in his mind, in producing he had lived for himself, remote from society, to which he had become indifferent; the practice of solitude had given him a love for it, as happens with every big thing which we have begun by fearing, because we know it to be incompatible with smaller things which we prize and which it does not so much deprive us of as detach us from. Before we experience it, our whole preoccupation is to know to what extent we can reconcile it with certain pleasures which cease to be pleasures as soon as we have experienced it.

Elstir did not stay talking to us for long. I made up my mind that I would go to his studio during the next few days, but on the following afternoon, after I had accompanied my grandmother to the far end of the sea-front, near the cliffs of Canapville, on the way back, at the corner of one of the little streets which ran down at right angles to the beach, we passed a girl who, hanging her head like an animal that is being driven reluctant to its stall, and carrying golf-clubs, was walking in front of an authoritarian-looking person, in all probability her or one of her friends' "Miss," who suggested a portrait of Jeffreys by Hogarth, with a face as red as if her favourite beverage were gin rather than tea, on which a dried smear of tobacco at the corner of her mouth prolonged the curve of a moustache that was grizzled but abundant. The girl who preceded her resembled the member of the little band who, beneath a black polo-cap, had shown in an inexpressive chubby face a pair of laughing eyes. However, though this one had also a black polo-cap, she struck me as being even prettier than the other; the line of her nose was straighter, the curve of the nostrils fuller and more fleshy. Besides, the other had seemed a proud, pale girl, this one a child well-disciplined and of rosy complexion. And yet, since she was pushing a bicycle just like the other's, and was wearing the same kid gloves, I concluded that the differences arose perhaps from the angle and the circumstances in which I now saw her, for it was hardly likely that there could be at Balbec a second girl with a face that was on the whole so similar and combining the same details in her accoutrement. She flung a rapid glance in my direction. During the next few days, when I saw the little band again on the beach, and indeed long afterwards when I knew all the girls who composed it, I could never be absolutely certain that any of them—even the one who resembled her most, the girl with the bicycle—was indeed the one that I had seen that evening at the corner of the street at the end of the esplanade, a girl who was scarcely but still just perceptibly different from the one I had noticed in the procession.

From that moment, whereas for the last few days my mind had been occupied chiefly by the tall one, it was the one with the golf-clubs, presumed to be Mlle Simonet, who began once more to absorb my attention. When walking with the others she would often stop, forcing her friends, who seemed greatly to respect her, to stop also. Thus it is, coming to a halt, her eyes sparkling beneath her polo-cap, that I still see her again to-day, silhouetted against the screen which the sea spreads out behind her, and separated from me by a transparent sky-blue space, the interval of time that has elapsed since then—the first impression, faint and tenuous in my memory, desired, pursued, then forgotten, then recaptured, of a face which I have many times since projected upon the cloud of the past in order to be able to say to myself, of a girl who was actually in my room: "It is she!"

But it was perhaps yet another, the one with geranium cheeks and green eyes, whom I should have liked most to know. And yet, whichever of them it might be, on any given day, that I preferred to see, the others, without her, were sufficient to excite my desire which, concentrated now chiefly on one, now on another, continued—as, on the first day, my confused vision had done—to combine and blend them, to make of them the little world apart, animated by a life in common, which indeed they doubtless imagined themselves to form; and in becoming a friend of one of them I should have penetrated—like a cultivated pagan or a meticulous Christian going among barbarians—a youthful society in which thoughtlessness, health, sensual pleasure, cruelty, unintellectuality and joy held sway.

My grandmother, whom I had told of my meeting with Elstir and who rejoiced at the thought of all the intellectual profit that I might derive from his friendship, considered it absurd and none too polite of me not to have yet gone to pay him a visit. But I could think only of the little band, and being uncertain of the hour at which the girls would be passing along the front, I dared not absent myself. My grandmother was astonished, too, at the elegance of my attire, for I had suddenly remembered suits which had been lying all this time at the bottom of my trunk. I put on a different one every day, and had even written to Paris ordering new hats and new ties.

It adds a great charm to life in a watering-place like Balbec if the face of a pretty girl, a vendor of shells, cakes or flowers, painted in vivid colours in our mind, is regularly, from early morning, the purpose of each of those leisured, luminous days which we spend on the beach. They become then, and for that reason, albeit idle, as alert as working-days, pointed, magnetised, raised slightly to meet an approaching moment, that in which, while we purchase shortbread, roses, ammonites, we will delight in seeing, on a feminine face, colours displayed as purely as on a flower. But at least one can speak to these young vendors, and this dispenses one from having to construct with one's imagination those aspects which a mere visual perception fails to provide, and to recreate their life, magnifying its charm, as in front of a portrait; moreover, precisely because one speaks to them, one can learn where and at what time it will be possible to see them again. Now I had none of these advantages when it came to the little band. Since their habits were unknown to me, when on certain days I failed to catch a glimpse of them, not knowing the cause of their absence I sought to discover whether it was something fixed and regular, if they were to be seen only every other day, or in certain kinds of weather, or if there were days on which they were not to be seen at all. I imagined myself already friends with them, and saying: "But you weren't there the other day?" "Weren't we? Oh, no, of course not; it was a Saturday. On Saturdays we don't ever come, because . . ." If only it were simply a matter of knowing that on black Saturday it was useless to torment oneself, that one might range the beach from end to end, sit down outside the pastry-cook's and pretend to be nibbling an *éclair*, poke into the curio shop, wait for bathing time, the concert, high tide, sunset, night, all without seeing the longed-for little band. But the fatal day did not, perhaps, come once a week. It did not, perhaps, of necessity fall on a Saturday. Perhaps certain atmospheric conditions influenced it or were entirely unconnected with it. How many observations, patient but not at all serene, must one accumulate of the movements, to all appearance irregular, of these unknown worlds before being able to be sure that one has not allowed oneself to be led astray by mere coincidence, that one's forecasts will not be proved wrong, before deducing the incontrovertible laws, acquired at the cost of so much painful experience, of that passionate astronomy!

Remembering that I had not yet seen them on some particular day of the week, I assured myself that they would not be coming, that it was useless to wait any longer on the beach. And at that very moment I caught sight of them. And yet on another day which, in so far as I had been able to conjecture that there were laws that guided the return of those constellations, must, I had calculated, prove an auspicious day, they did not come. But to this primary uncertainty as to whether I should see them or not that day, there was added another, more disquieting: whether I should ever set eyes on them again, for I had no reason, after all, to know that they were not about to set sail for America, or return to Paris. This was enough to make me begin to love them. One can feel an attraction towards a particular person. But to release that fount of sorrow, that sense of the irreparable, those agonies which prepare the way for love, there must be—and this is perhaps, more than a person, the actual object which our passion seeks so anxiously to embrace—the risk of an impossibility. Thus already they were acting upon me, those influences which recur in the course of our successive love-affairs (which can moreover occur, but then rather in the life of big cities, in relation to working-girls of whose half-holidays we are uncertain and whom we are alarmed not to have seen at the factory exit), or which at least have recurred in the course of mine. Perhaps they are inseparable from love; perhaps everything that formed a distinctive feature of our first love comes to attach itself to those that follow, by virtue of recollection, suggestion, habit, and, through the successive periods of our life, gives to its different aspects a general character.

I seized every pretext for going down to the beach at the hours when I hoped to succeed in finding them there. Having caught sight of them once while we were at lunch, I now in-

variably came in late for it, waiting interminably on the
esplanade for them to pass; spending the whole of my brief
stay in the dining-room interrogating with my eyes its azure
wall of glass; rising long before dessert, so as not to miss them
should they have gone out at a different hour, and chafing with
irritation at my grandmother when, with unwitting malevolence, she made me stay with her past the hour that seemed to
me propitious. I tried to prolong the horizon by changing the
position of my chair, and if by chance I did catch sight of one
or other of the girls, since they all partook of the same special
essence, it was as if I had seen projected before my face in a
shifting, diabolical hallucination a little of the unfriendly and
yet passionately coveted dream which, but a moment ago, had
existed only—stagnating permanently there—in my brain.

I loved none of them, loving them all, and yet the possibility
of meeting them was in my daily life the sole element of delight,
alone aroused in me those hopes for which one would break
down every obstacle, hopes ending often in fury if I had not
seen them. For the moment, these girls eclipsed my grandmother in my affection; the longest journey would at once have
seemed attractive to me had it been to a place in which they
might be found. It was to them that my thoughts agreeably
clung when I supposed myself to be thinking of something
else or of nothing. But when, even without knowing it, I
thought of them, they, more unconsciously still, were for me
the mountainous blue undulations of the sea, the outline of a
procession against the sea. It was the sea that I hoped to find,
if I went to some town where they had gone. The most
exclusive love for a person is always a love for something
else.

Meanwhile my grandmother, because I now showed a keen
interest in golf and tennis and was letting slip an opportunity
of seeing at work and hearing talk an artist whom she knew
to be one of the greatest of his time, evinced for me a contempt
which seemed to me to be based on somewhat narrow views.
I had guessed long ago in the Champs-Elysées, and had verified
since, that when we are in love with a woman we simply
project on to her a state of our own soul; that consequently the
important thing is not the worth of the woman but the pro-

fundity of the state; and that the emotions which a perfectly
ordinary girl arouses in us can enable us to bring to the surface
of our consciousness some of the innermost parts of our being,
more personal, more remote, more quintessential than any
that might be evoked by the pleasure we derive from the conversation of a great man or even from the admiring contemplation of his work.

I finally had to comply with my grandmother's wishes, all
the more reluctantly in that Elstir lived at some distance from
the front in one of the newest of Balbec's avenues. The heat of
the day obliged me to take the tramway which passed along
the Rue de la Plage, and I endeavoured, in order to persuade
myself that I was in the ancient realm of the Cimmerians, in the
country, perhaps, of King Mark, or on the site of the Forest of
Broceliande, not to look at the gimcrack splendour of the
buildings that extended on either hand, among which Elstir's
villa was perhaps the most sumptuously hideous, in spite of
which he had taken it because, of all that there were to be had
at Balbec, it was the only one that provided him with a really
big studio.

It was with averted eyes that I crossed the garden, which
had a lawn (similar, on a smaller scale, to that of any suburban
villa round Paris), a statuette of an amorous gardener, glass
balls in which one saw one's distorted reflexion, beds of
begonias, and a little arbour beneath which rocking chairs were
drawn up round an iron table. But after all these preliminaries
hallmarked with philistine ugliness, I took no notice of the
chocolate mouldings on the plinths once I was in the studio; I
felt perfectly happy, for, with the help of all the sketches and
studies that surrounded me, I foresaw the possibility of raising
myself to a poetical understanding, rich in delights, of manifold
forms which I had not hitherto isolated from the total spectacle
of reality. And Elstir's studio appeared to me like the laboratory
of a sort of new creation of the world in which, from the chaos
that is everything we see, he had extracted, by painting them on
various rectangles of canvas that were placed at all angles,
here a sea-wave angrily crashing its lilac foam on to the sand,
there a young man in white linen leaning on the rail of a ship.
The young man's jacket and the splashing wave had acquired

a new dignity from the fact that they continued to exist, even though they were deprived of those qualities in which they might be supposed to consist, the wave being no longer able to wet or the jacket to clothe anyone.

At the moment at which I entered, the creator was just finishing, with the brush which he had in his hand, the outline of the setting sun.

The blinds were closed almost everywhere round the studio, which was fairly cool and, except in one place where daylight laid against the wall its brilliant but fleeting decoration, dark; one small rectangular window alone was open, embowered in honeysuckle and giving on to an avenue beyond a strip of garden; so that the atmosphere of the greater part of the studio was dusky, transparent and compact in its mass, but liquid and sparkling at the edges where the sunlight encased it, like a lump of rock crystal of which one surface, already cut and polished, gleams here and there like a mirror with iridescent rays. While Elstir, at my request, went on painting, I wandered about in the half-light, stopping to examine first one picture, then another.

Most of those that covered the walls were not what I should chiefly have liked to see of his work, paintings in what an English art journal which lay on the reading-room table in the Grand Hotel called his first and second manners, the mythological manner and the manner in which he showed signs of Japanese influence, both admirably represented, it was said, in the collection of Mme de Guermantes. Naturally enough, what he had in his studio were almost all seascapes done here at Balbec. But I was able to discern from these that the charm of each of them lay in a sort of metamorphosis of the objects represented, analogous to what in poetry we call metaphor, and that, if God the Father had created things by naming them, it was by taking away their names or giving them other names that Elstir created them anew. The names which designate things correspond invariably to an intellectual notion, alien to our true impressions, and compelling us to eliminate from them everything that is not in keeping with that notion.

Sometimes, at my window in the hotel at Balbec, in the morning when Françoise undid the blankets that shut out the light, or in the evening when I was waiting until it was time to go out with Saint-Loup, I had been led by some effect of sunlight to mistake what was only a darker stretch of sea for a distant coastline, or to gaze delightedly at a belt of liquid azure without knowing whether it belonged to sea or sky. But presently my reason would re-establish between the elements the distinction which my first impression had abolished. In the same way from my bedroom in Paris I would sometimes hear a dispute, almost a riot, in the street below, until I had traced back to its cause—a carriage for instance that was rattling towards me—that noise from which I now eliminated the shrill and discordant vociferations which my ear had really heard but which my reason knew that wheels did not produce. But the rare moments in which we see nature as she is, poetically, were those from which Elstir's work was created. One of the metaphors that occurred most frequently in the seascapes which surrounded him here was precisely that which, comparing land with sea, suppressed all demarcation between them. It was this comparison, tacitly and untiringly repeated on a single canvas, which gave it that multiform and powerful unity, the cause (not always clearly perceived by themselves) of the enthusiasm which Elstir's work aroused in certain collectors.

It was, for instance, for a metaphor of this sort—in a picture of the harbour of Carquethuit, a picture which he had finished only a few days earlier and which I stood looking at for a long time—that Elstir had prepared the mind of the spectator by employing, for the little town, only marine terms, and urban terms for the sea. Whether because its houses concealed a part of the harbour, a dry dock, or perhaps the sea itself plunging deep inland, as constantly happened on the Balbec coast, on the other side of the promontory on which the town was built the roofs were overtopped (as they might have been by chimneys or steeples) by masts which had the effect of making the vessels to which they belonged appear town-bred, built on land, an impression reinforced by other boats moored along the jetty but in such serried ranks that you could see men talking across from one deck to another without being able to distinguish the dividing line, the chink of water between them,

so that this fishing fleet seemed less to belong to the water than,
for instance, the churches of Criquebec which, in the distance,
surrounded by water on every side because you saw them without seeing the town, in a powdery haze of sunlight and
crumbling waves, seemed to be emerging from the waters,
blown in alabaster or in sea-foam, and, enclosed in the band of
a variegated rainbow, to form an ethereal, mystical tableau.
On the beach in the foreground the painter had contrived that
the eye should discover no fixed boundary, no absolute line
of demarcation between land and sea. The men who were pushing down their boats into the sea were running as much
through the waves as along the sand, which, being wet,
reflected the hulls as if they were already in the water. The sea
itself did not come up in an even line but followed the irregularities of the shore, which the perspective of the picture
increased still further, so that a ship actually at sea, half-hidden
by the projecting works of the arsenal, seemed to be sailing
through the middle of the town; women gathering shrimps
among the rocks had the appearance, because they were surrounded by water and because of the depression which, beyond
the circular barrier of rocks, brought the beach (on the two
sides nearest the land) down to sea-level, of being in a marine
grotto overhung by ships and waves, open yet protected in
the midst of miraculously parted waters. If the whole picture
gave this impression of harbours in which the sea penetrated
the land, in which the land was already subaqueous and the
population amphibian, the strength of the marine element was
everywhere apparent; and round about the rocks, at the mouth
of the harbour where the sea was rough, one sensed, from the
muscular efforts of the fishermen and the slant of the boats
leaning over at an acute angle, compared with the calm erect-
ness of the warehouse, the church, the houses in the town to
which some of the figures were returning and from which
others were setting out to fish, that they were riding bareback
on the water as though on a swift and fiery animal whose
rearing, but for their skill, must have unseated them. A party
of holiday-makers were putting gaily out to sea in a boat that
tossed like a jaunting-car on a rough road; their boatmen,
blithe but none the less attentive, trimmed the bellying sail,

everyone kept in his place in order not to unbalance and cap-
size the boat, and so they went scudding through sunlit
fields and shady places, rushing down the slopes. It was a fine
morning in spite of the recent storm. Indeed, one could still
feel the powerful impulses that must first be neutralised in order
to attain the easy balance of the boats that lay motionless,
enjoying sunshine and breeze, in parts where the sea was so
calm that the reflections had almost more solidity and reality
than the floating hulls, vaporised by an effect of the sunlight
and made to overlap one another by the perspective. Or rather
one would not have called them other parts of the sea. For
between those parts there was as much difference as there was
between one of them and the church rising from the water, or
the ships behind the town. One's reason then set to work to
make a single element of what was in one place black beneath a
gathering storm, a little further all of one colour with the sky
and as brightly burnished, and elsewhere so bleached by sunshine, haze and foam, so compact, so terrestrial, so circumscribed with houses that one thought of some white stone
causeway or of a field of snow, up the slope of which one was
alarmed to see a ship come climbing high and dry, as a carriage
climbs dripping from a ford, but which a moment later, when
you saw on the raised, uneven surface of the solid plain boats
drunkenly heaving, you understood, identical in all these
different aspects, to be still the sea.

Although it is rightly said that there can be no progress,
no discovery in art, but only in the sciences, and that each
artist starting afresh on an individual effort cannot be either
helped or hindered therein by the efforts of any other, it must
none the less be acknowledged that, in so far as art brings out
certain laws, once an industry has taken those laws and
popularised them, the art that was first in the field loses
retrospectively a little of its originality. Since Elstir began to
paint, we have grown familiar with what are called "wonderful"
photographs of scenery and towns. If we press for a definition
of what their admirers mean by the epithet, we shall find that
it is generally applied to some unusual image of a familiar
object, an image different from those that we are accustomed
to see, unusual and yet true to nature, and for that reason

doubly striking because it surprises us, takes us out of our cocoon of habit, and at the same time brings us back to ourselves by recalling to us an earlier impression. For instance, one of these "magnificent" photographs will illustrate a law of perspective, will show us some cathedral which we are accustomed to see in the middle of a town, taken instead from a selected vantage point from which it will appear to be thirty times the height of the houses and to be thrusting out a spur from the bank of the river, from which it is actually at some distance. Now the effort made by Elstir to reproduce things not as he knew them to be but according to the optical illusions of which our first sight of them is composed, had led him precisely to bring out certain of these laws of perspective, which were thus all the more striking, since art had been the first to disclose them. A river, because of the windings of its course, a bay because of the apparent proximity to one another of the cliffs on either side of it, would seem to have hollowed out in the heart of the plain or of the mountains a lake absolutely landlocked on every side. In a picture of a view from Balbec painted upon a scorching day in summer an inlet of the sea, enclosed between walls of pink granite, appeared not to be the sea, which began further out. The continuity of the ocean was suggested only by the gulls which, wheeling over what seemed to be solid rock, were as a matter of fact sniffing the moist vapour of the shifting tide. Other laws emerged from the same canvas, as, at the foot of immense cliffs, the lilliputian grace of white sails on the blue mirror on whose surface they looked like sleeping butterflies, and certain contrasts between the depth of the shadows and the paleness of the light. This play of light and shade, which photography has also rendered commonplace, had interested Elstir so much that at one time he had delighted in painting what were almost mirages, in which a castle crowned with a tower appeared as a completely circular castle extended by a tower at its summit, and at its foot by an inverted tower, either because the exceptional purity of the atmosphere on a fine day gave the shadow reflected in the water the hardness and brightness of stone, or because the morning mists rendered the stone as vaporous as the shadow. And similarly, beyond the sea, behind a line of woods, another sea began, roseate with the light of the setting sun, which was in fact the sky. The light, fashioning as it were new solids, thrust back the hull of the boat on which it fell behind the other hull that was still in shadow, and arranged as it were the steps of a crystal staircase on what was in reality the flat surface, broken only by the play of light and shade, of the morning sea. A river running beneath the bridges of a town was caught from such an angle that it appeared entirely dislocated, now broadening into a lake, now narrowing into a rivulet, broken elsewhere by the interposition of a hill crowned with trees among which the townsman would repair at evening to sniff the cool air; and even the rhythm of this topsy-turvy town was assured only by the rigid vertical of the steeples which did not rise but rather, in accordance with the plumb-line of the pendulum of gravity beating time as in a triumphal march, seemed to hold suspended beneath them the blurred mass of houses that rose in terraces through the mist along the banks of the crushed, disjointed stream. And (since Elstir's earliest works belonged to the time in which a painter would embellish his landscape by inserting a human figure), on the cliff's edge or among the mountains, the path too, that half-human part of nature, underwent, like river or ocean, the eclipses of perspective. And whether a mountain ridge, or the spray of a waterfall, or the sea prevented the eye from following the continuity of the path, visible to the traveller but not to us, the little human figure in old-fashioned clothes seemed often to be stopped short on the edge of a precipice, the path which he had been following ending there, while, a thousand feet above him in those pine-forests, it was with a fond eye and a relieved heart that we saw reappear the threadlike whiteness of its sandy surface, grateful to the way-farer's feet, though the mountainside had concealed from us its intervening bends as it skirted the waterfall or the gulf.

The effort made by Elstir to strip himself, when face to face with reality, of every intellectual notion, was all the more admirable in that this man who made himself deliberately ignorant before sitting down to paint, forgot everything that he knew in his honesty of purpose (for what one knows does not belong to oneself), had in fact an exceptionally cultivated

mind. When I confessed to him the disappointment I had felt
on seeing the porch at Balbec:

"What!" he exclaimed, "you were disappointed by the
porch! Why, it's the finest illustrated Bible that the people
have ever had. That Virgin and all the bas-reliefs telling the
story of her life—it's the most loving, the most inspired
expression of that endless poem of adoration and praise in
which the Middle Ages extolled the glory of the Madonna. If
you only knew, side by side with the most scrupulous accuracy
in rendering the sacred text, what exquisitely original ideas the
old carver had, what profound thoughts, what delicious poetry!
The idea of that great sheet in which the angels carry the body
of the Virgin, too sacred for them to venture to touch it with
their hands" (I mentioned to him that this theme had been
treated also at Saint-André-des-Champs; he had seen photographs of the porch there, and agreed, but pointed out that the
eagerness of those little peasant figures, all scurrying together
round the Virgin, was not at all the same thing as the gravity
of those two great angels, almost Italian, so slender, so gentle);
"and the angel who carries away the Virgin's soul, to reunite
it with her body; or in the meeting of the Virgin with Elizabeth, Elizabeth's gesture when she touches the Virgin's womb
and marvels to feel that it is big with child; and the bandaged
arm of the midwife who had refused, without touching, to
believe in the Immaculate Conception; and the linen cloth
thrown by the Virgin to St Thomas to give him proof of the
Resurrection; that veil, too, which the Virgin tears from her
own bosom to cover the nakedness of her son, whose blood,
the wine of the Eucharist, the Church collects from one side
of him, while on the other the Synagogue, its kingdom at
an end, has its eyes bandaged, holds a half-broken sceptre and
lets fall, together with the crown that is slipping from its head,
the tables of the old law. And the husband who, on the Day
of Judgment, as he helps his young wife to rise from her grave,
lays her hand against his own heart to reassure her, to prove
to her that it is indeed beating, isn't that also rather a stunning
idea, really inspired? And the angel who is taking away the
sun and the moon which are no longer needed since it is
written that the Light of the Cross will be seven times brighter

than the light of the firmament; and the one who is dipping his hand into Jesus's bath, to see whether the water is warm enough; and the one emerging from the clouds to place the crown on the Virgin's brow; and all the angels leaning from the vault of heaven, between the balusters of the New Jerusalem, and throwing up their arms in horror or joy at the sight of the torments of the wicked or the bliss of the elect! Because it's all the circles of heaven, a whole gigantic poem full of theology and symbolism that you have there. It's fantastic, mad, divine, and a thousand times better than anything you will see in Italy, where for that matter this very tympanum has been carefully copied by sculptors with far less genius. Because, you know, it's all a question of genius. There never was a time when genius was universal, that's all nonsense, it would be more extraordinary than the golden age. The chap who carved that façade, you may take my word for it was every bit as good, had just as profound ideas, as the men you admire most at the present day. I could show you what I meant if we went there together. There are certain passages from the Office of the Assumption which have been conveyed with a subtlety of expression that not even a Redon could equal."

And yet, when my eager eyes had opened before the façade of Balbec church, it was not this vast celestial vision of which he spoke to me that I had seen, not this gigantic theological poem which I understood to have been inscribed there in stone. I spoke to him of those great statues of saints mounted on stilts which formed a sort of avenue on either side.

"It starts from the mists of antiquity to end in Jesus Christ," he explained. "You see on one side his ancestors after the spirit, on the other the Kings of Judah, his ancestors after the flesh. All the ages are there. And if you looked more closely at what you took for stilts you would have been able to give names to the figures standing on them. Under the feet of Moses you would have recognised the golden calf, under Abraham's the ram, and under Joseph's the demon counselling Potiphar's wife."

I told him also that I had gone there expecting to find an almost Persian building, and that this had doubtless been one of the chief factors in my disappointment. "Not at all," he assured me, "it's perfectly true. Some parts of it are quite oriental. One of the capitals reproduces so exactly a Persian subject that you cannot simply explain it by the persistence of oriental traditions. The carver must have copied some casket brought from the East by navigators." And indeed he was later to show me the photograph of a capital on which I saw dragons that were almost Chinese devouring one another, but at Balbec this little piece of sculpture had passed unnoticed by me in the general effect of the building which did not conform to the pattern traced in my mind by the words "an almost Persian church."

The intellectual pleasures which I was enjoying in this studio did not in the least prevent me from being aware, although they enveloped us as it were in spite of ourselves, of the warm glazes, the sparkling penumbra of the room itself and, through the little window framed with honey-suckle, in the rustic avenue, the resilient dryness of the sun-parched earth, veiled only by the diaphanous gauze woven of distance and the shade of the trees. Perhaps the unconscious well-being induced by this summer day came like a tributary to swell the flood of joy that had surged in me at the sight of Elstir's *Carquethuit Harbour*.

I had supposed Elstir to be a modest man, but I realised my mistake on seeing his face cloud with melancholy when, in a little speech of thanks, I uttered the word "fame." Men who believe that their works will last—as was the case with Elstir—form the habit of placing them in a period when they them-selves will have crumbled into dust. And thus, by obliging them to reflect on their own extinction, the idea of fame sad-dens them because it is inseparable from the idea of death. I changed the subject in the hope of dispelling the cloud of ambitious melancholy with which I had unwittingly shadowed Elstir's brow. "Someone advised me once," I said, thinking of the conversation we had had with Legrandin at Combray, as to which I was glad of an opportunity of learning Elstir's views, "not to visit Brittany, because it would not be whole-some for a mind with a natural inclination towards day-dreams." "Not at all," he replied. "When a mind has a tendency towards day-dreams, it's a mistake to shield it from them, to ration them. So long as you divert your mind from its day-dreams, it will not know them for what they are; you will be the victim of all sorts of appearances because you will not have grasped their true nature. If a little day-dreaming is dangerous, the cure for it is not to dream less but to dream more, to dream all the time. One must have a thorough understanding of one's day-dreams if one is not to be troubled by them; there is a way of separating one's dreams from one's life which so often produces good results that I wonder whether one oughtn't to try it just in case, simply as a preventative, as certain surgeons suggest that, to avoid the risk of appendicitis later on, we ought all to have our appendixes taken out when we're children."

Elstir and I had meanwhile been walking towards the end of the studio, and had reached the window that looked across the garden on to a narrow side-street that was almost a country lane. We had gone there to breathe the cooler air of the late afternoon. I supposed myself to be nowhere near the girls of the little band, and it was only by sacrificing for once the hope of seeing them that I had yielded to my grandmother's entreaties and had gone to see Elstir. For we do not know the whereabouts of what we are seeking, and often we avoid for a long time the place to which, for quite different reasons, everyone has been asking us to go; but we never suspect that we shall there see the very person of whom we are thinking. I looked out vaguely over this rustic path which passed quite close to the studio but did not belong to Elstir. Suddenly there appeared on it, coming towards us at a rapid pace, the young cyclist of the little band, with her polo-cap pulled down over her dark hair towards her plump cheeks, her eyes gay and slightly provocative; and on that auspicious path, miraculously filled with the promise of delights, I saw her, beneath the trees, address to Elstir the smiling greeting of a friend, a rainbow that bridged for me the gulf between our terraqueous world and regions which I had hitherto regarded as inaccessible. She even came up to shake hands with the painter, though without stopping, and I saw that she had a tiny beauty spot on her chin. "Do you know that girl, Monsieur?" I asked

Elstir, realising that he might introduce me to her, invite her to his house. And this peaceful studio with its rural horizon was at once filled with a surfeit of delight such as a child might feel in a house where he was already happily playing when he learned that, in addition, out of that bounteousness which enables lovely things and noble hosts to increase their gifts beyond all measure, a sumptuous meal was being prepared for him. Elstir told me that she was called Albertine Simonet, and gave me the names also of her friends, whom I described to him with sufficient accuracy for him to identify them almost without hesitation. I had made a mistake with regard to their social position, but not the mistake that I usually made at Balbec. I was always ready to take the sons of shopkeepers for princes when they appeared on horseback. This time I had placed in a shady milieu the daughters of middle-class people, extremely rich, belonging to the world of trade and industry. It was the class which, at first sight, interested me least, since it held for me none of the mystery either of the people or of a society such as that of the Guermantes. And no doubt if a preliminary glamour which they would never now lose had not been conferred on them, in my dazzled eyes, by the glaring vacuity of seaside life, I should perhaps not have succeeded in resisting and overcoming the idea that they were the daughters of prosperous merchants. I could not help marvelling at what a wonderful workshop the French middle class was for sculpture of the most varied kind. What unexpected types, what richness of invention in the character of the faces, what firmness, what freshness, what simplicity in the features! The shrewd old burghers from whose loins these Dianas and these nymphs had sprung seemed to me to have been the greatest of statuaries. Scarcely had I had time to register the social metamorphosis of the little band—for these discoveries of a mistake, these modifications of the notion one has of a person, have the instantaneousness of a chemical reaction—than the idea had already established itself behind the guttersnipe faces of these girls, whom I had taken for the mistresses of racing cyclists or prize-fighters, that they might easily be connected with the family of some lawyer or other whom we knew. I was barely conscious of who Albertine Simonet was. She had certainly

no conception of what she was one day to mean to me. Even the name, Simonet, which I had already heard spoken on the beach, I should have spelt with a double "n" had I been asked to write it down, never dreaming of the importance which this family attached to there being only one. The further we descend the social scale the more we find that snobbery fastens on to mere trifles which are perhaps no more null than the distinctions observed by the aristocracy, but, being more obscure, more peculiar to each individual, surprise us more. Possibly there had been Simonnets who had done badly in business, or worse still. The fact remains that the Simonets never failed, it appeared, to be annoyed if anyone doubled their "n." They were as proud, perhaps, of being the only Simonets in the world with one "n" instead of two as the Montmorencys of being the premier barons of France. I asked Elstir whether these girls lived at Balbec; yes, he told me, some of them at any rate. The villa in which one of them lived was precisely at the far end of the beach, where the cliffs of Canapville began. Since this girl was a great friend of Albertine Simonet, this was one more reason for me to believe that it was indeed the latter whom I had met that day when I was with my grandmother. There were of course so many of those little streets running down to the beach, and all at the same angle, that I could not have specified exactly which of them it had been. One would like to remember a thing accurately, but at the time one's vision is always clouded. And yet that Albertine and the girl whom I had seen going to her friend's house were one and the same person was a practical certainty. In spite of this, whereas the countless images that have since been presented to me by the dark young golfer, however different they may be, are superimposed one upon the other (because I know that they all belong to her), and by retracing my memories I can, under cover of that identity and as if through an internal passageway, run through all those images in turn without losing my grasp of one and the same person, if, on the other hand, I wish to go back to the girl whom I passed that day when I was with my grandmother, I have to emerge into the open air. I am convinced that it is Albertine whom I find there, the same who used often to come to a halt in the midst of her friends during their walks against the backdrop of the sea; but all those more recent images remain separate from that earlier one because I am unable to confer on her retrospectively an identity which she did not have for me at the moment she caught my eye; whatever assurance I may derive from the law of probabilities, that girl with the plump cheeks who stared at me so boldly from the corner of the little street and from the beach, and by whom I believe that I might have been loved, I have never, in the strict sense of the words, seen again.

Was it my hesitation between the different girls of the little band, all of whom retained something of the collective charm which had disturbed me from the first, that, combined with those other reasons, allowed me later on, even at the time of my greater—my second—love for Albertine, a sort of intermittent and all too brief liberty to abstain from loving her? From having strayed among all her friends before it finally concentrated on her, my love kept for some time between itself and the image of Albertine a certain "play" which enabled it, like ill-adjusted stage lighting, to flit over others before returning to focus upon her; the connexion between the pain which I felt in my heart and the memory of Albertine did not seem to me a necessary one; I might perhaps have been able to co-ordinate it with the image of another person. And this enabled me, in a momentary flash, to banish the reality altogether, not only the external reality, as in my love for Gilberte (which I had recognised to be an inner state wherein I drew from myself alone the particular quality, the special character of the person I loved, everything that rendered her indispensable to my happiness), but even the other reality, internal and purely subjective.

"Not a day passes but one or other of them comes by here, and looks in for a minute or two," Elstir told me, plunging me into despair at the thought that if I had gone to see him at once, when my grandmother had begged me to do so, I should in all probability have made Albertine's acquaintance long since.

She had continued on her way; from the studio she was no longer in sight. I supposed that she had gone to join her friends on the front. If I could have been there with Elstir, I should have got to know them. I thought up endless pretexts to induce him to take a stroll with me on the beach. I no longer had the same feeling of serenity as before the apparition of the girl in the frame of the little window, so charming until then in its fringe of honeysuckle and now so drearily empty. Elstir caused me a joy that was mixed with torture when he agreed to walk a few steps with me but said that he must first finish the piece of work on which he was engaged. It was a study of some flowers, but not those of which I would rather have commissioned a portrait from him than one of a person, so that I might learn from the revelation of his genius what I had so often sought in vain from the flowers themselves—hawthorn white and pink, cornflowers, apple-blossom. Elstir as he worked talked botany to me, but I scarcely listened; he was no longer sufficient in himself, he was now only the necessary intermediary between these girls and me; the prestige which, only a few moments ago, his talent had still given him in my eyes was now worthless save in so far as it might confer a little on me also in the eyes of the little band to whom I should be introduced by him.

I paced up and down the room, impatient for him to finish what he was doing; I picked up and examined various sketches, quantities of which were stacked against the walls. It was thus that I happened to bring to light a water-colour which evidently belonged to a much earlier period in Elstir's life, and gave me that particular kind of enchantment which is diffused by works of art not only delightfully executed but representing a subject so singular and so seductive that it is to it that we attribute a great deal of their charm, as if that charm were something that the painter had merely to discover and observe, realised already in a material form by nature, and to reproduce. The fact that such objects can exist, beautiful quite apart from the painter's interpretation of them, satisfies a sort of innate materialism in us, against which our reason contends, and acts as a counterpoise to the abstractions of aesthetic theory. It was—this water-colour—the portrait of a young woman, by no means beautiful but of a curious type, in a close-fitting hat not unlike a bowler, trimmed with a ribbon of cerise silk; in one of her mittened hands was a lighted cigarette, while the other held at knee-level a sort of broad-brimmed garden hat, no more than a screen of plaited straw to keep off the sun. On a table by her side, a tall vase filled with pink carnations. Often (and it was the case here) the singularity of such works is due principally to their having been executed in special conditions, so that it is not immediately clear to us whether, for instance, the strange attire of a female model is her costume for a fancy-dress ball, or whether, conversely, the scarlet cloak which an elderly man looks as though he had put on in response to some whim of the painter's is his professor's or alderman's gown or his cardinal's cape. The ambiguous character of the person whose portrait now confronted me arose, without my understanding it, from the fact that it was a young actress of an earlier generation half dressed up as a man. But the bowler beneath which the hair was fluffy but short, the velvet jacket, without lapels, opening over a white shirt-front, made me hesitate as to the period of the clothes and the sex of the model, so that I did not know exactly what I had before my eyes, except that it was a most luminous piece of painting. And the pleasure which it afforded me was troubled only by the fear that Elstir, by delaying further, would make me miss the girls, for the declining sun now hung low in the little window. Nothing in this water-colour was merely set down there as a fact and painted because of its practical relevance to the scene, the costume because the young woman must be wearing something, the vase to hold the flowers. The glass of the vase, cherished for its own sake, seemed to be holding the water in which the stems of the carnations were dipped in something as limpid, almost as liquid as itself; the woman's clothes enveloped her in a material that had an independent, fraternal charm, and, if the products of industry can compete in charm with the wonders of nature, as delicate, as pleasing to the touch of the eye, as freshly painted as the fur of a cat, the petals of a flower, the feathers of a dove. The whiteness of the shirt-front, as fine as soft hail, with its gay pleats gathered into little bells like lilies of the valley, was spangled with bright gleams of light from the room, themselves sharply etched and subtly shaded as if they were flowers stitched into the linen. And the velvet of the jacket, with its brilliant sheen, had something rough, frayed and shaggy about it here and there that recalled the crumpled brightness of the carnations in the vase. But above all one felt that Elstir, heedless of any impression of immorality that might be given by this transvestite costume worn by a young actress for whom the talent she would bring to the role was doubtless of less importance than the titillation she would offer to the jaded or depraved senses of some of her audience, had on the contrary fastened upon this equivocal aspect as on an aesthetic element which deserved to be brought into prominence, and which he had done everything in his power to emphasise. Along the lines of the face, the latent sex seemed to be on the point of confessing itself to be that of a somewhat boyish girl, then vanished, and reappeared further on with a suggestion rather of an effeminate, vicious and pensive youth, then fled once more and remained elusive. The dreamy sadness in the expression of the eyes, by its very contrast with the accessories belonging to the world of debauchery and the stage, was not the least disturbing element in the picture. One imagined moreover that it must be feigned, and that the young person who seemed ready to submit to caresses in this provoking costume had probably thought it intriguing to enhance the provocation with this romantic expression of a secret longing, an unspoken grief. At the foot of the picture was inscribed: "*Miss Sacripant*, October, 1872." I could not contain my admiration. "Oh, it's nothing, only a rough sketch I did when I was young; it was a costume for a variety-show. It's all ages ago now." "And what has become of the model?" A bewilderment provoked by my words preceded on Elstir's face the indifferent, absent-minded air which, a moment later, he displayed there. "Quick, give it to me!" he said, "I hear Madame Elstir coming, and though, I assure you, the young person in the bowler hat never played any part in my life, still there's no point in my wife's coming in and finding the picture staring her in the face. I've kept it only as an amusing sidelight on the theatre of those days." And, before putting it away behind the pile, Elstir, who perhaps had not set eyes on the sketch for years, gave it a careful scrutiny. "I must keep just the head," he murmured, "the lower part is really too shockingly bad, the

hands are a beginner's work." I was miserable at the arrival of
Mme Elstir, who could only delay us still further. The window-
sill was already aglow. Our excursion would be a pure waste of
time. There was no longer the slightest chance of our seeing
the girls, and consequently it mattered now not at all how
quickly Mme Elstir left us. In fact she did not stay very long.
I found her most tedious; she might have been beautiful at
twenty, driving an ox in the Roman Campagna, but her dark
hair was streaked with grey and she was common without
being simple, because she believed that a pompous manner and
a majestic pose were required by her statuesque beauty, which,
however, advancing age had robbed of all its charm. She was
dressed with the utmost simplicity. And it was touching but
at the same time surprising to hear Elstir exclaim, whenever he
opened his mouth, and with a respectful gentleness, as if
merely uttering the words moved him to tenderness and
veneration: "My beautiful Gabrielle!" Later on, when I had
become familiar with Elstir's mythological paintings, Mme
Elstir acquired beauty in my eyes also. I understood then that to
a certain ideal type illustrated by certain lines, certain arabesques
which reappeared incessantly throughout his work, to a
certain canon of art, he had attributed a character that was
almost divine, since he had dedicated all his time, all the mental
effort of which he was capable, in a word his whole life,
to the task of distinguishing those lines as clearly and of reproducing them as faithfully as possible. What such an ideal
inspired in Elstir was indeed a cult so solemn, so exacting,
that it never allowed him to be satisfied with what he had
achieved; it was the most intimate part of himself; and so
he had never been able to look at it with detachment, to extract
emotion from it, until the day on which he encountered it,
realised outside himself, in the body of a woman, the body of
the woman who had in due course become Mme Elstir and in
whom he had been able (as is possible only with something
that is not oneself) to find it meritorious, moving, divine.
How restful, moreover, to be able to place his lips upon that
ideal Beauty which hitherto he had been obliged so laboriously
to extract from within himself, and which now, mysteriously
incarnate, offered itself to him in a series of communions,

filled with saving grace. Elstir at this period was no longer at
that youthful age in which we look only to the power of the
mind for the realisation of our ideal. He was nearing the age at
which we count on bodily satisfactions to stimulate the force of
the brain, at which mental fatigue, by inclining us towards
materialism, and the diminution of our energy, towards the
possibility of influences passively received, begin to make us
admit that there may indeed be certain bodies, certain callings,
certain rhythms that are specially privileged, realising so
naturally our ideal that even without genius, merely by copying
the movement of a shoulder, the tension of a neck, we can
achieve a masterpiece; it is the age at which we like to caress
Beauty with our eyes objectively, outside ourselves, to have it
near us, in a tapestry, in a beautiful sketch by Titian picked up
in a second-hand shop, in a mistress as lovely as Titian's
sketch. When I understood this I could no longer look at
Mme Elstir without a feeling of pleasure, and her body began
to lose its heaviness, for I filled it with an idea, the idea that
she was an immaterial creature, a portrait by Elstir. She was
one for me, and doubtless for him too. The particulars of life
do not matter to the artist; they merely provide him with the
opportunity to lay bare his genius. One feels unmistakably,
when one sees side by side ten portraits of different people
painted by Elstir, that they are all, first and foremost, Elstirs.
Only, after that rising tide of genius which sweeps over and
submerges an artist's life, when the brain begins to tire, gradually the balance is disturbed and, like a river that resumes its
course after the counterflow of a spring tide, it is life that once
more takes the upper hand. But, while the first period lasted,
the artist has gradually evolved the law, the formula of his
unconscious gift. He knows what situations, if he is a novelist,
what scenes, if he is a painter, provide him with the material,
unimportant in itself but essential to his researches, as a
laboratory might be or a workshop. He knows that he has
created his masterpieces out of effects of attenuated light, out of
the action of remorse upon consciousness of guilt, out of
women posed beneath trees or half-immersed in water, like
statues. A day will come when, owing to the erosion of his
brain, he will no longer have the strength, faced with those

materials which his genius was wont to use, to make the intellectual effort which alone can produce his work, and yet will
continue to seek them out, happy to be near them because of
the spiritual pleasure, the allurement to work, that they arouse
in him; and, surrounding them besides with an aura of superstition as if they were superior to all things else, as if there
dwelt in them already a great part of the work of art which they
might be said to carry within them ready-made, he will confine
himself to the company, to the adoration of his models. He
will hold endless conversations with the repentant criminals
whose remorse and regeneration once formed the subject of
his novels; he will buy a house in a countryside where mists
attenuate the light, he will spend long hours looking at women
bathing; he will collect sumptuous stuffs. And thus the beauty
of life, an expression somehow devoid of meaning, a stage this
side of art at which I had seen Swann come to rest, was that
also which, by a slackening of creative ardour, idolatry of the
forms which had inspired it, a tendency to take the line of least
resistance, must gradually undermine an Elstir's progress.

At last he had applied the final brush-stroke to his flowers.
I sacrificed a minute to look at them. There was no merit in
my doing so, for I knew that there was no chance now of our
finding the girls on the beach; and yet, had I believed them to
be still there, and that these wasted moments would make me
miss them, I should have stopped to look none the less, for I
should have told myself that Elstir was more interested in his
flowers than in my meeting with the girls. My grandmother's
nature, a nature that was the exact opposite of my complete
egoism, was nevertheless reflected in certain aspects of my own.
In circumstances in which someone to whom I was indifferent,
for whom I had always feigned affection or respect, ran the
risk merely of some unpleasantness whereas I was in real
danger, I could not have done otherwise than commiserate
with him on his vexation as though it had been something
important, and treat my own danger as nothing, because I
would feel that these were the proportions in which he must
see things. To be quite accurate, I would go even further and
not only not complain of the danger in which I myself stood
but go half-way to meet it, and with respect to one that

threatened other people, try, on the contrary, at the risk of being endangered myself, to avert it from them. The reasons for this are several, none of them to my credit. One is that if, as long as I was simply applying my reason to the matter, I felt that I cherished life above all else, whenever in the course of my existence I have found myself obsessed by mental worry or merely by nervous anxieties, sometimes so puerile that I would not dare to reveal them, if an unforeseen circumstance then arose, involving for me the risk of being killed, this new preoccupation was so trivial in comparison with the others that I welcomed it with a sense of relief, almost of joy. Thus I find that I have experienced, although the least courageous of men, a feeling which has always seemed to me, in my reasoning moods, so foreign to my nature, so inconceivable: the intoxication of danger. But even if, when a danger arose, however mortal, I were going through an entirely calm and happy phase, I could not, were I with another person, refrain from sheltering him behind me and choosing for myself the post of danger. When a sufficient number of experiences had taught me that I invariably acted and enjoyed acting thus, I discovered —and was deeply ashamed by the discovery—that it was because, contrary to what I had always believed and asserted, I was extremely sensitive to the opinion of others. Not that this kind of unconfessed self-esteem has anything to do with vanity or conceit. For what might satisfy one or other of those failings would give me no pleasure, and I have always refrained from indulging them. But with the people in whose company I have succeeded in concealing most effectively the minor assets a knowledge of which might have given them a less paltry idea of me, I have never been able to deny myself the pleasure of showing them that I take more trouble to avert the risk of death from their path than from my own. As my motive is then self-esteem and not virtue, I find it quite natural that in any crisis they should act differently. I am far from blaming them for it, as I should perhaps do if I had been moved by a sense of duty, a duty which would seem to me in that case to be as incumbent upon them as upon myself. On the contrary, I feel that it is eminently sensible of them to safeguard their lives, while at the same time being unable to prevent myself from pushing my own safety into the background, which is particularly absurd and culpable of me since I have come to realise that the lives of many of the people in front of whom I plant myself when a bomb bursts are more valueless even than my own.

However, on the day of this first visit to Elstir, the time was still distant at which I was to become conscious of this difference in value, and there was no question of danger, but simply—a premonitory sign of that pernicious self-esteem— the question of my not appearing to attach to the pleasure which I so ardently desired more importance than to the work which the painter had still to finish. It was finished at last. And, once we were out of doors, I discovered that—so long were the days still at this season—it was not so late as I had supposed. We strolled down to the front. What stratagems I employed to keep Elstir standing at the spot where I thought that the girls might still come past! Pointing to the cliffs that towered beside us, I kept on asking him to tell me about them, so as to make him forget the time and stay there a little longer. I felt that we had a better chance of waylaying the little band if we moved towards the end of the beach.

"I should like to look at those cliffs with you from a little nearer," I said to him, having noticed that one of the girls was in the habit of going in that direction. "And as we go, do tell me about Carquethuit. I should so like to see Carquethuit," I went on, without thinking that the novel character which manifested itself with such force in Elstir's *Carquethuit Harbour* might belong perhaps rather to the painter's vision than to any special quality in the place itself. "Since I've seen your picture, I think that is where I should most like to go, there and to the Pointe du Raz, but of course that would be quite a journey from here."

"Yes, and besides, even if it weren't nearer, I should advise you perhaps all the same to visit Carquethuit," he replied. "The Pointe du Raz is magnificent, but after all it's simply another of those high cliffs of Normandy or Brittany which you know already. Carquethuit is quite different, with those rocks on a low shore. I know nothing in France like it, it reminds me rather of certain aspects of Florida. It's very curious, and

moreover extremely wild. It's between Clitourps and Ne-
homme; you know how desolate those parts are; the sweep of
the coast-line is exquisite. Here, the coast-line is pretty ordinary,
but along there I can't tell you what grace it has, what
softness."

Dusk was falling; it was time to be turning homewards. I
was accompanying Elstir back to his villa when suddenly, as it
were Mephistopheles springing up before Faust, there appeared
at the end of the avenue—like a simple objectification, unreal
and diabolical, of the temperament diametrically opposed to
my own, of the semi-barbarous and cruel vitality of which I,
in my weakness, my excess of tortured sensibility and intellectuality, was so destitute—a few spots of the essence impossible to mistake for anything else, a few spores of the zoophytic
band of girls, who looked as though they had not seen me but
were unquestionably engaged in passing a sarcastic judgment
on me. Feeling that a meeting between them and us was now
inevitable, and that Elstir would be certain to call me, I turned
my back like a bather preparing to meet the shock of a wave;
I stopped dead and, leaving my illustrious companion to pursue his way, remained where I was, stooping, as if I had
suddenly become engrossed in it, towards the window of the
antique shop which we happened to be passing at that moment.
I was not sorry to give the appearance of being able to think
of something other than these girls, and I was already dimly
aware that when Elstir did call me up to introduce me to them
I should wear that sort of inquiring expression which betrays
not surprise but the wish to look surprised—such bad actors
are we all, or such good mind-readers our fellow-men—,
that I should even go so far as to point a finger to my breast,
as who should ask "Are you calling me?" and then run to join
him, my head lowered in compliance and docility and my face
coldly masking my annoyance at being torn from the study of
old pottery in order to be introduced to people whom I had
no wish to know. Meanwhile I contemplated the window and
waited for the moment when my name, shouted by Elstir,
would come to strike me like an expected and innocuous
bullet. The certainty of being introduced to these girls had had
the effect of making me not only feign indifference to them,

but actually feel it. Henceforth inevitable, the pleasure of knowing them began at once to contract, to shrink, appeared smaller to me than the pleasure of talking to Saint-Loup, of dining with my grandmother, of making excursions in the vicinity which I would regret being probably forced to abandon in consequence of my relations with people who could scarcely be much interested in old buildings. Moreover, what diminished the pleasure which I was about to feel was not merely the imminence but the incoherence of its realisation. Laws as precise as those of hydrostatics maintain the relative position of the images which we form in a fixed order, which the proximity of the event at once upsets. Elstir was about to call me. This was not at all the way in which I had so often, on the beach, in my bedroom, imagined myself making the acquaintance of these girls. What was about to happen was a different event, for which I was not prepared. I recognised in it neither my desire nor its object; I regretted almost that I had come out with Elstir. But, above all, the shrinking of the pleasure that I had previously expected to feel was due to the certainty that nothing now could take it from me. And it recovered, as though by some latent elasticity in itself, its full extent when it ceased to be subjected to the pressure of that certainty, at the moment when, having decided to turn my head, I saw Elstir, standing a few feet away with the girls, bidding them good-bye. The face of the girl who stood nearest to him, round and plump and glittering with the light in her eyes, reminded me of a cake on the top of which a place has been kept for a morsel of blue sky. Her eyes, even when fixed on an object, gave the impression of mobility, as on days of high wind the air, though invisible, lets us perceive the speed with which it is coursing between us and the sky. For a moment her eyes met mine, like those travelling skies on stormy days which approach a slower cloud, touch it, overtake it, pass it. But they do not know one another, and are soon driven far apart. So, now, our looks were for a moment confronted, each ignorant of what the celestial continent that lay before it held by way of promises or threats for the future. Only at the moment when her gaze was directly coincident with mine, without slackening its pace it clouded over slightly.

So on a clear night the wind-swept moon passes behind a cloud and veils its brightness for a moment, but soon reappears. But already Elstir had left the girls without having summoned me. They disappeared down a side-street; he came towards me. My whole plan was wrecked.

I have said that Albertine had not seemed to me that day to be the same as on previous days, and that each time I saw her she was to appear different. But I felt at that moment that certain modifications in the appearance, the importance, the stature of a person may also be due to the variability of certain states of consciousness interposed between that person and ourselves. One of those that play the most considerable part in this respect is belief (that evening my belief, then the vanishing of my belief, that I was about to know Albertine had, with a few seconds' interval only, rendered her almost insignificant, then infinitely precious, in my eyes; some years later, the belief, then the disappearance of the belief, that Albertine was faithful to me, brought about similar changes).

Of course, long ago at Combray, I had seen how, according to the time of day, according to whether I was entering one or the other of the two dominant moods that governed my sensibility in turn, my grief at not being with my mother would lessen or grow, as imperceptible all afternoon as is the moon's light when the sun is shining, and then, when night had come, reigning alone in my anxious heart in place of recent memories now obliterated. But on that day at Balbec, when I saw that Elstir was leaving the girls without having called me, I learned for the first time that the variations in the importance which a pleasure or a sorrow has in our eyes may depend not merely on this alternation of two moods, but on the displacement of invisible beliefs, such, for example, as make death seem to us of no account because they bathe it in a glow of unreality, and thus enable us to attach importance to our attending a musical evening which would lose much of its charm if, on the announcement that we were sentenced to be guillotined, the belief that had bathed the evening in its warm glow suddenly evaporated. It is true that something in me was aware of this role that beliefs play: namely, my will; but its knowledge is vain if one's intelligence and one's sensibility continue in ignorance; these last are sincere when they believe that we are anxious to forsake a mistress to whom our will alone knows that we are still attached. This is because they are clouded by the belief that we shall see her again at any moment. But let this belief be shattered, let them suddenly become aware that this mistress has gone from us for ever, and our intelligence and sensibility, having lost their focus, run mad, the most infinitesimal pleasure becomes infinitely great.

Variation of a belief, annulment also of love, which, preexistent and mobile, comes to rest on the image of a woman simply because that woman will be almost impossible of attainment. Thenceforward we think not so much of the woman, whom we have difficulty in picturing to ourselves, as of the means of getting to know her. A whole series of agonies develops and is sufficient to fix our love definitely upon her who is its almost unknown object. Our love becomes immense, and we never dream how small a place in it the real woman occupies. And if suddenly, as at the moment when I had seen Elstir stop to talk to the girls, we cease to be uneasy, to suffer anguish, since it is this anguish that is the whole of our love, it seems to us as though our love had abruptly vanished at the moment when at length we grasp the prey to whose value we had not given enough thought before. What did I know of Albertine? One or two glimpses of a profile against the sea, less beautiful, assuredly, than those of Veronese's women whom I ought, had I been guided by purely aesthetic reasons, to have preferred to her. By what other reasons could I be guided, since, my anxiety having subsided, I could recapture only those mute profiles, possessing nothing else? Since my first sight of Albertine I had thought about her endlessly, I had carried on with what I called by her name an interminable inner dialogue in which I made her question and answer, think and act, and in the infinite series of imaginary Albertines who followed one after the other in my fancy hour by hour, the real Albertine, glimpsed on the beach, figured only at the head, just as the actress who "creates" a role, the star, appears, out of a long series of performances, in the few first alone. That Albertine was scarcely more than a silhouette, all that had been superimposed upon her being of my own invention, to such an extent when we love does the contribution that we ourselves make outweigh—even in terms of quantity alone—those that come to us from the beloved object. And this is true of loves that have been realized in actuality. There are loves that can not only develop but survive on very little—and this even among those that have achieved their carnal fulfilment. An old drawing-master who had taught my grandmother had been presented by some obscure mistress with a daughter. The mother died shortly after the birth of the child, and the drawing-master was so broken-hearted that he did not long survive her. In the last months of his life my grandmother and some of the Combray ladies, who had never liked to make any allusion in his presence to the woman with whom in any case he had not officially "lived" and had had comparatively sparse relations, took it into their heads to ensure the little girl's future by clubbing together to provide her with an annuity. It was my grandmother who suggested this; several of her friends jibbed; after all, was the child really such a very interesting case? Was she even the child of her reputed father? With women like that, one could never be sure. Finally, everything was settled. The child came to thank the ladies. She was plain, and so absurdly like the old drawing-master as to remove every shadow of doubt. Since her hair was the only nice thing about her, one of the ladies said to her father, who had brought her: "What pretty hair she has." And thinking that now, the guilty woman being dead and the old man only half alive, a discreet allusion to that past of which they had always pretended to know nothing could do no harm, my grandmother added: "It must run in the family. Did her mother have pretty hair like that?" "I don't know," was the old man's quaint answer, "I never saw her except with a hat on."

Before rejoining Elstir, I caught sight of myself in a glass. To add to the disaster of my not having been introduced to the girls, I noticed that my tie was all crooked, and my hat left long wisps of hair showing, which did not become me; but it was a piece of luck, all the same, that they should have seen me, even thus attired, in Elstir's company, and so could not forget me; also that I should have put on that morning, at my grandmother's suggestion, my smart waistcoat, when I might so easily have been wearing one that was simply hideous, and that I was carrying my best stick. For while an event for which we are longing never happens quite in the way we have been expecting, failing the advantages on which we supposed that we might count, others present themselves for which we never hoped, and make up for our disappointment; and we have been so dreading the worst that in the end we are inclined to feel that, taking one thing with another, chance has, on the whole, been rather kind to us.

"I did so much want to know them," I said as I rejoined Elstir. "Then why did you stand a mile away?" These were his actual words, uttered not because they expressed what was really in his mind, since, if his desire had been to gratify mine, he could quite easily have called me, but perhaps because he had heard phrases of this sort, in familiar use among vulgar people when they are caught in the wrong, and because even great men are in certain respects much the same as vulgar people, and take their everyday excuses from the same common stock just as they get their daily bread from the same baker; or it may be that such remarks (which ought, one might almost say, to be read backwards, since their literal meaning is the opposite of the truth) are the instantaneous effect, the negative exposure of a reflex action. "They were in a hurry." It struck me that of course they must have stopped him from summoning a person who did not greatly attract them; otherwise he would not have failed to do so, after all the questions that I had put to him about them, and the interest which he must have seen that I took in them.

"We were speaking just now of Carquethuit," he said to me as we walked towards his villa. "I've done a little sketch in which you can see the curve of the beach much better. The painting is not too bad, but it's different. If you will allow me, as a souvenir of our friendship, I'd like to give you the sketch," he went on, for the people who refuse us the objects of our desire are always ready to offer us something else.

"I should very much like, if you have such a thing, a photograph of the little portrait of Miss Sacripant. By the way, that's not a real name, surely?"

"It's the name of a character the sitter played in a stupid little musical comedy."

"But, I assure you, Monsieur, that I've never set eyes on her; you look as though you thought that I knew her."

Elstir was silent. "It couldn't be Mme Swann before she was married?" I hazarded, in one of those sudden fortuitous stumblings upon the truth, which are rare enough in all conscience, and yet suffice, after the event, to give a certain cumulative support to the theory of presentiments, provided that one takes care to forget all the wrong guesses that would invalidate it.

Elstir did not reply. The portrait was indeed that of Odette de Crécy. She had preferred not to keep it for many reasons, some of them only too obvious. But there were others less apparent. The portrait dated from before the point at which Odette, disciplining her features, had made of her face and figure that creation the broad outlines of which her hairdressers, her dressmakers, she herself—in her way of holding herself, of speaking, of smiling, of moving her hands and eyes, of thinking—were to respect throughout the years to come. It required the vitiated taste of a surfeited lover to make Swann prefer to all the countless photographs of the "definitive" Odette who was his charming wife the little photograph which he kept in his room and in which, beneath a straw hat trimmed with pansies, one saw a thin young woman, fairly plain, with bunched out hair and drawn features.

But in any case, even if the portrait had been, not anterior, like Swann's favourite photograph, to the systematisation of Odette's features into a new type, majestic and charming, but subsequent to it, Elstir's vision would have sufficed to discompose that type. Artistic genius acts in a similar way to those extremely high temperatures which have the power to split up combinations of atoms which they proceed to combine afresh in a diametrically opposite order, corresponding to another type. All that artificial harmony which a woman has succeeded in imposing upon her features, the maintenance of which she oversees in her mirror every day before going out, relying on the angle of her hat, the smoothness of her hair, the vivacity of her expression, to ensure its continuity, that harmony the keen eye of the great painter instantly destroys, substituting for it a rearrangement of the woman's features such as will satisfy a certain pictorial ideal of femininity which he carries in his head. Similarly it often happens that, after a certain age, the eye of a great scientist will find everywhere the elements necessary to establish those relations which alone are of interest to him. Like those craftsmen, those players who, instead of making a fuss and asking for what they cannot have, content themselves with whatever comes to hand, the artist might say of anything, no matter what, that it will serve his purpose. Thus a cousin of the Princesse de Luxembourg, a beauty of the most queenly type, having taken a fancy to a form of art which was new at that time, had asked the leading painter of the naturalist school to do her portrait. At once the artist's eye found what he had been seeking everywhere. And on his canvas there appeared, in place of the proud lady, a street-girl, and behind her a vast, sloping, purple background which reminded one of the Place Pigalle. But even without going so far as that, not only will the portrait of a woman by a great artist not seek in the least to give satisfaction to various demands on the woman's part—such as, for instance, when she begins to age, make her have herself photographed in dresses that are almost those of a little girl which bring out her still youthful figure and make her appear like the sister or even the daughter of her own daughter, who, if need be, is tricked out for the occasion as a "perfect fright" beside her. It will, on the contrary, emphasise those very blemishes which she seeks to hide, and which (as for instance a sickly, almost greenish complexion) are all the more tempting to him since they show "character," though they are enough to destroy the illusions of the ordinary beholder who sees crumble into dust the ideal of which the woman so proudly sustained the figment, and which set her, in her unique, irreducible form, so far outside, so far above the rest of humanity. Fallen now, situated outside her own type in which she sat unassailably enthroned, she is now just an ordinary woman, in the legend of whose superiority we have lost all faith. We are so accustomed to incorporating in this type not only the beauty of an Odette but her personality, her

identity, that standing before the portrait which has thus
stripped her of it we are inclined to protest not simply "How
plain he has made her!" but "Why, it isn't the least bit like
her!" We find it hard to believe that it can be she. We do not
recognise her. And yet there is a person there on the canvas
whom we are quite conscious of having seen before. But that
person is not Odette; the face of the person, her body, her
general appearance seem familiar. They recall to us not this
particular woman who never held herself like that, whose
natural pose never formed any such strange and teasing
arabesque, but other women, all the women whom Elstir has
ever painted, women whom invariably, however they may
differ from one another, he has chosen to plant thus, in full face,
with an arched foot thrust out from under the skirt, a large
round hat in one hand, symmetrically corresponding, at the
level of the knee which it covers, to that other disc, higher up
in the picture, the face. And furthermore, not only does a
portrait by the hand of genius dislocate a woman's type, as it
has been defined by her coquetry and her selfish conception of
beauty, but if it is also old, it is not content with ageing the
original in the same way as a photograph ages its sitter, by
showing her dressed in the fashions of long ago. In a portrait,
it is not only the manner the woman then had of dressing that
dates her, it is also the manner the artist had of painting. And
this, Elstir's earliest manner, was the most devastating of
birth certificates for Odette because it not only established her,
as did her photographs of the same period, as the younger
sister of various well-known courtesans, but made her portrait
contemporary with the countless portraits that Manet or
Whistler had painted of all those vanished models, models
who already belonged to oblivion or to history.

It was along this train of thought, silently ruminated over
by Elstir's side as I accompanied him to his door, that I was
being led by the discovery that I had just made of the identity
of his model, when this first discovery caused me to make a
second, more disturbing still, concerning the identity of the
artist. He had painted the portrait of Odette de Crécy. Could
it possibly be that this man of genius, this sage, this recluse,
this philosopher with his marvellous flow of conversation,

who towered over everyone and everything, was the ridiculous, depraved painter who had at one time been adopted by the Verdurins? I asked him if he had known them, and whether by any chance it was he that they used to call M. Biche. He answered me in the affirmative, with no trace of embarrass-ment, as if my question referred to a period in his life that was already somewhat remote and he had no suspicion of the extraordinary disillusionment he was causing me. But, looking up, he read it on my face. His own assumed an expression of annoyance. And, as we were now almost at the gate of his house, a man of less distinction of heart and mind might simply have said good-bye to me a trifle dryly and taken care to avoid seeing me again. This however was not Elstir's way with me; like the master that he was—and it was, perhaps, from the point of view of pure creativity, his one fault that he was a master in that sense of the word, for an artist, if he is to be absolutely true to the life of the spirit, must be alone, and not squander his ego, even upon disciples—from every circum-stance, whether involving himself or other people, he sought to extract, for the better edification of the young, the element of truth that it contained. He chose therefore, instead of the words that might have avenged the injury to his pride, those that could prove instructive to me. "There is no man," he began, "however wise, who has not at some period of his youth said things, or lived a life, the memory of which is so unpleasant to him that he would gladly expunge it. And yet he ought not entirely to regret it, because he cannot be certain that he has indeed become a wise man—so far as it is possible for any of us to be wise—unless he has passed through all the fatuous or unwholesome incarnations by which that ultimate stage must be preceded. I know that there are young people, the sons and grandsons of distinguished men, whose masters have instilled into them nobility of mind and moral refinement from their schooldays. They may perhaps have nothing to retract from their past lives; they could publish a signed account of every-thing they have ever said or done; but they are poor creatures, feeble descendants of doctrinaires, and their wisdom is nega-tive and sterile. We do not receive wisdom, we must discover it for ourselves, after a journey through the wilderness which

no one else can make for us, which no one can spare us, for our
wisdom is the point of view from which we come at last to
regard the world. The lives that you admire, the attitudes that
seem noble to you, have not been shaped by a paterfamilias or
a schoolmaster, they have sprung from very different begin-
nings, having been influenced by everything evil or commonplace that prevailed round about them. They represent a
struggle and a victory. I can see that the picture of what we
were at an earlier stage may not be recognisable and cannot,
certainly, be pleasing to contemplate in later life. But we must
not repudiate it, for it is a proof that we have really lived, that
it is in accordance with the laws of life and of the mind that
we have, from the common elements of life, of the life of
studios, of artistic groups—assuming one is a painter—
extracted something that transcends them."

Meanwhile we had reached his door. I was disappointed at
not having met the girls. But after all there was now the
possibility of meeting them again later on; they had ceased
merely to be silhouetted against a horizon where I had been
ready to suppose that I should never see them reappear. Around
them no longer swirled that sort of great eddy which had separated me from them, which had been merely the expression of
the perpetually active desire, mobile, urgent, fed ever on fresh
anxieties, which was aroused in me by their inaccessibility,
their flight from me, possibly for ever. I could now set my
desire for them at rest, hold it in reserve, among all those
other desires the realisation of which, as soon as I knew it to
be possible, I would cheerfully postpone. I took leave of
Elstir; I was alone once again. Then all of a sudden, despite
my recent disappointment, I saw in my mind's eye all that chain
of coincidences which I had not supposed could possibly come
about: that Elstir should be a friend of those very girls, that
they, who only that morning had been to me merely figures in
a picture with the sea for background, had seen me, had seen
me walking in friendly intimacy with a great painter, who was
now informed of my secret longing and would no doubt do
what he could to assuage it. All this had been a source of
pleasure to me, but that pleasure had remained hidden; it
was like one of those visitors who wait before letting us know

that they are in the room until everyone else has gone and we are by ourselves. Then only do we catch sight of them, and can say to them, "I am at your service," and listen to what they have to tell us. Sometimes between the moment at which these pleasures have entered our consciousness and the moment at which we are free to entertain them, so many hours have passed, we have in the meantime seen so many people, that we are afraid lest they should have grown tired of waiting. But they are patient, they do not grow tired, and as soon as the crowd has gone we find them there ready for us. Sometimes, then, it is we ourselves who are so exhausted that it seems as though our weary mind will no longer have the strength to seize and retain those memories, those impressions for which our frail self is the one habitable place, the sole means of realisation. And we should regret that failure, for existence is of little interest save on days when the dust of realities is mingled with magic sand, when some trivial incident becomes a springboard for romance. Then a whole promontory of the inaccessible world emerges from the twilight of dream and enters our life, our life in which, like the sleeper awakened, we actually see the people of whom we had dreamed with such ardent longing that we had come to believe that we should never see them save in our dreams.

The assuagement brought about by the probability of my now being able to meet the little band whenever I chose was all the more precious to me because I should not have been able to keep watch for them during the next few days, which were taken up with preparations for Saint-Loup's departure. My grandmother was anxious to offer my friend some token of her gratitude for all the kindnesses that he had shown to her and myself. I told her that he was a great admirer of Proudhon, and this put it into her head to send for a collection of autograph letters by that philosopher which she had once bought. Saint-Loup came to the hotel to look at them on the day of their arrival, which was also his last day at Balbec. He read them eagerly, fingering each page with reverence, trying to get the sentences by heart; and then, rising from the table, was beginning to apologise to my grandmother for having stayed so long, when he heard her say: "No, no, take them with you, they are for you to keep. That was why I sent for them, to give them to you."

He was overwhelmed by a joy which he could no more control than we can a physical condition that arises without the intervention of our will. He blushed scarlet as a child who has just been punished, and my grandmother was far more touched to see all the efforts he made (without success) to contain the joy that convulsed him than she would have been to hear any words of thanks that he could have uttered. But he, fearing that he had failed to show his gratitude properly, begged me to make his excuses to her again, next day, leaning from the window of the little local train which was to take him back to his regiment. The distance was, as a matter of fact, nothing. He had thought of going by road, as he had frequently done that summer, when he was to return the same evening and was not encumbered with baggage. But this time he would in any case have had to put all his heavy luggage in the train. And he found it simpler to take the train himself too, following the advice of the manager who, on being consulted, replied that "Carriage or train, it was more or less equivocal." He meant it to be understood that they were equivalent (in fact, very much what Françoise would have expressed as "coming to the same as makes no difference"). "Very well," Saint-Loup had decided, "I shall take the 'little crawler.'" I should have taken it too, had I not been tired, and gone with my friend to Doncières; failing this I kept on promising, all the time we waited in Balbec station—the time, that is to say, which the driver of the little train spent waiting for unpunctual friends, without whom he refused to start, and also in seeking some refreshment for himself—to go over there and see him several times a week. As Bloch had also come to the station—much to Saint-Loup's disgust—the latter, seeing that our companion could hear him begging me to come to luncheon, to dinner, to stay altogether at Doncières, finally turned to him and, in the most forbidding tone, intended to counteract the forced civility of the invitation and to prevent Bloch from taking it seriously: "If you ever happen to be passing through Doncières any afternoon when I'm off duty, you might ask for me at the barracks; but I hardly ever am off duty." Perhaps, also, Robert was afraid that I might not come alone, and, thinking that I was more intimate with Bloch than I made out, was providing me in this way with a travelling companion, one who would urge me on.

I was afraid that this tone, this manner of inviting a person while advising him not to come, might have wounded Bloch, and felt that Saint-Loup would have done better to say nothing. But I was mistaken, for after the train had gone, while we were walking back together as far as the crossroads where we had to separate, one road going to the hotel, the other to the Blochs' villa, he never stopped asking me on what day we should go to Doncières, for after "all the civility that Saint-Loup had shown" him, it would be "too rude" on his part not to accept his invitation. I was glad that he had not noticed, or was so little displeased as to wish to let it be thought that he had not noticed, in what a less than pressing, indeed barely polite, tone the invitation had been issued. At the same time I should have liked Bloch, for his own sake, to refrain from making a fool of himself by going over at once to Doncières. But I dared not offer a piece of advice which could only have offended him by hinting that Saint-Loup had been less pressing than he himself was impressed. He was a great deal too ready to respond, and even if all his faults of this nature were atoned for by remarkable qualities which others, with more reserve than he, would never have possessed, he carried tactlessness to a pitch that was almost maddening. According to him, the week must not pass without our going to Doncières (he said "our" for I think that he counted to some extent on my presence there as an excuse for his own). All the way home, opposite the gymnasium in its grove of trees, opposite the tennis courts, the mayor's office, the shell-fish stall, he stopped me, imploring me to fix a day, and, as I did not, left me in a towering rage, saying: "As your lordship pleases. For my part, I am obliged to go since he has invited me."

Saint-Loup was still so afraid of not having thanked my grandmother properly that he charged me once again to express his gratitude to her a day or two later in a letter I received from him from the town in which he was quartered, a town which seemed, on the envelope where the post-mark had stamped its name, to be hastening to me across country, to tell me that within its walls, in the Louis XVI cavalry barracks, he was thinking of me. The paper was embossed with the arms of Marsantes, in which I could make out a lion, surmounted by a coronet encircling the cap of a Peer of France.

"After a journey which," he wrote, "passed pleasantly enough, with a book I bought at the station, by Arvède Barine[28] (a Russian author, I fancy; it seemed to me remarkably well written for a foreigner, but you shall give me your critical opinion, since you are bound to know all about it, you who are a fount of knowledge and have read everything), here I am again in the thick of this debased existence, where, alas, I feel a sad exile, not having here what I left behind at Balbec; this life in which I can find no affectionate memory, no intellectual attraction; an environment which you would no doubt despise yet which has a certain charm. Everything seems to have changed since I left it, for in the interval one of the most important periods in my life, that from which our friendship dates, has begun. I hope that it may never come to an end. I have spoken of our friendship, of you, to one person only, to the friend I told you of, who has just paid me a surprise visit here. She would very much like to know you, and I feel that you would get on well together, for she too is extremely literary. Otherwise, to go over in my mind all our talks, to relive those hours which I never shall forget, I have shut myself off from my comrades, excellent fellows, but altogether incapable of understanding that sort of thing. This remembrance of the moments I spent with you I should almost have preferred, on my first day here, to conjure up for my own solitary enjoyment, without writing to you. But I was afraid lest, with your subtle mind and ultra-sensitive heart, you might needlessly torment yourself if you did not hear from me, if, that is to say, you still condescend to occupy your thoughts with this blunt trooper whom you will have a hard task to polish and refine and make a little more subtle and worthier of your company."

On the whole this letter, in its affectionate spirit, was not at all unlike those which, when I did not yet know Saint-Loup, I had imagined that he would write to me, in those daydreams from which the coldness of his first greeting had shaken me by bringing me face to face with an icy reality which was not, however, to last. Once I had received this letter, every time the post was brought in, at lunch-time, I could tell at once when it was from him that a letter came, for it had always that second face which a person assumes when he is absent, in the features of which (the characters of the handwriting) there is no reason why we should not suppose that we can detect an individual soul just as much as in the line of a nose or the inflexions of a voice.

I would now happily remain at the table while it was being cleared, and, if it was not a moment at which the girls of the little band might be passing, it was no longer solely towards the sea that I would turn my eyes. Since I had seen such things depicted in water-colours by Elstir, I sought to find again in reality, I cherished as though for their poetic beauty, the broken gestures of the knives still lying across one another, the swollen convexity of a discarded napkin into which the sun introduced a patch of yellow velvet, the half-empty glass which thus showed to greater advantage the noble sweep of its curved sides and, in the heart of its translucent crystal, clear as frozen daylight, some dregs of wine, dark but glittering with reflected lights, the displacement of solid objects, the transmutation of liquids by the effect of light and shade, the shifting colours of the plums which passed from green to blue and from blue to golden yellow in the half-plundered dish, the chairs, like a group of old ladies, that came twice daily to take their places round the white cloth spread on the table as on an altar at which were celebrated the rites of the palate, and where in the hollows of the oyster-shells a few drops of lustral water had remained as in tiny holy water stoups of stone; I tried to find beauty there where I had never imagined before that it could exist, in the most ordinary things, in the profundities of "still life."

When, some days after Saint-Loup's departure, I had succeeded in persuading Elstir to give a small party at which I should meet Albertine, the freshness of appearance and elegance of attire, both quite momentary, which were to be observed in me at the moment of my starting out from the

Grand Hotel (and which were due respectively to a longer rest than usual and to special pains over my toilet) were such that I regretted my inability to reserve them (and also the credit accruing from Elstir's friendship) for the captivation of some other, more interesting person, I regretted having to use them all up on the simple pleasure of making Albertine's acquaintance. My brain assessed this pleasure at a very low value now that it was assured. But, inside, my will did not for a moment share this illusion, that will which is the persevering and unalterable servant of our successive personalities; hidden away in the shadow, despised, downtrodden, untiringly faithful, toiling incessantly, and with no thought for the variability of the self, its master, to ensure that that master may never lack what he requires. While, at the moment when we are about to start on a long-planned and eagerly awaited journey, our intelligence and our sensibility begin to ask themselves whether it is really worth the trouble, the will, knowing that those lazy masters would at once begin to consider that journey the most wonderful experience if it became impossible for us to undertake it, leaves them arguing outside the station, vying with each other in their hesitations; but it busies itself with buying the tickets and putting us into the carriage before the train starts. It is as invariable as the intelligence and the sensibility are fickle, but since it is silent, gives no account of its actions, it seems almost non-existent; it is by its dogged determination that the other constituent parts of our personality are led, but without seeing it, whereas they distinguish clearly all their own uncertainties. So my intelligence and my sensibility began a discussion as to the real value of the pleasure that there would be in knowing Albertine, while I studied in the glass vain and perishable attractions which they would have preserved intact for use on some other occasion. But my will would not let the hour pass at which I must start, and it was Elstir's address that it called out to the driver. My intelligence and my sensibility were at liberty, now that the die was cast, to think this a pity. If my will had given the man a different address, they would have been properly had.

When I arrived at Elstir's a few minutes later, I thought at first that Mlle Simonet was not in the studio. There was cer-

tainly a girl sitting there in a silk frock, bareheaded, but one
whose marvellous hair, whose nose, whose complexion, meant
nothing to me, in whom I did not recognise the human entity
that I had extracted from a young cyclist in a polo-cap strolling
past between myself and the sea. Nevertheless it was Albertine.
But even when I knew it to be her, I gave her no thought. On
entering any social gathering, when one is young, one loses
consciousness of one's old self, one becomes a different man,
every drawing-room being a fresh universe in which, coming
under the sway of a new moral perspective, we fasten our
attention, as if they were to matter to us for all time, on people,
dances, card-tables, all of which we shall have forgotten by
the morning. Obliged to follow, if I was to arrive at the goal of
conversation with Albertine, a route in no way of my own
planning, which first brought me to a halt in front of Elstir,
passed by other groups of guests to whom I was presented,
then along the buffet table, at which I was offered, and where I
ate, a strawberry tart or two, while I listened, motionless, to
the music that had begun in another part of the room, I found
myself giving to these various incidents the same importance
as to my introduction to Mlle Simonet, an introduction which
was now nothing more than one among several such incidents,
having entirely forgotten that it had been, but a few minutes
since, my sole object in coming there. But is it not thus, in the
bustle of daily life, with every true happiness, every great
sorrow? In a room full of other people we receive from the
woman we love the answer, auspicious or fatal, which we have
been awaiting for the last year. But we must go on talking, ideas
come flocking one after another, unfolding a smooth surface
which is pricked now and then at the very most by a dull throb
from the memory, infinitely more profound but very narrow,
that misfortune has come upon us. If, instead of misfortune,
it is happiness, it may be that not until many years have elapsed
will we recall that the most important event in our emotional
life occurred without our having time to give it any prolonged
attention, or even to become aware of it almost, at a social
gathering to which we had gone solely in expectation of that
event.

When Elstir asked me to come with him so that he might

introduce me to Albertine, who was sitting a little further down the room, I first of all finished eating a coffee *éclair* and, with a show of keen interest, asked an old gentleman whose acquaintance I had just made (and to whom I thought that I might offer the rose in my buttonhole which he had admired) to tell me more about the old Norman fairs. This is not to say that the introduction which followed did not give me any pleasure and did not assume a certain solemnity in my eyes. But so far as the pleasure was concerned, I was naturally not conscious of it until some time later, when, back at the hotel, and in my room alone, I had become myself again. Pleasure in this respect is like photography. What we take, in the presence of the beloved object, is merely a negative, which we develop later, when we are back at home, and have once again found at our disposal that inner darkroom the entrance to which is barred to us so long as we are with other people.

If my consciousness of the pleasure it had brought me was thus retarded by a few hours, the gravity of this introduction made itself felt at once. At the moment of introduction, for all that we feel ourselves to have been suddenly rewarded, to have been furnished with a pass that will admit us henceforward to pleasures which we have been pursuing for weeks past, we realise only too clearly that this acquisition puts an end for us not merely to hours of toilsome search—a relief that can only fill us with joy—but also to the existence of a certain person, the person whom our imagination had wildly distorted, whom our anxious fear that we might never become known to her had magnified. At the moment when our name rings out on the lips of the introducer, especially if the latter amplifies it, as Elstir now did, with a flattering commentary—that sacramental moment, as when in a fairy tale the magician commands a person suddenly to become someone else—she to whose presence we have been longing to attain vanishes: indeed, how could she remain the same when—by reason of the attention which she is obliged to pay to the announcement of our name and the sight of our person—in the eyes that only yesterday were situated at an infinite distance (where we supposed that ours, wandering, unsteady, desperate, divergent, would never succeed in meeting them) the conscious gaze, the incommunicable thought which we were seeking have just been miraculously and quite simply replaced by our own image painted in them as in a smiling mirror? If this incarnation of ourselves in the person who seemed to differ most from us is what does most to modify the appearance of the person to whom we have just been introduced, the form of that person still remains quite vague; and we may wonder whether it will turn out to be a god, a table or a basin. But, as nimble as the wax-modellers who will fashion a bust before our eyes in five minutes, the few words which the stranger is now going to say to us will substantiate that form and give it something positive and final that will exclude all the hypotheses in which our desire and our imagination had been indulging. Doubtless, even before coming to this party, Albertine had ceased to be for me simply that phantom fit to haunt the rest of our lives which a passing stranger of whom we know nothing and have caught but the barest glimpse remains. Her relationship to Mme Bontemps had already restricted the scope of those marvellous hypotheses, by stopping one of the channels along which they might have spread. As I drew closer to the girl and began to know her better, this knowledge developed by a process of subtraction, each constituent of imagination and desire giving place to a notion which was worth infinitely less, a notion to which, it is true, there was added presently a sort of equivalent, in the domain of real life, of what joint stock companies give one, after repaying one's original investment, and call a preference share. Her name, her family connections, had been the first limit set to my suppositions. Her friendly greeting as, standing close beside her, I once again saw the tiny mole on her cheek, below her eye, marked another stage; finally, I was surprised to hear her use the adverb "perfectly" (in place of "quite" or "absolutely") of two people whom she mentioned, saying of one, "She's perfectly mad, but very nice all the same," and of the other, "He's perfectly common and perfectly boring." However little to be commended this use of "perfectly" may be, it indicates a degree of civilisation and culture which I could never have imagined as having been attained by the bacchante with the bicycle, the orgiastic muse of the golf-course. Nor did it mean that after this first metamorphosis Albertine was not to change again for me, many times. The qualities and defects which a person presents to us, exposed to view on the surface of his or her face, rearrange themselves in a totally different order if we approach them from a new angle—just as, in a town, buildings that appear strung in extended order along a single line, from another viewpoint are disposed in depth and their relative heights altered. To begin with, Albertine struck me as somewhat shy instead of implacable; she seemed to me more proper than ill-bred, judging by the descriptions, "she has bad manners" or "she has peculiar manners" which she applied to each in turn of the girls of whom I spoke to her; finally, she presented as a target for my line of vision a temple that was somewhat inflamed and by no means attractive to the eye, and no longer the curious look which I had always associated with her until then. But this was merely a second impression and there were doubtless others through which I would successively pass. Thus it can be only after one has recognised, not without some tentative stumblings, the optical errors of one's first impression that one can arrive at an exact knowledge of another person, supposing such knowledge to be ever possible. But it is not; for while our original impression of him undergoes correction, the person himself, not being an inanimate object, changes for his part too: we think that we have caught him, he shifts, and, when we imagine that at last we are seeing him clearly, it is only the old impressions which we had already formed of him that we have succeeded in clarifying, when they no longer represent him.

And yet, whatever the inevitable disappointments that it must bring in its train, this movement towards what we have only glimpsed, what we have been free to dwell upon and imagine at our leisure, this movement is the only one that is wholesome for the senses, that whets their appetite. How drearily monotonous must be the lives of people who, from indolence or timidity, drive in their carriages straight to the doors of friends whom they have got to know without having first dreamed of knowing them, without ever daring, on the way, to stop and examine what arouses their desire!

I returned home thinking of that party, of the coffee *éclair*

which I had finished eating before I let Elstir take me up to
Albertine, the rose which I had given the old gentleman, all
the details selected unbeknownst to us by the circumstances
of the occasion, which compose for us, in a special and quite
fortuitous order, the picture that we retain of a first meeting.
But I had the impression that I was seeing this picture from
another angle of vision, very far removed from myself, realising
that it had not existed only for me, when some months later,
to my great surprise, on my speaking to Albertine about the
day on which I had first met her, she reminded me of the *éclair*,
the flower that I had given away, all those things which I
had supposed to have been, I cannot say of importance only
to myself, but perceived only by myself, and which I now
found thus transcribed, in a version of which I had never
suspected the existence, in the mind of Albertine. On this first
day itself, when, on my return to the hotel, I was able to
visualise the memory which I had brought away with me, I
realised what a conjuring trick had been performed, and with
what consummate sleight of hand, and how I had talked for a
moment or two with a person who, thanks to the skill of the
conjurer, without actually embodying anything of that other
person whom I had for so long been following as she paced
beside the sea, had been substituted for her. I might, for that
matter, have guessed as much in advance, since the girl on the
beach was a fabrication of my own. In spite of which, since I
had, in my conversations with Elstir, identified her with
Albertine, I felt myself in honour bound to fulfil to the real
the promises of love made to the imagined Albertine. We
betroth ourselves by proxy, and then feel obliged to marry the
intermediary. Moreover, if there had disappeared from my life,
provisionally at any rate, an anguish that the memory of
polite manners, the expression "perfectly common" and an
inflamed temple had sufficed to assuage, that memory awakened
in me another kind of desire which, though placid and in no
way painful, resembling a brotherly feeling, might in the long
run become fully as dangerous by making me feel at every
moment a compelling need to kiss this new person whose good
manners, whose shyness, whose unexpected accessibility, arrested the futile course of my imagination but gave birth to a

tender gratitude. And then, since memory begins at once to record photographs independent of one another, eliminates every link, any kind of sequence between the scenes portrayed in the collection which it exposes to our view, the most recent does not necessarily destroy or cancel those that came before. Confronted with the commonplace and touching Albertine to whom I had spoken that afternoon, I still saw the other mysterious Albertine outlined against the sea. These were now memories, that is to say pictures neither of which now seemed to me any truer than the other. Finally, to conclude this account of my first introduction to Albertine, when trying to recapture that little beauty spot on her cheek, just under the eye, I remembered that, looking from Elstir's window when Albertine had gone by, I had seen it on her chin. In fact, when I saw her I noticed that she had a beauty spot, but my errant memory made it wander about her face, fixing it now in one place, now in another.

Whatever my disappointment in finding in Mlle Simonet a girl so little different from those that I knew already, just as my disillusionment when I saw Balbec church did not prevent me from wishing still to go to Quimperlé, Pont-Aven and Venice, I comforted myself with the thought that through Albertine at any rate, even if she herself was not all that I had hoped, I might make the acquaintance of her comrades of the little band.

I thought at first that I should fail in this. As she was to be staying (and I too) for a long time still at Balbec, I had decided that the best thing was not to make my efforts to meet her too apparent, but to wait for an accidental encounter. But even if this should occur every day it was greatly to be feared that she would confine herself to acknowledging my greeting from a distance, and such meetings, repeated day after day throughout the whole season, would benefit me not at all.

Shortly after this, one morning when it had been raining and was almost cold, I was accosted on the front by a girl wearing a little toque and carrying a muff, so different from the girl whom I had met at Elstir's party that to recognise in her the same person seemed an operation beyond the power of the human mind; mine was, however, successful in performing

it, but after a moment's surprise which did not, I think, escape
Albertine's notice. On the other hand, remembering the "well-
bred" manners which had so impressed me before, I now
experienced a converse astonishment at her rude tone and
manners typical of the "little band." Moreover, her temple had
ceased to be the reassuring optical centre of her face, either
because I was now on her other side, or because her toque hid
it, or else possibly because its inflammation was not a constant
thing.

"What weather!" she began. "Really the perpetual summer
of Balbec is all stuff and nonsense. Don't you do anything here?
We never see you playing golf, or dancing at the Casino. You
don't ride either. You must be bored stiff. You don't find it too
deadly, idling about on the beach all day? Ah, so you like
basking in the sun like a lizard? You must have plenty of time
on your hands. I can see you're not like me; I simply adore all
sports. You weren't at the Sogne races? We went in the 'tram,'
and I can quite understand that you wouldn't see any fun in
going in an old rattletrap like that. It took us two whole
hours! I could have gone there and back three times on my bike."

I who had admired Saint-Loup when, in the most natural
manner in the world, he had called the little local train the
"crawler," because of the ceaseless windings of its line, was
daunted by the glibness with which Albertine spoke of it as
the "tram" and the "rattletrap." I could sense her mastery of
a mode of nomenclature in which I was afraid of her detecting
and despising my inferiority. And the full wealth of the synonyms that the little band possessed to designate this railway
had not yet been revealed to me. In speaking, Albertine kept
her head motionless and her nostrils pinched, and scarcely
moved her lips. The result of this was a drawling, nasal sound,
into the composition of which there entered perhaps a provincial heredity, a juvenile affectation of British phlegm, the
teaching of a foreign governess and a congestive hypertrophy
of the mucus of the nose. This enunciation which, as it
happened, soon disappeared when she knew people better,
giving place to a natural girlish tone, might have been thought
unpleasant. But to me it was peculiarly delightful. Whenever I
had gone for several days without seeing her, I would refresh

my spirit by repeating to myself: "We don't ever see you playing golf," with the nasal intonation in which she had uttered the words, point blank, without moving a muscle of her face. And I thought then that there was no one in the world so desirable.

We formed, that morning, one of those couples who dotted the front here and there with their conjunction, their stopping together just long enough to exchange a few words before breaking apart, each to resume separately his or her divergent stroll. I took advantage of this immobility to look again and discover once and for all where exactly the little mole was placed. Then, just as a phrase of Vinteuil which had delighted me in the sonata, and which my recollection allowed to wander from the andante to the finale, until the day when, having the score in my hands, I was able to find it and to fix it in my memory in its proper place, in the scherzo, so this mole, which I had visualised now on her cheek, now on her chin, came to rest for ever on her upper lip, just below her nose. In the same way, too, we are sometimes amazed to come upon lines that we know by heart in a play in which we never dreamed that they were to be found.

At that moment, as if in order that the rich decorative ensemble formed by the lovely train of maidens, at once pink and golden, baked by the sun and wind, might freely proliferate before the sea in all the variety of its forms, Albertine's friends, with their shapely limbs, their supple figures, but so different one from another, came into sight in a cluster that spread out as it advanced in our direction, but closer to the sea, in a parallel line. I asked Albertine's permission to walk for a little way with her. Unfortunately, all she did was to wave her hand to them in greeting. "But your friends will be disappointed if you don't go with them," I hinted, hoping that we might all walk together.

A young man with regular features, carrying a bag of golf-clubs, sauntered up to us. It was the baccarat-player whose fast ways so enraged the senior judge's wife. In a frigid, impassive tone, which he evidently regarded as an indication of the highest distinction, he bade Albertine good day. "Been playing golf, Octave?" she asked. "How did it go? Were you

in form?" "Oh, it's too sickening; I'm a wash-out," he replied.
"Was Andrée playing?" "Yes, she went round in seventy-
seven." "Why, that's a record!" "I went round in eighty-two
yesterday." He was the son of an immensely rich manufac-
turer who was to take an important part in the organisation of the coming World's Fair. I was struck by the extreme
degree to which, in this young man and the other very rare
male friends of the band of girls, the knowledge of everything
that pertained to clothes and how to wear them, cigars, English
drinks, horses—a knowledge which he displayed down to its
minutest details with a haughty infallibility that approached
the reticent modesty of the true expert—had been developed
in complete isolation, unaccompanied by the least trace of any
intellectual culture. He had no hesitation as to the right time
and place for dinner-jacket or pyjamas, but had no notion of
the circumstances in which one might or might not employ
this or that word, or even of the simplest rules of grammar. This
disparity between the two forms of culture must have existed
also in his father, the President of the Householders' Association of Balbec, for, in an open letter to the electors which he
had recently had posted on all the walls, he announced: "I
desired to see the Mayor, to chat to him about it, but he would
not listen to my just grievances." Octave, at the Casino, took
prizes in all the dancing competitions, for the boston, the
tango, and what-not, an accomplishment that would enable
him, if he chose, to make a fine marriage in that seaside society
where it is not figuratively but literally that the girls are
"wedded" to their "dancing partners." He lit a cigar with a
"D'you mind?" to Albertine, as one who asks permission to
finish an urgent piece of work while going on talking. For he
was one of those people who can never be "doing nothing,"
although there was nothing, in fact, that he could ever be said
to do. And since complete inactivity in the end has the same
effect as prolonged overwork, in the mental sphere as much as
in the life of the body and the muscles, the steadfast intellectual
nullity that reigned behind Octave's meditative brow had
ended by giving him, despite his air of unruffled calm, ineffectual longings to think which kept him awake at night, for all
the world like an overwrought philosopher.

Thinking that if I knew their male friends I should have more opportunities of seeing the girls, I had been on the point of asking for an introduction to Octave. I told Albertine this, as soon as he had left us, still muttering "I'm a wash-out," thinking to put into her head the idea of doing it next time.

"Come, come," she exclaimed, "I can't introduce you to a gigolo! This place simply swarms with them. But what on earth would they have to say to you? This one plays golf quite well, and that's all there is to him. I know what I'm talking about; you'd find he wasn't at all your sort."

"Your friends will be cross with you if you desert them like this," I repeated, hoping that she would then suggest my joining the party.

"Oh, no, they don't need me."

We passed Bloch, who directed at me a subtle, insinuating smile, and, embarrassed by the presence of Albertine, whom he did not know, or, rather, knew "without knowing" her, lowered his head towards his neck in a stiff, ungainly motion. "Who's that weird customer?" Albertine asked. "I can't think why he should bow to me since he doesn't know me. So I didn't respond."

I had no time to explain to her, for, bearing straight down upon us, "Excuse me," he began, "for interrupting you, but I must tell you that I'm going to Doncières to-morrow. I cannot put it off any longer without discourtesy; indeed, I wonder what de Saint-Loup-en-Bray must think of me. I just came to let you know that I shall take the two o'clock train. At your service."

But I thought now only of seeing Albertine again, and of trying to get to know her friends, and Doncières, since they were not going there, and my going would bring me back too late to see them still on the beach, seemed to me to be situated at the other end of the world. I told Bloch that it was impossible.

"Oh, very well, I shall go alone. In the fatuous words of Master Arouet, I shall say to Saint-Loup, to beguile his clericalism:

'My duty stands alone, by his in no way bound;
Though he should choose to fail, yet faithful I'll be found.'"

"I admit he's not a bad-looking boy," said Albertine, "but he makes me feel quite sick."

I had never thought that Bloch might be "not a bad-looking boy"; and yet in fact he was. With his rather prominent forehead, his very aquiline nose, and his air of being extremely clever and of being convinced of his cleverness, he had a pleasing face. But he could not succeed in pleasing Albertine. This was perhaps to some extent due to the bad side of her, to the hardness, the insensitivity of the little band, its rudeness towards everything that was not itself. And later on, when I introduced them, Albertine's antipathy for him did not diminish. Bloch belonged to a social group in which, between scoffing at high society and at the same time showing the due regard for polite manners which a man is supposed to show who "does not soil his hands," a sort of special compromise has been reached which differs from the manners of the fashionable world but is none the less a peculiarly odious form of worldliness. When he was introduced to anyone he would bow with a sceptical smile, and at the same time with an exaggerated show of respect, and, if it was to a man, would say: "Pleased to meet you, sir," in a voice which ridiculed the words that it was uttering, though with a consciousness of belonging to someone who was not a boor. Having sacrificed this first moment to a custom which he at once followed and derided (just as on the first of January he would say: "The compliments of the season to you!"), he would adopt an air of infinite cunning, and would "proffer subtle words" which were often true enough but "got on" Albertine's nerves. When I told her on this first day that his name was Bloch, she exclaimed: "I would have betted anything he was a Jew-boy. Typical of their creepy ways!" In fact, Bloch was destined to give Albertine other grounds for annoyance later on. Like many intellectuals, he was incapable of saying a simple thing in a simple way. He would find some precious qualifier for every statement, and would sweep from the particular to the general. It irritated Albertine, who was never too well pleased at other people's paying attention to what she was doing, that when she had sprained her ankle and was lying low, Bloch said of her: "She is outstretched on her couch, but in her ubiquity has not ceased to frequent simultaneously vague golf-courses and dubious tennis-courts." He was simply being "literary," of course, but in view of the difficulties which Albertine felt that it might create for her with friends whose invitations she had declined on the plea that she was unable to move, it was quite enough to make her take a profound dislike to the face and the sound of the voice of the young man who said these things.

We parted, Albertine and I, after promising each other to go out together one day. I had talked to her without being any more conscious of where my words were falling, of what became of them, than if I were dropping pebbles into a bottomless pit. That our words are, as a general rule, filled by the people to whom we address them with a meaning which those people derive from their own substance, a meaning widely different from that which we had put into the same words when we uttered them, is a fact which is perpetually demonstrated in daily life. But if in addition we find ourselves in the company of a person whose education (as Albertine's was to me) is inconceivable, her taste, her reading, her principles unknown to us, we cannot tell whether our words have aroused in her anything that resembles their meaning, any more than in an animal to which we had to make ourselves understood. So that trying to make friends with Albertine seemed to me like entering into contact with the unknown, if not the impossible, an occupation as arduous as breaking a horse, as absorbing as keeping bees or growing roses.

I had thought, a few hours before, that Albertine would acknowledge my greeting only from a distance. We had now left one another after planning to make an excursion soon together. I vowed that when I next met Albertine I would treat her with greater boldness, and I had sketched out in advance a plan of all that I would say to her, and even (being now quite convinced that she was not strait-laced) of all the favours that I would demand of her. But the mind is subject to external influences, as plants are, and cells and chemical elements, and the medium which alters it if we immerse it therein is a change of circumstances, or new surroundings. Changed by the mere fact of her presence, when I found myself once again in Albertine's company, I said to her quite different things from what I had planned. Then, remembering her flushed temple, I asked myself whether she might not appreciate more keenly a polite attention which she knew to be disinterested. Finally, I was embarrassed by some of her looks and her smiles. They might equally well signify a laxity of morals and the rather silly merriment of a high-spirited girl who was at heart thoroughly respectable. A single expression, of face or speech, being susceptible of divers interpretations, I wavered like a schoolboy faced by the difficulties of a piece of Greek prose.

On this occasion we met almost immediately the tall one, Andrée, the one who had jumped over the old banker, and Albertine was obliged to introduce me. Her friend had extraordinarily bright eyes, like a glimpse, through an open door in a dark house, of a room into which the sun is shining with a greenish reflexion from the glittering sea.

A group of five men passed by whom I had come to know very well by sight during my stay at Balbec. I had often wondered who they were. "They're nothing very wonderful," said Albertine with a contemptuous snigger. "The little old one with dyed hair and yellow gloves—isn't he a weird-looking specimen, quite an eyeful, what?—that's the Balbec dentist. He's a good sort. The fat one is the Mayor, not the tiny little fat one, you must have seen him before, he's the dancing master and he's pretty awful too—he can't stand us, because we make such a row at the Casino and smash his chairs and want to have the carpet up when we dance, which is why he never gives us prizes, though we're the only ones who know how to dance. The dentist is a nice man—I would have said how d'ye do to him, just to make the dancing master mad, but I couldn't because they've got M. de Sainte-Croix with them—he's a county councillor, and he comes of a very good family, but he's joined the Republicans, for money, so no decent people ever speak to him now. He knows my uncle, because they're both in the Government, but the rest of my family always cut him. The thin one in the waterproof is the conductor of the orchestra. What, you don't know him! Oh, he plays divinely. You haven't been to *Cavalleria Rusticana*? Ah, I think it's marvellous! He's giving a concert this evening, but we can't go because it's to

be in the town hall. In the Casino it wouldn't matter, but in the
town hall, where they've taken down the crucifix, Andrée's
mother would have a fit if we went there. You're going to say
that my aunt's husband is in the Government. But what difference does that make? My aunt is my aunt, but that's no reason
why I should like her. The only thing she's ever wanted to do is
get rid of me. No, the person who has really been a mother to
me, and all the more credit to her because she's no relation at
all, is a friend of mine whom I love just as much as if she was
my mother. I'll show you her photo."

We were joined for a moment by the golf champion and
baccarat plunger, Octave. I thought I had discovered a bond
between us, for I learned in the course of our conversation that
he was some sort of relative of the Verdurins, who were quite
fond of him. But he spoke contemptuously of the famous
Wednesdays, adding that M. Verdurin had never even heard
of dress-clothes, which made it a horrid bore when one ran
into him in certain "music-halls" where one would very much
rather not be greeted with "Well, you young rascal" by an old
fellow in a frock coat and black tie, for all the world like a
village notary.

Octave left us, and soon it was Andrée's turn, when we came
to her villa, into which she vanished without having uttered a
single word to me during the whole of our walk. I regretted
her departure all the more because, while I was complaining
to Albertine how cold her friend had been towards me, and
was comparing in my mind this difficulty which Albertine
seemed to find in bringing me into contact with her friends
with the hostility that Elstir, in attempting to fulfil my wish,
seemed to have encountered on that first afternoon, two girls
came by to whom I lifted my hat, the misses d'Ambresac,
whom Albertine greeted also.

I felt that my position in relation to Albertine would be
improved by this meeting. They were the daughters of a kins-
woman of Mme de Villeparisis, who was also a friend of Mme
de Luxembourg. M. and Mme d'Ambresac, who had a small
villa at Balbec and were immensely rich, led the simplest of
lives, and always went about in the same clothes, he in an
unvarying frock coat, she in a dark dress. Both of them used

to make sweeping bows to my grandmother, which never led
to anything further. The daughters, who were very pretty,
were dressed more elegantly, but it was an elegance more suited
to Paris than to the seaside. With their long skirts and large
hats, they seemed to belong to a different race from Albertine.
She, I discovered, knew all about them.

"Oh, so you know the little d'Ambresacs, do you? Well, well,
you do have some grand friends. But they're very simple
really," she went on as though the two things were mutually
exclusive. "They're very nice, but so well brought up that they
aren't allowed near the Casino, mainly because of us, because
we're too badly behaved. You find them attractive, do you?
Well, it all depends on what you like. They're real goody-
goodies. Perhaps there's a certain charm in that. If you like
goody-goodies, they're all that you could wish for. There
must be some attraction, because one of them has got engaged
already to the Marquis de Saint-Loup. Which was a cruel blow
to the younger one, who was madly in love with that young
man. As far as I'm concerned, the way they purse their lips
when they talk is enough to madden me. And then they dress
in the most absurd way. Fancy going to play golf in silk frocks!
At their age, they dress more pretentiously than grown-up
women who really know about clothes. Look at Mme Elstir.
There's a well-dressed woman if you like." I answered that she
had struck me as being dressed with the utmost simplicity.
Albertine laughed.

"She's very simply turned out, I admit, but she dresses
wonderfully, and to get what you call simplicity costs her a
fortune."

Mme Elstir's elegance passed unnoticed by anyone who had
not a sober and unerring taste in matters of dress. This I
lacked. Elstir possessed it in a supreme degree, so Albertine
told me. I had not suspected this, nor that the beautiful but
quite simple objects which littered his studio were treasures
long desired by him which he had followed from sale-room to
sale-room, knowing all their history, until he had made enough
money to be able to acquire them. But as to this Albertine,
being as ignorant as myself, could not enlighten me. Whereas
when it came to clothes, prompted by a coquettish instinct and

perhaps by the regretful longing of a penniless girl who is able to appreciate with greater disinterestedness, more delicacy and discrimination, in the rich the things that she will never be able to afford for herself, she spoke very interestingly about the refinement of Elstir's taste, so difficult to satisfy that all women appeared to him badly dressed and, attaching infinite importance to proportions and shades of colour, he would have specially made for his wife, at fabulous prices, the sunshades, hats and coats whose charm he had taught Albertine to appreciate and which a person wanting in taste would no more have noticed than I had. Apart from this, Albertine, who had done a little painting, though without, she confessed, having any "gift" for it, felt a boundless admiration for Elstir, and, thanks to his precept and example, showed a judgment of pictures which was in marked contrast to her enthusiasm for *Cavalleria Rusticana*. The truth was that, though as yet it was hardly apparent, she was highly intelligent, and that in the things that she said the stupidity was not her own but that of her environment and her age. Elstir's had been a good but only a partial influence. All the branches of her intelligence had not reached the same stage of development. Her taste in pictures had almost caught up with her taste in clothes and all forms of elegance, but had not been followed by her taste in music, which was still a long way behind.

Albertine might know all about the Ambresacs; but as he who can achieve great things is not necessarily capable of small, I did not find her, after I had greeted those young ladies, any more disposed to make me known to her friends. "It's very good of you to attach importance to them. You shouldn't take any notice of them; they don't count. What on earth can a lot of kids like them mean to a man like you? Now Andrée, I must say, is remarkably clever. She's a good girl, though perfectly weird at times, but the others are really dreadfully stupid."

When I had left Albertine, I felt suddenly a keen regret that Saint-Loup should have concealed his engagement from me and that he should be doing anything so improper as to choose a wife before breaking with his mistress. And then, some days later, I met Andrée, and as she went on talking to me for some time I seized the opportunity to tell her that I would very much

like to see her again next day; but she replied that this was
impossible, because her mother was not 'at all well and she
did not want to leave her alone. Two days later I went to see
Elstir, who told me that Andrée had taken a great liking to
me. When I protested that it was I who had taken a liking to
her from the start, and had asked her to meet me again next
day but she couldn't, "Yes, I know, she told me all about that,"
was his reply, "she was very sorry, but she had promised to
go for a picnic somewhere miles from here. They were to drive
over in a break, and it was too late for her to get out of it."
Although this falsehood was of no real significance since
Andrée knew me so slightly, I ought not to have continued
to seek the company of a person who was capable of it. For
what people have once done they will go on doing indefinitely,
and if you go every year to see a friend who, the first few
times, was unable to keep an appointment with you, or was in
bed with a chill, you will find him in bed with another chill
which he has just caught, you will miss him again at another
meeting-place where he has failed to appear, for a single and
unalterable reason in place of which he supposes himself to
have various reasons, according to the circumstances.

One morning, not long after Andrée had told me that she
would be obliged to stay beside her mother, I was taking a
short stroll with Albertine, whom I had found on the beach
tossing up and catching again at the end of a string a weird
object which gave her a look of Giotto's "Idolatry"; it was
called, as it happened, a "diabolo," and has so fallen into disuse
now that, when they come upon the picture of a girl playing
with one, the commentators of future generations will solemnly
discuss, as it might be in front of the allegorical figures in the
Arena Chapel, what it is that she is holding. A moment later
their friend with the penurious and hard appearance, the one
who on that first day had sneered so malevolently: "I do feel
sorry for him, poor old boy," when she saw the old gentleman's head brushed by the flying feet of Andrée, came up to
Albertine and said: "Good morning. Am I disturbing you?"
She had taken off her hat for comfort, and her hair, like a
strange and fascinating plant, lay over her brow, displaying all
the delicate tracery of its foliation. Albertine, perhaps irritated

at seeing the other bare-headed, made no reply, and preserved a frigid silence in spite of which the girl stayed with us, kept apart from me by Albertine who arranged at one moment to be alone with her, at another to walk with me leaving her to follow. I was obliged, to secure an introduction, to ask for it in the girl's hearing. Then, as Albertine uttered my name, the face and the blue eyes of this girl, whose expression I had thought so cruel when I heard her say: "Poor old boy, I do feel sorry for him," lit up with a cordial and affectionate smile, and she held out her hand to me. Her hair was golden, and not her hair only; for if her cheeks were pink and her eyes blue, it was like the still roseate morning sky which sparkles everywhere with dazzling points of gold.

Instantly aroused, I said to myself that this was a child who when in love grew shy, that it was for my sake, for love of me that she had remained with us despite Albertine's rebuffs, and that she must have rejoiced in the opportunity to confess to me at last, by that smiling, friendly look, that she would be as gentle to me as she was ferocious to other people. Doubtless she had noticed me on the beach when I did not yet know her, and had been thinking of me ever since; perhaps it was to win my admiration that she had mocked at the old gentleman, and because she had not succeeded in getting to know me that on the following days she had appeared so morose. I had often seen her from the hotel, walking by herself on the beach in the evenings. It was probably in the hope of meeting me. And now, hindered as much by Albertine's presence as she would have been by that of the whole band, she had evidently attached herself to us, in spite of the increasing coldness of her friend's attitude, only in the hope of outstaying her, of being left alone with me, when she might make a rendezvous with me for some time when she would find an excuse to slip away without either her family or her friends knowing that she had gone, and would meet me in some safe place before church or after golf. It was all the more difficult to see her because Andrée had quarrelled with her and now detested her. "I've put up quite long enough," she told me, "with her appalling duplicity, her baseness, and all the dirty tricks she's played on me. I've stood it all because of the others. But her latest effort was really too much!" And she told me of some piece of malicious gossip that this girl had perpetrated, which might indeed have injurious consequences for Andrée.

But those private words promised me by Gisèle's confiding eyes for the moment when Albertine should have left us by ourselves were destined never to be spoken, because after Albertine, stubbornly planted between us, had continued to reply with increasing curtness, and had finally ceased to reply at all, to her friend's remarks, Gisèle at length abandoned the attempt and turned back. I reproached Albertine for having been so disagreeable. "It will teach her to be more tactful. She's not a bad kid, but she's so boring. She's got no business, either, to come poking her nose into everything. Why should she fasten herself on to us without being asked? In another minute I'd have told her to go to blazes. Besides, I can't stand her going about with her hair like that; it's such bad form."

I gazed at Albertine's cheeks as she spoke, and asked myself what might be the perfume, the taste of them: that day she was not fresh and cool but smooth, with a uniform pinkness, violet-tinted, creamy, like certain roses whose petals have a waxy gloss. I felt a passionate longing for them such as one feels sometimes for a particular flower. "I hadn't noticed it," was all that I said.

"You stared at her hard enough; anyone would have thought you wanted to paint her portrait," she replied, not at all mollified by the fact that it was at herself that I was now staring so fixedly. "I don't believe you would care for her, though. She's not in the least a flirt. You like girls who flirt, I suspect. Anyhow, she won't have another chance of sticking to us and having to be shaken off. She's going back to Paris later to-day."

"Are the rest of your friends going too?"

"No, only she and 'Miss,' because she's got to take her exams again; she'll have to stay at home and swot for them, poor kid. It's not much fun, I don't mind telling you. Of course, you may be set a good subject, you never know. It's such a matter of luck. One girl I know was given: *Describe an accident that you have witnessed.* That was a piece of luck. But I know another girl who had to discuss, in writing too: *Which would you rather have as a friend, Alceste or Philinte?* I'm sure I should have dried up altogether! Apart from everything else, it's not a question to set to girls. Girls go about with other girls; they're not supposed to have gentlemen friends." (This announcement, which showed that I had but little chance of being admitted to the companionship of the little band, made me quake.) "But in any case, even if it was set for boys, what on earth would you expect them to find to say about it? Several parents wrote to the *Gaulois*, to complain of the difficulty of questions like that. The joke of it is that in a collection of prize-winning essays there were two which treated the question in absolutely opposite ways. You see, it all depends on the examiner. One wanted you to say that Philinte was a two-faced socialite flatterer, the other that you couldn't help admiring Alceste, but that he was too cantankerous, and that as a friend you ought to choose Philinte. How can you expect a lot of unfortunate candidates to know what to say when the professors themselves don't agree? But that's nothing. It gets more difficult every year. Gisèle will have to pull a string or two if she's to get through."

I returned to the hotel. My grandmother was not there. I waited for her some time, and when at last she appeared, I begged her to allow me, in quite unexpected circumstances, to make an expedition which might keep me away for a couple of days. I had lunch with her, ordered a carriage and drove to the station. Gisèle would not be surprised to see me there. After we had changed at Doncières, in the Paris train there would be a carriage with a corridor, along which, while the governess dozed, I should be able to lead Gisèle into a dark corner and make an appointment to meet her on my return to Paris, which I would then try to put forward to the earliest possible date. I would travel with her as far as Caen or Evreux, whichever she preferred, and would take the next train back to Balbec. And yet, what would she have thought of me had she known that I had hesitated for a long time between her and her friends, that quite as much as with her I had contemplated falling in love with Albertine, with the girl with the bright eyes, with Rosemonde. I felt a pang of remorse, now that a bond of mutual affection was going to unite me with Gisèle. I could, however, truthfully have assured her that Albertine no longer attracted me. I had seen her that morning as she swerved aside, almost turning her back on me, to speak to Gisèle. Her head was sulkily lowered, and the hair at the back, which was different and darker still, glistened as though she had just been bathing. "Like a dying duck in a thunderstorm," I had thought to myself, and this view of her hair had induced me to embody in Albertine a different soul from that implied hitherto by her glowing complexion and mysterious gaze. That shining cataract of hair at the back of her head had been for a moment or two all that I was able to see of her, and continued to be all that I saw in retrospect. Our memory is like one of those shops in the window of which is exposed now one, now another photograph of the same person. And as a rule the most recent exhibit remains for some time the only one to be seen. While the coachman whipped on his horse I sat there listening to the words of gratitude and tenderness that Gisèle was murmuring in my ear, all of them born of her friendly smile and out-stretched hand; for the fact was that in those periods of my life in which I was not actually in love but desired to be, I carried in my mind not only a physical ideal of beauty which, as the reader has seen, I recognised from a distance in every passing woman far enough away from me for her indistinct features not to belie the identification, but also the mental phantom— ever ready to become incarnate—of the woman who was going to fall in love with me, to take up her cues in the amorous comedy which I had had all written out in my mind from my earliest boyhood, and in which every attractive girl seemed to me to be equally desirous of playing, provided that she had also some of the physical qualifications required. In this play, whoever the new star might be whom I invited to create or to revive the leading part, the plot, the incidents, the lines them-selves preserved an unalterable form.

Within the next few days, in spite of the reluctance that Albertine had shown to introduce me to them, I knew all the little band of that first afternoon (except Gisèle, whom, owing to a prolonged delay at the level crossing by the station and a change in the time-table, I had not succeeded in meeting on the train, which had left some minutes before I arrived, and to whom in any case I never gave another thought), and two or

three other girls as well to whom at my request they introduced me. And thus, my expectation of the pleasure which I
should find in a new girl springing from another through
whom I had come to know her, the latest was like one of those
new varieties of rose which gardeners get by using first a rose
of another species. And as I passed from corolla to corolla
along this chain of flowers, the pleasure of knowing a different
one would send me back to the one to whom I was indebted
for it, with a gratitude mixed with as much desire as my new
hope. Presently I was spending all my time among these girls.

Alas! in the freshest flower it is possible to discern those just
perceptible signs which to the instructed mind already betray
what will, by the desiccation or fructification of the flesh that
is to-day in bloom, be the ultimate form, immutable and already
predestined, of the autumnal seed. The eye follows with delight a nose like a wavelet that deliciously ripples the surface
of the water at daybreak, and seems motionless, capturable by
the pencil, because the sea is so calm that one does not notice
its tidal flow. Human faces seem not to change while we are
looking at them, because the revolution they perform is too
slow for us to perceive it. But one had only to see, by the side
of any of these girls, her mother or her aunt, to realise the
distance over which, obeying the internal gravitation of a type
that was generally deplorable, these features would have
travelled in less than thirty years, until the hour when the
looks have begun to wane, until the hour when the face,
having sunk altogether below the horizon, catches the light
no more. I knew that, as deep, as ineluctable as Jewish patrio-
tism or Christian atavism in those who imagine themselves to
be the most emancipated of their race, there dwelt beneath the
rosy inflorescence of Albertine, Rosemonde, Andrée, unknown
to themselves, held in reserve until the occasion should arise,
a coarse nose, a protruding jaw, a paunch which would create
a sensation when it appeared, but which was actually in the
wings, ready to "come on," unforeseen, inevitable, just as it
might be a burst of Dreyfusism or clericalism or patriotic,
feudal heroism, emerging suddenly in answer to the call of
circumstance from a nature anterior to the individual himself,
through which he thinks, lives, evolves, gains strength or dies,

without ever being able to distinguish that nature from the particular motives he mistakes for it. Even mentally, we depend a great deal more than we think upon natural laws, and our minds possess in advance, like some cryptogamous plant, the characteristic that we imagine ourselves to be selecting. For we grasp only the secondary ideas, without detecting the primary cause (Jewish blood, French birth or whatever it may be) that inevitably produced them, and which we manifest when the time comes. But perhaps, while the one may appear to us to be the result of deliberate thought, the other of an imprudent disregard for our own health, we take from our family, as the papilionaceae take the form of their seed, as well the ideas by which we live as the malady from which we shall die.

As in a nursery plantation where the flowers mature at different seasons, I had seen them, in the form of old ladies, on this Balbec shore, those shrivelled seed-pods, those flabby tubers, which my new friends would one day be. But what matter? For the moment it was their flowering-time. And so when Mme de Villeparisis asked me to go for a drive, I sought an excuse to avoid doing so. I no longer visited Elstir unless accompanied by my new friends. I could not even spare an afternoon to go to Doncières, to pay the visit I had promised Saint-Loup. Social engagements, serious discussions, even a friendly conversation, had they usurped the place allotted to my outings with these girls, would have had the same effect on me as if, at lunch-time, one were taken not to eat but to look at an album. The men, the youths, the women, old or mature, in whose society we think to take pleasure, exist for us only on a flat, one-dimensional surface, because we are conscious of them only through visual perception restricted to its own limits; whereas it is as delegates from our other senses that our eyes direct themselves towards young girls; the senses follow, one after another, in search of the various charms, fragrant, tactile, savorous, which they thus enjoy even without the aid of hands and lips; and able, thanks to the arts of transposition, the genius for synthesis in which desire excels, to reconstruct beneath the hue of cheeks or bosom the feel, the taste, the contact that is forbidden them, they give to these girls the same honeyed consistency as they create when they

go foraging in a rose-garden, or in a vine whose clusters their
eyes devour.

If it rained, although the weather had no power to daunt
Albertine, who was often to be seen in her waterproof spinning
on her bicycle through the showers, we would spend the day
in the Casino, where on such days it would have seemed to me
impossible not to go. I had the greatest contempt for the
Ambresac sisters, who had never set foot in it. And I willingly
joined my new friends in playing tricks on the dancing master.
As a rule we had to listen to admonitions from the manager,
or from some of his staff usurping directorial powers, because
my friends—even Andrée whom on that account I had regarded when I first saw her as so dionysiac a creature whereas
in reality she was delicate, intellectual and this year far from
well, in spite of which her actions were responsive less to the
state of her health than to the spirit of that age which sweeps
everything aside and mingles in a general gaiety the weak with
the strong—could not go from the hall to the ball-room
without breaking into a run, jumping over all the chairs, and
sliding along the floor, their balance maintained by a graceful
poise of their outstretched arms, singing the while, mingling
all the arts, in that first bloom of youth, in the manner of those
poets of old for whom the different "genres" were not yet
separate, so that in an epic poem they would mix agricultural
precepts with theological doctrine.

This Andrée, who had struck me when I first saw her as the
coldest of them all, was infinitely more refined, more affectionate, more sensitive than Albertine, to whom she displayed
the caressing, gentle tenderness of an elder sister. At the Casino
she would come across the floor to sit down beside me and
was prepared, unlike Albertine, to forgo a waltz or even, if I
was tired, to give up the Casino and come to me instead at the
hotel. She expressed her friendship for me, for Albertine, in
terms that were evidence of the most exquisite understanding
of the things of the heart, which may have been partly due to
her delicate health. She had always a gay smile of excuse for
the childish behaviour of Albertine, who expressed with naïve
violence the irresistible temptation held out to her by the
parties and pleasure trips which she was incapable of resisting,

like Andrée, in order to stay and talk to me. When the time came for her go to off to a tea-party at the golf-club, if we were all three together at that moment she would get ready to leave and then, coming up to Andrée, would say: "Well, Andrée, what are you waiting for? You know we're having tea at the golf-club." "No, I'm going to stay and talk to him," Andrée would reply, pointing to me. "But you know Mme Durieux invited you," Albertine would cry, as if Andrée's intention to remain with me could be explained only by ignorance on her part as to whether or not she had been invited. "Come, my sweet, don't be such an idiot," Andrée would chide her, and Albertine would not insist, for fear that she might be asked to stay too. She would toss her head and say "Just as you like," in the tone one uses to an invalid who is deliberately killing himself by inches. "Anyway I must fly; I'm sure your watch is slow," and off she would go. "She's a dear girl, but quite impossible," Andrée would say, enveloping her friend in a smile at once caressing and critical. If in this craze for amusement Albertine might be said to echo something of the old original Gilberte, that is because a certain similarity exists, although the type evolves, between all the women we successively love, a similarity that is due to the fixity of our own temperament, which chooses them, eliminating all those who would not be at once our opposite and our complement, apt, that is to say, to gratify our senses and to wring our hearts. They are, these women, a product of our temperament, an image, an inverted projection, a negative of our sensibility. So that a novelist might, in relating the life of his hero, describe his successive love-affairs in almost exactly similar terms, and thereby give the impression not that he was repeating himself but that he was creating, since an artificial novelty is never so effective as a repetition that manages to suggest a fresh truth. He ought, moreover, to note in the character of the lover an index of variation which becomes apparent as the story moves into fresh regions, into different latitudes of life. And perhaps he would be expressing yet another truth if, while investing all the other *dramatis personae* with distinct characters, he refrained from giving any to the beloved. We understand the characters of people to whom we are indifferent, but how can we ever grasp that of a person who is an intimate part of our existence, whom after a while we no longer distinguish from ourselves, whose motives provide us with an inexhaustible source of anxious hypotheses, continually revised? Springing from somewhere beyond our intellect, our curiosity about the woman we love overleaps the bounds of that woman's character, at which, even if we could stop, we probably never would. The object of our anxious investigation is something more basic than those details of character comparable to the tiny particles of epidermis whose varied combinations form the florid originality of human flesh. Our intuitive radiography pierces them, and the images which it brings back, far from being those of a particular face, present rather the joyless universality of a skeleton.

Andrée, being herself extremely rich while the other was penniless and an orphan, with real generosity lavished on Albertine the full benefit of her wealth. As for her feelings towards Gisèle, they were not quite what I had been led to suppose. News soon reached us of the young student, and when Albertine handed round the letter she had received from her, a letter intended by Gisèle to give an account of her journey and to report her safe arrival to the little band, apologising for her laziness in not yet having written to the others, I was surprised to hear Andrée, whom I imagined to be at daggers drawn with her, say: "I shall write to her to-morrow, because if I wait for her to write I may have to wait for ages, she's such a slacker." And turning to me she added: "You mightn't see much in her, but she's a jolly nice girl, and besides I'm really very fond of her." From which I concluded that Andrée's quarrels were apt not to last very long.

Except on these rainy days, as we always arranged to go on our bicycles along the cliffs, or on an excursion inland, an hour or so before it was time to start I would go upstairs to make myself smart and would complain if Françoise had not laid out all the things that I wanted. Now even in Paris, at the first word of reproach she would proudly and angrily straighten a back which the years had begun to bend, she so humble, modest and charming when her self-esteem was flattered. As this was the mainspring of Françoise's life, her satisfaction and her good humour were in direct ratio to the difficulty of the tasks imposed on her. Those which she had to perform at Balbec were so easy that she displayed an almost continual dissatisfaction which was suddenly multiplied a hundredfold and combined with an ironic air of offended dignity when I complained, on my way down to join my friends, that my hat had not been brushed or my ties sorted. She who was capable of taking such endless pains and would think nothing of it, on my simply remarking that a coat was not in its proper place would only boast of the care with which she had "put it past sooner than let it go gathering the dust," but, paying a formal tribute to her own labours, lamented that it was little enough of a holiday that she was getting at Balbec, and that we would not find another person in the whole world who would consent to put up with such treatment. "I can't think how people can leave things lying about the way you do; you just try and get anyone else to find what you want in such a pell-mell. The devil himself would give it up as a bad job." Or else she would adopt a regal mien, scorching me with her fiery glance, and preserve a silence that was broken as soon as she had fastened the door behind her and had set off down the corridor, which would then reverberate with utterances which I guessed to be abusive, though they remained as indistinct as those of characters in a play whose opening lines are spoken in the wings, before they appear on the stage. But even if nothing was missing and Françoise was in a good temper, still she made herself quite intolerable when I was getting ready to go out with my friends. For, drawing upon a store of jokes which, in my need to talk about these girls, I had told her at their expense, she took it upon herself to reveal to me what I should have known better than she if it had been accurate, which it never was, Françoise having misunderstood what she had heard. She had, like everyone else, her own peculiar character, which in no one resembles a straight highway, but surprises us with its strange, unavoidable windings which other people do not see and which it is painful to have to follow. Whenever I arrived at the stage of "Where is my hat?" or uttered the name of Andrée or Albertine, I was forced by Françoise to stray into endless and absurd side-tracks which greatly delayed my progress. So too when I ordered the cheese or salad sandwiches or sent out for the cakes which I would eat on the cliff with the girls, and which they "might very well have taken turns to provide, if they hadn't been so close-fisted," declared Françoise, to whose aid there came at such moments a whole heritage of atavistic peasant rapacity and coarseness, and for whom one would have said that the divided soul of her late enemy Eulalie had been reincarnated, more becomingly than in St Eloi, in the charming bodies of my friends of the little band. I listened to these accusations with a dull fury at finding myself brought to a standstill at one of those places beyond which the rustic and familiar path that was Françoise's character became impassable, though fortunately never for very long. Then, my hat or coat found and the sandwiches ready, I went to join Albertine, Andrée, Rosemonde, and any others there might be, and we would set out on foot or on our bicycles.

In the old days I should have preferred our excursions to be made in bad weather. For then I still looked to find in Balbec "the land of the Cimmerians," and fine days were a thing that had no right to exist there, an intrusion of the vulgar summer of seaside holiday-makers into that ancient region swathed in eternal mist. But everything that I had hitherto despised and thrust from my sight, not only the effects of sunlight upon sea and shore, but even regattas and race-meetings, I now sought out with ardour, for the same reason which formerly had made me wish only for stormy seas: namely, that they were now associated in my mind, as the others had once been, with an aesthetic idea. For I had gone several times with my new friends to visit Elstir, and, on the days when the girls were there, what he had selected to show us were drawings of pretty women in yachting dress, or else a sketch made on a race-course near Balbec. I had at first shyly admitted to Elstir that I had not felt inclined to go to the meetings that had been held there. "You were wrong," he told me, "it's such a pretty sight, and so strange too. For one thing, that peculiar creature the jockey, on whom so many eyes are fastened, and who sits there in the paddock so gloomy and grey-faced in his bright jacket, reining in the rearing horse that

seems to be one with him: how interesting to analyse his professional movements, the bright splash of colour he makes,
with the horse's coat blending in it, against the background of
the course! What a transformation of every visible object in
that luminous vastness of a race-course where one is constantly
surprised by fresh lights and shades which one sees only there!
How pretty the women can look there, too! The first meeting
in particular was delightful, and there were some extremely
elegant women there in the misty, almost Dutch light in which
you could feel the piercing cold of the sea even in the sun
itself. I've never seen women arriving in carriages, or standing with glasses to their eyes in so extraordinary a light, which
was due, I suppose, to the moisture from the sea. Ah! how I
should have loved to paint it. I came back from those races
wild with enthusiasm and longing to get to work!" After
which he waxed more enthusiastic still over the yacht-races,
and I realised that regattas, and race-meetings where well-
dressed women might be seen bathed in the greenish light of a
marine race-course, might be for a modern artist as interesting
a subject as the festivities which they so loved to depict were
for a Veronese or a Carpaccio. When I suggested this to Elstir,
"Your comparison is extremely apt," he replied, "since because of the nature of the city in which they painted, those
festivities were to a great extent aquatic. Except that the beauty
of the shipping in those days lay as a rule in its solidity, in the
complication of its structure. They had water-tournaments, as
we have here, held generally in honour of some Embassy, such
as Carpaccio shows us in his *Legend of Saint Ursula*. The ships
were massive, built like pieces of architecture, and seemed
almost amphibious, like lesser Venices set in the heart of the
greater, when, moored to the banks by hanging stages decked
with crimson satin and Persian carpets, they bore their freight
of ladies in cerise brocade and green damask close under the
balconies incrusted with multi-coloured marble from which
other ladies leaned to gaze at them, in gowns with black sleeves
slashed with white, stitched with pearls or bordered with lace.
You couldn't tell where the land finished and the water began,
what was still the palace or already the ship, the caravel, the
galley, the Bucintoro."

Albertine listened with passionate interest to these details of costume, these visions of elegance that Elstir described to us. "Oh, I should so like to see that lace you speak of; it's so pretty, Venetian lace," she exclaimed, "and I should love to see Venice." "You may, perhaps, before very long," Elstir informed her, "be able to gaze at the marvellous stuffs which they used to wear. One used only to be able to see them in the works of the Venetian painters, or very rarely among the treasures of old churches, or now and then when a specimen turned up in the sale-room. But I hear that a Venetian artist, called Fortuny, has rediscovered the secret of the craft, and that in a few years' time women will be able to parade around, and better still to sit at home, in brocades as sumptuous as those that Venice adorned for her patrician daughters with patterns brought from the Orient. But I don't know whether I should much care for that, whether it wouldn't be too much of an anachronism for the women of to-day, even when they parade at regattas, for, to return to our modern pleasure-craft, the times have completely changed since 'Venice, Queen of the Adriatic.' The great charm of a yacht, of the furnishings of a yacht, of yachting clothes, is their simplicity, as things of the sea, and I do so love the sea. I must confess that I prefer the fashions of to-day to those of Veronese's and even of Carpaccio's time. What is so attractive about our yachts—and the medium-sized yachts especially, I don't like the huge ones, they're too much like ships; and the same goes for hats, there must be some sense of proportion—is the uniform surface, simple, gleaming, grey, which in a bluish haze takes on a creamy softness. The cabin ought to make us think of a little café. And it's the same with women's clothes on board a yacht; what's really charming are those light garments, uniformly white, cotton or linen or nankeen or drill, which in the sunlight and against the blue of the sea show up with as dazzling a whiteness as a spread sail. Actually, there are very few women who know how to dress, though some of them are quite wonderful. At the races, Mlle Léa had a little white hat and a little white sunshade that were simply enchanting. I don't know what I wouldn't give for that little sunshade."

I should have liked very much to know in what respect this

little sunshade differed from any other, and for other reasons, reasons of feminine coquetry, Albertine was still more curious. But, just as Françoise used to explain the excellence of her *soufflés* by saying simply: "It's a knack," so here the difference lay in the cut. "It was tiny and round, like a Chinese parasol," Elstir said. I mentioned the sunshades carried by various women, but none of them would do. Elstir found them all quite hideous. A man of exquisite taste, singularly hard to please, he would isolate some minute detail which was the whole difference between what was worn by three-quarters of the women he saw, and which he abominated, and a thing which enchanted him by its prettiness; and—in contrast to its effect on myself, for whom every kind of luxury was stultifying—stimulated his desire to paint "so as to make something as attractive."

"Here you see a young lady who has guessed what the hat and sunshade were like," he said to me, pointing to Albertine, whose eyes shone with covetousness.

"How I should love to be rich and to have a yacht!" she said to the painter. "I should come to you for advice on how to do it up. What lovely trips I'd make! And what fun it would be to go to Cowes for the regatta! And a motor-car! Tell me, do you think women's fashions for motoring pretty?"

"No," replied Elstir, "but that will come in time. You see, there are very few good dress-making houses at present, one or two only, Callot—although they go in rather too freely for lace—Doucet, Cheruit, Paquin sometimes. The others are all ghastly."

"So there's a vast difference between a Callot dress and one from any ordinary shop?" I asked Albertine.

"Why, an enormous difference, my little man! Oh, sorry! Only, alas! what you get for three hundred francs in an ordinary shop will cost two thousand there. But there can be no comparison; they look the same only to people who know nothing at all about it."

"Quite so," put in Elstir, "though I wouldn't go so far as to say that it's as profound as the difference between a statue from Rheims Cathedral and one from Saint-Augustin. By the way, talking of cathedrals," he went on, addressing himself ex-

clusively to me, because what he was saying referred to an
earlier conversation in which the girls had not taken part,
and which for that matter would in no way have interested
them, "I spoke to you the other day of Balbec church as a
great cliff, a huge breakwater built of the stone of the country,
but conversely," he went on, showing me a water-colour,
"look at these cliffs (it's a sketch I did near here, at the
Creuniers); don't those rocks, so powerfully and delicately
modelled, remind you of a cathedral?"

And indeed one would have taken them for soaring red
arches. But, painted on a scorching hot day, they seemed to
have been reduced to dust, volatilised by the heat which had
drunk up half the sea so that it had almost been distilled,
over the whole surface of the picture, into a gaseous state. On
this day when the sunlight had, so to speak, destroyed reality,
reality concentrated itself in certain dusky and transparent
creatures which, by contrast, gave a more striking, a closer
impression of life: the shadows. Thirsting for coolness, most
of them, deserting the torrid sea, had taken shelter at the foot of
the rocks, out of reach of the sun; others, swimming gently
upon the tide, like dolphins, kept close under the sides of occasional moving boats, whose hulls they extended upon the pale
surface of the water with their glossy blue forms. It was perhaps
the thirst for coolness which they conveyed that did most to
give me the sensation of the heat of that day and made me exclaim how much I regretted not knowing the Creuniers. Albertine and Andrée were positive that I must have been there
hundreds of times. If so I had been there without knowing it,
never suspecting that one day the sight of these rocks would
arouse in me such a thirst for beauty, not perhaps precisely
natural beauty such as I had sought hitherto among the cliffs of
Balbec, but architectural rather. Especially since, having come
here to visit the kingdom of the storms, I had never found, on
any of my drives with Mme de Villeparisis, when often we saw
it only from afar, painted in a gap between the trees, that the sea
was sufficiently real or sufficiently liquid or gave a sufficient
impression of hurling its massed forces against the shore, and
would have liked to see it lie motionless only under a wintry
shroud of fog, I could never have believed that I should now

be dreaming of a sea which was no more than a whitish vapour that had lost both consistency and colour. But of such a sea Elstir, like the people who sat musing on board those vessels drowsy with the heat, had felt so intensely the enchantment that he had succeeded in transcribing, in fixing for all time upon his canvas, the imperceptible ebb of the tide, the throb of one happy moment; and at the sight of this magic portrait, one could think of nothing else than to range the wide world, seeking to recapture the vanished day in its instantaneous, slumbering beauty.

So that if, before these visits to Elstir—before I had set eyes on one of his sea-pictures in which a young woman in a dress of white serge or linen, on the deck of a yacht flying the American flag, put into my imagination the spiritual "carbon copy" of a white linen dress and coloured flag which at once bred in me an insatiable desire to see there and then with my own eyes white linen dresses and flags against the sea, as if no such experience had ever yet befallen me—I had always striven, when I stood before the sea, to expel from my field of vision, as well as the bathers in the foreground and the yachts with their too dazzling sails that were like seaside costumes, everything that prevented me from persuading myself that I was contemplating the immemorial ocean which had already been pursuing the same mysterious life before the appearance of the human race, and had grudged even the days of radiant sunshine which seemed to me to invest with the trivial aspect of universal summer this coast of fog and tempest, to mark simply a pause, equivalent to what in music is known as a silent bar—now on the contrary it was bad weather that appeared to me to be some baleful accident, no longer worthy of a place in the world of beauty: I felt a keen desire to go out and recapture in reality what had so powerfully aroused my imagination, and I hoped that the weather would be propitious enough for me to see from the summit of the cliff the same blue shadows as in Elstir's picture.

Nor, as I went along, did I still screen my eyes with my hands as in the days when, conceiving nature to be animated by a life anterior to the first appearance of man and in opposition to all those wearisome improvements of industrial civilisation

which had hitherto made me yawn with boredom at universal
exhibitions or milliners' windows, I endeavoured to see only
that section of the sea over which there was no steamer passing,
so that I might picture it to myself as immemorial, still contemporary with the ages when it had been divorced from the
land, or at least contemporary with the early centuries of
Greece, which enabled me to repeat in their literal meaning the
lines of "old man Leconte" of which Bloch was so fond:

> 'Gone are the Kings, gone are their towering prows,
> Vanished upon the raging deep, alas,
> The long-haired warrior heroes of Hellas.'

I could no longer despise the milliners, now that Elstir
had told me that the delicate touches by which they give a last
refinement, a supreme caress to the bows or feathers of a hat
after it is finished would be as interesting to him to paint
as the muscular action of the jockeys (a statement which had
delighted Albertine). But I must wait until I had returned—
for milliners, to Paris, for regattas and races to Balbec, where
there would be no more now until next year. Even a yacht
with women in white linen was not to be found.

Often we encountered Bloch's sisters, to whom I was
obliged to bow since I had dined with their father. My new
friends did not know them. "I'm not allowed to play with
Israelites," Albertine announced. Her way of pronouncing the
word—"Issraelites" instead of 'Izraelites"—would in itself
have sufficed to show, even if one had not heard the rest of the
sentence, that it was no feeling of friendliness towards the
chosen race that inspired these young bourgeoises, brought up
in God-fearing homes, and quite ready to believe that the
Jews were in the habit of massacring Christian children.
"Besides, they're shocking bad form, your friends," said
Andrée with a smile which implied that she knew very well
that they were no friends of mine. "Like everything to do with
the tribe," added Albertine, in the sententious tone of one who
spoke from personal experience. To tell the truth, Bloch's
sisters, at once overdressed and half naked, with their languid,
brazen, ostentatious, slatternly air, did not create the best impression. And one of their cousins, who was only fifteen,

scandalised the Casino by her unconcealed admiration for Mlle Léa, whose talent as an actress M. Bloch senior rated very high, but whose tastes were understood not to be primarily directed towards gentlemen.

There were days when we picnicked at one of the outlying farms which catered for visitors. These were the farms known as Les Écorres, Marie-Thérèse, La Croix d'Heuland, Bagatelle, Californie and Marie-Antoinette. It was the last that had been adopted by the little band.

But at other times, instead of going to a farm, we would climb to the highest point of the cliff, and, when we had reached it and were seated on the grass, would undo our parcel of sandwiches and cakes. My friends preferred the sandwiches, and were surprised to see me eat only a single chocolate cake, sugared with gothic tracery, or an apricot tart. This was because, with the sandwiches of cheese or salad, a form of food that was novel to me and was ignorant of the past, I had nothing in common. But the cakes understood, the tarts were talkative. There was in the former an insipid taste of cream, in the latter a fresh taste of fruit which knew all about Combray, and about Gilberte, not only the Gilberte of Combray but the Gilberte of Paris, at whose tea-parties I had come across them again. They reminded me of those cake-plates with the Arabian Nights pattern, the subjects on which so diverted my aunt Léonie when Françoise brought her up, one day Aladdin and his Wonderful Lamp, another day Ali-Baba, or the Sleeper Awakes or Sinbad the Sailor embarking at Bassorah with all his treasures. I should dearly have liked to see them again, but my grandmother did not know what had become of them and thought moreover that they were just common plates that had been bought in the village. No matter, in grey, rustic Combray they were a multi-coloured inset, as in the dark church were the flickering jewels of the stained glass windows, as in the twilight of my bedroom were the projections cast by the magic-lantern, as in front of the railway-station and the little local line the buttercups from the Indies and the Persian lilacs, as was my great-aunt's collection of old porcelain in the sombre dwelling of an elderly lady in a country town.

Stretched out on the cliff I would see before me nothing but grassy meadows and beyond them not the seven heavens of the Christian cosmogony but two stages only, one of a deeper blue, the sea, and above it another, paler one. We ate our food, and if I had brought with me also some little keepsake which might appeal to one or other of my friends, joy sprang with such sudden violence into their translucent faces, flushed in an instant, that their lips had not the strength to hold it in, and, to allow it to escape, parted in a burst of laughter. They were gathered close round me, and between their faces, which were not far apart, the air that separated them traced azure pathways such as might have been cut by a gardener wishing to create a little space so as to be able himself to move freely through a thicket of roses.

When we had finished eating we would play games which until then I should have thought boring, sometimes such childish games as King of the Castle, or Who Laughs First; not for a kingdom would I have renounced them now; the aurora of adolescence with which the faces of these girls still glowed, and from which I, young as I was, had already emerged, shed its light on everything around them and, like the fluid painting of certain Primitives, brought out in relief the most insignificant details of their daily lives against a golden background. Their faces were for the most part blurred with this misty effulgence of a dawn from which their actual features had not yet emerged. One saw only a charming glow of colour beneath which what in a few years' time would be a profile was not discernible. The profile of to-day had nothing definitive about it, and could be only a momentary resemblance to some deceased member of the family to whom nature had paid this commemorative courtesy. It comes so soon, the moment when there is nothing left to wait for, when the body is fixed in an immobility which holds no fresh surprise in store, when one loses all hope on seeing—as on a tree in the height of summer one sees leaves already brown—round a face still young hair that is growing thin or turning grey; it is so short, that radiant morning time, that one comes to like only the very youngest girls, those in whom the flesh, like a precious leaven, is still at work. They are no more than a stream of ductile matter, continuously moulded by the fleeting impression of the moment. It is as though each of them was in turn a little statuette of gaiety, of childish earnestness, of cajolery, of surprise, shaped by an expression frank and complete, but fugitive. This plasticity gives a wealth of variety and charm to the pretty attentions which a young girl pays to us. Of course, such attentions are indispensable in the mature woman also, and one who is not attracted to us, or who does not show that she is attracted to us, tends to assume in our eyes a somewhat tedious uniformity. But even these endearments, after a certain age, cease to send gentle ripples over faces which the struggle for existence has hardened, has rendered unalterably militant or ecstatic. One—owing to the prolonged strain of the obedience that subjects wife to husband—will seem not so much a woman's face as a soldier's; another, carved by the sacrifices which a mother has consented to make, day after day, for her children, will be the face of an apostle. A third is, after a stormy passage through the years, the face of an ancient mariner, upon a body of which its garments alone indicate the sex. Certainly the attentions that a woman pays us can still, so long as we are in love with her, endue with fresh charms the hours that we spend in her company. But she is not then for us a series of different women. Her gaiety remains external to an unchanging face. Whereas adolescence precedes this complete solidification, and hence we feel, in the company of young girls, the refreshing sense that is afforded us by the spectacle of forms undergoing an incessant process of change, a play of unstable forces which recalls that perpetual re-creation of the primordial elements of nature which we contemplate when we stand before the sea.

It was not merely a social engagement, a drive with Mme de Villeparisis, that I was prepared to sacrifice to the hide-and-seek or guessing games of my new friends. More than once, Robert de Saint-Loup had sent word that, since I had failed to come to see him at Doncières, he had applied for twenty-four hours' leave which he would spend at Balbec. Each time I wrote back to say that he was on no account to come, offering the excuse that I should be obliged to be away myself that very day, having some duty call to pay with my grandmother on

family friends in the neighbourhood. No doubt he thought ill
of me when he learned from his aunt in what the "duty call"
consisted, and who the persons were who combined to play
the part of my grandmother. And yet, perhaps I was not wrong
in sacrificing the pleasures not only of society but of friendship
to that of spending the whole day in this green garden. People
who have the capacity to do so—it is true that such people are
artists, and I had long been convinced that I should never be
that—also have a duty to live for themselves. And friendship
is a dispensation from this duty, an abdication of self. Even
conversation, which is friendship's mode of expression, is a
superficial digression which gives us nothing worth acquiring.
We may talk for a lifetime without doing more than indefinitely
repeat the vacuity of a minute, whereas the march of thought
in the solitary work of artistic creation proceeds in depth, in
the only direction that is not closed to us, along which we are
free to advance—though with more effort, it is true—towards
a goal of truth. And friendship is not merely devoid of virtue,
like conversation, it is fatal to us as well. For the sense of boredom which those of us whose law of development is purely
internal cannot help but feel in a friend's company (when,
that is to say, we must remain on the surface of ourselves,
instead of pursuing our voyage of discovery into the depths)—
that first impression of boredom our friendship impels us to
correct when we are alone again, to recall with emotion the
words which our friend said to us, to look upon them as a
valuable addition to our substance, when the fact is that we are
not like buildings to which stones can be added from without,
but like trees which draw from their own sap the next knot
that will appear on their trunks, the spreading roof of their
foliage. I was lying to myself, I was interrupting the process of
growth in the direction in which I could indeed truly develop
and be happy, when I congratulated myself on being liked
and admired by so good, so intelligent, so rare a person as
Saint-Loup, when I focused my mind, not upon my own
obscure impressions which it should have been my duty to
unravel, but on the words of my friend, in which, by repeating
them to myself—by having them repeated to me by that other
self who dwells in us and on to whom we are always so ready

to unload the burden of taking thought,—I strove to find a beauty very different from that which I pursued in silence when I was really alone, but one that would enhance the merit not only of Robert, but of myself and of my life. In the life which such a friend provided for me, I seemed to myself to be cosily preserved from solitude, nobly desirous of sacrificing myself for him, in short incapable of realising myself. With the girls, on the other hand, if the pleasure which I enjoyed was selfish, at least it was not based on the lie which seeks to make us believe that we are not irremediably alone and prevents us from admitting that, when we chat, it is no longer we who speak, that we are fashioning ourselves then in the likeness of other people and not of a self that differs from them. The words exchanged between the girls of the little band and myself were of little interest; they were, moreover, few, broken by long spells of silence on my part. This did not prevent me from taking as much pleasure in listening to them as in looking at them, in discovering in the voice of each one of them a brightly coloured picture. It was with delight that I listened to their pipings. Loving helps us to discern, to discriminate. The bird-lover in a wood at once distinguishes the twittering of the different species, which to ordinary people sound the same. The devotee of girls knows that human voices vary even more. Each one possesses more notes than the richest instrument of music. And the combinations in which it groups those notes are as inexhaustible as the infinite variety of personalities. When I talked with any one of my young friends I was conscious that the original, the unique portrait of her individuality had been skilfully traced, tyrannically imposed on my mind as much by the inflexions of her voice as by those of her face, and that they were two separate spectacles which expressed, each on its own plane, the same singular reality. No doubt the lines of the voice, like those of the face, were not yet finally fixed; the voice had still to break, as the face to change. Just as infants have a gland the secretion of which enables them to digest milk, a gland which is not found in adults, so there were in the twitterings of these girls notes which women's voices no longer contain. And on this more varied instrument they played with their lips, with all the application and the ardour of Bellini's little angel musicians, qualities which also are an exclusive appanage of youth. Later on these girls would lose that note of enthusiastic conviction which gave a charm to their simplest utterances, whether it were Albertine who, in a tone of authority, repeated puns to which the younger ones listened with admiration, until a paroxysm of giggles took hold of them with the irresistible violence of a sneezing fit, or Andrée who spoke of their school work, even more childish seemingly than the games they played, with an essentially puerile gravity; and their words varied in tone, like the strophes of antiquity when poetry, still hardly differentiated from music, was declaimed on different notes. In spite of everything, the voices of these girls already gave a quite clear indication of the attitude that each of these young people had adopted towards life, an attitude so individual that it would be speaking in far too general terms to say of one: "She treats everything as a joke," of another: "She jumps from assertion to assertion," of a third: "She lives in a state of expectant hesitation." The features of our face are hardly more than gestures which force of habit has made permanent. Nature, like the destruction of Pompeii, like the metamorphosis of a nymph, has arrested us in an accustomed movement. Similarly, our intonation embodies our philosophy of life, what a person invariably says to himself about things. No doubt these characteristics did not belong only to these girls. They were those of their parents. The individual is steeped in something more general than himself. By this reckoning, our parents furnish us not only with those habitual gestures which are the outlines of our face and voice, but also with certain mannerisms of speech, certain favourite expressions, which, almost as unconscious as our intonation, almost as profound, indicate likewise a definite point of view towards life. It is true that in the case of girls there are certain of these expressions which their parents do not hand on to them until they have reached a certain age, as a rule not before they are women. They are kept in reserve. Thus, for instance, if one were to speak of the pictures of one of Elstir's friends, Andrée, whose hair was still "down," could not yet personally make use of the expression which her mother and elder sister employed: "It appears the man is quite charming!" But that would come in due course, when she was allowed to go to the Palais-Royal. And not long after her first communion, Albertine had begun to say, like a friend of her aunt: "It sounds to me pretty terrific." She had also inherited the habit of making one repeat whatever one said to her, so as to appear to be interested, and to be trying to form an opinion of her own. If you said that an artist's work was good, or his house nice, "Oh, his painting's good, is it?" "Oh, his house is nice, is it?" Finally, and more general still than the family heritage, was the rich layer imposed by the native province from which they derived their voices and of which their inflexions smacked. When Andrée sharply plucked a solemn note she could not prevent the Périgordian string of her vocal instrument from giving back a resonant sound quite in harmony, moreover, with the meridional purity of her features; while to the incessant japing of Rosemonde the substance of her northern face and voice responded willy-nilly in the accent of her province. Between that province and the temperament of the girl that dictated these inflexions, I perceived a charming dialogue. A dialogue, not in any sense a discord. No discord can possibly separate a young girl and her native place. She is herself, and she is still it. Moreover this reaction of local materials on the genius who utilises them and to whose work it imparts an added vigour, does not make the work any less individual, and whether it be that of an architect, a cabinet-maker or a composer, it reflects no less minutely the most subtle shades of the artist's personality, because he has been compelled to work in the millstone of Senlis or the red sandstone of Strasbourg, has respected the knots peculiar to the ash-tree, has borne in mind, when writing his score, the resources and limits of the sonority and range of the flute and the viola.

All this I realised, and yet we talked so little! Whereas with Mme de Villeparisis or Saint-Loup I should have displayed by my words a great deal more pleasure than I should actually have felt, for I was worn out on leaving them, when, on the other hand, I was lying on the grass among these girls, the plenitude of what I felt infinitely outweighed the paucity, the infrequency of our speech, and brimmed over from my immobility and silence in waves of happiness that rippled up to die at the feet of these young roses.

For a convalescent who rests all day long in a flower-garden or an orchard, a scent of flowers or fruit does not more completely pervade the thousand trifles that compose his idle hours than did for me that colour, that fragrance in search of which my eyes kept straying towards the girls, and the sweetness of which finally became incorporated in me. So it is that grapes sweeten in the sun. And by their slow continuity these simple little games had gradually wrought in me also, as in those who do nothing else all day but lie outstretched by the sea, breathing the salt air and sunning themselves, a relaxation, a blissful smile, a vague dazzlement that had spread from brain to eyes.

Now and then a pretty attention from one or another of them would stir in me vibrations which dissipated for a time my desire for the rest. Thus one day Albertine suddenly asked: "Who has a pencil?" Andrée provided one, Rosemonde the paper. Albertine warned them: "Now, young ladies, I forbid you to look at what I write." After carefully tracing each letter, supporting the paper on her knee, she passed it to me, saying: "Take care no one sees." Whereupon I unfolded it and read her message, which was: "I like you very much."

"But we mustn't sit here scribbling nonsense," she cried, turning with an impulsive and serious air to Andrée and Rosemonde, "I ought to show you the letter I got from Gisèle this morning. What an idiot I am; I've had it in my pocket all this time—and to think how useful it can be to us!"

Gisèle had been moved to copy out for her friend, so that it might be passed on to the others, the essay which she had written in her examination. Albertine's fears as to the difficulty of the subjects set had been more than justified by the two from which Gisèle had had to choose. The first was: "Sophocles, from the Shades, writes to Racine to console him for the failure of *Athalie*"; the other: "Suppose that, after the first performance of *Esther*, Mme de Sévigné is writing to Mme de La Fayette to tell her how much she regretted her absence." Now Gisèle, in an excess of zeal which must have touched the examiners' hearts, had chosen the first and more difficult of these two subjects, and had handled it with such remarkable skill that she had been given fourteen marks and had been congratulated by the board. She would have received a "distinction" if she had not "dried up" in the Spanish paper. The essay of which Gisèle had sent a copy to Albertine was immediately read aloud to us by the latter, who, having presently to take the same examination, was anxious to have Andrée's opinion, since she was by far the cleverest of them all and might be able to give her some good "tips."

"She did have a bit of luck," Albertine observed. "It's the very subject her French mistress made her swot up while she was here."

The letter from Sophocles to Racine, as drafted by Gisèle, ran as follows:

"My dear friend, you must pardon me the liberty of addressing you when I have not the honour of your personal acquaintance, but your latest tragedy, *Athalie*, shows, does it not, that you have made a thorough study of my own modest works. You have not only put poetry in the mouths of the protagonists, or principal persons of the drama, but you have written other, and, let me tell you without flattery, charming verses for the chorus, a feature which did not work too badly, from what one hears, in Greek tragedy, but is a complete novelty in France. In addition, your talent, so fluent, so fastidious, so fine, so delicate, has here acquired an energy on which I congratulate you. Athalie, Joad—these are figures which your rival Corneille could have wrought no better. The characters are virile, the plot simple and strong. You have given us a tragedy in which love is not the keynote, and on this I must offer you my sincerest compliments. The most familiar precepts are not always the truest. I will give you an example:

'This passion treat, which makes the poet's art
Fly, as on wings, straight to the listener's heart.'

You have shown us that the religious sentiment in which your chorus is steeped is no less capable of moving us. The general public may have been baffled, but those who are best qualified to judge must give you your due. I have felt myself impelled to offer you all my congratulations, to which I would add, my dear brother poet, the expression of my very highest esteem."

Albertine's eyes never ceased to sparkle while she was reading this to us. "Really, you'd think she must have cribbed it somewhere!" she exclaimed when she reached the end. "I'd never have believed Gisèle could cook up an essay like that! And the poetry she brings in! Where on earth can she have pinched that from?"

Albertine's admiration, with a change, it is true, of object, but with no loss—an increase, rather—of intensity, combined with the closest attention to what was being said, continued to make her eyes "start from her head" all the time that Andrée (consulted as being the biggest and cleverest) first of all spoke of Gisèle's essay with a certain irony, then, with a levity of tone which failed to conceal her underlying serious-ness, proceeded to reconstruct the letter in her own way.

"It's not bad," she said to Albertine, "but if I were you and had the the same subject set me, which is quite likely, as they set it very often, I shouldn't do it in that way. This is how I would tackle it. In the first place, if I had been Gisèle, I shouldn't have got carried away and I'd have begun by making a rough sketch of what I was going to write on a separate piece of paper. First and foremost, the formulation of the question and the exposition of the subject; then the general ideas to be worked into the development; finally, appreciation, style, conclusion. In that way, with a summary to refer to, you know where you are. But at the very start, with the exposi-tion of the subject, or, if you like, Titine, since it's a letter, with the preamble, Gisèle has made a bloomer. Writing to a person of the seventeenth century, Sophocles ought never to have said, 'My dear friend.'"

"Why, of course, she ought to have said 'My dear Racine,'" came impetuously from Albertine. "That would have been much better."

"No," replied Andrée, with a trace of mockery in her tone, "She ought to have put 'Sir.' In the same way, to end up, she ought to have thought of something like, 'Allow me, Sir,' (at the very most, 'Dear Sir') 'to inform you of the high esteeem with which I have the honour to be your servant.' Then again,

Gisèle says that the chorus in *Athalie* is a novelty. She is for-getting *Esther*, and two tragedies that are not much read now but happen to have been analysed this year by the Professor himself, so that you need only mention them, since they're his hobby-horse, and you're bound to pass. I mean *Les Juives* by Robert Garnier, and Montchrestien's *L'Aman*."

Andrée quoted these titles without managing quite to conceal a secret sense of benevolent superiority, which found expression in a rather charming smile. Albertine could con-tain herself no longer.

"Andrée, you really are staggering," she cried. "You must write down those names for me. Just fancy, what luck it would be if I got on to that, even in the oral, I should quote them at once and make a colossal impression."

But in the days that followed, every time that Albertine asked Andrée to tell her again the names of those two plays so that she might write them down, her erudite friend seemed to have forgotten them, and never recalled them for her.

"And another thing," Andrée went on with the faintest note of scorn for companions more childish than herself, though relishing their admiration and attaching to the manner in which she herself would have composed the essay a greater importance than she wished to reveal, "Sophocles in the Shades must be well-informed about all that goes on. He must therefore know that it was not before the general public but before the Sun King and a few privileged courtiers that *Athalie* was first played. What Gisèle says in this connection of the esteem of qualified judges is not at all bad, but she might have gone a little further. Sophocles, now that he is immortal, may quite well have the gift of prophecy and announce that, according to Voltaire, *Athalie* will be the supreme achievement not only of Racine but of the human mind."

Albertine was drinking in every word. Her eyes blazed. And it was with the utmost indignation that she rejected Rose-monde's suggestion that they should have a game.

"Finally," Andrée concluded in the same detached, airy tone, a trifle mocking and at the same time fairly warmly con-vinced, "if Gisèle had first calmly noted down the general ideas that she was going to develop, it might perhaps have occurred to her to do what I myself should have done, point out what a difference there is between the religious inspiration of Racine's choruses and those of Sophocles. I should have made Sophocles remark that if Racine's choruses are impregnated with religious feeling like those of the Greek tragedians, the gods are not the same. The god of Joad has nothing in common with the god of Sophocles. And that brings us quite naturally, when we have finished developing the subject, to our conclusion: What does it matter if beliefs are different? Sophocles would hesitate to insist upon this point. He would be afraid of wounding Racine's convictions, and so, slipping in a few appropriate words on his masters at Port-Royal, he prefers to congratulate his disciple on the loftiness of his poetic genius."

Admiration and attention had made Albertine so hot that she was sweating profusely. Andrée preserved the unruffled calm of a female dandy. "It would not be a bad thing, either, to quote some of the opinions of famous critics," she added, before they began their game.

"Yes," put in Albertine, "so I've been told. The best ones to quote, on the whole, are Sainte-Beuve and Merlet, aren't they?"

"Well, you're not absolutely wrong," Andrée told her. "Merlet and Sainte-Beuve would do no harm. But above all you ought to mention Deltour and Gascq-Desfossés." She refused, however, despite Albertine's entreaties, to write down these two unfamiliar names.

Meanwhile I had been thinking of the little page torn from a scribbling block which Albertine had handed me. "I like you," she had written. And an hour later, as I scrambled down the paths which led back, a little too vertically for my liking, to Balbec, I said to myself that it was with her that I would have my romance.

The state of being characterised by the presence of all the signs by which we are accustomed to recognise that we are in love, such as the orders which I left in the hotel not to wake me whoever might ask to see me, unless it were one or other of the girls, the throbbing of my heart while I waited for them (whichever of them it might be that I was expecting), and, on those mornings, my fury if I had not succeeded in finding a barber to shave me, and must appear with the disfigurement of a hairy chin before Albertine, Rosemonde or Andrée, no doubt this state, recurring for each of them in turn, was as different from what we call love as is from human life the life of the zoophytes, in which existence, individuality if we may so term it, is divided up among several organisms. But natural history teaches us that such an organisation of animal life is indeed to be observed, and that our own life, provided we have outgrown the first phase, is no less positive as to the reality of states hitherto unsuspected by us through which we have to pass, even though we abandon them later. Such was for me this state of love divided among several girls at once. Divided, or rather undivided, for more often than not what was so delicious to me, different from the rest of the world, what was beginning to become so precious to me that the hope of encountering it again the next day was the greatest joy of my life, was rather the whole of the group of girls, taken as they were all together on those afternoons on the cliffs, during those wind-swept hours, upon the strip of grass on which were laid those forms, so exciting to my imagination, of Albertine, of Rosemonde, of Andrée; and that without my being able to say which of them it was that made those scenes so precious to me, which of them I most wanted to love. At the start of a new love as at its ending, we are not exclusively attached to the object of that love, but rather the desire to love from which it will presently arise (and, later on, the memory it leaves behind) wanders voluptuously through a zone of interchangeable charms—simply natural charms, it may be, gratification of appetite, enjoyment of one's surroundings—which are harmonious enough for it not to feel at a loss in the presence of any one of them. Besides, as my perception of them was not yet dulled by familiarity, I still had the faculty of seeing them, that is to say of feeling a profound astonishment every time that I found myself in their presence.

No doubt this astonishment is to some extent due to the fact that the other person on such occasions presents some new facet; but so great is the multiformity of each individual, so abundant the wealth of lines of face and body, so few of which leave any trace, once we are no longer in the presence of the other person, on the arbitrary simplicity of our recollection, since the memory has selected some distinctive feature that had struck us, has isolated it, exaggerated it, making a woman who has appeared to us tall a sketch in which her figure is elongated out of all proportion, or of a woman who has seemed to be pink-cheeked and golden-haired a pure "Harmony in pink and gold," that the moment this woman is once again standing before us, all the other forgotten qualities which balance that one remembered feature at once assail us, in their confused complexity, diminishing her height, paling her cheeks, and substituting for what we came exclusively to seek other features which we remember having noticed the first time and fail to understand why we so little expected to find them again. We remembered, we anticipated a peacock, and we find a peony. And this inevitable astonishment is not the only one; for side by side with it comes another, born of the difference, not now between the stylisations of memory and the reality, but between the person whom we saw last time and the one who appears to us to-day from another angle and shows us a new aspect. The human face is indeed, like the face of the God of some oriental theogony, a whole cluster of faces juxtaposed on different planes so that one does not see them all at once.

But to a great extent our astonishment springs from the fact that the person presents to us also a face that is the same as before. It would require so immense an effort to reconstruct everything that has been imparted to us by things other than ourselves—were it only the taste of a fruit—that no sooner is the impression received than we begin imperceptibly to descend the slope of memory and, without realising it, in a very short time we have come a long way from what we actually felt. So that every fresh glimpse is a sort of rectification, which brings us back to what we in fact saw. Already we no longer had any recollection of it, to such an extent does what we call remembering a person consist really in forgetting him. But as long as we can still see, as soon as the forgotten feature appears we recognise it, we are obliged to correct the straying line, and thus the perpetual and fruitful surprise which made so

salutary and invigorating for me these daily outings with the
charming damsels of the sea shore consisted fully as much in
recognition as in discovery. When there is added to this the
agitation aroused by what these girls were to me, which was
never quite what I had supposed, and meant that my expectancy
of our next meeting resembled not so much my expectancy the
time before as the still throbbing memory of our last encounter,
it will be realised that each of our excursions brought about a
violent change in the course of my thoughts and not at all in
the direction which, in the solitude of my own room, I had
traced for them at my leisure. That plotted course was forgotten,
had ceased to exist, when I returned home buzzing like a bee-
hive with remarks which had disturbed me and were still
echoing in my brain. Every person is destroyed when we cease
to see him; after which his next appearance is a new creation,
different from that which immediately preceded it, if not from
them all. For the minimum variation that is to be found in
these creations is twofold. Remembering a strong and searching glance, a bold manner, it is inevitably, next time, by an
almost languid profile, a sort of dreamy gentleness, overlooked
by us in our previous impression, that at the next encounter we
shall be astonished, that is to say almost uniquely struck. In
confronting our memory with the new reality it is this that
will mark the extent of our disappointment or surprise, will
appear to us like a revised version of the reality by notifying
us that we had not remembered correctly. In its turn, the facial
aspect neglected the time before, and for that very reason the
most striking this time, the most real, the most corrective,
will become a matter for day-dreams and memories. It is a
languorous and rounded profile, a gentle, dreamy expression
which we shall now desire to see again. And then once more,
next time, such resolution, such strength of character as there
may be in the piercing eyes, the pointed nose, the tight lips,
will come to correct the discrepancy between our desire and
the object to which it has supposed itself to correspond. Of
course, this fidelity to the first and purely physical impressions experienced anew at each encounter with my young
friends did not only concern their facial appearance, since the
reader has seen that I was sensitive also to their voices, more

disturbing still, perhaps (for not only does a voice offer the same strange and sensuous surfaces as a face, it issues from that unknown, inaccessible region the mere thought of which sets the mind swimming with unattainable kisses), those voices, like the unique sound of a little instrument into which each of them put all of herself and which belonged to her alone. Traced by a casual inflexion, a sudden deep chord in one of these voices would surprise me when I recognised it after having forgotten it. So much so that the corrections which after every fresh meeting I was obliged to make so as to ensure absolute accuracy were as much those of a tuner or singing-master as of a draughtsman.

As for the harmonious cohesion into which, by the resistance that each brought to bear against the expansion of the others, the several waves of feeling induced in me by these girls had become neutralised, it was broken in Albertine's favour one afternoon when we were playing the game of "ferret."[29] It was in a little wood on the cliff. Stationed between two girls, strangers to the little band, whom the band had brought in its train because we wanted that day to have a bigger party than usual, I gazed enviously at Albertine's neighbour, a young man, saying to myself that if I had been in his place I could have been touching my beloved's hands during those unhoped-for moments which perhaps would never recur and which might have taken me a long way. Already, in itself, and even without the consequences which it would probably have involved, the contact of Albertine's hands would have been delicious to me. Not that I had never seen prettier hands than hers. Even in the group of her friends, those of Andrée, slender and far more delicate, had as it were a private life of their own, obedient to the commands of their mistress, but independent, and would often stretch out before her like thoroughbred greyhounds, with lazy pauses, languid reveries, sudden flexings of a finger-joint, seeing which Elstir had made a number of studies of these hands; and in one of them, in which Andrée was to be seen warming them at the fire, they had, with the light behind them, the golden diaphanousness of two autumn leaves. But, plumper than these, Albertine's hands would yield for a moment, then resist the pressure of the hand that clasped them, giving a sensation that was quite peculiar to themselves. The act of pressing Albertine's hand had a sensual sweetness which was in keeping somehow with the pink, almost mauve colouring of her skin. This pressure seemed to allow you to penetrate into the girl's being, to plumb the depths of her senses, like the ringing sound of her laughter, somehow indecent in the way that the cooing of doves or certain animal cries can be. She was the sort of woman with whom shaking hands affords so much pleasure that one feels grateful to civilisation for having made of the handclasp a lawful act between boys and girls when they meet. If the arbitrary code of good manners had replaced the hand-shake by some other gesture, I should have gazed, day after day, at the untouchable hands of Albertine with a curiosity to know the feel of them as ardent as was my curiosity to learn the savour of her cheeks. But in the pleasure of holding her hand unrestrictedly in mine, had I been next to her at "ferret," I did not envisage that pleasure alone; what avowals, what declarations silenced hitherto by my bashfulness, I could have conveyed by certain pressures of hand on hand; for her part, how easy it would have been, in responding by other pressures, to show me that she accepted; what complicity, what a vista of sensual delight stood open! My love would be able to make more progress in a few minutes spent thus by her side than it had yet made in all the time that I had known her. Feeling that they would last but a short time, were rapidly nearing their end, since presumably we were not going on much longer with this game, and that once it was over it would be too late, I could not stay in my place for another moment. I let myself deliberately be caught with the ring, and, once in the middle, when the ring passed I pretended not to see it but followed its course with my eyes, waiting for the moment when it should come into the hands of the young man next to Albertine, who herself, convulsed with laughter, and in the excitement and pleasure of the game, was flushed pink. "Why, we really are in the Fairy Wood," said Andrée to me, pointing to the trees all round us, with a smile in her eyes which was meant only for me and seemed to pass over the heads of the other players, as though we two alone were intelligent and detached enough to

make, in connexion with the game we were playing, a remark
of a poetic nature. She even carried the delicacy of her fancy
so far as to sing half-unconsciously: "The ferret of the Wood
has passed this way, sweet ladies; he has passed by this way,
the ferret of Fairy Wood!" like those people who cannot visit
Trianon without getting up a party in Louis XVI costume, or
think it amusing to have a song sung to its original setting.
I should no doubt have been saddened not to see any charm in
this realisation, had I had time to think about it. But my
thoughts were all elsewhere. The players began to show surprise at my stupidity in never getting the ring. I was looking at
Albertine, so pretty, so indifferent, so gay, who, though she
little knew it, would be my neighbour when at last I should
catch the ring in the right hands, thanks to a stratagem which
she did not suspect, and would certainly have resented if she
had. In the heat of the game her long hair had become loosened,
and fell in curling locks over her cheeks on which it served to
intensify, by its dry brownness, the carnation pink. "You have
the tresses of Laura Dianti, of Eleanor of Guyenne, and of her
descendant so beloved of Chateaubriand. You ought always
to wear your hair half down like that," I murmured in her ear
as an excuse for drawing close to her. Suddenly the ring passed
to her neighbour. I sprang upon him at once, forced open his
hands and seized it; he was obliged now to take my place inside
the circle, while I took his beside Albertine. A few minutes
earlier I had been envying this young man, when I saw that his
hands as they slipped over the string were constantly brushing
against hers. Now that my turn had come, too shy to seek, too
agitated to savour this contact, I no longer felt anything save
the rapid and painful beating of my heart. At one moment
Albertine leaned her round pink face towards me with an air
of complicity, pretending thus to have the ring in order
to deceive the ferret and prevent him from looking in the
direction in which it was being passed. I realised at once that
this was the sole object of Albertine's mysterious, confidential
gaze, but I was excited to see thus kindle in her eyes the
image—simulated purely for the purposes of the game—of a
secret understanding between her and myself which did not
exist but which from that moment seemed to me to be possible

and would have been divinely sweet. While I was still enraptured by this thought, I felt a slight pressure of Albertine's hand against mine, and her caressing finger slip under my finger along the cord, and I saw her, at the same moment, give me a wink which she tried to make imperceptible to the others. At once, a multitude of hopes, invisible hitherto, crystallised within me. "She's taking advantage of the game to make it clear to me that she likes me," I thought to myself in a paroxysm of joy from which I instantly relapsed on hearing Albertine mutter furiously: "Why can't you take it? I've been shoving it at you for the last hour." Stunned with grief, I let go the cord, the ferret saw the ring and swooped down on it, and I had to go back into the middle, where I stood helpless, in despair, looking at the unbridled rout which continued to circle round me, stung by the jeers of all the players, obliged, in reply, to laugh when I had so little mind for laughter, while Albertine kept on repeating: "People shouldn't play if they won't pay attention and spoil the game for the others. We shan't ask him again when we're going to play, Andrée, or else I shan't come." Andrée, with a mind above the game, still chanting her "Fairy Wood" which, in a spirit of imitation, Rosemonde had taken up too, without conviction, sought to take my mind off Albertine's reproaches by saying to me: "We're quite close to those old Creuniers you wanted so much to see. Look, I'll take you there by a dear little path, and we'll leave these silly idiots to go on playing like babies in the nursery." Since Andrée was extremely nice to me, as we went along I said to her everything about Albertine that seemed calculated to endear me to the latter. Andrée replied that she too was very fond of Albertine, and thought her charming; nevertheless my compliments about her friend did not seem altogether to please her. Suddenly, in the little sunken path, I stopped short, touched to the heart by an exquisite memory of my childhood. I had just recognised, from the fretted and glossy leaves which it thrust out towards me, a hawthorn-bush, flowerless, alas, now that spring was over. Around me floated an atmosphere of far-off Months of Mary, of Sunday afternoons, of beliefs, of errors long since forgotten. I wanted to seize hold of it. I stood still for a moment, and Andrée, with a charming divination of what was in my mind, left me to converse with the leaves of the bush. I asked them for news of the flowers, those hawthorn flowers that were like merry little girls, headstrong, provocative, pious. "The young ladies have been gone from here for a long time now," the leaves told me. And perhaps they thought that, for the great friend of those young ladies that I pretended to be, I seemed to have singularly little knowledge of their habits. A great friend, but one who had never been to see them again for all these years, despite his promises. And yet, as Gilberte had been my first love among girls, so these had been my first love among flowers. "Yes, I know, they leave about the middle of June," I answered, "but I'm delighted to see the place where they lived when they were here. They came to see me at Combray, in my room; my mother brought them when I was ill in bed. And we used to meet again on Saturday evenings, at the Month of Mary devotions. Can they go to them here?" "Oh, of course! Why, they make a special point of having our young ladies at Saint-Denis du Désert, the church near here." "So if I want to see them now?" "Oh, not before May next year." "But can I be sure that they will be here?" "They come regularly every year." "Only I don't know whether I'll be able to find the place." "Oh, dear, yes! They are so gay, the young ladies, they stop laughing only to sing hymns together, so that you can't possibly miss them, you can recognize their scent from the other end of the path."

I caught up with Andrée, and began again to sing Albertine's praises. It was inconceivable to me that she would not repeat what I said in view of the emphasis I put into it. And yet I never heard that Albertine had been told. Andrée had, nevertheless, a far greater understanding of the things of the heart, a refinement of sweetness; finding the look, the word, the action that could most ingeniously give pleasure, keeping to herself a remark that might possibly cause pain, making a sacrifice (and making it as though it were no sacrifice at all) of an afternoon's play, or it might be an "at home" or a garden party, in order to stay with a friend who was feeling sad, and thus show him or her that she preferred the simple company of a friend to frivolous pleasures: such were her habitual kindnesses. But when one knew her a little better one would have said it was with her as with those heroic poltroons who wish not to be afraid and whose bravery is especially meritorious; one would have said that deep down in her nature there was none of that kindness which she constantly displayed out of moral distinction, or sensibility, or a noble desire to show herself a true friend. When I listened to all the charming things she said to me about a possible attachment between Albertine and myself it seemed as though she were bound to do everything in her power to bring it to pass. Whereas, by chance perhaps, not even of the slightest opportunity which she had at her command and which might have proved effective in uniting me to Albertine did she ever make use, and I would not swear that my effort to make myself loved by Albertine did not—if not provoke in her friend secret stratagems calculated to thwart it—at any rate arouse in her an anger which however she took good care to hide and against which, out of delicacy of feeling, she may herself have fought. Of the countless refinements of affectionate kindness which Andrée showed, Albertine would have been incapable, and yet I was not certain of the underlying goodness of the former as I was to be later of the latter's. Showing herself always tenderly indulgent towards the exuberant frivolity of Albertine, Andrée greeted her with words and smiles that were those of a friend; better still, she acted towards her as a friend. I have seen her, day after day, in order to give this penniless friend the benefit of her own wealth, in order to make her happy, without any possibility of advantage to herself, take more pains than a courtier seeking to win his sovereign's favour. She was charmingly gentle and sympathetic, and spoke in sweet and sorrowful terms, when one expressed pity for Albertine's poverty, and took infinitely more trouble on her behalf than she would have taken for a rich friend. But if anyone were to hint that Albertine was perhaps not quite so poor as people made out, a just discernible cloud would overshadow Andrée's eyes and brow; she seemed out of temper. And if one went on to say that after all Albertine might perhaps be less difficult to marry off than people supposed, she would vehemently contradict one, repeating almost angrily: "Oh dear, no, she'll be quite unmarriageable! I'm certain of it, and I feel so sorry for her." As far as I myself was concerned, Andrée was the only one of the girls who would never have repeated to me anything at all disagreeable that might have been said about me by a third person; more than that, if it was I who told her what had been said she would make a pretence of not believing it, or would furnish some explanation which made the remark inoffensive. It is the aggregate of these qualities that goes by the name of tact. It is the attribute of those people who, if we fight a duel, congratulate us and add that there was no necessity to do so, in order to enhance still further in our own eyes the courage of which we have given proof without having been forced. They are the opposite of the people who in similar circumstances say: "It must have been a horrid nuisance for you to have to fight a duel, but on the other hand you couldn't possibly swallow an insult like that—there was nothing else to be done." But as there are pros and cons in everything, if the pleasure or at least the indifference shown by our friends in repeating something offensive that they have heard said about us proves that they do not exactly put themselves inside our skin at the moment of speaking, but thrust in the pin-point, turn the knife-blade as though it were gold-beater's skin and not human, the art of always keeping hidden from us what might be disagreeable to us in what they have heard said about our actions or in the opinion which those actions have led the speakers themselves to form, proves that there is in the other category of friends, in the friends who are so full of tact, a strong vein of dissimulation. It does no harm if indeed they are incapable of thinking ill of us, and if the ill that is said by other people only makes them suffer as it would make us. I supposed this to be the case with Andrée, without, however, being absolutely sure.

We had left the little wood and had followed a network of unfrequented paths through which Andrée managed to find her way with great skill. "Look," she said to me suddenly, "there are your famous Creuniers, and what's more you're in luck, it's just the time of day and the light is the same as when Elstir painted them." But I was still too wretched at having fallen, during the game of "ferret," from such a pinnacle of hopes. And so it was not with the pleasure which otherwise I should doubtless have felt that I suddenly discerned at my feet, crouching among the rocks for protection against the heat, the marine goddesses for whom Elstir had lain in wait and whom he had surprised there, beneath a dark glaze as lovely as Leonardo would have painted, the marvellous Shadows, sheltering furtively, nimble and silent, ready at the first glimmer of light to slip behind the stone, to hide in a cranny, and prompt, once the menacing ray had passed, to return to the rock or the seaweed over whose torpid slumbers they seemed to be keeping vigil, beneath the sun that crumbled the cliffs and the etiolated ocean, motionless lightfoot guardians darkening the water's surface with their viscous bodies and the attentive gaze of their deep blue eyes.

We went back to the wood to pick up the other girls and go home together. I knew now that I was in love with Albertine; but, alas! I did not care to let her know it. This was because, since the days of the games with Gilberte in the Champs-Elysées, my conception of love had become different, even if the persons to whom my love was successively assigned remained almost identical. For one thing, the avowal, the declaration of my passion to her whom I loved no longer seemed to be one of the vital and necessary stages of love, nor love itself an external reality, but simply a subjective pleasure. And I felt that Albertine would do what was necessary to sustain that pleasure all the more readily if she did not know that I was experiencing it.

As we walked home, the image of Albertine, bathed in the light that streamed from the other girls, was not the only one that existed for me. But as the moon, which is no more than a tiny white cloud of a more definite and fixed shape than other clouds during the day, assumes its full power as soon as daylight fades, so when I was once more in the hotel it was Albertine's sole image that rose from my heart and began to shine. My room seemed to me to have become suddenly a new place. Of course, for a long time past, it had not been the hostile room of my first night in it. All our lives, we go on patiently modifying the surroundings in which we live; and gradually, as habit dispenses us from feeling them, we suppress the noxious elements of colour, shape and smell which objectified our uneasiness. Nor was it any longer the room, still with sufficient power over my sensibility, not certainly to make me suffer, but to give me joy, the well of summer days, like a marble basin in which, half way up its polished sides, they mirrored an azure surface steeped in light over which glided for an instant, impalpable and white as a wave of heat, the fleeting reflection of a cloud; nor the purely aesthetic room of the pictorial evening hours; it was the room in which I had been now for so many days that I no longer saw it. And now I was beginning again to open my eyes to it, but this time from the selfish angle which is that of love. I liked to feel that the fine slanting mirror, the handsome glass-fronted bookcases, would give Albertine, if she came to see me, a good impression of me. Instead of a place of transit in which I would stay for a few minutes before escaping to the beach or to Rivebelle, my room became real and dear to me again, fashioned itself anew, for I looked at and appreciated each article of its furniture with the eyes of Albertine.

A few days after the game of "ferret," when, having allowed ourselves to wander rather too far afield, we had been fortunate in finding at Maineville a couple of little "tubs" with two seats in each which would enable us to be back in time for dinner, the intensity, already considerable, of my love for Albertine had the effect of making me suggest successively that Andrée and Rosemonde should come with me, and never once Albertine, and then, while still inviting Andrée or Rosemonde for preference, of bringing everyone round, in virtue of secondary considerations connected with time, route, coats and so forth, to decide, as though against my wishes, that the most practical policy after all was that I should take Albertine, to whose company I pretended to resign myself willy-nilly. Unfortunately, since love tends to the complete assimilation of a person, and none is comestible by way of conversation alone, for all that Albertine was as nice as possible on our way home, when I had deposited her at her own door she left me happy but more famished for her even than I had been at the start, and reckoning the moments that we had just spent together as only a prelude, of little importance in itself, to those that were still to come. Nevertheless it had that initial charm which is not to be found again. I had not yet asked anything of Albertine. She could imagine what I wanted, but, not being certain of it, surmise that I was aiming only at relations with no precise objective, in which my beloved would find that delicious vagueness, rich in expected surprises, which is romance.

In the week that followed I scarcely attempted to see Albertine. I made a show of preferring Andrée. Love is born; we wish to remain, for the one we love, the unknown person whom she may love in turn, but we need her, we need to make contact not so much with her body as with her attention, her heart. We slip into a letter some unkind remark which will force the indifferent one to ask for some little kindness in compensation, and love, following an unvarying procedure, tightens up with an alternating movement the machinery in which we can no longer either refrain from loving or be loved. I gave to Andrée the hours spent by the others at a party which I knew that she would sacrifice for my sake with pleasure, and would have sacrificed even with reluctance, from moral nicety, in order not to give either the others or herself the idea that she attached any importance to a relatively frivolous amusement. I arranged in this way to have her entirely to myself every evening, not with the intention of making Albertine jealous, but of enhancing my prestige in her eyes, or at any rate not imperilling it by letting Albertine know that it was herself and not Andrée that I loved. Nor did I confide this to Andrée either, lest she should repeat it to her friend. When I spoke of Albertine to Andrée I affected a coldness by which she was perhaps less deceived than I, from her apparent credulity. She made a show of believing in my indifference to Albertine, and of desiring the closest possible union between Albertine and myself. It is probable that, on the contrary, she neither believed in the one nor wished for the other. While I was saying to her that I did not care very greatly for her friend, I was thinking of one thing only, how to become acquainted with Mme Bontemps, who was staying for a few days near Balbec, and whom Albertine was shortly to visit for a few days. Naturally I did not disclose this desire to Andrée, and when I spoke to her of Albertine's family, it was in the most careless manner possible. Andrée's direct answers did not appear to throw any doubt on my sincerity. Why then did she blurt out suddenly one day: "Oh, by the way, I happen to have seen Albertine's aunt"? It is true that she had not said in so many words: "I could see through your casual remarks all right that the one thing you were really thinking of was how you could get to know Albertine's aunt." But it was clearly to the presence in Andrée's mind of some such idea which she felt it more becoming to keep from me that the phrase "happen to" seemed to point. It was of a kind with certain glances, certain gestures which, although they have no logical rational form directly devised for the listener's intelligence, reach him nevertheless in their true meaning, just as human speech, converted into electricity in the telephone, is turned into speech again when it strikes the ear. In order to remove from Andrée's mind the idea that I was interested in Mme Bontemps, I spoke of her thenceforth not only absent-mindedly but with downright malice, saying that I had once met that idiot of a woman, and trusted I should never have that experience again. Whereas I was seeking by every means in my power to meet her.

I tried to induce Elstir (but without mentioning to anyone else that I had asked him) to speak to her about me and to bring us together. He promised to introduce me to her, though he seemed greatly surprised at my wishing it, for he regarded her as a contemptible woman, a born intriguer, as uninteresting as she was self-interested. Reflecting that if I did see Mme Bontemps, Andrée would be sure to hear of it sooner or later, I thought it best to warn her in advance. "The things one tries hardest to avoid are those one finds one cannot escape," I told her. "Nothing in the world could bore me so much as meeting Mme Bontemps again, and yet I can't get out of it. Elstir has arranged to invite us together." "I've never doubted it for a single instant," exclaimed Andrée in a bitter tone, while her eyes, enlarged and altered by her annoyance, focused themselves upon some invisible object. These words of Andrée's were not the most reasoned statement of a thought which might be expressed thus: "I know that you're in love with Albertine, and that you're moving heaven and earth to get to know her family." But they were the shapeless fragments, easily pieced together again, of some such thought which I had exploded by striking it, through the shield of Andrée's self-control. Like her "happen to," these words had no meaning save at one remove, that is to say they were words of the sort which (rather than direct assertions) inspire in us respect or distrust for another person, and lead to a rupture.

If Andrée had not believed me when I told her that Albertine's family left me indifferent, it was because she thought that I was in love with Albertine. And probably she was none too happy in the thought.

She was generally present as a third party at my meetings with her friend. There were however days when I was to see Albertine by herself, days to which I looked forward with feverish impatience, which passed without bringing me any decisive result, without any of them having been that cardinal day whose role I immediately entrusted to the following day, which would prove no more apt to play it; thus there rose and toppled one after another, like waves, those peaks at once replaced by others.

About a month after the day on which we had played "ferret" together, I learned that Albertine was going away next morning to spend a couple of days with Mme Bontemps, and, since she would have to take an early train, was coming to spend the night at the Grand Hotel, from which, by taking the omnibus, she would be able, without disturbing the friends with whom she was staying, to catch the first train in the morning. I mentioned this to Andrée. "I don't believe a word of it," she replied with a look of annoyance. "Anyhow it won't help you at all, for I'm quite sure Albertine won't want to see you if she goes to the hotel by herself. It would be against 'protocol,'" she added, employing an expression which had recently come into favour with her, in the sense of "what is done." "I tell you this because I understand Albertine. What difference do you suppose it makes to me whether you see her or not? Not the slightest, I can assure you!"

We were joined by Octave who had no hesitation in telling Andrée the number of strokes he had gone round in, the day before, at golf, then by Albertine, who came along swinging her diabolo like a nun her rosary. Thanks to this pastime she could remain alone for hours on end without getting bored. As soon as she joined us I became conscious of the impudent tip of her nose, which I had omitted from my mental picture of her during the last few days; beneath her dark hair the vertical line of her forehead controverted—and not for the first time—the blurred image that I had preserved of her, while its whiteness made a vivid splash in my field of vision; emerging from the dust of memory, Albertine was built up afresh before my eyes.

Golf gives one a taste for solitary pleasures. The pleasure to be derived from diabolo is undoubtedly one of these. And yet, after she had joined us, Albertine continued to play with it, just as a lady on whom friends have come to call does not on their account stop working at her crochet.

"I gather that Mme de Villeparisis," she remarked to Octave, "has been complaining to your father." (I could hear, underlying the "I gather," one of those notes that were peculiar to Albertine; every time I realised that I had forgotten them, I would remember having already caught a glimpse behind them of Albertine's determined and typically Gallic mien. I could have been blind and yet have detected certain of her qualities, alert and slightly provincial, in those notes just as plainly as in the tip of her nose. They were equivalent and might have been substituted for one another, and her voice was like what we are promised in the photo-telephone of the future: the visual image was clearly outlined in the sound.) "She hasn't written only to your father, either, she wrote to the Mayor of Balbec at the same time, to say that we must stop playing diabolo on the front as somebody hit her in the face with a ball."

"Yes, I was hearing about that," said Octave. "It's ridiculous. There's little enough to do here as it is."

Andrée did not join in the conversation; she was not acquainted, any more than was Albertine or Octave, with Mme de Villeparisis. She did, however, remark: "I can't think why this lady should make such a song about it. Old Mme de Cambremer got hit in the face, and she never complained."

"I'll explain the difference," replied Octave gravely, striking a match as he spoke. "It's my belief that Mme de Cambremer is a society lady, and Mme de Villeparisis is just an upstart. Are you playing golf this afternoon?" And he left us, followed by Andrée. I was alone now with Albertine. "You see," she began, "I'm wearing my hair now the way you like—look at my ringlet. They all laugh at it and nobody knows who I'm doing it for. My aunt will laugh at me too. But I shan't tell her why, either." I had a sidelong view of Albertine's cheeks, which often appeared pale, but, seen thus, were flushed with a coursing stream of blood which lighted them up, gave them that dazzling clearness of certain winter mornings when the stones sparkling in the sun seem blocks of pink granite and radiate joy. The joy I felt at this moment at the sight of Albertine's cheeks was as keen, but led to another desire which was not the desire for a walk but for a kiss. I asked her if the report of her plans which I had heard was correct. "Yes," she told me, "I shall be sleeping at your hotel to-night, and in fact as I've got a bit of a cold I shall be going to bed before dinner. You can come and sit by my bed and watch me eat, if you like, and afterwards we'll play at anything that you choose. I should have liked you to come to the station to-morrow morning, but I'm afraid it might look rather odd, I don't say to Andrée who is a sensible person, but to the others who will be there; if my aunt got to know, I should never hear the last of it. But we can spend the evening together, at any rate. My aunt will know nothing about that. I must go and say good-bye to Andrée. So long, then. Come early, so that we can have a nice long time together," she added, smiling.

At these words I was swept back past the days when I loved Gilberte to those when love seemed to me not simply an external entity but one that could be realised. Whereas the Gilberte whom I used to see in the Champs-Elysées was a different Gilberte from the one I found within me when I was alone again, suddenly in the real Albertine, the one I saw every day, whom I supposed to be stuffed with middle-class prejudices and entirely frank with her aunt, the imaginary Albertine had just been embodied, she whom, when I did not yet know her, I had suspected of casting furtive glances at me on the front, she who had worn an air of being reluctant to go home when she saw me making off in the other direction.

I went into dinner with my grandmother. I felt within me a secret which she could never guess. Similarly with Albertine; to-morrow her friends would be with her, not knowing what new experience she and I had in common; and when she kissed her niece on the forehead Mme Bontemps would never imagine that I stood between them, in the shape of that hair arrangement which had for its object, concealed from all the world, to give pleasure to me, to me who had until then so greatly envied Mme Bontemps because, being related to the same people as her niece, she had the same occasions to put on mourning, the same family visits to pay; and now I found myself being more to Albertine than was the aunt herself. When she was with her aunt, it was of me that she would be thinking. What was going to happen that evening, I scarcely knew. In any event, the Grand Hotel and the evening no longer seemed empty to me; they contained my happiness. I rang for the lift-boy to take me up to the room which Albertine had engaged, a room that looked over the valley. The slightest movements, such as that of sitting down on the bench in the lift, were sweet to me, because they were in direct relation to my heart; I saw in the ropes that drew the cage upwards, in the few stairs that I had still to climb, only the machinery, the materialised stages of my joy. I now had only two or three steps to take along the corridor before coming to that room in which was enshrined the precious substance of that rosy form—that room which, even if there were to be done in it delicious things, would keep that air of changelessness, of being, to a chance visitor who knew nothing of its history, just like any other room, which makes of inanimate things the obstinately mute witnesses, the scrupulous confidants, the inviolable depositaries of our pleasure. Those few steps from the landing to Albertine's door, those few steps which no one could stop, I took with rapture but with prudence, as though plunged in a new and strange element, as if in going forward I had been gently displacing a liquid stream of happiness, and at the same time with a strange feeling of omnipotence, and of entering at last into an inheritance which had belonged to me from time immemorial. Then suddenly I reflected that I was wrong to be in any doubt; she had told me to come when she was in bed. It was as clear as daylight; I pranced for joy, I nearly knocked over Françoise who was standing in my way, and I ran, with sparkling eyes, towards my beloved's room.

I found Albertine in bed. Leaving her throat bare, her white nightdress altered the proportions of her face, which, flushed by being in bed or by her cold or by dinner, seemed pinker; I thought of the colours I had had beside me a few hours earlier on the front, the savour of which I was now at last to taste; her cheek was traversed by one of those long, dark, curling tresses which, to please me, she had undone altogether. She looked at me and smiled. Beyond her, through the window, the valley lay bright beneath the moon. The sight of Albertine's bare throat, of those flushed cheeks, had so intoxicated me (that is to say had so shifted the reality of the world for me away from nature into the torrent of my sensations which I could scarcely contain), that it had destroyed the equilibrium between the immense and indestructible life which circulated in my being and the life of the universe, so puny in comparison. The sea, which was visible through the window as well as the valley, the swelling breasts of the first of the Maineville cliffs, the sky in which the moon had not yet climbed to the zenith— all this seemed less than a featherweight on my eyeballs, which between their lids I could feel dilated, resistant, ready to bear far greater burdens, all the mountains of the world, upon their fragile surface. Their orb no longer found even the sphere of the horizon adequate to fill it. And all the life-giving energy that nature could have brought me would have seemed to me all too meagre, the breathing of the sea all too short to express the immense aspiration that was swelling my breast. I bent over Albertine to kiss her. Death might have struck me down in that moment and it would have seemed to me a trivial, or rather an impossible thing, for life was not outside me but in me; I should have smiled pityingly had a philosopher then expressed the idea that some day, even some distant day, I should have to die, that the eternal forces of nature would survive me, the forces of that nature beneath whose godlike feet I was no more than a grain of dust; that, after me, there would still remain those rounded, swelling cliffs, that sea, that moonlight and that sky! How could it have been possible; how could the world have lasted longer than myself, since I was not lost in its vastness, since it was the world that was enclosed in me, in me whom it fell far short of filling, in me who, feeling that there was room to store so many other treasures, flung sky and sea and cliffs contemptuously into a corner. "Stop it or I'll ring the bell!" cried Albertine, seeing that I was flinging myself upon her to kiss her. But I told myself that not for nothing does a girl invite a young man to her room in secret, arranging that her aunt should not know, and that boldness, moreover, rewards those who know how to seize their opportunities; in the state of exaltation in which I was, Albertine's round face, lit by an inner flame as by a night-light, stood out in such relief that, imitating the rotation of a glowing sphere, it seemed to me to be turning, like those Michelangelo figures which are being swept away in a stationary and vertiginous whirlwind. I was about to discover the fragrance, the flavour which this strange pink fruit concealed. I heard a sound, abrupt, prolonged and shrill. Albertine had pulled the bell with all her might.

I had supposed that my love for Albertine was not based on the hope of carnal possession. And yet, when the lesson to be drawn from my experience that evening was, apparently, that such possession was impossible; when, after having had no doubt, that first day on the beach, that Albertine was licentious, and having passed through various intermediate assumptions, it seemed to me to be established that she was absolutely virtuous; when on her return from her aunt's a week later, she greeted me coldly with: "I forgive you; in fact I'm sorry to have upset you, but you must never do it again,"—then in contrast to what I had felt on learning from Bloch that one could have all the women one wanted, and as if, instead of a real girl, I had known a wax doll, my desire to penetrate into her life, to follow her through the places in which she had spent her childhood, to be initiated by her into the sporting life, gradually detached itself from her; my intellectual curiosity as to thoughts on this subject or that did not survive my belief that I might kiss her if I chose. My dreams abandoned her as soon as they ceased to be nourished by the hope of a possession of which I had supposed them to be independent. Thenceforward they found themselves once more at liberty to transfer themselves—according to the attraction that I had found in her on any particular day, above all according to the chances I seemed to detect of my being possibly loved by her—to one or other of Albertine's friends, and to Andrée first of all. And yet, if Albertine had not existed, perhaps I should not have had the pleasure which I began to feel more and more strongly during the days that followed in the kindness that was shown me by Andrée. Albertine told no one of the rebuff which I had received at her hands. She was one of those pretty girls who, from their earliest youth, on account of their beauty, but especially of an attraction, a charm which remains somewhat mysterious and has its source perhaps in reserves of vitality to which others less favoured by nature come to quench their thirst, have always—in their home circle, among their friends, in society—been more sought after than other more beautiful and richer girls; she was one of those people from whom, before the age of love and much more still after it is reached, more is asked than they themselves ask, more even than they are able to give. From her childhood Albertine had always had round her in an adoring circle four or five little girl friends, among them Andrée who was so far her superior and knew it (and perhaps this attraction which Albertine exerted quite involuntarily had been the origin, had laid the foundations of the little band). This attraction was still potent even at a great social distance, in circles quite brilliant by comparison, where, if there was a pavane to be danced, Albertine would be sent for rather than another girl of better family. The consequence was that, not having a penny to her name, living, not very well, at the expense of M. Bontemps who was said to be a shady individual and was anyhow anxious to be rid of her, she was nevertheless invited, not only to dine but to stay, by people who in Saint-Loup's eyes might not have had much distinction, but to Rosemonde's mother or Andrée's, women who though very rich themselves did not know these people, represented something quite extraordinary. Thus Albertine spent a few weeks every year with the family of one of the Governors of the Bank of France, who was also Chairman of the Board of Directors of a railway company. The wife of this financier entertained prominent people, and had never mentioned her "day" to Andrée's mother, who thought her wanting in politeness, but was nevertheless prodigiously interested in everything that went on in her house. Accordingly she encouraged Andrée every year to invite Albertine down to their villa, because, she said, it was a charitable act to offer a holiday by the sea to a girl who had not herself the means to travel and whose aunt did so little for her. Andrée's mother was probably not prompted by the thought that the banker and his wife, learning that Albertine was made much of by her and her daughter, would form a high opinion of them both; still less did she hope that Albertine, kind and clever as she was, would manage to get her invited, or at least to get Andrée invited, to the financier's garden-parties. But every evening at the dinner-table, while assuming an air of indifference and disdain, she was fascinated by Albertine's accounts of everything that had happened at the big house while she was staying there, and the names of the other guests, almost all of them people whom she knew by sight or by name. Even the thought that she knew them only in this indirect fashion, that is to say did not know them at all (she called this kind of acquaintance knowing people "all my life"), gave Andrée's mother a touch of melancholy while she plied Albertine with questions about them in a lofty and distant tone, with pursed lips, and might have left her doubtful and uneasy as to the importance of her own social position had she not been able to reassure herself, to return safely to the "realities of life," by saying to the butler: "Please tell the chef that his peas aren't soft enough." She then recovered her serenity. And she was quite determined that Andrée was to marry nobody but a man, of the best family of course, rich enough for her too to be able to keep a chef and a couple of coachmen. That was the reality, the practical proof of "position." But the fact that Albertine had dined at the banker's country house with this or that great lady, and that the said great lady had invited

her to stay with her next winter, invested the girl, in the eyes of
Andrée's mother, with a peculiar esteem which went very well
with the pity and even contempt aroused by her lack of fortune, a contempt increased by the fact that M. Bontemps had
betrayed his flag and—being even vaguely Panamist, it was
said—had rallied to the Government. Not that this deterred
Andrée's mother, in her passion for abstract truth, from wither-
ing with her scorn the people who appeared to believe that
Albertine was of humble origin. "What's that you say? Why,
they're one of the best families in the country. Simonet with a
single 'n,' you know!" Certainly, in view of the class of society
in which all this went on, in which money plays so important a
part, and mere charm makes people ask you out but not marry
you, an "acceptable" marriage did not appear to be for
Albertine a practical outcome of the so distinguished patronage which she enjoyed but which would not have been held
to compensate for her poverty. But even in themselves, and
with no prospect of any matrimonial consequence, Albertine's
"successes" excited the envy of certain spiteful mothers,
furious at seeing her received "like one of the family" by the
banker's wife, even by Andrée's mother, whom they scarcely
knew. They therefore went about telling mutual friends of
theirs and of those two ladies that the latter would be very
angry if they knew the truth, which was that Albertine repeated to each of them everything that the intimacy to which
she was rashly admitted enabled her to spy out in the household of the other, countless little secrets which it must be
infinitely unpleasant to the interested party to have made
public. These envious women said this so that it might be
repeated and might get Albertine into trouble with her patrons.
But, as often happens, their machinations met with no success.
The spite that prompted them was too apparent, and their only
result was to make the women who had perpetrated them
appear rather more contemptible than before. Andreé's mother
was too firm in her opinion of Albertine to change her mind
about her now. She looked upon her as "unfortunate," but the
best-natured girl living, and one who was incapable of making
anything up except to give pleasure.

If this sort of popularity to which Albertine had attained did not seem likely to lead to any practical result, it had stamped Andrée's friend with the distinctive characteristic of people who, being always sought after, have never any need to offer themselves, a characteristic (to be found also, and for analogous reasons, at the other end of the social scale, among the smartest women) which consists in their not making any display of the successes they have scored, but rather keeping them to themselves. She would never say of anyone: "So-and-so is anxious to meet me," would speak of everyone with the greatest good nature, and as if it was she who ran after, who sought to know other people. If someone mentioned a young man who, a few minutes earlier, had been in private conversation with her, heaping the bitterest reproaches upon her because she had refused him an assignation, so far from proclaiming this in public or betraying any resentment she would stand up for him: "He's such a nice boy!" Indeed it quite annoyed her to be so attractive to people, since it obliged her to disappoint them, whereas her natural instinct was always to give pleasure. So much did she enjoy giving pleasure that she had come to employ a particular kind of falsehood peculiar to certain utilitarians and men who have "arrived." Existing, incidentally, in an embryonic state in a vast number of people, this form of insincerity consists in not being able to confine the pleasure arising out of a single act of politeness to a single person. For instance, if Albertine's aunt wished her niece to accompany her to a not very amusing party, Albertine by going to it might have found it sufficient to extract from the incident the moral profit of having given pleasure to her aunt. But, being courteously welcomed by her host and hostess, she preferred to say to them that she had been wanting to see them for so long that she had finally seized this opportunity and begged her aunt to take her to their party. Even this was not enough: at the same party there might happen to be one of Albertine's friends who was very unhappy. Albertine would say to her: "I didn't like the thought of your being here by yourself. I felt it might do you good to have me with you. If you would rather leave the party, go somewhere else, I'm ready to do anything you like. What I want above all is to see you look less unhappy" (which, as it happened, was true also).

Sometimes it happened however that the fictitious aim destroyed the real one. Thus Albertine, having a favour to ask on behalf of one of her friends, would go to see a certain lady who could help her. But on arriving at the house of this lady—a kind and sympathetic soul—the girl, unconsciously following the principle of the multiple utilisation of a single action, would think it more affectionate to appear to have come there solely on account of the pleasure she knew she would derive from seeing the lady again. The lady would be deeply touched that Albertine should have taken a long journey out of pure friendship. Seeing her almost overcome by emotion, Albertine liked the lady even more. Only, there was this awkward consequence: she now felt so keenly the pleasure of friendship which she pretended to have been her motive in coming, that she was afraid of making the lady suspect the genuineness of sentiments which were actually quite sincere if she now asked her to do the favour for her friend. The lady would think that Albertine had come for that purpose, which was true, but would conclude also that Albertine had no disinterested pleasure in seeing her, which was false. With the result that she came away without having asked the favour, like a man sometimes who has been so kind to a woman, in the hope of winning her favours, that he refrains from declaring his passion in order not to deprive his kindness of its appearance of nobility. In other instances it would be wrong to say that the true object was sacrificed to the subordinate and subsequently conceived idea, but the two were so incompatible that if the person to whom Albertine endeared herself by stating the second had known of the existence of the first, his pleasure would at once have been turned into the deepest pain. At a much later point in this story, we shall have occasion to see this kind of contradiction expressed in clearer terms. Suffice it to say for the present, borrowing an example from a completely different context, that they occur very frequently in the most divergent situations that life has to offer. A husband has established his mistress in the town where he is quartered with his regiment. His wife, left by herself in Paris, and with an inkling of the truth, grows more and more miserable, and writes her husband letters embittered by jealousy. Then the mistress is obliged to

go to Paris for the day. The husband cannot resist her entreaties to him to accompany her, and applies for a twenty-four
hour leave. But since he is a good-natured fellow, and hates
making his wife unhappy, he goes to see her and tells her,
shedding a few quite genuine tears, that, dismayed by her
letters, he has found the means of getting away from his duties
to come to her and to console her in his arms. He has thus
contrived by a single journey to furnish wife and mistress alike
with proofs of his love. But if the wife were to learn the reason
for which he has come to Paris, her joy would doubtless be
turned into grief, unless her pleasure in seeing the faithless
wretch outweighed, in spite of everything, the pain that his
infidelities had caused her. Among the men who have struck
me as practising most consistently this system of killing several
birds with one stone must be included M. de Norpois. He
would now and then agree to act as intermediary between two
of his friends who had quarrelled, and this led to his being
called the most obliging of men. But it was not sufficient for
him to appear to be doing a service to the friend who had come
to him to request it; he would represent to the other the steps
which he was taking to effect a reconciliation as undertaken
not at the request of the first friend but in the interest of the
second, a notion of which he never had any difficulty in
persuading an interlocutor influenced in advance by the idea
that he had before him the "most obliging of men." In this
way, playing both ends against the middle, what in stage
parlance is known as "doubling" two parts, he never allowed
his influence to be in the slightest degree imperilled, and the
services which he rendered constituted not an expenditure of
capital but a dividend upon some part of his credit. At the
same time every service, seemingly rendered twice over, correspondingly enhanced his reputation as an obliging friend,
and, better still, a friend whose interventions were efficacious,
one who did not simply beat the air, whose efforts were always
justified by success, as was shown by the gratitude of both
parties. This duplicity in obligingness was—allowing for disappointments such as are the lot of every human being—an
important element in M. de Norpois's character. And often at
the Ministry he would make use of my father, who was a simple

soul, while making him believe that it was he, M. de Norpois, who was being useful to my father.

Pleasing people more easily than she wished, and having no need to trumpet her conquests abroad, Albertine kept silent about the scene she had had with me by her bedside, which a plain girl would have wished the whole world to know. And yet for her attitude during that scene I could not arrive at any satisfactory explanation. As regards the supposition that she was absolutely chaste (a supposition to which I had first of all attributed the violence with which Albertine had refused to let herself be taken in my arms and kissed, though it was by no means essential to my conception of the kindness, the fundamentally honourable character of my beloved), I could not accept it without a copious revision of its terms. It ran so entirely counter to the hypothesis which I had constructed that day when I saw Albertine for the first time. Then, so many different acts of affectionate sweetness towards myself (a sweetness that was caressing, at times uneasy, alarmed, jealous of my predilection for Andrée) came up on all sides to challenge the brutal gesture with which, to escape from me, she had pulled the bell. Why then had she invited me to come and spend the evening by her bedside? Why did she speak all the time in the language of affection? What is the basis of the desire to see a friend, to be afraid that he may be fonder of someone else than of you, to seek to please him, to tell him, so romantically, that no one else will ever know that he has spent the evening in your room, if you refuse him so simple a pleasure and if it is no pleasure to you? I could not believe, after all, that Albertine's virtue went as far as that, and I came to wonder whether her violence might not have been due to some reason of vanity, a disagreeable odour, for instance, which she suspected of lingering about her person, and by which she was afraid that I might be repelled, or else of cowardice—if for instance she imagined, in her ignorance of the facts of love, that my state of nervous debility was due to something contagious, communicable to her in a kiss.

She was genuinely distressed by her failure to gratify me, and gave me a little gold pencil, with the virtuous perverseness of people who, touched by your kindness but not prepared to grant what it clamours for, nevertheless want to do something on your behalf—the critic, an article from whose pen would so gratify the novelist, who asks him to dinner instead; the duchess who does not take the snob with her to the theatre but lends him her box on an evening when she will not be using it herself. To such an extent are those who do the minimum, and might easily do nothing, driven by conscience to do something!

I told Albertine that in giving me this pencil she was giving me great pleasure, and yet not so great as I should have felt if, on the night she had spent at the hotel, she had permitted me to kiss her: "It would have made me so happy! What possible harm could it have done you? I'm amazed that you should have refused me."

"What amazes me," she retorted, "is that you should find it amazing. I wonder what sort of girls you must know if my behaviour surprised you."

"I'm sorry to have annoyed you, but even now I cannot say that I think I was in the wrong. What I feel is that all that sort of thing is of no importance really, and I can't understand a girl who could so easily give pleasure not consenting to do so. Let's be quite clear about it," I went on, throwing a sop of sorts to her moral scruples as I recalled how she and her friends had scarified the girl who went about with the actress Léa, "I don't mean to say that a girl can behave exactly as she likes and that there's no such thing as immorality. Take, for example, what you were saying the other day about a girl who's staying at Balbec and her relations with an actress. I call that unspeakable, so unspeakable that I feel sure it must all have been made up by some enemies of the girl and that there can't be any truth in the story. It strikes me as improbable, impossible. But to allow oneself to be kissed, or even more, by a friend—since you say that I'm your friend . . ."

"So you are, but I've had other friends before now, I've known lots of young men who were every bit as friendly, I can assure you. Well, not one of them would ever have dared to do such a thing. They know they'd get their ears boxed if they tried it on. Besides, they never dreamed of doing so. We would shake hands in a straightforward, friendly sort of way, like good pals, but there was never a word said about kissing, and yet we weren't any the less friends for that. Why, if it's my friendship you're after, you've nothing to complain of; I must be jolly fond of you to forgive you. But I'm sure you don't care two hoots about me, really. Own up now, it's Andrée you're in love with. Besides, you're quite right; she's ever so much nicer than I am, and absolutely ravishing! Oh, you men!"

Despite my recent disappointment, these words so frankly uttered, by giving me a great respect for Albertine, made a very agreeable impression on me. And perhaps this impression was to have serious and vexatious consequences for me later on, for it was around it that there began to form that feeling almost of brotherly intimacy, that moral core which was always to remain at the heart of my love for Albertine. Such a feeling may be the cause of the greatest suffering. For in order really to suffer at the hands of a woman one must have believed in her completely. For the moment, that embryo of moral esteem, of friendship, was left embedded in my soul like a stepping-stone in a stream. It could have availed nothing, by itself, against my happiness if it had remained there without growing, in an inertia which it was to retain the following year, and still more during the final weeks of this first visit to Balbec. It dwelt in me like one of those foreign bodies which it would be wiser when all is said to expel, but which we leave where they are without disturbing them, so harmless for the present does their weakness, their isolation amid a strange environment render them.

My longings were now once more at liberty to concentrate on one or another of Albertine's friends, and returned first of all to Andrée, whose attentions might perhaps have touched me less had I not been certain that they would come to Albertine's ears. Undoubtedly the preference that I had long pretended to feel for Andrée had furnished me—in habits of conversation and declarations of affection—with, so to speak, the material for a ready-made love for her which had hitherto lacked only the complement of a genuine feeling, which my heart, being once more free, was now in a position to supply. But Andrée was too intellectual, too neurotic, too sickly, too like myself for me really to love her. If Albertine now seemed to me to be

void of substance, Andrée was filled with something which I
knew only too well. I had thought, that first day, that what I saw
on the beach was the mistress of some racing cyclist, passionately interested in sport, and now Andrée told me that if
she had taken it up, it was on orders from her doctor, to cure
her neurasthenia, her digestive troubles, but that her happiest
hours were those which she spent translating one of George
Eliot's novels. My disappointment, due to an initial mistake
as to what Andrée was, had not, in fact, the slightest importance for me. But the mistake was one of the kind which, if
they allow love to be born and are not recognised as mistakes
until it has ceased to be modifiable, become a cause of suffering. Such mistakes—which may be quite different from mine
with regard to Andrée, and even its exact opposite,—are
frequently due (and this was especially the case here) to the
fact that people take on the aspect and the mannerisms of what
they are not but would like to be sufficiently to create an illusion
at first sight. To the outward appearance, affectation, imitation,
the longing to be admired, whether by the good or by the
wicked, add misleading similarities of speech and gesture.
There are cynicisms and cruelties which, when put to the test,
prove no more genuine than certain apparent virtues and
generosities. Just as we often discover a vain miser beneath
the cloak of a man famed for his charity, so her flaunting of
vice leads us to surmise a Messalina in a respectable girl with
middle-class prejudices. I had thought to find in Andrée a
healthy, primitive creature, whereas she was merely a person in
search of health, as perhaps were many of those in whom she
herself had thought to find it, and who were in reality no
more healthy than a burly arthritic with a red face and in white
flannels is necessarily a Hercules. Now there are circumstances
in which it is not immaterial to our happiness that the person
we have loved for what appeared to be so healthy about her is
in reality only one of those invalids who receive such health
as they possess from others, as the planets borrow their light,
as certain bodies are only conductors of electricity.

No matter, Andrée, like Rosemonde and Gisèle, indeed
more than they, was, when all was said, a friend of Albertine,
sharing her life, imitating her ways, to the point that, on the

first day, I had not at once distinguished them from one another. Among these girls, rose-sprigs whose principal charm was that they were silhouetted against the sea, the same indivisibility prevailed as at the time when I did not know them, when the appearance of no matter which of them had caused me such violent emotion by heralding the fact that the little band was not far off. And even now the sight of one of them filled me with a pleasure in which was included, to an extent which I should not have found it easy to define, that of seeing the others follow her in due course, and, even if they did not come that day, of speaking about them, and of knowing that they would be told that I had been on the beach.

It was no longer simply the attraction of those first days, it was a genuine wish to love that wavered between them all, to such an extent was each the natural substitute for the others. My greatest sadness would not have been to be abandoned by whichever of these girls I loved best, but I should at once have loved best, because I should have fastened on to her the sum total of the melancholy longings which had been floating vaguely among them all, the one who had abandoned me. It would, moreover, in that event, be the loss of all her friends, in whose eyes I should speedily have forfeited whatever prestige I might possess, that I should, in losing her, have unconsciously regretted, having pledged to them that sort of collective love which the politician and the actor feel for the public for whose desertion of them after they have enjoyed all its favours they can never be consoled. Even those favours which I had failed to win from Albertine I would hope suddenly to receive from one or other who had left me in the evening with a word or glance of ambiguous meaning, thanks to which it was towards her that, for the next day or so, my desire would turn.

It strayed among them all the more voluptuously in that upon those volatile faces a comparative fixity of features had now begun, and had been carried far enough for the eye to distinguish—even if it were to change yet further—each malleable and elusive effigy. The differences that existed between these faces doubtless bore little relation to equivalent differences in the length and breadth of their features, any of

which, dissimilar as the girls appeared, might perhaps almost
have been lifted from one face and imposed at random upon
any other. But our knowledge of faces is not mathematical. In
the first place, it does not begin by measuring the parts, it
takes as its starting point an expression, a combination of the
whole. In Andrée, for instance, the fineness of her gentle eyes
seemed to go with the thinness of her nose, as slender as a
mere curve which one could imagine having been traced in
order to pursue along a single line the notion of delicacy
divided higher up between the dual smile of her twin gaze. A
line equally fine cut through her hair, as pliant and as deep as
the line with which the wind furrows the sand. And there it
must have been hereditary; for the snow-white hair of Andrée's
mother rippled in the same way, forming here a swelling, there
a depression like a snowdrift that rises or sinks according to
the irregularities of the land. Certainly, when compared with
the fine delineation of Andrée's, Rosemonde's nose seemed to
present broad surfaces, like a high tower resting upon massive
foundations. Although expression may suffice to make us
believe in enormous differences between things that are
separated by infinitely little—although that infinitely little
may by itself create an expression that is absolutely unique, an
individuality—it was not only the infinitely little of its lines
and the originality of its expression that made these faces
appear irreducible to one another. Between my friends' faces
their colouring established a separation wider still, not so
much by the varied beauty of the tones with which it provided
them, so contrasted that I felt when I looked at Rosemonde—
suffused with a sulphurous pink that was further modified by
the greenish light of her eyes—and then at Andrée—whose
white cheeks derived such austere distinction from her black
hair—the same kind of pleasure as if I had been looking
alternately at a geranium growing by a sunlit sea and a camellia
in the night; but principally because the infinitely small
differences of their lines were enlarged out of all proportion,
the relations between one and another surface entirely changed
by this new element of colour which, in addition to being the
dispenser of tints, is a great generator or at least modifier of
dimensions. So that faces which were perhaps constructed on

not dissimilar lines, according as they were lit, by the flames of a shock of red hair, with a pinkish hue, or, by white light, with a matt pallor, grew sharper or broader, became something else, like those properties used in the Russian ballet, consisting sometimes, when they are seen in the light of day, of a mere paper disc, out of which the genius of a Bakst, according to the blood-red or moonlit lighting in which he plunges his stage, makes a hard incrustation, like a turquoise on a palace wall, or something softly blooming, like a Bengal rose in an eastern garden. And so when studying faces, we do indeed measure them, but as painters, not as surveyors.

The same was true of Albertine as of her friends. On certain days, thin, with a grey complexion, a sullen air, a violet transparency slanting across her eyes such as we notice sometimes on the sea, she seemed to be feeling the sorrows of exile. On other days her face, smoother and glossier, drew one's desires on to its varnished surface and prevented them from going further; unless I caught a sudden glimpse of her from the side, for her matt cheeks, like white wax on the surface, were visibly pink beneath, which was what made one so long to kiss them, to reach that different tint which was so elusive. At other times, happiness bathed those cheeks with a radiance so mobile that the skin, grown fluid and vague, gave passage to a sort of subcutaneous gaze which made it appear to be of another colour but not of another substance than the eyes; sometimes, when one looked without thinking at her face punctuated with tiny brown marks among which floated what were simply two larger, bluer stains, it was as though one were looking at a goldfinch's egg, or perhaps at an opalescent agate cut and polished in two places only, where, at the heart of the brown stone, there shone, like the transparent wings of a skyblue butterfly, the eyes, those features in which the flesh becomes a mirror and gives us the illusion of enabling us, more than through the other parts of the body, to approach the soul. But most often it too showed more colour, and was then more animated; sometimes in her white face only the tip of her nose was pink, and as delicate as that of a mischievous kitten with which one would have liked to play; sometimes her cheeks were so glossy that one's glance slipped, as over the surface of a miniature, over their pink enamel, which was made to appear still more delicate, more private, by the enclosing though half-opened lid of her black hair; or it might happen that the tint of her cheeks had deepened to the mauvish pink of cyclamen, and sometimes even, when she was flushed or feverish, with a suggestion of unhealthiness which lowered my desire to something more sensual and made her glance expressive of something more perverse and unwholesome, to the deep purple of certain roses, a red that was almost black; and each of these Albertines was different, as is each appearance of the dancer whose colours, form, character, are transmuted according to the endlessly varied play of a projected limelight. It was perhaps because they were so diverse, the persons whom I used to contemplate in her at this period, that later I developed the habit of becoming myself a different person, according to the particular Albertine to whom my thoughts had turned; a jealous, an indifferent, a voluptuous, a melancholy, a frenzied person, created anew not merely by the accident of the particular memory that had risen to the surface, but in proportion also to the strength of the belief that was lent to the support of one and the same memory by the varying manner in which I appreciated it. For this was the point to which I invariably had to return, to those beliefs which for most of the time occupy our souls unbeknownst to us, but which for all that are of more importance to our happiness than is the person whom we see, for it is through them that we see him, it is they that impart his momentary grandeur to the person seen. To be quite accurate, I ought to give a different name to each of the selves who subsequently thought about Albertine; I ought still more to give a different name to each of the Albertines who appeared before me, never the same, like those seas—called by me simply and for the sake of convenience "the sea"—that succeeded one another and against which, a nymph likewise, she was silhouetted. But above all, in the same way as, in telling a story (though to far greater purpose here), people mention what the weather was like on such and such a day, I ought always to give its name to the belief that reigned over my soul and created its atmosphere on any given day on which I saw Albertine, the appearance of people, like that of the sea, being dependent on those clouds, themselves barely visible, which change the colour of everything by their concentration, their mobility, their dissemination, their flight—like that cloud which Elstir had rent one evening by not introducing me to these girls with whom he had stopped to talk, and whose images had suddenly appeared to me more beautiful when they moved away—a cloud that had formed again a few days later when I did get to know them, veiling their brightness, interposing itself frequently between my eyes and them, opaque and soft, like Virgil's Leucothea.

No doubt, all their faces had assumed quite new meanings for me since the manner in which they were to be read had been to some extent indicated to me by their talk, talk to which I could ascribe a value all the greater in that, by questioning them, I could prompt it whenever I chose, could vary it like an experimenter who seeks by corroborative proofs to establish the truth of his theory. And it is, after all, as good a way as any of solving the problem of existence to get near enough to the things and people that have appeared to us beautiful and mysterious from a distance to be able to satisfy ourselves that they have neither mystery nor beauty. It is one of the systems of mental hygiene among which we are at liberty to choose our own, a system which is perhaps not to be recommended too strongly, but gives us a certain tranquillity with which to spend what remains of life, and also—since it enables us to regret nothing, by assuring us that we have attained to the best, and that the best was nothing out of the ordinary—with which to resign ourselves to death.

I had now substituted, in the minds of these girls, for their supposed contempt for chastity, for their memories of daily love-making, upright principles, liable perhaps to falter, but principles which had hitherto kept unscathed the children who had acquired them in their respectable middle-class homes. And yet, when one has been mistaken from the start, even in trifling details, when an error of assumption or recollection makes one seek for the author of a malicious slander, or for the place where one has lost something, in the wrong direction, it frequently happens that one discovers one's error only to substitute for it not the truth but a fresh error. I drew, as regards their manner of life and the conduct to be observed towards them, all the possible conclusions from the word "innocence" which I had read, in talking familiarly with them, upon their faces. But perhaps I had carelessly misread it, and it was no more written there than was the name of Jules Ferry on the programme of the performance at which I had seen Berma for the first time, an omission which had not prevented me from maintaining to M. de Norpois that Jules Ferry, beyond any possibility of doubt, was a person who wrote curtain-raisers.

No matter which of my friends of the little band I thought of, how could the last face that she had shown me not have been the only one that I could recall, since, of our memories with respect to a person, the mind eliminates everything that does not concur with the immediate purpose of our daily relations (even, and especially, if those relations are impregnated with an element of love which, ever unsatisfied, lives always in the moment that is about to come)? It allows the chain of spent days to slip away, holding on only to the very end of it, often of a quite different metal from the links that have vanished in the night, and in the journey which we make through life, counts as real only the place in which we are at present. My very earliest impressions, already so remote, could not find any remedy in my memory against the daily distortion to which they were subjected; during the long hours which I spent in talking, eating, playing with these girls, I did not even remember that they were the same pitiless and sensual virgins whom I had seen, as in a fresco, file past between me and the sea.

Geographers or archaeologists may conduct us over Calypso's island, may excavate the Palace of Minos. Only, Calypso becomes then a mere woman, Minos a mere king with no semblance of divinity. Even the qualities and defects which history then teaches us to have been the attributes of those quite real personages often differ widely from those which we had ascribed to the fabulous beings who bore the same names as they. Thus had there faded and vanished all the lovely oceanic mythology which I had composed in those first days. But it is not altogether a matter of indifference that we do succeed, at any rate now and then, in spending our time in familiar intercourse with what we thought to be unattainable and longed to possess. In our later dealings with people whom at first we found disagreeable there persists always, even amid the factitious pleasure which we have come at length to enjoy in their society, the lingering taint of the defects which they have succeeded in hiding. But, in relations such as I enjoyed with Albertine and her friends, the genuine pleasure which was there at the start leaves that fragrance which no artifice can impart to hothouse fruits, to grapes that have not ripened in the sun. The supernatural creatures which for a little time they had been to me still introduced, even without my being aware of it, a miraculous element into the most commonplace dealings I might have with them, or rather prevented such dealings from ever becoming in the least commonplace. My desire had sought so avidly to learn the meaning of eyes which now knew and smiled at me, but which, that first day, had crossed mine like rays from another universe, it had distributed colour and fragrance so generously, so carefully, so minutely, over the fleshly surfaces of these girls who now, stretched out on the cliff-top, simply offered me sandwiches or played guessing-games, that often, in the afternoon, while I lay there among them,—like those painters who, seeking to match the grandeurs of antiquity in modern life, give to a woman cutting her toe-nail the nobility of the *Spinario*, or, like Rubens, make goddesses out of women they know to people some mythological scene—I would gaze at those lovely forms, dark and fair, so dissimilar in type, scattered around me on the grass, without emptying them, perhaps, of all the mediocre content with which my everyday experience had filled them, and yet (without expressly recalling their celestial origin) as if, like young Hercules or Telemachus, I had been playing amid a band of nymphs.

Then the concerts ended, the bad weather began, my friends left Balbec, not all at once, like the swallows, but all in the same week. Albertine was the first to go, abruptly, without any of her friends understanding, then or afterwards, why she had returned suddenly to Paris whither neither her work nor any amusement summoned her. "She said neither why nor where-

fore, and with that she left!" muttered Françoise, who, for
that matter, would have liked us to do the same. We were, she
thought, inconsiderate towards the staff, now greatly reduced
in number, but retained on account of the few visitors who
were still staying on, and towards the manager who was "just
eating up money." It was true that the hotel, which would
very soon be closed for the winter, had long since seen most
of its patrons depart, and never had it been so agreeable. This
view was not shared by the manager; from end to end of the
rooms in which we sat shivering, and at the doors of which no
page now stood on guard, he paced the corridors, wearing a
new frock coat, so well tended by the barber that his insipid
face appeared to be made of some composition in which, for
one part of flesh, there were three of cosmetics, and incessantly
changing his neckties. (These refinements cost less than having
the place heated and keeping on the staff, just as a man who is
no longer able to subscribe ten thousand francs to a charity can
still parade his generosity without inconvenience to himself by
tipping the boy who brings him a telegram with five.) He
appeared to be inspecting the empty air, to be seeking, by the
smartness of his personal appearance, to give a provisional
splendour to the desolation that could now be felt in this hotel
where the season had not been good, and walked like the ghost
of a monarch who returns to haunt the ruins of what was once
his palace. He was particularly annoyed when the little local
railway company, finding the supply of passengers inadequate,
discontinued its trains until the following spring. "What is
lacking here," said the manager, "is the means of commotion."
In spite of the deficit which his books showed, he was making
plans for the future on a lavish scale. And as he was, after all,
capable of retaining an exact memory of fine phrases when they
were directly applicable to the hotel-keeping industry and had
the effect of enhancing its importance: "I was not adequately
supported, although in the dining room I had an efficient
squad," he explained, "but the pages left something to be
desired. You will see, next year, what a phalanx I shall collect."
In the meantime the suspension of the services of the B. C. B.
obliged him to send for letters and occasionally to dispatch
visitors in a light cart. I would often ask leave to sit by the

driver, and in this way I managed to be out in all weathers, as in the winter I had spent at Combray.

Sometimes, however, the driving rain kept my grandmother and me, the Casino being closed, in rooms almost completely deserted, as in the hold of a ship when a storm is raging; and there, day by day, as in the course of a sea-voyage, a new person from among those in whose company we had spent three months without getting to know them, the senior judge from Caen, the leader of the Cherbourg bar, an American lady and her daughters, came up to us, engaged us in conversation, thought up some way of making the time pass less slowly, revealed some social accomplishment, taught us a new game, invited us to drink tea or to listen to music, to meet them at a certain hour, to plan together some of those diversions which contain the true secret of giving ourselves pleasure, which is not to aspire to it but merely to help ourselves to pass the time less boringly—in a word, formed with us, at the end of our stay at Balbec, ties of friendship which, in a day or two, their successive departures from the place would sever. I even made the acquaintance of the rich young man, of one of his pair of aristocratic friends and of the actress, who had reappeared for a few days; but their little society was composed now of three persons only, the other friend having returned to Paris. They asked me to come out to dinner with them at their restaurant. I think they were just as well pleased that I did not accept. But they had issued the invitation in the most friendly way imaginable, and although it came in fact from the rich young man, since the others were only his guests, as the friend who was staying with him, the Marquis Maurice de Vaudémont, came of a very good family indeed, instinctively the actress, in asking me whether I would not come, said, to flatter my vanity: "It will give Maurice such pleasure."

And when I met them all three together in the hall of the hotel, it was M. de Vaudémont (the rich young man effacing himself) who said to me: "Won't you give us the pleasure of dining with us?"

On the whole I had derived very little benefit from Balbec, but this only strengthened my desire to return there. It seemed to me that I had not stayed there long enough. This was not the opinion of my friends in Paris, who wrote to ask whether I meant to stay there for the rest of my life. And when I saw that it was the name "Balbec" which they were obliged to put on the envelope, as my window looked out not over a land-scape or a street but on to the plains of the seas, as through the night I heard its murmur, to which, before going to sleep, I had entrusted the ship of my dreams, I had the illusion that this life of promiscuity with the waves must effectively, without my knowledge, pervade me with the notion of their charm, like those lessons which one learns by heart while one is asleep.

The manager offered to reserve better rooms for me next year, but I had now become attached to mine, into which I went without ever noticing the scent of vetiver, while my mind, which had once found such difficulty in rising to fill its space, had come now to take its measurements so exactly that I was obliged to submit it to a reverse process when I had to sleep in Paris, in my own room, the ceiling of which was low.

For we had had to leave Balbec at last, the cold and the damp having become too penetrating for us to stay any longer in a hotel which had neither fireplaces in the rooms nor central heating. Moreover, I forgot almost immediately these last weeks of our stay. What I saw almost invariably in my mind's eye when I thought of Balbec were the hours which, every morning during the fine weather, since I was due to go out in the afternoon with Albertine and her friends, my grandmother, following the doctor's orders, insisted on my spending lying down with the room darkened. The manager gave instructions that no noise was to be made on my landing, and came up himself to see that they were obeyed. Because the light outside was so strong, I kept drawn for as long as pos-sible the big violet curtains which had adopted so hostile an attitude towards me the first evening. But since, in spite of the pins with which Françoise fastened them every night so that the light should not enter, and which she alone knew how to unfasten, in spite of the rugs, the red cretonne table-cover, the various fabrics collected here and there which she fitted in to her defensive scheme, she never succeeded in making them meet exactly, the darkness was not complete, and they spilled over the carpet as it were a scarlet shower of anemone-petals, which I could not resist the temptation to trample for a moment with my bare feet. And on the wall which faced the window and so was partially lighted, a cylinder of gold with no visible support was placed vertically and moved slowly along like the pillar of fire which went before the Hebrews in the desert. I went back to bed; obliged to taste without moving, in imagination only, and all at once, the pleasures of games, bathing, walks which the morning prompted, joy made my heart beat thunderingly like a machine set going at full speed but fixed to the ground, which can spend its energy only by turning over on itself.

I knew that my friends were on the front, but I did not see them as they passed before the links of the sea's uneven chain, at the far end of which, perched amid its bluish peaks like an Italian citadel, could occasionally be distinguished, in clear weather, the little town of Rivebelle, picked out in minutest detail by the sun. I did not see my friends, but (while there mounted to my belvedere the shout of the newsboys, the "journalists" as Françoise used to call them, the shouts of the bathers and of children at play, punctuating like the cries of sea-birds the sough of the gently breaking waves) I guessed their presence, I heard their laughter enveloped like the laughter of the Nereids in the soft surge of sound that rose to my ears. "We looked up," said Albertine in the evening, "to see if you were coming down. But your shutters were still closed when the concert began." At ten o'clock, sure enough, it broke out beneath my windows. In the intervals between the blare of the instruments, if the tide were high, the gliding surge of a wave would be heard again, slurred and continuous, seeming to enfold the notes of the violin in its crystal spirals and to be spraying its foam over the intermittent echoes of a submarine music. I grew impatient because no one had yet come with my things, so that I might get up and dress. Twelve o'clock struck, and Françoise arrived at last. And for months on end, in this Balbec to which I had so looked forward because I imagined it only as battered by storms and buried in the mist, the weather had been so dazzling and so unchanging that when she came to open the window I could always, without once being wrong, expect to see the same patch of sunlight folded in the corner of the outer wall, of an unalterable colour which was less moving as a sign of summer than depressing as the colour of a lifeless and composed enamel. And after Françoise had removed her pins from the mouldings of the window-frame, taken down her various cloths, and drawn back the curtains, the summer day which she disclosed seemed as dead, as immemorially ancient as a sumptuously attired dynastic mummy from which our old servant had done no more than cautiously unwind the linen wrappings before displaying it to my gaze, embalmed in its vesture of gold.

NOTES, ADDENDA
SYNOPSIS

NOTES

1 (p. 15) Bressant: a well-known actor (1815-1886) who introduced a new hair-style which involved wearing the hair
short in front and fairly long behind.

2 (p. 29) *O ciel, que de vertus vous nous faites haïr.* From Corneille's
Mort de Pompée.

3 (p. 29) *à contre-coeur*: reluctantly.

4 (p. 31) *Le Miracle de Théophile*: verse play by the thirteenth-
century troubadour Rutebeuf. *Les quatre fils Aymon* or
Renaud de Montauban: twelfth-century *chanson de geste.*

5 (p. 84) *bleu*: express letter transmitted by pneumatic tube
(in Paris).

6 (p. 148) The first edition of *Du côté de chez Swann* had "*pour
Chartres*" instead of "*pour Reims.*" Proust moved
Combray (which as we know was modelled on Illiers,
near Chartres) to the fighting zone between Laon and
Rheims when he decided to incorporate the 1914-1918
war in his book.

7 (p. 158) Indirect quotation from Racine's *Phèdre*, Act I, Scene 3:
Que ces vains ornements, que ces voiles me pèsent!
Quelle importune main en formant tous ces noeuds
A pris soin sur mon front d'assembler mes cheveux?

8 (p. 208) In English in the original. Odette's speech is peppered
with English expressions.

9 (p. 213) "Home" is in English in the original, as is "smart"
on p. 214.

10 (p. 268) *Reine Topaze*: a light opera by Victor Massé presented
at the Théâtre Lyrique in 1856.

11 (p. 269) *Serge Panine*: play by Georges Ohnet (1848-1918),
adapted from a novel of the same name, which had a
great success in 1881 in spite of its mediocre literary
qualities.
Olivier Métra: composer of such popular works as *La
Valse des Roses* and a famous lancers quadrille, and
conductor at the Opéra-Comique.

12 (p. 288) *Serpent à sonnettes* means rattlesnake.

13 (p. 321) *Pays du Tendre* (or, more correctly, *Pays de Tendre*): the
country of the sentiments, the tender emotions, mapped
(the *carte de Tendre*) by Mlle de Scudéry in her novel
Clélie (1654-1670).

14 (p. 371) The rather forced joke on the name Cambremer con-
             ceives of it as being made up of abbreviations of
             Cambronne and *merde* (shit). *Le mot de Cambronne* (said to
             have been flung defiantly at the enemy by a general at
             Waterloo) is the traditional euphemism for *merde*.

15 (p. 437) *Pneumatique* or *petit bleu*: see note to p. 84 above.

16 (p. 468) *Le seize mai*: constitutional crisis in 1877 which even-
             tually led to the resignation of the President of the
             Republic, Marshal MacMahon.

17 (p. 498) Singers' Bridge: headquarters of the Russian Foreign
             Ministry in St Petersburg.
             Ballplatz (more correctly Ballhausplatz): the Austrian
             Foreign Ministry in Vienna.
             Montecitorio: the Italian Chamber of Deputies in
             Rome.

18 (p. 501) The tomb of Tourville, the seventeenth-century French
             admiral, is in fact in the church of Saint-Eustache in
             Paris.

19 (p. 503) The word is *cocu*=cuckold. Norpois is being comically
             prudish.

20 (p. 549) August Wolf: German philologist (1759-1824) who was
             the most notable adherent of the view that the *Iliad* and
             the *Odyssey* were the work of a number of anonymous
             bards.

21 (p. 583) The letters p.p.c. stand for *pour prendre congé*=to take
             one's leave.

22 (p. 621) *Rachel quand du Seigneur*...: famous aria from Halévy's
             opera *La Juive*.

23 (p. 642) Vatel: chef, after the famous *maître d'hôtel* of the great
             Condé.

24 (p. 701) This is an imaginary work. No such Memoirs exist.

25 (p. 755) Baronne d'Ange: character in *Le Demi-monde* by
             Alexandre Dumas *fils*—a courtesan who tries to marry
             into high society without success.

26 (p. 793) *Concours général*: competitive examination open to all
             secondary schools at *baccalauréat* level. "People's
             universities" were established between 1898 and 1901
             with the object of raising the intellectual level of the
             workers and bringing different social classes together.
             They mainly consisted of evening lecture courses.

27 (p. 880) The reference is to Amphion, who, according to Greek
             legend, rebuilt the walls of Thebes, charming the stones
             into place with his lyre.

28 (p. 928) Arvède Barine was the pseudonym of Mme Charles
Vicens (1840-1908), a French woman writer who
published several volumes of critical and historical
essays.

29 (p. 980) *Le jeu du furet* is the French equivalent of "hunt-the-
slipper."

ADDENDA

Page 558. *The original manuscript has a more detailed version of the scene, which the Pléiade editors reproduce in their "Notes and Variants":*—

Odette was quite prepared to cut short her visit, but could not leave at once since she had only just arrived. Either to get round the difficulty, or as a studied insult to her niece, "I should be most interested to look over your house," Lady Israels had said to Mme de Marsantes, knowing that the latter had a great regard for her and an even greater need of her. Moreover Lady Israels, who was extremely beneficent and upright, was also very haughty. "I shall be delighted to show it to you," Mme de Marsantes had replied, and at once set off with Lady Jacob [*sic*] as though she felt she had no need to bother about Mme Swann who must be only too happy to be in her house, leaving the unfortunate woman standing there alone, kicking her heels for half an hour. Then Mme de Marsantes had returned and said curtly to Mme Swann: "Excuse me"; whereupon Lady Jacob had raised her lorgnette and looked at Odette as at a person she had not even noticed before and who must have arrived in the meantime, or as yet another feature of the house. This feature no doubt failed to impress her, for it was the only one on which she made no comment, and turning towards Mme de Marsantes she started up a conversation with her in which Odette was not invited to join. "I trust you won't go back there," Swann had said to her afterwards, and this single visit had not encouraged Odette to pursue her offensive in that direction. Let us hasten to add, however, that this was not the world that preoccupied Mme Swann. On matters concerning the nobility, on pedigrees and ducal houses, she lacked even the petty erudition that peaceful bourgeois citizens of Nantes or Tours cultivate night and day, although they may never know anyone from that world. When, as we shall see, it began to flock to the house of the aged Odette, it did not come to fill a void, to gratify a craving induced by the reading of old memoirs and the Almanach de Gotha; it was received without the slightest mental preparation. Mme de Guermantes was for Odette no more than a superior Mme Verdurin whom it was "smart" to have to one's house, and she was far less concerned about who the

Guermantes family were than a great many people who would
never know them...

Page 810. *The manuscript gives a longer and more detailed version of
this passage, reproduced in the Pléiade "Notes and Variants":*—

So Mme de Villeparisis, who when I used to hear my grandmother
talking about her in my childhood had seemed to me to be an old
lady of the same sort as her other friends and had always remained
so to me—that person who had once given me a box of chocolates
held by a duck and was now going out of her way to be agreeable
to us—was a member of the powerful Guermantes clan! This change
in the value of what we possess, like those old bundles which turn
out to be priceless treasures, is one of the things that introduce
most wonder, animation, variety and consequently poetry into
one's adolescence (that adolescence which, while gradually dwindling
until it becomes no more than a thin trickle that often runs dry,
is sometimes prolonged throughout the whole course of one's life).
The rise or depreciation of one's wealth, the weirdly unexpected
reassessments of one's possessions, the misrepresentations of
people we know, which make one's youth as fabulous as the
metamorphoses of Ovid or even the metempsychoses of the
Hindus, derive in part from ignorance—an ignorance that extends
to people's names as to everything else. My great-aunt had bought
for one of the rooms at Combray some crude painted canvases
(perhaps indeed they were only coloured paper) framed in coffee-
coloured wood, which represented scenes by Teniers. I had told
Bloch in perfectly good faith that we had a room full of Teniers.
In the vague world, innocent of any notion of discrimination, that
painting was to me then, I could see no difference between a five-
franc reproduction and an original work. Similarly in the Army,
where one has a captain called Lévy and another called Lévy-
Mirepoix: these two names, though the second is longer than the
first and therefore a little more ridiculous, appear otherwise interchangeable. When one is a child, certain words placed in front of
a name seem funny, except M. *l'abbé* which is respectable; but if
Mme Galopin is called Marie-Euphrosine Galopin, or Mme de
Villeparisis the Marquise de Villeparisis, this merely adds something
rather heteroclite to persons otherwise of the same ilk. For one
starts from the impressions one has received, and not from the
preconceptions whereby an educated man knows what a painting
is, and a man of the world what the Villeparisis are. People have
only to present themselves to our eyes in a particularly simple light

—which happens especially often with elegant people, like Swann who pushed the piano for my great-aunt and sent her strawberries, or Mme de Villeparisis who had given me a chocolate duck—while being otherwise indistinguishable from the other modest supernumeraries on the family stage, and they will seem to us if anything of a slightly inferior rank. One fine day we are amazed to hear someone we place very high, someone to whose level we seek to aspire, speak of them as people far superior to himself. Thus to ignorance is added, further to mislead us, the homogeneity in one's memory of impressions belonging to the same category, and their heterogeneousness in relation to impressions of another category. This heterogeneousness, in effect, makes it far more difficult for us to calculate value. In order to compare, to subtract, it is first of all necessary to reduce to qualities of the same kind. Those who start from preconceived notions can do so. Childhood, enclosed in its impressions, cannot. Mme de Villeparisis, an old family acquaintance, less brilliant and intimidating than the optician, was further removed from "the Guermantes way" than if she had been confined to "the Méséglise way." But these differences in kind, if they make the assessment of values impossible, are great sources of poetry (all the more so because those beliefs of our youth, like forces that need room in which to deploy, operate over the great, wide surfaces of time that stretch behind us). When we discover that the easy-going captain whom we treated with less respect than Captain Lévy, and who—not content with being nice to us every day—asked us to dinner before we finished our term of service, was the step-brother of the Duc de Fezenzac (once we have acquired preconceptions and know who the latter is), this sudden displacement—as of a ray of light shifting on the horizon—of a personage who rapidly switches from the vulgar and charming environment in which we have always situated him into a totally different world, acquires a sort of poetic charm. He had become almost unreal, like everything that we once knew in a place to which we have never returned, in a special life intercalated into our very different life for three years, like the officers in our regiment, or long ago the good people of Combray. To learn that these people, as different from real people as pantomime figures, took the train on Saturday, after removing their uniforms or their country clothes, and went to dine with Mme de Pourtalès—how interesting that makes it for us to know Mme de Pourtalès, how we long to get her to talk to us about them! But what she tells us will no more be able to enlighten us than what we ask of people who knew the real people on whom Mme Bovary or Frédéric Moreau were modelled. How could this information elucidate an inner charm which stems from a certain distortion of memory and certain transformations of reality? Thus Saint-Loup could have spoken to me indefinitely about his family without helping me to get to the bottom of the pleasure I had derived from the fact that suddenly, set free from a homely bourgeois prison that had been spirited away as in a fairy tale, Mme de Villeparisis was embarking—or rather (so swift had been the spell) was already awaiting me—on the Guermantes way.

"But how do you know the Château de Guermantes?" Saint-Loup asked me. "Have you visited it—or perhaps you knew my aunt de Guermantes-La Trémoïlle who lived there before?" he added, whether because, finding it quite natural that one should know the same people as he did, he failed to realise that I came from a different background, or because he was pretending not to realise out of politeness.

"No . . . but . . . I've heard of the château. They have all the busts of the old lords of Guermantes there, haven't they?"

"Yes, it's a fine sight . . ."

Page 834. *At this point in the holograph material the Pléiade editors found some loose sheets containing the following passage which Proust failed to complete and incorporate in his novel. (Santois was the name Proust originally gave to the violinist, Morel, who does not make his first appearance until Volume I of* The Guermantes Way.):—

N.B. *This, which was originally intended for the last Guermantes party, is for the evening in the Casino at Balbec, but may perhaps be changed. I might split it in two, keeping the quintet for the Guermantes party and the organ for Balbec?*

At the back of the Casino's dance hall was a stage from which some excessively steep and widely-spaced steps led up to an organ. The "famous Lepic Quintet," composed of women, came in to play *a quintet by Franck (insert another name).* Although this quintet was her favourite piece, the pianist executed it with the same feverish concentration both on the score and on her fingers as she would have shown had she been sight-reading, and with such a striving towards speed that she seemed not so much to be playing the music as catching up with it as fast as she could go. The piano might perhaps be shattered by the end of it, but she would get there. Since she was a distinguished lady, dressed with studied elegance, she gave her feverish attentiveness a knowing air which from a distance seemed almost mischievous; and indeed whenever she played wrong notes—which happened all the time—she smiled as though she were playing a joke on them, as one laughs when one splashes someone in order to pretend that one has done it on purpose. All the people there were sufficiently elegant and musical not to be paying attention to anything but the music, as would have happened at a bourgeois soirée . . . *Put in here the remarks made to me by Mme de Cambremer about the quintet, perhaps even put in here, to vary it a bit, my observations on art and love . . . and in that case perhaps bring on the man who says "It's devilish fine," who will be a character already introduced but who has gone grey. Before putting in Mme de Cambremer's reflexions during the interval, say:* Nevertheless the minds of all these people were preoccupied less with what they were listening to than with the way they were listening and the impression they were making all round them. They endeavoured with their boas or their fans to give the appearance of knowing what was being played, of judging the performers and waiting for the extremely difficult *allegro vivace* to compose a satisfying ensemble. The minuet set all their heads nodding and wagging, with knowing smiles which signified both "Isn't it charming!" and "Of course I know it!" Meanwhile my unintentionally ironical smile upset the head-wagging of a few intrepid listeners who replaced the knowing smile with a furious glance and abandoned the head-wagging, though— in order not to appear to be surrendering to a threat—not at once but rather as if under the pressure of Westinghouse brakes, which slow trains down gradually until they come to a complete stop. An artistic gentleman, anxious to show that he knew the quintet, shouted "Bravo, bravo" when he judged that it had reached its conclusion, and began to clap. Unfortunately, what he had taken for the end of the quintet was not even the end of one of its movements but simply a two-bar pause. He consoled himself with the thought that people might imagine that he knew the pianist and had merely wished to encourage her. When the end, longed for by the more musical members of the audience, came at last, I said to Mme de Cambremer. . . .

Meanwhile the organ recital had begun. At that moment a paralytic old man, who could walk with some difficulty but was utterly incapable of climbing the steps, conceived the strange intention of going to sit on a chair right at the top beside the organ, and three young men pushed him up. But after a while, as the organ's crisp keyboard notes were executing their pastoral variations, he got up again, with the three young men in hot pursuit. I thought he must have had a stroke, and I admired the obliviousness of the organist who, having ceased to uncoil the spirals of his rustic pipes, covered the descent of the unfortunate paralytic with a thunderous noise. Pushed and carried by the three young men, the old gentleman disappeared into the wings. The pianist, performer turned critic, had now come to sit on the stage. In spite of the suffocating heat, she had donned a white fur coat, of which she was evidently extremely proud. Moreover her hands, so active on the keyboard only a moment before, were buried in an immense white fur muff, either because she simply wanted to show how elegant she was, or in order to enclose the precious relics of her piano-playing in a shrine worthy of them, or to exchange the activity of the keyboard for the motionless but skilful exercise of the muff, which moreover dispensed her from having to applaud her colleagues. No one understood the rôle of this muff, about which Saint-Loup interrogated me in vain. But what surprised me more was that scarcely two minutes had passed before the paralytic old man, evidently warming to the very exercise of which he was all but incapable, returned, pushed by the three young men, to take his useless place beside the organ. He nodded off there for a moment, then awoke and climbed down again, and since the organist was invisible behind his instrument, the stage was to all intents and purposes occupied by the perilous exertions of the clumsy quinquagenarian [sic] squirrel. When the organist came down in his turn to take his bow, it was to him that the thankless task devolved of helping down the impotent dotard, whose every step made the frail executant stumble. But with a wiliness that is often characteristic of the moribund, the old man clung to the organist in such a way that it was he who appeared to be supporting the man who was more or less carrying him, to be protecting him, to be presenting him to the audience, and to be receiving his share of the applause, which out of pure modesty he seemed not to wish to take for himself by pointing to the organist, who, tottering beneath his human burden and afraid of falling down the steep steps, could not make his bow.

Meanwhile, I was looking at the programme to see what the next piece was to be when I was struck by the name of the soloist: Santois. "He has the same name as the son of my uncle's former valet," I thought to myself. I heard someone say: "Look, a soldier." I raised my eyes and at once recognised the young Santois, who was indeed now a soldier for a year, or rather disguised as a soldier, so much did he give the impression of being in fancy dress.

He played well, looking down at his instrument with that charming Gallic face, the open yet pious demeanour of some contemporary of St Louis or Louis XI, with the defiance of the peasant who feels that there would be little point in having had a revolution if one still had to say "Monsieur le Comte." To these

agreeable features there was added, after the first two pieces, as
though to complete the picture of the traditional young violinist,
a symmetrical adjunct to the redness of the neck at the spot where
the instrument rests (the product of the *allegro* although it was *non
troppo*), a curvaceous lock of hair, as round as if it had been in a
locket, . . . charming, belated, perhaps not entirely fortuitous, but
activated at the appropriate moment by a virtuoso who knew what
a contribution it can make to the seductiveness of a performance.

After he had finished playing, I sent a message round to him
asking if I could come and pay my compliments. He replied in a
few words scribbled on his card saying that he looked forward to
seeing me and assuring me of his "amicable regards." I thought
of the indignation Françoise would have felt, she who since she
had learned, fairly recently it was true, the use of the third person,
had prescribed it to the whole of her family, down to the most
remote degrees of kinship or descent, every time a young cousin
of hers came "to pay her respects to Monsieur." But if I found this
deference towards me of the whole of Françoise's family very
traditionally domestic, it seemed to me that, although it was at the
opposite extreme, there was something no less characteristically
French in the cavalier tone of the young Santois, scion of a race
that made the Revolution, implying that a peasant's son, educated
or not, considers himself nobody's inferior, and when a prince is
mentioned insists on showing by his demeanour that such a person
seems to him no better than his father or himself—though with a
tinge of hauteur in the way he manifests it that betrays the fact
that the age when princes were indeed superior is still fairly recent
and that he may be afraid that people still remember it.

After the concert I went round to congratulate him, and recognised him without difficulty, not from the face I remembered, since
there is always a certain discrepancy, a certain displacement in the
memory, but because his appearance accorded with the impression
he had made on me in Paris and which I had forgotten. He was
doing his military service near Balbec, and he too had immediately
recognised me. We had nothing in common save a few mental
images, and the memory of the things we had said to one another
during the short visit he had paid to me, and which were of little
moment. But it would seem that faces are fairly individual, and
moreover that the memory is a pretty faithful organ, since we had
remembered each other and our meeting.

Santois was presently joined by his colleagues, the other players,
for each of whom, as an aeroplane adds wings to an aviator, his
instrument was as it were the beak and the throat of a melodious

song-bird; a twittering troupe that had gathered for the summer season at this resort and would shortly, with the first frosts, take off elsewhere. I left Santois with his friends, but when I got back to the hotel I regretted not having asked him who the mountaineering paralytic was who had scaled the heights of the organ so many times, and also whether Santois, his father, had ever told him how my uncle had come to have the portrait of Mme Swann by Elstir. I resolved not to forget to ask him these two questions if I saw him again.

SYNOPSIS

SWANN'S WAY

Combray

Awakenings (3). Bedrooms of the past, at Combray (6), at Tansonville (7), at Balbec (8; cf. 717). Habit (9).

Bedtime at Combray (cf. 46). The magic lantern; Geneviève de Brabant (10). Family evenings (11). The little closet smelling of orris-root (13; cf. 172). The good-night kiss (13; cf. 24, 29-46). Visits from Swann (14); his father (15); his unsuspected social life (16). "Our social personality is the creation of other people's thoughts" (20). Mme de Villeparisis's house in Paris; "the tailor and his daughter" (21). Aunts Céline and Flora (23). Françoise's code (30). Swann and I (32; cf. 322). My upbringing: "principles" of my grandmother (cf. 11, 12) and my mother; arbitrary behaviour of my father (38). My grandmother's presents; her ideas about books (42). A reading of George Sand (44).

Resurrection of Combray through involuntary memory. The *madeleine* dipped in a cup of tea (48).

Combray. Aunt Léonie's two rooms (53); her lime-tea (55). Françoise (56). The church (63). M. Legrandin (72). Eulalie (74). Sunday lunches (76). Uncle Adolphe's sanctum (77). Love of the theatre: titles on posters (79). Meeting with "the lady in pink" (81). My family quarrel with Uncle Adolphe (86). The kitchen-maid: Giotto's "Charity" (86). Reading in the garden (90). The gardener's daughter and the passing cavalry (95). Bloch and Bergotte (97). Bloch and my family (98). Reading Bergotte (101). Swann's friendship with Bergotte (105). Berma (105). Swann's mannerisms of speech and attitudes of mind (106). Prestige of Mlle Swann as a friend of Bergotte's (107; cf. 444). The Curé's visits to Aunt Léonie (111). Eulalie and Françoise (115). The kitchen-maid's confinement (118). Aunt Léonie's nightmare (118). Saturday lunches (119). The hawthorns on the altar in Combray church (121). M. Vinteuil (121). His "boyish"-looking daughter (122). Walks round Combray by moonlight (123). Aunt Léonie and Louis XIV (128). Strange behaviour of M. Legrandin (129-145). Plan for a holiday at Balbec (141). Swann's (or the Méséglise) way and the Guermantes way (146).

Swann's Way. View over the plain (147). The lilacs of Tansonville (147). The hawthorn lane (150). Apparition of Gilberte (153). The lady in white and the man in white "ducks" (Mme Swann and M. de Charlus) (154). Dawn of love for Gilberte: glamour of the name "Swann" (157; cf. 447). Farewell to the hawthorns (158). Mlle Vinteuil's friend comes to Montjouvain (160). M. Vinteuil's sorrow (161). The rain (164). The porch of Saint-André-des-Champs, Françoise and Théodore (164). Death of Aunt Léonie; Françoise's wild grief (167). Exultation in the solitude of autumn (169). Disharmony between our feelings and their habitual expression (170). "The same emotions do not spring up simultaneously in everyone" (170). Stirrings of desire (170). The little closet smelling of orris-root (172; cf. 13). Scene of sadism at Montjouvain (173).

The Guermantes Way. River landscape: the Vivonne (182); the water-lilies (184). The Guermantes; Geneviève de Brabant "the ancestress of the Guermantes family" (187). Daydreams and discouragement of a future writer (188). The Duchesse de Guermantes in the chapel of Gilbert the Bad (190). The secrets hidden behind shapes, scents and colours (195). The steeples of Martinville; first joyful experience of literary creation (197). Transition from joy to sadness (199). Does reality take shape in the memory alone? (201).

Awakenings (203; cf. 3).

Swann in Love

The Verdurins and their "little clan." The "faithful" (205). Odette mentions Swann to the Verdurins (208). Swann and women (208). Swann's first meeting with Odette: she is "not his type" (213). How he comes to fall in love with her (214). Dr Cottard (217). The sonata in F sharp (224). The Beauvais settee (226). The little phrase (227). The Vinteuil of the sonata and the Vinteuil of Combray (233). Mme Verdurin finds Swann charming at first (234). But his "powerful friendships" make a bad impression on her (235). The little seamstress; Swann agrees to meet Odette only after dinner (237). Vinteuil's little phrase, "the national anthem of their love" (238). Tea with Odette; her chrysanthemums (239). Faces of today and portraits of the past: Odette and Botticelli's Zipporah (243). Odette, a Florentine painting (245). Love letter from Odette written from the Maison Dorée (246). Swann's arrival at the Verdurins' one evening after Odette's departure (247); anguished search in the night (249). The cattleyas (253); she becomes his mistress (254). Odette's vulgarity (263); her idea of "chic" (265). Swann begins to

adopt her tastes (268) and considers the Verdurins "magnanimous people" (271). Why, nevertheless, he is not a true member of the "faithful," unlike Forcheville (273). A dinner at the Verdurins': Brichot (274), Cottard (275), the painter (278), Saniette (285). The little phrase (288). Swann's jealousy: one night, dismissed by Odette at midnight, he returns to her house and knocks at the wrong window (297). Forcheville's cowardly attack on Saniette, and Odette's smile of complicity (302). Odette's door remains closed to Swann one afternoon; her lying explanation (302). Signs of ' distress that accompany Odette's lying (306). Swann deciphers a letter from her to Forcheville through the envelope (308). The Verdurins organise an excursion to Chatou without Swann (310). His indignation with them (312). Swann's exclusion (315). Should he go to Dreux or Pierrefonds to find Odette? (319). Waiting through the night (322). Peaceful evenings at Odette's with Forcheville (325). Recrudescence of anguish (327). The Bayreuth project (327). Love and death and the mystery of personality (336). Charles Swann and "young Swann" (337). Swann, Odette, Charlus and Uncle Adolphe (339). Longing for death (345).
An evening at the Marquise de Saint-Euverte's. Detached from social life by his love and his jealousy, Swann can observe it as it is in itself (351): the footmen (352); the monocles (355); the Marquise de Cambremer and the Vicomtesse de Franquetot listening to Liszt's "St Francis" (357); Mme de Gallardon, a despised cousin of the Guermantes (358). Arrival of the Princesse des Laumes (359); her conversation with Swann (370). Swann introduces the young Mme de Cambremer (Mlle Legrandin) to General de Froberville (373). Vinteuil's little phrase poignantly reminds Swann of the days when Odette loved him (375). The language of music (379). Swann realises that Odette's love for him will never revive (384).
The whole past shattered stone by stone (cf. 404). Bellini's Mahomet II (386). An anonymous letter (387). *Les Filles de Marbre* (392). Beuzeville-Bréauté (392). Odette and women (393). Impossibility of ever possessing another person (396). On the Ile du Bois, by moonlight (397). A new circle of hell (399). The terrible recreative power of memory (400). Odette and procuresses (401). Had she been lunching with Forcheville at the Maison Dorée on the day of the Paris-Murcie festival? (402; cf. 246). She was with Forcheville, and not at the Maison Dorée, on the night when Swann had searched for her in Prévost's (403; cf. 253). Odette's suspect effusions (405). "Charming conversation" in a brothel (406). Odette goes on a cruise with the "faithful" (406). Mme Cottard assures Swann that Odette adores him (408). Swann's love fades; he no longer suffers

on learning that Forcheville has been Odette's lover (410). Return
of his jealousy in a nightmare (410). Departure for Combray,
where he will see the young face of Mme de Cambremer whose
charm had struck him at Mme de Saint-Euverte's (414). The first
image of Odette seen again in his dream: he had wanted to die for
a woman "who wasn't his type" (415).

Place-Names: The Name

Dreams of place-names. Rooms at Combray (416). Room in the Grand
Hotel at Balbec (416; cf. 8). The real Balbec and the Balbec of dream
(416). The 1.22 train (418). Dreams of spring in Florence (419; cf.
423). Words and names (420). Names of Norman towns (422).
Abortive plan to visit Florence and Venice (423). The doctor forbids
me to travel or to go to the theatre to see Berma (427); he advises
walks in the Champs-Elysées under Françoise's surveillance (427).
In the Champs-Elysées. A little girl with red hair; the name Gilberte
(428). Games of prisoner's base (429). What will the weather be
like? (429). Snow in the Champs-Elysées (431). The reader of the
Débats (Mme Blatin) (431; cf. 448). Marks of friendship: the agate
marble, the Bergotte booklet, "You may call me Gilberte" (436);
why they fail to bring me the expected happiness (438). A spring
day in winter: joy and disappointment (439). The Swann of Combray
has become a different person: Gilberte's father (441). Gilberte tells
me with cruel delight that she will not be returning to the Champs-
Elysées before the New Year (442). "In my friendship with Gilberte,
it was I alone who loved" (446). The name Swann (447; cf. 157).
Swann meets my mother in the Trois Quartiers (449). Pilgrimage
with Françoise to the Swanns' house near the Bois (451).
The Bois, Garden of Women. Mme Swann in the Bois (453). A walk
through the Bois one late autumn morning in 1913 (456). Memory
and reality (462).

WITHIN A BUDDING GROVE

Madame Swann at Home

A new Swann: Odette's husband (465; cf. 550 sqq.). A new Cottard:
Professor Cottard (467).

Norpois (468); the "governmental mind" (470); an ambassador's
conversation (471). "*Although* is always an unrecognised *because*"
(472). Norpois advises my father to let me follow a literary career
(474).

My first experience of Berma (475). My high expectations of her
—as of Balbec and Venice (477). A great disappointment (480).
Françoise and Michelangelo (480). The auditorium and the stage
(481; cf. 79).

Norpois dines at our house (486). His notions about literature
(487); financial investments (489); Berma (492); Françoise's spiced
beef (493); King Theodosius' visit to Paris (495); Balbec church
(501); Mme Swann (501); Odette and the Comte de Paris (509);
Bergotte (509); my prose poem (511; cf. 491); Gilberte (513).
Gestures which we believe have gone unnoticed (514). Why M.
de Norpois would not speak to Mme Swann about me (516).

How I came to say of Berma: "What a great artist!" (518). The
laws of Time (520). Effect produced by Norpois on my parents
(521), on Françoise (522); the latter's views on Parisian restaurants
(523).

New Year's Day visits (524). I propose to Gilberte that we should
rebuild our friendship on a new basis (524); but that same evening
I realise that New Year's Day is not the first day of a new world
(525). Berma and love (525). Gabriel's palaces (527). I can no longer
recall Gilberte's face (528). She returns to the Champs-Elysées
(528). "My parents can't stand you!" (529). I write to Swann (529).
Reawakening, thanks to involuntary memory, in the little pavilion
in the Champs-Elysées, of the impressions experienced in Uncle
Adolphe's sanctum at Combray (530, 533; cf. 77). Amorous wrestle
with Gilberte (532). I fall ill (534). Cottard's diagnoses (536).

A letter from Gilberte (538). Love's miracles, happy and unhappy
(539). Change of attitude towards me of Gilberte's parents, unwittingly brought about by Bloch and Cottard (541). The Swann
apartment; the concierge; the windows (542; cf. 451). Gilberte's
writing-paper (543). The Henri II staircase (544). The chocolate
cake (545). Mme Swann's praise of Françoise: "your old nurse"
(547). The heart of the Sanctuary: Swann's library (548); his wife's
bedroom (549). Odette's "at home" (550). The "famous Albertine,"
niece of Mme Bontemps (552). The evolution of society (556).
Swann's "amusing sociological experiments" (561). Swann's old
jealousy (563) and new love (565).

Outings with the Swanns (566). Lunch with them (566). Odette
plays Vinteuil's sonata to me (570). A work of genius creates its
own posterity (572). What the little phrase now means to Swann
(574). "Me nigger; you old cow!" (577). Consistent charm of Mme
Swann's heterogeneous drawing-room (580). Princess Mathilde
(583). Gilberte's unexpected behaviour (586).

Lunch at the Swanns' with Bergotte (587). The gentle white-haired bard and the man with the snail-shell nose and black goatee (589). A writer's voice and his style (592). Bergotte and his imitators (593). Unforeseeable beauty of the sentences of a great writer (594). Reflecting power of genius (597). Vices of the man and morality of the writer (600). Bergotte and Berma (603). "A powerful idea communicates some of its power to the man who contradicts it" (605). A remark of Swann's, prelude to the theme of *The Captive* (607). Gilberte's characteristics inherited from both parents (607). Swann's confidence in his daughter (610). Are my pleasures those of the intelligence? (613). Why Swann, according to Bergotte, needs a good doctor (615). Combray society and the social world (615). My parents' change of mind about Bergotte and Gilberte; a problem of etiquette (618).

Revelations about love (619; cf. 100); Bloch takes me to a second-rate house of assignation (619). "Rachel when from the Lord" (620). Aunt Léonie's furniture in the brothel (622). Amatory initiation at Combray on Aunt Léonie's sofa (622). Work projects constantly postponed (623). Impossibility of happiness in love (625). My last visit to Gilberte (626). I decide not to see her again (629). Unjust fury with the Swanns' butler (632). Waiting for a letter (633). I renounce Gilberte for ever (634); but the hope of a reconciliation is superimposed on my resolve (636). Intermittency, law of the human soul (636).

Odette's "winter-garden" (637): splendour of the chrysanthemums and poverty of the conversation: Mme Cottard (641); Mme Bontemps (642); effrontery of her niece Albertine (643); the Prince d'Agrigente (645); Mme Verdurin (645). Painful New Year's Day (654). "Suicide of the self that loved Gilberte" (657). Clumsy interventions (660). Letters to Gilberte: "one speaks for oneself alone" (661). Odette's drawing-room: retreat of the Far East and invasion of the eighteenth century (662). New hair-styles and silhouettes (665; cf. 215).

A sudden impulse interrupts the cure of detachment (669); Aunt Léonie's Chinese vase (670). Two walkers in the Elysian twilight (671). Impossibility of happiness (672). The opposing forces of memory and imagination (673). Because of Gilberte, I decline an invitation to a dinner-party where I would have met Albertine (674). Cruel memories (675). Gilberte's strange laugh, evoked in a dream (678; cf. 628). Fewer visits to Mme Swann (680). Exchange of tender letters and progress of indifference (681). Approach of spring: Mme Swann's ermine and the guelder-roses in her drawing-room; nostalgia for Combray (682). Odette and the "Down-and-outs Club" (684). An intermediate social class (687).

Place-Names: The Place

Departure for Balbec (691). Subjectiveness of love (692). Contradictory effects of habit (692). Railway stations (694). Françoise's simple and infallible taste (698). Alcoholic euphoria (701). Mme de Sévigné and Dostoievsky (703). Sunrise from the train (704); the milk-girl (706). Balbec church (708). "The tyranny of the Particular" (709). Place-names on the way to Balbec-Plage (711).

Arrival at Balbec-Plage (712). The manager of the Grand Hotel (712, 716). My room at the top of the hotel (717; cf. 8). Attention and habit (717, 721). My grandmother's kindness (718). The sea in the morning (723). Balbec tourists (725). Balbec and Rivebelle (727). Mme de Villeparisis (728). M. and Mlle de Stermaria (730). An actress and three friends (731). The weekly Cambremer garden-party (733). Resemblances (736). Poetic visions of Mlle de Stermaria (740). The general manager (742). Françoise's Grand Hotel connections (744). Meeting of Mme de Villeparisis and my grandmother (746). The "sordid moment" at the end of meals (746; cf. 929). The Princesse de Luxembourg (740). Mme de Villeparisis, M. de Norpois and my father (753). The bourgeoisie and the Faubourg Saint-Germain (756).

Drives with Mme de Villeparisis (757). Different seas (757). The ivy-covered church (761). Mme de Villeparisis's conversation (762, 775). Norman girls (766). The handsome fisher-girl (769). The three trees of Hudimesnil (770; cf. 197). The fat Duchesse de La Rochefoucauld (780). My grandmother and I: intimations of death (781).

Robert de Saint-Loup (782). My friendship with him (790), but real happiness requires solitude (791; cf. 968). Saint-Loup as a work of art: the "nobleman" (791). A Jewish colony (793). Variety of human failings and similarity of virtues (796). Bloch's bad manners (799). Bloch and his father (800; cf. 825). The stereoscope (803). Mme de Villeparisis is a Guermantes (810).

M. de Charlus's strange behaviour (807). I recognise him as the man in the grounds of Tansonville (811; cf. 154). Further weird behaviour (815). Mme de Sévigné, La Fontaine and Racine (818). Charlus comes to my room (821).

Dinner at the Blochs' with Saint-Loup (824). To know "without knowing" (826). Bloch's sisters (826). The elegance of "Uncle Solomon" (829). Nissim Bernard (830); his lies (831). Bloch and Mme Swann in the train (835). Françoise's view of Bloch and Saint-Loup (835). Saint-Loup and his mistress (838). My grandmother's inexplicable behaviour (843).

The blossoming girls (845). "Oh, the poor old boy . . ." (849). The dark-haired cyclist: Albertine (851). The name Simonet (858, 865, 903). Rest before dinner: different aspects of the sea (860). Dinners at Rivebelle (865). The astral tables (868). Euphoria induced by alcohol and music (869). Meeting with Elstir (884). A new aspect of Albertine (887).

Elstir's studio (892); his seascapes (893); the painter's "metaphors" (894). Elstir explains to me the beauty of Balbec church (899). Albertine passes by (902). The portrait of *Miss Sacripant* (906). "My beautiful Gabrielle!" (909). Age and the artist (909). Elstir and the little band (914). Nullity of love (917). *Miss Sacripant* was Mme Swann (920) and M. Biche Elstir! (923). "One must discover wisdom for oneself" (923). My grandmother and Saint-Loup (925). Saint-Loup and Bloch (926). Still lifes (929; cf. 746). Afternoon party at Elstir's (930). Yet another Albertine: a well-brought-up girl (933). Albertine on the esplanade: once more a member of the little band (936). Octave, the gigolo (938). Albertine's antipathy for Bloch (941). Saint-Loup engaged to a Mlle d'Ambresac? (945). Albertine's intelligence and taste (946). Andrée (946). Gisèle (947).

Days with the girls (952). Françoise's bad temper (956). Balbec through Elstir's eyes (958). Fortuny (960). A sketch of Les Creuniers (962). The mobile beauty of youth (966). Friendship: an abdication of oneself (968; cf. 791). Twittering of the girls (969). Letter from Sophocles to Racine (972). A love divided among several girls (977). Albertine is to spend a night at the Grand Hotel (991). The rejected kiss (995). The attraction of Albertine (996). The multiple utilisation of a single action (1000). Straying in the budding grove (1006). The different Albertines (1009).

End of the season (1013). Departure (1016).

MARCEL PROUST

George D. Painter

With *A la recherche du temps perdu* Marcel Proust achieved a perfect rendering of life in art, of the past recreated through memory. It is both a portrait of the artist and a discovery of the aesthetic by which the portrait is painted, and it was to have a seminal influence on twentieth-century literature. George Painter's work has brilliantly captured the life of the great writer in a *tour de force* of scholarly research and literary craft.

"Mr Painter has done his work so well that it is hard to speak in moderate terms of his skill and unobtrusive wit" – Anthony Powell

"No biography has ever before thrown so much light on the making of a masterpiece" – Raymond Mortimer

"Brilliant and scholarly . . . Mr Painter's greatest triumph is in his depiction of place and people, his revelation of the raw material of the novel" – Angus Wilson